by a spell
...ing in Japan, subject
...Pictures from the Water Trade. Having
made his home in Munich, the focus of Morley's life has been in
Central Europe, where for twenty-five years he worked as a location
manager for Japanese TV and as a journalist for publications such
as *The Times*, the *Sunday Times Magazine*, the *Observer* and *Condé
Nast Traveller*. *Ella Morris* is his tenth novel.

*Also by John David Morley*

Pictures from the Water Trade
In the Labyrinth
The Case of Thomas N.
The Feast of Fools
The Anatomy Lesson
Destiny or, The Attraction of Affinities
Journey to the End of the Whale
Passage
The Book of Opposites

# Ella Morris

## JOHN DAVID MORLEY

Weidenfeld & Nicolson
LONDON

First published in Great Britain in 2014 by Weidenfeld & Nicolson
An imprint of the Orion Publishing Group Ltd
Orion House, 5 Upper St Martin's Lane
London WC2H 9EA

An Hachette UK Company

ISBN 978 0 297 87172 9

Typeset at The Spartan Press Ltd,
Lymington, Hants

Printed and bound in Great Britain by
Clays Ltd, St Ives plc

The Orion Publishing Group's policy is to use papers that are natural,
renewable and recyclable products and made from wood grown in
sustainable forests. The logging and manufacturing processes are expected
to conform to the environmental regulations of the country of origin.

www.orionbooks.co.uk

# CONTENTS

# BOOK I

## Exiles

# CHAPTER ONE

## The Will

### 1

Why was this?

Twisting a finger through long chestnut-coloured hair, the girl smiled as she listened to her friend talk. The listening girl was fair-complexioned. The girl doing most of the talking had black hair, black eyebrows he had seen when she turned to get the waiter's attention.

Alex could follow the gist of their conversation, audible to him three tables away. Mostly it was taking place in Serbo-Croat, with the occasional word in Albanian thrown in, dialect words he didn't understand.

It was the chestnut-haired girl who sometimes used Albanian. She listened intently to the dark girl telling her in Serbo-Croat about the restoration of a house on the Dalmatian coast. The dark girl was showing the chestnut-haired girl photos, presumably of the house. The house belonged to her parents. It had been destroyed in the war eight years ago, when her brother was killed. Now the house was rebuilt, but her parents preferred not to live there any more. In summer they let the house to tourists. When it grew too hot in Zagreb and they wanted to get out of the city they stayed at a pension, the same place every year, not far from the restored house, where the family used to spend their holidays before the war. During the winter the house was uninhabited.

The conversation interested Alex. Watching them from behind his newspaper, he could see that the girl with the chestnut hair always smiled. Odd, under the circumstances.

It wasn't a smile in the ordinary sense, something that came on and went off. Nor would he have described it as the dreamy smile of a person preoccupied with her own thoughts or the polite smile of someone not really interested in what the other person was saying. It seemed to be something in the grain of her nature rather than an expression of the girl's momentary feelings. She wouldn't have been smiling, not in the ordinary sense, while listening to the story of the destruction of a house, even a house that happily had been rebuilt – a house with a happy end, so to speak, meriting a smile from the listener. The dark girl passed the fair-complexioned girl photos of the restored house as she talked, which the fair girl held carefully as if they were a trust, the house itself, something fragile that might easily get broken again.

From the way she talked, the dark girl didn't seem to be too cheerful about her parents' house having been rebuilt. Now and again Alex heard her sniff as if she might have been crying, but perhaps she just had a cold, or an allergy, or something. He couldn't tell what sort of sniffing it was because the dark girl was sitting with her back to him.

Whether or not the dark girl was crying, and whatever she said, it made no difference to the reaction of the chestnut-haired girl, who was listening to her with a smile – smiling her way through the disasters the dark girl recounted. This was what puzzled Alex. It reminded him of the smile he'd seen on the face of a Japanese woman in front of the ruins of her house destroyed by the earthquake in Kobe, smiling as she talked to the TV reporter about the ruined house behind her.

Unexpectedly the dark girl turned and looked at Alex. She sniffed again, several times, but there was definitely no trace of tears in her eyes now. It must have been a cold or an allergy after all. The dark girl was also smiling, quite differently from the other girl. The dark girl wore the polite switch-on smile of a person who wanted something.

She held out her camera and said in English, 'Would you please take picture me my friend?'

Alex smiled as he took the camera. The two girls smiled as they looked towards the camera and Alex took their picture. All three of them were smiling when Alex took the picture, and each was a different smile, for a different reason.

'Thank you,' said the dark girl.

The other girl signalled to the waiter and asked for the bill. As she raised her arm to attract the waiter's attention he noticed the swing of her breasts inside her sweater, how the material there tightened, revealing the outline stirring underneath, coming alive. There was a Viennese

4

lilt to the way she spoke German. He guessed she was local, but did she live here? Alex wondered if it was right of him to listen in on the girls' conversation and not let them know that he understood what they were saying. He tried to think of some way of telling them without it seeming sneaky, really rather underhand of him to have sat beside them in the cafe for an hour and a half, eavesdropping on their conversation, but he couldn't think of one. It was too late now. He should have told them earlier.

The girls paid, got up and left. Alex watched them wander slowly out of sight up some steps along a gravel path that led between the trees. The chestnut-haired girl was apparently showing the dark one the local sights, and this was one of them, the former Palm House, the beautiful old wrought-iron and glass conservatory in the park, now a cafe, where he usually spent his Saturday mornings reading the newspapers over a late breakfast.

For the last three months, on those Saturday mornings when he wasn't away on some assignment but back home in Vienna and came here to read the papers, the girl with the chestnut hair had shown up too. The first couple of times she came later than him and sat down about as far away from his table as she possibly could have. The next time Alex arranged to arrive later than she did so that he could choose a table that was closer and get a better look at her. For an hour or two they both sat at their tables, drinking coffee and reading their newspapers. As she read her paper, the girl often twisted a finger through her hair, but until now Alex had never seen her smile. Occasionally he glanced over at the girl. Once, she looked up and caught his glance, held it for a moment, then looked away.

Today was the second time she'd looked at him, or at the camera he was holding, to have her picture taken. If she remembered him from previous occasions, and by now they had both sat in this cafe on quite a lot of Saturday mornings, she gave no sign of recognising him.

The smile was new. It must have been something about being in the company of the dark girl that made her smile. Not smile exactly. The company of the dark girl brought out in her friend's face something that resembled a smile but wasn't a smile in the usual sense but in the sense of the smile of the Japanese woman whose house in Kobe had just been destroyed by an earthquake. The smile had allowed a not otherwise expressible resignation to show on the woman's face. In Japan, or so a fellow IPA correspondent had once explained to Alex, people struck by some disaster and interviewed about it on television smiled in order to lessen the discomfort that might be felt by viewers. The smiling woman in Kobe didn't want to impose on the viewers. Whatever she privately felt about the disaster that was being shown in public, the woman kept it to herself behind the smile.

Seeing her smile in this way for the first time, and now taking her picture, Alex experienced a moment of déjà vu. He had done all this before: the dark girl and the girl with chestnut hair, both of them had been in a déjà vu picture taken at some other place and time and perhaps by someone other than Alex. While he couldn't remember ever having seen the dark girl, he now felt quite sure that he had seen the other girl somewhere else. The difference was the smile. She had not been smiling then.

He unlocked his bicycle and took the short cut through the park, following the direction the two girls had taken.

'But who's to say it wasn't *here* I saw her? After all, I've seen her here every other week for the last three months. Naturally she seems familiar. I mean, obviously so – it's here I must've seen her before.'

Living for the most part alone, Alex had got into the habit of talk-ing to himself. He talked out loud quite a lot of the time at home, sometimes in public too. Perhaps it wasn't a good habit, but it didn't necessarily seem to him to be a bad one either. It was a natural thing to do when you were on your own. He had lived in cities where talking to oneself in public was not at all uncommon, Washington for one, where it was ignored, perhaps because the people who talked to themselves were usually black vagrants on the streets, Vienna for another, where it was no kind of stigma; on the contrary, it might be understood as an invitation to other people to join in the conversation, often a grumble about something you liked to share, because everyone in Vienna enjoyed grumbling, had their grumbling rituals – almost a form of politeness. They even had their own local word for it.

He had got to know one of his best Viennese friends in this way. Alex and Roman, the grumbling man who was to become his friend, had both been standing in front of the sold-out opera house talking to themselves one night – neither of them with a ticket, both wishing they had one and complaining they hadn't because tourists had bought them all – until each had taken over the other's grumble, finishing the other's grumble for him, and they both laughed. Musicians playing duets could probably do something similar, thought Alex, reaching up and down the keyboard to take over each other's parts.

Vienna – a garrulous, frivolous, morbid, grand, cosy, ostentatious, backbiting and fraudulent capital that had remained provincial because it had never really moved out of the nineteenth century, a permanent state of theatre where strangers could pass the time of day on the street without suspecting one another of ulterior motives. The city, its people, their affable manners, even their affable buildings, celebrated a self-ironic sense of the theatrical, paying lip service to Vienna's claim to former greatness while in reality taking a much keener interest in the most recent gossip and scandal, the human comedy, or perhaps it was the burlesque, behind the scenes that was the true stuff of the city's life.

Doing his weekend shopping on a roundabout way to Spittelberg in the 7th District, where he lived, calling in at a favourite patisserie, an umbrella maker and a second-hand bookshop, Alex collected en route to the Kursalon Stadtpark, a yellow and white building resembling a cream cake, the neo-Greek buildings of parliament, a neo-Renaissance museum of natural history, neo-Gothic churches, the neo-baroque palaces of a long-defunct aristocracy – all this neo-frontage constituted the theatre sets of Vienna's often questionable not to say shady imperial past.

Ten years ago, when he first came here, many of these buildings had been on the verge of collapse, rotting on their foundations like the palaces in the once splendid and now sad old quarter of Palermo – in quite a few other towns he had collected on his travels too – their downward slide into beggary and eventual demolition apparently unstoppable. But then communism had collapsed instead, all of a sudden, and this city in what had become a stagnant backwater, the last outpost of the West before you reached the Warsaw Pact countries, regained its hinterland, its old but still loyal clientele in eastern Europe. Along with its former Habsburg allies, Bratislava, Prague and Budapest, Vienna began to be revitalised by investors who had withheld their capital for the last fifty years.

The building in which he lived up on the hill in the eighteenth-century Spittelberg quarter had so far escaped revitalisation. It had once been a palace, a rather modest one, then a hotel, with enormous if shabby suites, which were now let out as apartments. The neo-frontage of the former palace was provided by a facade painted in a colour known

7

as castle yellow and an imposing marble staircase at the entrance, but the moment you turned the corner at the top everything further up became narrow, dingy, malodorous, badly lit. It was the domain of Ciska, who spent all of his days and most of his nights in the glass-fronted concierge's office commanding a view of everything that passed in and out of his demesne.

Ciska fastened on Alex the moment he came in.

'Herr Doktor! I have a package for you, Herr Doktor ...'

The concierge stepped out of the gloom of his office and handed Alex the package.

'Thank you, Ciska.'

It went against the grain every time he said Ciska rather than Mr Ciska, but he had learned that local etiquette required this of him, just as it required Ciska to defer to the titles of his clientele, however hard his clientele tried or pretended to try to keep them hidden.

'How are you, Ciska?'

'One can't complain, one can't complain.'

'And how is your wife?'

'Ah!'

Ciska seized on this question, or rather it seized forcefully on him, propelling him out of his den into the corridor, where he stood rocking on his heels for a moment as if needing to adjust his balance to the thick carpet pile, which he didn't have on the floorboards of the concierge's office.

'Very poorly, I'm afraid to have to say, very poorly!'

Ciska reminded Alex of the antique receptionist who used to officiate out of a cupboard under the stairs of a dentist's practice the Morris family had visited once a year in Wimpole Street. Even then, in the London of the 1960s, that deferential Dickensian figure in an old frock coat had outlived the world around him by half a century. Ciska was dressed in a frock coat too, shiny from wear and no less threadbare, and also featured a high shirt collar, some sort of cravat and trousers hoisted halfway up his shins, drawing attention to a pair of old boots with bits of unsuccessfully blackened string improvising as laces. The larger part of what appeared to be a duster rather than a handkerchief was hanging out of his trouser pocket.

'I'm sorry to hear that.'

'She's back on the crutches, Herr Doktor.'

8

'I thought Mrs Ciska had a … had a …'

Alex felt a momentary twinge, a phantom pain that flashed through his body, for some reason reminding him of his mother.

'Unfortunately the new leg hasn't taken. The fit doesn't seem to be right. By the end of the day the stump is all sore and inflamed – a shocking sight.'

'Oh dear. Isn't there anything one can do?'

Momentarily Ciska seemed to brighten.

'Very good of you to enquire, Herr Doktor. I'm afraid not. But I don't want to detain you. How was the war?'

'War? Oh, well, not exactly *war*.'

'On the radio this morning I heard that hostilities still haven't entirely ceased.'

'Well, no, I mean sporadic fighting, here and there, but the war as such is over. Were there any messages?'

'The young lady came in this morning while the Herr Doktor was out. She left something in the Herr Doktor's postbox. Would that be all?'

'Thank you, Ciska.'

Ciska retired into his office while Alex continued down the corridor, opened the postbox marked MORRIS and took out an envelope. Inside it he could feel a key. With a sinking heart he climbed the stairs to his apartment on the floor above, took the key out of the envelope and opened the door. A piece of paper fell out of the envelope onto the floor. He picked it up.

'Sorry to have missed you. I can't manage dinner this evening after all, so I'm returning the key now. B.'

For six months it had seemed to be working, but then she started drifting away. The fair girls and the dark – for once, making a conscious effort, he had resisted the instinct that attracted him to fair girls and had become involved with the black-haired, moody-tempered, dark-complexioned Belinda, whose mother was from Granada, perhaps with Arab ancestors. But when for half of those six months he had been working away from home, what else could one expect, even if the dark Belinda had been as fair as she was lovely?

*How was the war?*

Ciska's question – he had been right to ask it. A war didn't end until the peace had begun.

Almost five years to the day since the NATO bombing of Yugoslavia began, yet another outbreak of violence in Kosovo only the previous week had shown up the fragility of the country's so-called peace, or rather its intermittent lack of war. A boy in a Serbian village near Prishtinë/Priština, depending on who was talking, had been shot from a passing car. Enraged Serbs had thereupon erected barricades on the main roads to Priština and Skopje and attacked an Irish KFOR contingent that arrived to dismantle the barriers. The following day thousands of Kosovo Albanians had demonstrated in towns around the country, and Alex flew in from Vienna to cover the story for IPA.

With the discovery of the bodies of two Albanian children found drowned in a river, hounded to their deaths by dogs set upon them by Serb youths, according to local Albanian TV and radio stations, a violent situation escalated into one of open warfare in the streets of Mitrovicë, with attacks taking place against Serb minorities by as many as fifty thousand Kosovo Albanians throughout the country. Alex had been unable to confirm the involvement of any Serbs in the drowning of the two children. He filed a report that did little more than present a tally of the dead and injured, the burned and looted houses after two days of what war correspondents writing at this late stage in the Balkan upheaval understated as 'an excess of violence', and flew back to Vienna three days later in time for the main fixture of his week, Saturday morning breakfast in the Palm House with all the furtive pleasures that entailed.

Feeling very tired when he let himself into the apartment, Alex sat down for a moment and at once fell asleep.

He was woken by the telephone ringing in the dark. He came to slowly, up and up, emerging from the anaesthetic of an almost sensual tiredness. Most of the day must have passed. The answering machine interrupted the ringing and he heard his own voice giving instructions in three languages, followed by the booming voice of his sister Felicity in London. She wanted to talk to him about his visit and the meeting planned at her house. Philip would definitely be there; Max thought he almost certainly would be too. For what that was worth. Felicity gave a dry little chuckle unlike her, who preferred a good hearty laugh. She said they should have a discussion among themselves. Probate had now come through, by the way. She didn't see the necessity of a lawyer being present. They could always go and see one if there turned out to be a problem. Which she didn't expect. They had Philip, after all. They would sort things out between themselves.

There was something else he had to do. Beyond this business Felicity was rambling on about but not unrelated to it. His head gradually cleared of the remains of sleep. He sat up. There was something he had to see to. What was it?

He stumbled over a rumple in the carpet in the dark and switched on the light. Standing, he started to take a pee in the lavatory at the end of the corridor, thought better of it, let down his trousers and sat down. Belinda had called it primitivism, the inconsiderateness and uncouthness of men. She wasn't joking. She got quite angry. There was no contradicting her. She had shown him the telltale splash marks of urine on the seat and the wall.

'Get into the habit of sitting to pee.'

The splash marks of urine and blood on the seat and walls, corpses with heads lolling and arms flung forward, still crouching on the toilet as they had been when shot, their bodies since bloated by the heat, covered with flies swarming over ripped-open intestines. Urinals as places of standing execution, preferably out of sight, with no witnesses, the victims lined up along the wall inside and shot in the back of the head. In any case death, whether sitting or standing. The inconsiderateness and uncouthness of men. Images of lavatories he had seen across the Balkans during the last ten years flashed through his mind. Belinda's objection was not trivialised by such a comparison; on the contrary, it seemed to Alex to be validated.

'Of course!'

He remembered.

It was the package handed to him by the concierge outside his office. Alex had only glanced at it then, seeing something he didn't want to see, which was why he'd put it out of his mind.

He walked back down the corridor to the table at the entrance where he'd left the package when he came in. Yellow wrapping, foreign stamps, three of them. He turned it over with a deepening sense of misgiving. The address of the police presidium in Madrid was printed on the back.

He opened the package. Inside it there was something wrapped in tissue paper, accompanied by a letter in a separate envelope. He slit open the envelope and took out the letter. For the second time that evening something fell out of a letter onto the floor. He picked it up and looked at in his hand. It was a piece of faded white cloth the size of a postage stamp, attached to a safety pin.

'What on earth is this?'

He read the letter.

He carried everything back into the living room, sat down at his desk and read the letter again. In the regurgitative polysyllabic style of Spanish officialese it informed him that the investigation by the responsible authorities in Santa Cruz de Tenerife into the deaths of his parents there in March the previous year had now been completed, and the tape recorder and the tape inside it, withheld by them as evidence bearing upon that investigation, were herewith returned to him as their rightful owner.

This restitution of his property had taken twelve months.

'His property' included the safety pin attached to the piece of cloth he was holding in his other hand. A postscript at the bottom of the letter explained that the police had found it in the dead woman's clenched hand, adding that forensic examination had failed to come up with any connection between it and the circumstances of her death. Well, what sort of connection had those forensic idiots expected to find between a safety pin and the cause of death? Alex sat looking at it, trying in vain to fathom its secret.

Then he unwrapped the tissue paper enclosing the Sony microcassette tape recorder that had accompanied him for ten years of his journalistic life. Evidence that he was its rightful owner was given by an aluminium plaque which, with an eye to thieving colleagues, his mother had paid to have engraved with his name and address and glued to one side of it. The recorder had been built to last. During the previous twelve months he had often wondered where it was and had since bought two replacements, both of them plastic and of inferior quality, and both already defunct.

'Well.'

He looked at it lying on his desk and wished it wasn't there.

Reconstructing the long-missing tape recorder's recent history, trying to remember where he had left it and on what occasion, the initial qualm he had felt on receipt of the package from Ciska, just a slight misgiving at first, now took shape as a foreboding.

He had left the tape recorder at his parents' house in Tenerife on his last visit there in February. Why hadn't Ella, so conscientious in all things, sent it back to him or at least let him know that it was there?

Because she hadn't found it.

Briefly he escaped into a sense of relief afforded by this explanation.

But unfortunately she had found it. Otherwise it wouldn't be here on his desk. During the six weeks between early February and the middle of March Ella had found the tape recorder and earmarked it for the particular use she already had in mind for it.

*Were there any messages?* he had asked Ciska in the passage downstairs, and now he knew that he had already been holding it in his hand, in the package Ciska had just given him: the taped message from his mother and father, the mysterious safety pin. They too were returning a key they had been lent.

The package from Madrid explained why no farewell letter had been found at the scene. Its absence had puzzled and grieved Alex.

Presumably the police from Santa Cruz, investigating within an hour the scene of what they had to assume might be a crime, having been informed by Paco, the gardener and general handyman who had found the bodies, chose to withhold the information about the existence of the tape until they had listened to it themselves. The evidence of the tape recording might be valuable, if only as a means of corroborating the evidence of other witnesses. But no other witnesses existed, or none would ever be forthcoming. For about thirty-six hours between some time on the Saturday afternoon and some time on the Monday morning the two old people had been lying there alone on the terrace overlooking the distant sea.

Somewhere within the police bureaucracy the cassette recorder had been lying around, probably mislaid, at any rate put on one side for twelve months and effectively forgotten, its existence never mentioned to interested parties such as the owner of the recorder or the children of the deceased.

Alex ejected the cassette. It had been played to the end and not rewound. The speed was set at the slower of the two speeds, giving a recording time of one hour on each side. The quality wasn't so good, but it doubled the recording length. Quite good enough for voice recordings close to the microphone without any background noise. It was the setting he automatically chose for interviews. For all its reliability, the ancient Sony had one fault, and that was the lack of a clearly audible signal that the tape had reached its end and needed to be taken out and turned round if you wanted to continue recording.

From the fact that the tape had not been rewound he guessed that there had been nothing more to listen to. Side B would be empty. Whatever the tape contained, the person who had set the tape speed must have calculated that half an hour might not be quite enough for what they had to say. They would have figured out that after half an hour, overdosed and already halfway to death, they might no longer be in a position to raise so much as a hand, let alone eject a tape, turn it round and press a button. They had given themselves sixty minutes for their final summation.

It would have been Ella who worked this out. Claude was useless with anything of a technical nature. But Ella was adept and curious and she had watched him using the tape recorder often enough. Maybe, being Ella, she had asked him about such details as playing speed and playing times, having already earmarked it for later use and wanting to be *prepared for all eventualities*. Ella always wanted to be ready. Alex wondered if her lifelong refrain about the necessity to be prepared for all eventualities was prompted by a fear of being caught unprepared.

What might Ella have been afraid of? Unprepared for what?

Ella had been a refugee.

Clear enough. The shock of those experiences remained in her bones.

He wound Side A back to the start of the tape. The fact that the investigators had not bothered to do this themselves was somehow as shocking a reminder of the callousness of the treatment surrounding the dead as the gruesome details of any death he had reported from the Balkans.

Now all he had to do was press PLAY and be taken into the last sixty minutes of his parents' lives. It was perfectly easy.

It was not by chance that the police had returned the tape recorder with the message on the tape to him rather than to one of his brothers or to his sister. Placing the recorder where she had, probably on the little white wrought-iron table between the two reclining chairs on the terrace, Ella knew the police could not fail to overlook it, would confiscate it as evidence and in the fullness of time would return it to its owner. It had been part of the arrangements. She was counting on this. It was a last message in a bottle his mother was sending personally, one that he might choose to share with the others or to keep to himself.

14

Prepared for all eventualities, Alex sat and looked with acute dis-comfort at the little machine on his desk. He waited a while, hoping something else would turn up, a phone call, an immediate assignment, so that he could defer doing this.

'So press the button and get on with it.'

The rustle of static first, or maybe it was the effect of wind blowing into the microphone and upsetting the balance. A tinkle was audible, then Ella's voice very close, a whisper.

'Will you ever hear this, my dearest Alex?'

He could hear it, her blood in his heart.


# 2


'My last surprise for you. Will it reach you? Will you be pleased to get it? I wonder. Will you want to share it with the others? I leave that for you to judge. That's the wind chime above the terrace door. It was the first thing I bought for the house. A cascade of glass beads. A cooling sound when it gets very hot. It's always reminded me of winter. Bells on the farmers' sleighs in Schlawe. What a beautiful morning! So peace-ful. Saturday, March the sixth. A haze hangs over the sea. La Gomera unrecognisable as an island. A blue haze, floating out there offshore. I can hear children playing in the village. Someone mending fences by the sound of it. Hear it? *Thock thock thock-ck!* The echo adds a syllable. Can you hear the sound? Someone must be putting posts in lower down the mountain. Probably on the Ferguson property. Your father tells me the new owners are rebuilding the terraces. Now and then I catch a scent of blossom on the breeze that comes up around the middle of the day. The plum and apple trees along the coast began to blossom in mid-February. Pink and white. It'll be another week or so before the colour arrives up here. I'm sitting on the terrace, looking down over the avenue of dragon trees leading up to the fountain. Claude will be coming out soon. We'll just let the tape recorder run. We've let you in on all our conversations in the past few years. You've joined us for meals. On one occasion even for a shower. So much more vivid to listen to than read in a letter. Even if I were still able to write letters. You get in all the background. You could hear we were having fun. I gave you the last update on my muscular dystrophy and Claude's Parkinson's in my new year tape. We know we won't be able to continue independently as we've been doing the last few years. Professional nursing, hospitalisation, separation. We don't want to get into that. Being dependent means having someone around all the time. The two of us like being on our own. So now's the time for us to leave ... Claude? Have you got the tray? – Coming! – I asked if you'd remembered the *tray* ... He's getting so deaf, Alex. – Yes, got the tray. Two bowls of apple purée on it, two glasses. Have I forgotten anything? – Spoons? – Long spoons, yes, they're on too. – And the hoods? – Squeezed under one arm. So we're all ready. Where shall I put this down? – On the table between us. I was just saying to Alex that we're letting the tape recorder run. – Well, the two of us did have a discussion about this, whether it was a good idea, and we decided it was all right. – This is a *fest* for us, Alex. That's how we'd like you to look at it. – In a no longer distant future we'll start becoming a burden, first to ourselves and eventually to you. – How can we expect you to cope with such a situation? All of you children living and working abroad. Two of you in England. Max in America. Alex all over the place. – In the old days everyone did their dying at home, with their nearest and dearest around them. I was at my Uncle Louis' bedside in Paris when he died, and it was ... I wouldn't call it a *happy* occasion, but Louis asked for us, and we were all glad to have been there and accompanied him at the end. – When my mother died in Hamburg just after the end of the war it was such a comfort to her to have me and one of her cousins to nurse her. Medically there was nothing to be done for her. And it's a consolation to Claude and me to know the four of you are sort of here when we make this recording, isn't it, Claude? Why should we hide our dying from you? There's so much hypocrisy about death. We all know it has to come. So why not arrange for it to happen before the suffering begins? Why not share it with the family as one used to? Before hospitals intervened. – I wanted to say something about that. Ella and I prefer to be going ... on our own terms, before one begins to ... leak, and the sense of shame sets in. We came to this decision years ago, in fact, soon after George died. But now we've reached this point we can see the risk of stalling. A week more or less, even a day more or less, makes a difference. You can go on putting it off. And then you find yourself in a rush. You need a leeway of ... how shall I say ... in which to improvise ... the right mood, the right occasion, and when it starts rolling you have to seize the moment. – What you children probably

16

don't realise is that the two of us here are kept more or less under *surveillance* by Alicia or Paco or one of their daughters in the village. Someone comes round to see how we are several times a day, often last thing at night. We hadn't realised what a problem it would be to find twelve hours at a stretch without someone checking up on us, which they've done very kindly and conscientiously for the last couple of years, and we're grateful to them for all they've done for us, but ... – So when we heard they were all going off today for a family christening in Santa Cruz, Alicia and Paco, all the children and grandchildren, and would be spending the weekend there, we knew an opportunity had come we were unlikely to get again soon. – They asked us if we'd like them to arrange for someone to look in while they were away, and we told them we had friends staying overnight. – When we saw the way things were going with us, quite some time ago, we wrote off to an organisation called Exit in Switzerland and they sent us a booklet listing the appropriate medications, the dosage, the time it would take, and so on. They recommend eating something light beforehand – apparently it helps you to retain the barbiturates – which is why we've got these bowls of apple purée on the tray ... They said about quarter of an hour between the purée and the pills, Ella, so maybe we should think about doing that soon. – It's easy starting with the apple purée. Often that's all I have for lunch. Only this time Claude has mixed in a sedative. We tried it out once to see what effect it had, and we slept through the whole afternoon! I'm glad we did a rehearsal. It makes me feel more comfortable with the procedure. – This time it's not a rehearsal. Once we've eaten it we're committed. We'll be going on to the barbiturates. Would you like me to put some music on? That bit of Schubert you once said you'd like? – I'd rather just be here with you listening to the garden. – Listening to the garden? What can you hear? – I can hear the palm fronds rustling. I can hear Paco's canaries in the aviary. I can hear the fountain. I can smell the water in the fountain. – Really? It must be all of fifty yards away. But then your senses have always been acute, Ella. Perhaps your sense of smell in particular. – It's because I haven't eaten anything the last two days. – What's that got to do with it? – Fasting makes all one's senses much finer. I found that out when I lay in my room for days without eating anything after George died. In my room I could smell the fountain outside. – Really? How did you know it was the smell of water? – It's something fleeting, a coolness, a shiver, a very fine edge to the air, betraying the presence of fresh water. – Now that you mention it … I remember long ago a monk in Japan who ate nothing for a week, and he told me the same thing, that he could smell the water in the temple spring, but he didn't say what the smell was like. – The smell of a wet stone may be what comes nearest to it. It's the smell of life. Has the quarter of an hour passed? – Another five minutes. – I want to thank the children for showing so much understanding. It wasn't easy for them … George disappearing when they were so young … Claude coming into the family and taking his place … the birth of Alex and the way they accepted him as their brother. Without that we wouldn't have got this far together. – No, we wouldn't. – And I also want to say that if George hadn't shown the understanding he did I would have faced an impossible choice. But we found a compromise, didn't we. Without their help we couldn't have done it. Claude and I wouldn't have had these last years together, which have been the happiest in our life. It wasn't an unhappy life we had before, but the strain of it for me is something you children may never have realised. Having to be there for everyone. Having to hold it all together. I think I did my best. I think we all did. We had a good life. And these years that Claude and I have been given at the end, after George died, when the two of us could be together on our own … I'm grateful for that. Do you remember marrying us in the little chapel on the col above Rémuzat? – I do. – Claude pretended to be the curé from Rémuzat, Alex. You know the story, a little old man, or young man as he then was. They'd sent him down south from some damp place in Belgium. – Liège. – Was it Liège? Anyway, they gave him a posting in Provence to cure his consumption fifty years before, and it did. He lived on and on. He must have been well over eighty at the time we were there. In Rémuzat. It must have been in the 1950s. – 1958. – The curé wore a pair of old-fashioned drawers under his cassock, full of holes – I know because I darned them for him. But that's another story. Can you still do his voice? – I can try. It wasn't so difficult, Alex, because he lisped. We're gathered here today to … thelebrate the joining of two people in holy matrimony … do you, Ella, take thith man, and so on, whatever it was I said. – But *exactly*! Spot on! The curé in Rémuzat. You gave us a sermon. You took him off *perfectly*. – The chapel on the col above Cornillac. – You fell out of a tree. – That was in the Bois de Boulogne. – Still, but for that tree. – But for the smell of leaking gas in my uncle's house. – But for that letter.

18

– In the pigeonhole of Room 7 of the hotel in Rémuzat. – Room 7? Really? You remember that? It was all make-believe, of course, the wedding in the chapel, but when Claude and I parted, he back to Paris, I to London, I felt no less committed to him than I had to George after exchanging our marriage vows in that cold little church in Hampstead in January 1948. I had a second husband. – It's time, Ella. – Before we drink the glass with the barbiturate solution and put on our hoods, I need to say it. I've always been honest and I'd like the children to know. – Time's up, Ella. We do the glasses now. I've given them a good stir. – I *would* have separated from George. Claude was the love of my life. I'd have gone anywhere, done anything to stay with him. I'm very glad I didn't have to, but it doesn't alter the fact that I'd have walked out on George and the children if that had been necessary. That's the truth. I want you to know it. There, I'm ready. How much longer have we got, Claude? – A few minutes. Then we should put the hoods on before we fall asleep. – And then? – Then about twenty minutes before it's all over. – Kiss me, my darling. Hold my hand! – What's that you've got in your other hand? – Just something I keep for comfort. Hold on to me tightly! Don't let me go! It's not dying I'm afraid of, it's having to part from you. – I'm here. I'll be there. – Will you be waiting for me? – We won't ever be parted again. – I'm going numb. Claude? Are you there? – I'll help you put it on ... If the hood feels too tight put a finger in and hold it away from your throat. – Kiss me again before I put it on! I'm frightened! Don't go away ... Promise me you won't go away without me. Can you still hear me in there? – Lay your head on my arm ... like that ... Ella? – I'm so tired ... Can you hear me, Claude? – My darling! – When ... all numb ... all over. – Ella? Ella ...?

# 3

Alex turned off the Kings Road down a side street leading to a square and let himself into the basement flat. Thanks to the reconstruction of the house after it was bombed in World War II, the flat had acquired half of the ground floor above. There was a large bedroom, bathroom and sitting-room suite upstairs, where someone was playing Janis Joplin rather badly on the piano. Max had arrived. Alex caught a whiff of hot water and soap. A trail of discarded garments, beginning at the burst-open suitcase lying on the sofa and leading along the passage up the stairs, indicated that his brother's first priority on getting in from New York a day earlier than arranged had been to get undressed and take a bath. Typical of him to take possession of the master suite upstairs and leave his brother to make do with the rookie bedroom in the basement.

Barely into the house, Alex decided he couldn't face Max at the moment. They hadn't seen each other since their parents' funeral a year and a half ago. Given a day or two to settle in, to change gears to an English environment that had become alien to him, Alex would enjoy sitting down with Max to have the talk that was long overdue. He'd been looking forward to meeting his brother. But Max breezing in like this annoyed him – Max and his graffiti of strewn clothes vandalising memories of the place that were precious to Alex. His mother and father had always kept this flat in such beautiful order. Max would sneer at beautiful order, and they would already be having their first quarrel.

Alex considered leaving with his brother a copy of the transcript he'd made in Vienna. He had edited some passages out of the tape, cutting the references to himself at the beginning because it might make the others feel he'd been given preference over them, ditto the sentences at the end because they were unbearable to read. Ella couldn't have anticipated how the end of the tape would affect the listener. No doubt that was why at the opening she had explicitly left it to him to judge. That sentence had to go out too. He had posted copies to Felicity and Philip. There wasn't enough time to mail one to Max in New York, so he'd brought it with him. He put it on the kitchen table, thought better of it and took it with him when he left the house. Otherwise his brother would know he had been here.

'So where now?'

After decades away from London he felt a stranger in the city where he was born and had spent the first eight years of his life. But after moving abroad and spending ten years at school on Tenerife, even longer in academia, and the next decade as a correspondent based in Vienna, he had become alien, didn't know anyone here any more, not one of his dozens of Morris cousins. Apart from the International Press Association's London news desk, there was no one here for him to look up. His dependable, pedestrian brother Philip in an office in Chichester, a conventional family life in a house in Emsworth overlooking the estuary ... Compared with the prospect of wrestling with war-torn Max, going back over old family battlegrounds in that memory-laden flat he had just turned his back on, the prospect of a trip to the seaside seemed appealing. It occurred to him that it was this staid, commonsensical accountant brother of his who was just the person he wanted to see at the moment

'Philip? It's Alex.'

'Alex! Where are you, you old IPA vagabond?'

Old IPA vagabond had been standard Philipese for ten years. It was an improvement, though not much, on having to hear himself addressed in the third person as the Brother, a mock-facetious name Philip had deployed throughout their childhood despite his objections – demeaning, but he put up with demeaning because he understood why.

'In London. Actually, I was wondering ... I was wondering if I might come down for a couple of nights to see you and Ann and the children.'

'I thought you and Max were staying in London.'

'Well, we are. We were. That was the original plan. But I thought: it's been ages since I last saw Ann and Hilary –' the names of the other two children momentarily escaped him '– and the whole gang down in Emsworth. Good opportunity to come and see you all.'

'Well what a nice idea.' This was more Philipese for subjecting an unexpected and maybe undesirable suggestion to tightened scrutiny. 'Can you hang on just a second?'

His enthusiasm for this rash move already waning, Alex lit and smoked half a cigarette while Philip put him on hold. Then his brother came back with approval from the board, no explanation for why he'd been off the line for so long. No doubt he had quickly called Ann. The pronoun gave him away.

'Well we'd be delighted to see you. As it happens, Denis and Darren are taking part in a regatta over at Wittering, so they won't be around, but the rest of us, we'd love to see you. Will you be down for supper?'

'I will.'

'Give us a call from the station. We'll come and pick you up.'

There was a click. Philip, the former stamp collector, bus timetable addict and trainspotter, now an accountant with a firm of auditors, didn't say goodbye, never had, thought of it as an extra word that didn't pay its way.

That left the best part of a day to kill. Alex got on a bus.

There was also his sister Felicity in Clapham, of course.

From upstairs on the bus he looked down at the streets of London with growing despondency. How shabby and dispiriting this city seemed to him now that he didn't know anyone here.

'I don't belong here any more.'

He spotted another bus headed for Paddington, jumped off, crossed the street and got on it. He was in a state of deep depression when the bus reached Paddington station. He got off with no particular plan in mind, just a vague idea that seemed to hold out a gleam of hope.

'There used to be a quite disgusting hotel here. Back of the station. Generous helpings of soot and grime, genuine mildew on the walls, as I remember. The smell of lavatories and smoke when you opened the windows. The soothing all-night racket of trains.'

This was the gleam of hope. It was the honest admission to himself that any alternative was preferable to spending the next couple of days with any member of his family.

The hotel had shrunk even deeper into decrepitude than he remembered it from their last acquaintance. It stood dark and uninviting at the end of an alley. At the sight of it his spirits lifted.

A sallow, foxy-faced man with thinning hair greased down onto his skull, Ciska's opposite number in London, stood behind his counter in the alcove that served as reception. A sign advertising hourly rates hung over a chequered board with keys slung around numbered pegs, reminiscent of an old-fashioned game of quoits. Alex said he would be staying two nights. The foxy-faced man caused a registration form to appear from somewhere beneath the counter and by another sleight of hand produced from his sleeve a ballpoint pen to go with it. Alex filled out the form, received a key and went upstairs.

Still on the landing outside his room, he sent a text message to Philip. *Urgent assignment Belgrade. Sorry. See you Sat at Felicity's.*

With a sense of long-awaited relief, the gradual release of blood staunched in microscopic arteries, a suffusion of something like peace of mind, he opened the door onto the tiny dark space he had just purchased, a linoleum-floored asylum with a bed and a phone on a chair, closed and locked it against the world outside. No place on earth more private than an anonymous hotel room.

For the next four or five hours, losing track of time as he jogged in and out of sleep, he mourned Ella. Claude too, but it was mainly his

mother, not his father, who flowed out with the late tears now unexpectedly shed after the paralysis of the initial grief. He had got that behind
him. Through the pinprick of the puncture he felt a slow leaking away
of the sadness that Ella was gone. He knew that she had sent him
that last tape to help him cry, and in crying begin to heal. He recited
sentences to himself, not ones he had made up, not quite quotations
either, but ones he roughly remembered having read somewhere, or
perhaps in several places.

'Roughly someone else's words in roughly this order ... In time everything heals. Kübler-Ross? Time heals. It's not possible to live for very
long with too great an unhappiness. We all know this from our own
experience. The passage of time on the clock marks the gradual retreat
of pain from the wound of memory. The hands of the clock are healing
hands. Either the wounded spirit heals with time or it dies.'

When he had listened to himself for long enough, perhaps to himself,
perhaps to someone else, it was getting on for midnight. He took a walk,
bought a sandwich and hung around the station, eating watchfully, as
if he were a late-night traveller with an elusive unscheduled train to
catch. The station surroundings, lacking any immediate urgency, this
moment of stasis between arrival and departure provided just what he
was looking for.

'Besides, maybe she's not gone. So long as Ella is in my mind, so
long as I can imagine her and resurrect her in dreams, she remains. I can
still talk to her. She is only gone when she's no longer passing through
anyone's mind, no longer the occupant of anyone's dreams.'

Returning to the hotel after his reconnaissance of the station, he
unlocked the door onto the dimly lit hallway, the now empty reception
with its keyboard game of quoits. Only four of twenty-one keys were
missing from the board. That made a 20 per cent occupancy, or rather
an 80 per cent vacancy, rate. Who were the three other people in hiding
here?

In his room he unplugged the phone jack and hooked up his laptop.

The file Dead or Alive opened up a portrait gallery of five hundred
people he had photographed across the Balkans in the course of the last
ten years. Some of them were corpses, some of them victims still alive,
the majority of them perpetrators of unimaginable but verifiable crimes
on the wanted lists of human rights watch groups with whom as a
journalist he collaborated. Few would ever be found. But still he did his

homework every night. In hotel rooms between Ljubljana in Slovenia and Pec on the Albanian border, Alex had spent hours scrutinising these images, scrutinising the faces of people who passed in the street by day, looking for a match that he had only once made.

The cursor drifted down to a file labelled Family & Friends. He preferred to enjoy the company of his brothers and sisters without the drawback of them being actually present. He looked at pictures of Philip standing in the sea. Philip and his sons in wetsuits, messing around in boats. Ann and Hilary wrapped up against an evidently cold wind, having a picnic on the beach. It gave him a snug, warm sensation to be looking at these pictures of his brother's family without having to join them on the screen, subject to his own interpretations without the harassment of their real-life intrusions. He was fortunately not in Emsworth with them, nor was he in Belgrade, he was hiding in a hotel at Paddington, a spy in reserve, waiting to be given his mission. He felt a surge of glee.

Roman and Andro in Vienna, Anton in Zagreb, Ivo in Belgrade. Belinda, Mirjana, Seada, Nadja, dark, fair, fair, fair. Whatever her name, the chestnut-haired girl would be the odd one out on this list.

For some reason all his male friends were wearing suits with open-necked shirts. For some other reason all his female friends from the past twenty years didn't have any clothes on. Every time he looked at them Alex was touched by the tenderness of their nudity. Every time he scrolled through these photos he was filled with regrets.

Ella had her own file, even her own sub-file, Hair.

She began with short ash-blonde hair in the early 1950s, wearing a short-sleeved pullover that looked as if it had shrunk in the wash, a faraway look in her eyes. From the lost look it was apparent to Alex that Ella, sitting safely in a back garden of St John's Wood with little Max ensconced on her lap, remained a refugee a decade after expulsion and flight.

In the mid-1950s, with still shorter hair, leaning against an open car at the kerb with her coat collar up and a *mondaine* style that identified the location as Paris even without the background of a slummy Parisian street, she continued as a refugee. Even at the parties held in chateau gardens in the company of Borowski, Kokoschka, Koestler, Nabokov, their smart female companions and their ever-smiling host Prince de

Broglie hovering at Ella's elbow, she remained within a space that was not shared by, and perhaps not admissible to, the people around her.

Ella's Paris period lasted about three months. Sasha Borowski drove her there from London in a Cadillac with the hood up and she had driven him back with the hood down. Or so George had written, but it was too symmetrical a sentence to be true. True or not, the claim had been made and entered into the family ledger. This was a few years after the birth of the twins. She told George she needed a break. But Ella's version was different. The Paris trip was a watershed. Nothing would be the same afterwards. On her return she brought Claude with her.

By the early 1960s Ella wore her hair long in thick clusters over her shoulders. Alex himself, aged four, had helped her measure it with the leather-bound retractable tape measure that lived in the bottom sewing drawer. Alex was allowed to unreel and retract the tape measure by turning the brass winch that folded out of the case and slipped snugly back in. Her hair was long, very long, he couldn't remember how many inches, but it had certainly reached down to her bottom. This was Ella's Hair, something given by nature, just as there was grass on the lawn, birds in the trees and clouds in the sky.

In the mid-1960s she wore her hair up. It was still long, but piled up on top of her head its length was no longer visible or even imaginable. Alex had regretted this loss. For no good reason that he could see, turbans and headgear he disapproved of were permitted by Ella to cover her hair up. Overnight, apparently, the hair came down again for a rest, but Alex seldom saw it because during the down phase of the hair he was asleep.

During the 1970s the up hairdo went through refinements and took accessories on board. By this time George had given up wearing ties and passed them all on to Claude. Ella took over George's tie rack on the two facing inside cupboard doors, where several dozen bands of variously coloured and patterned material hung, one fifth of an inch thick, three inches wide, and eleven inches long.

A compact bun of hair, Ella's own hairs that had got caught in combs, been plucked out and stored in a box until she had collected enough of them, provided the stuffing for the bun that was bound up in a hairnet. Ella pinned the bun slightly to the back of the crown of her head, lifted the long mane hanging down her back up over the bun, plaiting it over the crown and tucking wispy strands at the end of the plait into the hair on either side of her forehead where they were fastened with pins. White-gold clasps she had made to order held the upswept hair in place at the back of her head. The coloured bands chosen to match – how could it have been otherwise? – the outfit she was wearing would be drawn under the bridge-like braid on the crown of her head and buttoned at the nape of her neck.

Once this style of dressing her hair had been perfected to Ella's satisfaction it remained in place for the next quarter of a century. She had invented it herself. It was a hair architecture of unique complexity, and assembling it required a singular dexterity. How was it done? Impossible to figure out unless you'd watched her do it. A hairdo reminiscent of a woman from a remote past. A portrait on an Etruscan urn, from a shard of pottery in Troy, a wall in Byzantium, a beehive-coiffeured head of Nefertiti. There was nothing like it around.

Other qualities occurred to Alex in connection with the exacting procedural dressing of Ella's Hair, which he had watched many times: its formality and discipline, reminding him of her Prussian origins.

After the accident in which George had lost his life and Ella most of her health, Claude learned to braid her hair for her in two long plaits tucked inside her blouse. They still reached down to her bottom but she felt she was too old to allow plaits to be seen.

Gold brocade worn inverted, Claude called this hidden hair, referring to a proclamation of the shogun forbidding Edo's wealthy merchants the display of excessively luxurious apparel, with the result that they inverted their brocade and wore it next the skin.

But Claude had been defeated too. Under his increasingly shaky hands, as his Parkinson's deteriorated, Ella's fine long hair ran away through his fingers like threads of water. They took leave of her hair. *Snip snap*, shorn off just like that, it was the one occasion in Ella's life when she considered going to a hairdresser. In the end she had preferred Claude to cut off her hair. A few bound strands of it made their way onto the baize floor under the revolving pendulum of the glass-domed clock that even as Alex skulked in his Paddington hotel continued its silent revolutions, impartially shedding healing hours on his mantelpiece in Vienna. As for the rest – cremated, burned, ash on the wind blowing over the sea off the coast of Tenerife.

A late picture of Ella showed her with cropped hair much as she had worn it as a young woman fifty years before. Alex let this image rest on the screen while he went out for a walk.

It was half past five. Platforms were being swept by men driving hoover crafts. Sprinkler vehicles zombied through empty streets. Moist, metallic early-morning smells hung in the air in their wake, metallic sounds, the banging of dustbin lids, the hydraulic whine of waste disposal trucks and the clanging when they shuddered to some unseen climax of offloading. To this percussive accompaniment of the city gradually regaining consciousness, Alex wandered down Portland Place and Regent Street to St James's Park, fetching up by the river, where he finally saw the connection.

Long hair might once have been short.

Tomorrow was Saturday. While he was sitting in his sister's house in Clapham with Max and Philip, the girl with the marvellously spreading chestnut hair would be sitting in the Palm House, reading the news-papers over a late breakfast, unobserved by him.

On that still unremembered occasion when Alex first met her, the girl's long hair had been cut off, like Ella's.

Like Ella, he now realised, she was a refugee.

# 4

Felicity slept badly – unusual for her. Shortly before midnight, just when she had got through cleaning the house and preparing the next day's lunch, her older daughter Kim called and spent most of the next hour crying and yelling down the phone. That was on top of a long day at the hospital. Felicity mistrusted sleeping pills, but after a couple of hours, unable to get to sleep, she had taken a sedative and drifted off into uneasy dreams.

Kim was the first subject to come into her mind when she woke. Ratko, the new boyfriend, had beaten her up again. Ratko was only the most recent in a long series of violent boyfriends to whom her daughter was instinctively drawn. The boyfriends, who began in India and Pakistan, continued in the Middle East and eventually arrived in the West, were all woman-beaters. Most, though not all of them, were Muslims. Ratko wasn't, and he, who was also the Westernmost, seemed to be the worst woman-beater of them all. Ratko was Orthodox and came or rather fled from Bosnia after the massacre of his family there. He had been given a residence permit in Britain eight years ago and was still waiting for citizenship.

Did the violence in his background account for the violence in the man? Felicity doubted it, but then what motivation could she have for believing it? Should she inform the immigration board in charge of Ratko's case that woman-beaters made undesirable citizens, and try to have him chucked out? She was tempted to. But deporting Ratko wouldn't solve Kim's problem. Ratko's successor was already around the next corner. In the end, her daughter would always get what she wanted. In the end, her daughter would always turn round and remind her mother of the history of violence in their own family.

It began with Felicity and Stephen in the early years of their marriage. They quarrelled – she hit him – he hit her back – and the sex that ensued had been the better for it. Then they moved on to quarrels with violence but without sex. It was time to seek the help of a counsellor. Felicity thought about the pain that had once been able to give her pleasure in the subsequent reconciliation but no longer did, and that was not something she wanted, either for herself or for Stephen, whom she demeaned just as he demeaned her. After five years of marriage they got divorced. It hadn't been too bad a marriage while it lasted, and the divorce, coming at just the right time, a kind of coitus interruptus shot through with remorse and relief in equal parts, was even better, the stunted marriage's crowning achievement.

Felicity hadn't been tempted to try it again.

After Stephen moved out Janine moved in. A lodger was needed to help pay the mortgage. Janine was a nurse who worked at the hospital where Felicity was an administrator. When Kim and her younger sister Liz grew old enough to want their own rooms, Janine moved into Felicity's room and nursed in her landlady a different sexual preference, to which she succumbed with a sense of gratitude that she could now be shot of men altogether. Big and strong, Felicity's transition to becoming something of a butch character had turned out to be easy. She cut her hair short, favoured smoking cheroots and wearing big-buttoned red waistcoats, arriving at parties with her arm protectively around the thin shoulders of her companion, the petite and slender-hipped Janine.

And here was the problem with Kim – she didn't move on. Kim went back again and again to the boys who would beat her. In a disco

28

full of men she could smell out the ones who would, and she went and danced with them.

Then she was on the phone again to her mother, turning to her for comfort in her unhappiness.

What was this mystery, a girl committed to making herself unhappy? Making a life for herself out of misery?

The psychologist Felicity arranged for Kim to see told the parents that she lacked self-esteem, lacked it so fundamentally that only when abased did she feel something like herself. In Kim's abasement lay Kim's identity, said the psychologist. Well, there you were – or might be, thought Felicity. To her mind, six of one made half a dozen of the other whatever it was worth. Allowing abasement as a working hypothesis, what had triggered such a peculiar mechanism? What was the spring that set it in motion? What for? How did one get rid of it?

Both Felicity and Kim were suspicious of something schematic and predetermined in the categories enforced by psychological analysis, the way it pulled identical stuffed rabbits out of identical empty hats. They deplored the theoretical bias, the lack of closeness to individual life. The therapy sessions were discontinued.

Felicity resented the criticism of herself that was implicit in Kim's pursuit of unhappiness. Had Felicity managed things better, Kim wouldn't be in this condition – that seemed to be the message.

But it was wrong. It just wasn't true.

There was her other daughter, Liz – as even-keeled a young woman as you were likely to come across. Only thirteen months apart from her sister. Subject to the same treatment, same influences, same mother's love, same divorce. Felicity had no doubt that if two girls could turn out so differently, it must be because each of them had forged her own fate from the materials at hand – from something in herself, then, not something she'd got from her parents.

Could it be that Kim missed her father as Liz apparently didn't? That little bit older and more conscious of what was going on, had she been hurt more? Had she felt Stephen's departure from the family to have somehow been her fault? Or her mother's fault? Was it this that doomed her to continue re-enacting dramas of hurt, pain and self-punishment as ritual offerings on her father's altar? Was her daughter practising some kind of atonement for her mother's actions, even believing that she performed them on her mother's behalf?

These never-ending thoughts harried Felicity out of bed in the mornings without her having reached a conclusion, no prospect of consolation other than a long hot shower.

Sitting alone at the kitchen table with her coffee, Felicity missed Janine, the distraction of Janine's company allowing her to escape from herself. But Janine was tactfully spending the weekend with her mother so as not to be in the way of Felicity and her brothers.

It seemed to be an inescapable law that children made parents responsible for whatever went wrong with the children's lives. What Felicity had done to her mother, her own daughter was now doing to her.

Felicity had solved her problems with Ella by keeping them to herself. Ella was no longer required or, depending on the point of view, allowed to partake in her daughter's life. Effectively, Felicity had shut Ella out of her life.

And now, a year after her death, Ella was reaching out of the grave to take her revenge. There it lay on the kitchen table, the transcript of a tape recording Ella and Claude had made of their suicide on the terrace of the Arguayo house.

Felicity wept when she first read it. She read it a second time with dry eyes, a third time with rising indignation culminating in the anger that she needed for self-justification.

'What a tasteless stunt for the two of them to have come up with! Poor Paco! How grotesque! What a monstrous thing to do!'

It was the first thing Felicity said to her twin brother when she let him into the house. Philip knew without asking what she was referring to. He had been sent a copy by Alex too.

Interested but impartial, the same truth-testing frown on his face he had worn as a congenitally doubt-ridden constipated child – an expression that had regularly driven his father out of the room – Philip listened to his sister letting off steam. It was Claude's contributions – his *chiming in*, Felicity called it, always in Ella's slipstream, never venturing out to risk making the going himself – which had particularly irritated her. Philip picked up Felicity's copy of the transcript that was lying on the sofa and flipped through the pages.

'But it's really just the one passage here, isn't it? *I would have separated from George. Claude was the love of my life. I'd have gone anywhere, done anything to stay with him. I'm very glad I didn't have to, but it doesn't alter the fact that I'd have walked out on George and the children if that had been necessary. That's the truth. I want you to know it.* And so on. Well, we already did know, thank you very much. Nothing new about that. It's nothing new to me to learn the three of us were a disappointment to Ella. How can one's own children be such strangers? This was always the tenor of it, even if she didn't always trouble to say it to our faces. I hear her saying it, even when she didn't. Not good enough for her. Do you remember the word *kleinbürger* she used to hurl at me? Why at this late date does it upset you, Felicity?'

Following her own thoughts, Felicity was only half-listening as her brother paced up and down.

'We had it all out, years and years ago,' Philip continued. 'Everyone spoke their minds before that disastrous party we had on the island – and that was it. We were *done*, Ann and I. Finished! We were never truly on speaking terms again. Well, I wasn't. I know you and Max still went out to visit them after George died. All right, so it was Ella's sixtieth birthday, *and* the fortieth wedding anniversary of Ella and George, but so what? And the hypocrisy of it! What did Claude have to do with *that*? Forty years of what? Ella's bigamy with Claude, George dishonourably relegated to second place. His fault to have allowed it. Whose marriage was it? Never understood why he put up with that. He was Ella's puppet. What sort of a wedding anniversary worth the name are we talking about?'

'Ella always spoke her mind, Philip. One's used to *her* being judgemental. But coming from Claude – I felt really let down. What a sneaky thing to do – and not giving us a chance to answer back.'

Felicity snatched the file out of Philip's hands.

'Here. *And it's a consolation to Claude and me to know the four of you are sort of here when we make this recording, isn't it, Claude. Why should we hide our dying from you? There's so much hypocrisy about death. We all know it has to come. So why not arrange for it to happen before the suffering begins? Why not share it with the family as one used to? Before hospitals intervened.* A comfort to Claude and me! That was Claude saying goodbye to the three of us. Who's he to talk? He wasn't our father. And then they go and try to put the blame on Dad: they dump him, they dump us, with that stuff about … Here it is. *Claude and I wouldn't have had these last years together, which have been the happiest in our life. It wasn't an unhappy life we had before, but the strain of it for me is something you children may never have realised. Having to*

31

*be there for everyone. Having to hold it all together.* It wasn't an unhappy life we had before! Well thanks! That's us done!'

Felicity hurled the file across the room.

'I bet you it was Claude who put her up to it.'

'Anyway,' said Philip, unimpressed. He cracked his knuckles. 'The mover behind the scenes has so far managed to escape the full fury of your flail. Who do we owe all these revelations to? Who is the benefactor we have to thank for contriving this stagy end or at least bringing it to our attention? And what are his reasons for having done so?'

'You mean Alex?'

'The Brother himself. What is his role exactly? Do we take his word for it that the tape was sent to him by the police? Only now? Do we trust his transcription? Is it a coincidence that this thing has arrived just as we all meet here to discuss the terms of the will?

'I've no idea and frankly I don't care. I have no quarrel with Alex. Would you like some coffee?'

'No, thanks.'

Philip frowned, irritated by his sister's unexpected lack of interest in a subject close to his heart. 'Anyway. You asked me to come earlier so that we could talk about the houses before the others arrived. Well, go ahead.' He took a folder out of his briefcase and waited for her response.

The subject of George and his houses on Tenerife had caused a lot of soreness in the family. While the children were growing up they had lived in St John's Wood and then in Richmond, where they went to school and from where George used to commute to central London. George gave up his job at the Foreign Office and bought himself a writer's hideaway in La Orotava. The picturesque Spanish-colonial town looked down over Puerto de la Cruz on the north coast of the island. But Ella wanted something more suitable for the children when their father was readmitted to the family, so George had acquired in Ella's name a grand old house just outside a village called Arguayo, overlooking the west coast of the island, where the children spent their holidays. That was the second property. The third was the apartment in a new tourist resort near La Caleta on the north-west coast, which George bought so that he would be able to leave each of his children a property on the island. He distrusted shares and believed real estate to be the only dependable form of investment.

Back in England, after Max, Felicity and Philip had moved on to boarding schools and George was increasingly holed up on the island as a freelance writer, the family home in Richmond was occupied on a regular basis only by Ella, Claude and their son Alex. To keep down expenses, the big house was sold and they moved into a pied-à-terre – George's expense-down-keeping word – in Kensington. All four of the children except Philip had later lived in the flat while studying in London. George, Ella and Claude stayed there when they were in town.

Between George's purchase of the properties and the death of Claude and Ella forty years later the value of the investments had increased twentyfold. Each of George's three children by Ella would be left a house or an apartment on Tenerife. Alex, her son by Claude, would inherit the property his father had bought in San Cristóbal de La Laguna, where Claude became a professor at the university on his return from Japan. Which house should go to which child was a topic frequently discussed in the family, without the beneficiaries ever managing to come to an agreement. After George's death, it was left to Ella to decide who should get what and draw up a will that settled the matter.

Ella felt it was fair for the biggest house to go to the biggest family, represented by Philip, his wife and their three children. But the biggest house, near Arguayo, formerly a bishop's residence overlooking La Gomera on the west coast, had for many years been very much the family home away from home for all Ella's children, for none more so than Felicity. She was emotionally attached to the house and the neighbouring village, to the bricks and mortar, the oasis of a garden Ella had created on an arid hillside, the spirit of the place. Nothing else would do. No compensation to Felicity could make up for the loss of the house. Her daughters had partly grown up there and thought of it as their home. But Philip wouldn't back down. The quarrel with her twin brother led to rows between them – this was the subject Felicity wanted to get out of the way before the others arrived.

By the time Ella died – just after the perhaps more considerable impact made on her son by the late advent of yachts in his life – Philip was beginning to change his mind. Inland houses no longer interested him, and by island standards the Arguayo house was inland. A small flat like the one in La Caleta on the north-west coast of Tenerife, with two snug bedrooms the size of cabins, a dark cupboard of a kitchen that could only be improved by calling it a galley, above all by its access to the sea in two minutes – this was now the house after Philip's heart. How convenient it would have been if Felicity had been left this property — he and she could have just swapped houses. But Felicity had inherited her father's stylish apartment in an eighteenth-century colonial mansion in La Orotava, while the smallest property, the modest apartment in La Caleta that Philip wanted, had gone to Max, the brother who was still a single man — and Max wasn't interested in swapping with Philip.

'In any case, what does Max want that house for?'

Philip frowned.

'La Orotava would suit him much better. Urban, sophisticated — trendy little eateries, bars, all those things Max enjoys about living in New York, and with the best view in the world.'

Felicity shook her head.

'There's something about the La Caleta flat which Max gets a kick out of.'

'Gets a kick out of?'

'That may not be the right expression. I've no idea what it is. Something secretive. I don't think he ever spent more than a couple of days there. When I asked him he just shrugged his shoulders and gave me one of his nasty smiles.'

'And how did he respond to your suggestion that he might like to do a swap with one of us?'

'Well, I brought it up when I spoke to him on the phone last week. And he said he wouldn't dream of it. He didn't owe either of *us* any favours. That's what he said. Straight out like that.'

Philip mused.

'You know what? It was a mistake of me to let Max know just how much I would prefer to have inherited the place that's been left to him. He doesn't really want it for himself. It's only to spite me. That's what he gets a kick out of. Out of getting his own back on me for his failure to get on with George. As if that was my fault. Dad and I were never such a great team either come to that.'

'No, but you and I were. We were twins, don't forget. Dad thought we were adorable. For the first years at least. And Max was only two. He'd had the stage to himself and now he was suddenly out of it all. That's when things began to go wrong with Max, and between him and Dad. Jealousy got to him. He hated Dad for having passed him over in favour of us. Forget about doing a deal with Max. You swap with me instead. I get the Arguayo house and you get the apartment in La Orotava.'

Philip frowned.

'Look,' said Felicity, confronted with Philip's frown. 'You can get down from La Orotava to the marina in Puerto de la Cruz in, what, twenty minutes or so. Is that so different when accessing your yacht from the flat in La Caleta? A difference of fifteen minutes maybe.'

'Plus much more substantial harbour fees, plus parking, not to mention all the hassle of getting the boat in and out to sea from that jam-packed harbour. If it weren't for that clause in the will preventing us from selling the houses we've inherited within the first five years I'd get rid of it and buy something that suits me better. I can't wait five years.'

'Take my advice. Behave to Max as if you'd come round to finding the La Orotava apartment the very thing you wanted after all. And on the market it must be worth more than any of the other properties. Remember Tom Sawyer whitewashing the wall? Like it wasn't a chore he had to do but a lot of fun? Knowing Max, when he sees you enjoying life up there he may want to move there himself. Max likes having buzz around him. He'll soon get bored in La Caleta. Play your cards right and it'll be Max coming to you, saying he's changed his mind after all.'

Philip pursed his lips. The frown deepened into a scowl. He was about to say something carefully worded to his sister when there was a short impatient buzz at the front door several times in quick succession.

# 5

Max leaped through the door like a dog that had been kept waiting too long outside, nudging it open with its snout and rushing in at the first crack. Behind the haystack of hair confronting her and the advance guard of laughter that cleared Max's way into the room, Felicity could make out the dangling figure of Alex still short of the porch, reluctant, or perhaps it was just his shyness, hanging back several steps behind his brother. He's put on weight, Felicity immediately thought, and simul-taneously, *Could Aids be the reason why Max by contrast looked so thin?* So stringy and hard-ribbed his body when she came up against him — was that new or had it always been like that? And this bubbling over with inane merriment — was that genuine or did Max have some trick up his sleeve, some prank he was about to spring on them? All waggy-tail and dog-eager, he was already moving on to Philip as if set to lick him all over, his brother's bulk still rising, so sudden was Max's entry, from the sofa on which he'd been ensconced, Max bounding over and gripping Philip by the shoulders as if to haul him to his feet. He clapped him on the back, perhaps as a preferred alternative to giving him a hug, gargling cries of delight like a moaning halfwit incapable of coherent speech. This had been more or less standard greeting protocol for as long as Felicity could remember, ever since Max had been, in Ella's phrase, a rather highly strung or, in George's sterner words, a chronically overexcited child.

It took a while for this flurry to subside. Under cover of Max, Alex slipped into the room almost unnoticed, greeting his sister and his brother with more restraint than Max but also more warmth conveyed to the addressee personally. A welcome from Max was like being visited by a tropical storm, leaving you to sort out the pieces. Thwarted as ever by his own good intentions, overdoing things, Felicity thought. What a shame, dismayed by the oddness of Max, she saw more clearly than ever an unmanageableness that caused people to throw up their hands and back off Max as instinctively as they took to Alex.

'Taxi!' screeched Max.

They looked at him uncomprehendingly. Was he about to leave? He'd only just come.

'I get out of this taxi and the moment I open the door guess what I see standing right beside me? This little fellow, this little Alex of mine. Hello, brother mine, I say; where did you spring from then? And he says, off the 397 bus or something, takes you right to the door. Bus! He flies in to London from – where'd you fly in from, Pooky?'

'Belgrade.'

'From Belgrade and then gets on a bus, for Christ's sake.'

'Well what's so remarkable about that?' Felicity asked irritably.

Philip stirred in the background. 'Where did you fly in to, Alex? Heathrow?'

'Yes.'

'The 397 doesn't go anywhere near Heathrow.'

'True, Philip. How do you know that?'

Philip frowned. 'You forget that London bus routes used to be a bit of a hobby of mine.'

'And train timetables. Yes, I *do* forget. Well, since you ask, there's a coach service to Waterloo and you pick up the bus there.'

Philip smiled with a hint of malice. 'Correct. And how was Belgrade?'

'I found Belgrade pretty much as the NATO air strikes left it five years ago – still lots of bomb sites, destroyed Danube bridges still not repaired. It's a pity that Belgrade intervened. I'm sorry not to have got down to see you and Ann and the children. How did the regatta go for Darren and Denis, by the way?'

'They won.'

Felicity interrupted this shadow-boxing by asking them if they would like a drink before lunch, leading the way through the living room to the glass patio she had recently had built onto the back of the house. Max strode out into the garden as if expecting acreage, and seemed surprised to be brought up short by a wall with a plant growing on it.

'What's this thing? Surely it can't be cotton you've got growing in the garden, Fellatio?'

Felicity hurried out and took him by the arm.

'I don't want to be called by that name again,' she hissed into his ear. 'D'you hear? We've put all that nonsense behind us, Max. *Long* ago. OK?'

Max laughed. 'All right. So tell me about this seemingly innocent plant, its predatory feeding habits, its obscene nocturnal activities.'

'Well I don't know. It's just some sort of *bush*, and the dried stuff on it is what's left of last year's flowering, isn't it? Now what would you like to drink?'

'Diet Coke with a shot of tequila.'

'I haven't got tequila or Diet Coke.'

'Whisky and regular Coke will do.'

Philip and Alex looked on from the patio.

'D'you think he's on speed or something?' Philip asked.

'No no, just underslept, jet-lagged and on a jig, you know, the way Max so often is.'

Felicity came back inside and unnecessarily clapped her hands to get everyone's attention, declaiming in a loud voice as if there were a hundred people sitting there waiting for lunch.

'There's beer and wine in the fridge, buffet on the sideboard, plates and glasses here, so please help yourselves.'

Lunch drifted away on little puffs of small talk, dilatory exchanges of family news while everyone was waiting for some intervention from Max, some new stunt, but Max had gone quiet. He had his nose buried in the pages of something he'd picked up off the living-room floor. Felicity lit a cigarette, put the packet back into her pocket but had to take it back out again and pass it on to Alex and Max when they raised their hands to indicate they wanted one too.

Philip got up with a groan, picked up his chair and carried it outside. 'Can all you self-destructors in there hear me for as long as you remain alive? Good. Then if you don't mind I'll start.'

He sat formally facing his brothers and sister, who looked out from the smoke-filled auditorium of the patio at Philip, enthroned on his little stage lawn, their chorus, ready to unveil for them the Greek tragedy about to begin. He opened the folder on his lap, cleared his throat and adjusted his spectacles.

'As you know, probate has finally come through on our parents' will, and as the family accountant it is incumbent on me—'

'Objection!' It was Max making at last the move they'd been expecting. 'Our parents? What sort of incumbent language is this, Philip?'

'Objection sustained,' Alex felt bound to add in support of Max.

'Are we a board meeting or something?' Max continued. 'In which case, how about Mr and Mrs Morris? Who authorised you in any case? But since we are their *children*, how about something a little more – parent-friendly? – like Ella and George or Mum and Dad. What say, Philipino?'

'You know what I mean, Max.'

'No, I *don't* know.'

'It's just that in my capacity as accountant as opposed to son – and look, Max, you're all expecting me to deal with this fairly and objectively, which is what I'm trying to do, so if all the thanks I get is to have you hectoring me –'

'Hectoring you? D'you mean heckling you?'

'– from the moment I open my mouth, then you can get stuffed.'

Max pondered this as if he might take him up on an interesting offer.

'I'm on Philip's side,' said Felicity, getting red in the face. 'What's the slightest contribution you've made since Ella and Claude died, Max? Have you volunteered to help sort anything out – houses, rental arrangements, paperwork, publishing contracts, legal business, that endless

38

investigation of the Spanish police – what have *you* done about any of that? Or Alex for that matter. Of course you both live abroad, so Philip and I got lumped with it all. Now that's all right. But it's fucking well *not* all right when you start getting on your high horse and telling us how we should be dealing with a business that is no concern of yours. You've no right.'

'But it *is* my—'

'No, it's not. You've opted out. If it'd really been your concern you'd have shown you were concerned with it by taking on a responsibility for it, and your responsibility has been *nil*. So shut up and let Philip get on with it.'

'Max quashed,' said Max good-humouredly. 'Objection overruled. Apologies, Philippic. I won't butt in again.'

Philip pulled his ear lobe, as red in the face as his sister.

'As I was saying. The will covers three main items: the houses on Tenerife, the London flat and George's royalties. George and Ella suggest – they don't stipulate – that the London property is sold and the proceeds divided between us, the four beneficiaries from their will, according to the market value of the Tenerife properties at the time we inherit them – i.e. now. Those of us with more valuable properties on Tenerife would receive less, and vice versa. According to this scale, I would receive least, the flat in La Orotava being the most highly valued of the properties, and Alex would receive most from the sale of the London flat – that's minus 40 per cent inheritance tax, of course. As for the royalties on George's books, his agent Putnam & Hawkes tells me that over the last ten years, since the publication of his last book, the annual income from the books still in print has gone from a high of thirty thousand pounds ten years ago to a low of five the year he died, or an average of eight thousand for the last five years of his life.'

'Eight thousand?' queried Felicity. 'How on earth did they live on that?'

'They didn't. After George's death Ella and Claude lived off Claude's salary, later his pension. They had an investment portfolio with an offshore bank on the Channel Islands, which was managed by financial advisers based in Malta – all rather complicated due to European Union tax regulations I don't want to bore you with. Well, when Dad took me through the figures the year he died, that port-folio was worth half a million pounds. That was fifteen years ago. My understanding was, and I think this was what George wanted me to understand, that this sum was a stand-by in case of emergency; current expenses were generally covered by the earnings from his books, and the half-million would go to us when they passed on. Well, to cut a long story short, all that money's gone.'

'Gone? Where did it go?'

'It went on maintenance of the Tenerife properties and the one in London. Even that wasn't enough. Ella and Claude chose to die when they did because that was when the money finally ran out, is what I guess. A five-year trust in which the bulk of their money was invested matured in 2000, at a value of around one hundred thousand pounds, meaning a guaranteed annual income of thirty thousand in cash, plus whatever the declining royalties brought in, for the last three years of their life. Claude latterly had to borrow money and pay the interest from his pension. That was how they timed it. Keep up the properties, pay your way for $x$ number of years and then make an exit without a bean in the bank.'

'There was no life insurance?'

'No life insurance. Or rather, there was, but it was cashed in at a loss and the proceeds gobbled up by all those hungry properties.'

'But for years they had let the properties in La Caleta and Laguna,' Alex put in, 'and even the apartment in Orotava, after George died. They must have had a lot of money coming in from all those rentals.'

'The outlay for the renovations necessary in order to let those places cost more than what the rentals brought in. It'll be years before they start paying their way. And there was still another property unlet, don't forget, in London, draining away money, just standing there. Renewal of sewage pipe, for instance – that's x thousands gone for nothing you're ever even going to see. The idea of the Arguayo property as a going agricultural concern never stood up. The place has been haemorrhaging money for I don't know how long. Effectively, Paco and Alicia have been privately subsidised farmers more or less since George bought the place, and that's *way* back. Madness, in my opinion.'

Felicity got up to fetch another packet of cigarettes, evidently shaken by these disclosures.

'But – I mean – one had always understood George and Ella to be, well, if not exactly *rich*, at least very comfortably off.'

'I think that in George's heyday they were. But that was twenty years

40

ago. The illusion was sustained by the fact that after George's career went into decline they could still rely on Claude's salary. Claude's will left everything to Ella, by the way. As things stand now, it's not just that they left no money; as far as I can see, even the proceeds from selling the Kensington flat may not be enough to cover inheritance taxes. And it's all complicated by the fact that the properties we have been left are not in this country. I've no idea what debts they may have left here and on Tenerife. I can't say for sure, but we could wind up having to pay for our inheritance.'

A long silence followed this conclusion until Max put up his hand.

'May I cause trouble again?' He grinned. 'You should take a look at yourselves in a mirror. What downcast faces all round! No money left in the kitty! How dreadful! Wicked spendthrift parents – oh dear! What a miserable lot you are, brothers both and sister mine. We're hardly into the house and Philip gets his account books out, plus this and minus that, totting it all up, as if wills and stipulations and liabilities and whatnot were our most pressing concern, our *only* concern.'

Alex squirmed on his chair. 'I don't know about that.'

Max reached over and tweaked his ear.

'Then a pretty good imitation, I'd say. I mean, Philipino can take out the ledger and tot up the accounts, and you, Pooky, can sit there listening with your heart in your mouth, and that's a *choice* you've made. All right? It's the thing you do first because it's what matters most. Why aren't the three properties on the island making more in rentals than they cost in repairs? You brought that question up because it worried you. You've taken Philipino's budget-balancing to heart – tacitly maybe, not happily, to be fair, knowing you, but unless you're heard to object you assent to making this paltry business of squaring the accounts your own priority too.'

'I didn't hear you objecting, Max.'

'Because I'd just promised not to butt in again. Well I am now. I had to wait and see where all this was leading. *My* priority would have been *this*, which I found lying on the floor next door.'

Max held up the copy of the transcript that Felicity had hurled in exasperation across the room.

'Forget about the money that isn't there – *this* is what Claude and Ella left us. This is the final tally we should be talking about, not all that maturing portfolio boogie-woogie and market-value crap.'

41

Felicity lit another cigarette. 'All right. So why don't you make a start, Max. What d'you suggest? Sackcloth and ashes?'

'I've nothing to lose. You all know the record. Unlike you two, I was always on much better terms with Claude than I was with Dad. I didn't get on with George and George didn't get on with me. I was a bad son to him; he was a bad father to me, and we wisely went our separate ways. His death fifteen years ago didn't affect me in the least. No, I'm not doing myself justice. My reaction was: good riddance. For my part, I'm *glad* if George didn't leave me any money. I would've been tempted to take it – OK, I guess I *would* have taken it – but I wouldn't have been happy about it. I would've felt I'd been bribed. So having nothing in the kitty lets me off the hook of a bad conscience, and I can go on feeling comfortable with that conclusion. The apartment in La Caleta, well. I can't sell it for five years. What good is it to me now? How often is a photographer scratching a living in New York going to be flying across the Atlantic for vacations on Tenerife?'

'Well quite, Max. So why don't you do a swap with me?'

'I suppose I could let it,' said Max, avoiding a direct answer to Philip's question, 'but I won't because it's George's house and George still lives there.'

'How d'you mean, George still lives there?'

'Because for me Dad isn't dead. I wish he were. He goes on living in me and making life difficult for me. I'd much rather he didn't, but he does. I'm stuck with him. So why not make the most of being stuck together and torment him a bit? After the months I spent living in Fiji I know a bit about voodoo rites. Far more effective when carried out at a site intimately connected with the victim. The guy still spooks me. And that's *my* priority, what I've found out during the fifteen years George has been dead: I'm *not* shot of Dad after all. But if I can keep him in that house and give his spirit something nasty to think about it'll make things easier for me. That's Dad's place. I can handle him there. I can keep him under lock and key. And that's the other thing. Ella never lived in that house. Never visited it. Never even went near it. She *hated* that house. So all the hate residue lingering in the house doesn't contaminate Ella, if you see what I mean.'

'No,' said Felicity, put off by the voodoo business, 'I don't have a clue what you're talking about.'

'What about Ella?' asked Alex. 'Isn't she still around for you? Doesn't she live on?'

'Not really. I don't think so.' Max mused. 'Dad took it all and left nothing for Ella. She doesn't live in that house with Dad. She's not in the picture. She left it long ago and went to live in another picture with Claude. For me Ella's dead. But unlike George, Ella's death *did* affect me. I knew I'd lost something that mattered to me. I mourned her. I did miss her. I felt sorry for her, because George gave her a tough time. She had a tough life trying to balance all those things. She says so on the tape. She was happiest those last few years alone with Claude – she says that too. How close those two were together. How wise of her and Claude to have made their exit together. Whereas George is still around because he never went. That's what I heard on that tape you transcribed, and it was right of her to have said so.'

Unable to remain sitting a moment longer, Philip got up.

'Well you seem to hear some very peculiar things, Max. I only recall George's name being mentioned on that tape in a completely different connection. *I'd have walked out on George and the children if that had been necessary*, says Ella. What's she got to complain about? She could have her cake and eat it. All her life. Felicity and I were disgusted by that tape.'

'You've never forgiven her, have you, Philipino. You should think about it. Mum's nature was generous and forgiving. Your nature is small and narrow. We all know we sometimes found her impossible to deal with, a bit of a tyrant, a pedant who always knew better and thought she was right. But basically she was on our side, wasn't she? She was the one with the human interest, the genuine caring not just about us but about anyone and anything – Alicia's grandchildren, El Salvador and Somalia, the San Fernando postman's feet. She forgave us our bad behaviour on that disastrous occasion, as Claude rightly called it, fifteen years ago. She let go, and so I could let go too, and she was gone. But Dad didn't forgive. He didn't let go. He gave me no blessing. George is still holding on to me, still giving me hell – and now I'm going to move into his house and start giving *him* hell.'

Philip looked at Max with contempt.

'You're an acid head. You're completely crazy, you know. You're completely fucked up.'

Felicity put a hand on Max's arm. 'Holding on to *you* perhaps, not

43

to us. For my part, and I think Philip's too – I can't speak for Alex – George is long dead and gone.'

She got up and put her hands on his shoulders.

'Parents pass on, Max. Isn't it you that's not letting him go? You're fifty-four. If you're still not free of your father at the age of fifty-four then that's unfinished business you can only deal with yourself. Whereas for me … my unfinished business is with Claude.'

She wandered around the table, absent-mindedly dabbing at wine stains with her napkin.

'I felt Claude let us down. His moving in when we were children ruined life at home for me and Philip. That's why we wanted to go to boarding school. I felt disgust at his cowardice, his conniving with Ella on that creepy tape and scooting off without confronting me in person, not giving me a chance to respond.'

'Yes, he did,' said Alex. 'It was just that you didn't want to respond.'

'How can you respond to someone who's dead?'

'He gave you the chance before he died.'

'Really? I didn't notice.'

Felicity began clearing the table. Philip came in from the garden, flapping his hands to clear the smoke, and wordlessly helped his sister carry things into the kitchen. Max and Alex took the hint and moved out into the garden to smoke. No one said anything. There seemed nothing left to say.

# 6

Brothers – not that they really knew each other.

Max called to the barman from the table where they were sitting.

'More of the same for me, landlord. One with a bit more snarl to it. A stinker. And another of those feeble-minded Belgian piss-alley beers, what's it called – Grolsch – for my wee brother cutting his teeth here.'

Four words raised question marks in Alex's mind here: *landlord, stinker, wee* and *brother*.

He was still trying to gauge Max's use of English. During the years he'd spent abroad Alex found his own use of colloquial English slipping. Those noiseless changes of gear in conversational English, shifting from one plane of idiom to another, hedging your bets, foxing your opponent, playing hide-and-seek behind understatement or irony – Alex could no longer play this game unselfconsciously and wondered how well he had ever been able to.

Max was scrutinising him, thinking: *Always was a serious little bugger.*

'You always were a serious little bugger. You still take yourself too seriously. I'll do a workout with you. How about it? Help loosen you up.'

He gave his neck a friendly squeeze.

'What's on your mind, Pooky?'

'How strange it is to be listening to you acting up this English pub routine and doing so in an American accent. OK, after thirty years in San Francisco and New York. But I'm wondering where the real you is.'

A moody girl in jeans hung with chain mail arrived at their table with a Bloody Mary, Max's third, and a second pint of Grolsch for Alex. She asked if they were ready to order their food yet.

'No. And do try a smile for a change,' he said to the barmaid. 'The real me,' Max continued in the same breath, 'is in always saying what I think. Try me. Ask me another.'

'All right. Was there anything particular on the tape – in the transcript – that surprised you?'

'Yes, that stuff about the mock marriage. Claude doing the priest-bridegroom combo in one person. Didn't know about that. I'd have liked to have been around at that marriage and signed the register as a witness. I can imagine it. We didn't often get to see it, but Claude could be a lot of fun.' Max exhaled. 'The impression I came away with was that Ella felt she and Claude had been left in the lurch by us during their last years. As if right up until the very end there could be no reconciliation with the Morris family, no understanding for Ella having lived such an unconventional and independent life. I wish I'd called her more often, come over to visit more than I did. She's right when she complained she was writing her letters into the blue, an emptiness where no one was listening any more. I did listen, but – I don't know – maybe I no longer had much to say myself. She always had so *much* to say. I was the one who had got old, not Ella. I loved her letters, but they reminded me of my inadequacy.'

'What d'you mean?'

'Ella was always 100 per cent about whatever she did. She was a perfectionist, and she expected you to be one too. Well, none of us were, of course – fiddling around, half-measures, satisfied with less – like everybody. It was bound to be that she felt in the end she'd given an awful lot more to people than she ever got back from them. It was bound to be that she was going to feel she'd been hard done by. That becomes the refrain of the later years. It wasn't publicly aired, but I know that's what Claude had to live with.'

'I got to hear some of it too. That she'd been taken for granted, taken advantage of. That she didn't get what she deserved from life. And particularly from her children.'

'You always excepted, eh? I think, true enough. But beyond that – this is fine tuning, maybe *too* fine – I hear a disillusionment with people. *All* people – we can extend this. Mankind generically. Whose paltriness it had taken Ella most of her anything but paltry life to find out. Well, was that their fault or hers?'

'I don't know that it was anyone's fault.'

'Typical Pooky, always avoiding confrontation.'

'Typical *Max*, always seeking it.'

Max grinned again.

'Well, you remember, or maybe you don't – I'm sorry, but you've always seemed to me such a tiny little kid, hell, ten years younger is a *lot* – how George used to call Ella the Princess on the Pea. Or he did when I was a kid, but by the time you arrived maybe he'd quit calling her that. Princess Pea for short. That was the story, the Andersen story called "The Princess and The Pea", about the girl who told the poor folks who found her in the wood or somewhere that she was really a princess, and needed an awful lot of mattresses – like about, *twenty?* – piled on top of each other, in order to be able to get a good night's sleep. And this crafty old dame comes along and secretly slips a pea under the bottom mattress. OK? That's the *real* test. And in the morning she asks the girl how she slept, and the girl says just awful, there must have been something under the mattress and I'm black and blue all over. So the poor folks know she's the real thing.'

Alex looked at him blankly.

'Well,' said Max, 'that's Ella for you. Just too sensitive a design – and she did come from a very posh background.'

'Her grandmother used to tell Ella that she was the first commoner in the family in eight hundred years.'

'Eight hundred years! Well there you go, Pooky. She'd outlived her time. Overly fine-tuned, *un*paltry, too … *porous* for the knockabout conditions of ordinary life. She had no block function on her console; she couldn't screen stuff out. It was all so banal. It all got through to her – everything. That paltriness of people, that banality, as Ella felt it, and maybe *rightly* felt. But that's how it is, the middle-of-the-road, run-of-the-mill ordinariness of life – well, godammit, it *is* ordinary, and if you think it should be something else then the only choice you have in the end is to lump it or leave it, and Ella chose to leave it.'

'Princess Pea was still current when I was growing up and you had already gone to America. But I haven't heard it for twenty years. Funny you should bring it up. I found myself thinking of Princess Pea again just yesterday as I was walking along the Thames.'

Max leaned all the way over the table until his forehead was almost touching his brother's.

'Another regrettable case of collateral damage in unintended places, Mr Foreign Correspondent? Or just a slip of the tongue? Since when has the Thames flowed through Belgrade?'

Alex was stunned.

Max sat back with a smile. Leisurely, he drew a cigarette out of the pack on the table, groped for a lighter in his pocket and lit the cigarette without taking his eyes off his brother. He was going to enjoy this.

'International Press Association, eh. Famed for the accuracy of their reports. The truth, the whole truth and nothing but the truth. I'll tell you one thing, brother mine. It wouldn't have been good enough for Ella. She would have put it in that class of generic behaviour by which she felt so disillusioned that in the end she preferred to take her own life.' Max exhaled and raised his glass mockingly. 'To paltriness!'

Alex squirmed. He'd been found out. Sometimes he hated Max – what a smug bastard he could be!

'I could sort you out in two shakes,' Max went on. 'I could *destroy* you, if I had half a mind to. We all play our roles. In our family, you were the goodie and I was the baddie. Fellatio and Philipino are knocking around somewhere in the middle. You and I are the extremes. But does that make us opposites? What single idea matters most to you in your life? What's your headline?'

'Headline?'

'Ella had one: *Avoid paltriness at all cost! Die rather than live a banal life!*'

'And do you have one?'

'I do. *Say what you think! Never lie!*'

47

Alex felt miserable.

'Now if I were Ella,' Max went on, 'I'd tell you that you were in the wrong job. I'm not interested in your reasons for pretending to be in Belgrade when actually you're in London. No concern of mine. I'm sure they're banal reasons in any case. But if you think you can be Mr IPA in the morning and tell whoppers in the afternoon, Pooky, you're deceiving yourself. You're footing your life on a lie. Is this perhaps new to you? Did this connection never strike you?'

Alex said nothing.

'Do you concede that I have a point here? Isn't this something along the lines of what Ella might have said if she were sitting here?'

'I suppose it might be.'

'So what's your life motto?'

'Fairness, decency.' Alex fumbled. 'Respect for other people's dignity. Something like that.'

Max dismissed all this with a wave of his hand.

'How can you respect other people's dignity, as you call it, without respecting your own? And how can you respect your own if you have to tell lies to justify what you do? If you have reasons to be in London, why say you're in Belgrade?'

'Does it matter?'

'In the world of paltriness no, it doesn't matter, people in paltryland lie all the time.'

'Then I guess I live in paltryland.'

Max shook his head.

'You don't get out that easily. You can't live there and uphold a commitment to the truth at the same time. You *do* have a commitment to the truth, don't you? Hasn't sorting out the lies from the truth been the business of your life for the past ten years? Isn't that why you left your sheltered university life and became a war correspondent? Isn't that what you told me yourself at the time?'

'My professional life, yes. My private life is another matter. Look, I lie easily, habitually, and unless I'm caught out it really doesn't worry me, because it just makes life more manageable. They're small, unimportant lies. They make things easier for me without making things more difficult for someone else. The lies just slip away and I don't think twice about them afterwards. As you said, Max, that's how it is, the middle-of-the-road, run-of-the-mill ordinariness of life, where most of us live,

48

whatever you say, because we've come to terms with our contradictions, knowing there's nothing we can do about them. And why should we?'

Max nodded.

'So that's your motto. Don't think I like you less for it, Pooky. Don't think I'm criticising here. Just clarifying. Because we both go for accuracy, OK? The motto is *not* respect for other people's dignity. Allow me to correct you. It's: *Telling lies makes my life more manageable.*'

'One can do both. The one isn't in conflict with the other.'

'So do you respect other people's dignity easily, *habitually*, the way you tell lies? Which of these activities would you say you devote more time to?'

'Having to sit here and go on with this conversation makes me realise how you must have driven George up the fucking wall. I can understand the dislike he felt for you.'

'George. *But not Ella.*'

Alex tried to come up with a riposte and failed to find one.

'George spent all his life lying. And by your own account so do you. Almost everybody does. Apart from myself, Ella is the only other person I know well enough to say for sure that neither of us ever told lies. Serious lies. OK, we may have slipped up here and there. Which is why she respected me. And she did. She may not have loved me the way she loved you. But then she may not have respected you the way she respected me. What d'you think, Pooky?'

'I think all this is a detour around the subject of your envy.'

'We'll come to the envy. All in good time. Do you carry on with the things you were brought up to do? Do you make your bed in the morning before you leave the house, like Ella taught you to do on pain of death?'

'On pain of death, I still do. Or let's say I still have a bad conscience when I don't.'

'A made bed may be a good thing to have ahead of you at the end of the day. Who knows at the beginning of the day under what circumstances you'll be returning to it? You may be with someone you're hoping to share it with, or you may be required to show it to the secret police who turn up in your apartment without warning. An unmade bed may get you a life sentence. Such things have been known to happen. Remember Sasha? You should; you were named after him. Sasha's unmade bed stayed unmade for ten years. As Ella liked to think she said, readiness is all. But what use to anyone is a bad conscience? It's just a form of masturbation. Do you still jerk off? How often? What passes through your mind when you do?'

Alex said nothing.

'I take that to mean yes. Look, we can bring an end to this conversation, which is driving you up the wall, if you agree to answer one question. I will take yes or no for an answer and not press the matter further. Because my contention is that the small habitual lies that don't matter pave the way for the big one that does. The whopper that puts a bullet through your integrity, undermines your self-respect. Then you lose it all. Brother mine. Did you ever have sex with our mother?'

Again Alex was speechless.

'Come on, Pooky. Silence is the most infantile form of response. Yes or no?'

'For Christ's sake, no!'

'All right, all right. Don't get so excited about it. It's not that big a deal. It would *become* a big deal, however, if you had lied about it. Then you would be in denial of what you had done, which is the birth of evil. Then the serpent comes slithering into the garden.'

Max ordered a club sandwich with an extra side order of chips and laid into his meal with appetite. All that Alex could manage after Max had put him through the mangle was a cup of coffee.

On their way back through the drizzle of streets Max took his brother by the arm and tried to shelter him under his broken umbrella. He told him about the tenement where he lived in the East Village, the half-crazy Indian who lived opposite with a bad leg condition that confined him to his room, always badgering Max to call his son who lived in New Jersey to ask him to come and visit his father, the Chinese family of four, a litter of tidily industrious mice living in the single room down the corridor, the Hell's Angels chapter across the street, who ran the neighbourhood. He told him about the nearby loft studio, bought by a cooperative of freelance photographers to which he belonged, which they had set up in Tribeca twenty-five years ago, before it became fashionable and real estate prices soared. The studio was an asset, said Max, a gold mine in reserve for the day they put the property on the market, but that didn't alter the fact that he'd never cut it as a photographer.

'As a young man my lack of success troubled me. OK, I got some early breaks like the Aids series that ran in *Life* and lots of other places, but that had less to do with my being a great photographer than with my happening to belong to the gay community in San Francisco when the story broke. And then there was the war stuff I did all over the place. But I wanted to do straight pictures of ordinary people in ordinary situations in a style that was recognisably mine, and I didn't cut it. They weren't distinctive enough. I tried to compensate by spending money on the kind of lifestyle I associated with success – lots of boyfriends, restaurants, razzmatazz, an apartment in a chic neighbourhood, until I ran up debts I couldn't pay off, and I had to turn to Ella, behind George's back, for help.'

'I remember George and Ella talking about you buying into that Tribeca studio project in the late 70s when I was still going to school in Puerto, and there was a lot of money involved, and they were worried.'

'They had reason to be. I failed financially. But more serious than that, I was living a lie. I pretended to be one of the hip photographers doing fantastic commercial work in the 80s, but I wasn't. At least I realised that. So I pulled out of the Tribeca group and radically downsized, moving into the one-room studio on 1st and 3rd where I still live. Once I began living in a low-key style in keeping with my meagre income, *and*, it has to be said, my meagre talent, once that balance had been found between the way I was and the way I lived, my lack of professional cachet ceased to bother me. I enjoy taking pictures of people. Either clients pay me to do so or I do so for my own pleasure. These are ends I can just about make meet. I'm poor, but that has its advantages. Being poor gives you moral leverage. You get rid of illusions and a lot of ballast. The only thing that matters, Pooky, is not to get caught up in living a lie – that's when the rot sets in.'

The drizzle increased and became a steadily drumming rain on the canopy of Max's umbrella. A lot of it made its way through the holes. They were soaked by the time they got back.

It was cold in the flat. Max switched on the electric fire. He took off his wet clothes and wandered around the room, draping them to dry over chairs and lampshades. He sat on the sofa in his underwear, nursing a glass of whisky.

Watching him, Alex wondered about the bits of Max's New York life Max so far hadn't mentioned. The missing bits always interested him. This came out as a blurted question: 'Isn't there anyone you love in your life?'

'There used to be. He died a few years ago. Like so many of his predecessors.' Max winced. 'How about you?'

'There are girlfriends. They come and go; most recently go. I don't know ... I'm forty-five.'

'Time's wingèd chariot. That SUV is still on the roads, a lot more wingèd these days, I'd say. It all goes so much faster. The familiar middle-aged panic. You'd like a family, Pooky? Wife, kids?'

'I think I would. At least, I used to.'

'Strollers in the porch, mortgage on the house, hellish holidays on Tenerife? Wall-to-wall carpets of lies?' Max lit a cigarette. 'The whole package?'

'I don't know about hellish. Or about the lies. What is this with you, Max? You can't keep off the subject.'

Alex watched him and wondered about his brother's preoccupation with lying. He had observed that what people picked on to criticise in others often revealed their own shortcomings. Did Max only harp on about lies because his own life in New York had been founded on a lie – as he said, his pretending but failing to make a living as a photographer? Why had he left San Francisco and gone to ground in Tangiers? Did the lie only leave you when you were down and out? But why should it leave you? Perhaps it continued, or it came back in another guise and Max hadn't noticed it. Perhaps people short of everything but hope were more susceptible to illusions, more likely to splurge on dreams.

Max looked tired. His face was drained. So worn, so thin! Now the day's energy had gone out of him he looked ill.

'I don't know that you want to hear about this, Pooky. Isn't there something dry you can get me to put on?'

'There's an anorak of mine in the closet.'

'That'll do.'

Alex went and fetched it, his youth hanging there in the closet, mothballed by Ella. It was his old skiing anorak, bright red. There was a clip-on hood to go with it. He had been proud of the anorak then. He was too fat for it now.

'Dig the hood.'

Max clipped it on and pulled the garment over his head.

'Max the red rapper. How do I look?'

'OK. Have you got a cigarette?'

'Pants pocket, left.'

'How come you called Felicity Fellatio? And why was she so uptight about it?'

'I guess anyone would be, remembering how she used to suck her elder brother's dick.'

'She did that?'

'She wanted the sixpence.'

'What sixpence?'

'George used to give me a shilling a week pocket money. Kids were cheaper in those days. Well, I gave the sixpence to Felicity if she sucked my dick. Look, I was six or seven and she was five or something. It was the sort of game kids play at that age. But that wasn't how George saw it. He told me I was a nasty piece of work and thrashed the daylights out of me. And I got sent away to boarding school, for life. Well, the porn magazine that gave me the idea in the first place was hidden at the back of George's shoe cupboard. That makes sort of a dramatic story, with clear character outlines, plot development, motivation and so on, but it doesn't really count.'

'What does?'

'What counts is realising that the nasty piece of work was just a pretext. George didn't like me, never had. I was the wrong delivery. It only showed after Felicity and Philip were born. Here's that envy you brought up earlier. I could see the way he enjoyed being with them, but that it got on his nerves when I was around. George, as you know, or maybe you don't – you're not his son and in any case you got preferential treatment – was very good at disapproval. He could stand there like a lighthouse, not saying anything, emitting flashes of disapproval visible from distant points on the horizon. He could switch the deep freeze on and turn you into a block of ice. Naturally he had to pretend he liked me. If only for his own benefit. Much more of this pretending goes on than you seem to realise. Just put yourself in the guy's position. There's his first son, and he finds out he doesn't like him. I mean, that's tough. And it turned out I didn't like *him*. I don't think I didn't like him *in return*, tit for tat, as it were. I didn't like George for himself. Mutual antipathy. Fact of nature, perhaps unnatural. With Claude it was different. We got on well.'

'But didn't Ella stand up for you?'

'Sure she did. There was a terrific rumpus when I got bumped off to school against my will. She even threatened to leave George. In fact,

53

Ella's disappearance to Paris at the time was the upshot of that row. But George gave her the third-degree cold treatment, the full-frontal of English arrogance. This is just after the war, OK? Ella wasn't allowed to forget she was just a refugee. Worse. A *German*. A penniless displaced person, and but for the grace of the Morris family, et cetera. Who incidentally had been upstart Hungarian imports themselves only a generation before. I felt I had to rush to her defence. It was terrible to see her humiliated in this way. And so I said I'd changed my mind. About this boarding school deal. So that she wouldn't lose face having to back down.'

Max got up and went to the cupboard to get a drink.

'Like anything, Pooky? Not a wide range of choice.' He chuckled. 'Jesus, this is a museum of a drinks cabinet. How about a toddy of vintage port? A slug of Benedictine? Pimm's, for Chrissake!'

'I'm OK.'

Max wandered around the room in his brother's red anorak, clutching a small blue bottle. He took a swig, put it on the mantelpiece and performed a sort of dance in front of the fireplace, crossing and uncrossing his legs in the air, pointing his toes and doing little capers.

'Courtly old Spanish dance,' he panted, crashing onto the sofa. 'Executed by men within a floor space of about one square yard. May look easy, but it's a tough act. Dancing on one spot. Really takes it out of you. Guy from Salamanca taught me long ago. Old guy I met in New Orleans. A tailor. Still amazingly nimble. When he danced he reminded me of a tailor who could sit and sew cross-legged in mid-air. He told me he'd fought in the Spanish Civil War.'

'You looked like a goblin casting a spell.'

Max glanced at his watch. 'Christ! Four o'clock! Goblin's got to go before break of day.'

'What time's your plane?'

'Gate closes at seven thirty. How long in a cab to Heathrow?'

'At this time on a Sunday morning you'll be there in an hour. Are you packed? I'll make us some coffee.'

Max was already halfway up the stairs.

Alex went into the kitchen and looked in the fridge. The Nescafé in the tin looked years old. No one who had been here since Ella's death had bothered to replace it, and at one time or another all of them had been here. He put the kettle on and opened a tin of condensed milk he found in the cupboard. There was another tin in the cupboard with biscuits in an advanced stage of decomposition, wreathing fantastic cobwebs of mould around the inside of the tin.

Max came into the kitchen with a backpack over his arm.

'I suppose I always had a dirty mind, Pooky. I was always a degenerate. But then isn't that a wholly natural state of affairs?'

Alex put two coffee mugs on the kitchen table.

'No, I can't say that it is. I called a minicab, by the way. It'll be here in fifteen minutes.'

Max went to the back door and opened it.

'It's still raining. There's drizzledom for you. Goodbye, England, and good riddance.'

He stood looking out at the rain-soaked basement steps for a moment before shutting the door.

'The thing is, Pooky, people really have no idea who they are. George, for example, thought of himself as an honourable man, but he was a professional liar. We know he was a spy, one of his lesser renditions of lying, incidentally.'

'We don't *know*, but quite probably he was. And perhaps George thought the vocation of a professional liar was an honourable one. I don't know how you like your coffee. Help yourself.'

His brother sat down wearily at the table.

'He had a personality that was only viable as a forked existence involving endless self-contradiction. Lying is a forked existence, bifurcation. Whether it occurs deliberately or out of an innocent unawareness or willing collusion, our inexhaustible capacity for self-deception, lying is at the root of all things. And the family is the breeding ground of lies in human relations. Families are for teaching us to tell lies. The family lie is the prototype of all those habitual little lies – I seem to remember you calling them that – which grease the axle on which the world turns.'

Max showed no intention of spooning Nescafé into his mug and pouring water into it, so Alex did it for him.

'That rather sounds as if lies might be necessary.'

'It does or, rather, it would seem to.'

'So why have you been picking on me then?'

Max pulled the strings under his chin and tightened the hood.

'Because you are the one Ella thought of as her inheritor. In your flesh, not in mine, not in Felicity's or Philip's, she would live on. Know your own mind and don't lie. You are her trustee, the fiduciary of Ella's memory. She must have said something to you to that effect. There must have been something in addition to the will. Didn't she leave you a note or anything?'

Alex stirred his coffee and thought for a while.

'It's uncanny the way you suss these things out, Max. There was something, the wind chime.'

'Three hundred and sixty-five million, twelve thousand and thirty, three hundred and sixty-five million, twelve thousand and thirty-one, three hundred and sixty-five million, twelve thousand and thirty-two ...'

While Max sat mumbling to himself, Alex got up and wandered around the kitchen.

'I don't know if you remember the wind chime that used to hang over the door leading to the back terrace at Arguayo. Well, Ella recorded it on the tape. It's the first thing you hear.'

He looked at Max sitting bowed over the kitchen table, like a monk, a hooded figure in his anorak. What was this bowing business? What had he got up his sleeve this time? Alex looked at him warily and waited for him to interrupt as usual. He was so used to being interrupted by Max that he was expecting him to say something, but Max didn't. He just sat there with his head resting on the table.

'The sound of the wind chime is the first thing you hear on the tape,' Alex repeated, 'and then Ella talking. She says, *What a beautiful day.* At any rate, that's the edited version I gave you and the others in the transcript I made of the tape.'

His brother's continued silence made him uneasy.

'As a matter of fact Ella *did* say something, after the wind chime but before she says, *What a beautiful day.* I left it out because it was kind of a personal message. She says, *Will you ever hear this, my dearest Alex. I wonder. That's the chime above the terrace door. I wonder if you can hear it ...* That's all. But I felt ... embarrassed that it was addressed to me personally. She's speaking to me, by name. Otherwise, you know, it's as if we were eavesdropping on the conversation between the two of them. I left it out of the transcript and a couple of other things too, because I thought they were unnecessary, things that might hurt you, or Felicity or Philip. The fact that there was a personal message for me and not one for any of you ... So I suppose yes, I misrepresented what Ella actually says on the tape, if only by omission. You might call it a lie. I leave that for you to judge. Not that it was a secret or anything. I'm telling you about it now, after all. I just left out a couple of things in case they upset any of you.'

Max had nothing to say to any of this.

The buzzer rang in the hall at the bottom of the stairs. Alex went through and answered it.

'We'll be out in just a minute. Thank you.'

He came back into the kitchen.

'Max? The cab's here.'

His brother was still sitting bent over, his forehead resting on the table. Alex noticed his arms hanging down motionlessly beneath the table.

'Max? Are you all right?'

Alex put a hand under his shoulder and eased him into an upright sitting position. But Max immediately toppled sideways and crashed down onto the bench.

'Jesus, Max! What's wrong with you?' he implored his brother, knowing full well what was wrong with him.

Max was dead.

# CHAPTER TWO

—

# East of the Elbe

## 1

Ella had to stand on tiptoe on the balcony of her grandparents' apartment to see over the parapet. She looked down at a truck in the street. Bundles of clothes stacked on the pavement were being tied up and tossed onto the truck. Old clothes were being collected for the poor, Granny explained. Ella wondered why the poor were being given old clothes rather than the new ones she knew they needed. Poor people and old clothes went together. She'd seen them often enough, waiting in a line outside the employment exchange she passed with her mother whenever they went into town. Would the same people be waiting somewhere in another long line to be given the old clothes?

She had other memories of events that must have happened earlier, memories she might treasure more, but her life seemed to begin with this one in Berlin, on one of the rare visits to the Andrzejewski grandparents. Her mother and father had separated when she was a year old.

A bowl of fruit, exotic fruit, oranges and bananas, stood in a bowl on the table beside a plate of candies. They were on the same level as her eyes. Ella stood by the table with her hands behind her back and looked at them in awe. Don't touch. But she could look closely at them without touching them. Such fruit on the table! And in winter! Bowls of fruit and plates of candies! Luxuries unimaginable in the house where she lived with her grandmother Cosima von Sieres in the country far away from Berlin.

Ella never learned much about the Polish side of the family. What little she learned was confusing. Although they had bowls of fruit and candies and were well-to-do, they didn't have real traditions, time-honoured ways of doing things like her mother's family did. As Grandmother Cosima later explained to her: the Andrzejewskis were commoners.

Ella's father Leo thought the Andrzejewskis took their name from a place called Andrzejóws in Poland. Whether they had been the landowners of an estate there, or a peasant family who worked there, he could no longer say. Too long ago, said Leo. Not long enough, said Ella's mother. Maria thought definitely the peasant rather than the landowning family. Had the Andrzejewskis been the landowners of the Andrzejóws estate they wouldn't have forgotten. For a noble landowning family worth their salt, she said, nothing was too long ago. Nothing was forgotten. A camel in the family crest reminded you of ancestors who had taken part in the crusades. Andrzejewski listened to his wife tearing up his ancestry, rolling it into a ball and throwing it into the wastepaper basket, and he rubbed his chin.

All his father could say for certain was that his grandfather had moved from Andrzejóws to Danzig, where he became organist in the cathedral and married a half-German half-Polish wife. His father studied medicine in Danzig, opened a medical practice in Berlin and married a Silesian woman. Although they had retained their Polish nationality, the Andrzejewskis were 'to all intents and purposes' a German family. None of this meant much to Ella as a child. What mattered about her father was that despite her mother's differences with him she always described him as a warm person. She never spoke badly of him after their separation, even if she sometimes mocked his social pretensions.

Her mother used to work as a secretary in Potsdam for an officers' organisation formed by an aristocratic military clique at the end of the Great War. Then her brother had got her a job with Siemens. He shared an office with Andrzejewski, a physicist working in the company's patent department. Ella's mother Maria, a bright young twenty-something, came into the office one day, and for Andrzejewski that was it – he knew he'd just met his future wife.

Bouquets of roses sent by Andrzejewski arrived every day at the Mommsen house in Potsdam where Maria lived. She succumbed to his intense attentions, less a courtship than a siege, but from the way he put his tongue in her mouth when he kissed her she might have known that things would start going wrong. She should have known better. So why did she marry him? He was a hypnotist. Or she was a fatalist. Who could say why? She wouldn't have married him but for that encounter early one foggy November morning, not another soul around, when she was walking over a bridge in Berlin and in the shape of the figure approaching she recognised Andrzejewski coming towards her from the opposite end. At that point Maria knew she had no choice and that she was going to marry him. So whose fault was it after all if Maria knew she had no choice?

Within the month they got married at a register office in Berlin. Only her brother Benno was let in on the secret, signing the register as witness. 'I need a drink,' Maria said as they came out of the office, thinking to herself, *I must have been out of my mind to have married this man*. Somehow Andrzejewski had put Ella's mother under a spell.

At home again with her mother for Christmas, Maria received from the secret husband an envelope on which her maiden name was written, inside it a second envelope on which her married name was written. With aplomb, to Maria it seemed more like indifference, Cosima received the news of her daughter's marriage.

'It's in God's hands,' said Cosima, much to Maria's annoyance, who thought God's hands were the least reliable place to put anything. If it had been in God's hands she would never have married Andrzejewski.

Pah! She snapped her fingers in irritation. So much for God's hands.

Maria would have preferred her mother to have been angry, showing she was concerned about her, just as Ella would later wish the same of her mother. Cosima to Maria, and Maria to Ella — to both daughters both mothers appeared hurtfully unconcerned about them. They felt they were loved less than those children whose mothers made a fuss over them.

Her first child, a son, was a stranger to Maria from the moment he was born. There was something about his colouring, his odour, his wail, or perhaps it was just an instinctive shrinking from this evidence of a marriage she knew to be wrong. It was a difficult birth. He was a difficult child. Oscar had such bad eczema that his wrists had to be put in plaster casts to prevent him from scratching. So mother had no choice but to be concerned about the sick little boy, this troublesome child with whom she felt no bond.

Leo and Maria moved into a rented apartment. Ella's father was soon involved in rows with the landlord because Andrzejewski, who was a communist and believed property was theft, refused to pay rent. The landlord didn't share this view. He took him to court. Maria was shocked and ashamed for her husband. They had to move to another apartment.

Just a year after the arrival of this first child Maria again became pregnant, against her wishes. She went for wild motorcycle rides along bumpy roads in the hope of having a miscarriage. At Easter, in classic slapstick style, she slipped on a banana skin on her way back from the market and immediately went into labour. Her sister Helena acted as the midwife. Actually she was Maria's half-sister. Helena was the daughter of a countess who had married Oswald von Sieres and died in childbirth at the age of nineteen.

The widower married again. Within half a dozen years the second wife, Cosima, had given birth to four sisters and brothers for Helena – Charlotte, Ella's mother Maria, their brothers Benno and Max in quick succession, not counting a miscarriage in between. At eighteen Max attended a military academy and fell in love with a girl one of his fellow cadets had also fallen for. It was a question of honour. They agreed to settle it by drawing lots, a white ball or a black. Max drew the black ball and shot himself.

Things happened in God's hands – birth, death, suicide, divorce. One thought it was the end of the world, but such events passed and were forgotten – the story of all families.

This time the mother's birth labours were brief. At half past four in the afternoon Ella was there, ready-made, as quick and easy a birth as the child would prove to be. She was born feet first, which might have helped prevent the baby's face from acquiring the squashed appearance her brother's had. It may also have helped the mother to love this daughter intensely from the moment she was born, her motorcycle-ride attempts to get rid of the child notwithstanding. The girl who slipped effortlessly out of her this second time in the wake of the mother slipping on the banana skin was altogether different from her firstborn. At the sight of the baby girl who came into the world with shoulder-length coal-black hair, Maria was reconciled with the initially unwanted child.

Maria had Andrzejewski bring her the hare she had bought at the market and was carrying home for supper when she went into labour. Still in childbed, an hour after giving birth, she broke the hare's legs at the joints, cut off its ears, pulled the skin over its head and dispatched it downstairs for the cook to prepare. Born and brought up on a country estate, Maria knew that fresh meat couldn't wait to be skinned any more than a child could wait to be born. Andrzejewski was sent out with the hare's pelt and his wife's afterbirth in a bag to bury them in the grounds of the adjacent zoological garden.

Soon there were arguments between the young married couple. Maria failed to put her fox terrier on the leash when she visited the zoo and had to pay a fine because the dog ran up and down and barked hysterically at the lions, which led to a violent quarrel with her husband – all on account of a wretched little sum of money. It ended with him hitting her. In bed she refused her husband's advances, not wanting to get pregnant again. In a fit of pique at being refused by his wife, Andrzejewski poured a bottle of ink over the baby in its cradle. By the end of the year Ella was born, Maria had already left her unpredictable, choleric, hypnotist husband, taking her two children and going home to live with her mother.

Andrzejewski was very unhappy when his wife left him. His estranged and soon-to-be-divorced wife was the only woman he would ever really love. He never recovered his balance in life, Maria later told her daughter.

But she was a free spirit, and there were irreconcilable differences between them. He was an only child, she one of five. He was imperious, she was self-willed. He was a sophisticated city man, she a country girl. Her education had prepared her to be a wife equipped to run her husband's country estate; a husband resembling Andrzejewski had not been foreseen. He was a political, a communist. She had no political opinions at the time. And he ran after other women. The housemaid provided sufficient grounds for a divorce by admitting to having had sexual relations with Andrzejewski throughout the marriage.

None of this apparent incompatibility had led the couple unavoidably to a divorce. They might still have stayed together. The one difference between them that mattered in the end was that he loved her but she didn't love him.

# 2

Widowed early when her husband Oswald von Sieres died unexpectedly at a young age, Cosima moved from her old family home in Holm in Mark Brandenburg to a rented house in Herischdorf in the district of Bad Warmbrunn, a spa in the mountains of Silesia.

The town belonged to the estate of a count whose family owned ninety-nine villages and was famous for his saying that it was better to be a count of substance than a prince by the skin of one's teeth. And a prince, as Cosima reminded her granddaughter Ella, the count would have been by the skin of his teeth had he owned a single village more. In those days the title was automatically conferred on landowners possessing not less than a hundred villages. The history of the place and the love of it, the lore, the fairy tales, the gossip — all this flowed to Ella out of the inexhaustible repertoire of stories she was told by her grandmother.

Ella's first memories of her grandmother's house were Christmas scenes.

A toddler, she pulled a cart piled with Christmas presents around the second-floor apartment of her grandmother's rented house. There were dolls on the cart her mother had given her but Ella unloaded them in a corner and chose not to play with them. Maria tried to interest her in them without success.

'What a strange little girl, not wanting to play with dolls,' Maria said to her sisters Charlotte and Helena, seeking their endorsement, but they smiled benevolently and watched Ella trundling around with her cart. It was all the same to them if the child played with her cart or dolls. With a phalanx of aunts and uncles around her, Ella was surrounded by a warm, protective atmosphere. Mother was there too, her grandmother, her brother Oscar, whom she dearly loved. No one could ever harm her. She felt safe. Her family formed a cordon around her happiness that no one would ever be able to take away.

Her first views of summer were seen from the perch behind her mother on her bicycle, her arms around her waist, cycling down a path through cornfields, the tips of the corn brushing against her face and tickling her. Ella sneezed with delight. She liked motion. She preferred stillness. She enjoyed watching people do things. Pumping water, cooking meals, women doing needlework, wash days when the whole village was set to work in the wash house. The local farmers emptying the cesspool by hand with buckets, loading the night soil onto wagons and carting it away to manure their fields. The pungent smell of that. The mouldy, blunted smell in the cellar. A sense of excitement going down into the cellar, and up into the attic, piled with old things. The soft scent of the apples that were spread out to winter in the attic, a scent she found somehow painful. How could a scent hurt? When she closed the trapdoor on the specks of dust dancing in the cold air in a shaft of light, she wondered if they continued to dance in the dark.

Ella disliked dairy products, detested cream, couldn't drink milk or eat butter. Her mother said Ella screwed up her face even at the taste of the milk from her breast. Mother was a great believer in health food. What her allergy-prone children ate was prepared specially for them by the cook on her detailed instructions – apple or carrot purée, with a daily spoonful of medicine from a large brown bottle to strengthen their bones and prevent them from getting rickets. Only brown sugar was allowed. Otherwise sweetness was not on the menu. Sweetness became a preoccupation of Ella's. Something she craved was missing from her childhood.

Mother worked as a secretary for Mr Bipphardt, a manufacturer in Hirschberg – seven kilometres of hilly road away, which she cycled back and forth every day. Hirschberg was where Grandmother's ward lived, the man nominated by Oswald von Sieres to look after his wife's affairs in the event of his death. That was why the family had moved here. Mother was out in all weathers. She called it earning a livelihood and making ends meet. In order to make ends meet she had to work hard just to cycle from Herischdorf to Hirschberg and back.

In her mother's attic room stood a large soft mahogany bed. It was half of the marriage bed in which Cosima used to sleep with her husband Oswald. Grandmother now slept by herself in the widowed half of the bed in her room downstairs. On holiday afternoons Maria and Ella took their afternoon nap together. She lay behind her mother, clinging to her shoulders, covering her back, and listened to her long, often melancholy monologues. Then mother would announce, 'The first of us to fall asleep says piep!' and because Ella wanted to win the game she was always the first to say piep! But then she had to lie completely still and pretend to be asleep so that her mother wouldn't find out she had cheated. Often her mother fell asleep before Ella, uttering no piep! to announce she had done so.

The ruminations that Ella listened to in her mother's room were often sad. By nature her mother was a gay person, full of vitality. But things had gone unexpectedly. The course of her life – the early marriage and divorce, the return to Grandmother's house in the country, where she was cut off from the world that interested a young woman – had turned Maria into such a serious person, and the seriousness never left her.

What her mother wanted to talk about with Ella were grown-up subjects of conversation. Taking them upon herself, sharing her mother's concerns, a listener who had no choice about what she was given to hear, Ella absorbed her mother's seriousness from an early age.

Once, she woke up in the kitchen to find someone slapping her face, and the smell of gas made her feel sick. She saw her mother lying on the kitchen floor. What had happened? The cook threw open all the windows and rushed around flapping a blanket. A fire engine came. People ran in and out. There was a great to-do. Cook said mother hadn't switched the gas off properly.

Her mother was so petite and had such a dainty figure. It fascinated Ella to inspect her mother's hands. One of them was much smaller than the other. Why? Mother said she'd been born only eleven months after her sister Charlotte, and probably there hadn't been enough left over to finish her left hand the same size as her right. Why her hands and not her feet?

Ella became aware from half-sentences in Maria's monologues that she felt neglected by Grandmother. Although unspoken, Ella heard it as a reproach. This was what had made her mother a melancholy person. In solidarity with her beloved mother she became reserved with her grandmother. She slipped out of her embrace when Cosima wanted to cuddle her. It was always Ella who got into her mother's bed, always Oscar who climbed into his grandmother's.

In the bottom drawer of the chest in her bedroom Mother kept the presents she bought long ahead of the occasions on which they would be given. Sometimes she anticipated the occasions years in advance. Still a small child, Ella was unable to pull this drawer with its hoard of occasional presents out all at once. She had to toddle back and forth, tugging at one end of the drawer and then at the other. Placed by her mother on the potty in front of the chest, Ella had opportunities to investigate what was in the intriguing bottom drawer. There were extremely desirable things like a spinning top wrapped in liquorice, with pictures of laughing people around the side. There was never any trouble with getting Ella to sit on her potty, as it gave her a chance to take another furtive bite at the liquorice spinning top. Eventually the liquorice top would all be gone, but then another appeared in the drawer in its place.

Regretfully Ella graduated from the potty to the lavatory on the landing halfway down the stairs, where, instead of presents, her mother kept things for physical fitness. Ella desired physical fitness too. She sat with both arms struggling to lift one of the weights she had watched her mother repeatedly raise and lower when sitting on the lavatory. Sometimes Ella overdid the weights. They proved to be too heavy for her, and she toppled off the seat.

'I can't put up with this child any more!' Maria impatiently announced at intervals. The announcement wasn't directed at her son Oscar in person, it was more an airing of mother's views, a statement to the world in general, a public washing of her hands of the boy.

The boy had been influenced by Andrzejewski's physics and communism. He had red hair, freckles, eczema — things Maria found alien. There was no one in her family he took after. Where did he get his red hair? The pedantry of the boy, like his father, his slowness, his thoroughness, his persistence — these things drove his mother crazy. Whenever she took Oscar to Warmbrunn or Hirschberg to see the doctor, he never failed to say, 'There's an ice-cream vendor over there,' pointing it out for his mother's benefit in case she had missed it.

'There's an ice-cream vendor over there' entered the family language as a way of dropping hints.

The nursery where Ella and her brother lived led into the maid's room on one side, Grandmother's room on the other. Sitting astride her mother's lap, being washed by her when she was put to bed, standing in a footbath in the nursery to be soaped down, Ella felt cared for. In the children's bedroom she was always welcomed by the scent of the freshly aired room, where her bed was covered with a quilt incorporating a sampler embroidered by her grandmother as a young girl.

> *Spread wide your wings over me*
> *Oh Jesu, joy of mine.*
> *Should Satan take her in his power*
> *May angels watching over her*
> *Sing in their heavenly bower*
> *'No harm shall ever come to thee!'*

# 3

She went barefoot through her childhood summers, running out with a pannikin, down the road and into the fields, to fetch milk from the farmer or to pick blueberries for supper. The soles of her feet became so hardened that when she ran over the gravel of Countess Pfeil's driveway next door to deliver the newspaper she could do so without it hurting. Country girls' pastimes occupied her – sitting on the steps leading into the garden with her skirt full of phlox blooms she had plucked, sucking out the drop of nectar in each of them and singing to herself. Rain or shine, she and her brother always played outside.

It was women who peopled the house. At seven in the morning the children were got up and dressed by the maid. The monotony of the household peace, the routine of their days, this sameness reassured Ella.

She liked things to have their fixed place and to know where they all belonged. Her own spoon, for example. It lived in the sideboard drawer. No other spoon would do. When it got broken her mother had it repaired. Poor spoon! Along the seam where the silversmith had soldered it there remained a little bump, reminding her of the break, which she comfortingly ran her finger over whenever she held the spoon. Poor spoon was better now.

Grandmother shared her newspaper with Countess Pfeil, and it was one of the children's jobs to carry it from one house to the other. Their reward was to have Grandmother tell them instalments of the serialised newspaper novel every evening in words they could understand.

Grandmother was as much a presence in the children's life as the bricks and beams of the house, where she was always waiting at the window to wave to them when they came back from playing outside. In the winter she moved from the window to the tiled stove, and above the stove, on a string hanging from a nail, there would be two pretzels, one for each of the grandchildren, which they sat nibbling while she told them the day's instalment of the newspaper story. She made albums with collages of cut-out pictures pasted in, the same albums she had used for her own children, and she thought up stories about a brother and sister called Oscar and Ella, weaving into the stories events from their own lives.

Grandmother busied herself every morning with correspondence to friends and relatives. Every day there would be a letter or a postcard for Ella to put in the postbox. As she was too small to put the letter through the slit, her grandmother arranged for two bricks to be placed at the foot of the box for Ella to stand on and so be able to post her letters. She posed on the bricks by the postbox and had her picture taken with a chimney sweep beside her, and the picture appeared on a Christmas card sold in the local shop. The two bricks lay there for years, then there was only one left, and then came the proud day when she needed no brick at all to stand on to reach into the postbox.

A large number of elderly single women, many of them Grand-mother's correspondents, lived in retirement in the Silesian spa, widows of husbands who had fallen in the Great War. In winter they wore black clothes made of a heavy material. White muslin dresses were the rule in summer. Among the widows was one extremely ancient relative of her grandmother, an English countess. Ella's great-aunt Cathy lived to be a hundred. Aunt Cathy was famous for the scent of a perfume which she made herself according to a recipe handed down within her family by a French grandmother who had married in England, where Cathy was born at about the time Queen Victoria came to the throne. The secret of the perfume was never disclosed, but close friends like Grandmother were occasionally honoured with a tiny flask of it as a present.

From the age of three Ella was sent every day to Aunt Cathy to learn to speak English, or rather to listen to it, since Aunt Cathy did all the talking: stories which to Ella sounded like fairy tales, only they were peopled with princes and princesses and ladies-in-waiting. In fact, the stories were about Cathy's own life at the Prussian court after marrying a German prince and moving to Berlin. She told them to Ella in German first and then repeated them in English, and then in English only, so that by the time Ella was six or seven and Aunt Cathy died, Ella had unconsciously absorbed the language and could speak it almost without a mistake. She hoped some day to be told the secret of what was in Cathy's perfume, but Cathy took it with her to her grave.

In the afternoons Grandmother would lie on the sofa under a portrait of her sons Max and Benno and read books in English and French. Ella was impressed and decided she would learn to do so too one day. On the mantelpiece in Grandmother's sitting room stood the clock with the angel under a glass dome. On the stroke of the hour the angel brought his hammer down on an anvil where he was forging a sword. The angel fascinated Ella. She made up her mind that she would one day have a clock like it herself.

There was a baroque cupboard with a glass front, displaying knick-knacks in what Grandmother called her curiosities corner. This was Ella's favourite piece of furniture in the house.

On each shelf stood a collection of personal objects – *treasures*, Cosima said, put together by her in the course of her life. All of them had some sentimental value for her, such as a lock of baby hair of each of her five children, or their first tooth. Each lock and each tooth had a drawer to itself in a chest of drawers hardly taller than Cosima's thumb. The more sentimental the knick-knacks and the stories that accompanied them, the better Ella liked them, such as the pressed flowers that had lain on the graves of friends of Grandmother's who had died long ago. Grandmother took the objects out of the cupboard and told Ella their stories. Gold thimbles, inkstands, tiny knitting needles with which she had knitted as a child. Or the shell as big as Ella's hand, which she asked Grandmother to take out and show her. Grandmother held it to her ear and she heard the sea. What was the sea? She asked Grandmother for stories about the sea, and Grandmother said that in the rustling she could listen to the stories which the sea had to tell about itself.

All these objects were arranged on shelves, only the lowest of which Ella could see when she was little, such as the doll baby's milk bottle with its tiny teat and string of pearls, which had once belonged to Ella's mother. It had been given to Maria by her father to make up for his having forgotten her when she was just a few years old. Because she had been disobedient he put her on top of a cupboard and told her she was to stay there until he returned. But unexpected business took him out of the house and he remained away all day. A father's word was law, however. No one dared to take the child down from the cupboard, where she remained sitting sad and tired until whatever hour her father chose to return. On his way home her father thought of the child he had left on top of the cupboard. Feeling extremely guilty about having forgotten her, he went into a shop and bought her the toy with the pearls to make up for what he had done.

As Ella grew she could see into the next shelf, and then the next, and she grew also into the stories Grandmother could tell her about all the objects on the new shelves. On the top shelf stood a mirror with the back of it facing out. Grandmother told her a story about a beautiful girl who used to admire herself in the mirror every day, and every day, with each glance in the mirror, it had taken away from the girl a little bit more of her beauty, until there was nothing left, and one day the girl looked into the mirror and saw the wrinkled face of an old woman.

From this moment Ella avoided looking in mirrors. Never again, she vowed to herself. Even as a grown-up woman she continued to do her hair without a mirror.

Every morning Grandmother said prayers with her maid, Erna. Erna brought in the breakfast, porridge and coffee, and served it to Cosima in bed. Together they said their morning prayers, Grandmother lying in bed, Erna standing. Cosima read the lesson for the day. After that Grandmother got up and washed, and Erna dressed her and did her hair. She sat on a stool with a barber's cape over her shoulders to have her hair combed and put up by Erna in a plait, wound around her head and held in place with pins.

Each of the hairpins had a name, women's names, Louisa, Margarete, Elfriede, and Grandmother would refer to them while Erna was doing her hair.

'Elfriede seems to be giving you trouble this morning,' she would say, or, 'I think Louisa needs straightening out.'

She wore the same old-fashioned high-collared dresses with the same jewellery pinned to them year in year out, the jewellery made from her grandparents' wedding rings, beaten out by a goldsmith and reworked as brooches. There were rules about what was appropriate, or at least what had been considered appropriate at the turn of the nineteenth century. For the mornings a long dark skirt was considered suitable, worn with 'morning' jewellery and a high-collared blouse that became paler as the year advanced from winter to summer and darker again as the year passed back. Afternoons and evenings Grandmother changed into another skirt and blouse worn with 'evening' jewellery.

When the children were put to bed Grandmother came into their room wearing her evening jewellery and gave each of them her blessing. The Trembling Blessing, Oscar called it, because the hand she laid on top of their heads when she gave them her blessing always trembled. Ella found this trembling hand on her head disagreeable. After Grandmother had given them her blessing, Ella lay in bed and listened to her brother explain a very different world to her, involving lectures on physics and electricity, communism, the stars, all of which Oscar already seemed to know about by the time he was eight.

On Sundays during the summer Grandmother went to Warmbrunn to hear outdoor concerts. The spa had a bandstand in the park where a brass band played for the public in a building that curved inwards, shaped like a shell. On one side of the building stood a kiosk with a vending machine outside, known to Oscar and Ella as the Clucking Hen. The Clucking Hen was the main reason why the children were always willing to accompany Cosima to concerts in the park. Grand-mother never omitted to give each of them a coin to put in the hen to make it cluck and lay them a sugar egg.

During one concert the children pulled the lever without inserting a coin and, to their amazement, the hen clucked and laid an egg. After that there was no stopping them. They pulled the lever again and again, and each time the hen gave another cluck and laid another egg, which Ella collected in her apron. The noise began to disturb the audience and Grandmother waved her stick at them as a signal that they should stop, which they reluctantly did.

For years afterwards Ella had a recurrent dream about the hoard of unlaid sugar eggs inside the Clucking Hen.

Grandmother used to walk around the neighbourhood spearing rub-bish on the point of her stick and putting it in a bag she carried with her. Armed with her own stick and an old sack, Ella imitated her. Another of her habits that Ella copied was to count her steps when out walking. It was a walk of several kilometres to the park, the distance depending on which entrance one used. Grandmother knew the precise distance on all the routes she took, measured in steps. If she was late for a concert, she took the shorter route, if she had lots of time, the longer. To the postbox, the houses of neighbours – wherever she went she could tell one how far it was by the number of steps there.

Ella often crossed the park on errands for her grandmother, taking messages to her acquaintances in Warmbrunn. In the park stood a memorial to soldiers who had died in the Great War. Not more than a few years separated the end of the Great War from Oscar's birth. The Cry-Woman, Oscar called the statue of the stone woman with bowed head, her hands covering her face as she wept for the soldiers who had fallen. There were always people stopping at the Cry-Woman on their way through the park. The women bowed their heads, just like the Cry-Woman in front of them, and the men took off their hats.

Grandmother was a storytelling grandmother who kept the memory of past generations alive. Many of the things she passed on to Ella were about her own family, Ella's family, and in the stories Ella came to know her ancestors in such detail that many of them who had long been dead seemed as alive to Ella as the people around her. The family's past that Grandmother had lived in flowed into the same river of the present that Ella lived in now, reaching forward and back, constant and unchanging through the generations.

'Am I a countess too?' Ella asked her.

Cosima put her head on one side, looked at Ella and said, 'You're my first blood relative to have been born a commoner in eight hundred years.'

What was a commoner? Grandmother explained. Ella objected that if Cosima's blood flowed in Maria's veins, her own mother wasn't a commoner, so how then could Ella be? Because of her father, said Grandmother. Leo Andrzejewski was a commoner, and that made Ella one too. Leo Andrzejewski's blood flowed in her veins too.

Something about her grandmother's preoccupation with the subject of underwear intrigued Ella. She knew that it was in the drawer with her linen underwear that Cosima hid her money, hid all the things she wished to keep secret. Naturally, Grandmother concealed her money carefully. Money was valuable. Money was scarce. Ella heard the whispers about money creeping around the house at night, whispers the children weren't supposed to hear. There was never enough of it. Making ends meet was why her mother was condemned to cycle to Hirschberg and back every day to type letters in Mr Bipphardt's office, back and forth, back and forth, every day for the rest of her life.

# 4

Countess Pfeil, Cosima's neighbour, lived in a mansion set in extensive grounds. Her lodgers, the Acksteiner family, rented the ground floor of the house. It was separated from Grandmother's by a long driveway. In the days of coaches the drive had led up to the main entrance to the house, but it had since fallen into disuse. The old avenue was lined with linden trees. At the end of a dry autumn, the children waded up to their waist through a rustling sea of fallen leaves. The wrought-iron gate remained locked these days, but Oscar, Ella and her friend Medi Acksteiner were still so small that they could slip back and forth between the bars of the gate when they wanted to play in each other's homes.

The countess's property offered more opportunities for play than Grandmother's house. It had a wash house, a gardener's cottage, stables, coach yard and other buildings that in the old days had served various purposes on the estate. It was in one of these outhouses that a washer-woman laid out the corpse of an acquaintance of the Countess Pfeil, a Russian prince, before he was taken into the house to lie in state in an uninhabited wing of the house. Pressing their faces to the window, Ella and Medi could see him in a dark suit with his waxy face illuminated by candles, lying on a bier that seemed to be made entirely of flowers. The prince was their first corpse and they were deeply moved. After all the things they had heard about it in Sunday school they had not expected death to be so beautiful.

One year the linden trees were in bloom when the gardener came to prune them. The branches lay in piles in the avenue, thick with blossom, and out of nowhere a horde of Gypsies appeared to pick the blossom, with which they could make tea. They were swarthy people, all the men with moustaches, all the women in headscarves, dressed in strange clothes and speaking a language Ella didn't understand. The countess had given the Gypsies permission to pick the linden blossom to make tea. They came again the next year and were again given permission to pick the linden blossom, but then they stopped coming. Their encampments were closed down and they moved on. That was the last time Ella saw Gypsies.

Medi was the only daughter of the wealthy Acksteiner family and by Ella's standards she was spoiled. The Acksteiners had a car and even went abroad for their holidays. Medi was the same age as Ella. The two girls became friends. On Medi's birthday Ella was invited along. Mr Acksteiner had to stop the car twice to let Medi out of the car because she had diarrhoea. Her mother said the best way to stop diarrhoea was to eat chocolate. Mr Acksteiner pulled up at a shop in Hirschberg and bought her two bars of chocolate. Ella wished she had diarrhoea too. When she came home she told her mother she had, hoping to be given chocolate, but all she got from her mother was a dose of medicine from the brown bottle.

Ella grasped that behind the wrought-iron gate Countess Pfeil and the Acksteiners lived in a world of their own. Life outside was different. Growing up, ranging beyond house and garden with her brother or often on her own, Ella got to know the local people. How poor they were! How thin! They didn't have enough money for food. Beggars called at the house. Grandmother had them come into the kitchen. It was Cosima's policy to give them food rather than money; money they would just spend on drink, she said.

Money was why the carpenter came round to speak to Grandmother about her coffin. Looking out of the window, Ella overheard their conversation.

'Coffin?' asked her grandmother. 'What do I want a coffin for?'

The man stood twisting his cap.

'Well,' he said, 'let's face it, ma'am. We all know what we need a coffin for. Order it early and you get it cheap. A clean oak coffin. You'll feel better knowing you've got it done ahead of time.'

Grandmother understood the carpenter needed the order to earn some money. She agreed on condition that the coffin would be kept in the carpenter's workshop until she was ready for it.

On her visits to Else Zentner, her grandmother's seamstress, Ella went to the railway workers' estate, where many of these poor people lived. It was like crossing a border into a foreign country. Entering the bare hallway of the housing block, Ella had a prickling sensation down her spine. The Zentners, husband and wife, were what Grandmother called poor folk, and she always found odd jobs around the house for them to do. When Ella sat on her perch behind her mother and they cycled to the local town, she had seen a long line of men waiting outside the employment exchange, year in year out. But at about the time the Gypsies disappeared, the lines of men waiting outside the employment exchange disappeared too.

The novelty of their life, the smells in their apartment, the patterns on the curtains and chair covers, the way they talked: all of these things excited her interest because they were so different from her world at home. It was from these people, their children with whom Ella played, that she learned to speak the Silesian dialect, the different language poor people spoke, rough and sometimes rude expressions Ella never heard at home.

Many of the families who lived in the neighbourhood known as the Russian Colony were also poor people, down on their luck, but it was a different kind of poor. Ruined by the war, impoverished Russian aristocrats — after whom the colony was named — still lived there, with dwindling resources, a dozen years after going into exile from the Bolshevik Revolution.

Countess Pfeil offered hospitality to some of these people, among them an old count and his wife who did puppet shows for children, charging an entrance fee of a few pence. In the case of the deceased Russian prince, her hospitality extended to having him lie in state in circumstances befitting his rank, if not his purse. Baroness von Schwindt, an agitated and extremely thin woman whom the countess invited regularly to her house in order to feed her up, was also down on her luck and lived in the Russian Colony. The baroness suffered from delusions she was being pursued. She went around with a feather mattress strapped to her back in case someone tried to stab her. No reassurances could persuade her to take it off even in Countess Pfeil's drawing room. She eventually drowned in a mysterious deep pool in the mountains, known as the Giant's Spittoon. The police investigated, but whether she had fallen or thrown herself in was never cleared up.

The water level in this mysterious pool daily rose and fell. Ella imagined the body of the dead woman falling and rising with it, the feather mattress uppermost. Or would it have caused her to sink? Had it weighed her down? The changing water level aroused Oscar's scientific interest. They went to inspect the Giant's Spittoon for themselves and consulted their father in Berlin. Andrzejewski thought the explanation must be that the pool was connected via a subterranean channel to the tidal ebb and flow of the distant sea.

One of the familiar local eccentrics was Lisa, known as Black Ida in the neighbourhood for as long as anyone could remember. Was she called this because she didn't wash? Ella was fascinated by Black Ida and at the same time found her a little frightening. She was accompanied by a barrel-organ man on their rounds through the neighbourhood. Her barrel-organ companion was soft in the head. Sometimes he was drunk too. They made a living from begging. While the barrel-organ man stood outside the house and ground out his tunes, Lisa pushed an old pram from house to house and asked for alms. Ella once watched her squatting in a ditch to piss and was shocked that she didn't have any underwear. Wherever Black Ida appeared, she would be teased by the village children. Once, Ella saw them throwing stones at her. Not long after this incident Black Ida and the barrel-organ man disappeared from the district and never came back.

In the attic over Countess Pfeil's disused stables lived the widow of her old coachman, Zinkwart, with her two children Guido and Greta. The widow walked with a limp. Her son cultivated a crouching walk, taking long strides and swinging his long arms like a monkey.

Guido was a few years older than Ella and Oscar. They were impressed by Guido's monkey walk. It made him their undisputed leader. They idolised Guido, did anything he asked. He promised to reward them with sausages, later. One day, he said, he would inherit his uncle's butcher's shop in Hirschberg. Later they would get as many sausages from him as they wanted, but only on condition they brought him food now. Meanwhile Guido would show them how to do the crouching walk with the swinging arms.

Like the Zinkwart family, old Mr Engel lived in one of the rooms over the stables in which there were no longer horses or coaches. The tram conductor did Grandmother occasional extra favours, such as dressing up as Santa Claus. For decades he put in an appearance at the family Christmas, an imposing personage for the children until they saw him slip afterwards into the kitchen to receive from Cosima his Christmas box, money and cigars in recognition of his various services to her. Not the least of them were his kindnesses to her grandchildren. He showed them the barns and stables, which had fallen into disuse, the lofts piled with the discarded sledges that had once been in service around the Tannenberg forest throughout the winter months. Mysteriously he referred to them as his Winter Gallery, perhaps because he thought of the sledges as people and gave them names. Oscar and Ella learned from him all the sledges' names, from the giant sledge called Goliath, which had been used for carting fuel and fodder down the mountain, to the smallest one, a children's toy called David.

At new year, when the house was full of Ella's uncles and aunts, and the mountains were covered with snow, the old sledges were taken out of the lofts and tied together. A horse pulled the chain of sledges with all the family except Grandmother around the zigzag mountain roads

76

of the Tannenberg. Ella must have been only four or five, but persuaded her mother to let her sit on the last sledge in the procession. Being at the end of the chain, it was more wobbly than the others. On one sharp bend the sledge overturned and dumped her in the ditch. Ella got a mouthful of snow. Chattering and laughing, none of the others noticed. Ella's wail went unheard. Sitting all alone in the snow she listened to the bells fading into the distance and thought she would die. But her mother saw the riderless sledge trailing behind, asked them to stop the horse and went back to find her daughter.

'See, I told you – the last sledge was too wobbly for you!' her mother said, took her back to her own sledge and set her safely between her legs.

The house where Cosima was waiting to welcome them seemed so much more warm and inviting when they got back safely after this mishap. There were so many of them that they could all only just be seated round the old dining table, where candles were burning and the traditional new year dish of carp was served. Ella felt happy, snug and secure.

New years came and went but would always remain the same. Nothing would ever change.

But it did change. A few years later Ella's mother remarried and the family moved to Schlawe. Ella lost touch with Medi. In 1938, on her way from Berlin to Schlawe, she came back and visited Medi one last time. Ella was surprised to find the family living in an empty apartment, sitting on packing cases and eating dumpling soup in an atmosphere of deep gloom. They were put out that Ella declined their offer of dumpling soup, which she didn't like, but it was all they had to offer. It was inexplicable to Ella, for she knew in what style the Acksteiners were accustomed to live. The fact that the Acksteiners were about to move might explain why there was no furniture in the house, but the dumpling soup, their grim faces – something peculiar was going on.

Ella heard nothing more from Medi Acksteiner. Like Black Ida and the barrel-organ man and the Gypsies who used to come and pick the linden blossom from the trees along the driveway next door, the Acksteiner family also disappeared without trace.

# 5

Ella's daily walk to school took her along the path by the mountain stream with ice-cold water as clear as glass. About fifty children aged seven to fourteen attended the village school. They were all taught by the schoolmaster, Mr Mayer, in three classes in one large room. He moved around the room from class to class in a black suit, shiny from overuse, his shoes creaking to the accompaniment of the screeching noise of chalk on the slate tablets where the children wrote their lessons.

Absolute obedience was expected and absolute order had to be maintained if the teacher was to be able to do his job. The schoolmaster's complaints to the local council that the school was understaffed, or that he was overworked, which amounted to the same thing, went unheard during the penny-pinching Depression years. Disobedient children were put over his knee and spanked from time to time, if only to relieve the teacher's exasperated feelings.

Apart from poor local children, who formed the majority at school, there were also a few rich children like Medi Acksteiner. These privileged beings were collected from school and escorted home by their nanny. Ella sometimes managed to string along with them. When nanny asked them if they wanted anything from the village store, an Aladdin's cave of treasures ranging from halfpenny gob-stoppers and sherbet pyramids to boxes of chocolates individually wrapped, the rich children amazingly said no. But Ella nonchalantly tagged along with them, currying favour with nanny in case they said yes, and just occasionally there would be some of the rich children's gleanings for her too.

It was her mother who impressed on Ella the need for being absolutely truthful. Mother had given her money to buy a present for Medi Acksteiner, who had invited Ella to her birthday party. Perhaps you could get her some chocolate, Maria suggested. Ella calculated that, with the money her mother had given her, she could buy either one bar of good chocolate or two bars of not so good chocolate. She opted for the latter, giving one bar to the birthday girl, who already had more than enough chocolate in any case, and keeping the second bar for herself.

Somehow her mother found out. She confronted Ella and Ella lied. Ella's lie had made her very, very sad, her mother said. The most important thing in life was not to tell lies. Lies took away the value of a person. They lost their honour. Only a person who never told lies was a free person.

This lesson made a deep impression on Ella. She resolved she would never again tell a lie.

It wasn't easy. But for her craving for food, she might just have managed it. But in the lean Depression years of the 1930s, before she remarried and her financial situation improved, Maria didn't give her children what they would have liked to eat. Maria wouldn't buy food unless it qualified as health food – rye bread, porridge, brown sugar – disapproving of the 'cheap' sausage and sweet things her children wanted. Throughout their childhood Oscar and Ella took an obsessive interest in these forbidden foods.

While waiting for Guido Zinkwart to inherit his uncle's butcher's shop, Ella began raiding the box with her mother's store of pennies to buy sausages. Devouring them cold on the spot where she had bought them, feeling guilty and wanting to dispose of incriminating evidence as fast as possible, became a habit that remained with her long after her childhood ended.

Ella felt uncomfortable about the secret raids on her mother's piggy bank. She knew that Mother could only just get by on the salary she earned as a secretary, and Grandmother didn't have much money hidden in her underwear either. They talked a lot about the Depression. The Depression was something that made it particularly hard for families to make ends meet. Ella decided that she and Oscar should also make a contribution.

On summer evenings, she and her brother went through the woods of the Tannenberg picking blueberries, which they sold to the village shop. In the autumn, they spent days collecting chestnuts and acorns until they had filled their cart, pulled it home and put their harvest into sacks. By the end of the autumn they might have filled several sacks, which they took to the forester. He could use chestnuts and acorns as winter feed for the deer. He weighed the sacks and paid the children for them by the hundredweight. Earning her own money to pay for the sausages and the Clucking Hen's sugar eggs made Ella feel better.

Once, Ella's uncle Benno left his wallet on the train, which he failed to notice until after they had got off. But Ella remembered not only the number of the car; she even remembered the number of the seat where her uncle had been sitting. This information was passed on by telephone to the station at the end of the line, where the railway staff found the wallet exactly where Ella had predicted it would be.

'That child's always attentive,' said her grandmother admiringly. 'She has her eyes everywhere.'

This knack of finding things earned Ella not only a reputation but rewards for her sharp wits, so-called breath pictures, paper cut-outs of insects and birds which she laid on the palm of her hand and blew on, causing the paper bird or dragonfly to stir its wings as if about to fly. Breath pictures were welcome as rewards, but secretly Ella always hoped to be given something else.

A white pullover. How she longed for a white pullover with short sleeves.

When one of the local women gave birth Ella told her mother that the baby had been brought by a stork. 'Nonsense!' said her mother, and she explained to her how these things took place.

Ella never hesitated to entrust her mother with her own secrets either. What she had done with the boy who had told her he would show her something at the rabbit hutch was a secret. Ella had gone with him to the rabbit hutch, he showed her his, she showed him hers. His elder sister caught them at it and gave them a scolding. Puzzled about something she didn't understand, Ella confided this secret to her mother. Once again her mother explained what it was all about, and why the children had wrongly been scolded.

'Respect people, whoever they are' – 'Never do anything you wouldn't do in front of your children' – 'When one's hard up one can't afford to buy cheap!'

Ella took to heart such precepts of her mother's. From the practical woman her mother was, Ella derived a lot of advice that fitted into a short sentence and would later serve her well.

Happily she entrusted herself to her mother's love. On her birthday her brother turned up in the schoolyard with the white pullover with short sleeves her mother knew she was longing for. Maria had told Oscar to give it to her as a surprise during the mid-morning break. Ella felt the happiness of being in her mother's thoughts, of being looked after by her. Mother, not Jesu, was the presence that spread protective wings over Ella.

One autumn evening she was taken for a walk by her mother's old nanny along the foot of the hills. Caught by a sudden shower, they sheltered under a tree on the edge of a vast meadow. The meadow seemed to stretch out forever to the mountains in the distance. They saw a rainbow arcing down out of the sky.

'Look! A rainbow!' nanny said.

Ella ran off. She could see where the rainbow came down in the meadow, and at the end of the rainbow she would find the pot of gold pictured in one of Grandmother's story books. It wasn't far. She could run there and get it for her mother. She ran and ran, ignoring nanny's calls. It was further than she thought. She ran on through the fading light, but the end of the rainbow didn't come any nearer. It was hard to run through the tall grass. Ella began to get tired. Then the rainbow disappeared. She lost heart. She was so worn out that she lay down for a rest and fell asleep.

Nanny had soon lost sight of the little girl, swallowed up in the tall grass. Now it was dark, how would she find her way back? The old woman hurried home and reported that Ella had got lost running off to find the end of the rainbow. The child had been deaf to all her calls. It was in such pretty colours, nanny said in Ella's defence. Mother went round the neighbouring houses and got together a search party. The men went up the road into the hills. By the light of the flares they carried, they could make out the tracks which had been left by the girl in the long grass, showing the way she had taken across the meadow. And there they found her, asleep on the ground already wet with dew. Mother wrapped her in a blanket and carried her home, safe and warm in her arms.

Ella was happy her mother had been so worried about her that she had come out in the night with a search party to find her, and was not cross with her at all. Maria was touched by what her daughter had done, knowing Ella had run off to the end of the rainbow only in order to find the pot of gold that would help her mother to make ends meet.

# 6

In the early summer of 1936, when Ella had just turned eight, her mother married Carl Winter.

Maria met Carl at the public baths in Hirschberg. Both of them enjoyed sports. They were a fashionably sporty couple. In summer they swam together like two seals, twinned in sleek black bathing costumes.

At weekends they went for drives on Carl's motorbike in fashionable goggles and tight-fitting leather headgear. They hiked through the mountains wearing spectacular knickerbockers. In winter they went skiing together. For all this, Mother somehow managed to make ends meet, probably with a bit of help from Carl.

Oscar and Ella saw less of their mother.

Carl had a job as assistant to the district court judge. He was two years younger than Mother. He had just finished his law studies and was about to embark on a career as a civil servant. He was ambitious. To Ella's mother he confided the motto of the ambitious civil servant who wanted to get on in life. 'Live in a house beyond your means, dress according to your means and eat below your means.'

Maria was not quite sure about this, nor did she share Carl's enthusiasm for the National Socialists.

It wasn't long before her mother started calling her young admirer by his diminutive, Carlchen. Letters addressed to her mother in an unmistakable pale blue ink began to arrive almost every other day. Ella kept count. By Christmas her mother had received forty-three letters. Mother smiled over them. Sometimes she sighed over them too.

As an ambitious civil servant Carlchen didn't hesitate for a moment when offered a senior post in the city administration in Stettin, without even consulting Maria beforehand. 'It's only for a year,' he said, but before the year was out he would be given another posting.

If Carlchen got a job with the civil service in Stettin they would all move away from Grandmother's house in Silesia and go to live with him on the Baltic. If Maria married Uncle Carl, it meant that the family would have to follow him around wherever he was posted. It meant they would leave Herischdorf for ever.

Ella was glad that she liked Uncle Carl, because she could see how much her mother liked him. Ella realised that her mother felt more strongly for him than for any of the other men who arrived at the house to take her out. She wanted to please her mother by liking Uncle Carl. She was nonetheless taken by surprise when — it seemed to her all too soon after Carlchen's first appearance on the scene — her mother announced that she and Uncle Carl had decided on the date of their wedding. June was only a couple of months away.

The wedding was held in a little Protestant chapel tucked away somewhere in the overwhelmingly Catholic world of Silesia. Ella strewed flowers on the church floor for the bridal couple to walk over between the entrance and the altar. As if to make up for the modesty of the chapel, the reception was held in the ballroom of a great country house, rented for the occasion from the legendary count who would have been a prince had he owned one village more. Mother appeared for her wedding wearing a silver-grey costume. Ella found it so beautiful she was speechless. In the long summer twilight at the end of the day a horse-drawn coach rolled up to the house, and mother got in with Carlchen. Ella watched the coach drive off through the growing darkness to the station where they would catch the train to take them on their honeymoon.

'Now this day is over too,' said Ella to herself. She sat on the steps beside a marble lion at the entrance to the house feeling very downcast. 'Mama is gone!' she said, stroking the lion's mane.

The day was over and had taken with it something she knew would never come back. For the first time in her life she fell into one of those moods her mother called the Depression. Somehow, Ella realised, she too was now going to have to learn to make ends meet.

Until this moment Ella's childhood had known only an unchanging present in which past and future played no part. She lived in the here and now, with the reassurance that yesterday would be the same as tomorrow, and people and things around her which she had been familiar with for as long as she could remember would remain with her for ever.

For as long as she lived at her grandmother's house in Herischdorf, Ella didn't know what it meant to long for something. Her mother's departure, the family's going away from Herischdorf, left an absence in what Ella had used to feel as whole. From then on she was waiting for something or somebody to fulfil her, for she felt she was incomplete. A sense of longing had arrived in Ella's life that she was sure would never leave it again.

# 7

In 1938 the family moved to Berlin Lichterfelde-West on the outskirts of the city. Three houses stood in a row on a tree-lined street, and the one on the outside at the corner was theirs. Opposite lived a family related to Reichsmarschall Göring, well-bred people, according to her mother, but poor. She and Oscar played with the children. The father was a former cavalry officer, a tall, dignified gentleman who now worked as a shoe salesman.

In Berlin the ten-year-old Ella became aware of the presence of things that had not intruded onto her life until now – National Socialist youth movements, the Hitler cult. They had more days off school that year than ever before, as all schoolchildren were sent out to line the streets and cheer at the mass parades. Because Ella was a pretty girl with long blonde plaits representing the Nordic ideal, she was often chosen to recite a poem or hand flowers to visiting dignitaries. Once, for the fun of it, she jumped onto the running board of the car whose occupant she was to greet, and she was permitted to remain standing there until the car came to a standstill. Later she was told that the guest of honour was Goebbels. Such scenes found their way into newsreels.

Ella had her den in the attic, up a flight of stairs too steep for the younger children to climb, where on the pretext of doing her homework she could escape into her own world of books and not be disturbed by her family. 'You have become quite a bookish child,' her mother said, and from the tone of her voice Ella could tell that she didn't approve. The attic room was decorated in the most modern style, with clean-lined matter-of-fact Bauhaus furniture given to her by her father Andrzejewski.

'The only time I ever find the leisure to read is during my confinements,' her mother would say.

*How stupid*, Ella thought. And she made a vow that when she grew up she would always find time for the things that mattered to her.

Her mother being increasingly preoccupied with her two new brothers, Eduard and Nico, Ella was left to her own devices. Other interests began to absorb her, such as the housemaid Marlies with her intriguingly full-breasted figure, so different from Ella's petite mother.

Once a week Marlies was permitted to take a bath in Ella's parents' bathroom. On these evenings Ella arranged to sleep in her parents' bed adjoining the bathroom where Marlies took her bath. The moment Marlies had gone into the bathroom Ella got up, went to the bathroom door and spied on Marlies through the keyhole. She watched her standing in the tub soaping herself down, her heavy breasts, the dark patch of hair between her legs. Spying on a man wouldn't have excited her, but the sight of the naked Marlies did.

On one occasion Ella must have made a noise. Marlies, suspicious, came to the door and looked back through the keyhole. *It's light in there, dark in here*, the thought immediately crossed Ella's mind, *so Marlies won't be able to see anything*, and she scurried back into bed and pretended to be asleep when Marlies opened the door and came out. Ella's presence of mind in a tight spot made evident a cunning streak in her nature she wasn't sure she liked.

To get into her own bedroom Ella's mother had to pass through the children's room. One corner was furnished with a child-size desk and matching bench on which Ella would lie in contorted positions and try to fall asleep at night, waiting for her mother to look in and take pity on her, but she found it so uncomfortable that she usually gave up and fell asleep in bed.

When she woke up in the night, as she began to do frequently at this time, she imagined sinister figures in the shape of the clothes hanging on the door, imaginings Ella had never had before. She also began biting her fingernails. Mother noticed her lack of nails and said in her matter-of-fact way, 'You'd better take some calcium tablets, Ella.'

Once a week she and Oscar took the tram to visit their father. They got to know by heart all the advertisements they could see on their way through the city. They made a game out of the jingles, taking it in turns to tell a story using only the words in the advertisements. Whoever won got a wish. Oscar wished for a day without a single thought passing through his mind and Ella regretted such a wish hadn't occurred to her first.

Her father lived in an expensively decorated penthouse apartment that appealed to Ella's tastes much better than the homely style of her mother. The entrance hall downstairs, with a marble staircase and mirrors, was completely different from the houses Ella had lived in since her mother had remarried. She preferred the style in which her father lived. This made her uncomfortable. She felt that taking sides against her mother was disloyal. She didn't think she was a particularly good daughter to her father either. She liked him. But could she honestly have said she felt the same fondness for her father that he showed for her?

Ella understood Oscar's wish not to have to think. Sometimes Ella too wished that she could have just one clear feeling, not various contradictory feelings at the same time.

Andrzejewski was a tall, elegant man, always turned out in fashionably tailored suits. She liked his scent, his smooth clear skin. She liked the atmosphere of discreet luxury around him. She liked that he was an intellectual, a different type from all the other people in her world. Her father was a physicist employed by Siemens, testing their products for suitability for patenting. His apartment had a study full of gadgets where he pursued his private scientific interests, a dining room separate from the living room, and a lavish bedroom with a large brass bed, much larger, Ella thought, than a man needed who lived alone. The place was beautifully kept by a housekeeper who came every day and did everything for her father, from making his bed to washing his underpants.

Andrzejewski thought up games for the children when they came to visit him, usually demonstrating some physical law such as centrifugal force. Try putting a ball in a bucket and turning the bucket upside down without the ball falling out. Back at home, Oscar demonstrated to their mother how it was done, whirling the bucket over his shoulder and smashing a chandelier. Once, her father noticed Ella scratching her leg, took a pair of forceps to remove a tiny bit of skin from under her fingernail and put it on a slide under a microscope. With amazement she could see things moving that she didn't even know were in her skin. They ran outside to find leaves, bits of earth, anything their father could put under the microscope to show them more of these marvels. But for Ella the most memorable of the things her father taught her was the lesson with the stone.

The stone lay on the table in the laboratory where he did his experiments. It was just an ordinary piece of limestone, he said, giving it to each of them to hold in their hand.

'When you put your hand over something like this stone,' Andrzejewski said, 'you realise you can't close your hand, because there's something there filling out the space. You have the feeling of something pressing against your hand, so some force must be there. You look at what you have in your hand, but something stops you looking into the stone. Those are the two main impressions you get from this stone: that it has a force which resists you, and which prevents you from looking inside. But what if one breaks the stone with a hammer?'

He gave Ella a hammer and told her to hit the stone.

'So, it's broken into three pieces. Now we *can* look inside. Has something changed as a result of breaking it? Well, we can of course hold the three pieces and put the stone together again. Then it may look as if nothing much has changed. But we can't get back to the stone we started with. When I take my hands away it falls apart. The stone is no longer whole. We can hold the pieces in place, but they remain there only as long as we do so. The forces that held the stone together and gave it its wholeness are no longer there where you now see the break lines. So something has been destroyed, not life exactly, but a little bit like life.'

Oscar went over with Ella what they learned from their father, even if he couldn't explain to her how there was a force inside the stone that held it together. He gave her tests on why the sky turned red in the evening, why the moon changed shape and so on, but she knew the answer before he had even finished asking the question. She was irritated by her brother's slowness, explaining things to her that she had long since understood but not the things she wanted to know most, like the nature of the force that held the stone together. Why did the stone need such a force? Why didn't it just stick together by itself?

Andrzejewski usually gave Oscar some experiments to do in his study while he sat down for a chat with Ella in the living room. He wanted to hear what she had been doing that week. What had her mother been doing? He always wanted to hear everything about Mother as well.

Ella had once again been taking part in mass parades. One particu-larly long parade was held to celebrate Austria having become part of the Reich. For hours she waited in the huge crowd, unable to see what was happening because she was too small, and at last got so tired that she sat down on the ground. A man in a uniform picked her up and set her on his shoulders. She saw *him*, standing on the balcony to receive the applause of the crowd. How much more tired the Führer must be. In bed at night she imagined herself sitting on his knee and consoling him as he rested his head on her shoulder. *Yes, yes, of course you're tired. You work so terribly hard, so I will take care of you.* And dreaming up such fantasies she fell asleep.

In the youth movement she had joined, Ella told her father, she was required to keep a diary with the title: *My Führer and I.* Inside the cover there was a photo of him in an oval mount smiling at her whenever she opened the book. Underneath, Ella wrote out the official potted biography of Hitler in the old-fashioned script – *Sütterlin* it was called – which she had learned to write at school. Mother looked over her shoulder and helped her when Ella didn't know something. She had to write about her father and mother and the 'Aryan family'. She told Andrzejewski about it, thinking he would be pleased she had included him in her book.

But he frowned and asked irritably, 'You didn't have to join the girls' youth movement, did you? Do you even know what Aryan means?'

Although Ella had not in fact been obliged to join the local section of the Girl Pioneers, she lied to her father that she had. She joined because she had a crush on a girl who was a member, called Grete Hein, and sought opportunities to be close to her, but she could hardly tell her father that. At the age of ten Ella was far more likely to have a crush on a girl than a boy. One corner of the gold tooth Ella was so proud of in her mouth would be named after the girl of the moment; the other corner of the tooth was called by her mother's name. She said goodnight to each of them by passing her tongue first over one corner and then the other. Ella didn't think these were suitable subjects of conversation with her father and kept them to herself. It had to do with a certain reserve she had towards Andrzejewski, which in turn had to do with the loyalty she felt to her mother.

To prove herself worthy of membership in the Girl Pioneers she had to jump through a fire, hold a flag and swear an oath and do all sorts of things she found rather silly, but for Grete she would have done anything. Grete knew this and used the fascination she held for Ella to blackmail her, offering her honours such as carrying the flag at ceremonies if Ella would give her sweets or money. Ella went back to stealing from her mother's piggy bank to satisfy Grete's wishes.

As a Girl Pioneer she began to find out more about Hitler. They were given homework such as writing essays about him, listened to lectures about his youth movement and so on, which Ella found boring but put up with for the sake of Grete Hein.

In many situations Ella felt herself to be two people, one of them absorbed in whatever she was doing here and now, the other standing to one side, watching her other self doing these things.

Instead of telling Andrzejewski about Grete Hein, Ella told him about the dances the youth groups were preparing in celebration of Hitler's fiftieth birthday. All girls participating were let off school for the rehearsals. They were told to buy a white dress with wide skirts and a colourful bodice suitable for the folklorist sort of dances they were doing. But as usual Mother thought she would save the money and make it herself. Ella wanted one exactly like the one all the other girls had – these were school activities and she felt ashamed if she was different from everyone else – so she refused to wear the dress her mother made and in the end preferred not to take part in the dance at all.

'So you didn't do the dances for Hitler because you hadn't got the right dress?' her father asked. Ella shook her head unhappily, but Andrzejewski laughed and said it was time for their supper.

Before they went out to supper Ella wanted to ask him a question. It took her a little courage to ask him this question. It had been buzzing around in her head all that year in Berlin. Her father had never talked to her about Nazis, but he had to Oscar, and from Oscar she knew that he was against them. Oscar said Andrzejewski was a communist who had been opposed to Hitler from the beginning. She fidgeted before asking the question. Her father smiled, encouraging her to go on and ask. Well, said Ella. Was her stepfather a Nazi?

Andrzejewski put his head first on one side, then on the other, and said that her stepfather, with whom, as Ella knew, he was on friendly terms, which was just as well considering that father and stepfather often had reason to meet to discuss matters relating to the two children, was undoubtedly a National Socialist, but not a Nazi. What was the difference? Andrzejewski had already anticipated her question and began to elaborate in the pedantic way he did when explaining some scientific problem to the children.

The original National Socialists were people whose nationalism and socialism had brought them into the political movement they had given that name. He could not approve of their ideals, but it was as idealists, after a fashion, that they had started their movement. Whereas today's Nazis were merely opportunists, people without principles, only ambition, an interest in furthering their careers, if necessary over the dead bodies of those who stood in their way. That was why they had to be combated. That was why, said Andrzejewski, he would feel very much easier in his mind if he knew that when his daughter lay in bed at night she was imagining anything in the world, whatever she liked, anything other than that picture of herself sitting on Hitler's knee and consoling him as he rested his head on her shoulder. There and then Ella promised him that she would never again indulge in fantasies of sitting on Hitler's knee.

Her father was on the board of directors at Kempinski's, and he had his own table at the best restaurant in town. He always took the children there for an early supper before they caught the train back home after their weekly visit. The waiter brought Ella the ladies' menu, on which the prices were not listed. It made her feel very grown-up. Andrzejewski taught them how to study the menu, what courses went best together and what wines to choose with them, how to eat snails and dismember a lobster and other strange foodstuffs of deep interest to Ella, although her brother, like her mother, was indifferent about what he ate, preferring dishes he was familiar with, such as the stews he was given at home. The bill her father paid at the end of the meal seemed to her an unbelievable amount of money, and he told them it might be better for them not to mention it to their mother.

Andrzejewski took exception to Ella's clothes. He said she ought to ask her mother to buy her clothes more suitable for a girl who went to Kempinski's for her supper. Ella marvelled at her father's simple-mindedness. Money might be no object for *him*. He even had his own bust at his tailor to save himself the trouble of going there to be fitted. The reason Maria favoured the folklore patterns for her daughter's dresses which Andrzejewski disliked, with blouses and ornamental stitching round the shoulders in what was known as the Russian look, was that she could have them made up from clothes she had once worn herself. There wouldn't have been the money to buy the fashionable outfits her father wanted Ella to wear.

All one needed to go on holiday in Capri was a briefcase with room for a spare shirt and a pair of bathing trunks, Andrzejewski told her on one of her visits, and she watched him practise, walking around the apartment, briefcase in hand, as if he was already on his way.

Her father pushed open a door onto an unknown world that fascin-ated her. By comparison, her mother's world seemed plain and homely, lacking the intellectual sophistication Ella craved.

The number of children Ella knew who were suddenly having to leave the country was growing, although Ella didn't understand why they were leaving or why it made them unhappy. There was Ursula, a girl with beautiful glossy black ringlets. Ella had a crush on her too. Ursula cried bitterly because she was going to have to go away. How Ella envied Ursula's black ringlets! How she longed for an opportunity to break out of the narrow horizons of her family! And then there was the boy who sang in the choir in which Ella sang too. The boy was moving to America, it was rumoured, and when the rumour was confirmed and the boy sang his last chorale with them, many of the older choir members cried.

Why were they crying? Wasn't it wonderful to be able to go to America?

The Marx family, who lived a few blocks away, were among those who disappeared overnight without saying goodbye. It was rumoured of the Marxes that they too had gone to England. For a while Ella had a close friendship with one of the three Marx boys, Klaus. He was two years older and had fallen in love with her. Oscar told her Klaus had scratched onto his bicycle seat the words 'I love Ella' so that he could sit on them whenever he rode his bicycle. She found this embarrassing.

Klaus and Oscar were classmates. To do his friend Klaus a favour, Oscar fixed up a Morse apparatus connecting the Marx house with the house where he and Ella lived about half a kilometre away. He taught Ella how to say good morning and goodnight in Morse code, and for a while she and Klaus exchanged signals at the beginning and end of each day. When Klaus tapped out a message she couldn't read and her brother told her that the message meant 'I love you,' Ella firmly wrote back, 'Goodnight!'

She didn't like boys paying her that sort of her attention. It didn't interest her and it made her feel uncomfortable.

Next day Klaus and his brothers were not in school. The family had gone. The message Klaus had sent to Ella was the last she heard of him.

In November Ella's stepfather Carl came home in the middle of the day, which he otherwise never did, in a state of shock, and shut himself up in the bedroom to talk with her mother. What had happened? Jewish stores all over town had been raided by the Nazis, their windows smashed, the stores looted. In the residential suburb where Ella lived and went to school there had been no such signs of violence. How could there have been, for there were no shops?

Until quite recently Ella had no idea what Jews were, hadn't known they existed, let alone been aware of knowing any Jews herself, but it now turned out that she'd known quite a few, even if she didn't understand what made them different from herself. Families like Ursula's and the Marxes in Berlin and the Acksteiners she'd known in Herischdorf were now leaving Germany because they were Jewish.

'The writing's on the wall,' she overheard Andrzejewski mysteriously say in a phone call to her mother. What writing? On what wall? Her father explained it was because of the yellow star that Jews now had to wear. She had first seen people wearing the yellow star when she was walking down a street in Stettin. An elderly gentleman came towards her accompanied by a girl of her own age, dressed like a princess, more beautifully dressed than any girl she had ever seen. Ella heard the girl talking in a language she recognised as English, but it was different from the English she had learned from Aunt Cathy. Ella asked the man what language the girl was speaking, and he said she was from America and didn't speak their language. Ella said, 'How wonderful! America!' 'Oh no,' said the old gentleman, 'you don't understand. You don't know how lucky you are. Unlike my granddaughter, you're free to come and go as you please.' Ella stood and watched them walk down the street until they turned the corner and disappeared.

Did it mean the girl was Jewish and should never have come here because she wouldn't be allowed to leave again? Then why had the boy who sang in the choir been allowed to leave? Why could some children go but not others? This uncertainty troubled Ella, not least because it meant the little girl she'd always wanted to be, the protected child whose parents indulged her and worried over her, as Ella wanted to be protected and worried over, lost her magic power and no longer had a place in Ella's world of make-believe. That child ceased to exist.

# 8

In 1939 Ella's stepfather, Dr Carl Josef Winter, was appointed sub-prefect of the civil administration of Schlawe. That summer the family prepared to move from Berlin to their new home. Carlchen had already been living in Schlawe for several months before he was joined there by the rest of his family. Maria was now pregnant with her fifth child. Ella and her brother Oscar spent the summer holidays in a youth camp on the North Sea island of Sylt. Schlawe was far away, at the easternmost point of the country on the Polish border. In accordance with provisions laid down by the Treaty of Versailles to counter the threat of German rearmament and aggression, it was accessible by only a single railway track. The trip from Sylt to Schlawe took days. En route, the children changed trains in Hamburg and stayed overnight with their father in Berlin.

In the few months since they had last seen him Andrzejewski had changed. He had grown much thinner and offered them none of the usual experiments and quizzes to which Ella had been looking forward. He was not his usual cheerful self. The apartment was untidy and not very clean either. His housekeeper had given notice. Washing was piled in the basket in the bathroom waiting to be done. Even the Kempinski menu failed to animate him. Tired at the end of a long day, the children fell asleep in the guest room the moment they got into bed. When Ella woke up in the night she could see her father through the open door, pacing up and down in the living room.

Early the next day they got a taxi to the Stettiner Bahnhof to catch their train to Schlawe. At six o'clock on a Sunday morning Berlin was deserted. Ella and Oscar played their advertisement story game while Andrzejewski sat between them in silence, listening to their chatter. Was this a good idea at such a time, he remarked as they got out of the taxi, absent-mindedly handing each of them a ten-Reichsmark note, this trip to Schlawe so close to the Polish border? What did he mean? wondered Ella, a good idea at such a time, but in the excitement of holding more money in her hand than she'd ever been given she forgot to ask him. Her father escorted them down the platform and saw them onto the train. He kissed them goodbye and gave Ella a letter for her mother. Standing at the window to wave to her father as the train pulled out, she wondered why he was carrying a briefcase on a Sunday morning.

Ella had one of her premonitions.

Where are you going? she called down to him on the platform. To Capri, I expect, said Andrzejewski, waving as the train set off before he turned and walked back down the platform.

The railway station at Schlawe was outside the town. Mother and stepfather were waiting with two cars to meet the children when they arrived. One of the vehicles was a large official chauffeur-driven limousine in accordance with the sub-prefect's status. Oscar, the technical expert, climbed in enthusiastically. Knowing her stepfather would be hurt if they both chose to ride in the official car, Ella joined him in his own, more modest car, which he kept for his private use. They drove along cobbled streets through an imposing ancient gate at the one end of the old town – Romanesque, the sub-prefect said with pride – across the market in the centre and out through a second gate at the other end. It was a quiet country town of ten thousand inhabitants, fifteen kilometres from the Baltic to the west. To the east stretched the endless plains beyond Poland. From here came the prevailing wind, the cold wind from the Russian hinterland that was always blowing.

Ella was very excited by her first sight of the sub-prefect's enormous residence. It was an imposing vine-clad house that expressed the imperial ambitions of the Wilhelminian period. Most of it was taken up with offices and rooms required for the state business that went with the sub-prefect's job. These rooms were on the ground floor, the private apartments of the family on the floor above. The doors off the entrance hall opened up a perspective of eight large rooms with ceilings six metres high, leading into an enormous conference hall at the end. The building was so large that the children were given permission to cycle down the corridors.

Setting up a new home, one that this time was supposed to last, Ella's mother came into her element. All the curtains for the gigantic windows she would make herself. Maria redecorated and modernised, brought workmen in to install pipes and fit basins and water closets in the old-fashioned house, which had been built at a time before people bothered about hygienic requirements. In the stone stairway leading down from the attic the caretaker of the house had built an aviary for breeding canaries. The trilling and singing of these birds could be heard throughout the house. Listening to them at night, Ella could imagine she had moved to a tropical country

In the sub-prefect's Schlawe residence they lived on the grand scale to which Carl had aspired as an ambitious young civil servant whose axiom it had been to live beyond his means. Now at last he was living within his means. Here Ella's mother had room for all the furniture she'd inherited from relatives who lived in big country houses and which she'd never found space for in the civil service quarters the family had previously occupied. All the rooms for official entertaining faced north – as had then been common, Maria explained to Ella, to preserve the complexion favoured by the fashionably pale ladies of the empire. The maids' and children's rooms looked south. Ella had a corner room with a lot of light, and her mother chose for her curtains through which the light flooded with a warm pinkish glow.

Arriving a week late for the beginning of term at her new school, wearing long blonde plaits with a blue frock, Ella found that of the thirty or so children in her class there were only two other girls. It was almost entirely made up of the sons of local farmers. She stood at the front of the class while the teacher introduced her as the daughter of Schlawe's new district sub-prefect.

The appearance of the sub-prefect's daughter caused a stir. Ella had gone to so many different schools in the course of her stepfather's moves, from Hirschberg to Stettin, and from there to Berlin, that she had difficulty fitting in with the curriculum of each new one. In Schlawe she found herself back in a village school that presented her with no intellectual challenges, where chalk and slate were still in use and the farm boys who had got up early to milk the cows could sleep undisturbed at the back of the class. The country people here were heavy-set, broad-faced and thick-skinned folk, as reliable as they were taciturn, not the kind of schoolchildren among whom a girl as quick-witted as Ella could feel stimulated.

September the 1st was a school day like any other for Ella, but when she came home for lunch she found the house in a state of gloom. Her mother told her that Poland had gone to war with Germany early that morning and Germany had retaliated by invading Poland.

They sat around the table and her stepfather said, Don't worry, the war will be over in two weeks. Her mother got up. She went and stood by one of the high windows. Her silhouette against the window looked so frail that Ella had an impulse to go over and put her arm around her. Turning with a little shrug of her shoulders, Maria said to her husband, Before this war is over we shall lose house and home and Oscar will be taken for a soldier, you'll see. Oscar was thirteen at the time. Nonsense, her stepfather said with a dismissive laugh. No, Maria insisted, not nonsense. This is how it will be. We shall lose house and home, house and home – and she repeated it three times, like a witch's curse.

Ella was disturbed by this exchange. Which of them was right? She didn't know whether to believe her stepfather or her mother, who still had such vivid memories of the Great War, which had started when she was exactly the same age as Ella was now. Mother had been through it all before. That was why she was certain this war would also go on for several years like the last one. Ella tended to trust her mother's judgement more than her stepfather's. If only Andrzejewski had been there to ask; he would have known. Her brother Oscar might have known too, but he had been sent to boarding school, leaving his eleven-year-old sister to come to her own conclusions.

Later that day Ella went with her mother to the linen room to help her fold the laundry and put it away in the cupboards. The linen room was where mother and daughter had their private conversations. When they had finished folding the laundry her mother sat down and took out Andrzejewski's letter. Your father's been working on a secret project for the army, she said, and he's known for a long time that this war was coming. They'll need your father for his work, so probably he'll be safe. But for how long? After all, she said, you know your father's views, and it's his country that has been invaded. What will he do? Where will he go?

Maria didn't tell her daughter Andrzejewski had warned her of the dangers of living in a town as close to the Polish border as Schlawe. She put the letter back in the envelope and told Ella to burn it in the grate.

Ella thought of her father standing on the platform with a briefcase containing all he needed to go on holiday, a pair of bathing trunks and a few shirts, according to what he had told her in his apartment in Berlin.

He'll probably go to Capri, Ella said. She knelt down and put her arms around her mother, her head in her lap, and her mother stroked her hair.

Their house lay just outside Schlawe's northern gate, and from her corner room Ella saw the columns passing to the war, men and creak-ing horse-drawn carts covered with awnings, soldiers and their baggage marching east, old-fashioned infantry she imagined not so different from Napoleon's troops marching on Russia more than a hundred years before.

A few days after the war began she came home from school to find her mother in tears. She had received a telegram informing her that one of her favourite cousins had been killed in action. He was the seventeenth casualty of the war.

From then on followed a stream of official communications – the telegrams were soon replaced by letters – announcing that others from Ella's far-flung family or circle of acquaintances had fallen in the war. The circular published by an organisation of aristocratic families listing the deaths of their members grew longer and longer from one issue to the next. Ella and her girlfriends at school looked at the pictures of those who had been killed in action and wondered which of the young men in uniform they might have married if they had survived.

*Clip clop clip clop.* The sound of the hooves of the horses drawing the carts along the road that passed beneath Ella's window went on without interruption day and night – it was just a few kilometres to the

Polish Corridor. There were no armoured cars, let alone tanks, no motor vehicles at all. The horses were requisitioned from farming communities all over Pomerania.

Sometimes she was woken by a mournful drawn-out cry. *Po-o-land, Po-o-land!* That was what the voice seemed to be calling through the night. But why would someone be out there in the dark calling, *Poland?* What kind of person would do such a thing?

For months the columns kept trekking from west to east along the road. The horses and carts were still coming when her mother gave birth to a second daughter on the day that everyone in the house was called on to form a chain and pass the rifles stored in the attic of the sub-prefect's residence to the soldiers outside. Ella realised the rifles must have been there lying ready and waiting for the war before the family had even moved into the house. She wondered if this was why her stepfather had gone to Schlawe ahead of them. Thousands of recruits had been assembled from Pomerania's hinterland in Schlawe and were on their way to war. The children made extra pocket money collecting the empty beer bottles the recruits left lying around and taking them back to the shops. Glad of the windfall they were earning for the bottles, the children hoped the soldiers wouldn't be departing for the war too soon.

They had nothing much to do because the school was closed. There was no coal to heat the building. Classes wouldn't be resumed until the spring of the following year. Throughout the winter it served as a mustering point for recruits. Only the gym was heated. The rector of the school had made himself unpopular with his pacifist opinions, and as a punishment he had been transferred to the little town at the easternmost end of the Reich. But he was a kindly man with the schoolchildren's interests at heart. He'd somehow organised coal to heat the gym in order to give the children something to do while the school remained closed in the first winter of the war. The gymnasium was used by a group of children who preferred training sessions to hanging around with nothing to do at home. On her walk there Ella took a country road leading to the River Wipper and crossed the bridge into the park through which the river flowed.

The wholesale disappearance of able-bodied men had immediate and dramatic effects. One was the hurried, mismanaged harvest brought in by workers too old or too young, who didn't know enough about what they were doing. Another was the flooding of the river because all the lock-keepers had gone. With the autumn rains, the river burst its banks, putting much of the surrounding countryside under water. In November the flood water froze, providing the children with another welcome side effect of the war – a skating rink that ran to the horizon. Exuberantly they skated cross-country for hours before they turned back and headed home through the twilight.

When the first snow came, putting an end to the skating excursions, runners were fitted under the wheels of the farmers' wagons, converting them into sleighs. On Sundays the farmers had to drive wagons into the town centre, clear the snow and cart it off to the outlying fields. It was fun for the children to jump onto the runners of a wagon as it came through one gate, get a ride through town and a ride back on an incoming sleigh entering by the other gate. All deliveries were done by sleigh. Bread and buns sometimes rolled through the street, picking up snow and horse dung on the way. The children wiped them with their sleeves, put them in their pockets and took them home to eat. Food rationing had begun immediately after the start of the war. There wasn't much to eat in the shops, let alone the health foods her mother wanted for the new baby. To enlarge her kitchen garden, in the spring the sub-prefect's wife commandeered a platoon of recruits. She had them sent over from the garrison to dig up the lawn and cart off the turf, which could be put to use in the recruits' training exercises. They planted the former front lawn with vegetables.

School reopened at Easter. Coal was available in Stettin, and the building could be heated again. Knowing how badly shortages were affecting everyone by the end of the winter, the sub-prefect doubted whether coal freighted out of Stettin on the long journey by train to Schlawe at the eastern border of Pomerania would arrive safely. He went there in person, boarded the locomotive armed with a pistol and ensured that the coal wagons bound for Schlawe were not diverted en route.

The social order in the remote rural town was undisturbed by the war. The sub-prefect and a few top officials, with the doctor, the pastor and the commanding officer of the garrison made up the top layer of society, followed by the wealthier merchants, junior officials, craftsmen and farmers. The rituals of life in the small town continued with no change. One of these was the parade of young people that took place in the early evening when the market stalls were closed and the day's work was over. The boys assembled on one side of the square, the girls on the other, eyeing one another. The parade provided Schlawe's farming community with its only courting opportunity, a marriage market in which all young people over the age of thirteen took part – Ella included, although she was still under age. At first it was fun. She sensed the excitement in the air. But as the war went into its second year the ranks of the young men on the other side of the square were drastically thinned. Both Ella's classmates had sweethearts who were killed within six weeks of their departure for the front.

Within eighteen months of Ella's arrival at the secondary school in Schlawe all the young male teachers had been drafted for military service and been replaced by elderly men and women. History ceased to be taught at the school; it was replaced by briefings on the progress of the war. Yet despite the general mobilisation, despite the battles fought in distant places, life as people had always known it in Schlawe continued much as usual until Hitler's armies began their march on Russia.

# 9

On the first day the school reopened an older boy in her class walked up to Ella, gave her a pencil and a piece of paper and told her to draw a straight line. She didn't manage the task to his satisfaction. The boy said, Well, you'll never become an artist, that's certain. Ella had never had any intention of becoming an artist, but she felt snubbed nonetheless.

Ferdinand Zitzewitz was the boy's name. The sensual, over-refined and oversensitive product of an ancient aristocratic family, he was the son and heir of a domineering father and a cool mother who lived with his eleven brothers and sisters on the family estate some distance from Schlawe, too far for him to make the trip to school and back every day. During the week he stayed at lodgings in town and went home at weekends. Despite the initial snub Ella felt drawn to Ferdinand. He introduced her to his friends, opening a door on a world that until now had been closed to her. Discussions were his passion – about literature, art, aesthetics – and under his guidance they became hers too.

Ella was friends in a different way with a boy in the class above her who was a friend of Ferdinand. Jochen Wetzel's father was farm manager on the Zitzewitz estate. He was one of the boys in the clique which went to the gym every day. It was Jochen who asked her if she would like to join the group in the gym. He was the best gymnast among them and the best turned-out. She watched how he chalked his hands to give him a better grip, the way he bandaged his wrists with white tape, and she thought this professionalism looked stylish. On the parallel bars he performed a handstand and won her over completely. When Ella once came to the gym with dirty fingernails he sent her away to clean them. That firm discipline, making no allowances for anyone, impressed Ella. At the gym the boys sometimes put their arms around the girls they liked, but perhaps because Ella was the sub-prefect's daughter they were reluctant to do so with her. Jochen saw her home but he made no attempt to kiss her. Ella knew he had another girl. She had seen him with her in the town. She suspected that Jochen did things with her that he didn't dare do with Ella, and this made her envious.

At twelve Ella was considered too young by her stepfather to be allowed to go to dancing classes. She would have to wait until next year. Ella's clique – Jochen, Ferdinand, Micky and Ilse – were all going to the classes that year, meaning they would remain a year ahead and she would never catch up. But twelve months later, as the war spread, casting longer and longer shadows over their lives, the dancing classes came to an end in any case. Of the half-dozen boys whom Ella had got to know at the gym club in her first winter all would be killed in action within the year, including the gymnast Jochen Wetzel.

Ella began to grow independent. She was discovering herself as someone distinct from her family. She had a different name from her mother, whose name had changed to Winter while Ella's name remained Andrzejewski. She was becoming aware of her own feelings, of the fact that she was her own person, an individual with her own tastes and priorities, one of which was having time to do the things that interested her. She began frequenting bookshops. She no longer ran to her mother and shared everything with her. The things that interested her she now kept to herself. They wouldn't have interested her mother in any case. Maria's constant 'I haven't got the time for that!' began to get on her nerves. Was it necessary to turn the house upside down and clean it room by room with such pedantic thoroughness? Couldn't she delegate more of her work? Her mother's inability to find time to sit down and talk, to read a book or take an interest in anything beyond her household, began to bore Ella.

When she came home from school and saw her mother's tear-stained face she knew without asking that someone close to Maria must have been killed in the war. Ella's way of coping with the extinction of the young men who passed in and out of her life was not to allow herself to become attached to any of them. Keeping her distance became the pattern in Ella's relations with people, men or women, whom she found herself liking. Not wanting the pain of separation, the disappointment she already knew from her own experience was bound to follow – perhaps because of Andrzejewski's early disappearance from her life, perhaps because of her mother's remarriage and the betrayal, as Ella felt it to be, of her daughter, putting the interests of the younger children first – Ella forestalled disappointment by cutting her ties with others before they cut their ties with her.

Ferdinand was the natural partner for conversations of the kind Ella sought at this time. They became intimate friends. Over Christmas he invited her to come and stay in the castle outside the village named Zitzewitz after the family that had lived there for hundreds of years. Who is she? one of Ferdinand's sisters asked, pointing at Ella with her riding crop when he arrived with her. Degenerate aristocrats, her mother called them, and Ella thought she was right. Inflated with self-regard, of the twelve brothers and sisters, Ferdinand, the heir to the Zitzewitz estate, was the least infected with the family arrogance. So Ella was struck all the more by their poverty, the inhospitable atmosphere of the castle, the meagre food, the coldness of the rooms, the conversations obsessed with the increasing human toll of the war as in all homes with family members to mourn.

Ferdinand, too, was soon called up as a recruit. They kept up their friendship by correspondence. As if there had been no war, or as if to keep the war out of their privacy, they discussed literature and ideas that stimulated Ella's mind – religion, predetermination and freedom of the will. When he came home on leave, she introduced him to her parents before his arrival as a possible marriage candidate, but her stepfather didn't think he was the right man, too young and inexperienced. Ella herself was not yet sixteen. They should wait a few years. Ella's mother was principally against marriage between old aristocratic families on account of the inbreeding, she said. Ferdinand's own family provided an example of the unfortunate results. Ella accepted their veto because she was nagged by her own misgivings. It let her off the hook. She was relieved she could now write to him telling him her parents were not in favour of them marrying and that it would be better for them to wait. But with no end of the war in sight Ferdinand knew they couldn't afford to wait. Before he was sent to the front he managed to arrange leave to try and persuade Ella. They went for a long walk in the woods. Ferdinand pleaded his case, but Ella's mind was made up. All right, he said, since it's you who wants to leave, you go first, and he watched her go, leaving him standing there on the edge of the wood without looking back.

Deprived of the friendship with Ferdinand, her most intimate cor-respondent, the person who in many ways had been closest to her, to her mind if not her heart, Ella experienced the same emptiness she felt when told that boys she had known at school had been killed in action. Ferdinand was one of the few who survived the war, but she never saw him again.

As the tide turned at Stalingrad, civilians on the home front were mobilised to make their contribution to the war effort. Ella was assigned work as a hospital orderly in Schlawe. Wounded soldiers repatriated from the Russian front were among the patients, but Ella worked on the maternity ward. There she got to know a Polish woman with syphilis. Until she saw her, Ella didn't even know what syphilis was. Half the woman's vagina had already been eaten away by the disease. She had given birth to a child which she asked Ella to kill. It was already her third child, all of them illegitimate. Ella refused.

The family's situation became critical when a high Nazi official ar-rived in Schlawe to assess the civilian war effort on the Polish border. At the inn where the official was staying, he got drunk and made advances to the innkeeper's wife. When she refused his overtures he began to demolish the inventory. Called out in the middle of the night to deal with the troublemaker, the sub-prefect locked him in the wine cellar and kept him there until he had sobered up the next morning. Enraged by this treatment from a mere sub-prefect, the official complained to his superiors in Berlin, brought charges of insubordination against the offender and demanded that disciplinary measures be taken.

Carl Winter was relieved of his duties as sub-prefect and within six weeks had been drafted as a rank and file soldier to the eastern front. It was not deemed necessary to appoint a substitute. His family was permitted to stay in the sub-prefect's residence. By the summer of 1944 it was clear even to the diehards in Berlin that the collapse of the eastern front was imminent and that Schlawe would not be requiring a civil government any more, for the town would soon be in the hands of the advancing Soviet army.

At the end of the summer Ella walked out with her mother into the fields to pick flowers to decorate the house. The railway line ran past the field where they were, and if the train happened to be passing, the engine driver, an admirer of the sub-prefect's wife and her daughter, would slow down and blow the whistle in greeting. That day the women laughed and waved back. For a moment they were happy and forgot about the war. This image of the two of them, waving bunches of flowers as the train passed, was the memory of her mother Ella most treasured from that last summer of the war.

In the autumn she was sent hundreds of kilometres west to Thürin-gen. She was put to work washing bandages and cleaning out pigsties. Then she accompanied a team of itinerant butchers who travelled from village to village, slaughtering the remaining pigs on the farms, cooking and canning the meat for army provisions. All day she stood and turned the wheel that ground the butchers' knives. They shared with her snip-pets of pork directly out of the vats where the pigs were broiled. In a few weeks she ate more pork than she'd had in her whole life.

When she had completed her assignment with the butchers she was sent to a camp near Weimar to weave baskets for transporting munitions. Women from all over the country worked in this camp, including a contingent of whores from Hamburg, who cracked jokes and told sala-cious stories while the women sat making baskets from willow saplings soaked in water. The quarters where the women were accommodated were overcrowded: in each dormitory there was only one bed, which the women took it in turns to sleep in while the others lay on straw sacks on the floor. When Ella became ill and unable to work, unable even to eat, she was given the bed for the rest of her stay in the camp until she was fit to travel.

At Christmas she returned to Schlawe, so weak she barely managed the journey home. Her mother had saved up for her as Christmas treats little delicacies she knew Ella liked, but she was unable to eat anything. Ella's apathy made her mother sad. Only later was she diagnosed as having jaundice, probably the result of all the pork she'd eaten while working for the butchers. She stayed at home until she recovered. Early in 1945, shortly before her seventeenth birthday, her school was disbanded and Ella was again dispatched to Thüringen for another assignment in Weimar.

Just before Ella's departure news came that her grandmother had suffered a stroke in her house in Herischdorf. The old lady was moved to the family home at Holm in Brandenburg. There she was being looked after by two maiden aunts who were still living in the house. Worried about the crumbling eastern front, and what that would mean for her daughter's safety, Maria was relieved to see Ella leave for the west, thus escaping the threat of the Red Army's imminent arrival. In the event of losing touch, they agreed to meet in Holm.

Meanwhile Maria would stay in Schlawe with Eduard, Nico and Charlotte for a few more weeks to wind up the family's affairs before joining the refugees who had already set out on the trek west. Ella was uneasy at the thought of leaving her mother alone with the younger children.

'Will you be all right here on your own? I don't really have to go to Weimar, do I? I could stay and help you.'

'You go. You'll be safer there than here. The Russians will be coming soon, but don't worry. What harm will they do to a mother with three small children?'

# 10

Schlawe was still unscathed when it fell to the Red Army in the early days of March. On the night the Russians arrived they set the town on fire. Buildings burned everywhere, turning the sky red. Maria had been warned that the occupying troops would probably commandeer the sub-prefect's house as their *kommandatura*, so she sought shelter in a neighbour's house. There was no electricity. It was pitch dark. She got into bed with the three children, who were so tired they immediately fell asleep. Then people came into the house. She heard them striking matches. She listened to them rummaging around the house, apparently looking for something. She heard things being knocked over, glass breaking, but they didn't find what they were looking for and left.

She looked out of the window and saw soldiers with torches setting fire to the house next door. Realising they might be next, she decided to leave immediately. She woke the children and told them they would have to keep very quiet. She got their things together as well as she could in the dark because it was too risky to light a candle. She found only half of what she had prepared for the journey. Unfortunately Charlotte's doll was among the things she couldn't find, and later she would often have cause to be sorry for not having recovered it.

Elsa, the neighbour's daughter, went into the yard to fetch their push cart, but it had been stolen, so they had to leave the heavy suitcases behind. It was an icy moonlit night, the snow so slippery that they kept on falling over. Dragging their bags behind them, they headed for the hospital, hoping to find shelter. Dr Schmidt, one of the doctors she knew there, had told Maria she would be safer in the hospital than in her own home. It was he who had also warned her that the official residence of the sub-prefect would immediately be occupied by the Russian troops. The back entrance to the hospital was ominously still. It was so dark she had to light a candle, by the light of which she saw the amount of destruction that had already been done. There wasn't a single person to be seen. Maria remembered one of the doctors saying that it would be safer in the quarantine station than in the hospital itself, so she went there with the children, but it was the same desolate scene, everything destroyed, not a living person around.

The next place she tried was the old people's home, where she knew Sister Lina, a young woman on the staff there. Surely they'd be safe if they took refuge with the old people. When she got to the home she found all the doors open, everything in the rooms smashed. She lit another candle and crept along a corridor until she got to a room where an old woman was lying alone in bed. Furniture and bedding looted by the soldiers was piled up around her bed, which was buried in the wreckage around it. The old woman told Maria that all the old people who were able to walk had gone to the refectory. So she went on down the corridor until she reached the refectory, and there they were, about fifty old people, and she went in and asked for Sister Lina.

Here, said Sister Lina and threw her arms round her neck. How relieved Maria was to be among people again! It didn't matter that the room was overcrowded. They were made welcome like all the other refugees from the town who had made their way there too. The children lay on the floor; the grown-ups were given chairs. Elsa and two other women who said they had been through some bad experiences with the

Russians the previous night kept on going over to the basin in the corner to throw up. That was how shaken they still were.

Sister Lina said that the Russians had tried to rape Dr Schmidt's daughter too, but she resisted and they shot her on the spot. Dr Schmidt was out at the time. When he came back and found her dead he no longer wanted to go on living. His wife agreed. Things would only get worse. Dr Schmidt gave his wife and the three younger children an injection, and then himself, and within minutes they lay there dead with calm expressions on their faces, as if they had just fallen asleep. Some of us envied them, said Sister Lina. That was the end of Dr Schmidt. He was a good doctor and how we missed him.

All forty or fifty refugees stayed in the refectory for the next eleven days and nights. No one went outside except to go to the toilet, or when the Russians came and took the women out, first the girls and the Red Cross sisters and then whoever was left. Mostly they were drunk and violent, and they scared the patients out of their wits. Some of the old people went out of their minds and lingered on for a few days until they died. Some of them died outright.

After several nights of this Maria hid in the bed of an old woman in one of the wards down the corridor. The Russians came in every night, turned the place upside down, pulled the blankets off people lying in bed, but she was lucky: they didn't pick the bed where Maria was hidden under the old woman's blanket, half dead with fright. Then Lina went to the *kommandatura* in the sub-prefect's house and begged for protection. She came back with posters printed in large Cyrillic letters, warning of typhoid in the house, which they pinned up on all the doors and the refectory walls. That stopped the marauders coming. After that things quietened down and they were able to venture out again.

Maria was never frightened of going out on the streets in the company of her three small children in the daytime. Unless they were drunk the Russians respected mothers and children and sometimes stopped to play with them. Most of the town had burned down. The streets were full of rubble and it was difficult to get through. The inhabitants were slowly returning from the outlying villages, where they had fled. They were in a terrible state, exhausted, famished, and most of them came back only to find their houses gone. Thousands of other people had vanished. No one knew what had happened to them.

In May, when it got warmer, the first typhus epidemic broke out. The

Russians had got it into their heads to turn the old people's home into a hospital and the hospital into an old people's home. All protests from the people of Schlawe were to no avail. There followed an extraordinary procession through the town. Forty or fifty volunteers carried whatever they could out of the old people's home to the hospital and left it in the yard outside – loose drawers for which the chests were missing, cupboards that had been taken apart and bits of beds that had been dismantled at one end and could not be reassembled at the other. In the chaos it took the volunteers weeks just to get the old people's beds back together again, and in the meantime they had to make do with the floor.

Maria was allotted a pleasant room on the first floor of the home for herself and the children. She managed to borrow a cot for Charlotte and organised one big bed for everyone else, including a little girl who had somehow got attached to them during the move, so Maria now had four children to look after in addition to a bedridden old woman in the room next door. Bed and board was what they were supposed to be given, but for months there was hardly anything to eat. The situation only improved when they were permitted to leave Schlawe and go out to the farms in the surrounding countryside, where they were sometimes lucky and got a proper meal.

Maria decided to leave the old people's home and move into an empty cottage on the edge of the town. A mother and daughter she knew slightly had lived there until they killed themselves after being gang-raped by the soldiers who broke into their house. The cottage was painted blue and the children called it the Blue House. It had a garden with fruit trees and tall beeches that were good for climbing, so Eduard and Nico were happy there.

Meanwhile the Russians had handed over jurisdiction for Schlawe to the Poles. The first thing they did was to turn the Germans out of their homes and move in themselves. The occupants had to leave on the spot, get up and go, dressed as they were, allowed to take nothing. The streets of Schlawe were full of beggarly people with nowhere to go. Some of them found shelter in the residence where the sub-prefect's family used to live, as the Russians had moved their *kommandatura* elsewhere. From a distance Maria watched soldiers loading all their possessions onto lorries – their furniture, curtains, carpets, pictures and knick-knacks – and drive away. They left some linen and towels and kitchenware lying around outside the house, so Maria and the children gathered it all together and took it back with them to the Blue House.

Poles showed up at the Blue House and took whatever they wanted. They saw how comfortable the cottage was, and it wasn't long before Polish officers arrived and put the family out on the street. There were no more nice cottages available by now, just an outhouse in the back garden of a building that had burned down. Russian soldiers had been quartered there and had left the place full of rubbish. It hadn't been aired in months. The walls were covered with mould. The place stank. Maria cried when she saw the state this hovel was in, which started the children crying too. Once again there was no alternative but to set to, tidying and scrubbing and getting the place back into some semblance of order. Once she had arranged her furniture and the utensils they had retrieved from their previous home it began to feel almost cosy in the hovel. The advantage of living in a such a miserable-looking place was that no one who came past bothered to look inside.

Every day the boys walked out into the country and back to beg for food from the farmers while Charlotte helped her mother with the housework. Maria wondered whether to stay put in Schlawe or to join one of the treks heading west, as more and more Germans were doing that summer. It was hard to turn your back on your home and leave everything, but conditions had grown so bad that people had no choice, what with strangers arriving in your house in the middle of the night and turning you out of bed. Mothers didn't even have time to dress their children properly. Carrying them off in their nightshirts, with no other clothes, no food, nothing, they were herded through the streets to the station, where they were loaded onto cattle trucks, often in the rain. It rained a lot that summer.

Those who stayed ran the risk of dying in the epidemics of typhoid and diphtheria that were ravaging the population. Almost every day Maria went to mass funerals, eight or ten people buried in one grave. She was frightened she might get ill too, and what would happen to the children then? This finally persuaded her it would be best for them to leave Schlawe, which she had put off doing because she feared the children might not survive the journey. She felt isolated, cut off from her husband, her grown-up son Oscar and her daughter Ella, from all of whom she had heard nothing for months. But it was a very long way to the west, hundreds of kilometres, and she heard reports about how dangerous the journey was. Many people died on the overcrowded trains. Bandits were looting and raping and killing women and children. But the summer was already coming to an end and Maria knew it would be even more hazardous to attempt the journey in winter.

She made careful preparations for the journey. She bought food and organised warm clothes and packed them in two potato sacks to take with them. In all likelihood bandits would rob them, so she packed only things that were not in a good state of repair. She had saved over a thousand marks in notes, which she hid in a leather wallet in the cold ashes at the back of the oven in the cottage. But there must have been a residue of heat in the ashes she hadn't noticed, and when she took the bundle out the day before they were due to leave she found to her dismay that all the money had turned to ash. Desperate, she went around begging from people she knew, even those who were in hospital, and almost everyone gave her a small sum which added up to enough to buy provisions. She took her leave of these kind people with a heavy heart, doubting she would ever see them again.

It was already October when Maria and her three children set off, accompanied by two married couples, landowners who had been turned out of their estates in East Prussia and arrived in Schlawe only the day before. Maria took them into her house because they were travelling illegally and had to hide from the Polish authorities. She had been assigned a secretarial job in the Polish administration and had to sneak off in order to get to the station, where she had arranged to meet the others, but someone spotted her and followed her. This waiting and hiding to shake off her pursuer cost much more time than she had allowed to get to the station. She was so worried she wouldn't get there in time that she had painful stomach cramps. She only just managed to join the others at the station, climb into the cattle car and slide the door shut before the train jolted into motion.

As the train rolled slowly out of the station into open country, Polish-speaking bandits emerged from the bushes, ran alongside the train and jumped aboard. They tore the coats off the women and took their dresses and shoes, stripped the men down to their pants and threw everything off the train to be picked up by their accomplices. Maria had been forewarned of these attacks and had taken the precaution of folding their coats into bundles which they sat on with the rest of their things hidden underneath, so that the bandits overlooked them. The marauders must have been in cahoots with the train driver, because after passing the next station they blew whistles, the train promptly slowed down and the bandits began throwing people out of the cars onto the side of the railway track with an audible *crash, crash, crash*. Old people and children and mothers with their babies, one after another they flew off the train although it was still travelling at quite a speed. What screaming there was! Without the intervention of a Polish soldier who happened to be sitting with Maria's party, she and the children would have been chucked out too. But the soldier held up his arm and said to the bandits in Polish, I'm in charge of these people, and they left them alone.

Soon it grew dark and the Poles moved through the cars with torches, on the lookout for more loot. Somewhere in the dark ahead they heard the most terrible screaming. There was a commotion, shouts in a mixture of Russian and Polish followed by banging and thumping and then gun-shots. The train came to a halt. The Polish bandits had been chucking children off the train from cars at the front and preventing the mothers from jumping after them. But some Russians posted along the railway track saw what was happening, stopped the train and hauled the bandits out. The bandits began shooting at the Russians and the Russians shot back, killing several of them. The gunfight continued in the dark until the marauders had been expelled and the train moved off. The Polish soldier who was sitting beside Maria told her that the children who had been thrown off the train had been picked up and given back to their mothers – in what condition Maria didn't see, but the sound of women and children crying in cars further up the train troubled her through the night. At least they now had Russian protectors on board and peace had been restored, at least in their car, where she counted sixty people sitting crammed tightly together on the floor. Perhaps they would now reach Scheune safely, the station after Stettin. But in Stettin they came back under Polish jurisdiction, and the Russians got off the train, the friendly Polish soldier as well, leaving the refugee families defenceless.

It was only another quarter of an hour to Scheune, where they would change trains for the next leg of the journey to Berlin. What could go wrong in quarter of an hour? A lot could go wrong. Shortly after the train left Stettin at two o'clock in the morning a dozen marauders of the worst kind they had seen so far jumped into their car train while it was still gathering speed. At gunpoint the leader of the gang told the passengers to move to the other side of the car and hand over their baggage. They refused. So the bandits linked arms and formed a cordon to shove them across by force, but they were all sitting so tightly packed together it was impossible for them to move any further. A big young man who was in the car beside Maria kneeled with his back to the bandits and did his best to resist the pressure, but if the shoving had gone on for much longer the children lying between them on the floor would have been crushed to death.

Maria had Eduard in front of her, the two little ones behind her, and she could feel them being squashed against her back. She began screaming, all the other passengers screamed with her, and this had such an effect on the bandits that they left them alone. People were moaning and children crying all around her in the car, but the crisis was over. The moment the danger passed Maria felt so exhausted she had a recurrence of her stomach cramps. It was so bad that she couldn't move. The band of marauders threw everything they could lay their hands on out of the train and jumped off. Again by some miracle they overlooked the two potato sacks containing everything the family had left in the world. The two couples from East Prussia had lost all their possessions, but they helped Maria get the heavy sacks off the train when it reached Scheune, drag them along the platform and lift them and the children onto another train of cattle cars, which finally left Scheune at four o'clock in the morning. From then on the worst of their troubles were over, but without her doll Charlotte was inconsolable, and she cried all the rest of the way to Berlin.

# 11

The journey from Schlawe to Weimar took Ella a week. Trains were always being diverted and delayed. Sometimes no trains came at all. When and where would the next train be running? No information was available. Many stations had been abandoned by their staff. This collapse of the otherwise always reliable national railways provided Ella with unmistakable evidence that the war was really lost and the country on the verge of breakdown.

People congregated in the emergency camps that were improvised along the line to deal with stranded people, many of them children evacuated from the bombed cities to the west of the Elbe or refugees from the east, like Ella herself. The homes or boarding schools the children had been sent to had been closed, and there was nowhere for them to go. The orphanage in Weimar where Ella had been told to report for work was one of these institutions abandoned overnight. All the inmates had gone, leaving behind everything but food. With nothing to do, nowhere to stay, Ella decided to head back north in the direction of Berlin and make her way to her grandmother's house in Holm.

Her mother had a cousin in Weimar. Ella sought her out in the hope that this relative might be able to help her, but meanwhile the war had reached Weimar too. With five small children in the house – they were just getting ready to flee – the harassed woman already had more on her hands than she could handle. It was Ella rather who could help her. On her way out of the house she went through a list of things that had to be done before they could set out. What the children most urgently needed were their boots, otherwise they wouldn't survive the long journey she anticipated. Unfortunately the boots were at the cobbler's. She couldn't pick them up herself, she said, as she had to take her baby to the doctor, so she asked Ella to go and fetch them and take the children with her in case something happened in her absence. So the four older children – two of them still toddlers – accompanied Ella to the cobbler's to collect their boots.

They were making their way back from the shop when they heard the air raid sirens. Ella pressed on as fast as she could with four small children struggling to keep up. She was expecting the Allied bombers to fly over the city on their way to other targets as she knew they usually did – Weimar had no military installations or industry – but this time Weimar was itself the target. Bombs were already falling in the outskirts of the city. She and the children just made it into an air raid shelter in time. A bomb landed in the street overhead, the force of the blast sending everyone in the shelter hurtling across the cellar. The lights fused and went out; children screamed in the dark.

As soon as the all-clear was given they went back up into the street. Bombed buildings were burning all around them. The house her mother's cousin lived in was no longer there – it had ceased to exist. There was no sign either of the woman who had left the house to take her baby to the doctor half an hour before. What should Ella do? Refugees from the east were arriving in Weimar in such numbers that the camps couldn't take any more people in. With four small children in her charge, Ella thought it best to try to continue the journey to Holm. There she could be sure of help, somewhere for the children to stay, food for them to eat. All she had with her was a small wicker suitcase and an eiderdown.

She managed to get herself and the children aboard one of the trains still running – full to bursting with refugees, wounded soldiers, recruits travelling aimlessly around with no idea of where they should be going, the front in collapse, the divisions they were supposed to be joining already on the retreat. The train took them no further than the town of Halle. There, Ella thought, they might be able to get another train to Berlin, and from there to Holm, but she was told there wasn't any hope of reaching Berlin – the city was under siege. The town of Halle had been completely flattened and was in flames as far as the eye could see. People arriving were told to move on via Magdeburg to Wittenberge, from where Ella hoped to get a train to her grandmother's home in Brandenburg.

She spent the night with the four children in her care at the station, waiting for a train to come. But when the train finally came day was already breaking. Trains didn't run during the day because they were strafed by Allied aircraft – they could only travel without risk of air attack when it was dark. The train was shunted into a siding and everyone was told to get out and take cover for the rest of the day. But an hour later they were suddenly told to get back on the train. At intervals during the journey, Allied aircraft attacked, repeatedly bringing the train to a standstill, and everyone scrambled for cover to wait until the planes had gone. Then they all got back on board. And so it went on, stopping and starting – the panic-stricken rush of the passengers away from the railway track the moment planes reappeared – the hectic rush back to the train to make sure that they didn't get left behind when it set off again.

By nightfall they had reached Wittenberge, only to be told that from here no further trains were running. Ella and the four children spent the night in an underpass with hundreds of other refugees. They had nothing to eat, only water to drink from the tap in the station washroom.

At dawn the air raid sirens started blaring. Soldiers came into the underpass and told the people there it would be safer for them to take refuge in the air raid shelter on the other side of the railway line. At once everyone got up to go, but Ella had one of her premonitions of impending danger – perhaps it was her claustrophobia – and she refused to go.

The soldiers started pulling the children away. They were too strong for her — she only had two arms to cling to her four charges — and they dragged the children away from her. She kicked and struggled — refused to go with them — so they cursed and let her stay where she was. Within a minute the station underpass, where hundreds of people had spent the night together, was empty. Only Ella remained, hugging her knees, stopping her ears with her fingers. Bombs began exploding all around the station, there was one last terrific detonation and the entire station building shook and seemed to have exploded all at once. Screams from inside the earth — echoes through the underpass — a dreadful silence afterwards. Terrified, Ella remained curled up there for the rest of the day, clutching her counterpane for comfort, calling on her mother as she heard the planes roaring overhead and dropping their bombs — *boom boom boom!* — it seemed right on top of her. Not until it grew dark did she dare to venture out of the underpass. But once outside she found the night was as bright as day. Petrol wagons standing in one of the sidings had exploded and gone up in an inferno — houses on either side of the station had disappeared — flames flickering up out of cellars where three-storey buildings had stood. The air raid shelter where the four children had been taken for refuge must have received a direct hit. Only one wall of the station building was still upright and the railway tracks in both directions were ablaze as far as she could see. Nothing but rolling flames moved in this ruined landscape. Charred bodies — some of them still smouldering — lay twisted across the lines. A just legible sign on the platform pointed Ella in the direction of Berlin. This was where she had to go to reach Holm.

Making a detour around the burning tracks, she rejoined the railway further down the line and set off — stepping from sleeper to sleeper — stumbling along as best she could — carrying her counterpane and her wicker suitcase. She counted her steps, a habit she'd learned from her grandmother, but after an hour she forgot the total and gave up.

She walked all night without meeting a living soul — not daring to leave the railway line in case she lost her way — afraid of the solitude in which she found herself. When morning came she lay down for a while — falling asleep in a thicket on the embankment — and woke up shivering with cold. Later she passed a cottage. An old woman gave her some milk and bread. At nightfall she reached a small country station, where she slept as she waited throughout the following day. Finally a train arrived that took her to Zernitz, a halt rather than a proper station, provided for the convenience of visitors to her grandmother's estate. She left the railway track and headed for Holm.

Along the road to Holm in the early morning light poured an unbroken stream of refugees from the east, fleeing from the Russian army, all with one purpose in mind – to cross the Elbe – the natural frontier where the Red Army would halt – and reach safety on the west bank of the river. Ella joined the thousands pushing bicycles, prams and carts on which their possessions were stacked, making their way along the old tree-lined avenue that led to the estate. The jetsam of the thousands who had preceded them lay strewn on either side of the road. In the panic of their flight they had ditched not only their goods but anything that impeded them, leaving on the wayside people who had given up, the sick and enfeebled, the wounded and the dead.

About a hundred refugees had found shelter in the house at Holm. Ella was given an emotional reception by Great-Aunt Sophie and Aunt Charlotte, who was usually rather reserved. They had only recently arrived with Ella's grandmother after a long and arduous odyssey from Herischdorf in Silesia. Confused by the influx of strangers and unsure what they were doing there, the old lady wandered around the house with her eiderdown strapped to her back to prevent it from being stolen. Her great-aunt took Ella aside as soon as she arrived to warn her to keep a sharp eye on her things. Not a stitch of clothing – not a curtain – not a thread of material – nothing was left in the house; the swarms of people who had moved through the house had stripped it bare. Ella took the cover off a mattress and with the help of her great-aunt's sewing machine made herself a skirt and blouse. Sewing helped to keep her mind off the grim conditions around her.

She tried to get in touch with her mother in Schlawe, walking to the station and posting a letter to her every day, not knowing if her mother would ever read the letters or even if they were still being collected for delivery. One day the postbox had gone. The station premises had already been stripped of everything that might have been of use – door handles, light fixtures, taps – even the tracks in the sidings had been torn up and removed. There was no electricity and few trains – eventually none at all – just people waiting in the hope that a train would come. Perhaps it was as well she eventually stopped going to post letters. She risked her life getting there. Planes would roar over the tree-lined alley and strafe anything that moved. She soon learned that from the moment she heard the aircraft until it appeared directly overhead she had not more than ten seconds to seek cover or throw herself into a ditch at the side of the road.

Once she hid in a stable where refugees had sheltered. The place was full of things they'd left behind, among them a suitcase stuffed with money. All her life she'd dreamed of finding such a suitcase – she would give it to her mother so that she could make ends meet – but Ella left the suitcase where it was. What use was money now?

From an upstairs window she saw them arrive one morning – a group of foot soldiers, half a dozen men on horseback – smoking, chatting, making their way in almost leisurely fashion up the avenue towards the house. They might have been any visitors, on foot or horseback, as visitors had always arrived at Holm, but were recognisable by their uniforms as Russian soldiers. An advance guard of the Red Army had arrived, but such a humble one it seemed as if they might have stumbled across the place by accident. She had heard stories of the horrors that would come with the Russians, but these men looked harmless, not the conquering army they had all been expecting, more like refugees, ill fed, ill clothed, unwashed and tattered men at the end of their tether. Everyone huddled together in the vaulted cellar beneath the house, seeking safety in numbers. The Russians peered curiously into the cellar. They were not at all intimidating; on the contrary: their friendliness was almost encouraging.

On the next day the main body of the Russian troops arrived, accompanied by tanks and a motorcade of armoured cars. The officers requisitioned the grander of the two houses that made up the estate – Holm Two as it was called – for use as their headquarters. They turned the refugees out of the house and brought in the pigs and poultry they had brought with them. The animals were put in one of the best rooms of the house, a salon furnished in rococo style with old-fashioned satin-covered chairs on which, half a century or so before, ladies wearing hooped skirts and bustles could perch without disarranging their clothes. Chairs and sofas were tipped over to serve as troughs for the pigs' swill, gold-rimmed Sèvres soup bowls put down on the floor and filled with grain to feed the poultry. Geese, chickens and pigs were all housed together in this room, live food to provide the Russians with their meals.

Bedsteads hastily assembled from boards with straw pallets to lie on had been put up everywhere in Holm One to accommodate the influx from Holm Two, and everyone went to bed that night feeling relieved that the arrival of the Russians had passed off without the unpleasantness they had all been expecting.

Ella, the housemaid Erna, a Ukrainian family and a couple of other women bedded down upstairs in what had once been Ella's mother's dressing room. In the middle of the night Ella heard voices downstairs which seemed to be coming from her grandmother's room. The women spoke to each other in whispers. They thought they would probably be safe where they were, but the Ukrainian woman could understand what the Russian soldiers were saying and knew why they had come. She told them that they were taking first pick of the women in the house. Ella wondered if she had understood her correctly. *First pick of the women?* The soldiers were already in the corridor outside. The door opened with a crash – torches were shone round the room – *Dawaj! Dawaj!* – Come on! Come on! – fear in the pit of Ella's stomach. She and the Ukrainian woman and Erna were chased out of their beds and hustled downstairs. Ella had enough time to tuck into her stocking the little casket in which she kept her jewellery.

The women were led through the downstairs living room – her grandmother lay asleep on the sofa while Aunt Charlotte looked on helplessly – then taken across the entrance hall into the billiard room. Along the walls of this room stood several of the rough bedsteads that had been knocked together to provide the refugees with a place to sleep, and it was on these makeshift cots that the three women were raped.

Ella had been told by Aunt Charlotte to wear all the clothes she possessed in order to be able to leave immediately in case of an emergency, and removing her layers of clothing was such a time-consuming business it made the waiting soldier impatient. He did no more than unbutton his trousers; didn't even bother to take off his cap. She lay under this stranger thrusting himself down on top of her and looked up at her great-grandfather's portrait hanging on the wall above – a fine old gentleman, complete with all his military braid and ribbons and medals, his startlingly white beard and stiff white collar highlighted in the gloom of the old oil painting by the sheen of a candle burning on the sideboard below. With every thrust the rim of the soldier's cap struck her forehead, the buckle of his belt bored into her skin. She lay there quite passive.

The man repeatedly said, *Rabotta! Rabotta!* —meaning, she guessed, he wanted her to move with him — but she could only lie there and let this happen, looking up at her great-grandfather's whiskers while reciting to herself the words of the prayer her grandmother had embroidered in the quilt on her bed at home.

*Spread wide your wings over me*
*Oh Jesu, joy of mine.*
*Should Satan take her in his power*
*May angels watching over her*
*Sing in their heavenly bower*
*'No harm shall ever come to thee!'*

But reciting prayers didn't help — Jesu wasn't there to hear them. What the soldier was doing hurt — she was a virgin — and she began to whimper. The Ukrainian woman being raped in the cot beside her said the men were bothered by her making these noises. She told Ella to be quiet or they would stuff something into her mouth to shut her up, or just shoot her. Then Ella and the Ukrainian woman and Erna were told to get off the cots and lie on the billiard table; the men changed places, and the women were raped again. After that the men rested, talked and drank. The Ukrainian woman understood from what the Russians were saying that they wanted to change women again and do it a third time, but she thought the men were now so tired and drunk that the three of them should resist, and they screamed and kicked, and the Russians gave up. Before she went back upstairs Ella made a sign to one of the men that she wanted to go outside for a pee. Squatting down, she slipped the casket with her jewellery out of her stocking under her skirt and hid it in the bushes; everything of value the two other women possessed had already been taken off them by the soldiers before they were raped.

On her way back upstairs she again passed through the living room — the women there were now all wide awake, her aunt and her great-aunt down on their knees praying. Charlotte got up and made camomile tea. Ella thought she would be given the tea to drink but it was a prophylactic — the women had their recipes and knew what to do in such cases. The tea was to wash out her vagina. There was no receptacle other than an old coffee pot with a broken spout for this purpose, guided by Charlotte's wavering hand. The warm tea running over her legs felt like urine. Ella let all this be done to her as she had let the Russians do what had been done to her before – didn't feel she was fully there – only her body was present, her mind was elsewhere. The old ladies were crying and fussing over her. Then she went back to bed and lay awake for a long time before she was able to fall asleep.

The following evening the three women who had been raped went up to their room before it got dark. Her great-aunt gave instructions to the men in the house to barricade the women in by pushing a massive cupboard against the door, completely covering it. From inside their room later that night they could hear soldiers out in the corridor, but all the men could see was a cupboard; they couldn't find the door and so they left them in peace. Angry that they were unable to find the young women they'd been looking for, the soldiers took their revenge on women they had originally passed over, selecting young mothers among the refugees as their rape victims that night.

Even older women now knew it was no longer safe for them to be in the house at night. By bad luck the moon was full, the nights clear, so finding hiding places outside proved difficult. They hid in the hedgerows at the bottom of the field but the sparse bushes provided little cover. It was early spring; the bushes were only beginning to leaf. Under this meagre cover the women went into hiding before it grew dark and soon got extremely cold. The Russians drove lurching over the fields in trucks – headlights searching the hedgerows where they guessed the women were hiding – hauled them out of the bushes and raped them. Others lay terrified in the dark, praying they wouldn't be found. Night after night it went on like this, this hide-and-seek, each of the women lying alone in the dark. They crept back into the house at dawn, an hour at which the Russians had gone to bed drunk and were certain to be asleep. But sometimes they got caught. It was always Ella the Russians picked out. After several nights of this her nerves were at breaking point. Terrified, unable to bear it, she began to go out of her mind. Had Erna, her grandmother's loyal maid, an older woman she'd known all her life, not pleaded with Ella and put her arms around her to hold her back, she would have thrown herself down the well.

Among the human flotsam washed up in Holm by the tide of war was a wealthy industrialist from Berlin who before the war had bought the game rights to the estate. He rented an apartment in the house and drove out there at weekends to shoot and fish. Foreseeing the imminent collapse of Berlin, this man took refuge with his wife in Holm in the belief that their chances of survival would be better there than in the city. But they were now trapped in the same house as the Soviet army they had come there to escape. In the orgy of plundering, rape and killing that took place in the early weeks of the Soviet occupation, this couple were the victims of an atrocity committed under the eyes of the inmates of the house — they watched it through the windows looking onto the terrace where it happened. Soldiers approached the couple as they were walking there, pushed the man away, seized his wife and began ripping off her clothes. The husband went to the defence of his wife and was shot dead on the spot. The soldiers raped the woman on the ground beside her husband's corpse then took knives out of their belts and cut off her breasts. She rolled on the ground, screaming in agony — left to bleed to death in full view of witnesses inside the house. Not a person stirred, not an onlooker in the house dared to raise a hand in the couple's defence.

Ella could bear these unbearable experiences only by becoming dissociated from herself. She looked at the horrors — the terrifying games of hide-and-seek, the nightly rapes — as if they were happening to someone else — as if the onlooker and the victim of these events were two different persons — and dividing herself into these two distinct people, Ella learned it was possible to live through experiences she would not have imagined a human being could wish to survive.

# 12

Holm was where so many refugees ended up because the estate was very close to the Elbe, a last way station where they could rest before crossing the river. A lot of them had arrived there mistakenly, following the turning that led to the estate instead of continuing along the main road to the bridge over the Elbe. Getting across the river was the only certain destination they had. What lay beyond was unknown. But now it was too late in any case, and they found themselves trapped in the village under Soviet occupation. Before the Russians came, the remains of the retreating German army had still been making their way to the river. Ella had seen these soldiers when she first arrived in Holm. The German field hospitals had been disbanded, the wounded left to fend for themselves. The desperateness of their attempts to hang on to life — a life that Ella would willingly have thrown away many times after the Russians came — burned unforgettable images into her mind.

Knowing the Russians would soon be doing to the Germans what they had done to the Russians, hundreds of these soldiers set out for the west bank of the Elbe — some of them on foot, some on crutches, some of them crawling on their hands and knees — she had seen men with amputated legs rolling their way along the road as best they could — to get across the river, whatever the cost. Many had given up on the way. Soldiers who had shot themselves lay rotting in heaps on the roadside — pairs of comrades, dozens of them who had made a pact, met a better death shooting each other simultaneously. Ella was stopped by some of these wretches, who asked her for a drink of water before they killed themselves. And others came, mysteriously full of the joys of life. A flamboyant young man in a flowing red cape, an opera singer from Breslau, stood in the courtyard of the house one morning and sang Schubert lieder, giving a last performance for his fellow refugees before crossing the Elbe later that day.

For the same reason that attracted refugees to Holm — its strategic proximity to the Elbe — the village was where the Russian army established its westernmost positions in the early months of 1945. This was where the Russian advance came to a halt. The refugees in Holm were given work assignments by the occupation army. They were put to sweeping, cooking, cleaning, distributing Russian newspapers, working in the fields, whatever was required. Planting potatoes, following a machine pulled by a horse, Ella trod the fields barefoot like everyone else, for no one had any shoes; everything had been taken away. The machine bored holes in the furrow in which she laid the seed potatoes she carried in a sack. From morning till night she felt the coolness of the earth between her toes — something basic that reassured her. She was grateful to have work to do. Surrounded by people, she felt safe. By day the Russian soldiers were subject to strict discipline. At night the rules of the game changed and they could do as they pleased. Women were still hunted and raped at night, but it could no longer be done with impunity.

Within weeks of the establishment of an official Russian military command on the demarcation line along the Elbe agreed between the Soviets and the Western Allies, murder, rape and looting of the civilian population were decreed to be punishable offences. To check the rapid spread of syphilis in the Russian army, a notice was posted in Holm announcing that all women who had been raped would be taken to Soviet army headquarters in the nearby town of Kyritz to be examined by a medical officer. Ella was among the few dozen women who climbed onto the hay carts which lumbered over the country roads to Kyritz. She was also among the much smaller group of women, neither pregnant nor syphilitic, who were returned to Holm the following day. Ella didn't learn what happened to the women who remained in Kyritz. None of them came back.

Since her arrival in Holm Ella had been waiting anxiously for news of her mother. Imagining her stuck on her own with three small children in Schlawe, where the full force of the Soviet invasion down the Baltic coast had broken over the civilian population – under circumstances apparently even worse than here – she grew increasingly restless. A resolution to go in search of her mother took root in her mind. Refugees who had managed to escape from East Prussia and arrived in Holm spoke of the Soviet reprisals on reaching German soil for the first time – the mass executions, the raping, burning and mutilating, the crucifixion of families of farmers on the walls of their own barns. After the murder of the Berlin couple on the terrace behind their own house, Ella's aunts had forbidden her to attempt the journey back east on any account – into the thick of the conquering Soviet army, said Charlotte in tears – a fate worse than death awaited her there.

Despite these warnings and entreaties from her family, despite all that Ella had been through herself since the Russians arrived in Holm, the daughter's need to look for her mother became so urgent that it overrode all objections. She was so insistent on making the journey that her aunts finally had to give way. When Ella got on her bicycle at dawn one morning she was seen off by her grim-faced relatives. They had done what little they could – given her provisions and drawn a map for her to help her find her way – but watching her niece as she cycled off, Charlotte was convinced she would never see her again.

The late spring weather was sharp – the nights cold and clear, she had the Pole Star as her guide. Her brother Oscar had long ago taught her the constellations and how to find her way at night. She kept going east, following the list of places she would pass through on her way, which her aunt had written down for her on the map she had drawn. Ella's plan was to start every day before it was light – in June it got light very early – and to keep going until life began to stir in the surrounding countryside. Then she went into hiding in the woods.

She stayed in hiding until it was dark, when she could venture out again. Fortunately the weather was dry, making it easier to sleep out of doors. On her way she passed through burned-out villages, bombed towns where not one stone was left standing on another, not a living soul was to be seen. Whenever she came to a place where there was a church, she looked for the vicarage nearby. There she begged for food. One morning she crept into a vicarage garden while it was still dark and fell asleep among the blackcurrant bushes. The vicar saw her there and told his wife to give Ella a bowl of soup. As the sun was already high, and Ella was afraid of being seen, she bolted down the soup and crept away.

On another morning she overslept – started out too late, knowing the risk, knowing it was unwise, sick with the nausea of fear churning in her stomach. The road led through a small town, or what had been a town. It no longer existed except on the list her aunt had given her. The surrounding countryside had been devastated – the barns burned down, the cattle slaughtered on the pasture, men with their hands tied behind their backs hanging from the trees. In the desolation of this place she looked round and saw a man on a bicycle coming up fast behind her. She saw his face when he caught up with her – a Mongolian soldier – as he grabbed the handlebars of her bicycle and tipped her into the ditch. *Kommandatura!* she screamed at him, hoping the Russian word for army headquarters would discourage him, but it had no effect. He struggled with her and she hit him in the face – kicked and screamed so much that the would-be rapist thought better of it and left her alone.

So it was worth resisting, she learned, but the attempted rape by the Mongolian in an isolated spot where she might easily have been murdered gave Ella a shock. Her determination to get to Schlawe by whatever means, unshakeable until now, received a blow from which her self-confidence never fully recovered.

She came to another village where most of the houses had been burned down. The cows stood outside the deserted farms waiting to be milked, lowing with the pain of their bursting udders. She heard a voice through the open door of an intact house further down the village street. An old man dragged himself out followed by a dog, shuffling and muttering agitatedly to himself while the dog stood by and feebly wagged his tail. Ella asked if she could shelter in his house. The man didn't reply. He didn't take in what she said. He was completely out of his wits. She knocked at the door of another house. Another old man opened the door. Again she asked if he could let her rest there for the day, but he shut the door in her face. She knew why he had refused. Having women in the house meant Russian soldiers banging on your door, bringing you trouble.

The last house left standing was already full of refugees, including some girls of her age. But they turned her away too. Ella panicked. The sun had been up for hours and she still hadn't managed to find cover. She might as well have been out there naked for the whole world to see. She felt vulnerable in her aloneness. The starkness of fear was something terrible – that such fear could exist, such awful fear! – and it had already become such a natural part of her life. She pushed her bicycle as fast as she could across a field and plunged into a wood.

That night she came out of hiding with the moon. It cast enough light for her to follow the road. Before daybreak she had reached the outskirts of a place called Scheune – close to Stettin – she recognised her surroundings – where she had lived for a while as a child. Across the fields she saw a stream of refugees, a great surging mass of people pouring east. They could only be on their way back to their homes in Pomerania – from where they had fled just weeks before! Ella joined the throng – grateful for the warmth of companionship – wondering why all these people were risking their lives going east. Listening to them talk, she was astonished to hear that now the war was over they believed they would be safer at home than on the long trek to the west bank of the Elbe. Ella knew better – she wanted to warn them of the risks of staying on the wrong side of the Elbe – but who was she to talk? What could she have said? That she was heading east herself despite her better knowledge?

When the road went up a hill too steep to pedal, Ella got off her bicycle and pushed. Beside her walked a man; he was pushing a bicycle too. He had a suitcase he held in place on the saddle with one hand while he pushed his bike with the other. Where from? Where to? They fell into the usual exchanges as they walked up hill. The suitcase had been entrusted to him by a girl he had met on the westbound trek, he said, and he was looking after it until they met up again. When the war was over they were going to get married. Downhill, against the great stream of people on their way up, came a man riding a black horse. The horseman was a Russian officer. His gaze wandered over the refugees as they passed. He seemed to be looking for something, or someone.

When the rider reined in his horse and beckoned to Ella she immediately knew what it was he wanted. She knew the look, the way he beckoned. She heard the familiar command *Dawaj* that preceded every act of rape. But the command was addressed not only to her. It included the man with the bicycle beside her. She realised the officer was afraid that if he went off with Ella alone it might attract attention – she would resist, how she would resist! She would scream for help, and there were a lot of people around, hundreds of men in this stream of refugees who wouldn't hesitate to come to her aid. This might explain why the officer signalled to the man to come along too, to conceal the intentions she knew he already had in mind. But the man pushing his bicycle beside Ella refused to go. He had a suitcase he had promised to take care of for a friend and he didn't want to let her down. So the Russian officer took out his pistol – at gunpoint he waved the man out of the crowd, then Ella, as if his business was with both of them, with the man no less than with the girl. They stepped out of the no-longer-protective stream of refugees – stood apart from it – no longer had anything to do with it – and the stream disowned them, continuing on its course.

They turned off down a track that disappeared into the woods. Ella and the man went on ahead, the officer rode behind. Ella pushed her bicycle with a feeling of dread at what awaited them once they were out of sight of the road. They went a long way into the woods until they reached a clearing. Despite her deepening sense of dread, Ella was struck by the sight of this clearing in the woods in the morning light. How momentarily beautiful it was, as if she and her human anxieties didn't matter, didn't exist, the sun shining in a fuse of green through the transparent new leaves on the trees! A dozen soldiers had set up camp here – horses grazing in the clearing – carts with men lying under them – saddlery, kitbags, rifles standing in stacks – a fire burning in the middle – much as she imagined camps might have looked during the Napoleonic Wars. The officer told the man who had come with her to wait in the clearing. He went on with Ella alone into the woods until they were out of sight of the camp.

The officer was a young man in his early twenties, fair-haired, with a broad Slavic face and high cheekbones, a type familiar to her from the

Polish border country of Schlawe. He used no force but conveyed to her with a gesture that she should undress and lie down on the ground. He lay on top of her on the springy turf floor in a patch of wild strawberries. Ella could smell the scents of the wood around her. Remembering the terror and abuse she had been through on so many nights before, this happening – this place in this daytime – had something almost tranquil by comparison. The man thrust into her a few times – she looked up at the sky through the greening trees – and already he was done – it was over. While she was getting dressed he picked a bouquet of wild strawberries and handed it to her. She took the bouquet – understood the gift as an apology – as if the man had wanted to make up to her for what he had done.

They made their way back to the camp. From the gestures accompanying the conversation between the young officer and his men, Ella guessed that the men were bargaining with him – they expected they would now have their turn with the girl too. With one officer in the woods – that she had accepted – but all these other men queuing up to rape her – she looked at them in horror. Falling on her knees, she clung to the legs of the young officer, hung on to him as if he were the only support she had left, crying and begging in such scraps of Russian as she could muster, pleading with him not to turn her over to his men. Ella could tell the officer liked her, and now, seeing her distress – for she felt that if he had picked her a bouquet of wild strawberries he couldn't be a bad man – it seemed he took pity on her. All right, he said, conveying the meaning of his words with gestures, I shan't allow these men to touch you; instead you shall do it again with me. And they went back into the wood, and when the officer was finished with her he brought her back to the camp, where he lay down to sleep under one of the carts, having instructed one of his men to accompany Ella and her companion – the man had been waiting there all this time with his bicycle and only frowned when she returned – back to the main road, making sure that no harm was done to them.

When they got to the edge of the wood their escort pointed his rifle and told them to leave their bicycles there. They had no alternative but to do as he said. Then they walked back to the main road, merging once more with the stream of refugees – still flowing along the road as if nothing had changed in the interval they had been gone – as if none of these events had happened – and even had the people known about them, no one would have cared. The only person who cared was the man who had forfeited his bicycle on her account. It was all Ella's fault. She was to blame that he was now unable to keep his promise to the girl who had given him her suitcase for safekeeping. Angrily he pushed on ahead, and Ella soon lost sight of him in the crowd.

# 13

Like all the other refugees returning to homes they had left head over heels in eastern Pomerania, Ella first had to reach Stettin. There she should be able to catch a train back to Schlawe. But in Scheune, a few kilometres away, she was told that the border to Stettin had been closed the day before. Stettin under Soviet occupation had ceased to be a German city and become a Polish one. No trains now crossed this border. That was the official version given out by the Russians; Ella heard other versions to the contrary. Finding herself a corner in the ruins of the town, she sat down and waited for a few days with thousands of other refugees in Scheune to see what happened.

But days passed and nothing happened other than that Ella's health took a turn for the worse. Dysentery had weakened her. She had no appetite. She realised that, even it were still possible, even if she had the spirit, she no longer had the physical strength for the arduous journey back to Schlawe. She accepted she had reached her limits and accom- plished nothing. It would take all her remaining strength to get back alive to where she had started out with such hopes three weeks earlier.

Westbound trains to Berlin and Hamburg were still running at infrequent intervals. It was rumoured that a freight train standing in a siding would be departing shortly. Ella waited on the platform for days, keeping an eye on the train in case it suddenly started. The station had been stripped bare by the occupation army – taps, light fixtures, electric cables, door handles, lavatory bowls, all dismantled and freighted back to Russia. The platform was overflowing with refugees, who made themselves at home on the tracks, spread out such bedding as they had, made fires and cooked. Like Ella, all these people had given up the attempt to return to their homes in the east and were now heading back west once again. At night the Russians came and shone torches over the crowds of people. Ella was always expecting the worst, but in such a mass of people she felt safer. They slept wearing all the clothes they had with them, ready to move at a moment's notice. When there were signs that a train was preparing to depart, there was a rush for places. In the open freight cars, exposed to the elements, there was standing room only. When Ella eventually got a place on a train, it pulled out of the siding, stopped, started again, and so it went on for days and nights, stopping and starting at frequent intervals.

In Ella's freight car a peasant woman was travelling with her eight children, the youngest of them a baby eight months old. The woman made a fire on the floor of the car and cooked a pot of millet pap to feed the children. She offered some to Ella, but Ella's bowels couldn't retain anything she ate. She made friends with the woman, who was a Ukrainian of German extraction by the name of Luther. Seven of the children were her own, the eighth was an orphan she had found on the way. The family had been forcibly relocated by the Germans from the Ukraine to Riga in Latvia. When the first Russian troops occupied the area, Frau Luther told Ella, rape was only one of the torments the family had suffered. The Russians hated the German Ukrainians – or Ukrainian Germans – as traitors. They raped the woman in the presence of her husband and her children. Then they beheaded him before her eyes, turned the family out of their home and sent them packing. It was a miracle they had survived the trek to Stettin during the East Prussian winter. God had stood by them, she said. She was a firm believer, undeterred by her trials. Listening to what Frau Luther had been through and helping her to look after the children made it easier for Ella to forget her own troubles. Taking responsibility for the children, Ella found she was looking after herself much better than if she had been making the journey alone, in charge only of herself.

Eventually they reached the station of yet another town that had been badly bombed. The railway line had been hit too. Everyone was ordered out of the train until the damage had been repaired. They settled down on the platform: Ella, Frau Luther, the eight children, among the hundreds of other refugees. Russian soldiers walked up and down the line, looking them over. The two women felt uneasy. They decided it would be safer for them to go into the nearby community hall that served as the station waiting room.

Several hundred people had crammed themselves into the hall. Ella took refuge under a table with two of Frau Luther's boys. When soldiers came in at night and tried to pull her out from under the table she resisted with all her strength. She hung on to the table legs and yelled so loudly that people in the waiting room trying to sleep began to grumble. 'Better you go with them,' voices in the crowd muttered, but Ella refused to let go of the table. Frau Luther heard the Russians say they would take her two older boys instead, which they did, and she was angry with Ella for having been the cause of it. Fortunately the boys were returned to the station the following day, unharmed.

That night a freight train arrived, taking the refugees on to another ruined town. Again they were ordered out onto the platform. Not wanting to risk another encounter with Russian soldiers, Frau Luther and Ella thought it best for Ella to hide in the rubble of the bombed town, so the two women with the baby went to find a suitable hiding place while the other children waited on the platform.

Ella noticed a house where a queue of people stood waiting to be given milk by the woman who lived there. That anyone in the ruins of this town had milk, let alone was giving it away to strangers, seemed incredible, but they took their place in the queue. On hearing about the troubles of Frau Luther and her large family, the woman gave them a large jug of milk to take back to the children. She herself had just lost both her teenage sons in the last days of fighting, she said, one of them in front of the house, the other inside, shot dead right where they were standing. All she now had left to do was help the refugees. She advised Frau Luther that Ella and the two older boys would be safer spending the night on the floor of her shop, where they couldn't be seen from outside. All three of them were at an age when they might easily be deported to Russia to work. They did as she suggested. Ella felt warmed and cared for by the kindness this woman spread over them like a coverlet, and she fell asleep the moment they lay down on the floor.

Ella had arranged with Frau Luther that she and the two boys would come back to the station before it got light, but they overslept. Two freight trains had come and gone during the night, taking everyone else away. When Ella returned to the station as arranged she found the poor woman still sitting on the platform with her six other children, utterly exhausted and in despair of seeing her boys again. Not a single other person was left. So they sat and waited there all day. The platform filled up again with hundreds of other refugees, but by nightfall no train had come. Ella and the two boys again went to the milk woman and slept on her floor, only this time it was arranged that one of Frau Luther's daughters would come and fetch them in the event that a train arrived. In the middle of the night Lucy appeared, woke them to tell them a train had come, and they all ran as fast as they could back to the station. Frau Luther and the other children were already on the train – they scrambled onto the freight car and off they went.

At daybreak the train stopped at another station. The stationmaster told them to cross over to another platform, where the next train was waiting. It was a freight train with a barrel-shaped tank car attached, evidently for the transport of liquids. A boy climbed the ladder up the side of the tank car and put his head into the opening to see what was inside. It seemed to be some kind of syrup, the boy reported. By the smell of it the tank contained something treacly that might be edible. A group of people at once gathered. Someone passed him a bucket and told him to fill the bucket with whatever was in the tank. Ella stood in the open doorway of one of the freight cars further down, watching what the boy was doing, when without warning the train gave a jolt and started moving. The boy, who was leaning into the opening of the tank car to fill the bucket, fell in and disappeared. The train gathered speed. Ella and the two older Luther boys clambered along the the cars until they reached the opening where the boy had climbed in. He must still be inside. She put her head in and looked down into the tank but there was no sign of him. The boy had been completely swallowed up in the treacle.

Ella looked up at that moment and saw the mouth of a tunnel ahead. She yelled to the two boys to lie flat and hang on tight. There was a buffet of air as the train entered the tunnel. She felt the roof skimming over her head. It was cold and dark. In her mouth she had an acrid taste of the smoke rushing back from the locomotive ahead. A few minutes later they emerged from the tunnel into the blazing sunlight of a hot July day. From the top of the tank car she watched an empty landscape pass by – deserted farms – fields untilled – animals lying dead by the wayside. She looked again. Other animals, living ones, lumbered through the landscape. She saw what at first she took for an enormous cow, but it wasn't a cow, it was a rhinoceros. Elephants, zebras, giraffes – a menagerie of exotic animals which must have been abandoned in some circus or zoo had broken out and were roaming the countryside in search of food. Perched on the top of the train, Frau Luther's two boys looked in disbelief at these extraordinary creatures they had otherwise seen only in picture books.

That day they reached Zernitz, the halt for passengers for Holm. They didn't go to Holm, however, as Ella decided it would be too much of a risk to take Frau Luther and the children, who were Ukrainian nationals, to a place where there was such a strong garrison. Once in Soviet hands they could expect only deportation back to Russia. So instead of taking the road west to Holm, she would accompany the elder boys Hans and Matthias in the opposite direction to Melchow, where an aunt of hers lived, to ask her if she could find room for the family on her estate. Meanwhile the Luther family settled down in the shade of a huge old linden tree and waited for Ella and the two elder boys to return.

It was very hot. Ella's boots had been stolen, while the boys had never had any shoes at all. The three of them walked barefoot along roads littered with evidence of the mass exodus – burned-out carts, beds, crockery, pots and pans, jettisoned relics of households that the refugees had tried and failed to take with them. Here and there on mounds by the wayside a cross had been erected to commemorate the person who lay buried there. Sometimes names and dates gave a record of what had happened. Here lay an old woman who had collapsed of exhaustion; over there were the graves of a father who in desperation had shot himself and his five children – somehow he must have summoned the resolution and energy to erect a makeshift memorial to them before doing so. By now Ella had seen so many such things that she registered them without finding them remarkable, just the degree of instinctive attention that helped to keep her alive.

Ella's aunt had no objection to the Luther family staying in Melchow, she told her niece, but the decision was no longer hers. Together they walked across the estate to a row of cottages built to accommodate seasonal workers during planting and the harvest. A Russian-speaking farmer, himself a refugee from Silesia, had been entrusted by the Russians with the management of the estate. This was the man, said the countess with a downturned mouth, to whom one must now defer in all matters, even such a negligible one as the accommodation of Frau Luther and her eight children. It turned out that one of the cottages was vacant, and the man had no objection to the family moving in.

So Ella went back with the two boys the way they had come, another seven kilometres, and found Frau Luther sitting under the linden tree where they had left her. With the small children in tow, who had to be carried or needed to stop frequently for rests, it took the rest of that day to reach the estate. On Frau Luther's behalf, her aunt registered the family's arrival with the Russian command in the big house, explaining that like most refugees they had lost all their papers. Then they could take possession of their cottage.

With Frau Luther safely installed, Ella could finally return to Holm. Her grandmother, her Aunt Charlotte and two of her other aunts burst into tears when she came into the house. Erna and some women she didn't even know, who had been given refuge in the house, gathered around and cried over Ella until she started crying herself. How thin she was! How worn she looked! Ella began to tell her story, but suddenly dropped down where she was standing and lay like a stone on the floor. They covered her with a blanket and left her to sleep for twenty-four hours.

# 14

During the weeks Ella was away Holm had been used by the Russians as the centre of a major concentration of troops east of the Elbe. Considering it unsafe for her to stay there, Ella's aunts had made arrangements with a relative of the family, Ada von Klitzing, for Ella to go and live on her estate in Demertin. The road to Demertin passed through Melchow, where Ella had just deposited the Luther family, then on for another ten kilometres. Ella and Aunt Charlotte set off at daybreak one July morning, pulling a handcart on which her luggage was piled. On their way Charlotte taught Ella a hymn with a seemingly endless number of verses. They sang them together as they passed down the long poplar-lined roads, and by the time they arrived in Demertin at nightfall Ella had all the verses by heart.

They passed a Russian checkpoint on their way, a turnpike manned by a sentry sitting on an elaborately carved throne engraved with the coat of arms of the Klitzing family. Charlotte recognised it as belonging to the set of chairs that until recently had stood in Ada von Klitzing's dining room at Demertin. The sentry took no interest in the older woman and the girl, waving them through without asking to see their papers. Instead of a HALT sign, the barrier at the checkpoint sported a red flag improvised from the lining torn out of a mattress, which probably had originated in Demertin as well. Lazily the sentry lowered the leg he was resting on a stool and the barrier went up, tied to his foot with a piece of string.

The stench of rotting flesh hung over the fields. Herds of cattle had been rounded up for transport to feed the starving population of Russia, but many of the animals had died on the way. Their cadavers still lay where they had fallen. They passed a horse lying on its back in a ditch, unable to get up. The horse looked at Ella with an almost human pleading in its eyes. When she reached Demertin just a bit further on she asked a young Russian, who had nothing better to do than sit on the roof taking potshots at storks, to go back with her down the road and put the horse out of its misery. The Russian went to take a look at the horse, shot in the air instead and laughed, leaving the horse to die.

Ella remembered the Demertin estate from childhood visits there. A Russian command centre had been established in the house. The count-ess had been moved into a wing where servants and refugees were also quartered. Ella was given a room in the same wing. It was a vast castle of a place, once inhabited by a numerous family of three generations. Now it stood almost empty. Where is everyone? Ella asked. Gone, said the countess – four of my brothers and sisters, their wives and husbands, on the day the Russians arrived. Gone? Where did they go? Her aunt took Ella's arm as they went outside. They sat down, you know, all ten of them, she told Ella, and discussed it as if it was just another item of business, and decided they preferred to shoot themselves rather than to live through the wretchedness they knew would come with the Soviet occupation.

On Ada's insistence, the large kitchen was kept busy providing food for all the refugees quartered in the cottages of the estate. In the washing room adjoining the kitchen stood a mangle for pressing linen. It had stood there so long that everyone in the house had forgotten that when it was installed it blocked up the entrance to a larder. Faced with an extreme shortage of food and wondering where to get more with so many new mouths to feed, Ada remembered the larder hidden behind the mangle. Men were sent in to move it to one side and unblock the larder door. Inside they found racks of wines half a century old, jars of home-made marmalade, conserved fruit shrivelled to dust, cocoa that had turned white.

Demertin was one of the great country houses in Mark Brandenburg. Its turret-topped roof dated back to the Thirty Years War. Dogs were hardly less important than people in the feudal world of Demertin. Aunt Ada bred dachshunds. They were the passion of her life. The dogs had had their own salon in her apartments, equipped with an electric sunbathing apparatus. The portrait gallery in the castle showed Klitzing ancestors pictured with their favourite dachshunds going back several generations. If for some reason the dog had not been included in the picture beside his master then a separate portrait of the dachshund was hung alongside. In the cemetery adjoining the family burial ground behind Demertin's church the dogs were buried with their names and dates at the heels of their owners.

Ella had seen all these things before and paid them little attention during her peacetime visits, but under the circumstances of the Soviet occupation in the aftermath of war she understood her mother's radical point of view that estates like Demertin had become obsolete and should be done away with along with the degenerate aristocracy that had lived too well off them for too long.

However, Aunt Ada had ruled the estate since her husband's death decades ago and she intended to continue doing so despite the occupa- tion. An energetic, rather masculine and stern old woman, she was no more prepared to make concessions to the occupying forces than she had been to Adolf Hitler. 'I shan't take orders from that upstart house painter,' she was reported to have said of Hitler, a remark that had landed her in jail in Potsdam. Every morning Aunt Ada stood in her widow's black dress beside the Soviet commissar and participated in the daily briefing on the administration of her estate. During the harvest she was on her feet from daybreak to nightfall, a white-haired old lady with a riding crop in her hand, standing beside the Russians and giving orders when things didn't move along to her satisfaction, and the Russians, respecting her air of authority, let her be.

Demertin had been designated a food supplier to the Red Army in Berlin. Once a day a truck made the trip with potatoes, bread, meat and vegetables. Perhaps because of Demertin's status as official supplier to the Soviet high command, the estate was run on disciplined lines. The looting and rape that had taken place at Holm were not tolerated here. For the first time since she had left Schlawe Ella began to feel more at ease. She got to know a young soldier from Kiev, Sasha, who was frequently among those who sang and danced in the courtyard in the evenings. From Sasha, whom she liked and trusted, she quickly picked up Russian and was employed as an interpreter. Had it not been for the uncertainty of her mother's fate, she might even have begun to enjoy life again.

When Aunt Charlotte came from Holm on her regular visits to Demertin she was struck by the change in her niece. The dry, rather formal and increasingly shrewish Charlotte, now middle-aged, had never found a husband and lived instead for the profession she loved – inspector of farms. In their choice of rape victims the Russians had always passed over the unattractive spinster. Witnessing the abuse of the women around her, Charlotte's lack of attractiveness to men had at first been cause for her to feel grateful. She thanked God in his all-seeing wisdom for not bestowing on her the qualities she had wished for as a young woman. But gradually her disqualification even as an object of rape by not otherwise choosy soldiers with only one purpose in mind brought home to Charlotte just how much she must lack – even by this most brutish standard – what it was that men found desirable in women. This singled her out from most other women, and in some of them Charlotte's exemption from the Russian scourge became a cause of resentment. On the one occasion a soldier dragged her into the bushes and began undressing her, he subsequently thought better of it and left off before completing the act.

How had her attractive young niece survived the onslaught Charlotte had been spared? Why wasn't she traumatised? How had she even re-gained a degree of her former joie de vivre? Charlotte regarded it as her duty to bring up the subject with Ella in case her niece felt the need to discuss it – disguising from herself her own compulsion to talk about it.

Ella surprised her aunt with an ability to talk about her experiences of rape objectively, as if it had happened to someone else. The worst part, said Ella, wasn't the rape itself but the fear of it beforehand. The nights that she and the other women had spent hiding from the Russians in the fields, only to be sought out and dragged from their hiding places, had been terrifying experiences. But apart from the attempted rape by the Mongolian who had chased her on his bicycle, almost all of the soldiers had been very young men – a Slavic type, blond, broad-faced farm boys familiar to her from school in Schlawe. Rape was as unavoidable a consequence of war as looting, burning and the killing of civilians who had been spared the experience of personal combat. Germany had invaded Russia, not the other way round. In Ella's view, these were not personal acts of hostility directed against her. They belonged to the things you had to expect in the wake of a war. They were reprisals for what her country had done to others.

These views of Ella's had a disturbing effect on Charlotte. As she listened, she became conscious of the envy she had always felt for this niece. It wasn't just that Ella, ever since Charlotte could remember, had been an attractive girl with a forthcoming nature, making her an easy child for everyone to get on with. It was not only the lack of rancour Charlotte recognised in Ella and missed in herself; it was the opposite, the hardening of heart Charlotte recognised in herself and could discover no trace of in Ella. She had always looked on the bright side of things. But then how much easier looking on the bright side must have been for the niece than for her aunt, painfully aware of being an unattractive woman, lacking that appeal with which Ella had been blessed but also cursed, as these last months had shown. If this revealed some kind of even-handed justice in the world, by what dreadful law was it done? Charlotte would have chosen to go without such a justice. Her belief in God was shaken to its foundations.

When Ella's grandmother fell out of bed and broke her hip, Charlotte sent for Ella at Demertin to come to Holm. For the past quarter of a century the old lady had been accustomed to getting out of bed in Herischdorf on the side where in Holm there was a wall. Disorientated, one night Cosima found herself on the floor with a broken hip. All they could do for her was to put her leg in a splint. She was bedridden. Unable to comb and set Cosima's long hair, her daughters cut it off – the sight that shocked Ella most of all when she arrived to visit her grandmother. Within days of Ella's arrival the old lady contracted pneumonia and died – the quick and relatively painless death described as the blessing of the old. When she was buried in a makeshift box in the graveyard of the family church Ella thought of that beautiful bespoke coffin with brass handles that would still be lying in the shop of the out-of-work carpenter from whom her grandmother had ordered it in Herischdorf ten years previously just in order to give him a job to do.

Ella returned to Demertin and was put to work in the dairy. She came back from the dairy one evening to a surprise so overwhelming that in that first moment it caused her more of a shock than the happiness she had always felt whenever she imagined the scene.

She found her mother sitting in the bare and draughty entrance hall, a forlorn figure – much smaller than she remembered – much thin⁄ner – haggard – utterly exhausted. After the first tears and embraces they talked about all the events during the nine months they had been separated. Ella asked her about friends, relatives and their house staff in Schlawe. Her mother shook her head in response to the names of the first ten people she mentioned. All of them were dead. Of her brother Oscar, who had been taken for a soldier as her mother had predicted the day the war began, of her stepfather Carl Winter and her father Andrzejewski, who had disappeared from Berlin, there had been no news since the end of the war.

Like shadows they flitted across the room, the memories of them briefly summoned by their names before the conversation moved on and they faded away. There were too many of them. Too much had happened. The individual losses mother and daughter had sustained were all interred in one enormous graveyard of memory. All the men had gone. Only women were left. Ella had not understood the full extent of their loss until this conversation with her mother. East of the Elbe the old estates had been swept away after hundreds of years in the family, not just lands and possessions but traditions, an identity, a way of life.

Lying together in bed that night, her mother also confided thoughts about her own mother, Cosima, recently buried alongside her ancestors in Holm. The news of her death appeared to have made little impression on Maria, who had been through so much in the previous months. Had she been more concerned about me, Maria told Ella, had she kept more of an eye on what I was doing and given me advice, I would never have married your father, which was the greatest mistake of my life, you know. Grandmother's uncomplicated easy⁄going nature, as it had seemed to Ella, turned out in the version she was now receiving from her mother to have been an insufficiently caring nature. This lack of care, as Maria saw it, had been the cause of her unhappiness, and Ella had paid her grandmother back by withholding, or at least not fully showing the affection she felt for her. Cosima never learned the reason for this neglect, and now that she was dead she never would. Ella had heard similar thoughts from her mother before, but in the aftermath of her grandmother's death they took on a different significance, one that caused her to feel uncomfortable as she lay there in the dark – it had been wrong of her to act the way she had.

Barely arrived, her mother was already running through with Ella a list of preparations to be made for their flight. They must get across the Elbe as soon as possible, she said, first to Berlin and from there to Hamburg, where she had relatives who would take them in. If they stayed in Holm they wouldn't survive the winter. Her mother's *not survive the winter* still in her ears, Ella was already drifting off to sleep – so tired that she didn't even remember to say piep!

The refugees' trek began in Demertin after Ella, her mother, Eduard, Nico and Charlotte had collected the Luthers from Melchow. Ella had promised to help the family escape to the west. After the birth of another baby, Frau Luther now had nine children to take with her. Including Ella's mother, Ella and the three other children, they made a party of fifteen people. The first leg of the journey was made easy by Sasha, the young Russian who had befriended Ella during the months on her aunt's estate. Without asking for permission from his superiors, Sasha commandeered a truck and drove the party to Zernitz station.

Trains were still running at irregular intervals, but they were so overcrowded that it would be difficult to find room for fifteen people. It was Ella's idea to occupy the toilet as soon as the train reached the station. One of the smaller boys was lifted so that he could climb in through the window, locking the toilet from inside until the rest of the family had got on the train. Six of the children could squeeze in and sit on the floor; Frau Luther with her baby on her lap was installed on the toilet seat. Every few hours they exchanged places with the others sitting or standing in the corridor and guarding the luggage. People seldom wanted to use the toilet, because the train was continually stopping for one reason or another and passengers found it easier to get off and relieve themselves outside rather than squeeze through the packed corridor to the toilet.

At one of the endless checkpoints where the train stopped the Russians decided that their papers were not in order. All of them were ordered off the train and Ella's mother was sent to Red Army headquarters in the town to sort the matter out. The others waited for her on the platform, but Maria didn't come back.

It was November, getting cold for anyone having to sleep out of doors. The children were hungry and cried all the time. Their food was kept in a sack, which Ella sat on night and day to make sure it didn't get stolen. Once, she gave the children crusts to eat, but the people around them saw her doing so, snatched the bread out of their hands and ran away. So the children had to wait until it was dark before Ella could risk opening the sack to give them something to eat.

For three long days they watched one train pull in and another pull out, hundreds of passengers arrive and depart, and Ella began to worry that her mother would never return. But at the end of the third day she appeared on the platform again, thinner and more haggard than ever. Maria was so relieved to see them all that she broke down and cried, not having dared to hope that her family would still be there. She had all their papers and they were now in order. To get the papers validated she had been forced to spend three days cleaning the Soviet command centre in the town. Barely had she arrived when a train departed and they all had to run to catch it. In the hurry Ella dropped a glove. She didn't notice it until they were already on the train. It meant she would have to go through the rest of the winter with only one glove.

Frau Luther was unable to breastfeed her baby. She had a bottle of milk with her, but the milk was too cold and the baby refused it. So on one of the long stops the train frequently made, Ella ran up the line in the dark to the engine at the front. She climbed up onto the footplate and asked the driver to warm the bottle. The driver did as requested, but at that moment the signal changed and the train had to move on, and Ella had no option but to stay there in the cab. It wasn't until an hour later that the train stopped again, giving Ella the chance to run back to her carriage, but it was dark and she no longer knew which it was. She ran up and down the line, calling her mother's name. The family heard her voice outside and opened the door, and Ella yelled to the engine driver that she had found her car. He answered with a whistle to let her know that he had understood, Ella got back on the train and it set off again.

The baby drank the warmed milk all in one go. In their relief, overcome with exhaustion and anxiety, Frau Luther and Ella's mother cried in each other's arms while the children slept.

Few border transit points remained open. After a week of being shunted back and forth across the country the train reached Helmstedt. On the eastern side of the border the Russians boarded the train and interrogated passengers, wanting to know the names and addresses of those in the west with whom the refugees would be staying. Ella's mother gave them the telephone number of her relatives in Hamburg. The Russians said that until they were able to verify the details the family wouldn't be allowed to cross the border. They stayed cooped up in the train for another two days in what was apparently called no-man's-land, just a few hundred metres from the border. Ella had never been abroad, never heard of no-man's-land, and what she saw of it through the train window looked disappointingly like any other place.

At last the Russian emigration inspectors came back and confirmed that the relatives Ella's mother had named were waiting for them on the other side of the border. But Frau Luther's Ukrainian-German family, unable to name any contacts and having no papers to prove either their citizenship or their German origins, were classified as stateless persons who could not be allowed to cross the border. There was no time for protracted farewells. Then and there they had to leave the train. After all she had done for Frau Luther and her family, Ella felt grief and frustration to be thwarted at the last moment.

Ella's mother's relatives had organised a Red Cross van to meet them at Helmstedt. Purportedly Red Cross patients, they were driven across the border and put on another train bound for Hamburg. It was the middle of November. Winter had already set in. Hungry, dirty and cold, the family stood herded together in open cattle trucks in the falling snow, too worn out to be relieved to have made the border crossing safely, too exhausted even to be glad to be alive.

They arrived in a totally destroyed city. From the station they had a long trek through the ruins of the city, dragging all their possessions in a couple of sacks on the precious cart they had closely guarded all the way from Holm, before they reached the house in the outskirts where Maria's widowed cousin lived. It was her husband who had been number 17 on the list of war casualties, entitling his wife to a personal condolence telegram from Hitler. The widow opened the door. Ella's Aunt Ulia received the ragamuffin family with cries of pleasure and pain, pleasure to see them standing there on her doorstep, distress to see them in such a wretched state. They were so thin and filthy. Like all refugees they had lice, which she could see crawling in their hair. The children scratched their itchy scalps until the blood flowed. The only way of getting rid of them was to shave their heads and douse them in alcohol. Aunt Ulia submitted them one by one to the treatment. Ella additionally had worms. When she went to the lavatory and looked down into the bowl she saw what looked like maggots crawling in her faeces.

Oh, the misery!

Once she had delivered her family to Ulia's door, her duty done, Ella's mother fell into exhausted apathy and became ill. She was moved out of the single room in which the five of them lived with other refugees into a hospital nearby. Her health was disintegrating. She had reached the end of her tether. Ella was too inexperienced to read the signs that the strain of the last year had been too much for her mother. The doctor diagnosed pneumonia. No medicine was available that might have helped her. She dwindled over the weeks. Day by day there was less and less of her mother until finally life just went out of her. Maria was not yet fifty. Respiratory and cardiac failure, the doctor wrote on the death certificate, suspecting stomach cancer, but what difference did it make?

Grief for her mother made Ella ill that winter, a grief almost beyond her strength to bear. Had she shown Maria more attention, done more to take things off her hands, cared more for her, given her more love ... Ella felt she was partly to blame for her mother's death. It was not only her grandmother, it was her mother too to whom Ella realised she had not given as much love as she might have done. During her mother's pregnancy with her last child Maria had complained about Ella's cool-ness, an inconsiderateness uncharacteristic of her. There was a reason for her daughter's reserve. Ella believed that after her second marriage her mother had become far more preoccupied with her children by Carl than with Oscar and Ella. Ella no more confided in her mother the reason for having turned away from her than she had explained to her grandmother a similar change in her behaviour towards Cosima. Ella could give love greatly and she could forgive generously, but she could also punish greatly by withdrawing her love and not relenting once her mind was made up. It made her unhappy to recognise this trait as something in her nature over which she had no control.

Soon after Maria's death, Charlotte, now five years old, was diagnosed with polio and sent to a sanatorium where she would remain isolated for the next two years before she died of pneumonia. For Ella and her two half-brothers Eduard and Nico, nine and seven, sharing an attic room with a family from East Prussia, living out of cardboard boxes, sleeping in one bed, ducking washing lines hanging from the ceiling where the husband dried tobacco leaves, emptying their chamber pots into buckets every day and carting them off as manure for the vegetables her aunt raised on an allotment a couple of miles away, there seemed to be no future. The boys hadn't attended school for years and were running wild. Aunt Ulia had no time for them; she was beset by too many problems of her own. Her house was packed with dozens of other refugees. None of the grown-ups had any time for them.

Before she died, foreseeing the desperate situation her orphaned children would be left in once she had gone, Maria had told her daughter that if she didn't know who to turn to she should go to the British consulate in Hamburg and ask them to get in touch with Ella's great-aunt Hermine in London.

Hermine's mother, Countess Königsmarck, had died in childbirth, and Hermine had been raised with the Klitzing children in Demertin. Still in her teens she had married an Englishman, become a British citizen and moved to London. Her husband was killed in the First World War and she had lived there on her own ever since. Ella's mother hoped that Hermine would be able to do something for the three children. And so it turned out. Great-Aunt Hermine came to Hamburg to meet them, took pity on them and decided to adopt the three children. Fifteen months later, in the spring of 1947, just before Ella's nineteenth birthday, she and her two brothers took ship from Hamburg to Gravesend and went to live in London.

# CHAPTER THREE

## St John's Wood

### 1

His father had been an altogether more commanding figure than any of George's six siblings, of whom five were brothers, would be when their turn came. But then his father had belonged to the last generation in which fathers were still acknowledged as commanders. One generation further back, six sons, including George's own father Gábor, and seven daughters, a round baker's dozen of children, had populated George's grandfather's household in Budapest. George never made the acquaintance of the old patriarchindustrialist Bela Móricz himself, who had founded the family's fortune in steel, foundries spewing whitehot wealth strewn across half a dozen countries under the umbrella of the Habsburg empire at the close of the nineteenth century.

In 1900, at the age of twentyone, Gábor Móricz and his twin brother Miklós arrived in London and Manchester respectively to carry out their father's instructions to the sons he considered to have between them more business sense than the rest of the family put together. Bela Móricz had ordered them to establish a trading house for the export and import of industrial goods between continental Europe, Britain and the United States, a visionary undertaking ahead of its time, torpedoed fourteen years later by the outbreak of the First World War. At this point Gábor and Miklós adroitly switched to munitions production and supply to the government of the country of which they had already become naturalised citizens, emerging from the bonfire that incinerated Europe incomparably better situated men than their continental cousins. While the Móricz family of Budapest went into decline, soon to become as defunct as the AustroHungarian empire that had raised it, Miklós in Manchester and Gábor in London married into well-to-do English families and founded their own dynasty which flourished throughout the Depression years.

Gábor bought a large property that had originally been part of an estate in Hampstead. It comprised a residence built by a Victorian industrialist half a century previously, set in its own park with a circular driveway bordered by stables, a coach house, a cottage for servants, and a kitchen garden laid out in accordance with Victorian principles of domestic economy.

Gábor took possession of his English identity under the new name he adopted when naturalised, changing it by deed poll from Móricz to Morris. Nothing but the old brick wall between the grounds of the house and the surrounding world separated the seven Morris children, born and raised there between the wars, from what they were encouraged to see as their English heritage. Nannies drummed into them the nursery rhymes, cooks the puddings, expensive private schools the history, the etiquette and the class distinctions of their host country until they were indistinguishable from the real thing. Englishness was what the commander wanted for his sons, and Englishness was what he got, ordered from the best purveyors at the best prices and deliverable via the tradesmen's entrance.

That something else belonged to this identity which was not to be had for money may have escaped the commander but was enduringly brought home to his sons while running the gauntlet of public school. Mysteriously, knowledge of their Hungarian origins percolated through these closed institutions and was put to cruel use to teach them their places – teach them Englishness, come to that – for a refined cruelty belonged at its core. Despite all their father's investments and their mother's well-bred native Englishness, here at least they remained foreigners, associated with screeching violins, Gypsies and garlicky stews, too much hysterical enthusiasm and too little reliability, manners that were not quite *comme il faut*. Here at least they were reminded that they did not belong. *Not bankable* was the phrase that George particularly remembered as the neatest destruction of his half-bred self-esteem, rubbed in by the grudging concession of his fellows that his Hungarian cousins were sharp fencers.

George was the child in the middle of the pile, with three brothers older than him, two brothers and a sister who were younger – the sandwich boy was how he thought of himself. Two years separated

144

him from his nearest senior, two from his closest junior. He occupied a sort of no-man's-land in the cluster-like arrangement of alliances that defined the topography of the Morris family. Bookish, often alone, he did not take much part in their games, their passing enthusiasms, or later in their socialising with their neighbours in Hampstead and later beyond. Perhaps the niche suited his solitary temperament, or perhaps it was the niche that formed the temperament.

In the commander's study, where George as a small boy used to curl up like a puppy in one of the deep leather chairs where his father spent the evenings reading the newspapers and smoking cigars, he established his own society with a membership of just two, his father and himself. The society was never formed as such – no minutes were kept, no motions passed, there were no formalities like that; it was not even given a name. George couldn't have said if it was his father's study he liked being in because he enjoyed his father's company or because it offered a refuge from other more crowded places in the house that he liked being in less. But here inside the study, at any rate, he could approach the mountain of his father from its more approachable and gently inclined south side, otherwise seldom glimpsed, presenting a prospect that turned out to be quite different from the stern north face the commander presented to the world outside. Here he felt safe.

Here among the cigar smoke with its tropical Santo Domingo incense, the silver-medalled decanters that clanked when they were lifted and unstoppered by Barrington, the butler, to replenish his father's glass, there were ruminative noises and exotic lazily drifting smells that the boy breathed in with a keen sense of their luxury. Spilling through the room were also the sounds of a language his idling brain soaked up when his velvet-jacketed father read aloud to his secretary Kodaly something that had caught his attention in a Budapest newspaper or dictated letters to him in Hungarian, the use of which was otherwise banned from the house.

The boy could lie curled up for hours without him and his father exchanging a word, his presence there tolerated if not expressly welcomed or even acknowledged, allowed to eavesdrop on the ritual of the commander lighting one of his massive coronas and weighing it silently in his outstretched hand, like some divining rod for the precise gauging of Kodaly's briefing for the day, while the latter's lithe fingers hurried back and forth, back and forth, like nervous animals, smoothing his moustache as he talked and George listened, until the boy was seven years old and came out of hiding.

Last night there was an envelope on the desk here with a week's wages for the staff, his father said to Kodaly one evening; did he know what had happened to it? George raised his head over the armrest of the chair and piped up in fluent Hungarian, 'You put it in the enamel box on the mantelpiece, Father.'

Gábor looked at his son in astonishment, told him to come over, set him on his knee and scrutinised him as if taking notice of him for the first time.

'Well, this is a fine sort of Englishman, hiding in his father's study, eavesdropping on his father's language and keeping track of where he puts his money. What shall I do with him, Kodaly?'

He tweaked George's nose, kissed him on the head and told him to run along because it was time for bed.

To Kodaly he said as the boy went out, 'This one will be the flagship of the firm one day.'

But to the commander's disappointment the man that grew out of the boy lacked any business sense and took not the least interest in the family enterprise, not even in its chief article of faith, making money. In his father's view of the world such an attitude was deplorable. When George came down from Cambridge, where he read modern languages, two of his elder brothers had already been killed in action. George was then released from a brief and unhappy period of indenture in the family business by an authority not even his father could oppose. For the remainder of the war he disappeared into a department of the Foreign Office involving work with classified documents in German, Hungarian and Serbo-Croat.

A month after the war ended Gábor died at the age of sixty-six. His oldest surviving son, André, now titular head of the London branch of the Morris family, gave a speech in honour of the commander at the wake held in the Hampstead house. No fewer than twenty-four members of the Manchester branch had made the journey down to pay their respects.

During the long valedictory address, which began with a narration of events that had taken place in Hungary three quarters of a century ago and rehearsed in family chronicles many times, George had leisure to take stock of the Morris clan assembled in one place in greater numbers than they had probably ever been before or would ever be afterwards.

The overwhelming impression was masculine, a dark almost saturnine masculinity reinforced by the funereal turnout in black suits and hats on an already overcast day. Few women represented the family, three cousins among the Manchester contingent and his one sister alongside her four surviving brothers. It was the reverse of what he saw outside that room, as if the war had taken all the women and left all the men.

The other overwhelming impression, formed in an instant in that room and reversing a lifelong prejudice imposed on him, which he had taken upon himself and held for safekeeping without conviction but with a perverse loyalty he couldn't have explained, was that if there was one thing these lean, sober and rather angular men had in common it was their quality of being bankable.

Where did that leave him? For George didn't feel that he was one of these people any more than that they were of him. He saw them as the sandwich boy had always seen his family, in the middle of the pile but not of it, insulated from it, not particularly for or against, just missing a sense of kin. For the first time he realised with a shock the lack in him where his sense of family should have been. Recognition of shared kinship, something surely instinctive at the core of human life, profound in its ordinariness, one of nature's great commonplaces, was apparently missing in him.

George recognised this absence as a loss, but he didn't feel it was a serious, possibly even a vital one. The absence inside him, a hole almost, didn't cause him anxiety at the time. It was nothing one could see. *Hole* was just a figure of speech. But at the same time he knew this was one thing he could never share with another person, this secret of his life.

Did it follow that he was incapable of love?

What was the nature of his feelings for his father, his mother?

For his father it was perhaps not so much a fondness as a restful sense of familiarity with his father's study, George himself, the room and his father were of a piece. He could not recognise love in this picture of the room, neither love coming towards him nor going out of him. All he could see was a restful self-sufficient familiarity, linked perhaps with a vague hope or yearning for something in which both he and his father partook and in that sense were together.

He had difficulty with the words father and mother.

For his mother the lie of the land seemed to him to be this. It was not so much a question of having a particular feeling for her as of subjection to the habituation of such a feeling, to the expectation of there being such a feeling, which the unavoidable and irreplaceable mother word aroused. Without the word there would not have been the obligation of the feeling that was supposed to go with it. He was conditioned to have it, just as relationships were conditioned to follow from relations, meaning family. Family relations provided the blueprint for human relationships, the score on which all human notes were registered.

George's feeling about the feeling was that he had been duped. If he had once had such a feeling, when he saw through the word, the feeling simply disappeared. It left behind no rancour in him or disappointment. There might have been a bond of affection had it been with a person of his choice. But who was the person beyond his mother, beyond her merely biological relationship with him?

A self-effacing but for all that still tenaciously self-interested person of lukewarm emotions, superficial interests and vapid intelligence, with no claims upon his affections, or none that George could make out other than those mediated by that word mother – with only a spurious claim, then, founded on conventions that were the custodians of a womb-born nexus, a supposedly special relationship protected by the copyright of those mystical words: mother, son.

It was in these reduced, if not to say impoverished, circumstances of the heart that George met Ella, straight off the boat, so to speak, that brought her from Hamburg to Gravesend in 1947 in the company of her two brothers, Eduard and Nico.

## 2

Had it not been for Ella's mother's aunt Hermine, the three refugees might never have been allowed into the country. As they were all under age, however, and the aunt, who was a countess in her own right, now living in a semi-derelict bombed house in Clerkenwell, had agreed to adopt the three orphans, they were issued with residence permits until such time as they qualified for British citizenship. The tedious bureaucracy this involved was made easier by the intervention of George and his useful connections at the Foreign Office.

George knew Hermine well. For ten years, as a Great War widow fallen on hard times, she had spent the better part of a day at the mansion in Hampstead teaching the seven Morris children the piano. In winter she used to arrive in a feathered hat with a snarling fox flung around her neck and her hands held mandarin-style in front of her, enveloped in a black fur muff. She surrendered the fox and the feathered hat to the butler's safekeeping but kept the muff on all day, removing her hands only when they were required to demonstrate on the piano or to take snuff. She suffered from chronic chilblains, she said, muttering about the unheated castle where she had spent her youth.

Prompted by her pupils, she willingly allowed herself to be distracted during piano lessons, telling them stories about a closed courtyard in the castle where a tree growing out of the ground had been sawn off for its stump to serve as a table, a gallery in which the portraits of generations of pedigree dachshunds hung alongside their owners, an attic contain-ing a hundred linen chests that had been the dowry of generations of brides. George's favourite story concerned a beautiful but melancholic great-niece from a Hohenlohe branch of the family who lived confined in a wing of the castle, victim of the horrible delusion that she had swallowed a glass piano, which she was always trying to regurgitate.

'Wouldn't it have stuck in her throat?'

'Indeed it would.'

'But what … I mean how …?'

'My dear, I have no idea.'

Hermine herself possessed impeccable credentials as an eccentric. She blended completely into the English landscape.

Once her great-niece and her two great-nephews had been released from the detention centre where they were held for three months after their arrival, they moved into Hermine's bombed house in Clerkenwell. Another three months went by before George dropped in to see how his piano teacher and her three refugees were getting on. As he passed the railings in front of the house he looked down to see a small figure covered with a white sheet, banging on the dustbin in the basement yard and shouting 'Wheee! Wheee!' until a window opened and the form fled up the steps, disappearing through the open front door of the house above. A woman stuck her head out of the basement window and shouted furiously after him, 'I'll catch yer yet, yer rascally little furriner. You come down 'ere again I'll catch yer and give yer a good drubbin'!'

Hermine appeared frowning at the front door, holding the now unsheeted boy by the ear with one hand, in the other the stick with which he had been beating the dustbin.

'Now we are not Nazis here and not in the habit of striking *terror* into the hearts of our *neighbours*. So you be a good little ghost and go down and apologise to Mrs White *this instant*. Apologise and promise her you will never make such a nuisance of yourself again. What's a drubbing? Well, when you go down to Mrs White I dare say you'll find out. Good morning, George. Would you care for a cup of tea?'

Over tea in the kitchen Hermine explained the household situation to George. It was, she said, a little tight. Half the house had been blown away, most unhappily including the agreeable Mr Blennerhassett, a travelling gentleman from the north of England who had been her lodger for fifteen years and whose misfortune it was not to have been travelling at the time the house was hit. It seemed callous even to mention it, but it was not only her lodger she had lost; it was also the contribution he had made to her household expenses. Her niece and two nephews, all three of them, slept in one bed at one end of the drawing room, which had been curtained off. The countess retained her bedroom upstairs, if a little precariously, as portions of the wall on the stairs' side of the house were missing. They shared the bathroom on the landing. And there was the kitchen.

'If only' – and Hermine admitted she would have done better not to mention this to Ella in front of the two children – 'we had the base-ment. Unfortunately, in the contract I made with Mrs White when I let out the basement flat to her six years ago – and I was grateful to have found a lodger at all in the middle of the Blitz – I stupidly neglected to insert a clause that would have allowed me to terminate the contract with Mrs White in the event of needing the basement myself. Without some such clause, and I have taken legal advice on this matter, George, there is no means of evicting Mrs White. I have a sitting tenant down there, and not, it has to be said, a particularly agreeable one. My young great-nephew Nico no doubt believes he is acting in my interests by dressing up as a ghost and making all that hullabaloo to frighten Mrs White out, but of course that kind of thing won't do.'

George was given a tour. One half of the house was a pile of rubble, from which Mr Blennerhassett 'had to be extricated', the countess said, 'piece by piece', before he could be put back together again and given a Christian burial. Next of kin had not been traceable. His landlady was the sole mourner behind his coffin.

'And as you can see for yourself, the drawing-room *wall*, behind which my three refugees sleep,' Hermine declared with a dramatic fling of her arm, 'is now publicly *exposed* to the *elements*, for which occasion it was never suitably dressed, with consequences it's not difficult to foresee. Much more of this rain and the poor old wall will cave in.'

George was appalled.

'What about the boys? Don't they go to school?'

'Never been to school in their lives. I teach them at the kitchen table. History, arithmetic, calligraphy, basic cookery and above all the king's English.'

'And their sister – what's her name, Ella?'

'Has a temporary job at the centre for the repatriation of aliens, translating German. Her English, by the way, is excellent. My niece wisely employed an English nanny or some such individual when the children were growing up before the war.'

George discussed the situation with his elder brother André, keeper of the family purse now that Gábor was dead, and persuaded him to provide Hermine with an interest-free loan – a gift would not have been accepted – to do such repairs to the house as were necessary to prevent it from falling down. George pointed out that with two of their brothers dead and a half-sister married and now living in America, there was also no shortage of space in the Morris family home for three new residents. Ella, Nico and Eduard could come and live there.

'Perhaps we should meet them first,' said André. 'We could invite them over with Hermine for lunch.'

André being the businessman he was, or liked to imagine he was, cooked up a scheme that honoured philanthropy and 5 per cent at the same time, knowing there was not the slightest chance of Hermine ever raising enough money to pay off a loan. He made Hermine an offer for her house based on its pre-war market value in an intact state, with the understanding on her side that the money could be used only to restore the house, and with the understanding on his side that the house would legally belong to him while Hermine remained its nominal owner. She would become his rent-free tenant until her death, when the whole house became the de facto property of the Morris family, separate terms having been made with the sitting tenant in the basement, Mrs White. They would thus avoid the death duties they would otherwise have to pay in the event of Hermine leaving them the property in her will. As André, his lawyer Dickinson and the countess would be the only signatories to the deed setting out the terms of this purchase, it might as well remain a secret between the three of them, André suggested, even from George.

André was puzzled and intrigued by his brother's uncharacteristic helpfulness and involvement in the fate of three people who would ordinarily have been of indifference to him. If André was not being entirely honest with his brother, nor, he suspected, was George being entirely honest with him.

'And their sister, what's her name, Ella?'

George knew very well what her name was when he asked Hermine this question. Ella Andrzejewski, born in Berlin-Charlottenburg in 1928. Colour of eyes: green. Her papers, the transcript of interviews with her in the detention camp, the photographs taken of her and her brothers on arrival in England, had sat on his desk at the Foreign Office for a couple of weeks. He had Ella's details by heart. A few days before George dropped in on Hermine he had used his lunch break to pay a visit to the centre for the repatriation of aliens down by the river, not far from Millbank, where it had been installed at short notice in a warehouse immediately after the war.

The great yawning interior of the building had been partitioned into cubicles, each equipped with two chairs and a desk. On one side of the desk sat the applicant, on the other an employee of the centre who spoke the applicant's language, anything from Estonian to Cantonese. The place was a warehouse of Babel, an aviary of babbling sounds that rose all the way up and chased each other sibilantly around the ceiling thirty feet above. Queues of applicants, displaced and for the most part stateless persons, sat waiting on benches in corridors hung with signs indicating the language spoken in each cubicle. Thousands of people passed through this place; hundreds of individual fates were decided here every day. George could feel the great press of humanity, the collective energy of the applicants, their hopes and fears, a mass of overflowing urgency that could hardly be contained within the building's walls.

George sat on one side of the canteen watching a very striking girl on the other whom he could not have mistaken for anyone else. She sat with her colleagues, eating a sandwich and drinking a glass of milk. He had recognised her face at once from the photos he had seen at the FO. In life it was a much more animated face, with high Slavic cheekbones, full lips, large eyes, a small nose with flared nostrils, a high forehead from which her ash-blonde hair was swept back and gathered in a clasp at her neck. Ella and her two half-brothers had been destitute and half-starved when they arrived at Gravesend. She had celebrated her nineteenth birthday in a detention camp outside Aldershot a week later. Five foot seven inches tall and less than six stone at the time she was first measured, the girl had clearly put on weight during the intervening six months.

Ella's account of the previous eighteen months – a microcosm of the chaos that had engulfed central Europe – had begun with the horrors in East Prussia during the rampage of the first Soviet soldiers to set foot on German soil. 'They had it coming to them,' someone had pencilled in the margin of the interview with Ella conducted by the immigration officer in Aldershot.

An iron curtain had since come down across Europe, shutting off the east. The curtain hid from Ella's view the homes of her family in Pomerania and Silesia and separated her from all her relatives who might still be alive. All she and her two half-brothers had left were their great-aunt Hermine in Clerkenwell and a cousin who had emigrated to Canada between the wars. They now left their history behind them and acquired a new one as members of the Morris household in Hampstead, and, in time, of the family. One year after the refugees arrived in England, George Morris married Ella Andrzejewski.

Only a couple of months before they got married Ella had received a letter from Alex in Canada suggesting that she and her brothers might like to come out and join him on his farm in British Columbia. Ella read the letter to George and asked him what he thought of the idea. George asked her if she wanted to go. Ella said she hadn't made up her mind and was hoping that George would help her to do so. She knew nothing about Canada, nothing about anywhere. Until she boarded the ship that took her from Hamburg to Gravesend she had never left her country. George unexpectedly broke down. He cried. He put his arms around Ella and begged her not to go. He asked Ella to marry him, and Ella, surprised and moved by a sympathy for George that was reinforced by a keen sense of her indebtedness to him, said on the impulse of the moment that she would.

For the first year of their marriage the young couple moved into the

Hampstead coach house, where they could enjoy more privacy. The rooms upstairs had been used for storage, and George and Ella went through all the things, the cases full of old clothes, the odds and ends of furniture, the piles of photograph albums, to see what they could use, throw out or give to jumble sales. Inside the albums George came across photos of his uncle Miklós and his father Gábor taken on their arrival in England in 1900. Half a century ago they were still such young men, hardly twenty-one. In one overexposed shot of his father, Gábor looked out of the picture three-quarter-face at his son with a mischievous smile that had about it a charm the son couldn't remember having ever seen in Gábor.

'I wouldn't have recognised him,' said George. 'Odd. Somehow it's not my father I see. He reminds me of someone. I look at him and see someone else.'

Ella asked him who.

George said he didn't know. At the time he didn't. It was only much later he realised who it was. The photograph of George's father as a young man reminded him of Ella.

# 3

George was hardly less startled than Ella when he cried. George hadn't cried since he was a small boy, not since the first few times he was sent away to school. He learned to bite his lip, bang his head on a wall, go and sit on the lavatory, do anything but cry in front of other people. Once indoctrinated into the culture of boarding school, he had never cried again, not even when he was alone. Such was his anxiety about losing Ella, however, the crucial importance of not losing her, that for the first time since he was a small boy George had wept.

Instinctively George understood his weakness and Ella's strength. Yet otherwise George did not feel weak. In his even-keeled self-satisfaction, inside the little walled-off harbour he had made for himself where no ripples were left by the toing and froing of people outside, he did not feel inferior to anyone. But neither did he feel bound to anyone. I am me, he crowed to himself, and I am completely free! He could manage quite well without anyone – until Ella told him of her plans to emigrate to Canada.

That George cried and Ella comforted him, saying that instead of going to Canada she would stay in Hampstead and marry him, that this action/reaction was a trade/off, that in some sense George blackmailed Ella and she acquiesced – had the matter been put to him in such terms at the time, George would have considered the idea preposterous. George might have thought he could grow into marriage as he had grown into life, bit by bit, as a matter of course. George never liked to force the issue of anything by imposing a decision on it. In its self/sufficiency, his nature was quite passive. Until Ella no other person had been intimately involved in George's passage through life, no other person had been required. But when Ella spoke to him out of the blue about emigrating to Canada, it became clear to George that there could be no growing into marriage with Ella unless he first asked her. Ella talking about Canada seemed to establish beyond any doubt that she could not have been contemplating marrying George. Unlike George, she had not been quietly growing into marriage but into emigrating!

George felt something like jealousy that he had been overlooked for Canada. His feelings were hurt. He was disappointed and frustrated. All this had flowed into George's unexpected crying. But tears *had* flowed, the one immediate, incontrovertible display of emotion George had at his disposal. He could tell from Ella's reaction that it was his tears Ella responded to rather than his proposal. George realised that what Ella meant to him was more than what he meant to Ella. So was it blackmail? Or was it just an appeal to Ella's soft side, the side that took up most of her nature? From their first meeting George had at once appreciated the human warmth in Ella lacking in him. Eagerly he stretched out his hands to warm them at this vital fire. George took a decision, or rather a decision was wrung from him by the tears he shed. Ella would be the hearth in his life.

To his surprise, the response of his family, with one notable exception, to the announcement that he and Ella would be getting married was lukewarm. His elder brother André was suspicious. To André it was plain that for a destitute young woman, a German with two brothers in tow, there could be nothing more desirable than to marry into a wealthy family in England. His sister Tessa even took Ella on one side to tell her that in the Morris family they took a dim view of children being born out of wedlock – an insinuation that infuriated George, though not sufficiently to make an issue of it, as Ella had expected, and have a row with his sister. But for once George was supported by his mother, wielding her habitual two-edged sword when she gave her verdict in front of all the family at Sunday lunch. George could consider himself lucky if a girl of Ella's class looked at him twice, she announced over dessert – and that was that.

Like all her brothers except George, Tessa had a dark complexion and was tall and thin. She had a pinched face, a wrinkled forehead with a permanent suggestion of a frown from the effort to see despite her short-sightedness and exacerbated by her refusal to wear glasses. What one at first took for a quizzical expression, perhaps imposed on her face by the muscular strain of trying to manage without spectacles, gradually took on the appearance of disapproval or distaste. Tessa could find lots of reasons to be dissatisfied with the world, but all of them could be traced back to one source: her knowledge that she was not a prepossessing young woman. Men took no notice of her, and if they did she discouraged them, as there could then be only one other thing they had in mind.

Her father Gábor, looking for prettiness in his one daughter and not finding it, lost interest in her and failed to notice how intelligent she was. Intelligence in women was considered undesirable by the patriarch. He did nothing to promote it; she was encouraged to conceal it. She received erratic private tuition at home and never went to school except a finishing establishment in Lausanne, to which she was sent when she was seventeen. While Tessa was growing up in the 1930s, the need for qualifications equipping her for any role other than that of a society hostess was not foreseen by her parents. In the depressed Britain of the 1950s a spoilt rich girl like Tessa, lacking the slightest sense of social responsibility and with no qualifications to earn a living, was a drain on the family.

Denied a proper education, her mind pursued other avenues to satisfy her curiosity. She studied the people around her. Observant and astute, equipped with a sharp tongue, Tessa found an outlet for her thwarted energy in the scathing comments she contributed to family and social gatherings. Prompted at first by envy of girls more attractive than herself, then by a misanthropic cast of mind in which nobody found favour, Tessa instinctively sought out the weaknesses in a person's character and appearance, never their good points, and became incapable of recognising anything unless in the form of caricature.

Naturally she intrigued against Ella. Oh yes, Tessa knew them well – the bounty hunters, the women who beleaguered her brothers with an eye to a share in the family fortune. Wasn't she a woman herself? Couldn't she smell them out, the girls no less than the boys, the only ones who paid her attention?

'And if you think you can snare George by getting yourself pregnant, then think again, because that's not how we do things in this family.'

Ella was speechless.

Tessa turned against Ella an unspoken spite against her own mother for having done just that to bring pressure to bear on her child's father when she saw him beginning to waver. Decent is as decent does. Wherever the bones of her eldest brother now lay, shot down over the Channel in 1940, the memorial erected to him in their local church recorded a date of birth adjusted to be compatible with the date of her parents' wedding. These were among the skeletons shut away in a chock-full family cupboard of which Ella had no inkling on her arrival in the Morris home.

From Ella there had not been a murmur of promiscuity – no disporting herself, she might have retorted, nothing along the lines that Tessa had in mind since the last time she was raped by a Russian officer four years previously.

On the first occasion she went to the Morris house to meet the family for dinner the conversation had been dominated by Tessa's lament over a new litter of kittens, a litany that dragged on for most of the meal: how one of the kittens was too weak to survive, the vets she had consulted, what measures had to be taken on the kitten's behalf, how Tessa had been up all hours of the night and still the kitten had died. A kitten! Ella sat and listened in silence, thinking of her dead mother, who had lost everything, husband and son, house and home, everything except for the sack of potato meal and a side of bacon she had taken with her to feed the family on their flight to the west.

Elaine Morris, Gábor's widow, had no doubt it was her son's money rather than her son which had persuaded Ella to marry the least attractive of the brothers. And why not? In Ella's place Elaine had done the same. She thought back thirty years and saw another well-bred young blonde woman with no money, exchanging what she had got for what she had not – an acceptable arrangement upon which society had rested then as now. Elaine could sympathise with Ella. You had to make use of what you had. But she doubted whether Ella herself saw it like that. Ella was naive as Elaine had never been. Ella had illusions about love and integrity, genuinely believed in such things. Elaine could already pity her for the disappointments she knew lay in store. How anyone, even for money, would agree to marry her son George, particularly when two more eligible brothers were still available, was a mystery to their mother, she confided to Ella.

'I'm pleased for George's sake,' Elaine continued to Ella, 'but what you see in him, *as a man*, I just don't know.'

Feeling her way in a bristling family atmosphere unlike any she had ever known, learning to converse in a code entirely new to her, Ella heard the undertones in Elaine's rhetorical question and did not attempt to answer it. Elaine's candour astonished her, if candour it was, but she was not sure about that either. To have given a truthful answer to the question, Ella would have had to tell Elaine about her conversation with George after his unexpected breakdown, and to have done that would have been a breach of confidence.

None of the Morris family, including George, was in a position to understand what Ella had already been through by the age of twenty. They might know of it but they could not share it. They could not have conceived her bewilderment on entering the walled grounds of the Morris family residence to find herself listening to Tessa's lament for a dead kitten. Everything within these walls was still in its place; everything was available; everything was intact, and yet a divisive spirit ruled the house.

Despite outward appearances the house was not really cared for. It was not even particularly clean. It might just have been Ella's German meticulousness, or it might just have been that she looked more closely because she cared about details. For Ella's mother, care showed in the details or it was nowhere. Wherever things could be put out of sight in the Morris home, in chests of drawers and cupboards, there was no neat-ness or purpose in their arrangement as there had been in her mother's and grandmother's linen cupboards. They had simply been bundled in. The visible surfaces in the house – the mirrors, the silver, the furniture, the brass handles on the front door – maintained their sparkle for visitors. The hidden, humbler parts of the household inventory, however, were not looked after, the small things such as socks, hairbrushes and rubber bands, disparate bedfellows crammed into the same drawer, bedlinen that had not been folded properly in the airing cupboard, missing buttons that had not been replaced, burst seams or tears not darned, which spoke to Ella of their neglect.

Elaine, André and Tessa might wonder more or less spitefully why she had agreed to marry George. But their conjectures – and someone naturally made sure they got back to Ella – revealed more of the persons who made them than of the person about whom they were made. Ella married George because for the first time since her mother's death she felt needed by someone. This they had in common. Each of them needed the other in the awareness of an outsidership they shared, if for different reasons.

# 4

The maternity home where Max was born on a dark November morning had still been only provisionally repaired four years after it was hit by a flying bomb at the end of the war. Her mother-in-law had chosen the home for Ella because that was where she had given birth herself. What Elaine Morris remembered as a light and spacious place, built according to the most modern specifications, had gone into decline in the thirty-odd years since she had given birth there to the first of her seven children. The windows on one side of the building had been boarded up to meet wartime curfew regulations. The sanitary facilities had not been modernised since they were installed in the 1920s. None of the original beds had been replaced. Ten to fifteen were crammed into one room with the door always left open onto a draughty passage, so that Ella in the bed facing the door could see and hear the women in labour in the room on the far side.

An overworked midwife gave Ella an enema and told her to go to the lavatory before getting into bed and rushed off without saying where the lavatory was. Ella made her way barefoot down the passage but couldn't find the lavatory, winding up in a big room full of wounded soldiers who had been quartered in the maternity home because of lack of hospital space elsewhere. One of the soldiers got up and showed her the way to the toilet, and then she had to run to get there, what with the enema and the child in her she could feel was about to be born. The midwife came back and had a look at Ella, reaching with her fingers into her vagina, just like that, and said, Yes, it's a boy all right, I can feel his penis. Off she went again and Ella lay there whispering *a boy a boy a boy* to herself, and was very happy.

She could see the midwife darting to and fro in the opposite room and pregnant women coming and going, and she was so absorbed with what was going on there that she forgot to let the nurse on duty in her own ward know that her condition was changing, and that she should tell the midwife to come and have a look. Eventually the midwife came rushing back in, ripped the sheet off the bed and saw that Ella was in fact already giving birth. Couldn't you have let me know sooner? she snapped at Ella, but how was Ella to know? This was her first childbirth, and the midwife had told her when she arrived on the ward, what, only about half an hour ago, that she could expect to wait four or five hours before she went into labour. A woman doctor arrived to supervise the birth, a kind and gentle woman not in a hurry at all, unlike the midwife, and in next to no time Max was born. The doctor laid the baby with the umbilical cord on Ella's stomach, took a pair of scissors and said Bye, cutting the cord, picking up the little bundle and putting Max on a bedside table to be cleaned and swaddled by the nurse.

It was only after the birth that Ella realised how cold she was. While giving birth she had lain uncovered for about half an hour wearing only the nightshirt the midwife had given her, and she felt chilled to the bone. So she had a drink of hot coffee from the Thermos she had brought with her, as she had learned from her mother to do after giving birth, but she didn't seem to get any warmer as a result, so she drank off the whole flask of coffee all at once. After that she wasn't able to rest at all. The baby had been taken away somewhere; no one came, and in that tense, hyper-wakeful state brought on by the caffeine, she lay in bed unable to sleep for the next thirty-six hours.

Why hadn't George come? George would later explain to her that an emergency had come up at the Foreign Office requiring him to fly to Budapest during those thirty-six hours Ella had been left by herself in the maternity home on the other side of London. Why hadn't he at least telephoned to say he couldn't come? Why hadn't he called his mother and asked *her* to come? But for one reason or another none of the Morris family had been able to visit Ella to see if she needed anything in hospital until late on the evening of the second day, when Elaine turned up with apples and flowers and a murder thriller to keep Ella occupied until George arrived to fetch her and the baby home. It was the first blight on the marriage.

Within fifteen months the family had been enlarged by two more children, the twins Philip and Felicity, and the young couple moved into their own house in St John's Wood. Eduard and Nico moved with them. George took a tolerant if rather disengaged attitude to the presence of the two boys in the house, but he was used to living with a lot of people around him and he understood how important they were to Ella. He knew that Ella worried about them, particularly Eduard, or Edward, as he was now known in the family.

Two years younger than Edward, Nico barely remembered the trek in 1945 from Schlawe to Hamburg. More or less unconsciously he absorbed the new language and slipped into the new way of life. But Edward was already ten when they arrived in England, nine when his mother died, eight when the Russians opened their bombardment on Schlawe and the first soldiers arrived in the coal cellar of the hospital where they were hiding, and he lay mute with terror beside his mother while the soldiers raped her. The nightmares persisted. Edward wet his bed. He stole small sums of money, or appropriated them, as Ella defended him to George, since it wasn't only coins he kept in his magpie's nest under the floorboards but clips and pins and bits of wool, things of no value at all. He lied. He developed a stutter. People attributed it to his uncertainty with the new language, which he learned slowly and with difficulty. That was why he continued to go to the special school Hermine had found for him in Hampstead while Nico went to a local school off Abbey Road.

Later Ella would realise that Edward had been traumatised and blame herself for having let her brother down. She would see that the boy was in need of help beyond what she was able to do for him. She would also recognise that she had not paid sufficient attention to the signs that Edward was a disturbed child, for who knew about such things at the time? The main reason, however, for Ella underestimating the seriousness of her brother's mental disturbance was because Edward's problems and her own – the death of their mother, the loss of their home and most of their family – all these misfortunes of war were obliterated by the Pathé newsreel she saw in a cinema soon after she arrived in London. The film showed skeletal corpses in a pit being shovelled up by a bulldozer and tipped onto a pile in a concentration camp in Poland. Many of the corpses were children.

That the Nazis had organised concentration camps and gas chambers on an industrial scale for the mass production of death was not news to Ella when she saw this film. The subject had come up in conversation with refugees at the repatriation centre where she worked. It was talked about in the Morris family. She heard it discussed on the radio. It was not that Ella disbelieved what people told her. It was just not imaginable. What she saw in her mind's eye, what she sometimes saw in her dreams at night, was the road leading from Holm to the Elbe, corpses piled on the wayside, only more of them, covering the fields on either side as far as she could see. It was a horrific image, but it was one she knew, or thought she knew. She had seen death so many times and in so many forms, become so accustomed to the sight of it that she supposed the mass production of death organised by the Nazis must have been something like what she had seen of it herself.

But the Pathé news images showed her something quite unlike any-thing she had ever seen. Among the piles of corpses there had no longer been time to burn at the end of the war, Ella saw the bodies not just of children but of very particular children, Jewish boys and girls she had known and who had names: Medi Acksteiner, Ursula Loew, Klaus Marx. Others had no names but remained as alive in her memory as they had been when she met them, like the elderly gentleman accompanied by a girl of Ella's own age, dressed like a princess, whom she saw as she had last seen them in 1937, walking down the road in Stettin and turning the corner out of sight. Heading where? Whether or not they had managed to escape, those piles of corpses bulldozed out of the pit in the Pathé film were the destination for which the old man and the girl would have been heading. It was not killing as commonly understood. It was the factory processing of human beings, from the beginning of the production-line cycle with their delivery in wagons to the ovens where they were incinerated, the *Endlösung*, leaving nothing but smoke, rising in those baleful never-ending plumes from the crematorium chimneys.

The newsreel had a devastating effect on Ella.

It shocked her hardly less that people sat in a cinema looking at such things and chewing chewing gum and later walked out of the cinema as if nothing had happened. She found it shocking that the world outside the cinema to which she returned went on as normal. That ordinary life continued after seeing these things shocked Ella almost as much as the things themselves. She found no way to fit what she had seen into the rest of her life, which continued as usual with the cooking of meals, the washing and ironing of clothes.

'That such a thing could have happened!'

That it could have happened – as an avalanche struck, a typhoon blew up, a fire broke out – happened as such disasters happened, natural occurrences, as if like these the Holocaust had just happened. She was so stunned by the images she had seen that at first she didn't give much thought to the process of the happening, that the happening was indeed not a happening but a deed, and the deed had a doer or doers, and these were names, and the individual bearers of those names took on flesh in the Pathé news reports of the tribunal that was trying German war criminals at Nuremberg in the years just after the war. There was talk of the collective responsibility of the German nation, but Ella could discover no connection between such an abstraction and the skeletal corpses of Jewish children to whom she felt bound to give names, be-cause either she had a personal involvement with these dead children or she didn't have one at all.

Medi Acksteiner had been her first and maybe closest Jewish friend, but Medi's Jewishness had never entered into their friendship, for Ella didn't know Medi was Jewish, didn't even know what a Jew was. Yet Ella's mother had known. Thinking back to the Herischdorf days when the Acksteiners lived next door in Countess Pfeil's house, Ella recalled a scene she had previously forgotten.

It was at Easter. Medi came to Grandmother's house to bring Ella a present of chocolate, saying ruefully as she handed it to Ella that it hadn't been her own idea – she had wanted to keep the chocolate for herself – but she had been told by her parents that she should share it with her friend next door. Ella felt admiration for Medi's honesty, owning up to a feeling that didn't show her in a favourable light. Had Ella been in Medi's position she would have wanted to keep the chocolate for herself too, but would she have said so? The truth took courage.

Ella's mother and stepfather happened to be present at this scene in the sitting room, and Ella saw her mother nudge Carl and overheard her whisper, 'Typically Jewish!'

Ella wondered what her mother meant by the remark and asked her, but her mother gave her an evasive answer.

On several other occasions her mother had made remarks that Ella didn't understand at the time. At school in Berlin the prize for the best essay on 'A person I admire' was awarded to a girl in Ella's class called Barbara Schramm, who had written about her grandmother in a style evocative of the Nazi idealisation of the Nordic race. Where had Barbara got such ideas from? Ella asked her mother. From her father, no doubt, said Ella's mother with a wry expression. Dr Schramm was a well-known paediatrician, the head of a clinic specialising in the treatment of physically and mentally retarded children, run in accordance with Nazi principles of racial hygiene. What did racial hygiene mean? But her mother hadn't wanted to go into the subject with her ten-year-old daughter, and Ella didn't raise the matter with her again.

Later, in the course of a tour he was making around the country during the war, Dr Schramm had once called in at the sub-prefect's residence in Schlawe. After his departure Ella's mother remarked it was just as well that Dr Schramm had called on the sub-prefect in his official capacity and had done no more than pay them a courtesy visit while passing through. More would have been compromising. *That man gives me the creeps*, Ella overheard her mother say to Carlchen. It was better for them not to socialise or have anything to do with a man who had been charged with a task she considered *absolutely indefensible.*

These remarks were not meant for Ella's ears, so Ella did not learn at the time why Dr Schramm gave her mother the creeps, what the nature of his task was, or why her mother thought it absolutely indefensible. What did her mother's words mean?

It was only after the war that Ella realised what the purpose of Dr Schramm's journey to Schlawe on his way east into the occupied Polish territories must have been. Dr Schramm had been travelling throughout the Reich to visit hospitals and other institutions in order to select the children who would become victims of the Reich's racial hygiene or euthanasia programme.

The pieces began to fit together in Ella's mind.

Dr Schramm and his colleagues, or someone like them in the Nazis' racial hygiene organisation, would also have been responsible for the disappearance of other undesirable people like Black Ida and the barrel-organ man, and the Gypsies who used to come and pick the blossom in the avenue of linden trees behind Countess Pfeil's house. These people just vanished, and maybe no one had missed them because they were always on the move in any case. But then they had been followed by other people, like the Acksteiners, who had no business to be disappearing overnight, Ursula Loew, the Marx family – ordinary people like Ella – all of whom had disappeared overnight without explanation or a word of farewell.

Ella came to the conclusion that if people had talked openly about these matters at the time they would not have happened. That such a thing had happened was only possible because it was done in silence; more, because it had been kept a secret. Perhaps her mother had not known the full extent of what was happening, but Carlchen surely must have. As sub-prefect of a district on the Polish border surely Carlchen must have known what was going on, only he hadn't talked about it, he had kept it a secret. Ella wondered who else had known.

Had George known?

The discussions Ella began having with her husband in an attempt to answer the question of how such a thing could ever have happened placed George in an awkward position.

George had in fact known towards the end of the war what was going on in places east of the Elbe. As an analyst of central and east European affairs at the Foreign Office it was his job to evaluate intelligence information. From the middle war years on, there had been an increasing number of reports concerning the mass extermination of Jews and others in concentration camps on sites all over the Reich. It was and for the time being would continue to be his job to keep those reports a secret. George saw how these conversations distressed Ella and he found it distressing himself that he could not give honest answers to her questions. He understood exactly what she was talking about when she spoke of a conspiracy of silence in which so many people must have acquiesced, because George was one of them.

He remembered a dossier that had passed across his desk dealing with a breathtaking plan to trade Jews Germany didn't want for things it did, such as munitions, money and food. At the Majestic Hotel in Budapest in the spring of 1944 a meeting took place between Adolf Eichmann and Joel Brand, a German-Hungarian representative of the Jewish resistance organisation Sochnuth. Eichmann offered to sell Brand one million Jews in exchange for ten thousand trucks, but the deal never went through. By then it was public knowledge, after an article entitled 'A Monstrous "Offer"' had appeared in *The Times* in July of the same year. Brand flew to the Middle East, where he was held in detention by the British until the end of the war, his mission unaccomplished.

Whether any of these initiatives were feasible – whether militarily relevant goods needed by the Germans could in practice have been traded for the lives of people not needed by the Allies – merely by formulating such propositions in this way it became clear that they were *not* feasible, for the strategic reasons that had naturally been uppermost in the minds of those whose job it was to decide such matters. As the responsible British minister in Cairo, probably Lord Moyne, allegedly said to Brand after listening to his proposal, 'What shall I do with these million Jews? Where shall I put them?' As a private individual George found this attitude deeply regrettable, but as an analyst he agreed with the logic of the decisions taken at the time by his superiors. The mass murder of a substantial percentage of the civilian European population had taken place, however reluctantly, with the connivance of the Allies.

Here, to his dismay, George watched a rift opening up between himself and his wife, between his language of *deeply regrettable logic* and her giving the names of childhood friends to the children in a pile of corpses so dehumanised that to George they seemed more like objects than people.

Ella needed to talk against the silence in which her mother's generation had acquiesced. When she told her stepbrothers stories about the places east of the Elbe where their family came from and they had grown up, she found words to explain to eleven-year-old Nico why they could no longer live there now. Germany had invaded and occupied other countries and had been invaded and occupied by them in return. That was why they had had to leave their home. It had been hard for them but not unfair. One couldn't complain. Germany had brought its fate upon itself, of which their own fate was a part. She told them about the murder of millions of people. How could such a thing have happened? It had happened because it was done in silence. Only by bringing out into the open things that were hidden could one prevent them from happening again. She talked the brothers through her own childhood, reliving it from her perspective in the present, recognising the wayside signs she had not known how to read at the time and pointing them out to the boys – Black Ida and the Gypsies, the Acksteiners sitting on packing cases in an empty apartment, eating dumpling soup.

All those pieces from the mosaic of her life she now put together as part of a larger picture, talking the children, and above all talking herself, out of the silence that had soundproofed her own childhood, *because of which such a thing could have happened*. She drew a curtain of talk around her brothers, until they became aware of it themselves, a sound like a distant waterfall they would never be able to ignore at the back of their minds.

Once when George came back from the office he opened one of the kitchen cupboards to make himself a cup of tea and found himself facing a full-size newspaper picture of the railway tracks leading to Auschwitz. He ripped it out and took it into the next room where Ella was reading at her desk.

'What is this doing in my cupboard?'

'Our cupboard. As a reminder. Whenever we open the cupboard.'

'Well maybe *you* need a reminder, but *I* certainly don't. Don't you think you're overdoing it a bit, Ella? Is this your German conscience manifesting itself so busily after the event? There's quite enough of this stuff in my head already without needing to open cupboards and find it staring out at me there too, for God's sake!'

Ella turned pale. Then she stood up and snatched the cutting out of George's hands.

'You don't care, do you. You really just don't *care!*'

She walked out of the house and slammed the front door.

# 5

George sat alone in the house for the rest of the evening. The heating wasn't working. He had been planning to go to the theatre with Ella and take her out to dinner. The baby was spending the night with his grandmother in Hampstead. The boys had gone away on a school outing for the weekend. Ella didn't come back. George drank and brooded gloomily in the cold, silent house.

He picked up the book that Ella had been reading. It was a book of poems by Paul Celan. It lay open at the page with a poem that reiterated the phrase *der Tod ist ein Meister aus Deutschland*. George sat down, poured himself a glass of Scotch, read the poem and laid the book aside.

After the extermination of the European Jews one might have expected the deeply rooted anti-Semitism in these countries to have

167

withered away. Not so. Death might be a master from Germany, but he had apprentices everywhere.

In the Foreign Office reports on post-war developments in eastern Europe, which it was his job to analyse, George had discovered that, far from withering away, anti-Semitism was already flourishing again. In Poland, of all places, pogroms during the first couple of years after the liberation of Auschwitz had cost hundreds or perhaps thousands of Jews their lives. All of these eastern bloc countries, formerly under Nazi domination, now took their orders from the Soviet Union. In the 'anti-cosmopolitan' campaign organised by the Soviets at home and abroad it was unmistakably Jews who were being targeted.

Purges with anti-Jewish tendencies had taken place in almost all countries liberated by the Red Army. It was a phenomenon in which George took a close interest, and nowhere more so than in his own country of origin, Hungary, a personal interest fuelled by George's speculations about the possibly Jewish ancestry of his own family. From occasional disparaging remarks about Jews George recalled Gábor making to his secretary Kodaly during the sessions he had attended as a small boy in his father's study, George had gained an unfavourable impression of Jews early on in life. Gábor appeared not to approve of them. That Jews might once have been among his Móricz ancestors in Hungary had thus never occurred to George until the wake after Gábor's death. The overwhelming impression he had received from the massed Morris contingent down from Manchester on that occasion was of a dark, almost saturnine masculinity, reinforced by the funereal turnout in black suits and hats. He remembered his feeling that if there was one thing those lean, sober and rather angular men had in common it was their quality of being *bankable* people.

Two thirds of the country's Jews had been liquidated in the death camps, but a relatively high percentage was able to return to Hungary. They returned embittered towards their fellow countrymen, who had made the most of the Jews' disappearance in order to improve their own situation. The notion of the Jews that they were assimilated, on an equal footing with their fellow citizens, was shown up for what it had been from the beginning, an illusion. Many then emigrated. Many of those who stayed joined the Communist Party, embracing the principles of a class struggle that would inevitably jeopardise the existence of no section of the population more effectively than the Jewish community.

How Jewish communists made possible and in some ways even en-couraged anti-Semitism in Hungary was a question of particular interest to George. Like leading communists in other eastern bloc countries, they had survived the war in exile in the Soviet Union. They had not experienced the trauma of the Holocaust at first hand like their fellow Jews. A rift opened up between the Jews who had spent the war in concentration camps and those who had spent it in exile. The exiles did not think of themselves as Jews at all. By becoming communists, they ceased to be Jews – a putative change in identity that enabled them to implement anti-Semitic policies eventually leading to pogroms. Rakosi and other communist leaders' repudiation of their Jewish origins was thus an act of self-denial – more, of self-mutilation. Such was the cyni-cism to which their opportunism had led them. But the anti-Semitism cultivated by these Jewish leaders as a means of self-protection carried in it the seed of their own destruction as well as that of their fellow Jews. Here, for George, was the nadir of the Jewish tragedy played out in eastern Europe.

George was stung by Ella saying he didn't care. To prove to her how much he did care, he broke an absolute rule not to talk outside his office about anything he had learned inside. He shared with Ella some of his Foreign Office intelligence about ongoing anti-Jewish activities in Europe. Basing his judgement on the country he felt he knew best, not just the facts but the spirit of the place, the condition of the Jews in Hungary, he also attempted to answer Ella's question.

'But why?'

What was stronger than guilt? What fed hate? What poisoned human kindness? What was the most deep-seated, obdurate and unchangeable cause of unhappiness in the world?

'Envy,' said George in reply to her question, with an uneasy recol-lection of how, with his Morris money, tailored suits and the chauffeur-driven family car that came to collect him at the end of term, he had himself been the subject of envy at school.

Ella thought about Medi Acksteiner being fetched from school by her nanny. She remembered the abundance of chocolate in Medi's life, the beautiful clothes her mother bought for her and the fuss she made over her daughter. She thought of the protected child in the garden of the big house, the gorgeous black ringlets Ursula Loew had curled into her hair, the American princess, a fabulous little girl walking with her grandfather down the street in Stettin. Ella hadn't known these children were Jewish, but it was true that she had envied them, just as it was true she had herself been envied by others. She could still recall the words her mother had said to her when she was fourteen.

'You will have to learn to live with the fact that people, especially women, are always going to envy you, good-looking, well bred and intelligent as you are. Envy will bring you a lot of unhappiness in your life.'

Her mother hadn't mentioned money, thought Ella as Maria smoothed the hair down over her daughter's head, and she wondered why not, after all the struggles her mother had been through to make ends meet.

Perhaps at the root of envy, it occurred to Ella, lay a sense of injustice and of the need to redress it. Perhaps envy watched over the inequality of distribution of the things people wanted. And if no one had done more than Jewish thinkers to elaborate theories to counter social inequality, as Ella knew from her father Andrzejewski, then that was also not by accident.

If envy could not exalt those who were deprived, it could humble the mighty, at least in the eyes of those who felt deprived. Why should one woman be born plain, another beautiful? In the gap between them where Ella found no satisfactory answer, that was where envy flourished. By what law should an ugly woman not begrudge another woman her good looks? By what right? Morality might demand it, but morality could demand only what nature withheld. Begrudging the beautiful woman her beauty, the ugly one created a flaw in that beauty. Tagging it with the stigma of hate, she corrected or sought to correct an imbalance. A seed was sown and went underground to grow in the dark. One way or another, the plain woman's envy of the beautiful woman would some day cause her harm.

And so it was that Ella, a striking young woman people stared after when they passed her in the street, still had her grandmother's warning in her ears and avoided looking at herself in a mirror.

Whether it was on account of the sense of outsidership they shared – for George as the sandwich child in a family he had never felt he belonged to, for Ella as a child who no longer had the family to which she once belonged – or whether it was an awareness of the envy of other people who lacked and begrudged them what they possessed, her looks and his wealth – it was in the process of these late-night discussions,

exchanging confidences not shared with anyone else, that George and
Ella grew together as man and wife.

# 6

Paul Hartmann turned up one Saturday morning when the family had
gone on an outing to Regent's Park and George was alone in the house.
He was a neighbour, he said, introducing himself to George, just paying
a neighbourly call. George peered down at him at the bottom of the
steps, in the downpeering way that he had, which some callers found
intimidating. But Paul had no trouble with that. He lived six doors
down on the opposite side of the street, 'you know, in that thing that
looks like a barn', he boomed for the entire street to hear. The Morris
family had been installed in their house for three years, but apparently
Paul had only just noticed their arrival. Considering the scaffolding
that had covered the house for the best part of a year, the noise, dust
and amount of traffic in the street generated by work on it, George
was surprised to hear this. Come in, he said to Paul. Let me show you
around so that you can see what we've been doing to the place.

A large, sprawling man wearing a battered beaver hat, Paul heaved
himself up the front steps and overflowed unabashed into the hall.
George indicated a coat stand for the visitor to hang his hat on. Paul
waved it away.

The lack of clutter and the lightness of the decoration was the first
thing that struck him. In the basement, where there was least natural
light, the walls were the palest of eggshell blues. Catherine, the children's
nurse, had her room down here. Adjoining was the children's playroom.
Paul noticed the sturdy wooden toys and how tidy the place was for a
playroom. He picked the toys up in his large hands and stroked them
absent-mindedly, exploring their texture with his fingertips. Next door
there was a workroom, still in two minds, said George, whether to allow
itself to become the dustbin of the house where everyone just came in
and dumped their stuff. And there was a lavatory. He switched on the
light so that Paul could see into these darker places.

Coming back upstairs, George showed him into the kitchen and
adjoining dining room. A large wooden table with benches on either
side took up most of the room, with two high chairs at either end.

A bookcase occupied most of the wall, housing, to Paul's surprise, an entire set of the *Encyclopaedia Britannica*, dictionaries and reference books arranged alphabetically in several languages, covering subjects from architecture to zoology. Paul wondered at this library being accommodated in the dining room. George explained that eight people sat down to meals here every day. Discussions at mealtimes often gave rise to questions to which one wanted answers right away, so Ella had decided to put the books where they could be consulted to settle arguments on the spot.

He noticed Paul running his hand over the corners of the table, which had been rounded off as smooth curves. That was his wife's idea too, said George. She had asked the carpenter to take the corners off all the furniture in the house so that the children wouldn't hurt themselves if they fell. George opened the French windows of the dining room onto the garden. It was a lawn garden without any flowers other than the climbing plants that bloomed along the fences and some shrubs on the wall at the back; a garden for children to play in, thought Paul, and didn't doubt that this had been another idea of George's wife. A swing, sandpit and slide, all new, showed that children had staked their claims to this garden. Paul had to bend down and reach for a handful of sand as if to touch was to believe.

The kitchen was the most modern Paul had seen. He didn't know such kitchens with dishwashers, stainless-steel twin sinks and streamlined cupboard doors with inset handles existed in England. All the surfaces were of stained wood, the floor too; there were warm honey-yellow tiles on the walls between the kitchen units, and the ceiling was painted white. Two steps led up from here to a sitting room overlooking the street. This room was carpeted. The chairs and sofa had dark leather covers, modern lighting, a single large picture hanging on the wall, a portrait of a woman by the expressionist Beckmann, on which Paul's eyes rested for several minutes. George was too modest, or perhaps too haughty, to have pointed the Beckmann out to his guest. He saw it wasn't necessary in any case.

He led the way up to the next floor. Here George and Ella had their bedroom, with en-suite bathroom and separate lavatory, George a small study overlooking the back garden. 'That's our bedroom,' said George without opening the door to show the room to the visitor. Paul admired two small pictures by Klee on the wall over the desk in the study, wondering what pictures hung in the bedroom he had not been shown. 'Yes, well,' said George, as if he had been about to make an apology and then thought better of it. He smiled instead, a curious lopsided smile that was confined to the left half of his face, as if the right half had nothing to do with it.

Across the landing, a dark work by Lucian Freud faced a contortionist figure by Francis Bacon on the other side of a room that George rather quaintly described as 'our salon' perhaps because it had a piano. But to Paul's mind, any idea of cosiness in this room was banished by the two paintings. Ella sat here at an elegant escritoire in the corner when she read or wrote letters in the evening, while George sank into a deep armchair that had been his father's favourite, smoking a pipe and doing the crossword puzzle before going to bed. This room was the space they reserved for themselves, a retreat from tumultuous days full of children. It was the only untidy room in the house. On the sofa here in the afternoons Ella took her nap, which she would not allow to be disturbed on any account. This room Paul was given just a glimpse of.

The children's room was above their parents'. Built-in cupboards took up two walls. Three cots constituted the only furniture. The ceiling was papered with motifs from the stories of Babar the Elephant 'so that the children have something they enjoy looking up at when lying in bed', said George. 'Ella's idea too, of course. Rather a good one. Everything but the pictures in the house is her idea.'

On the same level as the children's room was their bathroom. The floor seemed to be made of something like cork, and the baths were covered on the outside and at the corners with the same material. Paul got down with a grunt and probed it with his thumbnail. The same care to prevent accidents that was evident in the sawn-off table corners downstairs had been taken here as well. The tubs had been let into the floor, or rather, as George explained, the floor had been raised to accommodate the small people who were the bathroom's sole users. Just the top part of the toilet bowl sprouted out of the floor, allowing the children to squat on it in a way that was natural to them.

'What happens when the children start growing?' Paul asked with a smile, amused by this doll's house bathroom.

'We take the floor out. Oh yes. Ella had already thought of that when the workmen put the floor in.'

Paul heard the pride in his voice.

Next to the bathroom was a room, housing two washing machines, a tumbler, a mangle, two ironing boards and a capacious airing cupboard. Then there was a boxroom. The two elder boys, his wife's brothers, shared the room at the top of the house.

'And that's it,' said George, 'apart from the attic. It's a bit poky, but we might have to convert it one of these days, to make space for the children. Who knows ...'

When George showed him out Paul said that he and his wife kept open house on Sunday evenings. He invited George to drop in with Ella.

'Don't bother to call beforehand. Just come along.'

George forgot to mention this invitation when he told Ella about the visitor. He was intrigued by Paul Hartmann. George liked to drop in at West End galleries during his lunch hour and had recently seen the sculptures of a Paul Hartmann, who must be the man he'd shown round the house. His work was reminiscent of Barlach but without the spirituality. George had noticed the peculiarity of the way his visitor had pronounced his *r*s, not German, as one might assume from the name, but Czech. In the biography of the artist at the back of the catalogue he came across the sinister statement, 'Paul Hartmann was emigrated from Prague to London in the 1930s.'

Their days, his days and Ella's, were so full of other people that George liked to reserve part of one day a week for themselves, and that was Sunday evenings. Fridays and Saturdays they went out to dinner parties, to official functions, to the theatre or the opera or to call on friends. On Sunday they stayed at home in the salon. Edward and Nico went to the cinema; Catherine put the three small children to bed and brought them in to say goodnight on their way upstairs. George and Ella had both grown up with maids. A measure of privacy even from their children was familiar to them from their own upbringing as something to which parents were entitled as a matter of course. The Sunday evenings in the salon were their privacy. It occurred to George that in this room he could recreate with his wife something of the atmosphere of intimacy, warmth of companionship and trust he had enjoyed as a boy in his father's study.

His marriage had transformed George. Against his own expectations, he was turning into a family man after all. During the years of home-building Ella began to thaw out of that condition of deep shock she had been in when she arrived in England, the extent of which had become clear to George only after they got married. She was terrified of fireworks. She hoarded food in caches all over the house. The children were not allowed to leave food on their plates. The clothes in her cupboards were on hangers all pointing in the same direction so that they could be taken out with a single sweep of her arm. She never left the house without a document proving her identity, never went into a shop or stayed in a room where there was a man on his own. Despite what had taken place east of the Elbe, she came to her husband as a virgin, as he did not to her, fumbling for all that, still with misgivings, even an uneasy conscience on his part, and a lack of participation, a neutrality, a sort of blankness on hers. That puzzled and grieved him, so out of keeping was it with Ella's nature, never lukewarm about anything, always completely involved.

The birth of Max and the twins seemed to have a stabilising effect on Ella, substituting a new family for the one she had lost, giving her anchorage in London. She hadn't cared for the city at first. She would have preferred to live in the country. When George showed her a house for sale in the quiet street off Abbey Road she had walked around without saying much, keeping her hands in her pockets. It had been the same with the coach house where they lived for the first year of their marriage. It would be the same with anywhere they lived, even if it were just for a few days in a hotel. She warmed to a place only gradually. Before she recognised it as her own she criss-crossed it many times, turned and turned in circles, treading the ground as her early human ancestors might have trodden down the grass where they made their lair. Only when she had put her own touches to it did a place become a home for Ella.

Ella at twenty-six had finally found herself. Her presence radiated a glow that shed warmth and light throughout the house. George saw himself and the rest of its inhabitants reflected in that glow, lit up by Ella's radiant nature. How different things had been in his parents' home, where his father, not his mother, had set the tone of the family. It now became clear to him what had been lacking in that tone. It had been the absence of his mother. There was no substitute for a woman in creating a sense of family. There was no substitute for a mother when it came to quite a number of things he had taken for granted until now. Willing as George was to get up in the night and deal with the changing of nappies once he had learned from Ella how to do so, he was unconvinced by himself in this new role, at least where Max was concerned. Changing Max's nappy in the middle of the night, George and his infant son looked at each other with what George felt to be a mutual distrust that disturbed him. Max did not like having his nappy changed in the night. He resented the intrusion, and he stared at the nappy-changing intruder with a coldness, hostility even, which troubled his father. George tried to babytalk his way around this discomfort, but it didn't fool Max. His infant son seemed to look straight into his father's heart and not to like what he saw. Did Max only see in him what he saw in Max? Ashamed of such feelings, he kept them to himself.

Gratefully, George followed Ella's lead in their home. He delighted in his wife. He woke up happy just to open his eyes and to see her again. He returned from work in the evening curious to see how she might have changed since he had left her in the morning. Fine shifts were constantly taking place within the outline that was no more than a momentary approximation to his wife, always subject to her seismo-graphic temperament, like a landscape taking on different aspects when ruffled by wind or overshadowed by cloud, the slightest disturbance of the parts that made up her equilibrium. She wore her hair at first short and straight, then, as she let it grow down to her shoulders, had it curled — a mass of ash-blonde curls with a greenish tinge, the most beautiful hair George could imagine to match her grey-green eyes. She had a tiny mark under her left eye, otherwise not a blemish on her face. Her skin had the same clear, warm tone as her mezzo voice. She was as agreeable to listen to as to look at. Still as small-waisted as she had always been but with broader hips after bearing three children, Ella's figure had filled out in five years of marriage. Neither too large nor too small, her breasts stood up without the help of a bra and pointed in clearly different directions. She thought this was a sign of good breeding. Just fine as they were, thought George, amused by Ella's notion that breasts pointing in different directions could be considered aristocratic. But her arms, she complained, her legs! For a woman of medium height, her legs were proportionately shorter than her torso, which accounted for the stockiness of her appearance. She thought her upper arms too thick and ungainly. She was conscious of lacking elegance. She wasn't tall or petite enough to be elegant. Clothes would never hang on her the way she wished.

Had she been an animal, Ella thought she might have been a penguin, an all-purpose amphibian equally at home on land or in the sea. For

George she had more the character of a pit pony, stoical, with unlimited stamina and heart. Unlike English women, she didn't use make-up. She hated the lipstick stains women left on her cups. Make-up would have required Ella to look at herself in a mirror, which she still would not do, not by choice. How do I look? she asked George instead. He was her mirror.

While they were still living in the coach house George told his young wife that she had sex appeal. At twenty-one, she didn't know what that meant. Despite what she had gone through in the war, Ella remained an innocent, as her mother-in-law Elaine recognised long before George. But George recognised other things about his wife that Elaine didn't notice, curious little observations that cropped up in what she said. If she chose to believe in aristocratic breasts, that was fine by George. Ascribing certain qualities to certain physical traits was part of what was understood by 'breeding' in old families with long pedigrees, the people, their horses and dogs. It was a form of eugenics that had been around for as long as domestic animals had been reared and trained to play their part in human life.

But when Ella expressed her annoyance with the bottom of baby Max's ears for being attached to the side of his face, explaining to George that it was desirable for an earlobe not to be attached at the bottom but distinctly separate from the face, George felt uncomfortable. As Max was growing she would periodically give a little tug at his earlobes, encouraging them to grow independent. With a frown of concentration she would examine the sleeping twins in their cradle, poring over their faces as if fearing to make some unwanted discovery and smiling up at George when she found none. The shape of a person's head, an upper lip that was too thin, eyes that were not set wide enough apart, provoked mistrust. The list of things in the category of attached earlobes was long, and she was dogmatic about them. These were ideas, propaganda in fact, along with a terminology specifying full Jews, half Jews, quarter Jews and so on, that had filtered through the conversations, films or radio broadcasts to which Ella had been exposed and which had taken root in her from the moment she was born; inklings in the mind, stirrings of the emotions, shadowy implants that grew unnoticed within the grain of her nature. When Hitler came to power a new eugenics had also come of age, a jinn, a demon let loose on the world and never to be confined again in the flask from which it had been released.

# 7

Edward spent the summer holidays with his Uncle Alex on a farm in British Columbia. After four months he came back to London full of enthusiasm for the mountains, the forests and the animals but above all the horses, which his uncle had begun breeding as a hobby and was now expanding into a business. London in the closed November weather to which he returned depressed him. He felt shut out of life. At seventeen he had left school with few qualifications and no idea of what he wanted to do. He hung around the house for a week, dissatisfied with his life, until Ella sat him down and had a talk with him.

She had a particular fondness for this stepbrother who was nine years younger than her, by now as much a son to her as a brother. She remembered the long struggle Maria had to give birth to this large baby, no less the long struggle the baby had to be born, pushing his battering ram of a head out of his mother's womb; a squat, glowering baby, his ugly beetroot face permanently screwed up ready to howl, who seemed to continue to batter his way out of one confinement or another throughout the early years of his life. That Maria had so obviously loved this child from the moment she first took him into her arms, immediately forgetting her labour, had astonished Ella then and still puzzled her now. That flood of love she had seen on her mother's face and heard in her voice she expected to feel herself when Max was born. But she had not, not after the birth of the twins either, and she wondered why.

For two years as refugees she had shared a bed with Edward and his younger brother. Nico slept like the child he was; Edward had nightmares, tossed and turned and tried to butt his way out of them, the dark places, the wombs, coal cellars and air raid shelters in which he was confined. But now Ella recalled other scenes in which Edward figured as a happy child, a hero admired by all, his back to the candlelit room where the family and their guests gathered at Christmas, showering the boy with praise.

Every winter Edward used to sit sentry on the window seat, looking out at the farmers' wagons driving by. The wagons were loaded with snow shovelled off the cobbles of the old town centre of Schlawe on the sub-prefect's orders and were now carting it away to dump in the river. After a heavy snowfall a few dozen teams would work through the night to clear the snow, each large hay wagon drawn by two horses. As they passed by his window, Edward at the age of six could already identify by name all of the thirty to forty horses in the shafts of the carts. He noticed when the farmer changed the near-side for the far-side horse in his team. Not believing the boy at first, his father once stood with him at their front door, asking each of the passing farmers if the names his son gave the horses were correct, and he was assured by their owners that they all were. Edward never made a mistake. Naming the horses became Edward's Christmas party piece, which the family looked forward to every year quite as much as he did.

'If Uncle Alex agreed, would you like to go and live with him on his farm?' Ella asked him.

The boy's eyes shone.

Ella sat down and wrote a long letter to her cousin, whom she had never met. Just before Christmas a telegram arrived. It read: 'Edward welcome to join the family here in the spring stop Alex.'

That Christmas of 1955, before the family began to disperse, was one of the happiest in Ella's memory.

Ella and her brothers had been brought up to celebrate on Christmas Eve. In Herischdorf, presents had hung on threads from the ceiling, but in the high rooms of the sub-prefect's house in Schlawe that hadn't been possible, and the presents were tied to the branches of the Christmas tree or put underneath it in the English manner. In St John's Wood, continuing the tradition she had learned from her mother, Ella introduced a two-day Christmas: on Christmas Eve for as many children as wanted to come, for people in the neighbourhood who lived alone and had nowhere else to go; on Christmas Day reserved for the family. Her great-aunt Hermine counted as family and was invited on Christmas Day, but she preferred to come on Christmas Eve because the celebrations with children were so much more lively.

The preparations for Christmas began a year before the event. At whatever time of year, if Ella saw something she thought suitable for someone she would buy it and put it in the present cupboard, just like her mother had done. Like her mother, she kept the key to the cupboard in the left toecap of a red shoe. When she came across things in shops that caught her fancy, her synapses seemed automatically to connect a particular gift with the particular person for whom it was intended. In her cupboard she also kept a stock of 'open' gifts in case the need for a present should suddenly arise. The children to whose birthday parties her own children were invited might be the beneficiaries of this store, or visiting friends, the postman, the milkman, the workers who did jobs for her about the house. All these people's names and the gifts they were to receive were noted down in the school exercise book she kept with a small reserve of cash hidden under the underwear in her lingerie drawer exactly as her grandmother had done.

The two teenage boys got up early on the morning of Christmas Eve to hide presents for the smaller children's treasure hunt. In the afternoon they lit the candles and turned out the lights in the living room while the children were kept occupied by Catherine in the nursery, until the signal was given and they all came rushing up. Max would always be first, his face fraught with excitement, followed by Max II, a playmate from the crèche down the street, and half a dozen other children from the crèche between the ages of four and six, with the three year-old twins Felicity and Philip, who were always bumping into each other and falling over, bringing up the rear.

As many as fifty small presents would have been hidden somewhere on the ground floor between the dining room overlooking the back garden and the sitting room, where the guests had gathered on the street side of the house. Under the Hot, Warm or Cold directions of Edward and Nico, who were in charge of the treasure hunt, a dozen children shot around the rooms whirring like toys wound up to the maximum and then released. They darted, shoved one another, did about-turns and froze, making little whimpering sounds of nervous impatience, giving shrieks of excitement when they found something. The older guests invited by Ella had as much fun as the children, occasionally interrupted by a restraining call of 'Gently now, Max!' from his father when Max cut in too roughly on someone's find or bowled over a smaller child in a state of excitement that made him oblivious to everything else.

Hermine, now eighty, came over from Clerkenwell every year and this year stayed for the entire Christmas week. But it was becoming rather too much for her, she told Ella, and this visit would probably be the last. It was Hermine who brought Giselle along to the Christmas Eve parties, a middle-aged Hungarian lady who eked out a living making dolls in her basement flat. Giselle became friends with Maureen, whom she met at the first of these parties, the woman who ran the crèche down the road, a widow like herself. George referred to them mockingly as the three graces, or sometimes as Ella's old trouts. At fifty, Maureen was without any physical attractions, which perhaps was why she dyed her hair red. Giselle, whose husband had died suddenly and left her without a penny, had the cobwebbed appearance of a once-beautiful woman left on the shelf, worn down by undernourishment and drudgery. When it was her turn to be given a present she threw up her hands in disbelief, looking questioningly around the company for confirmation there had not been a mistake, and that she really was entitled to her present.

Sensing her loneliness and that she would benefit from more company, Ella invited Giselle to join them for the open-house evenings held on Sunday by Paul Hartmann and his wife. Sometimes George came along too, but recently his work had kept him busy at weekends. Only a year or two ago they would sit together in the salon almost every weekend and have proper conversations, or at least exchange remarks, each of them busy with their own occupations, but these days the demands made by George's work were such that he preferred to settle down at his desk in the study across the landing. Left to herself, Ella began to get restive at home. Paul and Marta's open house on Sunday evenings soon became a regular fixture in her week. She would put her head around the door of George's study and tell him she was going over. Later she didn't even do that. She just reminded him not to let Max sit up too late.

George began the institution of Sunday evenings with Max when Max was five. Just as George from the age of four or five had once gone to sit in his father's study, so should Max, his father thought, now be encouraged to come and sit in his. For George, Gábor's study had been a sanctuary and his presence there a privilege. But George's study was not at all like this. It was a small room with a desk and a couple of hard-backed chairs. He had no cigars or decanters to offer, no interlocutor with whom he spoke in a code requiring to be deciphered by the third party in the room. It was not an interesting place for a child to be. George thought that Max would enjoy the special mark of favour, but Max got bored and fidgeted. George cleared a shelf for books he had bought specially for Max, the entire set of the adventures of Tintin in French, so that Max would derive some educational benefit from reading comic books just as George had benefited from listening to Gábor and Kodaly speaking Hungarian.

The rustling of pages being turned behind his back soon began to irritate George.

'Can't you turn the pages over more quietly, Max?'

Every quarter of an hour or so he could hear Max quietly putting one book back and taking out another. George turned round.

'You can't *possibly* have got through that book already.'

'Yes, I have. I looked at all the pictures. Honest. Every one.'

'Well why don't you try reading them. I mean, you could at least *try*.'

'I did try, Dad. But it's all in French.'

George spent half an hour showing Max how to use a dictionary, and told him to make a list of the words he looked up and learn them. Max settled down to his task on the floor. George settled down at his desk and resumed writing. Max was very quiet. Peace was restored to the room. George soon became so absorbed that he completely forgot about Max until Ella looked in on her way back upstairs three hours later and found Max lying asleep on the floor.

'Do you know what time it is? Eleven o'clock. You could at least have taken him upstairs and put him on his bed.'

'I didn't want to wake him.'

'You wouldn't have woken him. It just goes to show how little you know about children. You can carry a child this age all over the house, undress him and put him to bed without him waking up, he's so fast asleep.'

Ella proceeded to do so. He heard her go upstairs and come down again. George sat for another half-hour making notes. He listened to her rummaging in the room across the landing, getting ready to go to bed, before he went over and joined her. A trail of clothes led from the door of the bedroom to the bathroom where Ella stood naked at the basin cleaning her teeth. It was Ella's habit to discard her clothes as soon as she got into the bedroom, beginning with her skirt and stockings, letting them lie on the floor where they'd fallen. George picked them up and draped them folded over the chair on her side of the bed, with her underwear lying uppermost so that she could get dressed the next morning in the reverse order she had undressed the previous night.

Ella had finished cleaning her teeth and was putting on her nightdress. The silence from the bathroom was ominous.

'How were Paul and Marta?' asked George, broaching a safely neutral subject when Ella came into the bedroom.

'Giselle could give Max Hungarian lessons,' said Ella unexpectedly.

'Why Giselle? Why not me? And in any case, what does Max need to learn Hungarian for?'

'Giselle could do with the money.'

'Max learns Hungarian because Giselle could do with the money. I see.'

'Besides, you wouldn't have the time. You don't even have time to teach him French, not even when the two of you are sitting in the same room and you give him Tintin – a five-year-old child barely able to read and write English!'

'I have a report to deliver to the undersecretary's committee at nine o'clock this morning,' said George pompously.

'Then let Max play with the others and tell Catherine to put the three of them to bed while you get on with your report. Either that or sit down with Max and read Tintin together.'

George undressed and got into bed.

More gently she added, 'You can't do both, not at his bedtime, when he's too tired to concentrate properly.'

'You're perfectly right' said George, mollified by Ella's tone.

He felt guiltier about having neglected his wife than he had his son. Sundays were the only evenings that George and Ella got to themselves. Catherine went out on Saturday evenings, and on weekdays George didn't get home before eight or nine.

They resumed their visits to the theatre or the opera and had dinner out on Sundays. Whenever preparations for the undersecretary's committee meeting on Monday mornings made it necessary for George to stay in and work, Ella called on Paul and Marta across the street. The cosy study evenings George had hoped to establish with Max were quietly dropped. Instead, at Ella's suggestion, George put aside Sunday mornings to spend with his children.

Weather permitting, they went to Regent's Park and took a rowing boat on the pond. George felt grateful to Felicity and Philip for being obedient children who were easy to manage, leaving him free to deal with Max, who was not. Max was always running off somewhere, climbing a fence, stamping in puddles or stepping on dog shit, pretending to be blind, walking into lamp posts and giving himself black eyes. A thin, stringy boy with endless energy, he seemed physically incapable of keeping still, always rocking the rowing boat. Either you sit still in the boat, George warned him, or we stop going for boat rides altogether. Then we just come to Regent's Park for a walk.

Even so, out in the open air, given plenty of space and the freedom of his feet, Max was impossible to restrain unless kept on a leash. Max on firm ground was not much of an improvement on Max in a boat. Walking out with the twins in the pushchair, Max in reins held by his father or mother or Catherine, one person could negotiate the crossing of Abbey Road with three children in tow without risk. That was how their London neighbourhood could be explored, and was explored, until Max was about five. But Max at six was already tall for his age, too tall to be trailing reins out on the street. Children in traces were not a common sight. At that age, as Catherine said to Ella, it looked funny. It would make people think the child must be barmy, said Catherine. Ella felt ashamed.

Largely for this reason, after Max turned the corner of his sixth birthday, his father stopped taking the children out to Regent's Park on Sunday mornings. Weather permitting, George played with them, or at least supervised them playing, looking up from his Sunday newspaper to adjudicate differences of opinion in the back garden, laid out by Ella as the perfect children's playground. 'Invest in outdoor toys so that you can get on with the housework' had been another piece of her mother's practical home advice which Ella followed with her own children's upbringing. They were given a swing, a slide, a climbing cube and a bar for dangling upside down over a sandpit they could fall into without hurting themselves. The lawn was big enough for them to kick a ball around, with George in goal defending the wisteria on the garden wall, grenadier Max taking potshots at him.

Catherine giving notice in the spring of 1956, after five years with the family as nanny, came as a bombshell to the Morris family. She was apologetic, but there it was. Her young man in Yorkshire had finally taken over a farm and she was returning there to become his wife. Ella knew that Catherine was irreplaceable. An era had come to an end.

The week before Catherine left she accompanied Ella and the children to see Edward off from Southampton. In the children's excitement to be standing on the quay looking up at the enormous ship – their first ocean-going vessel – and the excitement of Edward to be embarking on it, Ella's undertow of sadness went unnoticed; at first, happy for Edward despite herself, putting a brave face on the hurt she felt on parting from her brother, she knew for ever, it was not properly registered even by Ella. But after seeing Catherine off from the station only a few days later and returning to an empty house for the first time in her life – the three smaller children at the crèche, Nico at school, George at work and Edward gone – Ella sat down in the kitchen and cried. Never had she been surrounded by such silence, such space; never had she felt so unnecessary in her own home.

She kept her promise to write to her brother once a week for the rest of the year to keep him in touch with his old family until he began to grow together with his new one, forty letters for Edward to look forward to, helping him to get over his initial homesickness. In fact she'd packed the first of the letters with a bar of chocolate inside his night case as a surprise when he opened it en route. The weeks passed and there was no word back from Edward. Her cousin wrote to say he had arrived safely, but the first Ella heard from Edward himself was the Christmas card in which he scribbled a few sentences eight months later.


# 8


After several years of being badgered by Paul, Ella agreed to sit for him. She disliked being the object of anyone's scrutiny, particularly an artist's. Ella made up a number of reasons for saying no to Paul's request. She wasn't used to sitting doing nothing. She didn't have the time. And she wondered what other designs Paul might have on her beside painting. Being painted by Paul was to Ella almost like being touched by him, and she disliked being touched.

There were few exceptions. Ella didn't mind being touched by her mother and her brother Edward, but as both of them had gone out of her life they couldn't be included. The others she could count on one hand. She could think of no one apart from her mother whose touch she actively desired, not even George. In this regard Ella was uncharacteristically passive, even aloof. She was always the touched, hardly ever, with the exception of her children and her husband, the touching one. So when Paul approached her yet again she put it to George, or rather she tried to pass Paul's request on to George and let him decide. Emphasising this last misgiving of hers, that Paul might use the opportunity to make a pass at her, she half hoped that George would place a protecting arm around her and say no. But George thought a portrait of Ella by Paul Hartmann a wonderful idea. It flattered him. He would buy the picture and hang it in his study.

Until that spring Ella had not given Paul's request serious consideration, but once she had done so she made up her mind quickly. Her giving in to Paul not long after Edward and Catherine had left and her great-aunt Hermine died coincided with moments when it could seem to Ella her own life was was already beginning to slip away from her. In this changed mood, the many reasons for her having said no to Paul were overruled by Ella's notion that a portrait of her could somehow reverse that process and give her a new lease of life. In the painting Paul made of her she would mysteriously be restored to life.

For two hours every morning, when the children were with Maureen at the crèche and the cleaner was at work in the house, Ella walked across the road and let herself into the life-restoring atmosphere of Paul's studio. His studio seemed to inhabit a different world from the house in which she lived. It began with the smells, the odours of paints and turpentine, tar and sawn metal that didn't belong in an ordinary house. Three quarters of the studio were taken up by Paul's workspace, canvases, pulleys, blocks of wood and metal, plaster of Paris and terracotta. A small bedroom for Paul and Marta squeezed in at one end of the studio, a bathroom and kitchen at the other, was the extent of the space allowed to a private life. Everything else happened in the space between.

The group of people who met here on Sunday evenings were different from the other residents of St John's Wood, different from almost everyone who had passed through Ella's life. She could imagine her intellectual father, the communist Andrzejewski, feeling at home among them, perhaps her idealistic school friend Ferdinand who had once wanted to marry her, but that was about all. There was a buzz of ideas in this space that seemed to Ella to be coming out of her own head. The ideas buzzed in several languages besides English – German, Czech, Russian and occasionally Yiddish. Very few of the visitors to the *jour fixe* in Paul's studio were people born and bred in England; Paul's wife Marta, for example. Most of them were foreigners in transit, birds of passage on their way from London to Paris, Berlin and Vienna. They turned up for a while and disappeared without warning, just as suddenly reappearing to resume the conversations they had begun there, finishing sentences interrupted months previously. The majority were naturalised immigrants who had made their lives in London just before or just after the war, and of these people all except Ella and Marta were Jewish.

In the early months of 1956 a visitor began showing up regularly at Paul's studio whom Ella had never seen there before. His name was Sasha Borowski. He came from a Yiddish/Polish/German/Russian/speaking family in Galicia. A committed communist and idealist, Borowski had studied physics in Kiev, Vienna and Berlin between the wars before pledging himself to the cause, joining the staff of the Technical Institute in Moscow as a young researcher in the early 1930s. Swallowed up in Stalin's Great Purge, Borowski spent years in the Gulag before he was released and deported from the Soviet Union in 1940, undertaking a perilous journey back to Poland. He surfaced in Warsaw as one of the ringleaders of the doomed uprising. He was caught and condemned to death.

Borowski's usefulness to the Nazis as a physicist with detailed knowledge of Soviet military research saved him from execution in the first instance. When he became expendable for the Nazis he was sent to a concentration camp just weeks before its liberation by the Red Army. Russian military interrogators aware of Borowski's record in the Soviet Union identified him as a renegade rather than a deportee. Suspected of espionage, he was detained for six months in a camp on the Polish–Russian border until he made his escape across the Baltic from Stettin the day before the city was closed by the Soviet forces and declared a Polish city.

Ella's story of her flight poured out of her. Here was someone who had been there, who knew what it had been like! They might almost have bumped into one another in the streams of refugees flowing in and out of Stettin at the time. On the evening they first met, she and Sasha sat talking together in the empty studio until it grew light. All the other guests had long since left. Even Paul and Marta had gone to bed.

Sasha began to show up at the morning sessions when Paul was working with Ella. Paul was delighted. Sasha was a wonderful talker, with an unlimited repertoire of stories of his Jewish/Polish childhood. They completely absorbed Ella. Paul was making studies for his portrait of Ella, who was lying with a book on a sofa in a printed cotton dress. Noting the look of absorption on her face, he drew up a chair and tried to capture it on paper. A morning might be spent on an ear, a week on her nose and eyes. Absorbed in Ella's expression as Ella was in Sasha's stories, Paul heard nothing of what was being said, just as she remained unaware of his scrutiny. Two hours passed like this every weekday morning. After a month there was still no flagging of Sasha's narrative, no sign of it moving beyond his poor but evidently happy childhood in the company of eleven brothers and sisters. Sasha had been the youngest, and Ella sensed his reluctance to leave their company and go out into the world that lay beyond his Galician childhood.

When Ella first met Sasha she saw a tall man in his late forties, six foot two but already beginning to stoop, big-boned, heavy-framed, with a ring of greying once-fair hair, tufty and never combed, an unruly laurel crown around his large bald head. The sadness of his eyes, dark brown pools in his hollow face, drew Ella to him. He wore pale silk polo-neck shirts inside cashmere suits, dispensing with ties as he did with combs, which in the world of conventionally dressed Englishmen would have raised a question mark over Sasha Borowski's *bankability*. That was George's verdict, and George knew about such things. Ella invited him to lunch. After lunch George and Sasha went out for a walk and didn't come home until supper.

'Well?' asked Ella excitedly when he had left.

George understood that Ella wanted not just his opinion. She wanted confirmation of her own feelings, which were obviously in Sasha's favour.

'What did you make of him?'

'That man should be working for us. But who knows,' said George, smiling that odd smile of his which still baffled Ella, riding up one half of his face but leaving the other half untouched, as if he suffered from some sort of nervous condition, 'maybe he already is. He knows so many things that, in this country at least, are state secrets, even information I don't have at all.'

'For example?'

'Some intriguing details, for example, of political unrest as a result of Khrushchev's speech denouncing Stalin. He predicted an uprising in Poland within the next few months.'

It was not that Sasha bore a physical resemblance to her father. It was the spirit they had in common, or rather the death of spirit, the atmosphere of resignation surrounding both men.

This resignation was shared to a greater or lesser degree by many at the Sunday evening gatherings in Paul's studio, the resignation of the homeless, people who had lost not just the places but the ideals to which they had been attached. Recalling vividly her father standing with his briefcase on the platform of the Stettiner Bahnhof in Berlin, seeing his two children off on the outbreak of the war in the direction Andrzejewski knew the war was coming from, Ella understood in retrospect the despair her father must have felt, with his marriage, his profession and his political faith already in ruins around him.

What prospects could there have been for a Polish-born physicist, a communist who at the time was a government employee, working against all his inner convictions in Nazi Germany on the eve of the invasion of Poland in 1939?

*He'll probably go to Capri*, Ella had told her mother after they had burned Andrzejewski's letter in the grate. Ella wept when she described the scene to Sasha.

'At least he wasn't a Jew,' said Sasha with a wince in reply to Ella's question about her father's prospects, and the deep pools of his eyes seemed to silt up, becoming entirely opaque.

They were sitting on the terrace at the back of the Ritz, with a view down over the Embankment and the Thames. When in London Sasha always stayed at the Ritz. He had invited Ella to join him for lunch, as he would be returning to Paris the next day.

'*Vielleicht war er doch Jude. Andrzejewski war ja auch Pole. Wer weiß – vielleicht weil Du mit meinem Vater Ähnlichkeit hast?*'

The conversation tended to drift out of one language into the other, according to what they felt comfortable with at any moment. In English it would've been unthinkable, Ella's extraordinary impromptu remark – that Andrzejewski might have been a Jew, that Sasha was like her father – this wouldn't have been possible for her in English; it wouldn't have conveyed what she was saying between the lines.

'It's been my experience,' said Sasha, 'that all close human ties originate at an early age in our feelings for people belonging to the surroundings we were brought up in. Family members, obviously. But also others. For me it was my teacher in my first class at primary school. She was fair and slim and wore her hair up, showing in profile the long line of her neck.'

He smiled.

'Once I see that neckline I begin to tingle, like an alarm going off, like one of Pavlov's dogs. There's no way for us to resist a conditioned response, however trivial the stimulus. What a tediously mechanistic background to our greatest feelings. One is delivered over, bound hand and foot.'

'George told me he fell in love with me because I reminded him of his father,' said Ella.

'There you are! And he? Who does he remind you of?'

'I don't know.' Ella hesitated before going on. 'But then I didn't fall in love. I never have. I'm not the type that does.'

'There is no type – with your acquiescence or without, there is no choice – it happens. And what is it, this falling in love that demands so much of our attention? It's falling into bondage. We welcome back something familiar but forgotten from far away in the early years of our lives, only we don't usually know it. Will this love be able to live up to the expectations raised by its ghostly prototype? No. It brings us disappointment and unhappiness.'

During their conversation Sasha had his hand on Ella's knee. She would have removed his hand under other circumstances, but faced with Sasha's sadness she didn't have the heart. Sympathy flowed into his hand on her knee. What was he thinking about? With gently circling motions he caressed her knee and thigh, until a flood rose in her and she came. It was the first time Ella had experienced an orgasm – caught completely unprepared, she would have felt embarrassed had Sasha not happened to be looking out over the river – otherwise he must have seen what effect his caresses were having on her.

Without Sasha talking in the background – and after Sasha left for Paris he no longer came to the studio – Paul Hartmann had to abandon his original picture of Ella. He lost the expression he'd been painting on Ella's face and failed to coax it back, leaving him with no alternative but to pose his model turned away from him. She lay curled up on the sofa, her left hand reaching around her right shoulder. Paul relished the flow of her curves, echoing the exuberant rococo lines of the gilt-edged sofa, but it was a compromise that reminded him of the portrait he'd been forced to abandon. Ella *en face* defeated him – never had he been confronted with such different flows of expression on one face.

# 9

When Ella went on from Paul's to collect the children from the crèche, she found Giselle there with Maureen and a dozen children. Maureen had a good way with children. There was always the bright firefly patter of happily occupied children in the crèche but seldom a racket, not even from Max. Ella wondered about this.

At home Max wanted everything to be done as he wanted, and in the end he usually got his way. He dominated the roost. But here he seemed content to fit in. The little ones were playing with blocks of wood. Felicity and Philip sat at the shoe rack, learning to lace and unlace shoes. The older children were carting large wooden letters around the room under Max's direction and laying them on the floor to form words.

Max would be seven in November. Ella realised he was getting too old for the crèche. She mentioned this to Maureen, who agreed.

'By the way,' she said to Ella, 'I was just wondering if Catherine's room is still vacant ...'

Giselle had been given notice by her landlord in Clerkenwell and was looking for somewhere to live. Giselle did her doll-making at home. She could do so just as well as anywhere else, thought Maureen, speaking on Giselle's behalf, in the bedsit in the basement of the Morris house that had recently been vacated by Catherine. It would help Giselle and perhaps Ella too.

Giselle moved in. Three taxi rides, quietly paid for by Ella, sufficed to move all of her worldly goods from Clerkenwell to St John's Wood.

On fine days the children played outside where Ella could keep an eye on them, checking on them from one of the windows overlooking the garden. Philip and Felicity, inseparable, always played together in the sandpit. Max was losing interest in them now and preferred to play alone. Ella had to go to one of the front windows to check on him. Her heart missed a beat if she looked down into the front garden and failed to see Max. How relieved she was when she caught sight of him! He usually hung over the gate and would swing on it back and forth, or he would be running along the top of the wall, testing his freedom to the limit. Going out into the street unless accompanied by a grown-up was strictly forbidden, and Max seemed naturally drawn to the forbidden. George had beaten him once for disobeying, putting him over his knee and spanking him hard. Ella, used to being spanked by her mother with a hairbrush, found that quite natural. Max had been taught his lesson, but he resented it and had not forgiven his father.

Max could feel the flaw in himself like a knot you rubbed up against in the grain of wood. Ella could sense what was going on inside him. He was all bunched up there, around that knot: stubborn, self-hating, intransigent. Why was he like that? Where did one get one's nature from? Was one accountable for it?

A mystery.

Then there were moments, no less mysterious, when she felt deeply moved by her son, like in the evening when he came in from playing in the garden, turned round on his way into the house and called back, 'Goodnight, garden! I'll come and play with you again tomorrow!'

On weekend mornings the three children came downstairs and got into their parents' bed. They weren't allowed in before half-past seven. There were two clocks on the wall outside to help them tell the time, a cardboard clock with the hands at half past seven which they could compare with a real clock showing the actual time. Often George and Ella were awake and heard them whispering outside the door. It was the moment of anticipation they liked best, the stage whispers of the children waiting on the landing before they came rushing in all at once, with their toys and their noise and their little warm bodies burrowing around under the bedclothes. Ella told them stories, resurrecting the people who had inhabited her own childhood, almost as much for her own benefit as for theirs. It was always Ella who told the stories, never George. He didn't seem to have any stories to tell.

One morning it was just Felicity and Philip who came in. Where was Max? asked Ella. Max was upstairs, reading. He said he didn't want to come down.

Ella wondered. Later she went for a walk with Max. Shall I tell you the stories you missed this morning? she asked him. Max gave a shrug. Or shall I tell you *why* you missed them? Shall I tell you *all* about it? Max stopped and looked up at her. How did his mother always know?

It was true that he was angry with his father. The deeper truth of that was that Max didn't like his father. And the deeper truth behind *that* was his father had spanked him, not, he knew, because he had broken the rule about staying in the front garden, but because his father didn't like him either. George made up rules for Max to break, giving him an excuse to hit him. It was the lie of the land in the Morris family that father and son didn't get on with each other. Why should they? It was just like that, for no reason.

With this secret Max was on his own. He couldn't tell it to his mother. He knew it would be unacceptable to her. So he pretended it was all on account of the spanking. Given a reason, it would be acceptable to Ella. He let her go on believing that he didn't get on with George because George had spanked him, even after Ella had promised him that his father wouldn't spank him any more.

'Giselle told me,' she said.

'What did she tell you?'

Max was at once fully alert, with a prickling sensation all over his body.

'That you came down early to the nursery while Felicity and Philip were upstairs with Daddy and me in our bedroom and that she heard you crying.'

'I *wasn't* crying. I was blowing my nose.'

'I'm sure you were. But *she* thought you were crying. That was why she wanted to comfort you. Besides, she said, you would have caught cold in those thin pyjamas. Well, I think it was very nice of her. But we won't tell Daddy. It will be our secret.'

How like her own brother Max was, Ella thought uneasily.

She remembered Oscar's eczema, his freckles and reddish hair, a physical type not unlike Max, so alien to her mother from the moment he was born. Ella now had an inkling herself how disturbing it could be for a mother to sense a strangeness about a child from the moment of birth. The strangeness was like a vacancy of feeling, which the mother waited anxiously to be filled. She felt let down by her mother's instincts.

That there was something worryingly wrong about Max and his relationship with his father had become clear to Ella when she picked up off the floor of the children's playroom an album of photographs of George's family she had given Max to look at. With a shock she saw that all the photos of George had been defaced with a large X.

# 10

Ever since he had found the magazines at the back of the cupboard in George's study Max had been curious about his parents' privacy. There was nothing private about the lives of children. They were all on display to see. They weren't very interesting. But his parents had a private life. It went on in their private sitting room, in their bedroom and bathroom and in George's study.

Sometimes they wanted a bit of privacy for themselves, his father said to him when he went into their sitting room one hot Sunday afternoon. What did that mean? Max waited for his mother to intervene on his behalf, as she often did with his father. His mother could overrule his father. Sometimes Max did things just to see if she would. He pushed his luck. But this time Max interrupted them in the middle of a conversation, and his mother flew off the handle in the way she unpredictably did. Flying off the handle was the expression his father used of her. It meant that Ella got extremely cross.

The magazines were in the same language as Tintin, so Max knew the captions under the pictures must be French. The pictures showed men and women doing the sort of things they did to each other in their privacy.

In the aftermath of discovering the French magazines, Max undertook a series of investigations into the privacy of the house. The safest time for this was when his parents went out on Saturday or Sunday evenings. The twins would be down in the nursery with Giselle – bless her, Ella used to add whenever she mentioned Giselle's name – giving them their supper. For an hour the coast was clear. For an hour Max had the run of the house.

In his parents' bedroom he went through all the drawers and the cupboards. He found a box labelled *Private Medicine* in his father's handwriting. It contained unexciting objects whose purpose he could not guess. He found nothing else of interest except his mother's underwear. Max got undressed and tried putting it on. He looked at himself in the mirror and laughed. He lay down on the carpet and rolled around, rubbing himself and laughing.

Investigating privacy gave him a thrilling sensation.

Next he investigated the sitting room his parents referred to as their salon, where they sometimes held what they called soirées. Soirées usually involved Paul's fat wife Marta singing, with his father accompanying her on the piano. Sometimes the songs would be followed by charades, giving Max the opportunity to dress up. He loved charades. He loved dressing up. He loved being in the salon when it was full of people. He loved showing off. But the salon empty of people became for Max a scary place, on account of the picture hanging there on the wall, the corkscrew man, all twisted up, pink and bleeding like a skewered pig, in punishment for something very bad he must have done.

Each exploration of the house ended with the French magazines in his father's study.

Max had come across them by chance. He was drawn to cupboards, climbing into them where possible, shutting the doors and sitting in the dark inside. To his surprise, the cupboard in George's study reached much further back than he had expected, ending in an alcove so low and narrow that he had to wriggle in on all fours. This alcove at the back of the cupboard was where his father kept the French magazines. Max settled in there with a swell of excitement and looked at the pictures by torchlight.

It was scarcely believable, the rude things grown-ups did to each other in their privacy. He put it in the fat woman's mouth for her to suck. He stuck it up the fat woman's bum. Sometimes three or four of them would be at it at the same time, fat ones and thin ones, men and women, all mixed up together. He couldn't believe his eyes.

He wondered if his mother and father did things like this to each other but couldn't imagine it. Max was fascinated by the pictures, the evidence they gave of the rude goings-on inside the grown-ups' private world. And all for what? Children, he was quite sure, would have been forbidden to do such things. After his first two or three investigations of the house had failed to turn up anything new of interest, Max now headed straight upstairs for the cupboard the moment his mother and father were out of the front door.

But one evening he had barely got into the cupboard when he heard the front door slam. The crash of the door slamming was followed by his parents talking loudly as they came up the stairs. It was his mother doing most of the talking, and by the sound of it she had flown off the handle. He could hear every word she said. He could even hear the angry rustle of her stockings as she came into the study, his father's tread on the floor as he came in after her, the click of the latch as he closed the door.

'Why didn't you tell me about this before?' his mother was saying, her voice quivering with anger.

George answered coolly, 'What was there to tell? That's just how things are done in this country. Only private schools count. Boys go to the schools their father went to. Order of the day. I went to Park House, so Max goes there too. I really can't understand why you're making such a thing of this, Ella.'

'I don't want to send Max away to school. Later, perhaps, if that's what he wants. But this autumn – he'll only just have turned *seven*. He's still a little child!'

'When I was sent to Park House I had just turned seven too. It didn't do *me* any harm.'

'But look at him. Max isn't ready to leave home.'

'Leaving home is precisely what Max needs. He needs to be taken in hand. He needs discipline.'

'No, he doesn't. He needs love and care. Difficult children do, especially them.'

Her voice cracked. There was a pause. Max could hear his mother breathing heavily as she did when she got excited. He knew the signs. Soon she would begin to cry. Max wondered what she meant by *difficult children*, and why they especially needed love and care.

There was a thud. What was happening now?

Max crawled stealthily forward so that he could look through the crack in the cupboard door. To his amazement, he saw his mother kneeling on the floor, her arms clutching his father's knees.

'Please,' she implored him. 'Please don't send him away!'

'Well,' his father answered, 'there's not much we can do about it now. And do get up from the floor, Ella. These histrionics! You don't know how ridiculous you look down there.'

This was said with a coldness that at once brought his mother back to her senses. Max was relieved to see her get up again.

George continued: 'The boy's already down for this Michaelmas term in any case. I put him down as soon as he was born. I've already paid half his fees.'

'*What?*'

'Well, it's like this, Ella. There are private schools – Park House is one of them, a very good school, one of the best prep schools in the country – that give you a rebate if you pay the fees in advance – as much as 15 per cent depending on when you begin doing it. When I went to school there it wouldn't have mattered. There was still a lot of money around. But the family business hasn't been doing so well since the end of the war. And with this Suez situation developing the way it is, we could find ourselves in trouble. A lot of André's investments are tied up there: oil refineries, shipping and of course dividends on the canal itself.'

'Suez! Max matters more to me than the family investments in *Suez*, for goodness' sake.' She sang the word out with astonishment.

Who was this Suez? Max wondered inside the cupboard.

'To you maybe. It's all very well for you to talk. You didn't bring a penny with you where you came from. But what sort of an education do you think we're going to be able to give our children if we find we're no longer in a position where we can afford to send them to private schools? *Three* of them. It's not just Max. With half his Park House fees already paid, which I've been doing bit by bit over the last six years, it would be lunacy not to send him there.'

'I'm sure there are perfectly adequate local grammar schools for the children to go to in London.'

'Yes, but they're state schools. That's just it. They're *not* adequate.'

'What's wrong with them?'

'Ella, you don't understand,' said George, beginning to sound exasperated. 'In our class, in this country, it's just not *done* to send children to state schools. It's not the English thing.'

'Well I don't care what's *done,* if it's not good for the child. Another child, perhaps, a more settled, robust child. But not Max. I'm not having it. We can talk about it a year from now and perhaps the situation will be different. A year from now, if Max really wanted to go away to school, and I felt it was the right thing for him to be doing so, then perhaps. But this year – it's out of the question. Park House! What is *Park House* to me? How could you even *think* of taking such a decision without consulting your wife? What am I? Just a cook and a nanny or what?'

Max heard his mother's stockings rustling again and the sound of the handle turning as she opened the door. She must have gone out onto the landing because her voice sounded further away.

'And I want you to write a letter to this Park House place first thing

197

on Monday morning, George, telling them Max won't be coming, definitely not this year and most likely never.'

'I have no intention of doing any such thing,' answered George in the tight voice Max recognised as a warning signal and wanted to tell his mother so. George was warning Ella not to push it. 'I shan't be writing any such letter,' he said.

'In that case,' said Ella, 'I shall be leaving this house, and you can look for someone else to be the mother to your children.'

'Then go!' shouted George, losing his temper, and he hurled the door shut so violently that the floorboards inside the cupboard shook. Through the closed door he yelled an afterthought: 'Try going back where you came from! Just see how far you get!'

Five minutes later George left the study himself. He must have gone downstairs because Max heard the slam of the front door shortly afterwards.

Max immediately slipped out of the cupboard and went up to his mother's bedroom, where he thought he would find her. But she wasn't there. She wasn't in her sitting room. Sometimes on nice evenings she went and sat out in the garden. He went down and looked for her, but she wasn't there either. He began to feel scared. So he went into the basement, where the twins were playing and Giselle was standing in the kitchen washing up. Max ran over and buried his head in her apron, beginning to cry despite himself, proud he was a tough kid and not a cry-baby.

By nine o'clock at night there was still no sign of either Ella or George. Giselle had put the twins to bed. She was still reading them a story, although they were already asleep. She continued reading for Max's sake. He lay on his back with his sheet in his mouth and his eyes open, completely still, which was most unusual for him. At last she put down the book and went over to him.

'Don't worry. They'll be back soon, I expect. They probably went out for a walk. People sometimes quarrel, you know. It's natural. And then they make up. They both went out and met up somewhere, and had things to talk over with each other. I'm sure that's what happened.'

She kissed him on the cheek.

'Now you go to sleep. Goodnight, dear child.'

Dear child. Nobody but Giselle called him that, and Max didn't know if he liked it. It sounded soppy. And he wasn't too keen on having the child bit rubbed in. But his mother called him Snippet, and was Snippet any better? Maureen at the crèche sometimes called him Captain Hook. He liked that. Different people had different names for him. Why? Whereas his father never called him anything but Max. Was that a good or a bad sign? So many thoughts were still tumbling through his head that Max lay wide awake for a long time.

*Try going back where you came from! Just see how far you get!*

Max sensed his father had shouted something terrible at his mother. But would she go back where she came from? And, if so, how far would she get?

In the morning Giselle came up from the basement to help George with the children's breakfast, although she didn't sit down with them at the table. She had never been there at breakfast before. She might have sat down with them if his father had invited her to. But his father didn't. He hardly seemed to know what was going on. The twins kept on asking when Mummy was coming back. George told them several times that Mummy had gone on holiday and wouldn't be back for a while, but when the twins asked him again he told them to shut up. Giselle said something to his father in a language Max didn't understand, which he had never heard her speak before, and George spoke back to her in the language, sounding extremely angry. Felicity began to cry. Giselle took her and Philip downstairs.

Max and his father sat in silence at the breakfast table. A fly was buzzing over the table. Max tried swatting it and hit a plate, which fell with a crash to the floor.

George looked at him with hatred. 'You did that deliberately, didn't you?'

'No, I didn't!'

'It's all because of you. It's your fault, you know.'

His father got up and left the house.

A minute later Max heard an engine starting. He ran to the window and watched his father's car drive off in the direction of Abbey Road.

Max spent the morning swinging on the gate. He wanted to be the first to see his mother when she came home. Giselle came out onto the front steps to call him in when it was time for lunch. Ella still hadn't come back.

Late in the afternoon his father returned to the house. He had just got in when the phone rang. He picked it up, listened in silence and made a note on a piece of paper. When he put the phone down he turned to Giselle, who was in the kitchen making supper, and began talking to her in the foreign language they had spoken the night before. They went on speaking for quite some time in this language the children didn't understand. It frightened the twins. They stood looking up at their father and began crying. Even Max found it scary how different George and Giselle sounded from their usual selves.

'Who was it on the phone, Daddy?'

'It wasn't anyone. It was a telegram.'

Then George got down on one knee and put his arms around Felicity and Philip.

'Mummy's gone on holiday. She sent a telegram to say she's arrived safely. And just to make sure everyone will be all right without her at home she's arranged for Catherine's sister Betty to stay here and help Giselle while Mummy's away. Betty will be arriving tomorrow. Daddy will be picking her up at the station after work and bringing her back home.'

On Monday morning everything seemed to be back to normal at first. George left for work; Giselle took the three children to the crèche and picked them up again at lunchtime. But when they came back to the house and saw no Ella standing smiling at the top of the steps, where she always stood to welcome them home, the twins began wailing again and even Max had to wipe a few tears out of his eyes with the back of his sleeve.

In the afternoon he sat on the wall in the back garden, kicking it with his heels. He didn't know what to do, what direction to go in, where to play. Why didn't he want to fly his paper plane? Why had he lost interest in it? Why all of a sudden had it become so difficult to play at anything? Inside the cupboard of his head he could hear voices getting mixed up, telling him all kinds of disturbing things.

In the autumn he would be sent away from home, to Park House. Why? Because his father had gone there. Because his father didn't like him and wanted him out of the house. Because his father had already paid a lot of money for him to go, and Suez had said he must.

*It's all because of you. It's your fault, you know. Just see how far you get!*

That was what came of sneaking into the cupboard to look at the French magazines. He knew he shouldn't have, but he still did. That was why he would be sent away to Park House. The only person who could help him had quarrelled about it with his father and now she had disappeared.

Max missed his mother very much. He spent his afternoons swinging on the gate, to be the first person to see Ella when she came back. But days passed and there was no sign of her. He wondered if she was dead.

Gradually it began to sink in. What his father had said was true. It was Max's fault that his mother had gone away, perhaps worse.

Perhaps she would never come back.

Perhaps his mother had died because of him.

# 11

It couldn't have been more than five minutes, ten minutes at most, since Ella had left the house. And she had left it for certain, as George confirmed with a glance into each of the rooms on his way out of the house. She hadn't taken the car. He looked up and down the street. He went down to the corner of Abbey Road to see if she was there or was waiting for a bus. On his way back down the street he tried calling on Paul and Marta in case she had gone to see them, but no one answered the door.

If she had decided to go over to Hampstead to see his mother she might have walked in the other direction and caught a bus from there, as she sometimes did. George got into the car and followed the route she would have taken. There was no sign of her. Where had she disappeared to? It seemed unlikely she would have gone to see her mother-in-law, but who could say? She might have resorted to her as a court of appeal in the Park House case. His mother always took Ella's side in her disputes with George, if only to annoy him. And it was Ella's way in these matters to get as many allies as possible. Having already come this far, thought George, he might as well go on and deal with it. André usually had dinner at home with his mother on Saturday evenings. A piece of unpleasant business with his brother, still unfinished, which he had already put off for long enough, had suddenly stumbled into George's mind.

When Ella's great-aunt Hermine died in her Clerkenwell house that winter he assumed that the property had been left to Ella. Hermine had never discussed the matter with her, but given that Ella was her sole surviving relative it would have been surprising if she had left the house to anyone else. When the will was opened, however, it transpired that some ten years previously the property had been made over to his brother André in exchange for an interest-free loan he had advanced Hermine to pay for the rebuilding of the house.

George was furious when he learned how Ella had been done out of her inheritance. What a dirty trick! It was just the sort of underhand thing André could be expected to do. There had been angry exchanges with his brother on the phone, but he had not yet sat down and talked it out with him. Now, for some reason, just after his wife had gone off, having this matter out with his brother suddenly became George's most pressing concern.

It was six months since George had last visited the family home in Hampstead. It was still light when he got there. As he drove through the gates he noticed that the gatepost that his younger brother James had driven into a year ago had not yet been straightened. George hadn't even noticed it himself. It was Ella who pointed it out to him. To his irritation, he found himself looking at everything through Ella's eyes: a dead branch left hanging in a tree and not removed, ridge tiles missing on the roof, a cracked pane of coloured glass in the fanlight over the door – evidence of decline all over the property he had overlooked until she drew his attention to it. Little steps on the downward path; not yet dramatic, but cumulative, leading to dereliction. Ella was right, of course, but was it her business to be pointing it out?

Even Barrington, who opened the front door without callers having to ring the bell – a piece of magic the ancient family retainer had been performing for as long as George could remember – fell foul of the new scrutiny to which George, under Ella's influence, submitted him. Barrington needed a new suit. He was wearing what appeared to be carpet slippers. That wouldn't do. And the unsightly bushels of hair now extruding from the dignified old man's ears and nostrils really had become too much. But it didn't seem to George to be his job to tell him so. He felt that would have been an impertinence.

'Good evening, Barrington.'

'Good evening, sir.'

George handed him his umbrella whatever the weather. He kept an umbrella in the car not for use but in order to entrust it to Barrington's safekeeping when he arrived at the house and to have it returned to him when he departed, a pledge given, a pledge received. It was a ritual that had to be honoured. His father's venerable butler expected it of him and he could not let him down.

'Lovely weather we're having, Barrington. Manage to get out at all?'

'A very pleasant afternoon at Lord's last Sunday, sir.'

'Ah. How was the cricket?'

'It was a draw, sir. Rather disappointing after such a cracking start.'

'So it was, so it was. Is Mrs Morris having dinner?'

'She is, sir.'

'Just about finished, I dare say. Still, I'll go in and join her.'

George crossed the hall and went on through the lounge into the dining room. How dark the place was! How old-fashioned! Over-wrought crystal chandeliers, dark heavy curtains and massive, rather sinister furniture dating back to the 1920s and 1930s in the kind of style that had been favoured by Mussolini. Over a quarter of a century had passed since anything in these rooms had been replaced. Lots of old acquaintances here. He knew them individually. He'd miss them. But they'd have to go some time. The whole place needed renovating.

Returning to his childhood home as an adult, George was victim of the same illusion that befell most people – namely, how much smaller everything had become than it had been when one was a child. The dining room, however, seemed to have got bigger. When he was growing up, there would have been at least a dozen people sitting down at his father's table. The members of the family alone accounted for nine, and there would always be guests staying, relatives or business associates of his father's. It was an enormous Regency table, very dark and heavy and twenty feet long. His father's partiality for dark heavy furniture was something he had not given thought to before. He wondered what that told him about his father's character and guessed it might have to do with power. Twelve or fifteen chairs would typically be drawn up at mealtimes and there was room for a dozen more, reinforcements held in reserve – as Gábor phrased it, whose hobby was the study of famous battles, Napoleon's in particular – along the short walls at either end of the rectangular room. Three or four maids might have been coming and going, serving at table on especially big occasions. Now that the extra chairs had gone, the maids with them – and these days there were never more than half a dozen people sitting down at the table in any case – the empty dining room appeared much larger than George remembered it as a child.

On this Saturday evening he found four people seated at the table – his mother, his sister Tessa, André and his wife Constance. The sight of them there, a forlorn encampment of diners clustered around one end of the great table which a single twin candlestick sufficed to illuminate in the dusky light, stirred feelings in George for which he was unprepared.

His mother put down her knife and fork to receive a kiss from George on the cheek, shook out her napkin and said, 'Your elder brother has decided to turn his old mother out of the house, George. What do you say to that?'

'What do *you* say to it, Mother?' parried George.

'I say that I don't have any choice in the matter. If André tells me I'm to be bundled off, then I suppose I'll just have to do as I'm told.'

André frowned. 'It's not what *I'm* telling you. I'm just passing on a decision that was taken by the board of the family trust, which as chairman of the trust it's my unpleasant task to have to carry out.'

André was in fact extremely annoyed, not so much on account of having to relate to his mother the decision that the family home was going to have to be sold, but because he had been manoeuvred into doing so by his sister Tessa at a moment that didn't suit him.

George's brother André, third in the line of succession but already titular head of the family, had shown no sign of interest in marriage until recently. However, that year he had secretly married at a register office a woman three years his senior whom none of his family had even seen and would only meet once, before being invited to the church wedding at Hampstead and a reception held at the family home, which even by André's standards had been so parsimonious as to shame the description hospitality. The married couple gave the impression of being pressed for time and anxious to get the celebration over as quickly as possible.

Perhaps that had to do with the fact that Constance was already thirty-seven. The proof of the good family from which she came was stamped onto her long, lugubrious face – like many members of the aristocracy, she resembled a horse. The evidence of the good family she came from also being a wealthy one was less obvious. The jewellery she wore, typically an old-maidish string of pearls, sometimes black opals, made quality statements with discretion. It also found expression in the understatement, if not to say flat-chestedness of her body, thin to the point of self-denial. With a resentful look she peered out of the cavernous hollows of her red-rimmed eyes at a world by which she felt insufficiently appreciated.

This middle-aged woman left on the shelf had astounded herself and her husband by her extreme alacrity of conception, becoming pregnant within weeks of initial insemination by her brand-new husband. Such was the news that pushed the retiring Constance into the limelight in her mother-in-law's house – should have pushed her, at least, had the happy announcement the couple planned to make at dinner not been sabotaged by Tessa.

Tessa at thirty could see in her sister-in-law the future that awaited herself a few years hence, a thin and arid future, perhaps without even the benefit of a husband. Unmarried, unprepossessing, doomed, it seemed, to a life of dissatisfied idleness because her parents had prepared her for nothing else, Tessa had been placed by the board of the family trust in the same category as her mother, Barrington and the bulk of the inventory of the Hampstead house – redundant items to be disposed of in a clearance sale as soon as possible. Soon Tessa was going to have to find another roof over her head.

A chance remark made by the family lawyer had alerted Tessa that something was afoot. Dickinson was on the board of family trustees of which André was the chairman, and his two brothers Joseph and James were members, along with a cousin from the Manchester branch who in practice never attended meetings – an all-male board reflecting the prejudices of Gábor Morris, who shortly before his death had nominated its members and equipped the body of trustees with powers even to overrule the wishes of his widow. That the family must take precedence over the individual was the law by which Gábor had lived and died.

Word was put out that the Morris family intended to dispose of its unique Hampstead property and would be open to serious offers made by interested parties. One of these offers, more generous even than anticipated by the estate agents, had been received and approved by the board only the week before. It seemed opportune to André to link the announcement of the dissolution of the family home to the significant sum of money that would be shared out among its members to compensate them for their distress at having to part with the house. A few details remained to be settled before he could make the announcement, however.

All the board agreed on the necessity of selling the property. In the old days Gábor had run his business from the house. Half a dozen employees had worked there. At least nine people had lived there year-round, looked after by four servants who until the late 1940s had all lived in. Effectively inhabited now by only two people, the place had become too expensive to keep up. George had been the first to move out, followed a few years later by his two youngest brothers. The last to move out had been André after he married Constance. That left just his mother Elaine and his sister Tessa occupying the main house, with one live-in maid and old Barrington accommodated in the coach house.

Confronted by Tessa during dinner with rumours he couldn't deny, André had come out cold with the facts of the matter – his favourite phrase. The fact of the matter was that they could no longer afford the house. The fact of the matter was that they had received an offer they couldn't refuse. The fact of the matter was that since the end of the war the fortunes of the family firm run by himself and his two brothers had been on the decline, and that this decline seemed likely to be hastened by the situation in the Middle East, where the firm held half of its investments. The fact of the matter was that Egypt's diplomatic recognition of China and purchase of arms from communist countries had led to the withdrawal of an offer by Britain and the US to fund the building of the Aswan High Dam on the Nile, which in turn had led Egypt to retaliate with threats to nationalise the Suez Canal to raise the revenue to fund the dam itself.

This lengthy chain of reasoning expounded by André in defence of his actions had taken up most of the evening prior to George's arrival. Arms purchases, the Suez Canal and investments in the Middle East meant nothing to his bird-brained mother, however. Grateful for the interruption provided by the arrival of George, she reached back to the beginning of the chain to seize on the one link that mattered to her.

'Your elder brother has decided to turn his old mother out of the house, George. What do you say to that?'

George deflected the question, leaving it to be fielded by André. Constance at André's side rose visibly to the occasion, clasping his hand as a sign of her support – this was to be their moment.

'Constance and I would be very happy if you came and lived with us, Mother. As a matter of fact ...'

André had been about to announce the happy news that they were expecting an addition to the household, but at the sight of the scowl on his mother's face he changed his mind.

'It's not *me* I'm concerned about; it's your sister. What's going to happen to poor Tessa?'

André hadn't thought about Tessa. Or rather he had and decided that, unlike his seventy-year-old mother, Tessa wasn't his responsibility. A young woman of modest independent means was capable of looking after herself.

'Tessa is *thirty*, Mother. The time has come for her to branch out on her own.'

'No one would argue with that,' said Tessa. 'It's just the coldness with which you sell up our family home, the despicable cowardice, the sneaky way you do it behind our backs. Mother and I *live* in this house, you know.' Tessa folded her napkin and got up. 'Yes, yes, I know you're within your rights. But how convenient for you, André, to have that little board of so-called trustees to hide behind. Trustees, my foot. You talk as if all this were a foregone conclusion, but it doesn't seem to me you've been making a very good job of running the firm.'

'That's hardly for you to judge. You don't know the slightest thing about running a business.'

'Nor it seems do you. You just told us yourself that the fortunes of the family business have been on the decline since the end of the war. In plain English, it's been losing money for the last decade. No, André, let's face it. You're incompetent. If it wasn't your own firm, if you were employed by someone else, you'd be given the sack. Certainly *I* would give you the sack, if only for the appalling way you've handled the sale of our home. Would you be selling if you were still living here? Of course you wouldn't. Dickinson told me that he had been in favour of selling the house years ago because it tied down capital that was needed for the business. The house should have been put on the market long ago, but you resisted. You only agreed to the sale after you had married Constance, and your wife conveniently provided you with an alternative place to live, a very nice one by all accounts, a mortgage-free property in her name so that in the event of the firm going bankrupt they can't touch it.'

André turned pale.

'How dare you sit there and make these offensive remarks! How dare you make such insinuations!'

'How do *I* dare?' shouted Tessa. 'How do *you* dare, André, to sit on *our* chairs at *our* table in *our* house and tell us you're selling it all without consulting us beforehand, even if *you* don't care, but as a gesture of courtesy to *our* feelings? Because you're a despicable louse, that's why!'

And with that she stormed out of the room, slamming the door behind her.

# 12

An urn of ostrich feathers sitting on the lintel over the door toppled and crashed to the floor in the wake of her departure. It had been quite a day of slammed doors. Elaine rang for the maid and asked her to sweep up the pieces.

As if that was all there was to it, thought George – impressed, despite himself, by the coolness of his mother. He looked with satisfaction at the three glum faces round the table.

Tessa's performance had surprised and impressed him with its profes-sionalism. It had been a neat demolition job, and he agreed with what she had said. André was a coward. That was true. And he should never have been entrusted with running the firm. His father should have foreseen that. For a moment George forgot that the old man *had* foreseen it and had wanted to nominate him over his older brother, but George had turned his father down. It cheered him to watch his brother being given a tongue-lashing by his sister. He had enjoyed every moment of it, the more so, he was well aware, after a similar treatment had just been meted out to him by Ella.

George was also fully aware that Elaine had spoken up for her daugh-ter as much as for herself. With that cunning question *What's going to happen to poor Tessa?* which incidentally had placed his mother on the high moral ground out of the rough and tumble of a family row, Elaine had pushed Tessa into the front line. The obloquy Tessa had taken upon herself left her altruistic mother untainted. A fool though she was in many things, when it came to family politics Elaine wasn't easily outmanoeuvred.

Warmed by the glow left behind by Tessa's attack on André, George realised that it was also an odd sort of warmth *for* André which he felt, solidarity with his brother, who had come out of the humiliation at his sister's hands a somehow more likeable person than he had gone into it.

Applying this to his own situation, when he and Ella had had a row about where Max should be sent to school, had that really been the issue? Or was there another one at stake?

André looked enquiringly across the table at him as if to say, *What are* you *doing here?*

'I know this may not be quite the right moment,' began George, and the three faces turned towards him expressed such open displeasure that he back-pedalled. All the animus intended for Tessa was by default being directed at him.

'Some other time, perhaps. Actually, I just came over because there were a couple of books I wanted to borrow from father's library.'

'Won't you at least have a cup of coffee, dear?'

George was familiar with the dismissals his mother couched in the form of such invitations.

'No, really, I must get back,' he said, and with a peck on his mother's leathery cheek he left the room.

Ignoring the library on his way back through the main hall, he went up the broad staircase and found Tessa packing in her room.

'Where are you off to?'

'I'll decide when I get to the station. One of the local shires – Hertfordshire, Berkshire, Hampshire. The country. A change of air will do me good. I have a choice of girlfriends with nice country houses.'

George settled in the window seat and watched Tessa packing – her unhurried economical movements, getting a job done without the least sign of emotion. She was obviously leaving because of the row she had had with André, but it looked as if she was simply getting on with a plan of action she had already made up her mind about beforehand.

'And you?' asked Tessa. 'What brought you here?'

'Oh, well. I was taken by surprise by all of this. I had a bone of my own to pick with André.'

'About Hermine's house in Clerkenwell, I imagine,' said Tessa.

George was astonished. 'How did you know that?'

Tessa held a blouse up under her chin and draped a couple of shawls over each shoulder.

'Which of the shawls do you think goes better with it? The pink stripy one or the plain white one?'

'The white.'

'I knew you'd say white.'

'Oh? Because of my conservative tastes?'

'No, because of your caution. Colours are a risk. White is not a colour. White is safe.'

'Why not take both?'

'I shall. Correct answer. But you should have said that first time round. Sorry, you only get one chance. Had someone's decision whether or not to marry you depended on your answer to the question, it wouldn't have gone in your favour. Go back to square one.'

'In other words, you would marry risk rather than caution?' asked George, who was getting interested in this conversation.

'Not risk so much as unpredictability. When men become too easy to read, women begin to lose interest in them. And vice versa, of course.'

George fell silent, thinking about the decision he had made the moment Max was born to send his son to Park House. Before Max was born, in fact. That a son of his would some day attend Park House school was implicit in the fact the George had been there himself. He wondered if this was a case of choosing white rather than a colour, and what implications the choice of white might have for Ella's degree of interest in him.

'I thought André and Dickinson were the only people who knew about the loan to Hermine and the terms of her will,' said George, coming back to the subject that had brought him to the house. 'The secrecy of the deal betrays how uncomfortable André must have felt about it. If it was the family's financial interests he had at heart, as he's now claiming, why wasn't the family consulted?'

Tessa tried on a hat and looked at herself in the wardrobe mirror.

'The family *was* consulted. Dickinson told me and asked me what I thought.'

'Why you?'

'Because I know things about Dickinson,' Tessa replied airily, trying on a beret in which she fancied she looked rather *gamine*, 'and Dickinson is in my pay.'

'What sort of things?'

His sister laughed.

'I can't believe you do that hush-hush work at the Foreign Office,

George. I suppose it's all just files you read. You don't *observe*. You're so *naive*.'

George let that pass. 'And what did you think of what Dickinson told you?'

'I thought that for once André was making a smart move.'

'Not to mention a heartless and opportunistic one.'

Tessa turned and looked hard at him.

'You're beginning to sound rather like Ella, you know. It's really not your style, George. Go back to square one.'

George lost his temper. 'Oh shut up!'

'Temper temper!' Tessa taunted him, just as she had when they were children. She knew exactly where she could needle him.

'Anyway,' she said, sitting down and lighting a cigarette, 'the question you should be asking yourself is: given André's poor record, why was he for once making a smart move?'

'Fraud isn't making a smart move.'

'It was your fault.'

'*My* fault?'

'Your snapping up Ella with such uncharacteristic panache really galled André. He was very jealous. Tricking the two of you out of the house Ella stood to inherit from Hermine was André's way of getting his own back.'

'How do you know?'

'I observe things, George. I keep my eyes open. I simply see more.'

George pretended to be unimpressed. 'Like what, for example?'

'For example André and Ella going out onto the terrace and kissing.'

'What? When?'

'At Christmas the year she came over – I think it was forty-seven. André pursued her. Seriously. He would have liked to marry her, but for some reason, I can't imagine what, she had set her sights on you. I happened to be out there too, unsuccessfully attempting to seduce the pretty little maid we used to have at the time. Do you remember dear little Clara? In the end I had to go up to her room and just, well, rape her. Imagine! In those days I still used to feel guilty about that sort of thing.'

'I didn't know you were a lesbian rapist.'

'But do you know *anything*, George?' She came over and straightened his tie. 'That your wife is quite as attracted to women as to men, for example. Did you know that, George?'

'I'm not sure she knows that herself, Tessa. I think that's just your wishful thinking.'

Tessa laughed.

'Touché. Move forward six squares. How is Ella incidentally? Isn't it about time another child was on the way? Doesn't she need topping up? Have the two of you stopped breeding?'

George frowned as he walked to the door.

'Some time you must tell me your recipe, Tessa. What it is that gives you your unmistakable tang. The aftertaste, you know, the *je ne sais quoi* that lingers acridly in the mouth after just a nibble of you. Not now. Some other time. There are more important things I have to get on with now.'

For once he left his sister with nothing to say. Leaving the door of her room open, he walked away down the landing.

Barrington was waiting downstairs to present him with his umbrella on his way out.

'A very good day to you, sir. I hope it won't be too long before we see you again here.'

Not too long, come to that, before the place was sold up and disappeared, lock, stock and Barrington. George wondered if the old man had been told that his fifty years of service in the house were about to come to an end. He realised he knew hardly anything about the family retainer who had been living in the house since before he was born. What provision had been made for him? Where would the custodian of umbrellas go and live? Who *was* Barrington? Did he have a life of his own? Friends, relatives? His father's old butler anywhere other than here was unimaginable. A life apart from this house did not exist for him.

Whereas for George himself visiting home was like catching a disease. He arrived there fit as a fiddle and left feeling under the weather.

Not that Ella hadn't told him at the time about his brother's interest in her. In the interval it had slipped his mind. Not, as far as he knew, that she hadn't told him everything in the almost ten years they had now known each other. She had no secrets from him. More, she volunteered them. Her absolute trustworthiness was founded on an absolute honesty that frightened him.

Did he have secrets? Not exactly. Not yet. But there were things he chose not to tell her. He was more likely to suppress information than volunteer it. He wasn't a communicative human being. Certain things remained unspeakable for him. He didn't tell her about that cold stare, for example, which used to pass between him and Max when he changed his nappies in the middle of the night.

So far this imbalance of communications hadn't appeared to present a problem, but George sensed that it was now beginning to.

It was getting on for midnight when he arrived back at St John's Wood.

There was a light on down in the basement, but Giselle seemed to have gone to bed. Inside, he leaned into the stairwell and listened for a moment before switching off the light at the top of the stairs. Sounds of the house, its night breathing. George remained standing in the kitchen and took note of what sounded like a chest complaint of the refrigerator as it sought to maintain the equilibrium of its chill. Two clocks, Fat and Thin, Hampstead heirlooms Gábor had brought over from Budapest, keeping four-handed time, fractionally out of sync, in the darkness of the dining and the living rooms. The sound of them running on different *tacks* was familiar to him from the long evenings he used to spend listening to them in his father's study, waiting for the *tacks* to coincide, providing him with a sense of satisfaction when they briefly did before they began to diverge again. He looked for a note in the kitchen. Ella always left a note for him on the sideboard in the kitchen if she went to bed before he got back to the house.

The lack of a note troubled him.

He went upstairs and looked into the children's room. Here too he remained standing in the middle of the room, listening. The night-time of children reminded him of being in church. Their inaudible sleep, like a mantle of frost, touched him by its kinship with death. He might have mentioned it to Ella. If not, why hadn't he shared such a thought with his wife? She would have told him.

George found this question worried him too.

Perhaps there were more holes in the fabric than there were places filled in. With just a slight shift of perspective, one found oneself contemplating a life consisting mainly of gaps.

In the bedroom he looked through Ella's things to see if anything was missing, notably one of her bags. If she had gone off anywhere, she would at least have taken her bag. She had four more or less similar shoulder bags, red, blue, black and beige. The bag in use would normally be hanging over a chair. The ones she wasn't using hung on the inside of the cupboard door. The blue, black and the beige ones hung there now. He found nothing important in any of them.

Anything essential to her she would have transferred to the red bag, which was clearly currently in use. Essential was above all her passport. Even going out to the local shops the passport would be in her bag, not necessarily her purse. Payment could be deferred; identifying yourself could not. In Germany she had learned that her passport might save her life, and she hadn't forgotten the lesson. George remembered the red bag hanging over the back of the chair the night before. It wasn't there now.

Two weeks, he had told the children, but he knew no better than they did how long their mother would be away. Two weeks was the measure of an ordinary holiday. It was just George's wishful thinking.

He stretched out on the bed and dozed fitfully until a thought made him sit up.

What was Ella doing in Paris, from where she had apparently sent the telegram that afternoon? He had no idea why Ella would have gone to Paris, or where she would be staying, for she didn't have enough money for a hotel and she didn't know anyone there with whom she might have stayed.

Or did she?

Or not anyone George knew.

Or did he?

# CHAPTER FOUR

## Pogrom

### 1

As the cold war was coming to an end, Dr Alex Morris was appointed to a lectureship in south-east-European studies at a small university in Austria, not far from the Yugoslav border. Quite quickly, much sooner than anyone expected, the Soviet Union would cease to exist; the wall dividing Europe would be breached. Something familiar, indestructibly solid, it had seemed; an overarching political structure that had always been there was crumbling and would not be replaced. Alex sensed the vacuum in the continent surrounding him, the shapelessness of some-thing else that was already in the making, about to be born.

On a weekend trip to Osijek he sat with friends in a restaurant on the bank of the River Drava, eavesdropping on the buzz around him. In white shirts or blouses, dark trousers or skirts, the girls with flowers and garlands, groups of freshly graduated high school students were celebrating all over the Croatian town. A party of them sat in the restaurant, laughing and singing. In twos and threes they strolled along the riverbank, others lay on the grass. None of them got drunk; there was no disorderly conduct, not even much noise. It was a peaceful happy scene, lasting through a lunch that continued all afternoon.

In the early evening groups of students began to gather along a stretch of water branching off the river, ending in a swamp at the edge of the town. It was still warm enough to sit outside in shirtsleeves, still too early in the year to be troubled by the mosquitoes that would drive everyone indoors later in the summer. In the gradually failing light more and more students congregated by the swamp. Perhaps there were as many as two or three hundred of them down there in the end. What was audible at first as a gentle murmur in the background grew louder and louder until it became a furious buzz of flies, a cauldron of voices boiling over in the dark with what sounded to Alex like anger.

Seven years had passed since Tito died, and yet until very recently his birthday continued to be celebrated all over the country he had held together as if the old magus were still alive, still around to acknowledge the accolades in his honour. Relays of torch-bearing runners, young people like these school graduates in Osijek, set out from all corners of Tito's six republics to converge like the spokes of a wheel on the hub of the Yugoslav nation in Belgrade. Apprehensive of what would happen without him, they wouldn't let the old man go. But when even these young enthusiasts finally lost heart the dead man's birthday celebrations were discontinued. It was as if he had died a second time.

There was no doubt about Tito's achievement as unifier of a country, divided many times over, which until its creation in 1918 had existed only in the dreams of a few pan-Slavic nationalists. There was also no doubt, in Alex's mind, that unification had been achieved by gloss-ing over underlying differences that remained unreconciled. Catholic Slovenians and Croatians, formerly subjects of the Habsburgs, still claimed allegiance to a central European culture and history. Orthodox Serbs maintained traditional ties that linked them to Byzantium in the past and to Moscow in the present. The Muslims among the Slav popu-lation, whose history had lain within the Ottoman empire for hundreds of years, were still orientated to their old lodestars Mecca and Istanbul.

It was no more than a couple of hours by car from the Austrian–Slovenian border to Osijek in the heartland of Yugoslavia, but this heartland remained terra incognita to visitors from western Europe, whose interest in Yugoslavia was confined mainly to the coastal resorts of the Adriatic. From Osijek one might have walked in a couple of days – as Alex did during those years on his reconnaissance of a country he had studied at a distance for so long – into most of the entangled six republics, back west into Croatia and Slovenia, south into Serbia, south-west into Bosnia-Herzegovina, north into the autonomous prov-ince of Vojvodina bordering on Hungary.

Within each of these territories he found himself crossing and re-crossing islands of minority ethnic groups isolated within the larger population, identifiable by sometimes hardly perceptible changes in the local language, the choice of food, the brand of slivovitz, the style of

houses, the shape of a church tower, the number of cars parked in a village street, the relative shadings of affluence and poverty. The car journey
from the Austrian border through Slovenia and Croatia was a journey
through those shadings, beginning with affluence in the north-west and
ending in poverty in the south-east. Money earned in the Slovenian
north-west and paid as fiscal dues to the government in Serbian Belgrade
was spent on projects in the country's poorhouse, Kosovo, an autonomous province in the south corresponding to Vojvodina in the north.

No amount of minority representation in this federation or confed-
eration – a distinction to which Slovenes and Croats were becoming
increasingly sensitive after Tito's death – of patchwork nations with
their different languages, cultures and religions could alter the fact that
of the population of the six Yugoslav republics over a third counted as
Serbs. Alex had given a course on demographics at Graz University
and come to his own conclusions.

With the exception of Slovenia, there were Serbs with more or less
long-established rights of domicile living in all parts of the country. The
lack of an indigenous Serb population in Slovenia, taken in conjunction
with local revenues they felt were being disproportionately plundered by
federal politicians, plus the threat posed by the nationalist ambitions of a
new president of Serbia, Slobodan Milošević, encouraged the members
of the Slovenian delegation to walk out of the national congress of the
Yugoslavian Communist Party, taking the Croatian delegation with
them. The question of what the Croats would do with the half-million
Krajina Serbs living in their midst if Croatia seceded was shelved for
the time being, as no one had an interest in asking a question to which
no one had an answer.

The fourteenth party congress that saw the walkout of Slovenia and
Croatia – witnessed by Alex, who had been permitted to attend as an
observer – turned out to be the last. Communist regimes had already collapsed in half a dozen former satellites of the Soviet Union. The time was
ripe for declarations of independence all across Europe, and the republics
of the Yugoslavian federation would be among the last to follow suit.

In the borderland where Alex was then living there were still people
who had been born as subjects of the Habsburgs at a time when Slovenia and Croatia had belonged to the Austro-Hungarian empire. There
was no mistaking the prejudice of the Austrian and German press in
favour of their old friends and allies and against their common Serbian

foe, who had been on the other side in two world wars. Alex had no personal bias one way or the other, or rather, he had two, and they cancelled each other out. His soft spot for the Croatian cause went by the name of Slavenka, a woman he was seeing at the time. She came from a Croatian family living in Zadar. But before Slavenka there had been Mirjana, a major influence on the life of Alex during his teens and again much later, whose presence still remained with him. If she hadn't been killed, he would have married her.

Brought up in an Orthodox Serb household in Novi Sad in the early years of Tito's Yugoslavia, Mirjana emigrated with her family to Cádiz, where they eventually became Spanish citizens. She qualified as a teacher, married and moved to Madrid, divorced and moved to Puerto de la Cruz on the island of Tenerife in response to a job offer from the newly established British school there. Alex got to know her under the maiden name she reverted to after her divorce, Mirjana Stepanovic. She taught geography and history to A-level students, and for the two years he sat in Mirjana's European history classes he was her greatest admirer. Perhaps there had been too much emphasis on the history of Serbia and its contribution to the new nation created after the First World War, but who was Alex to judge, ignorant and infatuated as he was with the tall, sensual woman with the tousled auburn hair and an absent-minded almost surprised air, who looked as if she had just got out of bed in a hurry, still trailing the intimate scents of sleep – so different from the small, trim, sleek-headed women of Spanish stock who defined femininity on the island. That Alex Morris had gone on to specialise in Balkan studies at university was due to the influence of Mirjana Stepanovic, a commitment he had undertaken in the spirit of redeeming a lost cause, with all the hope and desperation of a young man's unrequited love.

Slavenka worked for Yugotours, a state travel agency with its head office in Belgrade and outlets in all major Austrian towns. Alex met her at a party in Klagenfurt, a cool, elegant but for all that forceful young woman in her late twenties who looked clearly at him out of her large brown eyes. This clarity was missing in the Austrian girls he knew, with whom Alex played charming if inconsequential games of hide-and-seek. There was no pretence of any kind with Slavenka. She would have had no use for irony if she had known what such a thing was. She kept her sense of humour well concealed. On her not so good days a matter-of-factness, even bluntness in her manner one could have taken for rudeness if one chose, was very much to the fore. But this brusqueness stood at one end of a scale that ran in the opposite direction to that complete openness and receptiveness of Slavenka's being which Alex found so attractive, generous to the point of brimming over, too full to be able to contain itself. In bed it manifested itself in a feverish sexuality, consuming Slavenka so utterly that she seemed to undergo a personality change into a devoted, even servile woman whom Alex didn't recognise and felt uncomfortable with. She kissed his feet, apologised for being inadequate, waiting to be contradicted, wanting to be reassured.

The events that were beginning to unfold in Yugoslavia went largely unnoticed by much of the outside world. The international media were occupied with bigger stories that made stronger headlines: the disintegra- tion of the Soviet Union, the fall of the Berlin Wall, the Gulf War. Who outside Yugoslavia recognised the significance of a speech made by Milošević at a rally in Kosovo attended by a million Serbs? Who cared about the separatist ambitions of Slovenia and Croatia, tiny places that many people had never heard of? Who knew the background of the new Croatian president, Franjo Tudjman, or had even heard his name? Who had the slightest idea about the old scores he began to settle with his Serb enemies as soon as he came to power, elevating a long-standing tribal feud to the status of an official programme of anti-Serb discrimination, the articles of which were written into the new Croatian constitution that replaced the constitution of the federation of the six republics yoked together by Tito? Who cared?

Alex knew about these things because he was a Balkan specialist. He was aware that the subject of the secession of the six national republics from the Yugoslav federation was the only topic of conversation among people everywhere in the country, even more important to them than the disastrous state of the economy. With the loss of former export markets in the now defunct and bankrupt communist states that had been Yugo- slavia's main trading partners, the collapse of the country's economy exacerbated the political disagreements, allowing the old ethnic rivalries to erupt on the surface as outright hatred. A spirit of fatalistic gloom had taken possession of all the people Alex spoke to, whatever their ethnic affiliation. Everyone he spoke to on his forays into the country assured him that the break-up of the federation could only be achieved at the cost of enormous bloodshed, but that it would come nonetheless. He knew of these dangers, but he still didn't believe them. The country still seemed to be functioning as normal. If everyone saw so clearly the disaster ahead of them, surely it could be averted, surely they would change course to avoid confrontation?

But Slavenka was reluctant to discuss such matters with Alex. She always managed to come up with some reason not to accompany him on his trips across the border. During the two years he had known her they had not once been to Yugoslavia together.

'You're not being honest with me,' he told Slavenka sadly. 'There's something you're hiding from me. And that's so uncharacteristic of you.'

Something, whatever it was, had got under the skin of their tight little cocoon. Some invisible irritant had come between them.

# 2

Alex was invited by Andro and his wife Mirsad, the friends with whom he had attended the graduation ceremony of their niece in Osijek four years earlier, to go down and stay with them at their home in Zadar over the May Day holiday. Alex had put off visiting the popular Adriatic city in the hope of going there some time in Slavenka's company. Zadar was where Slavenka came from, after all. It was her home town. Having meanwhile given up on that ever happening, and knowing that he would be leaving the region in the summer when his contract with the university, already extended for a year, finally ran out, Alex decided to accept his friends' invitation and go without her. But with the thought still at the back of his mind that she might come with him after all, he mentioned it to her a couple of weeks before he was due to leave, and to his surprise she agreed. Yugotours had a hotel in town, she said, where company employees could stay free of charge. Wouldn't that be preferable to each of them living in separate apartments, Slavenka said, she at her parents' cramped place, he with his friends, where it probably wasn't much better? And so the matter was arranged.

Slavenka's life revolved around her company, which was a Yugoslavian state enterprise. She travelled constantly up and down the Adriatic, staying in company hotels, eating company meals, driving a company car, a Fiat with a Belgrade numberplate on permanent loan from Yugotours headquarters in the capital. Her work always took precedence, and it intervened the day she and Alex were due to leave, so that they didn't set out until after midnight. Thus Alex saw nothing of the Dalmatian coast with its myriad islands until the sun came up and they were already within an hour of their destination. Slavenka parked the car in a street behind the hotel. It was half past five when they finally got up to their room, and they both fell asleep the instant they lay down.

Alex lay drowsily, fragments of a fading dream somehow entangled with his feet in a swaddle of sheets, all mixed up with roaring sounds and a smell of smoke. He thought of fire and woke up, it seemed only moments after he had fallen asleep. The rumpled other half of the bed was empty. A note from Slavenka lay on the pillow with a phone number at which he could reach her. He went to the window and looked down at the surprisingly sparse traffic pounding across the square. He could see the smoke he had smelt in his dream, the kind of drizzle of smoke that rose from an already extinguished fire. It came from the street-level window of a store on the opposite side of the square. The fire brigade must have come and gone. Perhaps that explained why nobody apart from a few bystanders seemed to be taking much notice of what had happened.

He called the number Slavenka had left. She answered immediately. She was at her parents' house. She had to go out, she said rather tersely, gave him the address of a restaurant where they could meet later that afternoon and hung up without saying goodbye.

Puzzled, Alex had a shower and got dressed.

At the hotel reception he picked up a city map before leaving. Outside, a cloudless blue day spread out before him. He wandered over the pedestrian bridge, taking in the view of the peninsula reaching out into the Adriatic, and wandered contentedly back before crossing the square to investigate the burned-out premises he had seen from his hotel window. It turned out to be a shipping company office. At close quarters it didn't look like the usual fire damage, more as if a bomb had exploded. The glass shopfront had burst outwards, buckling the window frame and showering the pavement with splinters. Its still-smouldering tables and chairs covered with traces of foam, filing cabinets with all the drawers ripped out, fixtures ripped from the walls – the office looked to Alex as if it had been ruined by a deliberate act of demolition rather than accidentally by fire.

The shipping company office was only the beginning. On his way across town to the address where Andro and Mirsad lived, Alex passed dozens of offices, shops, a hairdresser's, a car rental agency, sometimes isolated sites in blocks of otherwise intact buildings, sometimes in rows on a single street which had been targeted for destruction. Alex looked around in disbelief. All had been gutted, windows smashed, shops looted. Here and there stood burned-out cars, still smouldering at the kerb. Yet no one was taking any action to deal with this vandalism, no firemen or policemen, no shop owners cleaning up or truckers hauling wrecks away. Even passers-by who were evidently local walked on through these scenes of destruction as if they had nothing to do with it and wanted to have no part in it, not even to give any indication of surprise at what they saw.

I'm the only person just standing here looking, Alex said to himself, unnerved as he watched the people hurrying past. It struck him how few pedestrians were out in the streets at all. Not many cars, come to that. Of course, this might be due to the holiday. The shops were shut. There was no one working in the office buildings. So why would he expect there to be anyone in the city? They must all have gone to the beach or stayed at home, leaving the buzzing centre of Zadar deserted, he told himself, knowing this to be nonsense, knowing how unnatural this emptiness was.

No one was at home, either, in the apartment block on the Bulevar where Andro and Mirsad lived. He pressed the buzzer several times but got no reply. After hanging around outside the building for half an hour in the vague hope that his friends might still show up, he set off for the restaurant where he had arranged to meet Slavenka.

It was on the way to the restaurant in the old quarter of the town that Alex registered the graffiti on the walls he passed. It was everywhere. He must have passed much more on his walk through town after leaving the hotel, but being so preoccupied with the extraordinary scenes he was encountering en route, he had failed to notice it. SRBIMA SMRT was one of the slogans frequently daubed on the wall, TUDJMAN = BOG another. Death to the Serbs. Tudjman is God. Who was responsible for writing these signs? The omnipresent letter U standing for Ustaša, sprayed on doors and windows everywhere, brought home to Alex the truth of what had happened here. A pogrom had taken place in Zadar during the last twenty-four hours. It had been carried out by Croatians and the target had been Serbs.

Of course!

How could it have taken him so long to realise something so obvious, a full hour during which, at every other street corner he had turned in the course of his walk, he had been confronted with evidence he should have taken in at a glance? Tripping over a corpse with a slit throat and a battered head, one would be justified in seeing this as evidence of a murder, wouldn't one? Then why had he been so slow? Because it went against all his instincts, ran against the grain of every judgement about what was possible here in Zadar on this beautiful spring day, because it was impossible, and he had been unable to believe it – that was why.

Reaching a little square, Alex checked his map and confirmed that he was just off the Kala Larga, the main artery in the maze of alleys in the old town where he had arranged to meet Slavenka. It must be here. Looking around, he read the name of the restaurant she had given him over the entrance to a place on the corner of the square. The restaurant was full, with only one vacant table at the back by the house wall. It was much busier here than everywhere else he had been in the city. The place was a hive of bustle and noise. People were coming and going across the square as if they had urgent business and were in a hurry to get wherever it was they were heading. He sensed excitement in the air. Something was up. You could hear it, the tide of sound in the distance, the thousandfold footsteps that were approaching. The sound reminded him of the rising murmur of the crowd of high school graduates on that evening by the river in Osijek four years ago. He was so preoccupied with his own thoughts that he didn't see Slavenka. She materialised out of nowhere and was already sitting down beside him.

'It would be best for us to go somewhere else,' she said agitatedly. She must have been walking fast. Alex noticed the sweat on her forehead as she leaned across the table and spoke urgently in a low voice. 'There's probably going to be more trouble here. It could get dangerous. People have gone crazy.'

But the vanguard of the procession making its way along the Kala Larga had already reached them, a group of muscular young men in jeans and white T-shirts, carrying banners on long poles bearing a chequerboard of red and white squares, the symbol of the Croatian fascist Ustaša movement during the Second World War, another

223

swastika, suppressed under Tito, which had now come out of hiding to become once again the national flag. They were followed by a priest bearing a cross and a huge man in some sort of folk costume, holding high over his head on a lectern a book the size of a placard, its pages open. Boys wearing cassocks and surplices followed the giant with the book, church dignitaries in gold-embroidered vestments and hats, some of them swinging incense burners, others carrying elaborate staffs or vessels of gold and silver in which the host was displayed, crowds filling the street behind them. The tail of the procession must have been several hundred yards long, men and women, old and young, muttering a never-ending paternoster as they made their way down the Kala Larga.

The moment the priests carrying the monstrance came level with the corner of the restaurant where Alex and Slavenka were sitting, everyone else there got to their feet to show their respect. The two people who remained sitting at the back table by the wall soon attracted attention, scowls and hisses.

'Don't,' said Alex, when he saw Slavenka getting to her feet. She had gone white. Her eyes were fixed on the crowd shuffling along in the wake of the priests. It was as if something or someone she had seen in the crowd had given her a shock, and it wasn't in honour of the procession that she now got up; it was to slip away from the restaurant unnoticed. Within minutes of arrival Slavenka vanished as mysteriously as she had come.

Once the procession had passed, animated conversations sprang up at tables all around him. Realising that he was a foreigner, the other customers left him in peace. Alex ordered something to eat, but when the food came he found he had lost his appetite. He sat there for a couple of hours, the food untouched, drinking wine and coffee, hoping that Slavenka would come back, full of uneasy feelings caused by what he had seen that day, and among them was a premonition that Slavenka would not just fail to come back to the restaurant; she had gone for good, he wouldn't see her again. What had happened in Zadar would be taking place in other places as well, and all this had happened before. His mother had been in Berlin at the time of the pogrom in 1938 and told him about it, an introduction to the subject of the Holocaust, a refrain that began in his early childhood and would remain with him throughout his life.

On his way back up the Kala Larga Alex came across more ruined shops, right there on the main street in the old quarter or in malls just off it, a popular tourist shopping centre, where clothes stores, boutiques, jewellers, had been vandalised and looted. A rampage on this scale, which must have gone on for hours, was only possible with official approval. The demonstration by the Croatian Catholic Church he had just witnessed made clear that the pogrom could have taken place only with the backing of the local authorities; more, the chain of responsibility must reach back to President Tudjman, that old Ustaša man now in power in Zagreb.

With extreme unease, halfexpecting some provocation or challenge from the people he passed, Alex made his way back across town. He began to feel safer once he reached the Bulevar, a dual carriageway for longdistance traffic in transit from Rijeka in the north to Split in the south. Here the passing cars travelled at speed and there were fewer pedestrians. Reaching the block of flats where his friends lived, he pressed the buzzer and was relieved to hear Mirsad's voice answer immediately over the intercom. There wasn't a moment to lose, she said, telling him the elevator was out of order and that he should come up by the stairs to their apartment on the fourth floor.

A small dark woman opened the door and let him in.

'Are you all right?'

She put her arms around his neck and clasped him to her. Two little girls stood behind her, waiting their turn to be kissed by Alex.

'Where have you been all day? We were so worried about you.'

Alex was starting to tell her that he had called in the afternoon but nobody had been at home when an older woman came out of the living room. This was Mira, her motherinlaw, said Mirsad. The stout silverhaired woman whom he had never met embraced him hardly less warmly than her daughterinlaw had done. She had come from Krajina yesterday to spend the holiday with her grandchildren, only it had not turned out to be a holiday at all. In the background Alex could hear two separate voices, one of them a man on television, the other a woman on the radio, talking incessantly and at cross purposes, it seemed.

'Where's Andro?'

'At the office, doing a late edition of the paper. He thought he'd be back about nine or ten. Come in and have something to eat.'

Mirsad was interrupted by the telephone ringing. While she was answering it, her motherinlaw bustled around Alex at the table with bread, salad and a pot of stew she ladled into a bowl for him, while the two little girls stood by to supervise him eating it. As soon as she had finished on the phone, Mirsad came and sat down at the table beside Alex to tell him what was happening.

She had heard reports on the radio that day about the murder of a policeman in a place called Polače in northern Dalmatia, a Croat allegedly killed by a Serb. People she had talked to on the telephone who lived in the area put this report in a different light, however. According to them, a delegation of Serbs had gone under truce to speak to the Croatian police chief in Polače about recent hostilities in Borovo between the two ethnic groups. Outside the police station they had been ambushed by Croats and fired back. In the course of this skirmish the policeman had been killed. The dead man was a native of Bibinje, just outside Zadar. Enraged by the murder of a local man, a group of friends, colleagues – and the kind of people who were always around whenever there were any heads that needed bashing in, Mirsad said with a rueful face – had caught a train early that morning to carry out a pogrom against Serbs in Zadar in retaliation for the murder in Polače.

'You must have seen for yourself what happened.'

'Was anyone killed?'

'That's one of the things Andro has been trying to find out. Not that the paper can be relied on to print the truth, even if Serbs have been killed. You've no idea what pressure is being put on the media to support Tudjman's nationalist line. Just take this business with the candles.'

'Candles?'

Word had gone around Zadar that day, later endorsed by an exhortation on local radio, that people were expected to get home that evening before it got dark and place a lighted candle in a window as a sign of mourning for the murdered man from Bibinje – effectively in solidarity with the Croatian cause and approving the pogrom. Well, she and Andro and their relatives and friends, no one was going to tell them what to do. She had spent the whole evening on the phone. The consensus of the people she had spoken to was that they must make a stand against this kind of intimidation and not put a candle in the window. In half an hour it would be dark, and as if to bring home to Alex how the tension was rising as the minutes passed, the telephone never stopped ringing.

One of the calls was for him. It was Slavenka calling from her parents' place.

'Have you heard about the candles?' she asked at once.

'We were just talking about it.'

'And what will they be doing, your friends?'

'They've decided not to put a candle in the window.'

'They're crazy. Tell them what danger they're in. I know. Alex, I never talked to you about my parents —' she lowered her voice '– espe, cially my father. He's involved with the cause. He has powerful friends, Alex; he knows. He's not here at the moment or I wouldn't be talking to you like this. My mother's in the kitchen. But from the conversation she had with my father before he went out I know what the consequences will be for people who fail to put a candle in the window, so tell your friends, it's a witch hun—'

The line went dead. Alex imagined her mother coming out of the kitchen and Slavenka immediately hanging up.

He was shaken by this conversation. Many more such conversations followed during the evening, with friends of Andro and Mirsad calling from places all over Yugoslavia.

About an hour and a half after nightfall Andro arrived home with the news that he had run into groups of Croatian nationalist vigilantes on their way through the city, checking street by street to see where no candles were burning in windows. He had watched them climb over walls to look at the backs of buildings, and according to a conversation he overheard they were even going into blocks of flats and up the stairs, checking floor by floor the names on the doors of the apartments.

'This is a country where all the southern Slavs live together,' Andro said to Alex, his voice rocky with anger. 'This is what we have achieved in the last forty years. This is what Yugoslavia means.' He took his passport out of the hall table drawer and thrust it in Alex's face.

Mirsad came out of the living room and said, 'Snjezana just called to say that she and Zoran will be doing the candle after all. She says a colleague of Zoran just lost his job because one of his grandmothers is a Serb. If there's the slightest rumour of someone not being one hundred per cent in support of a Croatian state they'll take it as an excuse to fire them. Zoran's job is on the line, and they don't want to risk it. So where does that leave you?'

Andro's mother came out of the room where she had put the two children to bed and closed the door. She caught the tail end of what her daughter-in-law had said and must have realised a row with her son was in the making. He was already beginning to shout back at Mirsad. Why were they all standing around in the hall? she asked. They would wake the children up, and was that the sort of hospitality one showed to a guest? Saying which, she shepherded the three of them back into the living room.

They went out onto the balcony and looked at the buildings across the street. In many windows the lights were out so that the burning candle could be clearly seen. Where there were lights on it could be assumed there were no candles. In apartments where no lights were on and no candle was burning either, people were not at home, but that wouldn't help them the next day.

Vigilantes were already beginning to appear at the far end of the Bulevar. They could be heard shouting to one another across the street. As Andro and Mirsad looked out into the night they knew there would be some sort of reckoning with the people who lived in the apartments displaying no candles.

'An hour ago it was still only about half the windows that had a candle,' Mirsad said. Alex heard the anxiety in her voice. 'Now it's more like three quarters.'

'More people like Zoran,' Andro answered contemptuously, 'people who think it's just their jobs that are on the line, not their principles. Come in and have a drink, Alex. We'll drink a toast to Yugoslavia.'

So the four of them sat down and the bottle went round a couple of times, and then just back and forth between Andro and Alex, as the two women said they'd had enough and got up to go out onto the balcony, where they could be heard talking quietly with each other as they kept watch on what was happening on the street. The shouts of the men below, carrying out the survey of candles, were now distinct enough to be intelligible.

'It's now up to eighty or ninety per cent,' Mirsad called.

Mira came back in, sat down on the sofa opposite her son and looked squarely at him. Alex watched her broad face, a peasant's face, tanned and wrinkled, the serious but calm manner of a woman who didn't easily lose her composure and knew just what she wanted to say. Between the stout mother and her barrel-like son, the family resemblance was evident not just in their physique but the force of personality they had in common.

'This Zoran, whose grandmother was a Serb, like the colleague who already lost his job, what would have happened to him if his mother had been a Serb?'

She waited for Andro to answer, but he said nothing.

'Would they drive him out of town? Would they kill him? Such things have happened before, and they will happen again. When your father died I went back to live with my brother in Krajina. I know what is happening there. They treat Croats there no differently from the way Serbs are being treated here. In Krajina the Serbs are already preparing for the war they know will come when the Croats try to drive them out of their homes. People on both sides will die. And this will happen, Andro, whether you put a candle in your window or not. But if you do not, not only will you lose your job, other things will be done to your family.'

Mirsad came in from the balcony and sat down on the sofa beside her mother-in-law.

'They will find reasons to shut your daughters out of school and to dismiss Mirsad from the kindergarten,' Mira continued, 'if only because of her name. Schools, doctors, youth organisations, all those things that are in the hands of the state to give are also in the hands of the state to take away. It's not worth risking losing these things for the sake of a candle you don't want to put in the window, Andro. What use is this principle of yours if it brings you so little and takes away so much? I have no respect for it. It's just a vain and selfish thing.'

The two women, his mother and his wife, looked at Andro as if it was now in his hands to give or take away, and Andro knew what both expected of him. He made a gesture with his arm as if brushing something away, and his mother got up and went into the kitchen. She returned with a candlestick and a tall white votive candle like the ones people bought to burn in churches, placed it on the windowsill and put a match to the wick.

Just that one little action. But one of many, thought Alex, and collectively they would tip the balance.

As he watched this scene in the apartment, a scene that was taking place in many other apartments that night, Alex was reminded of Ella's instruction to him as a child on colder evenings in Tenerife to go indoors and light the candles. This had happened many times, and what happiness it had given him, knowing that it made his mother happy. But on this night the act of lighting a candle in this place brought no one pleasure and shed no illumination; in this flame Yugoslavia would be consumed.

# 3

Alex stayed on in Zadar. He had made up his mind. He would work for a news agency, and the only question was which one. He called David Evans, a colleague of George who had retired to Malta, and caught him on his way out of the house to play golf. Yesterday's man will do what he can, quipped Evans on his sunny island off the coast of Africa. He thought he still had some pull with former Foreign Office colleagues who were not yet in retirement. Evans had been a friend to Alex when he was a student in London. He said he'd see what he could come up with and call back.

There was no hotel bill to pay as Slavenka had sorted out everything before she left. She was no longer in Zadar. Alex spoke to her mother when he called her parents' house and was told by her that Slavenka had gone to Zagreb. He spent the days after the pogrom reading the local newspapers. The most impartial accounts of events were broadcast by a local radio station for an hour or two in the middle of the night, an indication of their reliability and of the risks the broadcasters must have been taking.

As for the international press, with the exception of one Italian paper he found no mention anywhere of what had taken place. It was conspicuously ignored by the German and Austrian press, which usu-ally kept close tabs on developments in Yugoslavia and shouldn't have missed something this important. Had it really been missed, or was it deliberate editorial blindness in the interests of the pro-Croat anti-Serb case favoured by the mainstream media in those countries? The interests of the news media determined what they told you. You only saw what others chose for you to see. How wars were presented to the spectators had become a more important strategy issue than how wars were fought by the participants. After Zadar this came to Alex as an epiphany – the revelation of a truth which until now he may have thought he had known but which he had not understood. First-hand experience was really everything.

Overnight it led him to change the plans he'd been making for an academic future and to launch into a career in journalism. But he wasn't going to sit in an office far away from what was happening and write editorials about it; he would be here, establishing the facts, what was happening at ground level, or so he hoped – for the pogrom in Zadar demonstrated to him how difficult that was. The reconstruction of this one pogrom in this one city was daunting enough. One thing led to another, but where did the leading begin? Before the events in Zadar there had been other events in Bibinje, relating to still other events in Polače, which in turn were connected with an incident in Borovo, and so on, taking you back weeks or months – six hundred years if necessary, as the pilgrimage, reportedly of a million Serbs, to a medieval battlefield in Kosovo had recently shown.

He didn't tell Andro of his plan, anticipating that Andro might be envious of a freedom that was denied him. Andro's articles were now scripted by others. *Slobodna Dalmacija* toed the official Croatian line. The paper continued as if nothing out of the ordinary had happened. Daily life continued everywhere as if nothing had happened. People went to work and came home. They sat out in cafes, chatted and laughed. Children ran around and played football in the street. Candles had disappeared from windows.

What had changed wasn't necessarily noticeable to an outsider. Andro told Alex that people in the building where he lived avoided looking at each other in the elevator, no longer greeted people known to be Serbs.

'After what happened, you know, it was awkward. I found I was no longer able to look certain colleagues in the eye,' Andro confessed to Alex. 'I gave in. I betrayed them. But you know the situation here.'

The situation was that a Serb minority eighteen thousand strong lived in Zadar. Some of the families had been there for centuries, but that still hadn't protected their property rights. Over a hundred Serb business premises had been destroyed in the pogrom. So had Slavenka's Yugotours car, vandalised because of its Belgrade numberplates. With no independent judiciary to appeal to, the victims had no hope of restitution.

'What else could I have done?'

Between them Andro's mother and his wife had undermined his self-esteem. Quite casually that night, with a gesture that Alex thought was open to interpretation – a dismissive gesture with his hand that might have been as much a reluctant concession as it was a refusal, an expression of resignation and anger – Andro had surrendered what mattered to him most, his pride in his vocation, doing a job he believed mattered. He'd allowed his mother to tell him what to do. Among the first casualties of a war still months away was Andro's loss of self-respect, just as people everywhere were losing their bearings, coming off the beaten paths of previous lives, not speaking to neighbours in the elevator, not saying good morning to people they used to greet every day. The women knew family came first, and family in this country was already difficult enough. Mirsad was a Muslim from Sarajevo. The children were mixed Croatian and Bosnian, as much or as little Catholic as they were Muslim, and their paternal grandmother was a Serb. All this need not be complicated further by Andro unnecessarily losing his job.

Then the nightly explosions began.

Two or three times Alex was woken in the night when the houses destroyed were in the neighbourhood. One beautiful old house set in a garden a couple of blocks from the hotel stood there the next morning looking oddly truncated. It took a few moments to realise that while the upper storey and the roof had survived the explosion, they had sunk a storey to replace the no-longer-existing ground floor. The two-storey house had become a bungalow. The demolitionists simply pumped gas into the houses of people on their list and ignited it, to encourage them to go. The blowing-up of houses soon became a part of ordinary life in Zadar, as if removing houses considered a hazard had been launched as a municipal project in the interests of public safety.

The evening before Alex left Zadar for an interview with the International Press Association in London set up for him by David Evans, he went with Andro to a party in a big house near the sea. It belonged to Aida, a woman from a wealthy family with property interests all over the city, a pure Croat family, as far as Andro knew, but these days who could tell. These days a hint of Serb blood a couple of generations back might be seen as an unforgivable racial impurity.

Alex got into conversation with Aida's husband, Zlatan, a tall athletic figure with a resemblance to Goran Ivanisevic. It came as a surprise to learn that Zlatan was a Muslim. Alex caught himself out in a prejudice he held that – for some reason he couldn't even have named himself – tall tennis-star-type men were unlikely to be Muslims. What *did* make Zlatan a Muslim? Was he a believer? Did he practise his religion?

'It's just something I inherited from my father,' he said. 'Like the colour of my eyes. Like my name.'

'So it doesn't really affect your daily life?'

'Not in the slightest!' Zlatan sounded amused. 'I'm an atheist. I never prayed to Allah or anyone else for that matter for a single day in my life.'

He was in the YNA, the Yugoslav National Army, an officer on the teaching staff of the military academy in Zadar. Zlatan was full of praise for this most Yugoslav of institutions, a democratic army reflecting the balance of the country's six nations.

'Well, this is the point,' said Alex. 'If the referendum goes in favour of Croatia declaring its independence, and Croatia really does secede from the Yugoslavian Federation and declares itself a sovereign state, where does that leave you and the army? Surely it becomes by definition an occupation army in a foreign state where it has no right to be.'

'Theoretically, I suppose that situation might arise,' Zlatan said with a frown, 'but it's in the power of the army to set a positive example. Look, a representative cross-section of this federation of states makes up the YNA – Serbs, Croats, Bosnians, Macedonians and so on – with each nation free to practise its own religion, and yet there is harmony. Perhaps the military discipline helps, but really, you see, we're the model of what Yugoslavia is all about. We show that it works, in military bases dotted all over the country in all of the national republics.'

'Of course,' interrupted Alex, 'and, as you say, that's an admirable thing. But if Slovenia and Croatia declare independence, the fact is that in YNA barracks all over Croatia there will be soldiers whom the Slovenian and Croatian governments must regard as hostile forces. Simply by being there they constitute an occupation army. The Yugo-slavian Federation, or what's left of it, won't even need to invade the seceding republics, if that's what they decide to do. They're already here. What will you do, for example, as a Croatian Muslim, if the Croatian government tells you to quit the YNA and to join their army, while Belgrade orders you to remain at your post and repel attempts to dislodge you from your barracks? I mean, that could result in your having to shoot at almost any of the men you see in this room.'

'Fortunately, I don't see that likelihood arising,' Zlatan responded tersely, already turning as his wife called to him from across the room. 'Can I get you another drink?'

They make a handsome couple, thought Alex, watching the tall blonde Aida and her dark-haired husband, their three beautiful children in tow, moving out into the garden to join their guests, but how can't they see that the party's not going to last? The flawless early summer weather heightened the garden party atmosphere, the laughter and chatter, propitiatory gifts of banality, a reckless celebration of the lightness of life, not just here but everywhere in Zadar an act of collective forgetting in the face of all the evidence to the contrary, the frightening reality Alex had got to know on arrival in this town, which intruded on his view of everything he had experienced here since.

Elections in Yugoslavia had never been a reliable indicator of the people's will under Tito, while doubts about the fairness of the referendum held in Croatia later that month were justified. Andro, for one, could confirm to Alex that the atmosphere in the polling booths had been one of intimidation. Under whatever circumstances, 93 per cent of the population supposedly voted in favour of seceding from Yugoslavia, whereupon foolhardy politicians in Germany and Austria, two countries that might have exercised a restraining influence, pressurised the European Union into too-hasty recognition of Slovenia and Croatia as independent states.

What if Scotland were to behave like this, or Wales, wondered Alex, unilaterally declaring their independence from the United Kingdom? Would the European Union hurry to recognise them as sovereign states, branding Britain an intolerable aggressor for any action it took to prevent secession?

Within a couple of months of the events in Zadar, the break-up of Yugoslavia began with military action in Slovenia. From the campus of his former university on the Austrian border, Alex looked up into the clear summer sky and saw jets of the Yugoslavian armed forces come streaking in from the east, violating Austrian airspace in order to turn for their attacks on targets in Slovenia. He saw the same pictures on TV that night. It was the beginning of a war fought with extraordinary savagery, although it was no worse than the war fought by the previous generation – no better was really the point – which escalated as it spread to the rest of the country. Europe might have thought it had got such upheavals behind it, but the war in Yugoslavia would continue for the next ten years.

Andro and his family went into exile in Vienna three years after the hostilities in Slovenia began. They were fortunate to receive funding for an NGO called Vienna Watch, which they helped to set up to monitor crimes against humanity committed in the Yugoslavian civil war. A constant stream of guests flowed through their Vienna flat, refugees from the war en route to some other place to live. A year after Andro's family moved into their apartment Alex met Zlatan there, a thin stony-faced man who seemed to have aged ten years. The Croatian Muslim he remembered from that last evening in Zadar as a good-looking tennis star, a relaxed confident man with a happy family life, was so changed that Alex didn't recognise him, as much a ruin of the man he once was as the ruins of the beautiful houses Alex had seen after they'd been blown up by Croatian fanatics in Zadar. On Alex's first visit back to Zadar after the war ended these ruins were passed off to him and the other journalists on the city tour as collateral damage, the result of shelling by Serbian artillery.

Zlatan had briefly remained loyal to his employer, defending the army base in Zadar against Croat attackers, until the impossibility of the situation forced him to change sides. He joined the army of Croatia and was permitted to go to Bosnia and fight the battles of his fellow Muslims there, although officially Croatia had no part in that war and denied it had any military personnel involved. Zlatan took photographs of massacred Bosnian Serbs, which he showed to Andro and Alex, assuring them that he himself had taken no part. Why did he take the pictures? To document what was happening, said Zlatan, otherwise no one would believe such things. Seeing them through a camera helped him to objectify them. They illustrated why, as soon as the nature of the Bosnian war became clear to him, Zlatan had returned to Zadar, only to learn that he had been relieved of his duties in the Croatian army because he lacked the ethnic purity qualifications now required.

The family moved north and tried without success to get established in Rijeka and Ljubljana. Zlatan had left his family with friends in Klagenfurt and was now in Vienna en route for the western European countries that ran relief programmes for refugees from the former Yugoslavia to see what opportunities he could find. Andro later heard from him in Germany and Sweden, but in none of these places did the family settle for long. After a long odyssey across Europe, Andro heard nothing more of Zlatan and his family until a postcard arrived from New Zealand, to which they had emigrated. They had managed to make a new life for themselves there, Aida wrote, and things were beginning to look up for them again at last, seven years after leaving their home in Zadar.

# CHAPTER FIVE

# Nadine

## 1

On the day after his brother Max's funeral, Alex returned to a message on the answering machine in his apartment in Vienna. The message was from Andro.

'You must have got caught up in something, Aloisha, or I would have heard from you. We missed you last Sunday. Perhaps you'll be able to make it Sunday next. There'll be at least one new person coming you'll be interested to meet. Give us a call when you get back. Or just come over. One of us is always in.'

Sunday evening was the *jour fixe* hosted by Andro and Mirsad in their apartment in the 8th District. It had begun as a weekly information evening open to anyone interested when they set up Vienna Watch ten years before, transforming into an informal gathering of friends, usually though not always including something on the agenda concerning what was now known as ex-Yugoslavia.

It was warming to have such friends. It was warming to be welcomed home by such a message.

Home!

Yesterday he and his sister Felicity had buried Max in the family plot in Hampstead in the red anorak Alex had lent him after they got drenched on their way home on the morning of his death. Max had no money, or none that could be found at such short notice, leaving his siblings to split the costs of the cheapest funeral a local undertaker had to offer. Philip contributed his share but declined to attend, adding a bonus of five hundred pounds, what he called toll money – one of those odd actuarial phrases Philip had in his keeping – saying that he and Max had never had much in common in life and nothing at all now. So it was Alex and Felicity, just the two of them, who had deposited Max in the unlikely company of his grandparents Gábor and Elaine. It was less a burial than a disposal of leftovers, a body to be got rid of that nobody wanted. Philip's toll money paid for the tips Alex gave to the four pall bearers and a wake for two at the Ritz when the meagre ceremony in the Hampstead churchyard was over. There was complete agreement between the two of them that such a treat was the barest necessity, the minimum required by the desolate circumstances that had preceded it.

These thoughts drifted in and out of his dreams, a whorl of strange unpleasant shapes coming to no conclusion. But a sentence rose in Alex's mind the moment he awoke. The solitariness of Max in life was reflected in his death. Perhaps it would have been different in New York. Perhaps people who cared about Max would have rallied round, but from what he had said about the person closest to him having died of Aids a few years ago, no other person he found worth mentioning since, Alex got the impression there were few such people in New York either. Whereas the young Max, with whom Claude had shared the London flat for a couple of years in the late 60s, had opened his life to so many friends – they streamed in and out – the place was a hive, Claude said, Max very much the queen bee, with many courtiers and admirers. So why did he take himself off to America if it was all happening in London? It was that self-destructive streak in Max coming to the fore again, said Claude, Max bent on giving up his belonging, throwing away what was most precious in his life.

As he cycled down Spittelberg on a mild May evening on his way to the apartment where Andro and Mirsad lived, Alex thought of Max giving up his belonging and wondered how far family resemblances went. Like Claude, Alex was not a gregarious person either, but unlike him he lacked an Ella he regarded as home. *One of us is always in.* A Croatian family in exile in Vienna came close to it for Alex, but not quite.

Uncertain burial was the fate of exiles, people without belonging, no claim to land, the body thrown over the city wall or into a ravine to be eaten by jackals by order of a council of elders, stern-faced and bearded men in togas – this was the image that had come to him uncomfortably in his dream. Burial was an end restored to its beginning. He remem-bered something similar Ella had said on the tape. Or was it a line from

238

Eliot? The symmetry of life and death. The homing instinct to return. Completing the circle. In earlier days Chinese immigrants to America, unable to make it back home to die, arranged to have their bones dug up and taken back to the old country for burial.

It was Max's good fortune to have been among kin at the moment of his enviably sudden death. But it could have gone otherwise. He might have been on an assignment in Montevideo or Valparaíso, places that existed only on cargo labels. It would go otherwise for many of the displaced persons Alex would be seeing at Vienna Watch that night, some of them more voluntarily rooted here than others, but displaced and relocated persons for all that. Wasn't this the condition in which more and more people found themselves, a minority that was increasing all the time?

Alex could derive some reassurance from such thoughts, but it didn't stretch far enough to disguise what was missing from his own life, the sort of commitment Ella would have called *having a responsibility for another person equal to the responsibility one had for oneself*. He agreed with Claude, or rather he would like to have been able to share his father's ideal that exile from a place meant nothing as long as there was a person with whom you had your belonging. It put him to shame that at the age of forty-five he carried responsibility for no one in his life apart from himself.

The chestnut trees had already put out pink and white candles, raising hopes of soon lighting up summer. The roar of traffic on the ring road was distant. The side streets in the residential neighbourhoods of the 8th District were deserted. On a mild Sunday evening people would either still be out, in the Wienerwald, perhaps in Grinzing, in a restaurant on the Danube, or already back home – the collective spring airing of a population that had spent the winter mothballed in dark, mouldy apartments built a century ago. Alex wheeled his bicycle through the gateway into a courtyard and chained it to some railings. The building had no elevator. He climbed three flights of creaking stairs, admiring the exuberant scrollwork of the wrought-iron banisters, to the gradually swelling sound of cello music coming down the gloomy stairwell to meet him.

The music emerged from the open door of an apartment with a VIENNA WATCH sign on the wall on one side and the name Bobic in much smaller letters underneath, as if the Bobic family were no more than caretakers appended to the organisation that had come to define the locus of their belonging. Alex could recall very few occasions on coming up these stairs when the door had not been open. He had come an hour early to catch up with Andro before other people started to arrive, on the off chance that the door would be shut. But no, it was already open. He walked down a long passage towards another always-open door that led into the Vienna Watch office where Andro would invariably be sitting at the long desk with the three computers that were always on.

'Aloisha.'

A wave of the hand from Andro, acknowledging his presence, just a wave, indicating that he didn't want to be disturbed for the moment. Alex sat down on a swivel chair behind him and listened to Andro's daughter playing a Bach suite in the room next door. A printer at his elbow spewed out sheets of paper, hurling them into a tray, and stopped again just as suddenly. Alex took out the top sheet, the first of twelve. It was an abridged transcript of the trial in 1999 of Goran Jelisić, who had been sentenced to forty years' imprisonment by the International Court of Justice in The Hague. Probably this was what Andro was looking at on the computer. Alex already knew the case. In just eighteen days during May 1992, the then twenty-three-year-old Jelisić had personally murdered over a hundred prisoners, the majority of them Muslims, at the police station in Brčko and the nearby detention camp Luka. And Jelisić was only one of many.

Leafing through the transcript, Alex came across the testimony of a witness at the Jelisić trial whom he remembered hearing in the courtroom on one of the many visits he had made to the tribunal.

His eyes had a strange expression. It was like looking into turbid water. He must have taken drugs or something. You looked him in the eyes once but never again. The way he looked at you made you feel afraid, especially after he had introduced himself. I don't know what to call it. I mean the fear we had, which was already considerable. The way he looked at us made it much worse. His eyes didn't smile, only his mouth did. The sort of thing you see in movies.

*Introduced himself?*

'Sorry,' said Andro, swivelling round from his screens. 'I've been asked to do a piece about war trials for a German magazine and I wanted to get it in before my guests started to arrive.' He grinned. 'Friends can be kept waiting, but not guests.'

'Jelisić. "Introduced himself". What's the significance of that?'

'It tells you lower down. Bottom of the next page. "Hitler was the first Adolf. I'm the second." That's how he used to introduce himself to prisoners. Then they knew that they were going to die.'

'What's your piece about?'

'Evil. My contention is that Hannah Arendt's famous "banality of evil" misses the mark.'

'What's your mark?'

'The ordinariness of evil.' Andro put his feet up on the desk. 'Take young Goran, aka Adolf. Nice kid. General agreement on that. More Muslim witnesses spoke up in Goran's defence than for any other defendant, and yet it was mostly Muslims he murdered. He had nothing against Muslims, nothing against any sort of person, whether they were old or young, male or female, whatever nationality – he murdered them all impartially. That's why they had to drop the charge of genocide; otherwise he would have been put away for even longer. Fishing was his great hobby. The prosecution expected they'd get some mileage out of that, and so did I, his being cruel to fish, enjoying watching them die slowly, the sort of thing you find with Landžo, who roasted his prisoners alive, but there wasn't any evidence of exceptional cruelty in young Goran's case. Just that one remark he volunteered when someone asked him if he didn't feel pity for the fish. Pity? What a question. Fish were lower creatures. Law of nature. Eat or be eaten. If it were the other way round, the fish would be eating us. Well, nothing much to be made of that. Perhaps a bit odd, the notion of the fish eating us. Still. Not all that abnormal an attitude for an uneducated young mechanic brought up in a backward rural area. And yet it raises a doubt. Something in me begins to nag when I hear about the fish.'

'And?'

Andro had paused for such a long time that Alex thought that the nagging fish would be the end of the matter, but there was more to come.

'The problem is,' he went on, 'that until those eighteen days in May he *was* the model boy next door. Helped people in difficulties, even at his own expense, putting himself out for them, even putting his life at risk. Goran may just have gone through the motions of what they took for compassion. I don't think he felt compassion. He was just doing what people expected. He was fulfilling a norm. They offered a prompt and he came up with the response, thinking to himself, When I behave like this people take me for the nice boy next door. Slightly retarded people do this – has it ever struck you? Pay attention next time you meet a mentally defective person. They do a pretence of someone involved in a conversation without being involved or quite sure of what they're saying. They talk a lot, rather hastily and rather loud. They want to be *taken* for someone involved in a conversation. They want to be one of the crowd. Retarded is a good word because there's a slight time lag involved here. They're just slightly out of sync. I think of the fish as Goran is doing one of these impersonations and I see a lack of compassion at the core. But the nice lad from next door, the neighbours said, that's our Goran. It remains a mystery. They all lined up in the courtroom and said the same thing. It's not possible he did those things, even if he's admitted he has. All right, he'd forged a few cheques and been sent to jail, and it was the chance of getting out of jail that persuaded him to sign up with the Croatian police. He had an impersonation of a volunteer wanting to sign up as a policeman just as he had impersonations for everything he did.'

Andro reached for a cigarette.

'Things only really change with young Goran after his first murder. It's then he starts talking about the beauty of killing, standing in front of the prisoners, taking his pick – *You, you and you*, as easy as that – and they kneel down and he shoots them, the lower creatures, in the back of the head. He's enjoying himself. This is also another impersonation, the executioner, only he hasn't bargained for how it affects him. It's the ease of it he calls the beauty. And then another twist. The more someone pleads for his life, eyewitnesses tell us, the more he enjoys taking it. Think of Dostoyevsky reporting from the *The House of the Dead*. The ritual of flogged prisoners screaming for mercy, the flogged screaming to please his flogger, knowing he won't be satisfied unless he hears the evidence of the flogging taking effect. Screaming won't make him give you less, you see, but it may stop him from giving you more.'

Andro pointed at the page of the transcript open in Alex's hands.

'That's the drug the witness assumed Jelisić to have been taking when he looked into his eyes. Pleasure. The pleasure of killing another human being. Of transgressing that prohibition. Unimaginable. To imagine it you have first to do it. An impersonation will be required of you. The fisherman has to wade in to such experiences. Out of your depth, you have to let yourself go. Kneel down! Won't take a second. So easy, so momentous. Bang! The first time it must have taken him by surprise, the report of that first shot. It must have burst his eardrums. It must have burst his mind. Just a step away but until now unreachable, out of your depth. Now it is, and so *easily*. It's allowed, more, it's *ordered*, the defence will indefensibly argue – there's almost no proof, by the way, that refusing orders leads to penalties commensurate with the magnitude of the crimes committed – but this is how the defence always argues none- theless. Killing is what Goran's become a policeman for. The drug is the power that releases the enjoyment, the thrill, a chemical transformation of the cells in his burst mind on a ricochet throughout the executioner's body, the executioner's own magically untouchable life, which until now has been slipping away from him in the little town on the river where he lives without excitement, without significance, without compassion, not for fish, not for people. Such is the narcotic of power. His own life is magically exempt who can take the lives of others.'

'Isn't Jelisić simply a psychopath?'

'Simply? What is this "simply"? The problem begins with those Greek words, as if we needed a special word to segregate people with sick minds from the rest of us. But it's my contention that so-called sick minds are nothing out of the ordinary. After ten years of war in Yugoslavia it turns out that tens of thousands of psychopaths have been living undiscovered in our midst all the while. For all I know, maybe I'm one of them. I started thinking about all this after reading Browning's book about the German police battalion in World War II who went in after the army to do the dirty work in the areas that had been – what's the word – *subdued*. Browning researched the biographies of all the members of that police battalion.'

'I remember the book. *Reserve Police Battalion 101 and the Final Solution in Poland*, I think it was called.'

'Well remembered. But that's the subtitle. You've missed the import- ant part. The title is *Ordinary Men*. It was Browning's title that grabbed me. That's what got me thinking about ordinary as opposed to banal. Until the war exempted them from moral restraints, they were ordinary people leading ordinary but not necessarily banal lives. Banal for whom? Banal is a value judgement. Most of these men came from Hamburg, one of the least Nazified cities in Germany. They were working class or lower working class, petty officials whose political culture was socialist rather than national socialist. These men, as Browning says, do not seem to have been a very promising group from which to recruit mass murderers. Yet when it came to it, not more than about 10 per cent of them refused to go in and kill. Put it like this. Among ordinary but not necessarily banal people there are those, like Jelisić, who sign up to do the dirty work and go in and do it, and there are those who don't, and those who don't sign up or sign up but don't go in are less ordinary individuals than those who do.'

'Less ordinary, meaning?'

'Meaning those who have compassion. This is where I part company with Arendt and her banality of evil. Imagine calling Browning's book *Banal Men*. If you speak of banality, it suggests you might have been expecting to discover something not banal – a demonic energy of evil perhaps, a psychopath – and you're disappointed how commonplace the embodiment of evil turns out to be. She writes herself about the lack of any evidence of the demonic in Eichmann, the greyness of the man. It's not banality, but the apparently ordinary lack of compassion, the courage that compassion in certain situations demands.'

Andro took his feet off the desk.

'I've found myself in such situations and failed the test.'

Alex wondered if this might be a reference to the candle, Andro's admission that he could no longer look his Serb colleagues in the eye, or whether he was admitting to darker moments Alex didn't know about, when there had been no light at all.

'The ordinariness of evil is a reminder of how much more of it there is around us, and in ourselves. To demonise evil is to deny its ordinariness and put a safe distance between it and us. Arendt's banality of evil is really a critique of the lack of style or poor taste of certain manifestations of evil. She was confusing the grey person of Eichmann with the grey deeds committed at his desk out of sight of the people they would affect. It tells us nothing about the frequency of its occurrence or the assured place evil has and must have among the universal constants of the human soul. As must compassion. Where would we be without compassion? Where would we be without evil? Which for me in practice will always come down to lack of compassion. Between the two is where humans have their being. Evil is ordinary because pleasure in trespassing onto forbidden places is an ordinary pleasure, but not a banal pleasure, of human beings. Generically, one might say. This is the fascination of monsters, serial killers, and so on. They're much closer to us than we would like to admit. Just a step away. But they've dared to make that step, whereas we haven't, which is why we hold them in awe.'

The cello playing in the next room broke off, and voices could be heard from the end of the corridor.

'There's nothing reprehensible in taking pleasure in what is forbidden.'

'Then why the pleasure when the forbidden is allowed?' objected Alex.

'Because the prohibition is entrenched as a lifelong experience and sits much deeper than the brief holiday of exemption. Ship's leave for twenty-four hours, and what do you do? You go on furlough and get smashed. In war people go on vacation from an excess of peace.'

Alex was appalled. But Andro, long familiar with his own thoughts, seemed unconcerned by them.

Roman and his girlfriend Brigitte, friends of Alex, were among the guests to have just arrived. Andro went to meet them as Mirsad was showing them into the salon, a large room with a balcony overlooking the street with two chestnut trees below, one pink and one white, already in bloom.

'Is that their scent I can smell?' wondered Brigitte, who had a reputation as an intellectual woman, which in Vienna was definitely a criticism. 'Or is it just my mind suggesting scent in association with the bloom I see?'

Roman was an orientalist, a match for Brigitte, used to questions like this from her even over the breakfast table.

'Well, contrary to what generations of poets have written about the scent of cherry blossom, the most common type of Japanese cherry blossom has no smell. The discrepancy goes back a thousand years or so, when poets in Japan were imitating their Chinese colleagues' verses about the plum tree blossom, which *does* have a scent. When the Japanese poets began to celebrate their own national tree, the cherry tree, *very* much a symbol of *their* national culture, they got rid of the Chinese plum tree but kept its scent, as it would have been a poor sort of national tree that didn't have a scent to offer, wouldn't it?'

'I suppose it would. But what about chestnut trees? You've not answered my question. Andro, Mirsad tells me you're doing a piece on Hannah Arendt for the *Spiegel*. How did that come about?'

'It's not exactly a piece on Hannah Arendt, just that dictum of hers about the banality of evil that I discuss in a piece I'm doing on war crimes trials ...'

Andro had found another listener. They wandered back inside.

Alex looked down and said to Roman, 'So what about the chestnut tree?'

'I'm not sure I'd call that sickly-sweet aroma a *scent*, would you? A smell, perhaps ... It becomes more noticeable in the evening and at night, by the way, so we really ought to sample it.'

They leaned over the balcony and sniffed.

'Doesn't do anything for me,' said Alex. After a pause he went on, 'My impression is that after ten years of Vienna Watch Andro needs a break from all that war. It's infected his mind. He's become obsessive. He talks of nothing else. *La guerre est finie*. Why don't he and Mirsad go back?'

'They can't. Not as long as they've got children here in school. Besides, Mirsad says that they no longer feel at home there. Same with lots of their friends, apparently. Zadar may still be there, she says, but it's no longer in Yugoslavia. The Serb minority has gone. The mixed society they grew up in no longer exists. Don't underestimate the amount of brainwashing that genial populist Tito needed to bring it into being in the first place, beginning with his own image as a father figure acceptable to all Slavs whatever their ethnic allegiance. Was he a Serb? Was he Croat? Nobody seems to know for sure.' Roman glanced across at Alex. 'Isn't it really yourself you're talking about?'

'Me?'

'Needing a break from all that war. How many concerts at the Musikverein we had arranged to go to have you missed as a result, because you had to dash off to some place of massacre at the last minute? To mention only one of the casualties of your private life. I know that sounds cynical. But your friends seem to see less and less of you the longer you live here. Let me fill your glass while you think about how to apologise for your neglect of the living people to whom you matter, in the interests of the dead people to whom you don't.'

For the second time that evening Alex was left speechless.

Roman fetched a bottle of wine from the table inside, where he bumped into Andro's daughter Snzejana in full flight with a sheet of music.

'Oh dear,' she said breathlessly. 'I'm so sorry.'

'My pleasure, dear girl. At last we've managed to get in touch. Are you going to play something for us?'

'Later. Please excuse me.'

Smiling, with a wave to Alex, the girl sped off in pursuit of something more urgent on the far side of the room.

Roman went back out onto the balcony.

'Completely Viennese, that girl in flight with her music – the sound of her, the look of her, as if born to live here. There's no question of her or her sister wanting to go back and live in Croatia. Home for them is here. That's the divide between the children and their parents, who, however well they have settled down here, will still in some way remain exiles from a remembered life that continues somewhere else, a tune that never quite goes away.'

He filled Alex's glass.

Alex said, 'It's difficult to explain why I've stuck with this job when I can clearly see the cost of continuing to do it. Tunnel vision, like Andro – seeing everything through the prism of war. You could say it's become a habit, an unbreakable habit, a drug. The excitement, the urgency, even the sense of vocation, things I guess I would lack if war was taken away from me. I feel that what I do matters. That's how I got into it in the first place. I got bored with academic life because it didn't really engage me. The motivation has to come from inside yourself to do academic work. I don't have it. It seems I'm dependent on some outside stimulus to get me going. But maybe the time has come for change.'

'Well,' said Roman in his languid way, 'take me, if you must. I'd be the first to agree that the comparison of Chinese and Japanese aesthetics I'm employed to make is a dispensable occupation. No one needs it. It's a piece of embroidery, a sampler, a charming trivial pursuit in accordance with the best Viennese traditions. But that is really where culture begins, isn't it, with occupations that aren't necessary. Perhaps I see it this way because that's my temperament. Rousseau thought that by the Neolithic Age we'd already got about the right mix – you know, enough to eat but not too much, enough safety but not debilitatingly so, enough leisure but not too much so as to make us feel bored, the occupational disease of all leisure societies. I don't know what they had in the way of music in Neolithic days, but speaking for myself, I'd say we've got not a bad mix now. Unlike you, I don't feel and I don't need to feel that what I do matters. It's as pleasant a way of spending one's life as any other occupation. Urgency, excitement, vocation ... to my ears those are excruciating words, Alex.'

The sound of cello and piano tuning up for one of the musical interludes that punctuated evenings in the Bobic household interrupted this conversation. The two men came in from the balcony just as Snzejana, a violinist and a woman at the piano launched into a Haydn trio.

'Who's that at the piano?' Alex asked Roman.

'I've no idea.'

'Where's Adriana?' wondered Alex, as it was otherwise always Snzejana's elder sister who accompanied her on the piano.

'In New Zealand at the moment. She's taken a year off to travel round the world. *Months* ago. See what I mean about not keeping up with your friends?'

# 2

When the musical interlude was over, and the unknown accompanist at the piano, who had been sitting with her back to the room, stood up and turned round, Alex was shocked to find himself looking at his fellow breakfaster from the Palm House.

There she was, with her smile and all. She was taller than he remembered from his last visit prior to leaving for London, with a bigger build. Her physique suggested she might do a lot of swimming. The strong back and shoulders he'd been looking at for the past quarter of an hour he realised he already knew very well from much longer study sessions over breakfasts at the Palm House. He was already quite an expert in the view of her from the rear, which on some mornings was the only one available of her for a couple of hours. In fact she was the first woman he had fallen for entirely on the evidence of how she looked from behind. Now it was time to get to know her other side. This was the first occasion he'd seen her wearing her long chestnut hair up, revealing a rather full round face, and it triggered the memory that had been missing until now. It was as if an identikit assembly of different features had taken over a woman with short hair as the default option. The reversal from misleading long hair back to short hair caused a frisson, setting in motion an instant memory retrieval of the circumstances under which he had met her the first time.

It had been in a refugee camp at a place called Kukës in Albania in early May 1999. In the aftermath of the Serbian invasion of Kosovo the month before, a million people had fled from their homes and made their way through the mountains to places of relative safety across the border in Montenegro, Albania and Macedonia. It was from Blace on the Macedonian border that the pictures of fifty or sixty thousand people crammed together under appalling conditions during the Easter week of 1999 had been broadcast around the world, drawing attention to the catastrophic failure of humanitarian aid agencies, notably of the United Nations. There had been lots of committees and observers but not much in the way of help on the ground. As a Human Rights Watch representative, Andro had been admitted to the camp in Blace, going on from there to Kukës in Albania, where Alex had accompanied him for an interview with a doctor from the United Arab Emirates working for Médecins Sans Frontières. Alex was given permission to speak briefly with a party of refugees who had recently arrived from Zur in Kosovo, to where they had been taken in buses by the Red Cross, making their way on foot across the border to Kukës.

To Alex's surprise, the spokesperson for the party from Zur was an Austrian citizen, an articulate and to all appearances calm young woman who turned out to be from Vienna. It was from her that Alex first learned of the events that had taken place in a village in the Suva Reka municipality in Kosovo two weeks earlier. When Serbian security forces arrived there nearly all the men in the village had disappeared into the surrounding hills to seek reinforcements from the Kosovo Liberation Army, leaving behind them a small group of elderly men and two or three hundred women and children. The elderly men and a few younger men who had stayed to defend the village were shot and thrown into a well, the well grenaded. The women and children were divided up into three groups and herded into private houses, where they were held prisoner. For three days, the young woman said, they were subjected to terror, maltreatment and sexual harassment before being forced to walk to another village, where they were held captive for two days in the local school without food or water. As far as she knew, the spokeswoman said, no further abuses had taken place there. Then the Serbian Red

Cross arrived in the village and arranged for the refugees to be taken by bus to Zur, from which they had made their way on foot across the Albanian border.

Had any of the women and children been killed by the invaders? Alex wanted to know. An aunt had been shot before her eyes, said the woman. What was to be understood by the term sexual harassment? Alex continued. Did that mean rape? Yes, it meant rape, the woman answered, or more precisely degrees of molestation usually culminating in rape. How many women had been victims of rape? the journalist in Alex was always obliged to ask, never without a feeling of extreme discomfort. Although the spokeswoman answered his questions in Viennese-accented German, apparently her mother tongue, she translated the questions into no less fluent Albanian for the benefit of the other women in the room where the interview took place, and heard their views before replying. Several women had been victims of rape, she said after consulting with them, shaking her head when asked by Alex to be specific about the number of occasions on which rape had taken place, and the doctor from Médecins Sans Frontières intervened, bringing the interview to a close.

Alex was the only journalist given access to the refugees in Kukës, thanks to the presence of Andro. Still, the entire time Alex was allowed to spend in the camp, including this interview with the villagers and a subsequent conversation with the doctor, amounted to barely an hour. The doctor was able to confirm some of the figures relating to the incid- ent, but he declined to disclose any details concerning the raped women. The full extent of traumatisation that had gradually become evident in the years since the war in Bosnia made this a sensitive subject he thought it wiser not to discuss after so short an interval. For many victims trauma would remain with them for the rest of their lives. To the question that had subsequently interested Alex most – how a sophisticated Viennese city girl, an Austrian citizen to boot, managed to get caught up in the mass exodus of Kosovo's rural population over the mountains after being driven from their homes by Serbian forces – he had never received an answer.

And here she now was in Andro's living room.

Already she had spotted him on the other side of the room and was making her way over; naturally she recognised him from their encounters at the Palm House, even if they had exchanged no more than a few words in the past six months, and was intrigued to find him now in the house of a mutual friend. Alex had no time to consider whether or not he should refer to their first meeting at the refugee camp in Albania, whether that was a good or a bad idea, or to wait for her to bring it up. Already she stood smiling in front of him, a little bit taller than him, extending her hand and shaking his, her substantiated presence filling out the space in front of him just as it seemed to be entering and beginning to fill out his mind too, putting all reflections there on hold.

'My name is Alex,' was the best he could manage.

'And mine is Nadine.'

She at once started talking about the Palm House, where she went to have breakfast on Saturday mornings, how she had been keeping an eye out for him since that time when he had taken a photograph of herself and her friend, and that she had missed him the last couple of weekends. All this was said directly and artlessly, and Alex felt at once that he could take this woman completely at her word.

He explained he had been in London, adding that he was English, as if his being in London rather than at the Palm House needed justifying to Nadine.

'It seems you travel quite a bit,' she said, stepping out onto the balcony. 'Does that have to do with your work?'

'I'm a journalist. But what gives you the impression I travel quite a bit?'

'I was just guessing. Because you're one of the Saturday morning regulars, one of the dozen or so people one always sees at the Palm House, only you're often not there.'

'I spend more time in other places than I do at home in Vienna. My friend Roman – that's him over there, fellow wearing a striped jacket he rather fancies himself in – has just been taking me to task for neglecting my friends here. I think he's right. It's time to settle down. But that sounds so depressingly middle-aged, doesn't it.'

He stood facing her as she leaned back against the railing.

'What sort of journalism?'

'For most of the last ten years I've been a correspondent on the Balkans for the International Press Association, so mainly I've been covering the war in Yugoslavia.'

'Ah.'

When he told people he was a war correspondent it usually led to

251

further questions, but with Nadine it went nowhere. Evidently this wasn't a subject she wanted to pursue.

'What about you?'

'I've just finished my doctorate and am wondering what to do with it. I'm rather wishing I'd stayed with music, like Snzejana, only I don't have her talent.'

'What's your subject?'

'South-east European history. First at the University in Graz, then here in Vienna.'

'I must have just missed you in Graz.'

Nadine's eyes flickered.

'I was on the faculty there for several years,' explained Alex, 'until I left to work as a journalist in the summer of 1991. It's a small place and we would have been working at the same institute, perhaps even in the same classroom.'

'I matriculated there in the winter semester of 1991.'

'Well, there you are.'

But before this promising avenue could be explored any further, Snzejana came out onto the balcony and asked Nadine to take her place at the piano as they were ready to do the next piece.

During the time he had been standing with Nadine on the balcony the large room had filled up, and more people kept on arriving, packing into the adjoining dining room and spilling over into the passage, groups of them clustering in the kitchen and in Andro's office. Regulars at the *jour fixe*, acquaintances whom Alex had not seen for months as a result of his frequent absences from town, wanted to catch up on what he had been doing in the interval, and although he was much more interested in tracking down Nadine there was really no way of shaking them off without being impolite. When the apartment began emptying towards midnight he went in search of her and ran into Mirsad.

'I've hardly exchanged two words with you all evening, Alex,' she said. 'Not your fault, I know, and not mine either, so why don't you come for a quiet dinner *en famille* on Thursday? Not this Thursday, the week after.'

'I'd love to,' said Alex, not having a clue where he would be on Thursday the week after next. 'Actually, I was just looking for Nadine ...'

'Nadine left half an hour ago.'

'Left? Where did she go?'

'Where did she *go*? Home, I expect. But I don't keep track of guests once they leave, you know.' Mirsad was amused.

'Where does she live?'

'Nadine? I don't really know. Somewhere in Leopoldstadt, I think.'

It was only on his way back to Spittelberg – the thought of Nadine having gone anywhere other than home in Leopoldstadt causing jealousy to flare up in him – that Alex realised what kind of trouble he was in.

Oh week, pass!

Fortunately, trips to cover unexpected political developments in Montenegro and Romania distracted him from his life in Vienna for Tuesday, Wednesday and most of Thursday. That still left all of Monday, however, half of Thursday and a wholly empty Friday to get through before he saw her again at the Palm House on Saturday morning. He was up at five, had a shower, fell asleep again and woke up at seven, had a second shower, a cup of coffee before leaving the house at eight, making a long detour on his bike and still arriving at the Palm House twenty minutes before it opened. He went for a walk through the park and came back just as the doors were being opened by a waitress, carrying an easel with a board announcing the day's specials, which she put up outside on the terrace.

By ten she still hadn't arrived. By ten thirty he began to feel uneasy. By eleven fifteen the Palm House was as good as dead, shorn of life or anything he could take the least interest in. He waited miserably until twelve, against the possibility of a late breakfast at half past or a brunch at one, on an outside chance even at two. Completely crushed, he left at last, riding out through Leopoldstadt across the Danube, following the riverside paths, seeing nothing, thinking of all the thousands of eventualities that might have intervened to alter her Saturday morning breakfast routine.

He returned home with the firm intention of calling Andro for Nadine's phone number and calling Nadine to find out what had happened to her. But putting himself in her position, imagining himself receiving such a call, he realised that she might feel it an unwanted intrusion. He hardly knew her, or rather, she hardly knew him. They had made no appointment, after all. He might expect it, but they hadn't *arranged* to meet at the Palm House. She wasn't accountable to him for how she spent her Saturday mornings.

He reminded himself of Ella's advice on courting: *Show interest, be attentive, but don't pursue her too actively. Make yourself scarce.*

A telephone call under these circumstances undoubtedly qualified as a too-active pursuit.

At least to be close to people who were close to Nadine would have been a consolation. But as bad luck would have it, Andro and Mirsad had gone away for the weekend, so the Sunday *jour fixe* had been called off. But who knew, perhaps they had changed their plans too and would be in town after all. Alex called their number and got Snzejana on the line.

'They've gone away for the weekend. Can I take a message?'

'Actually, it was just a phone number I wanted ...'

'Oh. Whose?'

'A colleague of Andro's. No one in particular. I mean, not someone you'd know. No hurry. I'll call again next week.'

Alex hung up, appalled at himself. In five sentences he'd told five lies.

The conversation about lying which he had had with Max on the morning Max died returned to trouble him. At the first opportunity he'd slipped back into the facile, cowardly habit of telling convenience lies. He'd let Max down. Worse, he had let Nadine down. A convenience liar wasn't worthy of such a woman. His penance would be to put her out of his mind.

Much more at ease once this resolution was fixed, he arrived at Mirsad and Andro's house for the dinner *en famille* they had arranged on the Thursday evening of the following week. It was just Snzejana and a nephew of Mirsad who was passing through en route for London, a meal with the sort of intimate atmosphere and conversation Alex liked, with Mirsad reading aloud bits from Adriana's letters, Andro bantering with the nephew, who obviously had an eye on his cousin Snzejana, the four of them swapping news of an extended family living in the diaspora which Alex felt he now knew as if he were a member of it himself. Andro had to take a call just as Alex was leaving, so it was Mirsad who saw him to the door.

'How was your weekend, by the way?' he asked on his way out.

'Yet another family wedding,' said Mirsad, 'this one in Holland. It was fun. A small world. Everyone seems to be everywhere these days. Imagine, on our way into Amsterdam airport we bumped into Nadine with a friend on her way out.'

Having regained his balance, got through the evening without any mishaps that might have cropped up in that connection, Alex was thrown by this last-minute guest appearance of Nadine.

So while he had been waiting in the Palm House, Nadine had been on her way out of Schipol airport *with a friend*, presumably but of course not necessarily, on her way back to Vienna. Of course, what Nadine was doing in Amsterdam was no business of his, but he would have been happier if that last gratuitous sentence at the door hadn't slipped out and he hadn't found out about these alternative arrangements for the Saturday morning she had spent *with a friend*. But there it was – he had – and having come this far he found it impossible not to go on. Why stop at morning? Why not wrap up the whole weekend between Friday evening and Sunday night in the company of this airport friend?

Oh week, stick around! Do not pass!

For if his penance was to forget her once and for all, it meant no more visits to the Palm House, no more leisurely Saturday morning breakfasts, which had become the brightest feature of his week. He had just that one intervening Friday to decide if he could or would take such a penance upon himself.

On Friday morning the first sign of improvement he found in himself was that he could see the ridiculous figure he was cutting and laugh at it. How feeble! How puerile such behaviour in a forty-five-year-old man!

But by the evening he was in a more belligerent mood.

'Why should I change my habits for someone I don't even know? In aid of what, some theatrical gesture? You've got the whole business out of proportion. What's it to her? What's it to me?'

On Saturday morning he lay in bed feeling ill, numb with indecision.

It was the phone ringing that got him out of bed.

'Hello?'

'I hope I didn't wake you up.'

It was Nadine.

'No no, I was already on my way ... literally halfway through the door.'

'See you there in about half an hour?'

Thirty-five minutes later Alex walked into the Palm House.

# 3

Nadine had discussed with Dr Jelinek the rendezvous, and when it turned out that Dr Jelinek had never been inside the Palm House, described to her the venue in detail. Imagine a conservatory, she told the psychiatrist, all glass and plants and light, with no corners where something ominous might lie in waiting, no cubbyholes where murder or anything could be committed – just this one open space, *lots* of space, with everything in full view, everything under control. At the sight of the cautious smile, a rare enough occurrence, creeping out across Dr Jelinek's face as if first having to get used to itself before going public, Nadine laughed, something she couldn't remember having done for a long time.

'I suppose it *does* sound a little obsessive,' said Nadine.

'Not at all. It makes me happy to hear you talk like this. And laugh. This will be your first date, and you will have set it up yourself. What does he look like?'

'He's got a trustworthy face, which has to do with the expression in his large brown eyes. I go with the eyes. He's not very tall and probably rather shy, possibly a bit lonely. He doesn't clean his shoes, but he looks after his hands. Quite good-looking in that small French way. He seems to be someone who thinks a lot. But I've only talked to him for ten minutes so I can't really say.'

Nadine noticed that Dr Jelinek was watching her as she combed her fingers through her hair and twisted the ends.

'I can't really say anything at all,' she blurted, letting go of her hair. 'What can I say?'

'There's nothing you need to say.' Dr Jelinek got up to draw a blind over the window through which the sun was shining into her face. 'Listen and ask questions. If you pay attention and draw someone out by asking them the sort of questions they like to answer, they'll never notice they're doing all the talking. They'll go away thinking, What an interesting person that was! They won't even notice they're doing all the talking themselves. Come back and tell me about it next week. Believe me. It works.' Observing the doubtful expression on Nadine's face she added wryly, 'I've been doing it for most of my life.' And for the second time that afternoon the cautious little smile came out of hiding on the older woman's face.

Not wanting to leave anything to chance, Nadine was already installed in the Palm House when she called Alex on her mobile. The choice of table was hers, her choice of seat, back to the glass wall at one end of the conservatory, giving her a full view of everything going on inside. The rather gruff sound of his voice when he answered the phone had caused her a momentary setback, but when she heard the gruffness change to unmistakable pleasure she began to feel more comfortable. Half an hour later he arrived, still damp from the shower he had evidently just taken, still with a trace of shaving soap on both earlobes, suggesting he must have got up and dressed in a hurry.

They discussed breakfast, toast versus rolls, waffles versus pancakes, coffee versus hot chocolate or tea.

While waiting for breakfast to arrive they talked about the Palm House, and just as that subject was almost exhausted, the meal put in a timely appearance, for which she was most grateful.

She asked him about his job at the university. Inevitably that led on to her question as to why he had left, and for the next hour she felt reasonably secure, listening to him talk about events in Zadar more than ten years ago, a *pogrom*, as he described it, anticipating all the horrors that were to come in Yugoslavia's civil war, giving a twist to the conversation Nadine had no desire to pursue further. Only the past was safe, the long-buried, long-distant past, preferably of other people, containing no surprises, or if surprises then only those that had been well marinated in memories and were out of harm's way.

You seem to have had such a full and varied *past*, she said to Alex: brought up in London, then sent to school in Tenerife, your father from an Anglo-French family, your mother from Germany, and studying at universities in different countries. But he didn't rise to this question; he got sidetracked and began talking about a much older brother called Max, with whom he had got drunk in London a few weeks previously. Max had done a dance for him in their parents' flat and died of a heart attack, literally on the spot, probably from the exertion of doing that dance minutes before he was due to leave for New York, just as they were getting to know each other properly for the first time in their adult lives.

257

'And he began to cry, and apologised, said he had to go and suddenly left, just like that. It made me feel *awful*.'

Dr Jelinek thought about this for a while.

'And he didn't ask you about yourself? Not once?'

'Well, he asked me about things I liked and disliked, but no ... not really about *myself*. Not because he wasn't interested, I think. But somehow I had the sense he knew more about me than he was letting on and refrained from asking me out of tact.'

'What about *your* feelings? For him?'

'My feelings?' Nadine pondered. 'My feeling was that he was honest, and that unlike me he wasn't hiding anything. Do you know what he did when he arrived at the table? He emptied his pockets. He took out the things he had in his trouser pockets and put them on the table. What do you think is the significance of *that*?'

'Interesting,' said Dr Jelinek, glancing at her watch. 'I've no idea. But I look forward to you telling me next week.'

Secretly she was extremely satisfied that Nadine had spent an hour with her and not spoken once about herself.

The coming Saturday there was Alex standing again at the table in the Palm House, turning out his pockets and placing the contents on the table as if Nadine were a customs officer and wanted to see if it was true that he had nothing to declare. She kept a sharp eye on what was coming out, if only to be able to report faithfully back to Dr Jelinek. A pack of Lucky Strikes and a Zippo lighter came out first, a packet of tissues, loose coins, a whistle, and a ring to which several keys were attached. The keys were of no interest to her but the safety pin piercing a tiny piece of white cloth aroused her curiosity.

'What's that?' she couldn't resist asking.

'Well, to be honest, I have no idea. Do you?'

'May I?'

She reached over the table and picked the key ring up.

'It's the little bit of cloth that's rather odd,' she said. 'What's it for?'

'I don't know.'

'Where did you get it?'

'From my mother.'

'Didn't *she* tell you what it was for when she gave it to you?'

'Well, she didn't give it to me herself, you see. It was ... handed on, officially, as it were.'

'Oh.'

Nadine would have liked to know under what circumstances someone had officially handed on to Alex a safety pin attached to a bit of material that had belonged to his mother – in a little jeweller's box presented on a cushion, perhaps – and for what reason they might have done so, but she thought it would be impolite to continue this interrogation. The conversation wandered harmlessly from productions they had both been to see at the Burgtheater and the opera to concerts that month at the Musikverein.

The third time they met at the Palm House, and the pocket-emptying ritual was carried out as usual, she couldn't resist asking the question that had been preoccupying her.

'Why *do* you do that?'

'The thing is, I always find myself having to delve into my pockets to get out whatever it is I want, and that's not so easy when one's sitting down. One has to squirm around, you know, and one keeps on pulling out the wrong thing, so I find it easier just to plonk it all down on the table where it's within easy reach.'

'The whistle, for example.'

'Admittedly, there's not much call for the whistle, but you never know. I mean, I've been stuck in places I wouldn't have got out of again if I hadn't blown the whistle to attract the attention of people who helped me out.'

This notion amused Nadine.

'Were you stuck up a tree or something?'

'I was under the rubble of a house that had collapsed on top of me.'

Nadine guessed where this was leading, but there was no way out now and she had to press on.

'While you were covering the war in Yugoslavia.'

'In Kosovo, during the NATO bombing in the spring of 1999.'

He saw Nadine turn pale.

'Were you injured?'

'Nothing serious. But if it hadn't been for the whistle ... My mother gave it to me just before I left – it was her own. Being the sort of person she was, she had a supply of them in the house, and I promised her I would always keep it with me. And although there's little chance of my ever finding myself under a collapsed house again, a promise is a promise, so I suppose I'll carry it around with me for the rest of my life. Who knows? She was right once. She might be right again.'

Nadine reported back to Dr Jelinek. She told her about the whistle and the story of the collapsed house, and that on the key ring he regularly turned out of his pockets there was a safety pin with a piece of cloth attached that used to belong to his mother.

'So what does that tell you about this man you are seeing?' asked Dr Jelinek. 'Do we have a name for him, by the way?'

'Alex.'

'What does this tell you about Alex?'

'Well, if I knew what that safety pin with the funny little bit of cloth was for—' Nadine began, but Dr Jelinek interrupted her.

'Don't worry about what it's *for*. Ask yourself what it *is*.'

'What do I know? It's just something he keeps in his pocket?'

'Exactly. So?' She waited, smiling over her spectacles while Nadine searched vainly for an answer. 'It's a keepsake,' said Dr Jelinek after a pause. 'That makes two things that Alex always has on his person that are keepsakes of his mother. Two things. Have you worked out the percentage?'

This was the oracular all-knowing Dr Jelinek who sometimes seemed to enjoy letting her grope in the dark, thought Nadine.

'A third of the things this grown man carries around with him in his trouser pockets were given to him by his mother.'

A sort of amazement touched Nadine, and in the wake of this illumination an unexpected surge of tenderness.

The following weekend she met him two days in a row, at the Palm House as usual on Saturday and on Sunday evening at the *jour fixe* given by Andro and Mirsad. It was Mirsad who met them as they came in, not greeting them in the usual way, just saying 'Oh good!' and giving them a little smile as they passed through the living room apparently without seeing any of the people who were gathered there, as if they themselves were invisible, and went straight out onto the balcony where they could talk alone together.

At breakfast in the Palm House they had just chatted about things that hadn't interested her, marking time, not moving forward to the places Nadine began to realise she would prefer to be but never would unless she initiated the move herself. He's very reserved, she thought with passing irritation before qualifying this judgement with the admission that his reserve only reflected her own.

More of the same kind of desultory conversation followed on the balcony. At ten o'clock Alex excused himself, saying he had to leave as he had a plane to catch early the next morning.

We've reached an impasse already, Nadine told herself unhappily, and it's all my fault. She sat for another half-hour in the living room, not taking in what people were saying to her, before she tried to slip away unnoticed, but Mirsad caught her on the landing.

'Dear Nadine, I know what a difficult time you've got ahead of you. Andro and I think you're brave. We're your closest friends and would do anything, anything if it would help you to go through with it. I know that Alex would too, if only you'd let him. It's quite obvious how much he likes you. And it's no less obvious how much you like him.'

Nadine gave a start. Mirsad took her by the hand, led her into the bathroom and shut the door behind them.

'This is a conversation you should really be having with Alex, but unless I tell you certain things that only I and Andro know, you never will. No, don't go. Stay and listen to what I've got to say.'

Nadine sat down on the edge of the bath, gripping it with both hands as if worried about falling in, while Mirsad stood beside her and stroked her head.

Nadine began to sob.

'How *soft* your hair is,' said Mirsad. 'I've always wanted to feel it, you know. I'm a little jealous. My own is so coarse.'

She put her arms round Nadine and rocked her gently until the sobbing had passed.

'About this Alex of yours. You probably won't remember this, but he came to the camp with Andro and had an interview with you and the other refugees. He knows who you are. He knows what happened to you. You don't need to be afraid of him finding anything out, because he knows about it already. And there's one other thing I think you should know about him. His parents killed themselves a year ago. He seems to have been very attached to both of them. He's still not over it. And then his brother died a few weeks ago. Not that he and his brother ever had much to do with each other, but they were in the same room when he died and Alex has this notion that his brother somehow brought it on, actually died on him because Max was afraid of something and wanted to die in his company. Since his parents' death Alex rather keeps to himself. He's as much on his own as you are, Nadine.'

All of this preoccupied Nadine over the next few days.

She had a tiny room in a garret in the 1st District not far from the Hofburg, a short walk away from the museum of anthropology, where she had a temporary job in the archives, transferring handwritten documents onto a digitalised retrieval system. The job didn't interest her, but she didn't want a job that interested her, so this one suited her fine. A day spent in the museum archives, computer-gazing, exchanging an occasional word with two spinsterly old creatures there who seemed to be part of the museum inventory, was as soothing as going under an anaesthetic.

The extreme quiet and solitude of this occupation, the unvarying regularity of her museum days, the secrecy of her little garret room, accorded perfectly with Nadine's expectations of life.

Reluctantly, she sometimes locked up her room and stayed at her mother's house in Leopoldstadt for a few days. Her mother believed Nadine came because she had need of her company, and Nadine made these dutiful visits home in the belief that her mother was lonely and looked forward to her daughter's visits. Neither of them particularly needed the other, however, and lived quite happily on their own. Nadine had her museum, her mother the patisserie she had inherited from her parents and still continued to run after reaching retirement age.

When Nadine tried to imagine her mother giving her a whistle to blow in case she needed help – and there would have been no better time to have given her a whistle than the day she left home with her father five years ago – she understood the difference between her own mother and the sort of woman Alex's mother must have been.

*I wonder what your mother needed a whistle for*, read the first sentence of the letter she sat down to write to Alex in her bedroom in her mother's house. She spent the next half-hour looking out at the rooftop scenery in Leopoldstadt, just roofs and the swallows circling overhead in the summer twilight.

The second sentence continued,

*A few days after your visit to the camp in Kukës, which is completely erased from my mind – the camp itself, your visit there, everything – I was taken by car on a long journey to a town I don't remember either. I don't remember what it looked like, I don't even remember its name, although I have since been told. All I remember is the name of this clinic or institute, which was called Medica. By the time I arrived at Medica I knew I was pregnant, like most of the other women who were there. Some of them had already given birth to their children, like Natasa, who had been living in the clinic for three years. Medica specialised in cases like ours, short-timers, women like me, who had been caught on the run, and long-timers, girls like Natasa, who was sold into sex slavery for months and had been raped by dozens of men hundreds of times. She was the girl who asked you to take our photograph in the Palm House. That was the only time I met Natasa afterwards. We don't see each other more often because we don't want each other's memories. Natasa lived in the clinic with her little boy, who was almost three. She was one of the women who wanted to give birth to the child. Some of them kept the baby. Others delivered the child and then asked for it to be given away for adoption. And then there were women like myself who chose to have an abortion. The abortion was done at Medica two months after I got pregnant. My mother visited me there and stayed for several weeks. She also wanted to know just what had happened to my father, of course, but I was no more able to talk about that than I was about what had happened to me. It was my mother who persuaded Dr Jelinek, my psychiatrist to come and talk to me in Medica. My mother wanted to get me back to Vienna, away from surroundings she felt were bad for me, and Dr Jelinek agreed to take me on as a long-term patient because she has a lot of patients with experiences like mine, so after three months I was able to leave Medica and come home. My mother cared for me and did everything possible to help me get back to normal life. Yet there is no real bond between my mother and myself like the bond I had with my father. When I left for Kosovo with my father five years ago, my mother would never have thought of giving me a whistle to blow in case of danger, as your mother did when you set off for Kosovo, and the coincidence of us both having gone to the same place at the same time, and then meeting again at the Palm House, is obviously not a coincidence at all but a prior arrangement with which we have no choice but to concur . . .*

What an odd sort of sentence that was to have escaped her, had slipped out under her guard. She thought of deleting it but let it stand. She couldn't decide how to go on, went back instead, wondering whether to delete the gratuitous opening sentence about the whistle as well but couldn't make up her mind about that either, so she left the letter for a few days before posting it, still in two minds, to the Spittelberg address Alex had given her.

# CHAPTER SIX

—

# Paris

## 1

Not that Ella had anything particular in mind when she left the house – flew off the handle, as George might have said. She was too busy with her indignation. She didn't so much leave as – *wham* – hurtle out of the house. Beside herself, she walked out into the middle of the road and barely noticed the enormous sky-blue car, hardly paid any attention when she heard her name called. What was Sasha doing in such a car? Driving, as it happens, he said, and asked if he could give her a lift. I don't mind, said Ella and got in. Sasha wondered if she wanted to go anywhere in particular and Ella said no. She noticed that he hadn't shaved, and thought, That's unlike him. Sasha continued, Well *I'm* going to Paris, in case you want to come along for the ride, and Ella shrugged, and said, All right. The ingrained sense of fatalism in her was not displeased with Sasha being bound for Paris. This woman is distraught, Sasha might have recognised, but naturally he didn't say so, not – all this being so to speak very fluid – until after the event, when things still liquid had settled down into a shape.

Only after the event, otherwise preoccupied as Ella was at the time, did quite a number of coincidences strike her mind. In some way, their previous lives, which had already almost met once in Stettin in 1945, a possibility foregone in Stettin, however, a mere warming-up, as it were, for the reality accomplished later, conspired to intersect in this time at this place – a redundancy of speech one still hung on to as one hung on to so many other habits, as the physicist in Sasha would explain to Ella on a later occasion. He thought there was nothing remarkable about this meeting. The whole idea of coincidence was unfounded. Coincidence was remarkable, for all that it was the norm. Perfectly ordinary life was remarkable in all its happenings, Sasha told Ella on that later occasion – only for the most part what was remarkable about it went unnoticed. Paul Hartmann, in his capacity as the painter of the picture which Sasha had bought and just picked up from his studio across the street from Ella's house, was also party to this self-arranged meeting of their lives. Sasha had stowed the picture in the boot of the enormous car he was now, via Belgravia, Dover and Calais, in the process of driving to Paris.

It was one of those London squares paradoxically built in the round, a cake of a square, cream-coloured houses that curved around a plot of thin rather candle-like new trees, replacing the ones that had been bombed, under lock and key behind railings in the middle. The rooms inside, at least on the ground floor of the house rented by Sasha, were oval, and Ella assumed, with no interest in the assumption, that oval would also be the case on the floor above. Sasha walked through oval rooms shouting, or so it seemed, an effect of the oval echo in hollow marble-floored rooms that still lacked any furnishing. We only moved in the day before yesterday, Sasha said, and the question rising in Ella's mind was answered by the appearance of an ample turbaned woman wearing an ankle-length pink gown who had come to find out what the noise was about. She was holding a chow in her arms with a matching pink bow tied chignon-like on the animal's head to keep the hair up out of its eyes.

Hanna set the little dog down on the floor and drew Ella to her bosom instead. She had heard *so* much about her already, she said, although she did not know Ella, not even her name, sensing only that this young woman needed some motherly comforting, while the dog yapped at Ella's heels.

Sasha having disappeared from the evening as mysteriously as he had entered it, taking the dog with him, the two women settled on the sofa with a bonbonnière of chocolates and talked. Ella had no clear memory of what the talk was about, only an impression of it enclosing her like a curtain in a small space where she felt comfortable, indeed cosy, so much at home that when Hanna left her – to take a bath, it seemed – she stretched out on her side on the sofa with one hand hanging over her shoulder and fell asleep. Sasha, passing through the room on his way briefly back in, mistook Ella asleep on the sofa for a replica of *Ella Asleep on the Sofa*, the picture by Paul Hartmann he had just bought, portraying

266

the recumbent subject viewed from the rear with a hand draped over her shoulder. In both cases the sleeper dreamed the same recurrent dream, that she was back at her grandmother's house in Herischdorf, waiting for her mother to come home. It *was* the house, no doubt of it, but Ella couldn't quite believe that it was grandmother's. Perhaps she had made a mistake and was in the wrong house. She stood on the balcony to wave to her mother as soon as she saw her coming along the path by the stream, only it wasn't the stream. It was a flow of refugees in a column that stretched to the horizon, and her mother failed to come.

Ella woke up in the dawn light to a feeling of unbearable sorrow, an immense, deep vault of a place, and caught Hanna and Sasha red-handed, tiptoeing like burglars through the room as they lugged valises out to the street. How fortunate you woke up by yourself, dearie, said Hanna in her odd mixture of East End and Polish-accented English. I would have hated having to wake you. And she brought Ella a cup of coffee while Sasha packed the car, and ten minutes later they left for Paris. But I haven't got any clothes, said Ella as she got into the car, and Hanna smiled and said, We'll see about that, dearie, patting her hand, something Ella had otherwise seen people do only in films.

It was raining, Sasha had closed the roof of the sky-blue car, which looked to Ella as if it was ten yards long. It had plenty of room for all three of them in the front, four overfed beige suitcases bound crosswise with leather straps bulging on the back seat like portly uniformed schoolchildren in need of exercise, perhaps on their way to a playing field. Hanna glanced over her shoulder from time to time to reassure herself they were still there, while Ella made not-merely-polite enquiries about the functions of the array of switches and knobs on the dashboard in front of her. Sasha knew them all. A swanky Cadillac, he said, doing an American accent, a show-off and proud of it, with flashy fins mounted like twin rocket exhausts over the rear fender; a more un-English car was not to be had. It was the newest convertible model, shipped over from the States just a week ago. He'd collected it from the docks himself, he said, and with barely a pause, he began singing.

His voice inclined more to the full bass end of the baritone register, but could surprise Ella, just as she thought she had got used to it, with lyrical passages softly traversed in a sweet light tenor. The songs that Hanna could join in and sing with him, the standard Polish repertoire, were exhausted while they were still on the outskirts of London. The Yiddish ones, however, an apparently unlimited supply of them, needling, caress-ing, plaintive, which Hanna as a Polish Gentile was unfamiliar with, accompanied them as far as Maidstone, where they stopped for breakfast. Thereafter the songs moved across the border, beginning in the Ukraine, moving gradually north-east into Russia as the car travelled south-west and rolled to a halt on the deck of the Dover–Calais ferry.

In blustery weather they retreated to drink pitching coffee from thick white cups in the saloon bar. Ella felt queasy. She was put off the coffee by the crudeness of the cups it was served in. Hanna smoked greedily all the while. Sasha didn't smoke, he said, had done time, he said, in regions of the Soviet Union from Kiev to Novosibirsk, first as a technician on building sites and then as a prisoner in camps where trading tobacco rations for food and telling stories had probably saved his life, and as he was saying this Ella noticed Hanna looking down at the ashtray where she had just stubbed out her cigarette.

From Calais Sasha told stories against the rain driving at them without interruption until they reached Amiens. To all appearances it was one story, about the two and a half months he had spent one summer with twenty-nine men in a cell measuring four by two metres in a prison in the Ukraine, but in effect it folded out into twenty-nine separate stories about each of his companions, for each had brought with him his own story from a far-flung region of the Soviet Union: Turks, Tatars, White Russians, Assyrians, Latvians, Macedonians, Koreans and Chinese impossibly crammed into this one tiny, stifling locker averaging 0.267 square metres of space per prisoner, where their collective sweat – according to the inmates at the bottom of the pile who measured it by sticking in a finger – accumulated on the floor several centimetres thick. While they remained bodily confined in this hole, the stories they told each other helped to take their minds out of it, said Sasha, in particular the fables related by a Persian Armenian called Gewondian, whose name Sasha remembered among the many he had forgotten because he remained indebted to this man for having helped to preserve his sanity.

Like all Assyrians and Armenians in the Soviet Union, said Sasha, Gewondian was a cobbler and shoeblack. As a boy he learned his trade in Baghdad, where he must have picked up the fables of caliphs and courtesans, as they were still being told in the oral tradition of the *Arabian Nights* at the end of the nineteenth century. Beyond two arcs kept open by the windscreen wipers to give a limited view of the road ahead, the surrounding countryside passed them by as an irrelevant green blur while Sasha related to Hanna and Ella the stories related to him by Gewondian in their prison cell, which in turn had been related to Gewondian half a century before by mendicant storytellers sitting cross-legged on the streets of Baghdad. Slotted between husband and wife on the front seat, Ella felt warm and safe – privileged, like a child, just to be. She needed a story. Sasha was giving her a book of them. The couple had adopted her. They would look after her. She wasn't responsible for anything. She wasn't required to do anything in return, not to answer questions or give an account of herself, not to speak or even to think.

If only this gliding state of mind, drifting along between one bit of rain and the next without having to arrive anywhere, could have continued for ever – but then the rain left off, the hypnotic motion of the windscreen wipers switched off, and with the onset of silence Ella came reluctantly out of her trance. For a while she resumed her life. That she would have to speak to Catherine in Yorkshire was one thing. She checked that her address book was in her bag. A roadside sign they had passed a little while ago said it was only another fifteen kilometres to Paris. They were in imminent danger of arriving after all – that was another. That she would have to let George know was yet another. Preferably by telegram. Sasha pulled in at a lay-by with a cafe so that Hanna could go to the lavatory and have a smoke and he could stretch his legs.

They reached the outskirts of Paris in the late afternoon. The rain had come and gone, leaving a gleam on the streets. Their arrival in the city prompted Hanna and Sasha to commence a discussion in Polish which Ella was unable to follow. It reinforced her sense of isolation as she looked out at unfamiliar streets, all of them laid out somehow in Sasha's mind like a map with the route marked by heart in coloured ink that led to a particular tree-lined street no different from a hundred others along which they had passed. This sense of being vulnerable, a sense of exposure, could induce in Ella a hypersensitive state of mind. Where were they heading? Somehow they were already there before they had arrived. Things might not be as unfamiliar as at first sight they appeared. Not that it mattered. But a certain curiosity, perhaps native to Ella's location on the bright side of things, and to her always active mind, pushed her into guesswork despite herself. In a mood of precognition, as if momentarily able to share the view from Sasha's mind, Ella had already anticipated the house where the car eventually pulled up – a pretty large sort of place, it seemed more like an institution, she thought, than a private residence – some time before the car actually got there, and before they fell she had heard the sound of spattered drops, little paws scurrying across the car roof, falling from the still rain-wet canopy of branches in the boulevard trees under which the car came eventually to a standstill.

It might be on the small side for a *palais*, as Sasha said it was, but it was quite big enough for a house. His Excellency Monsieur de Marsay, the French ambassador to Argentina, a student friend of Sasha from his Sorbonne days back in the 1930s, lived here when he was in town, a likelihood that was remote after his recent appointment to the embassy in Buenos Aires. Sasha was welcome to use the *palais* as his own home during its owner's absence. A nephew of Monsieur de Marsay lived in the mansard apartment where servants were quartered when the ambas- sador was in residence, but as the mansard could be accessed from the street via a back staircase, which the *domestiques* were required to use in order to avoid being seen by their employers whenever they left or returned to the house, the nephew upstairs remained a phantom Sasha had never yet set eyes on.

The front door opened a wedge of light into a dim entrance hall with a broad staircase circling up on either side to a mezzanine. Momentarily it reminded Ella of Demertin in Mark Brandenburg. She had not been inside a house on this scale in the ten years that had passed since her last visit there. But even with the door wide open as Sasha went back and forth to the car to fetch the suitcases, this house remained a dark place. Ella ran upstairs ahead of her hosts and drew the curtains of the windows in the gallery overlooking the street to let in more light, but it still remained full of the shadows that were apparently native to the place, claiming rights of residence that would not be dispelled. The *palais* was not surrounded by a park, like Demertin, not even like the house in St John's Wood, where the sky filled all the windows from the ground floor up. She couldn't see the sky here without bending down and looking up through the windows of the mezzanine. A line of boulevard trees closed in the house on one side; on the other it appeared to be more or less bricked in, looking out onto an avenue with a frontage of tall buildings as far as her eye could see. She followed the interior through a series of half a dozen rooms en suite that overlooked the avenue running parallel outside, drawing the heavy curtains in each of them. She would have liked to open all the windows too to let the air in and the musty odour out, but checked herself. This was not her responsibility. This was not her house.

But nor did it seem to be Hanna's. Hanna took no responsibility, not for the house, not for her own life. What should she put on? Where should she go? No shortage of places. She loved to eat out on the boulevards and watch life go by, she said; she loved the museums of Paris no less than its restaurants; she had friends in the Polish community, she said, with whom she had gone to school, but until she had made a choice about where to go she couldn't decide what to wear. She stood in front of her wardrobe unable to make up her mind. Sometimes the anxiety of having to make a decision actually made Hanna incontinent. She stood on the spot and leaked, wailing while the pee ran down her legs. Sometimes she managed to find the situation comic, and the problem dissolved in laughter. Sometimes she went back to bed to reconsider. Paralysed by indecision so severe that she was unable to do anything, the nominal mistress of the house might spend days on end in her bedroom with the curtains closed, shutting out the world and leaving Monsieur de Marsay's residence to look after itself. But for the need to attend Mass she might not have left the house at all at such times of crisis.

When Hanna was suffering from one of these bouts of inability to do anything, a form of catalepsy – a *pathological* paralysis, she confided to Ella, as diagnosed before the war by an eminent Viennese specialist – Ella would bring food up to her room on a tray. She picked at the food. She was secretly eating too many chocolates, until Ella found out and hid them. Ashamed by her weakness, disgusted by her obesity, she wept. The only food that nourished her during one of her bouts of indecisiveness was talk. Ella put the tray on Hanna's lap and settled at the end of her bed to listen to the older woman unburden her mind, just as she once used to lie in bed listening to her own mother.

Her attacks afflicted her, Hanna explained to Ella, only when her husband was not in the house, which often seemed to be the case. When Sasha was at home he told her what she wanted to do, and she got on with it. But, for whatever reason, Sasha might not come home for days at a time. Hanna's first husband Borowski had stayed away from home for weeks before Hanna gave him up as dead. Borowski was one of the

Polish army officers murdered by the Russians, thousands, it later turned out, buried in a mass grave at Katyn. When Hanna gave Sasha refuge in her house in Warsaw she also gave him her dead husband's name, his papers, his complete identity, including a certificate of marriage to Hanna. The successor even bore a certain resemblance to his predecessor, Janek. Both men were quite a few years younger than their wife. The two identities overlapped. Hanna sometimes caught herself thinking it was almost as if Janek hadn't died. Even the dead officer's shoes fitted the living Sasha's feet, and he stepped into them, resurrecting Hanna's husband to begin a new life as her second first-husband. Together Hanna and Sasha went underground, into the sewers, after the uprising in the Warsaw ghetto. Food was passed down to them through a manhole in the street by members of the Polish resistance. Splashing through the sewers, they eventually escaped to Stettin, from there across the Baltic to Malmö, and spent three years in Sweden before they took up their peripatetic post-war life in the capitals of Europe.

Poland was not closed to Hanna; she still had a sister there whom she could visit. But Sasha no longer had any relatives left alive in eastern Europe. As a communist renegade condemned to death in his absence by one of Stalin's kangaroo courts, he was in any case unable to go back behind the Iron Curtain, to what was now known as a Warsaw Pact country, without risking his life. He had lost his home, his political faith, his family and many of his friends, murdered by the Russians and the Germans between them.

West of the Elbe, the network that remained for Sasha was made up of disaffected fellow communists and Jews in a similar position to his at the end of the war: destitute, deprived of their past and with nothing but their wits to live on. Nothing as definite as a company was formed, but within this circle of like-minded associates Sasha laid down the agenda that would earn them their living. First, reasoned Sasha, what people most needed was food. Coordinating supply and demand on the food market became their business in the late 1940s. By the early 1950s people had become used to being better fed and now wanted to be better clothed. Sasha diverted his energies to cultivating textile markets for the masses. By the mid-1950s what people most needed was better housing, and Sasha, the once passionate communist who had believed property was theft, began buying up real estate in London, Paris, Berlin and Vienna.

Business interests and business acquaintances filled the holes in Sasha's gutted life. Still escaping from the terrors of his past, still driven on by them, it was as if he needed to keep moving, instinctively spending little time at home, nights least of all, because home was where you most ran the risk of being arrested, usually just before dawn. Sasha was out all day and for many nights too. The habits of fear remained even when its causes had gone, said Hanna, and she knew from her own experience what she was talking about. But this vagrant life of Borowski's outside the house meant nothing to her. The people her husband dealt with were not people she knew. She was neither Jewish nor a communist nor an intellectual like Sasha. She spoke foreign languages badly. She was a domestic creature, a harmless fat woman for whom Parisian or Viennese society held more anxieties than attractions.

Her only ambition in life had been to raise a family in her own home, an ambition that was never realised. Ten years older than Sasha, all she now wanted was to live quietly at home. But how could she be at home in four cities at once? She didn't expect her husband to share the life that would have suited her. He did not expect her to share his. He was a husband only in name, which under the circumstances at the time, she had lent him only in order to save his life. He supported her. More she could not expect and did not ask of him. She knew that more would have bored him. She missed him nonetheless. She missed her chow, from whom she was separated by British quarantine laws she considered heartless. Just the dog would have helped; Sasha's presence somewhere in the house, unseen, unheard, would have been more than enough.

'He's a good man,' she told Ella. He was decent to her and fair. He had paid her back what she had given him, but he was not a husband who held her in his arms and comforted her when she cried. Waking in the middle of the night, Hanna would go into Sasha's adjacent room and feel better, she told Ella, just by being able to sit in a chair and look at her husband asleep. But sometimes days passed when Sasha didn't come home at all. At first his absences were justified to Ella as business trips, but when Hanna knew Ella better, she confided that he was with what he called one of his cubicle women or on a gambling spree at 'the club', or both, and days later would return to her without a penny.

During Sasha's longer absences, Hanna would take a taxi to the Île de la Cité to attend early Mass in Notre Dame and tenaciously enforce his return by prayer. Every Sunday without fail, she visited a church in

273

a poor neighbourhood where Mass for an expatriate Polish community was held by a young priest with a pale face and beautiful hands.

Receiving the sacrament every week from the priest's beautiful hands, the obese, rheumatic, unhappy old woman fell in love with him by degrees, from his hands and arms and on up to the rest of the person who was attached to them. He listened earnestly to Hanna's confession in her native language, absolving her of her sins of ingratitude and littleness of faith. When pressed by her pale-faced father confessor if there were truly no other failings than these two she recited to him in the confessional week after week, Hanna took her life in her hands. With an abject sense of her own worthlessness, she admitted to having committed in addition the sin of gluttony more times than she cared to remember. But what was closest to her heart was the thing she kept most secret, in time it also became her guilt, the love aroused in her by this young priest.

Ella's need for something to wear halted temporarily the annual downward plunge of Hanna's spirits that coincided with her removal from London to Paris. With a mixture of motherly concern and conspiratorial womanly glee she took Ella shopping at the stores along the Champs-Elysées and the Boulevard Saint-Germain, where Hanna bought her own clothes and everything could be put on Borowski's account. Ella bought underwear, two frocks, three blouses and a skirt, an evening dress, a cardigan, a jacket, a pair of trousers and a pair of shoes and was horrified at the prices – the absolute minimum, Hanna insisted. Not to worry, her husband would pay. He was the most generous man she knew. He liked paying. He didn't care about money. What else did he have left? Once you had lost your soul, as had happened to Sasha, declared Hanna breezily, money no longer possessed any value. Ella was reminded of Andrzejewski. She thought unhappily of the suitcase full of money she had found and left untouched in a ruined building in Holm at the end of the war because she had believed money was no longer of any use.

The shopping spree anticipated Hanna's departure for Poland to stay with her sister. The moment she got home and tried the clothes on again Ella, as always, felt unhappy about her purchases. Why was this? The wish fulfilled was a wish less. Perhaps it was better for the wish to remain unfulfilled. She had read in a women's magazine that to be in two minds was a symptom of schizophrenia. When she bought things, clothes in particular, and took them home, it was as if she could hear a chuckle behind her back, mocking the absurdity of her shopping efforts, of all efforts, of her entire existence. Shopping could have this drastic effect on her. Was this schizophrenic? Such thoughts depressed her. And then Hanna was suddenly gone too, an older woman such as she had missed since the death of her mother, a woman friend, a companion Ella had grown fond of despite her maundering and chocolate guzzling and pessimism, away in some unpronounceable place in Poland.

At around the same time Sasha left for Rouen on a business trip that would last several days. That at least was what he said, but you could never be quite sure with Sasha. After Hanna's departure Ella had intended to start courses at the Alliance française. She even walked the long way to the address in the Boulevard Raspail to register, but at the last minute she changed her mind. She couldn't settle anywhere, couldn't make up her mind about anything. For hours she wandered around the city. Paris cast no spell on her. She found it more dirty and downtrodden than she had expected, in summer hot and dusty, with corners that her sharp sense of smell found malodorous. Certainly she didn't regret having walked out on George, but she was not sure she wanted to remain in Paris. She was neither here nor there. For she didn't want to return to London either.

A heatwave provided her with an excuse to stay all day in the house. Ella now welcomed the shadowy rooms for their coolness, the imprecision of contours she had no desire to see more clearly. She sat with her legs tucked up on a chair under a lampshade in a corner of the *palais* library, reading whatever came to hand, beginning with *Tales of Ariosto* under A. The library housed several thousand leather-bound books, most of them in French, catalogued in old-fashioned italic handwriting on cards in a filing cabinet. She had to force herself to sit down and read a book in the middle of the day. Her grandmother Cosima used to, and she had read French, awaking in Ella an ambition that had led her to the Alliance française. But Ella felt she ought to be doing something more useful than reading a book in the middle of the day. Again she heard her mother's voice saying that the only time she found to read was during one of her confinements. It had annoyed Ella then and it annoyed her even more now, coming unbidden into the library to disturb her peace of mind. She had a whole house to herself, a beautiful house in the middle of a beautiful city, and she was unable to enjoy it.

Given the opportunity for the first time since she was a child to do just as she pleased, Ella felt uncomfortable, ill at ease with herself and the notion of her own pleasure. She was conscious of all the unfinished business of the war now beginning to catch up with her. At the same time she told herself how privileged she had been in comparison with millions of others. She had no reason to feel dissatisfied, but a voice that came out of nowhere still nagged her.

'Of course I love my children!' she announced out loud to herself, contradicting what the voice was saying. But the voice that came out of nowhere was not saying that Ella didn't love her children; it was saying that she wasn't really interested in them. It was suggesting that if she could start again she would choose another life, possibly one without either George or children.

This was an impossible voice to listen to. It drove Ella out of the house. She took long walks across the city, through the Tuileries and all the little parks around the Palais Royal and back and forth along the banks of the Seine. In the August tourist crowds on the *quais* of the Left Bank, she felt crushed by a sense of her own anonymity, oppressed by the chatter of people around her in the cafes. Always, men tried to encroach on the privacy of her space. She just shook her head, and something in her face must have told them it was better to leave her alone. How anonymous she was. She felt weary and empty and didn't care. One afternoon when she got back it was there to welcome her, the emptiness of the house in person, a stark figure reaching out to her and drawing her inside as she stood for a moment at the entrance, dreading to go in. 'What am I alive for?' she heard a voice asking again and again, apparently prompting her to action. Sometimes it was Hanna's voice, sometimes Sasha's. Ella went into the kitchen as if this had been decided long before by someone acting on her behalf, leaving her no choice, turned the gas on and put her head in the oven.

It was Ella's acute sense of smell that brought her back to herself a minute later. She found the odour so unpleasant that she responded to it with an upsurge of nausea from her stomach. The sickly-sweet stench of gas filling her nostrils would eventually also seep through into the houses on either side, she realised, at the risk of causing an explosion. People might be injured or killed. A sense of responsibility for these people reclaimed her. Already there was a pervasive smell of gas in the house. Feeling sick, she switched off the gas and opened the downstairs windows. She retched into the bowl of the toilet in the hall. Then she went upstairs to open the windows there as well. As Ella walked along the gallery of the mezzanine a door disguised as part of the wall at the far end flew open, and a young man, misjudging the high step, came tumbling out.

'Excuse me for disturbing Mademoiselle,' he said rapidly in French to an astonished Ella, 'but is it possible there is a gas leak in the house?'

She told the young man she didn't speak French and he repeated his question in English. He could quite definitely smell gas in his room upstairs, he said. There *had* been a gas leak, said Ella, through her own fault. She had been in the kitchen preparing dinner for the first time and was unfamiliar with how the oven worked — it was a different system from the one they had in England – but she had switched the gas off and now it was all right.

The young man stood there taking this in with a slight frown on his face, unsure in the first instance if he had correctly understood Ella's explanation and if he believed it once he had. Of course her paleness could be attributed to shock, but there was something about her manner that didn't convince him that what she said was true. His doubts found expression in solicitude.

'Is Mademoiselle quite sure that she is feeling all right? Is there something one can do? Perhaps a glass of tea?'

He was so young, so earnest, thought Ella, not more than twenty, if that. He was slight. His eyes were blue. His hair stuck up in tufts at the back as it did with small boys when they got up in the morning. *She, her* – how curiously he addressed her, as if she were someone else.

'I'm quite all right, thank you. I was giddy for a few moments but that seems to have passed.'

'Well, then ...' He hesitated. 'It is inconsiderate of me, disgorging like a burglar into your house. It must be quite upsetting for you, such a dramatic appearance through the wall. Unbelievable. I can imagine!' He laughed at the memory of falling out of the concealed staircase. 'Allow me to introduce myself. My name is Claude. My uncle has allowed me to live in the apartment upstairs while I am completing my studies at the Sorbonne,' the young man declared formally, and held out his hand.

When Ella gave him hers he did a quaint little bow, stooping to touch her fingers with his lips, and an electric current passed through her body.

'Well then,' said Claude again, 'if everything is all right and there is nothing I can do ... But if you change your mind, you know, I live just up these little steps ... There is no handle from this side, but here, see, there is a little – how do you say – a spring. Just press on this spot and *voilà* – the door jumps open like in the puppet show and I descend with the rapidity of a fireman.'

'Thank you,' said Ella, the least she could say.

The smell of gas lingered in the house for the rest of the day. Sasha commented on it the moment he returned from Rouen that evening. Expecting him back after a rare phone call telling her he was on his way, Ella had already closed the windows and was hoping he wouldn't notice. She didn't want to have to answer his questions. She would have preferred him not to find out as much about her as the gas incident had betrayed. She was upstairs in her bedroom writing a letter to George when she heard the door. Not wishing him to come upstairs, to discover that she was writing a letter – Sasha would want to know who to, and being inquisitive wouldn't hesitate to ask – she went down to meet him.

'What's that smell of gas?' he asked.

'I turned it on, but then I forgot about it and went out,' said Ella matter-of-factly. 'The gas must have been on for a couple of hours.'

Sasha could tell she was lying.

'It seems I've misjudged you, Ella. I took you for a person who'd never have forgotten a thing like that. Leaving the gas on and going out. You're too organised, too responsible. Your attention doesn't wander. You're always aware of what you're doing. You should know that I'm highly allergic to the smell of gas, not just the smell; the mention of it is enough.'

The look he gave her that accompanied these words hurt even more.

'Would you like a drink?' she asked.

She went through into the library without waiting for an answer. Sasha followed her. She knew that once he wanted to know something there was no escape from cross-examination. He could be very persistent. He could become cruel. She wondered if Sasha wanted revenge. The interrogations he had been subjected to, he now imposed on others. They provided a legitimate outlet for his sharp aggressive intellect. There was something about his argumentativeness that Ella thought of as characteristically Jewish, or perhaps the thought wasn't hers – it had probably been implanted by her mother – a hint dropped in one of her sarcastic asides.

'So I hope you'll not be angry with me for saying that I don't believe you,' said Sasha.

'The usual?'

She took a bottle of crème de menthe out of the cupboard, poured him a glass and handed it to him.

Sitting down, she spoke with detachment, almost casually: 'I didn't want to go on. I wanted to put an end to it all. Not for the first time.'

'Put an end to all what exactly?'

'Making an effort that never ends and seems to have no purpose.'

Sasha came over to her and anxiously took her hands in his.

'Perhaps because you're separated from your family. Aren't you needed by your children? Would it be better for you to go home?'

'No — at the moment — it would be worse.'

Ella took her hands away. She was irritated by having to continue this detestable conversation.

'I've been thinking,' she said. 'There has to be something apart from family, you know. Something quite different. Family can't be the whole purpose of a woman's life. As a person you remain alone, after all, apart from your family, even as a mother. You're a person *besides* being a mother and having a family. There has to be something in *you* and for you *alone*. That realisation can escape you as long as you're in the treadmill, because you're busy all the time. But I know now that I lack something I need. And it's my mind that lacks, my mind that needs.'

Waiting for her to go on, not wanting to interrupt and risk irritating her again, Sasha watched Ella get up and walk around the room with her hands in her pockets, following a pattern in the carpet.

'My brother Oscar and I used to share a room when we were children. He used to tell me about things that interested me — about communism, for instance, or about the stars, or the physical laws explaining why things are as they are. I found all that very interesting and I would have liked to take it further. I remember my father showing us a stone and asking me to break it with a hammer. The stone broke into three pieces. It was no longer whole. We could hold the pieces together, he said, but the forces that had held the stone together were no longer there to keep it in place. He said we might think the stone was inanimate, but it could lose its wholeness and never be the same again — and in that sense die. I've always wanted to know what those forces were that held the stone together, but I never learned because the war came and put a stop to those lessons with my father.'

'Well, if that's the sort of thing you're curious about,' said Sasha, 'perhaps I can help. There's nothing I'd be happier to do. I trained as a physicist and I used to teach at the Technical Institute in Kiev before they threw me into prison during the Great Purge. And believe me, I've spent much of my life trying to be a communist, even if in the end I failed, or perhaps it was communism that failed me. But if that's what you'd like, shall we resume with the stone that broke into three pieces when you hit it with a hammer?'

Ella nodded.

'I'll tape these conversations and have a stenographer type them out for you so that you've got a record,' said Sasha, pressing a switch on a machine conveniently sitting on the lower tier of the glass trolley at his side before sitting back in his chair and crossing his legs.

'We have a tendency to take things apart in order to understand them better. The question we're seeking to answer is: what are the parts a thing is made of? Because we have this idea that things are made of parts. It's a useful idea, but in the end, I think, a misleading one. So we keep on dividing a thing into ever smaller parts, until all that's left of your stone are grains of sand, like the sand you find on the beach, the result of stones having been pounded by the sea. And it was once believed that all matter finally consisted of such grains of sand. But there comes a point – when we reach atoms – when one can no longer go on breaking things up indefinitely into ever smaller parts as we've been doing until now.'

Sasha took a piece of paper from the table drawer, made a sketch on it and handed the paper to Ella.

'Here's a diagram of the atom with the simplest structure, the hydrogen atom. Because it turns out the atom has an inner structure, you see, and nearly all the actual matter in an atom is contained within a nucleus one hundred thousand times smaller than the atom as such, which is itself an immaterial cloud. So matter itself is largely immaterial. The nucleus of the atom is tiny, a pinhead surrounded by Notre Dame, relatively speaking. At the beginning of this century the physicists Rutherford and Bohr pictured the structure of an atom as a mini planet system, with one or more negatively charged electrons orbiting a positively charged nucleus and constituting its shell. And this was a surprise, as it seemed there was no such thing as a smallest particle, but an endless series of particles contained one within the other like those sets of Russian dolls. Are you familiar with the periodic table of the elements?'

Ella shook her head.

'Then let's make a start there,' said Sasha, 'because there are different atoms corresponding to different chemical elements, and while there are different atoms based on these different elements, such as iron atoms, an iron atom always remains the same. So you see, matter is significantly characterised by both difference and sameness at one time.'

He made rapid notes and sketches as he talked, which he passed over for Ella to see.

Sasha was immediately absorbed in his subject, and Ella came over to the table and drew up a chair beside him, happy to have deflected the conversation from personal matters she didn't want to talk about. She was afraid that admitting to even the tiniest crack of doubt about her future with George would encourage Sasha to advance his own suit, personalising their relationship in a way she didn't want.

Perhaps her fears were unfounded and ungenerous. Preoccupied with himself, Sasha preferred to talk than to listen and have to preoccupy himself with others. With her it was the reverse. He kept his word. From then on they spent an hour or two in the library together every morning. The transcripts of the lessons were delivered to Ella as promised, so that she could go over them again. If he was out of the house at night he would come back in the morning specifically for that purpose, but now that he and Ella could spend the evenings alone he tended to spend more time at home. In the library in the mornings Sasha expounded some aspect of the nature of matter. He presented a problem and showed Ella how to solve it. Doubtful at first, he left her tasks to solve for her homework and was impressed by her quick grasp of the subject. It surprised him how much she seemed to be enjoying these physics lessons. It surprised him how much he enjoyed them himself.

Sasha had been separated for more than ten years from what had been the subject of his life. He had left it behind him, as he had left everything else that made up his old identity. After imprisonment, war and exile, he had to earn a living somehow, so he turned himself into a businessman. His ventures made money. He was successful. He acted like a big shot and made sure he was seen to be one – lived at the most fashionable address in a city, stayed in the best hotels, ate in the best restaurants, gave the biggest tips. But Sasha had lost his self-regard. He despised the charade of his post-war existence.

If he wanted to attract Ella, all he needed to do was to engage her mind. Had he not lost his self-regard, he would have understood this. But as it was he felt the need to impress her, and this was done in the usual way Sasha set about impressing women he took an interest in, because it coincided with the way he sought to persuade himself of his own worth. Two or three times a week they dined out at three-star restaurants such as Maxim's, Ledoyen or La Tour d'Argent – where they sat by a tall window watching raindrops dimple the Seine. To impress Ella with the cachet he enjoyed in political circles Sasha took her to Chez Lipp, a belle époque brasserie in Saint-Germain-des-Prés frequented by ministers with whom he was acquainted, or to La Closerie des Lilas, a rendezvous for *le monde* on the Boulevard du Montparnasse. But Ella had no idea who any of these people were, which rather spoiled the effect.

As an intellectual, a communist intimately acquainted with life in the Soviet Union, but no less as a cosmopolitan of considerable if apparently intermittent wealth and having the buzz of a man with a past that aroused curiosity, even if in some circles his family background was not *comme il faut*, Sasha had access to very different worlds within a small area in central Paris, and he moved between them with ease. The nobility and old money, families such as the de Broglies, clung to their *hôtels particuliers* – once majestic, now moth-eaten mansions with distempered walls, flaking shutters and rotten windowsills discreetly camouflaged in the leafy side streets of the Faubourg Saint-Germain. Sasha was welcome in these houses as a raconteur. When he went to meet the intelligentsia on their own ground at Les Deux Magots and de Flore, a cafe on the corner of the Boulevard Saint-Germain and rue Saint-Benoît where Sartre held court and Sasha was known by his *nom de guerre* 'le russe', he became a different person. He sat down with Sartre to argue with him the economic and moral bankruptcy of Stalinism, still stubbornly defended by Sartre after Stalin's death and denunciation by Khrushchev. The debate went on until the early morning, when they agreed to differ. Sartre's equal as a Marxist dialectician, better informed than Sartre about the realities of life in the Soviet Union, Borowski was reckoned to have emerged from this encounter the winner on points.

Ella watched and paid attention, a largely passive participant. She had little to say on such occasions, sometimes not even a speaking part at all. But that wasn't the role Sasha had in mind for her. Ella's role was as Sasha's ornament, to be admired for herself by other men and giving them cause to envy him, benefiting Sasha's self-esteem. How was I? he might have been tempted to ask Ella when they went offstage and he drove her home. He wasn't vain, she decided, but insecure. She welcomed that he neither smoked nor drank. Addicted to his car, he was always fit to drive, and by preference he drove everywhere. Sasha liked to freewheel in the small hours of soft summer nights with the roof down, cruising through the emptying streets of Paris. They had some of their best conversations while night-cruising in the Cadillac, listening to *le hot jazz* steaming on the car radio until the sun came up and traffic began to pick up again as it grew light. Usually, however, Sasha dropped Ella off at the ambassador's residence off the Champs-Elysées around midnight before continuing to the Upper East Side, as he called it, to keep what for Hanna's benefit were described as his business appointments.

The *nouveaux riches* of Paris resided in large bourgeois apartments in the impersonal 16th arrondissement, the parallel, as Sasha saw it, of Manhattan's Upper East Side. Weinstein and Nabarro, two of Sasha's *confrères* in the *schmatters* and real estate business, ran a private gambling club in one of these apartments as sophisticated as anything found in New York. He shuttled between Paris and New York, the link between the couturiers' studios in the one city and their high-end market in the other. The club was Weinstein's idea, to create an informal venue for potential investors, professional financiers as well as idle rich men with nothing to do but prop up the decor, elevating the tone of the place. Members might be interested to talk money and enjoy themselves at the same time, mixing business with a little gambling, with a little jazz, a little sex, a little grass. The club mixed a new breed of gyrating black people, who were called hip, with the broad-checked buyers of the *schmatters* trade, high-rollers Weinstein flew in from America and blended with mannequins who were on catwalk call by day, metamorphosing at night into what were known as *grandes horizontales*.

Weinstein represented the short bow-legged ebullient type of Ashkenazim who originated from the Polish border area where Ella had grown up. Turn him away from the front door, Sasha told Ella before introducing him to her, and he would come straight round to the back. Resilient as a rubber ball, you could bounce him; nothing could dent him, nothing deflate his chutzpah or his optimism. You might not trust him, said Sasha – he might cheat you, he might even put the boot in when you were down – but you liked him for doing so in the friendliest possible manner. His sidekick Nabarro, a lean and sombre Spanish Jew, a funereal man with the discretion of a Mafia bookkeeper whose figures one did not question, represented the checks and balances department in the partnership, the man who took care of the small print in the wide-open deals breezed through by Weinstein. You might mistake them once for a comedy act, said Sasha; next time round you were dead.

From an elevated armchair in the background, unnoticed himself, Nabarro kept a watchful eye on everything that went on in the joint, on the barman and the hostesses, on the croupiers at the roulette and baccarat tables, above all on the cashier behind the grille and whatever passed back and forth between him and the club members who went to cash in their chips on their way out. Weinstein was seen to socialise, a man always on the move, setting an example of how to enjoy oneself, laughing and glad-handing, abhorring any kind of void, matchmaking empty glasses and refills, single male guests and house girls, making the introductions that might later lead to the deals.

In the characterisation of his partners Sasha seemed to Ella to de-liberately purvey anti-Jewish stereotypes. She wondered if this was the rationale of Jewish jokes. Ella knew Sasha well enough to ask him and he said yes, by bringing hidden resentment out into the open, Jew-debunking jokes could lance the resentment festering in Gentile minds and let out the poison before it got corrosive. She wondered if his bad-mouthing was also a form of mockery of herself, if Sasha took pleasure in denigrating his fellow Jews because to do so was to flaunt a privilege the goyim didn't have, as if challenging the goyim by giving expression to things they might be thinking but wouldn't dare say.

Weinstein and Nabarro were the people Sasha spent most of his nights with, his business associates, thought Ella, with mixed feelings when she first took in the scene at the club, unaware that just as she was vetting the pair of them she was being vetted in turn. They chaffed Sasha about his girls, if necessary warned him, protecting Sasha from his own good nature when it was obvious to them the girls were on the make. It was impossible for any girlfriend of Sasha's to fool the instincts of his two business cronies regarding what sort of person she was. They knew his weaknesses. Sasha was careless about money, a soft touch. They weren't. They had no objection to him losing money at their baccarat table, but they resented him throwing it away on women they could see were taking him for a ride. They might not be as clever as Sasha, but they were more shrewd. They could tell whether a girl was wearing her own outfit or one that had been paid for by Sasha, for they knew his tastes, which ran to full figures in loud colours. Weinstein could name the designer of the outfits and the price within ten francs.

This girl was different from the others. She wore an expensive but simple evening dress she had bought to please herself – Sasha would not have chosen it. She wore no jewellery, hardly any make-up. Her hair was cut short and she obviously coiffed it herself, meaning she did nothing more than brush and comb it. This wasn't Sasha's preferred style when he was paying, and when he was paying for a woman's clothes he wanted to be tucked snugly in with her in the shop, as Weinstein knew, with direct access to the cubicle, because clothes viewed coming on and off were something of a fetish with Sasha, especially under restraint in confined spaces, even more so when accompanied by a whip. The new girl wasn't one of his cubicle girls. She was a free agent and pleased herself.

The thousand francs that Sasha slipped her on arrival at the club so that she could play the tables, the equivalent of two to three times the wage that a working man earned in France in a month, went straight into Ella's purse. She saw through the role Sasha envisaged for her there and she didn't like it. She was nonetheless glad to have visited the place. She understood that she had been shown it so that she could see it and judge for herself, the other side of Sasha, the man who didn't drink or smoke but was addicted to gambling, paid women and whatever might be left over in the dregs of the night. She appreciated the honesty implicit in him showing her that. She gave him credit for it, even if the honesty of the admission had itself been a calculated move. It was an admission that redeemed their friendship, made it possible at all. Sasha had grasped that Ella was incapable of maintaining personal relations with someone she didn't respect.

As a token of their friendship and in encouragement, he hoped, of something more, Sasha gave her an emerald ring – to match your eyes, he said, dripping sentiment as he watched her open the jeweller's blue velvet box and hold the ring up against the light. Thanking him for the ring, she kissed him on both cheeks, slipped the ring over her finger to see how well it fitted and was so pleased with it that she kept it on.

Sasha raised the stakes. On one of their night cruises in the Cadillac with the top down he coasted alongside an illuminated showroom on the Champs-Elysées where luxury cars were on display costing the equivalent of an apartment in central Paris. He would buy her any one of these cars she chose, he proposed to Ella, if she left her husband and came to live with him. Ella put a knuckle to her mouth, as if about to bite it, and said nothing. She remained silent while Sasha drove on up the Champs-Elysées and headed for the Pont de la Concorde. He asked if his offer had offended her. If it had, he apologised, said Sasha, beginning to realise he had blundered, and promised not to speak of it again.

'*Da hast Du meine Antwort!*' she called out as they were crossing the Seine, took off the ring he had given her and threw it into the river.

She went, without the ring or any jewellery at all, to spend a weekend with Sasha at a chateau outside Paris. The Rothschilds invited guests there during the summer. This was another Borowski ruse. Having been refused admittance at the front door, in his own figure of speech, Sasha came right round to the back. An invitation to the Rothschilds couldn't fail to impress Ella. But if she allowed herself to be impressed she would not be overawed. Fame alone was not enough. At a *fête champêtre* in the chateau gardens Sasha introduced her to friends or nodding acquaintances of his, famous artists and writers who were either resident in Paris or happened to be passing through. She knew the painters' pictures and had read the writers' books, mostly with admiration. Sasha was a contemporary and shared the Viennese-Habsburg-Jewish background of some of them, could talk politics or science or art or society gossip with anyone there with equal ease in half a dozen languages. In Ella's company these famous older men tended to preen and talk mainly about themselves. She was a good listener, good at sizing up such men and distilling character from remarks made off the record. The casual remarks, she said to Sasha, the ones not meant for publication, were what gave a person away. Canetti disqualified himself in her eyes with a cavalier manner, the callous attitude he revealed toward women. She admitted to a soft spot for Chagall, despite his bottom-pinching. She thought Nabokov charming but conceited, she added, completing her report to Sasha afterwards. Ella gave him the impression of enjoying the post-mortem more than she had the event itself.

A downpour washed out the *fête champêtre* and everybody fled.

'The trouble with you is that you're judging people all the time, you know? Judge Ella, always judging,' said Sasha with irritation, struggling to put up the Cadillac roof for the drive back to Paris, his desire to criticise Ella already weakened by how sexy she looked in a soaking dress that clung to her body.

'I form an opinion about them,' countered Ella. 'Don't you? They may be able to do something particularly well, but they're still just people, aren't they? Or are your famous acquaintances just props for your self-esteem?'

'I may form an opinion about people – we all do more or less – but I leave them be. I'm not *opinionated* like you. I don't expect them to come up to a certain standard, as you do. You measure and criticise if something doesn't fit. There's a dogmatic streak in you, Judge Ella. You have a weakness for axiomatic truths. You have a reverence for the axiomatic.'

'What's wrong with that?'

'The zealot's conviction in his own truth prevents him from acknowledging the truth of others. The Reformation may be at fault. Or militarism. Or maybe that mother of yours you're always quoting. It comes with the evangelical German background, at any rate.'

It didn't sound convincing, not of a woman in a see-through dress.

Meanwhile this was the extent of the only contretemps the two of them had had since Hanna's departure three weeks before. Ella thought about Sasha's criticism and conceded there was some truth in it, but that didn't alter the direction from which Sasha's criticism came – his exasperation with her for still refusing to go to bed with him.

As for any dogmatic streak she might have, she felt this was no worse than the obsessive preoccupation with sex that obscured most men's view of most women. It leered at her wherever she went. How about *that* for a dogmatic streak?

Sasha was not as put out by Ella's rejection of his advances as he pretended to be. To himself he could admit almost good-humouredly what a relief it was not to have to wind up the machinery for a performance of which the outcome was dubious in any case. Without the stimuli provided by the cubicle girls there was no guarantee of sexual consummation, and the long passage to that briefest moment led through degrading scenes.

This side of sex, abstinent, unperformed, he could enjoy an uncomplicated friendship with Ella that remained stable from day to day. Whereas on the far side – waking up in the morning in the same bed but not the same people of the previous night – lay the terra incognita of relationships between men and women. Often this had unpleasant surprises in store: recriminations, charades and lies. Stability went out of the window, domestic peace was in jeopardy. Sasha felt he was getting too old for all of that.

This side of sex, at any rate, Ella was the most engaging, companionable and efficient woman he had ever lived with. If she had come with sex, even if only once a month and on her terms, she would have been the perfect wife – a pity!

When she was doing something around the house he could hear her singing. She didn't have a good voice and sang out of tune, but Sasha found it heartening just to hear. When had he last lived in a house where someone sang? His sisters used to once. That had been fifty years ago. Like the sound of workmen hammering, bright sounds on metal, dull sounds on wood, singing around the house was for Sasha the sound of peacetime. How had a harmless drudge like George managed to get his hooks into such a woman? She was not for sale. She would be tempted by no bribe. She must have a weakness somewhere, but Sasha had been trying for months to find it and had not yet succeeded.

From time to time Sasha gave her housekeeping money, which she accepted. Without him even being aware of it, she ran the household. A housekeeper's work was something taken note of only when it was not done, said Ella, quoting her mother, a bon mot retailed by Sasha in Saint-Germain salons, where he took the credit for it as his own. She wrote detailed lists of chores for the woman who cleaned the house. Defective light bulbs and soiled towels were replaced without delay. He could always count on there being a roll of toiler paper ready for use on the reel in each lavatory. She could disappear into the kitchen, shake a food tree and come out with a meal in ten minutes. There was always some cheese and pâté in the larder, white wine in the fridge, apple juice for Sasha, chocolates in the bonbonnière in his room.

She never had moods. She never asked him for money. She never bored him. Although not funny herself, she was the accomplice of humour, aiding and abetting those who perpetrated it. And she was game for anything – with that one irritating exception.

If he had a few bad evenings at Weinstein's, Sasha could count on Ella to tide them over with the surplus housekeeping money she squirrelled away between books in the library. Once, when he was completely broke, she surprised him with the thousand francs he had given her to splash out on her visit to the club – typically, she had not spent them. She was never caught short of either money or time. She never kept him waiting. He had never lived with a woman who managed to get by so economically. Still more astonishing about this virtually anonymous woman he had picked up in a dazed state on the street outside her London house and brought to Paris, her effortless grasp of Sasha's household was developed in tandem with an instinctive understanding of the elusive ideas behind the new physics that Sasha expounded to her in his morning lectures in the library.

Having established in detail the Rutherford–Bohr metaphor of an atom as particles constituting a miniature planetary system, Sasha told Ella to rub the slate clean and start anew. The particle picture posed problems. If the electron jumped from higher to lower orbits, higher to lower energy levels, as happened whenever it emitted light, why didn't it jump down the rest of the way, into the nucleus? The way around this difficulty was to change the picture of the electron as a particle to a picture of it as a wave.

'Particles at a sub-atomic level virtually disappear and are replaced by waves. The world breaks up,' said Sasha, adding, 'it's as if matter disappeared and only mind remained.'

It turned out, according to de Broglie, that between the inner orbit and the nucleus in the old picture there was just room for half a wave, a wave crest or a wave trough, to undulate. The new picture Sasha now gave her was of a standing wave, like a wave at sea on a windless day. No more falling down went on here; no rotation was needed. The picture of the electron orbiting the nucleus without falling into it was replaced by the picture of a standing wave or a cloud of non-oscillating electrons standing around the nucleus. The standing wave could be in a state of higher agitation, corresponding to the old picture of the higher-energy-level electron, or it could shrink to a condition of lesser agitation, less energy, and in so doing it released an electric charge, which in turn generated a wave of light.

But what was it, whatever it was that waved? Sasha said that one had to imagine an oscillation without a carrier, like a vibrating string only without the string, or a long-playing record only without the grooves into which the music had been etched. The wave in the world of the new physics was no longer something wavy; it was a probability wave.

Ella's vision of the probability wave was strangely confident and at the same time obscure. She could imagine but not begin to explain it.

# 2

For quite some time now, without a word to Sasha, Ella had been attending classes at the Alliance française for several hours a day. She left the house at midday and came back in the early evening. She ate at the same restaurant off the Boulevard Raspail every day, where she got to know the regulars and was soon sitting down to lunch with them at the same table. During lunch she practised the structures she had learned in the morning, and what she learned in the afternoon would be tried out in the bistro where she went for a drink before returning home. At home she started accompanying the maid on her round of duties – making beds, washing up or cleaning the silver – asked her to give a running commentary on whatever she was doing and repeated the maid's words. The maid was happy to oblige with hour-long coffee breaks during which she sat down with Ella so that her employer could listen to the ins and outs of her private life. Syllables that at first ran together and were unintelligible were gradually distinguished as single words she understood. There were no half-measures with Ella. Learning the language became her project, and she immersed herself in it as she immersed herself in whatever she undertook. After six weeks of this self-prescribed intensive study she went out to dinner with Sasha, this time at her invitation, ordered the meal, approved the wine and exchanged pleasantries with the waiter in quite passable French.

Sasha looked on in astonishment.

'But you speak French. When did you learn to do that?'

At the Alliance française she had made friends with a young Persian woman in her class. Bibi, as she was known, had been sent to Paris by her rich parents to complete the education they considered desirable for the marriage Bibi would make to an older diplomat or businessman with international interests to be chosen for her by her family.

Bibi at twenty-two was a voluptuous dark beauty with an electric sexuality that charged any room she sat in and sent shock waves down any street she walked along. Ella was not immune to this force field herself. Bibi stirred her. To protect Bibi from the collateral damage of her sex appeal she was sent to Paris with a beefy maiden aunt as her chaperone. The aunt escorted her to the Boulevard Raspail in the morning and collected her again in the afternoon. For the first couple of weeks she chaperoned Bibi during her lunch hour as well. But after the aunt had met and approved Bibi's friend – an older married woman, after all, already with three children to her account – the chaperone delegated her lunchtime duties to Ella, leaving the two women to make their way to the restaurant alone, or so she thought. But word of the blonde and the brunette soon got around the neighbourhood. Before Bibi and Ella reached the brasserie a few minutes' walk from the institute a swarm of young men would already be there waiting for them to arrive.

Ella had no ambition to compete with Bibi for the attention of these admirers; in fact she was grateful to leave the brunt of it to her and concentrate on her language practice. Young men primed her with questions about where she came from, what she was doing in Paris, and so on, and Ella answered them. Different young men asked the same questions, giving her the opportunity to try out other answers. Among the young men involved in this game it was a matter of honour never to let the flow of questions or the witty backchat flag. It was an ideal arrangement all round.

Some of them pressed for more. The cinema, *le hot jazz* at Le Bal Nègre, a trendy new restaurant on the Seine, an outing to the races or to the Bois de Boulogne were trailed as bait. What were the girls doing after classes this afternoon? This evening? Tomorrow evening? At the weekend?

Ella eventually related these lunchtime doings to Sasha while they were cruising around in the Cadillac at night.

'And what answer do you give them?' asked Sasha.

'I tell them I'm too busy studying French and physics.'

'They won't believe that. They will feel you are insulting their intelligence. Why aren't you studying French and physics with *them*? Tell them you are married and have three children to look after at home.'

'They won't believe that either. They think I'm younger than Bibi.'

'Tell them you have a fond, elderly, jealous husband, and if you betrayed him it would break his heart.'

'But that would only whet their appetite.'

Sasha rubbed his chin.

A dapper young man of slight build with a lock of thick dark hair hanging down over a forehead angled at much too flat a slant for Ella's taste showed up in the lobby of the Alliance française one day. Ella and Bibi knew him by sight. He was one of the faces in the background at the restaurant where they went for lunch. His first name was Alain. Someone had pointed Alain out to Bibi because his second name was de Broglie. For Ella he was the relative of a physicist who had recently figured in Sasha's lectures. For Bibi he was the nephew of a prince and belonged to *le monde*, which for Bibi held a greater fascination than anything. She would have liked nothing better than to make Alain's acquaintance. Until now, however, the nephew of the prince had shown no interest in making hers. He had not even looked in her direction. But here he now stood waiting for them in the lobby in a pearl-grey polo-neck sweater with a bold, easy confidence Ella found smug, twirling car keys back and forth over his knuckles and smiling as if all this had long since been arranged.

'Let's go somewhere else for lunch for a change. Wouldn't it be fun to give them all the slip?'

He laughed, his lips parting, showing his teeth. His deep voice sent tremors through Bibi's body. For her there was no question of not giving the others the slip. A low-slung Jaguar XK stood half on the kerb directly in front of the institute in a no-parking zone. The three of them squeezed in, with Bibi in the middle, one of her large breasts nudging each of them.

If it was a restaurant he took them to, it seemed to be a very private one. There were no other customers visible, no bill of fare. They sat on a terrace overlooking a garden. An elderly woman in an apron and headscarf came out to announce what was on offer, *le fricandeau*, a cold terrine of braised veal and bacon coated in aspic, to be followed by quenelles of pike or turbot poached in butter.

'And what did you choose?' asked Sasha, when Ella recounted this curious lunchtime episode to him during one of their night drives.

'The quenelles,' said Ella. 'I'd never eaten them before. I love pike, and it was absolutely delicious.'

'What about the wine?'

'Sancerre, very clean and crisp. The three of us got through a bottle and a half. Bibi drank most. She was a bit tipsy.'

'Hmmm ... Bibi must have been in bibible-beddable form by the end of lunch. The old dame who served the meal no doubt officiates also as bawd and had a freshly made bed upstairs awaiting the young master's pleasure.'

'Well, that's maybe where Bibi's eventually headed. But young Alain is already an experienced operator. He won't spoil his chances by hurrying her.'

'I'm not so sure he won't spoil his chances by taking too *long*. You say *her* by the way with such confidence. How d'you know it's not you he's after? Or maybe a threesome?'

'*Aber Sasha, so was weiss doch eine Frau.*'

But *how* did a woman know that? wondered Sasha.

'Besides, he knows he's not my type. Alain has this flat forehead he's aware I dislike, which is why he combs his hair forward to cover it up. I mistrust flat foreheads, just as I mistrust thin lips.'

'Poor Ella, you're a victim of those Nazi phrenologists and not even aware of it. I know, you were a child at the time.' Sasha took his left hand off the steering wheel and involuntarily put it to his forehead. 'Besides, if he *does* comb his hair forward to cover his forehead, then it must be because he wants to please you. What you say isn't logical.'

Ella didn't bother to reply to this.

'So you wouldn't marry a man with a flat forehead or thin lips,' continued Sasha, changing tack.

'No, I wouldn't.'

'And not a Negro either, I take it.'

'No.'

'What about a Jew?'

Ella hesitated.

'Marrying is one thing, having children is another. Under certain circumstances I might have married a Jew.'

'Under what circumstances?' demanded Sasha.

'Under Hanna's circumstances, for instance.'

293

'Hanna would have borne my children, if she hadn't been past childbearing age. But you wouldn't have.'

'No,' said Ella softly.

Sasha abruptly pulled up at the side of the road and pounded the wheel with clenched fists. 'Why the hell not?'

Ella thought for a while.

'There's a feeling of strangeness, of not belonging together.'

Sasha was appalled. 'But that's racism.'

'Maybe it is. But if it is, then it's part of all established family tradi⁄tions. Ours go back eight hundred years. It's called breeding. Breeding is another word for race. People from the same class marrying and having children and if possible staying in the same place, in Silesia, in Branden⁄burg, in Pomerania, with the same beliefs, the same culture – the family has a pedigree. Either that or you dilute your traditions and lose your heritage. What Orthodox Jewish family, after all, would want to take in an outsider, to marry their sons and daughters to non⁄Jews? So you marry within your own people, your own background, your own class.'

'On principle? But these are the most appalling beliefs! You can't be serious. What if you had decided you wanted to marry a man and have his children and then found out he was Jewish?'

'You can be a *Jew* and not be Jew*ish*,' said Ella emphatically. 'If I was unaware of his Jewishness then, for me, he would not *be* Jewish. It's not what he *is*, it's how I *perceive* him to be. I mean, I don't have any evidence, but I can't rule out that George comes from a Jewish family. After all, he comes from a wealthy industrialist family that rose through the ranks in the late nineteenth century when Hungary was part of the Habsburg empire and Jews who wanted to move up had to assimilate, change their names and become indistinguishable from everyone else ... It's altogether possible they *were* Jews.'

*Aber Sasha, so was weiss doch eine Frau.*

How cunning she can be, thought Sasha. She had foreseen she could only lose an argument about general principles and make a fool of her⁄self, so she had reshaped the conversation to fit that one brute fact, that saving grace of her husband's possible Jewish ancestry. Unfortunately, there could be hardly any doubt about it. Sasha had made enquiries among his Budapest friends about the Móricz family. Quite probably George *was* Jewish, and Ella, damn it, had married him. But he had found the chink in Ella's character he had been looking for.

A flaw! However well hidden, a streak of opportunism ran through her after all. She knew what side her bread was buttered on. She could juggle with the facts and make them fit, if need be to fool herself. *Not how he was, but how she perceived him to be!* Ella had gone to London in that starvation winter of 1947 and married George Morris and borne his children, not out of love for the Jew who mysteriously was not Jewish, but because it was the best solution to her problems at the time.

The stigma remained and she had fleshed it out with words.

*There's a feeling of strangeness, of not belonging together.* Was what Ella had said a slander? Worse, it was Ella telling him her truth.

She hadn't said it to offend him. She hadn't even sounded deprecating. This was Ella telling Sasha honestly why she would not want to bear his children, and it hurt, even if, like Hanna, and he didn't doubt Ella's word on this, she would have married him to save his skin. All this made what she had said about the feeling of strangeness even more painful for Sasha. Without doubt she would have been a friend to a fugitive Jew in Sasha's circumstances, shared her last crumb with him, but would she have *loved* him? And was such altruism perhaps as much for the benefit of the saviour as the saved?

Had she loved George, come to that?

Sasha recalled his conversation with Ella on the terrace of the Ritz in London, and a remark she had made at the time: *But then I didn't fall in love. I never have. I'm not the type that does.*

Sasha wavered in the awareness of quite what it was he was feeling, between the profound revulsion he felt for nationalism or racist discrimination of any form, and an impulse just to hurt Ella back for having hurt him. But then, what if not a Jewish cliquishness or sense of their shared race or the sheer necessity of solidarity bound him to the Koestlers and Canettis on the one hand, the Weinsteins and the Nabarros on the other?

*There's a feeling of strangeness, of not belonging together.*

Sasha felt depressed, doomed in the ghetto of his Jewishness, it seemed, without hope of getting out. It was a racist remark all right. But after all, she was German. What else would you expect?

The next moment he felt that the crudeness of his reaction did Ella an injustice. That was racism no better than what he charged her with himself. Then he changed his mind back again, and so it went on, back and forth, until Sasha was exhausted with the whole subject and grew sick of it, sick of his self-preoccupation, which maybe was another characteristically Jewish trait. The next day, without a word to Ella, he got into his car and drove angrily to Deauville to spend a few days at a boarding house he knew there, right on the beach, where the ceaseless crashing of the waves succeeded in driving all thoughts out of his head.

When Sasha returned to Paris he checked into the small hotel in Saint-Germain-des-Prés where he used to stay on his first visits to Paris in the 1920s. He was not yet ready to return to the *palais*, not yet sure if he wanted to go back to living there with Ella until he had made up his mind about her.

Sasha's hotel stood in the rue de Tournon, which ran between Saint-Germain-des-Prés and the Jardin du Luxembourg. At the top end of the street, near the gates to the gardens, was a cafe called the Tournon. Seedy and run-down compared to the more fashionable cafes on the Left Bank, the Tournon's decor was garish, its fare coarser and cheaper. Although patronised during the day by the odd tradesman and book dealers from local shops, at night the Tournon turned into a cafe frequented by foreigners, judging from the English Sasha heard spoken around him, rather than by locals who liked to spend an evening at their neighbourhood cafe.

The place was run by a Monsieur and Madame Alazar. Monsieur worked in the kitchen out of sight, of no account; it was Madame up front at the counter, a large blowsy woman with a big red voice and big red hair, in every sense the figurehead of the Tournon, leaning full-bosomed over her counter displaying a deep cleavage, as if on offer herself along with the drugs you could get at night from Madame in person, big bags of ganja and hard drugs like horse, straight over the counter in brown paper bags. No precautions seemed to be taken with these transactions. Sitting up at the bar where the stuff was traded right under his nose, Sasha couldn't help but know what was going on, and Madame, watching him, knew he did. He looked at Madame, taking her all in. She stared back at him boldly, as if challenging him. She flaunted herself. She was gross, she was vulgar, and she fascinated him.

On the wall behind the proprietress, for all to see, was a large photograph of a naked woman with a shaven head walking down a Paris street, followed by a jeering crowd. Sasha spent a good part of his evenings in the Tournon trying to figure out what such a photograph was doing in the place. It was over ten years since the liberation of

296

Paris. What was a picture of the ritual punishment of a woman who had slept with the enemy still doing here displayed on the wall? As if to help Sasha make up his mind, Madame came over to where he was sitting, leaning forward to wipe the counter in front of him and give him the full benefit of her cleavage.

'Well, little one, would you like to come upstairs with me for five minutes? Go outside and I will let you in the back. A quick one. No one need see.' She smiled and blew smoke in his face. 'Of course, my body is no longer what it used to be.' She looked over her shoulder at the photo behind her and then back at Sasha. 'But still not bad.'

Finally Sasha realised. 'So it's you in that photograph.'

She made a moue, jutting out her chin, petulant, dismissive.

'That's what they did with *collabos* then. But what's the difference between going to bed with a Gestapo man in your room and serving him a meal in your restaurant or selling him a bouquet of flowers in your shop? Aren't they all personal services?'

'But why do you keep that photograph on the wall, Madame?' asked Sasha. 'Why do you go on reminding yourself?'

She spat on the counter and rubbed it vigorously with her cloth.

'*Collabos* are bad but hypocrites are worse, Monsieur. I detest all those people who became *résistants* overnight. I despise those cowards. I do not despise myself. Why? What did I do?'

She shrugged.

'I did my job. I'm not ashamed of that. That is what the photo declares. I am not a coward. I am who I am. That is why my picture hangs on the wall.'

Sasha walked up the street to the gates and went on into the Jardin du Luxembourg where he could hear the huddled whispers of invisible lovers around him in the night. He thought of Madame Alazar. At least you knew where you were with her, even in the dark. Sasha agreed with her about the hypocrites. Even after she had told him about her Gestapo lover she remained sexually arousing in his imagination; whispering. she led him on through that dark. He found the prospect of such continuing dependence humiliating. His having remained alive against the odds, hanging on to his bare existence in no other sense than of its mere physical continuation, merely a relic, losing everything that had mattered to him before the war, to become after it – what? An importer of canned food and *schmatters*, posing as a bon vivant, participating in charades of luxury and extravagance that didn't interest him, a gambler, a wastrel, an unloving husband. As he walked around the gardens he clearly saw the worthlessness of this life.

Leaving the gardens he got into his car and drove back to the ambassador's *palais*. He noticed Ella had put vases of flowers on the two marquetry tables in the entrance hall. The light was on in the library. He walked down the corridor, his footsteps still echoing in the hall he had already left. Ella sat in the library reading, her legs tucked up under her, a rug on her lap, a sliced apple in a glass bowl at her elbow.

'Have you eaten?' she asked.

'Let's go for a drive,' said Sasha. 'How's Bibi?'

'Bibi's gone back to Teheran. Her father died.'

'So the bird has flown. And Alain? Did he wait too long, as I predicted?'

'There was one afternoon …' Ella hesitated.

There was one afternoon, said Ella, after another mysterious visit to that empty house where the old woman served them lunch – it must have been the third or fourth time – when Alain drove them to the *hôtel particulier* in Faubourg Saint-Germain that belonged to the de Broglie prince who was his uncle.

While they circled the loop of the bright lights, Sasha's favourite diversion, so insecure of himself, thought Ella, showing off his big car on the Champs-Elysées from the Place de la Concorde down to the Arc de Triomphe and back up again a dozen times, she told him about the dreamlike events of that afternoon, beginning with a white-faced footman in livery, rouge on his cheeks – would you believe it – a sort of fancy-dress costume, wig and all, who opened the door into a world Ella had imagined no longer existed.

'There's something he will show you that may amuse you,' Alain said to her as they went in, not even crediting the mute footman with a name. They wouldn't be long, he added, and he disappeared with Bibi up a flight of stairs.

Ella followed the footman down long corridors across a courtyard into an *orangerie* full of tropical plants and paradise birds with long bills that matched their long scooping cries. There was a pool and a series of waterfalls, where dragonflies and hummingbirds hovered, and glistening thick-leafed shrubs with whitish branches, from which a pair of mottled green and orange snakes hung intertwined, arched out over the water.

'*Les serpents ne font pas du mal, pas du tout*,' the footman reassured her, making an unexpected foray into speech when Ella started at the sight of them. He followed her at a distance around the *orangerie*, carrying a tray in case she wished to take some refreshment. She spent an hour in this tropical garden, until it became too warm and she went back across the courtyard into the house. This way, directed the footman with a wordless gesture. She wished she could think of something to say to him. He showed her into another corridor. It was a portrait gallery of de Broglie ancestors, the footman informed her, all of them women, beauties cele‑ brated in their time, said the footman, two, three and more hundred years before. But Ella didn't find them beautiful. The women looked down at her out of their extraordinary plumage with cold, disdainful, seigneurial faces she thought hateful. When she arrived back at the front door about two hours had passed, and Alain and Bibi were already waiting for her outside. Ella looked at Bibi and could tell at once from the flush on her face that she and Alain had been making love. It was her first time, she was a virgin, Bibi told Ella afterwards.

'And the next day Bibi phoned me to say that her father had died and she was flying back to Teheran the same evening. Perhaps it's just as well. Alain would have had his pleasure and thrown her away. Now he has left her with a dream.'

'Or a nightmare,' said Sasha, pulling up outside the Ritz. 'Perhaps he has left her with another de Broglie bastard in her belly. In Persia they used to stone unmarried women for that kind of thing; I don't know if they still do. Would you like a drink?'

Inside, just across the way from the affectedly rakish Club Bar where the regulars, all of them men who liked to gamble for their drinks, sat throwing dice in dome‑shaped cubicles resembling hourglass cages, was the large rectangular bar for the Ritz's fashionable clientele: mostly wealthy women, their hair dyed platinum, pink and green, their dia‑ mond earrings and necklaces flashing under the chandeliers, setting off a shimmering and a tinkling in accompaniment to the bright swarm of chatter that rose from the crowd. At the sight of them Sasha changed his mind.

'Do you mind? It's rather noisier in here than I'd expected. Let's wander down the road and find somewhere quieter.'

'If it's not too far. I'm having trouble with one of my shoes.' Ella took his arm. 'And you must tell me what *you've* been up to, Sasha. Where have you *been* these last few days?'

As he told her about the beach at Deauville, not telling her why he had gone but what it was like – the charge of the cavalry of a big sea, great roaring breakers you could lie in bed and listen to crashing on the beach at night, and how he wished she could have been there to listen to them with him – Sasha's heart flooded out. Disengaging from Ella, he had set in motion a process that would eventually end with his death. Between himself walking here with her arm in his and that moment of extinction stretched a level plain, bare of any expectation or desire. Ella's appearance on that plain had briefly given hope back to him. Her youth, her incorruptibility, the brightness of her being with its power to dispel bad thoughts – foolishly Sasha had thought he could fasten the talisman that was Ella to himself. He wished he could have transformed himself on the spot into someone who would have been more suitable for her. The last thing he wanted was to play the role of the tedious older man who has become an embarrassment. He would find some excuse and slip away.

'I'm thinking of getting out of Paris for the rest of August. There's nobody in town,' he said to Ella as they went into a *hôtel particulier* that had been converted into a casino and restaurant, 'so not much point in staying anyway ...' He paused for a moment but she said nothing to contradict him. Without a hiatus Ella would have noticed, Sasha continued, 'Perhaps with Hanna for a holiday in Switzerland. You don't mind being on your own in the house, do you?'

'I was thinking—' began Ella.

Sasha interrupted her to tell the waiter who came forward that they were going upstairs for a drink.

'There's a terrace up there overlooking a beautiful eighteenth-century garden you'll like,' he said to her.

Ella stood at the bottom of a broad sweep of red-carpeted staircase and took off her shoes.

'Strap's broken. I was thinking of going back to London quite soon anyway,' she said. To Sasha's delight and the waiter's astonishment she ran up the stairs in her bare feet, shoes in hand.

Sasha left early while Ella was still asleep. He hadn't said goodbye the previous evening. She was disappointed he hadn't at least left her a note.

But when she came home that evening she found a parcel had been left for her with the concierge. Inside the parcel a note from Sasha was attached to a pair of shoes identical to those she had been wearing the night before.

'*To replace the ones that got broken,*' said the note in Sasha's hand.

He must have been to the shop and bought them himself. He had remembered the make. He had even got the size right. She took one of the shoes in her hand and felt a prick in her heart.

'*Wie liebevoll er doch ist!*' she said to herself. 'How loving he can be!'

The subject of going back to London had come up because soon she would have completed her course at the Alliance française. In three months she had done the work of six. If she passed her exams in early September, she would receive an impressive document bearing the crest of the institute and signed by its director, certifying that she had reached an intermediate level of proficiency in the French language. How she coveted that certificate with its crest and signature. She might not yet be able to sit down and read a French book as comfortably as Cosima had done, but she was on her way to fulfilling a wish that had accompanied her since she was a child in Herischdorf and used to look over her grandmother's shoulder, trying to make sense of the mysterious books Cosima was reading.

The other reason was the letter that arrived from George.

'*First things first,*' the letter began. '*How much we all miss you and wish you were back at home with us.*' Then there was a bit about the weather, the '*rather poor sort of summer we're having*' and what a treasure Catherine's sister Betty had turned out to be '*in the event*', and about a trip George would be making to Hungary in October, concluding with the sentence: '*On reflection, Park House may not be the best solution for Max after all. Another option we might look into is a private school off the Marylebone Road that's been recommended to me by parents who have children there.*'

It wasn't this sentence that Ella reread again and again, taking in a word at a time, treasuring it. It was the bit about being missed and everyone wishing her back home. True, until now they had hardly ever been separated. Perhaps that was why in the seven years of their marriage Ella had been taken for granted. Now for the first time George had found words of recognition for Ella, told her, in so many words, that she was needed and that she was missed. The mention of the trip in October was George's way of hinting that with him absent she should be back in London by then at the latest.

The summer weather lingered on during the early days of September. Ella spent her weekends at the Bois de Boulogne with her notebooks, memorising vocabulary lists and irregular verbs. Some kind of fair was taking place on the edge of the Bois. She strolled along the stalls where children shot at balloons with miniature crossbows. If they punctured a balloon they won a prize. The prize for bursting one balloon was a little French toy, a bag the size of a child's fist, with coloured paper streamers attached and a piece of string to whirl the sack up into the air. Whirling boys were dotted all over the Bois, streamers attached to bags fluttering in the sky. One of them thumped down at Ella's feet and burst. Sand spilled out. The child came running over and picked it up in dismay.

'It's broken!' the boy exclaimed indignantly.

He handed it to Ella, no doubt hoping she could repair it on the spot. But the seams of the material used to make the bag were sewn with such poor thread that after the bag had fallen to the ground a dozen times it was bound to break. 'Without a needle and thread there's nothing I can do,' she told the child. 'But if you take it home and put in some new sand I'm sure your mother will be able to mend it for you and it'll be as good as new.'

In the middle of the day it became too hot in the sun. Ella picked herself a tree where she could sit down in the shade.

She studied irregular verbs for half an hour, but gradually, as people went home for lunch and peace settled on the park, her eyes glazed over and she dozed off. She found herself wandering along an avenue lined with trees to a fountain at the end where a unicorn was standing in what seemed to be some kind of tapestry. A unicorn! If you can see it, she told herself, it must be there, even if it's only in a tapestry, even if it isn't quite real.

How strange!

Something landed with a thud beside her, waking her up.

The man who had jumped down out of the tree under which she was sitting rolled over to break his fall, laughing at the little boy who came running up and was now standing beside him.

'Excuse me if I gave you a fright, Mademoiselle,' he said, holding up one of the paper streamer toys by way of explanation. 'It was caught in the tree, so I had to climb up to get it.'

'And descend with the rapidity of a fireman,' replied Ella in English. 'I beg your pardon?'

She held out her hand. 'How nice to see you again, fireman. The gas leak. Remember?'

It took Claude a moment to register where he had met Ella before, and it took Ella a while to recall the occasion before *that*, as it now amazed her to realise there *had* been an occasion before.

How bound to happen, that magical appearance from the tree! As predictable his appearance from that tree as her mother's would have been at whatever moment she appeared in whatever place, however unlikely the coincidence on the face of it, unmissable and unmistakable — having to be just *so* to the tip of his small round nose — having to be just as he was — just as *she* was — with the colour in his cheeks, the slightness and litheness of his figure, the duplication of an outline from the top of his head to the nape of his neck that caused Ella to tingle all over. Like an alarm going off, Sasha had said during that lunch at the Ritz — her foot in the glass slipper, a perfect fit, unalterable, irreversible, the close-fitting touch of fate, a lock snicking shut, the bolt sliding snugly into the socket — the flood of recognition in her heart.

# CHAPTER SEVEN

## The Cold War

### 1

There was an uncertainty about his name – it kept changing, according to whether he was in England or France – which Claude thought didn't matter much, as the people in one country who knew him under one name generally didn't meet the people in the other country who knew him under a different name. Claude itself was something of a *nom de guerre*, not to be faulted in writing, irreproachably the same on any official document, such as a passport, but shifting its allegiance in the spoken language, pronounced this way or that as required by an undercover agent having to adapt to changing circumstances – he could imagine the words *Dilute to taste* in the instructions for use on the packet in which his soluble name had been delivered at his baptism.

Either way he didn't feel comfortable with the name. Somehow it didn't fit him. Claude as in 'clawed' already sounded a bit old-fashioned in wartime England, perhaps a little prissy, at risk of being associated with cavalry twill trousers, conceivably even with knickerbockers. You could get by with it in a London drawing room, but in the rough and tumble of the village where he grew up in post-war Somerset it made you a sissy, and other children made fun of you.

Claude rhyming with 'glowed' presented no obvious problems in France: you were acceptable currency at whatever address in society, almost run-of-the-mill, Tom, Dick or Harry, at risk of no more than being overlooked. But then, what was true of his name was true of the language in general: the French spoken in Les Halles or Saint-Germain remained basically the same, whereas the English of his godfather, who had belonged to the same social set and flown in the same squadron as his father, was not the language of the barrow boys at Covent Garden. And while Gifford, his father's name, was neither here nor there to the French, the second syllable metamorphosing without fuss into a familiar *fort*, all the insular barriers of Britain went up instinctively at the appearance of a de Marsay.

This was the name to which his mother reverted after her husband was killed, reverting Claude with her when she took him back home, as she impressed on him, home to *la France*. But then his mother went off with an Argentinian millionaire and returned Claude to her husband's sister Dorothy at Little Compton on the edge of the Mendips. Nevertheless de Marsay stuck with him for the next seven years, rolling with Arsy-Marsay in the mud where the 'de' was quickly obliterated. But when Claude ran out of such village schooling as was available, and the next step required removal to a grammar school in Bristol, meaning that Claude would have to board there during term, his aunt lacked the means to pay for this, and she wrote to Claude's French uncle asking him for help. For another seven years, at the *lycée* in Paris, the name de Marsay served Claude well; that he could ever have been a Gifford was forgotten. By some oversight, perhaps deliberately perpetrated by his mother, the *carte d'identité* Claude used in lieu of a passport inside France was issued in the name of de Marsay, omitting any mention of Gifford at all.

He remained a British citizen for all that, returning to spend his school holidays with Aunt Dot in Little Compton, travelling on a British passport issued in the name of Gifford. Aunt Dot was his mother, and his affection for her was undiminished by distance. The woman who had technically given birth to him had not been seen in ten years. On her brother's appointment to the embassy in Buenos Aires he contacted the millionaire she had gone off with when Claude was four or five, but this grandee hadn't seen her since her affair with an American some years previously, whom he believed she had married and gone to live with in California. Here lay the reason for Claude's vacillation in the matter of his name — Gifford or de Marsay?

Sometimes when called on in France to give his name on the telephone, for example, he said Gifford apparently on a whim, when in a passing mood of anger or frustration he could flare up, resenting the selfishness and high-handedness of his mother so strongly that he preferred not to be associated with her even by name. As he grew older, this mood came upon Claude more frequently, and he preferred to arrange a delivery or reserve a table in the name of Giffort, with the final 't' established in writing, scotching de Marsay for good and all. It was under the name of Giffort that he matriculated at the faculty of French literature at the Sorbonne before he turned eighteen.

Claude's uncle Louis, who had become his nominal father in France as Dot had become his mother in England, happened to find out about this and drew his nephew's attention to a problem he had overlooked, quite apart from the matter of him having perpetrated a fraud which the university would be entitled to punish by expelling him. If he matriculated as Giffort, it was as Giffort he would have to graduate, which meant that when de Marsay presented his credentials he would be unemployable with the degree bestowed by the university on a person called Giffort, a person absent from the official record who therefore did not exist. A second passport as a French national could be arranged for him by his uncle without difficulty, but it would have to be made out in the name of the bearer of the English passport. Claude couldn't be Gifford in England and de Marsay in France. He could not have a *carte d'identité* according to which he was known by the name of de Marsay and a British passport in the name of Gifford. It was not allowed. He would have to settle for one or the other.

The dual passport, or rather the single-name but double-identity, issue was on Claude's or at least his uncle's agenda the summer that Ella arrived in Paris. It had in fact become urgent. With his uncle's intervention, the university had agreed to waive action against Claude for matriculating under a false name, but insisted that the continuation of his studies at the Sorbonne in his second year depended on him presenting documents by October at the latest establishing that he was the student he officially purported to be.

One way or another, as Claude recognised in uncomfortable moments, he had done a fair amount of lying on account of his name. Perhaps it wasn't quite lying, more like confabulation, but this was just another case of dodging the issue by substituting one word for another, one name for another, a habit Claude had got himself into because he didn't know who he was.

Naturally he had started out as a Gifford, the proud son of the man killed in action and posthumously awarded the Distinguished Flying

Cross, displayed with a photograph of the hero in a frame that hung over the mantelpiece in the front sitting room in Little Compton.

'That's your dad,' said Aunt Dot pointing. 'That's him in his uni-form. A fine-looking man, he was: kind, compassionate, with a spiritual turn of mind. But for the war he would surely have taken holy orders, like our father before him.'

Every evening before he went to bed, she took the picture down for little Claude to see, never failing to rub the glass with her sleeve.

'And am I a Gifford too, Aunt Dot?'

'Course you are.'

The airborne father, who would have taken holy orders had he not been shot down and posthumously decorated, possessed unlimited potential for an imaginative boy. On the whole Claude had reason to be thankful for his death. The flying-Gifford legend upheld Claude's honour when the boys at the village school baited him by calling him Frenchie. He was no less of service to Claude at the *lycée* in Paris. But there Wing Commander Gifford underwent the first of many transformations in which Claude would eventually lose sight of him altogether. How could the father be called Gifford if his son was de Marsay? The Somerset background had to be abandoned, all connection with the Anglican church erased.

In the French version it was accordingly as de Marsay that Claude's father made his way to England and enrolled with De Gaulle's Free French, sacrificing his life for his country, for the honour of France. He became a hero of *la Résistance*, of which the English war effort had been hardly more than an adjunct in the view of the French, a minor affair on the side of the Channel that had the advantage of being unoc-cupied. Claude was uneasy about these developments to the story, but it had passed beyond his control. All this was his mother's doing. It was she who had smuggled Claude into a French identity with a passport application incorporating him under her name, an act of revenge on her husband for having inveigled her with his handsomeness into a hasty marriage, dumped her with Aunt Dot in Little Compton and gone off to enjoy the war. From the point of view of a Parisian society lady, what was a brief heroic moment of death in comparison with a life of ennui?

Claude felt or at least used to feel most like himself in Little Comp-ton. But from the age of about thirteen, getting off the train at Temple Meads station in Bristol and catching the bus that trundled out to

Little Compton, where he regularly spent three or four weeks of his *lycée* holidays every summer, Claude's return to what he still loyally thought of as home caused his heart to sink a little lower each time. The woods and fields full of big wet cowpats and nettles it had once been fun to explore no longer interested him. He saw the grey slate huddle of houses in the rain at the end of the road, which had once seemed to welcome him with the promise of cosiness and affection in dear Aunt Dot's house, for the dismal little village it was. Claude no longer saw himself as belonging to these circumstances. Since he was powerless to change them, he would have to change himself.

He began to shorten the time with Aunt Dot down in Somerset by breaking his journey for a couple of nights on his way in and out, staying with his godfather Cornelius Marsden-Smith in London. Cornelius lived with his mother over the shop in a two-storey house in Camden where they ran an antique business, or what in the England of the time was still known as a curiosity shop. The up and down Marsden-Smith Camden establishment kept Claude in two minds, intriguing the mucky Gifford boy still buried in Claude, while the fastidious de Marsay boy turned up his nose at it.

Nothing was to be done about remaining the familiar boy who was Aunt Dot's nephew in Little Compton, where he had spent his childhood and everyone knew him inside out, but in London he was unknown. There was room for improvisation. The first time Claude presented himself at the curiosity shop in Camden he spontaneously walked with a limp, the result, he said, of poliomyelitis contracted as a baby from which he had never properly recovered. He spoke English with a strong French accent and often paused to search for words. He explained that after a long absence from his native country he was gradu-ally forgetting its language.

Cornelius had last met his godson, their one and only meeting since Claude's baptism, when he had left England to go to school in France. He didn't remember Claude limping on that occasion or speaking with a French accent, but then there were lots of things he didn't remember these days. The boy lived in Paris after all; it seemed reasonable enough. Mrs Marsden-Smith made a great fuss over Claude, giving him mugs of hot Ovaltine every night, putting hot-water bottles in his bed and helping him out with the words that constantly escaped him. How awful it must be to lose one's own language! Tears came to her eyes when she watched him gamely negotiating the stairs with his bad leg.

Mother and son were slow-moving, absent-minded people who both seemed to Claude, as he for his part watched them groping their way tentatively up and down the stairs, to be very old and musty indeed, much older even than Aunt Dot. She would have been at least the same age but not at all musty; *au contraire*, lean and spry. He put it down to the fresh milk and broths, the scones and spinach pies served up by Aunt Dot, the exercise she took in the brisk country air, while in the Marsden-Smith house in Camden, in an atmosphere of damp encircling gloom, they lived mainly off sweetened tea and bread with jam or dripping. The food was disgusting. He found it difficult to imagine that not so many years ago Cornelius had been participating in dogfights with German planes over the English Channel and squeezing into the gun turrets of the Lancasters flown by Claude's father on night bombing sorties over enemy territory.

Had his father been a hero? No question of it, Cornelius confirmed, but also a bit of a scamp, and he had to explain to Claude what the word scamp meant. He had lots of stories to tell Claude about the missions he had flown with his father, about the mess life they shared, the fun they had. He had been something of a practical joker, had Claude's dad, and something of a ladies' man, come to that.

Putting together a picture of his father quite different from the one he had grown up with in Aunt Dot's house, Claude realised this was the bond between them. His father too had evidently been different people. When Claude brought up the holy orders his father had forgone in order to fly and die for his country Cornelius fairly quaked with laughter.

'I think somebody's been pulling your leg, old boy.'

Fat, balding Cornelius wheezed with asthma, forgot where he had left the latchkey and couldn't have found it in any case because he had mislaid his glasses. He put on a grey work coat before he went downstairs to his dusty shop, where he spent the day from nine to six, closing for an hour for lunch, among the discarded relics of an empire on which until quite recently the sun had never set: the carved camphor chests from the Far East, travelling utilities in leather, hampers, cases and boxes of every description, paintings on canvas, silk and glass, toiletry articles inlaid with mother-of-pearl, clocks, jewellery, buttons, fans, Victorian stationery articles, chinaware, weaponry from all countries, assegais, kukris, crossbows, a scimitar, a blunderbuss, a waste-paper basket made from an elephant's foot. After a day standing in his shop he sat upstairs with his feet in a bowl of hot water laced with Epsom salts. Claude wondered how all the stuff had found its way into the shop.

'Well the thing is, old chap, my father was a colonial man himself, spent his life in the service, d'you know, and picked up a lot of ... well, I s'ppose these days you'd call 'em souvenirs in all the various places he was posted. He was just fond of ... things. Bric-a-brac. Isn't that a French word? Didn't cart it all around with him, Lord no. Shipped it straight back home. Went into storage in a warehouse in Deptford. His life insurance policy, he said. Something to build on when the show's over and we all get sent back to Blighty.'

'Bu-la-i-té?' enquired Claude in his Frenchified accent.

Cornelius blinked.

'England, old chap. Well, anyway. Rather far-sighted of the pater, in the event. Sooner than he thought. Always was a great drinking man. Not quite feeling myself, dear, he said to my mother in the Tiffin Room at Raffles, and those were his last words. Dropped dead with a large pink gin in his hand. Twenty-five years ago, youngish for the final drop. Tough on his wife. Not much of a service pension for the widow. But she had all that stuff in the warehouse in Deptford, didn't she; had to make a living somehow, and so she started the business. Still tons of it knocking around in lots of old houses all over the country.'

'Tons of what?'

'No staff these days, you see. Too big to keep up. So they're all having to be sold. When the houses come onto the market, the stuff inside gets auctioned off in lots, pot luck, you know – tusks, totems, camel-riding crops, tiger skins, Tibetan prayer flags, opium pipes and whatnot – five quid a hundredweight, just as it comes. Flogging off the British empire, we call it.'

The following summer Claude did not visit the Marsden-Smiths in Camden. A postcard from Lourdes announced that he had gone on a holiday arranged by his school instead. He didn't mention that the *lycée* in Paris was run by priests, a fact that Claude had learned to keep to himself when in England, after the word Jesuits once happened to crop up in Little Compton. Aunt Dot had reacted with revulsion. The power of prayer and the healing properties of the sacred spring in the famous grotto in Lourdes had achieved a miraculous healing of his withered leg. His polio was cured. He could run and jump like a normal happy child, wrote Claude.

The following summer he returned to Camden to give the Mardsen-Smiths proof of his cure in person. He ran and jumped and pulled up his trouser leg to show them his smooth straight leg. But this time Claude had miscalculated. Cornelius and his mother remained sceptical. Perhaps the whole Lourdes business was just too foreign to them.

'Odd little blighter,' said Cornelius to his mother as he soaked his feet in the Epsom salts while his mother sat beside him knitting mittens for her son, regretting she had no more mugs of Ovaltine to make now that Claude was gone.

They couldn't put a finger on it, but they felt there was something about Claude they no longer trusted.

# 2

Claude befriended Pierre, the son of the concierge, because he would have liked to have been befriended by an older brother himself. Books had yielded older-brother substitutes for him as a small child, boys with magic powers like Mowgli or *le petit prince*, who had not been forthcoming in real life. He discussed tricky situations with his invisible companion, and allowed himself to be guided by his advice. Older brother's presence gave Claude self-confidence.

The outings with the concierge's son were usually to the Bois, where they played games for which there was no room in the city. On their first outing after the summer vacation – Claude had spent August with Aunt Dot in Little Compton; Pierre had accompanied his parents to the resort in Brittany where they went every year – they had found the fair, and Pierre had won the sack with streamers and a piece of string, which, on his third attempt, Pierre whirled into the chestnut tree promptly climbed by Claude. Jumping down from the tree, he had avoided landing in Ella's lap only by a narrow margin.

It was not until she addressed him in English that he remembered who she was: the somewhat flustered Englishwoman who had forgotten to turn off the gas downstairs in his uncle's house at the beginning of the summer. At that time she had not spoken any French at all; he was surprised by how fluently she spoke it now. Caught off guard, without time to consult his elder brother, Claude had slipped into the Frenchified English he was in the habit of speaking with tourists in Paris. It was fun, just a game he enjoyed. But he now found himself stuck with it for the long, always interesting conversations with Ella that followed during her last few days in town, and, already bored by having to keep up the act, Claude regretted it. He could see himself speaking to her through a veil of what might be taken for mockery, which she would resent once she found out, making Claude feel extremely uncomfortable. He didn't know how to extricate himself without losing credibility.

When he paused and seemed to be searching for a word, she always came up with what he was looking for, and maybe it was to help him when he got stuck that she switched to French to continue the conversa-tion. Claude happily switched with her, letting him off the hook of having to keep up the deceit of his broken English. But one day, when they took a *bateau mouche* and spent the morning drifting on the Seine and somehow got onto the subject of the war, Ella began telling him about what she had experienced as a refugee. Claude was appalled. Beside his revulsion at what had happened to her – a feeling so strong and unpleasant that it almost made him wish not to have to listen, which in itself raised additional uncomfortable questions – Ella's French, quite adequate to deal with the topics of everyday life covered by the institute's intermediate certificate, proved unable to cope with this subject. She began to flounder, and Claude in a state of dreadful pity found himself having to prompt her, having to put into her mouth himself the often hateful words that escaped her. The shame of the ordeal was so unbear-able that he burst into tears, which occasioned his confession and tears in turn from Ella.

There they sat, both of them weeping, on the largely deserted boat, wondering for a while if they had come up with a bang against the end of the world. Someone had put a record on a gramophone on board, and as the boat slid under the Seine bridges, the Bach chorale 'Jesu, joy of man's desiring' played again and again. How strange! People crossing the bridges looked down at the boat and stopped to listen. At the sound of the music Ella broke down completely. But after crying her eyes out she rallied more quickly than Claude, and to his surprise – as she had every right to be angry with him and to have reckoned with his sympathy at the very least – perhaps under the influence of the music *she* now began consoling *him*. Incapable of moving under their own steam, they did another round trip on the *bateau mouche*, the Bach chorale included, which took up the rest of the afternoon.

It was now Claude's turn to account for his past life, something he had never done before – to be managed only hesitatingly in either language, it turned out – all about the flying Gifford who had landed in an early grave, the absentee mother who had landed in alien beds in the Argentine and California, the top-secret older brother, his somewhat formidable Uncle Louis in Paris, Aunt Dot in Little Compton, the *soi-disant* miracle of Lourdes, the Marsden-Smiths fog-bound in the Camden curiosity shop and the indefensible and inexplicable trickery they had been treated to by him. He had turned into a compulsive *liar*, he told Ella, choosing the hardest of possible words in self-punishment. Why? He had no more idea how to stop it than to explain what had got him started telling lies.

Ella got off the boat and went more or less directly to the airport to catch a plane back to London the same evening, so their conversation was continued by correspondence. For a while the business of Claude's confabulations receded in the face of their mutual astonishment at having taken one another into their confidence so quickly and so deeply. For a while the letters marked time, as if coming to terms with the measure of that surprise.

'*I have not told anyone about those things that happened at the end of the war, with the exception of George, and even to him not everything,*' wrote Ella to Claude, teased by an afterthought she suppressed which did not find its way into the letter: and yet here I am telling it all to a nineteen-year-old boy. For Claude it was no different. How was it possible for him to have poured out his inmost thoughts to a woman who was almost a stranger?

Propped up on his desk was the black and white photo he had taken of Ella with her camera on the boat. After she had the film developed in London she enclosed the picture in one of her letters. It had been a drizzly autumn day, accounting for the lack of tourists on board and the dark leather or mock-leather coat, brown with black spots, which Ella had worn with a scarf. The picture showed her standing slightly turned away from the camera, hands in pockets and the belt drawn tight, narrowing her waist and accentuating her hips. It reminded Claude of a photograph of Françoise Sagan, whom he had met a couple of times as a student at the Sorbonne and whose picture seemed to look out at him from every magazine he had opened since the publication of her book two years before.

Claude decided that he didn't want to be reminded of Sagan and he wrote to Ella saying so, asking her to send him another photo. The second photo showed Ella in a summer frock, leaning over a gate and smiling at the person taking the picture. In fact, she was not quite smiling. Claude liked this picture much better and studied it carefully. What defined Ella's appearance, he decided, was not the expression on her face but in it, something latent in her nature, not the smile but the readiness to smile.

A remark of a philosopher's that Claude had recently stumbled across came to mind, as if in anticipation of him soon needing it, ready to hand, one of those many queer little coincidences that Claude had already marked down – coincidences in general – as belonging to the greatest and most significant mysteries of human life. The philosopher had remarked that a good overall picture of something, however clear the picture, was of no use if you wanted to see it close up; only here it was the other way round. Claude couldn't get far enough away from Ella to see her properly. He had an impression of her being too near, *crowding the lens*, so that he couldn't see the overall picture. Claude thought there was a problem with getting up really close to your subject and at the same time keeping it clearly in focus, in both a technical and a philosophical sense.

There was a sense of Ella brimming over, shining in at him from the entrance to his cave. Until now Claude had not thought of himself as inhabiting a cave, just of being distinct from everything around him. But now he lay open to inspection and saw around him the lair that was his self, into which Ella was shining, and he was no longer distinct from everything around him.

He spent Christmas and the new year at Little Compton. From there he wrote to Ella telling her that he would be passing through London on his way back to Paris after the holiday, and it was arranged for Claude to stay overnight at the house in St John's Wood to meet the Morris family.

Claude was unprepared for this visit. During the short week he had spent with Ella in Paris that autumn he had had her entirely to himself. He had seen her at rest, like a cat, alone, curled up on one of the library chairs in his uncle's house, reclining by the gunwale of the *bateau mouche*, sipping her aperitif on the terrace of Chez Dupont, the cafe frequented by Sorbonne students in the Latin Quarter. In Paris, only Claude had concerned her.

Now, visiting Ella in her own home, Claude realised with dismay how many other people had competing claims on her attention. He kept on counting them, more and more, as they emerged from rooms upstairs or popped up from the basement. It was a warren of a house. Including Nico, Ella's brother who had just moved out but came round every day over the holiday period, Claude counted eight people in the Morris household, and during the holiday Ella cooked for all of them. They sat down to lunch and dinner in the dining room as one family, including the nanny Betty, who lived in a converted attic, and a mysterious Hungarian tenant who inhabited the basement – unthinkable in the Paris households Claude was acquainted with.

In his imagination Claude had remodelled the reclining catlike Ella of Paris as a solitary odalisque inclined to melancholy, remaining latent throughout her nature, not scrutable, a person about to happen, like her withheld smile. He now saw her in action – the centre of a household that orbited in overlapping ellipses around her, complex human interactions taking place all the time – sometimes in a hurry though never with a sense of rush.

There were always little people to be got up, fed or put to bed, busied, listened to, scolded, consoled and loved; there were arguments to be arbitrated; there was cleaning, washing and cooking to be done; there were shopping lists to be written and supplies to be purchased, things broken to be replaced or mended, household accounts to be settled – all this while keeping an open ear for the individual needs of her children, her brothers, her husband, the nanny or the tenant, and now of Claude himself. She nonetheless always seemed to have time and to be able to create time for others in an atmosphere of leisure, providing it with a purpose, such as when she contrived to bring George and Claude together in the upstairs salon and make sure they were undisturbed there.

George had been friendly enough to Claude when Ella introduced them to one another in the rough and tumble of family life downstairs. But it was a formal sort of friendliness, without personal interest, without any real content. There had been something a bit distant, a bit too English about George. Compared with Ella's vitality, her glowing personality, her husband seemed a lacklustre, even stuffy figure. The moment George was ensconced with Claude upstairs, however, and

began speaking to him in French, his personality came alive – quest-
ing, witty, streaked with mischief. In the downstairs English-language
George, Claude encountered a man who belonged to his uncle's generation, a man who made him feel the fifteen years difference between them
and might almost have been his father. The upstairs French-speaking
George was more like a graduate student friend of his. They talked
animatedly about this personality shift brought out by switching to
another language, a subject that was close to both their hearts.

Claude said he felt more adult when speaking French and that he
reverted to childhood when he spoke English. George said French allowed him to be intellectual without being ashamed of it. It put pepper
in his mind. He felt more liberated in the French language than he did
in English or Hungarian, respectively his first and second tongues, both
of them nursery languages. French was at the furthest remove from
the childish thoughts and feelings that had grown with the nursery
languages. The words and feelings expressed in those languages were
embedded inextricably in the tree rings of his still-forming personality,
whereas French had been superimposed on the finished product of
himself. Words in French carried no comparable responsibility. Thus
the sense of freedom it gave him, explained George, to explore a new
incarnation, to acquire a new personality.

Claude rejoiced when he heard George say all this. It described
exactly his own experience, only expressed it much better. Armed with
such analytical tools – the phrase *the tree rings of his still-forming personality*
had particularly impressed Claude – the whole unfortunate business of
his confabulations, his hasty self-designation as a liar, would have to be
revised. For an hour the conversation bubbled along happily like this,
with Claude feeling better and better, when out of the blue George asked
him if he had taken a fancy to his wife. That was the unmistakable gist
of *un petit béguin pour ma femme*, the phrase that George had smilingly used.

Claude was taken aback.

George spoke fluent and idiomatic French; still, he spoke it like a
foreigner. He made occasional blunders that a native speaker wouldn't.
Perhaps George had misjudged the connotations of this phrase, and
Claude intimated as much when, in reply to George's question, he said
that *un petit béguin* would not have been his choice of words. George
laughed and said he had just been pulling his leg, a put-down that
made Claude feel he had been shown up for a stupid boy, lacking

sophistication. Ella came into the room with her daughter shortly afterwards and the conversation reverted to English.

But in the first letter Ella wrote to him back in Paris, she referred to this *petit béguin* episode. She told him how *pleased* George had been with Claude's answer. George had in fact been *testing* him. Claude's response to the lure of the *petit béguin* question had convinced him of Claude's honourable intentions regarding his wife. Altogether he had taken a liking to Claude, which made Ella happy. It was important to her that George and Claude got along with each other.

A parcel arrived from Ella in London containing woollen vests for Claude, to ensure that he didn't catch cold during the Paris winter. Claude was touched by her consideration and at the same time irritated.

In the meantime, with Ella's help, the question of what name Claude should register under had been settled with the Sorbonne administration. Ella persuaded him to overcome his emotional resistance to de Marsay for the sake of practical considerations. What sort of career would be open to Claude with a degree in French literature and philosophy? Not inconceivably an academic one. In which case a job application in the name of de Marsay had better chances than an application from a candidate called Gifford or even *Giffort*. The difference might be a merely cosmetic one, but it mattered.

Ella was already thinking years ahead. Claude was reluctant to think even a week ahead about such things, but under the pressure of the deadline he had been given by the university he conceded Ella's point and re-matriculated under the name of de Marsay.

In his correspondence with Ella long letters were devoted to the old issue of Claude's Gifford father versus his de Marsay mother. Claude's position was still that of the abandoned child. He had been rejected by his mother, therefore he rejected her in turn. On what evidence? Ella wondered. Claude's only evidence for the events of his early life was what he had learned of it from the gospel according to Aunt Dot, which Claude transcribed, filling a dozen closely handwritten sheets. Ella responded with commentaries and more questions.

After pondering the evidence, Ella wrote a letter to Claude which concluded that Aunt Dot probably had her own Gifford axe to grind. She had lost her only, beloved brother to an attractive young woman. She had never married herself. It was quite likely she had been jealous of Claude's mother. At Aunt Dot's house doubtlessly very few good words had been put in for the de Marsay side of Claude's family, while the Gifford side had been glorified. In modern parlance Claude might to some extent have been *brainwashed* by his aunt in Little Compton.

Apropos his mother, Ella suggested that Claude should try to put himself into the position of a very young woman, hardly more than a girl, whose husband had been killed only a couple of years after she married him, leaving her with a small child in a foreign country in time of war, a dependant in the house of a seriously churchgoing sister-in-law who was probably jealous of her, possibly even hated her, a fashionable young lady grounded in the mud of rural Somerset, naturally homesick and, even worse, bored, deprived of all the diversions to which she was accustomed. It was no wonder she had taken off at the first possible opportunity.

With what justification did Claude assume any woman had a vocation for motherhood because she had given birth to a child? Claude's mother, recognising the lack of it in herself, had perhaps done the next best thing under the circumstances: handing her child over to a woman she knew would bring him up lovingly. As Aunt Dot had done.

So had Claude been abandoned by his mother in Little Compton, or had he been judiciously placed there? What was the alternative? Would Claude have done better to have gone traipsing off round the world with his mother in pursuit of a series of stepfathers? Did he think that would have given him a better life?

Claude was astonished by this letter.

For a while it irritated him. He thought of it as meddling. He resisted the drift of Ella's argument, but a crack had opened up in the gospel according to Aunt Dot, which began to crumble.

Ella didn't point out the similarities between her own position and that of Claude's mother, although she could hardly have been unaware of them. Ella too had left her home and married young, giving birth to her children in a foreign country. And while she hadn't abandoned her children, she had taken herself off to Paris on an impulse and left them to be looked after by someone else. Naturally she could put herself in the other woman's position. She was like Claude's mother in some ways, only heading in the opposite direction. It was this that made Ella's presentation of the case convincing to Claude.

How unexpected her train of thought! *Quelle originalité!* Once he had cooled down and allowed the dust of broken ideas to clear, Claude felt admiration for Ella.

Before Christmas letters had gone back and forth between him and Ella a couple of times a week. In the new year, after Claude returned to Paris, they were writing to each other every day. There was too much to say, too much life they hadn't spent together which they had to catch up on. Driven by a sense of urgency regarding the terra incognita of the past, vast virgin tracts of their lives needing to be made known to one another, they could hardly cram enough additions into the margins of pages already exuberantly overcrowded. Dashed-off letters sped back and forth, trembling with expectation, hurrying on the passage of time that separated them until Easter, when Claude again stayed with the family for a few days, and then until the summer holidays in August in Biarritz, where George rented a house by the sea and invited Claude to join them. George had recently taken a new job, which required him to return to England after a couple of weeks, but Claude stayed on to help Ella with the children during his absence.

George was away travelling a lot on account of his new job, so Claude would often miss him on the regular visits he was now paying to St John's Wood, to what Claude was already coming to think of as his home. In fact, this was where Claude had always belonged, he concluded, and but for an unfortunate oversight at the child sorting office that had resulted in him being forwarded during his infancy to the wrong address, this was where he would have arrived long ago.

# 3

Seconded quietly by the Foreign Office to the British Trade Mission in eastern Europe, George was travelling frequently these days to capital cities behind the Iron Curtain. His trip to Budapest turned out to be longer than planned when he and his colleagues found themselves trapped in the middle of the uprising that broke out in Hungary in late October.

The uprising began as a spontaneous student march through the city to the national assembly, gathering supporters on the way. A delegation entering the state radio building in an attempt to broadcast their demands was detained. When its release was demanded by the crowd outside they were fired on by the State Security Police. The revolt spread across the country. The airport closed. The members of the trade mission were stuck, taking refuge in the British embassy when a large Soviet force invaded Budapest in early November. Thousands of Hungarians died, hundreds of thousands more made their way abroad as refugees. It was a bad week for British diplomats. Days later, as a result of Nasser's nationalisation of the Suez Canal earlier that summer, a coalition of British, French and Israeli troops attacked Egypt, an ill-fated venture which, in the wake of declarations of independence from a clutch of new African states, sounded the death knell of the British empire.

In December of the year prior to these events George had received a note from Major Trevor Phillips, who had been chief of his sections at the Foreign Office and at MI6 respectively during the war and early post-war years, inviting, or more accurately summoning, him to a meeting at the Ministry of Supply, where Phillips now worked. On his first meeting with him almost ten years before, George had been overawed by the major, or the Old Man, as he was known in-house when George worked under him. He was old enough to have been George's father, as in point of admiration, trust and even affection he did indeed eventually become.

George owed his introduction to espionage to the Old Man. Two years after the war officially ended, when MI6 took over from the Swedes full control of the émigré agents infiltrated into the Baltic countries, it was Phillips who transferred this operation, code-named Jungle, to Hamburg. Phillips was in charge of Jungle and arranged for the training of its agents to be moved from Stockholm to London. They lived at 'the school', a rambling Victorian house in Chelsea rented from a retired British officer. There they were taught Morse code, surveillance methods, dead-letter drops, the use of small arms and guerrilla tactics. Issued with forged passports, ID cards and work permits and cyanide suicide pills known as L-tablets, they were sent on their missions.

The Old Man succeeded in making himself something of a father figure not only to George but to the entire motley group that lived in the school, people for the most part a generation younger than him, who came to regard themselves as his family. The agents' contact officers, known as controls, remained at home, while the graduates from the school were transported to their destinations in a supercharged ex-Kriegsmarine

E-boat – another of the Old Man's ideas, one he was particularly proud of. On a trip with him to Hamburg George was given a joyride in this boat and was enthralled. Powered by twin Mercedes-Benz 518 diesel engines, stripped down to increase performance, it could outrun any vessel afloat. A trip up to the Swedish coast and back home for tea was all in a day's work. War like this was exhilarating. George had fun.

A former German E-boat commander by the name of Klose was hired to skipper the boat. Operating under cover of the Fishery Protection Service, it was maintained by the Royal Navy in Hamburg, nominally to protect the German fishing fleet from interference by Soviet naval vessels. Its crew came to know every inch of the Baltic coast. During operations Klose had instructions to set to sea from Kiel for the five-hundred-mile journey to shelter at the Danish island of Bornholm before hoisting the Swedish flag at Gotland. This branch of Special Operations conducted in the Baltic seemed to the people who participated in it, sustained as they were by the romantic flair of adventure that youth brought to it, bound to succeed.

George's area of responsibility was the German Baltic coast from Rostock up to Königsberg and the Lithuanian border. The Russian occupation of East Prussia from 1944 allowed operations there only under unavoidable circumstances, such as the emergency withdrawal of agents at risk of being caught and shot. As the coastline of Lithuania in turn became an increasingly risky place to infiltrate, Latvia and Estonia were chosen as the destinations for agents. The agents operating in these countries were run by a woman, Julia Manning.

Julia's mother was Estonian, her father an Englishman who had spent most of his life working in the lumber industry in the Baltic. The Mannings had lived in Tallinn, and Julia graduated from school there before the impending war forced the family's return to England. She and George took to each other instantly and became close friends. In the hothouse atmosphere of the school, where enormous work schedules and strict security might keep them confined for days without any off-duty time, and an awareness of the shortness of life was brought home to them by reports of agents killed or missing, people they had followed through the school only weeks before, it wasn't long before the colleagues who were close friends metamorphosed into lovers.

She was a small, dark woman with pleasant rather than pretty features, a perfectly proportioned figure and with what seemed to George, a few years younger than Julia and not yet initiated into the mysteries of sexual intercourse, considerable experience in the art of making love; experience that took him by surprise, demure and unapproachable as at first she had seemed to be. Julia's apparent modesty, the chaste atmosphere surrounding her, was what George found beguiling when he first met her at the school. Thinking he had won her over, George realised it was she who had won over him.

George was no less surprised when Julia told him she was a communist. How could she be? It was communists after all they were fighting.

Julia disagreed. 'No, George, the people we are fighting are first and foremost imperialists. What business have they got taking over the Baltic states and suppressing their national cultures, their languages even? No, it's the old tsarist dream of a pan-Slavic state dominated by Russia in another guise, with naval bases at both ends of their empire, on the Baltic and the Japan Seas.'

The big strategic ideas of the little dark woman impressed George, even more so now that she had chosen to make a conquest of him. This inflated his appreciation of his own worth. He began to see why Phillips had taken her on.

'Did you tell the Old Man you're a communist?'

'Of course I did. I'm not ashamed of it or anything, so why should I keep it a secret?'

The first Operation Jungle group was sent into the Baltic in the early summer of 1948 and had what seemed to be a perfect infiltration into Lithuania, but the mission had been betrayed and ended in disaster. The agents were massacred. Information began to trickle back to the school about the atrocities that were taking place throughout the Baltic region. George was among those in the family who began to have second thoughts about what until now had gone unquestioned, the infallibility of the Old Man. In reality, they saw with hindsight, the first phase of the struggle had already ended in Lithuania. By 1949 the revolt in the woods was over; the last battle in Latvia took place in February the following year, and Estonia followed into virtual surrender to the Soviet occupation.

The school was dismantled, the staff disbanded, George back to intelligence analysis at the Foreign Office, Julia to a humdrum life in Civvy Street, where he soon lost track of her. With the end of their professional collaboration their personal relationship ended too. It was one of those love affairs that were typical of the time, a sudden flowering under circumstances encouraging an intimacy that would probably not have come about in the normal course of life. This at least was the explanation George with all his twenty-five-year-old wisdom offered Julia by way of consolation when they parted, keeping to himself the true reason why he had broken with her: in the meantime he had met Ella.

The old battles they had fought together from the Chelsea school were ritually recalled and fought again when George went to meet the major in his room at the Ministry of Supply. In the course of these recollections, perhaps aware of something in their shared past that had yet to be made good, Phillips got on to the subject of Kim Philby.

'Well, he's been cleared by the commission of enquiry and even reinstated, our man in Beirut now, but I don't know, when I think of so much unfinished business in the past ... Still, I will say this for him: it wasn't so much Philby passing on information about our activities to the other side — and there's little doubt in my own mind he did — that scuppered the Baltic operations, as some people are now claiming. It was the manoeuvres of the MGB and the NKGB at their end, deceptions they had cooked up themselves which fooled us, without necessarily the benefit of whatever intelligence they were receiving from our side. Either that or Philby must have had a whole team of helpers at this end, which on the face of it is unlikely. No, my reluctant conclusion is they just made a better play of it than we did. By the summer of fifty-two it was clear that all other special operations against the Soviet Union had also failed. We lost all across the board.'

The major sounded a little truculent to George as he sat at his desk twiddling a paperknife, and the sporting metaphors George did not remember or hadn't noticed in the past now jarred with him.

'I mean, it became open knowledge, didn't it,' Phillips added, 'with the Soviets ensuring that the reports they leaked of the capture of Western agents and the success of their deception campaigns, notably in this country, were given prominent coverage by the newspapers. Both over there, where it boosted morale, and over here, where morale was in the dumps.'

With a sense of puzzlement he couldn't quite place, George remembered both the habit and the knife, recognisable by its distinctive inlaid mother-of-pearl handle, from many long knife-twiddling sessions with

323

the Old Man at the school. In his mid-fifties now, he was quite unchanged, mysteriously unaffected by the passage of almost a decade, the same slight figure with sandy hair thinning around the temples, so quietly spoken that one had to pay close attention to catch what he said.

'Anyway, George, what do you do with yourself these days?'

'Well, Major ...'

George knew that the major expected a short answer to this question, for he was less interested in what George was currently doing than in the something else he would shortly be doing at the major's instigation. There was no other reason for his having summoned George to this meeting, at the Ministry of Supply of all places. In the absence of a Ministry of Defence and with the War Office being phased out, the Ministry of Supply provided a stopgap administrative umbrella for projects related to national defence. George was aware of that. The Old Man's authority still went unquestioned then, and it seemed to extend throughout Whitehall. On both sides it was already being assumed that whatever Phillips asked him to do, George would have no choice but to comply.

'Now you must get out of this habit of calling me Major,' he said, holding up his hands theatrically in a gesture of defencelessness and smiling to indicate this was no fault of his own. 'Better stick with "the Old Man". I know you see me sitting in this building and naturally you think, So that's what the Old Man is up to these days. But my military career is over and I'm just a civil servant these days. The truth is, George, I need your help. There are two prongs to this particular fork I'm about to hand you. The first of them is the BTM, which is short for British Trade Mission, an organisation that has recently been proposed to seek outlets for British exports in eastern Europe.'

Phillips got up and began to walk up and down in the space between his desk and the tall windows looking out onto an enclosed courtyard.

'With the forthcoming creation of the European Economic Community, as envisaged by the Treaty of Rome, this country must take care not to get left behind by political and economic developments taking place on the continent. Whatever our insular misgivings, we must establish a foothold allowing us to build a much stronger presence in Europe, or we will find ourselves bypassed by the new order of things. Europe, which has been so much a concern of ours in the two wars of the past half-century, will increasingly become a concern of ours in peace. Western Europe. It may be early days to want to include eastern Europe in the equation, it may even be controversial to do so, but if we want to pay our bills, and this is no longer a wealthy country, we can't afford to be choosy about where we get a foot in the door – in the opinion of the people who have come up with the idea of the BTM, and of course I can only concur. So …'

Phillips slowed his walk and dipped his head as he looked sidelong at George, a characteristic scooping movement with his head and shoulders as if shaking something off. George was familiar with it and knew what would follow: a change of rhythm in his pacing, a change of tack in the line of the argument pursued.

'The notion that the BTM needs a political department has been my modest contribution to this discussion. We are thinking of incorporating a small unit of what might be described as liaison officers, three or four people at most, with its own secretariat, which would help to smooth the path, and on occasion there will be a lot of smoothing to be done, for BTM's approach to markets in the Warsaw Pact countries. You have the requisite background for a job of this kind, George. So, with your permission, I would like to suggest your name.'

How effortlessly the approach was always crafted by the Old Man, thought George, and how artless it managed to seem. Phillips had now delivered the sentence George had been waiting for, coming full circle to retrieve that 'So' left hanging in the air at an earlier point in the conversation.

'Here comes the part that's more fun.'

He interrupted his sentry duty in front of the now-darkening windows, rubbing his hands and chuckling as he made his way back to his desk. He switched on a lamp, and the increasing darkness in which the two men were beginning to lose sight of one another yielded them up suddenly into the light again.

'There's a sort of unspoken protocol about these trade missions, you know. It's respected on both sides. Both sides benefit from trade missions, which is why the missions benefit from more relaxed standards of security than one commonly expects. At immigration, for example, when a trade mission is coming through, they won't do more than open and shut the delegates' luggage, just as a matter of form, you know, before giving it their chalk mark of approval. I don't suppose you have recently done much travelling on the dark side of Europe's borders,

George, but if you had, you would appreciate how exceptional such treatment is. Now this tolerance only applies when the delegation is in officially sanctioned areas, cordoned off from the messy coincidences of life on the street outside. Once a member of the delegation leaves the privileged area, however, and goes out of his hotel for a walk around the block to stretch his legs, then his immunity is suspended. Surveillance is complete; any perceived infringement immediately subject to drastic penalties.'

The Old Man reached forward to pick up the paperknife, which was lying in the pool of light on his desk, leaned back into the shadow outside the light cone and began twiddling the knife as usual.

'The question thus is: how does a cachet reach the delegate inside his area of immunity? To which the answer is: the cachet is already inside the area.'

He continued twiddling in silence for a while. Then he laid the paperknife aside, put his feet up on the desk and began filling his pipe.

'Well, how has it got there? What do you think, George?'

George was thinking how idiosyncratic the cachet terminology of the Old Man was, where he had got the word from and why he still favoured it while everyone else had moved on. It sounded like something from a bygone age, something that Foucault or Metternich might have come up with.

'I would imagine that a member of the delegation must have brought it in,' answered George, 'having taken delivery of the, er, cachet on some prior occasion in the usual way.'

'Good. Then what happens?'

'The member of the delegation on one side has an opposite number on the other, and the cachet is passed to this person.'

'How?'

'How? I can imagine any number of ways.'

'One will do.'

'A place for handing the cachet over has been prearranged, for example in the toilet of the building where the trade delegations meet.'

'A toilet is the worst place for a transfer. We know from experience that any place where an individual is doing something separated from the group will be kept under close surveillance. Try again, George.'

At this moment the telephone on his desk rang. Phillips transferred his pipe to his right hand so that he could pick up the phone, which was on his left.

'Phillips. Look, I'm in a meeting, so if you could … Who? Yes, of course.'

Phillips took his feet off the desk and sat upright, rolling his eyes at George.

'Yes, sir. In ten minutes. Of course. I'm already on my way.'

He put the phone down and stood up.

'I'm afraid we'll have to resume this conversation some other time, George. I have been summoned upstairs, as you will have gathered. The great man himself. An emergency, he says, but you know how top brass like to exaggerate things to justify their own importance. Look, it really has been grand to catch up with you again after all these years. I'll see you out because I'm going that way myself. How's your wife, by the way? Wasn't your first son on the way when we last …'

In a flurry of small talk they parted at the end of the corridor. As George went downstairs he looked back, and the Old Man, who was on his way up, waved to him from the turn of the stairs and called out something that George didn't catch. Wondering what it might have been as he made his way out into the street, it occurred to George that Phillips had never got round to telling him what the second prong of the fork was. George also wondered whether he was pleased to have renewed his acquaintance, and whether he was really suited for the kind of work he suspected the second prong held in store for him.

# 4

To all appearances at least George was no longer employed by the Foreign Office. He had seen a more desirable post advertised by the BTM, applied for it and been accepted, terminating a twelve-year record of service with the FO. Such was his wife's understanding of the situation. This was George's first deception of Ella. *Einmal ist kein mal*, as George got into the habit of telling himself at this time.

He moved to a new office, the modest if not to say nondescript premises of the British Trade Mission on the Edgware Road. The floor was linoleum and the chairs were collapsible. It was a comedown after the mahogany surroundings he had been accustomed to at the FO, but it didn't matter, as it turned out that he wouldn't be spending much of his time there. His duties took him abroad for several months a year, notably to the places where he spoke the local languages and could draw on the expertise he had assembled during his years with the Foreign Office, the three Bs, as George's domain was known – Budapest, Belgrade and Berlin (East).

For the first twelve months he and his colleague David Evans had to make do with a glass cubicle for an office – the cage, Evans called it. This stood at one end of an open-plan space on which they looked out and from which they could in turn be viewed, as they had no choice but to be, by the two dozen civil servants who sat there facing them. An office where they could work more discreetly had been promised but was still not forthcoming a year after they moved in. Underequipped and overworked, they were still waiting for a secretariat as well.

A Welshman, David Evans was the second of the two political liaison officers employed by the organisation. It was their job to keep their colleagues at the BTM, all of whom had a background in business and economics, up to date on the changing political and social under-currents of the countries targeted for the British export drive. Sceptics by profession, the political officers' view of the world was that it was the product of an always temporary arrangement, one of many alternative possibilities that could break into reality at any time. Everything was inherently unstable. Nothing could be taken for granted. Clear-headed and cool-hearted analysts, unencumbered by personal preferences, they had no illusions about one ideology being superior to another and shrank from any mention of ideals.

Evans and George made it their business to know how power was structured in the countries within their domain, what individuals cur-rently had influence there and the channels through which they could best be approached. It was their job to identify the particular deficiencies in the economy of a target country and pinpoint its specific needs. The broader political context concerned them as well. There had been armed Soviet interventions in Berlin in 1954 and Hungary in 1956. Where and when were such interventions likely to occur again? How combustible might Czechoslovakia, that still relatively recent creation of the Treaty of Versailles, turn out to be? Not to mention that suppurating wound in the centre of Europe, the divided city of Berlin. How dependable was the neutrality of Austria, stagnating in the backwaters of central

Europe and bordering Hungary and Bohemia, two former Habsburg territories, now satellites in orbit around the USSR? And what about Tito's Yugoslavia, which had broken out of, and so far managed to resist re-inclusion in, the Soviet bloc? All this information was fed to the organisation's trade administrators who brokered the actual deals.

After a year and a half the BTM came up with an annex to the main building on the Edgware Road, where the political analysts were to be housed. They were to remain on display in their glass cage no longer. The annex had its own back-street entrance so that they could come and go, and more importantly their visitors could pass in and out, without attracting unnecessary attention. Isolating the politicals from office gossip was belatedly recognised as what it was – the essential security measure which they had been insisting on from the outset. Evans and George carved up the Warsaw Pact countries according to their expertise, flipping a coin in borderline cases such as Romania. Bucharest joined George's three Bs. Like George, David Evans was on secondment from the Foreign Office, where he specialised in the politics of the fringe countries of the Soviet Union, Bulgaria, Czechoslovakia and Poland. Another six months later, two stenographers with half a dozen languages between them turned up at the office to replace the sturdy but old-fashioned typists on loan from the Ministry of Supply. Within a week of their arrival, Helen Frobisher, another recruit from the Foreign Office, had moved into David Evans' office as his personal assistant.

On Monday morning the following week George walked down the corridor to his office and was greeted by a familiar voice saying, 'Good morning, Mr Morris,' even before he was through the door. It was a manoeuvre of tact and delicacy of feeling, not to mention presence of mind, George realised with hindsight, allowing him the grace of a couple of seconds to absorb the shock of discovering his former colleague Julia Manning in the room.

'My God, Julia! Where have you been all these years?' he blurted out at the sight of her standing at the window.

'Oh, here and there, you know. Nowhere particularly exciting. A company called British Non-Ferrous Metals during the day, my old place in Pimlico at night. Nothing much has changed.'

For the first couple of days they spent together in George's office almost no work got done. They at once became so immersed in memories of their mutual past and the accounts of what they had been doing since they had last seen each other, carefully exempting their private lives, that it seemed scarcely credible seven years had meanwhile passed.

His uneasy conscience – knowing he had treated Julia badly and it seeming only yesterday – agitated George when he saw how she had changed despite what she said to the contrary. The young woman he remembered, unlike the Old Man, on whom the intervening years had left no visible mark, was a young woman no longer. She had become a little fuller in her figure, in the face too, framed by shoulder-length hair that curled inwards under her chin, whereas previously it had streamed in a straight black jet down her back. A little crease which hadn't been there before curved down from either side of her mouth. Her blue eyes were rather larger than George remembered, but the expression in them was new and all her own, something diffuse, no longer the frank, amused eyes with which Julia used to look out at the world.

George wondered if the change was in some way his doing. Looking at Julia with a sense of remorse prompted by a troubled conscience, he expected the reproaches from her he would have considered justified, but no reproaches came. Julia seemed perfectly relaxed. Either she really was relaxed or she had her feelings under complete control. George couldn't tell, but either way the effect on him was the same. It put him back at ease, into that calm unruffled state of mind he considered himself entitled to, in just the way he could rely on a physical constitution that, beyond the occasional indigestion after an extravagant evening meal with too much to drink at his club, had never caused him the slightest inconvenience.

Within a few weeks of Julia's arrival they had settled into a quiet professional routine, functioning as the well-oiled machine that had already proved its efficiency in the years of their earlier collaboration. George enjoyed his new duties in a way that he had not enjoyed his recent work at the FO. He enjoyed the sense of anticipation, even of excitement, with which he arrived at his office in the mornings, a mysterious, unfathomable contentment he felt when he sat at his desk, looking up from time to time at Julia opposite him, a woman with an unwavering disposition he knew he could always rely on.

Helen Frobisher and Julia Manning were not the usual kind of secretaries – the stenographers and typists who staffed the offices of the 1950s. They were researchers, planners and information organisers, hardly less dispensable than their bosses. In their mid- to late thirties, loyal, self-effacing, discreet, equipped with good family backgrounds, women devoted to their work and to not very much else in life, it seemed, they made ideal material for the civil service, and the civil service gobbled them up. Together the four annexites, as they were referred to in the main building where their colleagues had more important things to do, constituted the British Trade Mission's think tank. From time to time they were issued with broad strategic guidelines by the BTM chairman. Otherwise they were left to their own devices.

It didn't often happen that all four of them were present in the annex at the same time. Usually, when one team was travelling, the other stayed at home. Each team made half a dozen trips abroad a year. Home or abroad, they spent a lot of time in their partner's company. The two people on each team had to get on well with each other. This was one reason why they had been selected from a common background. Travelling in the often chilly atmosphere prevailing in communist bloc countries at the time naturally brought them still closer together. Nothing induced intimacy so quickly as the desolation of east European capitals, the forlorn hotels to which they were confined. Within eight months of his assistant joining him at the BTM, George had probably spent as many waking hours with Julia Manning as he had with his wife in the eight years of their marriage.

In a once-sumptuous hotel in Bucharest, now as run-down as everything else, the initials GBH in the floral stucco mouldings in the corners of the dining-room ceiling were an anachronism from pre-communist days. Once the place had been known as the Grand Boulevard Hotel. George happened to know this because he had stayed there in the 1930s, as he told Julia when he drew her attention to the monogram, and by some untraceable process of association, the moment seemed right for the conversation with Julia that had long been in the offing but which so far they had both avoided.

'It was the Old Man who talked me into this job. I suppose he must have talked you into it too,' he said.

'I didn't take much persuading. I was bored with my job and felt in need of a change.'

'Did he tell you that you would be working with me?'

'Yes, he did. Did he tell you?'

'Yes, as a matter of fact he did,' lied George without hesitation and wondered why. He wondered if Julia had lied too.

'He knew we had made a good team in the past,' said Julia, 'so why shouldn't we make a good team again?'

She smiled, stretching, and as she stretched the tight-fitting pullover she was wearing accentuated the contours of her breasts underneath.

'Well, why shouldn't we, George?'

In Julia's cavernous unheated bedroom in the former Grand Boulevard Hotel that night they shrank into the warm refuge of her bed and resumed their relationship as lovers.

*Einmal ist kein mal*, George sought to reassure himself when he woke up the next morning, but it was too late. Once had already become twice.

Beyond the fact that George was married, and that Julia briefly had been too, neither of them made any mention of their lives at home. It was an unspoken agreement in which they both acquiesced.

George didn't ask David Evans about his relationship with Helen. He guessed it might be the same as his own with Julia. Both David and Helen were married, but in the mitigating circumstances of their semi-nomadic life, what difference did marriage make? A sexual relationship with one's professional partner seemed almost to come with the post – *a fringe benefit*, as a recent coinage of the job advertisements in *The Times* amusingly put it, a flying saucer laden with little goodies, as George imagined it, zooming in when required from outer space. George remained an avid reader of both science fiction novels and the Situations Vacant column all his life, fantasising about other galaxies and other lives he might have led. At some point the step into a more intimate relationship with Julia just happened, a natural extension of their already established intimacy, nourished by loneliness and boredom in bleak hotel rooms that became less depressing simply for being shared with another person. It was like a second marriage. In effect his job made a bigamist of George. And something else.

There were no conspiratorial rendezvous with people from the opposite side, none of the usual MI6 skulduggery. No clandestine, risky meetings outside. It was a beautiful thing. They never met their opposite number anywhere alone, never exchanged a word with them, likely didn't see them and wouldn't even have recognised them if they had.

The couriers on either side remained complete strangers to each other. What they recognised were each other's briefcases.

The transfer was made under the enemy's nose. The idea astonished George for being so bold and simple.

Whose idea was it? Something like it had been broached in the discussion with the Old Man when George first went to see him at the Ministry of Supply, but the discussion had reached no conclusion at the time and had never been resumed.

A supply of briefcases was ordered to MI6 specifications. Although new, they were not to look new. They gave away nothing as to their place of manufacture. Well preserved, a little scuffed at the corners, they might have been passed down from previous users. They had to be rugged, roomy, and but for two inconspicuous rectangles under the lock on the front, the small one contained within the larger one and in a slightly lighter leather than the rest of the dun-coloured briefcase, there was nothing about them to attract attention. George was given one of these briefcases, with instructions to put in it only dispensable papers relating to the meeting he was attending, as he would not be seeing them again. It was not what George took out with him that mattered. That would be in the briefcase he brought back.

Political liaison officers attended conferences as observers, not as participants. They could be seen but not heard. During the breaks between sessions they might consult or be consulted by members of their own delegation, and they made a point of being seen with their colleagues for this purpose, justifying their presence. That was the apparent extent of the contribution they had to make at trade conferences. However, somewhere in the room there would usually but not always be a contact. This person had to be identified, which was easily done – the bearer had been provided with a briefcase belonging to the same custom-made batch ordered to MI6 specifications. Not more than a dozen such briefcases existed in the world. There could be no mistake.

For each of the cities visited by the BTM contingency plans were made after a delegation had attended a conference there and it was established how things were arranged. During coffee or lunch, which in one or the other case would be consumed on the conference premises, the contact would leave his briefcase in the conference room, unattended on the floor by his chair, and during that time it was up to the liaison officer to locate it, take it and substitute his own.

Ideally, the switch would be carried out in such a way that if seen and challenged, the political liaison officer could explain it away as something he had done inadvertently. He was given training in various ways of making the switch, so that such an explanation would sound credible, but George knew, and the people behind him knew, that once asked to account for the contents of the briefcase he had exchanged for his own, he was probably done for. He had a small margin of safety in which to manoeuvre, the margin of his own instincts. If for some reason George lacked confidence about exchanging the briefcases without being detected, or if any unexpected problem should come up, he was to refrain from performing the switch. It was left to his judgement whether to break off or go through with his mission.

On the first few occasions George went through the procedure it seemed child's play. He even felt a bit foolish to be involved in such ridiculous games. But when he thought seriously about what he was doing and realised the consequences if he were caught, he found his first thoughtless sangfroid seeping away, and once it was gone he never recovered it.

That such a trivial piece of funny business could generate such adrenaline took George by surprise. Sometimes his heart began beating faster even before he entered the building where the conference was taking place. The longer he continued doing it, the stronger the surge of adrenaline that accompanied the switch. Knowing the penalty he could expect if he was caught, his initially mild attacks of stage fright got worse and worse. He would disappear for many years. Possibly worse. The only way out might be to agree to work for the other side.

The risk of what he was doing, George realised, was reflected in the salary he was now being paid, which was considerably higher than what it had been when he had spent his days as a junior analyst in the back rooms of the Foreign Office. The higher pay had been a major inducement to leave the FO and join the BTM. All this appeared to have been taken for granted by the Old Man, who had not even asked to see him again after that one meeting.

George didn't know what the briefcases he took back with him to England contained. It didn't interest him to know. His responsibility was as the courier. He and David Evans supplied the pipeline for agents to deliver cachets – it was only the Old Man's cosy euphemism that made them seem harmless – containing secrets from all the Warsaw

Pact countries and latterly Yugoslavia as well. Perhaps the few minutes required to make a switch five or six times a year were the most valuable contribution he had to make. He had no illusions about how dispensable he was. In the regrettable case of him being caught, another courier using another method would be substituted for him. At the Foreign Office George had always been able to persuade himself that his work mattered, but in his new career with the BTM he realised that the rest of his work achieved little more than to provide the camouflage for those brief moments when he was centre stage. It probably counted for not very much.

It was in the cynical frame of mind accompanying this insight into his worth to his employers that George began to take less interest in his work during the off phases back at his London base. He found he was now living largely for those moments every couple of months when he went over the top, as he dramatised this form of trench warfare to himself, taking his life into his hands, no less. George wasn't a back-room boy any more. He was in the front line.

The adrenaline kick generated by the switch lingered for the rest of the day as a sensation that became smooth and soothing as it wore off. The intense experience of sex he enjoyed on the crest of this sensation with Julia Manning after a successful switch turned into a craving, and satisfying the craving was what provided the secret essence that had unexpectedly come to flavour his life. But for that, but for the woman who made it possible for him to satisfy that craving, George would have given up his job, recognising that he really didn't have the nerves for it.

George thought he had learned to perfection how to compartmentalise his life during a decade with the Foreign Office. The routines of deception had long since anaesthetised conscience into connivance. Somewhere on his way to work he changed into another person and, returning to his wife and family, he changed back. But speaking French with Claude on that first Christmas visit, the language which allowed him to explore a new incarnation, acquire a new personality, as he had so glibly explained to Claude, the home-George momentarily got confused with the away-George, and *un petit béguin* slipped out. Once released from the bottle, that imp became so much of a preoccupation with the other George that it had soon turned the tables on its master and could do with him just as it pleased.

It was one more example of an increasing number of instances of

crossover and leakage between the lives George led. Compartmentalisation was proving to be far from perfect. The essence that flavoured his
life had turned out to be addictive. He needed it more often than
those four or five times a year, riding the aftermath of adrenaline in
a hotel room with Julia Manning after a successful switch. But sex
alone was not enough. Clandestine meetings with Julia in London
hotels or her depressing bedsit in Pimlico failed to recreate the conditions that made sex so exciting in the decadent bourgeois remains of
the Grand Boulevard Hotel in Bucharest or even the soulless new
Intercontinental skyscraper in East Berlin, built especially to impress
foreign delegations.

By chance, routed back to London via Paris, where they spent a
night on the way home from one of their trips to East Berlin, they had
stumbled across a cafe near the Jardin du Luxembourg and discovered
that drugs were available over the counter in brown paper bags. Back in
their hotel room they used the ganja to kick-start a sex experience almost
as good as boarding the Berlin–Budapest express. They were now in
business all year round, and George found that life was beginning to be
more fun than it had ever been before.


# 5


It never occurred to George that any of this concerned Ella. It took place
in a world uninhabited by Ella, a world to which she didn't belong. It
changed nothing in their relationship as man and wife, or so George
thought. Nothing in that other world jeopardised their marriage. He
remained, in his own view, a loyal husband.

He was as proud of his wife as he had been from the beginning.
Aware of her attractiveness to other men, George liked to show her off.
He encouraged her to spend money on clothes. He bought her expensive
jewellery. He was vainer about Ella than she was herself, although this
was as much a vanity on his own behalf. He was aware that he was
shown off by her in a better light.

Paul Hartmann did a series of nude portraits of Ella. It was like
painting Sleeping Beauty, Paul said, and he meant her unawareness.
Paul didn't know about the vow Ella had taken not to look in a mirror,

but this was the quality he sensed when he said it was like painting Sleeping Beauty.

At about the time Paul was painting his Sleeping Beauty series Ella was thawing out of the rape trauma, the state of permafrost she had remained in for over ten years. Those Russian soldiers apart, Ella's only experience of sex had been with her husband. She could not be expected to know that George's poor performance as a sexual partner – his premature ejaculation – was not normal. Three children in seven years was so far the sum of what Ella had got out of having sex with her husband. Sasha stimulated her, but stimulation was a state of switch-on, switch-off ambivalence. He had pursued her in Paris, perhaps pushed a little too hard, and all Ella's old fears had flared up. As soon as Sasha began pushing, Ella switched off. He had misjudged his chance and would never get another. The thought of having sex with him filled her with disgust.

But once awoken, Ella began to demand more satisfying sex with George. She read up on the subject and found that George's condition had a scientific name. She wanted him to consult a specialist at just the time George was secretly discovering more satisfying sex with Julia Manning. George's sex drive was weak, like all his appetites. Resistant to the attractions of sweets, liquor, tobacco, George had no particular cravings, or none that Ella could see, not even for other women; an extraordinary partiality for potatoes, true, but she felt that really didn't count. In general, things mattered less to George than they did to Ella. Sometimes Ella wished he would show greed, a raw desire for something – anything – as long as it mattered passionately to him. But George went on enjoying his potatoes and otherwise stonewalling, sealing any leaks, putting off making an appointment with a specialist until Ella finally gave up. The idea of talking to a stranger about his sex life was repellent to him.

Unknown to Ella, to her reference manuals and the specialist she herself went to see without telling George, sex had become another subject for the compartmentalisation of George's life. Sexual arousal and the fulfilment of what might be described as normal sex relations now belonged in the Julia Manning compartment. Ella sensed the change. In bed with Ella, George was no longer coming too quickly. The problem was that he wasn't coming at all.

One of the sentences from the mouth of the specialist that stuck in Ella's mind was that the penis never lied. She asked George if he was seeing another woman. George said he wasn't. He reassured her, and above all he reassured himself, that he loved her as he always had. These days, said George, at least for him, love just didn't lead on to sex as automatically as it had done earlier in their marriage. A couple could take a break from sex, couldn't they, George said, without their marriage suffering. He went on the attack. There was no law *obliging* them to do it for Christ's sake, he declared to Ella one night in bed – an unfortunate sentence that made Ella laugh. Abashed and not amused, George switched off the light. He didn't like talking about sex in any case.

George's vanity in wanting to be shown off by Ella in a better light was responsible for a feeling Ella harboured from the beginning of her marriage. Being to some extent on display, paraded in public, having attention drawn to her attractions, Ella sometimes felt she was being put on offer to other men. She did not feel protected by her husband. She was not enclosed in a conjugal cordon of safety. In Paris she had perhaps been expecting George to come and fetch her back. An energetic George, showing up in Paris and taking her home, perhaps even against her wishes, was a figure she would have liked to discover in her husband. But George had done no such thing, of course. What Ella thought of as protection George would have regarded as interference. Enclosing his wife in a cordon of safety would for George have been like tying a dog to a post. He would have considered jealousy vulgar, beneath his dignity. His self-regard went first.

George would have defended his values as belonging to the best patrician British tradition. Patrician British values went with a lukewarm temperament that George was vaguely aware of and idealised as self-control. All human beings were entitled to their freedom, so the ideal ran, and there was no greater freedom given a human being than in the exercise of self-control. All passions that led human beings to be unable to help themselves from doing something were undesirable and belonged to a plebeian way of life. As for the rest, he counted absolutely on Ella's loyalty and tact. Only discretion mattered. Confident that Ella would always come back to him, George would not even have objected to her having an affair with Sasha. That George himself was caught up in an affair he could no longer control was one of those inconvenient facts he had learned to filter out of his consciousness.

He had no objection to her correspondence with Claude, now into its second year. Ella made no secret of it. Secrets were not in her nature. She read bits of letters aloud to George. Had he asked to see the letters for himself, she would have given them to him to read. She included Claude in her conversation, just as she included other absent members of the family, Edward in British Columbia and Nico, who had joined the merchant navy. Every other day there would be a letter from Claude in the post. In two years, despite his absence for much of the time, Claude had become an established quantity in their life.

By the naturalness with which she handled the situation she accustomed George to Claude. Whenever he passed through Paris, George would arrange to meet Claude, and whenever Claude came to England during the vacations, he stayed with George and Ella for a couple of weeks in St John's Wood. Ella was pleased and at the same time felt a little tug of jealousy to see how well the two of them seemed to get on with each other.

Until the arrival of Claude, the misdirected parcel that had eventually washed up on his doorstep, there had been no friends in George's life. In a social setting George gave a good imitation of a gregarious person. There was the family in Hampstead. There were old acquaintances that lingered on from university days, people George met for lunch at clubs or caught up with at old boys' reunions. And there were colleagues, some of whom George was intimate with in a quaint sort of English way, intimate at arm's length. But, as Ella remarked, none of them were really *friends*.

The friendship between George and Claude, as George remarked, might equally have been a mutual antipathy. Grounded in what they had in common, the stake that each of them had in Ella, George and Claude might well have considered the other to be his rival, but they became collaborators instead. That was Ella's doing. Both of them were solitary by nature and, but for Ella, would have remained so, bound neither by friendship not enmity, preserving their neutrality.

That summer Claude would graduate from the Sorbonne. He was thinking of applying to London University to take a higher degree, which would keep him in London for several years. In the meantime he invited George and Ella to join him for a holiday in Provence.

The three of them had been on holiday together in France before, once in Biarritz with the family, once in Brittany without. There they had stayed in a house with three bedrooms, one for each of them, remarked George with his lopsided smile, and given first choice he picked for himself the room with the best view of the sea. On that occasion Betty had taken the three children back home with her to Yorkshire to stay with her family on the farm. The children loved it, and Claude assumed it could be arranged for them to stay there again. His written examinations would be over in early June. He suggested meeting George and Ella in Paris and driving down in the recent acquisition of which he was so proud, the little Citroën 2CV which his uncle had given him for his twenty-first birthday. They would need a car to get around, one with good suspension and ground clearance, he wrote, in the remote and sometimes trackless places of Haute-Provence. Ella was amused by Claude's untypical interest in such technical matters.

The snag with this plan was Max. The twins could be packed off with Betty to Yorkshire whenever, but Max's school didn't break up until the middle of July. Max might have been left in Giselle's charge, Giselle willing, as she always was, having a soft spot for Max, but she had arranged to visit her sister in Switzerland in June. So George came up with another solution.

Ella should go on holiday with Claude, and George would remain in London to look after Max. Max would stay on for the extra prep hour at school to do his homework and George could either pick him up there when it was over at six or arrange to be home by seven to cook the two of them supper. It would give him the chance to devote more time to Max than he had done recently. They had a few fences to mend. He hadn't always been the best of fathers where Max was concerned.

This suggestion roused conflicting feelings in Ella.

What was behind it?

The simple answer George gave her was that it would be good for her to get away completely – from home, family, everything.

Only the simple answer wasn't simple. It raised a lot of other issues, of which Ella was keenly and George dimly aware, configurations he couldn't make out or simply didn't want to see in the dark even if he knew they were there. For different reasons it suited both of them not to go into those other issues, so they let the simple answer stand.

Never at a loss when it came to preserving his own peace of mind, shutting out whatever threatened it, George seemed content with this solution that was none. It was Ella who lost her equilibrium so easily, turned and twisted, had second thoughts, changed her mind, Ella who needed clarity at whatever cost, but this time couldn't find it and for once was lost for words.

Was George being generous and noble or was he trying to get her out of the way for some reason to suit his own convenience?

Ella wrote to Claude that June was a problem, explaining the position. July or later would be preferable. Claude wrote back that he had to return to Paris in early July to attend a colloquium where he would be orally examined by his professors.

Ella had one more try.

Was George sure he didn't mind her going on holiday with Claude for a couple of weeks? Wouldn't George feel left out? Wouldn't he be jealous?

Why should he mind? asked George with unfeigned surprise. They both liked Claude. Claude was their friend. Why should he be jealous? What was more natural than for Ella and Claude to go on holiday together?

Ella had nothing to say in reply to these questions, nothing she could put into words, and so the matter was finally settled.

A fortnight before Ella was due to leave, Giselle received a telegram informing her that her sister in Switzerland had died. The visit proposed for June was cancelled. So Giselle would be at home to look after Max after all.

'That means you'll be able to join me and Claude,' said Ella eagerly. 'Doesn't it, George?' She almost felt relieved.

But George told her he was now tied up with too many other things. His diary was already booked up for the whole period she would be away.

Ella again felt almost relieved, but differently.

Ella was particularly attentive to George during the week before she left. Feeling in advance that she had to make up for going away and enjoying herself while George was stuck at home, she pampered him, cooking all his favourite meals, buying him a box of the Santo Domingo cigars his father used to smoke, a partiality he shared for reasons of nostalgia but seldom indulged because of the expense.

In a tender, rueful mood on the eve of her departure Ella made love

341

to George as she had never done before. She who had always waited for the first move to come from her husband chose now to seduce him, artfully and boldly, as if a different woman had taken Ella's place in bed beside her husband. As they lay with their arms and legs intertwined, how new and tender that husband word seemed to Ella, how tender and precious such possession, and he rose with her, full of unspoken remorse, flooded on the tide of desire that washed over them.

# 6

For no clear reason Ella could see, Claude changed his mind. He didn't meet her in Paris and drive down to Provence with her as arranged. At the last minute he asked her to take the train to Avignon, where he would pick her up at the station. He wanted to check out the house he had rented before she arrived, he told her — to make sure that it was *all right* and to look for something more suitable if it wasn't.

Claude had rented in Cornillac from the same owner two years before and had already been shown round the house, or rather the upper floor of the building in which the ageing, though still buxom, landlady with bold mischievous eyes lived downstairs with her partner. It was the first of the ruined houses in Cornillac to have been rebuilt by Madame's partner, fifteen or twenty years her junior, a taciturn, sinister Belgian with a chiselled, angular face and an extraordinary physique. Gosselding was a lean blond man in his mid-thirties of apparently unlimited energy and strength, who had shown up in Cornillac, no one knew from where, and moved in with Madame, only recently widowed, soon after the war ended.

Cornillac's population had drifted away after the two world wars that had bled the village of its youth, leaving the older generation with no one to pass their properties on to. On their deaths the houses remained uninhabited and gradually fell apart. In the post-war decade Gosselding single-handedly set about rebuilding many of the ruins in the tumbledown village perched on the top of a hill. As each house was rebuilt, the businesslike Madame Gosselding-Verseé rented it out to the visitors, most of them Belgian, who found their way to Haute-Provence once a year for a cheap holiday between May and October. In season the moribund village came back to life.

Whenever Claude dropped in he would find Madame with her bare arms encircling her smooth white bust at a desk by a window overlooking the village. There she sat making entries in her ledgers as if it were her intention to resurrect all the dead houses of Cornillac into the columns in her books, and perhaps some day – or so she seemed to be saying with a smiling sideways glance up at Claude – revive lapsed matriarchal rights that included having all her male lodgers for lovers on the first night they slept in her demesne.

The upper storey of the Gosselding house had its own entrance, accessed by an outside stairway, and a spacious terrace extending like a protruding jaw over a slope that fell away steeply to the Oule river valley with the church and the half-dozen or so houses that made up the village of Rémuzat. It was the terrace that caught Claude's heart, a semicircular platform suspended in mid-air, offering a view in the round of mountains on all sides, isolated and for the most part ruined farmhouses tucked away among straggling groves of olive and walnut trees, slopes of wild poppies and unkempt fields of lavender deepening from a pale mauve to a darker purple colour as the summer advanced.

This terrace was what Claude remembered from his previous visit at a time when he had not yet met Ella. The terrace filled his memory to the exclusion of everything else. Behind the terrace, in the narrow wings of the house that came with it, as it were, there was a kitchen, a bathroom and a living room, but what about the bedroom, or bedrooms – had there been one bedroom or two?

A week before Ella was due to arrive this question had broken and entered Claude's mind. He couldn't remember. The Gosseldings had no telephone. A letter there and a letter back with a reply to his question might take longer than a week, Claude reckoned. To be on the safe side, he called Ella in London and arranged to meet her at Avignon station instead. This would allow him to go down beforehand and check out the lie of the land, as Claude told himself in the odd, reassuringly non-committal phrase which came to mind in the wake of the bedroom question. When Claude thought of showing Ella around an apartment he had rented for them with only one bedroom, leaving her no choice, such a scene caused him to burn with embarrassment.

Seven years at the Jesuit-run *lycée*, in an atmosphere as tacitly homo-erotic as it was misogynist, had sown in Claude a seed of guilt prior to any sexual experience that might have occasioned it. He developed an instinct for the rapacity that came by stealth with certain people under certain circumstances and he learned to avoid them, at the price of leaving school and entering adult life with an extreme secrecy about sex that overlapped with feelings of self-loathing and disgust.

When Claude was eighteen his uncle took him to have dinner with a little friend of his, as he put it, who wanted to make Claude's acquaintance. His uncle's little friend turned out to be an able-bodied and very handsome woman in her mid-thirties, who lived alone, apparently, with only an aquarium of tropical fish for company, in a sparsely furnished, but still sumptuous apartment in one of the quieter side streets of the 16th arrondissement. She was an interior designer, Madeleine said coolly in reply to Claude's maladroit question as to what she did for a living, giving him a look that actually made him blush. Claude's uncle suffered an attack of such acute indigestion while they were still on the hors d'oeuvres that he got up from the dinner table, apologised to his hostess and left the two of them to it while he disappeared hurriedly into the night in search of a doctor.

Claude had none of his uncle's social ease, least of all in the company of the beautiful woman for whom his uncle's departure now made him alone responsible, and the candlelit dinner would have dragged on insufferably had Claude not drunk quite a few glasses of wine in rapid succession. In the resulting anaesthetised state of mind Claude could look at Madeleine without any misgivings and find her extremely desirable, which he knew was the whole purpose of the charade she had arranged with his uncle. Willingly he followed her into the bedroom, let her undress him and gave himself over to the pleasure of her caresses, but that was as far as it had gone. Despite all her efforts, Claude remained unable to perform.

Had Madeleine reported back? From the way his uncle looked askance at him, Claude reckoned she had. The shame of his failure was compounded by embarrassment that his uncle knew about it. It was on the rebound from this painful experience that Claude discarded de Marsay and matriculated at the Sorbonne under the name of Giffort.

Girls were unavoidable at the university. In lecture halls and seminar rooms, sitting in knee-to-knee proximity with them, he still tried to keep his distance, but the more reserved Giffort's behaviour in his dealings with them, the opposite of the riotous behaviour of his imagination, the keener they seemed to be to make friends. They carried him off to clubs

344

to listen to *le hot jazz* where they taught him to swing, pressing their bodies snugly up against his crotch when the house lights were brought down for the slow dances, until Claude, stiff with desire, ejaculated inside his corduroy trousers and had to beat a retreat to the lavatory to inspect the damage.

Was this messy business progress of a sort? Claude doubted it, but lacking the courage for a second attempt he had no means of finding out. Until further notice he was impotent. The burden of having to carry around with him this secret seemed almost worse to Claude than the secret itself.

With Ella the business of sex hadn't come up.

They maintained their friendship at a distance, and it was perhaps thanks to this distance that the friendship had lasted without the dread intervention of sex. Face-to-face meetings had been few. They had always taken place in the presence of others. She was a married woman and therefore off limits, a naked white hand that perfectly fitted the Jesuit glove of sexual hygiene with which Claude had been taught to approach women.

The one-bedroom apartment in Cornillac changed all that. The accommodation was *not* all right. The apartment had only the one bedroom, after all, just the one. The nervous but happy excitement with which Claude had been looking forward to Ella's arrival turned into anxiety from the moment he established the *lie of the land*. He wished he could wave a wand over the obstinate one-bedroom apartment and give it two bedrooms – ideally over his landlady with her white bust and knowing smile as well, causing *her* to disappear. Afraid of being found out in the dark secret places of his thoughts, he wished that Ella wasn't coming.

It was this Claude who drove to Avignon to meet the early-morning train from Paris. Even the bright green colour of his little 2CV, drawing attention to itself among the dowdy dust-streaked cars in the parking lot by the station, embarrassed Claude when he looked at it from the platform. Look at me! Here I am! Guess where I'm going! Joyfully, her face full of smile at this moment she had been looking forward to for months, Ella stepped down from the train into Claude's arms and felt the flame of her happiness snuffed out by the stiffness of his unwelcoming embrace.

345

Something's the matter with him, thought Ella at once with a contraction of her heart. It was as if the sun had gone out.

Wondering about the peremptory change in the travel arrangements at short notice – Claude's early departure from Paris for no good reason – the inconvenience to herself – Ella guessed that he had probably got involved with another, no doubt younger, woman. A frost settled on her soul. It felt like dying. She wished she hadn't come.

Unhappily they headed up the road into the mountains. The further they went, the worse things got. Dutifully, in a tight voice, Claude pointed out sights en route he thought might be of interest to Ella; but Ella had no eyes for sights, struggling to keep back her tears. I shan't give him the satisfaction of shedding any tears for *him*, she thought with growing anger, and felt the anger giving her new energy.

Claude pulled up under the plane tree outside the general store in Rémuzat.

'I must just pick up a few things,' he said as he got out of the car. 'Is there anything you want?'

But Ella didn't deign to answer.

Claude wandered in a daze around the store, trying to remember what he had been meaning to buy. Paraffin? Wouldn't they be needing paraffin for some reason? He unhappily bought cigarettes, a newspaper, vegetables, a shoulder of lamb and a loaf of bread.

When he came out of the store Ella was not in the car.

He wandered around the little square looking for her. There weren't many places she could have gone. He peered through the window of the little dressmaker's shop, but it was still closed. Then he went into the church to see if she might be there. Beside the church stood the house where the curé lived, but she obviously couldn't be in there. He walked back to the other side of the square into the bar beside the store. She wasn't in there either. The only other place she could be was the hotel next to the bar. Claude went in and asked the man at the reception if he had seen a woman in a straw hat and a blue dress.

'The lady already checked in, Monsieur.'

'Checked in?'

The man gave a shrug. 'I carried her suitcase upstairs for her.'

'What room is she in?'

'In Number 7, Monsieur.'

Claude slipped the man a few coins and went upstairs. Number

7 was the first room on the right. He tried the handle. The door was locked. Claude knocked. There was no reply.

'Ella? Please let me in. There's been a misunderstanding.'

He raised his voice and hammered on the door.

'I can explain. Please!'

The door behind him opened and a bald man with bloodshot eyes and a waxed moustache stood there in his underwear, cursing Claude for making such a noise at this unreasonable hour of the morning. In case it had slipped the young man's mind, he was in a hotel. People here had paid good money to sleep. He slammed the door angrily in Claude's face.

Claude asked the clerk for hotel stationery to write a letter he wished to leave for the guest in Number 7.

For an hour he sat at one of the tables under the plane tree outside the bar, smoking and drinking coffee and writing a long letter to Ella. He recapitulated what he had already told her about his Jesuit schooling in Paris, broached for the first time the fiasco with Madeleine, the habitual self-abuse he had fallen into as a result of his failure to have normal sexual relations with girls, the nightmare of the one-bedroom apartment, the awkwardness and embarrassment that had followed from it, the shame in which he found himself caught up and which Ella had misinterpreted as coldness. He suffered from the same condition as Octave, the unspeakable hero in Stendhal's *Armance*. I cannot love women. Octave had said it in the code required by his time, concealing more than he revealed. Believing Claude to be suffering from neurosis, his uncle had arranged for him to see a psychoanalyst, whom he had visited once a week during his first year at the Sorbonne, but the consultations hadn't helped. Claude discontinued the sessions, feeling more of a failure than he had before he started. He should have told her all these things before, Claude admitted to Ella, but like Octave he had lacked the courage.

In the middle of the day there was no one on duty at the hotel reception. Claude went behind the counter and slotted the letter to Ella into the pigeonhole for Number 7 himself.

In the afternoon he went for a walk up the valley, picked sprigs of lavender and a bouquet of wild flowers and carried them back to the house on top of the hill. No one stirred outside in the mid-afternoon heat; Madame and her families of lodgers, even Gosselding – *le monstre sacré*, as he was known locally – had retreated into the shade for their siesta. Claude put the flowers in wine bottles and distributed them round the living room, the sprigs of lavender in the bedroom on the pillow and between the sheets to scent the single sour-smelling bed where a first generation of Belgian holidaymakers had already slept.

He looked at the bed with revulsion.

When the heat of the day had passed he walked down to the hotel in Rémuzat. Without entering the hotel he could already see the white envelope still tucked into the pigeonhole under the hook, from which the key was missing.

He sat for a couple of hours drinking pastis at a table outside the bar. Now and then he got up and glanced through the hotel door. At about half past nine, as it began to grow dark, he retrieved the envelope, sketched a map on the back showing the way to the house in Cornillac, slipped his key into the envelope and replaced it in the pigeonhole.

With a dull heart, breathing in the uproariously scented dark, immune to all its excitement, he walked back up the hill and knocked on his landlady's door. Disturbed in the middle of his evening wash at the sink in the passage, Gosselding flung open the door, an act of hostility rather than a welcome, one arm raised as if ready to bar the entrance, bare-chested, drying his armpit with a flannel. Claude couldn't help noticing the tattoo there.

His guest would not be arriving until later that night, Claude explained, maybe not even until tomorrow morning. To cover both eventualities he had left his own key at the hotel in Rémuzat. Perhaps Madame would be so kind as to let him have a second key. Gosselding bawled into the dark passage behind him and vanished without another word. Madame herself appeared at the door a minute later, handed Claude the key and wished him goodnight.

But what goodnight was there to be had, tonight or ever again? How dismal his greeting of her at the station had been! What a small and mean reception to have given her! How he had let her down! He felt miserable. Already, at the first opportunity that had presented itself, Claude had ruined his life.

From the terrace he looked down at the village in the valley. He could see the garland of coloured lights outside the bar in Rémuzat. He could hear the laughter of the customers sitting out under the plane tree. Above the entrance to the hotel next door an old-fashioned coach-lamp fixed

348

high up on the wall shed a slanting, elongated shard of light, reminding Claude of a fallen leaf. How sad! What strange perceptions came with changed moods. Yesterday he had looked down at exactly the same scene and thought how snug it all looked down there. What a cheerful sight! How warm and welcoming that light in the dark!

If only one could be fixed and still, like a rock, a tree. If only one could switch off all thoughts and sensations and just be!

He went into the kitchen and opened a bottle of wine, drank a tumbler straight off and poured himself another.

'All because of the second bedroom that wasn't there,' he said aloud, the sad mood receding, becoming angry with himself.

When he went back onto the terrace the village lights had gone out. Even the lamp over the hotel entrance had been switched off. Without any lights there was no trace of Rémuzat in the valley below him. It was as if the village itself had been extinguished.

A wind rose and swept up out of the valley. Wine glass in hand, shirtsleeves billowing, he sat cross-legged on the parapet – a fortification almost, but against what, this massive bulwark that Gosselding had built with stones quarried from the ruins of Cornillac – and stared down grimly into the dark.

A light, a solitary light!

It waved at him when the wind rustled the branches of the plane tree in front of the hotel. A light was fluttering in one of the windows. It came and went with the wind. The light must be on in Ella's hotel room, Claude was sure, for by that light she was reading his letter. She could hear what he was saying. On a surge of exultation that lifted him to his feet he stood on the parapet, raised his glass and shouted defiantly into the night, 'To impotence!'

Claude drank off the glass, threw it over the parapet, heard it smash on the stones below, and in the same instant understood everything about Gosselding: his looks, his secrecy, his mysterious origins, the fortifications he built, the narrative of his life. Fear was what he and Gosselding had in common, sounding an unexpected chord of sympathy for this dungeon of a man he had disliked from the moment he met him. The measure of the stone bulwark the Belgian had erected was a measure of the defences demanded by his fear to keep the world at bay.

Afraid of discovery – of the things he might have done during the war being found out – if only having joined the SS, that warrior elite whose members had their blood group tattooed under the armpit — Gosselding had gone underground in the rubble of Cornillac, buried himself in a backwater of Haute-Provence. Gosselding's was one of the many wartime lies people were still living, the many secrets they carried around with them.

Now Claude understood the icon of the square-jawed helmeted soldier in a corner of Madame's parlour he had noticed while waiting for her to write out a receipt for the deposit he had been asked to pay on arrival, the significance of the motto, the text of the narrative of Gosselding's life printed in brazen copperplate Gothic lettering underneath the picture.

> *Der Gott, der Eisen wachsen ließ,*
> *Er wollte keine Knechte*

Who had hung that motto there, or allowed it to be hung, about the god who caused iron to grow and despised serfs? Whose parlour was it, after all? What light did this shed on Madame? Was this her mockery of him, her labourer, lover, footman, whatever service she wanted of Gosselding, a factotum who had become Madame's serf after all?

She was in collusion with him. She had power over him. He was at her mercy. But perhaps she was also at his, most of all in bed. What was the price of their mutual mercy, the nature of the punishments mutually exacted? Was it paid in love or hate or something between the two?

Claude at last gave up his vigil on the terrace and went back inside, stretched out on the bed without undressing and in seconds fell asleep.

The dawn chill came through the open door with the scent of a perfume that seemed familiar, something other than the fragrance of lavender strewn between the sheets, brushing his face and whispering, opening a crack of light in the stone-cold room where he lay shivering while a dog barked somewhere nearby, covering him up with a blanket until he grew warm again, and, groping half asleep in the half light, sparring with his dreams, entangled in cobwebs and trying to break out, Claude imagined that Ella was lying in bed with him, and when he woke up, broad daylight streaming in through the window, he found her there asleep beside him.

# 7

In the early mornings, when Claude was still asleep, she felt as if she lay on the surface of a pool, floating on the surface and looking down into the transparency of the pool that was herself. It brought back the salt taste of Biarritz, where she had snorkelled the previous summer in the shallows of a calm warm sea as smooth as glass. Floating in the watery warmth, half an hour at a stretch, she watched tiny fish scudding between wavy plants on the seabed, her mind empty of movement, so relaxed in this feeling of emptiness that she sometimes fell asleep.

On the first morning, her mind still busy with new impressions, she made an inventory of everything she saw in the little room. This room, this space around her, was an extension of herself.

'I am all these things I see.'

On her side of the bed stood a dresser with a swing mirror which she had turned to the wall. On his side there was a chair and a table. That was all the furniture. Objects hung on the wall or stood on a ledge that ran around the room below the ceiling. Old farming tools, bits of pottery, a horseshoe, dried sprigs of lavender. Then there were the wine bottles Claude had put on the ledge, in which he had arranged bouquets of wild flowers to welcome her. The ledge didn't seem to serve any other purpose. It was apparently just an accident of the building, a bump or a scar, something that might have taken a knock and not got straightened out during Gosselding's renovation of the house. The flowers had since withered, but wanting to keep everything as it was when she arrived, Ella had resisted her first impulse and chosen not to replace them.

Looking at each one in turn, she memorised all the objects in the room, then shut her eyes and recapitulated them.

*Liebes Zimmer*, dear room, she said softly to herself to imprint the memory of the moment better, Claude still asleep beside her, I shall want to come back here at some time in the future when I no longer can – for even if I could, all this will be over then, it will have gone, except in my mind. This room is the fulfilment of a wish in the absence of a wish, the place and state of mind of having nothing to long for, which is all there is to happiness.

She would wake early, eager to look at Claude and memorise all the details of his face. He was the last thought to occupy her mind when she went to sleep, the first when she woke. That was the answer her mother had given when Ella asked her how one knew if one was in love – first thought in the morning, last one at night.

Somehow privy to Ella's self-conversations – as if anticipating the fulfilment of a wish in the absence of a wish, intuitively understanding what that meant – Claude was already awake one morning and looking at Ella, memorising her face in turn. Were he not, had Claude continued day to day to sleep on beside a waking Ella, there would no longer have been that absence of a wish which Ella understood as happiness. Sometimes she would wish for it to be the other way round, wish to find him already awake for her, receiving her when she came out of sleep. Had he not been there to receive her, she would have wished he had – and then there would no longer have been that absence of a wish in which Ella's happiness lay.

With nothing to long for, this having been settled to their mutual satisfaction, they had no inclination to go anywhere, not even to leave the house. They went through the motions – they got ready, made as if to go out – but somehow they never got round to it. Conveniently, Claude lost the car keys. The bright green 2CV remained backed up a steep slope in the shade of a chestnut tree, gathering dust and bird droppings which gradually dulled its shine. Barefoot, they wandered back and forth between the bedroom, the bathroom, the kitchen, the terrace in the mornings and evenings, the cool recess of the tall sandstone cavern of a living room during the heat of the day. Clothes they had shed on arrival were not put on again, books with place markers were not reopened.

Claude whistled, Ella hummed – now and again she pursued a few notes that led to a bit of song. Between smokes and drinks – between one occasional nibble and another – meals as such were dispensed with. In the absence of a wish, in Ella's bare room of happiness they felt no particular need for anything except just to be with each other.

Claude seemed to have something stuck in his throat. He made throat-clearing noises and was unaware of it. Frequently he leaned over the parapet and spat. When he went to the toilet he would spit into it. He spat into the basin and let the water run, although there was nothing in the basin that Ella sitting alongside on the toilet cleaning her teeth could see.

Claude is getting rid of something, she thought. A phrase came to her mind that George often used in connection with Max. Max was getting this or that *out of his system*. All the anxieties about sex that Claude confessed to in his letter seemed to have dissolved that first morning they lay in bed together. *Pouf!* Vanished in a shimmer of bliss. He was so happy when he found her beside him that he had forgotten to think about being anxious. She had praised the rampant size and splendour, above all the stamina of his cock. Claude realised he was not like Octave after all. He must make up for lost time. Now he could love women he would not stop molesting her, Claude promised Ella, kissing her all over in ardent gratitude, particularly her breasts, praising them in turn for their size and splendour but above all for the fragrance of her nipples, surprising him with a sense of their vulnerability, the painful tenderness of his response when he chafed them between his lips.

Having nothing to long for – in the aftermath of lovemaking Ella called it *having arrived*. What does that mean, asked Claude, nibbling the lobes of her ears, having arrived?

It meant you didn't search any more, you had arrived where you fitted – the foot in the slipper, unalterable – she extemporised on the flow of associations that had come to her with Claude's descent from the tree – irreversible, the lock snicking shut, the bolt flush with the socket, the close-fitting snickety sound of fate – where you were always bound to be. With this other you felt complete. Not feeling yourself complete was what one experienced as longing. Arriving where she fitted, Ella told him, had taken her all her life.

'So is it just a matter of chance?'

When she talked of having arrived at such completeness Claude became aware of a distance between them that worried him: Ella's difference from him – he had not arrived at Ella with the degree of surety that she had arrived at him – an awareness that shivered togetherness. Momentarily they ceased to be in the same room. Momentarily it seemed he had fallen out of it. The bare room of happiness he lived in with Ella, one side of that room opened onto an abyss.

If he had shared her confidence of having arrived, if he had partaken in equal measure in that sense of arrival she claimed for herself, then Claude would not have felt this difference from Ella. But such definiteness of knowledge of arrival he did not share. Lacking her commitment, he felt shut out from Ella's certainty.

Was there a higher degree, a different quality of love, which Ella knew about but he didn't?

353

Jesuitical self-doubt tugged at his heart.

No sooner had one uncertainty been scotched than another took its place.

'I think I understand what you mean by having arrived,' Claude said to Ella, 'but I don't know if I've arrived there too, and that troubles me. Because maybe I'm not ready yet to commit to the finality of arrival. Maybe I'm not able to.'

This honesty cost him a big effort. He knew he was close to the abyss, had taken his life in his hands. How would she react?

She lit a cigarette and looked at him – a disengaged look, as if moving away from him the better to size him up.

'You're only twenty-one,' she reassured him. 'Your life is still used to being by itself, just there for you, a one-room apartment for your sole convenience – no brother or sister, no father, no mother – not an establishment to speak of, no maintenance of anyone but yourself. It may take time to make room for someone else and you may not find it easy. One is familiar with one's solitude, gets into the habit of oneself – for a long time I used to live like that too.'

She passed him the cigarette.

'Give yourself time. I've had to wait until I was over thirty.'

Made aware as he had not been aware before of their difference in age, how much younger he was, how much he still had to learn, Claude felt relieved that he might yet be capable of love after all.

'Is that what it is? Just a question of time? But why me all of a sudden?'

'When you jumped down from the tree in the Bois I was over-whelmed by all the reminders of my mother – your bright eyes and your complexion, the uptilt of your nose, your litheness, the spring of your movements – I was wide open to them and they came straight into me.'

'But doesn't that mean it's your mother you recognise, not me? Don't I owe my presence to another presence you see in me?'

'Perhaps you do. Perhaps this is how it has to happen. Familiarity can trip you up, you see, and you fall in love. Perhaps without that trigger of familiarity it doesn't happen. But that's only the beginning – the engagement of two bodies. But then we slough off that first skin, making way for deeper, more lasting forms of recognition. The marriage takes place between minds.'

She could make such statements with a solemnity that in anyone else he would have found ludicrous.

What proof did she have? How did Ella know about the sloughing-off of a first skin? What skin? Where did it come from? Where did it go?

Claude thought that if duplication of some foregone familiarity was the nature of love it was just a matter of chance whether you would ever experience love or not. It wasn't something you could go and seek. It came to you. Love either happened to you or it did not.

'One is left with no choice in the matter,' he objected. 'One might as well just sit and wait.'

Perhaps it was an illusion that your goings and your doings took place on your initiative. Perhaps you only appeared to initiate, whereas in reality all your so-called initiatives were happenings to you, only apparently performed by you, in reality just taking place through you, or not even that: they merely involved you. Perhaps it was an illusion that you were you, not the subject of your own going and doing but the object of someone else's or at least of a collaboration with someone else.

'Perhaps you analyse things too much; you can just live them,' she told him, kissing Claude to put an end to these obsessive reflections before slyly getting in the last word: 'But then maybe you are not you, after all, not the person you believed yourself to be.'

Absorbed with taking Ella into himself and thus forgetting himself, liberated from the solitary confinement of his doubts by being given access to another being, happier than he could remember ever having been, Claude experienced the exuberance of a second childhood, or perhaps just the childhood he felt he had always missed. He played pranks on her, standing in the bathroom and peeing – he calculated it would sound like that to Ella – a stream that didn't come to an end, until curiosity drove her in to take a look and she found him emptying a watering can into the lavatory. On the terrace he entertained her with imitations, Gosselding's lunging stride, Madame's waddle, the curé's splayed-leg gait as he walked with folded hands across the village square. He could do their voices too, cameos that captured the speaker's characteristics: the square-jawed neck-jerking bark of Gosselding, straining like a dog on a leash; the curé's thin trickle with just a trace of a Belgian accent still audible half a century after being posted south from Liège as a consumptive young priest given not more than a year to live; the gesticulations that accompanied the slow rumblings of old farmers in their characteristic *accent du midi*; and people Ella had never met but recognised from Claude's previous descriptions, including Cornelius Marsden-Smith, Claude's curiosity-shop godfather besieged by the fog-bound dampness of Camden, his head wrapped in a towel when recounting his day to his mother upstairs in nasal tones punctuated by explosions of sneezing.

She noticed that Claude often steered the talk round to one of his favourite discussions, first impressions. What had they made of each other on the first occasion they met, when Claude burst out of the door at the end of the mezzanine in the de Marsay *palais*? But Ella seemed to have no clear recollection of Claude on that occasion. Her otherwise precise attention to detail was missing — the first five minutes of Claude's existence in Ella's life appeared to have gone unrecorded. For Ella, Claude began with his descent from the tree in the Bois de Boulogne.

'So but for that *tree*,' said Claude, revelling in imagining all the things that would not have happened but for the tree. He still found it curious, though — surely his appearance from the secret door had been more dramatic, more memorable? He kept on returning to this scene until Ella told him what had happened before he burst out of that door, starting with the row she had had with George in London — how this had led to the trip to Paris with Sasha and his wife — her deepening depression alone in the big house — trying to gas herself — her state of mind at the time explaining why Claude's emergence from the door in the wall had not left any lasting impression. It was only later she realised a significant difference between the appearance of Claude in her life and the appearance of George — Claude emerging from the hidden staircase and coming towards her, George going away from her on his way up the stairs at the Hampstead house where she had first set eyes on him.

Ella's admission of her attempted suicide shocked Claude; he would never have believed of the Ella whom he had since come to know that it was in her nature to be at such a low ebb that she no longer wanted to live. Given the evidence at the time, however — the smell of gas in the house — Ella's flustered appearance — her extreme paleness, the first thing about her that had struck him — how had he failed to guess what had been going on? All of this had to be *shored up*, according to Claude, this still-tentative edifice which was the history of their beginning. He wanted to go over it again and again, looking at it from all angles. *But for the tree* came to be reinforced by *But for the smell of gas* in an obsessive list of things identified by Claude as dead-end streets that would have failed to lead to his meeting Ella. A private mythology of events that had taken place grew out of a parallel universe in which they had not happened. In Claude's mind the events that had not happened continued to exist as an alternative reality that had only narrowly been averted. With the help of such constructions, which cast fleeting shadows of terror across his mind, Claude sought to give expression to his amazement at the extreme improbability of a meeting between him and Ella ever having come about. The improbability of its coming about inspired in Claude a particular joy, shared by Ella, no less susceptible to the same amazement – they had taken on the universe and beaten the odds – a first step in his idealisation of their relationship, the marriage taking place between minds as Ella had predicted.

Ella in turn wanted to know from Claude what first impression she had made on him.

'You looked to me as if you were in need of help,' began Claude, wondering where he was heading.

Unsatisfied with this answer, Ella gave him prompts. Had she struck him as slim? Did he think the outfit with horizontal stripes she was wearing had suited her, or did it make her look a bit ... dumpy? Would vertical stripes have been more flattering to her figure?

Definitely not dumpy, Claude reassured her, which was truthful even if he couldn't remember what Ella had been wearing at the time. As for slim, she had too much of a woman's body – a waist that you thought of as narrow but in terms of the hips around it and breasts above it – both of these features being, to Claude's mind, generous helpings, not stinted – the proportions were what counted, and Ella's were classic.

Ella pondered this.

'Don't you prefer the figures of those petite French women? Be honest; I won't mind.'

'But I'm unable to love those petite French women, remember? I tried and didn't succeed. It's you I'm able to love, Ella.'

There – he had said it, surprising himself, and with a sense of liberation he had never experienced until now, Claude realised that he had finally left Octave behind him for ever.

Two weeks later, a couple of days before they were due to leave the house and the car keys would become indispensable, Ella conducted an armchair search for them while Claude ran around ransacking the apartment – and without even having to get up from the chair she found them in a flower pot on the terrace. Don't run around if you want to find something, she told Claude, *think*.

The 2CV sputtered, cleared its throat a few times and went bouncing down the steep cobbled streets to Rémuzat. Claude pointed out to Ella the table at which he had sat while writing his letter to her. She told him of the great happiness she had felt when she crept downstairs and found the letter in her pigeonhole. She had felt cared for. In that anonymous place she had felt so grateful for the presence of the envelope with her name on it in Claude's writing, giving her a belonging, that she forgave him even before she opened it. Tears came to her eyes. Both of them were so moved by what they had been through – the narrow escape from another dead-end street – that Claude stopped the car so that they could seek comfort in each other's arms.

'But for that letter,' said Claude, and she laughed.

He was amazed at the speed with which Ella could move out of one mood into another.

They drove up the valley past the lavender field they could see from their bedroom window, reached the top of the pass where the road petered out into a grassy track and lurched down into the next valley. Negotiating the hollows and bumps, one side of the little car seemed to go up while the other went down, as if it was being stretched in opposite directions. Claude selected this elasticity of the 2CV, its suspension, for particular praise. Another was its ground clearance. But for the ground clearance, he told Ella, they wouldn't have been able to get over the col, and he stopped the car for Ella to get out while he drove over a particularly bumpy bit so that she could see for herself the remark-able ground clearance of the 2CV. Ella made herself comfortable on a patch of springy heather for the demonstration and commended the car's performance.

'My goodness,' she declared.

'It's quite something, isn't it?' he called to her, grinning through the window. 'Really, I mean, but for the ground clearance—'

She smirked, tried to hide it, but was unable to keep a straight face and started laughing.

Claude was miffed, genuinely, she saw, before he pretended to be.

'Oh, Claude,' said Ella, 'come over here.'

He followed her along the ridge of the col to a rocky outcrop where Ella stood with her arms outstretched, turning in a circle between the two valleys.

'Look! I can see our house.'

In a hollow not visible until one got to the outcrop stood a little stone chapel, in good repair and apparently still in use judging by the fresh flowers in the alcoves on either side of the door. She pressed down on the old brass handle and pushed the door open. Claude followed her in.

The chapel was hardly bigger than the bathroom in their apartment down in Cornillac. Not more than half a dozen people could have stood in there at one time. It had no seats, only an altar rail with a cushion in front of it for people to kneel on when they received the sacrament. Two steps led up to a stone jutting out of the wall to serve as a lectern. On an impulse Claude took possession of this lectern and extemporised an address.

They were gathered here, he said in the perforated voice of the old Belgian curé, which occasionally crumbled, to celebrate the joining of two people in holy matrimony, despite the many obstacles that had been put in their path. But for the sufficient ground clearance of the wedding car with its remarkable suspension – but for a timely letter in the pigeonhole of Room 7 of the hotel in Rémuzat – but for a tree in the Bois de Boulogne and the smell of leaking gas in a Paris house – but for that singular possibility emerging from an infinitude of other possibilities and breaking surface to become the reality of these two people's lives, they would not be in this place for this purpose today.

Do you, Ella Maria, he said, with a sign to her to kneel at the altar rail, take this man, Claude William, for all his faults, his past omissions and in ignorance of the many more you yet have to discover, cognisant of all this, do you nonetheless take him for your wedded husband? I do, she said. And do you, Claude William, take this woman, Ella Maria, et cetera et cetera, for your wedded wife? Claude stepped down and took his place beside her on the altar rail. I do, he said in his own voice, looking up at the lectern. Holding her right hand with his left, he stood again on the other side of the altar rail, and with his other hand, the hand of the curé, which he laid on top of their joined hands, he made them man and wife, giving them his blessing. Claude kissed the bride, offered her his arm and escorted her out into the sunlight.

Twenty-four hours later they arrived in Paris. By the evening of the same day Ella was back home in St John's Wood.

# 8

In a vague sort of way George and Ella – Ella perhaps more than George – had been on the lookout for a new house for the past year, but it was only with Ella's pregnancy that the search began in earnest.

With three children growing up fast and no doubt clamouring to have rooms of their own sooner rather than later, the house in St John's Wood that had served them so well for the last ten years had become too small. Moving house – leapfrogging to a better address – came naturally to the English, Ella had learned, but it remained a distasteful notion to her. A better address was poor compensation for uprooting one's family and discarding one's home. To do so seemed disloyal. But they needed a place with five or six bedrooms, thought George; at least that, thought Ella, and ideally it would be somewhere out of London – not too far, since George had to commute and needed quick access to the airport, but in the country surroundings that Ella, with clear memories of her own happy childhood in Herischdorf, considered indispensable for her children's upbringing.

That George had backed down over the issue of sending Max to Park House, that he had not felt unduly troubled about Ella in a house with Sasha in Paris or with Claude in Provence, had partly to do with his diffident temperament, partly with his his assessment of Ella. She showed her affections freely and took what life had to offer. But her loyalty was absolute. It was beyond doubt.

However, observing how ingeniously Ella could talk herself out of going to a dinner party she didn't want to attend, or just the devious strategies she could come up with in an argument, enabling her to wriggle out of admitting defeat, George found traces of cunning in his wife. But this was not at all the same thing as the outright lies that he had become accustomed to fabricating when covering up the deceptions that now took up quite a lot of George's life. Ella might be cunning, but he had no evidence she was dishonest.

Self-discipline, a dominant will, an absolute loyalty and a refusal to compromise, coupled with the kind of instinctive deviousness and presence of mind Ella showed on occasion, capable, last but not least, of accommodating apparently conflicting interests – in George's opinion this all added up to a pretty fair description of what made for a born spy.

When Ella told him she was pregnant she also said, 'and I don't know if it's your child or his'.

Having gone back over the dates, she concluded that she could either have conceived on that last night she was together with George in London or at the beginning of the holiday she had spent with Claude in Provence. She hadn't yet spoken to Claude, she said, who was in the middle of exams, but she would be doing so now that she had told George.

George took the news in his stride, apparently unperturbed. He told her that was her affair, and for a moment it wasn't clear to Ella what 'her affair' referred to. But the child could only have one father, he went on, and as long as Ella and the child remained part of the Morris family, he, George, would 'to all intents and purposes' be that father.

Ella had calculated that George would not disown a child that might not be his, but she was grateful for and rather surprised by the unexpected show of firmness with which he accepted responsibility for the child, or pre-empted Claude, denying him the chance of claiming responsibility for it – whichever. It clarified the issue.

'That was her affair' referred to Ella's part in it, which was conceiving and giving birth to the child for which he, George, accepted the responsibility at the price of ousting Claude. Even if there was something about the matter-of-fact way George had responded to the news of her pregnancy which disappointed Ella, something dismissive and joyless in those words 'that was her affair', handing her pregnancy back to her as if he didn't know what to do with it, Ella now knew at least what she had to do, which was to find a bigger house for the family as soon as possible.

So the house in St John's Wood was put on the market. Within six weeks they were made an offer they accepted, just as Ella found and put in an offer for a house on the river in Richmond, exactly the sort of house she had imagined, with a big garden and lots of cupboard space. There were good schools nearby, green surroundings that made it like living in the country even if wasn't the country, and the commute into central London would be manageable for George. The house also had no less than seven bedrooms, or at least rooms that Ella on her first inspection of the premises had decided could serve as such. George thought the house too large and expensive to heat. What did she want with all those surplus bedrooms?

Ella threw herself into the house-moving project with enthusiasm. She needs to have goals, thought George, who was abroad for most of the summer. She packed off the children to Yorkshire for the remainder of the holidays and in the few weeks before they went back to school that autumn organised the move more or less single-handedly, with just a little help from Giselle. For Ella it was a matter of course that Giselle would be moving with them. The children had become attached to her; she was part of the family, so much a part of it that George had overlooked her, but he raised no objections. Mentally, he ticked off one of the surplus bedrooms for occupancy by Giselle.

Ella stood alone outside the empty house in St John's Wood and looked at it for the last time through the gate. She couldn't help shedding a few tears.

'Goodbye, house. Thank you for being a good home to us. I hope your new owners will look after you.'

Claude crept into London without being seen, quietly beginning the research for his DPhil in the Reading Room of the British Museum. Even Ella didn't learn of his arrival until he was already established in digs near the museum in a house owned by a friend of his uncle.

Ella was hurt. 'You behave as if you were here on a secret mission. Why didn't you tell me?'

'Because I knew you were very busy with lots of other things. I knew you would want to arrange my move as well as your own, and so I thought it better to make my own arrangements. Besides, I didn't know what the position was.'

'Position?'

'All you said in your letter was that you didn't know for sure who the father was, but that George didn't mind as he recognised the child as his and would officially be the father in any case. Well, I suppose one of us has to be. Officially you're his wife. So it may be better for him to be officially the father. But where does that leave me, the unofficial father? Leave *us* – having this sort of hateful conversation about official and unofficial fathers.'

Ella put his arms around him and kissed him.

'Does it make any difference for you and me? What other way can we stay together? With three children. Where would we go? How could we afford to live? Why should things have to be any different from the way they've been for the last two years? You and George get on so well. Why should that change? Because of the child? We're free of those conventions, aren't we? We're free individuals. We can live as *we* see fit, not to suit other people and their ideas of what's fit. It might be different if we knew for certain whose child it is. Under the circumstances perhaps it's better we don't. But if you want to go ...'

'No, no.'

It was true she didn't know for certain, but there was a clue to the fatherhood of the child, an instinctive affinity, a magnetic attraction, which Ella couldn't overlook. Claude was as drawn to her pregnant body as George seemed repelled by it. Not once since she returned from Provence had he wanted to sleep with his wife. All that swelling and stretching, he said, put him off, but Ella remembered he hadn't been put off the last time she was pregnant with the twins. Even more restless at night than she usually was, wanting to get up and do things likely to disturb George's sleep, Ella suggested she move into a separate room.

'I think it might be better for both of us,' she said to George, and George concurred. There's another bedroom accounted for, he thought, keeping that thought to himself.

For Claude, by contrast, the swellings and stretchings of Ella's body worked as an aphrodisiac, something he would ideally have ingested and swallowed whole. I am your boa constrictor, he said, sucking at her with tooth and tongue, vacuum-cleaning her body all over. He couldn't keep his hands from stroking and squeezing her. During the three hours Ella spent in his room he made love to her three times, taking her from behind on the sofa and *topping her up*, he said, sex with an almost violent tenderness, expressed in a direct language that both excited and estranged Ella. She could guess what Claude felt when he spoke of *topping her up*, the phrase spilling over into other words he poured over her when making love, *fecund*, *fructify* and *fuck*, delivered in a slurred speech that Ella felt was alien to Claude even as she assented to the necessity of the rituals of lovemaking and possession that apparently had a part to play here. What George had laid claim to with the declaration of his fatherhood, an agreement between them covering what he would give and what he expected the mother to give in return while treating the woman as if she wasn't there, Claude reinforced with the urgency of his

363

desire, his cock bringing it home to her, his hands laying claim physically to the mother's body.

Claude didn't visit the house in Richmond until Christmas. Five and then six months pregnant, Ella made the journey to Claude's room in Bloomsbury once a week, indulging his new preference for doing it on the sofa, receiving his adoration in the poems he dashed off with his hands on her body and the words he made up for her in his desire, sucking her swollen nipples and bouncing her breasts enthusiastically, pushing his penis into her up to the hilt, pounding with a slap-slapping sound the buttocks fleshed out over the back of the sofa. In the late after-noon or early evening she took the train back to Richmond, packed with commuters, her body still glowing in the aftermath of Claude's desire.

'We thought you were avoiding us for some reason,' George said to Claude when he arrived at last to spend the Christmas holiday with the family, 'didn't we, dear?' he said, turning to Ella for confirmation.

'No, of course we didn't. We thought no such thing. Don't pay any attention, Claude.'

After one or two of these sallies, indulging his desire to do mischief, perhaps to get at Ella by making a few double-edged remarks to Claude, George settled down. The enjoyment he found in Claude's company, despite his intentions to the contrary, was now reinforced by the pecu-liar pleasure George took in the awareness of being in collusion with Claude, of their being fellow conspirators.

'Meet Claude,' George would say with that unsettling smile confined to the left half of his face, leaving the other half expressionless, when he introduced Claude to the guests who came to the house-warming party they gave in the new year, 'an old and intimate family friend.'

In early February Ella received a call from Hanna, telling her that Sasha had died over Christmas. 'He didn't die for three days and all the time he was asking for you, but I couldn't get hold of you,' Hanna wailed down the phone. 'Where have you *been* all this time?'

Ella had neglected to send the Borowskis a card with their change of address; neglected, not forgotten. She had made the same clean break with Sasha in Paris she had made with Ferdinand, the friend of her schooldays in Schlawe, the same irrevocable break she made with all people who came too close to her inmost self.

On a cold February morning she drove Hanna in the Cadillac to the cemetery in Golders Green where Sasha had wanted his ashes to be interred on a plot of land set aside for the anonymous dead, where there would be no memorial except for a sign with the words MEMENTO MORTUORUM.

Hanna looked at the nameless memorial and made an odd remark: 'It's just more of the same kind as far as the Borowski family's concerned.'

Ella supposed Hanna was referring to the fact that almost all Sasha's family had been murdered in concentration camps.

Apart from Hanna and Ella and the man carrying the urn with the ashes, no mourners attended the ceremony, for there was no one to come back out of Sasha's past. The life of a now-extinct Jewish family that had scraped by in Galicia at the time of the Austro-Hungarian empire, the unimaginable, unrecorded sufferings Sasha had endured in Stalin's Great Purge and shared with only a few friends like Ella, the years of post-war exile and the emptiness of the life of a man who had survived all his murdered relatives – these were the ghosts of Sasha that came to Ella's mind as she watched his remains being laid to rest in the anonymous grave, ghosts that had long been homeless even during his lifetime.

At the end of the month she gave birth to her fourth child, a boy whom she named Alex after Sasha. It was an easy birth. The child slipped out as if assured by the great wave of love on which he came into the world.

This fullness of joy, touching her in all parts, was the difference between the birth of Alex and of the three children before him, and Ella understood why. This joy had infused her from the moment of conception, as if her body had realised it even before she knew she was pregnant. She loved the child as she loved his father, as she had not loved the other three children by the other father she had loved not necessarily less, she told herself, perhaps more with her head than her heart, but this thought she buried in herself.

In the months after the birth George noted a sort of placidity about Ella he had not seen before. He wondered if it was the child or the proximity of Claude, who came out to visit two or three times a month, or even if it marked a change of life – Ella on the threshold of the early middle period of life, becoming generally more settled, less turbulent, more predictable in her moods, as by degrees she was ceasing to be the headstrong young woman she had been. There remained an inscrutable Ella, about whom he could only guess.

She had made provision, it did not escape George, doing a mental tally of all the rooms in the house, beginning with Giselle's in the base-ment and ending with Max's crow's nest in the attic. Perhaps it was just a matter of time before Claude stayed in Richmond for a longer visit – a week, a month – until at the end of the summer he had become a full-time resident and given up his digs in town. Perhaps it was just Ella's need to look after the baby without disturbing George at night, as a result of which they had got into the habit of sleeping in separate rooms – a habit that then lingered on for no particular reason, as habits did, George noted, even after the baby's cot was moved to the little dressing room adjacent to Ella's, and husband and wife could have moved back into a room together. Whatever, within a year of the move to Richmond all that surplus space George had criticised when Ella bought what he considered much too large a house had been mopped up. There were now full-time occupants of all seven bedrooms in their heavily mortgaged new house.

# 9

On his way back from school Max found a dead cat on the rubbish dump behind the garage. COACH & BODY WORK DONE TO ORDER, NO CHEQUES, read the sign on the garage, but no one was there. He climbed in through a broken window and explored the place. The building seemed to have been empty for a long time, but the lavatory in the washroom still flushed when he tried pulling the chain. It was an ideal hideout for a gang. Max went round the back, where he discovered the dump, full of rusting machinery and piles of ripped tyres. And the dead cat. The head of the cat had been crushed. Its tail was missing. It had begun to rot. Then the cold weather came and refrigerated the cat, including the rot. Max covered it with a tin box so that no one else found it. Every day he came to look at it on the way home from school. When the cold weather passed the cat began to rot again. And to smell. With interest Max watched the maggots crawling inside the cat's body.

'Why d'you always go round by the lane?'

'Because.'

'Can we come too?'

'No. You go down to the end of the road and I'll meet you there.'

Just because he was in charge of Philip and Felicity on the way to school and back didn't mean he had to share the cat with them. It would frighten them, anyway. They were too little.

Philip tried to blackmail him. 'We're not allowed to walk down Fenbury Lane. Mrs Blondin said so. If you don't let us come too, I'll tell her.'

'No, you won't.'

Max twisted his ear and Philip cried.

In London Max used to walk alone down their quiet street to the main road and proudly catch a bus to his school off the Marylebone Road. He was growing up. His brother and sister had still gone to Maureen's crèche down the street, the babies' place, Max called it. But after moving to Richmond they all went to the same school, more or less, since the schools were in two buildings side by side, Kennington Hall for boys and Kennington House for girls. They walked there and back through the park. Max was the eldest. His mother put him in charge of the twins.

He didn't think much of them. Philip was a wet, Felicity a cry-baby and a sneak. But there was no help for it. Max didn't think much of the new house, didn't think much of anything he had so far seen of Richmond. He missed London. Above all, he missed the hour of freedom that was his once a day on the journey to school. Most days it was the same conductor on the bus, a Jamaican called Jim. Max liked the way Jim talked, his accent, his jokes, his hair, the funny little jingles he sang. He liked the hard smell of the three coppers he put into Jim's hand, and he liked the way when Jim opened his hand and stretched out his palm it was a different colour from the rest of his skin. It was like an animal coming out of hiding.

When they first came to see the new house, Max immediately bagged the rooms at the top. There were two, and Max used them both, one of them to sleep in, the other for the deployment of his soldiers, over a hundred of them, in wars on terrain that changed according to the way he arranged the folds in the rug. He could make a flat space for pitched battles requiring cavalry and artillery, like Waterloo, dunes for desert tank warfare against Rommel in Africa and canyons for commando action in mountainous country. But then Mrs Johnson arrived and Max had to move all his soldiers out so that she could move in.

'Mrs Johnson has come to help in the house,' his father announced the day she arrived. She set to work right away in a blue tunic with a white pinafore and a starched white napkin folded back over her head. She did the washing-up, cooked their meals and gave them their baths while their mother was away. She was a big fat woman with curly grey hair. She had spent the war working as a nurse and then as a matron in a school. She was a no-nonsense person with an unexpected melodramatic side, evident in the way she sometimes put her hand to her heart and rolled her eyes.

'I was one of the first into Bergen-Belsen in forty-five. Lord!' said Mrs Johnson with another of her theatrical gestures, pulling down one side of her mouth. It made her look funny.

Belsen was a concentration camp. Max knew Belsen. He knew the names of the concentration camps because his mother had told him all about them and what they were for, but she hadn't been in one like Mrs Johnson.

'What was it like?' Max asked with interest.

'It was terrible,' said Mrs Johnson. But it wasn't a suitable subject for children, she said, so she wouldn't tell him more.

Concentration camps belonged to the Rude Things reserved for adults, like the magazines his father hid inside his cupboard.

There had been a bomb site with an old Nissen hut in one of the streets behind Abbey Road, where Bernie and his gang used to meet. Bernie was a common boy like all the others except Max, and Max had been told by his father not to play with common boys. Bernie was twelve, quite a lot older than Max, and he taught him things like how to smoke, spit to hit a target, and swear in very rude language. Bernie had swagger. He knew about life. Common boys were more interesting than the official friends his own age he could bring back home to play soldiers with.

Once, Bernie had brought a girl to the hut, slapped her a few times and told her to lift her skirt and show them her sights, and then he took out his willy and tried to stick it into her, but it wouldn't go in and the girl ran away. Bernie said Max could join the gang once he was nine. He would brand Max with a hot wire on his arm and then Max would be a member, like all the others.

'This ain't for kids. We're perfeshunnels,' Bernie told him, tapping the side of his nose.

Max was impressed. He didn't understand what perfeshunnels were and had to ask his father. But before Bernie could burn the mark on his arm, the Morris family moved out of London to the new house in Richmond. His mother wanted the children to be surrounded by nature, to go for walks and explore the country, but Max wasn't interested in nature and didn't want to explore the country; he wanted to explore the city with the burn mark on his arm proving he was a member of Bernie's gang. Instead, he was put in charge of the twins, the babies, on the daily walk through the park to school.

Soon there would be a third baby in the house.

While his mother was away in hospital to have the baby, his father took time off from the office and stayed at home. Every evening, after Mrs Johnson had given them their baths, they all put on their dressing gowns and went to his father's study where he read to them. The new study was bigger than the old one. It didn't have a cupboard like the study in the old house, but it had a drinks cabinet, a fireplace and big comfy chairs you could swivel, only George had told them not to.

'Don't swivel, Max. You'll wear the bearings out and break the chair.'

Sometimes they sat with their father on the sofa and looked at old photo albums of the family. Max asked why there weren't any pictures of his mother as a child. Because his mother was a refugee, said George, and refugees couldn't carry photo albums with them; all they could bring were a few things to keep them warm and something to eat.

'What did they have to eat?' asked Philip.

'Meat and potatoes, I expect.'

'*Potatoes*?'

'Couldn't they go back and fetch the photo albums later?' Felicity asked.

'No.'

'Why not?'

George explained to them it was because of the war. The war was over now, but in a way it wasn't over, either. What they had now was something called a cold war.

Philip frowned. 'How can the war be over and not over at the same time?'

Patiently George tried to explain another way, but Philip still went on frowning. Inwardly Max smirked. He knew how persistent his brother could be. He knew how Philip's frowning exasperated his father, because it reminded him of his younger sister, Tessa, who Max knew his father had always disliked

Sometimes when his father was reading a babyish story like *The Water Babies* to the two younger children Max sat on the floor and went through the old Morris family photo albums by himself. There were pictures of his father as a boy, playing cricket against a wicket chalked on the wall surrounding the school quadrangle. Another picture showed boys in white shorts setting off on a run down the street outside the school. Opposite the school stood a gasworks. Tall chimneys were visible in the distance.

'Is that Park House?' he asked his father.

'Yes, it is,' George said.

'Where is it?'

'On the edge of Putney Heath. Those are the chimneys of Battersea Power Station you can see in the distance. It had still been built only recently when I went to Park House. The school was almost in the country in those days.'

'So it's in London now. Can we go and see it?'

George tipped his glasses and looked down over them at Max in surprise.

'We'll see,' he said.

After an absence of a week his mother came home with the new baby wrapped up in a pink blanket. The three children gathered round to inspect their new brother.

'What tiny fingernails he's got!' said Felicity and asked if she could hold him. Philip wanted to know what his name was and how much he weighed and went away and wrote this information down in his diary.

'Alex, his name is Alex, after the other Alex, Sasha,' their mother said, and they knew who the other Alex was because she had told them all about him when Sasha died just a few weeks ago. Sasha had almost been in Belsen too, his mother had told them, and Max thought what a coincidence it would have been if he had run into Mrs Johnson there. Max noticed the look that passed between his mother and father. He could tell that something between them had changed, but he couldn't say what. He wondered if it had something to do with the other Alex.

In the new house his mother had moved into her own room, with a cot for the baby beside her bed, so as not to disturb their father. The door of the room was always left ajar so that any of the children could come in whenever they wanted to. Max always managed to drop in whenever his mother was feeding the baby. He enjoyed watching the baby's lips tugging at the nipple on the plump white breast that reminded him of the turkey his father had carved at Christmas. His mother didn't mind him watching, but he knew his father wouldn't have approved.

His mother asked him what he had been doing while she was away in hospital. Max told her about the battles his soldiers had fought and won, but from her questions he could tell his mother wasn't as interested in his battles as he was, so he told her instead about the different routes they walked through the park to school every day, he and his brother and sister, knowing that this was the kind of thing she wanted to hear. This was why his mother had brought them to live here, in *natural surroundings*.

'Can I too?' he asked at last.

His mother looked up at him and smiled.

'Of course you can, Max,' she said, because she always knew without asking what he was thinking. Max knelt beside the chair on which she was sitting and she gave him her other breast, slipping the moist nipple into his mouth, cupping his head with her hand.

'Well? What does it taste like?'

'A bit like condensed milk.'

At weekends when the weather was fine, he took himself off for walks in the park, and saw with a sense of guilt how happy this made his mother. On fine weekends a skiffle group showed up regularly to play at the war memorial, tonking away on their banjos and guitars and tapping their pointed shoes in time with the music. The skiffle group was why he went to the park.

Pointed shoes were on display in a shop window in Richmond.

'Winkle-pickers is what they're called,' said the shop assistant when Max went in to enquire about the shoes he coveted, 'but I'm afraid we don't stock 'em in your size, young man.'

Max wandered down the high street, lingering outside the open door of the public bar of the Royal Oak, his nostrils twitching when he caught a whiff of the thick fug of smoke and farts and stale beer that came blasting out of the pub entrance, past the booky, closed on Sundays, the pavement still littered with scraps of paper from the day before, and on to the Gaumont, where a matinee would be showing at twelve o'clock. He stopped for a look at the pictures in the display case outside. There wasn't much else to do. Not much happened on a

Sunday. Sundays in Richmond in particular filled him with a sense of desolation that seemed like a view down the corridor leading to his later life. He caught a glimpse of himself reaching the end of the corridor and about to turn out of sight, a red blob disappearing in the distance.

Cinemas, pubs, dance halls, public lavatories, bus terminals and transport cafes, in the end even the station, Max liked to hang out and watch people in public places pursuing activities that for the most part were barred to him. There weren't many places of interest in Richmond, however, nothing compared to real London, and even when there were he usually found himself coming up against someone saying, Now you move along, sonny. This is no place for you. He began to comb Brylcreem into his hair to give it a quiff like the lads in the skiffle group, learning from them, copying their habits. Precocious little blighter they called him, not without affection, always trying to look older than he was. Scram, nipper, they said, though not unfriendly, and as soon as Max turned the corner he didn't forget to comb the quiff out again and part his hair neatly before arriving home for Sunday lunch.

# 10

At the beginning of the Easter holidays Mrs Johnson moved out of the room next to his and Claude moved in, vacating his own room downstairs for the nanny who had temporarily joined the household. Max was compensated for the continued loss of his battleground to these occupation forces by the present Claude gave him. Claude called it a whirligig. It was a little cloth bag weighted with sand, with streamers and a piece of string attached to whirl it around and hurl it up into the air. The two of them went into the park to try it out. Too risky in the garden, Claude thought. The whirligig might land in the river.

When the seams of the sack broke on impact with the ground after Max had whirled it up into the air for the twentieth time, he took it unhappily home for his mother to mend. She had a thousand other things to do but she smiled when she caught sight of him. Max loved it when his mother smiled. Her smile shone into his heart.

'Oh I know them,' she said, taking a closer look at the sack and laughing for no good reason Max could see. 'It just needs a stiffer fabric and a stronger thread for the seams.' And she promised to mend it for him by the next day. He found it on his breakfast plate when he came down the following morning. It was like new, with a neatly stitched dark blue sack that didn't burst when it hit the ground, just as his mother had said. She always kept her promises.

Interesting things were happening in the house, more interesting, except for the whirligig, than anything going on outside. Max hung about at home for once.

Apart from Claude, there were four other guests staying. Two of them were foreigners, who had come all the way from Paris. They were different from anyone Max had ever met. He studied them with interest, knowing he would learn something useful. They lay around even in the middle of the day, smoking and talking in English and French. One of them had long hair like a girl's, all the way down to his shoulders, although he was a grown-up man. His name was Jong Jack. Max was extremely interested in Jong Jack and his long hair, which wouldn't have been allowed at Kennington Hall. He would have been expelled. There wasn't enough space so the visitors had to share rooms and bed down on the floor, where they might be found lying at all times of the day, even when they weren't sleeping, even when they must have guessed that George didn't approve.

'What are all these layabouts doing here?' he asked his wife.

'They've come for the march, of course.'

'Oh I see. So that's why they're having a good rest before they start.'

Max too would have preferred the floor to his usual boring bed, and at breakfast the morning after the guests had arrived he offered them his, explaining that he often slept in the cupboard in any case.

'Cabór? Why jew slip in ze cabór?' Jong Jack asked him.

'It feels safer sleeping in a cupboard,' said Max, fidgeting on his chair.

'True. It *is* safer slipping in cabór. I cannot dispute. No person is ever assassin who is sleeping in a cabór. *Tu comprends?* You are clever boy. One day, when I become *président* of France, I remember zis advice and make you prime minister, *hein?*'

All the people in the house were Protestants, his father said with the lopsided smile that appeared on his face whenever he said something he considered witty. They were heretics – in the old days they would have been burned at the stake. But Ella didn't think what George had said was clever or funny, and they had an argument. Always interested in arguments between his parents, Max paid close attention and kept the score, hoping his mother would win.

The argument was once again about war. Ella said the bomb should be banned. George said it all depended.

In the week before Easter dozens of people came and went. They were all CND volunteers, helpers and protesters, or what George to Ella's annoyance continued to call Protestants. George was the only person there who wasn't one.

In the conservatory overlooking the lawn, where the garden furniture was stored during the winter and Max had a corner for his hobbies, a committee, an office and a workshop were set up for making leaflets and badges. Some of them had CAMPAIGN FOR NUCLEAR DISARMA- MENT written on them, some of them just the letters CND, but they all had the sign of a circle around a rocket, or what they called the CND symbol. Claude told Max that the peace sign was a combination of the letters N and D, but Max didn't see that; what he saw was a rocket on a launching pad inside the circle. It was a war sign, he said to Claude, not a peace sign.

Jong Jack, who was standing nearby, overheard this conversation and said something to Claude in French.

'What did he say?' asked Max.

'He said you should do a Rorschach test.'

'What's that?'

'They show you blobs of ink and you have to say what the blobs remind you of, what pictures you see in them.'

Blobs of ink? Max had a flashback of the red blob that was himself fading from sight at the end of a long tunnel. But why red? Perhaps the blob at the end of the tunnel was red because he was wearing something coloured red, or perhaps it had something to do with blood.

'Is it a game?'

'Sort of.'

What Jong Jack had said to Claude in French had been much longer, however. Max could tell that Claude was only telling him part of what Frenchie had said. He would remember the word and what it meant. Rorschach test. Things you saw in blobs of ink.

The previous year Ella had gone off to spend Easter with Claude while George stayed at home with the children. Ella and Claude went on a march which took them four days. Four days! There was a picture of them on the television, marching along in the rain with hundreds of other bedraggled people who all wanted to *ban the bomb*. Max wished he could have gone with them. His mother wouldn't have minded, but his father wouldn't allow it. George was against banning the bomb, which was why he hadn't gone on the march with the Protestants. Besides, if everyone went off marching, he said, who would there be at home to look after the three children?

'Giselle!' said Max, quick as a flash.

This year there were endless arguments about whether they should do the same march again, from Trafalgar Square to Aldermaston, as in 1958, or the other way round, from Aldermaston to Trafalgar Square, as in 1959. In the end the committee decided they would do the latter. At the end of March they all went off, Claude and all the other Protestants, and to Max's regret the usual quiet settled again. He missed the all-too-brief period of anarchy that had taken over the Richmond house. This time his mother stayed at home – to look after the baby, she said. His father said it would be too much for her, going off on a long march just a few weeks after giving birth. He wouldn't put up with it, he said.

A craze for making ban-the-bomb signs swept the house. The year before last there had been a fad for submarines in the bath powered by baking powder. Last year they had gone through a craze of making harpoons after seeing the film *Moby Dick*. This year it was the CND sign. Felicity made drawings of it with coloured crayons and hung them up all over the house. They all had a starboard list, her father said, meaning that they were crooked, he explained with a grin when Felicity asked. Starboard list yourself, thought Max at the sight of his father's one-sided grin. Philip, very methodical and neat, cut his CND signs out of cardboard and cunningly handed them in at school as his project of the week for his handicraft class.

'Typical Philip,' his father commented.

Max shut himself up in his hobby corner in the big room where all the meetings had been held. It must be at least the Crown Jewels Max kept under lock and key down there, his father said, which in a way was true, as the crystal set, the fretsaw and the soldering iron he had been given for Christmas were among his most valued possessions. Using the special soldering wire that came with the iron, he made a circle with a rocket on a launching pad inside it – just one, because it took him such a long time to do.

'It looks like a stick insect wearing a monocle,' George said.

This was an extension of his parents' tit-for-tat arguments about war and banning the bomb, taking potshots at each other. In Max's war games this was the job given to camouflaged snipers positioned in shoes or on top of the cupboard. George had mainly cutting things to say about the three children's peace-sign efforts, Ella nothing but words of encouragement. There was a sense of relief throughout the house when Easter was over and George went back to work.

The house was full of secrets. Max could hear them whispering when he lay awake in bed at night. Even the sense of relief everyone felt when George went back to work was a secret of sorts.

'Perhaps we won't tell the others,' his mother said after she had let Max taste the milk from her breast.

'This is our secret, Max, just between you and me,' his father said.

They got off the bus at Putney Heath and went in the direction of the gasworks, following a long brick wall all the way down one side of the street. A large green gate in the wall stood open, leading into a quadrangle. This was where the boys had played cricket in his father's time, and still did, judging by the wickets chalked on the red-brick wall. On the far side of the chalk wickets, hissing and clanging sounds came from a pub, the Barley Mow, where some of the masters used to pop over for a quickie between classes, his father told him. The windows of the school buildings overlooking the quadrangle were covered with metal screens, to prevent the windows from being smashed by balls, George said. Probably the same screens that had been there in his day, he added with satisfaction. Probably he had whacked a few balls against them himself.

They entered the main building and walked down a passage lined with pictures of warships and school photographs, some of them going back to the beginning of the century. George pointed to himself in one of them, a boy the same age as Max, sitting in the front row wearing a cap. Max didn't recognise him.

They had an appointment with the headmaster.

Mr Colquhoun had a false leg. He had lost his real one in the war – with Slim in Burma, he remarked to George as he stomped off to show them the school. Max wondered who Slim was, and how odd it would have been if he had been fat. They marched through classrooms, a library, a masters' common room, a dining hall, dormitories and changing rooms. This is where this, and this is where that, the headmaster said, only there was nobody there for the this or the that, as all the boys were away on holiday.

Yes, they still had their reputation for Latin and Greek, he said in reply to George's question, largely thanks to old Hardcastle. Now there was tradition for you, the headmaster said. That was the sort of continuity the school prided itself on. The classics master who had taught George was still with the school a quarter of a century on, although he would be going into retirement next year. The two men sat in the headmaster's study and reminisced. Max's gaze wandered over the room, taking in the trophies, more photographs, three slender white canes standing sinisterly in the corner behind the door. Max found it odd. Although they were about the same age, George addressed Mr Colquhoun as Headmaster all the time, as if he were still a boy at school there himself. Then they wanted to be left to have a talk on their own.

Max wandered down the passage into vast empty kitchens, sculleries and outhouses, back into the dining hall again, where dark wooden panels covered two walls of the room. The panels on one side commemorated in gold lettering the names of old boys who had given their lives in the two world wars, the panels on the other the boys who had won scholarships to famous schools.

'You won a scholarship to Winchester, didn't you, Dad?' Max said with some pride on their way out of the school.

'Yes, as a matter of fact, I did.'

'Was it difficult?'

'Not particularly. Now we don't breathe a word of any of this, not to anyone, Max. Where we've been today. You know how your mother feels. All right? This is our secret.'

So Max had secrets with both his mother and his father. He had a secret with Felicity. And now he had a secret with Kirby too.

They lit a fire on the dump behind the garage. Both of them came with pockets full of coal they had stolen from a heap by the railway. Max had also brought along a jar of honey and bandages he had taken from the first aid kit his mother kept in the kitchen cupboard.

In half an hour they had a good fire going.

Kirby was the first friend Max had made at Kennington Hall, the only person with whom Max had shared the dead cat. He was a tall boy with red cheeks and front teeth that stuck out like a rabbit's. Otherwise he wasn't a bit like a rabbit. Kirby was tough. He was the best boxer under ten in the school. He had been tried and proven in a number of dangerous situations. He and Max had crossed the electric railway lines dozen of times together, even in the dark. If you touched the rail you were dead. Max had selected Kirby for the honour of being the first member of his gang.

Max took the stick insect with the monocle out of his pocket and laid it carefully on his handkerchief. Mrs Johnson had said hygiene was important.

Why on earth did he want to know *that*, she had asked archly, raising her eyebrows when he enquired about the treatment for burns. Grown-ups were always suspicious and Max was prepared for her question. He told her it was homework for a first aid project at school. If it was a light burn, Mrs Johnson said, rolling her eyes, hold it under running water for ten minutes, let the wound dry and put some honey and a sterile gauze bandage on it. Hygiene is the be-all and the end-all of first aid.

At the time he asked Mrs Johnson about treating burns he had been thinking of the burn mark you got when you joined Bernie's gang. He had seen it done to others in the Nissen hut on the bomb site where Bernie's gang used to meet. Max was allowed to watch, but he had been too young to join.

His mark wouldn't be just a mark. It would be much better, a sign with a hidden meaning known only to insiders, like the sign in the Rorschach blob of ink.

Kirby chewed on a straw and asked what the gang was called.

'It's called the CND gang,' said Max. 'I'm the chief, and when we're in the gang my name is Jong Jack, and everyone's got to call me that.'

Holding one end of the stick insect with a pair of tweezers, he put the monocle end into the embers of the fire.

Kirby watched the soldering wire begin to glow. 'Does it hurt?'

'Course it hurts. What a daft question.'

Max took off his shirt, gripped the end of the wire with his hand-kerchief and without hesitating pressed the glowing monocle into the flesh of his upper arm.

He almost fainted from the explosion of pain that went searing through his body. He clutched his arm and began to cry, kneeling with his head on the ground, whimpering and sobbing. The sobbing eased down into a low moan.

Then he got up and ran to the garage. He climbed in through the broken window, went to the washroom sink, turned the tap on and let water trickle over his burning arm until it felt cooler.

When he got back he crouched down by the fire and looked at Kirby.

The other boy saw the contortions of pain in Max's smudged and tear-stained face as he put the wire back in the embers. Kirby watched the circle of wire in the fire become red-hot.

'Go on,' said Max. 'Your turn.'

Kirby stared into the fire without moving.

'Dare you,' said Max.

Slowly Kirby unbuttoned his shirt.

A few days after the summer term began Ella got a phone call from Mr Hone, the headmaster of Kennington Hall. He asked her if she could come to the school to have a talk with him about her son Max.

'Is it something serious?' Ella asked.

Mr Hone said it was. Ella told him she would come right away.

Max was having a meeting with his generals in the mop cupboard in the hall adjacent to the kitchen where his mother took the call, and he overheard her end of the conversation. He heard her say, Yes, Mr Hone two or three times, and when he saw her get on her bicycle and head off down the road he knew he was in trouble, and he knew why.

It was Kirby's fault.

'Don't pick the scab,' Max told him a dozen times, but stupid Kirby had gone and done it again; dirt had got in, and the wound became infected. Kirby showed it to his mother and she took him straight to the doctor.

That's a nasty burn you've got there, the doctor said, and asked him how he'd come by it.

Kirby said he'd been stoking the fire and fallen on the tongs.

No, you didn't, said the doctor, who was examining the wound with a magnifying glass in order to get all the grains of dirt out, that's a ban-the-bomb sign you've got on your arm.

But Kirby wouldn't budge. He'd fallen on the tongs, he said.

When Kirby's dad got home from work he went with his son into the room where the fireplace was and shut the door. Then he took the tongs from the grate and held them up in front of Kirby's face.

Go on then, tell me what you see, Kirby's father said.

Tongs, said Kirby.

Don't give me any lip, you little bugger, or I'll give you what for, Mr Kirby told his son. *I* can't see any bleedin' ban-the-bomb sign on these tongs, can *you*?

Kirby agreed he couldn't either. In fact, to tell the truth, he'd made the mark himself with a bit of wire he'd heated up in the fire, he said to his father, and he was sorry he'd told a lie.

According to what Kirby told Max afterwards, he'd done his best to keep Max out of it. He wouldn't have betrayed him for anything in the world. Max believed him. But his dad was a very persistent man, said Kirby. He told his son he would get to the bottom of it even if it meant thrashing him every day for the next month. Show me that bit of wire, he demanded. Kirby said he'd thrown it away. All right, said his dad. We'll go and look for it, shall we, you and me, and Kirby had shown him the dump behind the garage, knowing they didn't have the slightest chance of finding or not finding anything, let alone a little bit of wire, in all the piles of old stuff.

Unfortunately Kirby's dad worked in a metal factory and knew a thing or two about wire. He made his son give him an exact description of the bit of wire, and then he got him a piece of wire just like it. Go on then, make me a ban-the-bomb sign, Kirby's dad said, and Kirby knew the game was up. He had to tell him he'd borrowed a soldering iron from a boy at school, but Kirby's dad had seen through that too, because Kirby couldn't tell him how a soldering iron worked.

That morning during break Mr Hone had asked to see Max and Kirby in his study.

'Who made the ban-the-bomb sign?'

'I did,' said Max.

'Where is it?'

Max took the stick insect out of the handkerchief in his pocket and handed it to the headmaster. Mr Hone looked at the wire, and then at Max and Kirby, and then at the wire again.

'Do you mean to say you *made* this thing for the sole purpose of using it to *brand* your *skin*?' he asked them in astonishment.

Max nodded. The headmaster looked at Kirby. Kirby nodded too.

380

'Whose idea was it?'

'It was my idea, sir,' replied Max at once before Kirby had a chance to get a word in.

Mr Hone rubbed the top of his bald head as if he was dusting it. 'But what on earth *for?*'

But to answer this question Max would have had to betray a secret, and he clammed up. Mr Hone couldn't get a word more out of him. He sent Max out but kept Kirby behind. Max waited for Kirby at the school gates when it was time to go home for lunch, but there was no sign of him.

After lunch Max called a meeting of his general staff in the mop cupboard to plan what to do. He must get hold of Kirby at all costs and find out what he had told the beak. Then the phone call from Mr Hone came through and his mother left on her bicycle. After she had gone he went out and climbed a tree overlooking the road along which his mother would come.

'Ahoy!' he called out when she came at last, sitting bolt upright the way she did when she rode a bicycle, as if she was playing the piano.

'I'm up here in the rigging, Mum. Look! The very top!'

His mother got off her bike and studied a patch of grass while waiting for Max to climb down the tree.

'What are you looking for, Mum?'

'A four-leafed clover. Come and help me find one.'

They knelt down by the clover patch. Max waited for his mother to tell him about her visit to the headmaster, but Ella said nothing. Combing through the patch with their fingers, they carefully sorted the clover.

'There's one! No, it's only a three ...'

Max couldn't contain himself. 'Mum, what did Mr Hone say?'

'I really don't know, Max. He didn't tell me, did he. I went all the way for nothing.'

'Didn't *tell* you?'

'Well, what could he tell me, if you had nothing to tell him yourself? So I said you'd tell me, and then I would go back and tell him.'

Max said nothing.

'I *promised* Mr Hone I would,' said his mother. 'You wouldn't like me to break my word, would you. Don't let me down, Max.'

Somehow his mother always managed to get it out of him. Max relented and told her the whole story, beginning with Jong Jack and the CND sign, in which he saw a rocket on a launching pad, which was different from what other people saw. She didn't understand how gangs came into the Rorschach test, so he had to double back and tell her first about Bernie's gang in the Nissen hut on the bomb site, which was where it had all started. Worst of all, he had to show her the gang mark on his arm. When she saw it she gave a shriek, put her arms around him and began to cry. Max felt dreadful.

'Have I done something wrong, Mum?'

'No, dear. I just wish you'd let me in on all this before.'

They didn't look for any more four-leafed clovers after that.

Max and the other children had gone to bed by the time their father got back that evening. George and Ella ate alone in the conservatory with the doors open into the garden. She recounted the day's events, saving the conclusion for after supper, when George was settled with his brandy and cigar.

'Mr Hone told me he doesn't think Kennington Hall is the right sort of school for Max.'

'More like Max isn't the right sort of boy for Kennington Hall,' said George wearily.

'Well.' Ella paused. 'He did as a matter of fact say something like that. He thinks Max is a bad influence and he would like us to take him away from the school.'

'Meaning he's being expelled,' said George, blowing out a plume of smoke. 'Well, what a great start to Max's schooldays. But for all that Aldermaston nonsense, those bloody anarchist friends of Claude's ...'

Realising she was on weak ground, Ella ignored the interruption.

'Talk has already got around, apparently. Mr Hone thought it would be in Max's best interests if he went to a school away from the Rich-mond area.' With a heavy heart she said, 'He thought a boarding school would be best.'

George caught the sadness in her voice.

'A boarding school isn't the end of the world, you know, Ella. Max will still be able to come home at half-term. We won't lose him. But at this short notice, a week into the summer term ...'

Under the circumstances, there was no alternative.

Three years after the row that had led to Ella disappearing to Paris she accepted defeat, not so much at the hands of the alien educational system that she had originally rejected as by her recognition of Max's nature, the strangeness to her of her own child, and a week later he left home for Park House.

# 11

George stepped uncertainly into the mews and peered around for Number 8. Was this the place?

It looked rather run-down. Houses needed a coat of paint, the street repaving. The wooden staircase, half-strangled by honeysuckle, leading up to the second floor of the house at the end of the mews was on the verge of collapse. Not watching where he was going, he stepped into a hole where a cobblestone was missing and twisted his ankle. He stooped to massage his ankle, feeling annoyed with Julia, as if she had twisted it for him.

Not the choice he would have expected Julia to make. He would have thought she would have gone for something more practical, less romantic. She wanted a home of her own, she told him. She had spent her mother's inheritance on this place. George doubted it was worth what she'd paid. The location was what had decided her in the end. Close enough to make it worth popping home for lunch, to meet George when they got away from the BTM for a couple of hours.

George had glanced back when turning into the mews. The notion someone might have been following him – was that just stuff his nerves served his imagination? He knew that occasional surveillance of staff was carried out. Routine procedures, or not so routine, keeping tabs on who went where to do what. It would once have made him uncomfortable. It was not that he had become careless; he had ceased to care. He had become cynical, or perhaps it was just that he didn't mind.

Besides, his intimate relationship with Julia had been sanctioned behind the scenes. Their previous affair was no doubt why the Old Man had picked them. He and she were collaborators. Their intimacy was part of their job. Wasn't it?

There was always a moment of anticipation between ringing the bell and the door opening. What if someone he had never seen before opened the door and claimed she was Julia? What if she insisted she was her, taking all the liberties to which as Julia she would be entitled? Where would that leave him? But the petite woman with short dark hair who stood in the doorway was undoubtedly Julia, casting a tiny shadow of disappointment. It was undoubtedly her perfume, Julia's identification tag, which rose to meet him when she kissed him as he came in.

'How was Easter?'

'It was terrible.'

George's life at home only really came into focus for him when he began editing the version of it he gave Julia. There were things he omitted, things he changed. Often not sure what version he would give her until he heard himself telling her, he observed this process with curiosity. The main omission was Claude. He hadn't told Julia about Claude's existence in his marriage.

Until recently, the phrase *Claude's existence in his marriage* would not have come to George. *Outside* their marriage Ella had a lover – that would have been his view of it. The family's fourth child, possibly Claude's child, had brought the lover inside the marriage. It was just a matter of time before it brought him permanently into the house. That George still hadn't worked out the consequences of what was going on, in fact not even *what* was going on, was one of the reasons he hadn't broached the subject in his conversations with Julia. For George to be able to do this, it would first be necessary to undertake a reappraisal of himself.

But was this a matter of how he saw himself, or how he wanted to see himself? That *grand seigneur* of his imagination, a man who considered jealousy to be a plebeian instinct – was there any reality to such a figure, or did he stand in for that other figure George might equally be or that might claim to be George, a person of lukewarm temperament, an emotionally crippled man who hid his deformity behind the charade of the *grand seigneur*?

George couldn't say. What he could say with certainty after ten years of marriage, however, was that in comparison with his open hearth of a wife he generated hardly more heat and light than the glimmer of a candle. There was that much less of him. He could see a justification for Ella having two husbands.

Once the nest-building was done, once that first spree of togetherness was over, Ella had begun to take stock of George just as George had taken stock of her.

'Don't just lie down and fall asleep. Talk to me! Tell me something interesting!' she would demand when they got ready to go to bed, because naturally she was still wide awake while George was already half asleep. 'There's nothing you have to tell me that I couldn't read in the evening paper' was another remark that had become a regular contribution to such bedtime skirmishes in the latter years at St John's Wood. The wish to avoid such scenes was why George readily agreed to her suggestion that they should sleep in separate bedrooms in the new house.

In the course of these differences with Ella, George had discovered that she was not armed to deal with superciliousness. It was easy to beat her. All he needed to do was maintain a lofty silence. This led to scenes that humiliated Ella. She actually got down on her knees and clung to him. 'Please! Please talk to me!'

George was in two minds in such situations. He felt such humiliation intolerable and he suffered with the woman subjected to it. It was his own humiliation as well. But in seeing her humbled like that there also lurked a queer sort of satisfaction. 'Serves her right' were the words that might have been put in a bubble coming out of his mouth.

She could go off to Paris with Sasha and at the same time reproach him with throwing her in the direction of the men who fancied her. She could blame him for the extramarital affairs she claimed he was forcing her into. She knew, she *knew* she wasn't in his thoughts as he was in hers – that he didn't carry her inwardly and cherish him as she did him even when she didn't seem particularly to love him – even when she went off to Paris.

Ella had her self-dramatising moments. 'Is there no one who will wake with me?' She thought this question of Christ's to his sleeping disciples in the Garden of Gethsemane was the saddest thing in the Bible. Coming from her mouth, to George it bordered on the absurd.

For all that, there remained that imbalance between them which had been there from the beginning. George knew and she knew that he loved her after his fashion, but that she didn't love him after hers, deep down. He gave her all he had, but there was much more love in Ella's pipeline than had ever come his way. George wondered if she thought of this imbalance as a blemish, that it was her fault and was always having to try to make up for it, and that this provided her with one more reason to feel bound to aggravate him.

George was aware of the difference in the kind of love they had for one another, but it took Claude to bring the full implications of it home to him. Ella loved Claude with the same squandering instinct that George loved Ella. All the taps were open; the vat was brimming over. There was nothing she could do about it. She told George of her conversation with Sasha at the Ritz about meeting a type of woman who resembled his piano teacher, blonde and slim, with her hair up, showing in profile the long line of her neck, and what Sasha had said of meeting such women: *One is delivered over, bound hand and foot.*

Relationships were easier when neither of the two people involved was bound hand and foot like this, tied to the imprint of a ghost they glimpsed in the features or manner of their partner. It was his own father George saw in Ella, always beckoning, always fading the moment one came near for a closer look. It had become easier for George to spend a weekend in the company of Julia Manning, without hurt feelings or the urge to quarrel intruding, than it was with his own wife.

This irritated him. How tiresome this whole business was! He wished he could be shot of it all. It was in this frame of mind that he had opened the door allowing Claude to slip into their life.

He followed Julia into the small upstairs bedroom and watched her undress with just a suggestion of the routine that habit had brought into their sexual relationship. She sat on the bed in her underwear.

'Well, what do you think?'

George looked around, taking in the wallpaper, some items of furniture familiar from her last flat and some that weren't, including an enormous new bed.

'It's certainly an improvement on Pimlico. I like the colours.'

She laughed. 'I meant me. My naughty underwear.'

This note of forwardness in Julia's exploration of intimacy was something new in her manner with him, and George didn't welcome it. The reserve, even the note of chasteness that accompanied his demure secretary into bed, was what George had always found exciting about Miss Manning. Unless he was mistaken, the signs she was giving him now were becoming a little proprietorial. She had started taking it for granted that she was entitled to make claims on him. He wondered lazily if this qualified for a spanking and was briefly aroused by the thought.

'It looks very beguiling.'

But beyond taking off his tie he didn't get undressed; he preferred to talk, and having just fobbed her off with a word that had slightly embarrassed even himself, he remained sitting in an armchair near the window with his legs crossed, as distant from Julia lying on the bed as it was possible to be in that small room.

If Julia was disappointed by this coolness on his part, George was puzzled by it, for it had been his abstinence from liberating bedroom sessions with Julia that he held responsible for his irritability at home over Easter.

She got off the bed and came to sit on his lap.

'You're being rather unsociable today. Aren't you going to join me?'

'It's hardly worth getting undressed. I've got to leave in half an hour.'

'We've got hours. Your train doesn't leave until half past eleven.'

'I'm catching an earlier train and staying overnight at my club. I've got a guest coming there for dinner.'

Julia tied his tie for him and called a taxi. Whatever she felt about his change of plan – that it might have upset her own, or that he might at least have shown her the consideration of letting her know earlier – she showed no trace of it. If she had to efface her own personality in order to fit in with him, naturally she would do so.

That Julia made no demands on him was what George particularly appreciated about her. He felt safe with her, relaxed, as he no longer really could with Ella. With Ella you never knew when she was going to fly off the handle. Neglect in a word, a glance, in some as it seemed to George quite trivial omission of his, could cause her to take disproportionate offence.

But recently, for some reason or other, George found Julia's conciliatory nature had begun to jar. Something about her passivity put George on his guard. There was a contradiction here – a petite, gracious, self-effacing woman but with a steel spring of resolution, which he could sense coiled up inside her.

'Shoot them,' she had said at a meeting when the subject had come up of what to do with people like the Aldermaston marchers. The others laughed, but George knew her well enough to tell that she meant what she said.

On her father's side Julia Manning came from an old family of landed gentry and was a patriot beyond what George saw as the call of duty. She had done the training course for special agents and was a first-class shot. She had been through the war in the cold outside while George had stayed warm and safe indoors. This was the code on which she had been brought up. Traitors – and in her eyes those marchers, who were saboteurs of the national interest, counted as traitors – were shot.

In many of the countries she travelled to with George such people *were* shot. Recently, when he was in bed with her in a hotel on their last trip, just about to doze off, the uncomfortable thought had entered his mind that Julia would be capable of cutting his throat in his sleep, and this thought had kept him awake.

This was why he had not mentioned Claude to Julia. *Claude's existence in his marriage*, a Trojan horse in the citadel, might set a precedent for Julia to follow. It might put ideas into her head. She might see an opportunity to divert George from the channel of his marriage with Ella, the river to change its bed. She might see an opportunity to blackmail him, to make George pay back in kind what for the past couple of years she had paid him. A spinster-in-waiting who would come to see herself or perhaps already saw herself as having deferred her own life in order to advance his – what furies might be unleashed in such a disappointed woman?

The cabby slid back the glass and called over his shoulder, 'What number, sir?'

'Drop me at the corner of Waterloo Place.'

This meeting was long overdue. It had been Ella's idea. She had even outlined some of the things George could say.

He got out of the taxi, paid off the driver and walked across the pavement to the entrance of the Athenaeum.

# 12

Claude detached himself from the shadow of the portico and emerged from behind a column as George came up the steps, taking him by surprise.

'God! You don't mean to say you've been waiting out here for me, have you? Why didn't you go in?'

'It looked rather intimidating.'

George noted with disapproval that Claude was wearing the leather waistcoat Ella had given him for Easter. It wasn't appropriate. Leather waistcoats were not for the Athenaeum.

'Well, there's nothing to be afraid of in *here*,' he said as someone ceremoniously held open the door for them, 'is there, Stubbs?'

'Good evening, Mr Morris.'

'I think we'll be dining in the Picture Room, usually a bit quieter there,' George said to the pink-complexioned whiskered man who had greeted him, handing him his coat and overnight bag as he breezed through the entrance.

'This way, Claude. And do take a look at the staircase on our way in ... Rather splendid, don't you think?'

Professionally, he said to Claude as they made their way to the Picture Room, he really belonged in the Travellers Club. But this had been his father's club, and of several uncles too, so by family tradition he belonged here. To the accompaniment of more such patter, they installed themselves in the less populated, smaller of the club's two dining rooms. It was already after nine.

'Well here we go,' he said to no one in particular as the waiter handed him a menu.

'What have you got in the way of fish tonight?'

Claude observed with interest this other George in conversation with the waiter, talkative, ebullient, characterised by a bounce and bonhomie he lacked at home. His guide to Pall Mall clubland, what it had once been and now was, provided them with a backdrop to the choice of hors d'oeuvres and a scrutiny of the wine list. George did the talking, periodically lapsing into French, Claude the listening.

George never discussed his work. If Ella hadn't told him, Claude wouldn't have known what he did. Politics was off limits too, partly because the government's claim on George's discretion made the subject unrewarding, partly because George was an Establishment man and Claude wasn't. His values were old-fashioned, patrician and authoritarian. It wouldn't have seemed that they had an awful lot in common. George didn't sympathise with Labour, with the trade unions, with Aldermaston marchers or any of the protest movements and alternative cultures that in the late 1950s had begun to stir up what Claude and his friends balefully regarded as the West's somnolent post-war miasma.

It would have been unsurprising if the rump figure of George that was left after subtracting the issues over which they differed had held not very much of interest to Claude. That it did interest him was due to the secretive atmosphere surrounding the apparent ordinariness of

George, and to Claude's perception of him as a person who led two different lives. Claude owed that perception to the fact that George frequently switched between languages when in conversation with him. It was thanks to this ambidextrous use of language that Claude had first become aware – when that odd little phrase *un petit béguin pour ma femme* slipped out – of an ambiguousness about George, leading Claude to wonder about another side of him.

By the time they were ready to place their orders, it was getting on for half past nine. To George's chagrin the Dover sole was off. While they sat waiting for their beef to arrive, George suddenly asked, 'Did Ella ever tell you about her father?'

'She did. She brought him up several times, but of course not nearly as often as she mentions her mother. Unsurprising, I suppose, considering how seldom she saw him. What was his name?'

'Andrzejewski. He came from a Polish family, you may remember. I don't know what sort of a man he was, but his people were Slavs from the Russian border country. I never met him but imagine he might have been a bit like Sasha Borowski, whom I did. A type of man one doesn't really come across in this country. There really does seem to be something like a ... an *extravagance* of the Slav soul, going to extremes in either direction, magnanimity and recklessness, real warmth but also a lachrymose sentimentality. Anyway, the point is that Ella's father provided the one lineage and her mother the other, which came together in their daughter – those two very different types, you see, the slapdash munificence of the Slav and the almost neurotic order of the Prussian, not cold necessarily, but stern, correct and frugal. Little wonder. A poor country. Look at the meagreness of Prussian court life. Saving crumbs off the supper table to go into tomorrow's lunch. The kaiser as the foremost servant of the state, pulling on sleeve protectors to economise on linen costs when he sat down to work at his desk. That sort of thing.'

George collected his thoughts and Claude lit a cigarette, curious where this was leading.

'Well, just before the outbreak of war, Andrzejewski escapes from Germany to Russia, doesn't he, where he presents himself as a card-carrying communist wanting to put his knowledge as a physicist at the disposal of his Soviet comrades. From the frying pan into the fire, you might say. I think there must have been both something of a realist and an idealist about him, but quite a bit more of the latter. Apropos

frying pans and fires, in Germany he had been working for the war
ministry on heat-seeking devices, research that eventually would filter
through into the design of Soviet anti-missile arms. He joined the staff
of the Industrial Academy in Moscow. Later he disappeared into the
Soviet military establishment in Kazakhstan, apparently to do missile
research using the technology that had led to the development of the
German A-4 rocket, or V-2 as it was more commonly known. When
they occupied Germany the Russians dismantled a captured A-4 and
transported it back to the Soviet Union, where …'

George paused to allow the waiter to place on the table a tray with a
selection of sauces in little silver bowls.

'How do you know all this?' Claude asked.

'Because I make it my business to. Would you like some bread?'

'No, thank you.'

'Now, most of the scientists who had been working with Wernher
von Braun at the missile base in Peenemünde chose to surrender to
the Americans rather than the Russians because they believed that the
realisation of von Braun's dream of sending a rocket to the moon would
more likely be achieved by the Americans. The moon! Lunatic! But that
was the criterion which decided their choice. Cornered in a mountain
village on the Austrian border, with enemy troops advancing from all
sides, they sat in the village hotel thrashing out the pros and cons of
which enemy to surrender to, which enemy would pay for their rocket.
Imagine!'

For once George laughed on both sides of his face.

'Maybe after the launch of the sputnik into orbit they're now wishing
they'd opted for the Russians. One of them did. His name was Gröttrup.'

At this point the beef arrived ceremoniously on a trolley manned by
a burly waiter in a long white apron and a chef's hat, but George was
in full swing and paid him no attention.

'Now here's the interesting thing, Claude. Why did Gröttrup plump
for the Russians? Because he preferred Soviet communism to American
capitalism? No. It was because von Braun's affair with Gröttrup's wife
in Peenemünde still rankled. Von Braun had snitched his wife and he
hadn't forgiven him. So you could say that he threw in his lot with the
Russians simply out of spite.'

However briefly, George now had to give his attention to the waiter,
who was standing by, waiting to get on with the carving.

'Gröttrup was a fuel specialist,' he continued as soon as the beef matter had been dealt with, 'but he was familiar of course with the overall concept of the A-4 and the details of its inner workings. Thanks in large part to him, then, thanks to this little domestic squabble, you see, the Soviets got a boost in the space race that enabled them to catch up with the Americans and, as the launch of the sputnik shows, even to outstrip them.'

George poured himself and Claude another glass of wine.

'So in von Braun's affair with Gröttrup's wife you have one of the points of origin of the threat to world peace,' he said, aiming one of his lopsided grins at Claude, 'which gets a movement like the Campaign for Nuclear Disarmament marching back and forth between London and Aldermaston and generally making a bloody nuisance of itself. Isn't that instructive?'

But Claude wouldn't let himself get sidetracked. 'What's the connection between Andrzejewski and Gröttrup?'

'They worked together in Kazakhstan on the Russian prototype developed from the A-4. That was in about forty-seven or forty-eight. Then Andrzejewski disappeared. He would either have been eliminated or sent to die more slowly in one of Stalin's labour camps in Siberia. All this information became available to us when Gröttrup was allowed to return to Germany a few years later, having spent most of that time in quarantine, meaning he was excluded from the ongoing research in Kazakhstan, so that he took no secrets home with him. Some of Gröttrup's information is still classified, but of course not the bits I've just told you.'

'And presumably Ella too.'

'No. As far as Ella's concerned, what I've told you about her father remains classified information. This is a confidence between you and me. It would be different if I had something more definite, if I could tell Ella her father was dead. Ella is not afraid of the truth, of any truth. But she cannot live with uncertainties. She has to know one way or the other. Her mother has long been dead, and she has made up her mind that her father is too. In the twenty years since she last saw her father in Berlin she has buried him, and in her mind she has built him a sort of monument where her thoughts of him have come to rest. Why disturb it for no good reason?'

Claude hesitated for a moment before making the leap.

'Then how is she living with the present uncertainty?'

'Ah! There's the question. What do you think, Claude?'

'I think we all have to live with uncertainty one way or another. There's no escaping it. Perhaps your exemption of Ella is wrong.'

'There's always that possibility, of course.'

George told the waiter, who was standing by, that they wouldn't be wanting further helpings of beef but that they might like more vegetables a little later, and handed him a shilling.

'Much obliged, sir.'

The man wheeled his trolley away.

When George turned back to address Claude, his voice had shed its usual ironic twang. 'The other possibility is that you're wrong about what you call the present uncertainty. Perhaps it is not an uncertainty.'

Claude looked perplexed. 'But Ella has told both of us that—' he began.

'Yes, yes, of course,' George interrupted him. 'That may be what she has told *us*. But what is she telling herself? As far as I can see, which is as plainly as I see you sitting there, Ella is telling herself: this is Claude's child.'

Claude was nonplussed.

'What you can't see, because you weren't around before,' George went on, 'but *I* can, is the difference in Ella after this birth compared with the births of her other three children. She is more relaxed. She feels at one with this child. She is happier. I hear her in that room singing as she nurses the child. She didn't sing for any of her other children, my children. Why?'

George reached unexpectedly over the table to grasp Claude's arm as he was about to tap his cigarette into the ashtray, causing Claude to deposit the ash onto the tablecloth instead.

'I'll spare your blushes. Let *me* tell you. She sings for the child because she is singing for the child's father. Can't sing for toffee, but, as they say, it's the thought that counts. She's happier with this child because she loves the child's father more than she loves the father of her other children. Well, why not? It's not as if there were any law forbidding such a thing.'

He half-rose from his chair, pushed it back and sat down again.

After a while he resumed eating, his eyes on his plate, saying nothing until Claude poured him another glass of wine, when he looked up and

393

said sharply, 'But this gives you no reason to feel pleased with yourself. It's not as if it were your doing that, as a result of which, you know, Ella was unable to prevent herself from — well, to some extent it *was* of course your doing — but wholly disproportionate — I mean, Ella's reaction — quite out of the blue, she hardly even *knew* you at the time in Paris. I mean, it doesn't add up, does it?'

He seemed to abandon the question, threw it angrily away with his napkin as he realised how incoherent he was becoming. It wasn't clear to himself just what it was he wanted to say and changed course abruptly.

'Coming back to the Russian border country, Andrzejewski, the Slav side of the question. There's all that *soul*, of course, with a capital S, but there's also a queer sort of unreliability. You can't quite make 'em out. Treat you as if you were the best fellow in the world, you know, with every conceivable kindness. You get drunk as a skunk together, and then suddenly they take off, leaving you high and dry. Do you remember the little ginger cat?'

'Ginger cat?'

'Neighbour's cat at the house in St John's Wood. It was always sneaking over to see what was in the offing. As if it knew that Ella couldn't help herself. If she sees an animal, a child, perhaps a postman she thinks looks too thin, she has to feed it. There's an instinct to provide. She's a provider, like that woman in the Sherwood Anderson story, you know, who goes out to feed the animals and dies in a blizzard. But if the ginger cat didn't take what Ella put out for it, she would round on it, I mean get really quite angry with it, even take a kick at it and tell it what a stupid, ungrateful little beast it was, fully expecting the cat to understand. Well, the cat learned the drill of course. Looked hurt and slunk off, but came back the next day as if nothing had happened. Never any hard feelings on Ella's side either, of course, always standing there waiting to provide as usual. This is the leeway in which you'll have to learn to live, Claude, with the imponderabilities of that Slav soul of hers, although — who knows — perhaps there are two of them, or three, or more, each of them arguing their case behind her back.'

George put down his knife and fork and leaned back.

The waiter, who had been keeping solitary watch from the far end of the otherwise deserted dining room, took this as his cue to wheel his trolley forward once again with the vegetables George had mentioned as an option earlier in the evening.

'What about you, Claude? No? Thank you, I think we're finished here. Just a coffee for my guest. And put it on my account, will you?'

Claude watched another bright new shilling pass across the table, the gleaming little coin between George's thumb and finger catching the light full on as it lay heads up for a moment in the outstretched palm where he placed it.

Naturally George paid. It hadn't occurred to Claude that he would not, but with the appearance of actual money a thought struck him. Until now Claude had never been much concerned with *who paid*. That was the privilege of youth. But now a list of the things that George naturally paid for began unreeling in Claude's mind at an alarming rate. The list began with Ella's travelling expenses to go on holiday with him in Provence last year. It took in the mortgage on the new house in Richmond plus various dependencies such as the Hungarian woman who had moved in with the family, not to mention the hospitality extended to a ragbag of Aldermaston marchers, complete strangers to George, whom he didn't approve of in any case, and had been brought up to date only yesterday with the purchase of a set of adorable new bedclothes for little Alex that Ella had been unable to resist, although they were overpriced, as she had told him herself over the phone. Remembering now in the context of *who paid* the stricken look on George's face, the way he had pushed back his chair and then sat down again, as if the proximity of *It's not as if there were any law forbidding such a thing* and those extraordinary claims to which he'd given expression just before that had been more than he could take sitting down, Claude said on impulse, to offer him some crumb of comfort, the first thing that came into his head.

'I don't know that you can quantify it George, I mean, as if you could have more of it or less. What you have are different kinds of love.'

George looked hard at him, searching his face for evidence that Claude was not just making this up to please him.

'Do you think so?' His expression softened. 'A different kind of love?' he asked incredulously, with a childlike need to be reassured. 'Is that it?'

'Why else does Ella always come home?' Claude asked.

'Well yes. Why indeed? A good question. Perhaps you're right.'

George got slowly to his feet, patting his pockets to make sure he wasn't missing anything.

'Sorry about this,' he said to Claude as they made their way back to the entrance. 'Boring for you. Bloody early start tomorrow morning. Train at half past five, can you imagine.'

'I don't have far. It's only back to Bloomsbury for me tonight.'

'Oh is it? Well, that's all right then.'

They stood in the portico outside and shook hands.

'Thanks for that, Claude,' said George.

He turned quickly and went back inside.

# 13

*Because I make it my business to* may have been George's disingenuous reply to Claude's question about how he knew all the background to the V-2 story, but this wasn't quite the truth – it was the Old Man, when he found the time was ripe to touch on the second prong of the fork he had mentioned to him at their first meeting, who made it George's business for him.

For a year and a half after that meeting Phillips had melted back into the obscurity from which he had briefly re-emerged for his discussion with George at the Ministry of Supply. George heard nothing from him. Then he received the most friendly of notes, as if it was not eighteen months but as many days since that last conversation, asking George to come for an evening meeting at the unlikely address he gave him, the premises of a business called Johnson's Dry-Cleaning on Goodge Street.

The place was on the third floor of a drab house that still bore the scars of bomb damage. The door was opened by a sharp-faced man George hadn't seen before and took an immediate dislike to. The room he entered, with a drinks cabinet, wall-to-wall carpet, kidney-shaped table and deep armchairs, looked like a private residence, but taking his cue from his taciturn guide he didn't volunteer any comment. Still without a word of introduction, the man took him through into a series of other rooms fitted out like offices. In one of these he found the Old Man waiting for him. The foxy fellow who had shown George in disappeared down the corridor.

If George had thought at their Ministry of Supply meeting that Phillips had not changed in the seven or eight years since they first parted company, that deferred change had caught up with him dramatically in the intervening eighteen months. His now sparse, once sandy hair had turned completely grey. He was thinner, his face and frame apparently eroded from within as if wasted away by some disease.

'Hello, George,' said the Old Man, looking up from the desk where he was sitting, extending a hand to shake without getting up. 'How are you? Oh, meet Hawkin, by the way. Probably didn't introduce himself. Leaves that to me. Bit of a secretive fellow, but don't take that personally. Where is he?' He turned and bellowed through the open door, 'Hawkin!?

'No reply. Must have gone off somewhere ... Anyway, he's the man in charge here, so if you need anything, Hawkin will see to it for you. Not much of a conversationalist, it has to be said, but a first-rate man. Very tenacious, never lets go. Known as the terrier. Practically lives here. You seem to have settled down very well at the BTM,' he continued seamlessly, 'in all departments. Wouldn't like you to get the impression that what you're doing isn't appreciated. But I don't believe your talents are being harnessed as fully as they could be. The time has come for us to move on to phase two.'

'The second prong?'

'The second prong. Or, if you like, the second hat you will be wearing while continuing your invaluable work with the trade mission.'

During their conversation that night in the Goodge Street house the Old Man proposed putting George's name forward as a delegate to the recently established Euratom, or European Atomic Energy Community, a position that would additionally allow him access as an observer to the fledgling International Atomic Energy Agency in Vienna.

To George's objection that he had absolutely no qualifications for such a job, Phillips answered there was now a perceived need for what he called interpreters, people to mediate between nuclear energy suppliers on the one hand and customers on the other. It was not the technical background of nuclear energy but its marketing that George would be expected to familiarise himself with, its strategic role in a potentially vast new nuclear industry devoted to exclusively peaceful purposes.

Euratom had been set up to develop nuclear energy and create a specialist market for nuclear power – to distribute it through the EAEC and sell surplus power to outside states. The idea was to initiate a process that over time would develop into a gigantic industrial operation with more than a thousand so-called FBRs – fast breeder reactors – and dozens of large-scale civilian reprocessing plants all over Europe. The world's first commercial nuclear power station, Calder Hill on the coast of Cumberland, had opened only recently. In the first couple of years of its life it had been primarily used to produce weapons-grade plutonium, with electricity production as a secondary role. Those priorities were now to be reversed. In Europe Britain had a head start in FBR technology, which it must not lose at any cost, said the Old Man, thumping the armrest of his chair to emphasise these words.

A desk lamp was switched on in one of the adjacent offices separated by glass partitions from the booth in which they were sitting. Hawkin must have been working in the obscurity of the gradually enclosing evening light, and his angular face was suddenly lit up, catching George's attention.

'The nuclear-exporting states,' the Old Man went on, 'are currently restricted to the Soviet Union, Britain and America, but we can expect them soon to include others, perhaps Canada, France – who knows, even West Germany. All of us scrambling to pay our oil bills, you see, which can be expected to increase as the world's fossil fuel reserves are depleted. The salesmen of half a dozen competing nuclear supplier nations will be tripping each other up on their rounds in search of buyers. You'll be kept on your toes, George.'

Thus began the tutorials at Harwell. Two or three times a month George made the train journey to Oxford, where he was picked up and driven to the Atomic Energy Research Establishment. He spent the afternoon closeted with a Dr Jennings, a retired physicist. George was intrigued by the view through the door that Dr Jennings opened on to an Aladdin's cave of energy derived from non-fissile uranium, but, ever the pragmatist, he remained sceptical. He kept to himself his view that a perpetual nuclear fuel cycle, supplying mankind with limitless energy, sounded too good to be true. No one ever got something for nothing, George told himself, long before Dr Jennings got round to addressing this point.

'Atoms intended for peace,' Jennings told George, echoing Eisenhower's phrase, 'can also be used for war.'

A nation with a functioning nuclear reactor and a reprocessing facility could produce plutonium for the manufacture of explosive devices. As little as five or six kilograms were required to make a bomb of the order of the devices that had destroyed Hiroshima and Nagasaki. Small reprocessing plants for weapons-grade plutonium could be built fairly quickly at moderate expense and were difficult to detect. It had been calculated that within the next two decades the world's nuclear reactors would produce as much as half a million kilograms of plutonium.

'So the nuclear reactor that powers the fridge is at the same time our Pandora's box,' quipped George.

'So to speak,' conceded Dr Jennings, a furrow in his brow registering disapproval of George's facetiousness.

On his way back from Scotland to London, George stopped off for a tour of the Calder Hill nuclear power station, close to the village of Seascale on the Irish Sea coast. The site had been renamed Windscale to avoid confusion with the uranium processing factory near Preston. Later it became Sellafield. The Windscale piles were shut down following a fire which destroyed the core and released radioactive material into the environment. Milk and other farm produce from the surrounding area had to be destroyed. For the past decade radioactive waste had been diluted and discharged by pipeline into the Irish Sea, making it one of the most heavily contaminated seas in the world.

All this information was made available to George in the classified documents he received from Dr Jennings. George must be familiar with the drawbacks attached to the second prong, the Old Man had judged, so as to be able to weigh the pros and cons when responding to objections that might be raised by Euratom's future business partners.

During the year he was groomed for his job with Euratom, George was given the use of a desk in the Goodge Street office, a phone and a safe in which to lock the classified documents he was given. Only here was he authorised to study them. He had his own key and the code required to access the building. At whatever time of the day or night he came in, George would almost always find Hawkin there, who acknowledged his presence with no more than a nod. There was never any sign of Phillips.

From the start George had got into the habit of discussing his work with Julia because his visits to her flat followed his trips to Harwell. The opportunity was too good to miss. The Oxford train didn't get in to London until nine or ten in the evening, and he went straight on to Julia's, where he spent the night.

Privately, George thought the margin between civil and military use too narrow for comfort, and when he imagined the thousand reactors projected by Phillips, and multiplied the accidents at the Cumberland facility by a factor of a thousand, those doubts began to cause him unease. Julia brushed them aside.

'In the long run there's no alternative,' she said. 'Reactors will become safer. It's still a new technology. Give it a chance. Think of the benefit to the masses who *can't* afford heat and light at the current prices.'

'I'd prefer to think of their safety.'

'Why not give *them* the choice?'

'God forbid.'

It always came down to politics.

Julia was still a member of the British Communist Party. She clung to what George considered not only the naive belief, but also a wrong and dangerous one, that the only viable society of the future was present in the form of the Soviet Union.

'How can you possibly believe that? Sometimes I think you say such things just to be provocative and make yourself interesting. It's the most frightening God-awful place imaginable. People there lead absolutely miserable lives.'

'How do you know? Have you been there to see for yourself?'

'No, but friends have and I know what *they* saw. Have you?'

'I went there on a school trip when I was fifteen, and again about six years ago on an official visit of the British Communist Party. There was tremendous energy and enthusiasm. You could sense it everywhere. The new society was all around you and it was so *alive*. How dead everything seemed after we returned here, back in the rut of our class-ridden society. What do you really care, George? You don't even *see* these things from the privileged world you live in.'

George was sure that the British communists had been given the usual selective tour and completely taken in by Soviet propaganda. But where, after all, lay the truth in these things? And what answer could he honestly give to the charge that he didn't really care? It was exactly the same charge that Ella had levelled against him the day he ripped those Auschwitz cuttings out of the cupboards.

George wondered why they had built the reactors he had visited on his tour in such out-of-the-way places, so inconvenient to reach, and he came to the conclusion it could only be because the authorities understood the scale of the catastrophe if something went wrong with a fast breeder reactor in a built-up area.

'If they were confident they were safe they wouldn't have put them where they are, would they, in the back of beyond?' he challenged Julia the evening he got back from his trip to Scotland.

Julia had been listening to the news and switched it off. She went and stretched out her legs at the hearth, where a fire was burning.

'What's at the bottom of this U-2 affair, George?'

'I wouldn't tell you even if I knew.'

She sat on his lap and put her arms around his neck.

'Yes, you would. You would tell me lies, just as the Americans have been telling lies to the Russians. But the Russians found the spy plane and the pilot and showed the Americans up for the liars they are.'

'Everyone lies in this business,' said George, 'and the best liar wins. In this case the Russians.'

'So how can I believe you when you say you love me?'

George made a show of scratching his head.

'Did I say that?'

'Yes, you did!' She drummed her fists against his chest. 'You'll have to prove it to me. I want proof!'

'All right. Throw your ring into the embers of the fire and I'll get it out for you.'

'Would you do that?'

'I could give it a try. But then I'd burn my fingers, darling, and I'd have to go to hospital, and that would be the end of our quiet evening here together, wouldn't it?'

'Yes, it would. I've got a much better idea.'

It was the first time they had been to bed together in the mews flat. Julia sat George down in the window chair and told him to shut his eyes, and when he was allowed to open them again he saw the result of what he had already heard. Julia had pulled back the cover and sprinkled out-of-season dark red rose petals over the pink sheets, imported Italian roses for which she had paid a shilling apiece, on which her petal-strewn body now lay spread out naked for his inspection. Drowsy from the two bottles of claret they had drunk with their supper, his desire thickened and slowed down, they went dreamily through the otherwise urgent lovemaking motions and came together as was possible only for such relaxed bodies, in a perfect coincidence, as rarely happened, of mutual pleasure. When Julia rolled off him George must have already been asleep as he didn't notice her get up, only realising she wasn't beside him when he woke up later in the night; but he soon went back to sleep, surfacing briefly again when Julia got back into bed.

'Where've you been?' George murmured sleepily.

'Where women sometimes have to go in the night more often than men do, darling.' She snuggled up beside him. 'Ours has less capacity, you know. And I only have one kidney. You don't want the technical details on *that*, do you? Go back to sleep, George.'

And he did.


# 14


At the end of July 1961 the BTM flew to East Berlin for its fifth trade conference in the capital of the German Democratic Republic. Machine tools, agricultural machinery and construction equipment were the main items on the agenda.

The by-now-familiar security bus with its usual blank-faced driver picked them up at the airport and took them to the Intercontinental. It was still light when they arrived. George and Julia had adjacent rooms on the top floor, giving them a view down the full length of the gargantuan Stalin-Allee. East Berlin's bombastic main boulevard with its ornate, even richly decorated ceramic facades, had been built from scratch out of the ruins of the bombed city. It was the communist retort to the Kurfürstendamm, a glitzy shop window where the wealth of West Berlin was on display.

It was a fine July evening, the only evening they would have, as it was a one-day conference and then they would be flying back to London. A stroll down what their chaperone called the prestige boulevard and dinner in one of its prestige restaurants had been laid on for the delegates. This was effectively obligatory for them all, but George had to go without Julia. She had been kept up by a sick cat most of the previous night, she said, and had one of her migraines coming on, so she wanted to go to bed early. When George got back later in the evening he knocked at her door, but there was no reply.

George couldn't sleep. He sat up late, drinking and doing *The Times* crossword while he thought about his last meeting with the Old Man.

A file concerning an East German facility known as WISMUT, perhaps the single most important item of information to be passed on to the British in all the time George had been acting as a courier, would be in the briefcase he exchanged in East Berlin. This was what the Old Man had told him at a late-night meeting at the dry-cleaners in Goodge Street the day before he left London. This was only the second occasion that Phillips had told him in advance of the contents of a cachet, impressing on him the need for particular vigilance. When a routine became habitual, he had drummed into his pupils back at the school, one became careless and made mistakes. One should always approach a task as if doing it for the first time.

'Does the name WISMUT ring a bell?'

'No,' said George.

'Well, that's no surprise, considering that it's one of the most secret facilities in eastern Europe outside the Soviet Union. Let me fill you in. What you are about to hear is for your ears only, needless to say.'

Phillips went on to explain that WISMUT referred to a uranium mine or rather an area of mines in East Germany, one of a number of uranium sources developed by the Soviet Union, which lacked uranium resources itself. It appeared that by far the most important of these were the WISMUT mines just north of the Czech border in a large area extending north-west into Thüringen.

Indirectly substantiated reports put the number of miners employed by the WISMUT facility in the tens of thousands. These figures were deduced from statistics gleaned from hospitals in the area, where a disproportionately high percentage of the population had been treated for lung cancer during the previous decade. Thousands of miners, it seemed, had met painful deaths after years of heavy labour in the poorly ventilated dusty tunnels.

WISMUT was the first uranium mining facility to pass into Soviet hands after the occupation of eastern Europe in 1945. No expense had been spared, it appeared, not even the lives of thousands of miners, to extract and transport back to the Soviet Union the raw material crucial to its atomic programme. If one could establish the percent-age contributed by WISMUT to the entire uranium supply going to the Soviet Union, Phillips said, it would be possible to deduce fairly accurately the quantity of weapons-grade plutonium that was being produced there, thus answering questions of crucial interest to military strategists in the West.

'How many atomic bombs have they got?' The shadow of a smile briefly haunted the Old Man's face. 'Are theirs bigger than ours?'

This question sounded as if it might be leading on to a joke. George said nothing, waiting.

'More than we have? Or less? Or does it matter as much as everybody seems to think? What do *you* think, George?'

'I'm afraid it wasn't on my Harwell curriculum. I wouldn't have the slightest idea, sir.'

'Well, with a bit of luck we soon will.'

Phillips looked and sounded very tired. George watched him getting with some difficulty to his feet. How old would he be now? In his early sixties. Not really so old, thought George, but already he was beginning to live up to the name they had given him at the school, in those days more out of affection than in deference to his seniority. But in the meantime he had actually become the Old Man.

'Are you all right, Major?'

He had meant it as a general enquiry into the Old Man's health. But then George thought he saw him about to stagger, and rose quickly from his chair to put a supporting hand under his elbow.

'Thank you for your assistance.' For a moment Phillips leaned on the table before straightening up. He put a hand on George's shoulder. 'You know, George, you can sometimes have a real *tenderness*. Hope your wife appreciates it.'

It was an extraordinary remark. It took George so completely by surprise that it left him with nothing to say.

That night George slept poorly and had bad dreams which he couldn't remember, slipping away like fractured patterns in a kaleidoscope the moment he moved his head. When he called on Julia to go down for breakfast the next morning she told him she had slept 'like a top' and was feeling herself again.

In a hall a few minutes' walk down the Stalin-Allee, built and fitted out in the monumental Stalinist style of the 1950s that George found unpleasantly reminiscent of fascist architecture, the conference began punctually at nine o'clock. He wondered how a building could have such an unsettling effect on him. He realised it might remind him of the style of Mussolini's Italy, no less grandiose, no less intimidating to a small boy, which had left its imprint on the Victorian house in Hampstead his father had bought and converted at that time. The fascist bombast of those columns and floral drapes in stone had always remained cold and uninviting, even when he encountered it in such an idyllic setting as D'Annunzio's villa on the Lago di Garda.

He drifted off along a chain of thought that led from dictatorships to the cult of monuments. The conference proceedings bored him, as conference proceedings usually did. The more democratic the state, he concluded, the less need it had for monuments. It agreed with his own tastes to live in a city that lacked the ostentation of most European capitals. He realised it was just as well that Wren's reconstruction of London had not been put into effect, for it would have been out of character. The character of London was as makeshift and understated as its political traditions and the British constitution, such as it was.

He felt pleased with these thoughts until he remembered why he was sitting there. Such thoughts were merely blinds to divert him from the business in hand.

George and Julia were sitting on their own at a table a few yards behind the British delegation, who were seated at the conference table proper, a huge disc which appeared to be made of solid steel, facing an East German delegation that outnumbered them two to one. It was as if they were re-fighting the war on their own terms. Punctually at half past ten a squad of blue-uniformed women marched into the hall and served coffee at tables to one side of the room. Delegates drifted over, some remained sitting, others wandered around, cups of coffee in hand, joining groups where conversations had been struck up. George knew the procedure and still felt perfectly relaxed. There was a good hour and a half to go before he was on.

Nothing was in jeopardy for the time being. To savour a sense of innocence, knowing that in a couple of hours he would have lost it, was a poignant, extraordinarily vivid sensation.

The conference resumed at ten to eleven. When George found himself involuntarily looking at the clock over the door every quarter of an hour, his pulse had already risen, his calm beginning to unravel. A few minutes before half past twelve the conference had got itself entangled in a knotty discussion from which it seemed unlikely to extricate itself in time for lunch. The chairman, who should have had his eye on the clock, was the most deeply embroiled of them all.

The meeting dragged on. George found it unbearable.

Somebody with responsibility for the conference schedule made a great show of opening the main doors at five past one and leaving them open as an admonition to the delegates to put their papers in order and come out for lunch. There were different rules in different places, in some places no rules at all, but the rule in East Berlin was that during the lunch break all documents had to stay in place behind locked doors. Reluctantly the delegates got to their feet, still in animated discussion.

This was the moment for George and Julia to get up too and do what they called the funny business. They had rehearsed what to do. On side tables brochures about the industries that were the subject of the conference had been laid out. George had browsed through these during the previous coffee break, giving him the opportunity to identify the two inconspicuous rectangles on the dun-coloured briefcase that was the twin to his own. It stood facing out on the floor behind the last but one chair on the East German side of the table.

As the delegates stood, continuing to talk as they sorted their papers, George and Julia wandered past, chatting, stopping at the side table a few yards behind the chair in question for George to pick up one of the brochures and put it into his briefcase. Julia then drew his attention to the fact that his shoelace was undone. Placing his briefcase on the carpet a foot behind the chair, George knelt down in order to tie his lace and got to his feet again, this time holding the briefcase for which he had just substituted his own. He and Julia sauntered on around the conference table, pausing here and there to glance at brochures, until they reached their own place again, where George deposited the briefcase on his chair. On their way out of the hall they mingled with the members of their own delegation.

It was this apparently straightforward routine which had led to George taking up cigarettes again, a habit he had previously had only for the duration of his work at the Chelsea school. He had always enjoyed an occasional cigar, but now he was a confirmed cigarette smoker. He admitted to Ella that he couldn't give it up. He didn't mention to her that he was also drinking more than he used to, as Ella had already noted with surprise. Addiction was out of character with the George she knew. Lunch for him at a conference, with the switch behind him, consisted of more coffee and Turkish cigarettes – keying himself up, he said to Julia, in order to bring himself back down. They never sat together at lunch, mixing judiciously with other members of the delegation.

At two twenty the conference reconvened in the hall for the afternoon session. George's thoughts were wandering, already anticipating the evening ahead with Julia, when a man in a grey suit appeared at his elbow and whispered to him that he was wanted on the telephone.

George felt his stomach suck in. 'Who is it wants to speak to me?'

'This way, please,' said the man, indicating to George with a sharp gesture of his hand the end of any discussion, that he was to get up immediately and leave the room.

George hesitantly rose to his feet.

'It appears I shall have to leave this in your hands for the time being,' George said, exchanging glances with Julia. They didn't have time for more. George was already on his way out.

There was no sign of a telephone anywhere in the marble corridor outside the hall. Two men, who were lounging by the street exit, took their hands out of their pockets and moved slowly down the corridor towards them. As they came level with George and the official who had fetched him out of the conference, his grey-suited escort continued walking on past the entrance in the direction of the cafeteria where the delegates had been taken for lunch, mumbling something over his shoulder to the two men that George didn't catch, before he hurried off down the corridor.

'*Kommen Sie mit,*' one of the two men said to him.

This wasn't an invitation. The lack of the word *bitte* made it sound ominous.

George asked them where they were taking him.

'*Sie sind des Landes verwiesen worden. Wir haben Anweisungen, Sie unverzüglich zur Grenze zu bringen.*'

George understood that he was apparently not being arrested, but simply deported. Still bad enough. Under the circumstances it seemed better for him to say nothing.

A car was waiting outside the building. George got in, the two men sitting on either side of him.

'*Friedrichstrasse Ecke Zimmerstrasse,*' one of the men said to the driver, and the car drove off down the almost empty boulevard at top speed.

Within a quarter of an hour the car pulled up at a corner. George recognised the border crossing, one reserved for visitors from the West, which he had made use of several times previously himself. The two men escorted George to the checkpoint on the East German side and told him to walk the fifty yards over to West Berlin.

'*Gehen Sie*,' they said simply, and stood there watching until he had reached the American checkpoint, where he showed his diplomatic passport and was allowed through.

'Well, I suppose I'm out,' George said aloud to himself when he arrived in West Berlin a minute later, but what the hell was going to happen to Julia? 'What the hell happened?'

His instinct was just to get out of sight, and he plunged into the nearest bar.

# 15

Within three quarters of an hour of crossing into West Berlin George got out of a taxi and walked up the steps to the entrance of a house on Savignyplatz. It was a quiet residential neighbourhood with large leafy trees along the pavement. The little glass-covered brass name plaque under the button that George pressed identified the occupant of one of the apartments on the third floor as P. Strachan. George had called on Strachan a couple of times when passing through town on earlier occasions. From his West Berlin apartment he ran a one-man operation representing several organisations, among them the BTM.

The front door clicked open without George being asked over the intercom to identify himself. He entered a dark, panelled vestibule with a wooden floor. Even in the daytime it remained so dark that only the permanent yellow glow of the switch at the bottom of the stairwell showed visitors where they could turn on the light. Despite the panelling and the elaborately scrolled woodwork of the newel post, testifying that it must once have been an affluent sort of building, the place now had a run-down appearance, like so many of the buildings in this exhausted city. George took his time on the way up the stairs, already framing in his mind the coded message he would send by telex from Strachan's office.

He had not yet reached the landing of the third floor when the stairwell light went out. That's a very short timer, thought George; the landlord must be economising. He had to wait a few moments for his eyes to get accustomed to the dark before he located another yellow glow indicating the next light switch at the top of the stairs on the wall to his left.

At that moment a door opened somewhere down the landing to the right.

'Is that you, Morris?' called an unfamiliar voice.

George was taken aback.

'Yes, it is. How did you guess?'

'I never guess. I make it my business to know.'

He came up the last few stairs and looked down the landing, where to his disagreeable surprise he saw Hawkin waiting for him in the doorway of Strachan's apartment.

'Come on in, said the spider to the fly,' chuckled Hawkin in a jovial, almost gleeful manner George found sinister. This man was very different from the taciturn grim-faced curmudgeon who had opened the door to him on his first visit to Goodge Street.

They didn't shake hands. Hawkin ignored even the courtesy of showing him in. He barged ahead, leaving George to follow.

'Where's Strachan?'

'In Rimini, I believe.'

'On holiday?'

'Something like that.'

George was alerted by these words. Something disagreeable was undoubtedly in the offing.

'I expect you could do with a drink. I'm afraid Scotch or vodka is all there is.'

'Vodka.' George sat down wearily. 'You probably know that I've just been deported from East Berlin.'

Hawkin handed him a glass. 'We were informed a few hours ago.'

George was nonplussed. 'A few *hours*! That was *before* I was deported. What exactly is going on here?'

'What a coincidence. I was getting round to asking you just that question myself.'

With chopping movements of his hands Hawkin squared off the loose papers lying on the coffee table in front of him and called, 'Pritchard?'

A short, balding man of about thirty came in immediately from the next room, as if he had been standing behind the door waiting for this instruction, and pulled out a chair at the desk to one side of the table. Obviously knowing from past experience of similar situations that

Hawkin wasn't going to bother with the formalities of introductions, Pritchard didn't even look at George. He took out his stenographer's pad and switched on a large tape recorder that George only now noticed was standing on the desk.

'A number of questions, in fact.'

Hawkin rubbed his hands, and George realised with stupefaction how much this odd man was enjoying himself.

'We need to take this right from the beginning, your meeting with Phillips at the then Ministry of Supply early in 1956 ... I assure you this debriefing is just a formality, if an unavoidable one, in view of what has happened.'

'It was in December 1955,' George corrected him, realising as he did so that Hawkin did not need to be corrected, because he already knew and had laid his first little trap, trivial as it might seem. Hawkin had more than a formality in mind.

Throughout a long afternoon George did his best to give as full and accurate an account as possible of his activities for the BTM during the previous five and a half years. Night had come on by the time he was finished. Now and then Hawkin quizzed him on some point or other, but didn't interrupt him. George trod carefully around the subject of Julia Manning, and told a lie only once, when Hawkin asked him about what they had talked about when he had last met Phillips. George remembered what Phillips had requested of him on that occasion and what he had promised him. *What you are about to hear is for your ears only, needless to say*, the Old Man had said, and George now felt bound to honour his word.

'On the evening before I was due to fly to East Berlin.'

'What did you talk about?'

It crossed George's mind that Hawkin had been present at the Goodge Street office on the evening in question and might have overheard something, but he decided to take a chance.

'I had asked to see him because I no longer felt confident about the courier work I was doing for the BTM, and wanted to terminate that side of the business in order to devote myself full time to the Euratom position I had been prepared for over the last eighteen months or so. Phillips agreed. He said the East Berlin trip was one of the last, if not the last he would be asking me to make.'

'No longer felt confident about what?'

410

'By temperament I felt unsuited for such work.'

'Unsuited?'

George hesitated.

'My nerves were going to pieces. My family life was suffering as a result.'

Hawkin gave Pritchard a sign to switch off the tape recorder. Pritchard then got up and left the room.

At that moment the telephone rang. Hawkin went over to the desk, picked it up and stood there listening for ten minutes without moving or saying a word, not even 'Hello' when he took the call.

He came back to the coffee table and poured them both another drink. George offered him a cigarette. Hawkin declined.

'Well of course we're as concerned as you are, Morris, about Julia Manning. The fact is, she wasn't on the plane that landed at Heathrow this evening with the rest of the trade delegation.'

George's heart sank. 'She's been detained in East Berlin, then.'

'So it seems.' Hawkin tapped his teeth with a fingernail. 'Or rather, she is still there, under whatever circumstances.'

'What do you mean?'

'I really don't know *what* I mean. I'm just stabbing in the dark, Morris. Aren't we all? Isn't that, so to speak, the very nature of our business?'

George was beginning to resent this cold fish, this queer fellow he hardly knew, presuming to call him Morris in such a familiar way. He might be George's superior, and he was quite a few years older than George, but that still didn't justify the patronising, even impertinent manner with which Hawkin was treating him. He felt as if Hawkin was baiting him. It might equally be a ruse to intimidate him, thought George, for as he had belatedly realised it was quite evident that, if through no fault of his own, he had now come under suspicion himself.

'A flight has been booked for you to London, by the way,' said Hawkin as if this was something he had just remembered, 'the last one out of Berlin this evening. A car will be arriving in a few minutes to take you to the airport. Your colleagues are currently being questioned to see what light they can shed on the events that transpired in East Berlin this afternoon. Did Miss Manning leave the conference hall and return with them to the hotel? Was she on the bus that took the delegation from the hotel to the airport? And so on. We still don't know what happened, you see. In London I'm afraid they will want to hear again from you what you have already told me here about the twenty-four hours, not even that, you spent in East Berlin, and to piece it together with whatever information the other members of the delegation have been able to gi—'

The longest speech by far that George had ever heard from Hawkin at one stretch was interrupted by the buzzer. He went to the front door and spoke briefly through the intercom.

'Your taxi's downstairs,' he called to George, and as George came through into the hall he opened the door for him. 'Bon voyage.'

'Bon voyage?' echoed George incredulously.

'Didn't you have anything with you? A coat or something?'

'I did, but not any more.' George walked out onto the landing. 'A briefcase. Remember? Unfortunately I had to leave it in East Berlin. Even more unfortunately I left it with Julia Manning. One of those little mishaps. I mean, what sort of a man are you, Hawkin?'

Quite openly angry now, George thought the time had come to give Hawkin a piece of his mind.

'What may be professionally required in the line of duty is one thing, Hawkin. Common decency is another. The consequences this business is going to have for Miss Manning apparently don't concern you much, whatever you say to the contrary. Well, they do concern me. When the Stasi open that briefcase and find what one of our agents was intending to get out of East Berlin, it's her head that will be on the block, not mine. I take the strongest exception to what I consider your extraordinarily callous attitude, not to mention the high-handed way you have treated me here today, and I shall say so when I get back to London.'

George had already started down the stairs when he heard Hawkin chuckling behind him.

'Oh dear. You *have* got the wrong end of the stick, haven't you, and the trouble is you still don't realise it,' said Hawkin gaily. 'I rather think you're in the wrong line of business, my dear fellow. But then your nerves are going to pieces, as you say. Look to your own head, Morris. It may be closer to the block than you imagine. It's not a problem of what Miss Manning and you were intending to get *out* of East Berlin or half a dozen other places during the last couple of years, come to that. It's what she's been getting *in*. Oh yes!'

Whereupon Hawkin went back into the apartment, leaving George staring up from the stairs at the door that had just closed in his face.

# 16

George returned to debriefings in London which gradually unfolded to him the full extent of the disaster that had taken place.

On the same day that the BTM had left for East Berlin a senior secretary in the recently established Ministry of Defence had defected just before he was about to be arrested. Julius, as the Russian mole was known, had long been running a network of agents in Britain, perhaps since the end of the war. MI6 had suspected Julius for some time but, as was so often the case, had been reluctant to intervene, preferring to bide their time in order to uncover his network as fully as possible.

Hawkin's unexpected appearance in West Berlin was only coincidental with George's deportation from East Berlin. The disappearance of Julius led to an unusual amount of human intelligence traffic passing through the needle's eye of a divided Europe in the one city where this still presented no undue problems. As one of the immediate repercussions of Julius's defection, half a dozen British agents still out in the field and now in imminent jeopardy were brought in through West Berlin on the same day Julius absconded. But this withdrawal was prompted by larger considerations than the defection of a Soviet mole.

Exactly when it would happen was still unclear, but that it would happen and soon — the blocking up of this loophole so exasperating to the German Democratic Republic in particular and to intelligence operations in all the Warsaw Pact countries generally — was in no doubt. And within thirteen days of Julia Manning being detained in East Berlin the wall that Khrushchev had demanded, and the possibility of which Ulbricht had publicly denied right up until the last moment, was indeed built between the two halves of Berlin along the demarcation line where Soviet and American tanks had rolled to a halt in 1945.

The Allies looked the other way. President Kennedy was on board the cabin cruiser *Marlin* when the news reached him, and communicated only briefly by telephone with the secretary of state before he resumed his vacation, while Dean Rusk was watching a ball game. De Gaulle was at his country house in Champagne, on holiday, as were his prime minister and foreign minister. Macmillan was on holiday in Scotland with the foreign secretary, Alec Douglas-Home. Adenauer castigated the mayor of Berlin, Willy Brandt, but otherwise did nothing. The connivance was complete. The Berlin Wall, prearranged to go up in circumstances that suited everyone, did so with little fuss.

For George, it was as if Julia had been immured in a tomb – irrecoverably, as he now discovered. Julia would never be exchanged, never let out; she had voluntarily decamped, gone over to the other side rather than face trial and imprisonment at home on charges of treason. She must have been forewarned by Julius, probably in the course of that evening when she had pleaded a migraine. In all likelihood, Julia had already been recruited before she left Estonia. As one of Philby's collaborators, she was co-responsible for the disasters that had beset British operations in the Baltic from the time she and George had begun working at the school. Not a few of the agents they had helped train there and controlled in the field were sent out on Klose's supercharged boat to deaths that had been arranged for them by Julia Manning, probably others as well.

How had it been overlooked that at the age of eighteen Julia Manning was already a member of the Communist Party? Partly because it would have been difficult for intelligence recruiters to take seriously a threat from a girl still so young and apparently innocent, a misguided idealist, perhaps, but inconceivably a traitor. Yet the SIS also had good reason to overlook this eccentricity in a candidate so qualified for the job at the time, with her intimate knowledge of the Baltic region and fluency in two of its languages. They had needed her.

With her post-war career, matters weren't so simple.

After the school, Julia had been employed as a secretary by British Non-Ferrous Metals, a company by no means as humdrum as its name suggested. She had mentioned this job to George at the BTM annex on the day he walked in and discovered that they would be working together again. George would come across this company later in the classified material relating to nuclear production facilities. British Non-Ferrous Metals was a manufacturer of components for nuclear weapons. But George had failed to make the connection. He had taken Julia at her word that she had left her job with the company because she found it boring.

She had in fact left on the instructions of Julius because her security clearance had been suspended, and without access to sensitive documents she was of little use to him. For the two years that Julia Manning was permitted access, however, she had photographed classified documents, using the Minox camera provided by Julius, and passed them on to her control by means of a dead drop that MI6 had latterly kept under surveillance. The damage done during the eighteen months that had escaped surveillance was inestimable.

It was on the instructions of her control that she accepted the job she was offered with BTM. At first there was little apparent benefit to be derived from her work there, but as Julius recognised, presumably with the advantage of inside information, in its political intelligence unit there was potential that could be developed for more rewarding purposes.

George went through the worst experiences of his life when his unwitting contribution to the Julius network was brought to light in the following months – shame, anger, sorrow, hatred, an embarrassment so humiliating that it made him groan aloud.

From the time of his first tutorials with Dr Jennings, every document relating to the British nuclear programme, which he had so conscientiously locked in the safe in Goodge Street the morning after he returned from those trips to Harwell, had been taken out of his briefcase by Julia the night before, photographed with the Minox and passed on to her control in Moscow. Sometimes he had not even noticed her absence from bed; sometimes he had woken up when she got back in, murmuring something about women's bladders which he didn't question, because it belonged to the *comme il faut* for a man with George's background that to question a woman about such things was indelicate.

This was the truth of the matter, at least for George, but to have admitted it at his debriefings by a military intelligence committee would have sounded so inane that George offered the classic line of defence, the blindness of a man infatuated with a woman. This did nothing to mitigate the extraordinary carelessness his superiors condemned him for, but male susceptibility to the attractions of a devious woman was a scenario familiar enough from the annals of spycraft to appear not unreasonable to them, and was even met with a degree of sympathy.

Had George been infatuated with Julia as he claimed, her betrayal of him might have been easier to bear. It was the betrayal of his trust that hurt. As the victim of an abused trust, or so at first it seemed to George in those never-ending conversations he held with himself, he came out of the affair more honourably than he did in the role of a victim of blind passion. But this too was just another self-deception. His abused trust was in reality wounded vanity – he had allowed himself to be completely taken in by a woman and shown up for a fool. His *amour-propre* had taken a beating. Chiefly for this reason, George told his wife nothing about the entire affair.

The building of the Berlin Wall provided a plausible explanation for his trips abroad suddenly ceasing. In this climate of hostility, he told Ella, trade delegations to eastern Europe made no sense. In fact, for the foreseeable future the BTM had lost its *raison d'être*. Under cover of this timely pretext, George's superiors could reprimand him and suspend him from his duties without attracting attention. After a couple of months' ostracism, during which George was left to kick his heels at home in Richmond, he was moved quietly back to the FO as a back-room analyst of American affairs, working with colleagues unacquainted with his recent record.

The U-2 Affair, in which the Soviets had shot down a high-altitude US reconnaissance plane over Russian territory, had apparently terminated such flights for good, but it was another U-2 flight – over San Cristóbal in Cuba in October 1962 – that produced the crucial photographs proving the installation of Soviet missile bases on the island. The CIA prepared a memorandum on the Soviet SS-4 missile identified by the photographs and compared the pictures with material from a GRU officer who had recently begun to provide the Allies with secret material from inside the Soviet military establishment.

The officer's material was so extraordinary that MI6 and the CIA, both of which had been approached by him, had initially suspected a trap and ignored his overtures. In 1961 this officer led a Soviet trade delegation to London, but his real mission was to set up a GRU spy network. A British businessman and MI6 agent by the name of Wynne arranged for him to meet SIS officers, resulting in the Russian being set up as a double agent, pretending to conduct Soviet espionage while sending reports to the West. It was only after his information about mis-siles on Cuba was corroborated by the U-2 photographs that Western intelligence services took him seriously.

In the US affairs department at the Foreign Office, George was one of the few to learn the name of this remarkable informant, a bona fide GRU colonel at the highest level of military intelligence with access to the Kremlin, who had first offered his services to the West in 1960. Penkovsky demolished the myth, assiduously propagated by Khrushchev, that the Soviets had more intercontinental ballistic missiles than the US and that these missiles were capable of precision attacks. In the vividly colloquial style characteristic of Penkovsky's communications, he told the Allies that the type of missile installed on Cuba couldn't hit a bull in the backside with a balalaika. With such reassurances to back him up, Kennedy felt confident calling Khrushchev's bluff, forcing the Soviet leader to back down. The Cuban missile crisis was over. It was a rare example of one man's spying having a direct effect on the fate of the world.

However, on 20 October 1962, the day after the crisis began, Penkovsky was arrested outside Soviet military intelligence headquarters. The KGB had entered his apartment and found the Minox camera he used to photograph the documents he passed on to the Americans. The following year, a few months before the Test Ban Treaty prohibiting all nuclear weapons tests in the atmosphere was signed in Moscow, Penkovsky was tried and shot.

In the aftermath of Penkovsky's exposure a number of moles in the intelligence establishments on both sides were arrested. The British businessman and MI6 agent Wynne was sentenced to a long term of imprisonment in Russia. And Caesar, the code name of a highly placed Soviet source inside British military intelligence, who Penkovsky claimed had been passing on secrets for the last twenty years, was identified as Trevor Phillips, or the Old Man, as he was known to George and to so many other young people who had learned from him the business of espionage.

At the kangaroo court where he was tried and convicted by his peers good reasons were put forward for handling the Phillips case as a family affair which it would be in nobody's interests to bring to public attention. Phillips had cancer and didn't have much longer to live. He was held in a room without bars in the infirmary of the army base at Aldershot and treated with morphine to ease him through the last couple of months of his life.

George went to visit him there two weeks after the signing of the Test Ban Treaty. It was a mild October afternoon, the dry leaves crackling underfoot on the pavement as he walked from the station to the infirmary. Recalling the Old Man's fondness for oranges, he had brought half a dozen and a blue plate from Provence that Ella had given him to put them on.

Phillips was lying on his bed, propped up with pillows and dressed in old-man clothes, baggy grey trousers and a cardigan that hung in folds once filled by his now emaciated body, exuding an unpleasant, indefinable old-man odour. He didn't get up when George came in, but raised an arm in greeting, and smiled.

'Peel me one,' he said when he saw the oranges.

George pulled up a chair, tucked the napkin which Ella had wrapped the plate in under the Old Man's chin and placed the plate on his lap.

He ate a segment and exclaimed 'Delicious!' but then pushed the plate away. 'It's the weight,' he said, and George understood that the plate pressing on his chest caused him pain.

The Old Man said he would answer any questions George wanted to ask because he had a right to know.

'The whole briefcase rigmarole,' said George. 'I can guess but I'd like to hear it from you. What purpose did it serve?'

'To take the heat off me. Hawkin had caught Caesar's scent and was damned if he wouldn't run him to ground. He did too. Dogged little bugger. Although, had it not been for the exposure of Penkovsky...' Phillips closed his eyes. For a long while he lay so still that George wondered if he'd dozed off.

'So anyway, the KGB and I came up with the BTM charade – political officers acting as couriers, all that business. A major operation. Pawns, even some really quite valuable pieces, had to be sacrificed to save the king. Julius to protect Caesar. But what does *sacrificed* mean? He got out all right – state pension, an apartment in Leningrad. Worse things can happen to a man. It all stays in the family. They're bad boys, but they belong to the family. You give us ours back and we'll give you yours. We're all in this together. There's a good German word for it, *Scheingefecht*. Wynne will be exchanged. Count on it. And Julia chose to go back home to the Baltic, to Tallinn, where for her it all began. So we did right by them. And it gave me a couple of years more, giving me what *I* wanted, the Test Ban Treaty, thanks in large part to a brave Soviet physicist whose very name is a state secret. So things balanced out in the end.'

'Not much help to the dead. It didn't bring the dead back to life.'

Phillips opened his mouth and laughed soundlessly. 'Who can possibly want to be brought back to life?'

'The young people we trained at the school, for example,' said George angrily, 'who you sent out to be slaughtered?'

418

'A general who sends his men into battle doesn't count the dead. If he did, he wouldn't be a general.' Phillips picked a thread off his sleeve.

'But they weren't your men,' snarled George, infuriated by the Old Man's stoniness. 'You and they weren't wearing the same uniform, only they didn't know that.'

'So what is it you hold against me? That I was responsible for their deaths? Or that I betrayed them?'

'Both.'

'People get killed in wars because killing people is the business of wars,' the Old Man answered without hesitation, looking squarely at George. 'For all I can see,' he went on, 'from the recurrent nature of war throughout human history, war is no less indispensable to us than peace. War is not a necessary evil, it is necessary; and what is necessary is not evil. The drums are sounded, warpaint or uniforms are put on civilians to turn them into soldiers, and off they go to war. Loyalty to your own side, what is called patriotism, is taken for granted. Still, it is basically a tribal instinct. It is not something that most people question in time of war. Nor do they question the sources of the intelligence they need to fight their war. Soldiers sent into war without the benefit of intelligence are wasted soldiers. Other things being equal, intelligence decides the outcome. Our side demands it. The other side demands it. As long as it is our intelligence, intelligence to our advantage, the man or woman who procures it is a hero. For one side Philby and Phillips are traitors, for the other they are heroes; they are given the Order of Lenin, in some cases *in absentia* ...'

The Old Man smiled.

'A state pension and a dacha. For one side Penkovsky is the greatest intelligence windfall in the fifteen years since the war ended. For the other side Penkovsky is the scum of the earth, fit only to be shot and thrown on the dung heap. Don't you admit, George, that without relativity it becomes meaningless to talk of these things?'

'Leaving you to sneak out the back door,' said George, struggling with a very lopsided expression on his face, 'washing your hands of all responsibility? No, it won't do.'

'Ah, so in the end it is the issue of responsibility, after all, and this is the noise of sheep bleating, George.'

The Old Man offered him the plate of orange segments. George declined and watched Phillips slide one into the grey cavity of his mouth, break it with his teeth, suck and swallow it in one go. George found the sight repulsive.

'The sheep bleat because it is the nature of sheep to bleat. They do not make choices. They follow their tribal instincts. The ones who make a choice, because they do *not* follow the tribal instinct, are the purveyors of intelligence, the spies. True, there are mercenaries among them, a minority, and I don't hold that against them. I don't regard it as dishonourable per se to do *anything* for money. The mercenary sees the reality of war, stripped of all sentiment and propaganda, and acts according to his judgement. In all cases, however, the double agent is more intimately acquainted with issues of morality than the herd that unthinkingly follows the tribal instinct. The business of purveying intelligence, and the reason why, are both beyond the ken of the herd, of anyone who unthinkingly follows. The motivation of spies – what goes in – is immaterial within the greater scheme of things. Money, ideals, greed, desire – irrelevant. What comes out is all that counts, the result. And the most important result is the levelling of the odds. It's a deeply egalitarian business. The contribution of spies is to help to achieve balance. They are the vessels through which this aim much greater than themselves is achieved. If there is loyalty in human nature it is only because it is definable in terms of disloyalty. Peace because it is distinguishable from war. And so on. And the levelling of the odds can only take place, of course, because this spectrum of human behaviour and the moral values attached to it are the same on either side. Spies are the personification of the ambivalence in all things. It's almost a law that on either side there will always be spies in roughly equal numbers. They are the referees who blow the whistle when the game gets too one-sided; they are damned and extolled in absolutely reciprocal measure – all depending on the point of view.'

The Old Man sat up. 'Here's the punchline, George. Forget tribes. Join the human race.' He cautiously lowered his legs over the side of the bed. 'Would you like to accompany me on my perambulation? Doctor's orders. Up and down the corridor three times a day. As it's such a nice afternoon, perhaps we might even venture outside.'

George put the blue plate with the remaining oranges on the table by the window where the Old Man took his meals, lighting a bonfire of colour in the whitewashed room lacking anything but the bare necessities.

The Old Man leaning on him, George steered him along the paths beside lawns kept clipped as closely as an army haircut. Two gardeners in khaki overalls were tending them. Leaves were not allowed to litter, and were apparently removed the moment they fell. The Old Man wanted to rest on a bench still touched by the last rays of the afternoon sun, so they sat down to enjoy the scene without feeling the need for any more talk. George looked at the rows of exfoliated trees and was reminded of the similarity between trees and men, both balding from the crown down, then thought of the frailty and the treachery of the sick man beside him. After all he had said, Phillips remained as unfathomable for George as he always had been, leaving him sad and deeply puzzled, irritated that his affection, though badly battered, still remained in place for this man who had seen into his inmost soul, used him as a marionette, manipulated and betrayed him.

'In the end there's been a high price to pay,' said the Old Man, who seemed to catch the drift of these thoughts. 'It's been a solitary life. Never married. Might have at one time, but didn't in the end. Don't see there's any way of reconciling this sort of life with a marriage, family and so on. Most of yourself is cut off. You're not on the level with your wife – can't be, can you, having to conceal things from her all the time. Having to lie all the time. Dishonesty and distrust are the death of love. No, I think my advice to a married man, if he were in our line of business, you know, would be to get out of it as soon as possible.'

The sky was clouding over. They sat in silence for a while until it began to get cool, when the Old Man held up the crook of his arm as an indication that he would like George to take him back inside. George left when the staff nurse brought the Old Man's supper in at six o'clock. It was already dark when he walked through the gates of the infirmary, and by the time he reached the station it had begun to rain.

# BOOK II

## Life Is Elsewhere

# CHAPTER ONE

## The Witness

### 1

It was only Alex, of course, with the books she'd asked him for. She knew he'd be coming – she was expecting him – but the shrill summons of the buzzer nonetheless startled Nadine. During the year she'd been living in her room near the museum where she worked, she'd not heard the buzzer more than a couple of times, and then always for a parcel delivery on mornings she happened to be in. The buzzer was an unwanted intruder, threatening. She took the phone off the bracket on the wall by the door, heard Alex's voice and pressed the button to let him in, biting her lip when she replaced the phone without having managed to say anything.

Nadine went out onto the landing and listened to him come scrunching up the stone steps and across the stone floor of the lobby before the sound muted on the wooden stairs, hollow, giving off an occasional creak. The sound of approaching steps reminded her of games of hide-and-seek at her grandparents' house, the excitement flaring with the terror she felt at the seeker's coming. Not wanting to be caught, afraid of that moment, she used to prefer to come out of hiding and confront her seeker before he found her. What are you doing, Nadine? You're supposed to be hiding. You're spoiling the game. But of course Alex said nothing of the kind, just handed her the books while he glanced over her shoulder into the room behind her, raising his left eyebrow, telling her he had to rush. Won't you ... But already he was on his way back downstairs, releasing Nadine, she knew he knew, from the dilemma of whether to ask him in or not.

Observing the curiosity of that glance over her shoulder, she took a step to the spot on the landing where Alex had been standing, to see what he would have seen. The sofa on the near-right wall. The corner cupboard where the photograph of her father stood in a silver frame. Part of the desk by the opposite wall, not the bed, which remained out of sight behind the half-open door. Nothing incriminating then, nothing that might have given her away.

Unless it was the size of the photograph of her father, and the fact that there was no photograph of her mother, at least not visible from where Alex stood. The smaller snapshot of her mother stood on her bedside table. What conclusions might he have drawn from that?

Years of therapy with Dr Jelinek had made noticing such things and asking questions of them second nature to Nadine. Such arrangements, however casually they might appear to have been made, could tell you a lot about yourself if you drew them out, the psychiatrist said, and encouraged them to speak. She went through Nadine's dreams with her like this. You are this shoe, Nadine, this door handle, this house; you are all the objects that appear in your dreams, and we must give them a voice because they have things to tell you about yourself.

The size of the photograph of her father — many times larger than the snapshot of her mother in its cardboard stand — the expensive frame Nadine had chosen for it and its proximity to her desk obviously reflected his continuing presence in her life five years after his death, still a much larger presence than her mother had been or would ever be. No mystery about that.

A mystery remained about him, however.

She glanced through the pile of documents Alex had brought, files downloaded by Mirsad from the Internet, bound in black and stencilled VIENNA WATCH in white on the cover. They now took up an entire room in Andro and Mirsad's apartment. Proceedings of the International Criminal Tribunal at The Hague. She preferred to hold the proceedings in her hands rather than to sift through them on the Internet. To look at them on her own computer meant letting them into her room, and she didn't want that. Whereas books were manageable, less threatening. Volumes on Rwanda, the former Yugoslavia, the Sudan, the Lebanon. She took comfort from the reach of the tribunal while at the same time it spooked her. Wherever they were hiding, the tribunal would get them. Wherever the witnesses were hiding, the tribunal got to them too.

The tribunal had followed her trail from her first officially recorded appearance at the camp in Kukës on the Albanian side of the Kosovo border to the practice of Dr Jelinek in Vienna. Undeterred by the pseudonyms she had given herself, the long time and the circuitous routes she had travelled in between, shaking off any pursuers and effectively losing track of herself – despite those precautions, despite the immense self-swallowing gulf in her memory that had opened up between who she had been before and who she was now, making useless whatever she might have said in testimony even had she wanted to, the tribunal's spies had not lost track of her, presenting their credentials in a letter to Dr Jelinek. The International Criminal Tribunal for the former Yugoslavia had requested Dr Jelinek to use her influence on her patient, insofar as this did not conflict with her professional obligations, to persuade Nadine Kelani to stand witness at a trial, currently in preparation in The Hague, concerning events that had taken place in the hamlet of Beli Atas five years previously.

All this jumped out of the slit envelope Dr Jelinek handed Nadine, which Nadine opened a year after the letter had originally arrived, two and a half years after she had left the refugee camp in Kukës.

'I didn't show you the letter because there was no point. It was premature. You wouldn't have been ready,' Dr Jelinek said. 'But now, if you choose to be, you are. This is not something you have to do, but have to want to do.'

Have to want to do – it was out of the question.

Nadine didn't have to want to do anything. She could do nothing. Nothing was what she did. This remained a secret between herself and Dr Jelinek and the ICTY, she thought for ever.

But then, just as she thought she was getting it all behind her and the whole thing would indeed, in her mother's irritatingly facile phrase, blow over, a tiny envelope showed up at the house in Leopoldstadt, a square bedraggled midget of an envelope from a poor country with her name and address on it in tall sloping letters, introducing the shadow of a premonition into Nadine's mind the moment she saw it lying on the hall table.

The letter came from her cousin Drita, formerly a member of the Kelani family household in Beli Atas, since extinguished, who was now married and living in Tirana, where the tribunal had finally got to her too. Drita had discussed it with her husband – he was an understanding

husband; if he hadn't been, he wouldn't have married her in the circum/
stances – and agreed to comply with the tribunal's request to testify as a
witness in the investigation of the war crimes committed in Beli Atas.
Drita's sister/in/law and one of her Kelani aunts had also agreed. Other
members of the family who were traceable had apparently refused to
cooperate. Drita didn't know about the many more refugees, mostly
women and children, who had sought refuge in Beli Atas shortly before
NATO began air strikes over Kosovo and the hamlet came under attack
from Serb ground forces. 'So that makes three of us, four if you agree
too. We're only women, but this we can do for the dead and the honour
of our family.'

Drita's letter caused Nadine to reconsider her position.

She discussed it with her father's photograph, then on the desk in
her room in her mother's house in Leopoldstadt, where Nadine was
living at the time.

'But for you, we would never have got ourselves into this mess. I'm
not saying it was your fault, but you completely underestimated how
dangerous the situation was. It was irresponsible of you. I had been
relying on you to look after me, even if I thought I was going along to
look after *you*. I know what you'd say. You had no choice. It was a matter
of family honour for you to attend your father's funeral, and it will be a
matter of family honour for me to give evidence in court. That's the law
of the clan. It's easy enough for you; you're dead. As for me, I still have
a choice. I can make a written deposition for the tribunal and retract it.
I can exercise my free will and step away from this at any time.'

Her father said nothing to contradict Nadine, continuing to smile at
her out of the photograph.

Nadine said a little sharply, 'Mother used to complain that you didn't
give her enough guidance, and that went all the way back to the dance
floor in the Volkspark where the two of you had your first date. You
were very light on your feet, she said, a good performer, but you were no
good at leading. Hardly surprising, given the kind of dancing you men
were brought up to do at Beli Atas. Even your father, Shehu, couldn't
resist stepping out to remind the women what a fine sort of man he still
was at eighty. But here you dance *with* the women, not for them.'

Nadine hadn't understood what her mother meant about guidance
until she was grown/up herself. Until she was grown/up, adoring her
father, who always indulged her and but for her mother's intervention

would have spoiled her completely, she had always carried a candle for him, protecting him from her mother, making allowances when her mother's judgement of him seemed to Nadine too severe.

'You have to put yourself in his shoes,' she was already telling her mother at the age of fourteen.

'Ugh!' said her mother, on the plump side but still attractive, arranging the cakes in the display case of the patisserie with dainty white hands encased in clear cellophane gloves. 'What shoes? His dancing shoes or his work boots? His boots were the last place I want to put myself.'

'But what else can you wear if you're working on a building site?'

'Ugh!'

Before Nadine was born Selim lived in a dormitory for foreign workers just down the street from the small business premises in Leopoldstadt that had been run by Nadine's family since Habsburg times. He came into the shop every morning for his breakfast, a cup of coffee and a pastry. Nadine had cross-examined her mother about these first encounters a thousand times.

'After he'd been coming for a year I gave him two, the second one for free. Your father had this way about him, you see.'

The tenth of twelve children, who lived with their parents, their uncles and their cousins and all their children – fifty people making up the *zadruga* or multifamily cooperative in Beli Atas – Selim herded goats as a boy. Until he was twenty he helped farm the land for the meagre living which was all that could be earned in the mountains of southern Kosovo. Like several of his elder brothers, he was sent away by his father to earn money to support the family at home, some south to Macedonia and Greece, some north to Serbia and Slovenia and places outside the territory of Yugoslavia.

Selim was taken on as an unskilled labourer by an Austrian construction company in Vienna. Kosovo-Albanian workers, the majority of them Muslim, enjoyed a reputation as sober and reliable workers. Selim was an exemplary worker who left a good impression from the day he began work at the construction site. Tall and spare, quick on the uptake, punctual and ambitious, he ate and smoked moderately and didn't drink. Within a week of his arrival in Vienna he had begun to attend evening classes in order to learn German. He sent most of his pay home to support his mother and father, his aunts and uncles, his brothers and sisters and their multitude of children, the always hungry mouths of the household in Beli Atas. What little remained he invested in furthering his education. He attended courses offered by the Chamber of Industry and Commerce on basic measuring and surveying, drainage, bricklaying, statics, tensile strengths of commonly used building materials – not too much of any one subject but a good working knowledge of everything – which got him a position as foreman in charge of a construction crew of foreign workers by the unusually young age of twenty-six.

In the late 1960s foreign guest workers in Austria knew their place and trod carefully, aware they were subject to the whims of a hostile bureaucracy still infected with notions of racial hygiene, of superior and inferior people in the greater German scheme of things to which the Austrians had until recently subscribed. Not a few of them still did. Despite the second free pastry the girl in the patisserie gave him, and continued to give him for the next couple of years, Selim made no advances to his benefactor. But for that summer evening in the Volkspark it might have gone on like this for much longer, she giving and he taking his extra bun, with nothing much else to speak of.

'He was so thin, I had to feed him up.'

If the weather was fine on a Saturday evening, Annemarie Lersch and her old school friend Ditta Mayer, the fat butcher's daughter from next door, dressed up and caught the tram to the Hofburg, from where they would walk across the former imperial lawns to the pavilion on the far side, now the people's side, with a restaurant, a bandstand and a dance floor. The two girls often went to the Volkspark to dance and flirt, leaving when they liked, fluttering in and out with no strings attached, beyond the range of parental radar.

Parental radar would immediately have picked up the tall spare figure of Selim, identified the sunburned foreign worker with one of those detestable moustaches and declared him out of bounds for daughters. But to Annemarie, when she first saw him by the bandstand, the man, familiar to her as the early-morning labourer she knew only in his working clothes, was a revelation. He stood in front of her transformed in suit and tie and patent-leather dancing shoes, smiling as he made a formal little bow. Before Selim had even opened his mouth she took his request as already spoken, offering him a little corner of herself, the crook of her arm, so that without more ado she could lead him out onto the dance floor.

'He is handsome,' fat Ditta conceded, smoothing down her dress, unable to conceal the envy in her voice.

With Ditta as chaperone, stringing along when Annemarie and Selim went out together, then just in name as an alibi, the secret couple spent their weekends the way most courting couples in Vienna did, in cinemas and coffee bars when it was wet, amusing themselves at the Prater, taking rides out to Grinzing or the Wienerwald when it was dry. It was in a nook in the woods there that they first made love. Selim had nowhere else to take her, no private room with a bed, and he knew without asking that he would not be welcome in Annemarie's parents' house. The prospect of cold winters ahead, enforcing months of abstention from the pleasures of sex Annemarie first got to know in Selim's arms, preoccupied her more than it did him. An only child, she was used to getting her own way. Why did he have to live in that awful dormitory with all those other men in boots? Why didn't he rent his own place? They had their first row. Selim hesitated, reluctant to incur an expense that would take a big chunk out of his remittances to the household in Beli Atas, but other considerations forced his hand.

Annemarie became pregnant.

Wary of anything put down in writing, the long memory of official documents in particular, and foreseeing problems that might arise from the form he was asked to fill out by the municipal clerk of the register office where they got married a month later, Selim thought it wiser to tick the box for NONE rather than MUSLIM in the list of religious denominations which the applicant for a marriage licence was asked to choose from.

Only after they were legally man and wife did Annemarie inform her parents. But Leopoldov wasn't short of gossipmongers and somebody, Annemarie couldn't help suspecting her friend Ditta, must already have put the word out. Her mother heard the rumours that her daughter had got herself knocked up by a Turk. A Turk! Vienna had never quite got over the invasion of the Turks three hundred years ago.

Annemarie had disgraced her family and betrayed her people, no less. What she had done was unforgivable. Her father ordered her to leave the house and to tell Selim that never again would he be allowed to darken the door of their shop. But Annemarie knew her parents better than they knew themselves.

'Once the baby's here they'll change their tune, you'll see.'

2

Not until Nadine was five or six did she realise that on the occasions when she was alone with her father he always spoke to her in a different language. He liked to sing and tell stories, which he could do by the hour when he took his daughter fishing or they just stood watching the river traffic. She grew up with the mountain people who formed the background to all Selim's stories, unaware that she was listening in her father's native language to the folk myths of the Albanian highlands and to accounts of his Kosovo childhood. The stories and the language belonged together. They had been a part of her world for as long as she could remember, although not of the world in which she otherwise lived.

Selim only ever used this language when speaking to Nadine, which may have helped her to understand that she in turn could only ever use it when speaking to him. It was a sound that went with herself and her father, their tune. Her mother wasn't included in the tune. Her mother's tongue included everyone, so it wasn't a tune in the same sense as her father's tongue, more a sort of background music. With the people who spoke them, the inclusive mother tongue and the exclusive father tongue, Nadine found that she lived on a different footing.

With her mother, her grandparents, the neighbours, the people of Vienna in general, Nadine lived in the ordinary world, but with her father she lived in a world inhabited by the mountain people of Selim's stories, and if this world was not ordinary and belonged to a different reality then that was because her father was not ordinary either. Ordinary things might occupy her mother around the house or in the patisserie, the firm reality in which she and they were anchored, but her father in another reality was occupied with extraordinary matters such as the fate of Salja Ramusaj, one of the, last, if not the very last, man-woman in the mountains, to whom Nadine was distantly related, so Selim said.

Salja's father died when she was seventeen, leaving her mother to bring up Salja, her three sisters and her three brothers, the youngest of whom had only just been born, without the help of a husband. So

Salja decided to become a man-woman, a *virdjin,* or *mashkullore* as they were known in the Drim Valley, in order to help her widowed mother bring up her children.

In the presence of six men as her witnesses, Salja swore that she would never marry. She vowed to remain a virgin all her life, to ex-change her woman's clothes for a man's, to take on the responsibilities of the head of the household and provide for the welfare of the family. She cut off her hair and changed her name to Sali. As Sali she lived a man's life. In Sali's presence women covered their faces just as they did in the presence of all men who did not belong to the house. Sali represented the interests of her family in public; she took part in tribal councils, carried weapons and connived in blood feuds, permitted to kill others but not to be killed herself. As a revered man-woman, Sali continued to carry out her duties as head of the household until the day she died.

Nadine was in two minds about emulating Salja-Sali and becoming a man-woman herself, for while the life of a *mashkullore* seemed in many ways admirable, the circumstances under which it could come about presupposed the death of her father.

From the age of six Nadine accompanied Selim every summer on his visit to the Kelani household. Beli Atas belonged to the world of her father's language, which may have been the reason her mother couldn't come with them. Her mother, at any rate, said she preferred to remain in her own world with Nadine's grandparents, happy to accompany them and their three dachshunds to the same spa in Carinthia where they had been going on holiday all their lives.

In her grandparents' house over the patisserie in Leopoldstadt (as Annemarie had foreseen, she and her spurned husband had been invited to move in within a year of their daughter's birth) Nadine grew up an only child, but in her grandfather's house in Beli Atas there were more children than she could count, so many that eventually two extra houses had to be built to accommodate them.

In the first house lived the patriarch, Shehu, with his wife Igballe. Long ago Shehu had moved out of his father's house at the bottom of the valley and built his own in a deserted place near the top. No road went there, not even a track, just marks made by the feet of the people and animals who walked there. Selim and his two younger sisters had been born and grown up in this house. At about the time he left Beli Atas to go and work in Austria, Selim's eldest brother Pllumbi built the second house for his wife and their six children because it was getting too crowded in Shehu's house, and not long after that Pllumbi's younger brother Baci built himself a third house for the same reason. Selim began telling or, one might suppose, crooning all these things to Nadine in the singsong voice he used when he rocked her to sleep in her cradle when she was still a baby, and no doubt Selim repeated them many times, impressing the stories on her mind, for by the age of four she would correct her father if he changed so much as a tiny detail.

What Selim told Nadine was true. She discovered it for herself. It took you all night and much of the day to travel by bus from Vienna to Beli Atas, passing a thousand sights en route, but the moment you got out of the bus at the turning off the main road you could see them on the mountainside, the three houses built by Shehu, Pllumbi and Baci. This scene was fixed, not passing like all the other sights. At least one or two of Selim's brothers or nephews, perhaps as many as four or five, would be waiting at the bus stop with a donkey, and they fastened the suitcase to the panniers slung across the donkey's back, set Nadine on top and off they went, exactly as her father had described it.

Selim at home in Beli Atas was a more talkative man than he was in Vienna, and a more cheerful one, it seemed to Nadine. She understood why. He was as much an only father in Vienna as she was an only child. It was different for her mother, who always had customers in the shop downstairs with whom she could gossip. But in Beli Atas there was no shortage of fathers and mothers with whom Selim could pass the time of day, brothers and sisters, nephews and nieces in abundance, not to mention the uncountable, because always growing, number of children. Nadine stayed with the children in the third house, because her uncle Baci's younger children were the same age as her and they could play best together, especially Nadine and her cousin Drita, who became her closest friend.

Baci's house was the first on the right as you crossed the stream and reached the hamlet. Baci and Pllumbi's houses flanked their father's, which stood in the middle of the yard. They were all built of the same stone in exactly the same way, only Shehu's house was a little bigger and Pllumbi's stood on higher ground than the other two. The well stood midway between Baci's and Shehu's houses. The yard behind was taken up with farm buildings, a cattle shed, a hen coop and a large barn.

Nadine was asked to recapitulate these memories of Beli Atas by the assistant prosecutor at the ICTY in The Hague on the first of three visits she made there while the trial was under preparation. When she began to describe in detail what the place looked like he interrupted her to suggest she draw a diagram of the hamlet – the three houses, the barn, the well and so on, because of the crucial part this would play in the testimony she would give at the trial. He left Nadine alone in the room while she got on with the drawing.

When the assistant prosecutor returned he went over the diagram with her, asking questions about it.

What was the distance between the barn and the well? How big was the well? Did the well have a cover? Was the water drawn up by a winch or hauled up by hand in a bucket? Did the barn have windows and if so what could you see from them? Was there a window at the back of Shehu's house from which you could see the barn, and so on, questions to which Nadine could in some cases give only tentative answers. The assistant prosecutor noted them on the copy he had made of Nadine's drawing and asked her to continue with her recollections of the Beli Atas she had got to know as a child, omitting nothing.

In some years, said Nadine, depending on the weather, the family would already have gone from Beli Atas by the time she and her father arrived, leaving only the old people and a couple of young women behind to look after them in Shehu's house. Sometimes Selim stayed on at Shehu's house while Nadine went on up the mountain alone. For most of the way the path led through the forest that began just above the hamlet and covered the side of the mountain right up to the open grassland on the plateau at the top.

The assistant prosecutor interrupted her to ask if this was the forest where the men of Beli Atas had hidden when the Serb forces arrived, and Nadine confirmed that it was.

It took a couple of hours, she said, to reach the pastures where the family spent the summer with their flocks of sheep and goats. The mothers and younger children lived in the wooden huts Shehu had built half a century ago; everyone else slept in lean-to sheds, made of branches and covered with sheets of corrugated iron, the men and boys in one lot of sheds, the women and the girls in another. Nadine herded goats with her cousins Drita and Solok. They could play, but they were also required to work. Fuel and water had to be fetched several times a day. When Nadine was a little older she was taught to milk the goats and cows, to churn milk to make butter and cheese.

Until she was about twelve and her periods began, Nadine used to long for the summers in Beli Atas. She liked having so many cousins as friends; she enjoyed being in the charge of the older children, the girls and the young women, particularly those who came into the household from outside as the wives of Pllumbi and Baci's eldest sons. However much her male cousins boasted of the ties of the bloodline, the patrilineal kinship that ran from Shehu's ancestors through his male children to his grandchildren, the bond between the Kelani women, what was called the milk line, seemed to Nadine a more precious, fine-tuned and intimate link. Among themselves the Kelani womenfolk were more demonstrative of their affections than Nadine was used to. She felt prized by them. They touched and kissed her and held her hand when they talked to her. No one she knew in Vienna did that, any rate not after she ceased to be a little girl.

But on reaching puberty Nadine became uncomfortably aware of the primitive sanitary conditions in the Beli Atas household that didn't use to bother her. Squatting on the ground to do your business, wiping yourself with leaves and grass, at least when you were up on the high pasture, had seemed fun to Nadine as long as she was a little girl, an adventure which her cellophane-gloved mother would definitely not have allowed. The facilities in the three houses in the valley weren't much better – no baths or flush toilets, no running water at all. Either she hadn't noticed this or it hadn't troubled her during the previous summers she had spent there, but from a certain age Nadine became aware, particularly for the first couple of days after she arrived in Beli Atas, of the smell of her Kelani relatives who embraced or brought their bodies close to her when greeting her.

Nadine felt uncomfortable when she reached this part of what she had been asked to tell the assistant prosecutor. She wondered if it was necessary. In the normal course of things she wouldn't have mentioned personal reflections with no apparent relevance to the issues at hand, but for Nadine there was no longer any normal course of things; nothing could be omitted. So after the disclosures she had already acquiesced in and was bound under oath to repeat in her evidence later to the tribunal, the notion that the smell of unwashed people qualified as a personal reflection would have struck her as not merely quaint but ludicrous. It was necessary, or so she told herself, or was reminded by the assistant prosecutor. Of necessity she learned to keep nothing to herself; she put herself and her dirty linen out for public inspection, and by doing so had committed herself to lowering the threshold of shame. But lowering it had not proved to be a therapeutic opening-up of herself, as Nadine had been encouraged to think it would by Dr Jelinek and the psychiatrist on the support team in The Hague. Far from her residual self-esteem recovering, as they had predicted, it disintegrated to a vanishing point where Nadine wished only that the rest of herself could have vanished with it.

The washing issue touched on a couple of sore points. There was the question of smell she had mentioned and felt ashamed to have mentioned to the assistant prosecutor because it seemed like a betrayal of her people. Then there was the issue of having to take your clothes off in order to wash, which got her into the larger and difficult question of gender segregation in the culture of her Kosovo relatives.

This had never sat easily with Nadine. The older she got the more impatient she became with the monopoly of privileges held by the men. She never understood why the milk line put up with it. The men ate first, the women and children separately in the kitchen only after the men had finished eating. They ate the men's leftovers. The men spoke first at family meetings, the women not even second; the women spoke only if they were asked a question. Younger brothers took precedence over elder sisters. This knuckling-under from childhood prepared girls for marriages in which the men held all the rights and the women none. It rankled with Nadine, and it came to a head in the incident with Sokol when Nadine was sixteen.

Sokol was her cousin, Pllumbi's son, two years older than Nadine. They had known each other and spent the summers together on the high pasture for many years. She herded goats with Sokol and admired him for the accuracy of his stone-throwing. He could throw a stone at a goat to head it off from some place it wasn't supposed to be going, hitting it from a distance smack on the bridge-bone between the animal's horns.

For several years Nadine lost sight of Sokol. He had been sent to help farm the land of a relative living in another part of the country who had been disabled in a car crash. During what would turn out to be the last summer she spent on the high pasture Sokol showed up again, now a tall young man, the best-looking among Nadine's many cousins, all of them now in their teens. Unlike the other boys, who knew only Beli Atas, Sokol had lived in other places, towns such as his cousins had never even seen. He had met other people and gained experience of life, particularly of girls, and he boasted to his cousins about these experiences. Maybe the boasts were true. Maybe Sokol had turned a lot of girls' heads, including Nadine's. Maybe it was just something in the air on the high pasture when you found yourself sitting together on the grass looking up at the night sky and your arms brushed unintentionally in the dark. It was impossible to say who had touched whom, who kissed or was kissed. Certainly it was his hands on her breasts, but had she put them in his way or had he sought them out? All she could say was that when she felt his hands on her she pushed them away and got up.

What Sokol told his brothers was that after they had kissed she allowed him to put his hands under her blouse and feel her breasts. For how long? Had he touched her nipples? What else had he done or had she let him do? And so on. The other boys plied Sokol with their many questions, and naturally their many questions put many answers into Sokol's mouth.

This brush between Sokol and Nadine came up before the family council. His version of what had happened was told to a gathering of men of the bloodline, who cuffed and knocked Sokol around a bit in order to get the truth out of him, whatever, who could say, but they must have known this would only have the opposite effect, causing Sokol not to change but to confirm the version of events he had been giving them all along. It was the girl who had led him on. Meanwhile Nadine was telling her version to the milk line of the family, all her assembled elder cousins and aunts. Nadine tried to tell the truth. It was impossible to say who had touched whom, Nadine told them, who had kissed whom – and in the end it was none of their business anyway, she added, her temper characteristically flaring up. This bold, rash answer was conveyed to Shehu's wife Igballe, who chewed it up and conveyed it to the patriarch out of the side of her mouth, kneeling behind Shehu on the divan and whispering into his ear, prompting the sometimes forgetful old man when he laid the matter before the family council.

Shehu may have been inclined to believe Nadine's version of events rather than Sokol's, if only because she took some of the blame on herself whereas Sokol took none. However, he chose to attach more weight to the display of insubordination Nadine had given in her answer. Such behaviour was unseemly, casting doubt on how seemly her behaviour was in other situations. Nadine had admitted to an ambiguity in the situation between herself and Sokol, but for a girl whose behaviour was seemly such ambiguities did not exist. Nor did they exist for Shehu himself. The *kanun* by which the household lived had no use for ambiguities. What was a woman worth? Less than a goat and more troublesome. In his youth, said Shehu, in the old days, he had known a father kill his own daughter for infidelity to her husband. Therefore the two of them must be separated. Either Sokol could be at Beli Atas, or Nadine, but not both of them at one time. It was Sokol the family presently needed to work with the flocks on the high pasture, so it was Nadine who would have to go.

This incident particularly interested the assistant prosecutor, and the detailed questions he asked about it embarrassed Nadine.

There remained a gap in Nadine's account of the Kelani household in Kosovo which she was unable to explain to the satisfaction of the assistant prosecutor, a gap of ten years between her departure from Beli Atas in the summer of 1989 and her return there in the spring of 1999. He asked her to think carefully. Perhaps something had happened which Nadine had forgotten to mention.

Nadine shook her head, getting the hair out of her eyes, perhaps getting the question out of the way too, at any rate leaving the assistant prosecutor to conclude that she had given him a negative answer.

# 3

'We can of course double-check, if necessary. Should we need to refresh our memories.'

Nadine had no idea what he was talking about.

'Details that have slipped your mind in the meantime. It's part of the process of traumatisation that you now don't remember things that you may have remembered when you were closer to the events, and of course vice versa.'

'I still don't follow what you're saying, Mr Grey.'

The assistant prosecutor clasped his knee and began bouncing the crossed leg up and down. It was a habit that irritated Nadine.

'Statements that you may have made to personnel at the refugee camp in Kukës; your case history as tape-recorded by the psychiatrist who treated you during the weeks you spent at Medica; last but not least, the records kept by the doctor you have been consulting in Vienna for the last few years, Dr Jelinek. A comparison of all that data to test it for inconsistencies.'

Nadine frowned. 'What's that got to do with anything?'

'In the end it's got to do with a rather grey area of the law.' The assistant prosecutor got up and went over to a filing cabinet. 'There was a ruling in a case we had here a few years ago. Here we are. Prosecutor versus Anto Furundzija.'

He read from the blue filing card he was holding in his hand.

'The Trial Chamber found that the prosecutor had breached Rule 68 by failing to disclose material considered to be relevant to the issue of credibility of Witness A's testimony. When the defence moved to strike the testimony of Witness A, a rape victim, or, in the case of a conviction, for a new trial, the Trial Chamber re-opened the proceedings in connection with, quote, medical, psychiatric or psychological treatment or counselling received by Witness A after May 1993, unquote. The Trial Chamber ordered, under the circumstances, that all related documents be turned over to the defence. In addition, a subpoena was issued to the nongovernmental counselling organisation in Bosnia, forcing them to turn over all relevant documents, which were reviewed by the judges *in camera*, and then disclosed to both the prosecution and the defence.'

'But that's outrageous!'

'I know, I know, and yet that's what happened.'

The assistant prosecutor shut the offensive blue card away in the cabinet.

'Let me assure you, there are lots of people in the legal profession who share your sense of outrage. They are aware of the history of rape trials in judicial systems all over the world – of the bias against the credibility of the victim, of the many instances of cases dismissed for insufficient evidence that the victim did *not* concur in the act forced upon them. No victim of murder, theft or fraud, or of any other crime for that matter, is viewed by the law in quite the way that it views rape victims. In rape trials there's a fundamental shift in the legal status of the victim. A violation has not been committed until the evidence of the victim, not the accused, establishes beyond any reasonable shadow of doubt that the victim was in no way a willing party to the act and that therefore a violation was committed. The onus of the evidence is shifted twice. It is shifted once from the perpetrator to the victim. It is shifted a second time by the unspoken assumption you come across in many rape trials that the victim has to establish her innocence before the court will acknowledge that a crime has been committed. You see?'

'No, I don't. I just find all these legal twists and turns despicable and disgusting.'

'I can sympathise with that, believe me.'

'There are too many men in the legal profession, not enough women.'

'I can sympathise with that too.'

The assistant prosecutor sat down and clasped his knee and again began jigging his leg up and down.

'I'm sorry, but would you mind not doing that?'

'Doing what?'

'Jiggling your leg around like that.'

'Ah! I'm so sorry. I don't even notice I'm doing it myself. I'm trying to give up smoking. I've come out with a rash of nervous tics instead, by way of compensation, as it were.' He withdrew his legs out of sight behind the desk. 'That said, the incontrovertible legal requirement remains that the accused be given a fair trial. The defence has to be able to call into question the truth of what the victim is telling the court. But how do you draw a line between calling into question and harassing the victim? It's up to the judge to decide. For a judge the legal provision exists to protect a witness from harassment. But if a judge looks at the actual situation in court and concludes, 'That's not harassment,' then there isn't anyone else to tell him he's wrong. There's a margin of human error here that can't be ruled out of the judicial process altogether. Misjudgements can and do occur, and throw the victim right back into a trauma from which she was just beginning to recover...'

The assistant prosecutor leaned over his desk and folded his hands.

'This is why it's imperative to have complete openness between prosecution and witness during their preparation for the trial. If there are any inconsistencies, the slightest chance of an opening, the defence will exploit it. So our best strategy is to have everything out on the table between us – everything. Then, if it turns out that the witness has a weak side, we can deal with it beforehand. You understand? The nightmare of the prosecution is to be taken by surprise. From your point of view it may be despicable and disgusting for the other side to demand access to information that was given in confidence. From their point of view it is just doing their job. It's their job to doubt the truth of what you say, to come up with devious strategies to trip you up somewhere, involve you in contradictions – and bang goes the credibility of the prosecution's key witness. So you see how much is riding on this.'

Nadine put her head in her hands.

4

On a warm August night Alex was standing on the balcony of his Spittelberg apartment, looking down over the neighbourhood, when the phone rang. He went into the living room and picked it up.

'Alex? It's me, Nadine.'

Her voice whispered out of the receiver.

'Don't say anything. Just listen to my instructions. Two men are on the landing outside my door. I overheard them talking. They think I'm in, but they aren't sure. I'm calling from the bathroom so that they don't hear me. I've no idea how they got into the building. But now they're inside I can't get out. So I want you to come round as soon as possible. Can you do that? Press the buzzer of the basement flat with the name Lobwein. That's the caretaker. I have his phone number, but it's in the other room. Tell him the lock on my door is stuck and ask him if he could try opening it from the outside. Ask him to come up with his master key. Perhaps you should give him ten euros. Is ten enough? I'll pay you back. Don't on any account mention the men I think are waiting here. Just keep a lookout. The two of you together ought to be perfectly safe, however ...'

Alex called a taxi.

Within twenty minutes he was standing outside the apartment block where Nadine lived. It was just after ten o'clock. At the bottom of the list of residents beside the buzzers on a poorly illuminated panel he made out the word CARETAKER in capital letters, followed by a name he couldn't read but which might have been Lobwein. He pressed the buzzer. There was no answer. He pressed it again. A distorted voice came blaring out of the speaker grille on the panel.

'Yes, who's there?'

'The person on the fifth floor is apparently stuck in her room because

442

she can't unlock her door. She wonders if you could bring up your key and try opening the door from the outside.'

The intercom crackled.

'Hello? Mr Lobwein? Are you there?'

'Wait. I'll be up in just a moment.'

A minute later the light went on in the entrance hall. The door was opened by a man in tracksuit pants and a vest with one arm in the sleeve of a dark blue work coat he was still struggling to put on. A lock of thin greasy hair hung forward over his forehead. He was wearing slippers. Caretakers were early risers. Probably he had been getting ready to go to bed.

Alex apologised for the disturbance when the man let him in. Lob-wein had his coat on now, even if it hung open, revealing a big slack belly beneath a hairy chest, above it the pasty, tired face of a type of ageing basement resident who seemed to represent the only caretaker option available in Vienna. The sight of him wasn't reassuring. Refracted by the strong lenses of his spectacles, his eyes had a trick of looming up oddly out of focus when the caretaker turned his head and looked at Alex from a different angle.

'The fifth floor? You mean Kelani?'

'Yes.'

Alex handed him a five-euro note, which Lobwein slipped without comment into his pocket as if collecting an entrance fee. Pressing the light switch, he shambled down the hall and set off up the stairs.

No one was in the stairwell. Alex took a look down the corridors on each floor as he followed the caretaker up. No doors stood open. There was no sign of the two men Nadine said she had heard on the landing outside her apartment. There was nothing out of order with the lock either, but then that had just been a ruse to get the caretaker to come upstairs with Alex.

'If I may be so free, Mrs Kelani,' said the caretaker in a loud voice before he unlocked the door and let himself into her room.

He locked and unlocked the door on the inside as well, to show Nadine there was nothing wrong with it. Perhaps it needed oiling. He would see to it in the morning, the caretaker said, receiving the second five-euro note Alex handed him and letting it glide into his coat pocket with practised ease.

She stood in the middle of the room, hugging her shoulders as if cold.

Alex put his arms around her. 'Are you all right?'

'Thank you for coming so quickly. I was terrified. I think we ought to leave at once in case they come back. I've packed a few things.'

At the sight of the little blue overnight case Alex immediately found himself reminded of Ella. Her emergency suitcase, which also happened to be blue, had stood ready in the cupboard downstairs throughout his childhood on that safe and friendly mid-Atlantic island where they lived. What had she been ready to flee from? What safer place had she imagined she could flee to?

'There's a spare room at my place,' he said, picking up the suitcase. 'We can go there.'

They sat out on the balcony of Alex's apartment until the early hours. Nadine showed no sign of wanting to go to bed. She still hadn't touched on the subject of the mysterious men she had heard outside her door, as Alex had been expecting her to do, so he didn't bring it up either. By five o'clock the dawn had begun to pick out the shapes of buildings in the darkness below them, and Alex got up, saying he wanted to get some sleep. He had a plane to catch in a few hours.

'Will you be gone long?'

'Just a day trip. I'll be back tonight.'

He cleared the things from the balcony table and carried them into the kitchen before going to bed.

'In case you think I'm imagining things ...' Nadine stood in the doorway frowning. 'The men I heard outside my door were speaking Serbo-Croat. Is it just a coincidence that the two men who came out of the terminal building behind me were also speaking Serbo-Croat? Or is it possible they were the same men, who followed me into town and found out where I lived?'

Alex hesitated.

'It's possible. But they don't know where you are now, do they. They could only have followed us here in a car. Besides, Ciska or Ciska's deputies, one of them is always on duty downstairs, and as I know from my own experience of living here for so many years, no one can get past Ciska's office without being seen. So really there's nothing for you to be worried about.'

'Thank you. Thanks for everything you've done, dear Alex. Did you give the caretaker five or ten euros, by the way?'

'I gave him five to get him upstairs and five to get him back down. That's more than enough.'

'When is it more than enough? What is enough?'

Nadine kissed him on the cheek, already turning on her way out of the kitchen as she said goodnight, not to him but to the empty hall.

When Alex left the house in the morning the door to Nadine's room was still shut. He left a note for her on the kitchen table telling her where to find the breakfast things, what number to call if she needed to speak to Ciska, and reminding her she could put the chain on the door if that made her feel more comfortable.

He flew to Klagenfurt for a political party conference that didn't interest him. It was the sort of brief he was getting increasingly often these days, now that the war in the Balkans was over, and it made Alex think it was time to start looking for another job. It made him think of his house in Tenerife and how he could arrange his life so that he could move there.

In the restaurant in Klagenfurt where he went for lunch he ran into Zoran, an old colleague who worked for a newspaper in Zagreb, a tall, untidy journalist with a look of permanent exasperation on his face. Wherever there had been big news stories to follow during the war in Yugoslavia, in Sarajevo, in Srebenica, in Priština and Belgrade, Zoran belonged to the group of journalists Alex could always count on meeting, and despite his look of exasperation Zoran would always be happy for Alex to pick his brains.

'Tell me, Zoran, the witness protection scheme operated by the ICTY. Does it protect them effectively?'

'I think it does. The trouble is, it's expensive, and as you know, the ICTY is chronically underfinanced. So some people who would like to take advantage of the scheme don't get accepted because their risk rating isn't high enough.'

'What's rated high enough?'

'Well ... a real risk of being murdered. Nothing less than that will get a witness protection. But how do you measure real risk? How real does the risk have to be before the murder is committed? Witnesses going back to a village somewhere in the boondocks can sometimes be given such a rough time that they're forced to move out of their ethnic enclave.

So where do they go? How do they pay for it? Imagine a rape witness trying to go back and live in Foča after the trial of the crimes committed there. Witnesses run all kinds of risks, from murder to ostracism to re-traumatisation. I spoke to a woman who went back to her village in Bosnia recently after testifying in The Hague, and what she told me was appalling. She said she still received anonymous phone calls threatening her and her family. Even on the street people spat at her and called her names such as Alija's whore—'

'Referring to the Bosnian president?'

'Yes. And she had lost everything. They had killed her son and her husband and burned down her house. But that still wasn't good enough to get her witness protection status. The protection scheme may look good on paper, but the reality on the ground looks different.'

When Alex flew back to Vienna, his view of the events the night before had changed. Then he'd been confident that there were no men on the landing outside Nadine's door; Nadine's imagination had put them there. *But how do you measure a real risk?* Alex no longer felt so sure.

The witness protection scheme came into effect when a trial was over. The witness received a new identity and disappeared. In Nadine's case, however, it wasn't a question of what might happen after the trial, but of before. Multiple rape was one of the charges. Many women had been raped, and several of them would be testifying. But Nadine was the only living witness of the crime that was the focus of the trial – the multiple murders with which three of the rape defendants, a policeman and two paramilitaries, had also been charged.

The men who would be put on trial in The Hague in a couple of months' time were a representative cross-section of the Serb forces that had fought the war – Yugoslav National Army troops, paramilitary, police – all Serb nationalists despite their mixed ethnic backgrounds, with roots that could be traced back to Bosnia, Montenegro and Albania. It was policemen recruited from the local population who posed the greatest threat to the key witness for the prosecution in the forthcoming trial. They knew the area, the families and the names. They would have kept tabs on individuals suspected of being KLA sympathisers in the Kelani household in Beli Atas long before the Serb forces moved in for the kill on that morning in March five years previously.

And for years before that Nadine and her father had been travelling down there every summer, and travelling back to Vienna, Alex thought as the lights of the city became visible through the plane window, where a not inconsiderable number of Yugoslav nationals had made their home. Suddenly Alex had a glimpse of that village on the hill he had visited six weeks after the massacre had taken place – visible from far off, exposed and vulnerable in its isolation – and it occurred to him that the key witness for the prosecution was no less exposed and vulnerable. There was a very real risk that some of the men who had killed and raped in Beli Atas, and were still on the run, would attempt to silence the witness before she could give evidence in The Hague. They had the strongest possible motive for doing so – to protect themselves. With luck their names might not yet have been betrayed to the prosecution, but once the trial approached and negotiations to commute sentences in exchange for information began in earnest, the accused would put their own interests first. So now was the time to act.

The connection between the hamlet in the Kosovo mountains and the Leopoldov house where Selim Kelani had lived, a well known figure in the expatriate Yugoslav community in Vienna, was easily established. It would be easy for someone to walk into the patisserie in Leopoldstadt and pass themselves off to Nadine's mother as one of Selim's countrymen with a message for Nadine they wished to convey to her personally. Nadine's account of the men talking in Serbo-Croat on the landing outside her door the previous night began to sound plausible to Alex.

She wouldn't have been so rash as to put her own name on the street door of her apartment, would she? Alex tried to visualise the panel with the residents' names he had been looking at the previous night, but he had been so preoccupied with finding the caretaker that he couldn't recall under what name the fifth-floor resident had been listed. Then he remembered the caretaker's question when he opened the door: *The fifth floor? You mean Kelani?*

Alex remembered the way the caretaker had pocketed the money as a matter of course. His casualness about receiving tips made Alex wonder whether Lobwein distinguished between a tip and a bribe. He'd not asked for identification or asked any questions. If someone came along and gave Lobwein a hundred to let him in, the caretaker would probably oblige.

As soon as he got off the plane Alex called his own number, letting it ring once before he broke off the call and rang again, as arranged with Nadine so that she knew who was calling. But she didn't pick up.

He tried her mobile. It was switched off.

Beginning to panic, Alex called Ciska's office downstairs to find out if Nadine had gone out at all that day. She had left just five minutes ago, said Ciska. She had mentioned she was going down the road to buy a few things at the supermarket in Spittelberg.

'Even if the name Kelani was on the door there, nobody can have traced her to where she is now,' Alex said out loud to reassure himself.

'Sorry?'

'Can't you drive a bit faster?' he asked the taxi driver.

'Not unless I want a ticket, which I don't. I'm already over the speed limit.'

It was getting on for eight o'clock when the taxi rolled up the steep cobbled street leading to the entrance of the former Palace Hotel. The headlights picked out a woman in a white blouse holding a carrier bag, and Alex told the driver to draw up beside her as they passed. Alex let down the window and called, 'Nadine!'

She stopped and looked round.

Alex got out. 'Is everything all right?'

'I got the supper ready and then saw that we were out of wine. So I went out to buy some before you got back. Is anything the matter?'

'No, no.'

Alex paid the driver and walked into the building with an arm around Nadine's shoulders.

'Everything's fine. It's just wonderful to come home and ... find you here. I've been looking forward to it all day.' He laughed.

He didn't tell Nadine what a scare he'd had, what a relief it was to come home and find her safe and well.

# 5

Her father had had a small stroke, apparently nothing serious, according to Nadine, and he was back at work within a month. But then he had another, and that was much worse. It left him partially lame on his left side and affected his speech. He learned to walk and talk again, but he wasn't the same afterwards. At fifty-eight he was no longer fit to work. He had to take early retirement. It was all right in the summer, she said; he could go off and spend the day fishing. Sometimes she went with him, as she had done as a little girl. Winters were the problem. He wasn't used to sitting about indoors. He regarded it as a disgrace for a man to hang around the house with the women. He might have helped out in the shop but no, he was too proud for that. Instead he started going to the Turkish Bazaar, a coffee house near the Naschmarkt. It was a meeting place for people like her father, mostly older men with nothing to do – Bosnians, Serbs, Turks and Kosovo-Albanians, all of them with the same pride that didn't allow them to stay at home during the day. Then, in March 1999, Selim's father Shehu died. Serb forces and the Kosovo Liberation Army had already been fighting running battles against each other for two years.

'What I ask myself now is how, under the circumstances, Mother and I could ever have agreed to let him go. There's no stopping a son going to his father's funeral, you could say, particularly with the sense of honour involved in a large patriarchal family such as the Kelani in Beli Atas. But we could have locked him in his room for a week. We could have put a heavy dose of sleeping pills in his coffee. If you *have* to stop someone, that's the sort of thing you've got to be prepared to do. Quite apart from the journey down to Beli Atas being dangerous at the time, my father wasn't very well. The physical strain of the journey on top of the emotional stress was more than he could manage. His doctor told him that he risked bringing on another stroke, and this time it might be fatal. But there's no stopping a son going to his father's funeral, or so you tell yourself, because this is what the moral blackmail of muddle-headed custom *makes* you tell yourself, as if the respect due an old man's death matters more than the respect due his son's life. The best thing we could come up with to do was for me to go with him. So I had a look at the map and decided the easiest way to get there would be to fly to Skopje, hire a car and drive back up north into the mountains. Can you imagine? That's how naive I was.'

Nadine still hadn't got over the fact that she had made the wrong decision. The tirades against herself went on. Without noticing it she would manage to take a turn in any conversation, whatever it was about, and find her way back into the danger zone, like an insect drawn into a glue trap then attempting to extricate itself but only getting more and more stuck. Ignorance wasn't a plea she could make. As a student of the Balkan region, her course in south-east European studies at the University of Graz running concurrently with the war in Yugoslavia,

Nadine followed events closely and knew exactly what was going on in the country. Naive was one thing she was not. This forced her into recognising that she might have been impelled by unconscious motives, the terrifying notion that she could somehow have acquiesced in the risks she and her father were taking. How else to explain why she had acted against her better knowledge?

This exacerbated her sense of guilt. It was like the sore Alex had noticed on the inside of one of her fingers, which she kept chafing with the nails of the other fingers. When he asked her if picking at it didn't make it hurt more, she snapped back at him that of course it made it hurt more; that was why she did it.

The drift of her self-interrogations gradually became clear.

'It was all my fault.'

Alex was astonished.

He noticed that when he left a room and switched the light off, Nadine would soon find a reason to go back into the room, switch the light on again and leave it on when she left the room. Dark places were one of her phobias. Now that she had stopped working at the museum, partly at Alex's insistence, and had no reason to go out, or rather had a reason to stay in, Nadine spent all her time in the apartment. She took a shower every morning and evening, half an hour or even longer, sometimes in the middle of the day too.

Should he bring up such things with her or let them pass? He decided it was for Nadine to talk about them if she wanted to, so he said nothing.

One night he woke up to find her sitting in a chair by the open bedroom door in a stream of light from the living room.

'Nadine! Can't you sleep?'

'I'm frightened of what I might dream when I sleep. Somehow it's better in a chair. I doze off, and the dreams I have aren't proper dreams, perhaps because I'm nearer the surface and can come up at any time.'

She got up and came and lay on top of the bedclothes, curling up beside him.

'Oh Alex! You've no idea how tired I am. I manage the days all right, but I can't deal with the nights alone any more.' She let out her breath in a long sigh, and by the end of it she was already asleep.

This became the routine of their nights. She could have settled down on his bed – it was on rather than in – when she went to bed, but something still held her back. So she went to bed in her room, woke up in the night and came to his. Sometimes he slept through her arrival and woke up in the morning to find her lying there beside him. Morning hours, when it was light, gave Nadine the best sleep, she said, the cream of the night, the lightest dreams. He could see the lightest dreams reflected in her face. They could even cause her to smile in her sleep.

When he looked at her in their morning bed his love of Nadine shifted key into desire for her, into his hands and his loins. In the months they had been together they had barely touched each other. Did she miss that as much as he did? In bed in the mornings the ache to touch her became more than Alex knew he could control, so he got up and did things quietly in the background while she had her best sleep.

Dr Jelinek, whom he had gone to see with Nadine's blessing, had advised him to wait for Nadine to make the first move. Not only the sexual act, just being touched could still trigger off fear and loathing in Nadine, or she might welcome it and respond, but there was no saying when or why.

'Don't be discouraged,' Dr Jelinek said, seeing Alex's downcast face. 'You've already accomplished miracles. Until you arrived it was quite unthinkable for Nadine to be alone with a man in the same room. She wouldn't even go into a shop with a man behind the counter unless she saw other people there.'

And within a few weeks of arrival it seemed to Alex that Nadine, molested by nothing other than bad dreams, was beginning to settle down, at least by day. He discovered how much he had diverted into sex with all the previous women in his life flowed in the mainstream tenderness of his love for Nadine. The instinct to protect a woman wasn't something he had known before. Perhaps he hadn't known any women who needed protecting, or perhaps they had needed it and he hadn't recognised this. Here it formed the strongest bond between him and Nadine. For of course it wasn't all on his side; it was she who brought out of him what he had long had in him but never used. Feeling more fully himself with Nadine than he had with any other woman, Alex began to understand why none of the relationships with them had lasted. There had been too narrow a base on which to build a lasting relationship. The ties that bound him and Nadine were strong and clear. He was there for her, and already she was there for him. How simple! How happy that made him!

'The Hague is such a dreary place. Do you know what they call it?

The widow of Holland. It'll be even more gloomy in the autumn. I dread the thought of coming back from court on dark afternoons to an empty hotel room. I won't even be able to see Drita and my aunt. They keep witnesses at the same trial in different hotels because they're not supposed to talk to each other. Will you come with me, Alex?'

'Of course I will! I'll be there, Nadine.'

'It could go on as long as two or three weeks.'

'Then I'll take a holiday!'

His confident enthusiasm infected Nadine.

'If only it could all be over quickly! Tomorrow! If only I could get this whole business behind me! I refuse to go on being a victim! I refuse to be stigmatised like this! I refuse to let them take away my life from me! Once I've testified I'll be all right, I promise.'

She put her arms around him and kissed him, moulding her body against his in a way she had not done before.

'No, perhaps I won't be all right until those men have been sentenced and put away behind bars. Will that take long, do you think?'

'A couple of months, at the outside,' Alex told her, although he suspected it might take quite a bit longer.

'So by Christmas then? I'd like to see your apartment in La Orotava. Could we spend Christmas there? It would be something for me to look forward to – you know, *after*.'

And so it was arranged. In October they would travel to The Hague for what Nadine called *my trial*, and they would spend Christmas together in Tenerife. Alex thought how much he would like to have gone and lived there happily with Nadine, but it seemed too much to hope for, contingent on too many other yet unknowns, so for the time being he kept that thought to himself.

# CHAPTER TWO

## Ella's House

### 1

Ella's mother had taught her daughter a simple secret of good house-keeping: tidiness counted most where you thought it mattered least. It lived in the places where you thought no one would see it. A cupboard was there to show, not hide. It might have doors, but God could see through them. Long after Ella was grown up and had stopped believing in God she went on believing in his X-ray eyes. They could see through her and into all her cupboards.

No threat of punishment was implied by what her mother said. There was nothing to be afraid of. Why should there be? Ella had nothing to hide. The inside of a cupboard or the inside of herself, keeping things in order came to her naturally. Until she saw the struggle that other people had to manage, their cupboard doors bulging with all the stuff that wanted to spill out, it never occurred to her as being any sort of merit, merely her own preference. She threw out things she didn't need. Mess – she frowned at the thought of it. Fuzziness – how she detested fuzziness! Whatever the choice was, she wanted to have it clear: the inside of her cupboards, the parting in her hair, the symmetry of her plaits, the crease in her slacks, the enunciation of her words, the answers to her questions, the white of her socks.

The first of the seven pine cupboards Ella had ordered from the ship's carpenter and chest maker in Santiago had gone to Alicia six months ago as her wedding present. The cupboard contained her trousseau: a set of six sheets, light down coverlets, pillowcases, bolster covers, fine linen hand towels and napkins, all of them with the bride's new initials, AS, embroidered on them by Ella. On giving her this trousseau, Ella had also passed on to Alicia Serra the obligations that went with it, the correct treatment of household linen and the principles of household order, notably the management of her cupboards.

Together they had viewed the trousseau spread out on the marriage bed item by item, Ella drawing the girl's attention to details such as seams, corners, reinforced buttonholes, how to deal with a loose thread end or sew on a button so that it wouldn't come off again, not in her lifetime. Together they stocked the cupboard, which stood against the bedroom wall in Alicia's house, its doors open, something of a bridal cavity itself, it had occurred to Ella as they laid in it the first of the linen, white, cool and crisp.

Paco called up from the courtyard below and Ella told him they would be done in about half an hour.

Three of the new cupboards stood downstairs, still awaiting their attention. The other three stood against the walls between the doors leading into the bedrooms off the corridor that ran around the buttressed gallery overlooking the courtyard, where Paco was sweeping together the debris of twigs and leaves deposited by the dragon tree, which had stood there, legend had it, since the house was built in the seventeenth century. The courtyard was open to the sky, the sun and the rain and the fog that occasionally descended from the mountain in winter.

With a renegade sheet put firmly back in line at the bottom of the pile, the second of the cupboards had been done to Ella's satisfaction, and they moved on to the third.

'When will the others be coming, Señora?' Alicia asked.

'Well, said they'd be here tomorrow.'

Ella sometimes found very convenient this omission of the subject in a Spanish sentence. *Said they'd be here.* There were times she couldn't say, or preferred not to know, exactly who was saying or doing what, such as how many guests would be arriving tomorrow, how many the day after. She took the two corners handed to her by Alicia, folded the sheet once and held it up for the girl to straighten the creases before taking the sheet back to fold it a second time, handing it back to Ella to repeat the procedure and fold it once more so that it fitted neatly into the space it had been allotted in the cupboard.

This was no different from the procedure Ella had followed with her mother thirty years ago in the sub-prefect's residence in Schlawe, where they had folded linen the day war broke out. Each cupboard held the linen for the room on either side of it, the left half of the cupboard for the room on the left, the right half for the room on the right. The linen was taken out of the broad-bottomed washing basket, ritually folded and placed in the cupboard according to function and size, with the fold always facing out, making it easier to handle the linen without disarranging it. Alicia could now be entrusted to do cupboards without Ella's guidance, but it was easier for two people to fold linen together, and both women enjoyed the opportunity this task allowed them for undisturbed conversation.

Alicia had been married to Paco for only six months, but she already showed signs of anxiety that she was not yet pregnant. Enviously if ungrudgingly, almost as happy for Ella as she would have been for herself, she monitored the older woman's pregnancy with curious eyes and exploratory hands whenever Ella invited her to touch. Ella was in her fifth month, with her fifth child. There's no hurry, she liked to tell Alicia; enjoy your husband while the marriage is still new. The wear and tear, the chipped corners of use, will come to it of their own accord.

It didn't rain. The clouds dispersed. Heat built up within the en-closed courtyard where Ella lay in the hammock slung between the dragon tree and one of the pillars supporting the gallery, sleeping a heavy sleep in the sag of the afternoon. She dreamed the dream of the child she had forgotten to tend, found unfed in its cradle, neglected in a corner or buried in a snowdrift. It was a recurrent dream, her only bad dream, or the only one she remembered. It came and went. Sometimes it left her alone for years. Now it was back, with the difference that she hadn't forgotten the child but couldn't find it. She wandered through a labyrinth of ill-lit places, searching for the child and dreading finding it, knowing it would be dead.

Disturbed by the anxiety of the dream she woke up to discover her son Alex sitting close to the hammock with his chin resting on the back of a chair, looking into her face.

'My darling ... you always come at just the right moment.'

Ella held out her arms. The boy got up and kissed her, and she put her arms around him. He remained standing by the hammock, squirming a little inside his mother's clasped hands.

He touched her forehead with his fingertips. 'You're sweaty, Mum.'

'Am I?' She pulled a handkerchief out of her sleeve and dabbed her face. 'So I am.'

'Are you all right?'

'Don't I look all right?'

'Your face looks sort of hollow.'

'I haven't been sleeping very well. That often happens with women before they have their babies. Did you have your lunch with Felipe and the others?'

The boy nodded.

'What were you and Felipe doing all morning then?'

'We helped his father repair a water pipe.' Hardly missing a beat he went on, 'Mum, what's a half-brother?'

'A half-brother has the same mother or father as you, but not both. Why do you ask?'

'Max said I was his half-brother.'

Ella moved her head to one side so that she could see into his face better.

'When did Max say that?'

'When he came out to the house the day before we left.'

'What else did he say?'

'He said that's why I was called Alex, after my father, because his name was Alex too.' The boy squirmed a bit more and rubbed his crotch with his knuckle. 'He said Dad wasn't my real father.'

'Well, Max has got some of it right and some of it wrong.'

Ella paused, wondering how Max, who must somehow have worked out for himself that George wasn't Alex's father, had come up with this nonsense about Sasha. However distressing she found it to have been forestalled in her choice of the moment when she judged it would be right to tell Alex that Claude was his father, there was no help for it; that moment had now come.

'It's true that Dad isn't your real father. But nor was Sasha. You were named after him, however. In some languages, you see, Sasha is a version of Alex. This Sasha after whom you were named died just before you were born. I called you after him because he was a very good friend, and I wanted to keep his name alive so that we'd always remember him.'

She took the tissue out of her sleeve and wiped away the prickle of sweat she felt under her eyes. Her son watched her, waiting for her to go on.

'Your real father is Claude. I know we used to call him uncle, but actually he's your father. We made you – Claude and I did. But not the

456

others, Max, Felicity and Philip. I made the other children with George. The way I told you men and women make children, remember?'

The boy nodded, his mouth still open, swallowing whole the enormity of what his mother was telling him.

'Well, that's what Claude and I did, you know, to make you. So you have the same mother but not the same father as your brothers and sister, so they're only your half-brothers and your half-sister, you see, because you only share me, your mother, not the other half, your father.'

Ella watched her son's face working, tiny movements of his facial muscles as he listened to her words and fitted their meaning together. From the faintest blush that spread across his cheeks she could see this imposed a strain, the pull of some liminal feeling inside him trying to work its way outwards. It might have been embarrassment, it might have been a stirring of shame.

'But how?' his face yielded up at last.

In the trace of a whine she heard the protest.

'How what?'

'How did you and Claude make me, and not Dad?'

'Because I loved Claude no less than I loved Dad.' Ella didn't hesitate. 'So Claude and I wanted to make a child too. That child was you, darling.'

The boy stood twisting his wrists, rubbing each of them with the other hand.

'Did Dad mind you and Claude making me?'

'No.'

'How do you know?'

'Well, he doesn't mind you calling him Dad for a start. Wouldn't he mind if he minded me and Claude making you?'

Alex stood still, looking at his mother as if she would take upon herself the load of the question and relieve him of it.

'Dad loves you as much as he loves the other children. He loves you just the same as if you *were* his child.'

'But I *am* his child, aren't I?'

The whine was out in the open now. His lip quivered.

'Of course you're his child, sweetheart. But you're not his own son in the same way that Philip is, because he didn't make you. Claude did, so you're Claude's son.'

'But how do you *know*?'

Ella knew this sound. It signified bafflement, when Alex was thwarted, a toy out of the child's reach, a thing beyond his understanding.

'Because I can see him in you. I can see it here –' she touched his nose '– and here –' she touched his chin '– and here and here –' she added, taking hold of him by both earlobes and wiggling them.

'Don't!' he protested, but still unable to suppress a giggle. 'You're tickling!'

'Tickling? You call that *tickling*? Oh, we'll see about that,' Ella said laughing, and began tickling him in earnest. Alex wriggled and shrieked, and she tickled him up and down his ribs, playing his pianoforte she called it, until he began thrashing around and suddenly fell with a wail onto his mother's breast, lying there sobbing while she stroked his head, saying, 'There, there,' until the sobs passed and at last the boy grew quiet. His breathing became even. His clutching hands let go. Pitched sideways across her body, Alex fell asleep.

She sniffed him. The downy odour of a puppy, hay and earth and all the outdoor scents he had gathered on his rounds, came off the boy's hair. She liked his scent, just as she had liked Claude's and not liked George's, right from the beginning. The way an attraction was always divided, with wedges of dislike driven into the core of one's liking for a person, posed something of a conundrum, but it was a normal, an entirely human one. It wasn't a problem. Nothing was the same all over.

Go in and light the candles, she told Alex, but it wasn't necessary to tell him. He had done it already. By nightfall a storm was brewing. Big winds blustered in from the Atlantic. It made for snugness indoors, where they ate their supper, in the brick-floored room with a vaulted ceiling which they used as a dining room and kitchen. Alex stoked the fire in the grate and lit the candles. They ate à la carte, Alex his baked beans on toast, Ella her prawns. She built a warm enclosure of words around her nine-year-old son, lit up in retrospect by the sunshine that afternoon in the Bois where Claude retrieved the whirligig that had landed in the tree under which Ella lay asleep – all the things they had done together, Claude and Ella and George in the thickets of their past, the houses they had lived in for a few days in Brittany and Biarritz and for as many years in St John's Wood and Richmond, not to be overruled by convention, remaining true to themselves if a little different from other families. Every day should be a Sunday. Life was made up of many small moments; the whole reflected the quality of all its parts. However modest the meal on the table, make a ceremony of it and light the candles, she had drummed into Alex since he was born, because every day was a Sunday, and her fourth child was more receptive than any of the others to the things that were closest to her own heart.

A couple of years back she had suffered a breakdown. There were reasons other than physical exhaustion for her collapse, arising from the fissure that ran all the way through her marriage with George and which had come to the surface five years ago when he resigned from the Foreign Office. George had taken the Old Man's advice that he should get out, and confessed to Ella his long affair with Julia Manning.

It wasn't the presence of another woman in George's life but Ella's exclusion from it that upset her. It was his keeping the secret from her for so long. How many lies that must have required of him, how many elaborate deceptions, how many times she must have talked to a man who wasn't there, how many thoughts, anxieties, cares, explanations to herself she must have expended on illusions concocted by a husband whose only concern was to keep his wife in the dark. That was the place of humiliation where she had been put by George, the cellar in which she'd been dumped. The initial shock of discovery was brief; the deeper ache of the injustice she felt done to her remained, for although Ella's temper subsided as quickly as it rose, the smart of the humiliation to which she'd been subjected continued to torment her.

Five years later it still did, long after the anger had evaporated. Her belief in George and her trust – long after she'd forgiven him and the crack across the marriage had apparently been patched up – continued to be undermined by a process of erosion of which she was intermittently aware. She could forget it for a while, but never quite. It was easy enough for her to forgive George, but there were instincts beyond her control, runaway feelings for George that came and went – pleas for and against – not of Ella's conscious accord but of their own doing in the overflowing wellspring of herself. George might be forgiven but not what he had done, and it seemed to Ella that what George had done was steal her innocence. She had wanted him out of her way. She hadn't wanted to know anything about him, where he was or what he was doing. She just wanted him to dissolve.

So George went away.

It'll blow over, he had said to himself, an emotional flatness finding expression in words as flat as the emotions were, betraying a reassertion of the other George at just the moment he thought he had got that aberration behind him. It revealed that his vows of self-renewal were already empty. Ella told him he no more understood the real nature of her feelings now, after she had explained to him that what he had done were actions above all against her integrity, than he had at the time of the events that prompted them.

The notion that a violation of *her* integrity had taken place had eluded George's understanding. What had it got to do with *her* integrity? It was as if she wouldn't even leave him what had been, after all, *his* transgression, *his* loss of integrity, but was laying claim to it for herself. What Ella saw as his *stealing of her innocence* — the very idea escaped him, let alone the psychology in which it was grounded. He could not stand outside himself and look in. Therefore he lacked empathy, she said, and would never be able to care genuinely about anything.

This, in Ella's view, was a limitation of his nature which he couldn't transcend. Could she hold him accountable, then? She could and she did, whatever she said to the contrary. There were also moments when, aware of the impositions Claude's presence imposed on the marriage, her heart softened and she would have forgiven George everything. It was the way George shrugged things off, however, that always succeeded in provoking her again, the impenetrability of his nature, a smooth monolith with no way in.

When George remained silent with folded arms, she would go over and batter him with her fists.

'Speak to me!'

After moving to the island there were fewer such scenes than before, but they still occurred. George learned to gauge when these storms were brewing and made himself scarce. Sometimes he stayed away from the Arguayo house for a couple of weeks. The flat in La Orotava, conveniently close to La Laguna airport, provided a jumping-off point at short notice when he came down with a particularly bad case of island claustrophobia and had to catch the next plane to London to recuperate.

# 2

George made one of these trips to attend the funeral of a wartime colleague whose subsequent career he had followed with close interest and not a little envy. Ian Fleming was still only in his fifties, a victim not of SMERSH or SPECTRE but of too many of the Macedonian-blend cigarettes with the three gold rings around the butt made for him, or so Fleming would claim on his hero's behalf, by Morlands of Grosvenor Street. He was among the first popular writers to appreciate the significance of image, anticipating the concept of product placement far ahead of its time. Toothpicks were by Steradent and mouthwash was by Rose, long before Fleming's contemporaries had ever used a toothpick or heard of mouthwash. A mere Rolls-Royce didn't cut it. It had to be an old black basketwork Rolls-Royce coupé-de-ville, with as much pedigree piled on as the chassis could carry. Even a lift got a bit part as a Waygood Otis. Not just Otis. It was the Waygood that did it for George.

In the icon of James Bond's life Fleming enshrined the Morlands that killed him just as he enshrined other everyday products, elevating them from banality to cachet by giving them a name. Banality was lack of distinctiveness; lack of distinctiveness was lack of a name; lack of a name was lack of an identity. Writing such stuff might seem to be a trite business, but thanks to the author's chuckling, which could be heard offstage, it was triteness rendered with humour – even, in George's view, with a touch of clairvoyant genius. Innocent of the slightest interest in brand names until Fleming smuggled them into his consciousness, George began a collection of them that would occupy him for the rest of his life.

From Taittinger champagne to Saxone golf shoes or asparagus with mousseline sauce, the James Bond icon was made up of a collage of labels that Fleming draped around the tailor's dummy of his hero, all the way down to Floris Limes Bath Essence for men and the Memmen's Baby Powder applied to the infant Bond's buttocks. Toiletry had a special fascination for Fleming. The prurient lists of toilet articles induced in his prose the same sort of overheated red-faced pleasure a certain class of Englishman – George, for instance – might have taken in administering a spanking. Even a humble bar of soap was elevated into that most desirably English of soaps, Pears Transparent, and in Fleming's ideal bathroom there was sure to be a bottle of Mr Trumper's Eucris beside *the very masculine brush and comb by Kent*. Such touches George found irresistible. This was the measure of the world according to Kent, whoever Kent was, a world that in future they were all going to have to live in.

In what lay the masculinity of a comb?

Such thoughts distracted George from his marriage crisis.

He had followed Fleming's post-war career with a reluctant admiration he would not have admitted even to himself. He read a few of Fleming's books, said flattering things about them to the author when they occasionally met at his club for lunch, keeping to himself the thought that if he paid the same attention to product image as him, meaning no less than an author's pedantic love of detail, he could do this sort of thing as well.

Why did George think this? He wanted to be free of complications, to live at his ease in the untroubled surface of things. Who didn't?

During the couple of months he had been suspended from his duties after the BTM disaster George had dashed off a thriller about love, espionage and mutual betrayal of lover-spies against the background of the 1956 Hungarian revolution. Under the pseudonym George Smythe, he even made it into the bestseller lists. He didn't have Fleming's flair for sex and luxury, but he knocked his ridiculous plots for six. In George's hands the politics of the cold war that Fleming travestied became as bleak as they were in the reality underneath the tracing-paper on which George's novels were traced with the precision of a seismographic needle. After Fleming's Caribbean antics the temperature with Smythe dropped to freezing point, earning him the sobriquet the Graham Greene of thriller writers.

Thrown out of his marriage, turned out of the Richmond family home, jobless, George had hung around gloomily in the London winter for a couple of weeks before his eye was caught by a one-line advertisement on the front page of *The Times*. 'Spend the winter in the sun!' the advertisement said, and gave a phone number. George's call led to a conversation with the Islington owner of a two-room apartment in La Orotava, which in turn led to George buying an airline ticket, and a week later he flew to Tenerife. The old Spanish town overlooking Puerto de la Cruz on the north coast of the island had steep cobbled streets and terraces shaded by trees, where he could sit outside to take his meals within view of the crumbling seventeenth-century house in which he lived in a garret overlooking an enclosed patio or courtyard on one side and on the other a view reaching far out to the big blue horizon of the Atlantic Ocean.

Within a month George had sketched out the first of what would become a trilogy of novels unravelling the scenes behind the scenes in London, Washington, Berlin and Moscow during the critical cold war years of the early 1960s. He wrote the initial draft in the first person, a narrative of his own experiences as a courier for the British Trade Mission, divulging some of his trade secrets. Before publication of his debut thriller, *Budapest '56*, he had received specific guidelines from the Foreign Office regarding infringements of the Official Secrets Act, with which his book had to comply before it could be published. With these guidelines in front of him George did a second draft excising actionable material and transforming his first-person into a third-person narrative.

Much of himself and much of Julia Manning, whose disappearance he still regretted, lingered on in the fictional characters that grew out of the originals. The trade secrets were watered down, adapted or dropped. The background against which the espionage story was set, the agent's family life and marriage troubles, was sketched in as only the faintest of outlines. George felt unsatisfied with this weakness at the heart of the book but didn't know how to give it more substance without incurring penalties in his personal life, which he feared more than any that might arise from an infringement of the Official Secrets Act. He dispatched this acceptable second draft to his publisher in London, and within the week he had received back an enthusiastic telegram offering him a respectable advance.

Confident he could handle his own finances better than any agent, George flew to London to negotiate a more opulent deal by embedding the book in the trilogy of thrillers he had already mapped out in his head, a synopsis of which he dictated on his arrival to the secretary he hired, with instructions to type and deliver it to his club on the same day.

He was exhilarated by the speed of recent developments in his life – that marvellous lucky find in La Orotava, the no less marvellous dependable December sunshine, writing his book outside on the terrace of a cafe in the old town up on the hill, a breeze rustling the paper, a glass of wine in one hand, a pen in the other, lancing with his writer's needle a furuncle full to bursting, experiencing a joyful catharsis in the telling of secrets that had festered so long inside him. It was only the day after concluding the deal with his publisher towards the end of a drunken three-hour lunch – a deal that would give George the freedom to do whatever he wanted over the next few years, and he found himself on the culmination point of the breaking wave, cruising euphorically on top of the world – that the flow of energy which had carried him along deserted him, leaving him stranded in the surroundings of a club that was no longer the haven it had been when he went to bed. The hangover left by euphoria gone stale the next morning was far worse than the ravages of alcohol. On waking he found himself in the most desolate place in the world.

Claude came as Ella's emissary. They met for dinner at the Athenaeum. If it weren't for Claude, thought George with mixed feelings. Although nothing was clear-cut, nothing engraved on a tablet of stone. He might be dependent on Claude's goodwill, but so was Claude on his.

It was quite a reversal of the tables, he thought ruefully, since their last meal at his club five years previously, with Claude now inside the marriage, George out. What George feared most was that Ella might want a divorce, but he doubted she would. Ella still believed in the integrity – that word again! – of the family. He considered the position from which he would bargain. Claude might be the man in at the moment but until there was a divorce George still had a say. He weighed up the prospects. Ella already shared her life with Claude, so there was no need for her to divorce George in order to marry Claude. And unless George was willing to support her beyond the requirements of the law, which he hadn't yet made up his mind about, she wouldn't be able to afford a divorce settlement without drastic changes to the family's lifestyle. On Claude's pay as a junior lecturer at London University they wouldn't get far. Private education for the children would have to be abandoned. If they lived in a decent London area they would have to make do with a flat rather than a house, or move out to the commuter belt in one of the Home Counties. If Ella wanted a property on the scale of the Richmond house, she would have to head up north or down to the West Country.

Just thinking through such matters caused George distress no different from what he was sure Ella must also feel. Neither of them was made for divorce. So where did that leave them in their rudderless marriage? Within the profound sense of responsibility she had for the family there was also an unreckonable Ella with an impulsive streak who could run to extremes with an absolute resoluteness George had glimpsed once or twice and of which he remained in awe. It could run to suicide, he knew. It might run to violence against others, as he'd already experienced himself.

But for Claude – a stabilising influence, his dependable ally on the inside – George thought Ella might well have gone for broke.

According to Claude, she nearly did.

It was a close-run thing.

For a trial period of three months George was allowed to spend a weekend at home once a month to see the children. Ella had covered up for him to the extent that she had told them he was currently working abroad. True enough, as George had meanwhile made Tenerife his base while writing the trilogy for which he had been paid a large advance. But Ella remained distant, at best neutral.

'Don't deceive yourself I told the children that for your sake,' she said, not sparing him the sarcasm of *deceive yourself*. 'Don't think I was being noble.'

'Why did you, then?'

'I told them for my own sake, because I don't want to lose respect for myself, my self-respect – not my respect for you, because there is none to lose, but for choosing you when I now know that emigrating to Canada would have been the better option.'

*Wham!*

Not until Ella wheeled out *Canada would have been the better option* did George realise what he was up against. For him Canada was Precambrian – measureless past, an infinitude of time ago – but that was how far the shock waves reached back from the upheaval his affair with Julia Manning had caused, cracking the bedrock of his marriage. But how far was far? Such things were relative. For Ella, with her elephantine capacity for recall, which reached back to relive as now a moment from her earliest childhood as if not one intervening jot of time had passed, the Canada option might have been yesterday.

Was this harping on about the Canada option justified? Or was it the pride of a woman who couldn't bear the prospect of herself as a loser? Fuck the Canada option, George wanted to say to Ella but wouldn't have dared. Didn't things even out with the Claude option you got instead?

During his second dinner with Claude at the Athenaeum George gave voice to these questions, which had preoccupied him over the last few months, but Claude had no more of an answer to them than George.

'She has a way of pulling emotional rank, if you know what I mean,' George said to Claude. 'As if your stripes, so to speak, your sore feelings, counted for less than hers.'

Claude didn't commit himself beyond saying that he thought he understood what George meant. 'It's up to Ella to decide.'

But who was Uncle Claude to judge matters between a wife and her husband, as George still was, even if he'd been relegated? Claude still needed him no less than he needed Claude.

# 3

During his first few years at London University Claude kept in touch with the two closest friends he had made at the Sorbonne, Henri Gloaguen and Jean-Jacques Petit. He spent a few weeks one summer with Gloaguen in his native Brittany, where Henri had returned to become a schoolteacher, but their contact thereafter was generally confined to letters. The journey across to Brittany took up more time than was available to Claude on his trips to Paris, paid for by his uncle, usually in connection with some de Marsay family event. These trips however did give him the opportunity to keep up with Petit, who had stayed on at the Sorbonne to study for a doctorate in sociology while Claude was at London University doing his. Twice during the five or six years since Claude had departed for England, Gloaguen joined him and Petit for one of their all-night sessions in Paris, revisiting old haunts, reliving student memories. For a while such reunions seemed to be the continuation of a friendship that would remain indestructible, but when they ceased it slipped away and disappeared without any of them taking much notice.

Gloaguen, the teacher-poet who had preferred a life in the provinces to Paris, an introspective and gentle man who lacked ambition, was the friend after Claude's heart. But this was the friend he lost first. Over the years the letters they exchanged became fewer, written only on the pretext of some anniversary or other, until eventually they dried up too. There was no substitute for two human beings meeting in the flesh. Unless warmed periodically at the common hearth of friendship, meeting face to face, seeing, hearing and touching one another, it seemed that close ties could not be maintained for long. Almost incidentally, as a result of this neglect, without his even registering it happen, the French side of the old Gifford–de Marsay ambiguity, the bifurcated existence Claude had led for as long as he could remember, withered away in all but the family name that Claude had hung on to at Ella's instigation, without the rest of Claude becoming more English as a result.

What Claude had become since moving into Ella's orbit reflected perhaps more of her personality and history than of his. That diffuseness about the young Claude who had vacillated between Gifford and de Marsay, Little Compton and Paris, whose lies grew out of an indecision regarding who he was or where he belonged, solidified gradually into the certainty that his only belonging lay in a symbiosis with Ella, for which no country, no language, no culture, no loyalty to other human bonds could be substituted.

Strength lay in such certainty, but by exclusion, also narrowness. Determining this mainstay of his life at so early an age, a decade before he would have done so in the normal course of events, gave Claude a head start over his contemporaries in London and Paris, allowing him to concentrate his energies on fewer things, such as his doctorate, which he gained by the age of twenty-four. The rivalry between Claude in London and Jean-Jacques Petit in Paris only fuelled their interest in what the other was doing and did no harm to their friendship. The first stage of their competition was won easily by Claude, who had already been offered a post in London a couple of years before his friend in Paris had even completed his dissertation.

While Claude trod an unwavering path that led from libraries to lecture halls and committee rooms and not really anywhere else, Petit was advancing by the principle of trial and error, which is the natural, perhaps the only teacher of life – poking his nose into the wrong places and having to backtrack, falling in and out of love, into debt too and not always back out, acquiring that connivance with the ways of the world which for him was required experience. Claude might be on the faculty staff in London while his friend was still slumming it in student digs in Paris, but JJP, as Petit now styled himself, had meanwhile travelled overland to India, been cited in a divorce case and arrested several times, organised student protests and begun to move in political circles after being invited by JJSS – Jean-Jacques Servan-Schreiber – to contribute a critique of the education system in France to his newspaper *L'Express*. In the thick of life, even if that was a political jungle where Claude had no desire to be, Jean-Jacques had already begun his career before he had completed his education. *Round Two goes to JJP*, he scribbled across the top of the *L'Express* article he sent to Claude, and without envy Claude agreed.

By his mid-twenties Claude had acquired a family not of his own founding, not so much an environment he had grown as been plunged into, acclaimed as an instant uncle by children who were already well-established individuals when he came into their lives. Claude was not a resident of the Richmond house until after the birth of Alex in February 1959, at which time Max was a little over nine. George's departure a few years later then produced an ambiguous status of fatherhood which took him completely by surprise. What Claude had gone along with, in the way a man might continue along any stretch of road he happened to be travelling, thinking it would be a temporary arrangement that would change one way or another when he got round the next bend, was turning out to be permanent.

Claude began to appreciate the nicety of Hegel's definition of freedom as insight into necessity. Before George's actual departure but with his absence for so much of the time, away on trips to eastern Europe, many of the duties of a father and householder devolved on Claude. He had not sought them out and certainly felt unprepared for them, but as they came in Ella's wake he had no alternative but to take them on if they were to continue living under the same roof. With Alex he found himself in an increasingly delicate situation, required to act as surrogate father, and be recognised as such by the outside world, to a boy who was in fact his biological child, his own flesh and blood, whom he was disowning even as he took him in his arms. The child he pushed in a pram and who toddled along holding his hand on walks through the park, was the Morris boy as far as the neighbourhood was concerned. This was the agreement reached by Claude with George and Ella when the child was born, and this was how it would remain while Alex was growing up. He was five when George disappeared from the Richmond household. After a long absence George came back periodically for weekends, but the house had ceased to be home for him. A writer living primarily abroad, the absentee father who was at first something of a mystery for his four children – a hurtful mystery they never quite understood, for all Ella and George's explanations and reassurances – dwindled into a secondary figure in the background of their lives. He concerned them less and less. Claude had to take up the slack, to try with only partial success to fill the space George had left.

<h1 style="text-align:center">4</h1>

Recognising that this imposed greater obligations on Claude than he could cope with, which in turn strained their own relationship, and having gradually relented to the point of being ready to take George back into the family, Ella came up with the idea of selling the Richmond house and moving the family base to Tenerife. To everyone's surprise but his own, Max had had a successful career at Park House, winning a scholarship to Winchester as his father had done before him. By their own choice, Philip and Felicity also went on from their local school to become boarders at Sherborne. Thus, after George had departed and Giselle had died, for the eight or nine months of the year when the children were away at school, Ella, Claude and Alex were the only occupants – one might have called them squatters – of the damp rambling house on the Thames, a corpse the old family spirit seemed to have slunk out of, too expensive to keep up. It seemed a more economical and attractive idea to find a suitable house on a sunny island where the children could come and stay during the school holidays.

It was Ella who reconnoitred the island, with a little help from George, found and for tax reasons bought in her own name the property in the hills overlooking La Gomera on the west coast, with enough left over from the proceeds of the sale of the Richmond house to cover the purchase of a small London flat as well. George had insisted on maintaining a pied-à-terre in London, in part out of snobbery, in part out of reluctance to sever his ties completely, rationalising it as an investment and as a base later on for any of the children who might be studying or working in London. In the meantime George did not seem to mind the flat he had paid for being used primarily by Claude during term time when he was teaching at the university, which was just as well, considering how things turned out in practice. For the first couple of years after the purchase of the Kensington flat Claude shared it with Ella and Alex, the three of them flying out to Tenerife to spend the holidays with George and the other children when their schools broke up.

In the more intimate basement flat Ella found herself living with Claude a second and more intimate marriage than the one with George that had preceded it. Lack of space made spending more time together inevitable. Long before Alex began to wonder who his father was, he knew that Ella and Claude slept together in the same bedroom. Sometimes he was in there with them, lying in the middle. Perhaps it never occurred to Alex that there was anything contradictory or puzzling about this arrangement because for Ella and Claude there was nothing contradictory or puzzling about it either. They never made it a secret so Alex had no reason to find anything mysterious about it. This was just how things were. It was all part of family life at close quarters, an animal sharing of the same trough, having baths together, walking around the flat without clothes on or sitting on the lavatory with the door open, sharing private noises and smells while carrying on conversations – a rather different life from the one that Alex remembered from Richmond or would get to know at the house where they went for their holidays on Tenerife.

Inside the extended family Alex joined on the island he had to adjust to a different way of doing things – core family life melted away and was absorbed inside the larger family in the much larger house. Even though he could not have put it into words, Alex experienced this as a loss of intimacy. He shared a room with his half-brother Philip; Felicity one with her schoolfriend. Max had a room to himself. Probably because of the presence of the two girls on the same corridor, the lavatory door was kept shut when someone was inside. Instinctively, Alex knew that shared baths or walking about with no clothes on was not possible here, and it also belonged to that clear, if inexplicable rule of *not possible* that Claude, George and Ella would sleep in separate but adjoining rooms along the corridor on their side of the house.

For about three years Ella did not sleep with George. A sporadic resumption of sexual relations came about only after his rehabilitation in the family, a part of the resumption of the rest of her life with George, almost a habit laid aside and picked up again as his wife and the mother of their three children. It was not merely a question of her relenting because forgiveness was in her nature; it was due also to her awareness of an equilibrium she wished to preserve. She was not, as George liked to believe she was and tried to impose on her, an either/or woman. What came naturally to Ella was both/and. Given the space, she used it. Within the scope of her nature there was room enough for George and Claude, and there would still have been room for more.

As the moment approached when Alex would start prep school, Ella saw the balance of the larger family life in jeopardy. Recognising that she and she alone bore responsibility for it, she knew she was going to have to come up with some way of keeping the balance. She recognised that Claude's ambiguous status, his hidden role within their quasi-marriage, was untenable in the long run. It all needed to be thought through, but as neither George nor Claude seemed to recognise any such necessity, the thinking was left to Ella, giving rise to the impression in the family that she was always the one who imposed her way of doing things.

As long as Alex wasn't going to school, Ella could divide her time more or less equally between London and Tenerife. But if Alex went to school in London, it meant that for at least the next half-dozen years she would be tied up there for eight or nine months every year. At first there seemed to be no alternative to sending Alex to school in London, and for a while that was what happened. The more intimate life of the threesome there appealed to Ella, and she enjoyed the opportunity it gave her to study on the side for some A levels. But keeping George and the larger family together was unmanageable in these circumstances. It was unfair to them, and knowing it was unfair caused Ella restlessness, undermining the happiness of the life with Claude and Alex she instinctively preferred – for all her self-reiterations to the contrary in the interests of keeping the balance.

At the same time she detected a restlessness in Claude that ran in the opposite direction. For Claude it was not all roses living with Mrs Morris and her son Alex in a basement flat off the Kings Road. While the arrangement did not bar him from inviting friends home, the complications of explaining the situation or indeed of not explaining the situation, passing over it without comment, were such that Claude chose to keep his private life to himself. It was not something he shared with friends and colleagues at the university. Thirty now, inevitably invited to dinner parties it was as difficult for him to go to as not to, being seen as rude in either case – going and being obliged but failing to invite people back, or continually refusing for no good reason – Claude followed the only natural way out of the dilemma by cultivating an image of himself as a recluse. People got the impression that Claude de Marsay was an unsociable sort of fellow who didn't seem to belong to any circle. Since he was never seen in the company of women, either, *recluse* wasn't the only conclusion his colleagues were left to draw.

The too-narrow base of Claude's life was recognised by Ella before Claude himself became aware of the source of his discontent. She saw him growing moody and uncooperative and understood the reason why. But a truthful account of their relationship, involving George and three other children, could hardly be shared in the normal course of socialising with other people – not because it was anything to be ashamed of, not in the least, in their view – but because it was too much, too much stuff to have to unravel. There were no short cuts to the heart of the matter, a living arrangement which in their eyes represented too great a burden of information to offload in casual conversations between refilling glasses, between coming into a room through one door and leaving it through another. As neither felt the need to justify themself to other people, and neither was prepared to resort to a subterfuge, the only option was to continue in this way of life that isolated them from society – and people around them who would otherwise have wished them well came to resent that.

A way out of this dilemma presented itself with the opening of a British school, called the Yeoward, in Puerto de la Cruz. Before mooting with George the idea of sending Alex there, Ella discussed it with Claude.

Claude came to the point straight away: 'It means you and I will have less time together.'

'On the contrary. Why don't you listen first? I haven't told you my plan yet. But why does my time always have to be for someone else,' countered Ella, moving off on another tack. 'Why aren't I entitled to my own time for myself, to spend as I choose?'

Claude was taken aback by the question, although it was justified. 'Of course you're entitled to time for yourself. What are you proposing to do with it?'

'Now that I've got a couple of A levels, I'm thinking of taking a degree, a BSc in biology. You can do it by correspondence, so it doesn't mean I would have to be in London all the time. Still, I need libraries, books. And those books aren't available on Tenerife. I'd have to take

472

them with me if I went over, but it wouldn't be for more than a few weeks at a time.'

Ella reached over and took Claude's hand.

'Here's how it can be done. During term time Alex goes to the British school in Puerto. There's a bus down from Orotava and back up again. George writes; I do my course, and we go over to Arguayo for the weekends. So I'm away for a month or so at a time. And for the rest of the term I can be here with you in London, just the two of us, you see. George can take care of Alex while I'm away. It's not as if he doesn't know how to cook and things. And when I'm away from here ...' Ella stroked the back of Claude's head. 'What was the name of that woman you said you rather liked, the PhD student you got to know last year?'

'Nina. Nina Ivanovna. Nina Rubinstein.'

Ella wondered why Claude gave her three different versions of this woman's name.

'Perhaps you might like to get to know her better. You could ask her out to one of those parties you're always finding an excuse not to go to.'

'I wouldn't enjoy it.

'How do you know if you've not been to one?'

'I have.'

'But alone. You might find it more fun if you were with this Nina. Is she attractive? You could do other things with her. I mean, she could get you out a bit. Out of libraries and academic hiding places.'

Claude said nothing.

'You're still young, Claude, but you've begun to live a middle-aged life. There's us and the faculty and that's about it. Sometimes I feel that you're getting a bit ... dry. These are your best years, and they're being spent in musty corners. There's not enough going on in your life. You should be growing, and sometimes I think you seem to be shrinking.'

'Is that necessarily my fault?'

'Of course it is. Who else's? There should be more input in your life, new interests, other people. I don't want you to turn round ten years from now and tell me it was *my* fault that you got into a rut. *I'm* not holding you back, Claude. It's your freedom, but only if you use it. Otherwise it goes stale. *Du bist deines eigenen Glückes Schmied.*'

Claude was irritated by Ella's fondness for these sayings she trotted out. You forge your happiness on your own anvil! All that Schiller and Goethe, all that German poetry she knew by heart and seemed to treasure more as a recipe book for moral guidance in life rather than as literature for its own sake.

He had also taken exception to Ella's belittling *this Nina*, not to mention the charges of being dry and shrinking. What annoyed him was not so much Ella telling him these things as his suspecting her to be right, and particularly what she had said about *this Nina*. He had thought of asking Nina out several times, during Ella's absences in Tenerife, but he had not done so, feeling that loyalty to Ella, and thereby Ella, was what held him back. But here she now was telling him she was *not* holding him back, as if she had read his thoughts, telling him it was his freedom only if he made use of it. Freedom to do what?

*Is she attractive? You could do other things with her. I mean, she could get you out a bit.*

Which led them back to where their conversation had begun, with her telling him about moving more of their life to Tenerife and him telling her that would mean having less time together, as if behind that spoken thought lurked Claude's thought it had been left to Ella to bring out into the open, with the name of Nina Ivanovna Rubinstein written all over it. Thus the two of them together conspired to sow a seed intended by neither of them alone.

# 5

She woke at five in the belfry, her bedroom, and went barefoot down the stone stairs to the kitchen. A short corridor led outside to the terrace on the west side of the house. A glimmer in the distance betrayed the presence of the ocean, waiting out there in the dark. She walked up and down the lawn, treading the dew that had gathered on the grass. Then she went back inside to make some coffee. She sat down at the table, took a notebook out of the drawer and wrote down the list of things that had occurred to her while she had been walking the lawn.

The fish and the meat George had brought with him from Puerto had already gone into the freezer. Fresh vegetables Paco would bring down from the Santiago valley in the course of the morning along with wine, tomatoes, almonds, figs and bananas. There were other things in the wine cellar. She put on slippers and went down into the foundations of the house, thankful to the seventeenth-century bishop, its first occupant, for a large dry storage space that remained cool all year round. She kept her home-made preserves in the cellar, the tins and jars arranged by category on the shelves Paco had put up to her specifications, sweet, bitter, grain, paste, dairy, dried fruits, half a dozen different kinds of potato in open sacks, all of them labelled, with a basket to carry upstairs the particular kind required for a particular meal. Over the next ten days to two weeks she estimated she would be serving up twenty or thirty meals, anything between two hundred and two hundred and fifty individual portions.

By a quarter past six, having written out the menu for a dozen guests, with a rough estimate of the quantities of foodstuffs required each day, a blue pencil for what she already had in the house, a red pencil for diminished stocks to be replenished, she went back upstairs. She washed quickly in the room behind the kitchen. Her used pyjamas went into the empty bin for white fabrics, which Alicia had washed the day before, dried outside and then left for Ella to deal with in one of the broad-bottomed wicker baskets on the counter. Two of Claude's shirts were among the white fabrics, two blouses of her own, T-shirts that belonged to Alex and George. Naked, she stood on the wooden slats covering the washroom floor, ironing the blouses and shirts. A shirt took her two minutes, a blouse a minute or two more. She noted a button missing on the cuff of one of Claude's shirts, a loose thread in the collar of a blouse, a tear in Alex's T-shirt. The articles needing attention lay on top of the basket containing the laundry she carried back upstairs.

Depositing the basket at the top of the stairs leading out to the gallery, she went on up the steep spiral staircase to the belfry, made her bed, slipped on a kimono and went back down to the gallery. It was getting light. She picked up the basket and walked past the two linen cupboards she had fitted out with Alicia's help to the sewing room in the north-west corner of the house, from where she could look up into the Teno mountains. Her sewing machine folded out of the middle section of a cabinet with drawers on either side containing a complete haberdashery: spools and threads, needles, pins, scissors, thimbles, buttons, stretch tape of different widths, skeins of wool of many different colours. She picked out a needle for drawing the loose thread through to the reverse side of the collar on her blouse, knotted and trimmed it, darned the tear in Alex's T-shirt, selected a button that matched the one on the other cuff of Claude's shirt and sewed it on.

475

By the time she had dressed and gone down to the kitchen again it was getting on for half past seven. She switched on the oven, took the mixing bowl and beater out of the cupboard, put the flour, butter, eggs, almonds and other ingredients on the counter and began making herself a birthday cake it would largely be left to Alex to eat. While making the cake she listened to the news in Spanish from a local radio station, news from the Canaries mainly, no more than outlining the events in the world beyond the haze of their Atlantic island cluster – events that here seemed to matter less. A daily half-hour programme on agricultural topics followed the news, and Ella timed her day so that she could get on with some work while listening to it.

With keen interest (she sometimes took notes), Ella listened to the tips on crop management, reports on what species of plants did best in what areas of the island. Once a month there would be a detailed bulletin on the current ventures of the cooperatives responsible for maintaining Tenerife's water supply, boring new wells to tap the aquifer resources of the island, sinking ever longer and deeper water galleries that now totalled over a thousand kilometres in length. She and George had invested in the Santiago cooperative that guaranteed their local water supply. During her first long stay at the house many weeks of listening to the local news passed before Ella realised that there were no conventional weather forecasts because there was no need of them, only drought or storm warnings when big seas were running or flooded *barrancos* might be dangerous to pass.

Alex was the first down at eight. He found his mother sitting at a table outside on the terrace, armed with a pair of scissors as she worked her way through the pile of magazines and newspapers Claude had brought with him from London and George from Santa Cruz. He gave her a perfunctory good-morning kiss and wandered off, not sulky exactly, but non-committal, more interested in a pair of mating dragonflies he was curious to investigate. It disappointed Ella that he hadn't remem-bered it was her birthday – her first on the island – the fortieth of her life. It disappointed her that his entry into her day had given it a note of such ordinariness.

George and Claude came downstairs at the same time as Paco and Alicia appeared in the courtyard, she with an enormous bundle of flowers in her arms, he leading a soft-footed mule laden with panniers full of produce he had brought down from the valley that morning.

Ella told Paco where to put it all: in the kitchen, the cellar or the cool room – a niche off the stairs on the way down to the cellar that she used as a larder. She took an apple she had already put on one side, knowing they were coming, and fed it to the mule, who seemed to be expecting it just as the ginger cat who lived next door had learned to expect food in St John's Wood. Alicia arranged the bundles of flowers, her birthday gift to Ella, in vases around the patio. When all these things had been done Claude produced with a magician's flourish an already burning candle from his pocket, to the astonishment of Alicia and Paco, who stood watching, and laid a flat black box on the table in front of Ella beside the lighted candle, kissing her on both cheeks and wishing her happy birthday.

'I know what it is!' she exclaimed. 'In the window of that shop with antique jewellery we walked past off Kensington High Street ... Is it? Is it?'

Smiling, Claude watched as she took out of the box a necklace made of flat gold studs and tried it on. It was months since they had passed the shop and seen the necklace in the window, but she knew at once what was in the black box. Even while she was looking at it in the shop window she experienced a sensation of its transference from her eyes to her skin, the dulled odour of old gold in her nostrils. She could almost feel the coolness of the studded necklace, heavy like chain mail, passing over her collarbones, fitting snugly around her neck, as now it did, just as she had imagined, knowing it would find its way to her – a synaesthetic déjà vu involving all her senses.

George's present was on the tray he brought out to the table, he claimed. On it lay an assortment of knick-knacks beside a bottle of Spanish sparkling wine and three glasses, but that ruse didn't work. She had in her head a complete inventory of all the house chattels, and a round silver tray wasn't on the list.

'It's the *tray*!'

'A salver, of Berber manufacture I'm told, for presenting assayed food to the king, which in Africa was apparently the done thing ...'

Intrigued by the salver for presenting the poisoned chalice, the glimpse this gift gave her into George's subconscious life, Ella asked him to fetch two more glasses so that Alicia and Paco could join in the toast.

While George was giving Ella his present, Claude stood looking out through the *portada sillería* at Alex running up and down in the street.

The elaborate gateway on the fourth side of the traditional Canarian patio consisted of a two-storey portal and entrance hall. The boy was playing with a paper boat, letting it sail down the gutter on a trickle of water that had attracted a squadron of dragonflies, picking it up when it reached the drain at the bottom and repeatedly carrying it back up to the top again.

Ella heard Claude call the boy and watched the two of them disappear into the enclosed staircase leading up to the first floor of the *portada sillería*. Even at a distance she couldn't help noticing the same slightness of build and the similarity of their movements. Surely it must be obvious to everyone that the boy was his son? She heard their footsteps on the gallery, wondered what they were doing upstairs and then forgot about them as she listened to George telling her what he was planning for lunch.

# 6

They whiled away the morning with a game of hide-and-seek in the courtyard. George and Claude had hidden presents for Ella the previous evening. Two or three more surreptitiously made their way down later that morning with Claude and Alex, to be given their hiding places while the boy thought his mother wasn't looking. Following the Hot, Warm and Cold directions called out by the three of them, Ella retrieved from caches all over the patio a series of small gifts, from practical things like the egg timer George had come across in Santa Cruz to less practical but very pretty ones like the seashells given her by Alex, candidates for Ella's curiosities cabinet in her room in the belfry. The three shells had identical dark brown spots on top, paling off into beige along the sides and bone-white underneath, and they were of proportionately diminishing size – a family of shells, as Alex said when his mother had found all three of them, lining them up on the table so that she could see the unmistakable family resemblance despite them having originated from three different beaches where he had found them the previous summer. Three shells, she noted, so it was Alex's core family he had given her.

In the middle of the day they got into the jeep and drove off. There was a good tarmac surface as far as Santiago del Teide, but proper roads leading up into the mountains beyond were still under construction.

Only in a jeep could one negotiate the mountain trails, from which one had views down into the dark green clefts of the valleys below. Mist floated up out of these wooded ravines and sometimes shut out the view. Almond trees already in full leaf on the coastal slopes of Adeje were still in blossom up here. Nowhere but on the north-west corner of the island could one find such richness of green lavished on the landscape.

The jeep followed a track that traversed below the ridge until they arrived at an isolated farmhouse overlooking the valley. It was a popular weekend destination for the islanders, *chicharreros* as they were known, and in very recent years for an increasing number of hiker tourists, as a place where good local food was served. No fish was available; it was all chicken or goat's meat and rabbit in *salmorejo* sauce served with *papas arrugadas* and *gofio*, flour made from roasted grains baked into small cakes, eaten with serrano ham, cheese and garlic olive oil, or as a dessert sweetened with sugar-cane honey. But what lured most visitors up to this place was its verdancy on an island they knew otherwise mainly for its arid brown landscape. Here it was pristine in its green emptiness, greener by far than the fertile and much more densely inhabited Orotava valley.

There was a lot of speculation at lunch among the four of them, for they were the only guests at the restaurant, as to what was happening on the hillside across the ravine.

A man wearing a hat stood on a ladder, boarding up the side of a farm outhouse. It was difficult not to watch him, for he attracted attention, the sound of his hammering punching echoes across the valley. The sound conveyed the resonance of the nails sinking into the posts, tightening as the nails became gripped by the wood in which they were being embedded, first *thock-thocking* and then singing higher and higher up the scale as they were struck straight and true. Picking the sound up as it came out of them, amplifying and multiplying it in overlays of echoes, the valleys provided a giant anvil on which the hammering was beaten out, hugely magnified as if orchestrated by the workman's tiny baton, cut off at will, falling silent the moment he lowered the hammer and climbed back down the ladder. Once he had reached the ground, the man in the hat turned and faced down the hill, put his fingers to his mouth and whistled.

As far as they could tell at that distance, the man was cupping his mouth with both hands. A long high whistle was followed by a swoop down and a trill, a complete musical phrase sounding very like an imitation of a bird call. There was a pause. Then a second whistle followed, a series of rapid upward slides ending in one long note at the highest pitch. He let his arms drop and waited. From somewhere below him, out of sight at the bottom of the ravine, a bird began singing in response to the whistling man in the hat, or so it seemed. One could make out four or five distinct phrases with pauses in between, with scoops, slides and trills again not unlike a bird singing, only more sustained and across a much broader and more exotic spectrum of sounds.

When the song coming up out of the valley broke off, the man in the hat put a hand up to his mouth and piped a high-pitched three-note call, up-down-up, before turning back to the ladder and climbing to resume boarding the wall.

'What on earth was *that*?' asked George.

He put the question to the small hunchbacked man standing in the door of the house, shading his eyes as he looked out into the brightness.

The man stepped out onto the terrace, where they were lolling in the sun, and said, 'Oh, that's Joaquín.'

'Can Joaquín talk to the birds?'

'Not to the birds. Not as far as I know. That's his son you heard down in the valley. It's the whistling language of La Gomera. Maybe they were talking about stopping to have lunch. That's how they communicate on the island.'

'A whistling language?'

'The *silbo Gomero*.'

'Could you understand what Joaquín was talking about? Stopping work to have lunch?'

The hunchback ducked his head as if the question startled him.

'I was guessing. Only people who were born and live all their life on the island can understand the *silbo Gomero*.'

Every now and then, he said, Joaquín came over from the island for a couple of days to do odd jobs for his sister, who had married a Tinerfeno with a small farm up here in the mountains, where she had been living on her own since her husband's death. That was as much as the man could tell them.

'I wish they'd whistle some more,' said Alex. 'I wish I could whistle-talk like that.'

On the drive back they talked of nothing else. Whether a meaning was coded in a tune, whether the sounds imitated language patterns and had a grammar, how the *silbo Gomero* had originated, how it could be learned, whether one could find a way of writing it down, over what distances a conversation could be carried on, and so on: they argued until they agreed that the best solution would be to take the ferry over to La Gomera and find out.

And we might never have known, thought Ella. How fortunate they were to have gone up there today – on her birthday! She felt something like grace had been bestowed on them up there in the mountains – but to say so would bring them bad luck.

Later George brought the tea out onto the terrace on her birthday salver – Claude put forty candles on the cake – Alex lit them – and Ella blew them out. Then she went up to the belfry with her son to find a place for the shell family in her curiosities cabinet. There was still room in one corner of the lower shelf alongside two products of her children's handicraft classes: a matchstick model of the Arguayo house built by Philip and a glass thimble on a little white doily crocheted by Felicity. Alex got on a stool to investigate the top shelf.

'There's *tons* of room up here.'

'Well, we'll need it. It'll fill up quicker than you think. Alex, come and sit here for a moment.'

He looked round, recognising from the tone of his mother's voice that something was up. He got off the stool and sat down beside her on the bed.

'Why were you such an old grumps when you came down this morning?'

She smoothed his hair across his forehead. 'I *wasn't* an old grumps.'

Denial came as the instinctive response. Ella ignored it.

'Did you have a bad dream?'

He sat there with crossed wrists, twisting his arms as if wringing out the answer. 'I didn't know what to give you for your birthday.'

Ella was taken by surprise. 'But what about the shell family?'

Alex blushed. 'That wasn't my idea,' he said in a small voice.

'Whose idea was it?'

'Claude's.'

'It may have been his *idea*, but it was your *find*, darling. They were among the most precious possessions in your treasure trove, weren't they? They're *beautiful* shells, and it was very sweet of you to give them to me. Come and give me a kiss.'

He sat facing her on her lap and put his arms around her.

'Mum, as it's your birthday, can I stay up late?'

'Of course you can.'

He gave her a kiss on the cheek. 'And can I have some more cake?'

Ella laughed. 'Oh I see. *That's* what all this is about.'

She put on a cardigan before she went back down. It was almost too much happiness to sit out in the soft air on the flower-scented terrace with the night sky for a roof, reading the newspapers with George and Claude beside her, cutting out items to put inside her cupboards, her eye caught now and then by Alex in the yellow lamplight as he ran tirelessly up and down the street, floating his paper boat down the drain.

'It was a lovely birthday,' she said to George and Claude when she said goodnight at midnight and went upstairs, telling herself to overlook the fact that her three other children had failed to call.

Only in that premonition *And we might never have known* lay something outside the day's happiness, not belonging to it but still intruding on it – a shadow across it from outside.

In the night she was woken by a knife cutting inside her, swishing across her stomach. She remained curled up, whimpering in the dark, calling for her mother as she still did when she was afraid. When the pain eased, she got up and went to the bathroom and found she was wet with some sticky liquid on the inside of her thighs. She washed and changed her underwear, went back to bed but couldn't sleep. So she got up again, wrapped a blanket around herself against the morning chill and made her way downstairs to tread the dew on the lawn beside the terrace. The terrace and the lawn were all that they had managed in the couple of years since they had bought the house. Now she had a vision. Now that the house was done inside, she would give it the setting, the garden it needed, the green lung for it to breathe. On the arid hillside she would create an oasis of blooming shrubs and flowers, a stepping stone between the ocean, which lay below to the west, and the mountain exhaling to a volcanic white peak in the east – a beacon, already lit up by the first rays of the rising sun while the rest of the island gathered around its slopes remained shrouded in darkness.

# 7

Tessa's arrival with the twins, plus a schoolfriend of Felicity they had invited, plus a girlfriend of Tessa's they had not, brought a bubbling commotion to the house which Ella and Alex had been looking forward to. Claude didn't seem to mind either way. George liked the twins coming for the holidays but could happily have done without the other guests.

'Why did you have to invite my sister?' he grumbled to Ella.

'I didn't invite her. She invited herself, and her friend too. Why not? Why should I have said no? It's nice to have the house full of people. I don't know what you've got against Tessa.'

'She used to be such a bitch and now she's become so *butch*. Lesbian – all right, if that's her thing – but she has to make a show of it. And that simpering itsy-bitsy friend of hers, what's-her-name, Miriam, writhing and mincing her way all over the place – I'd like to put her across my knee and give her a good spanking.'

George complained of people behind their back. In an ideal world he would have given quite a few of them spankings. George was a spanker by conviction, and but for Ella's veto he would have applied his hand more frequently to his children when they were growing up, particularly to Max. Outwardly George could be charming to his guests when he felt so disposed; his sister wasn't fooled, though. She knew him too well.

So her brother didn't like Miriam. We'll see about that, Tessa said to herself.

She wandered past as George was sitting on the patio doing *The Times* crossword one morning.

'I'm surprised you don't get bored, George, spending so much time by yourself on this island. What is there to *do*?' She gave a little squeal of a laugh. 'Apart from crossword puzzles.'

'Ah, but I have myself, Tessa, and my own company is very convivial. The two of us never get bored.'

'That must be reassuring for Ella, knowing you're in good hands when she's away. And how reassuring for *you*, knowing *she* is in good hands. How cleverly the two of you have arranged things.'

Tessa drifted on through the gate to join Miriam, who was waiting outside.

George wasn't happy with this first skirmish and what it boded for the rest of the holidays. He wasn't too happy about the sleeping arrangements either. His daughter Felicity and her Sherborne friend Jennifer were sharing a bedroom on the same corridor as Tessa and Miriam, with a view looking east to El Teide.

'Tessa's a barracuda,' George said to Ella as they stood at the kitchen sideboard preparing lunch for nine. 'She told me herself that she once raped one of the maids we used to have at Hampstead. She'll have those two little girls for breakfast. She'll gobble them up.'

But Felicity was going on eighteen now, a big strong horse of a girl, captain of her house tennis and lacrosse teams. Ella didn't share George's worries but wondered, as she often did with him, what put such ideas into his head. She looked at Felicity and thought rather, How can that girl be my daughter? It was odd. Neither of the twins resembled the other, but both of them were so like their father. Their father was what they had in common, allowing the rest of them to remain distinct.

'Where's Claude?' was all she said by way of an answer.

'I think I saw him drive off somewhere with the boys.'

There was a distinct sound of coughing.

'Oh no!' exclaimed George. 'Not *that* again.'

In the wake of the coughing George and Ella heard a burst of girlish giggling as clearly as if it came from somewhere inside the kitchen.

'I wish we could do something about those ... those *vents*,' Ella said. 'One can hear every word they're saying upstairs.'

As if in confirmation of what she had just said, Felicity's voice came booming down the air shaft: 'Helen's got a crush on Miss Thorpe.'

'No! How d'you know?' This was Jennifer, identifiable by her Scottish accent.

'She told me herself. She even invited her to the Buttery for tea on the day we broke up.'

'Well, if you ask me, I think Helen's just sucking up to Miss Thorpe because she wants to be head girl. But Miss Thorpe has her own secret pash for Mr Jenkins, if you can believe it, that bald little man in the chemistry department ...'

Jennifer's voice trailed off as she moved away from the window towards the door.

This mysterious soundbox in the kitchen ceiling — a relic of the Inquisition, George was fond of telling gullible guests — was one of the curiosities of the house. According to local records, it had originally been commissioned as a residence for a Spanish bishop, Bartolomé García Jiménez, who in the late seventeenth century had sponsored the idea of a new parish in Santiago del Teide and a new church to celebrate it on an old pilgrim site dating back to pre-Hispanic times. The vents, as Ella called them, had most probably been chimney flues in the east wall of the original house, but in the course of many reconstructions and additions, undertaken in the eighteenth and nineteenth centuries, all the fireplaces on that side of the house had been taken out, the truncated flues leading up to the upper floor sealed off. But when a person happened to be standing talking near the outside wall of one of the two upstairs rooms facing east, whatever they said could be picked up as clearly as if they were speaking into a microphone connected to a speaker in the ceiling of the kitchen below. George and Ella had had workmen in to take a look at it, but it seemed that without a major masonry job there was nothing to be done.

George, a self-confessed voyeur – an *auditeur* too, come to that, he admitted, never one to pass up the chance of a pun – was in favour of leaving things as they were, although perhaps 'in the interests of fair play' putting up a sign to warn people they might be overheard.

He was overruled by Ella. She had the furniture switched around, moving the beds, which had stood in the sensitive area under the windows, to the gallery wall, and the table and chairs that had been there to the space by the windows. It was her house. Any changes to it were her prerogative.

'Well, if we have to eavesdrop, at least we won't be party to people cavorting in bed,' said Ella, deploying one of her aunt Hermine's favourite words as she surveyed the new arrangement of the furniture. First-time visitors to the house were warned when shown up to their rooms.

George knew why he had been overruled. Ella's view was her mother's – another of her mother's old sayings on the tape she still heard going round and round inside her head, still determining so much of what Ella did. *Anything you said behind a person's back you should also be able to say to their face.*

'So now we all know about Miss Thorpe and Mr Jenkins, and who was invited to the Buttery for what reason,' was the first thing she said when Felicity and Jennifer came down into the kitchen for some breakfast.

'What?'

Ella pointed a finger up to the ceiling.

'Oh no!'

'Well I did warn you. Not for the first time.'

'Can't you have something done about it?'

'Yes,' said George. 'You can watch your tongue, even when you think no one's listening. Be discreet. A useful quality to acquire in life.'

Felicity went over to her father, who was mashing anchovies in a bowl with boiled egg yolk and paprika, pecked his cheek and laid her head on his shoulder.

'What's that?'

'A new *mojo* variant I'm trying out.'

Felicity put her finger in and sucked it.

'Mmmm ... are we having that for lunch?'

Felicity giving her father a kiss but not her mother. Ella made a point of not seeming to notice. She knew her daughter did this deliberately.

'Wouldn't you like to help yourself to some tea or coffee?' she said to Jennifer. 'The kettle's over there, and you'll find everything else you need in the corner cupboard.'

While Felicity talked to her father Ella chatted away with Jennifer, and neither mother nor daughter took any notice of each other.

# 8

Felicity and her brother Philip had inherited their father's build, compact and strong, not the typical Morris family build – André, Tessa and the younger brothers, the Manchester relatives, were all tall and spare and dark-complexioned. Both had George's fairer complexion, a robust-ness that squared up into rough-hewnness and a lack of sensitivity, of anything resembling finesse. Inside and out, Ella didn't recognise much of herself in either of them.

Until Felicity was about twelve, she had been her mother's closest companion. In a family of five males, Claude included, Ella and Felicity had naturally teamed up. How sick Ella got of all those males, their games and all that porpoising life, those outward qualities that seemed to exhaust themselves in their outwardness, which George and even Claude sometimes shared with the three boys. At times they could be no less like children than the boys were. How childish men could be when they got up to their games! And how enjoyable it was for Ella to be closeted with her daughter at such times, with small personal things in a small personal room, as her old room at the Richmond house had been, so rich in its detail, its cosy inwardness. In this seclusion she had often passed the same time of day with Felicity but differently from her, combing through the entanglements of her daughter's adolescent personality, her moods and what they arose from, and the things that mattered to Ella in the upbringing of her child – truthfulness, clarity, a responsibility to help people born of an urge to kindness as natural (Ella took this for granted) as the humanity that all people had in common.

But with Felicity's departure from home that intimate companionship ended. Ella's daughter slipped away. How mysterious! Perhaps Felicity had just grown more and more into what selfish genes had long since dictated she was bound to become – more of herself, just that, a robust rough-hewn altogether larger girl whose emergence was not due to, but had merely been accelerated by, removal from her mother's influence and exposure to the *corps d'esprit* of a traditional girls' public school. These days Ella didn't know where to begin with Felicity – what they had in common – what she could ask her – what she should avoid.

Four years previously, when Felicity and Philip had gone off to boarding school, Ella, George and Claude had sat down with them in Richmond to put into unmistakable words what until then had never been spoken about except to Max, who had previously been provided with confirmation of a fact he had already divined for himself. Alex's real father – his *biological* father, George sought to clarify, perhaps only muddying the issue for two thirteen-year-old children – was not George but Claude. The twins had a younger brother who was in fact their half-brother. For Max this disclosure had not presented a problem. Why should it be one for the twins?

George thought it was he who should be the one to tell them, speaking on behalf of *your mother* and *Claude* – the *uncle* had been dropped – and laying out the facts without a hint of there being anything the least bit intimidating in store for the children. George smiled as he talked; he even put an arm round Claude when introducing him as *your younger brother's father*. Claude and Ella smiled as if it were the most natural thing in the world – as far as they were concerned it *was* the most natural thing in the world. Smile-wreathed, the three of them might have been having

487

their picture taken. She was still the mother of all three children – or rather four, George said, perhaps moved to that odd choice of *still* by the exasperatingly wooden expression of the twins as they listened to this recital. Ella put in a word; Claude chipped in too. It didn't change anything, they said. Everything was just as it had been before, which from the point of view of George, Ella and Claude it was. But their encouraging adult smiles had failed to coax smiles onto the twins' faces, and when Philip's brow began to crinkle into a furrow, heralding his famous frown, it was clear that George's pitch hadn't worked.

'Is that why you left us, Dad?'

George threw up his hands in exasperation. 'That's got absolutely nothing to do with it, Philip.'

George then had no alternative but to give them an account of the events that had taken him away from his family, an account very different from the version that had initially been posted by Ella. And here something unexpected happened. Both Felicity and Philip accepted their father's infidelities and lies to their mother, resenting more the fact that she had not taken them into her confidence about George.

'Why didn't you tell us?' Felicity demanded. 'You're always telling *us* that we've got to tell the truth.'

'Because I didn't want you to feel let down by your father,' said Ella.

'Let *us* down? But it was really *you* he let down, wasn't it?'

'Don't answer back to your mother like that! I let the whole family down –' George came to Ella's defence '– and the only reason you didn't know about it at the time was because your mother covered up for me.'

Feeling helpless, Claude said nothing.

'So that you wouldn't lose faith in your father,' George added, wondering if *lose faith* wasn't a bit over the top.

But after this conversation Philip's *Is that why you left us, Dad?* remained hanging in the air, despite everything George said. However much he explained that he had had an affair with a woman he had met long before Ella even came into his life, the twins were given or perhaps helped themselves to the impression that their father's departure from home had more to do with the presence of another father already established in the house – their younger brother's father, their one-time uncle, Claude. His standing with them immediately fell. This uncle who was really their brother's father had been lying to them all the time – that was the view they took. They felt betrayed by Claude. And

Ella became party to that betrayal too, the target of the same resentment directed against Claude for conspiring with their mother to oust their father from their home.

The unfairness, as Ella felt it – worse, the stupidity – of the twins' judgement in their father's favour and against herself fairly took her breath away, coming over her in tearful squalls of anger and frustration. Who is it that has seen you through life, day by day? she would have liked to shout at them. Who has always been here for you when you came home from school, here in this house every day, actually here, coping with your needs, your wants, your hopes and troubles, played with you, laughed and cried with you?

Not George.

George had flown in from Tenerife just for the occasion, Ella would have liked to remind the two children who made up his fan club. Meanwhile she was busy packing their trunks with a school uniform she found conventional and drab and which could be ordered only from one expensive London shop and a long list of first-term requirements.

Between this maladroit conversation, intended to be about their younger brother's father, but which turned into an indictment of their mother, and the children's departure from Richmond for Sherborne – during the last week of the holiday before Philip and Felicity left for boarding school – they could hardly conceal their impatience to get out of the house.

Ella looked at their closed little faces with their smug expressions and flared up. 'Your father leaving the house has got *absolutely nothing* to do with your brother having a different father. Didn't you hear him tell you that himself?'

'Then why do you keep on about it?' said Philip stolidly.

'Because you stand there and judge me. Yes, you do! As if I'd done something wicked. As if I'd been a bad mother, a bad wife. That's what you think, *du kleiner Kleinbürger*! Isn't it?' She took him by the shoulders and shook him. '*Isn't it?*'

'No, it's not,' mumbled Philip, cowed by this outburst.

'Now you listen to me, Philip. And you listen too, Felicity. Nothing has taken place in this house that anyone need feel ashamed of. I am a free woman. Do you understand? I may make mistakes – I'm sure I do – perhaps it would have been better to have had this conversation sooner – maybe it would – but I act according to my conscience in the interests of everyone in the family, including my own. I will not have you stand there and judge me as if I had done something wrong when no wrong has been done. *I will not have it!'*

This was more than their mother flying off the handle, an always dramatic event they were familiar with and feared; this was Ella taking a stand and fighting for her life, and the conviction with which she did so left an impression on the twins they wouldn't forget. They believed what she said. They saw her strength. They knew she was right, even if they couldn't understand why, and they acquiesced in the state of things as they were in the family, even if they did not approve of them. They respected their mother, but they no longer quite loved her, not with the same unquestioning acceptance with which they had loved her before.

# 9

Ella returned to these subjects constantly. Claude knew them by heart. She got tangled up in them and couldn't find her way out. What he could do was talk her through these matters she fretted about until she was clear of them and free to move on again. George was no partner for this kind of conversation. It was Claude's task, listening to Ella telling him over and again the things she said he didn't have any idea about. But his support was given at one remove from dealing directly with the children as Ella did. It was true that she was the one who provided them with the guidelines for life. Their upbringing was in her hands. What Claude and George had to contribute was marginal.

They went back into the courtyard to work on her newspaper cut-tings.

Ella laid a portfolio on the table, a pair of scissors and Sellotape. She opened the portfolio and took out variously coloured folders. The bulkiest was a red one marked VIETNAM. Since the beginning of the Tet Offensive the war had been more in the news than ever. Ella spread out half a dozen of the more recent war pictures she had cut out of newspapers. The most arresting was a photo of a man shooting another man in the head at point-blank range.

'The man on the left is the chief of police,' said Ella. 'The man on the right is a Viet Cong prisoner responsible for the murder of some American soldiers. Or so we are told. There were reporters standing right there on a street in Saigon, you know, when the police chief shot the prisoner. This is what we do with people like you, he said, and shot him as a demonstration to the reporters of what was done with Viet Cong prisoners.'

It was a shocking picture. The hair of both men seemed to be standing on end, as if electrified by the tension. You could almost hear the report of the gun and see the bullet in mid-air. It was that close to capturing an instant.

'I think this should go into one of the kitchen cupboards, where people are most likely to see it. This is a picture everyone should see.'

'Just about everyone has seen it already.'

'Why shouldn't they go on seeing it?'

Claude hesitated.

'Just this one picture,' Ella pleaded. 'All right? We'll leave the others. Perhaps you're right. There are too many pictures. People look at them once and forget them. Just this one will stand for all the rest. Against forgetting the Vietnam War, which isn't even its name. You know what the Vietnamese call it? They call it the American War. In the cupboard. It will keep going on there even when it's over.'

She took the newspaper cutting into the kitchen. She opened one of the cupboards there and held the picture up against the inside of the cupboard door while Claude taped its corners.

'George will scoff, but I don't care. This is my house.'

They looked through the crop of cuttings Ella had reaped from the last batch of papers Claude had brought with him from London. Ella laid out a patchwork of them on the table.

Spring coming to Hyde Park. A town in Sicily in ruins after an earthquake. Sheepdog trials. Picture of an unidentified old woman. Flood victims in Brazil. Entire folders were devoted to Biafra, the Six Day War, thalidomide. Ninety-eight per cent of the pictures never made it out of the folders onto a cupboard door. Sometimes Ella spent an evening looking through the rejects. The pile grew and grew. She had nowhere to put them. The size of the pile distressed her. None were thrown away, and crates of them were left behind when Ella sold the Richmond house and the family moved to Tenerife.

'All this is taking place along the same wave. It's the same wave breaking and throwing up all these things,' she said to Claude. 'They're all connected.'

Putting the wave connection aside for one minute, Claude told Ella he wasn't in favour of having pictures of Biafra or thalidomide victims pasted into the guest-room cupboard.

'It's an imposition. Every time they open the cupboard to take out a towel they see misshapen children or people starving in Biafra. You can't dictate your values and your priorities to other people. You'll come across as moralistic and dogmatic. People will be irritated. They'll think you're preaching at them. It'll have the opposite effect of what you intend.'

'It's not an effect I intend.'

'Yes, it is. You want to draw attention to the pictures. You want them in there as a reminder. With your own children it's different. You can talk to them about the pictures and why they matter to you.'

'It's part of their upbringing.'

'But it might be better if you handed them the folders and suggested they make their own choice.'

Ella listened reluctantly, but this was why she'd wanted Claude to do the cupboards with her. Even if she didn't agree with what he said, it gave her another point of view. Conversations of this kind no longer took place with George. He took no interest in the pictures in her cupboards.

'So what should I do in the guest-room cupboard?'

'Something more cheerful out of the Tenerife file. Don't you think? Something of local interest. Here, for example, this picture of an aviary, the old fellow in Icod de los Vinos who wants to breed canaries to restore the bird population. Or the dolphins off Santa Cruz.'

They laughed.

Ella had a spasm. The pain came so suddenly she was hardly able to conceal it from Claude. She wondered whether to tell him. But she was happy doing the pictures with him. She didn't want to spoil it.

Having talked it through, they decided one tough picture was enough in each of the new linen cupboards outside the children's rooms. Biafra would go into the boys' cupboard, thalidomide into the girls'.

'Why not the other way round?'

'Because it's the girls who will be giving birth to children and will have to look at what comes out of their wombs.'

Claude had no answer to this.

That left the three cupboards downstairs. The one in the dining room was stocked with things for laying and decorating the table, a dozen salt and pepper cellars, one for each guest, napkins, napkin rings and table mats. In the cupboard in the winter lounge, where there was a huge old fireplace they sat beside on cold January nights, Ella kept her stock of replacements: candles, matches, incense sticks, light bulbs. There were caches of a variety of such articles tucked away in cupboards all round the house in case of an emergency. This was why Ella had seen fit to order no less than seven cupboards from the Santiago carpenter.

The connection between Ella's box fetish, her cupboard pictures and the caches of emergency rations squirrelled away around the house was her experience of being a refugee. All the war pictures, the disasters that grabbed her attention when she opened a newspaper, were stories about the homeless. This was the condition of the refugee, increasingly a condition of ever more people, having become a nobody and having nowhere to go. It was impossible for Ella not to sympathise with such people, not to want to reach out to Bahia or Biafra or wherever the refugees happened to be, and share with them her own experience of what it would be best to do. To have a receptacle was to be equipped for flight – something in which to carry the essentials you would need – something to put in it. Readiness was all.

# 10

Naturally, Tessa took a different view.

They were in the middle of dinner on the terrace after another day spent at the beach, when Tessa got up, striking the side of her glass vigorously with her fork to quell the babble of nine voices all talking at the same time. 'Try breaking it while you're about it!' George heckled. Tessa must have caught too much of the sun, he thought, and perhaps too much of the bottle. Her burning red face, glistening with *après soleil*, was puffed and blotchy, setting off starkly the whites of her eyes under her black eyebrows, making her look as if she was wearing some sort of carnival mask.

'I won't keep you from your dinner for long,' Tessa said, her face swivelling a lighthouse beam around the table out of this coruscating mask. 'I want to propose a toast to George and Ella for inviting us and for all the hospitality they've given us here. But first a toast in retrospect

493

to Ella's birthday, which unfortunately we just missed. Happy birthday, Ella!'

They raised their glasses and drank to Ella, expecting Tessa to sit down again, but she remained on her feet, striking her glass a second time to show that she wasn't done yet.

'Speech!' called Miriam.

'Your beautiful house. I've been looking around it, you know, taking a good look at everything. The view rather steals the show, of course. It's so stunning that it takes a while before you really notice the house. And then I read the fascinating history of the house framed in the downstairs loo, about the bishops and kings who owned the land and the old pilgrimage sites that date back long before the Spanish came and took it all away from those poor cave dwellers who once used to live here. And I used to think it was tourists who invented the Canary Islands!'

'Well it was,' interrupted George. 'The British started it off when they began wintering in La Orotava during the second half of the nineteenth century, all those rheumatic curates and ladies who suffered in our damp climate. Four quid return fare from Bristol. And you lived more cheaply here than in England.'

'Oh, much earlier than that,' Claude pitched in. 'Once America had been discovered, ships made the Canaries their last port of call to take on fresh food and water before crossing the Atlantic. Columbus, just across the water over there, at La Gomera. That put the islands on the map, and that was really the beginning of the tourist trade.'

'But it's a rather different—'

'Who cares about all that old rubbish,' snapped Tessa, her face glowing with increased intensity, irritated by the discussion that had interrupted her speech. 'I was about to say it was that framed history of the old kingdom of Adeje I came across in the loo that drew my attention to the regular little *library* of information posted in unexpected places all over the house. I mean, what an original idea! It can hardly have been your idea, George ...'

'As a matter of fact—'

'It was Ella. It *must* have been your idea, Ella.'

'Yes' said Ella, 'it was.'

'I was wondering what happened to the troglodytes.'

'Troglodytes?'

'Yes, the cave dwellers, the original inhabitants – Comanches or whatever they were called.'

'Ah, you mean the *Guanches*,' said Ella.

'Of *course* I do. Guanches, not Comanches. They're Red Indians, aren't they? John Wayne and Co. How silly of me to have got them mixed up.'

Alex caught sight of Felipe darting past outside the gate. Bored by what his aunt was saying, he decided it would be more interesting to go and play with Felipe and asked his mother if he could get down.

'Well, there's still pudding to come,' she said absently, already turning back to what Tessa was saying. 'I don't understand your question about what happened to the troglodytes.'

Alex took the opportunity while she was preoccupied to slip out and join Felipe.

'Well, I just thought they would have deserved a mention, as they obviously fit in with the others.'

'Fit in?'

'Well, let's see now ...' Tessa struck a theatrical pose, her index finger on her chin like a schoolgirl who had forgotten her lines. Miriam laughed. 'Offhand, I can think of five. Starving Africans in the kitchen loo downstairs, flood victims in the hall loo ditto, and then in the cupboards along the gallery upstairs those poor islanders evacuated to Britain at taxpayers' expense when their volcano erupted. What else?' She counted them off on her fingers. 'Oh yes, the thingamajig children with no arms and legs. And that quite horrible execution picture in Vietnam. All victims, which is where the troglodytes fit in, you see, those poor cave-dwelling natives who were exterminated when the Spaniards took over the islands.'

There was silence after Tessa had finished.

'Oh, have I said something out of place?' She sat down and dabbed her lips with her napkin.

Ella put her elbows on the table and leaned forward to face Tessa. 'Perhaps you *have* said something out of place. It all depends on how you meant it.'

'Meant it?' Tessa did her piglet squeal of laughter, pleasurably wriggling her little corkscrew tail.

'In what spirit you said it, seriously or in mockery.'

'Isn't it time we had a bit of both around here? Isn't this house already top-heavy enough with seriousness?'

'Mockery has its place, I agree. And I don't mind you making fun of me, which I think you were doing when you brought up the troglodytes. But not *thingamajig children*. That won't do. That expression is inexcusable.'

'Hear hear,' said Claude, rapping the table with his hand.

Claude's unexpected intervention persuaded the three children, who were still at the table but had been about to get up and leave, that a showdown was in the offing between the grown-ups, with fireworks which might be worth sticking around for.

Miriam was drawn in too. 'Really, I don't know about *inexcusable*. We're not in a classroom.'

Tessa threw her napkin onto the table. 'I mean, what's the point of sympathy with people if sympathy doesn't help them? Sticking a picture of starving Biafrans into your cupboard doesn't put food in their mouths. It doesn't bring back to life the man being shot on the Saigon street, does it? Or am I wrong about that? What good is it making a great show of solidarity with the suffering in the world if it's not going to alleviate it one little bit? All right, I hear on the news that a bus has gone off the road in Peru and twenty-seven passengers were killed. But why do I need to be told that? What has that got to do with me? What have those wretched, ungrateful little people from Tristan da Cunha got to do with *me*? Bereaved families after the Aberfan disaster, all right, if you must. At least that's closer to home. I still think it's in poor taste, but I can relate to that. Frankly, I don't particularly care. But if I did care, like you, Ella, I'd want all that caring to *achieve* something. I mean, if all you do is to paste pictures in your cupboards, darling, one wonders what for? It's almost like you were advertising what a caring person you are. I'm sure you *are*, darling, and that you're *not* advertising, but that's the impression some people might get, you see. Just ordinary people like not-particularly-caring-little-me, for instance. This is the thing about you, Ella, that does rather get my back up: your making this display of your pity or compassion or whatever you like to call it. Why can't you just get on with it quietly in your own little corner?'

'But this house *is* my own little corner. And how much quieter can you get than inside a cupboard?' Ella smiled. 'You got up to thank me and George for inviting you here, but we didn't, Tessa. You invited yourself. As for Miriam, I didn't know she was coming until the moment she arrived in our little corner. No one was brought here against their will.'

The promptness of this reply and the calmness with which it was delivered took Tessa aback. She was anticipating a fight, not to be disarmed as coolly as she just had been. Ella saw her hesitate and took advantage of it.

'As for my making a *display*, as you call it, I can only say that none of the cupboards you opened were cupboards you needed to open. They're all household cupboards for household things. You opened them because you're nosy. In the cupboard and chest of drawers for your personal use in the guest room there are no pictures anyone would find offensive, unless you consider the pictures of El Teide and the dolphins in Santa Cruz harbour to be offensive ...'

George considered this unexpected counter-attack on his pugnacious sister with the objective interest of a boxing referee. Tessa had gone in with fists flailing, intent on downing her opponent with the fury of her first onslaught, but Ella had sidestepped. Not a word in reply to the main charge, the pointlessness of sympathy unless it had more than just feelings to offer, but that was a tricky one to deal with. Evading rather than answering it had been the right move. Still better, the deflection of that patronising phrase Tessa hurled at Ella, the way *your own little corner* had been boomeranged right back at Tessa, who had tripped up over that invitation business. She'd thought Ella was a softy and would be a pushover, underestimating her toughness. It was gratifying for George to see his sister discomfited – Tessa who had herself discomfited so many others in her time.

Tessa yawned demonstratively as if she'd lost interest, as if all this was beneath her, announcing in her cut-glass vowels, 'Well *anyway*, I shall be turning in early. All this sun and fresh air have been a bit much for big-city me. How about you, Miriam?'

Miriam took the hint, announcing that she was rather tired as well, and the two of them made a leisurely retreat, trooping upstairs to the gallery without wishing anyone goodnight.

Disappointed by the anticlimax, Felicity pulled a face. 'The trouble with Arguayo is that there's absolutely *nothing* to do at night.'

'We could play Monopoly,' said Alex.

'I'll play,' Philip seconded him.

'I'm sick of Monopoly.' The girls moved off in a huddle. 'Jennifer and I are going for a walk,' said Felicity, linking arms with her friend as they left the terrace.

'Then we'll play with you,' Claude said to the boys. 'You get things set up and we'll join you as soon as we've cleared the table. It's our turn. You and the girls did your bit beforehand.'

Claude carried a tray into the kitchen, where he found Ella stacking the dishwasher.

'I suppose it *is* boring up here for young people at night,' she was saying to George. 'That didn't occur to me when we bought the house. The twins were only twelve at the time, and I didn't realise how quickly they'd turn into teenagers and that of course they'd want to go out and have fun in the evenings.'

'Well, as it happens,' said George, 'I was just talking to Paco, and he told me that a disco will be opening in Puerto de Santiago this summer, by which time with a bit of luck Felicity and Philip will have passed their driving tests, so they can take the jeep and drive down when they want to go out for a bit of fun. They've just started building *another* hotel, if you can believe it. The municipality want to turn Los Gigantes and Playa de Las Arenas into the main tourist resorts on the west coast. So thank God we're up here.'

Claude noticed that Ella was leaning over the sink, evidently in pain. 'What's the matter?'

'It's the …' Slowly she straightened up, white in the face. 'I don't know, I don't know what it is – a pain, not the usual pain … It passes, but it keeps on coming back, and it gets worse.'

'Perhaps you could do with a brandy, old thing,' said George. 'You're as white as a sheet.'

'Perhaps I could.'

'We'll join you.'

Claude steered her over to the kitchen table and sat her down while George fetched a bottle and three glasses.

'You shouldn't take any chances, Ella. I think you've got to see a doctor.'

'Oh no, please, not during the holidays, not when the children are here – I see so little of them as it is.'

'Naughty naughty!' Tessa's voice rang out of the soundbox in the ceiling.

The three of them at the kitchen table looked up, startled. They were sitting under the truncated chimney flues leading up to the two rooms on the east side of the house.

'Don't mind me, darling. I've run out of cigarettes. Could you let me have one?'

'Dad doesn't really mind if we have the occasional puff, but not in front of Mum.' It was Felicity's voice.

'So you're asking me to aid and abet you in unlawful pursuits, you wicked girl.'

Felicity giggled.

'Still, we're all in favour of wicked girls. *We* won't tell. Do you want one too, Jennifer?'

'Thank you, I don't smoke.'

'Sensible girl. Porridge is much healthier. Can you give me a light?'

A chair screeched as someone pushed it back, followed by rummaging noises and voices talking indistinctly in the background.

'I think one of us should go up and tell them,' said Ella. 'It's unfair, eavesdropping on them like this.'

'Well I did warn Felicity,' said George.

Tessa's voice could be heard again overhead. 'It can't always be easy being your mother's daughter, Felicity. Such a forceful personality. You must sometimes feel she's a bit overbearing.'

Ella got up to go but felt a recurrence of the pain and remained standing where she was.

'Well, she's strict about some things and can get really cross, but she is fair. She's actually quite liberal-minded. And she's always got time for us. The trouble with Mum is – she's so *good* at everything. She's so clever. She's so quick and well organised. A model housewife, I suppose. Model everything. She makes one feel conscious of one's inadequacies.'

'She makes us *all* feel that, dear,' purred Tessa.

'She puts people in their place,' said Miriam.

'I wouldn't say *that*. The trouble with Mum is she has such high expectations of you.'

'Well exactly, that's what I mean.'

'You can't live up to her expectations. You can't just be you and muddle along. It's all got to be just *so*. You've got to live up to *her* standards, *her* way of doing things – she always thinks *her* way is best.'

'Poor dear. You make her sound a bit of a tyrant.'

'Well, not a *tyrant* exactly, but too bossy for her own good. That's the reason I wanted to go to boarding school. To get away.'

Ella sat down again. George started to say something, but she cut him off with a wave of her hand.

'It used to be different when I was little,' Felicity went on. 'We were always doing things together. I could talk to Mum about *anything* and she'd understand. She was always there for me, perhaps more for me than Philip. Everything was different before Alex came along. Of course, I mean he was only a baby, so obviously she had to spend a lot of time looking after him. But from then on Philip and I took second place. And maybe she thought that now we were growing up we should be coming up to her expectations more, but we were muddling along as per usual, at least as *she* saw it — that's what she calls it — she's got a thing about muddling along. But so what? I don't want to live *her* life, I want to live *mine*.'

The telephone began ringing in the sitting room. George got up to answer it. As he was crossing the terrace Felicity came out onto the gallery with a cigarette in her hand. 'I can hear the phone ringing,' she called.

'So can I. I'm just getting it. Do watch what you say up there, darling. The soundbox, remember? The Inquisition will be on to you. We can hear every word down in the kitchen.'

'So what? You can hear what you bloody well like.'

George picked up the phone.

'Mr George Morris?' The voice came through muffled.

'Speaking.'

'Sorry to trouble you on holiday, sir. This is Sergeant Forbes calling from Brixton police station. We've got your son and another young man here, sir, whom we picked up while attempting to steal the tyres off a vehicle. He wanted to have a word with you. Shall I put him on, sir?'

'What do you think, Sergeant?' George swore under his breath.

'Beg pardon, sir?'

'I suppose you better had. Call me back and reverse the charges. This might take a while. Number you just called.'

He repeated his number, replaced the receiver and sat down to wait for the call.

# 11

It wasn't as if it hadn't become clear to Claude that there was some-thing seriously wrong with Ella. What he hadn't worked out was the all-important question of timing, choosing the right moment to win Ella's consent to a move she'd just resisted with that *not during the holidays, not when the children are here — I see so little of them as it is.* She would always come up with one reason or another. But that was before Tessa's *Naughty naughty!* had opened the conversation to which they'd all just been listening. Now George was waiting over in the sitting room for a call from a police station in Brixton, which was taking longer than expected to come through. Why hadn't he taken the police station number and phoned back himself? Ella asked Claude irritably. Why this rigmarole of reversing the charges? Naturally she wanted to speak to Max herself, even if she was telling Claude she didn't — she was still hurt by Max having failed to call her on her birthday. But by the time the call from Brixton came through — the sound level of the argument George was having with Max made the drift of what he was saying in the living room clearly audible to Claude and Ella in the kitchen across the courtyard — Claude had made up his mind on Ella's behalf that a conversation with Max was one more thing she didn't need on top of everything else. This was the moment to get her out. Ella never let on that there was anything wrong with her — if it had already got this far she ought to be taken to hospital immediately, with or without her consent. Claude went upstairs to the belfry room to fetch Ella's emergency suitcase, slipping their two passports into his pocket as an afterthought. It was the best prompt he could have given her. At the sight of the battered blue suitcase Ella's resistance broke down. She acquiesced, leaving a note on the kitchen table, and they slipped out of the house without saying goodbye to anyone.

How to interpret that sound she was making when they set off in the car — a sound that might equally have been a crooning or a moaning? Fearing the answer, he didn't dare ask. Ella? He just put a note of query in her name. *Mutti Mutti Mutti Mutti*, she wailed in response. Ella called on her mother only in direst need, only when she was at her wits' end. This may have been the reason why he didn't take the turning off to Adeje but continued on the road to the better-equipped hospitals he

501

knew they would find on the other side of the island in Santa Cruz. Ella now sat beside him in silence with her knuckle to her mouth, as she often did when she had something on her mind, resting the bone against her teeth. The pain or distress or whatever nameless unease it was that had made her call for her mother seemed to be on hold.

What I respect about Tessa, she began out of the blue, is that she says to your face what other people say only behind your back. Was malice any the better for being on show? Claude wondered, and Ella said not malice but envy – malice was only the visible warping of a deeper-seated envy in Tessa. Her father had crippled his daughter with false ambition. Rancour had filled the places left empty in her life by a bad upbringing. Naturally Tessa was envious, particularly of women who had what she lacked.

To keep Ella distracted – anything rather than those pains that made him feel so helpless – Claude prompted her now and again, without participating in her prolonged discussion with herself. Giving expression to musings about Tessa seemed to have a calming effect on her. She needed a post-mortem to regain her balance. She'd left her house in disarray. Now she was putting it back in order.

They didn't seem to be getting anywhere. Claude saw a sign to Candelaria. He recalled that there was a hospital there too, but the sight of broken buildings huddled in the night, the thought of leaving Ella in such a place, urged him to press on to Santa Cruz as fast as possible. No apparent deterioration, no pain to speak of, to Claude's relief. So far Ella had seemed to be all right. It was hubris even to have the thought – the pain returned immediately. He looked in alarm at Ella doubled up in the seat beside him. What sort of pain is it? he asked. A cutting pain, she said, a knife *swishing across my insides.* Try and hang on for a bit longer. It can't be much more than half an hour, three quarters at the most.

The options he'd blithely discarded on the road behind them at Adeje, even at Candelaria, seemed terribly desirable now. Should we go back? What do you think, Ella? No. There was a place called Nuestra Señora not far from the Mencey in Santa Cruz, she said. She remembered passing the sign when she visited Dr Vargas the previous month; she'd asked him about it and he spoke well of it. They reached the outskirts of Santa Cruz sooner than Claude expected and Ella gave him directions to the Mencey Hotel. They found their way without difficulty to the Nuestra Señora hospital nearby.

It was one o'clock in the morning, the place deserted but for a solitary night porter. He put a call through to someone and showed them into a consulting room, where a doctor would presently see them. About ten minutes later a small neat-looking man wearing a white coat and slippers came into the room. Tell me about the pain, he said to Ella, and Ella told him about the knife cutting inside her, swishing across her stomach. Where exactly? The doctor asked her to lie down on a couch and moved his hands across her stomach. Here? Ella shook her head. She could smell toothpaste on his breath and wondered if it was to cover up that he'd been smoking. Intolerance of the smell of cigarette smoke, which didn't otherwise trouble her, had for Ella always been the first infallible sign that she was pregnant. Or here? said the doctor, pressing her abdomen. She gasped. How old was the señora? the doctor asked. Forty. In what month of pregnancy? The fifth. Other children? Four. How long had she had this pain? The doctor's questions meandered in a relaxed conversational manner while his hands surmised and probed. Without saying what conclusion they led him to, he sat down at the desk and wrote for a few minutes. It would be best for the señora to remain in the hospital overnight, he said without looking up from his writing. A private room was available if required. In the morning they would arrange for the usual blood and urine tests, examination by specialists, non-invasive diagnostic methods to ensure insofar as possible the safety of the unborn child. In short, they must establish the cause of this recurrent pain and reunite the mother with her family as quickly as possible.

This last sentence of the doctor's was accompanied by a smile, such an unexpected and kind gesture from a stranger who'd been woken up in the middle of the night to attend to a patient that Claude and Ella began to have more faith in the healing powers of Nuestra Señora than the unprepossessing appearance of the hospital had given them cause for.

But several days passed and nothing happened. Several doctors examined Ella and failed to come up with a diagnosis on which they could agree. Two of the doctors diagnosed a ruptured appendix. In pregnant women, they argued, appendicitis was masked by the frequent occurrence of mild abdominal pain associated with nausea. The house gynaecologist took the view that the pain was from pregnancy-related causes and had nothing to do with appendicitis. It would pass. And indeed it did seem to be passing. Ella felt better. The bouts of pain subsided in intensity and frequency. Eventually the two other doctors deferred to their dissenting colleague's opinion. To be on the safe side, however, they advised keeping the patient under observation for a couple of days.

George drove over from Arguayo to discuss the situation. The children would be there for another week before the holidays ended and they went back to school. Ella was all for driving straight back with him, all for seeing the children. I'm much better, she said, reading the doubt on Claude's face. For Claude didn't like the way she looked, her quite untypical yellowish complexion – he still heard the cry she had uttered in the kitchen – Ella who was the most stoic and uncomplaining person he knew. Troubled by the doctors' disagreement, his initial lack of confidence in Nuestra Señora came creeping back, a continuously growing unease. Leaving George and Ella alone for an hour, he walked a couple of blocks until he found a travel agency, where he bought two tickets for a flight to Heathrow leaving La Laguna that evening.

On his way back to the hospital he ran into the doctor who had first examined Ella the night they arrived. The doctor asked if he could have a word with him, and Claude followed him into the same consulting room as before.

An indiscreet question, with permission, for there were certain imponderables regarding the condition of Señora Morris, but – the doctor coughed – had attempts been made to terminate her pregnancy prematurely? Certainly not, said Claude. Señora Morris was looking forward to this new addition to the family. The doctor was happy to hear it, for it confirmed the impression they had formed themselves. There was a moment of mutual awkwardness before the doctor went on to explain to Claude that mysterious complications during pregnancy could often be attributed to bungled abortions – the introduction of foreign objects into the womb – knives, razor blades, screwdrivers. Truly, Señor, it was incredible what objects had been found in the wombs of determined women. For this reason they had deemed it necessary to X-ray the patient to establish that this was not the case. But she might have taken other substances – herbs, liquids – that left no trace on an X-ray ... No? The doctor apologised. It was important to rule out any such possibility, he explained, which was why he had to ask these questions.

Claude kept to himself this interview with the doctor. It helped to explain why Ella's treatment was proceeding so lethargically. This was a Catholic country. It confirmed Claude's view of the necessity of flying

Ella back to London while she was still in a condition to travel. The docility with which she submitted to Claude's arguments was further evidence of Ella not being her usual self. George agreed. The three of them went to the hotel where Claude was staying, and Ella spent the day resting until George drove them to the airport in the evening. He called an old friend who was a senior consultant on the staff at St Luke's Hospital in Chelsea and was advised that if in any doubt Ella should go directly there on arrival at Heathrow.

During the course of the day Ella's condition once again deteriorated. It was so bad when they got to Heathrow that Claude arranged for her to be taken to St Luke's by ambulance. Within hours of arrival there, her condition was diagnosed as acute peritonitis. An emergency operation was carried out the same night. Despite arduous hours of surgery the patient was stable, the surgeon reassured Claude when he left the hospital at six o'clock in the morning. It was just as well they had acted when they did, he added, as even twenty-four hours later they would probably not have been able to save her.

# CHAPTER THREE

## Les Événements

### 1

The origins of the peritonitis from which Ella nearly died lay in a ruptured appendix that was wrongly diagnosed when she was a twelve-year-old girl. Growing pains, the doctor told her mother at the time, reassuring her they were harmless and would pass. And so they did, in their fashion. Ella's recollection of this incident during her late-night examination by the doctors at St Luke's alerted them to what might be wrong with her. When the appendix ruptured, the detritus from the infection could become encapsulated, as had apparently happened with Ella as a child. The inflammation could subside and remain dormant for as long as a quarter of a century, poisoning the system all the while, before it erupted again, as had happened the week before, causing the infected contents of the appendix to spill into the abdomen. Once the lining of the abdominal cavity got infected, the patient became critically ill. Surgery was necessary to remove the abscesses. *But for your prompt action*, said the surgeon. Claude added this to the list of *But fors* that bound together his life and Ella's with hoops of steel, the many apparently minor contingencies but for which their life together wouldn't have taken place.

What the surgeon at St Luke's chose not to tell Claude was how extensive in this patient's case the infection had been. Had it been cleaned up sufficiently to ensure there would be no recurrence? The pregnancy, the risk of damage to the unborn child, made it necessary to proceed with great circumspection, perhaps less thoroughly than the extent of the infection required. Claude asked him what the prospects were for a safe delivery of the child. As a precaution against them opening again when

506

the mother delivered her baby, the long incisions left by the operation had been stitched up with a synthetic material, the surgeon said; one could think of it as a sort of wire. This notion of stitching up a pregnant mother with wire was a nightmare that pursued Claude for as long as Ella remained in hospital. Whether the child would survive – the mother – no one could say. One would have to wait and see.

He went to the flat off the Kings Road to find a couple of friends of Max asleep on the floor in the living room. A fug of marijuana hung in the air. Bottles were strewn over the carpet. Ashtrays overflowed. Piles of unwashed dishes stood on the kitchen sideboard. Claude went into what used to be Alex's room, where Max lay asleep fully dressed on top of the bed. Claude shook him gently. He had woken Max many times in his life, to get him off to school in the Richmond days, and he knew that Max would be fully there as soon as he woke up, whatever time he had gone to bed and in whatever state, never groggy, never grumpy, as if instantly flipping a switch from a sleeping to a waking state.

'How's Ella?' were his first words. 'George called last night to say that you were on the way to London and that she would have to go into hospital.'

'Just as well we went there rather than here.'

'I waited up for you until about midnight, and then I went out and bumped into a couple of guys I knew, and well ...' Max yawned. 'One thing led to another, as you see. Sorry it's a bit of a mess.'

'Your mother nearly died last night.'

'What's this? A moral lecture?'

'You asked how she is, and I'm telling you – she's very ill.'

'What's wrong with her?'

'A ruptured appendix, complicated by pregnancy. After they operated they had to stitch her up with wire.'

'All this beastly baby business.'

'That's not how she thinks of it.'

'Can I go and see her?'

'Give it a few days. She'll come through.'

'Oh God. Poor Ella.' His face screwed up. Claude saw how upset he was.

'How did that car business go, by the way?'

'Car business? Oh, Brixton. I hated having to call George – not that I minded him finding out about it – I just don't like asking him for any

507

favours. But the thing is, if the police brought charges I'd get a record, and the Americans don't give visas to people with police records.' Max scowled. 'So George had to call one of his old mates at the FO to square it with the cops.' Max threw his head back on the pillow. 'Just nicking a tyre, for Christ's sake. What a fuss about a measly tyre.'

'I didn't know you were planning on going to America.'

'Well … eventually. I'm doing a photography apprenticeship on a magazine, and when that's finished in about a year or so from now … Yeah, goodbye London, hiya San Francisco.'

'Why? London's where it's all happening now.'

'London's OK, but London's also family, and family's what I have to get away from.'

'How come? George now lives full time on the island; Ella's there much of the time; your brother and sister are at school and you hardly ever see them, so what family do you have to get away from?'

'It's the constant expectations they have of you. The threat of them descending on you. People just not minding their own business. Letters, phone calls. Weddings and christenings and stuff I'm expected to go to. There are all these Morris cousins I keep bumping into in London. More and more of them seem to be turning up here from Manchester almost every week – people I'm really not interested in but who think they have a right to meet me. It's scary how much they know about you – getting expelled from Winchester. Next it'll be this tyre business. The family keep tabs. They have long ears. Things get around. I just don't feel comfortable living under surveillance. Whereas nobody knows me in America, where I'm free to be my own person, do my own thing without having anyone breathing down my neck.'

Claude could sympathise with all this. The surveillance Max spoke about was associated for Claude with the de Marsay family in Paris, Lyons, Dijon and elsewhere, a herd of far-flung relatives whom the imperious head of the family, his uncle Louis in Paris, would summon to family reunions in remote country places in much the way a huntsman brought a pack of hounds to heel. Claude's departure from France had largely exempted him from these duties, but now and again they were inescapable. There had been no way of getting out of the invitation to his uncle's seventieth birthday in April. Claude was due to go to Paris the following week.

At the time these arrangements were made the trip to Paris for his uncle's birthday had tied in conveniently with a summer-term exchange. Claude would teach at the Sorbonne while a junior lecturer from there took over his duties in London. Ella's illness meant that Claude would have to pull out of this agreement. Previously George might have been able to stay in London to look after Ella while Claude was in Paris, but now that Alex had started at the school in Puerto de la Cruz George couldn't leave the island. Obviously Claude would have to stay in London. A lot of telephone calls, explanations and apologies would result from this change in plan. And here an old problem returned to humiliate him in a particularly insidious way.

While his uncle and the university faculties in London and Paris would show understanding for a decision to stand by a seriously ill wife, a relationship for which there wasn't a word as acceptable to social convention and as bound up with natural sympathy, let alone legal status, as *husband* or *wife,* would stretch their sympathy. To explain that he was unable to attend his uncle's seventieth birthday or to fulfil the duties he had undertaken to perform at the Sorbonne in order to nurse a partner or woman friend wouldn't meet with much understanding. They wouldn't let him. He would be in breach of his contract with the Sorbonne, with his uncle in breach of his promise. Unforgivable. So Claude decided that *wife* was the word it would have to be.

'My wife is ill,' he explained in telephone calls to his uncle Louis in Paris, the dean of the faculty at London University and his opposite number at the Sorbonne. 'I'm afraid I shall have to cancel.'

Only Louis questioned his word, remarking sarcastically that it was the first he'd heard of his nephew having a wife. The news of Claude's wedding hadn't reached him in Paris. My belated congratulations, Claude. And the uncle hung up on the nephew to show him what he thought of such behaviour.

This unavoidable ruse brought on a bout of extreme frustration, anger at his helplessness, forced into a misrepresentation that offended most of all the conjugal truth of his relationship with Ella. None of this could be allowed to reach Ella, however. In the room where she lay it passed her by, entirely absorbed as she was with the effort to remain alive; the children she had left on the island, Claude's problems, Claude himself, responsibilities that otherwise shored up her existence, were blotted out by the intensity of the present of the illness she was now living, the

509

effort demanded by that illness for her lungs to breathe, for her heart to pump, for the will to live.

After a few days on a ward her condition deteriorated again and she was moved back into the intensive care unit where she had spent a week after the operation. Patients there could be monitored twenty-four hours a day by staff sitting at panels of instruments behind a glass screen. Here too it was only by using the *wife* word that Claude was allowed access to Ella. Not long after he left her one evening the extremely low blood pressure and failing pulse of the patient were noted by the duty nurse, who informed a cardiologist and the anaesthetist who had been on duty in the theatre when Ella was rushed in for her emergency operation.

'We're losing this patient,' the anaesthetist said to his colleague after checking the monitor screens, then got up and went into the intensive care unit to stand beside her bed, taking her wrist in his hand, gently shaking her by the shoulder.

Ella felt herself moving down a dark tunnel towards an unbounded lighter space of deep blue, which held out for her the promise of freedom from all the things that still adhered to her in the tunnel. Not yet quite out of the tunnel, not yet untrammelled and free to go, on the brink of the deep blue and already, as she began to merge with this blue vastness, letting herself go with a grateful sense of release, she was pulled back by the anaesthetist's hand on her wrist, his voice as he leaned forward and spoke urgently into her ear.

'You're not leaving us, are you, Mrs Morris? Think of the baby in you waiting to be born.'

She lay very still in a small room on her own. I'm lying still for the baby, she told herself, as if stillness could cocoon the baby and ensure its becoming. For she had felt a familiar stirring, a feeble kicking inside her. Joy touched every fibre in her body. Knowing the baby to be alive, perhaps even well, she believed in her own recovery. For her own sake alone she would have felt too tired. She would live for the baby's sake, if not her own.

Claude looked in every evening when his teaching day was over, and in the mornings before it began. He found Ella apathetic, lacking the strength to take any interest in anything outside the room. Inside her capsule of stillness she didn't want to listen to the radio and asked for the phone to be disconnected. Events in the outside world didn't interest her, only Claude's coming. She lay facing the door so that she would see him the moment he arrived.

When Claude entered the room he switched off the news headlines in his head. There were momentous events taking place in France, which he followed on the radio night and day, but even thinking them here meant a distraction from Ella she would at once have picked up on and felt as an intrusion. Her eyes hovered round him with an acutely sharpened perception from which nothing was hidden, as if she could look inside him. She might have guessed about the news headlines in his head, but if she did she suppressed that knowledge, wanting to keep all such things out of her way, the clutter of the world out of the capsule in which she lived with the baby.

Her heavy-lidded eyes looked up at him out of dark-ringed hollow sockets.

'Are you eating properly?'

'I eat lunch and a light supper in the staff canteen before I come.'

'Is it any good?'

'There's a minestrone of sorts. The meat pies aren't bad. Three veg. Salad. Custard pudding.'

'What's that you've got hanging from your belt loop at the side?' Claude stood by the bed and turned so that she could get a better look at it. 'It's a laundry tag. From the Chinese dry cleaners round the corner. When did you take these trousers to be cleaned?'

'Oh, some time last week, I think.'

'I didn't notice it under your jacket. You forgot to take the laundry tag off the loop. You must have been walking around with it on ever since.'

Ella took it off, a pink piece of cloth with a number on it, the ends stapled together round one of the belt loops.

'Give me a safety pin from the bedside-table drawer.'

She pierced the cloth with the pin and attached the pin to the strap of the hoist hanging over her bed. She gave the bar of the triangle a tap, setting it swinging, and fell back exhausted. During the day, when she lay in her room mostly alone, she would give the bar a tap and look up at the laundry tag swinging there. At night she unpinned it from the strap and fell asleep with it clasped in her hand.

One afternoon she woke up to find Max sitting on the chair by her bed.

'*Wie schön, daß du gekommen bist!*' She smiled and put out her hand.

Max was moved by her pleasure to see him. 'Why did you say that in German?'

'I'm alone here a lot. I spend most of my thoughts trying to retrace people who've disappeared. My grandmother, my mother, also my father and brother, both of whom went missing at the end of the war. Trying to remember just what they looked like – what they said on some occasion. I have conversations with them, you see, so I suppose that's why.'

'Do you miss them?'

'Miss them? No. I had them when they were here. Now they have gone. I miss you, Max.'

'But I'm here.'

'You're here, but I don't have you, and that's why I miss you.'

'What do you mean, you don't have me?'

She took his hand.

'I've not been able to get through to you as much as I would have wished, Max. You're in some place on your own.'

He grimaced. 'I *am* on my own, it's true.'

Ella stroked his head.

'I wish I wasn't,' said Max.

'Then you must let people know that.'

An obstetrician examined Ella and came to the conclusion that she might be nearing her term. The baby would be born three months prematurely.

He offered no prediction about the chances of its survival, and Ella asked for none.

When Claude visited her on the Friday evening he was supposed to have been spending in Paris to celebrate his uncle's seventieth birthday, Ella had been moved into a room on the gynaecology ward. A little woman in a white uniform sat on the edge of an examination table swinging her legs and reading a magazine. She looked up when Claude came in, said she would leave them alone and to call immediately if she was needed.

'What's this? Who is this miniature person? Why have they moved you in here?' asked Claude agitatedly.

Ella was calm. 'That's Margaret, the midwife. The obstetrician thinks the baby might be born any minute, and Margaret's on duty in case of an emergency. She's here just for me. They don't want to take any risks, after what's already happened, you see, and to give the baby the best chance of survival my bed has been wheeled in here.'

Claude waited until three o'clock, but as Ella showed no sign of being about to begin labour he went home.

'Have them call me as soon as it starts and I'll be here in fifteen minutes,' he said when he left. Claude had moved into a hotel just round the corner from the hospital.

Not long after Claude left the room and Margaret returned, Ella felt a sudden wetness between her legs.

'Something's happening,' she said to Margaret.

'I don't think so, dearie. We'd have had early warning.'

A moment later a muffled squawk came from the bed.

The little woman jumped up from her chair, pulled back the bed-clothes and said, 'Goodness me! The baby's here.'

She removed the wet bundle from the bed and, sure enough, the baby gave another squawk, not much of one, but undeniably a sign of life. The little woman hurried out of the room and returned ten minutes later with the baby wrapped in a cloth.

'Here you are, dearie; you can hold her. You've had a little girl.'

Ella gave her a phone number and asked her to call Claude.

She took the little girl and held her in her arms. Everything seemed to be there, everything perfectly formed. She had matted black hair, as Ella's own had been at birth, beautiful little ears, the tiniest fingers Ella had ever seen. Her large opaque eyes rolled around, looking up at the ceiling.

'But you're just lovely, you tiny little thing,' Ella said, and a feeling rose and ran through all her body, an orgasm of pleasure, of unalloyed love. She swam with her child in a stream of happiness.

After what seemed a long time there was still no sign of Claude, but in his place stood Dr Jennings with a serious expression on his face. Ella guessed what that look meant before he opened his mouth to tell her that for an infant weighing eight hundred grams there was little hope of survival.

'But look at her; she's perfect,' objected Ella.

Dr Jennings nodded and smiled and said he would leave Ella alone with her baby for a while.

Completely absorbed in the child in her arms, she did not realise time went by, did not even wonder why Claude had failed to come.

An hour passed, and within that hour the child was born and died.

At last the midwife came in to take the dead child from her arms, and Dr Jennings sat down to talk to her as the mother began to wail, almost to howl, a sound that came out like a piece of something that had been broken off inside her. Nevertheless she heard what the obstetrician said about the deceptiveness of the child's newborn perfection, how underneath that outwardly immaculate form irreparable damage had already been done by the anaesthetics, the X-rays, the medications and so on to which the foetus had been subjected during the past weeks. Even had the child been born a few weeks later, said Dr Jennings, seeking to console the mother, even had there been enough of it to survive, it would have come into the world with such handicaps that to be stillborn would have been a blessing.

When the doctor had gone, the midwife came in to clean up the mother and transfer her to a fresh bed. Margaret asked if she would like to see the baby for a last time before she wheeled her bed back to her room, and Ella, beyond wanting or not wanting anything, shook her head. Claude hadn't come.

Back in her room she was no longer in the cocoon she had left, for the cocoon was now empty.

Claude arrived to take her home.

'I called the hotel. Why didn't you come?'

'They wouldn't let me in.'

'Wouldn't let you in?'

'I asked for Ella Morris and said I was Dr Morris, the husband, and they asked for identification, and I showed them my driving licence identifying me as de Marsay. Well, it *was* in the middle of the night. Sorry, they said, you're not next of kin.'

Daffodils bloomed in London's squares and parks. The rich scent of hothouse flowers, red roses and white lilies, filled the basement apartment. Max had bought the flowers and done all the arrangements himself. He was at home waiting for his mother when she arrived. Ella was touched. From then on she seemed to recover rapidly.

# 2

With decidedly undecided mixed feelings — pleasure to have spent serious time with his sick mother for the first time in six months, guilt to be going, anger and relief to be shot of her when she started getting moralistic on him — Max kick-started the Lambretta at the kerb and cruised off into the London night.

When he bought it three years ago with the money left him by his recently deceased grandmother Elaine, the brand-new machine had been a two-tone silver-and-purple street stratocruiser with half a dozen decks piled one on top of the other, crash bars, four rows of lamps, horns and fog lights up front, chrome luggage racks gleaming at the rear, the handlebars festooned with a total of twenty-six wide-, wider- and widest-angle mirrors.

MAD MAX read the owner's logo in Algerian type across the bottom of the windscreen. It was Max's present to himself for having been kicked out of Winchester and terminating his school career. Now here's something like life starting, Max had said, taking delivery of this Marvelion from the Hackney specialist in customised mod machines, handing him a wad of five-pound notes with a foaming sensation of glee.

Remembering Jim, the long-ago Jamaican bus conductor who took his fare on the bus of his daily ride to school, who once happened to tell him that he lived in Brixton, Max had toured the neighbourhood on the new monster and found on the off chance a little place not to his disliking for a couple of thousand quid. The one-up one-down semi-detached off Coldharbour Lane, thin as a rake after being shorn by a V-2 and only half put back together, overlooked a pub across the road and backed onto a cemetery.

The very thing, said Max.

The purchase of these premises had cleaned out what remained of Elaine's legacy. Max now needed a job.

A year or two before, *lifestyle* magazine had begun seeping sporadically onto the market. Back issues of it had piled up on the floor of the study he shared at Winchester with Piers. At weekends, in the middle of the night, Max and his study-mate crept down from the dormitory, bolted their door and sat reading *lifestyle* dressed in velvet smoking jackets, puffing Sobranie Black Russian cigarettes and burning incense to camouflage the smell. One of the first issues of the magazine had a piece on the rude boys of London's Caribbean community, photographed in their sharp suits with button-down-collar shirts, thin ties and pork-pie hats. Max studied these individuals at close range in the flesh and added a few touches of his own before presenting himself at the Putney warehouse overlooking the Thames.

You give me a job, said Max to Pete Prescott, the editor of *lifestyle*, and I will render my services to your magazine, and you will value them for I am the incarnation of style and know what I'm talking about.

Pete looked him over, cheeky little bastard, went out into the yard to look over the flagship stratocruiser in the yard as well – *Whoo* – with its twenty-six mirrors, and said, Very nice, flicking his fag end over the wall of the yard with a skill that came from much practice, Three quid a week is the best I can do.

Oh what joy to be back in the thick of it, the familiar scum of London, part of the refuse the river threw up on its banks, relishing the daily ride on the Marvelion through the grimy streets of Clapham and the smoke of Battersea to Wandsworth in all its glory of grimness, within spitting or at least swearing distance of dubious former haunts on Putney Heath, thumbing his nose as he swept past it with horns blaring and all four rows of lights switched on, flashing the gaunt ribcage of a cracked and broken-windowed building that not so long ago had been Park House preparatory school, condemned at last, a vacant hangar slated for demolition.

*Yah!*

Once a month or so the chaos in the Putney warehouse resolved itself long enough to get out an issue of the magazine. Max made jokes and coffee, ran his machine around town on errands for the staff, acted as Fred the house photographer's assistant on achingly slow location shoots and sat in on meetings to give them the benefit of what his ears had picked up that week, close to the asphalt of south London, the fume in the cellars of Soho discos, the gossip, the gags, the trends, the ways and means and ends but always above all the *style* of young people he watched in coffee shops all over town.

At weekends he joined the exodus of a bored sub-London youth frantic to get off the Monday-to-Friday treadmill, the rallies that surged out from mod strongholds in Welwyn Garden City, Hemel Hempstead,

Basildon, heading for the coastal resorts to pass the time of the day, perhaps bash a few rocker heads or just scandalise the locals and put terror into the day trippers on the promenade. Hang on, Kirby, he said to a big bugger in black leather who was about to sock him one, it's me, your old chieftain Jong Jack.

The former second-in-command of the CND gang in Richmond, now a head taller than his chief, followed the Marvelion meekly on his Frances-Barnett motorbike to a neutral-territory coffee shop at the square end of the Southsea promenade. Max subjected Kirby's machine, stand- ing abjectly at the kerb, to the kind of detailed critique he had learned at *lifestyle* meetings. Beneath the dirt the machine was dark green, showing pretensions to trad British racing green, which for a 125cc two-wheeler was laughable. It was a piece of muck, standardised industrial crap without any personality statement. Rather like you, in fact, he said to Kirby. Look at you with that unwashed, ungroomed hair traipsing all over your collar leaving stains and dandruff. Where's your *style*, Kirby?

I can't afford style, said Kirby, incapable of taking offence, nine years old again and back on the dump where Max had handed him a red-hot wire to burn the CND brand on his arm. Yes, you can, said Max, this time putting twenty quid on the table instead of the wire. Ask no questions, tell no lies, just for Christ's sake get yourself a Vespa on the HP and come back in a suit and a tie. Then we'll work on the gear, big lapels and wide cuffs for what you wear. You're a big bloke, big heavy body-panelling for what you ride, out of them drainpipes, OK. With all that hulk up top you look like Battersea Power Station upside down, know what I mean? Individualise. That would be my humble advice. Blimey, said Kirby. He wouldn't have dreamed of arguing with Max or of questioning his advice, not under any circs, certainly not when it came wrapped up in a couple of tenners.

At fourteen Kirby had left school and home and become an ap- prentice mechanic at a garage in Hammersmith. Two grimy years had passed with little more to show for it than free oil in his hair and the piece of muck he now traded in for a shiny new Vespa bought on the HP, having put down a deposit of forty quid, half of it the money he'd been given by Max.

Forty quid! He'd never held so much money in his hand at one time.

And he needed it, what with the gear, the all-nighters at The Disco- theque in Lower Wardour Street or The Scene at Ham Yard and the quantities of speed they took on board to get them through it. Max hired Kirby, Kev these days, as his bodyguard, five bob plus expenses, a big bloke it was good to have around in the sometimes rough-and-tumble wasted early-morning exits from The Scene. The Scene crowd was elitist and prickly, took offence – Look at me, am I not a face – an edgy place with violence always lurking just below the surface, which often erupted in Ham Yard. Big Kev was still in training as a middleweight boxer, had a reach that came in handy when cracking heads together with good old British craftsmanship. It didn't do his apprenticeship with the Hammersmith garage much good, however, when he fell asleep over his spanner, forgot to tighten the bolts on the wheel he'd just changed before replacing the hubcap, Kev told Max, and the wheel spun off the governor's car, didn't it, before it done half a mile down the Goldhawk Road.

He was chucked out.

This episode led to some reflection on Max's part. He had to make it up to Kev. His old chum was his responsibility. So he called another old school chum, Piers, who happened to live just round the corner from the former Morris family pile in Hampstead, and said to Piers, Correct me if I'm wrong, but isn't your dad a big cheese at French, Kline and Smith? Piers confirmed he was. Max wondered if Piers could get his hands on some free samples of, what was the word, amphetamines. Piers thought he could.

Max ran the cushy top end of the production line, relishing his queen beeship, with worker bees like Kev, who toiled as a pusher with his evening shopfront south of Shaftesbury Avenue and doing nights in the doorway of Revels the shoe shop in Wardour Street. By the age of seventeen Kev had become a successful entrepreneur. The mechanic they had chucked out of the Hammersmith garage, prematurely terminating a five-year apprenticeship with the prospect of starting pay of fifteen quid a week on another production line at Dagenham a couple of years hence, was doing all right for himself, thank you very much, a lot better than the former boss who had hired and fired him. Easy as falling off a log. Money for stale jam. They sold like hot cakes – sold themselves, the dubes, the blues, the purple hearts or whatever you liked to call the colour of the speed of the day. Chief Inspector Max came by and looked over the candy-flake scooter at the kerb, the seventeen-inch bell bottoms flaring out over the boots with Cuban heels, and said that's more like it. *Style*. You're doing all right for yourself, Kev, he said, revving the Marvelion, and he sped on to supervise the half-dozen other outlets making honey for him in the West End.

Max Morris and Kevin Kirby, that was a team.

Scum, ponces, layabouts, not done a honest day's work in your life, said the smelly old pensioner farts ensconced in the envy of their muggy old pre-war overcoats, seeing the injustice of life, the shameless ostentation of the nation's grandchildren flaunted by the banderole Max wore around his mohair-net top hat reading MONEY IS THE ROOT OF ALL FUN.

Meanwhile, *lifestyle* was broadening Max's horizons beyond south London.

The magazine sent him off on a ferry with Fred to do pictures of a new group of anarchists in Holland called Provos. When he came back to London, he had the silver-and-purple Marvelion resprayed anarchist white. For Max the styles were a-changin' so fast that like the queen bee in *Alice in Wonderland* he was having to fly all the time just to keep up.

Hello, I'm getting tired, thought Max, need a rest cure, must be getting old, and caught himself humming the melody of 'My Generation', The Who's theme song of the long-ago battlefields of 1964, when he had still been a mere disaffected upper-class mid-teen, an overworked and underprivileged Winchester brat. Alive, still young, he spared a thought for his benefactor, his dead grandmother, whoever she was. Thanks.

He had a recurrent vision of a man in red at the end of a tunnel.

Getting deeper into provocation, as suited his nature, he began to discard the mod accessories, for this was now serious stuff, no longer the laugh-up-your-sleeve natty outfits and groomed hair that caught the square old folks in two minds, kept 'em guessing, is he or isn't he taking the mick, I'll give him what for if he is, I'll learn him, in much the way that the Marvelion was beginning to discard its mirrors and lights, left, right and centre. They were constantly being nicked off the monster and until now Max had immediately replaced them. Not any more. Sod it, he said, coming out of his toast-rack semi-detached one lunchtime to inspect the damage after a bad night in Coldharbour Lane. At the corner newsagents he had puttered past every day without noticing what it said on the stand outside, he now read the banner US TROOPS TO PULL OUT OF VIETNAM.

No less momentous was the mass scooter charge of the mods up the Mall to Buckingham Palace, or his first glimpse of John Lennon's Rolls-Royce decorated with a paisley print. Between the eyes it hit him. *Smack!*

The East is where it's all pointed – India, Tibet, Vietnam – he said wisely to Pete in the editor's office overlooking the river, so go with the flow. The suit had gone with the flow one week, and when he took off his parka the next, Max revealed he was wearing a paisley shirt with sea urchins, or perhaps they were crooked tears, patterned in lavender, red and gold on white and brown, with big pointy lapels and wide cuffs, velvet trousers, a high-collared Regency jacket. The new Max embodied the peacock wing of mod culture, which was evolving into the bohemian style of the London hippie scene, so different from the frenetic energy of the mod ethos, and Max, older now and beyond bratdom, felt more comfortable with it. What's that funny whiff, then? asked Pete. Max took the Woodbines off the editor's desk, threw them out of the window and handed Pete the joint he was smoking.

In a cafe in Ladbroke Grove he met two beautiful people, androgynous and very thin beings dusted with starlight, unlike any two beautiful people he had met before. Sheldon and Roxanna came from California. They had in person attended the human be-in in San Francisco. What are you doing in London? We're in London because it's on our way around the world. Max liked that *because*. Have you got anywhere to stay?

Instantly caring, instinctively providing, like his mum, Max ushered them back to his Brixton home. Then he took them round to *lifestyle* for Fred to photograph, and the pics Fred took of them slowly in subdued light in his studio succeeded in catching the starlight. Where's that light coming from then? wondered Fred, checking his meter. Max did a longish caption to Fred's photos, his writer's debut, introducing *lifestyle* readers to flower power, pot, psychedelic rock and the Jefferson Airplane.

The psychedelic period with Max, Sheldon and Roxanna shacked up together in the one-up one-down off Coldharbour Lane was fun. There was more laughter than at any other time of Max's life. Wafted on a gentle unrelenting high, things moved slowly. Half a day passed in bed devoted to a platoon of thirty toes the three of them pooled at the end of the mattress for inspection. Hadn't old Ben Jonson once done the same thing, long long ago, imagining battles taking place around two fortresses, his two big toes? Max seemed to remember. Sex wandered this way and that, one on one, two on one, a foursome. What was the difference? His lovers were so thin it wasn't easy to say. It didn't matter. He liked it skeletal. He could fancy Twiggy. A preference for spaced-out sex, physical hollowness rather than protuberances in the body he held, hollow bones thinly fleshed, remained with Max thereafter.

Back on firm ground, Sheldon cooked vegetarian meals. Roxanna strung beads and made necklaces she sold on the streets of central London. They taught Max to strum chords on a guitar, the recitation of mantras, the technique of tie-dying, the art of astrology, tarot and I-Ching divination. Now and then he had to get up and go out to work.

Naked, they lay stoned on the mattress and watched Max getting dressed. Something was actually happening for once. Through a haze they watched it happen. The wash was brief, putting on the deo and the gear a bit longer, getting the make-up right longest of all. These days Max was experimenting with eyeshadow, eye pencils and lipstick – tricky, putting on the finishing touches, fancying himself, until the peacock had his tail up, preened, and was ready to go.

Hey man, said Sheldon, mellow down! What you putting all that crap on for?

They laughed themselves silly.

Back on their way around the world, Sheldon and Roxanna eventually moved on from Coldharbour Lane to the Afghanistan leg of their overland trip to India, and then, if they lived long enough, maybe down under, end up there some time in any case. See you man, said Sheldon, in another karma, peace brother, and the two of them drifted off. Shalom, said Roxanna, making a rare appearance in speech. She was a great dreamer, never had been much of a talker.

A Barbados boy from Notting Hill moved in with Max for a while, but then, well, he was knifed in a pub, wasn't he, and he died in the ambulance on the way to hospital. Max cried, soon forgot him.

These days things were getting very confrontational, things were toughening up generally, there was an acute shortage of peace, brother, and riots all over the place. Oh yeah, Kev would've loved it, in cities and campuses all across the US, with flags and department stores going up in flames, bombs and little red books going off *boom*, in China, in Japan, in Bolivia, in Mexico, in Frankfurt, Berlin, Prague and Paris.

All of these places came off the map for real and burst into London cafes, real places, I mean *real*, said Fred, scratching his head, actually there. Old Fred was in his late thirties, antique, old enough to have been Max's dad. He had never seen anything like it, he said, staring at a magazine with a picture of a man about to be executed on a Saigon street, internalising the image, becoming part of it, until he heard the report of the shot and saw the bullet leaving the barrel of the gun.

Max worked as his assistant, learned a lot about photography and a few things more which would later also come in handy – the patience, the slow circumspection with which Fred approached whatever he was photographing, whatever he took it in hand to do, even drinking a cup of tea or smoking a cigarette, nudging the top of the packet open with his knuckle and tapping the butt of a cigarette against the box, scrutinising it every time before putting it in his mouth. Go on, Fred, dare you, take a sip, go on, have a puff, the staff would say, watching these rituals during coffee breaks, chaffing him because they were fond of him and knew what a good photographer he was if just given enough time.

Fred's Notting Hill pad was where Max was heading on the much-depleted Marvelion, a lean, mean machine stripped of all its former fripperies, when he left the Kensington flat where he had spent two days with his mother while Claude was away in Manchester, and went cruising off into the long May twilight, en route for Paris in the minivan with Fred and Piers.

# 3

Everyone was going to Paris. Word was that all grievances would be given an airing in Paris. The United States, had they thought about it, might have sent a Civil Rights delegation to march down the Champs Elysées, flanking a replica of the coffin of Martin Luther King, murdered in Memphis that spring. Paris had something of a name for itself when it came to revolution – and it was coming to revolution everywhere, because there were grievances, grievances of which all revolutions were born, and they needed airing. There was a consensus about a universally detested war, black and white wrongs that needed redressing. Draft protesters arose all over the country, students who had hijacked their universities for serious misdemeanours such as the involvement of their scientists with military research projects or for merely venal, all too human weaknesses such as decrepitude, their musty-dusty, old-fashioned, maybe just old, at any rate their no longer acceptable ways of doing things – lots of air needed to be let into all these dark, smelly places.

At London University, noticeboards in all faculties boiled over with incitements to break the rules. – Boycott lectures! – Occupy classrooms! – Take student strikes out onto the streets! – Mobilise the working class!

So far none of these measures had been carried out.

On a noticeboard that Claude passed in the corridor of the Faculty of French Literature at the University of London, the bulletins issuing from someone's erratic typewriter on the situation in the French capital were updated at least twice a day, sometimes every few hours. Written in French, the bulletins were concise and exhortatory, signed in the name of a movement called Action Directe. The most recent one read:

Comrades! The decision of the unspeakable Paul Roch [*sic*], rector of the Sorbonne, to call in the police to close the university and to remove students from the premises if necessary with force has led to an escalation of violence that is unacceptable. A show of solidarity with our beleaguered fellow students in France is essential! Two coaches on the train departing Vivtoria [*sic*] this coming Friday have been reserved for those who wish to join a London University delegation that will be spending the weekend in Paris in order to get first-hand impressions of *les événements* at Nanterre and the Sorbonne of which there have been such conflicting reports in the media. *Roche à la broche! À bas le capitalisme! À bas la société de consommation!*

Claude made the events in France the topic of his first class discussion that week. He outlined the situation at the desolate new campus of Nanterre outside Paris. An old friend of his, a sociologist, was on the Nanterre faculty and had been keeping him in touch with developments there. Across-the-board reforms of an outdated and authoritarian educational system were required at schools and universities throughout France. Critics at a recent convention at Amiens had described the universities as factories for misfits and drafted an agenda of what needed to be done, but there had been little recognition of student concerns on the part of the authorities.

Student dissatisfaction resulted in the occupation of the administrative tower at Nanterre by a hundred-strong body forming the core of the so-called March 22 Movement. One of their leaders, Dany Cohn-Bendit, was arrested. In Paris students gathered in the front square of the Sorbonne to discuss the issue. The university authorities lost their nerve and called in the CRS riot police. Fights broke out between police and students, leading to the arrest of students and injuries on both sides. Over the demand for the release of the arrested students the violence escalated and rector Paul Roche decided, for the second time in the Sorbonne's seven-hundred-year history, to close the university.

This persuaded Claude to appeal to the dean of the faculty for absence of leave for members of staff and their students to go to Paris in support of the cause of academic freedom at the Sorbonne. The dean turned down his request. Anyone who left the university during term without permission would be in breach of its regulations and risked incurring penalties. Thus Claude couldn't recommend a trip to Paris because that would be irresponsible. All he could do was to draw students' attention to the noticeboard outside, where there was an announcement concerning travel arrangements to Paris later that week. He himself would be going. It was impossible to say how long he'd stay in Paris, but it seemed likely he wouldn't return in time to resume work next week.

A vote taken at the end of this class showed roughly half of the students in favour of action, whatever the cost, the other half against. That was on 6 May, the day after Ella flew back to Tenerife to see Alex settled in his new school. Claude called Ella and told her about the forthcoming trip to Paris. She was all in favour. She wished she could have come along too.

Because of emergency military transport priorities, requiring trucks and tanks to be moved by rail to the outskirts of Paris at short notice, the Calais train was delayed for six hours. It didn't get into the Gare du Nord until five o'clock in the morning. It was only when the London University contingent, some fifty strong, piled out and began to disperse that Claude noticed Nina Rubinstein walking towards him from the far end of the platform. How could he have missed her during the journey from London?

'Nina! Where have you sprung from?'

'I met up with some old friends and was travelling with them at the other end of the train. Have you arranged for somewhere to stay?'

'Yes, as it happens, I have. What about you?'

'Most of the students seem to be headed for a youth hostel in Montparnasse, but I don't know.'

Claude sensed her reluctance.

'Well, if you like, I can suggest an alternative you might find more attractive. A house owned by an anarchist on the Boulevard Raspail and run along the lines of a commune. He's something of a celebrity in left-wing circles here. I've met Grandjean a couple of times in the past, and other friends of mine will be staying there too, so if you want to come along ... It should be interesting.'

Over the taxi radio they listened to the voice of Cohn-Bendit appealing to the students to go home. Nina told the taxi driver *les événements* were the reason they had come to Paris. The driver said that because of the fighting in the Latin Quarter the bridges over the Seine to the south had been closed. He would have to make a detour via the Place de la Concorde. A squat bristly man sitting bunched at his steering wheel, he spoke with a Corsican accent, deploring the brutality of the police and praising the student demonstrators. He expected students and workers to make common cause against this government – more, he demanded it. Nothing less than a revolution that did away with this hated political system would satisfy him. He drove furiously through the empty city as if he had declared war on it.

The taxi driver pulled up outside the Montparnasse Cemetery and told them to walk a block down and turn right in the direction of the Place Denfert-Rochereau. They would find the house on the corner. Road blocks prevented cars from entering the Boulevard Raspail but pedestrians could get through, he said, refusing to charge them the fare, and wished them good luck.

His reluctance to drive to the house struck Claude as exaggerated until they saw the remains of the still-smouldering barricades, the blackened shells of burned-out cars. Bulldozers were in the process of scooping them up and dumping them in trucks. An acrid pall of smoke hung over the street. They reached the house at the same moment as a group of young people coming from the other direction, ragged and red-eyed, their clothes torn and blackened. They had just returned from the barricades in the Latin Quarter. As they walked up the front stairs and entered the house they were already telling Claude about their experiences the previous night, still on an adrenaline high, their voices unnaturally loud, their gestures oddly overwrought. Within minutes they had disappeared and the house fell silent. They must have gone off to sleep. Claude wondered where. He and Nina were standing reading the noticeboard in the entrance hall in the hope of gleaning some information about sleeping arrangements when Grandjean came thumping down the stairs with his game leg and scowled at them from the landing above.

'What are you two doing down there?'

Claude began to explain, but Grandjean cut him off gruffly and told them to come up and join him.

They followed him along the glassed-in corridor of what must once have been a conservatory to a room overlooking a garden at the back of the house. A small thin woman lost in a much-too-large kaftan, lying on a hammock and knitting, smiled as they came in. The smile lit up a dark leathery face that had been exposed too long to the sun, surprising Claude with its beauty. Grandjean settled back into the chair he had vacated to investigate the noise downstairs. He took a pull at a water pipe, causing an uproar of tiny bubbles in the apparatus standing on the floor a couple of yards away at the end of a tube curling snakelike across the carpet. Incense was burning. Smells wafted. Light reflected from fragile shimmering things hanging by the window. The dry sound of hands softly slapping tabla drums whispered along the walls of the room.

'So what identifies a foreigner, my friends? What sort of ... *hmargh!* ... monster have we got here?'

Grandjean's hookah, chortling away contentedly, had a soothing effect on the old man, smoothing out his bad temper.

'It's a piece of paper. That's all it is. A so-called identity card. An *official* person. As if one could not be a person, not *exist*, unless officially recognised. Even in your own country. Without an identity card you are nothing – that's where our troubles begin. Unless the state gives you an identity card – officially acknowledges you – you do not exist. Otherwise I wouldn't have married Aurelia. Would I, my dear?'

His wife held up her knitting and examined it. 'Just as well then.'

'We don't believe in the nonsense of marriage. But if I had not done so, my friends, the French state would not have recognised her, she would not have existed in this country she entered illegally, she would not have had the rights to which all French citizens are entitled – the right to vote, to pay taxes to the state, to speak out and demonstrate against the state, and so on, as these students are doing now. They would have deported her, just as they will deport this young German – you wait and see! In France, where the revolution inscribed those words equality, liberty and fraternity on the nation's heart two hundred years ago. A scandal!'

Grandjean interrupted himself to consult his water pipe, which wheezed and gurgled as if in approval of what he had just said.

'You mean Cohn-Bendit,' Claude interposed, warming to the old anarchist, in his seventies now, still with no sign of losing the grand indignation for which he was celebrated. Claude hadn't forgotten his own troubles with identity cards when he was a student at the Sorbonne.

'And now they have the impudence to call him a German *Jew*,' rejoined the old man, 'this Red Dany, as if they had put the clock back a quarter of a century and were themselves behaving just like the Germans when they occupied Paris. He *is* a Jew – a French one and a German one too, as it happens – but when *they* call him that it's rabble-rousing. Shame on them – our so-called government – a scandal!'

'Théophile,' his wife interrupted, 'you're forgetting yourself. You haven't introduced me to our guests.'

'Haven't I? Yes, I have. I told them you're my wife.'

'You haven't told me who *they* are.'

'All right. So tell her who you are, my dear children.' This was said affectionately, without condescension.

'We're from London University,' said Claude. 'This is my colleague Nina Rubinstein, and my name is Claude de Marsay.'

Grandjean took his pipe out of his mouth.

'No relation to the abominable Giscard de Marsay, I hope.'

'He's my uncle. We may not agree on a lot of things, but I will say one thing for him. He took care of me after my father died and made sure I got a good education. To his nephew, at least, he has always been very generous. He has views that may be abominable but he's not an abominable man.'

'Well said, well said. I didn't mean to sound offensive. Would you like to have breakfast?'

'I think we'd like some sleep before we have breakfast.'

'Of course, my friends. You have just come from London and must be very tired. Just go back down the corridor and look into any of the rooms where you see a spare mattress on the floor and make yourselves at home.'

'No no, let *me* show you,' said Aurelia, swinging her legs and getting out of the hammock with a nimbleness remarkable for the elderly lady she was. Holding the hem of her kaftan above her knees, she led them up another two flights of stairs.

'You'll be much more comfortable in here,' she said, showing them into an attic room that was mainly taken up with an enormous double bed.

'My son and his wife sleep here when they're home, but that's not often since they moved to Bolivia.'

'Bolivia?'

'Inspired by Che's shining example. There's still much work to be done. I hope you sleep well.' She clasped Nina's hand and left the room.

Nina turned to Claude and said, 'Any particular side?'

'I don't mind. The one you don't choose.'

Nina patted the nearside of the bed. 'This'll do for me. It may be rather bourgeois of me but I'd like to get out of these clothes and have a shower, or at least a wash.'

Claude wondered about that *bourgeois*.

'I noticed a bathroom down the corridor.'

While Nina was in the bathroom Claude undressed to his underpants and got into bed. She spent a long time in the bathroom. He was already half asleep by the time she came back and slipped into the other side of the bed, bringing with her a scent of camomile soap, a pleasant, homely scent that reminded him of fresh apples on which Claude drifted down into a deeper sleep.

He was woken by the full brightness of the afternoon sun shining through the window into his eyes. He turned away from the glare and saw Nina facing him across the bed. What's she doing here? he wondered for a second. She was lying naked on her side, one arm tucked under her head, the other stretched out and resting on her hip. A faint residue of apple scent surrounded her in her sleep. Light brown hair streaked with blonde covered her face. He was surprised by the even tan on her skin from her shoulders down to her belly, the fullness of her breasts, the rich pink of her nipples. Where did she get a tan like that in London? The question of the tan uppermost in his mind, as if this was the question he would have to get to the bottom of, Claude got up and went to the bathroom, washed, dressed and went downstairs in the direction of the babble of voices coming up out of the basement.

A slight tremor shook the floor. Claude looked through a glass-panelled door into a room where the presses of Grandjean's printing business were running under the supervision of three men in blue overalls. He went in the other direction, through a warehouse where bales of newsprint were being stacked, to the canteen at the far end of the basement. This was packed with boys and girls in their teens, unwashed, their long hair unkempt, wearing ratty clothes, but their faces all lit up with the enthusiasm that had brought them to Paris. The mattress sleepers were from out of town. In the babble of languages around him Claude picked out Catalan, Spanish and English, provincial French ac-cents from Provence to Brittany, and the face to go with the last, the only person in the room over thirty, unchanged since Claude had last seen him four or five years ago – Henri Gloaguen, his best friend from his student days at the Sorbonne. He was talking to a group of youngsters sitting around him at a table, but the moment he saw Claude he got to his feet and spread out his arms with a cry of pleasure.

'My dear Claude!'

'Dear Henri!'

The two men embraced.

'You've brought half your class with you, I see,' said Claude, laugh-ing with sheer pleasure at seeing his old friend again.

'Exactly half. Jean, Armand, Jean-Luc, Marie, Marie-Ange, Hor-tense, Régis, Annette, Pierre ... this is my old Sorbonne friend, Claude Giffort when I first met him, who later mysteriously transformed himself into de Marsay. We were impressed by this transformation. Think of it! That a fellow could have one name on Monday and another on Tuesday – to us it seemed he took liberties that in those days were very original and daring.'

Claude sat down with the group of seventeen-year-old boys and girls and listened to the discussion. Armand, a tall boy with a rash of acne on his face it was painful even to see, was arguing the case of those who saw the schools and universities as ill equipped and understaffed, in need of more teachers, lecture halls, bigger budgets and guaranteed jobs at the end of it all. What use was it to the student and to society if they graduated only to find they were unemployable? This critique saw the educational system as not adapted to modern life, but its inadequacies capable of reform.

Hortense, a dark-haired and intellectual-looking girl in glasses, listened to Armand's arguments with a frown and shook her head. 'No,' she said decisively when he had finished. 'It's not what place we do or do not achieve in society when we finish our education. It's modern society *itself* that we reject.'

Once the students had left to revisit the battlegrounds of the previous night, Henri and Claude could reclaim the private space of their friendship. Claude was touched to see how little Henri had changed, attired in the same style of plaid shirt, baggy corduroy trousers and shaggy beard he had worn ten year ago as a student. He made no attempt to disguise his provincial accent.

'Have you seen Petit at all?'

'Once – on TV. You know that Jean-Jacques is one of the Nanterre faculty members who have come out in support of their students? People like he and Alain Touraine have become stars. He said he would be staying with Grandjean in Paris but he hasn't shown up. I doubt he'll have much time for the likes of us ... well me at least. He'll be too busy. But anyway, how about yourself and your *ménage à trois*? Is it still holding up?' A slightly superior smile played around his lips as he gestured at Claude's tweed jacket and tie. 'You've acquired a rather English style, you know. You look as if you're prospering. I'm not sure that it suits you.'

Claude's attention had been wandering, but this last remark brought him back. Now that Henri had brought up his *English style* he began to look more closely at his friend's unkempt appearance, the grimy and broken fingernails, the hair that wasn't combed and the beard that wasn't trimmed, and he wondered if habits that might have passed without comment when Henri was a student weren't in need of change for a professional man in his early thirties. But perhaps I should be looking at myself, thought Claude. He may be right: without even noticing it perhaps I've gone over to the camp of the shopkeepers from Rennes. Perhaps I'm really on the other side. Henri's offhand *the likes of us ... well me at least* and that question he posed had driven in a wedge, setting off a train of uncomfortable thoughts, and it was with some confusion that he watched Nina come into the room wearing a sky-blue trouser suit in which she looked so radiant that Claude wondered how he had failed to notice until now what a beautiful woman she was.

# 4

People were carrying suitcases and cardboard boxes and pushing cart-loads of possessions through the streets. They were hoarding food and household necessities in expectation of shortages. Place Maubert looked a wreck, as if Paris had regressed to that shabby, dispirited city no one back in 1945 had bothered to clean up. A pile of rubbish smouldered in the middle of the square. The traffic lights were smashed. Burned-out cars littered the roadside. Broken street signs lay in the gutters. The iron grids around the trees had been torn out, the trees flattened. Claude walked down the Boulevard Saint-Michel with Nina and Henri, hand-ing out leaflets to people they passed. They stopped at a corner coffee shop, where they found themselves talking to a group of students next to some riot police. We're making the world a better place for you as well, one of the girls in the group said, perhaps a little aggressively; a policeman as young and perhaps as scared as the girl during the long nightly battles they had fought with each other replied cautiously, And we're just doing our job.

There were no signs of impending battles that night. It was after midnight when they returned to sensational news at Grandjean's house. Pompidou, the prime minister, had overruled his ministers of the interior and education, giving orders for the police to withdraw from the Latin Quarter and for the Sorbonne to be reopened on Monday, the day planned for a twenty-four-hour general strike. The authorities would reconsider the case of the students arrested the previous week. If these were politicians' ploys to gain time, perhaps to persuade the unions to reconsider the proposed stoppage, which in any case would be in breach of the law requiring five days' notice before a strike could be held, they betrayed only the loss of confidence inside a French Establishment that had been shaken to its foundations.

Discussions of the consequences of the illegal strike went on all night in the basement. Grandjean and his wife sat up with the others, listening to what the young people had to say, particularly to the views of his own printers, who were constantly dodging back and forth between the presses, where they continued working throughout the night, and the canteen discussions. Hopes that the government was on the verge of collapse found expression in the certainty of most of the young people that it had already imploded – that a new society, a new republic, even a new world order was now within their grasp. But Claude thought of the people like the young CRS man who were just doing their jobs, of the vested interests that powerful sections of French society had in maintaining the Fifth Republic – people like his uncle, whose views were not represented in the opinions aired in Grandjean's house that night, and he wondered. Only after the events of the coming Monday would it be possible to make any predictions.

The day began with crowds gathering at six o'clock outside the gates of the giant Renault works at Boulogne Billancourt. By noon, in response to the unions' call for a strike, the streets were already packed. A phalanx of young people walked up the Boulevard de Sébastopol towards the Gare de l'Est on their way to the Place de la République, from where a march would pass through the Latin Quarter to the Place Denfert-Rochereau. Not a bus or a car was to be seen. The police were conspicuous by their absence.

Propitiously, it seemed to the demonstrators, it was another bright, sunny day. The girls wore summer dresses, the men were in shirtsleeves. A red flag was flying over the railway station when Claude and Nina arrived with Henri and the remainder of his class. Red and black flags, the banners of the Jeunesse Communiste Révolutionnaire, portraits of Castro, Mao and Che Guevara, spread like a canopy over the columns of assembled marchers. They handed out the last of Grandjean's leaflets. Sellers of revolutionary literature were doing brisk business. Some of the demonstrators climbed onto walls, the roofs of bus stops and the railings in front of the station in order to get a better view.

At two o'clock the students set off, singing the Internationale, twenty to thirty abreast, arms linked. In their exuberance, the young people laughed as they marched. Grandjean and Aurelia chose to march under the banner *ÉTUDIANTS, ENSEIGNANTS, TRAVAILLEURS, SOLIDAIRES* so that they could take their place alongside the young people they had sheltered in their house, Claude, Nina and Henri among them. Grandjean and his Spanish-Jewish wife began chanting *Nous sommes tous juifs allemands* in support of Cohn-Bendit, who had been the subject of anti-German and anti-Semitic abuse in right-wing newspapers that morning, and the marchers around them took up the refrain. The Boulevard de Magenta seethed, a boiling mass of humanity.

An hour later they reached the Place de la République. The crowd was so dense that people were fainting and had to be carried into cafes to prevent them from being trampled underfoot. Finally the first sections moved off. Although the demonstration had been announced as a joint one, the communist-dominated Confédération Générale du Travail had stewards on either side of the demonstrators to keep students and workers apart. It was a couple of hours more before the first students' and teachers' contingents were able to leave the square. Hundreds of thousands had preceded them, hundreds of thousands followed, but the left-wingers the CGT regarded as troublemakers had been bottled up. Some student groups cottoned onto this manoeuvre and broke out, taking short cuts and infiltrating the marching columns ahead. The CGT marchers assimilated the newcomers, if unsure what quite to make of them and what was going on. The students' dress and speech didn't make it as easy to distinguish them from workers as it would have been in Britain. Meanwhile the main student body proceeded in a disciplined formation. Only their slogans contrasted with those of the CGT. The students shouted, *Le pouvoir aux ouvriers!* or *Le pouvoir est dans la rue!* and *Libérez nos camarades!* while the trade unionists chanted, *Pompidou, démission!* The students chanted, *De Gaulle, assassin!* and *Non a l'Université de classe!* to which the CGT and Stalinists replied, *Université démocratique!* Occasionally the slogans united in *Dix ans, c'est assez! – A bas l'état policier! – Adieu, de Gaulle!* – to a waving of handkerchiefs amid general laughter.

As the main student contingent crossed the Pont Saint-Michel it stopped to pay tribute to the wounded of the previous street battles. In the sudden silence Claude and Nina could sense the anger, the united strength and determination of the students. They wondered if some of the dreams that had been voiced in Grandjean's house the previous night might become reality after all. At the top of the Boulevard Saint-Michel, the two of them dropped out of the march, climbed onto the parapet of the Luxembourg Gardens and watched the vast tide of humanity wash past. A million people? Two million?

Groups otherwise indistinguishable identified themselves by the banners they carried – union banners, student banners, non-political banners, banners of the French CND, the Mouvement contre l'arme

Atomique, the Conseils des Parents d'Élèves. There was an artists' union banner depicting parts of the human anatomy – hands, eyes, ears, head, the dissected and merchandised human being on display on the hooks and trays of a butcher's shop, with a price tag attached to each article. There were sections of hospital personnel wearing white coats and carrying posters that read OÙ SONT LES DISPARUS DES HÔPITAUX? There were factories and companies marching by industry or under their own name, railway workers' unions, postmen, printers, Métro workers, metal workers, sewerage workers, bank employees, construction workers, electricians, lawyers, waiters, municipal employees, painters and decorators, gas workers, shop girls, insurance clerks, road sweepers, bus drivers, film studio crews, fed-up workers and frustrated taxpayers in mile-long columns, the flesh and blood of modern capitalist society – the leviathan aroused, millions of individuals merged in one giant body.

Wearied by the sense of isolation in their withdrawal from the leviathan body, unable to resist its pull, the two onlookers perched on the parapet of the Luxembourg Gardens rejoined the march on its way to Denfert-Rochereau, passing statues of sedate gentlemen on horseback bedecked with red flags and wrapped in banners with slogans. Claude was struck by traffic lights continuing to alternate between red and green at the same fixed intervals, a reminder of the city's normal life, unaffected by the extraordinary events that had put everything else on hold. As they passed a hospital the crowd fell silent until someone began whistling the Internationale. Others took it up and it spread, rippling like a wind over the enormous human expanse.

The first of the demonstrators were now reaching the final point of the march and the CGT had begun to disperse its members. Word was put out that there was to be no fraternisation with the students, no indiscipline that might lead to disturbances at the end of what had been a peaceful march. De Gaulle's anti-chaos dictum – *La réforme oui; la chienlit non* – Reform yes; shit-in-the-bed, no – might have been written by the CGT. The union bosses detested unscripted student solutions. They preferred to isolate their members from dangerous doctrines, sending them quietly back to the safety of the powerless existence they led as individuals. The contribution of the students was welcome as an expression of a collective will to be manipulated by the union leaders; actions going beyond that mandate were undesired. The students remained determined to follow their own leaders' call for a meeting on the Champ de Mars, however. They wanted to sit down and discuss with the workers what they had gained from the march, encouraging CGT members marching alongside to join them. *Aux armes, citoyens! Formez vos bataillons!* The students took up the refrain from the Marseil-laise and the workers around them joined in.

This was just what the union stewards had orders to prevent. Arms linked, they formed lines five or six deep to stop individual marchers breaking out of the column, instructing them to disperse down the Boulevard Arago in the opposite direction to where the students were heading. Claude heard workers around him protesting at being ordered what to do. Some offered resistance. Why should they go home and revert to being nobodies? Here in the mass they were a power to be reckoned with. The collective will of a million-strong crowd could achieve much more than the routine demands put forward by trade union leaders. It wasn't an opportunity to be passed up. The clash of student and union intentions over what the workers should do led to punch-ups. Stewards moved in swiftly to deal with these skirmishes. The union leaders' message of restraint, coupled with their characterisation of students as provocateurs, adventurers and troublemakers, but above all the strong arm of the CGT's stewards eventually took effect. Most of the union members dispersed along the Boulevard Arago as instructed and went home. Thus it was thousands rather then tens or hundreds of thousands who made their way on to the discussion planned at the Champ de Mars, where the march petered out.

'Why don't we go to the Sorbonne instead?' said Claude to Nina.

'Where else?'

They hugged each other and laughed as they fought their way out of a crowd reluctant to let them go.

The riot police guarding the entrance to the Sorbonne had been withdrawn in the early hours of the morning. Students living nearby saw them go and immediately moved in, at first in small groups, then in large numbers. By midday the occupation was complete. Every tricolour was hauled down, every lecture theatre occupied. Red flags were hoisted on the official flagpoles and on dozens of improvised poles sticking out of windows. Giant red and black flags fluttered from the chapel dome. When Claude and Nina arrived that evening the Sorbonne was already in the process of being transformed from the fusty academy Claude had known into liberty hall, an open space where any person could express any opinion they chose.

Everything was up for discussion. A noticeboard at the entrance announced what subjects were being discussed where — the organisa-tion of the struggle, political and trade union rights in the university, university crisis or social crisis, a dossier of police repression, student self-management, opening the university to everyone, dormitories for both sexes in student halls of residence, free love, free distribution of the pill, equal rights for women, abortion, drugs, methods of teaching, the tyranny of exams. Some of the lecture theatres would be reserved for the organisation of a student—worker liaison committee while in others camp beds were being set up for students from out of town. In the main auditorium, discussions were still under way at three o'clock in the morning on sexual repression, the colonial question, on ideology and mystification, the rights of children, the role of women in the new society, the goals of the new education — the rejection of everything in the antiquated and useless system of values of the older generation. There were no taboos — in corners of the building couples made love without attempting to conceal it. All this had come about in the twenty-four hours since the police withdrew from the university.

It was growing light when Nina and Claude returned to their room to get some sleep. They found Grandjean and his wife sitting on the front steps outside the house. Aurelia said it was already too warm to be able to sleep in their room upstairs. The old man was snatching at the mosquitoes that came out at dawn from the dank shrubs around the house.

'Well, my dear,' he said to Nina, putting an arm around her shoul-ders, 'was it a good day we had?'

'It was the most wonderful day of my life.' At half-past five in the morning Nina was still ecstatic, her eyes brimming with all the things they had seen. 'And for you?'

'For Aurelia and me it was a grand day too. A grand consolation for many small humiliations. It does one's heart good.' The old man sighed theatrically and clasped his wife's hand. 'Hope is a mysterious movement of the human soul, so tireless to rise out of resignation again and again, only to be duped, deaf, blind and stupid — but how would we manage without it, this marvellous dumb instinct that in the end turns out to be wise? The only question my wife and I are asking ourselves at the end of this day is: Where is de Gaulle?'

'Isn't he making a state visit to Romania?'

Grandjean smiled at the naivety of this response. 'I didn't mean the general's whereabouts. I meant his state of mind. His silence – it's too loud. His invisibility – it's too palpable. He isn't there, yet the shadow he casts is long.'

'De Gaulle is biding his time,' said Claude.

'Exactly. He is biding his time.'

Grandjean made a grab at a mosquito buzzing around his head and crushed it between thumb and forefinger.

'Contrary to the old adage, very often the best form of defence is not attack; no, it is to do nothing, to go underground, disappear. Wait for the enemy to come to you. This is the strength of all guerrilla movements, in Algeria, in South America, in Vietnam. Did you read any banners supporting de Gaulle today? No. De Gaulle's people were not on the streets today. A million people out there, perhaps more, chanting, *Adieu, de Gaulle, au revoir, mon général!* Impressive! But misleading. Ten million votes have not been accounted for. Think of all those officials tucked away in provincial town halls dependent on Gaullist patronage, embedded in Gaullist sleaze. Think of the craftsmen, the little shopkeepers, the lawyers and the apothecaries who in their turn are dependent on the goodwill of the officials in those town halls and feed off that sleaze. Think of the farmers in the vast somnolent tracts of rural France. None of those people were here today.'

Claude could imagine the kind of people who made up that silent majority, and he feared that Grandjean was right.

'De Gaulle's allies are not these people as such,' the old man went on, musing as much for his own benefit as for the others, 'but Chronos and Saturn, the gods to whom they are all bound. The given order of things is what holds them fast. They resist change because inertia is the law that governs them, the unchanging and unchangeable trajectory of their lives on the path of least resistance – the natural path of all social organisation, all civilisations that have endured. De Gaulle doesn't need to pray to those gods because he knows he already has them on his side. All he need do is bide his time.'

'Knowing that the energy of the forces of change will dissipate and eventually peter out,' Aurelia put in.

'Perhaps not so much *knowing*, my dear, as reaching a conclusion by deducing from similar events in history. The Paris Commune in 1871, the revolution of 1848, the restoration of the monarchy in 1830. *Enrichissez-vous!* Then and now – what's the difference?'

'Democracy,' said Nina.

'Pah! Power in the end always reverts to those who have or want to have the money, and it deserts those who have the ideas. When the idealists begin to lose themselves in their ideas and quarrel, as they inevitably do, when the forces of change break up into factions, that's when de Gaulle will make his move. The propertied classes will be issued an ultimatum: close ranks around me or else. If he loses power, a pro-Soviet French Communist Party will take over. This argument will be understood by the socialists, who have co-opted a section of the student movement under the guise of supporting their revolt, and who are more afraid of communist domination than they are of Gaullism. The communists too will back-pedal, calculating that a revolt against Gaullism will not give them the share of power they are currently seeking in an alliance of the left, and they will be wooed tenaciously by the Gaullists to help them change their minds. De Gaulle will tell them France must be protected against the socialists, because they will subordinate French policy to American interests, leaving the French Communist Party and their self-serving alliance with the Soviets out in the cold. Thus all the established parties, right and left, will agree that the choice is either de Gaulle or disaster. *Voilà.* The outcome of *les événements* is surely not so difficult to predict.'

Claude felt himself brought back to earth by this analysis.

'Then how does that marvellous dumb instinct, as you described the hope you allowed us just a few minutes ago,' asked Nina, 'turn out to be wise in the end? What's wise about a hope if it's going to let us all down?'

'I've no idea,' said Grandjean, getting up. He gave his arm to his wife and helped her to her feet. 'Let's go to bed, Aurelia.' On his way up the steps he turned round. 'Hope abides. But it's unaccountable. It depends on how much you ask of it.'

Upstairs, on the big bed in the Bolivian room, as Nina called it, where the air was sticky and close, they lay without bedclothes on, no clothes at all, and talked through the day that still went on and wouldn't stop, until Nina leaned over Claude and put an end to the talk by kissing him on the mouth. Sensing Claude's hesitation when she put her hand on his cock she said, 'It's just butterflies,' and without his own doing he flew up to her and miraculously stuck fast, somehow hovering with Nina in mid-air – just butterflies, as she said.

# 5

The young guests in Grandjean's house, their ageing host and his wife hardly less, despite what they may have said to the contrary, lived throughout that Paris month in a state of euphoria, in expectation of the great and even more marvellous things yet to come. A gigantic lid had been lifted off the social pressure cooker, allowing thoughts, desires and aspirations that had been kept down for too long to escape and find expression. The spark ignited by a radical student minority set alight the consciousness of young people hitherto uninterested in politics. An exhilarating sense of freedom breathed in the marketplaces of new ideas, in the occupied Théâtre de l'Odéon, in the courtyard outside the Sorbonne and the sessions of the General Assembly inside. It spread from the Latin Quarter and the city via the suburbs and dormitory towns of the capital, to provincial towns throughout the country. It transformed people. The shy and inhibited discovered in themselves what it meant to be able to communicate; the loners, the pessimists, the cynics and the hitherto apathetic formed alliances in hundreds of action committees, loosely coordinated with the assembly at the Sorbonne. With a common purpose – reforms not imposed from above but which they could bring about themselves – social cohesion and community solidarity became tangible things imbued with real meaning.

At its first session the General Assembly instituted an occupation committee of fifteen members to be made up of students, professors and workers, who would be nominated on a daily basis. This committee declared the Sorbonne an autonomous university, open day and night to all workers. It made a number of fine-sounding appeals for solidarity in the common cause, but factions which had failed to get their representatives elected had already begun sabotaging the committee. By the end of the week it was clear that the occupation committee would be unable to get any of its proposed actions discussed and voted on, notably its appeal for the occupation of factories. However, factories were already being occupied by workers, making the deliberations of the General Assembly appear not merely irrelevant but out of touch. Faced with a combination of indifference and interminable squabbles between rival and always very vociferous political minorities, the occupation committee resigned. At just the moment the example of occupation first set by the students began to be followed in the factories, the spirit of revolution was beginning to dissipate at the source of *les événements*, at the Sorbonne itself. The students found themselves left behind. It was the workers who had taken over the leadership of the revolt, and the outcome of the crisis lay with them.

However, when workers occupied a Sud-Aviation plant in Nantes, locking the management in their offices and fortifying the plant against police attack, a burst of new enthusiasm broke out at the Sorbonne. Strikes hit other factories throughout the country. The General Assembly at the Sorbonne voted to send its own student deputation to an occupied Renault works, a move which the CGT did its best to thwart. Watching this depressingly familiar spectacle of infighting on the left undermining an alliance that might yet pose a credible alternative to the government in power, Claude was reminded of Grandjean's prescient remark that all de Gaulle need do was bide his time.

An estimated ten million workers were already on strike in France, paralysing the country. All those people who had marched with their union banners from the Place de la République only a week before made good their threats and deserted their posts – the gas, petrol and electricity suppliers, the national telephone company, the entire public transport system, even the undertakers, went on strike. Mines closed, banks and the stock exchange, shipyards, government offices, a nuclear plant, the town of Nantes in its entirety, where a central strike committee was elected which occupied the town hall for a week, even introducing the town's own currency. Students organised workers' councils and action committees to run essential services, providing electricity, manning petrol pumps for doctors to run their cars, organising convoys of free food to urban centres, occupying the national radio and television organisation, keeping the country informed of what was happening until the police broke in and ejected them. A state of anarchy prevailed for some time in some localities.

But then de Gaulle gave an address to the nation, warning of the imminent danger of civil war and dissolving the National Assembly with a view to holding imminent elections. In response to the president's address, hundreds of thousands of the bourgeois majority, which until now had kept away from the streets, came out in support of the government with a mass demonstration on the Champs-Elysées.

When the armoured vehicles of the state began rolling into those industrial centres still on strike, the will to continue the fight went out of the people. Thousands of troops were sent into the Flins Renault plant outside Paris. By mid-June the police were back in the Sorbonne too. Again the streets of the Latin Quarter went up in flames. But with the government's belated acknowledgement of the justness of some of the complaints, the concessions originally rejected as falling far short of the social revolution envisaged had to be accepted, the unity of the socialists, the French Communist Party, the unions and the student radicals collapsed, and the brief heyday of *les événements* was over.

At the beginning of June, Claude and Nina were still trying to get back to England. Train and ferry services were disrupted, air travel too expensive. Claude was coming out of a travel agent on the Boulevard Saint-Michel when he collided with a man coming in.

'Claude!'

'Jean-Jacques!'

It was his old friend Petit.

They went around the corner and settled down in a cafe. Claude gave an account of how he had spent the last three weeks in Paris, then it was Petit's turn.

'You may know that some of the faculty members at Nanterre came out in support of the March 22 Movement, and that I was one of them? Well, I spoke in their defence in front of the disciplinary committee at the Sorbonne too. We all lived in a commune in the rue le Goff. We were a team. All that street fighting in the Latin Quarter, we did it together and built our own barricades. We marched together from the Place de la République.'

Claude watched him toy with the paper doily on the table in front of him, then roll it into a little ball and flick it across the room.

'I was at the march too, but didn't see you,' said Claude, 'and I could hardly have missed you.' Petit's huge physique, his shoulder-length hair and beard modelled after those of nineteenth-century revolutionaries had always made his name seem ridiculous.

'Well, I was there. But I went back to Nanterre and joined the skeleton staff that kept things running during the general strike. I can't say that I regret that, when one sees how meagre the upshot of it all has been.'

*Meagre* and *upshot* left an unpleasant impression on Claude, arousing vague memories of the weights and measures of the old-fashioned grocer's he used to go to with his Aunt Dot in Somerset. He felt that one of them must be completely out of touch.

'How do you think the elections will go?' he asked.

'The Gaullists will sweep it, of course.'

Petit glanced at his watch, and even if he had not, it was already clear to Claude that his friend would prefer not to be sitting in the cafe having this conversation, and would perhaps rather not have run into him at all.

The day before Claude and Nina left Paris they took their leave of the Sorbonne, wandering along the corridors and reading the graffiti. Afterwards he took her to one of his old haunts in Saint-Germain-des-Prés, and there they got into conversation with one of the organisers at the Sorbonne during the May anarchy. Petit's name was familiar to him from the events in Nanterre and from the pages of *L'Express*, in which he had read some of his articles. He was quite sure he hadn't seen Petit at the Sorbonne General Assembly, nor had he come across his name on any of the ballot lists that had passed through his hands at the time.

Why would Petit have lied? wondered Claude.

After an absence of three weeks they arrived back in London. The depression that came over Claude when they landed in Dover grew worse as the train lurched its way between the soot-covered run-down buildings backing onto the track on the approach to Victoria. When you drink too much at a party, he told himself, you wake up with a hangover.

Nina hadn't drunk too much. Nina didn't have a hangover. Bright and happy, she was as radiant as she'd been when she appeared in the canteen wearing the sky-blue trouser suit on that first morning in Grandjean's house. The train got into London an hour late. Nina lived just around the corner, she said, five minutes in a cab, let's go to my place, and naturally they did, naturally they went to bed together and made love, just as they'd been doing every night for the past three weeks.

# 6

Claude returned to London to find a letter from the university disciplinary committee on his desk. He had absented himself without
permission from his duties during term and was accordingly in breach of
contract with his employer. He had failed to appear at the two hearings
of his case arranged for the previous week and the week before that. His
contract with the university was terminated forthwith. He was required
to vacate his faculty office and remove his belongings by the end of the
month.

'I've been fired,' he said to Nina.

Their initial reaction was to go straight back to Paris, to that asylum
at the top of Grandjean's house, to the discussions, the demonstrations,
the euphoric sense of universal belonging, the freedom they had enjoyed
there during a break from real life. But when the results of the elections
in France were announced it was clear they no longer had that option.
At the polling booths conservative France was re-established with a large
majority, a mandate to restore law and order to a country that had been
on the brink of civil war. Troops and armoured cars moved in. The
dream of May evaporated.

Due to the strikes Claude had been out of touch with Ella during the
Paris weeks for a longer period than ever before in their life. Mail had
not been delivered; calls were not put through. When he tried to reach
her from London with the news of his dismissal, no one answered the
phone in Arguayo. So he called George's flat in La Orotava, and got
Alex on the line. George wasn't here, his son told him; he was with
Ella in Santa Cruz, where she had been taken in a hurry to have an
operation on her tummy. Another operation? Alex said the operation
had been done a week ago and his mother had come through all right.
Daddy said – *George*, said Alex, correcting himself – she would be
home by the end of the week.

George is your dad, too, said Claude, grateful for him, as George
had been for Claude five years previously. But for George ... he thought.

Nina was a great comfort to Claude. She encouraged him. She went
through the possibilities open to him on the job market. She made lists
of situations vacant. He more or less moved into her flat. She cooked
for him. She slept with him. The delirious days and nights of sex with

Nina distracted him from his other worries, making it easier for Claude to agree with her when she assured him that everything would turn out all right.

It was only now he learned that Nina's family, wealthy Russian Jews living in Switzerland, were extremely well connected thanks to the work of the Rubinstein Foundation set up by her grandfather when the family left Bolshevik Russia in 1917 and moved to Zurich. London University was among the beneficiaries of the foundation. It might not be possible to have Claude reinstated by arranging for the foundation to intervene with the chancellor, Nina thought, but surely it should be no great difficulty to provide him with favourable letters of reference, glossing over his dismissal. Offhand she could think of one or two universit, ies, in Zurich, for example, or in Geneva, likewise beneficiaries of the Rubinstein Foundation, where a teaching position could be found for Claude to take up in the autumn.

Against the background of this information Claude began to look differently at Nina. It explained her casualness about the outcome of her ongoing PhD thesis on Dostoyevsky during their absence from London. She had neglected her own work no less than Claude had his. It helped explain her lack of concern about a situation that for Claude was critical. It did not explain why she was interested in him and doing so much to help him.

Nina was drawn to Claude for the reason that, although he seemed to enjoy her company, he had never given any evidence of being attracted to her as a woman. Why was this, when other men were falling over each other to get her into bed? She was a sexy woman, a modern woman: she liked men. Claude's chasteness amused her. How quaint! Out of curios, ity she had made the first moves with Claude, but he hadn't responded. He didn't turn her down as such, just seemed oblivious of the signals Nina was giving him. Her vanity had been piqued.

She had guessed there was another woman, but as Claude kept him, self to himself and never talked about his private life she couldn't tell. Claude had blocked all her attempts at personal conversations. Until chance brought them together in the room in Grandjean's house, the places they met and the things they talked about remained confined to London University. He hadn't even given her his phone number. Where Claude went home, and who, if anyone, was waiting for him there at the end of the day – this remained his secret.

She was surprised by the ready sexual passion of this withdrawn, secretive man. Expecting an inhibited partner in bed, and that it would be up to her to make the running, she was unprepared for the openness of his desire and the hungry way it took possession of her body. The things he said to her when they made love poured over her in a violent welter of words, and the cries he uttered when he came excited her by the sharp immediacy of arousal she heard in them. Nina had not had a lover like Claude before. It was like sleeping with a virgin every time, Grushenka with Alyosha, ripping the white shirt off his narrow back and watching his modest cock swell in her hand. She had the power to bring about this transformation without fail every time they went to bed together, and this power of sexually enslaving Claude in order for the enslaved Claude to enslave her masterfully in turn – this double edge gave Nina a more subtle and satisfying pleasure than the lovemaking she had known with other men.

During the early-morning hours in the Bolivian room Nina also got Claude to talk about Ella: their beginnings in Paris, Ella and George and the children in St John's Wood, Claude's grafting onto the new home the family moved to in Richmond, the *ménage à trois*, Ella's child by him, George's betrayal of Ella, the rift between them, his departure for Tenerife and gradual re-inclusion in the family – bit by bit the complex picture of Claude's unknown life was put together.

'Am I the first woman you've had beside Ella?'

'Yes.'

'And are you going to tell her about our relationship?'

'I don't have any secrets from Ella.'

But this *tell her about our relationship*, which Nina slipped in so matter-of-factly, made Claude uneasy. *Our relationship* suggested a status Nina was claiming for herself that Claude wouldn't have acknowledged. He went to bed with Nina, but that didn't mean he had a relationship with her. Claude didn't have relationships. He disliked the word. On the other side of a relationship he might expect to find some sort of possession – an investment perhaps, a pet or an aquarium, or an institution such as London University – but not a personal human attachment.

Nina was already mooting *our* summer holiday plans, until Claude bluntly told her that there weren't any *our* holiday plans. He had long since arranged to spend the vacation in Arguayo with Ella and the family.

'Couldn't I come over too?'

Claude was appalled by her suggestion. Realising what he had let himself in for, he moved out of Nina's place back to the Kensington flat.

'I've got some thinking to do,' he said to Nina, and told her he was going away for a few days. The trip provided him with the pretext for a note to Ella he chose to keep short, letting her know where he was going and that a proper letter to her would soon be in the post.

He went down to Somerset to visit Aunt Dot at her house in Little Compton, as he did at least once a year, even if it was just for a day trip. He remained fond of her, and once he had started to earn a living he gave her a monthly allowance. He had kept up with her over the years, albeit with an increasing sense of discomfort which overcame him when he entered the house. While his life had moved on, Aunt Dot's seemed to have gone backwards. Everything in the house remained in the place it had been assigned thirty years ago when his father was killed. She kept it as if it was a museum. The Distinguished Flying Cross was still on display in the front sitting room, the photograph of the hero who was Claude's father hanging above it on the mantelpiece framed by newspaper cuttings. Every evening before he went to bed she used to take the photo down for little Claude to see, never failing to rub the glass on her sleeve. Grown-up Claude was taken aback when she carried out this ritual on the evening he arrived.

'That was your dad,' said Aunt Dot, pointing as if Claude were still a child, 'that's him in his uniform. But for the war —'

'— he would surely have taken holy orders, like our father before him.'

Claude finished the sentence for her. Dot's gestures and the words that accompanied the ritual hadn't changed one bit over the years, whereas Claude's reaction to it had. Claude found it tiresome, the lie his aunt nourished about his father irritating.

Ella had been down with him to visit Aunt Dot on a couple of occasions. The two women had taken to each other. It was Ella who had suggested the monthly allowance. When the family moved into their new home in Richmond, Ella had even thought of asking her if she would like to come and live with them. Claude told her there was no point. He knew his aunt. She wouldn't budge. In the museum Dot had created Ella saw the loneliness of an old woman who had made her home in the past because she had nothing to live for in the present. Ella caught a glimpse of herself in the older woman, and wondered for the first time if Claude, ten years younger than her, would still be loyal to her when she reached Dot's age. Claude thought Ella was being sentimental. Of course he would. Incidentally, Dot was quite happy where she was. Claude wasn't ungenerous or insensitive. Such ideas just wouldn't have crossed his mind; no more Ella's misgivings, least of all the grounds for her identifying with Dot.

'This is my woman,' Claude had told Aunt Dot when he first introduced Ella. It seemed as solid and true a description as any at the time. But as the years passed, Dot grew restless and even reproachful that Claude's woman still hadn't become his wife. If Ella could see herself in Dot's position, Dot could see herself in Ella's too.

'If she's your woman, do right by her and marry her.'

'These days you don't necessarily have to get married to do right by a woman you love.'

'Nonsense. Course you do. Who do you think you are? What if something happened to you, like it did to your dad? What claim to a pension would she have as an unmarried woman?'

Dot's question pulled him up short. The silver sixpences George had tipped the waiters at their Athenaeum dinner ten years ago flashed into his mind, trailing the question, Who pays?

Claude had no answers to these questions. Nor did he want to get involved in explanations about the nature of his arrangement with Ella and George. He resented being required to give an account of himself that inevitably sounded like a justification. He wished people would mind their own business. Dot wouldn't have approved or understood in any case. So he said nothing to the person who had once been closest to him, slipping deeper into a habit of silence that became indistinguishable from concealment, nourishing an uneasy awareness that if it troubled him it must be because he had done something wrong.

In the woods and hills where he went for long walks Claude repeated to himself the question that had come up many times in Paris: How much revolution could one expect from a man who had let himself be stopped by a night porter from going to the room where his woman was having their baby? Because he didn't have a document – just a piece of paper, Grandjean had called it – proving he was next of kin? Why hadn't he ignored the porter and gone in? How could he have allowed himself to be deterred so easily?

No revolutions were led by such a man, no medals awarded in recognition of valorous conduct. Claude's sense of shame went deep.

He concluded that in the course of adapting to the ambiguities of his role in the Morris family he had been accommodating to the point of self-denial. Ella's name wasn't his, nor was his son's; his son had the name of the man who wasn't his father; Claude was the man in the marriage, but it wasn't his name on the door. He had erased his name. He'd got used to tradesmen in Richmond and Kensington, and now even in Arguayo, calling him Mr Morris. How were they to know? Claude had become so accommodating as to edit himself out of existence.

The exposition of this loss took up the first couple of pages of the letter he began drafting to Ella in his schoolboy room in Dot's house while she slept downstairs in front of the telly. *I feel that I haven't built my life for myself, but moved into a life that was ready made. I want to have my own life, my life, which has so far escaped me. Life is elsewhere.* He realised he was echoing the graffiti he had read on a wall of the Sorbonne: *la vie est ailleurs*, itself an echo of lines in Rimbaud's *Une Saison en Enfer*.

Without the experience of Paris he doubted he would have had this insight, not with this clarity, nor with the courage to put it into words. This brought Claude to *the liberating affair with Nina*. His pen wavered over these words, astonishingly out there on the page, almost without his doing, before striking out *liberating*.

Liberated from what?

He had had sex with Nina, he was even obsessed with having sex with her, but he didn't love her, did he? Therefore he would not take advantage of Nina's offer to help him find a job. In the making of his life he would not be beholden to anyone. Finding a new job was his immediate concern. It was only another three months before the new academic year started. He didn't have much time. Until he found a job he would not be able to join the family in Arguayo.

*These changes in the circumstances of my life have no effect on my love for you,* wrote Claude, underlining this sentence as if by doing so he could lift it out of its banality, before he went on: *What I am asking you is to let me go for a few years to live a life of my own making.* He added that he would naturally continue to pay her and Alex an allowance, as he had been doing until now.

He went to bed more or less at peace with the outline of this letter, but when he read it through in the morning he was appalled. What a heartless letter — all about himself and his brave new world, not one sentence in tribute to their thirteen years together, just those feeble and inadequate words about the changes in his circumstances having no effect on his love for Ella — circumstances, effects! What sort of drivel was this?

The truth, unfortunately, a truth — of sorts.

He meant to go away just as he meant to come back. He *wanted* to come back, to pick up again what he was now about to throw away. But did he? What guarantee could he give her he would?

He couldn't. Claude wanted it both ways — in both directions, going and coming — the tacit assumption being that in the meantime Ella would sit and wait for him while he made up his mind.

He got on the bus from Little Compton to Temple Meads station in Bristol and caught the train back to Paddington, his sense of dread mounting the nearer the train got to London.

There was no such letter to be written, no such letter for the asking, not from him, not to her. How had he got himself into this mess in the first place? Claude couldn't remember. The little gleam of hope that flickered up for a few seconds in the wake of this absence of memory was immediately extinguished again.

By the time the train drew in to Paddington a decision had been taken, not quite by Claude but by default — on his behalf, so to speak — instructing him to go to straight on to Heathrow and get the first flight to La Laguna. But it was the height of the summer holiday season; flights to Tenerife were booked solid. All that was available was a seat on the last flight to Madrid that night and the possibility of a vacancy on an internal flight to La Laguna first thing the next morning. No vacancy was available until that afternoon, however, and when Claude called George in Puerto de la Cruz to come and pick him up from the airport there was no reply. He wondered whether to try him at the other house and decided not to; it seemed an imposition to ask him to drive all the way across the island and back. By the time he had hired a car and set out on the road to Arguayo, his body aching with desire for Nina, his heart with its sad burden of baffled love for Ella, it was already getting dark.

# 7

Damp with sweat, exhausted, Ella lay on her bed in the belfry room and looked at the cracks in the ceiling. They had got bigger. The architect who had advised her during the restoration of the house was coming over to look at the repairs that already needed to be done – an ominous bulge in the wall of Claude's room, some re-plastering on the *portada sillería*, damp spots on the walls of the cellar stairs she had noticed only when she came back from hospital – there was no end to the demands of the unpredictable old house. She felt sympathy for it, for her body and her house; they were both patients in need of attention. But while the house could get by as it was, if need be for another ten years, she had ten days to recuperate. In ten days the children would be arriving for their summer holidays. She felt porous, transparent. One could have passed a needle through her body without resistance. She wondered what message her body was giving her.

'I don't regret it.'

'What?'

'Buying this house.'

'Well … as long as we can afford to keep it up.' George got up. 'Would you like me to bring you some more coffee?'

Money had never particularly interested George, if only because he had always had enough of it, but recently the subject had begun to surface in their conversations. George's last few books hadn't sold well. Money was making itself felt by its shortage. Ella was becoming aware of the cold undercurrents that had begun to flow through their life.

She remembered a trip to Salzburg with her mother before the war, standing outside an old country house that had been converted into a hotel, where they'd stayed, and looking up at the inscription over the entrance.

> DIES HAUS IST MEIN UND DOCH NICHT MEIN
> ES WIRD AUCH KEINES ANDEREN SEIN
> DIE VORDERN TRUG MAN AUCH HINAUS
> NUN FRAG ICH DICH WEM GEHÖRT DIES HAUS

Ella wondered about translating the lines into Spanish and having them inscribed on the *portada sillería*. The Spanish bishop who commissioned the building of the house three hundred years ago would have perfectly understood that sentiment about its ownership – how many of its owners during the last three hundred years had been carried out of the house up to the little walled cemetery on the hill outside the village?

She spent most of her morning in her corner sewing room, the view of the Teno mountains still in the shadow. She had an odd sort of cramp, a sort of tugging. Something wouldn't let her go.

Later she went downstairs to see what Alicia's sister Dolores was preparing for lunch. The sound of George's typewriter pattered clack-heeled around the courtyard. She watered the plants. The tug here was stronger. With a premonition of where it came from she looked into the little alcove, formerly a sentry box, and there on the little round table where the Adeje postman left their letters she saw it, a pale blue envelope from the stationery she used in London, with her name and address on it in Claude's small, meticulous handwriting. Reaching out to pick up the envelope, she became aware of an aura around it – so reluctant was the letter to be touched that she withdrew her hand and left it lying where it was.

On her way back upstairs she looked into the kitchen again and asked Dolores to check if there was any mail and to bring it up to her sewing room. Ten minutes later Dolores put her head around the door, the letter in her hand. Ella asked her to leave it on the windowsill. There it sat for the rest of the morning.

Alex came up to tell her lunch was ready. So she went down to join the others, and after lunch, when Alex went out to play with Felipe, and George wandered back across the courtyard to his typewriter, she returned to her sewing room and pulled herself together.

'It's not as if it's going to jump out and bite me, or anything.'

She slit the envelope open with her pattern-cutting scissors, took out the folded piece of paper and smoothed out the creases. Sit down to read a letter and open it properly, show the writer that much respect – she'd often enough heard that from her mother, who found the sight of Andrzejewski standing at his desk, ripping an envelope open with his fingers quite unbearable.

*Dearest Ella,*

*The aftermath of last month's upheaval in Paris has disappointed all of us who were there and had hopes of the great things that would follow from it. The police are back in the Sorbonne, the Gaullists are back in power, the shores of the new society that seemed almost within our reach have receded into the distance. I have been dismissed by the university for absenting myself without permission for three weeks in May and June. I don't regret it. This was a contribution I had to make, and I know many others who are now having to pay for the consequences of their enthusiasm. I will have to do my best to find another job as soon as possible, which may mean I shall be coming over for the summer holidays later than expected. I have tried so often to get hold of you in Arguayo but there was never any reply. It was only when I called George in Orotava that I finally got Alex on the line and heard about your having gone through yet another operation, poor darling. I'm about to go down to Aunt Dot's for a few days and will call or write to you with more news as soon as I get back from Somerset.*

*Your ever loving Claude*

Ella read the letter a second and a third time. She could just decipher the London postmark on the envelope. She worked out that the letter had taken a week to reach her. So Claude must be back in London now. She wondered why he still hadn't called.

She carried the letter over to the ironing board, sniffed and ironed it. Then she scrutinised it. The customary neat flow of Claude's hand-writing was deceptive, the skimped tops and bottoms of the *f*, *g*, *p* and *y*, the short cut he had taken with the elision of the double *m* in summer, the inward slope of his handwriting getting progressively further away from the left-hand margin as it moved down the page – all this suggested to Ella not just that Claude had written the letter quickly but that he had written it with more general omissions at the back of his mind.

Why this haste?

From a shelf in the cupboard she took out the green file with stencils of birds and butterflies and a photograph of Claude she had trimmed so that she could paste it on the spine. All the letters he'd written her that year were kept in this file. The last batch were the postcards he'd sent her from Paris, half a dozen of them, between the middle of May and the beginning of June, which had only recently arrived, weeks after they'd been written.

She read through them again, but to Ella's disappointment there wasn't a single reference to their own Paris days. Surely there must have been some spot he'd passed on his way through Paris that brought back memories of himself and Ella there in the 1950s. In spirit she was back there with him now, but Claude gave no indication of having been aware of any of that — all traces of Ella had been edited out.

Whereas in the letter she'd just ironed — what was the phrase? — in that phrase *all of us who were there,* right up there in the first sentence. No one who shared with Claude back in London their disappointment about the election results in France — how else would he have known about their disappointment? — was mentioned by name. They too had been edited out, and she wondered why, for obviously Claude was refer-ring to Nina, particularly to Nina, or even to Nina alone.

It was not as if the individuals hidden in *all of us* particularly con-cerned Ella. What could be more natural than for Claude to have had an affair with Nina while they were in Paris, as she immediately guessed? But for the aura surrounding the envelope, something akin to an electric charge, she might not even have noticed something wayward in Paris, no doubt in London too, little oddities in Claude's letter which told her all this in as many words.

But as it was ...

It was the drift of concealment. The omissions revealed themselves in the aura, the negative charge emitted by the letter. Without the omissions, no aura; without the aura, no omissions.

As it was, Ella already knew that Claude was going away from her twenty-four hours before he arrived in Arguayo to tell her so in person, and that nothing he or she could say would be able to prevent it from happening.

# 8

A few hours before Claude landed at La Laguna, George drove there in the jeep to pick up the children. Max nineteen, the twins going on eighteen, they were hardly children any more. For all the scrapes he kept on getting into, Max had landed himself a job and was supporting him-self without any help from his father — for once George could grudgingly approve of what his eldest son was doing. He'd recently returned from a photo assignment in Paris, and even as Max was shaking his father's hand with his right – George stuck to Gábor's rule of shaking hands with sons, only daughters got a hug – he was handing him the latest issue of *lifestyle* with his left. George could see how proud Max was of the magazine, and was secretly proud of his son in turn. Perhaps Max would get his life sorted out, after all – not that George put any of this into words.

In the front seat beside his father for most of the long drive across the island to Arguayo, Max talked animatedly about Paris.

'Claude was there too, you know,' said George. 'You didn't happen to run into him, did you?'

'No,' said Max, wondering what Claude had got to do with it, and carried on with his account of the night of the barricades. The twins in the back, not in the least interested in events in Paris, continued swapping Sherborne stories, still unsure if they were relieved or sorry to have got their schooldays behind them. As the jeep turned inland off the coast road, George told them not to expect too much of their mother. She'd been very ill, two major operations and a miscarriage within the space of a few months.

'Poor Mum!' sighed Felicity, more with the lost baby in mind than her mother, feeling sorry that she wouldn't have the little sister she'd been so looking forward to.

But for all their father's cautions they saw little outward sign of what their mother had been through in the last few months. Ella seemed to them to be her usual self, as bright and present as ever. Only Felicity noticed how much thinner she had become, and that she left all the preparations for the evening meal to Alicia's daughter Inma and George without intervening once. Mother and daughter sat out on the terrace talking, Philip coming and going, torn between the game he was playing with Alex and anxiety he might miss out on something interesting in the conversation, but when he found Felicity with her arms around her mother he slipped away without disturbing them.

Whatever new found sympathy it was that brought Ella and Felicity together, the gay atmosphere in the patio, where they all sat down to supper under the dragon tree, had something to do with the harmony between mother and daughter. It even rubbed off on Max and George. Father and son sat next to each other and talked merrily away with each other, as Philip couldn't recall having seen them before. He was a good natured boy, pleased to see his family assembled happily around him because this was how he expected families to be. He didn't mind if he was a bit left out – he could make a contribution from the middle, Philip realised with pride, persuaded that if they were now a united family this was partly due to his efforts as peacemaker in the disputes between his siblings and parents.

This was the scene on the patio, the ideal family portrait Philip had glimpsed in his mind, when Claude arrived. He walked in out of the night like a ghost. Where had *he* sprung from? Nobody was expecting him, and from the momentary silence on his appearance, so brief that no one but Claude himself would have noticed it, one might have chosen to suppose that nobody was missing him either. The very slightly delayed outbreak of expressions of pleasure, Alex running up to put his arms around his father, Max clapping him on the back, failed to dispel the vestige of reluctance Claude had sensed before it. Even without looking in Ella's direction – she was sitting somewhere towards the back – he could pinpoint the source of unwelcome, perhaps in his imagination, perhaps something he had brought himself.

Ella went to bed early, with no more than a general wave to them all by way of a goodnight. Later, when Claude went up to her room, he found the door locked. It was still locked when he went up again in the morning. He looked into George's room, but George wasn't there. Claude found him drinking coffee and reading the newspaper on the terrace.

'She's not been quite herself since the hysterectomy,' said George. 'She needs time to recover. It was only a couple of weeks ago. I'll go up a bit later and see if she wants anything.'

Around lunchtime, when the children began drifting down into the kitchen to see what was in the offing, George announced that their mother was still recovering from her tummy operation and would be spending the day in bed. The more she rested, the sooner she would be over her illness. It might be better if they didn't disturb her. He would give them their lunch.

For the first time the children could remember, their mother wasn't there for them when they came home for the holidays. They weren't even allowed to see her. Yesterday she'd been there, sitting out with them having supper and seeming perfectly all right. In fact, until Claude's unexpected arrival ...

Claude became aware of a vague general feeling in the house that the overnight decline in Ella's health had something to do with him. Even George appeared to share this view.

'Have you and Ella had some sort of tiff?'

Claude told him about the events in Paris, his affair with Nina, which was over now, his dismissal from London University and his so-far-unsuccessful attempt to find a new job.

'You mean to say you took off for Paris without leave of absence? Wasn't that rather a rash thing to do, old man?'

Claude tried to argue mitigating circumstances in the extraordinary revolutionary spirit of Paris that spring, but George was unsympathetic.

'Revolutionary? It was no more than a flash in the Gaullist pan. Just look at the majority that returned the ruling party to power.'

'But if you'd been out there on the streets—'

'Claude, being out there on the streets is what gives you a subjective view of events, the myopia of direct action, leading you to draw completely the wrong conclusions. The people on the streets see what they want to see. The overall picture is something you get only from outside.'

Claude spent the day fishing with Alex and Philip in a wobbly boat off the rocks of Los Gigantes, pondering the implications of what George had said. He wasn't used to criticism from George. It made him less sure of his ground. Behind it all he detected criticism of Nina, but who was George to talk?

Or Ella, for that matter.

He woke the next morning to find her sitting in a chair in his room.

'For a man who's just lost his job, you sleep very soundly. I've been sitting here for an hour and a half, wondering.'

'Wondering about what?'

'How impenetrably you sleep. Were you dreaming about Nina?'

'No.'

'But you'd be thinking about her if I weren't here.'

'So that's why you're here. To censor my dreams. To police my waking.'

'All I'm asking for is honesty.'

'You know you can ask me anything you like, and I'll always give you an honest answer.'

'Are you thinking of leaving me? Is that the deal you've done secretly with Nina?'

'I haven't done any secret deals with Nina.'

'You're infatuated with her. That's why you so carefully avoid talking about her. Not one word about her in your letter. *The aftermath of last month's upheaval in Paris has disappointed all of us who were there*, and so on. As if you gave twopence about last month's upheaval in Paris. You're too obsessed with this woman to care about anything else. Is she orgiastic? Is she good in bed?'

'I don't know what you mean by orgiastic. But yes, since you ask, she's very good in bed.'

'Well, you've had enough opportunities to find out, I dare say. These Russian women can be very orgiastic. I expect you talked dirty to her as you used to do to me. I expect you wanted to do it with her in odd places and at odd times, the way you used to do it with me. Stolen sex, out of greed, not love, because that's the only sort of sex you know. I dare say she led you on. I'm not saying it was all your fault. Conveniently, I was out of the way in hospital. It must have made it easier for the two of you to spend a lot of time in bed together.'

'That's under the belt, Ella. It's cruel and it's unfair.'

'But true.'

'And of course you home in on this one subject because this is what matters to you most. We could be talking about the fact that I've lost my job, but no. Because despite the rights you've allowed yourself in the past, you're jealous the first time I look at another woman. Your jealousy comes first.'

'What rights?'

'How about George?'

'I kept nothing from George.'

'So you think keeping nothing from George gives you the right to go ahead and install a second husband in the house?'

'George accepted that.'

'Perhaps he accepted because he had no other choice. Does George turn up in the mornings and ask you if you've been dreaming about me? Does he ask you if I'm good in bed? Is there one rule for you and another for me?'

'You should have told me.'

'You already knew. Who was it suggested I should see more of Nina to get me out a bit – compensate me for my celibate life while you were away from London? Who first brought that up, because I was getting dry and dull before my time? Who did that plan suit then?'

Claude got more and more angry, raising his voice as he shouted these questions at Ella, until she got up and left.

Contrary to Claude's expectation that Ella would disappear to her room as she had done the day before, she was up and about and busy with the children, rather ostentatiously so, making a kite with Alex and Philip, helping Felicity with a piece of needlework, laughing at Max's stories and even smoking pot with him when she and George sat talking with their son after lunch on the terrace. Claude found it difficult to get a word in edgeways, to fit in with the family at all. Not a word was exchanged between him and Ella, but none of the others seemed to notice. Lively and talkative, Ella monopolised the family's attention, broadening the base of her support for an impending struggle as Claude had often seen her do in the past, and the family responded to her miraculous recovery with gratified surprise. Claude was successfully marginalised, manoeuvred, as Ella intended, so unobtrusively outside the family circle that no one but Claude was aware of it being done. So he took off for the afternoon with Philip and Alex to fly the kite lower down the hillside.

When Ella came to his room the next morning, he was already awake.

'Come on,' he said as she saw her about to settle on the end of the bed. 'Slip in here or you'll get cold.'

She crept into bed and began to sob. 'I was so mean to you yesterday. Will you forgive me?'

'Of course I will.'

He took her in his arms. For a long time they lay without talking, as much caution as contentment in this silence neither of them wished to break.

'You'll have to go away,' she said at last. 'It'll break my heart, but you will. It has to be. I've tied you down. I've asked too much of you. You've got to go out into the world, I know. But then, after a while, a few years perhaps, you'll come back to me, won't you? I shall wait for you, and you'll come back to our island of your own accord. I know you will.'

She got out of bed, bent down and kissed him softly on the lips.

'Ella, don't go. There's so much more to say.'

'There's nothing more to say.'

Claude knew she was right. He felt a tear in his heart, a shiver where the fissure ran, and he understood that what had once been whole no longer was.

# 9

Claude applied for several jobs advertised in the *Times Educational Supplement*, one in Bristol, one in Grenoble, one in Nairobi, one at the University of Kyoto, the ancient capital of Japan. To his surprise, he received responses to all four applications. In early August he left Arguayo for interviews in Bristol and Grenoble, followed by two interviews in London conducted by boards acting on behalf of the universities in Kenya and Japan. At the end of the month he was offered jobs in Grenoble and Kyoto. The offer from Nairobi had been mysteriously withdrawn and Bristol had turned him down.

To Claude it seemed a foregone conclusion that he would accept the post in Grenoble. He liked the university. He liked the location in the French Alps, and he knew a few people there. He would remain in Europe, close to the family, whom he could join during vacations. The position was for an initial two years which could be extended by mutual agreement. Nina agreed that Grenoble had to be the choice.

But in the letter Ella wrote to Claude in London she argued that Kyoto seemed to her the better alternative. With a university in Japan there would be no half-measures, as there would be with Grenoble. It was about as far away as it was possible for him to go. The job there committed Claude for three years. If going out into the world to make a life for himself was what Claude wanted at this juncture in his career, giving him an opportunity to start anew, then the Kyoto position was the one he should accept. He would have to make his own way in a completely alien culture. The further away he went, the better it would be for her, wrote Ella. It would be easier for her if for the next three years she and Claude didn't meet at all.

Claude was stunned by this letter. But after he had turned things over in his mind, he saw how wise Ella's advice was. If clarifying their situation was what he and Ella wanted, his removal to the other side of the world answered that purpose far better than a halfway house in

Europe. He recalled what George had said to him on his return from Paris. The overall picture was something you got only from outside.

Claude cabled Kyoto University accepting the job.

Nina realised she had been outmanoeuvred by Ella and was furious.

'She's still got you under her thumb, you know. You can go away as far as you like, and you remain still tied to her apron strings. You do realise that, don't you? If you think this shows you are being strong, you're wrong. She's the strong one. You're little more than her puppet.' In bed Nina could be very persuasive. 'What about me? Don't I mean anything to you?'

She used a combination of sex and tears to soften him up, until Claude began to waver.

'I can't back out now. I've given my word.'

'Break it.'

Nina massaged his scrotum and took his cock in her mouth.

Claude went back to the Kensington flat, again in two minds as to what he should do. He found an envelope with a Tenerife postmark waiting for him on the mat. As he bent to pick it up, Ella's scent rose to meet him. It was in all her cupboards and the clothes that lay in them with the little sachets of lavender she still wrote off to a shop in Nyons for. In the envelope there was a dry old sprig of lavender too, almost an antique. Claude recognised it. It stood in a corner behind the glass front of the curiosities cupboard in Ella's belfry room. He had picked it from the hillside by Cornillac and used to decorate the apartment where he had stayed with Ella.

It was accompanied by a note. *I shan't be seeing you again before you leave. I couldn't bear it. Nor could you. I would say things to you better left unsaid. So I'm sending you this memento to take with you and bring back to me when you're ready to come home.*

Claude packed the sprig of lavender at the bottom of the large old trunk that had travelled with him from Paris when he moved to London to do his PhD. Now that Ella had taken leave of him, he would be departing for Japan a couple of weeks earlier than originally planned.

There was an ugly farewell scene with Nina when he told her of this decision. She called him a scumbag and he knew she was justified in doing so. He had misled her, not so much by what he had told her as by what he had failed to say. An incidental catalyst of developments in a drama concerning solely Ella and himself, Nina had been sacrificed in their interests, an expendable character whose misfortune it was to have crossed the stage during a play that had nothing to do with her. She never had a chance.

Claude had a bad last week in London and then moved on.

He took up his duties in Kyoto in the autumn. He had to work harder than he had in London. More language teaching was required than he had anticipated. It was drudgery compared to his lectures on French literature. His speciality was Rimbaud and Mallarmé, both poets on whose work he had published monographs. The translation classes he had enjoyed most in London were less satisfying here. He had to give his students English texts of which they didn't understand the nuances well enough to make translations into French a fair challenge for them or a rewarding task for himself. Claude spent all his spare time learning Japanese, hoping within a couple of years to offer a course in translating from Japanese into both French and English. The oral skills of his students were generally poor, the standard of their written language high. The enthusiasm of his students was far greater than in London, however.

The revolts that had paralysed universities throughout the West that year had reached Japan too. Ritualised confrontations between police and the national student association known as Zengakuren, with its banners and loudspeaker motorcades, disrupted the campus and neigh-bouring parts of the town. It was difficult to establish what the student demands were. The act of demonstration seemed to be an end in itself. As a teacher who had gone to Paris to support *les événements* and was dismissed from his post as a result, the faculty's new assistant professor acquired a mystique that gave him an immediate popularity among the students enjoyed by no other teacher on the staff.

It was not for that reason alone he felt more appreciated as a teacher and got greater satisfaction from his job than he ever had before. Teach-ers generally counted for much more in this country. He was astonished by the deference he was shown as a teacher, unthinkable in Europe, particularly as a *sensei* of the French faculty at Kyoto State University, reputedly the best such department in the country. *Kyodai no sensei* was a visiting card that made him persona grata with the people of Kyoto, known elsewhere in Japan as not very welcoming but rather haughty and reserved, aware of their former imperial status.

In the spring of his second year he moved out of the apartment he had been allotted in the residence for faculty members near the campus to a suburb in the foothills of the surrounding mountains. It was a quiet place, a village almost, still untouched by the encroachment of the city, with pine trees around a shrine, where he found a room for rent in an outhouse of the shrine administration building. It lacked any amenities beyond an old-fashioned squat toilet and a single tap with cold running water. He lived there for almost nothing. Half his salary could now go to Ella and Alex every month.

He learned the spirit of the place from the pages of Kawabata and other novelists of the time, whose books he read in translation side by side with the original texts. It was the slow world of natural objects that didn't change, like rocks, or which changed gradually, like trees, now and then yielding the kind of little epiphanies celebrated by Kawabata in his novel *Yama no oto*. Perhaps epiphanies wasn't the word, as Claude appreciated when he began to read haiku; commonplace events registered as slight elevations in the flatness of their context, taken in at a single copious glance. Nothing was celebrated as such. Something happened and was perceived, and the perception of it was the event.

It took him half an hour to reach the university from his village. A bicycle was the best way to get around. The city lacked urgency, carrying a cyclist gently with the flow of the traffic, or against it if need be, with no need of any such thing as a highway code, the flow managing to make way for him and his bicycle and putting him down at whatever point he wished. It was an exercise in Zen. Monks performed it on mopeds. In the Gion district he saw them with girls in flamboyant kimonos riding pillion, sometimes stopping for an iced tea at the cafe where Claude went for breakfast. He watched them pop with aplomb the plastic wrappers of the *oshibori* rolls, shaking out the hot, white flannels to wipe their smooth faces and shaved skulls. He liked the insouciance of these motorised monks, setting off to work in their robes with the same matter-of-fact air as the office workers in their suits. He liked the worldliness of some of the temples where these well-fed monks went to work. When they squatted smoking on the floor during a break in their duties, or chatted on the blue payphone in a corner between the postcard rack and the Coca-Cola vending machine next to the prayer tree at the entrance, they seemed to cordon off a part of the public domain and claim it as a private space, oblivious of everything around them, as if they were invisible. Claude amused himself imagining such scenes at St Paul's or Notre Dame.

The lack of urgency in the spirit of the city reflected its lack of ambition. Content to continue in its traditional ways, it had no ambition to grow, to industrialise, to modernise like other Japanese cities. The rituals of courtesy elaborated to give precedence to the wishes of others discouraged self-advancement, neutralised potential sources of friction and contributed to the preservation of the status quo. This you-go-first code led to scenes of virtual paralysis in the old quarters of the town, when two old ladies who met on the street were unable to stop bowing to each other, or customers arriving at the same moment at the door of the same premises were effectively prevented from entering. More time and more care was taken over these rituals of courtesy than with procedures of greeting in the West, which often required no more than a slackening of one's stride and a nod as one passed. Two people greeting one another here would step out of the flow of time. They would create an event, it seemed to Claude, a slight elevation in the flatness of the context of their meeting – a haiku written by a moment of stasis in the flow of the street.

When the ritual street protests were over, pupils continued to defer to their teachers at the university, and that sudden switch in their behaviour puzzled Claude. But the convoluted forms of intrigue under the guise of courtesy displayed by his colleagues relied on subtle gradations in the use of the language that completely eluded him. He stood outside this mysterious circle. None of his colleagues became his intimate. Conservative, they were suspicious of the escapades in Paris that had caused his dismissal and they were jealous of his popularity with the students. It was from the student rather than the teaching body that Claude recruited his friends. They emerged from the group of graduates who participated in his long-term project to translate works of Rimbaud into Japanese and English.

In the eighteen months since his arrival in Kyoto Claude had abstained from sex. It was made easier by his lack of erotic interest in Japanese women. If there were signs, he couldn't read them. He was not drawn. With the move to the room in the shrine outhouse Claude prized his celibacy, at first mistaking the tranquillity around him for a new quality of calm within himself. When going, go; when sitting, sit; but above all don't hesitate. This Zen precept began to work like a yeast in Claude. Like the monk at the temple in his corner between the blue payphone and the vending machine, he created an interstice he could inhabit, only bigger.

Japan itself was a place of non-involvement where he thought of himself as invisible. Here he could starve his endless self-chatter into silence, bring to a halt the never-ending rotations of the inner monologue with all its loose ends twitching, the thinking about thinking, the brunt of which was brought home to him by the sight of those monks popping the plastic wrappers of their *oshibori* flannels with the insouciance that so impressed him – Claude realised that until he had learned just to sit when sitting, just to go when going, he would never be able to pop wrappers as if in the moment of doing so nothing else existed. He persuaded himself he was at last beginning to achieve this.

But with the advent of the summer of his second year in Kyoto Claude found himself ambushed by the collusion of humid nights and the erotic attractions of Kyoto women. Hitherto he had overlooked their sexuality, camouflaged as it was by that most Japanese of all properties, a quality of absence, which was first brought to his attention by his friend Javier, a Jesuit priest.

In Kyoto, where many women still wore the kimono, he registered it with a shock in the nape of the neck left naked, cool and fragrant by upswept hair held in place with glossy lacquered combs. On his way home in the early evening he sometimes followed it up the hill in the defining figure of the woman who disappeared into a small bar festooned with red lanterns, where she apparently worked, a makeshift place tucked away at the end of a leafy cul-de-sac. But for the lights, it might have been taken for someone's garden shed. Later in the evening laughter was audible from this place, singing and occasionally women's shrieks. Curiosity eventually got the better of timidity. A sign on the door asked him to press the buzzer. A panel in the door slid open and the woman's face appeared. Recognising on it an expression of reluctance which had to do with his being a foreigner, Claude decided his business card would make a better introduction than anything he could say himself, and handed it wordlessly through the opening in the door.

This overture led to Claude's affair with Kimiko, which continued for as long as he remained in Japan. Much of what he learned during his stay there he owed to Kimiko, a bar hostess, and Javier. Through the mediation of these two people he formed a stronger affection for the country and rootedness in the culture to which he had been transplanted than for any place he had lived. He owed to it an education beyond anything he could have learned as an intellectual whose horizons were confined to the West, gradually coming to discern the quality of absence in which he recognised her presence the longer they were separated. *La vie est ailleurs* became something other than a nomadic longing for an elsewhere that he used to hear in those words when he first encountered them as a young man. For the object of the nomadic longing had yet to be found. Wherever the longed-for place or person might be, its doom was to be never here. But Claude now knew the elsewhere had an address in Arguayo where the longing whose name was Ella lived.

# CHAPTER FOUR

## The Trial

### 1

When Nadine and Alex came through immigration at Schipol airport, they were supposed to be met by a representative from the International Criminal Tribunal. They had been notified of this in a letter accompanying Nadine's plane ticket, sent to her weeks in advance, along with an offer to send someone to Vienna to collect her from her residence, escort her to the airport and fly with her to Amsterdam. Astonished by the thoroughness of these arrangements, Nadine had written back that she already had an escort. Alex looked at the placards held up by the drivers waiting at the exit, but the name Kelani wasn't on any of them.

'Here we go,' he said. 'Even international tribunals are human.'

They were about to head for the exit to get a taxi when a man detached himself from the crowd of people waiting outside immigration and came up to them.

'Mrs Kelani and Mr Morris from Vienna?'

'That's right.'

'Welcome to Holland. My name's Jeff Calloway? I'm here to meet you on behalf of the Victims and Witnesses Section at the tribunal and to drive you to your hotel in The Hague?'

Alex identified a trace of what he took to be a New Zealand accent, wondering at the spread of this mannerism among English-speaking people of making statements sound like questions.

'I notice you're not carrying a placard with our names,' said Alex, intrigued. 'How did you know how to identify us?'

'We have a policy at the VWS – the Victims and Witnesses Section? – of not using placards. We take a good look at the photographs of the people we're picking up from the airport beforehand, make sure we know what they look like, so that we don't have to stand around with placards displaying names for other people to see?'

'Interesting,' said Alex, the journalist in him making a mental note of a detail for the story he was thinking he might file for IPA. For the past couple of weeks he had been wondering why, in the tribunal's reply to Nadine's letter about already having an escort, she had been requested to send a photograph of the person who would be accompanying her from Vienna to The Hague.

'You say policy. Is it a security measure rather than a courtesy?'

Jeff hesitated. 'Put it like this. We do have a lot of people coming in whose presence in town isn't something we necessarily want to advertise?'

'I understand.'

Alex continued to ask questions and talk to Jeff for the hour or so it took them to drive to The Hague. Partly it was journalistic habit to pick up information as soon as you got to a place; partly it was to ease Nadine's passage to a destination he knew she wasn't looking forward to reaching. The talk ranged from the work of the VWS in The Hague to the fruit farm in Tasmania where Jeff's father grew up before going to sea, ending up in Rotterdam, where he got a job at the container port, met his Dutch wife and settled in Holland.

Nadine held Alex's hand, looking out of the window at the flat landscape they passed, and contributed nothing to the conversation. She had placed her hand in his as soon as they got into the car, entrusting herself to him, going with Alex wherever he found it necessary to take her.

For the time being, that was a small hotel in a side street off a broad avenue leading to the old palace grounds where the international court was housed. They could walk there in quarter of an hour, but a car would always be sent to pick up Nadine to make sure that she arrived on time, said Jeff's VWS colleague Wendy, the South African woman who took over from Jeff once he had delivered his passengers safely to the hotel door.

Wendy looked after witnesses while they were in town. She was already waiting for them when they got to the hotel. She was a large, comfortable, warm woman in her forties, with broad shoulders and an open face without make-up, her hair beginning to go grey, a reassuring presence in chequered slacks and a big blue pullover with a floppy neck, filling the niche in the corner of the lounge where she settled down with them to brief them on their stay in The Hague. Nadine looked out onto a courtyard where the wind was chasing leaves in spirals as the dull October afternoon began to close.

'The staff member from the VWS who welcomes you on arrival will look after you throughout your stay from start to finish,' said Wendy, smiling encouragingly at Nadine, 'and that's me, and the first thing I'm going to do is give you my card with four numbers you can call at any time, day or night, if there's anything you need. We assign every witness a special code number. We've booked your hotel room under that code to guarantee your anonymity. I'm also giving you an assistance card, which tells you how to contact the tribunal. You don't need to give your name. The code number on your card identifies you for us. Your witness assistant – me – will provide you with your daily allowance and ask you to sign for it, so why don't we just get that out of the way now ...'

Nadine took the envelope and signed the chit Wendy handed her.

'Your accommodation and meals are covered by the tribunal. All hotels offer their guests a minibar, phone in their room and pay-TV. These services aren't free of charge and won't be reimbursed by the tribunal. I've also got some general information leaflets about the court-room you may already have been sent, but in case you didn't bring them along with you. We have to remind people coming here to testify before the tribunal, and it's my job to particularly emphasise this point, that they're not allowed to discuss their testimony with other witnesses.'

'Not even to see them? My cousin will be here next week, and I really wanted to ...' Nadine's sentence remained dangling. 'Besides, she's got my mobile number. I can't stop her calling me if she wants to.'

'Of course you can't, and I don't mean to impose any sort of veto on you and your cousin meeting.' Wendy took a piece of paper out of the file on the table. 'Well now ... the revised schedule just posted by the court chancellery has an appointment for you to come in and see the assistant prosecutor at nine o'clock tomorrow morning.'

'Is that Mr Grey?'

'Yes. He'll be going through your evidence with you before you go on the stand. This could be Tuesday, it might not be until Wednesday, depending how quickly they can move things along.'

Nadine frowned. 'Again? But I've already been through it with him several times.'

'I know. But witnesses coming into court are always prepared by their lawyers a day or two in advance of giving testimony – you could call it a dress rehearsal – and this is done for a good reason. Many say this preparation time before they testify in court is the most difficult and emotional of the whole experience, but with their lawyer they can go carefully over all their statement and all the events that happened, and if they get flustered or break down in an empty courtroom then it doesn't matter. Maybe they *need* to break down and yell at the lawyer. That's what the rehearsal is for. It's been our experience that, once witnesses get into court, it's the formality and the ritual of the procedure that seems to give them some emotional distance from their story. There are no hard and fast rules about this, of course, but ... the emotional distance becomes much easier for the witness if they've already told their story under conditions as close as possible to those they'll find in court on the day.'

This introduction to the notion of *emotional distance* alarmed rather than reassured Nadine. In the event, however, the dress rehearsal in one of the empty courtrooms in the complex of tribunal buildings on the Monday morning turned out to be much less intimidating than she feared.

All that week the prosecution would concern itself with just one event confined to one place for the duration of about an hour and reliant on the testimony of just one witness – Nadine. This made the coordination of procedure, as Mr Grey called it, much simpler than when the testimony of a number of witnesses with conflicting accounts of events that might have continued in a number of places for as long as a year – as was often the case with war crimes – had to be sifted for the points on which they were in agreement or contradicted one another.

Apart from the perpetrators of the crime and the victims, the silent dead on whose behalf she had come to testify, no one but Nadine had been in the hamlet of Beli Atas on the afternoon in March 1999 when a dozen members of the Kelani household, including Nadine's own father and five of his brothers, were murdered and their bodies thrown down a well which was subsequently mined.

Five men were on trial for the murder – an officer of the Yugoslav National Army, two members of the so-called Free Serbian Militia, and two Serb policemen who served in the town of Prizren. Nadine had positively identified the first three but was unsure of the two policemen, although she had watched them for the best part of an hour as close as a few metres from her hiding place in the barn overlooking the yard. What uniforms the two policemen in particular had worn came to play an important part in the efforts made by the defence to shake the confidence of the prosecution's key witness and therewith her credibility.

'Imagine we are going through the choreography of a ballet together,' the assistant prosecutor said to Nadine, astounding her with the inappropriateness of this comparison.

'First, we have the arrival on stage of the three main characters,' Mr Grey said in pursuit of his analogy, 'the army officer Stojkovic and the paramilitaries Kvočka and Djilas. Here are photos of how those men look now, probably very different from the faces you remember, and I want you to study them so that when you are in court you will be able to name them confidently. They arrive in the yard in a jeep. For a while they have the place to themselves. This is what I call the first movement. From the hayloft in the barn you've got a clear view of what they're doing in the yard, and when they come into the barn to look at the coffin, which is standing there on trestles, you can hear clearly what they say. The two paramilitaries are right under you, taking a look at the coffin. The officer is still standing out in the yard. The prosecutor is going to want to hear from you what you heard one of the paramilitaries say.'

'You want me to tell you now?'

'Please.'

'He says, The lid's screwed down.'

'And what does the officer say to that?'

'He says, Open it, see what's inside.'

'And what's the response of the paramilitary in the barn to that?'

'These may not be the exact words, but the gist is that it wouldn't be a good idea to open it because then the smell of the corpse inside would become even worse.'

'Whose corpse is it lying in there?'

'The corpse of my grandfather, Shehu Kelani.'

'Who died of natural causes?'

'Yes. He was due to be buried that day, but owing to the arrival of the Serb forces the funeral never took place.'

'Which is why the paramilitary comes to the conclusion he does, after

570

making that comment about not taking the lid of the coffin because of the stink, and you recall his exact words, don't you?'

'He said, Seems they were all set to have themselves a funeral here.'

'And what did the other say in reply to that?'

'They still are.'

'And then the *coup de grâce* of this first movement involving the three main protagonists, the remark made by the officer, who's remained stand/ ing out in the yard while his co/workers have been taking a look at the coffin inside the barn just below they hayloft where you are standing. You heard and can still recall the exact words he said. What was it he said?'

'Let's get to work. This is a nice quiet place. We'll do it here.'

'Let's get to work. This is a nice quiet place. We'll do it here. Very good, Nadine. And then we have that piece you dug out from the tran/ script of the tape that was played at the Krstić trial, Wouters, relating to the word *work*.' Mr Grey snapped his fingers impatiently. 'During the Srebenica massacre. Have you got it there, Wouters?'

The young man who was sitting on the podium, representing the judge, took a piece of paper from the file on the desk in front of him and passed it down to the assistant prosecutor.

'The following is from a conversation between General Krstić and his adjutant Major Obradovic that took place during the massacre of seven thousand civilians at Srebrenica. We hear the same word *work* used that the witness has just told us she heard used by the commanding officer in the yard at Beli Atas minutes before a group of men were murdered there.'

Mr Grey put on his spectacles and read from the paper Wouters had handed him: 'Krstić: Are you working down there? Obradovic: Yes, of course. Krstić: Good.' Mr Grey looked up at his assistant on the podium. 'In both cases they call it *working*. Have you checked the Krstić original and compared it with the expression used by Stojkovic in Mrs Kelani's testimony?'

'It's the same word in both,' said Wouters.

The assistant prosecutor resumed reading: 'Obradovic: We've got a few others, with firearms or in the minefields. Krstić: Liquidate all of them! Obradovic: Everything's going to plan. Krstić: Not one of them is to remain alive!'

Mr Grey took off his glasses and handed the paper back to Wouters. 'The same *work* was done in Beli Atas, and not one of the men there remained alive either. The chief prosecutor, my colleague Mr Rasmus-sen, will read that transcript at the trial.' He turned to Nadine. 'Having done so, he will resume with the second movement, exactly as we have already rehearsed it, Nadine, and if you are as word-perfect tomorrow as you were today, then –' the lawyer held up his open hand and snapped it shut '– we'll have them in the bag.'

# 2

Alex reached into his coat pocket for his ID on arriving at the visitors' entrance to the tribunal at nine o'clock on Tuesday morning and realised that he had left his wallet in the hotel room. He had run upstairs to fetch a packet of tissues for Nadine, who was already ten minutes late and sitting in the car that had been sent to take her to the witness centre at eight o'clock. Handing the tissues to Nadine through the car window, he had gone back inside to drink a cup of coffee and then set off for the tribunal on foot. Both of them had overslept – on this morning of all mornings – and in the rush to get ready in the forty minutes before the car arrived for Nadine, she had forgotten her tissues and he must somehow have managed to leave his wallet behind.

There are no mistakes for no reason, Ella used to say to him when he mislaid things, and as he got into the taxi to take him to the hotel and bring him back again to the court, he wondered what objective was being pursued contrary to the apparent intention in his mind. The answer could only be that he didn't really want to listen to Nadine giving evidence in court, knowing how reluctant to do so she was herself.

Back at the tribunal building the smell of wet paint painfully re-inforced that thought with a memory of redecorating his apartment with Nadine earlier that summer – wiping paint off their fingers, a happiness he had never before seen in her – when she had completely forgotten what awaited her in The Hague.

Having passed through the metal detector, obliged to leave his camera and tape recorder in the safekeeping of the guard there, he ascended marble stairs and then the narrow iron staircase that led up to Room 3. After the tedious walk along the uniform white corridors of the build-ing, the immeasurably longer approach of the months preceding this moment of arrival, arousing both their expectations, Room 3 was an anticlimax, a paltry little room. How preoccupied he and Nadine had been with the day when she would give evidence at the ICTY, how big and significant that day had loomed in their lives – and now he found himself in a space not much larger than his own living room with not a single other visitor present.

A presumably bulletproof window separated the visitors' auditorium from the courtroom. On his side stood rows of blue plastic chairs, on the far side a room with white walls. There was nothing to distinguish it from any ordinary room in any ordinary building, no dark panelling, pictures, emblems, flags or anything of the kind one might have expected in a traditional court of justice. It might have been the waiting room of some nondescript government office.

Alex sat down in the middle of the front row. Over the tannoy he followed an exchange between one of the judges and one of four men sitting on the left. The judge spoke English, the official language of the court, his interlocutor Serbo-Croat, allowing Alex to dispense with the interpreter's translation over the headphones he had been issued at the desk downstairs and to follow proceedings in the original languages of the participants.

The men sat not more than a few yards away from him; the podium where the three judges presided was at the centre of the room, the defendants and the counsel for the defence to their left, the prosecution to the right – huddled together as if there wasn't enough space. Interpreters' booths flanked the courtroom on both sides. In front of the judges' podium was the registry bench, and in front of that, almost close enough to reach out and touch, was the witness stand where Nadine was giving evidence.

Not that he could see Nadine. A white plastic screen between the witness stand and the public gallery made her invisible. She was visible to the defendants, however, and they to her. The information sheet Alex had picked up at the press room identified them by name: Dragoljub Stojkovic, Anto Kvočka, Radomir Djilas and Zoran Kovac. Four very ordinary-looking men, they might have been travelling salesmen taking a break from their rounds, sitting on a bench and comparing notes. Looking at them in their unaccustomed suits and ties, Alex was reminded of the view put forward by his friend Andro about the ordinariness of evil and the ordinariness of its perpetrators. Charged with the murder of a group of civilians they took captive in southern Kosovo in March 1999, these four were the defendants in Case IT-937/10 being tried by Justices Roberts, Brundtland and Dallachiesa of the International Criminal Tribunal for the former Yugoslavia, convened to hear the evidence of witness FWS-309, whose testimony was scheduled for that morning. A fifth defendant by the name of Stepanovic was absent.

Chief Prosecutor Rasmussen got up to continue his questioning of the witness, which had been interrupted by Judge Roberts to clarify a point raised by the defence on behalf of their clients.

'You have described to us how you overheard three of the defendants, Stojkovic, Kvočka and Djilas, talking in the yard about the *job of work* they proposed to do. Then they got back into the jeep and drove away. How did you react to what you heard the three men discussing?'

'I was scared. I realised the danger I was in.'

Nadine's voice came over the tannoy clear and firm, if rather subdued.

'Did you take measures to protect yourself in any way?'

'I looked for a better hiding place. I climbed out of the hayloft into a space, about a metre high at the tallest point, between the roof beams of the adjoining cowshed and the ceiling, where I couldn't be seen and felt safer.'

'What happened next?'

'The back door of Shehu's house opened and some soldiers came out.'

The prosecutor walked over to an easel displaying a diagram of Beli Atas. He picked up a cue and pointed at Shehu's house in the middle of the hamlet.

'The soldiers came out of this house here?'

'Yes.'

'And you watched them from your hiding place under the roof of the cowshed adjacent to the barn, here?'

'Yes.'

'What do you estimate the distance to be between the house and the barn?'

'About twenty to twenty-five metres.'

'What were the soldiers doing whom you saw come out of the house?'

'They were guarding the men who had been kept prisoner in the house and they were now bringing out into the yard.'

'How many men?'

'My father and five of my uncles were among them, and then there were a few more I didn't know, so … I suppose there would have been about ten or twelve in all.'

'Where were these men taken when they were brought out of the house?'

'They were lined up along the wall of the cowshed.'

The prosecutor indicated the spot on the diagram on the easel.

'Here? So if you were positioned in this space between the roof and ceiling of the cowshed, they must have been standing directly underneath you.'

'Correct.'

'What happened after the men had been lined up along the wall?'

'The commander came into the yard, the man they addressed as Captain.'

'Do you see him in this room?'

'He is the second on the left over there.'

'Are you sure? Would you stand up, Stojkovic?'

There was a pause as the man got to his feet.

'That's the man,' said Nadine.

'Did the defendant Stojkovic come out of the house?'

'No, he came into the yard from the left, from the gap between Shehu's house in the middle and the house of his son Baci to the left.'

'Was he armed?'

'He was carrying a pistol. He walked up and down the line of men, shouting at them and waving the pistol. He said he knew the villagers were all KLA supporters—'

'Kosovo Liberation Army,' interpolated one of the judges.

'Yes, and the captain – Stojkovic – wanted to know how they were getting arms into Kosovo. Pllumbi, my uncle, said he didn't know anything about it, and this made Stojkovic so angry that he called him an Albanian swine and shot him in the face. Then they searched all the men and collected the money they took off them in a bucket.' Nadine hesitated. 'Shall I go on?'

'Please.'

'While this was going on the commander conferred with the two paramilitaries in a corner of the yard. One old man—'

'Could you be more precise?'

'About the old man? I don't know who he was.'

'Who do you mean by the commander and the two paramilitaries?'

575

'I mean the defendants, Stoj—' Nadine stumbled over the name. 'Stojkovic ... Kvočka ... and Djilas.'

'Thank you. Please continue.'

'One old man couldn't produce documents to identify himself, and he was told to step forward out of the line. He must have been beaten before. I could see blood on the top of his bald head. He was marched across the yard to the truck where the captain – Stojkovic – and the others were standing. But Stojkovic walked straight past the old man as if he didn't see him, and went over to the men who were still lined up against the wall of the shed. He was followed by Kvočka and Djilas and an MUP man, judging by his blue uniform, and they—'

'MUP, meaning a military policeman? Was this the defendant Zoran Kovac sitting on the extreme right? Stand up, Kovac.'

'Was it this man?'

Nadine hesitated again. 'I can't say for sure. He was too far away for me to see his face clearly and he was wearing a cap.'

'Very well. You were saying that Stojkovic walked across the yard and was followed by Kvočka and Djilas and someone you identified as an MUP man by his blue uniform. What happened then?'

'The three who had followed Stojkovic stood by while he told the men lined up along the wall that they were all swine and that they were helping the KLA to kill Serbs in Kosovo, which made them traitors guilty of insurrection against the state. Then, without another word, he returned to the truck where the old man was standing and ... shot him in the back of the head, and then the three other men opened fire with machine guns, shooting all the men who were lined up against the wall. Soldiers, Yugoslav Army men, dragged the bodies over to the well in the middle of the yard and tipped them in. Then everyone left the yard. After a few minutes the back door of Shehu's house opened and a blond man wearing faded fatigues with the word MILICIJA printed on his back – he had long hair at the time but he has since shaved his head—'

'Is he present in the courtroom?'

'He is sitting beside Stojkovic.'

'To his left or his right?'

'I mean the man on the right, Kos or Djilas, I don't know which because I keep on getting their names muddled up.'

One of the three judges on the podium cut in sharply: 'The man to the left of Stojkovic is Anto Kvočka, the one on the right is Radomir

Djilas. Is the man on the right the man you saw come out of Shehu's house after the bodies had been thrown down the well?'

'That was the man,' Nadine said with a slight quaver in her voice.

'I would ask the witness not to use descriptions to identify the defendants but always to refer to them by name or the number displayed above the chair on which the defendant is sitting.'

'But the names I heard them called at the time were different. The man on the left was called Mirko and the man on the right Tuta.'

'Never mind that now,' said the judge testily. 'You're only confusing the issue.'

'And what did this Tuta, or as you now know him to be called, and as we must continue to call him to avoid confusion, this Radomir Djilas do?' asked Rasmussen gently, resuming his examination of the witness after she had been reprimanded by the judge. 'What did you see him do?'

'He threw a hand grenade down the well.' A sob broke from Nadine and she began to cry.

Alex squirmed on his seat as he listened to her weep over the tannoy. Poor Nadine!

The judge who had interrupted Nadine must have come to a similar conclusion. Witness FSW/309 had already been on the stand for over an hour and a half that morning, he said, and he suggested that the court adjourn for a break to allow the witness a respite before she was cross-examined by the defence in the afternoon.

# 3

During the adjournment Wendy was on hand with comfort and cups of coffee in the witness waiting room, where Nadine arrived distraught after coming out of court.

'I was a disaster,' she said, flinging herself onto the sofa.

'Now don't you worry. That's what they all say when they come back here. I'm sure you did fine.'

'I did *not* do fine,' exploded Nadine. 'Were you in there yourself? How can you even *say* I did fine when you've no idea what happened in court? I got names mixed up and failed to recognise a man I'd positively identified during a line-up when I was here six months ago! Do you think I should tell them I had some sort of a mental blank when I go back in there? What sort of a witness will they take me for?'

But it was no good talking to Wendy or asking her advice. She wasn't allowed to say anything that could have an influence on the evidence a witness gave in court. Wendy tried to distract her with amiably banal conversation that Nadine wasn't in the mood for. She asked her to shut up. So for the next ten minutes the two women sat side by side in silence, until Nadine apologised, giving Wendy the opportunity to offer words of consolation acceptable to Nadine. That's what she was here for, Wendy said humbly, just someone around for witnesses to work off their feelings on, but this offering of the other cheek only made Nadine even more irritated – and then the twenty minutes for the break were up, and an usher came into the waiting room to announce that the court was ready to continue.

Had Mr Grey put in an appearance to offer a few words of reassurance, Nadine would have felt happier about going back into court for what she had been warned might be a tough session on the witness stand, the crossexamination by the counsel for the defence. As it was, she took the stand with the unpleasant feeling that she'd let Mr Grey and Mr Rasmussen down. She convinced herself that their dissatisfaction with her was shown by the fact that they'd neglected to come and see her in the break.

The counsel representing the four defendants was an unusually tall, knobbly GermanIrish lawyer by the name of Kuensberg. Mr Grey had warned her that he was very 'sharp'.

Nadine had taken stock of Kuensberg and his deficiencies when she came into court that morning, noting disapprovingly the way his black gown flapped around his skimpy frame. It was a stained and tattered little gown, really a disgrace to the court, much too short for a man of his height. Did appearing like this in public reflect a lack of vanity or a lack of modesty? It certainly showed lack of respect, and that offended her. The gown should have been taken to the cleaners or replaced. She knew the international court in The Hague cost millions of public money. Wasn't there someone at the tribunal responsible for little things like decent gowns?

With an absentminded air, apparently quite unconscious of his unsatisfactory appearance, the shabbygowned middleaged Kuensberg could hardly have been a married man, thought Nadine, for what self-respecting wife would have let her husband go to work looking like that? Wanting vaguely to do something to make the counsel for the defence more favourably disposed to her, she caught herself thinking that Kuensberg was thin and needed feeding up, just as her mother had once thought of feeding up the construction worker Selim – an almost inarticulate foreigner, as her father was when he began showing up for his coffee and bun at the patisserie in Leopoldstadt.

Her unfavourable impression of Kuensberg changed from the moment he opened his mouth, surprising Nadine with a lilt to his speech she found attractive. The soft-spoken lawyer had intervened only a couple of times and with apparent reluctance in the prosecutor's questioning of the witness that morning, predisposing Nadine to make allowances and do her best to like him.

Having requested the usher to turn off the lights in the courtroom, Kuensberg went shambling over to the easel and, with a touch of a button on the remote he was holding, transformed it into a screen onto which a photograph of a huddle of buildings was projected.

'Does the witness recognise this scene?' the lawyer asked in a tone of voice that sounded as if he was preparing to tell her a joke.

'Yes,' said Nadine.

She wondered how a photograph of Beli Atas could have found its way to The Hague after the hamlet it showed had been razed to the ground and everything in it destroyed during the war five years previously.

'What are we looking at?'

'The houses in Beli Atas.'

'Where do you think the picture might have been taken from?'

'Well, we are looking at Shehu's house in the middle—'

'Would you mind stepping over here and illustrating what you're saying to make it easier for the court to follow?'

Another invitation to Nadine to conspire with him in a forthcoming joke. She got up and went over to Kuensberg, who handed her a cue.

'Please use the cue to indicate the buildings you are talking about.'

'Here on the left you can see Baci's house,' said Nadine, pointing, 'with the tree growing at the corner adjoining the yard. The building at the centre is Shehu's house, and in the foreground is the well.'

'And where was the picture taken from?'

'From the opposite side of the yard, where the barn is, beside the cowshed.'

'So would this have been the view you had from the barn at the time of the events you described to the court this morning?'

Nadine pondered.

'My point of view was lower than this. It's confusing ... because there are no windows in the barn where this picture could have been taken from, so I don't know how it was done.'

'Ah.'

Kuensberg proceeded to illuminate the court: 'According to a member of the family who used to live in Beli Atas, who took this photo ten years ago before leaving home and going to live abroad, the picture was taken from a ladder propped up against the side of the barn. So was the next.'

It showed a view of the yard to the right, looking along the barn, against which the ladder was leaned, with the cowshed adjacent and Pllumbi's house visible in the background.

'Can you indicate the place where you were hiding, from where you watched the execution of the men in the yard?'

Nadine pointed the cue at a spot under the cowshed roof.

'About here, in the space between the roof and the ceiling.'

'You were lying there looking over the edge, were you?'

'Yes.'

'So you were very close to the events you have described – the firing squad by the wall of the shed – perhaps just a few metres? Don't you think?'

'It took place directly below me.'

'The problem with this bird's-eye position,' said the lawyer in his amiable sing-song way, 'was that while it gave you a good view of the yard, it prevented you from seeing what was happening directly below. Don't you think? The upper part of the wall of the shed juts out here, you see, creating an overhang which would have prevented you – what am I saying – which *must* have prevented you from seeing the lower part of the wall where the men were lined up who were subsequently shot. This picture taken from a ladder surely makes evident that it would have been a physical impossibility – don't you think?'

Kuensberg indicated the lower wall of the shed along which the men had been lined up for their execution, the tip of the cue tracing an imaginary line up the wall to the overhang, then one or two metres sideways, following the jutting overhang out before arriving at the top of the wall under the eaves of the roof where Nadine had been hiding.

'An impression, no doubt unintended by you, may have arisen in this courtroom that you actually *saw* what you so vividly described. But when we consider in detail the viewpoint from which you say you saw those men executed against the shed wall, we are bound to ask, *Can* the witness in fact have seen that?'

'It was obvious they were being executed.'

'But did you *see* them being executed.'

'No, I didn't actually see the——'

'Thank you. You may return to the stand.'

Furious to have been cut off and not permitted to have her say, baffled that anyone could stoop to such hair-splitting in such a serious matter and be allowed to get away with it, Nadine resumed her seat in a state of agitation.

The defence lawyer had remained standing where he was, the upper half of his body swaying slightly as he contemplated the screen now showing again the first of the two pictures the court had seen of the yard in Beli Atas.

'How good is the witness at estimating distances?' Kuensberg asked, and in what Nadine had taken for his courteous manner she caught for the first time a tone of mockery. 'This morning you told the prosecutor that you estimated the distance from the barn to the house on the far side of the yard to be twenty to twenty-five metres.'

He drew an imaginary line with his cue across the image on the screen.

'In fact, this distance between the barn and the back door of the house from which the prisoners emerged is thirty-one and a half metres.'

The lawyer drew another line, from the barn to a car standing at the entrance to the yard.

'The car in this picture is on the spot where the jeep and later the truck were parked, must have been parked, because driving any further into the yard would have been obstructed by the well, so thirty-four metres *minimum* from the point where witness FWS-309 was watching. And some of the events she watched would have been taking place even further away from her hiding place under the roof of the shed.'

'Where is this leading us?' one of the judges asked.

'The distances relate to the problem of making accurate identifica-tions,' said Kuensberg, 'particularly in the case of the defendant Kovac, sitting here within ten metres of the witness, who by her own admission she had difficulty identifying with certainty as the man who followed Stojkovic from the truck – here – to a point in front of the wall – around here – where three men opened fire with machine guns. The witness positively identifies two of the men as Kvočka and Djilas, but what about the third? *He was too far away for me to see his face clearly and he was wearing a cap* is what she told the court in the evidence she gave this morn-ing. Those were her words. And yet at an identification parade eighteen months ago she positively identified the defendant. This discrepancy has to be clarified.'

He returned to his desk, where his colleague handed him a document, which Kuensberg held up for everyone to see.

'Interpol has developed a procedure for identifications under the conditions obtaining in closed rooms. Reproducing in closed rooms the conditions under which identifications were originally made of people seen outside at a distance of thirty yards and over raises problems because there aren't many courtrooms of that size. At a closer range one has to show a proportionately smaller identification target, and there's a mathematical formula for the distance–size ratio, which has been tested by the Interpol specialists who concern themselves with such things and found to be fair and reliable. In this courtroom, for example, the distance from the witness stand to the screen is fifteen metres, half the distance at which the witness saw the MUP in the yard at Beli Atas, so an image of the MUP reproduced in this courtroom has to be correspondingly smaller. This is the case with the holograph image that will now appear on the screen. The image was put together by Interpol specifically for our purposes. The man in a cap you are about to see has been scaled down in proportion to the distance from which the figure is being viewed in this room.'

He pressed the remote, and a man shown three-quarter face appeared on the screen wearing a blue uniform and a cap.

As Nadine looked at the figure an irritating feeling came over her that she knew this man on the screen but couldn't quite place him. She didn't know where she had seen him but felt confident it had been quite recently.

'Well?' Kuensberg, all conjurer now, had a jaunty manner betraying he had something up his sleeve and that he was about to produce it at last. 'Can you tell us who this person is?'

'I have seen him before – I *know* I have – but ...'

The lawyer waited for a while before he sauntered over to the witness stand. 'Shall we enlarge the image and take a closer look?' The bottom half of the figure disappeared; the head and torso were brought into close focus. 'This is now larger than life, the sort of memorable proximity one has to a person only under close if not to say intimate circumstances.' Adding in an undertone audible to Nadine but not intended for the rest of the court, 'Hasn't that been your experience, my dear?'

Nadine looked at the man standing in front of her, then up at the man on the screen, and realised with a shock that they were the same person. It was Kuensberg himself.

# 4

The insolence of that question Kuensberg tagged on, the outrageousness of the lawyer's gratuitous rhetorical twitch at the end of his crossexamination – that *my dear* sting in the tail – didn't fully sink in until it woke Nadine up in the middle of the night, causing her to repeat the question aloud to herself.

*Hasn't that been your experience, my dear?*

Only then did she realise what the lawyer must have been referring to with his obscure phrase *the sort of memorable proximity one has to a person only under intimate circumstances*: It applied to the three defendants Stojkovic, Kvočka and Djilas, on trial this week for murder, regarding whom Nadine had never wavered in the confidence of her identifications. Why did it apply to them but not to the military policeman in his cap and blue uniform, Zoran Kovac? Because Nadine had not been in the same proximity to him as she had to the three other men. These men, and two others, would be on trial again during the second week on charges of rape. She had not seen Kovac at close enough quarters – so the lawyer had been insinuating – to remember his face as well as she remembered the faces of the men who had raped her on several occasions.

But if it had been Kuensberg's intention to undermine Nadine's resolve to carry on by intimidating her, then he had calculated wrongly. Bewildered on the first day by the array of arcane technicalities he brought to the case, staggered though she was by so much irrelevance to the reality of what she had experienced, the idea of wanting to see justice done persisted so stubbornly in Nadine that during the second and third days of the murder trial she refused to allow herself to be discouraged again.

*This is my experience and I shall not let anyone take it away from me* became the mantra she heard inside her head when she sat in the waiting room before being summoned into court. The defence could come up with whatever tricks they liked. It made no difference to the strength of Nadine's determination that the defendants she saw sitting in court would be found guilty of her father's murder, and if that firmness had been momentarily shaken by the unarguable contention that she could not have seen what happened to the men lined up against the wall, it only served to reinforce the memories of the executions she unarguably *had* witnessed — the killing of her uncle Pllumbi and the old man with crusted blood on his head, both of them shot by Stojkovic at close range.

So what was the point of the attempts made by that mercenary defence lawyer she now despised for daring to equivocate with the truth she had in her keeping, and for which she alone was responsible? So what if she hadn't seen men falling down at the exact moment they were hit by bullets? One minute she had seen the executioners firing with machine guns, the next she had seen the bodies of their victims dragged across the yard and thrown down the well. Where had those dead bodies been conjured from? Did they have nothing to do with the bullets that had been fired at them? Had they already been dead and lying in a pile before those shots were fired at the wall? Ignoring a question she was asked during one of the interminable hair-splitting exchanges she was subjected to by Kuensberg, Nadine couldn't resist letting fly with one of her own.

'Tell me, *dear* Mr Kuensberg,' Nadine said, interrupting his cross-examination. 'Did all those dead bodies have nothing to do with the bullets fired at them?'

For a moment the world stood still. Pins could be heard dropping in court.

'Ha ha!' jeered Nadine. 'So where did they spring from then? Were they lying there ready in a pile by the wall?'

The presiding judge intervened to reprimand the witness, warning her of the consequences of contempt of court.

Hours were spent reconstructing the events of that afternoon in March. The lawyer for the defence and the witness for the prosecution stood side by side while they argued the choreography of the killings step by step, indicating with their cues the exact points on the photograph projected onto the screen what persons had been standing where and when before moving with whom to what other spot in the yard at Beli Atas.

It had all once seemed clear enough to Nadine but now it became so confusing she began to lose track – and this disorientation was just what the defence intended. Had Nadine really seen all that? How could she remember it so well five years on? How could she say with certainty that one man at this spot had worn a green uniform and another man at that spot a blue one?

Because she had been required to go through the sequence of events so many times already in the course of her preparation by the prosecution. Because the details were like scars in her mind it was impossible to explore without pain. This deep structure in Nadine's memory, scoured by so many questions repeated in endlessly different forms, hammered away at by Kuensberg in an attempt to crack not so much the truth as the witness's confidence in the truth, only hardened as a result of his battering. *This is my experience and I shall not let anyone take it away from me.* The mantra reminded her to see it as she saw it with ever greater clarity, not to allow herself to be diverted by obfuscation.

In the defence counsel's view, however, the witness had become only the more inured to errors the further they became ingrained. Repetition was not a servant of truth. It merely compounded those errors – burned them deeper into her brain. He had demonstrated such errors with his argument about the impossibility of the witness having seen the execu-tion of the men by the wall. He had shown that an identification at a distance of thirty metres was a matter of opinion rather than of fact. He sought out other weaknesses, and by a process of attrition in the course of hour-long cross-examinations, he found them.

He established that in the aftermath of the salvo of machine-gun fire, Nadine must have kept her eyes closed for several minutes and that she had mistaken the military policeman Kovac for the fifth defendant Stepanovic, who was prevented by illness from taking part in the trial. And so on, a trail of corrections that gave rise if not to doubts then to reservations about the credibility of the witness. Whenever hesitation occurred in her narration of the sequence of events, the obliging imagination of the lawyer supplied her with alternative readings as plausible as her own. That the defendants named had been present in Beli Atas during the events that took place there in March 1999 was not at issue. Too many other witnesses testified to having seen them there to allow denial of that charge to have any chance of holding up in court. But what the defendants did deny was the perpetration of a massacre, and the plain and simple strategy followed by their defence counsel was to argue mistaken identity.

The defence took advantage of the fact that marauding bands had killed and burned and disappeared again in Kosovo without ever having been brought to justice. Often the bodies of the dead supplied the only facts verifiable in the aftermath of the chaos, evidence of crimes but not of their perpetrators. What if the bodies of the old men had already been lying at the bottom of the well in Beli Atas at the time of the defendants' arrival there? Where was it written that such a possibility could be ruled out? As the prosecution lawyers reminded Nadine when they met at the end of every day to review the position, if the defence succeeded in eroding the credibility of the sole witness of that massacre, then the prosecution risked losing its case. She must not waver again as she had during Kuensberg's first cross-examination. She must stand firm.

'It's your word against theirs.'

The defence would step up the pressure day by day. They would impute base motives to explain why the witness was testifying against the defendants at all, argue that she was producing testimony out of thin air, insinuate within the discretion allowed by the judges that she did so to get her revenge on them for their repeated abuse of her in the course of the three days they spent in the hamlet. They did not deny those and related charges outright, although they had yet to be substantiated, but as for this murder of a group of old men they had never seen before in their lives – they had not done what they were charged with having done. Why should they have done so? What possible interest, even interest in an enemy, could they have had in some feeble old men? Whereas the witness had compelling reasons for bringing against the defendants, alleged to have raped and tortured her and many others, charges of crimes against humanity that could put them behind bars for the rest of their lives.

In the course of the week Nadine became aware of a burden she thought she had placed irremovably on the shoulders of the defendants being transferred back to her own. It was her testimony *and hers alone* that had made it possible for the murder charge to have been brought against the defendants. This was the status quo on which the court's formal position rested. Denying that charge, the defendants' formal position in court was that they had done nothing. She accused; they denied. The accuser was required to be active in the prosecution of any accusations upheld by the judges, to bring that burden of proof which until now Nadine naively assumed to have already been brought clearly enough by the mere presence of the defendants in court. But they merely shrugged and held up their hands, protesting their innocence. It astounded Nadine to discover the brute power of the disclaimer, the denial, not just of responsibility for an act, but of the commission of any act at all. That *nothing* – which constituted the ground staked out by the defence counsel – proved to be more easily maintained than that *something* which was being insisted on by the prosecution – namely three specific acts of murder. The defence continued to challenge these acts on one point or another, forcing the prosecution to substantiate the charges over and over again.

It seemed to Nadine that not one trial but two trials were taking place in the same courtroom. The defence substituted a set of hypotheses for the set of events she had experienced, changing all the protagonists and spinning a web of arguments based on the premise that nothing in the world was as unreliable as what a witness claimed to have seen – and it felt to her as if the floor of the world on which she stood had been taken away, leaving her dangling in mid-air.

# 5

A taxi pulled up sharply on the other side of the street.

'Nadi! Oy! Nadine!'

Drita unfolded her long legs out of the taxi and came screeching across the road, all flying arms and scattering heels, ignoring the traffic and only narrowly avoiding getting herself run over.

'It's me!'

Nadine embraced her cousin through a fog of perfume and pecked at her cheek through an entanglement of spiky hair. She wore a denim miniskirt, black leggings, a black leather jacket, large earrings the colour of her burned-red hair and high-heeled red shoes that made her even taller than she already was.

'No pearls?' She pulled at the collar of Nadine's camel-hair coat and peered inside. 'Aren't you wearing a string of pearls with a coat like this?' She cackled. 'Is this the idea of fashion they have in Vienna? Are they as conservative as *that* over there?'

'I don't think so. It's just me who's become rather conservative over the last few years.'

'And you've put on weight.'

'And you've got even skinnier.' Nadine took Drita's thin arm and set off down the street. 'At least *you* seem to have remained yourself.'

Drita laughed.

'Up, up.'

'Up?'

'Higher than I used to be.' Drita stopped, took out her purse and squeezed it open. 'Try one. It'll make you feel good.'

Nadine took out a yellow pill, looked at it and dropped it back. 'Where do you get this stuff?'

'Ibrahim. He's a businessman. He deals in just about everything. If you know how to look after yourself, life in Tirana isn't as bad as you might think.'

'He's stood by you, hasn't he? Through all of this. He looks after you.'

'Me and a few others.'

'Shall we go in there?'

Nadine followed Drita into an Italian restaurant just down the street. 'What others? What d'you mean?'

'He has other women. One of them even has a child by him.' Drita slung herself around the corner table into the niche. 'I don't blame him. If his wife can't have children ...'

'But you *had* a child.'

'That was before I had an abortion, stupid.' Drita hurled the menu across the room. 'For God's sake! One can't even sit down and order a meal before all this has to start coming up!'

A waiter picked up the menu and brought it back, and to Nadine's surprise Drita — suddenly all smiles again — spoke to him in fluent

Italian, apparently some story about chucking a menu around, which made the waiter laugh.

'I told him we had a bet.'

'I missed that bit. Where did you learn your Italian?'

'It's just a couple of hours across to Bari in a speedboat. Ibrahim's business often takes him over there, and he takes me along with him. He's in with the 'Ndrangheta – they run Calabria, you know – and he handles the Albanian side of the connection for them.'

'Drugs? Isn't that rather dangerous?'

'Dangerous?'

Drita took the cigarette out of her mouth and screeched, 'It's fun! Whatever's happened to you, Nadi?'

'I guess I've just calmed down.'

'But you're only thirty-two.'

'You and I had fun together when we were kids, but I was never wild like you.'

'So I suppose this boyfriend you're here with is a quiet type too.'

Nadine smiled. 'I took him to a disco this summer. It was the first time for him. In the ten years he's been living in Vienna he'd not been to a disco once.'

'Doesn't sound as if he's a lot of fun.'

'No, I don't think you could say he is.'

'Is he good in bed?'

'I could imagine he might be.'

'You mean you haven't slept with him? How long have you known him?'

'About a year, on and off.'

'And didn't he ever want to make love to you?'

'He does make love to me. Only he does it in a different way.' Nadine fiddled with the oil and vinegar bottles on the table. 'I haven't wanted to be with a man since then ... You know.'

'And he accepts that? He doesn't complain?'

'He understands. Maybe because he's a bit older.'

'How old is he?'

'Forty-five.'

The waiter arrived at the table to take their order. Drita enjoyed flirting with him in Italian. He enjoyed it too, so the ordering took a long time. Nadine began to regret having arranged for the two of them to meet on their own, and she wondered what they would find to talk about for the rest of the evening. She was caught off guard when Drita said after the waiter left, 'You know they got one of those men.'

'What men?'

'It was in a bar in Tirana. Two years ago. I was there with Ibrahim and some of his Italian friends. A dirty little weasel of a man got drunk and started bragging about the women he'd had. The voice, the Kosovo accent – it took me a while to remember where I'd heard it before. When he mentioned the Kosovo war to one of the men he was drinking with, I was quite sure. I went over and asked him for a light so that I could get a closer look at him – and there he was, the man the others in Pllumbi's house called the Gypsy. *Gypsy*, they said, *here's one for you! Take her away and do what you like with her!* Maybe he *was* a Gypsy. I don't know. But it was him, all right. I knew that. I remembered everything he'd done to me upstairs in Pllumbi's house – how could I forget? Now that I think of it, I never found out his name. I suppose we could have asked him his name before he died. Anyway, we didn't. His name didn't matter any more. With or without a name, that was the end of him.'

Drita lit another cigarette, her hands shaking, and took a deep drag.

'Aren't you going to ask me what they did to him? Ibrahim and his Calabrian friends?'

'I can guess.'

'No, you can't. They cut off his balls. They soaked his prick in petrol and set fire to it. They shoved a poker up his arse and left him skewered to the floor.' Drita exhaled a thin wraith of smoke. 'They did it to him in a warehouse at the docks. I waited outside and heard his screams through the walls. When they came out, they told me what they'd done. In case you're wondering, here's what he did to me.'

She pulled up her T-shirt and exposed her midriff, pitted all over with blotches and scars.

'Cigarette burns and bites, and not only here. God! My poor breasts, what little there is of them – my groin – my thighs! The burns – when they go deep enough – leave the skin discoloured. The bites leave scars. In court they showed pictures of what it looked like two weeks after – taken by people at Medica, much much worse than they are now. They've faded since, but they're still there. We can go into the toilet – I'll show you if you want to see the rest. Ibrahim made me undress and show my scars to the Gypsy so that before he died he'd admit what he'd done and know why they were doing what they did to him. They left a note with *VENDETTA* on it on the shaft of the poker so that when the body was found and taken to the morgue they'd also know there why the man died. Good riddance to him. At least they nailed one of them.'

Drita stubbed out her cigarette savagely.

'I spent all yesterday in the witness box. It was me in the morning and Minavere in the afternoon, my own mother. Her sister Majlinda is on tomorrow, and it'll be your turn the day after. Not that anything will come of it. This trial is a farce.'

'No, it's not. The men charged with the murders of Baci, Pllumbi and Selim will be convicted and sent to jail.'

'Jail! Pah!' Drita pulled a magazine out of her bag. 'I saved this to show you. Here's where they're going, this … jail by the sea. What's it called? Here. Scheveningen. Look at it! It's a holiday camp.' She ripped angrily through the pages. 'Order in groceries delivered to the jail – cooking facilities for the prisoners so that they don't miss their home food – fitness room and sauna – swimming pool, table tennis – TV, films – all the magazines they want – healthcare beyond the dreams of their victims back in Bosnia. Some of them get off with eight or ten years. They get remission – the first murderers and rapists they got in Croatia and Bosnia back in the 90s will be out in a couple of years from now.'

'But not these ones, Drita. There were some Bosnian Serbs convicted here a couple of years ago for the rape of women in Foča, and they were given much longer sentences – twenty-five, thirty years – because that's no longer just rape, that's now classed as a crime against humanity.'

'Nadi, what good is that to you and me or to the thousands of other girls who don't qualify for a crime against humanity because there were only two or three of us and we were raped only a couple of times? And what about all the other beasts who got away? There must have been twenty of thirty of those animals in Beli Atas. Look how many of them are on trial here – five! Thousands, tens of thousands of those animals are still on the loose, lounging around in small-town cafes, and they'll never be made to pay for what they did.'

Even the waiter arriving eagerly with their orders, ready for another round of flirtatious banter, failed to get another smile out of Drita. He hovered with offers of Parmesan, pepper, another bottle of mineral water, but he was no longer wanted.

Popping another of the yellow pills and smoking one cigarette after another, Drita didn't take any interest in what was on her plate. Neither of them spoke for a while. Nadine twirled her fork slowly in her food with no intention of putting it in her mouth.

'How was it for you, giving evidence yesterday?' she asked eventually. 'But maybe you don't want to talk about it.'

'What difference does it make? It was a joke, Nadi. That creep, the blond jerk with a long knife who used to cut himself and drink his own blood – did you see him doing that?'

'Yes.'

'What a jerk. Who did he think he was impressing? But he was shooting heroin as well – Tuta I remember them calling him – he was one of the men in the dock and I had a few things to say about him. Only about him. Two others I remember raping me weren't there, so those bastards are probably sitting around in Priština or Zagreb or somewhere. But as I sat in the waiting room thinking how disgusting it was going to be to go into court and tell all those men about being forced to have sex with those animals, I only had to remember the Gypsy's screams to start feeling good. That's what got me through, that more than the pills or anything. I told Minavere about the Gypsy, hoping it would do her good, but she was horrified. How could we have done such a thing? It made us as bad as they were. And so on. Well, as you know, my mother and I haven't been on speaking terms for a long time. But they put us in the same hotel, despite the witness rule, us being mother and daughter – after all, how are you going to prevent *them* from talking? How could they know we didn't talk in any case? And I went and knocked on her door to find out how she was and I heard her crying in her room, but she refused to let me in. After what I'd told her about the Gypsy she said she never wanted to see me again. So what happened in Beli Atas has finally done for my mother. It really has. She's moved in with a cousin in Suhareka, but I don't see her putting a life together for herself ever again.' Drita swept cigarette ash off her skirt. 'Do you see *any* of us, come to that.'

Nadine put down her fork. 'Let's leave, shall we? What's the point sitting here pretending to have a meal neither of us wants?'

Nadine called for the bill, paid and walked with Drita back to the hotel.

'Would you like to come in and have a drink?'

'What would we talk about, Nadi?' She put her arms round Nadine and hugged her tightly. 'Maybe in ten years. I know there's no chance of you making it to Tirana, so I'll come and visit you in Vienna.'

She got into a taxi waiting at the kerb. Nadine watched her waving from the rear window until the car was out of sight before she turned and walked back into the hotel.

# CHAPTER FIVE

## In Kosovo

### 1

Alex was caught up by the dynamic of events that had swept him along since he began to work as the IPA's Balkans correspondent. The 1995 Dayton Agreement provided a brief respite in the relentless Yugoslavian conflict, but like many other observers of the ceasefire Alex didn't overlook the fact that one word missing from the agreement mattered more than all its provisions. That word was Kosovo. Retaining control of Kosovo was of enormous emotional significance to Serbia. In order to achieve at least an end to the ethnic cleansing that had been carried out in Yugoslavia with such savagery for the last four years, the accord brokered under the aegis of President Clinton and signed by Slobodan Milošević in Dayton, Ohio omitted any mention of Kosovo.

The summer of the year following the Dayton Agreement Alex flew down to Priština with a Viennese radio journalist on a second trip to the capital of Kosovo. Bit by bit, the Serb government in Belgrade had been dismantling Albanian institutions in the autonomous province for years. The process of Serbification had been initiated in 1989 by a famous speech given by Milošević before a crowd of half a million people on the site of a medieval battlefield sacred to the national memory of the Serbs. Discrimination against the majority Albanian population began in the immediate aftermath of this speech. The transfer of real estate between Kosovo Albanians could take place only with the permission of the Serbian authorities. Albanian personnel in the state hospitals of the province were dismissed for incompetence. The statute that allowed teaching in secondary schools and at the university to take place in ac, cordance with an Albanian curriculum was repealed. Albanians in the

594

local administrative, media, education and health services were replaced by Serb nationals.

The Kosovo Albanians responded to this by withdrawing into political negation, what they called inner emigration. They boycotted the Serb-dominated administration, replacing it with a shadow government which duplicated all the organs of the official state. They founded their own schools, health service, business institutions and services, creating an economy that circumvented Serbian banks. The shadow state and its institutions were supported in the main by Kosovo-Albanian workers living in Switzerland, Holland, Germany and Austria, who sent their pay packets back home from abroad. In 1990 this shadow administration acquired legal status under the name Republic of Kosova, with Ibrahim Rugova as its elected president and a presidential office in humble wooden barracks in the shadow of Priština's giant football stadium.

Alex parted company with the Viennese journalist at the barracks, where the latter had an appointment for an interview with Rugova, and set off across the market to visit the primary school that was the purpose of his own visit. The school was closed for the summer holidays, but the school janitor, or rather janitors, had agreed to show Alex around the school, or rather schools, for there were two of them in one building — the official school conducted by the state and attended by Serb children, and the shadow school run by the shadow state and attended by Kosovo Albanians. This particular building demonstrated better than anything the apartheid system in Kosovo which Alex was investigating.

First it was the Albanian janitor's turn to show the visitor the half of the school that came under his jurisdiction, or rather less than half, for the Serb administration had built a wall across the premises which gave the Albanians about a third of the space. The wall cut across corridors, staircases and classrooms. All the passageways in the building were dead ends sealed with steel doors to which each of the janitors possessed a key in the event of an emergency. The apartheid school had two entrances for its two nationalities. The school bells rang at different times in the two divisions to ensure that children didn't intermingle in the playground during breaks. Timetables were coordinated to make sure that pupils didn't meet in the gymnasium either. Each school had its own curriculum and language of instruction, Serbo-Croat and Albanian.

Two and a half thousand children were taught here, said the Kosovo-Albanian janitor to Alex, showing him into classrooms that had been

divided from the Serbian side of the school and subdivided again
with thin partitions to create additional rooms. Desks and chairs were
crammed in so tight that children sitting at the back had to climb over
them to get to their places. Because there were so many pupils and so
little space for them, the janitor said, teaching was done in shifts, beginning early in the morning and continuing until evening. The classrooms
were bare of ornaments or decoration of any kind.

On the other side of the wall six hundred Serbian children, or one
fifth of the total number of pupils, had been allotted almost twice as
much space, but it was with reluctance rather than proprietorial pride,
perhaps embarrassed by an inequality it was impossible to overlook,
that the janitor there showed Alex around. Pictures of Serb dignitaries
and historical heroes hung in the corridors. The bright and spacious
classrooms had been freshly painted. The windows had curtains; pot
plants lined the windowsills.

Secondary-school pupils and students who enrolled for higher
education had the choice of accepting Serbo-Croat as the language of
instruction or boycotting state institutions and improvising their own.
A network of Albanian shadow state schools held in private homes,
workshops and premises put at their disposal by Kosovo-Albanian busi-
nessmen, reached out from Priština to isolated villages in the mountains.
Albanian teachers dismissed from state schools resumed the instruction
of their former pupils under these makeshift circumstances, but as the
state refused to recognise the diplomas issued by such schools, their
graduates had no prospect of finding employment. A generation of
educated Albanians was thus lost to Kosovo society.

Early the following year, before the Kosovo negotiations were resumed
in Paris, Alex made a last trip down to Priština to see for himself the
situation on the ground just as the conflict there was escalating. Tanks
rolled across the border into northern Kosovo as the Yugoslav Army
shelled houses and turned the local population out of their homes. Their
villages destroyed, tens of thousands of refugees made their way south
and south-west to cross into Albania and Macedonia. Unable to verify
this exodus as long as he remained in Priština, Alex took up the offer
of a Kosovo Liberation Army recruiting agent he met through his local
contacts to accompany him on a tour of small towns and villages in the
mountains where they were preparing for the Serb onslaught. It was only

after he and Bardhyl left Priština that he realised he had left his mobile in the cafe where they had breakfasted that morning.

# 2

Selim Kelani's father, Shehu, the patriarch of the multi-family household in Beli Atas, died at the age of ninety-three. On the same day in March the peace negotiations in Paris between the Serbs and Kosovo Albanians, which had reopened only days before, were broken off and never resumed. There was no advance warning of Shehu's coming end, no faltering, Pllumbi told his younger brother Selim when he called him in Vienna; just a clouding, which their mother remarked on during the last months of his life, of his pale blue eyes. In the cold weather they had been having, Pllumbi said, Shehu's body could lie in state in Beli Atas for the four or five days until the funeral was held. It would take that long for the members of the far-flung Kelani clan to assemble, some of them flying home from places as distant as Kuwait, others coming on foot through the snow over the mountains from Albania. Counting family and old friends in the Drenica region, Pllumbi reckoned there might be as many as a hundred and fifty to two hundred people at their father's funeral. Selim assented to everything Pllumbi said. The first of Shehu's sons, Pllumbi was now the patriarch of the clan. His word was now law.

Nadine naturally questioned Pllumbi's word, just as she had opposed Shehu's before. She took the phone out of Selim's hand and spoke to her uncle herself. Her father had not been well since his second stroke. His doctor had warned against undue exertion. It would be better if he didn't attend the funeral. Personal problems apart, to arrange a large-scale funeral – any sort of gathering in Kosovo at this time – was an unnecessary provocation. It was madness even to contemplate it. This was not the moment for displays of solidarity by Kosovo Albanians, however legitimate the cause might be. The Serbs would only see a large funeral as a cover for the KLA to get its message and perhaps weapons distributed, or rather it would suit them to represent it as that, and so it risked being used by the Serbs as a pretext for another massacre.

By the time she and her father reached Macedonia, the delegations of the Organisation for Security and Collaboration in Europe stationed in

Kosovo, where Nadine and Selim were now bound in the car she hired at Skopje airport, had already been withdrawn in the opposite direction. Before they crossed the Macedonia–Kosovo border at Blace, Nadine spoke to the members of an OSCE contingent on the side of the road from Skopje, who did their best to dissuade father and daughter from continuing their journey. Surely the fact that they too were now leaving was the clearest possible sign of the imminent danger – it was no longer a question of whether but when NATO would fly the first bombing missions over Yugoslavia.

It was no use.

It seemed that Château de Rambouillet was somewhere people had never heard of in the Kosovo mountains, despite the fact that for months the name of the place was repeated daily on the Deutsche Welle and BBC satellite broadcasts, which could be received with the modern technology paid for by expatriate clan members like Selim. Not the slightest hint seemed to have reached Beli Atas of the storm that immediately began to brew on the breakdown of the talks in Rambouillet, even though the Kelani household was already bursting with refugees from Suhareka, all of them women and children. Their husbands and fathers had sent them away from the towns into what they persuaded themselves was the safety of isolated country regions. Nothing would happen to them out here.

The notion that Beli Atas would be unaffected by the build-up of Serb military and police along the Kosovo border – during the preceding weeks it had already led to the expulsion of tens of thousands people from their homes in the north of the province – seemed to Nadine to be somehow bound up with the authority still wielded by Shehu even in death, lying in state in an open coffin in the middle of the big room upstairs in his house. Had it been a woman lying there, Nadine felt, there would have been no need for macho sabre-rattling; in the altogether more flexible Yugoslavia she imagined run by women, one would have settled one's differences and reached a peaceable settlement.

Bundles of dried ferns had been laid along the walls and covered with blankets to make sitting on the floor of the large unheated room more comfortable for those like Nadine who were not accustomed to it. A collection of mattresses in one corner provided the children with a nest where they could settle. Normally only the men gathered in the vigil room, sitting smoking on the floor in their socks, their shoes left at the door, while the women bustled around bringing tea and refreshments.

Nadine didn't mind doing her bit on behalf of the household, but she would not be prevented from sitting beside the men in the room where the vigil was taking place.

This room held for her the fascination of the first corpse she had ever seen. She paid most of her visits at night, when she could be with her grandfather undisturbed by the presence of others, the room lit by candles – Pllumbi and Baci had long since had electricity installed, but the old man had never permitted it in his house. Lying with his head slightly raised in the open coffin, Shehu seemed prepared to rise and reassert his authority at any minute. Standing alongside the coffin – supported on trestles that raised it to the height of her breast – Nadine needed only to lean over and incline her head slightly had she felt disposed to kiss the corpse, which she most certainly did not, though she had seen many of her relatives doing so when they came to take their leave of him – just watching them made her shudder.

It was not Shehu in death that repelled her, it was Shehu hardly changed from her recollection of him in life. Ten years had passed since she had last seen him. Now she committed to memory the high forehead under his still-flourishing head of white hair, a shrivelled white scar on the lid of his left eye, the prominent hook nose and thin-lipped mouth that had always carried for her the imprint of his absolute will. That nose and mouth above the patriarch's flowing white beard were the particular seals of office of the *zadruga*'s patriarch, the beaky features of his asperity formed into an expression of disapproval or cold disdain, which Nadine had feared as a child and still feared when she stood alone with the corpse in the room at night.

On the second night she went to pay a solitary visit to her grand-father's corpse Nadine was struck by an unpleasant smell in the room which she hadn't noticed the day before. Standing at the open window, seeing flashes on the horizon followed by a thunderous rumbling, it took her several moments to realise what the light was: NATO had begun bombing Serb military positions in northern Kosovo. And as for the other thing, well, there was no help for that either. She held her nose. In the couple of days since Nadine and her father had arrived in Beli Atas the last cold days of winter had given way to the first warm days of spring. The body of the patriarch had begun to stink.

Nadine went back downstairs to the room with the big stove where the men sat smoking and drinking coffee after the women had cleared the supper table before retiring to eat their leftovers in the kitchen. Standing at the door she managed to catch her father's eye and indicate to him that she wanted to speak to him outside. Selim got up and followed her out.

'NATO have begun bombing.'

'We heard it on the radio,' said Selim.

'And Shehu's corpse has begun to smell. You can't wait any longer. He's got to be buried first thing in the morning.'

Selim rubbed the back of his neck, as he always did when he felt awkward.

'Pllumbi has just been discussing it with us. Three brothers still haven't arrived. We've agreed to give them until the day after tomorrow before we bury our father. In the meantime, we'll bring the coffin down and set it up in the barn tomorrow.'

'Set it up in the barn? Tomorrow? You're crazy. Bury him immediately or the Serbs will be here before you get the old man under the ground.'

'Nadine, I'm not having you speak of your grandfather in that disrespectful way. You make things hard enough for me here as it is. Do you realise the sort of things I have to listen to my brothers say about you?'

'I can imagine what they say about me and I don't care. You should be ashamed for your brothers, not for me. Bury him tomorrow, and then let's leave right away. Please, Selim! I promised Mother. The Serbs will be coming from the north, and Drita says that the road south to the border is still clear, but who knows for how much longer.'

Drita was Baci's youngest daughter, who had left home against her father's wishes and gone to work in Tirana. About the same age as Nadine, Drita and her Viennese cousin had always been the rebels in the Kelani clan, self-willed girls who Shehu had felt were a personal affront to the traditions of family dignity founded on women's respect for the prerogatives of men that were in the patriarch's safekeeping. In her father's house Drita made a show of penance while she laughed up her sleeve.

The women had been put in Baci's house for the duration of the funeral, not just the Kelani women but in-laws from elsewhere. Then there were the refugees from Suhareka and villages in its immediate neighbourhood who had been moved into the mountains for safety after the murder of a Serb policeman had led to reprisals among the local Kosovo-Albanian population. Baci's wife Minavere counted over fifty guests in her house, a quarter of them girls under fourteen. They slept on beds of hay and dried ferns in all the rooms of the house, romping around because they had got out of school early in order to leave Suhareka for what they were told was a holiday with their cousins in Beli Atas.

The boys and the men were quartered in Pllumbi's house, but during the night the NATO bombing began most of them left Beli Atas to join the KLA fighters who had taken up positions in the forest above the hamlet. The remainder made their way up as soon as it got light. With Serb army and police forces flushing the KLA out of their strongholds in Budakovo, Vraniq and other places to the north, the Kosovo-Albanian militias were moving into new positions along the main routes leading south to Albania, Macedonia and Montenegro. The older members of Shehu's immediate family, both men and women, had been put up in the patriarch's house under the nominal supervision of his widow Igballe and his eldest son, Pllumbi, but it was Shehu's unmarried youngest daughter Emina who really ran the house – a woman who, without ever having taken the formal step, came close to being acknowledged as a *virdjin*. She dressed like a man, wore her hair cropped short like a man, and she was reputed to possess a gun. It was Emina who catered for the guests and kept track of their numbers. She told Nadine that a hundred and fifty people were accommodated in Beli Atas during the week leading up to Shehu's funeral.

With the younger men all gone overnight, it was a group of the patriarch's older sons, Selim at sixty-two the youngest of them, who closed the coffin the following day, carried it downstairs and set it up in the barn while the women burned herbs to clear the air in the room where it had stood. Nadine took a photograph of her father and her five uncles in the barn beside the coffin in a trapeze of sunlight that swung through the open door – all of them lean men with bony close-cropped heads, all wearing dark suits with a white shirt and black tie. They stood motionless in silence for a few minutes, as if waiting for the old man to issue instructions. Only when their eldest brother moved to the door after what he judged to be an appropriate interval did the others follow suit.

As they came out of the barn they saw puffs of smoke in the valley below and seconds later heard explosions on the mountainside behind them, almost as if the Serbs had been waiting for them to appear in the barn door as a signal to open fire. Nadine could make out armoured personnel carriers and tanks moving up the Suhareka–Prizren road near the junction with the track where the bus stopped for passengers getting off for Beli Atas. Stupidly she wondered what the Serbs thought they were doing, firing shells over the hamlet to detonate only a few hundred metres away in the woods above. Some of the shells fell short, exploding on the fields below Beli Atas, where they grazed livestock. Nadine stood beside her father and uncles at the entrance to the barn, unable to believe what was happening.

'What are they doing? They can't do that!'

They dashed across the yard into Shehu's house.

Emina at the kitchen door was already issuing instructions to her two sisters-in-law to assemble the younger girls in Pllumbi's house. The older women should accompany the girls, slip them out at the back into the woods and take the trail up to the summer pastures. They could shelter in the huts. It would be cold up there, but they would find blankets and supplies of food to see them through the next few days.

'It's dangerous for them here. Get them together and go. Follow the gully that runs to the east; it'll be safer than the woods to the west where the KLA are probably taking cover. Go now! Go, go!' she said, opening the back door and pushing the two women out.

A shell exploded within a stone's throw of Shehu's house, rattling the window panes. The older men ran back out into the yard to gather the small children who hadn't understood what was happening and were still playing outside. A pack of barking dogs streaked off over the fields in the direction of the firing, but one of the men put his fingers in his mouth and whistled them back. The mothers of the playing children came running out of the two other houses, swept them up into their arms and carried them into safety inside the house.

'Are they trying to kill us, or what?'

'It's the KLA they're gunning for, not us. They're still finding their range, you'll see.'

The old men crowded around the narrow windows to follow what was going on outside. The barrage was now continuous but the impacts sounded further away – to the west, as Emina had said, where the KLA were returning fire from a wooded ridge that curved down into the valley and ended in a shorn-off promontory overlooking the road where the Serb artillery was now located.

'See? That's our boys! They're giving away their own positions in order to draw the fire away from us.'

'Go on! Give it to 'em!'

A cheer went up from the group at the window.

Hurrying past on her way upstairs, where she had heard Emina calling for someone to come and help, Nadine noticed the eager expressions on the old men's faces, including her own father's, the same tense eagerness she had seen on his face, leaning forward in the upright chair where he sat watching football on TV at home in Vienna. To them this was still a game, she thought with astonishment, struck by the contrast with Emina's efficiency in the bedroom upstairs, where the mattress was turned back to reveal a row of flat fish-shaped packages on the bed board wrapped in white cloths and tied with string. Her aunt Emina was taking them two at a time and stowing them as fast as possible in a wicker washing basket.

'Take off your grandmother's jewellery for her – the earrings, necklace. Quick! The comb in her hair. Hurry!'

Igballe sat upright on a chair by the wall, her eyes open but almost blind, deaf depending on who was talking to her, and gave no indication of having understood what her daughter had said. But she put her hand up to resist when she felt Nadine unclasping the necklace at the back of the neck.

'We must put your jewellery away, Mother,' Emina said, 'because you won't be needing it now. The funeral has been postponed.'

'Where shall I put it?' Nadine asked, holding up the necklace.

'Just lay it on the coverlet there.'

Carefully Nadine extricated the long-toothed comb from the crown of her grandmother's head, admiring the mass of upswept silvery hair, its vitality undiminished, as full as Shehu's had been until the day he died. She recognised the ornamental comb as a present Selim had bought at a sale of bric-a-brac in the Dorotheum in Vienna and given his mother for her birthday. She held it up to watch the colours change in the sheen of the mother-of-pearl.

'Don't dawdle. We don't have much time.'

Nadine looked out of the window. With a sinking heart, she saw a convoy of trucks had turned off the road and was driving up the track that led across the fields to Beli Atas.

'They'll be here in five minutes,' said Emina.

She took the comb from Nadine, wrapped it up with the other items in a linen cloth and placed it on top of the rest of the packages, unfolded the mattress back into place and smoothed the bed.

Emina picked up the washing basket and handed it to Nadine. Then she arranged a rug over her mother's knees, draped a shawl around her shoulders and patted her hand.

'You sit quietly here. I've got one or two things to see to downstairs, but I'll be back in a minute in case there's anything else you want. All right?'

Igballe indicated she had understood with a nod of her head.

At the bottom of the stairs Emina opened the back door leading into the yard. Nadine followed her out.

'Go around behind the chicken coop and enter the barn from the back,' Emina told her. 'You'll see a cross-beam running the length of the hayloft. Lay the packages on top of the beam. No one will be able to see them there, even if they're standing in the hayloft. This is all we have – money, jewellery, pieces of silver – everything of value the Kelani family owns. Hurry!'

'What shall I do with the basket?'

'Leave it lying on the floor.'

Emina turned back into the house.

Clasping the precious basket, Nadine made her way around the back of the chicken coop into the cowshed and on through a connecting door into the barn. Across the yard she heard trucks driving up out of sight on the far side of Shehu's house – doors slamming – men shouting. She ran up the flight of wooden steps to the hayloft. Taking two packages at a time, she stood on tiptoe with her arms above her head and placed the packages on the top of the beam just as Emina had said – fifteen of them in all – how long it took! – bending and stretching eight times in succession. At last the basket was empty.

'Only just in time!' Nadine said to herself, her heart beating very fast. Kicking the basket away from the wall, she turned and pressed her face against a crack in the boards that gave her a clear view of what was going on outside in the yard.

# 3

The view from the hayloft was framed by a corner of Baci's house to the left and part of Shehu's house to the right. Between the two houses there was a gap of thirty to forty metres, looking down through the still-leafless orchard trees around the houses over a grassy expanse that ended a couple of kilometres down in the valley, where the Prizren–Suhareka road marked the boundary of Kelani land. For quite some time, to Nadine's irritation, nothing appeared in this gap that might have given her a clue as to what was going on. Several more vehicles had meanwhile come up the track. They must have stopped somewhere in front of Pllumbi or Shehu's houses to the right, but she couldn't see them or any of the Serb soldiers who had presumably arrived in the trucks. All she heard was a lot of men shouting, women shrieking and children crying. Then there was a salvo of gunfire and in the silence that followed she heard shouts of, 'Go down onto the grass! Everyone onto the grass!' The order was given in Serbo-Croat first and then in Albanian.

A soldier in the green camouflage uniform of the Yugoslav Army backed into the gap holding a machine gun. It was pointed at the people who now began to appear from the far side of Shehu's house. Two more Serbs were with them, one wearing army uniform, the other the blue camouflage gear worn by Serb MUP police units – outfits familiar to Nadine from the many hours of coverage of the wars in Croatia and Bosnia she had watched on TV in Vienna. They stood with their backs to the barn, waving the women and children past with their guns, making sure that no one tried to slip off through the yard. More soldiers appeared on the far side of the crowd of people, forming a cordon to keep them all together and herd them down the hill away from the houses. 'Go down! Go down!' they shouted at intervals when their prisoners hesitated, unsure whether to stop or keep going. The women carried the smaller children, the older ones held the hands of mothers and aunts beside them. Nadine could make out the cumbersome figure of a Suhareka woman who was heavily pregnant. Emina was immediately identifiable by the light blue dress Nadine had noticed her wearing that morning, incongruously hitched up and tucked into the tops of her boots. There was no sign of her grandmother, however, or her father – not of any men, come to that. In the crowd making its way down the slope Nadine spotted only boys not yet in their teens.

At a distance of a hundred to two hundred metres from the houses the crowd came to a halt. It was too far for Nadine to make out what was happening. She could hear the soldiers' shouts but not what was being said. Little by little, however, the clump of people grew smaller as some of them moved to the left, others to the right, while others remained where they were. It looked as if they were being divided into groups.

At this moment two jeeps drove into the yard, obscuring Nadine's view of what was happening on the meadow below. Three men got out. One of them, judging by his uniform and the stars on his cap, must have been an army officer. The two others were different from any of the Serbs she had so far seen. One of them had a shaven head and wore a black singlet, showing tattoos on his muscular neck, chest and arms. He carried a machine gun slung over his shoulder. A knife, perhaps as long as thirty centimetres, hung in a sheath at his belt. The third man was dressed in faded camouflage fatigues with the word MILICIJA in Cyrillic letters on the back. He had long blond hair and a moustache that drooped at the corners of his mouth. This man too wore a long knife, but unsheathed, dangling from a loop attached to his belt. He remained standing by the jeep after the others had got out, busy with something she couldn't make out until he held up his arm and Nadine saw to her surprise that he was injecting himself.

The officer leaned against the front of the jeep, knocked a cigarette out of a pack and lit it. He said something to the blond man, who in turn spoke to the man in the black singlet, and the three of them laughed. A conversation ensued which lasted about ten minutes. From where Nadine stood listening it wasn't possible to follow what they were saying. Only the officer faced her. He was looking towards the open barn so he must have seen the coffin standing on trestles inside it, but he didn't seem to register it. But then he pointed at it and said something that caused the two other men to turn. Both walked in to take a look, passing directly underneath Nadine standing in the hayloft.

'The lid's screwed down,' she heard one of them say.

'Open it,' called the officer leaning against the jeep. 'See what's inside.'

'I don't think that would be a good idea,' said the voice that had spoken before. 'Even with the lid shut it stinks. Seems they were all set to have themselves a funeral here.'

'They still are,' put in the other man, and they both laughed.

'Right,' said the officer, flicking his cigarette butt across the yard. 'Let's get to work. This is a nice quiet place. We'll do it here.'

They got into the two jeeps and drove out of the yard, parking both vehicles outside Baci's house. Nadine saw them cross the gap, heading in the direction of Shehu's house.

But they would be back soon, and Nadine realised what danger she was in. If someone climbed the steps they would see her in the hayloft. She looked around for a place to hide.

The roof of the barn dovetailed with the roof of the adjoining cowshed. There was a gap of about a metre between the concrete ceiling of the shed and the timbers of the roof. Long wooden poles for constructing hayricks were kept in the space between. Gouges in the main upright beam provided finger- and toeholds making it possible for Nadine to climb up from the hayloft and crawl into this space. If she lay flat up there she would probably be invisible even to someone standing in the hayloft. On her hands and knees she moved further in and lay down by the wall. She had been up here as a child, playing games of hide-and-seek with her cousins. She was on an overhang directly above the entrance to the cowshed. Although Nadine could see the area just in front of the entrance, she couldn't see the entrance itself. She could hear the couple of cows the family kept for their milk scraping the floor with their hooves and rattling their chains when they moved their heads over the trough, and she found the warm brew of smells that drifted up to her in her hiding place reassuring.

Nadine had been installed there for only a few minutes when the back door of Shehu's house opened and two soldiers came out. They stood aside to let out the men they had been keeping under guard inside the house. The men emerged in single file with their arms raised – her father and her five uncles and a few other older men she didn't know. They were followed by two more soldiers, or rather policemen, judging by their blue uniforms, who poked their machine guns into the men's ribs, herded them across the yard to the cowshed and told them to line up facing the wall with their arms above their heads.

To Nadine the men lined up against the wall of the shed were invisible under the overhang. She sensed it was just as well she couldn't see everything because if she had she couldn't have failed to recognise it as a firing squad. She didn't dare look over the edge of the overhang. All she could see was the part of the yard onto which Shehu's back door opened, the well in the middle and the area to the left in front of the barn. It was from here that the officer with the stars on his cap reappeared. Pistol in hand, he walked up and down looking at the men lined up against the wall a few metres away and yelled at them in Serbo-Croat.

'We know you pigs have been sheltering the KLA,' he shouted at top speed in Serbo-Croat. 'We know you've been providing them with arms as well. Where did the arms come from? Albania? What kind of arms? How did you pay for them? Where do you keep them hidden?'

Silence.

'Well?'

'No arms,' Nadine heard Pllumbi say gutturally. 'No KLA men.'

The officer put the back of his hand to his cap and nudged it on to the top of his head.

'Step up here, you Albanian swine, and tell me that to my face.'

Pllumbi shuffled forward.

'Go on. Repeat what you said.'

'No arms.' Pllumbi hesitated, perhaps regretting the words already out of his mouth, as if he sensed what might be coming. 'No KLA men here.'

'You think I'm a complete idiot?' the officer asked with a frown. 'Then think again.' He raised his pistol and shot Pllumbi in the middle of the forehead at point-blank range.

Pllumbi staggered back. Nadine heard him crash against the wall as he fell.

Her heart pounded in her mouth.

A soldier came around the corner of the house and stepped up behind the officer as he was lighting a cigarette.

'We're ready with the women and children, Captain.'

'Wait. Keep them in the field. We aren't finished here yet.' He jerked his head at the corpse. 'Search him for money, documents.'

An MUP policeman came forward. Nadine could see one of his heels as he knelt down to search the corpse. When he rolled Pllumbi over, one arm flopped out. She saw a hand and a white sleeve sprinkled with blood. The policeman stepped back and dropped a wallet into the bucket someone held up.

'Let's have a collection,' the officer said.

The man with the bucket disappeared into the fast-lengthening shadow under the eaves of the cowshed. The two men Nadine had seen arrive with the officer reappeared in the yard and stood with their backs to her talking in low voices with him. Below her, the man carrying the bucket hovered in and out of her vision as he passed down the line, saying, 'Come on, old man, faster,' taking from the men out of sight under the overhang a jumble of keys, wallets, loose coins and paper money and tossing them into the bucket, which he then emptied onto the back of a truck behind where the officer and the two men stood talking.

One of them reached into the pile, fished out the identity cards, counted them, counted the men standing against the wall and called out, 'Before we brought you out here you were all told to have documents ready to prove your identity. But one man hasn't. Let him step forward.'

No one moved in the yard.

The policeman who had searched Pllumbi's corpse came up to the officer and the two paramilitaries with the knives and said, 'Some of these old men don't understand Serbo-Croat too well. Perhaps I should repeat what you said in a language they do.'

The officer nodded without looking up from the stack of documents he was flipping through, and the MUP man translated his order into Albanian. By the sound of it, he was a local man. Nadine guessed he was a Kosovo Serb.

A man who must have been in his late seventies or early eighties stepped out from beneath the overhang directly below Nadine. Strands of white hair lay sparsely over the crown of his head and a patch of dried blood where something must have struck his skull. He trembled.

With his machine gun the policeman motioned him forward to the truck where the officer was standing. The officer paid the old man no attention, walked past him as if he wasn't there. The MUP man and the two men with knives followed him across the yard. Stopping some distance from the cowshed, the four stood facing the prisoners still lined up against the wall.

'All you swine come from Beli Atas and belong to the Kelani clan, a family known to support the aims of the KLA. Many members of that family are themselves active in the KLA. All of you are guilty of insurrection against the Serb state and of the murder of members of its armed forces.'

The officer turned around, walked swiftly up to the old man waiting by the truck and shot him in the head. While the shot was still echoing around the yard the three other men opened fire — overlapping bursts of deafening machine-gun fire that ended as suddenly as they began, leaving a shattered silence in the yard. Nadine pressed her hands over her ears, pressed her mouth against the concrete floor to stop herself crying out – froze for what seemed a long time in this position so as not to give herself away.

When she lifted her head and looked down into the yard she saw soldiers dragging the bodies of the men who'd been shot across the yard. Two other men picked the corpses up and tipped them into the well. Nadine stuffed a handkerchief into her mouth – the cry not allowed to escape her mouth detonated inside her, convulsing her body.

The soldiers left. Minutes passed. It was still in the yard. Nadine lay gagging silently into her handkerchief.

Then the back door of Shehu's house opened. The blond man in the faded fatigues with MILICIJA printed on the back came out, followed by the man in the black singlet, who said something to him and laughed. Leaning against the door smoking a cigar, the man in the singlet watched the blond man walk across the yard. The blond man took an object out of his pocket, gave it a pull and tossed it casually into the well as he passed. Moments after he had disappeared between the two houses there was a terrific roar underground and the well exploded, leaving a smoking hole in the middle of the yard.

# 4

Nadine lay where she was for a long time without moving. She grew numb with cold. Even if she had dared she doubted she would have been able to move, or that she would ever again wish to. All the old men, her father among them, had been murdered. But when she heard men shouting again and the voices of women and children, the instinct of self-preservation got the better of her and she raised her head to find out what was happening. In the gap between the two houses the people who had been taken down to the fields were passing back and forth, some of them going into Baci's house, some of them into Shehu's. There were no men among them. The only men she'd seen since Emina sent her into the barn with the basket were the old men who'd been shot in the yard. Thinking back to the early morning before the Serbs arrived, she couldn't remember having seen any men except for her uncles. Why hadn't the younger men carried the coffin to the barn? Because they weren't there. All the younger men had gone up into the hills before the Serbs arrived. Perhaps that was just as well. The Serbs would have killed them just as they had killed the older men.

It was getting dark. Cold and uncomfortable though her hiding place was, Nadine felt there a measure of safety that made her reluctant to give it up for another. She wouldn't be able to spend the night here, however. When she had considered her options she had tended to assume – without giving the matter closer thought – that she would head up into the hills and alert the KLA to the massacre that had been carried out in the hamlet. The men must come back and rescue the women and children.

But for the time being it seemed preferable to Nadine to remain where she was and do nothing. So she stayed put. She watched the lights going on in the houses, the slow glimmer of the oil lamps in Shehu's, the switching on of electric lights in Baci's. Four soldiers came out of Baci's back door. One of them pointed and explained and the other three listened then set off in different directions. The other man went back into the house. Nadine heard the soldier setting off through the gap between the houses call out something that sounded like *midnight* to the man who was taking the path between the chicken house and the cowshed leading up the hill into the woods. Perhaps this meant that sentries had been posted and that the first watch lasted until midnight.

Turning this over in her mind, Nadine realised she might not be able to get past the sentry into the woods without getting shot. To attempt to leave the hamlet in the opposite direction and head down to the road was no less dangerous. The safest place for her was with the women and children in the house. But how to get into one of the houses? Naturally, the doors would be guarded. She lay and brooded over this problem until she happened to look up and saw the branches of the tree outside Baci's house silhouetted against the window as they stirred in the night breeze.

Of course!

How many times during summer nights at Beli Atas had she and Drita climbed out of that window and down the tree outside the house! How important it was for the games they had played! The friendly tree was easy to climb – once up it she could sit and look through the window to see if the coast was clear before getting into the house.

Nadine crawled back to the notched beam and let herself down into the hayloft. There she waited and listened. In the darkness she could see nothing. Then she climbed down the steps into the barn. Her bladder was bursting. She squatted to pee. She heard sounds coming from the houses, the cows rumbling in the shed below her, but in the yard it was quiet. As she made for the outline in the dark that she recognised as the frame of the barn door her foot caught on one of the trestles supporting the coffin and she stumbled. – What a noise! – She froze, one hand on the ground where she had fallen, expecting someone to challenge her, switch on a light. Kneeling in the dark on the barn floor, she resigned herself to dying. She could smell Shehu in his coffin and felt sick. After all that she'd witnessed they would shoot her without giving it a second thought.

But no voice called out. No one challenged her. No light went on. Gingerly she moved forward to the lighter patch in the dark that was the barn door, crept across the yard outside and hid by the trunk of the tree growing up the wall of Baci's house. There was a risk that when she got up to the window she would become visible to someone standing at the edge of the woods above the cowshed, but that was a risk she would have to take.

'There are always risks.'

She pulled herself up into the branches and put her face to the window to see what was going on in the room where she and Drita had spent the last few nights with a dozen other girls – family, friends, refugees from Suhareka. The room was empty.

'I can't risk staying here and being seen at the window. It's either back down or in.'

Nadine reached up to the top of the window. It had never closed properly, not for as long as she had been coming to Beli Atas. Give it a good tug from outside and the window would open, which it did, and she scrambled in. Just as she did so she heard someone coming upstairs. She squeezed behind a cupboard in the corner of the room.

Emina came in carrying a long sack filled with straw. She stooped to lay it on the floor along one of the walls.

'Emina!'

She swung around as Nadine came forward. 'Nadine!'

'Where is everybody?'

'Downstairs having supper. We'll talk later. Come down at once. If you mix in with the others you may be able to get away with it – they may not notice you've not been around until now – but if they see you on your own they're bound to ask questions and then you're in trouble. Don't tell anyone anything. Act as if you've been here all along. Always stay with the others. We've been divided into groups and all the young single women were put here.'

Nadine followed her downstairs. Emina picked up a basket lying on the chest in the hall and handed it to her. 'Here's some food I brought from Shehu's. If anyone asks, tell them you brought it. Take it inside and pass it around. I have to go back and cook for them over there. On no account go outside on your own. All right?'

Emina's calm instructions gave her confidence.

Nadine opened the door into the large room where guests were customarily received. The stove in the middle had been burning all day, so the room was warm. It was full of girls of around Nadine's age, her unmarried cousins in their late teens and twenties, a lot of children who were much younger. Three soldiers lounged at a table in the corner, their automatic weapons slung over the chairs where they sat drinking and playing cards. Nadine took care not to look in their direction, as if accustomed to the sight of them and she had just left the room for a few moments. It was strange to see tables and chairs and girls in the room around the stove. Normally this was where the men congregated, sitting on the mats along the walls and being served by the women, who otherwise stayed out of sight in the kitchen. She moved around the room, handing out little loaves of bread from the basket Emina had given her, before she went through to the kitchen where Baci's wife Minavere was chopping vegetables with her daughters under the bored supervision of a policeman sitting on a bench drinking beer.

'Emina brought over some bread which I've handed around,' Nadine said casually to her aunt. 'Can I give you any help in here?'

'I don't think so. We'll be eating in an hour or so.'

Minavere gave her a look. 'Why don't you go in and talk to the girls? I know they've been looking for you.'

'The girls' were Minavere's daughters, Drita, Fadballe and Merita. Nadine had seen them in the room but avoided going to where they were sitting as she mistrusted Drita's excitability, fearing it might give her away. Catching Drita's eye this time, Nadine put a finger to her lips as she made her way over to where they were sitting, her heart heavy with the things she had seen but knew she would have to keep to herself. For safety's sake, she decided not to tell her cousins anything until all this was over.

Until all this was over – now Nadine knew positively what *all this* entailed, she was expecting the worst. It had happened the previous year to the Ahmeti family in Qirez – the majority of the people murdered there had been old people, women and children – and fifty-eight Kosovo Albanians had been killed in a second massacre in Prekaze a few days later. How many people were there in Beli Atas? A hundred at least, perhaps as many as a hundred and fifty. After the massacres of thousands in Bosnia, what would it mean to these people to kill a few hundred?

From the conversation among her cousins Nadine got the impression that excitement had taken a stronger hold on them than a true apprecia-tion of the danger they were in. She fobbed off their questions, telling them that she had had to stay with her grandmother in Shehu's house in order to look after the old lady, now more or less bedridden and reliant on a wheelchair if she had to be moved. She learned that all the older women and married women with children were being kept in Shehu's house, the boys in Pllumbi's. In their descriptions of two of their captors who had left a strong impression on her cousins Nadine recognised the men she'd seen in the yard – the tattooed man in the black singlet and the heavy-set blond man. There were more paramilitaries, the girls said – a dozen of them came in a truck while they were being kept in the field. They drove down into the field to watch what was going on, leering and whistling and firing their guns. Some of them were already drunk when they arrived. They'd been quartered along with the rest of the soldiers and policemen in Pllumbi's house. It was there that some of the girls had been taken when they were all brought up from the field – four or five of them, Merita said, who'd watched them go in. They'd not been seen since.

When it was ready the cousins ate their soup in silence, not knowing what to talk about. Generally the buzz of voices died down as the evening wore on. When anyone wanted to go outside to take a pee, they had to ask one of the soldiers to accompany them. The girls put off going for as long as possible, because it was unpleasant squatting outside with a guard looking on. They were tired but too frightened to go upstairs to sleep. They felt safest when they were all together in one room. And it was here that they eventually began to nod off, sitting in their clothes. When Minavere turned out the main light and the soldiers left, locking the door behind them, it was past midnight and most of the girls were fast asleep.

Nadine didn't sleep. Terrible images of the day roller-coastered through her mind. She was awake when the men came in the middle of the night. She heard them roaring and bellowing outside, saw the beams of torches jigging around in the dark. The door opened with a crash and several shadowy figures stumbled in. They shone their torches over the room, whooping and shouting as they came in. They were big, heavy men, all of them wearing black ski masks, giving them a terrifying appearance.

'Which of you little KLA whores wants to be first?'

They moved from group to group, shining the lights into the girls' faces and shaking them if they weren't already awake.

'Show me your face, darling. Don't try to hide. Up you get. And you, and you. Come on, get your arse off that chair!'

Drita tried to cling to a chair, but the man chopped her arm with his hand, grabbed her by the hair and hauled her screaming to the door.

'Bitch! Cunt! Just wait till we really start working you over! Just wait till you start getting really fucked!'

Nadine didn't resist when someone pulled her to her feet. She was given a shove in the back that sent her flying across the room.

'Move, you cunts!'

Someone shoved her through the door and someone else pulled her outside the house, where another group of men was waiting.

'How many cunts have you got?'

'Five, six, I don't know.'

'That won't be enough for all our pricks.'

'There's plenty more cunt inside. Go and help yourself.'

Some of the girls whimpered and pleaded. Nadine felt as if every-thing had dried up inside her.

They were herded down the track past Shehu's house. Where were they being taken? Into the woods to be disposed of, like the old men they had thrown down the well that afternoon? But the gun in her back nudged her off the track into Pllumbi's house. Men in Yugoslav Army and MUP uniforms were waiting inside. Nadine saw a bucket with a purse in it and a bundle of banknotes in several currencies. She noticed a big blue hundred-Deutschmark note among them and knew this meant they were going to be searched. The girls waited in line at the bottom of the stairs, where a fat man in a white T-shirt stood with a cigarette in his mouth feeling them over before they were taken upstairs. He didn't ask if they had jewellery or money, just stuck his hand up their bras, ripped down their pants and stuck his hand between their legs. Nadine tried to pull her pants back up when he let her pass.

'Don't bother, they'll be coming off again upstairs. Welcome to the Beli Atas whorehouse.'

Drita went up ahead of her. Serb rock music was blaring out of a CD player on the landing. The doors to all the rooms stood open. In the middle of the landing stood the tattooed man in the black singlet – this was where selection took place. He jerked his head to the right – signifying to Drita that she was to go into the room there – his thumb over his shoulder to indicate that Nadine should go into the room behind him. Walking past him, Nadine registered with surprise that he was no taller than she was. Looking down from the roof of the cowshed he had seemed to her much bigger. It terrified her even to have such a thought – betraying where she'd been and what she'd seen – but then she had no more time for any thoughts of her own – she was inside the room – a small dark man lay in his underwear on the bed – the officer with the stars on his cap sat fully dressed in his cap and uniform on a chair behind the door.

'Close the door and take off your clothes.'

She closed the door and remained standing there.

'Either you take them off or Gypsy rips them off.'

Nadine undressed and hung her clothes over the closet door. It was cold. She was shivering.

'Come over here.'

The small dark man patted the bed beside him. Nadine went over and sat down with her back to him.

The officer lit a cigarette and stretched out his legs. 'Show her your cock, Gypsy.'

The dark man rolled off the end of the bed, took off his vest and pants and stood naked in front of Nadine. She saw the thin long penis and loose baggy scrotum dangling between his legs.

'Take it and suck it,' the officer said.

Nadine automatically did as she was told. Within a minute, not even properly erect, the man's penis had already ejaculated inside her mouth.

'Well, how does Gypsy taste?'

She spat on the floor.

The officer laughed. 'So much for you, Gypsy. Get out.'

The naked man picked his underwear off the floor and started to get dressed.

'I said get out. Send Tuta in.'

The big blond man she had seen in the yard that afternoon came in with a bottle in one hand, the one-piece camouflage fatigues he was wearing rolled down to his waist, massaging his midriff with the other hand. Two or three other men crowded into the doorway and jeered. The officer got up, pushed them out and shut the door.

The blond man took off his belt with the knife attached to it and tossed it onto the bed. He looked at Nadine. 'I haven't seen this one before. Where did she come from?' He rolled his fatigues down to his ankles and stood naked in front of her. He chucked Nadine under the chin. 'Where did you come from all of a sudden?'

'I was here – with the others. I was here all along.'

The blond man sat down on the bed beside her and squeezed her breasts.

'Where is your husband, whore?'

'In Vienna.'

'Earning money he sends home to support the KLA, right? Like all the rest of the Albanian scum who prefer not to work honestly and pay their taxes in their own country, right?' He pinched her nipples so hard that she gasped. 'Don't worry, I'm not going to hurt you. Just have a little fun with you while your husband's away. Lie down.'

Lying down as she was told, Nadine could see the officer sitting with crossed legs by the door watching the blond man running his hands over her body.

'White and smooth, a fresh-plucked chicken, nice and plump. It would be fun to truss her up and cut her a bit, eh? Send you home with some souvenirs for your husband to remember us by. What's your name?'

'Katarina.'

'Katarina? That's not a Muslim name.'

'I'm not Muslim. We – my husband and I – are Catholic.'

'Whoa! You'll be telling us you're Orthodox next. I think you're full of shit, you Catholic bitch. I think you're telling us lies, Katarina, my plump little chicken, and I think I'm going to have to cut you a little to teach you a lesson before I fuck the shit out of you.'

He backhanded her across the face.

'Turn over and give me your arse. Oh, that's good, that's a nice piece of arse just full of shit, my chicken. Bring it up a bit. OK, up. Kneel.'

When she felt his penis probing her backside she instinctively contracted her anus.

'Shit ... tight fucking arsehole on this chicken.'

'Maybe you should soften the position up a bit beforehand, Tuta?' came the voice of the officer still sitting in the corner watching it all. 'Let the artillery give it a pounding.'

Tuta slapped and punched her buttocks. 'C'mon, bitch. Open up your tight chicken arsehole and let me get my poker in here!'

She couldn't. She wouldn't. Spasms of contraction drew hot wires through her body.

'Shit! Bitch!' He pulled off her and rammed his knee hard into her backside, sending her flying across the bed. 'Out! Get out of here, slut!' He grabbed her arm, pulled her off the bed onto the floor and yanked her to her feet. 'Take your clothes and get out! Get out before I *kill* you!' He was red in the face and very angry.

She hurried to pick her clothes up off the floor and get out of the room before he changed his mind.

Out on the landing she tried to stand as she got dressed. She was trembling so much she had to sit on the floor. She sat and wept, tried to put on her clothes and couldn't, no longer knew how to, unable to find the arm and leg holes – her clothes or her body twisted out of familiarity – all coordination gone, where she was, who she was – what had happened to the reliable framework that used to make sense of a world in which until now she had got along without having to think about it – for Nadine this unthinking ease of being in the world had gone.

# 5

Her most urgent need was to be out of sight of other people and for other people to be out of her sight, but there was nowhere she could hide, nowhere she could go to be alone. Her hearing and vision seemed to have become blunt, as if a layer of padding had been placed over her ears and eyes. One look at her cousins who had been taken with her to Pllumbi's house in the night was sufficient to tell her that they had been through similar experiences, which she had no desire to be reminded of.

The blank horror of it still stood in their faces. None of them talked about what had happened. They didn't even want to sit together. They avoided looking at each other. Nadine sank into lethargy. Nowhere to hide, nothing to say, no desire to eat – just sitting with all the others in the dark room, not wanting anything, not waiting for anything, afraid that anything would only turn out to be more of what had already happened.

Emina came over from Shehu's house later in the afternoon, gaunt-faced, her hair combed back – a reminder of the sinewy vigilance and discipline she expected of herself. The older women had been molested too, women with children, women without, but not Emina herself, it seemed. Emina brought with her the charges she had taken into her special care, the young Suhareka woman in an advanced state of pregnancy and a two-year-old child. For some reason she seemed to think they would be safer in Baci's house, perhaps because she hadn't seen for herself what had happened there.

The events in Shehu's house must have been violent enough to impress themselves on her half-blind, half-deaf mother, penetrating the old woman's self-protective mantle of senility and bringing on a heart attack, of which she had died in the early hours of the morning. Emina tried to lay her mother out in the room vacated by her father twenty-four hours before, but the Serbs wouldn't have any corpses in the house and carried Igballe out to the barn where Shehu's coffin still rested. Minavere claimed that Igballe's body had been laid on top of the old man's coffin and, much worse than that: from the glance into the barn she was given on her way from Baci's to Shehu's house, she had made out a huddle of what seemed to be human bodies lying under the coffin on the barn floor.

While everyone else lost track of what happened in Beli Atas during what already felt like the week-long occupation of the hamlet, Emina and her sister-in-law Minavere were keeping their own tallies of events. They did not forget that Serbs were already being held accountable by a tribunal in The Hague for crimes committed in Croatia and Bosnia five or six years before, just as in the fullness of time they would be held accountable for the killing of Albanians in Qirez and Prekaze not twelve months since. In the absence of their menfolk, the only means of retaliation available to the women who survived the massacres was to remember as exactly as possible the circumstances under which the crimes took place. Watching and counting, Nadine's aunts hadn't overlooked the absence of the four younger girls who'd been with the rest of them when they came up from the field while the Serbs were dealing with the old men in the yard, and who'd not been seen since they disappeared into Pllumbi's house the previous day.

How those four had failed to be included in the group of girls taken out of the hamlet before the Serbs arrived was another matter, one which had already led to bitter recriminations among the women. Leaving that aside, Emina in Shehu's house assumed the four girls had been returned to Baci's house, where all the other young single women were being held, while Minavere in Baci's house thought they were still being detained in Pllumbi's house along with a group of small boys. But after the events of the previous night, when what had gone on in Pllumbi's house became clear, *detained* took on another significance, and the question as to the whereabouts of the little girls suddenly received a plausible answer in Minavere's contention that what she'd glimpsed on the barn floor was not a pile of old sacks or clothing or whatever but the bodies of the four missing girls.

Nadine sat in the kitchen listening to this conversation between her aunts without contributing to it – tongue-tied, in fact, because to Emina's suggestion that it might have been clothing her sister-in-law had seen Minavere answered that if it *was* clothing lying on the barn floor that hardly improved the situation, for whose clothing would it be, and why was it lying there instead of being worn by the people to whom it belonged? And everyone in the room understood what her question meant because everyone had been asking themselves the same thing. What had happened to the eleven or by Emina's count twelve elderly men from whom they'd been separated when the Serbs arrived – a question to which Nadine was the only person, apart from the perpetrators, who knew the answer.

It was frightening that four girls and a dozen men could have disappeared without trace, as if a trapdoor had opened in the ground and swallowed them up, which was why everyone moved with caution, preferably didn't move at all. As long as you all stayed together in the big room, traps in the ground were less likely to open, as they had a tendency to do on the short walk from Baci's to Pllumbi's house. But Nadine was already excluded from even this desperate solidarity by knowing something that nobody else knew, still more so by her reasons for continuing to want to keep that knowledge to herself. Once what had happened to the old men did the rounds among the girls, the likelihood of it being picked up by one of the Kosovo Serb policemen became almost a certainty. They sat there in the room apparently just playing cards, but actually with their ears open for information about KLA activities. No one believed the reassurances they gave when they took a girl out for questioning, as they called it. This was always a dangerous situation, the outcome of which depended not simply on what information the girl might volunteer under duress but on what the guards happened to feel like at a particular moment. The consequences of all such scenarios that passed through her mind resulted in a death sentence for Nadine the moment the girl opened her mouth.

# 6

When they came the third night, not turning on the house lights as any normal visitor would, but bringing in their own to tease out the secrets of the petrified room, they stirred up the nest of blankets Emina and Minavere had arranged around them to hide the thirteen-year-old Suhareka girl her aunts had so far managed to keep from the rapists' attentions. There she lay uncovered by the flashlights they shone down on her, a pale little girl who might indeed have been two years younger, as Emina claimed she was when pleading with the men on the girl's behalf. She received her answer with the butt of the machine gun one of the men rammed into her chest, knocking her over, while two others dragged out the screaming girl. Emina got to her feet, pulled out of the sash around her midriff the big revolver that had belonged to Shehu and shot her assailant in the face. The two other men dropped the girl and opened fire with their machine guns. The whipcord streams of bullets fired at close range spun Emina up and around and cut her in pieces. Other men rushed in from outside with drawn knives in their hands – the paramilitaries who came every night for their pick of the room. They hacked and mutilated the corpse, kicking it and stamping on it before they opened the window and bundled it out.

All the lights went on now.

One at a time the women were taken outside, stripped and searched. As they stood naked and shivering the soldiers combed through their clothes, ripping seams open if in doubt, before returning them to the wearer and allowing her to get dressed but not to go back inside until all the inmates of the room and the room itself had been searched for concealed weapons.

Under the light bulb hanging over the entrance to the door stood a bald soldier and three paramilitaries with long hair, looking at the women as they filed back into the room. They pulled out Drita, who was in front of Nadine, and Minavere, who was behind her, and then, it seemed as an afterthought, Nadine herself. But unlike the other women pulled out of the line, they weren't sent back outside, presumably to be taken to the brothel, as Pllumbi's house was known. They were led upstairs.

Three faces very familiar to Nadine now – faces she wouldn't forget – the triumvirate of the officer, the tattooed man in the black singlet and the blond brute who had tried to sodomise her in Pllumbi's house – turned to look at the women as they came in.

The room overlooked the yard with the tree outside the window that Nadine had climbed to get into the house. To be taken into this room – of all the rooms they might have been taken into in the three houses of Beli Atas – seemed to Nadine to be an ominous coincidence. Here was the evidence – the window, the tree, the barn – one thing led to another – establishing a chain of connections which they would now proceed to uncover, linking her with the crime she had witnessed these men commit on the day they arrived.

They had brought in chairs and a table, on which piles of unwashed coffee cups were stacked, scraps of food, bottles and glasses half full of slivovitz, a machine gun that happened to lie or was being used as a paperweight to hold down the map curling up over the edge of the table, where the officer sat chain-smoking as usual. For the first time Nadine saw him without his cap. The two other men slumped on chairs pulled back from the table, their legs wide apart exposing their crotches as if even sitting was something they managed to do obscenely.

'You three are the ringleaders in this house,' said the officer, singling out Minavere as the oldest and thus the most responsible of the three. 'You and that bitch who just shot one of my men. Was she your sister?'

'My sister-in-law.'

'Where did she get the weapon?'

'It belonged to her father. He always had a weapon in the house. All the men had a weapon in the house in case of the blood feud, since long ago, hundreds of years ago, long before any of this started. It was the custom here.'

'Then there must be more weapons in the house. And valuables. Where are all the valuables? We know that you Kosovo animals don't trust Serb banks. Don't think you can fool us. You peasant animals keep all your money at home. We've searched the whole place but we haven't found any and this is making us angry. No guns, no money. Where are they?'

Minavere shook her head. 'I don't know. It wasn't my responsibility. The only person who knew was my sister-in-law, Emina.'

'You peasant women are not only very obstinate but very stupid if you expect us to believe lies like that.' The officer motioned impatiently with his hand. 'Bring the pregnant woman in.'

The Suhareka woman, eight months pregnant, was brought into the room.

'Take off your clothes.'

Reluctantly, with slow, awkward movements that tried to keep her nakedness hidden from the watching men to the very last, the woman got undressed. She stood with one arm covering her breasts, the other across her distended belly. The officer got up from the table, walked over to her and looked her up and down with an expression of disgust.

'All you're good for is to open your legs and make more children than your miserable country is able to feed. Well, we're tired of paying subsidies for this surplus of Kosovo children. Where's your husband?'

'I don't know. In Suhareka. I don't know!'

'Here we are instead of him. What do you think?'

'Please, leave me alone!'

'Perhaps we'll leave you here with a few more bastards to look after, who at least can be proud of having Serb blood in their veins.' The officer ran his hand over the pregnant woman's belly. 'Or perhaps we'll cut this cow open and take out her calf to persuade you to tell us what you've been keeping from us. Prick her, Mirko. Show us the colour of the Albanian sow's blood.'

Mirko removed the knife from its sheath, took a whetstone out of his side pocket and began sharpening the blade.

'What do you say, Tuta? Are we going to cut the cow?'

'Sure,' said the blond man sitting beside him at the table, 'let's take the baby out.'

With the tip of his knife he made a snick in the crook of his arm and sucked the blood.

The two men got up and the woman shrank back. 'Please! Don't hurt me!'

'Which would you prefer first? To be fucked or cut?'

The woman got down on her knees and sobbed.

'Leave her alone!'

The men looked round in astonishment at Nadine.

'I can tell you what you want to know! The money's in the barn – the money and the jewellery and everything of value in the house – it's all hidden in the barn!'

The officer frowned. 'How do you know about this?'

'Emina – my aunt – told me where she had hidden it.'

'Ah!' The officer lit another cigarette and walked up to Nadine. He stood right in front of her but gave no indication of remembering her from their encounter the previous night.

'And why did she tell you that?'

The question flustered Nadine. 'Why?' she echoed. 'In case some-thing happened to her, I suppose. So that someone else knew. So that it wouldn't be lost.'

How stupid to have added that *I suppose* – didn't that make it ring false?

The officer grabbed her arm and stubbed out his cigarette on it.

Nadine cried out angrily, 'You monster! That hurt!'

'It was intended to hurt, bitch! Why didn't you tell us about this before, saving us the trouble of turning these three filthy hovels inside out?' To the guards standing at the door he said, 'Take the bitch into another room. Work her over. Do what you like with her. One of you go and check the truth of what she says. If she's lying, kill her. On no account let her into the barn.'

Nadine was pushed across the corridor into the small room that had been Minavere's and Baci's bedroom. To her relief, the blond man called Tuta and the bald man in the black singlet whom she especially feared disappeared. Two policemen were sent in to question her about the hiding place in the barn and report back. It took Nadine less than a minute to describe where the packages were hidden. One of the police-men then went downstairs. The other one told her to undress and lie down on the bed. Nadine refused. The MUP man took out his pistol and said he would shoot her if she refused.

'Shoot me then. I don't care.'

The man hit her across the side of the head so hard that she fell back onto the bed. He crashed on top of her and pinned her arms down. She kicked and screamed. At that moment the second policeman returned with two other men. Between them they ripped off her clothes, stuffing her underpants into her mouth to stop her screaming.

'Me first! I was here first!'

Two of them forced her legs apart; another held her arms, twisting her head down into the bed. She could hardly see out of the eye on the side of her head where the man had hit her, just the shape of the figure looming over her as fingers poked her crotch, then the weight of him on her chest and the rapid thrusts of his penis. Then he was off her and the next took his place. Dimly she could make out several men standing in the doorway looking on. She heard laughter and jeering voices while she was being raped, but they didn't come from the onlookers at the door; they seemed to come from under the bed, a whole gang of them, shouting abuse and obscenities while the four policemen took her one after the other. Many more must have been waiting their turn – she could hear them hooting and screeching under the bed. Somehow these voices must have got into her head – the fear that she was never going to get them out again drove her crazy. But when the last of the men got off her, he crawled under the bed and took out the two-way radio they had hidden there. He spoke into it, laughed, flicked a switch, and the sewer of noise pouring out of it was cut off. Enjoying Nadine's total bewilderment, the four men stood there laughing.

'They've got two bitches cooking for them down in the kitchen,' one of them said to the others. 'Why don't we go in the next room and have this one make us some coffee?'

They dragged her back into the room where she had first been taken with Minavere and Drita. There was no sign of her cousin and aunt. She wondered what had happened to them and the pregnant woman tortured with threats to cut out her baby. The room was full of the smoke and sweat and stink of unwashed men, some of whom she recog-nised – the paramilitaries with their terrifying knives at their belts – the tattooed Mirko – the man with the long hair whose name was Tuta – the small dark man the officer called Gypsy – the two policemen who had questioned her in the next-door room before they raped her. A bulb flashed in her mind and she photographed the scene. Naked and cold and dirty, she was forced to make coffee for them, clearing their trash off the table, the bottles and glasses and ashtrays, carrying the cups to the sink and washing them up, boiling water, making coffee, taking the cups around. Then they gave her a dustpan and brush and told her to get down and sweep the floor, then a bucket and a rag to wipe it clean for their entertainment. Someone grabbed her by the hair and pulled her up.

'Show us your black eye then, slave,' Mirko said, twisting her head to get a closer look at it. 'It suits you. Would you like another to go with it?'

A burst of machine-gun fire outside sent some of the men running downstairs. Mirko and Tuta ignored it. Now that they had got hold of Nadine they weren't going to let her go. They settled down at the table with slivovitz and coffee, Nadine sitting on Mirko's knee with one arm clamped behind her back while with his other hand he fondled her breasts.

Far away from what was happening to her in this room Nadine could hear a conversation between the two men about a rock band called Muslim Grief they played for in Belgrade. Mirko was bass guitarist; Tuta played the drums. They sat and talked about this band as if they'd forgotten about the war that had brought them here – all the things they'd done to her family in Beli Atas – were doing now – she heard the machine-gun fire still going on outside – the murder of the men, of Selim and Emina, the torture and rape of women and children. She wondered how this could be, how it was possible for these two men after what they had done to be talking about a rock band as if they were sitting in a Belgrade cafe – Mirko unzipping his fly and taking out his penis, telling her to work it with her hand and put it inside her – saying, Move, move, move, as she sat rigid on his lap, dehydrated, feeling the emptiness as if this emptiness were in someone else, until her passivity made him angry and he bit her neck, her armpits, her breasts, and the pain made her cry out.

Then the room was again full of men, and she had to clean up and make more coffee for them. KLA men had killed one of the sentries and tried to storm Pllumbi's house. The Serbs had shot two of them. Where was the captain? The women and children in these hovels were a liability they must dispose of, they urged Mirko; they must get out of this stinking hole immediately. They crowded around the map on the table, pointing and arguing, forgetting about Nadine in their excitement.

She slipped across the passage into the room where her clothes, or what was left of them, were still lying on the floor. She gathered them up, crept downstairs into the washroom, went in and locked the door. She shook uncontrollably. She tried to dab herself with a sponge at the big stone basin where the household washed its clothes but the water was so cold, she felt so weak and began shivering so much that she couldn't grip the sponge properly and had to give up. She was unable to stand. Sitting on one of the washing baskets in the adjacent linen room to pull on her trousers, she rummaged through the shelves for some garment as a substitute for the blouse that had been ripped to shreds. She found an old blue work coat and put it on.

Through the window she saw it was getting light. She wondered whether to wait in the washroom or go back into the big room to join the other women, but it was too late for that. She heard the men coming down the stairs, the sound of the door across the passage being opened, voices shouting, Get up! Get up! followed by a hubbub from the frightened women in the big room. People were running up and down the passage. She heard men shouting outside, doors slamming and trucks starting up. So they were leaving!

Nadine opened the door a finger's breadth and peeped through the crack. One of the Serbs was standing directly outside, hustling the women as they came out of the big room, telling them to hurry, shoving them down the corridor and out of the house. Shouting began in the yard. When the man went to see what was happening, Nadine slipped into the file passing the door, pushing up against the woman in front, ducking to make herself small, using the woman as cover, folding herself into the file so as to attract no attention. The column crossed the gap between the houses as soldiers started firing white phosphorus rounds into the buildings at the back of the yard. The cowshed and the barn immediately went up in flames with a great whoosh of hot air that Nadine could feel across the yard. The two houses in front of her were already on fire. The heat was so intense the refugees had to leave the track and make a detour across the field below. She looked back as the ridge beam of Pllumbi's house caved in and the roof came crashing down, sending out showers of glowing embers which stragglers at the back of the column leaving the hamlet only managed to dodge by running down onto the meadows.

In isolated knots of two and threes, the ragged column of women and children stretched from the outskirts of the village to the Suhareka–Prizren road at the bottom of the valley. Soldiers and policemen marched on either side. An open truck with a machine gun brought up the rear. The convoy swelled the already dense traffic on the road to Prizren, cars and tractors and people on foot with carts for their few belongings – even a wheelbarrow to transport an old woman wrapped in a blanket.

Nadine fell in with a family – it felt like a release to be caught up in their lives – driven out of their home in Suhareka and their house set on fire. Offered the choice of staying or going to Albania, they had naturally opted for the latter. They'd been on the march all night. She didn't rejoin the refugees from Beli Atas until they reached the outskirts of Prizren. The soldiers, policemen and paramilitary units who had torched Beli Atas and expelled its inhabitants disappeared when they reached the main road, apparently back in the direction of Suhareka. Others took their place. The refugees were approaching Prizren's old mosque when a contingent of Serb soldiers barred their progress and told them they couldn't go through the city centre. They would have to take a diversion. When it led them off the road into fields Nadine feared they were all being taken somewhere to be shot, but it turned out the diversion was due to a pile-up down the road that made it impossible for traffic to pass. After a few kilometres the diversion took them back onto the main road.

From dawn to dusk the trek south to the border continued, the adults taking it in turns to carry the children, stopping now and then to rest by the wayside and share the little food they'd brought with them. Nadine found her cousins Drita and Merita. The three girls roamed up and down the column looking for Minavere – Drita and Merita's mother – their aunts and cousins, fathers and uncles they hadn't seen in Beli Atas since the day it was occupied by the Serbs. They had to be somewhere in this mass of people, they told themselves, for there were thousands, tens of thousands of refugees streaming towards the Albanian border. The women talked through all the possibilities of where their missing loved ones might yet be found, if not in Albania then in Macedonia, if not in this border camp, then another – any subject other than what they had gone through in Beli Atas.

When Nadine left the refugee camp in Kukës for the clinic where the child she was carrying would be aborted, hiding from her friends and relatives, she continued to live with the humiliation of her absolute helplessness – a sense of having absented herself from her own body, wishing she could make herself disappear, walk out of the clinic and dissolve into thin air. A dirt she would never be able to wash out had got under her skin and polluted her being. In the end she avoided the company of those who had been closest to her because she was afraid of contaminating them. She made up her mind that she would be able to survive only by isolating herself from everything that she had loved and trusted – everything that made up the world to which she no longer felt she belonged.

# 7

The last news Alex heard before leaving Priština was that the Serbian delegation had rejected the draft resolution presented in Paris, and talks had been broken off. All non-combatants were advised to leave the area. Official OSCE observers currently stationed in Kosovo were pulled out to Macedonia in anticipation of the air strikes threatened by NATO in the event of peace negotiations failing.

The day before the NATO bombing was scheduled to begin Alex waited in their house in the town of Suhareka while his KLA contact Bardhyl accompanied his sister-in-law and her three children to stay with relatives in a remote mountain hamlet, where they would be safer during the coming conflict. Bardhyl returned the same evening. According to radio reports, NATO would commence bombing strategic military targets in Serbia and Kosovo the following evening. The two of them left the house in the afternoon and made their way on foot to a rendezvous with KLA representatives in Bukosh, a village ten kilometres away.

It was quiet. People stayed at home because they felt safer there. Avoiding roads, the two men made their way along forest paths and reached the village before nightfall. Most of the night was spent discussing KLA tactics and coordinating opposition to the Serb forces. Bombing was audible throughout the night. It was hard to tell whether it was NATO planes attacking military targets or the Yugoslav Army shelling towns. When Alex and his companion headed back towards Suhareka the next morning they could see smoke rising over the town. They met residents in the woods who told them that Serb paramilitary units had burned their houses down. More Albanians arrived. They reported that fighting was taking place in the town and it was unsafe to return there.

For late March it was warm in the mountains, making it possible to sleep out in the woods, if necessary for days. The refugees headed east through the woods to Bukosh. They decided to stay in the village overnight and return to Suhareka the following day. Bardhyl and Alex were given a lift by car to Vraniq, fifteen kilometres from Suhareka. Vraniq was under the control of the KLA, who walked around in the streets openly carrying rifles and bazookas, ignoring occasional sniper fire from the surrounding hills. They continued on foot to the next village, Budakovo, the local KLA headquarters. There they met people who had just arrived from Suhareka and told them to avoid the town – all hell was loose – a massacre had taken place. Bardhyl was worried by the news. He told Alex that he had an uncle who lived in a solitary house down by the river just outside Suhareka. Possibly the house had escaped attention and his uncle was unharmed, but Bardhyl wanted to go back to see for himself. Given the choice of staying in Budakovo and fending for himself or risking the journey back to Suhareka together, Alex opted for Suhareka.

Since it was impossible to go through Suhareka they had to bypass it, requiring the two men to pass an outlying farmhouse on the edge of the forest, but as they did so they were spotted by soldiers who immediately opened fire. Bardhyl dived into the house to take cover and Alex followed his example, throwing himself down on the floor. When he looked up there was no sign of Bardhyl. The house seemed to have swallowed him up. Seconds later he felt the air being sucked out of his body and heard a detonation that seemed to come from inside his own head. The shock wave of the explosion picked him up off the floor and hurled him across the room. The ceiling crashed down – beams and showers of plaster, a thundering torrent of rubble. Eyes and nose and ears filled with dust, but registering this meant that he wasn't yet dead, apparently not even seriously injured. Groping around cautiously in the dark, he established he was lying under a table, which must have saved him from the falling debris.

He called Bardhyl's name, but no reply came. When his eyes got accustomed to the darkness, he started to clear the debris around him but was unable to move the larger beams and blocks of stone. He was safe in the hollow under the table yet at the same time trapped there, with no possibility of getting out by his own efforts. The house appeared to be empty. The owners had probably fled, and who apart from the owner was likely to investigate a solitary ruined house on the edge of the forest? He had nothing to eat and nothing to drink. Within a few days he would be dead.

From time to time he called for help. The table seemed to be standing by a wall. The other sides were blocked by masonry and a tangle of collapsed beams. He tried to squeeze out between them. He made repeated efforts to shift them. Sweating and lying still after these exertions, he began to get cold and thirsty. It was better not to waste energy on these futile attempts. He fell asleep, woke up freezing in the dark. From his watch it was half past three, presumably in the morning. He lay and thought of the people who would miss him and how they would set about finding him, and realised there wasn't the slightest chance of anyone doing so because no one knew where he was. When he last contacted IPA before leaving Priština, he had told them only of his intention to head south into the mountains. And what could they do anyway? The day he left Suhareka with Bardhyl he had heard on the radio that all journalists had been ordered to leave the country. He had stayed at his own risk. There would be no special search party for a stranded journalist. His fate had now ceased to matter, swallowed up in a war that was producing tens of thousands of casualties and hundreds of thousands of refugees.

He lay awake until the pitch-black sameness of the dark around him broke up into a grainy texture that suggested it must be getting light. He looked at his watch again and saw that it was a few minutes after six. As he did so, he heard a faint knocking, or rather tapping. After a pause he heard it again, and so it went on for about twenty minutes, a series of taps followed by a pause, and then the taps again. Perhaps it was Bardhyl sending a message to let him know he was trapped in the same house. He shouted his name a dozen times at intervals of a minute, but he had a cold – his throat hurt and his voice was too hoarse to carry far. He could hear his shouts rebound back on himself, confined as he was in the little pocket under the table in a mantle of debris that probably absorbed most of the sound. It was unlikely that anyone outside would hear him.

Around the middle of the day a shaft or rather a needle of light miraculously penetrated the gloom, illuminating the massive leg of the table he was lying under – a leg of roughly hewn wood about six inches thick to which he undoubtedly owed his life – and his mind swung off on an orbit of life-saving tables he had heard about as a journalist, stories he had heard from Ella about hiding under tables in air raids, the table Hitler had been leaning over studying maps in the barrack in East Prussia when Stauffenberg's abortive bomb went off – until, via these meandering thoughts about bombs and instances of people who had survived under collapsed houses against all the odds, he was brought back to something in his pocket that had hitherto escaped his attention. It was the whistle Ella had given him – foreseeing a situation in which it might one day come in useful – when he started covering the Yugoslavian war back in 1991.

Why had it embarrassed him to be given a whistle by his mother? Why had he felt obliged by his promise to her to carry it around always attached to his key ring? Why had he objected? For he soon got used to it; indeed, it became a talisman he would have wanted back if he had been without it. Now, in serious need of rescue, he blew it for the first time – a high-pitched, fugitive sound he continued to hear moments after it left the whistle. Every hour or so he blew the whistle. Gradually it began to get dark again. He was hungry and cold. He slid into sleep and jolted back out. When the tapping started again, he guessed it might be about to get light. He looked at his watch. Convinced it was Bardhyl's wake-up call, sure he was with him somewhere in the house, he blew his whistle in response. At half past five it was still dark, but it now wouldn't be long before the complete blackness began to disintegrate into the grainy textured semblance of day that crept into his space.

The next thing he waited for was the needle-prick of the sun putting a spotlight on the table leg in about another six hours, time he marked off with whistle blasts at intervals of an hour. But before that happened somebody arrived. He could hear them rummaging around, wrenching and banging sounds, as if they were pulling things out of the house and throwing them outside. He blew several long blasts on the whistle. He heard voices. Someone called, and he blew another blast in response. The shuddering and banging resumed. They were pulling out debris. I'm in here, he called, but they didn't hear, didn't answer, at least, and he blew another few blasts. He could hear blunt heavy sounds, as if someone was pounding wood and masonry with a sledgehammer, and then the snarl of a chainsaw, and outlines he hadn't seen before became visible. Are you in there? a voice called out in Albanian. I'm under a table up against the wall here, he answered, but half the ceiling seems to be on top of it. Don't you worry, the man said, we'll have you out in no time at all.

His rescuers were the owners of the house, father and son. The first thing they passed him while he still lay under the table was a bottle of water. They had hidden in the woods until the Serbs moved on out of Suhareka. Their faces were still covered with the dirt they had rubbed into them. They had watched the house being shelled. After two days they came back to start clearing up. The shell had taken out a chunk of the front of the house, but the roof was still largely in place. A mass of bricks had filled up the stairway to the cellar.

Cellar! That was where Bardhyl must have gone. That was where the tapping must have come from. The men sat Alex down on a chair outside the house, gave him a piece of bread and a bottle of slivovitz to help him stop shivering. Then they began shovelling the rubble out of the cellar stairs. Now and then they called Bardhyl's name. Halfway down the stairs they could hear him answer. He told them to be careful with their shovels. He was lying with a leg trapped under the rubble.

Alex's rescuers began to clear the debris by hand, the older man filling a bucket, which he passed up to his son, who emptied it outside and told Alex what was going on. The explosion had hurled Bardhyl down into the cellar and blocked the stairs. His leg was lacerated and swollen but apparently not broken. They carried him up the stairs and set him down beside Alex in the afternoon sun on the edge of the forest. The two men laughed and sobbed as they embraced each other after two days under the collapsed house. After Bardhyl had rested, their rescuers put him in a wheelbarrow and carted him through the outskirts of Suhareka to his brother's house.

His brother had not been home since the beginning of the year, when he joined the KLA in Budakovo. When Bardhyl left the house with his sister-in-law and her three children it had still been intact. The house they now found had been burned to the ground. The ruins of other houses they passed on their way through Suhareka were still smouldering. A trail of household articles documented the passage of refugees who'd abandoned them for greater speed. A cafe near the centre of the town was open. A group of people stood talking outside. Women cried when they saw Bardhyl with the two men and told them what had happened. People had been hauled out of their houses and brought here to be murdered, the corpses thrown on a truck and driven away when the Serbs left town. Bloodstains on the floor of the cafe testified to the massacre.

Bardhyl wanted to find out how his sister-in-law and her children were faring in the hamlet where he'd left them. Trolli, the owner of the cafe, offered to take him and Alex there on his tractor if he could get it started. The tractor sputtered to life at the eighth attempt and they set off, following the Prizren road for a few kilometres before turning off onto a track. From here a plume of smoke rising from the razed hamlet at the foot of the mountain was already visible. Bardhyl covered his face with his hands.

'They've burned Beli Atas!' Bardhyl was baffled. 'Why didn't you tell me, Trolli? Why did you bring me here?'

'I wanted you to see for yourself.' He took a pipe out of his pocket and began stuffing it. 'Things have been done here – people don't believe unless they see things for themselves.'

'What happened to everyone?'

'I heard they left for Prizren a few days ago, heading for Zhur on their way to Albania. Thousands of people have fled in the last few days – on foot, on carts and tractors – an old woman on a wheelbarrow – all of them heading for the border. On the radio they said the refugees have been given shelter in a Red Cross camp in Kukës.'

'Can you take us there?'

Trolli lit his pipe. 'The tractor wouldn't make it. Better turn back and wait for someone in a car who's going in that direction. You and your friend can stay at my house, if you like.'

# 8

Bardhyl's leg swelled up alarmingly in the night. The next morning he was running a temperature and suffering a lot of pain. It seemed his leg was broken after all. Trolli asked around and improvised transport to the hospital in Prizren on a pickup truck, squeezing the sick man and Alex in among the sacks of potatoes piled in the back. At the hospital entrance Bardhyl gave Alex a photo of his sister-in-law, and the jounalist made a note of the names of Bardhyl's relatives and promised to look out for them in Kukës. After their extraordinary weeks together, he and Bardhyl took an emotional leave of one another.

It was a silent Sunday morning – eerily silent. Alex stood feeling drained in a cold drizzle on the side of the empty road, waiting for a car to come along, and found it hard to imagine the mass of vehicles and people heading for the border that had passed this way over the last few days. Only the litter they had left behind them – cardboard boxes, plastic bottles and articles of clothing – scattered along the roadside, supplied poignant evidence of the exodus that had taken place. An hour passed before a farmer came by and offered him a lift on his tractor as far as Zhur. From Zhur he could cross the border into Albania at Merina and walk to Kukës. In the event, he had no problem getting hold of a taxi to take him to Merina. The refugees appeared to have caused a business boom at this otherwise desolate frontier post. Several taxi drivers and hawkers selling cigarettes and drinks were waiting there, offering to change money.

Alex arrived in Kukës in the early evening as it was beginning to get dark. He had lost his mobile in Priština, and paid the taxi driver to let him use his so that he could touch base with IPA for the first time since early March. The driver told him that foreign journalists and relief workers in Kukës hung out at the America Bar. For a couple of hundred Deutschmarks he could rent an apartment from the man who owned it. On their way there Alex asked to be dropped off at a school near the mosque. According to the taxi driver, many of the refugees who had arrived from the Drenica region during the Easter week had been given shelter there.

He entered a poorly lit building with an unpleasant odour he immediately recognised, familiar to him from Croatia and Bosnia. An elderly man, incongruously dressed in a suit and bow tie, sat at the entrance reading a book behind a table piled with blankets. He didn't look up when Alex came in. The cries of children rippled sharply up out of the muted background murmur washing over the floor of the entrance hall. Everywhere there were people sitting or lying wrapped in quilts or blankets. A group of men in anoraks sat drinking coffee and playing cards. It was cold, although the sheer number of people crowded into the school helped to raise the temperature a little. Even the corridors were packed. Bodies lay huddled against the walls. Alex picked his way carefully up and down the corridors from one end of the building to the other, the photograph of Bardhyl's sister-in-law in his hand, asking if anyone recognised this woman, if anyone knew of the whereabouts of her family or the other refugees from Beli Atas. Some of the women took the photo and looked at it more closely before shaking their heads. Most people ignored him. He looked into blank faces that didn't seem to register his presence. Other faces he couldn't see at all, people who'd gone into hiding, sitting with their blankets over their heads. The dense odour in the building reminded Alex of many other overcrowded shelters lacking sanitary facilities he had visited during the wars in Yugoslavia. These places always provoked the same response of pity and revulsion.

Having done a tour of the building and got no response to the picture, Alex arrived back at the entrance, where the old man still sat reading behind his table of blankets.

'I wonder if you could help me,' he began. 'I'm looking for a family from a place called Beli Atas. This is the mother of the three children ...'

The old man laid down the book he was reading, held the photograph flat on the palm of his hand and studied it for a long time.

'I may have seen this woman,' he said eventually. 'I can't rule the possibility out. But unfortunately I have no recollection of her. In the old days we used to keep lists of the people who passed in and out, but with all these thousands arriving here now that has become impractical, I dare say impossible. But for all that we must continue to make an effort to keep up appearances, mustn't we.'

He returned the photo with an odd little bow, as if his failure to meet Alex's request required some form of apology. Alex was as intrigued by the old man's quaint dress and manners as puzzled by his answer.

'In the old days you used to keep lists of people?'

'I was the rector of this school for thirty years. When the communist regime came to an end, I went into retirement. Things have gone from bad to worse in this country. In the old days we kept lists and discipline was strict. We used to keep an eye on people. We knew how many we had and where they were. We looked after them. But now people come and go as they please; nobody keeps lists, and so one loses track of them. This family you're looking for, for example. I started keeping a list, but I had to give up. There were too many of them. Now I just give them blankets.'

'I'm sure people are grateful for them.'

'If they are, they don't say so. Not that one expects it. Who can tell?'

'Then let me thank you on everyone's behalf,' said Alex, already anxious to move on but wanting to say something encouraging to the old man, so that it wouldn't feel like he was abandoning him when he walked out the door.

When he left the school it was only half past nine. Wondering what his next move should be, whether to go back to the Red Cross reception centre he had passed on his way into Kukës or first get himself a room, he set off in the direction of the America Bar, where the taxi driver had told him he would be able to find accommodation. He walked a couple of blocks until he spotted an illuminated hotel sign.

He went in and asked if they had anything free. A small room was available in the attic. He could have it for a hundred and fifty Deutsch-marks or the equivalent in dollars. Alex went through the pretence of taking a look at the room before accepting this outrageous price. He was so tired he would have taken the cupboard of the room he was being offered, whatever they were asking. He told the man in the white shirt and dark waistcoat, who showed him upstairs, he would come down and fill in the registration form in the morning, gave him a tip in exchange for the key, collapsing on the bed as soon as the man shut the door.

He wondered what the old schoolmaster was reading.

Suddenly this seemed an important matter he would have to clarify first thing in the morning, but when he stretched out and asked himself why it was important he instantly fell asleep.

There was a great deal of rubble to be cleared before Alex could even think of getting up. He pushed and pulled in the dark place where he was trapped, twisted himself free of the counterpane he was entangled in and tumbled onto the floor. It was half past five. When he next looked at his watch it was eight o'clock. He was still lying on the floor. Even fully dressed, he felt extremely cold. There didn't seem to be any heating in the room. He got up. Through the raindrops on the windowpane he could see a mosque and wondered where he was. What was the name of the place? He got back into bed, just to warm up a little, and fell back to sleep.

He was woken by someone knocking on the door, told them to go away and tried to doze off again. But the knocking continued in his sleep. It came through the door and laid hands on him. Someone was standing by his bed shaking him by the shoulder.

'What is it?'

He looked up at the man who had shown him up to the room the previous night.

'It's eleven o'clock. The room has to be vacated by this time.'

'I'm not vacating the room. I'm staying another night.'

Alex reached into his pocket. All he had was Austrian money. He fished out a hundred-schilling bill and handed it to the man.

'Now go away and leave me in peace.'

When he came downstairs feeling very hungry it was half past one. The man who had woken him had been replaced at reception by a woman. He filled in a registration form, turned over his passport to the receptionist and left the hotel to get something to eat, almost colliding with his friend Andro Bobic on his way in.

'Alex!'

'Andro!'

'What are you doing here?'

'The same as you.'

They laughed and hugged each other.

'I must just pick something up from my room. Then we'll go out and have something to eat. I'm starving,' said Andro.

'Me too.'

Over lunch in a cafe across the street the two friends exchanged news of what they had been doing since their last meeting. The Vienna Watch representative had arrived from Blace on the Kosovo–Macedonia border the previous evening, where he had seen for himself the makeshift plastic shelters and complete lack of sanitary facilities with which the refugees arriving in the rain were still having to live while the UN belatedly began organising accommodation for them. Andro had applied to the Red Cross for permission to take a look at the situation at border crossings in Albania. He was now on his way to their reception centre in Kukës and agreed to take Alex with him.

'They may not let you in as a journalist, but if I introduce you as a colleague from Vienna Watch, there shouldn't be a problem getting you in anywhere you want. I'm not just here to inspect refugee facilities, you see. I'm also here to document war crimes. Earlier this week I spoke to a doctor from Iran who's working here for Médecins Sans Frontières. He told me that a group of women and children had just arrived who'd been beaten and raped and survived a massacre in their Kosovo village. He said he'd find out if they're prepared to talk to NGOs about their experiences. Kosovo women, Muslim women – it was the same in Bosnia – are reluctant to admit to having been raped, but it's important they do, otherwise it'll be impossible to bring these cases before the International Court of Justice. The tribunal have got their people here too, of course, and don't want the victims talking to the press because the defence may argue that jeopardises a fair trial.'

They got a taxi to a military barracks on the outskirts of town which had been put at the disposal of the Red Cross for their headquarters in Kukës. Other organisations such as Médecins Sans Frontières were also quartered in the barracks, and tents with room for several thousand refugees were pitched behind the buildings. Andro presented his credentials at the entrance and asked to see Dr Alemi, the Iranian doctor he had spoken to on the phone.

They were directed up a bare concrete staircase to the first floor. The walls of the corridors were whitewashed, the doors painted brown. They knocked on one of them and it was opened by a middle-aged man in a white coat. What immediately struck Alex about Dr Alemi were his eyes, large sad eyes such as he'd often noticed in people from the Middle East.

'The group I mentioned to you on the telephone,' the soft-spoken doctor said to Andro after the three of them had sat down, 'arrived here three days ago with the surge of refugees across the Kosovo border that began with the NATO bombardment in March and continued until Easter. Over a hundred people – all of them related, I gather – were held captive for several days in their village in the Suhareka municipality. The younger, able-bodied men left the village and joined up with the Kosovo Liberation Army before the Serb forces arrived. A dozen elderly men were the only males left behind to look after the women and children, and they were massacred soon after the Serbs – regular troops as well as police and paramilitaries, according to the women's reports – occupied the village. During their occupation seven of the women were molested, tortured, repeatedly raped. Probably the number was much higher, but –' Dr Alemi shrugged '– seven is the number in the official report I've written about this particular incident.'

Andro shuffled on his chair. 'Did these women agree to be medically examined?'

'Yes.'

'Did you carry the examinations out yourself?'

'Yes.'

'How much time elapsed between the events described by the women and your examination of them?'

'Between forty-eight and seventy-two hours.'

'What evidence did you find in support of their allegations of torture?'

'Bruising, burns and bite marks on the torso with all of the women, particularly wounds inflicted on breasts and nipples, the groin, the genital areas, and thighs. Two of the women were virgins. In both cases the hymen had been ruptured. All seven women were traumatised.'

'How long after the event can rape be proved?' Andro asked.

'We take swabs to look for the presence of sperm DNA up until seven days after a vaginal rape on post-pubertal women and up to seventy-two hours in the case of a pre-pubertal girl.'

'Seven days? In an earlier rape case in Bosnia tried at The Hague the defence successfully contested forensic evidence that was gathered only five days afterwards.'

'It always depends on the circumstances. Seven days is really the maximum time possible in cases where the victim has not moved – because she's unconscious, for example – and a result is more likely to be obtained if the woman has not washed.'

'Is the whole point of your report to provide evidence that will stand up in court?'

'Perhaps not the whole point, not from my point of view, but in practice it usually turns out to be a large part of it. One has to bear in mind that finding sperm is a criterion indicative of sexual activity, not a criterion of rape. In the absence of injuries, it can be difficult to secure rape convictions in court. The fact that in this instance we have been able to document injuries with all seven women much improves the chances of upholding the rape charge in court.'

'So have the women agreed to testify?' Andro continued.

Dr Alemi hesitated.

'That doesn't necessarily follow. Perhaps it's still premature to put the question. Certainly it's not one I wanted to ask. My job is to heal. My medical examination of the women was undertaken to assess the damage in order to heal it, not to provide evidence for use in court. Giving testimony in public is an ordeal. In their present state they wouldn't even want to contemplate it.'

'Would it be possible to see the women and ask them questions about their experiences?' Alex asked, the journalist in him anxious to get the first-hand quotes he needed for his copy.

'They've agreed to that. They're expecting your visit. I can go over to the hospital wing and see if they're ready. If you would like to wait in the meeting room just down the corridor I'll bring them there. It's up to them of course what they're prepared to tell you, but I'd be obliged if you could go easy and avoid asking too-direct questions.'

After a few minutes Dr Alemi appeared in the meeting room accompanied by four women. All but one of them wore scarves leaving only the upper part of the face visible, and were tall and spare, as in Alex's experience Kosovo Albanians often were. The exception was a woman in her mid-twenties. Alex was astonished by the appearance of this woman. While the other women seemed to be in hiding in their clothes she was completely out in the open. She had an athletic build, the shoulders of a professional swimmer. Her dyed-blonde hair was cut very short. She wore a tracksuit and clearly had no use for a headscarf. While the other women were all tanned from a life spent out of doors, this woman was white-skinned. She was the one who took the initiative after Dr Alemi introduced Andro and Alex. The other women remained silent and left her to do the talking.

To Alex's surprise, she was an Austrian citizen. The articulate and to-all-appearances calm young woman turned out to be from Vienna. It was from her that Alex learned of the events that had taken place in their hamlet the previous week. When Serb forces arrived, nearly all the men in the hamlet had disappeared into the surrounding hills to seek reinforcements from the Kosovo Liberation Army, leaving behind them a small group of elderly men and over a hundred women and children. The elderly men plus the handful of younger men who had stayed to defend the village were killed and thrown into a well, and the well blown up. She had witnessed the execution of her father and several of her uncles. The women and children were split up into three groups and herded into three houses, where they were held prisoner. For four days, the young woman from Vienna said, they were subjected to terror, maltreatment and sexual abuse before setting out on a forced march to Prizren after seeing Beli Atas burned to the ground. As far as she knew, no further abuse had taken place after leaving the village. Then the Serbian Red Cross had arrived and distributed milk, bread and canned food, arranging for some of the refugees to be taken by bus to a place called Zhur. She herself and a party of others had made their way on foot across the border to Kukës.

Had any of the women and children been killed by the attackers? Alex wanted to know. An aunt of hers had been machine-gunned right in front of her, said the woman. Andro made notes. Could she name the victims? Dr Alemi intervened to say that all the victims were members of the same family, and that beyond identifying this family by the initial K it was better if no names were given, including the first names of the women present.

What was to be understood by the term sexual abuse? Alex continued, picking up what the woman had said earlier in the conversation. Did that mean rape? Yes, it meant rape, the woman answered, or more precisely degrees of abuse usually culminating in rape. How many women had been victims of rape? the journalist in Alex felt obliged to ask, not without a feeling of discomfort. Although the spokeswoman answered his questions in Viennese-accented German, apparently her mother tongue, she translated the questions into no-less-fluent Albanian for the benefit of the other women in the room and listened to their views before replying – unaware that Alex understood what they were saying. Several women had been victims of rape, she said after consulting with them, shaking her head when requested by Alex to be specific about the number of occasions on which rape had taken place, and the doctor from Médecins Sans Frontières again saw fit to intervene, bringing the interview to a close.

To the question that intrigued Alex most but felt unable to ask at the time – how a sophisticated Viennese city girl, an Austrian citizen to boot, had managed to get caught up in the mass exodus of Kosovo's rural population over the mountains after being driven from their homes by Serbian forces – he never received an answer. All he had was the name of the spokeswoman for the group of refugees, Natasa K, and 'a village in the Suhareka region', the location he was asked by Dr Alemi to use in his piece to protect Beli Atas from unwanted publicity.

\*

Five years would pass before Alex saw Natasa again. The hair that had then been cut short had since grown long, and it turned out her name was not Natasa but Nadine.

Thanks to Andro's ruse, Alex was the only journalist to be given access to this group of refugees in Kukës, enabling him to send IPA an exclusive report on the events that had taken place in Beli Atas. The deception of Dr Alemi would subsequently cause Alex unease. In the pursuit of news he had become used to sanctioning whatever means it took, often overstepping the bounds of what he knew to be fair and decent. The interview in Kukës proved to be a turning point in his career. He realised how callous he'd become during the decade he'd spent reporting on the war on the Balkans, and decided to get out of journalism before it burned him out. He had liked to think of himself – had even prided himself on being – an impartial observer, a mere recorder of events that happened to other people in other places, and he was puzzled by how long it had taken him to find out that there was no such division. All these events were his personal concern. They had a belonging in his life. His eye had seen and his hand had intervened, rearranging the landscape through which he passed just as it had rearranged him.

# BOOK III

## The Island

# CHAPTER ONE

## A Delicate Balance

### 1

In the French and English books her grandmother used to read in the house at Herischdorf, peering down over Cosima's shoulder at words on the page she couldn't understand, Ella had stood at the first of those windows, not even that, a peephole, hardly more than a crack, through which she saw something briefly flash past belonging to a world she found intriguing because it was so different from the one in which she lived. Another flash sparked up from the stone which, thanks to the mysterious forces inside it that held it together, her father said, remained whole until, on her father's instructions, she hit it with a hammer and it broke into three pieces. Something had gone out of the stone. A loss, something like a loss of life, her father suggested. If in some way the stone had died, Ella thought at the time, it must also in some way have lived.

Until she had sat down with Sasha in the house in Paris, and he began to tell her about the foundations of physics, such windows had played no part in Ella's adult life, perhaps because Ella herself had ceased to play and no longer had the time to look for them. Preoccupied with war, flight, exile, marriage, establishing a home and having children, no more windows presented themselves to her until she arrived at that house in Paris. Physics offered a new window, the flashes she glimpsed through it no less mysterious and quite as enticing as the words she couldn't understand in the books she had watched her grandmother read. She thought that by coming closer, pressing her eye right up to the peephole as it were, it would give her a better view of what was on the other side. But the physics she studied and passed for her O level failed to open up this view of another world. So for her A levels, which she did by correspondence course, she switched to chemistry and biology, and it was in biology that she went on to do her BSc at London University.

To Ella's disappointment, in all the pages of the textbooks she read during her first year she came across no more such windows giving her a glimpse of the goings on in worlds hidden to her; this did not occur until her second year, when she picked up Rachel Carson's *Silent Spring*.

Carson's description of the transformation of matter into energy in the cell as one of nature's great cycles of the renewal of exhausted energy, like a wheel endlessly turning, carbohydrate fuel in the form of glucose being fed into the wheel molecule by molecule, broken up and transformed by enzymes — this metaphor of the great wheel gave Ella a rare glimpse into the hidden workings of reality she had wanted to understand all her life. It was her own life she saw in the metaphor of the great wheel. Carson described how at each step in the cycle energy was produced, shedding waste products of carbon dioxide and water, until the wheel had turned full circle and the stripped-down fuel molecule combined with a new molecule entering the cycle to start it anew.

The minute scale of this operation, visible only with the aid of a microscope, was among the marvels that impressed Ella. The work of oxidation was carried out in a magic box even smaller than the cell, the granules inside it known as mitochondria, boxes within boxes, tiny packets containing all the enzymes necessary for the oxidative cycle arranged in precise and orderly array along the wall and partitions of the cell. After the initial steps of oxidation had been performed in the cytoplasm, the fuel molecule was taken into the mitochondria and the process of oxidation completed, releasing enormous amounts of energy — a system of marvellous compactness, efficiency and tidiness in which Ella recognised the principle she followed in the management of her cupboards.

The energy produced at each stage of the oxidative cycle occurred in a form known as adenosine triphosphate, or ATP — the universal currency of energy, Carson called it — a molecule containing three phosphate groups found in all organisms from microbes to human beings. The role of ATP in furnishing energy arose from its ability to transfer one of its phosphate groups to other substances along with the energy of its bonds of electrons shuttling back and forth at high speed. This initiated another cycle within the main cycle. A molecule of ATP gave up one of its phosphate groups and retained only two, becoming a diphosphate molecule, or ADP. But with the turn of another segment of the wheel another phosphate group was coupled on and the energy of the potent ATP was recharged, and so on in never-ending revolutions of that great wheel of life.

The charging of the battery in which ADP and a free phosphate group were combined to restore ATP was coupled to the oxidative process. But if the combination became uncoupled, the means of providing usable energy was lost. Each step in oxidation was directed and expedited by a specific enzyme. When any of these enzymes was destroyed or weakened, the cycle of oxidation within the cell came to a halt. If the ATP content was reduced below a critical level, cells ceased dividing and organisms died.

In the third year of her BSc course Ella was required to do a field project and write up her findings. For her final written exams she would of course be required to come to London. As a field project would have been difficult for her to carry out in England, however, with a son at school in Tenerife whom she was having to continue to look after at the same time, a special dispensation allowed Ella to carry out the project under the supervision of the university at La Laguna not far from where she lived.

The death of an unusual number of birds on the islands had tentatively been linked to the use of fertilisers for intensive agriculture. Inspired by Carson's pioneering work on the disastrous results of introducing DDT into the environment, Ella chose as the subject of her field project an investigation into the connection between fertilisers and the birds' deaths. The thesis she hoped to back up with evidence from her work in the field was that, when links in the chain of the oxidative cycle became uncoupled, the cause might be found in chemical fertilisers that killed the enzymes, thus separating oxidation from the energy production needed to promote cell division and continue the cycle of life.

Such was the project she outlined in the letter she sent off to the university at La Laguna. She received an answer from the director of the Ecology Research Institute, to whom her letter had been passed, inviting her to come and discuss her work with him. This meeting between Ella and Dr Eduardo Rodriguez went to their mutual satisfaction, and the project was carried out under the supervision of his institute as requested by London University.

But shortly before she took her finals, Ella became ill again. It was a recurrence of her old thyroid problem, which had never been properly diagnosed. She was increasingly short of breath, as if something was pressing on her lungs. Her neck felt as if it was bulging. She measured it at intervals with her sewing tape measure, and found it had grown an inch and a half in six months. George persuaded her to go and see a specialist in London.

In the X-rays he made of her neck the specialist identified a massive ingrowing goitre. Ella would have to stay in a London clinic to have it surgically removed, he said, sooner rather than later. But before Ella agreed to go into hospital she wanted to see Felicity's first child safely born. She wanted to give her daughter, who at nineteen was even younger than she herself had been when Max was born, the family support that Ella had not received in the bleak hospital where she gave birth to her first child at the end of the war.

Felicity's husband Stephen was away much of the time, travelling in France and the Benelux countries as the representative of a British pharmaceutical company. He was at the hospital with Ella throughout the twenty-odd hours it took for his daughter to be born, but then flew to Brussels, leaving his wife and child in his mother-in-law's safekeeping. During the week before the birth Ella spent happy days with Felicity browsing in babywear shops. Ella wondered about the biological plan in the pleasure a woman took handling these tiny articles, the surge of happy warmth she felt just touching the miniature outfits a baby would wear. Smallness itself was beautiful. In this nexus nurturing instincts naturally flourished.

She kept Felicity on her feet right up until the moment the child was due. This was the received wisdom among the women in Ella's family.

'My mother always used to say—'

'I'm *fed up* with what your mother used to say!' Felicity flared up, just as Ella used to when she was younger, but apart from that one outburst the day before Felicity went into hospital, mother and daughter passed the week together very amicably.

While Stephen was away from the Kensington flat George had let to the young couple for a nominal rent, Ella moved in with her daughter and granddaughter, tiny Kim, in the big upstairs bedroom. Already well disposed to her simply for being a girl rather than a boy, Ella was satisfied with critical points such as her forehead and ears, which told her of nothing untoward in the child. She loved her large serious eyes, saw herself in her granddaughter's nose, George in her ears; her parents were represented about equally in the rest of her, with the same set chin Felicity had shown as a child auguring later stubbornness.

While Ella brought some sort of order to the chaos inside cupboards she had left behind in perfect order she thought about her daughter. On the tree of Felicity's stubbornness there was one fruit-bearing branch, her trustworthiness and loyalty, more to her father than her mother, perhaps, but still. The blighted branches of the same tree bore grudges with great perseverance — a reluctance, generally, to yield up what she carried in herself. What she thought and felt, these things remained hoarded inside her and were not available to her mother. Her daughter's slowness seemed to Ella to be an expression of that intransigence. How long it had taken her to deliver herself of that child! The ages she used to brood on the lavatory before assenting to empty her bowels when she was a little girl! Felicity On the Loo entered the family language as a euphemism for A Very Long Time. The patchwork quilt Felicity began six months ago was still not ready when the baby was born, while even in the first week Ella was there a collection of little woollen garments had already grown out of her knitting needles. Everything that came effortlessly to herself took root reluctantly in her daughter. While Felicity went plodding on, Ella seemed to be flying. Knitting flew off her needles, work off her hands, thoughts in showers of sparks off the anvil of her always-busy mind. She could hear a bright sound ringing away inside herself and wondered how one's own son and daughter could be so different.

Philip came up to London and spent the day with them. He had chosen his wife early, but, sensible as he was, wanted to be articled as a chartered accountant before he and Ann got married. They had met at the Sherborne school-leaving ball, and he had followed her down to Portsmouth. He took his two-week-old niece on his arm and weighed her up, pursing his lips while working out a rough estimate of what she might be worth.

'What's the daily cost of feeding a child this age?'

'Philip!'

His mother and sister laughed, pulled him down onto the sofa and pummelled him, kissed him and pulled his ears. Philip got red in the face but came out of the tussle looking pleased.

When Stephen returned from his trip abroad, Ella moved back into the spare bedroom downstairs. A couple of days later she went into hospital to have the goitre removed. For the operation it was necessary for her to lie with her neck pushed back at an unnatural angle, exposing her throat to the surgeon's knife. Lying in this position for a couple of hours overstretched the tendons and left her with chronic pains in her neck and shoulders. The operation also left her with a long scar at the base of her neck. The surgeon had the hypertrophic goitre preserved in a jar of formaldehyde and kept it as a specimen to show medical students. The scar would fade in time. Worse was what happened to her voice, the warm mezzo that was as much a part of Ella's identity as her face. Her skin remained almost as smooth in her forties as it had been in her twenties, but during the removal of the goitre irreparable damage was done to her vocal cords and she was left with a crack in her voice.

'Never mind, old thing,' said George, seeking to console her. 'What you've got to say matters more than how it sounds.'

But for her youngest son it was the other way around: how Ella sounded mattered more than what she said. Alex was disturbed by the change in his mother's voice. It disfigured her. Her whole appearance had somehow changed. With a different sound she no longer seemed to be the same person.

In the letters Ella wrote to Claude in Japan she wondered about all the illnesses that had befallen her in the last couple of years. She wondered why she had not been taken up into nature's great cycle of the renewal of energy, carried forward by the wheel she helped turn to carry forward others. She regularly sent off parcels to all her children living abroad, to people she remained fond of in St John's Wood, to the old aunt in Hamburg who had taken in the family of refugees that arrived on her doorstep back in 1945. But the parcels Ella secretly still hoped to receive herself, perhaps from her dead mother – for who else had ever sent her a parcel? – failed to arrive.

Ella reached her own conclusion in a letter to Claude: *I think I go into hospital in order to rest. That's why I get ill. The burden I've had to carry has been too much for too long.* She now knew why her mother's life had flickered out at so young an age, and she wondered now how she had failed to recognise something so obvious, the exhaustion that had caused her mother's death before she turned fifty.

# 2

Dr Rodriguez offered Ella a job with the team of researchers compiling a survey of the island's endemic species. Rodriguez' vision was that the survey would provide data for a map of the island's biological diversity, grounds for extending the areas that could be classified as national parks. It surprised Ella to learn that on a dry, in many parts extremely arid, island, heated by the proximity of the Sahara and benefiting from only scant rainfall, there were reckoned to be hundreds of times as many endemic species as there were in Britain. But although it rained seldom on Tenerife and the island lacked natural rivers, in a ravine on the island's northern tip an area of tropical forest flourished. Mossy tree limbs dripped with water in a humid climate sustained almost entirely by condensation from the low clouds pinned against the mountainside. This tropical forest region known as Cruz del Carmen provided one of those unusual evolutionary habitats, of which there were many on the Canary Islands, revealing a new species or subspecies to biologists every other week – more endemic species per square kilometre, Rodriguez calculated, than anywhere else in Europe.

The Ecology Research Institute situated outside San Cristóbal de La Laguna was still a recent and little-known addition to the university. When Ella made her first trip there in the early 1970s to discuss the supervision of her thesis with Dr Rodriguez she had difficulty finding the place. Local people she asked for directions hadn't heard of it. Even the university's buildings commission, whose job was to provide suitable premises, had only a vague idea what the Ecology Research Institute was for. Under the impression that it had some sort of connection with the environment, the commission housed the new institute in natural surroundings in a villa outside town on the road to Las Mercedes that led north-east into the mountains.

El Bronco was the name of the village, or rather settlement, a cluster of houses assembled along the country road. You could easily drive through it without noticing you had been there. Many visitors did. Set back half a kilometre from the road was a spacious two-storey villa with architectural pretensions quite different from the humble dwellings surrounding it, including a portico with columns at the entrance, a swimming pool and a grass tennis court at the back. The builder of this folly was a Santa Cruz businessman who went bust before he completed his extravagance in an out-of-the-way place with an undesirable name and little chance of ever finding a buyer. The buildings commission waited until the property had gone stale on the market and got it for half the price the owner was asking.

Eduardo Rodriguez walked into the empty premises and told the man from the buildings commission just how he wanted it: this here, that there, offices on the ground floor, laboratories and archives on the floor above. The swimming pool was to be turned into a salt-water facility to accommodate marine life.

'We are a small department, so small that there are people at the university who deny that we exist,' he told Ella as he showed her around the institute.

Then he introduced her to his faculty of three, the biochemist Julio, the marine biologist Domingo and the statistician Agrippina, who doubled as the institute's secretary. All were in their early thirties.

By the time Ella was invited back as a researcher on the endemic species project the faculty had grown by two members, Inma and Conchita, both in their late twenties, plus a number of students who drifted in and out on assignments. Eduardo must have been in his late forties, which would make her the second-oldest person on the staff. Sometimes he brushed through the villa and swept them all out onto the lawn at the back for a game of badminton. Sometimes the mood came on him, and the seven of them piled into his enormous black car. Eduardo's love of his 1948 Dodge grew out of memories of hitchhiking around Spain as a student and getting rides from teams of toreros travelling from fiesta to fiesta in just such cars. He drove them into La Laguna for lunch, or in the other direction for a picnic in the mountains. It would all be there in the boot, and Eduardo was the magician who had put it there with a shake of his wand, the food and drinks, the plastic plates and paper napkins. It had been planned in advance, of course, but with Eduardo such arrangements seemed to arise on the spur of the moment.

Conferences were apparently called on the spur of the moment too. Eduardo moved through the offices, clapping his hands. 'Everyone outside for a discussion. There are a few things we might sit down and talk about.' It was always *might* or *could*, never *must* or *should*.

'Eduardo started life as a Marxist-Leninist and has metamorphosed into a Maoist,' Julio confided to Ella. 'He doesn't want people to get into ruts; he's always shaking them up, getting intellectuals out of doors – it's part of his private Cultural Revolution.'

At Eduardo's bidding a couple of hours might pass with everyone ordered out to the pond to look at the fish. He believed such sessions of doing nothing in particular turned the group in on itself and nourished team spirit. The coming of all such moods on him was part of his natural spontaneity, or perhaps, as Julio said, his Maoism.

'Once I become predictable I risk losing your interest, and your interest is something I can't afford to lose.'

Such words made his staff conscious of their worth. He primed them with praise where praise was due, making them smart even more under the reprimands he was also capable of handing out. On their return from a field trip on the neighbouring island of La Gomera, so far barely touched by tourism, Julio and Domingo described the people and their living conditions as poor.

'Not poor – frugal,' Eduardo said sharply. 'People are poor when they don't have enough to go round. On La Gomera there's enough to go around and they're satisfied with what they've got. They're satisfied with less, but that doesn't mean they're poor.'

It might have helped that he had the same name as Ella's brother. It might have been his liking for axioms that put her in mind of her mother's home truths. But most of all it was his naturalness that drew Ella to him, a horn of plenty from which his life seemed to spring, nourishing the people around him. It was his likeness to herself.

'Eduardo's a provider,' Ella realised with surprise. In her own family, perhaps in most families, the lineage of providers ran on the women's side. It wasn't something men seemed able to do as well as women. Providing wasn't about bringing home the bacon, it was a condition of being unable to help oneself, taking into shelter, being bound to nurture, to keep in one's thoughts and guard over with spread wings – like the angel invoked in the sampler embroidered by Cosima and worked into the quilt under which Ella had slept as a child. Ella's grandmother, her mother and Ella herself were the providers in three generations of their family.

But the Rodriguez family was evidently an exception to this rule. The director of the Ecology Research Institute of La Laguna University was the first male provider Ella had met in her life. He had provided her with her first job. He had made it possible for her to live a dream. Weeks of fieldwork in Cruz del Carmen alternated with laboratory analysis back at the institute in La Laguna. Both kinds of work absorbed Ella equally. Reluctant to leave the field at the end of the day, she took to living on the site in a tent. No less reluctant to leave the laboratory, she rented a room in La Laguna so that hours wasted on commuting back and forth by bus every day between home and work could be more usefully spent.

With the transformation of matter into energy, the metaphor of a great wheel endlessly returning, carbohydrate fuel being fed molecule by molecule, broken up and transformed by enzymes, Ella had arrived at a very narrow window – not even that, the surmise of a window, initially no more than a crack of light. The closer she approached it, however, the clearer the view through it became – the window itself no longer formed part of her field of vision, only the view opening up further in width and depth, until she found herself looking at the scheme of life itself. The enabling constraint of the scientist's window – its very narrowness – was what opened up the view. Without the frame around what one was looking at, one wouldn't have seen the view.

These were thoughts she could share with Eduardo Rodriguez. He introduced her to other ideas which had a profound impact on Ella. On the wall of his office hung a framed piece of paper on which was printed the following declaration.

The basic behaviour mode of the world system is exponential growth of population and capital, followed by collapse. As we have shown in the model runs presented here, this behaviour mode occurs if we assume no change in the present system or if we assume any number of technological changes in the system. The unspoken assumption behind all of the model runs we have presented is that population and capital growth should be allowed to continue until they reach some 'natural' limit. This assumption also appears to be a basic part of the human value system currently operational in the real world. Whenever we incorporate this value into the model, the result is that the growing system rises above its ultimate limit and then collapses. When we introduce technological developments that successfully lift some restraint to growth or avoid some collapse, the system simply grows to another limit, temporarily surpasses it and falls back. Given that first assumption, that population and capital growth should not be limited but should be left to 'seek their own levels', we have not been able to find a set of policies that avoids the collapse mode of behaviour.

When Ella read this framed document on the first occasion she visited the institute, she asked Dr Rodriguez who had written it.

'The authors of *The Limits to Growth*, a study of global projections recently commissioned from MIT by the Club of Rome. They ran sets of different projections based on different hypotheses through computers, and that was the result they came up with.'

'I haven't read it.'

'Then you should.' Rodriguez reached for a little book on the shelf behind him and handed it to Ella. 'Here you are. It's only a hundred pages or so, but what pages.'

Two days later she returned it to him.

'It's stunning.'

'Terrifying, for anyone with the slightest imagination.'

'What is the alternative to runaway growth on the one hand and stagnation leading to collapse on the other? Equilibrium, they say. Well, we could live happily with that.'

'Fine in theory, but in practice difficult to achieve. There's no such thing as an equilibrium that endures. Systems change; the equilibrium shifts, however slightly. In theory all very well, but who's controlling the balance? The answer's up there.'

He pointed at the framed document behind his desk.

'Population and capital *seek their own levels* – meaning cycles of uncontrolled upswings and downswings, depending on whether the forces causing population and capital stock to increase – high reproductive fertility, low birth-control effectiveness, high rate of capital investment – or the forces causing them to decrease, which are the opposite of what cause them to increase, plus famine, plus pollution – i.e. on whether upswings or downswings are the prevalent conditions in the world. Allowing economies to be run by market forces provides a paradigm of a world where growth is left to seek its natural limits.'

'So it's a roller-coaster ride on an open-ended circuit, a circuit not even built.'

'Either that or someone intervenes, sets the agenda, closes the circuit.'

'Who would that be?'

'Who would that be. Some kind of world council it would have to

657

be. In the long run there'll be no alternative to a global government. Naturally the authors can't say this, but if you ask what the consequences are of leaving things to seek their own level you will have to answer that things *cannot* be left to seek their own level. This may mean the erosion of democracy. Lovelock may speak metaphorically of Gaia *culling excess population*, i.e. causing partial extinction, by making large areas of the earth too hot for habitation, but in the short term the task of determining how many of us there should be and the size of our footprint on earth rests with human beings. The elimination of excess population. By war? By natural or unnatural selection? No one wants to spell this out because it isn't something that can be achieved under anything like the existing political conditions in the world today.'

'People can be expected to exercise self-restraint, to submit to unwelcome measures if it's understood they're essential.'

Rodriguez laughed as he knocked a cigarette out of a pack.

'That may be an answer in the tradition of the humanist eighteenth-century Enlightenment. The modern answer given by our consumer society is different. People encouraged, more, *required* to consume, can *not* be expected to exercise self-restraint. And however rational your assumption that one can expect people to give up smoking if they know how bad it is for them, it's not a realistic one, because these days human behaviour isn't based on what you quaintly call rational considerations, Ella, it's based on consumer desires masquerading as needs.'

'So where do we go?'

Eduardo lit his cigarette and exhaled.

'We could ask first where we've already been. The world population grew from one billion to two billion in about a hundred years. The fifth, sixth and even seventh billions may arrive in less than thirty years from now. Although the rate of technological change has so far managed to keep up with this accelerating pace, we have come up with almost no new discoveries to increase the rate of social change. Applying technology to improve conditions in a natural environment hostile to growth or even to life itself has been so successful that civilisations have evolved around the principle of fighting against limits rather than learning to live with them. Why have less if you can have more? Only if you're forced to. Of all the exponential growth curves none is as steep as the one tracking the development of rich versus poor. More goes to the rich in inverse proportion to the less that goes to the poor. There *is* no equitable distribution in a growth society, and there will be even less of it in the society that emerges from the collapse of the system and tries to recover the pieces left. Fortunately, this is still a long-term perspective and it's not going to concern us personally. The perspective of the majority of people doesn't extend beyond next week. Very few people think about what's going to happen in a hundred years, let alone do they think about it being as urgent as what's going to happen next week. This is the doom with which we can most easily live by putting it out of our minds. Certainly I do. When I leave this office and drive home, burning up the highway in my beautiful old six-litre Dodge convertible, I shut the door on such thoughts. Don't we all?'

# 3

Ella thought about all this. She puzzled painfully over it. It continued to be thought and puzzled about inside her without her own doing even after she had shut the door and gone home for the weekend.

She got off the bus at the depot in La Orotava and walked up the hill, turned through the gate into the courtyard of the house and climbed the staircase to the third floor. The GONE FISHING sign hung on the handle but the door opening onto the gallery of their apartment was unlocked. Ella was annoyed. Anyone could just walk in. She'd warned George and Alex often enough. It might have been all right in the 1960s, when George first arrived, but by the 1970s, with the increase in tourism, crime had reached even La Orotava.

As she made her way along the gallery overlooking the well of the courtyard she put a hand in the flower boxes. They needed watering. She picked up the can in the corner niche and watered them. There was a watering can in each of the four corner niches, enough for the boxes all the way round. Making sure they were always full was Alex's job. Watering during the week was George's. She wondered how long it was since he'd last done them. Neglect of the flowers that were his chore, a casualness about money, forgetting to keep receipts, even a neglect of his own person, going for days without shaving, not caring what he wore – she wondered if George was beginning to let himself go.

*Making an effort that never ends and seems to have no purpose.* That was what she had told Sasha after she had tried to gas herself in the house in Paris.

The rooms off the gallery opened on to a view of the ocean to the north and the mountains to the south or the growing sprawl of Puerto de la Cruz along the motorway, which now ran visibly and sometimes audibly, when the wind came in from the ocean, west–east all the way around the island down to the projected new airport on the south coast.

A rather dainty sofa of St John's Wood vintage with scrolled armrests filled the glassed-in alcove facing inland. Ella liked to settle there between chores, to have a drink and still occasionally a cigarette, pursing her lips and squeezing out little puffs of smoke. The serious smokers in the family – George, Claude and recently Max – teased her about this technique Ella had developed to avoid inhaling and wondered why she bothered.

'To sit down for ten minutes and give myself a break.'

Before the botched attempt to take her life in Paris there had been an incident, allegedly an accident, involving a gas oven and her mother in Herischdorf when Ella was about three years old. Someone had come into the kitchen and switched the gas off, rescuing mother and child. The matter wasn't spoken of afterwards, but Ella knew what other uses ovens could be put to and, in the Depression of the 1930s, not infrequently were. The year after the war broke out she had once solemnly prepared for death, kneeling on the floor with her head and shoulders thrust into the cavernous oven of the Schlawe house, getting the feel of it and in her imagination already joining the mourners at her grave, halfway to committing herself to her extinction, before she changed her mind.

What kept the great wheel turning?

The collaboration of many small parts, those tiny packets of enzymes, arranged in precise and orderly arrays on the walls of the cell, charging the battery in which ADP and a free phosphate group combined to restore ATP – and the close enmeshing or coupling of this combination with the oxidative process. In her ignorance she had just taken all this for granted. It was only recently that Ella's knowledge of the micro-scopic cellular world and its labours on her behalf elicited something like admiration, gratitude, a reluctance to let these loyal collaborators down. Until then she would have called such reluctance the instinct of self-preservation, threatened only by an occurrence biologists described ominously as uncoupling.

Here was the puzzle the conversation with Eduardo left her with. How could someone dedicate themself to their life's work and at the same time acknowledge this work to be fruitless, as Eduardo apparently did? How could Eduardo seem to be so full of life, so vigorous and enthusiastic about his work as an ecologist, while convinced that what the MIT study called the overshoot mode and future collapse of world growth was inevitable, the hypothesised state of equilibrium untenable, the ecologist's goal of a sustainable environment unrealistic?

*When I leave this office ... I shut the door on such thoughts. Don't we all?*

The discomfort this parting shot still gave her had to do with the fading of the Holocaust from her mind. Meanwhile there were indeed periods in Ella's life when the Holocaust slipped her mind. Preserving it was the task that had been given her as a personal trust. Never forget! And yet forgetting, for a couple of days, even a week – after the Pathé newsreel she had seen with George of bulldozers piling corpses in a concentration camp she would have thought it impossible to forget even for a minute – this had come to pass in the quarter of a century since. Eduardo's question about natural or unnatural selection had just reminded her of it again.

Alex stayed down on the harbour wall, grilling fish with the local boys who went fishing there, so Ella and George had supper alone. She waited until George was finished with his account of the afternoon's fishing before she asked him her question. 'Do you think human beings can come to terms with anything? Can we get used to *anything*?'

'If we can get used to living with ourselves,' George said without hesitation, 'and most of us do, I suppose the answer is yes.'

'Seriously.'

'It depends on the person and the nature of what they're being asked to get used to. Are we talking about torture? Concentration camps? The standard of living in the world's poorest countries? Or the usual concerns of life? I, for example, have found out that I can come to terms with a rather low standard of honesty which you might find intolerable. And you would find it very difficult to live with a sense of failure, which most of us learn to accept.'

Ella became interested. 'You live with a sense of failure? Since when? You've never talked to me about this before.'

'How else to describe a career that ended in ignominy? Or another career I feel I've grown out of, and not just because of declining sales. All right, I get along. I've no complaints. I know how fortunate we are to live here. Just living here looking at the sun always shining almost imposes an obligation to be content. That makes me reluctant even to bring the subject up. But somehow I'm not quite ... hitting the mark, you know. I'm trying my hand at something else, something completely different from all the other stuff I've done before. I think too much about the bow in my hand, or is it the target, that marvellous little book by Herrigel, what was it called? Yes, *Zen in the Art of Archery.* I gave it to you to read in Biarritz, remember? Anyway, my aim isn't so good. Looking at me sitting here on permanent holiday in my T-shirt and shorts, you wouldn't necessarily see that I'm not really relaxed. Most people doing nine-to-five jobs would say my aim was fine. And perhaps I'm a bit envious.'

'Envious of what?'

'Of the way you've found something that suits you so well, how quickly your professional life has taken off. Perhaps not so much of your success as of you having found your vocation. I can't say that I ever really had one.'

It was the sort of throwaway remark into which she had learned to read the deeper feelings that George had difficulty talking about. She sometimes wondered if he had them. What actually went on in his mind? It was difficult to believe in other people's consciousness the way you believed in your own. Ella warmed to his candour, evidence of a human concern which it was otherwise left to her to draw out of him. There was now at least this much. The old George would never have made such an admission, never talked about himself in this way.

What to do about George had lain uneasily on Ella's mind for some time. She wondered if the state of the world in a hundred years could preoccupy her in the same way as the state of George. After fifteen years of living on the island he had become uncoupled. His books were no longer selling as they used to. What had once come easily to him he now found laborious. Reluctant to sit down to sustained work, George escaped into the distractions he invented for himself and Alex. They learned windsurfing and went sailing together, also fishing, at least nominally, even if George took the trip down to the harbour mainly as an excuse to settle in at the bar of the Marquesa or the Monopol in the

Calle Quintana, where he met his cronies for a game of chess, leathery old locals and expatriates in retirement in Puerto. Why not? Because more was needed. He didn't seem to understand that he couldn't just go on being an expatriate.

The financial situation that had begun to worry Ella a few years ago was back under control. Even if George's books brought in little these days, the salary she was earning went some way towards covering their decline in income. And that was before the bonanza. It had been another of Ella's ideas to sell the pictures that used to hang in their St John's Wood home. At a Sotheby's auction in the mid-1970s a work by Beckmann, one by Klee, two each by Francis Bacon and Lucian Freud, which George had bought when the Morris family was still rich in the late 1940s, fetched prices ten or twenty times higher than the sums George had originally paid for them.

Bringing to mind another sentence she had retained from Eduardo's rapid delivery on the subject of exponential growth curves before he shut the door on such thoughts: *More goes to the rich in inverse proportion to the less that goes to the poor.*

This mental intervention led to one of those sudden twists in the conversation that George had learned to expect from his wife. 'As it is, we're living far too comfortably. We can't have all this and give nothing back in return.'

'Anything particular in mind?'

'You need to engage with people here more, George. You must come out of yourself. You receive so many benefits from the island but what does the island receive from you? You're well informed about international affairs. You know lots of languages. You could teach. You do have things to give, you know.' She got up and looked absently around the room, forgetting what it was she had been meaning to do. 'Sometimes I wonder if it's my fault.'

'What's your fault?'

'You must remind Inéz to stock up on toilet paper,' she said to George as she shut the cupboard.

'I'm afraid Inéz has given notice.'

'Given notice? But she only started working for us six months ago.'

'She's moved to Gran Canaria. She's been offered a job working in a hotel over there.'

'I sometimes wonder about Claude. If you'd ever said, you know, years ago, when Claude moved in with us in Richmond, if at the time you'd said with any sort of force that you would have preferred him not to ...'

'I don't believe any person has an absolute claim on another person. That's one of the few things I *do* believe, Ella. Besides –' George folded his napkin into a triangle as he got up from the table '– Claude is my closest friend.' Continuing to fiddle with the napkin, as if trying to get something straight, George added, 'Claude is frail. I have to look after him. One of us does. He's vulnerable. I miss him, you know, holed up there in Japan. I'm looking forward to him coming home. In fact, I recently wrote to tell him so. I get the impression he isn't very happy there. I've come to the conclusion that things go more smoothly between me and you, you know, when Claude's around. You're so busy with other things these days. Maybe I miss him more than you do. Yes, that's my impression. In the old days you were always wanting to talk to me about Claude, but you've hardly mentioned his name recently. I only bring it up because you've always prided yourself on covering all your bases – everything on your radar screen, you like to think – but this is something you may have overlooked.'

This observation took Ella so completely aback that for once she was short of an answer.

# 4

With Ella away during the week, George had decided he needed some domestic help and hired a housekeeper called Inéz. A compact, self-assured and handsome widow of around thirty, Inéz had a bold way of looking at her employer with her black eyes that kept George in two minds. A challenge to his authority? An invitation to discover the woman in his employee? Or perhaps both? She came one morning a week from eight to two. She cooked and cleaned, washed and darned, went out and did the shopping armed with the list she was given by George.

She challenged his lists – not the right season for this or that vegetable, not the right day for fish, they were short of light bulbs and tissues but had more than enough toilet paper – in short, the list always needed revision.

George gave in. His housekeeper took charge.

One hand on her hip, the other waving the shopping list she objected to, Inéz stood leaning against the doorway to her employer's study. He would usually be sitting at his desk working on translations of United Nations reports, the kind of job he took on these days to make up the decline in his earnings as a writer. She debated the choices George had made. Inéz could inject a personal note into articles such as soap, shampoo, shaving cream, the particular aroma of WC deodorant and triple-layer toilet paper she recommended as substitutes for the brands George had been using to his satisfaction until now. In praise of the qualities of the products she wanted to buy instead of the cheaper ones on her employer's list, she would use words such as tang, softness, discretion – even chastity. These descriptions George found unsettling not so much because they surprised him, coming from an uneducated working woman like Inéz, as because they had an erotic effect on him for which he was wholly unprepared.

George could see where this might lead and he didn't want to go there, at the same time realising that he would be powerless to resist what had been set in motion by Inéz' arrival. It was this unhappy preoccupa-tion that led him to broach the subject, in the vaguest and most general terms, to the first suitable person who came along. This happened to be Ella's boss, Eduardo Rodriguez. George found it easier to discuss his inner life with strangers than with members of his own family. With Rodriguez it was particularly easy because he was an intelligent and cultivated man. 'These days,' he confessed to the stranger who dropped in to enquire about Ella, who was away on a trip to London, 'the feeling overcomes me that under the appearance of choosing – or so I used to think – a particular path for myself, what really happens is that I just find myself on it. I just sort of slip into it. All that apparatus – will, choice and so on – has it ever crossed your mind that all that may be no more than the props of a grand illusion we devise in an attempt to give meaning to our lives?'

'You mean we merely go through predetermined motions?'

Feeling the pressure of an exactness required of him which he wasn't capable of, George tried to squirm his way out.

'No, that's not quite the sort of thing I have in mind. Strings being yanked rather than things being prearranged. That's more like it. A grand illusion seems to me to require a grand puppeteer. These days, having given up the illusion of myself being the mover of what moves me, I've become susceptible to a feeling of being ... tugged, you know, urged on a course of action I'm not sure quite what to make of. Maybe not tugged. Slipping into things is really more a being *nudged* into them, you know? When I was younger I didn't have such feelings, but these days ... I'm aware of pressures to which I'm involuntarily subject – *forces*. I've no idea what those forces are. But I do understand that being subject to them means I don't have the freedom of will I used to assume I have ...'

A disconcerting series of nudges in connection with his housekeeper had led George to this conclusion.

There was the business with the latchkey. When George left the house he didn't take the key with him. He hung it on a nail one couldn't see but only feel behind a beam above the door opening onto the gallery at the top of the stairs. But when he came back from buying a newspaper on the Saturday in question the key wasn't there. He had no idea why it wasn't or where it might be. He retraced his steps to the newsagents. He searched the street outside the house. He even lifted the grid off a drain and looked in there. The concierge could have lent him her key, but she wasn't in. Nor were the two residents on the lower floors, both of whom had been given spare keys by Ella, making assurance doubly sure, mainly for the benefit of Alex, the family's notorious forgetter of keys. Ella and Alex had already left for Arguayo the previous evening. Meaning that George was stuck.

The missing key caused him a degree of unease that seemed disproportionate, as if the source of the unease had long since been conniving with a thought that only now surfaced in his consciousness: Inéz will have a key.

He felt that he could hardly ask her to come up on the bus to La Orotava and bring him the key. He would have to go down to her in Puerto de la Cruz to fetch it. They still didn't have a telephone at the Orotava apartment. George called from the newsagents to find out if she was in and asked her for the address.

Inéz lived in a block of flats on the ring road marking the limits of the old town clustered around the harbour before rising steeply up to the gardens of Parque Taoro. The bus down from La Orotava stopped across the street from the building. The building was accessed via an entrance in one of the alleys that criss-crossed the old town between the ring road and the ocean. There was no elevator. George walked up to the fourth floor and pressed the buzzer.

The door was opened by a little girl of about nine or ten, who stood rubbing her hands as if drying them while she smiled up at George without shyness. Inéz looked out of a doorway beyond and said to George, 'The key's hanging on that row of hooks to the left as you come in. But won't you stop for a few minutes and take some refreshment? This is my daughter, Estela.'

She came up and stood behind her, hands on the girl's shoulders, presenting her to George. He was struck by the likeness between mother and daughter.

George hesitated in the doorway. 'Well, if it's not too much trouble … if this isn't holding you up.'

'Why should it be too much trouble?' Inéz asked in her easygoing way. 'Or do you mean trouble for yourself, holding you up, not me?'

Her employer's curious ideas amused Inéz. Standing not more than two or three feet away from him, still holding her daughter between herself and the visitor, she took stock of George with a smile.

The entire window front of Inéz' living room, looking north-east to the ocean, could be folded into recesses in the wall on either side. It was like sitting on a balcony, bringing the brightness of the big surrounding day into the small space. Inéz placed her guest on the sofa, stage-centre of the sea view, and sat with her back to it. The ploy surprised George with a memory of Julia, how she would seat herself artfully to avoid light falling directly onto her face – if it did traces of acne became visible under the powder – in the vast mournful dining rooms of those hotels where they used to stay on the trade missions to eastern Europe.

And why would he think of Julia here?

Mother and daughter seemed dressed to go out.

'You're sure I'm not holding you up?' George asked again, needing to be reassured that he was not causing inconvenience, and again Inéz smiled her odd little smile.

The girl had red shoes and white socks on, red bows at the end of her plaits. Her mother wore a white blouse with soft blue patterns like faint smudges of ink rather like the cotton gowns Claude had sent over from Japan as a present for George to wear in hot weather, white shorts and blue sandals with gold trim. She sat facing him with crossed legs, shaking the bangles down her forearms with an occasional flick of a

667

wrist, drawing attention to the beautifully bronzed clear, smooth skin of bare arms and legs he couldn't help admiring. The brilliance of mother and daughter quite took George's breath away.

'I didn't know you had a daughter.'

'You never asked.'

Realising how little he knew about his housekeeper, George decided he must talk to her to find out more about her life. He must take more of a personal interest in Inéz.

When he got home and took out of his pocket the spare key she had lent him to open the door, he found his own key sitting in the lock. This nudge knocked him off balance. It was beyond explanation. It verged on the frightening.

'I can't have left it in the lock. I would have seen it if I had. So how did it get there? Someone must have found the key on the ground and put it in the lock for safekeeping.'

Things were happening beyond his control.

He bought himself an 8-millimetre film camera for no reason he could think of. He saw it in a shop window and just went in and bought it. Who knew what for, might come in handy, George told himself, but at the back of his mind he did have a rough idea, just as he had a rough idea that he might after all have managed to leave the key in the lock himself.

He read through the instruction manual until he could name all the camera's parts and understood what they were for. He filmed around the house and up and down the street, the girls playing hopscotch and the old women leaning on their sticks. Venturing further afield, he filmed boats leaving and coming into the port and a carnival parade on its way through the old town. Watching these images flickering on a screen back in his living room, George was as touched by their innocence as he was surprised at his own naivety. He had always scorned the tourists making their holiday movies, and now he had become one himself.

But the very particular home movie George had a craving to see was one that would capture the spruce freshness of Inéz and her daughter Estela dressed as they had been on that day when he called on them to pick up the housekeeper's latchkey. The light flooding that room airy as a balcony, the bright appearance of Estela in her white socks and red shoes, the gold bangles slithering down Inéz' bronzed bare forearms, sitting with crossed legs in white shorts, such touching harmony of mother and daughter in the surroundings of the otherwise very ordinary little flat where they lived – George had a craving for a kitsch image that held such lightness of being, sweet and addictive, like the craving for ice cream that periodically ambushed him these days.

Inéz stood in the doorway looking at the moving images the projector threw on the screen rolled down over the bookcase in the living room, then looking at her employer as he explained just what it was he wanted from her. He wanted mother and daughter to be dressed exactly as they had been before, and to be ready at the same time he had visited them the day he had forgotten his key, ten o'clock in the morning, with the sun coming into the room from the side. Inéz smiled and said no trouble; it would be arranged as George wished.

In pursuit of the *spruce freshness* he had been so struck by on that earlier occasion George arranged them in many different poses, sitting, standing – the mother standing behind her daughter, the daughter behind her mother seated with her legs crossed or sitting on her mother's lap with one arm around her neck – in the kitchen getting lunch ready, talking and laughing as they set the table. George was so naturally expected to stay for lunch that Inéz didn't even ask. In fact they had such fun together he stayed all day, getting home so late that he postponed driving to Arguayo until the following morning.

At George's invitation Inéz and Estela came up to the Orotava apartment a few days later to see the film that George had made. They watched it in respectful silence, not so much disappointed by the sight of themselves on the screen as perhaps not quite able to believe it. At any rate, they showed a more lively interest in the film sequences shot in their neighbourhood, the carnival parade through the old town and the boys fishing on the pier whom Estela went to school with and knew by name.

Inéz asked George if he would mind her showing Estela around the apartment. The mother gave her daughter an official tour of the premises, with names for all of the different rooms that Inéz appeared to have borrowed off the doors of the suites at the Casino Hotel where she worked as a chambermaid, upgrading George's lopsided if charming eyrie at the top of the old house into a grand residence he would have hardly recognised himself.

'And this is the Carrara Bathroom ...'

In the days when he was flush George had ordered marble from Carrara for a bathroom to be built by local masons to his own design, or rather to his memories of a bathroom in a Miami hotel where he stayed in the early 1960s at the time of the Cuba crisis. The bathroom was an impressive if vulgar statement, featuring an outsize round tub, matching twin basins with gold taps, and floor and wall tiles in the same beautiful white marble.

Estela asked the question a child didn't hesitate to ask.

'Can we have a bath?'

'Estela!'

But what her mother had to say didn't count here, and Estela already knew what George would say.

'You can have a bubble bath if you like.'

'Oh yes!'

'Would you like a green one or a blue one?'

'Blue!'

George put the plug in and turned on the taps.

'It'll take a while to run. I'll go and see what towels I've got in the cupboard.' He went out and came back with two large white towels. 'I brought one for you as well,' he said to Inéz, 'just in case.'

'For me? Am I going to have a bath too?' she asked with mock surprise.

'Oh yes, Mama, please! Please have a bath with me!' Estela jumped up and down.

'We don't have a bath in our apartment,' Inéz explained to George, 'only a shower, so this will be her first bath.'

'So you'll have to go in with her then. You can't let Estela down, can you.' He stirred the bathwater. 'What do you think? Is it about right?'

Inéz reached into the tub and their hands stirred alongside one another, testing the water, fingers accidentally touching.

With a big splash that washed over the rim of the bath, she lowered herself quickly into the water. 'Look at you! I've made you all wet!' Inéz laughed.

'My mistake – I shouldn't have clothes on in here.'

George handed a pile of bath toys to Estela, pulled off his canvas shoes and rolled up his wet trouser ends, aware of preparing for his life to change. He began to feel shipshape – getting back into the swing of things – granted permission to come aboard and set off on a cruise.

'I'll just hang these things up to dry,' he said, padding out, a shoe in each hand. A minute later he returned with only his shorts on, bringing the camera with him.

'No!' protested Inéz.

'Well, you never know,' said George, knowing full well. 'But I'll stick it in the cupboard so that it doesn't get wet.'

'I bought some new sponges,' said Inéz, pointing. 'There on the bottom shelf. You've not even taken them out of the wrapping!'

'I'm leaving them for Alex to try out. I thought they looked a bit too fierce for my tender skin.'

Inéz chortled. 'There's a rough side and a smooth side to those sponges, and probably to you too. Pass me one and I'll try it out.'

Estela stood up in the bath to have both sides of the sponge applied to her body, the smooth side to her front and the rough side to her back. The little girl squirmed.

'Stand still, Estela!'

George quietly retrieved the camera from the cupboard and shot the scrubbing sequence without protest. Once George's camera was back in the cupboard of course they didn't spare *him* with their splashing either. George got soaked and eventually everything ended up as it was bound to, with the employer discarding his shorts and joining the staff for water games in the tub, where they had a good go at him and he at them with the patent two-sided sponge, splashing and shrieking with laughter until the phone ringing in the adjacent bedroom brought these activities to an end. Dripping naked as he answered the telephone, George listened to his neighbour below, who had rung up to complain that water was coming through her ceiling, turning the plaster soggy and ruining the furniture. George apologised, accepted full liability and promised he would be down immediately to inspect the damage.

# 5

Longer conversations between Ella and Eduardo took place at night in the El Bronco institute building after everyone had gone home. The two of them liked to turn a subject inside out – it kept them on the move – most recently Eduardo's new hobby horse of compiling a terrestrial database of the fauna and flora of all the Macaronesian Islands – the Azores, Cape Verde, Madeira, the Savage Islands and the ten Canary

Islands. They followed the subject physically from one office to another – getting a perspective of it across desks and along corridors – eventually down the stairs and out of the building, ending up in Domingo's shed on the far side of the lawn. There were adjustments to be made to the concentration of toxins being drip-fed into tanks along the walls – one of Domingo's less cheerful long-term experiments designed to monitor the levels at which fish continued to live or at which they began to die. Eduardo made the adjustments last thing before going home at night, Domingo first thing when he arrived early in the morning. In the centre of the shed stood a glass tank, a walk-around aquarium big enough for humans to swim in, which close-quarter observations periodically required Domingo to do, and if the conversation took a particular turn Ella and Eduardo might sometimes end up skinny-dipping there too.

A line of chairs stood sentry around the aquarium, a couple of plain wooden straight-backs, a steel and leather cantilever, plus a beaten-up sofa and ditto armchair. On these the members of the institute would distribute themselves when their in-house marine biologist wanted to illustrate a talk with live action in the big tank behind him.

Dripping after a dip in the aquarium, Eduardo would plonk his wet naked bulk on the battered but still serviceable cloth-covered armchair. Ella would wrap a towel around herself and settle for the wooden straight-back chair beside him. There they sat and looked and talked while his hand scored conversational points on her back from time to time, tapping out some emphasis between her shoulder blades, or, when activities in the aquarium seemed to warrant it, giving her shoulder a conspiratorial nudge.

Eduardo's terrestrial database analysis module was designed to determine the zones of greatest biological wealth on the island that were not currently Protected Natural Areas. This was strictly a conservation project. Ella turned it into something else. It occurred to her that the module data – using a few fixed values such as the unit of water consumed, the unit of waste generated per day by unit of tourists or unit of forest required to absorb unit tons of $CO_2$ per annum generated by the consumption of so many gigajoules of fossil fuel burned up by unit of aircraft on take-off – could equally serve as a database for a more ambitious project. It would allow comparison between different island environments with many characteristics in common within the same subtropical to tropical belt of the Macaronesian Islands, all of which were coming under increasing threat from the effects of mass tourism.

'Given significant natural affinities in the environment of two or more islands,' she pronounced, 'it ought to be possible to introduce variables into a controlled experiment and come up with a meaningful result about the sustainability of the island environments.'

Nodding in agreement, Eduardo waited for her to develop the idea.

'In this way one might come up with a yardstick for determining the maximum tolerable number of take-offs per year or number of road vehicles registered at any one time on an island, establishing criteria to regulate human activities in a representative cross-section of world holiday resorts with the highest visitor frequency. What that means is testing the variables in the limits-to-growth models – at MIT they could only be simulated using computer projections – in *a real-life experiment*. You can establish the ecological footprint of passing island visitors with less difficulty and more precision than you can with resident earthlings on the planet. You can put an island into decline mode, analyse the collapse and pull the island back out of it without causing irreparable damage as you could never do with collapse on the global scale. You can play God, but responsibly, without causing God's damage.'

Eduardo grunted. 'Wonder what God would think about that.'

The problem was how to get lots of people with lots of different ideas to agree on a common course of action. As yet none of the islands even had such a thing as an environment agency. That would have to happen first. Once you had the appropriate bodies you could bang their heads together until they came up with some such trans-Macaronesian socio-environmental experiment. The idea had potential. They played with it, enjoying their enthusiasm, and Eduardo felt reluctant about raising an objection that dampened it.

'The problem of science is that the piecework procedures which experiments involve – changing the variables, more of one and less of the other – dismantle the integrity of what they investigate, treat it as an assembly of parts. Scientific investigation fails to take into account the holistic element, the moving spirit of integration, life, itself irreducible, immanent in all biological systems only as long as they are *not* reduced to their component parts. There's the dilemma. What's most real about the real world is something unreal, not identifiable in the material terms of the real world. The whole that matters most is not itself material. Break a stone with a hammer, and the life goes out of it.'

'*What?* Did you use to do that too?'

'We had a physics professor at school in Madrid who gave demonstrations like that.'

'He broke a stone with a hammer and told you the life had gone out of it? Amazing! With me and my brother Oscar it was my father. I've been waiting – well, perhaps not *waiting* – all my life to meet someone else who's taken a look inside a broken stone.'

'This calls for a celebration then.'

Eduardo disappeared naked into the bathroom and returned with his shorts on, placing his feet with the toes turned out and the legs stretched straight, taking deliberate dancer-like paces, quickening, the dramatic walk of a dancer coming out of the wings onto the stage.

Stopping in front of her, he performed an elaborate bow. Then he leaped, drawing in his legs and bending his knees before straightening them again and landing on the same spot. He carried out another scraping bow, extending his left leg with the toes pointed as he did so, then the right, following it with another odd little leap, seeming for a moment to be cycling while suspended in mid-air. So he continued these leaps and landings, bowing and turning and extending his legs with oddly dainty movements, all on one spot, until he was out of breath and concluded the performance with a final bow.

Ella clapped and laughed with delight. 'But you're a dancer!'

'Well ... not really, not any more. These days I'm a bit out of shape.' Eduardo looked down ruefully at his middle-aged bulk. 'There's all that, for a start. And then I smoke too much. But when I was a schoolboy I used to go to a dancing academy run by a little old man – I say old, but I suppose he was no more than fifty. It was just a few boys and girls in a room with a mirror and a bar for exercises. I went on dancing until I was a student and then for various reasons had to give it up. Nobody knew about it, not even my mother or later Aurelia, my wife. I would have been ashamed to tell anyone, so I kept it a secret. Apart from the dancing master in Madrid, who taught it to me, no one has ever seen me perform what I just performed for you. It's an ancient court dance that used to be danced by men to demonstrate their prowess.' He laughed. 'Such as is left of it. By the way –' Eduardo padded off towards the bathroom '– a job has come up that might interest you.'

674

'I already have a job.'

'But one below your abilities. I think you'll find this one more challenging. And you would be doing me a favour. With your permission, I'd like to put your name forward. I'll explain when I come out.'

She heard him whistling in the shower as he got dressed and smiled when she thought about the curious display she had just seen. 'It was a peacock strut, of course, a mating display to impress me.' And she was impressed, at the same time amused, and touched by an intimacy Eduardo had shared with her in the secret of that odd little dance he had never shared with anyone else.

# 6

You could stand under a bus shelter with Santana for a few minutes, waiting for the rain to pass, and fall into a conversation that would continue for the rest of your life. Just a drop or two of him, and Santana would go on spreading until his listener thought he had reached saturation level but still clamoured for more. 'He's one of the most interesting men I ever listened to in my life,' Claude wrote to Ella towards the end of his teaching assignment in Kyoto, where he first met Santana and became an instant addict.

When the American in the wide-brimmed white hat sitting alongside him at the counter in the noodle shop got down from his stool to go to the toilet, he left a manuscript on the counter that caught Claude's eye. *Nogyo Zensho*, said the title in Roman letters on the cover, with the name of the author, Miyazaki Antei, and the first date of publication, 1697. It was a treatise on silviculture from the Genroku period, excerpted in a handwritten English translation.

Claude was still looking through the manuscript, reading an underlined passage, when its owner returned to his seat and matter-of-factly began quoting it back at him as if in seamless continuation of a conversation he had been having with Claude before it was interrupted by his visit to the toilet.

'We have lost the measure of things,' he announced to Claude at that first meeting in the noodle shop. As a self-professed naturalist, a biologist by training, a self-taught ecologist, archaeologist, social anthropologist, and a few other things besides, not in any order, he preferred particulars rather than averages, individuals to genera. A geophysical system always began with the action of an individual organism – and there was no doubt that Santana liked to think of himself as an individual organism whose actions turned out to be beneficial to his local environment, thereby setting an example that would be followed by other organisms, in the long run resulting in what he called a global altruism. Species that improved habitability flourished, those that harmed it were set back and became extinct.

Only as a result of Claude's questions was Santana led back to the reasons for this trip he had made to Japan, which was to see for himself the conditions under which one of the world's first documented experiments in large-scale forest cultivation had taken place. 'Take nothing on trust without first having seen it for yourself,' was another of Santana's shibboleths. Nothing counted like personal experience. He liked to sit in this particular noodle shop, he said to Claude, because of its smooth counter made of *hinoki*, such a pale shade of beige it was almost off-white – even in the early 1970s this most beautiful of hardwoods was becoming rare, too precious to be used for counters in noodle bars or even in the sushi shops where it was more commonly to be found. Santana travelled to remote forest areas where the trees grew, delighted to discover the same detailed inventories still being made as they had been three hundred years earlier – the number of trees, how many and of what kind, the height and circumference, the straightness or crookedness of thousands of individual specimens. He spent months as the guest of a traditional timber merchant with workshops and a showroom for high-quality furniture in the old Gion district and a sawmill in the mountains outside Kyoto. The cabinetmaker's apprentices spent a year or two just handling wood, learning the look, feel and scent of it, before being allowed to cut it, and during his stay Santana and his interpreter often sat alongside them.

All of this flowed into the lifetime project that occupied Santana between other commitments to short-term research projects, books, teaching, travel. It was a study of the collapse of civilisations. As deforestation and forestry mismanagement were in Santana's opinion the salient factor in all recorded cases of societal collapse, beginning with the well-documented civilisations of the Mesopotamian Basin over five millennia ago, the subject held a particular interest for him that ran to whimsicality, manifesting, on closer acquaintance, an obsessive streak. In academia he was known disparagingly as the Tree Man, but colleagues who affected contempt for Santana's Warehouse Foundation may just have been envious of the publicity and the funding he managed to raise for his projects.

Mutations in thoughts that travelled around the world could often be attributed not merely to mistranslation but to incompatibility, the inability of one language to accommodate another, Claude said in reply to a belated question from Santana about the nature of the project that had brought him, Claude, to Japan. How did core language untranslat-ability differ from unknowability in another language? Were there things in every language that couldn't be said in other languages, explicable but not reproducible, and perhaps understood as something quite different?

Enjoying the challenge of a question he had never thought about, Santana asked Claude for specific examples of what he meant.

'If the concept of the self in Japanese and in other Asian languages requires differentiation by as many as a dozen or more distinct words for the first personal pronoun, isn't that a case of language speciation com-parable to the speciation of animals and plants? The number of words for self testifies to the bandwidth of the idea of self, and therewith surely to a different approximation to the understanding of self, a rubber-band elasticity of the self, for which there are only rough equivalents in other languages. They are singularities. All languages have these singularities, and they constitute the language's soul, for which there is no substitute.'

Claude was struck by the happy analogy that in the meanwhile defunct language of the natives of Heligoland, a bare rock inhabited by fishermen in the North Sea, where seeds dispersed by birds or winds from the mainland might have resulted in no more than the occasional shrub or tree, one wouldn't find and didn't expect to find a word for forest, just as in other environments, easily imaginable though they might not actually exist, one could not assume words for time or love or humour or even any idea of these things.

'Hmm!'

As Santana picked up the tab at the noodle shop for both of them he wondered in passing what the archaeological record was for a hy-pothesised forest that might once have flourished on Heligoland and was now extinct, and whether there might once have been a time for the Ik people in northern Uganda when the solitary dark internecine existence they now led had been illuminated by the light of a mutually

677

supportive society since lost, and with it the words of tenderness, concern and collaboration and the banter folks shared at the village well that one would have come across as a matter of course in those pre-collapse days of Ik life. The conversation with his new friend animated him. A project he would like to recommend to a protolinguist of Claude's sensibilities was the reconstruction of a language that might have been spoken in the Garden of Eden, said Santana in all seriousness, taking off his hat to wipe his mainly bald head with a large handkerchief as they stepped out of the noodle shop into the midday sun, quoting verses from the *Epic of Gilgamesh* as he did so.

*In the wilderness she made Enkidu the fighter,*
*His whole body was covered thickly with hair,*
*His head covered with hair like a woman's;*
*The locks of his hair grew abundantly, like those of the grain god Nisaba.*
*He knew neither people nor homeland;*
*He fed with the gazelles on grass;*
*With the wild animals he drank at waterholes;*
*With hurrying animals his heart grew light in the waters.*

Dawdling on his way home to Europe, perhaps apprehensive of returning at all, Claude travelled the wrong way around the globe, south-east across the Pacific rather than north-west via the pole. By a combination of boats and planes he drifted from the Solomon Islands down to Fiji and Tonga, taking in the Cook and Society Islands before landing up on statue-ridden and treeless Easter Island, catching a plane to Chile, from where he flew to San Francisco to visit Santana and, incidentally, Max, who had settled there after abandoning England. The writings of Bougainville were responsible for this detour across the South Pacific. Original eighteenth-century editions, occupying the last shelf devoted to the letter B in his uncle's elegant library in Paris, they had sewn into Claude's schoolboy mind dreams of an escapist island paradise that did not stand up to the reality he visited as a man. Once the dreams had been supplanted they were not recoverable – there was no longer anywhere to store them – leaving Claude to regret not merely the loss of paradise but the idea of it that had lived in a possibility now for ever gone.

Santana's San Francisco-based Warehouse Foundation had found its ecological niche in a converted warehouse on the waterfront. Some of the people who worked in the building lived there as well, graduate students for the most part. In their spare time they grew vegetables on the roof and cultivated the Santana legend.

He was famous for the eccentricity of his methods. On a joint visit to Tokyo Claude had personally witnessed Santana's glee to have reached, during the morning rush hour at Shinjuku station, what was arguably one of the half-dozen points of greatest human density on the planet. He told Claude about a day he had spent as an observer in a little glass information booth at Grand Central Station in New York, to get the measure, he said, of the density of modern human life. During an eight-hour shift he logged over a thousand contacts with people requiring information, all of them strangers wanting something in a hurry from the booth attendant and never offering him anything in return.

Santana thought evolution had not designed human beings for exposure to so much contact and that it would need thousands of years for evolution to catch up, but by that time the world population would already have imploded under its own weight. This was a disequilibrium of modern life that worried him. Santana's day shift at Grand Central Station was followed by periods spent in isolation without human contact at all, without light or sound, by way of preparation for a project researching the limits of human resilience. The need to experience everything personally led Santana to the extremes of the globe, from hot deserts to the Arctic Circle, not to mention the mind-altering drugs he regularly took with his friends on the roof garden of the Warehouse Foundation. He could have done with a few more words for self, he told Claude, wondering if a language as rich in first-personal pronouns as Japanese could maybe help out.

In his handling of people Santana had a directness indistinguishable, at least by people like Claude who were touchy, from crassness. In his presence you were as likely to feel invigorated as threatened, some might have gone as far as to say physically endangered. That Santana had accidentally shot his first wife was part of the legend that happened to be true, an episode that rattled his friends and associates and led them to treat him warily, although the court in California had found unequivocally in his favour. His eccentricity grew more pronounced as he got older. In a conventional teaching capacity at any university he

679

eventually ceased to be employable. This had led him to found his own institute, where he could do as he pleased.

An apparent perverseness in Santana's self-subjection to inconvenience, bordering on extreme discomfort and welcoming mortal danger, had to do with the need he perceived to keep on reinventing himself, discovering himself anew in order to grow rather than merely to just go on living. That was a lesson he reiterated again and again. People had to keep on coming up with new reasons for their existence. Only in the perception of his own growing could a man be content. It was part of what he called the battle to control reality.

Santana's belief that a man was his own best laboratory didn't stop at occasionally kidnapping and coercing others in the event of needing them for experiments in that laboratory. His approach to others was an extension of the there's-no-substitute-for-personal-experience rule he applied to himself — bluntness was a tool to be used to catch them off balance, dislodging them from a prepared state and stripping off the mental make-up people put on, the mask he saw as disfiguring them. The things that people didn't intend, the throwaway remarks and the body language they weren't even conscious of, were what revealed most about them, he told Claude, who wondered how Santana could quote Ella without ever having met her. This sort of talk was instinct with Santana. Critics called it irresponsible. With Santana around, a loose cannon gratuitously firing off broadsides as the mood took him, heated exchanges often took place. Some of the projectiles might turn out to be smash hits, spot on; or, just as likely, way off target and very wounding. People found it upsetting to be shown these X-rays of their inner life, but if they had the courage to look, as he did, Santana complacently assured his victims, they might find what he had to say revealing.

'You know, that criticism you just made of Bob is actually a criticism you're making of yourself,' was the sort of lunge Santana might make at someone in the group he was talking to. 'If duty is in there without heart your character is probably better than your nature,' was a barb he directed at Claude when Santana happened to observe him taking out his wallet with evident reluctance to pick up the tab for someone Claude felt it his duty to treat. Irritated by what he saw as Santana's presumption, Claude told him to mind his own business.

Ignoring Claude's angry retort, Santana continued the deconstruction of his new friend with that calm, disinterested rigour which characterised

all his discourse. If Claude honoured what was his duty without putting his heart into it because at bottom he had a grudging nature, as
Santana had gone on to surmise — not just from that one incident in the
cafeteria but from previous observations at the noodle shop in Kyoto
where Santana had picked up the tab for both of them — what was it
that Claude begrudged and how had it got there? These were questions
for Claude to grow on, not resent, said Santana, leaving Claude with no
choice but self-examination. And he began to wonder about the silver
shillings he had once watched pass between George and the waiter in
the Athenaeum.

*Who pays?*

During the Kyoto years, when he had no one to suit but himself, did
an idea of another, a better and more desirable life than the one he had
led begin to take shape in Claude's mind? Did he have trouble facing
up to the undesirable consequences which that other more desirable life
would inevitably also bring with it? Feeling unfulfilled, was Claude on
that account grudging, reluctant, as Santana had not only observed but
persuasively acted out for him in an astonishing replay of the cafeteria
scene, mimicking Claude's body language? Or did it all run much
deeper than that, linked to a resentment he had put aside at the time,
a grudge on which pleasurably to brood in later years, sitting over his
own dank deposit inhaling the smell that rose out of the toilet bowl, an
odour having to do with a dead father and a reckless absentee mother
who between them had managed to mislay Claude's childhood? Had he
remained entranced at that spellbound moment of development in his
youth when all paths were, or had at least still seemed to be, possible?

Whatever the answers, the questions seemed to point to some kind
of denied consummation, for instance Claude's state of half-marriage, a
sort of spare wheel put onto an already running system, or the modesty
of his professional ambition to be a professor at a university most people
had never heard of on an island known only as a mass tourist resort,
to which he had sent off an application before leaving Japan. Did an
old ambiguity arising from a youthful desire to keep his options open,
even including an alternative life on a South Pacific island, where he
had looked into the possibility of teaching elementary school in New
Caledonia as a fallback position in the event of being turned down for
the job at La Laguna, still linger at the back of his mind? Was it conceivable that Claude had hitherto begrudged George his first-husband

status and that this showed through in the reluctance he felt to go back to accepting his old status as Ella's second-best husband?

These were the things that passed through Claude's mind during the weeks in limbo in San Francisco, watching Santana setting examples and wondering where he himself was heading. Santana suggested to him it might first be Monterey, from where they would get a boat out to San Nicolas island and back to the mainland on a roundabout route to LA airport for Claude to catch his plane to Europe. There was a plan to repopulate the island with the sea otters that had once lived there, explained Santana, one of the many local environment projects being monitored by students at the Warehouse Foundation. The otter population, and incidentally a few hundred individuals making up the Indian population they had shared the island with for hundreds of years, had been wiped out in the nineteenth century by Russian trappers, seal hunters hailing from the Aleutian Islands. One woman had escaped and had lived alone on the island for twenty years before she was found by another party of hunters and brought to the mainland. They never found out her name, never understood a word she spoke during the seven months she survived her removal from the island before succumbing to some ailment for which her immune system had been unprepared. Various Indians from tribes native to the California coastal region were brought to the woman to see if they could figure out the woman's language, but none of them had been able to understand what she was saying. With the woman's death a culture became extinct – her tribe, its language and its history.

Mindful of apparently irrelevant things such as the scent of frangipani on the cool gust of wind that had tugged at his bare shins in the sun-dappled corridor of the elementary school in New Caledonia where he had stood waiting for an interview with the principal, Claude saw how imminent meanwhile his own extinction was, how much more so it had become during the time that he and Ella had been separated. Made uncomfortable by the desolation of the Indian woman's solitude, seeing it in the perspective of innumerable other islands he had passed on his way across the South Pacific, one as dispensable as the next, Henderson and Pitcairn Island, volcanic drops that had one day congealed in the ocean and would one day disappear back into it, not least the disappearance of the island that was himself, Claude told Santana he would rather skip San Nicolas and just go straight to the airport. Seeing a school of dolphins sporting in the sea below just after take-off, he remembered Santana quoting from the *Epic of Gilgamesh*, and with the hurrying animals he watched disappearing under the wing as the aircraft banked, he felt his heart grow light in the waters.

# 7

Claude returned after six years. He had been away for too long and was no longer in touch with the changed Europe to which he came back. Feeling himself a stranger, almost an impostor, he wondered if he would ever be able to make up this deficit – continuing, as he did, to miss Japan, where he would always have remained a foreigner but had never thought of himself as a stranger. So where did he now belong? Like all foreigners in Japan, he had occupied the neutral status of an outsider. Unlike many who became frustrated by the failure of Japanese society to absorb them, felt they were being discriminated against, their love of the Japanese unrequited, and left the country in a huff, Claude was content not to be involved, didn't seek acceptance by the Japanese or expect them to love him. A loner like Claude could live comfortably with this semi-official outsider status. It absolved him of responsibility for what in his own country would be regarded as self-segregation. When nobody expected anything of you or you of them, nobody was disappointed. This was an evasion of the real business of life, as Ella had warned him in her reply to the letter he wrote her when his contract expired after three years and he told her he was thinking of renewing it for three more.

In his years living on the temple premises on the outskirts of Kyoto, surrounded by silence, slowness, the rituals of priests, his private space reserved entirely for himself, deprived above all of Ella's influence, Claude had become more of what he was by nature, a rather formal, non-involved man who kept his feelings to himself. Claude appreciated living in a country where people avoided touching each other. Bowing in preference to shaking hands, they kept their distance. They took their shoes off at the door to avoid desecrating your floor. Body language was minimal. People didn't gesticulate when they talked, didn't kiss or hold hands in public. Women covered their mouths with their hands to hide their laughter, the unsightly hole it came out of in the middle of their face. It was possible to make a virtue of such diffidence, nowhere more so than in Japan's haughty old capital, and to cultivate it as an aesthetic of obliqueness – of things withheld, hinted rather than stated, reflected rather than directly seen – and Claude had embraced it, celebrating non-involvement as an expression of his true nature, choosing to overlook its other function as a carapace for the vulnerability it concealed.

He returned to a Western world that had become shrill and merciless in its pursuit of the false intimacy of a new egalitarianism. The strait-jacketed society he'd grown up with had unbuttoned to become a pervasively and indiscriminately touching culture. Everywhere hands reached out to touch, wanting to connect, seeking togetherness he didn't want, violating his private space. He thought back with distaste to that euphoric sense of oneness with the crowds that he'd experienced during the uprising in Paris. Nothing Western found favour with Claude any more.

Claude had adapted to his Japanese environment more easily than the foreigners whom he got to know in Kyoto, but he was unprepared for the reverse culture shock that awaited him on his return to Europe, where there was no one with whom he could compare his experiences. His adaptation to what he found on his way back in proved to be much harder than it had been on the journey out. Passing through London and Paris, he was horrified by the size of people, the volume of their bodies and their voices – enormous houses, built of stone rather than wood – intimidating cathedrals – the appearance and taste of food – smells in general – all contributing to the gross intrusive physicality of everyday life around him. It was above all women who embodied the difference. Blonde women, large women, women with big breasts and blue eyes, brought out his sense of estrangement from European culture most strongly. Not merely had he ceased to find European women desirable. They fell barely short of disgusting him.

When Claude renewed his contract in Kyoto, Ella had come out to a resort in Thailand to spend Christmas with him. How bulky she seemed in comparison with the delicately boned Asian people! How strange her green eyes, the fairness of her skin and hair! Her body so scarred from all the operations she'd been through that she didn't want to be seen in a bathing suit! Claude felt her physical presence had become alien to him. Premonitions of the long-term effects of his conditioning in Japan first came to him on this occasion before he returned to Europe, filling him with unease. It seemed he had become – the odd new word Ella had brought out with her – uncoupled. He wondered if he was still equipped to deal with European life.

They spent three weeks in a small beach hotel on an island. For the first couple of days Ella felt so estranged from Claude she told him she wondered how she could once have been so close to him. Was it possible she could have lost the intimacy with a person she knew and loved so well?

It seemed it was.

'We've grown out of practice with each other,' she told Claude.

But as the days passed they gradually got back into practice without too much difficulty. The strangeness that had grown on each of them during three years of separation rubbed off within a week. Under the layer of new strangeness felt by both of them, the older familiarity remained intact. Neither of them particularly sought it, whatever it was; it sought and found them, not of their making, but making them. All it required was trust. Claude's future didn't lie in Japan, they realised, nor did Ella's lie in a life without him. This was less a decision than an undertaking negotiated on their behalf by a mysterious third party, for both of them still shrank from renewing an emotional commitment to one another in as many words. They would wait and see. But when Ella flew back west and Claude back east it was with renewed confidence in their entangled destiny. They accepted it as no less than their due. Somehow or other he would be back in Europe within the next few years. Somehow their lives would be linked again. Ella believed they owed this to each other, such was the nature of the obligation, as she understood it, to something greater than them – to Claude's discomfort she called it grace – which they had been given when fate brought them together and to which they remained indebted.

# 8

A post in the faculty of French literature became available at the university of San Cristóbal de La Laguna, where Ella worked at the Ecology Research Institute. Claude had been waiting for some such opportunity in Spain, but he hadn't anticipated finding it on Tenerife. In two minds as to whether he really wanted the appointment, he didn't expect he would get it and was surprised when they offered him the job. His

French name probably helped, as Ella had long ago anticipated, not to mention the references provided by some distinguished academics and men of letters in Paris.

During the years Claude and Ella were separated they had exchanged letters every other day. Thus, although he and she had met only once during those years, they were hardly less attuned to each other's state of mind than they would have been if he had remained in his job in London. Perhaps more so. Ella's letters brought her very close to his ear, making the slightest shift in her day-to-day feelings and thoughts audible in Kyoto. It was as if she were sitting and talking to him from the other side of the paper screen that divided his room. His letters to Ella gave her the same sense of closeness to Claude. Time and distance had no effect on this proximity, a measure of their spiritual closeness that seemed almost to thrive in the physical absence of the other. It puzzled them to discover that the spiritual closeness which had worked so well at a distance didn't bring them any nearer once they were together again. On the contrary, it seemed rather to have deserted them.

Ella was not happy with the Claude who came back to her. She found him emotionally regressed to the person he had been when she first met him, not long after his release from the Jesuit lycée in Paris. She noticed the same mixture of detachment and awkwardness about him on his return from Kyoto. But this Claude was twenty years older. A reserve she had once attributed to his youthful uncertainty, attractive to her then, now seemed to Ella a deficiency, a lack of growth in a man approaching middle age.

What had he got to show for those years in Japan? A trilingual edition of the poems of Miyazawa Kenji and a philosophical treatise on translation, both of them published to barely audible acclaim within the academic world.

'They're a remarkable achievement,' said Ella after she had appraised the books and admired the poems, 'but it's all in the mind of an academic. What have you brought back as a human being?'

'It's more than an academic question. More than ever the world needs people who can mediate between cultures. I've recognised – and overcome – the innate sense of Western superiority over the rest of the world, which is so deeply ingrained that Europeans of my generation and older aren't even aware of it. I've arrived in the post-colonial world. I learned from my students no less than they did from me. A deep affection had grown up between us by the end. We remained friends after they graduated and came to visit me with wives and children.'

Claude hesitated, aware of sounding pompous, put off by the inquisitorial manner Ella seemed to be bringing to this conversation.

'I've learned what it means to live in a society that offers you a choice of half a dozen different words to differentiate what in the West is lumped together under the single word I. Imagine living in such a language. It's impossible to determine who you are without reference to the persons you are with. What the language represents is a more socialised individual within a more strongly knit society. I like this individualism founded on the community. I prefer it to our brand of selfishness. I think their way will give them better prospects of survival in an increasingly fragmented world lacking the cohesion – family, school, workplace and so on – that holds things together in other societies.'

Ella brooded. 'And for us? What does it mean for you and me?'

'It means what it's always meant. Without you I'm missing from myself. Your new word – uncoupled. When we were separated I longed for you. Now you are here, but I still long for you. How is that? It's easier to imagine being with you than to be with you.'

'Then why did you come back?'

'I told you – without you I'm only half alive.'

'Not much more when you're with me. You've hardly touched me since you came back.'

To both of them it was becoming clear that they wouldn't be able just to pick up where they'd left off when Claude went away. They weren't chiming. Often they didn't even seem to be striking the same anvil.

They would have to start over and find out where they stood, said Ella, but *start over* already caused Claude discomfort. He wondered if it was just Ella who had picked up this Americanism or whether it had entered the language in his absence. It showed how out of touch he'd become.

Without discussing with Ella the implications it had for the continuation of their life together, Claude used the double inheritance he'd been left by Aunt Dot and his uncle Louis to buy a tumbledown house in one of the back streets of La Laguna. His main reason for choosing this property was its equidistance. It was within ten minutes' walking distance of the university in one direction; in the other it was a symmetrical ten-minute walk to the house for retired nuns where Ella had a room in the administrative wing of the building.

Ella had been meaning not to intervene in the setting-up of Claude's house, but when it came to it, and she saw how uncertain he was about managing everything, knowing nothing about local contractors, prices, where to go for what, she couldn't resist organising it for him and put him in touch with all the necessary people. Once the house had been renovated, she took him shopping in Santa Cruz. Claude looked around the shops they went into and announced he saw nothing there he wanted in his house. Ella took so strong an objection to this possessive pronoun that she walked off and got onto the first bus that came by.

'Ella, wait!'

But Ella didn't wait, and Claude had to run to catch up with her, squeezing onto the bus just before it drove off.

'Leave me alone,' she shouted at him as he lurched down the gangway after her. 'Go back to Japan! So much for that social education you preached to me about! Go and live in your house on your own!'

'I didn't mean it like that.'

'But it's what you said! *My* house! Since when has any house we've lived in been mine or yours?'

Claude flared up at her. 'Houses we've lived in have always been *yours*! Who cares who owns them! But you put your mark on them. It's your personality they reflect, your cupboards with their inlaid messages – not George's, not mine. What say in them could I expect to have had in any case, the houses in St John's Wood and Richmond and here? I was the hanger-on who came in late. But not in this house! I've provided it! I've paid for it! And if I've acquired a taste for as little furniture as possible, ideally no furniture at all, then that's how it'll be. It so happens the deeds to this house are in both our names. Where's this bus going anyway?'

'I've no idea.'

She laughed and they got off.

Claude followed her off the bus, couldn't follow Ella's laughter, the speed of her transitions from one emotional state to another. He recalled the conversation he had had with George in the Athenaeum, something George said about the leeway in which Claude would have to learn to live with the imponderabilities of what George called that Slav soul of Ella's. Who knew, perhaps there were two of them, or more? George added, getting into the spirit of things, each of them arguing their case behind her back.

*Claude's house*, as she pointedly called it in front of George and Alex, remained in the no-man's-land where the quarrel on the bus had left it. Alex sometimes spent a night there out of solidarity with and curiosity about a father he felt he no longer knew but who, he sensed, might be more in need of his son's support than the son needed the father's. Ella effectively boycotted the house, didn't acknowledge its existence. Claude had bought it despite them, breaking the rule that everything in their life should be shared. George was hurt too.

'I'm sorry you're moving out, old man. I was looking forward to you coming back and living with us.'

'Why am I always expected to come and live in *your* house? I do so at weekends. When Ella's in Laguna during the week, she can come and live in the house with me. *Any* of you can come and live in it. It's a house for *all* of us. Ella doesn't have to keep that room she's rented in the house for retired nuns. Why does she have to live with *retired nuns*?'

Calling it *the house* didn't help at this late date. There were no takers for *the house*, and not for *our house*, either. Whatever Claude called it, whatever he said to make them welcome there, that faux pas of *my house* still stood between them and wasn't easily undone.

Reabsorbing Claude into the skein he had absented himself from for so long apparently wasn't something so easily done either.

Ella found it difficult to admit to herself that Claude's purchase of a house in La Laguna didn't suit her. Worse, his coming there at all didn't really suit her. George had divined it in that remark about him missing Claude more than she did. But there was more riding on this than either of them understood.

What Claude and George didn't understand was the self-evident freedom they had been given but Ella denied. For them freedom was the ordinary state of affairs. Unlike his sister Tessa, George's life had been his to do with as he pleased because he was a man. When he declined to take over the family firm from his father because he preferred a career at the Foreign Office, no obstacles were put in his way. No obstacles were put in Claude's way when he took off for Japan and left Ella to look after their son. Everything was given them. They could chop and change. She couldn't. Nothing was given her. To arrive at that place where George and Claude had always been, Ella had to struggle. For her, freedom was an extraordinary state of affairs, even if it might not look like that to them.

Sometimes it took the form of the tent where she camped during her field trips to Cruz del Carmen, or her corner of the office she shared with two other researchers at the institute, her workbench in the laboratory, her microscope, her eye at the aperture revealing a hidden world, her room in the house for retired nuns in San Cristóbal de La Laguna – she wouldn't let anyone get away with mocking those little old ladies she had grown fond of and felt the need to speak up for, even if she only ever saw them at a distance from her window overlooking the garden where they walked. Perhaps she identified with them because she thought of herself as one of them. The great wheel she had always put her shoulder to so that others could be carried forward – liberated from that bondage, she felt it was now her turn to be carried forward.

Claude and George saw this exhilarated Ella, and recognised they had been left behind. Ella *was* exhilarated. She who hadn't once been paid in twenty-five years for the work she had undertaken as mother and housewife was now being paid a salary to take her place at a microscope and record what she saw there. She could spend days combing through the forest of Cruz del Carmen and be paid for enjoying herself. She was paid to get on the bus and spend the weekend at home in La Orotava just as she was paid to get on the bus to La Laguna and go back to work on Monday mornings.

The institute was her world. It existed independently of George and the rest of the family. She had earned it entirely through her own efforts. She was proud of the institute, and everything connected with it was shot through with her sense of gratitude for what it had given her, was still giving her, would continue to give her in the future. This was her other family, and the joy was that she didn't have to run it – that wasn't her responsibility, and when had she ever been able to say that before? All she had to do was play her part.

She had got used to the idea of La Laguna as being in some way *her* town, her room there an asylum where she could detach herself from family and become her own person. La Laguna didn't need to concern any of the others. She felt they could leave it for her. But Claude now lived and worked in the same town. If she gave up her room and moved in with him, she would surrender that freedom to be just herself in her own space.

Knowing Claude was hurt by the cold reception she and George had given the house, Ella explained the importance to her of the room she had rented. This was her space, she told Claude, and because she needed it she would not be giving it up until she took up her new job in Santa Cruz.

'And perhaps you need your space too,' she suggested to Claude, 'after living on your own for so long.'

'Perhaps. But aren't we missing something here, Ella? Is it necessary for me to point out that we need *our* space no less than you need yours and I need mine? It doesn't have to be either/or. You can move back and forth between your space and our space, can't you?'

'But I don't want to move back and forth. Don't you understand? Why should I be the one moving back and forth? I want to stay in one place, I always have. You should know that better than anyone, Claude. I arrived there with you. The trouble is, I'm no longer sure where that is.'

Claude was unhappy with this conversation, with the direction conversations had generally taken since his purchase of the house. If he sounded rather ham-fisted to himself, it was because Ella was being uncharacteristically obtuse. He wondered if it had anything to do with the role that the director of Ella's institute now evidently played in her life. He wondered what might be left in the unfinished-business bin. Was he going to be required to do penance?

He returned to the subject of their living arrangements a couple of days later from an unexpected angle, that irritating little word *any* for some reason cropping up.

'If it's Eduardo or other friends you're thinking about, you're welcome to bring *any* of them to the house, you know. I'm not sure where you and I stand, for that matter. We've never kept *anything* from each other before, Ella. I'd be sorry if we were to begin doing so now.'

Days went by when they didn't see each other.

'But why should I see Claude every day? What for?' Ella asked herself, and failed to come up with an answer.

She lay awake at night with thoughts that troubled her in the absence of where Claude used to be. Not missing him was what troubled her. But she couldn't bring herself to admit it was over. She waited for the thought that it was all over between them to come floating along of its own accord, presenting her with a release note in unambiguous language, absolving her of what she still felt as her responsibility for

Claude. Envisaging some such release note as not being a problem at all, just a piece of paper with a few clear and straightforward sentences written on it, she decided to write him a letter. If need be, she wouldn't write it herself but just copy on paper the words she saw in her mind.

She opened the drawer of the desk in her room and took out a piece of paper and a pencil to write a first draft of this letter. Searching for the pencil sharpener, she put her hand into the back of the drawer and pulled out a little plastic tray, the souvenir of some airline meal she had kept for her stationery – clips, an eraser, pencils of various lengths – and among the bits and pieces she found a curious little object she didn't immediately recognise. It was the London cleaners' tag fastened with a safety pin. She had taken it off Claude's trousers when he had visited her in hospital.

When Ella took the safety pin in her hand she felt a prick in her heart – the same stab she had felt in the Bois de Boulogne when Claude landed in front of her at the foot of the tree. She saw the first space she had shared with Claude, their bedroom in Cornillac, committed for ever to memory. She remembered what she had said to herself at the time: *Dear room, I shall want to come back here at some time in the future when I no longer can, for even if I could, all this will be over then, it will all have gone, except in my mind.* The pity of it! The waste of those years!

A tenderness touched with sorrow for herself and Claude, which she thought her heart might have lost for ever, came back to her now. Grateful, she took hold of it and began to write what it dictated to her. The tenants had left Arguayo, the house stood empty again and was waiting for the family to move back in: George, Alex, Claude and herself at the weekends, Felicity with her two babies in the holidays, Philip and his wife Ann. The house might not yet know, but its best days lay ahead of it, yes they did. *Darling Claude*, she wrote, all that was needed was the will not to let go – and trust – and love – remembering where they had once been, where else they still had to go.

# 9

At Los Rodeos airport Felicity was met by her father. George hadn't seen his granddaughters for almost a year.

'How they've grown!'

It was a stereotypical reaction Felicity found irritating. Liz was almost four and Kim already five. What else did children that age do but grow?

'Where's Ella?'

'Your mother's at work. These days I'm the one who does the house and runs the errands.'

From the time she left home for boarding school Felicity had referred to her mother as Ella. George in his old-fashioned way hadn't approved then, and he still didn't. Correcting Felicity whenever she called her mother Ella served as a reminder of this.

'Your mother won't be coming over from La Laguna until Friday evening. She lives there during the week, you know, got her own room —'

'Her own room? I thought Claude had a house there.'

'— to save all that back and forth on the bus. She'll be coming with Alex.'

'And Claude?'

'Claude comes over for the weekends too, only he's away at the moment, some conference or other, I believe in Cameroon. Who in Cameroon can possibly be interested in structuralism? I don't know if he'll be back by the weekend.'

It was only Tuesday now. The thought of four days ahead alone with her father put Felicity in a good mood.

She let George show her over the house to see how it had been refurbished. With surprise she commented on the changes that had been made to the place since her last visit to Arguayo five years previously, keeping to herself her approval of the things that had stayed the same. A rich, lazy sense of contentment settled on her as she sat with her father after lunch on the patio while her daughters ran up and down the stairs and galleries, rushing into all the rooms, shrieking with excitement as they took possession of the place, peopling it with favourite make-believe characters, including one called Mooki, whom George later discovered to be their father Stephen, who no longer lived at home.

'When Mooki comes, he can sleep in our room.'

'And Thingums, but only if he promises to be good.'

'Who's Thingums?'

'It's a secret.' Liz squirmed, badly wanting to share the secret with her grandfather, but not in front of Kim.

George looked at these little girls — twisting and turning as they pranced around the table — with a tenderness which reminded him of his feelings when he first set eyes on Estela.

It puzzled and saddened him that his wife should so seldom have been the beneficiary of such feelings. Perhaps they had been too well hidden in his formal English upbringing. He had discovered them too late in life. Perhaps he had been too much on the defensive with Ella, too much in awe of her, for those stirrings in him to show themselves. Had it not been for the interlude with Inéz and Estela, he wondered if he would ever have discovered such feelings. It pained him that it wasn't his wife but a chambermaid from the Caribbean who should have been able to draw them out. That channel which might have flowed from him to Ella had never been used to convey such feelings; that sluice had not really ever been opened. Perhaps he would now make good the deficit in his balance with his wife by lavishing on their grandchildren the surplus of love that George felt he still had in him.

The elder girl, Kim, had very pale skin set off by her Snow White colouring, red lips, bold eyebrows, deep brown eyes, coal-black hair down to her shoulders. She was striking to look at, and if you some- how missed that, she commanded attention with her liveliness and self-assertive manner. She didn't resemble anyone in the Morris family, no one he knew on Ella's side either, so presumably she took after her father, whom George had met once and immediately forgotten. Liz was a placid child with the warm tones of Ella's skin, her grandmother's fair hair, small nose, green eyes and a surprisingly broad back for a girl who was not yet four. All the excitement and flurries of noise which had accompanied the two sisters on their exploration of the house and seemed to come from both of them had in fact been caused by the excit- able self-propagandist older sister, Kim. Withdrawn but not shy, a little girl with all the signs of what George would have called a contemplative nature, Liz seemed to live shut off inside a bell jar, surrounded by a calm that perhaps immunised her against the intrusions of her sister.

The two girls were put in the room with the built-in intercom via the chimney flue to the soundbox in the kitchen ceiling, their mother in the room next door. For George this early-warning system was most conveni- ent. Breakfasting in the kitchen, he could hear the girls chirruping away in their room as soon as they woke up. Moments later they were down in the kitchen, and George was already giving them their breakfast.

'Can we go and see the donkey?'

'Can we play with Rosalia and Inma?'

'Can they come with us when we go for a swim?'

After five barren years of marriage, Alicia had surprised the village by producing twin boys, followed in quick succession by two girls. Rosalia and Inma were a few years older than Kim and Liz. Sometimes the two older girls borrowed their house donkey to give Kim and Liz rides, but they preferred carrying Liz around the village themselves, taking up a stance on doorsteps, the little girl planted on one arched hip, gossiping away like practised women.

Felicity could let go. She sat up late talking to her father, lay in bed reading most of the night and slept until noon. The tiredness she was allowed to give in to here pulled her down like an anaesthetic. Alone with her father, taken care of and made to feel special, she spent the first days in drowsy contentment. When her mother arrived for the weekend with Alex and Claude, that mood was disturbed; Felicity was afraid she might have lost it altogether. But she woke up to something much better, a clearly defined sense of belonging, feeling herself back at home as she had not really felt since the time they lived at St John's Wood.

Relations between her mother and father were amicable, with Claude apparently more than that. A touch, a look – she noticed the signs exchanged between the two of them, the constant awareness of one another's presence – and she felt a pang of regret for what she had missed in her own marriage. Her much younger half-brother Alex, whom she still didn't really know, had grown into a quiet and good-natured young man she took an immediate liking to. Felicity admired his way with her children. Even with Kim, whose attitude to people bordered on the aggressive, overwhelming and taking possession of them, Alex remained calm. He handled the girls gently, as if afraid they might get broken, resisting Kim's attempts to provoke him and get him to roughhouse with her. Once Kim's combativeness was deflected, she settled down. Soon she was playing happily with her sister instead of seeking attention, as she usually did when adults, particularly male adults, were around.

But it was her own mother who surprised Felicity most. She was expecting Ella to want to talk about her marriage, to ask her probing questions about Stephen and herself – what future was there in their relationship, things that her daughter didn't want to discuss. She was ashamed the marriage had failed, not so much on her own account as because she felt she had let her parents down. But Ella didn't touch on any of these things. During the hour the two of them sat out on the terrace, the only time they were alone together that weekend, Ella surprised Felicity by talking about herself.

'I'm happy for you, darling, even though this is a difficult time for you, because there's a place for you here where you can always come. That's one of the things I've missed in my life.'

'What is?'

'A place to go.'

'A place to go? But you've got tons of places to go.'

'They're not home for me, not in the sense that this is home for you. When we had to make that trek with all the other refugees at the end of the war I didn't realise there'd be no going back. Home was gone. All those estates east of the Elbe were lost for ever, relatives one could drop in on at any time and be welcome. People led isolated lives in those big old country houses, and visits brought a little variety. In the summer my mother used to do a round of her relatives with me and Oscar. That stopped after she remarried. And there was no going back after the war. If my mother had lived she might have made a new home for us in Hamburg. But she died, and my sister died, my father and my brother went missing, and the three of us who were left went to live in London, and since Edward and Nico emigrated it's only me left of the family in Europe.'

'Do you still miss them?'

'Perhaps not any longer. But so often I've thought I'd like to be able to just let go. To have someone look after me instead of having to look after other people. To go somewhere I feel cared for whenever I want. Where I have my own room with my own things in it, waiting for me just as I left it. My grandmother's house, for example. Being able to turn up without forewarning or explanation – just being myself and accepted there because I'm part of it and it's part of me – which is out of the question, of course ... but I still wish I had it.'

'Is that why you haven't moved in with Claude in Laguna? Is that why you've kept your own room there?'

'I have moved in with Claude.'

'So why keep the room?'

'Because it's my freedom. So I can go there if I want to.' Ella stroked her daughter's head. 'This house is here for you whenever you and your children need it.'

For the time being Felicity said nothing about the plan that was taking shape in her head. After listening to what her mother had to say she could see the advantages a place like Arguayo had to offer. For herself the place would be something different, however — not with the sentimental attachment it had for her mother, just an option to escape. The sort of longing Ella described to her was not something Felicity wanted for herself or could even imagine. She had never felt homesick.

Certainly life was pleasant enough in Arguayo, where she woke up every morning to the sun and the blue sky. It was a luxury to be able to sleep in, knowing that her father would be giving the children their breakfast and keeping an eye on them when they went out to play. Trips down to Puerto de Santiago were fun, lying on the beach soaking up the heat and imagining a late-winter afternoon in London. And the arrival of Ella, Claude and Alex to spend the weekends in Arguayo provided a welcome distraction after the quiet weeks she spent there with her father and the children. For Felicity realised with dismay that, after a month of this uneventful life, she was beginning to get bored. The world was passing her by. She felt left out. With the worries she had in London now taken care of, she realised how much unused energy she had.

'I'm twenty-four!'

The slow pace of life in the village up on the hill, far away from the coastal resorts, where at least there was always something going on, made Felicity restless. Of course she loved her children, but they did tie her down. She longed to return to the London life she had fled but now realised she was beginning to miss.

Felicity hadn't realised how busy Ella would be at the institute. Her new job would apparently be even more demanding. Clearly she wouldn't have the time to look after two small children. One weekend Ella had to fly to Cape Verde with the institute director for a conference on the environment. George told Felicity that weekend trips in connection with a major project involving all the Macaronesian islands took Ella away a couple of times a month.

'She's taken on a new lease of life since she started working for the institute,' he said. 'I've not seen her so happy in years.'

'Have you met the people she's working with?'

'Some of them. They're a nice bunch. All of them quite a bit younger than she is. That took her a little getting used to. Eduardo, the director, is the only person there older than she is.'

'What's he like?'

'Eduardo? About my age. He's an interesting man, nothing much to look at from a woman's point of view. I've had some good conversations with him and took to him immediately, and Ella clearly has too.'

'Well, that's good.'

The tug of envy that her mother's late venture into a professional career had turned out to be so successful shamed Felicity, and she made an effort to suppress it, just as George suppressed the temptation to share with his daughter what Ella had recently shared with him. She and the institute director had had an affair. With Claude's return it had ended. George didn't doubt that the conferences Ella went off to with Eduardo were what she said they were, but it would be only natural if they made the most of the opportunity these business trips gave them.

In her place I'd have done the same, thought George before correcting himself: I did the same. Yet he hadn't been able to resist taking a stab at Eduardo with that *nothing much to look at from a woman's point of view*. He wondered about this. None of the men Ella had been attracted to were anything much to look at, not Sasha or even Claude – least of all himself, George added ruefully. Claude had had more difficulty accepting Ella's affair with Eduardo than he had, or so it had seemed to George until now, but in that gratuitous comment he had just made to Felicity he was confronted with evidence of his own jealousy. Why otherwise would he have made a bitchy remark like that?

The plan Felicity had already made up her mind about before broaching it to her parents meant leaving her daughters in their care in Arguayo for the three years it was going to take her to qualify as a hospital administrator. She had already been along for an interview and offered a place on a course beginning that autumn. She would need an allowance, and it would be a help if she could live in their London flat. It was a full-time course involving a six-month hospital internship and it required her to do night work as well. Having two small children at home would be impossible under these circumstances. So everything depended on their grandparents. Would Ella and George be prepared to take the children for that long?

To Felicity's surprise it was her mother, not her father, who responded without hesitation.

'Of course we will, darling. But more to the point, what do Kim and Liz think about it?'

'Well, actually...'

Felicity admitted she'd already started getting the children used to the idea when it first came to her six months ago. In fact she'd told them before they left London that this wasn't just a holiday they'd be spending with their grandparents. They wouldn't be coming back to London until it was time for them to go to school a few years hence.

Ella looked at George.

'I say we, but it's really up to your father. After all, with me being away so much of the time he'll be the one mainly responsible for the children.'

George sat there for a while with a bemused expression on his face while his wife and daughter looked at him expectantly.

'You could do nothing for me that would make me happier.' To her astonishment, Felicity saw tears in her father's eyes. 'It makes me feel I've come back to life.'

# 10

Travelling frequently to Europe as he did, and being the gregarious sort of man he was, full of curiosity, always willing to go one further bend in the road if he thought it might give him a different point of view, Santana took Claude up on the open invitation to visit him and showed up on Tenerife within the year.

Show up was just what he did. There was no letter or call. He arrived in Arguayo by taxi, walking through the *portada sillería* into the courtyard as everyone was sitting down to lunch. Even without the presence there of Claude, who happened to have gone down into the cellar, Santana seemed to be perfectly sure he knew where he was, recognising these people he had never seen before. 'You have to be Claude's son Alex,' he said, grasping him by the shoulder as if to get the measure of him. 'I'm a friend of Claude's.' Passing on to George and Ella, he took possession of them in the same easy way with the remark, 'That's a very fine dragon tree you have here in your yard, must be a few hundred years old,' clasping the hands they offered him in both of his as he explained his sudden appearance there: 'I was in the locality so thought I'd drop by.'

Ella would recall this arrival scene when she later watched Santana arrive in many other places on their long journey from the Malay

Peninsula via the Indonesian archipelago to the Solomon Islands, notably in those places where there were no people waiting – too remote, even by Santana's global standards of locality, to be just dropping by. He would advance with much the same look of expectation on his face, ready for anything, lifting his hands and spreading his arms, greeting the empty landscape around him – it might equally well have been grieving with it – as if coming across a gathering of old friends, entire forests that had been waiting for him on previous visits having meanwhile been cut down. Ella noted that he seldom smiled. There was no such thing as a broad smile with Santana. One inferred the smile from a generally favourable disposition of mien, a tuck at the corner of his mouth, a barely raised eyebrow that seemed to hold out hope of some pleasant surprise in the offing.

It wasn't until his second visit the following year that Ella had an opportunity to talk to Santana alone. She brought up the subject of family, which Santana had so far not touched on. In reply to her question, he took photographs of two women out of his wallet and passed them to Ella. 'My sister,' he said, 'and ...' without finishing what he had begun. Nor did he need to, for Ella had already guessed from the likeness to the sister that the other woman could only be Santana's wife.

There was another similarity between the two women that couldn't be seen in the photo and which you could know only if you had been told, as Ella had been told by Claude. Both women were dead. Ella knew how the wife had died but knew nothing about the sister beyond that marker she instantly spotted – a phenomenon she'd seen many times in her life, the likeness you were likely to find between a person who belonged to the given inventory of your early life and the person you would later choose yourself, in her own case between her mother and Claude. The emotionally more significant matriarchal lineage that had led Ella to Claude recalled the slighter build and fairer colour of her mother, Maria. Claude wasn't a man in the way that the other men were who belonged to the patriarchal lineage – men not necessarily big but strongly built and of virile appearance. This was particularly so in Santana's case. The large head and broad face with its copper-coloured complexion and the powerful torso atop the relatively short legs gave him the compact – one might have said squat – figure of the Mexican Indian. Typically Santana stood with his weight mainly on one leg, the other relaxed, bent slightly at the knee and put forward as if to draw attention to the row of ornamental silver buttons running down his calf. Ella was intrigued by the buttons and wondered what they represented. She preferred him sitting down facing her in any case. Then she could pay more attention to the features of Santana's she liked best, his high forehead and straight nose, the firm line of his mouth, the not-quite-fathomable liquid-black eyes.

It was on this second visit to Arguayo – Santana standing, as he talked to Ella in the kitchen, with one leg forward in this posture he seemed to think showed him to advantage, she sitting at the table looking at the photographs he had just taken out of his wallet to show her – that he announced, 'Now that my wife Miriam's picture is out on the table I feel bound to tell you how it happened. Perhaps we should get it out of the way. It's become the thing in my life nobody likes to bring up but everyone is curious about. Well, there were no witnesses.'

'Witnesses?'

'To the scene on the factory roof where I shot her. So it was my word against nobody's. In the whole universe the only version of what happened is mine. It's all I have to offer.' He spread his hands. 'Interested?'

Ella nodded.

'In the course of the subsequent inquest, which went on for months, the police reconstructed the scene. Not in a courtroom, but on the roof itself. We had tables and chairs in the roof garden up there, even a bed where we used to sleep in fine weather. Miriam was lying on the bed while I sat at the table cleaning the gun I had bought only the week before. People had attempted to break into the factory at night, you see. Two or three times. Not just burglars. There was an attempted rape of one of my researchers on her way out of the building. The area has since been spruced up and become an expensive neighbourhood, but there was a lot of crime around at the time we moved in.'

'Why are you telling me this?'

'Because it was an issue at the inquest.'

That wasn't the answer to the question she had asked, but Ella let it pass, as it was obvious Santana wanted to talk about it.

'Why would a peacenik biology professor with such an abhorrence of the taking of life of animals and even of many plants that he kept to an extreme vegetarian diet followed only by sectarians like the Jainists, why would this man have found it – I won't say necessary, I would ask rather, as the inquest went to great lengths to, how could an undertaking

701

have presented itself to this man's mind, under whatever circumstances, entailing the necessity of him going through all the requisite actions, each of them small enough in itself but cumulatively substantial, as is the case with any complex choice, which have to be gone through in order to buy a gun, without that abhorrence objecting loud enough to be heard, and for that objection to be sustained, if the word *abhorrence* is to be taken at face value? Isn't that a very reasonable question to ask? Rather more than a question, isn't this already an elaborately constructed hypothesis of a man's ultimate responsibility for all the actions preceding the action and conniving to serve as its pretexts, one might as well go ahead, mightn't one, and call such responsibility by another name – guilt – even if the enquiry eventually came to a different conclusion?'

Hedged around with so many qualifications as to blur the edge of quite what he was asking, this was apparently not a question he expected Ella to answer, and Santana continued at top speed without leaving a pause long enough to encourage her to attempt to do so.

'So now the gun is there. There is now a gun in the space where there was no gun before, ideas in the mind where there were no such ideas before. The gun was not my choice. My choice would have been a stun gun or some such device, and I told the dealer so, but Miriam insisted on what she called a proper gun, a gun that killed, and so I bought it. In fact, Miriam accompanied me to the store and bought it for me. It was she who told the dealer what we wanted, and he recommended a couple of models, and Miriam chose the one she liked best, because it was really Miriam we were buying the gun for. If anyone, she was likely to be the one who would use it. Miriam was a meat eater, in case you are wondering –'

Ella looked up, wondering what on earth he was talking about.

'– and she liked her meat rare. This has to be said vividly if it is to be said at all, the blood seeping from the meat and collecting visibly on the plate. So she wasn't involved in any sort of ethical conflict here, as I would have been. I only bring this up because it was brought up by my lawyer at the inquest, constituting what he considered a strong line of defence. The lawyer arranged for the gun dealer to give testimony, an exact account of the way the conversation went between Miriam and himself, with me standing by, not much more than an onlooker. That pretty much spiked the guns the opposition had pointing at me, said the lawyer. They still insisted on that action replay on the roof, however, or maybe that was precisely why they wanted it done as closely as possible to how it had been done on the day. Nothing is as elusive as the motive for doing a thing—'

'Maybe it's something other than a motive we're looking for,' interrupted Ella.

Santana looked at her sharply.

'What is it we're looking for then?'

'A justification.'

'How would you distinguish the two?'

'By the time lag. The motive for doing the act is unconscious and inseparable from the act; it only becomes evident afterwards, in the justification for what can no longer be undone. We feel bound to rationalise it to claim it as our own. If we want our actions to be our own we need to come up with a reason for them.'

'I'd never thought about it like that. Are you saying that whenever we act we give hostages to fortune?'

'I'm saying that we often act without knowing why we do so.'

'So we find a justification for it after the event? To claim it as our own? Well, the hostile atmosphere surrounding the inquest certainly had to do with the fact that Miriam came from a very wealthy family and that her family had never approved of her choice of me as a husband, a Mexican immigrant, which was why they retained the best attorney in California – to make an actionable case out of what at that stage was still an inquest into a tragic accident, and to pin a murder charge on me. That best lawyer's guns weren't yet spiked, by no means. I could have put Miriam up to it – buying a gun to protect herself – or I could have seen in her own insistence on buying the gun a golden opportunity to get rid of her – maybe her doing so was what put the idea in my head. Because I would benefit from the will, as the best attorney in California argued on behalf of Miriam's family. Over ten million dollars in a complicated trust, difficult but manageable over time. And so on. You see? You had a motive, therefore you did it. No end to the spin you can put on anything you want, and what the best attorney wanted was a murder conviction, because this was how he was professionally disposed to see the case and how he had already arranged it in his mind long before we got anywhere near the roof.'

Santana shifted his weight onto the other leg.

'It's night on the roof. A beautiful summer night. A photographer

703

friend has installed an umbrella-shaped cone of light for us, positioning it over the table where we read and write and listen to music. Moths whirl around in the cone, fumble and crash against the light but they don't burn because of the gauze in front of the bulb. Seen at a distance across the roof, the site resembles a hive, a whirring colony of life. All this finds its way into the reconstruction, including the weather. Including the conversation, so far as I can recall it. An aide from the San Francisco Police Department is standing or rather lying in for Miriam. She says, "Did you show the gun to Jerry? Did he clean it for you?" "No, but he checked it out, took it down into the basement and fired it a couple of times and said it was OK – didn't have time to clean it as he had to catch a plane but he showed me how. I've got all the stuff I need here. I'll deal with it just as soon as I've added up these figures." Miriam takes the book she's reading at the table and moves to the bed, but she lies down the other way around to get the full slew of the light. Her head is right on the edge of the mattress, tilted toward the light over the table where I'm sitting. Once I'm through with adding up the figures, I pick up the gun lying on the table. I have it in my hand and am pointing it at the ground in front of me. The bed Miriam is lying on is to my right, about five or six feet away. I've thought about that before I even pick up the gun. No way is a gun going to fire round a ninety-degree angle. The first thing I have to do is to check the safety catch – this is what I'm thinking when the gun goes off. "There's a really loud detonation followed by a *ping* and Miriam seems to have fallen asleep. Her head just lolls over and she goes to sleep, the book still in her hand lying flat on her breast." This is what I say as the caption to what I'm doing when we reconstruct the scene on the roof, and I look over and see the head of the policewoman loll over, the open book fold and close on her breast. Someone asks me to show them what I did next. So I get up and kneel at the bed with my arms on Miriam's shoulders and then on her head, only it's this policewoman's head, and when I lift it up off the mattress there's no blood, as there was with Miriam. Again someone asks me to show what I did next, so I get up and sit on the edge of the bed cradling the policewoman's head on my lap. At the time of the actual happening I just sat like that, it must have been for hours, because in the meantime it had grown light, but when we did the reconstruction I only held the position long enough to take the policewoman's pulse, I suppose because they wanted to see if I could do it properly, having told them in my first statement that I had taken Miriam's pulse. I don't recall having done that, but there it was in my original statement so I suppose I must have, and when I went through the same action at the reconstruction I remembered having done this before. It wasn't as if I took her pulse to verify that she was dead. It seemed to me rather to be something I ought to do in view of the fact that I otherwise wasn't doing anything for her other than sitting there with her head on my lap. Why had I waited for six hours before calling an ambulance? How could I presume? For there might still have been a chance, however slight, said the attorney hired by the family, of an emergency operation saving her life. *Nothing* could have saved her life. How could it have happened? Didn't I give a thought to that? they asked me. But I sat there with the dead burden of my wife on my lap and couldn't think about anything, not for hours. People came up onto the roof, eventually, people who worked in the building, and they lifted her head off my lap and took me away. They had to leave Miriam lying as she was until the police had investigated the site. But there was never anything that could have been done for her. She was dead the instant the bullet entered her right ear and passed into her brain.'

Santana paused to take a turn around the kitchen, his fingers riffling through the streamer of a wind chime hanging by the window, agitating it into sound before he began talking again at top speed, the chiming he left behind him jangling into the words already pouring out of him as he took up his position in front of Ella at the table.

'You'll be wondering how that could have happened. Part of how it happened was gross negligence on the part of Jerry, who'd fired the gun a few times earlier that day and neglected to remove the clip with the remaining bullets or to warn me they were still in the gun, I guess because he was in a hurry to catch his plane and had a lot of other things on his mind. So there's that bad start to the whole freakish incident, and on the roof it gets a lot worse. When the gun goes off it's pointing down at the ground three feet away. The bullet strikes a curving iron clamp shaped like a handle screwed to the floor – part of a structure that used to be there. I don't know why it didn't get removed when the structure itself was dismantled. The curve of the handle gives the bullet a new trajectory, a bit like a ski jumper descending a chute and leaving it on a trajectory that rises before it begins to drop – that was the analogy of the ballistics expert who did the analysis. A billion other trajectories would have been possible, depending on the angle of the clamp relative to the direction from which it was approached by the bullet, the point on the curve at which the bullet struck the clamp that had no business to be still screwed down there in any case, the velocity, and so on. Naturally the bullet leaves a mark where it strikes the clamp and receives its new direction and velocity, the trajectory of the ricochet that will embed the bullet in Miriam's brain. These are the milestones that bear out its story. There's no way for that freak trajectory to have been intended and put into effect by any mere human being. Only an all-powerful, all-malicious and all-evil providence could have pulled off such a stunt.'

# 11

Had George and Claude not happened to have come into the kitchen as if on cue Ella might have been at a loss to find the right words to break the silence that followed this extraordinary rapid-delivery account. By some protective instinct that it might be better to cover up for Santana, she hid the two photographs inside a memo pad lying beside them on the table and slipped the pad into his pocket at the first convenient moment.

The following morning, when they again happened to find themselves in the kitchen on their own, she and Santana both being early risers, he returned the memo pad to the table and asked her why she had done that.

'I felt the urge to cover up for you.'

'Cover up what?'

Ella was undeterred by the gruffness of his manner.

'It was as if the whole story of that terrible accident with your wife lay spread out there with the photographs. You hadn't bargained on George and Claude coming in suddenly like that. You were so caught up in what you were saying. They must have overheard the tail end of it. It didn't seem to me that what you'd chosen to tell me personally, in confidence, should unintentionally reach anyone else. Or have you told Claude about it too?'

'I only told you because you asked about my wife.'

'I also asked about your sister.'

'What's this interest you have in my wife and my sister?'

'Because of the sympathy I feel for you.'

Santana frowned. 'How come?'

'Because I could identify with everything you've been telling us about what it was like to be a Mexican family arriving in California in the 1940s.'

This was a bond between them. Ella was persuaded of it, and when she had told him about her wartime experiences she was confident Santana would be persuaded of it too. He was an immigrant and she a refugee. This was the connection that had a particular fascination for her. Both of them had lost their families when young; both had needed looking after at an early age, but instead had made a life for themselves by looking after others. Ella took comfort from having her own experiences shored up by people who had undergone similarly harsh fates. *Only an all-powerful, all-malicious and all-evil providence could have pulled off such a stunt* were not the words she would have chosen to describe the loss of family and home and total destitution at the end of the war, but she shared Santana's disillusionment about the absence of any sort of benevolent principle working in the interests of human life.

In her teens Ella had lost a sister; so had Santana, an asthmatic girl who hadn't taken well to the Los Angeles climate or the proximity of a cement factory in the neighbourhood where the family lived. Cement dust hung in the air. Apparently that was the problem. Her eyes were always sore; she had headaches and chronic breathing problems. They moved to another area, but she didn't get any better. It seemed the trouble might be not the cement factory but something they had everywhere in the Los Angeles basin known as smog. In the early 1950s the high school Santana attended was often closed on account of the smog levels. There would be radio announcements advising children and old people to leave the house as little as possible. Staying indoors didn't help Santana's sister, however. She developed a condition that was not identified as emphysema until she suffered a paroxysm and was rushed to hospital. Santana, sitting beside her in the ambulance, watched her die of asphyxiation before they got her there.

Santana's interest in science began at that point. He wanted to know about smog and went to the public library. The article he read there described the reaction of sunlight with air containing hydrocarbons and nitrogen oxides that reacted to ground-level ozone, none of the words he understood at the time. So he began his own studies, branching out from the chemistry they were teaching him at school. If his resolution sometimes wavered, he made a trip out to the Golden Gate Bridge to see for himself the best view of smog available – an ominous brownish cloud bank piled up behind the bridge. How come it had that particular colour? His chemistry book told him it was due to the nitrogen oxide element in it.

By the time he graduated from college he knew a lot more about smog and the properties of ozone. There was ozone up in the stratosphere, mostly produced by the sun's ultraviolet rays reacting with oxygen. There was also a lot of it around on the ground, where it was an atmospheric pollutant that interfered with the process of photosynthesis, stunted the growth of plants and increased the risk of lung disease – in Los Angeles by as much as 30 per cent. By the laws of thermodynamics, the energy used by man must ultimately be dissipated as heat. That heat would result in warming the atmosphere, either directly or indirectly through radiation from water used for cooling purposes. Locally, waste heat around cities caused the formation of urban heat islands, within which many meteorological anomalies such as smog occurred. Waste heat released over the vast area of the Los Angeles basin, for example, amounted to about 5 per cent of the total solar energy absorbed at ground level and by the year 2000 was projected to amount to around 20 per cent, a figure that would prove to be not far off the mark.

The projections published by Sherwood Rowland and Mario Molina in *Nature* magazine in 1974 were even more sensational. Chlorofluoro-carbons, the authors claimed, were contributing to a massive destruction of the earth's ozone layer. On the basis of evidence of an exponential growth in pollution rates, it was being concluded by many scientists at the time that the length of life of the biosphere as an inhabitable region for organisms was to be measured in decades rather than hundreds of millions of years, but they had too little knowledge about where the upper limits to the earth's absorption capacity of pollution lay to make such conclusions anything more than informed guesses.

That *length of life of the biosphere* and its measurement in *decades rather than hundreds of millions of years* was a quote from the Club of Rome report. Santana was among those consulted for his response to the projections of the report. He saw it as a call to arms and gave it his full support. But for many of his colleagues at UCLA and elsewhere that contraction of hundreds of millions of years into decades was irresponsible hyperbole, the sort of thing that shouldn't have found its way into a scientific analysis.

Here the *battle to control reality* was joined that Santana would continue to fight for the rest of his life.

# 12

In the course of history, as Santana never tired of reminding his students at the Warehouse, people had utilised about seven thousand kinds of plant for food, notably wheat, rye and maize, yet there were known to be at least seventy-five thousand edible plants in existence. Of the several thousand utilised by mankind, only about a hundred and fifty had become important enough to enter world commerce. Less than twenty species on that list of staples accounted for 85 per cent of the world's food. The four major carbohydrate crop species – wheat, corn, rice and potatoes – fed more people than the next twenty-six most important crops combined. What lay behind this imbalance?

He believed passionately – and he made a dogma of this passionate belief – that people and the economic decisions they made were an integral part of the ecological system. To treat the two things separately was a consequence of the idea of objective knowledge, the Western standard of science that had come to dominate as the globally valid truth of the new colonialism. The false premise of its neoclassical economic model, namely that gains would result from the shifting of production activities for which they had a comparative advantage, had been a major contributing factor to the extinction of species because it failed to take into account that biological species were less able to adapt to different activities than the people who carried them out. That mankind had come to rely on less than one per cent of plant species for its existence was a consequence of such a doctrine.

Question 1. Who were the people responsible for this state of affairs?
They were the Corporation.
Question 2. How were they getting away with it?
The artificiality of the collective legal person fiction, which made it possible for corporations to remain faceless and unaccountable, and the legal requirement that it was above all the duty of boards to make money for their investors and that they were punishable by law if they failed

in this duty — these were the drives behind the evolution of a narrow socioeconomic culture into which the biosphere with all its diversity was being compressed for the short-term profit of the few to the long-term detriment of all.

Santana thought there was no better illustration of corporate irresponsibility than the logging industry, which he had come to know well from his study of island environments past and present, and there was no better illustration of this industry than the US Weyerhaeuser corporation's recent alliance with PT Tri Usaha Bhakti, owned by the Indonesian armed forces, in order to extract wood from a concession of some six hundred thousand hectares of virgin forest on Sumatra.

That so-called wood extraction on Sumatra, as if it were some kind of anodyne dental treatment being administered by the logging companies, was still going on at the time Ella accompanied Santana and a team of his colleagues on a Warehouse Foundation tour. Santana invited her along in the months between Ella leaving the institute and starting work at the environment agency on Tenerife. She was in Arguayo with George, looking after the grandchildren Felicity had left in their care while she returned to England to do her training. George assured her he could handle the children on his own, making it possible for Ella to take off on a tour that began with the first of the south-east Asian countries to have been inveigled by the lure of money into sacrificing its virgin forests.

The money came from international logging corporations in the guise of those neo-colonialist advisers who had already commandeered world food production and made it a global industry. The world's diet today, like so much else, had been determined by exploitation patterns developed when tropical countries were European colonies. A few key species were selected for export, and the establishment of a market for the chosen species had determined their cultivation until the present day. The corporations were the successors of the former colonial powers, only more dangerous. While you could chuck out colonial oppressors, corporations eluded your grasp. Almost none of the forest resource exploiters big enough to matter were local operators, making it easy to remove the cheap raw timber to sawmills overseas and transform it into far more valuable semi-finished products, cutting the host nation out of any share in the profits and keeping it all for themselves.

Advised and encouraged by agencies such as the World Bank and the Asian Development Bank to target timber as their major export, *seduced and corrupted to do so*, as Santana described it in the articles he wrote denouncing these organisations, the governments of many developing countries exploited their forests recklessly at the cost of the aboriginal peoples who lived in them. What was good for the loggers turned out to be not so good for the local people, who lost their source of forest products and suffered the consequences of soil erosion and stream sedimentation. It was also bad for the host country as a whole, which lost much of its biodiversity and its foundations for sustainable forestry, not to mention the consequences for the rest of the world.

Corporations such as Weyerhaeuser, MacMillan Bloedel, Georgia-Pacific, the Scott Paper Company, Mitsui, Mitsubishi and Sumitomo and a slew of firms associated with a powerful cartel of Japanese trading companies carried out what their PR described as the commercial harvesting of tropical rainforests all over the world. From Burma down, they had already harvested most of the lowland forests of the Malay Peninsula, then of Borneo, then of the Solomon Islands. The sites visited by Santana's team in Indonesian Sumatra were operated by two other Japanese companies, Shin Asahigawa and Ataki. Typically, such companies took out short-term leases and cut down the trees on all the forest land in one country before moving on to the next. As soon as the loggers had paid for their concessions they removed the forest as fast as possible, reneging on any agreements that might have been made to replant trees, before high-tailing it out of the country.

The names of the exploiters and the places exploited might change but the same procedure was used everywhere. The return on investment was around 30 per cent. Stumpage fees and taxes were minimal or non-existent. The fees charged the harvesting companies amounted to only a very low percentage of the real cost of tree replacement and forest management. The drawback for the representatives of governments selling trees they didn't own to line their own pockets was that licences tended not to be renewed. When the logging companies left, the area had usually been deforested to such an extent that it no longer paid to continue operations. What had been taken away from the land wouldn't be replaced in the foreseeable future, perhaps not for ever.

Admittedly, things might conceivably take a different course when the logging company owned the land, anticipated repeated harvests and found a long-term perspective to be in its own interests as well as in those of the host country. But such cases were rare. More frequently the forest was subjected to a 'clear cut', which didn't leave a tree standing, a slaughter that Santana described as mass murder, leaving land that had always been protected by dense forest cover denuded, raped and shamed. Despite this rhetoric, which caused Ella considerable discomfort, nothing she heard from Santana in advance of the trip prepared her for the reality of the logging site she first saw or rather heard in one of the ancient forests in northern Thailand on the Burmese border.

Tipped off by a local tree watch organisation, Santana's party made its way along a track leading deep into the forest to the already large clearing where illegal loggers had begun cutting only the day before. In the silence after the buzz of chainsaws left off she heard, as they approached the clearing, a slow cracking and wrenching followed by a sound like a gust of wind, something sweeping or brushing, before a gigantic thud made the ground on which she was standing shake, then more explosions one after another, the repeated splintered wrenching of things being twisted off – an unbearable sound, the groans, as they seemed to Ella, giving voice to the death agony of those huge old trees as they wrenched themselves free of their trunks and went crashing down – bursting their bonds with the earth in which they had stood rooted for hundreds of years, breaking that seal of a sacred trust which until now had remained intact.

## 13

As a Mexican immigrant, Santana had grown up with an awareness of the degree of US intervention in Central and Latin America. The United States had supported Somoza in Nicaragua – keeping the dictator in power suited US commercial interests just as US commercial interests lay behind their opposition to Arbenz – the land reforms he was planning to introduce to Guatemala would have been injurious to the United Fruit Company. Dictators such as Pinochet in Chile and Vileda in Argentina, who were more amenable than their predecessors, received support from the World Bank and the International Monetary Fund.

It was a particular coincidence of events in the late 1970s and the early 1980s that caused Santana and his team to analyse this familiar background in more detail. Taking advantage of the recent deregulation of financial markets in Latin America and Asia, short-term capital was pumped into these markets and suddenly withdrawn again. As a result their currencies collapsed. A sudden rise in the dollar and interest rates led to the devaluation of the peso – a major debt crisis in Mexico – and the foreign speculators cleaned up. Within a decade the debts of Latin American countries had risen from sixteen to one hundred and seventy-eight billion dollars. Comparable debts were being incurred by developing countries all over the world.

The so-called Washington Consensus – intervention disguised as aid – provided the means for the subjugation of former colonial territories that only nominally had become sovereign states. Under the auspices of the Washington Consensus, the old domination of former colonies by former colonial powers, now reconstituted as a consortium of global capital interests, could be resumed with greater effectiveness than ever before.

Consultancy agencies were set up by the US National Security Agency to act as advisers to governments in Third World countries. Collaborating with the International Monetary Fund and the World Bank – a US-dominated institution conveniently located a block away from the White House – these agencies would make recommendations about the infrastructure a country needed or could be persuaded it needed – large expensive projects they couldn't afford such as the construction of dams, power stations, airports and highways. The NSA would also arrange loans from financial institutions set up to service American interests. Often the money would not even be remitted to the states, but go directly to the US contractors in New York, Houston or San Francisco that were providing the infrastructure for which the loans had been granted.

Typically, the developing nation was unable to service the debt in the long run. Using this leverage, the World Bank and the IMF dictated political terms that suited American economic interests. Santana had personally investigated one such scenario in Ecuador, a country that had been forced to buy its way out of the debtor trap by granting Texaco oil rights in an area of the Amazon. The deforestation of the rainforest was what initially attracted the attention of the Tree Man, but he later returned to document its familiar consequences – the lasting pollution of the area, the loss of their homes for the thousands of indigenous people who had previously lived there.

Before returning home to take up her job as director of the newly created Department of the Environment in Santa Cruz, Ella stayed as Santana's guest at the Warehouse in San Francisco. Without her realising it at the time, the seminars at the foundation were giving her a preview of aspects of the job which her training as a biologist had not prepared her for. She learned to analyse political events and look for signs of a global conspiracy of which she hadn't previously had the slightest notion. Could it be true that respected international institutions such as the United Nations, the World Bank and the IMF supplied the channels through which the richer nations dictated the terms of the loans to the poorer countries primarily to benefit themselves?

Having to service their debts at increasing cost because of higher interest rates, Third World countries were paying as much as seven times more interest on loans than richer countries with far greater debts themselves. Many of the debtor nations were spending more on debt repayment than they earned from the goods they produced, with no prospect of ever finding a way out of this trap. As one speaker at the seminar phrased it, the repayments from the poorer countries to the richer resembled a blood transfusion from the sick to the healthy. At the donor end, only a small elite surrounding the presidents of countries subjected to this kind of aid attrition benefited from the transfusion.

'Doesn't this get you down? How do you cope with it all?'

The question she put to Santana the evening before she was due to leave for Europe was the same one she had asked Eduardo after he had presented her with the pessimistic conclusions reached by the Club of Rome report.

The two of them were up on the roof of the Warehouse overlooking the waterfront, Ella sitting on a bed, Santana sprawled in a hammock.

'By reducing it.'

'Reduce how?'

'Ignoring most of it and concentrating on a few things it's possible to fix. Some of them are in this locality, part of our environment here. There are cooperative ventures we have been involved in on a small scale in Mexico and Central America. The introduction of simple, inexpensive do-it-yourself technology. Even banks and currency schemes based on exchange that bypass the need for conventional money. Ideas outlined a long time ago by Silvio Gesell, ideas that work. I have a paper on the subject downstairs, if you're interested.'

'I am. But these are … pinpricks.'

'All individual actions are pinpricks as long as they remain isolated. But if they're performed in a spirit of altruism and set an example that others follow they can create a community of mind. This will always be an idealistic venture at the beginning. All you or I can usefully care about is our immediate environment – you and your circle in Arguayo, me and my circle here. All we can do – *what* we can do – is set an example of caring beyond personal advantage. Actions undertaken merely for personal advantage will always be accompanied by disadvantages in the end. Natural selection will see to that. Neo-liberalism may be here to stay for a long time yet, but not for ever. An institutional vacuum has arisen in the wake of globalisation. As I see it, the vacuum can only be filled by a government equipped by a worldwide electorate with a global mandate to bring to an end the rule of these robber barons who are making the running now.'

'The successors to the robber barons might just be other robbers of another rank.'

'They might be. But I envisage the problems we'll soon have in common, all of us without exception – consider just water resources – as becoming the source of the new solidarity we shall also have in common if there's to be a chance of solving the problems. Unconfined egoism either of individuals or states doesn't have a future. All solutions lie within the world community because all problems lie within it. I don't deny that this may only take place under extreme pressure. Maybe we'll reach a very bad pass before we turn the corner, but turn it we will.'

'You say that with such confidence I can almost bring myself to believe it.'

Santana got up out of the hammock, sat down beside Ella and put his arm around her. 'Are you nervous about taking on this new department in Santa Cruz?'

'I wasn't until now. Until now I'd seen only my own ideas of what needed to be done and the organisational problems of implementing them – I felt capable of dealing with that. But I'm not sure how well I shall manage with graft and greed and all the manoeuvring that goes on inside the tourist industry. Tourism poses *the* problem for the environment of the islands, but it also generates the income for the measures we need to take to alleviate the problem.'

715

'Strike a compromise, Ella. Do a deal with them. Let them have their pound of flesh.'

'Have you ever had to do a deal with anyone?'

'All the time. The main ones with myself. Remember that about half the running costs of the foundation are covered by interest on the income from Miriam's estate. You may also remember how much opposition I faced from her family at the time of her death.' Santana put his hand on the bed they were sitting on. 'Right here. This is where she died. I was sitting in a chair just there.'

Ella looked down at the roof for the clamp from which the bullet fired by Santana had made the fatal ricochet that killed his wife. There was no trace of it. He showed her where it had been.

'I had it removed. That endless self-interrogation – I had to put an end to it – profitless self-obsession – anything that reminded me of it – had to be got out of the way. So I came to a decision about Miriam's estate. I would have nothing to do with that either. It was converted into a trust for the foundation. There's a board, a lawyer, an accountant, a representative of the foundation, a couple of other people. I have nothing to do with it, no personal entitlement, no personal benefit beyond the benefit to the foundation. Had I retained control it would have looked like I was benefiting personally from Miriam's death. And that was something I had good reason to want to avoid at all costs.'

Santana got up and ran his hand over his bald head.

'How is the trust money invested? I have no idea. I *ought* to know because it's a fair guess that some of the money that funds the foundation derives from investments I wouldn't sanction if I knew about them. But in order to dissociate myself from any personal interest in the trust I've chosen not to know where the money comes from. It's not a good choice, but in my circumstances it seemed to me to be the lesser of two evils. My dear Ella, these choices aren't easy, and I can tell you now that you will face them when you go back to your new job on the island.'

He offered her his hand to help her up.

'Let's go down, shall we? I have a surprise for you, by the way.' Santana smiled and kissed her cheek. 'Your son Max is in town and will be joining us for dinner.'

# CHAPTER TWO

## Son and Father

### 1

In the toilet at Madrid airport Max popped a couple of pills and snorted the last line of coke wrapped in the foil-lined spearmint-chewing-gum paper before boarding the flight for Tenerife. The plane made a lunge up and then froze, cool at twenty thousand feet, with puffball clouds stand-ing still in the sky and a violent purple sea smeared out below. What seemed to Max no more than a few minutes later they were beginning their descent. A chunk of flaming-red mountain trailing smoke flew up into his porthole window. Wow! Max ducked the disintegrating asteroid and made a feint at it with his camera. He grinned at the old lady in the seat beside him, snapped her instead, lit a cigarette and was immediately asked by the stewardess to extinguish it and fasten his seat belt. We're landing in five minutes, she said. Pretty damn *yellow* down there, Max called after the figure swaying down the aisle to the front of the aircraft. You sure this is a good idea?

Briefly he stepped out into a nice broad breezy heat — *ka-a-a-rumph!* — before passing into the cooler terminal of Los Rodeos airport. He remembered the pictures he'd seen on TV a few years back but didn't recognise this place — must have fixed it up since. Passengers milled and shoved. After a long emptiness of what looked to Max like nothing more to come on the conveyor belt, the squalid green camouflage US Army-surplus kitbag containing everything he owned in the world apart from his Leica M-Series camera arrived as an afterthought, the last item to be dredged up out of the bowels of the airport.

'Whoa!'

The belt with his bag came to a halt right in front of him. He hefted it onto his shoulder and headed for the exit.

'Max!'

And there was Claude, grown stouter since their last meeting, in a short-sleeved pastel shirt with coordinating blue trousers, a bit on the twee side for a guy his age and size. Claude clasped Max to him and pulled back and surveyed him in his ragged shorts, T-shirt, once-white headband and Ray-Ban sunglasses. Max could hear him thinking beat, gay, junkie, malnutrition, needs a bath, all the usual stuff on the tape, but it turned out Claude was saying something different.

'Good to see Max still occupying his familiar space.'

'Good for *you*, venerable Claude. Spot on. You know, you wrote me some venerably good letters from Japan. But the figure I still see most often in my mind is the one-legged painter of those temple screens, remember? Turning the electric hairdryer onto the waterfall he'd just painted coming out of the mountain, you standing by and looking on, he saying to you as he plugs the hairdryer in to blast the wet paint, *Gotta get the waterfall dry by lunch before the carpenters come to put it up*. Man, I've *dreamed* about that guy.'

'Where do you think it all is now?'

'In the sea?'

'In the sea? Oh … waterfall in the painting, OK. That river eventually leads to the sea.'

'At some point it all winds up in the sea – the trash boats take it out and dump it there.'

They came out of the terminal and walked across the car park. As they got into Claude's car Max said with a casualness long mastered, 'Oh, forgot to change money. Would you take a cheque?'

'Sure. How much do you want?'

'Couple a hundred bucks. Local currency?'

'I'll let you have it when we get home.'

'Thanks.'

Max slumped and fell asleep.

He awoke inside what seemed to be a cave. It took him a while to register it was a courtyard closed in by old dark walls. Claude wasn't in the car. Nor was his bag. Max got out at the foot of an outside staircase leading up to a door that stood open. He stood marvelling.

'C'mon! Jesus. The belt stops the bag right where I'm standing *every time*. Delivery to the door. Cash on the fucking nail.'

It was hot in the courtyard, but the moment he entered the house through the open door at the top of the stairs it turned cool. He was standing in a gallery overlooking a brick-walled room with an identically sand-coloured brick floor dappled by sunlight slanting in from a high window, which filled the top right-hand corner of the facing wall. A staircase to the left led down from the gallery to the room. To the right the gallery continued as a passageway, almost a tunnel, through a slab of masonry several yards deep.

'Whoa!'

He ducked as he made his way into the tunnel, emerging in a lofty, airy room with a window that let in the branches of a tree growing up the wall outside. Beyond the branches he heard birds singing. The passage led on to a third room at the same height as the gallery before steps led down again to one more room at street level.

Max was delighted with this little puzzle box of a house. It reminded him of a misassembled Rubik's cube.

'Or maybe a misassembled *me*. Ho ho! Dig this, man, really *dig* this Hobbit hole, tree roots and all, neat. Claude!'

'Up here.'

Max passed back through the tunnel and made his way up a very steep flight of winding stairs.

At the top he found himself in a bedroom.

Claude was sitting with his back to him, counting money in his counting house, laying the bills out fanwise like a deck of cards on the coverlet of a bed beside a window. Max stretched out on the bed near the door, put his hands under his head and took stock of the room.

'Great little higgledy-piggledy space you got here.'

'Two houses knocked into one. Three, if you count the fishmonger's shop converted into the downstairs room you passed on your left as you came along the gallery.'

'Yeah, not to mention that *tunnel*. That gave me the creeps. I only just scraped through.'

Along the facing wall cross-beams formed ledges on which a miscellany of small objects had been placed: a line of cups hardly bigger than thimbles, a flask, an inkwell, a set of books three inches high, silver and enamel boxes, a flaxen-haired doll in a blue dress sitting with her legs dangling over the edge, a steam engine made of matchboxes and a matchbox house, a family of identically speckled shells of diminishing size. In a niche formed where the beams intersected stood a stone figurine beside what looked like a cloth purse with streamers for a tail hanging down to the floor.

'What's that?' Max asked, pointing.

'Don't you remember it? At the Richmond house ...'

'The whirligig! You brought one as a present for me from Paris that Easter you came over with some friends for the Aldermaston march. I remember one of them – his name was Jong Jack.'

'Jean-Jacques.'

'I told him I sometimes slept in the cupboard.'

'I remember that, but I've forgotten why you did.'

'Because it felt snug there. He thought that was a clever idea for people at risk of being murdered in bed, and he said he would make me prime minister when he became president of France, but I've not heard back from him, so I suppose he never did.'

'Not president, but he did become a minister.'

Max got up to take a closer look at the things on the shelf. 'Felicity's doll – what did she call it? *Miss Emma Jenkins.*' He put back the doll and picked up the matchstick house. 'Philip and I had a competition making things with matchsticks. He did the engine and I did the house. Dad was the judge. The house won because it was better constructed, but Ella said it was easier, just up and down, much easier than the engine, with the tender, wheels, footplate and all that stuff, so Philip was awarded extra points for difficulty and in the end it was a tie.'

Claude chuckled.

'It's like being in one of Mum's curiosity cupboards,' said Max, 'you know, not just looking in, I mean in*side*. So I suppose they've all got stories to tell.' He flung himself back down on the bed. 'Go on, tell me one. Has the inkwell got a story?'

Claude took the inkwell, caressing it lightly with his fingertips before handing it to Max.

'It belonged to my father, and after he died it sat unused on my aunt's desk in their house in Somerset. Ella admired it, and my aunt gave it to her, and of course she *did* use it. To write letters to me, hundreds of them, when she was living in London and I lived in Paris.'

Max put the inkwell on the bedside table.

720

'And the cups?'

'The cups, the flask and the netsuke I brought back with me from Kyoto. They were a present from a woman I grew rather fond of who ran a little bar where I usually spent my evenings for the best part of three years.'

'Must've been a lotta booze. In those cups?'

'Well, you order by the flask, so ... twenty, sometimes thirty. Cups.'

'Thirty! Must have turned you into an alcoholic.'

'It almost did.'

'Ella won't have liked *that*.'

'No, she didn't.'

'How long were you over there?'

'Six years.'

'Why did you guys get back together again? Why didn't you stay put with the bar floozie you –' Max scratched his chin '– were *rather fond of*.'

Claude put the cups back in place on the ledge. 'I don't think I ever had the choice.'

'C'mon!'

Absent-mindedly Claude raked in the rainbow-coloured fan of notes on his bed and handed them to Max. 'Well, look at it from my point of view and then tell me what you think.'

Claude perched on the windowsill, looking slightly to one side of Max as he talked, a habit of his that Max noticed the time he first came to the house in St John's Wood.

'What happens back there in the Bois de Boulogne? The whirligig lands in a tree. I climb up one side of the tree to retrieve the whirligig, jump back down on the other and find myself at Ella's feet.'

'When's this?'

'In 1956. Ella's twenty-eight. I'm ten years younger, a neurotic product of a Jesuit school in Paris, abused and self-abused, self-hating, lacking all confidence, least of all when it comes to women.'

Max squeezed a pack from his pockets and took out a cigarette.

'Wow! You checked pretty much *all* the boxes on the list. And this broad whose feet you've landed at looks good, eh? You've just, like, landed yourself a home run and can't quite believe it, right?'

'Mm ... she has a tune to her that's catching. She is apparently so poised and self-sufficient, but I sense how vulnerable she also is. I hear the catch in the tune, a catch in her voice, the break in her, and I already know it will be my fate to listen to her and mend her whenever she breaks, because this is the one thing I seem to have a specialised aptitude for. I'm not generally a sympathetic person; she is. My empathy is tailored just to one particular human case. Hers knows no limits, enters into an ant, a blade of grass. Had she not happened to be sitting under the whirligig tree I doubt that this aptitude would ever have developed, this one flourishing branch on the otherwise stunted whirligig tree.'

Claude brought Max an ashtray.

'Well, the world stands still. We spend the rest of the day talking and talking and the same evening she flies back to London. And then we write letters, hundreds of them, thousands, and finally I follow her to London myself. From Paris to London to get a doctorate in French letters! Imagine! But of course it's not the doctorate that takes me to London, it's Ella. I follow her lead. I follow her lead, and overall that becomes the pattern. I'm passive. I'm reacting to something she did there – her tune, not mine. And Ella is already putting this into a story she's telling me over and again. It's hypnotic. The foot that fits the glass slipper. It fits so perfectly she never has the slightest doubt. She's very persuasive when she tells me about the snugness of the fit. I just felt it go *click*, she says. It fell into place of its own accord. And this account is reiterated so often that I come to hear that click myself, even though it's something falling into place inside her and not inside me. But if it was she who was making the sound, it was me who heard it. How could there have been the sound of her without the listener who was me? As I said, had she not happened to be sitting under the whirligig tree, this listening aptitude wouldn't have developed. Without her I might never have lived. And this dependence eventually gets to be something of a problem.'

'Wait a minute. The foot and the slipper, who's what?'

'It doesn't matter. The click is the sound of recognition, the foot the slipper, the key the lock – whatever – but in all these pictures there's an active part and a passive, one moving, one stationary, it's not a docking manoeuvre of two capsules approaching at uniform speed or twin particles balancing out their total predictable spin. Symmetry like that isn't what's happening here.'

Max flicked ash into the ashtray on his chest.

'You've patented some kind of theory on this? Some kind of *law*?'

Max grinned at Claude, and Claude, despite himself, grinned back at Max. This was almost an event.

'You know,' said Max, holding the Leica up at arm's length and viewfinding Claude with his rare-event grin on, 'this is an interview, right. You and Alex look so alike that I wonder how anyone could ever have bought the idea he was George's son. People must have *seen*. I mean, they must have told you this and that about George's son and you had to stand there listening to this crap, and he's your kid and how did you all feel about that? Off the record.'

This finally dislodged Claude from his perch on the windowsill. He got up and walked around the room, his hands on a reconnaissance of his pockets exactly the way his son Alex did.

'Well, it's never worried me here. But in England, before I left for Japan, I felt bad about it, frustrated and sore. But it goes back to what I said before – I didn't have a choice.'

'Course you did. You could've said this is *my* kid, and he's going to have *my* name.'

'That's too simple, Max. With three people living as George, Ella and I have done for the past twenty-five years, things don't work like that. The alternatives you're offering me exist in another world where *my* husband, *my* wife, *my* children are the conditions of people's lives. Either you're my husband or my wife or somebody else's and there's not much leeway. These days the breaking point is quickly reached and it's called divorce. But we don't live in that world.'

'How come?'

'Because each of us needs freedom as much as we all need commit-ment. Ella went to Paris but came back home. George took off into a secret life, but he came back out of that too. My years in Japan. The equilibrium is always shifting, and it always requires attention, a lot of thinking. You have to work on it, talk things out. You only have the privilege of the leeway if you have a consensus about things the balance won't tolerate.'

'Mmm, mmm ...' Max massaged his stomach. 'Yeah, I get that. Yeah, yeah – OK, I mean that balance stuff could just be a load of crap, a *huge* load. You could be conning yourselves and not even know you were standing up to your *knees* in bullshit, but, on consideration ... Herumm! ... Hand it to you guys, seems to work. Like you say, have to *work* on it. Personally don't know that I'd ... But no, that's cool, Claude.'

Claude sat down on the bed, where Max was rubbing his stomach with circular motions, and peered at him over his glasses. 'Maybe you need something to eat.'

Max saw a softness wrinkling around Claude's eyes and passed his camera over it before it disappeared.

'Is that the camera you always work with?'

'Always. This Leica – my bird. Nestles in my hand, broods there, eats, sleeps, does its poo there. We never part. *Never.* Should you find me dead without my bird you can be sure there's been foul play. I can take pictures with it in my sleep. So small and light and ... quiet. Listen to it rubbing its feathers.'

The shutter action was hardly audible to Claude sitting just a few feet away.

'Only camera you can use in a courtroom – that's the law in the state of Florida. No other camera operates beneath the admissible noise level. No clicking from this little one here. Ideal for work in churches. You hang it around your neck like a tourist and squeeze pictures so softly out of it that nobody notices. The tears in the women's eyes, the fingers in the kids' noses, the old men with their eyes shut. Only picture of the Pope celebrating Mass in the cathedral in Buenos Aires. All the other guys toting around Canons and Nikons, no good. Too big, too noisy, not allowed in, not after that attempt on the Pope's life. I had the bird clasped in my hand. I can take pictures with my hand held up to my forehead like I'm about to faint or I'm trying to make something out in the distance. Give the bird a little squeeze and off it flies, unseen, unheard. From the sound of it so do you, Claude. Listen again.' He lifted the Leica and released the shutter within a foot of Claude's face. 'No click.'

Max knocked another cigarette out of the pack and put it between his lips.

'I mean, that was you, wasn't it?'

Claude got up and walked over to the window, settling on his perch on the sill again.

'Well ... it clicked for Ella while we were still under that tree in the Bois de Boulogne, but it didn't for me. It has since but it didn't then, not for years, and all the time I was aware of having to catch up. I was a parasite. I lived off the certainty of her feelings for me, not of mine for her. There was a … deficit on my side, too much thinking, too few spontaneous emotions, and such as got through were subjected to the kind of self-inquisition only an obsessed neurotic is capable of. You feel unqualified to love. It's taken most of my life to learn that I am. But for Ella, I never would have. That's the most convincing thing about me and Ella. There's no alternative. It's either her or nothing. Me or nothing. That's what I meant by not having a choice – a meagre, defeatist little sentence, I know, so maybe the pop song version is better – only you. Ella was already handed this certainty on a silver tray under the tree in the Bois de Boulogne – why under a tree, I still wonder – whereas I had to work my way slowly towards it over the course of many years.'

'So how does George fit in with this arrangement?'

'Slightly to one side of it.'

'Does he carry a grudge because of it?'

'I've talked to him about it. He knows that but for me coming along he'd have lost Ella completely. She would have gone out of his life. As it is, she remains within it because she recognises that but for George being prepared to accommodate me in the same house and to bring up in the family a baby that wasn't his, she and I wouldn't have stayed together either. Because, as I said, I wasn't ready for the silver tray, didn't know what it was. Ella knew, but I didn't. I was still too young. That was why I took flight to Japan, the choice that Ella wanted and George made possible because in the end he knew that I made *him* possible. But it was never thought out like that, something we planned.'

'Maybe Ella did.'

'No. She let it grow, trusting in something that George and I didn't yet know but Ella already did.'

# 2

But while all this interested Max in a way, always on the lookout for coordinates to help him establish his own position, it wasn't what first returned to him when he woke up in the middle of the night on the couch in his father's study, where he was sleeping for the duration of his stay as all the bedrooms in the house were full; and as she had reminded him often enough, what first came to your mind out of sleep was what mattered.

It was the question *Where do you think it all is now?* which Claude had slipped in, referring, so Max had chosen to think, to the wet paint of the waterfall coming out of the mountain. But Claude had been asking about much more than that. *It* referred to the scene in the temple described in Claude's letter in its entirety, the chain-smoking one-legged painter applying the hairdryer to the wet paint of the waterfall on the painting so that the screen would be ready for the carpenters to install after lunch – carpenters in the offing, so to speak, who remained permanently in the wings of Claude's imagination – for Claude visiting the temple had been part of that scene too. His question wondered about a context in which to continue to see the one-legged painter of temple screens, his whereabouts after he had left the temple in question, his whereabouts now, a continuity of the one-legged painter's existence both inside and outside Claude's one-off memory of him.

One of the one-legged painter's whereabouts was in a dream Max had had under the influence of hashish on the roof of Santana's Ware-house Foundation building in San Francisco. It was like Claude had slipped him a counterfeit with that question about *it*, not the kind of straight question Max thought he'd been asked and replied to, not legal tender but, when he turned it over in the middle of the night to take a second look, something that belonged to a frame of reality different from the one in which Max had answered it, even if he'd begun to get into Claude's frame with that off-the-wall afterthought. *The trash boats take it out and dump it there.* Here it emerged, the matter in common between two people who initially seemed to have been talking at cross purposes.

There was always a good reason for understanding something some-one had said in a way other than how they meant it, and in this case Max had no doubt what it was: he had misheard the question he'd been asked because it was one he didn't want to answer. *At some point it all winds up in the sea – the trash boats take it out and dump it there.* He'd already looked down into that no-go trash-tipping area when the aircraft banked and began its descent to Tenerife. What Max had chosen to see scorching past the porthole window was not just the smoking black volcano but an asteroid disintegrating on its approach to earth. After that haul halfway around the world from San Francisco, disintegration was how *he* felt, an extraterrestrial bursting into flames as he entered the earth's atmosphere, burning up, scattering away his body before the moment of impact, all but a small hard asteroid chunk at the heart of himself, all the excess accumulated during ten years he'd spent in a place he once thought he'd never leave and where he now knew he'd never go back.

Everett, Jamie, Caramba – where were they now? Claude might have been asking him *that*. Everett and Jamie dead, Caramba an illegal immigrant to the United States, deported back to the Caribbean island he came from. From the late 70s and early 80s a mysterious dying began all around him. On top of his perch, his life fairly singing out of him, running up and down the trills for the sheer piercing pleasure of living close to the bloodline pressured up by the spuming geysers of his exuberance, Max watched other birds in the bright twittering San Francisco aviary drop dead off the branches. It was a mass killer, like bubonic plague, only it took longer and at first it took only the men. The men Max lost to Aids and US Immigration had all been his lovers, not the only lovers in his promiscuous sex life with slippery greased partners, but the main ones in whom he had most frequently sheathed his never anything but horny little ramrod cock.

In too short a time he'd lost too many of them to the plague. The streets he walked were their memories. Max was no longer enjoying his life in San Francisco. When one day he ran into his Winchester school friend Piers in a waterfront bar Max was ready for a change.

He hadn't seen his old study mate since Paris in sixty-eight. Piers had grown plump and soft, a rotundly perambulating middle-aged queer now, with a heavy-jowelled face and a big quivering arse that gossiped obscenely behind his back when he toured the crannies of the Tangiers medina in search of suitable Arab boys. Piers flaked with laughter and wheezed asthmatically when he quoted to Max this description of himself by a malicious competitor before adding, 'I'm only in Tangiers for the benefit of the climate, of course. Incidentally, I've got a very nice little whorehouse there where friends are always welcome to come and salivate.'

Max thought news stories with photo opportunities first before committing himself to Africa. What was big in Africa? Aids was big, famine was always around, and so were wars. The Lebanon and all that never-ending Middle East conflict just around the corner. Max had cut his teeth as a war photographer in El Salvador and Grenada during the US invasion of the island where he had met Caramba. Throw in

European stories a hop away across the Straits of Gibraltar and he was in business. Within striking distance of his parents too, he belatedly realised as he was buying a one-way plane ticket to Tangiers, and he re-routed it to include a stopover in Tenerife.

It was five years since he had seen his mother, but the Ella they went to pick up at the new airport on the south coast of the island hadn't noticeably changed from the Ella Max remembered from their last meeting in Vancouver. She was as energetic and sharply present as ever, a woman not at risk of being overlooked in a crowd. She was parading a pink trouser suit with flared bottoms that didn't really go with her stocky figure and short legs, and now looked rather dated in any case. She wore a matching pink silk scarf drawn under the braid of hair on the crown of her head and held in position with a gold clasp at the back. When she saw Max she shone with pleasure, a real shining that left Max in no doubt about how pleased she was to see him.

*How long will you be staying?* was her second question to him, and Max, who had been intending to leave in two or three days but hadn't yet booked the flight to Tangiers said, *Oh, coupla weeks or so, I guess*, caught off balance by the freshness of her scent when she took his face in her hands and kissed him on the lips. So she still wore the same Guerlain Mitsouko perfume, but that was only a part of it. It was the native scent of her complexion, a background clearwater freshness that seemed to go with the skin tone of a blonde woman, unassertive but unmistakable, the same aroma that came out of the jars in which she kept the vanilla-pod-and-sugar mixture used in the puddings she had made for them as children. In her mid-fifties she looked no different from the mother Max remembered at St John's Wood. She had always left him in a bind as to whether he should play where he really wanted to, swinging on the gate in the front garden, or on the lawn at the back, where he was less interested in playing but could watch his beautiful young mother through the ground-floor windows.

Wherever Ella appeared he had the impression of lots of things happening in her wake, as if an invisible crowd of attendants were being kept on their toes to see to the several and not seldom pernickety things she wanted done her way and preferably all at once, like the technique of flat-palm portage she demonstrated to Max before entrusting to him the bulging carrier bag, full of mostly edible presents she'd bought in Madrid for the grandchildren, which on no account should be crushed, and in the same breath the ticket she gave Claude with instructions to go and locate the counter where he could pick up the *bulky luggage* she'd checked in separately at Madrid airport.

'I knew you'd be here, my darling' she said to Max as Claude set off on his errand. 'I *knew*,' giving the word an emphasis which seemed to express the true intention that had been in her mind all along, the purpose of her having made the trip to Madrid at all, namely to find Max waiting for her at the airport when she got back to Tenerife.

Within an hour they were climbing the mountain road to Arguayo. Ella had been away for a week and was more excited at the prospect of seeing all the family who'd arrived in her absence than was Max, who had not been back to Arguayo in ten years. But when they reached the house they found only George and his daughter-in-law there, playing chess in the shade of the *portada sillería*.

'The others are all down at the beach in Puerto del Santiago,' said the sister-in-law Max had never met, detaching herself from the shade where she'd been sitting with George, willowy and wraith-like, something of a shadow herself, offering Max a limp, damp hand for him to shake.

'We've never met but I've heard so much about you. I'm Philip's wife, Ann.'

Ann had a long pale face made even longer by a receding hairline, a virtual lack of eyebrows. Irritated by that ubiquitous and overworked commonplace *heard so much about you* Max was already halfway to disliking her. Watching her pull back slightly from the hug that Ella gave her, Max guessed that Ann probably wasn't his mother's sort of person either.

'They'll be back for supper in a couple of hours. Would you like some tea?'

Ann brought out a tray with sandwiches she must have made, pouring the tea with languid grace.

The conversation batted around the table, with Ann and George reporting on the family's doings in Arguayo, Ella giving an account of her trip to attend a conference in Madrid and Claude chipping in with comments from time to time, leaving Max to look on and listen without volunteering any contributions. It wasn't that he found it hard to keep track of names and references that meant nothing to him. It was the tone of this cosy family *parlando* in the courtyard, including the doilies, napkins and miniature knives and forks Ann put out with the cake. All of this reminded him of the issue of *Punch* he'd picked up and read on the plane over to London from San Francisco, the first he'd seen since he'd left England. Nothing about that old fart of a magazine had changed during the fifteen years since: same layout, same typeface, same cartoons, above all a style of writing that struck him as so antiquated that he wondered if without anyone noticing it the whole thing had turned into a pastiche of a long-obsolete British way of life.

His brother and sister and five nieces and nephews Max also hadn't met until now added to this sense of estrangement on his arrival back in the Old World. With incredulity he encountered his thirty-three-year-old brother Philip in short-trousered boyishness, a schoolmaster on holiday, team leader for twins Denis and Darren. Philip demonstrated his sons to Max as if he were throwing a ball around for performing seals to catch.

'What world-famous monument stands in Pisa?'

'The leaning tower!'

'That's two—five to Denis. What hero stands on top of a column in Trafalgar Square?'

'Nelson!'

'Two—six to Denis. Come on, Darren, you're slipping. Don't let the team down.'

Max repeated these dialogues to himself with disbelief when he lay on the couch in George's study, recalling a language he had once learned but no longer spoke.

The boys had spookily good manners, little old-fashioned twitches like calling Max uncle and saying good morning when they saw him first thing in the morning. He liked their wide-eyed frank expressions, hair that stood up in identical uncombable tufts at the backs of their heads, their wriggling bodies when they wrestled with him, but their father wasn't so sure.

'Now come on, boys, leave your uncle in peace.'

Uncle Max knew what this meant. His wrestling matches with the kids were adjourned until their father wasn't around.

Their elder sister Hilary didn't seem to fall within Philip's jurisdiction. She flitted alongside Ann, her mother's attachment, the shadow of a shadow. Hilary is *delicate*, Ann explained to Max as they stood under the archway while Philip was backing up the car. She had had falls as a toddler and suffered concussion, leaving a hairline crack across her skull. Ann's hand rested lightly on her daughter's head as if to ward off any threat of falling masonry from the *portada sillería*.

The five children had all been born within a few years of one another, but Hilary already seemed to belong to another generation. As a result of her lifelong invalid status, by the age of ten she was a wizened little old lady with a pinched asthmatic face and the secret habits of the solitary child. She looked on at the games of her elder cousins Liz and Kim with admiration but no desire to join in. These two hardy girls were bronzed within a week of arrival, swam like dolphins, spoke Spanish like the Tinerfenos and could roller-skate down cobbled streets without a wobble. Well no *wonder*, darling, said Ann, scotching any suggestion of Felicity's daughters being in any way superior to her own; they did *live* here, you know, for several years before they went to school in England, so they jolly well *should* speak the language. As for roller-skating and the athletic sort of swimming Liz and Kim went in for, Ann considered them to be vulgar accomplishments it wasn't worth taking the trouble to deflate.

So Ann looked on with her rather superior smile in readiness when the bulky package Ella had brought with her from Madrid was unpacked in the courtyard that evening. Philip's team had been assigned this task, which required the deployment of advanced penknife work to slit open the parcel without damage to the string or the wrapping paper. The twins folded the paper and rolled the string into a ball while their father laid out on the ground five sets of poles and cross-pieces whose function and the way they all fitted together he had grasped within seconds of opening the parcel.

'They're box kites,' Philip said with evident satisfaction. 'My good-ness, *five* of them, and they're *huge*. They must have been incredibly good value.'

George and Claude laughed, even Max joined in, and the three of them crowded round Ella making the old jokes that had accompanied her from the day she arrived back at St John's Wood in a taxi and had the cab driver carry into the house bulk-bought parcels of clothing she had bought in a clearance sale — thirty-two children's vests, ten pairs of shoes to fit children between the ages of four and nine, socks, shorts, jumpers, shirts, skirts and knickers for Felicity by the dozen. But what on earth is all of this stuff *for*? cried George in alarm as the parcels filled up the living room around him. *For*, echoed Ella, what do you mean *for*; all this is *for* ten *pounds*, that's *incredibly* good value, George.

Naturally there must be a story to the kites, and there was, and Ella told it to the delight of her family.

She happened to have been walking past the department store El Corte Inglés in Madrid, she said, when they were changing the window displays. The five kites were being removed and dismantled, apparently to be put into storage in case needed again but more likely to be trashed, the window decorators told Ella when she intervened on the kites' behalf. There were five children, she told them, up on an empty hillside in Tenerife with nothing but wind, so she would take all five kites and give one to each child; the children and the kites would be served much better if given a new lease of life and a chance to get airborne than if stowed away in some basement. An assistant manager fetched by one of the window dressers was persuaded by this argument no less than he was by the señora's striking appearance. Smoothing with his forefinger a glossy managerial moustache, he took Ella on one side and explained that for tax reasons the sale of effects in window displays wasn't allowed, but in this case, he said, he would be happy to make an exception.

Most afternoons a breeze came up from the ocean stiff enough to raise a box kite launched on the hill behind the house. Max sat and watched in the shade of a tree on the terrace. As kitemaster general, his brother was out there for all the children, but the only one who needed his help was Hilary. Philip held up the kite for his daughter, or she held it and he ran and the two of them guided it together as the kite soared. Usually Hilary seemed content to caper around flapping her arms, shrieking with pleasure as she sprouted wings and pretended to become a kite herself, leaving her father to handle the string. Ella had fitted them all out with different-coloured streamers so that when the children came in for tea, anchoring their kite strings with stones, they could look up from the terrace and tell which was theirs and how it was doing, if need be dash up to save it when the wind flagged.

Max was content to spend whole afternoons watching the children flying their kites, just as he spent whole mornings with them down on the beach in Puerto del Santiago. All the family but Alex were there for the August holiday. Felicity and her friend Janine had gone off by themselves for a week to tour the island, and were away when Max arrived. Max lay on the sand under a sunshade beside his mother and talked to her while watching the children play on the fringe of the sea. Claude, Philip and George were usually in the water with them, George giving directions and filming the children with a camcorder. Max was amused and surprised. The camcorder must have been a recent acquisition, he said to Ella, as they had only been on the market for a couple of years.

'How come George suddenly wanted a camcorder? What got him interested in filming?'

'Well, that goes back to when we had Kim and Liz living here with us in the 70s. He had an ordinary 8-millimetre film camera then. The two girls made an ideal subject for a hobby filmmaker, of course. He completely documented those girls' childhood. He *loved* it. I was glad when he found something to do that gave him focus. He must have reels and reels of film in storage in the La Orotava flat. Perhaps we could screen some of them while everyone's here. I'll ask George to make a selection.'

Max rolled over and looked around. 'Where *is* George, by the way? I haven't seen him for the past hour.'

'He went for a swim with Kim to the sandbar out in the bay.'

Max broached the new camcorder, a safe neutral subject between father and son, when they were alone in George's study. George discoursed on the technical differences between video and film. The latter was more *eloquent*, as he put it, video harder and flatter, and already he could see its influence in the way news clips were put together. In time it would probably influence the way feature films were made as well.

'But it's just games for me,' said George, 'whereas you have to make a living from photography. How's it going?'

'It's going OK. But it's precarious. The ideal margin of comfort remains thin. Work in America is tougher than over here. There's no welfare state to pick you up when you stumble.'

Four ways of saying the same thing, all contradicting his first statement. Ella would have picked up on it, but George didn't.

'Then why don't you move back to England?'

'To Mrs Thatcher's Britain? You must be joking.'

'Are you faring better with Mr Ronald Reagan? Mrs Thatcher is the best thing to have happened to the country since the end of the war.'

'No, she isn't. She's killing the country, knocking off all its corners, castrating it, destroying the national character. Soon they'll take the lions off the coat of arms and put on sheep.'

'You've no idea what you're talking about, Max. When have you ever even *been* in the country during the last ten years?'

'How about you, Mr Early Retirement? How many Hyde Park benches have *you* slept out on lately?'

This exchange ended the conversation. George left the room abruptly without saying goodnight.

# 3

Max knew that his father's disappointment with his son, the son's with his father no less, stood in the way of a relaxed relationship. To the long-standing mutual dislike, the list of objections each of them had to the very existence of the other, there had since been added George's horror of Max's homosexuality. Max had the notion that if this so evidently repelled his father, it might actually hold attractions for him he found it intolerable to have to admit, which would go some way towards explaining the virulence of the revulsion. Generally, Max had observed, people were prone to criticise in others the things they disliked in themselves, and this was truer of no one more than his father.

*George took off into a secret life.*

The statement lingered with Max. That was how Claude had described George's affair with the woman who had betrayed him just as he had betrayed Ella, a deception on various fronts that eventually led to George disgracing himself and having to resign from the Foreign Office. But once you'd acquired the taste for a secret life, how easy was it to kick the habit? The question of whether he had genuinely come back out of it or merely disappeared into another remained. Max resented the fact that Ella had treated George so leniently after he had been deceiving her for so long. Why had she forgiven him? Why hadn't she chucked him out? The conversation with Claude at his house in La Laguna had gone some way to answering such questions.

On the morning after the late-night brush with his father Max went up to his mother's bedroom in the old bell turret of the house. He perched on the end of her bed and sat watching her sleep, listening to the little blathering patter of noises leaking out of her nose and half-open mouth, not quite snoring, he decided, but close. A scarf was wrapped around her head like a blindfold, covering her eyes, so that she wouldn't be disturbed by the early-morning light when it came through the facing window, heavily curtained though it was. She lay with one hand resting on the side of her head, a third defence line to ward off intruding waves of light. Max grinned. So the princess still remained sensitive to the pea underneath all the mattresses she slept on, even if she did snore these days.

'Max?'

The hand by her head moved to the bandanna and hooked it up with her thumb. One eye peered piratically at him before it was covered up again. Max wondered how she had known it was him. Eventually, when the ritual of the removal of the earplugs was under way, he would ask her. But before he could put to her his question she got hers in to him.

'Something's making you sad. What is it?'

She patted the side of the bed, where there was room for one more, and Max lay down beside her. Soon he began shaking, giving himself away; the tears he had been crying silently to himself became audible to Ella too. She drew him to her and laid his head against her breast. '*Wein' dich aus, mein Kleiner, wein' dich aus*,' she said, telling him to let the tears out, and he did until he lay quietly in her arms and even for a moment fell asleep. It was up to him to talk, but he was reluctant; talk would take him out of this peaceful hollow timelessness of a place, start the clock again, slip him back into the race. So for a long while they lay there in silence and let the race go on without them.

Eventually he said, 'While I still had them – two or three people who mattered to me – I thought that if they moved on I'd still be able to manage without them; other friends would replace them, in time. And that's how it was. A few months after Everett died Jamie showed up, and not long after Jamie died I met Caramba. I had these *replacements*, you see. Until a year ago I thought I was invulnerable. Whatever happened, I would bounce back. But when they deported Caramba, something in me changed. I was no longer as resilient as I had been – I didn't *want* to be. This whole idea of *replacements* shamed me. My thirty-fifth birthday was sort of a watershed. Bounce had gone out of me. Not necessarily a bad thing – bounce is really a sort of hubris. Other people may fall by the wayside, but not you. What you see as your vitality is really just a knack of not letting things get to you, and you're good at doing this because you're closer to yourself than to anyone else, the shameful secret of your resilience. So when I'm here and see the kind of family base Felicity and Philip have built for themselves, I realise that's a reliance pattern I'd roughly speaking like for myself, and from the way it hurts to watch them enjoying something they've got and I haven't I guess I'm envious, and this discovery comes as a surprise. But that's nothing compared to the surprise I've got coming for you. I'm tired of my freedom. If all it's given me by the age of thirty-five is to be able to manage on my own without people who matter to me, then I don't want it – I'm trading it in. But for what? In the world I live in it's hard to find same-standing same-age partners with a long-term perspective they're willing and able to share with you. The kind of thing you have with George and Claude, respecting each other's freedom but also your mutual responsibilities – Claude has been telling me about it – that would be *ideal*. I mean, here I am with a bag of T-shirts and a spare pair of jeans, and that's it. Apart from the real estate in New York, the sum of my possessions is in that crappy bag in my room – Christ, isn't even that – I'm camping in my father's study. Here we are, Ella. After ten years stateside nothing seems to have stuck – *nothing*. I've come out with no more than I had when I went in.'

Ella was there right away.

'Yes, you have. What you've just been saying – those experiences, that insight you came out with you didn't have when you went in.' She took his hand. 'You've grown up, Max.'

'OK. But that may have been the easy part.'

'But you never wanted an easy part. You've always made the difficulties for yourself. You always stuck out like a sore thumb.'

'The thumb was sore *because* it stuck out.'

'Well, if you live your individualism beyond a certain point, you'll be doing so at other people's expense. You were often *reckless*. And thought that was a good thing. You were full of admiration for yourself. And maybe the impressionable boys you used to go around with then admired you for your recklessness too. Maybe you can build gang loyalties on that sort of admiration. But friendship calls for something else. All that space you used to claim in those houses where we lived in England – the attic, the cellar. Your toys even managed to spill over into Philip's cupboard. Well that's a picture of how you are, your own pushing ego first, not respecting other people's space. How can you expect something to stick that someone offers you unless you're ready to welcome it and make space for it?'

736

'But you're forgetting, I did, and in that space two people *died* within a couple of years of each other. If they hadn't, I wouldn't be here; we would never have had this conversation.'

Ella sat up. 'So who's running your life? Are *you* running it? Or are you going to let Aids run it for you?'

'That's unfair.'

'All of us are up against something, Max. People can lose their homes and their families. They lose their countries and become stateless persons. They get ill and they lose their means of making a living. What's unfair? One can always come up with a reason for regarding oneself as a victim. Is that how you want to continue on your way through life?'

This harsh question from Ella pulled Max up short. 'I guess not.' Said more with defiance than conviction.

'So let's see what we can do. What is it about Tangiers that made you decide to go there?'

'Its reputation, I guess. Bowles and Burroughs, that community of gays and junkies who hung out there in the 1950s, I found that inspiring, far out. Not mechanical life. Life as experimentation and adventure, uncertain of your ground, taking risks every day, *making* the ground. That's an ideal of life I believe is worth trying – maybe with a better chance of doing so in Tangiers than anywhere else.'

'Thirty years is a long time. Tangiers has changed since then, Max. Claude and I were over there not so long ago and found it very run-down.'

'I'll have to go to find out. Besides, unlike you and Claude, *run-down* is what I like. An old school friend of mine has a house there and invited me to stay. According to what Piers told me ...'

Max gave his mother an edited version of what Piers had told him about the old town where he lived in Tangiers, dwelling more on the Janus-headed city looking east—west, the harbour, the medina, the labyrinthine entanglement of the poor Arab quarters, ideas and descriptions he borrowed from the American writers he had mentioned, talking himself into a state of excited persuasion that as a photographer at this moment in time there no was no other place in the world he would prefer to be.

'This is what you want, isn't it?'

'It is, it is!' crowed Max.

*Action!*

'Have you got enough money? Will you get enough work?'

'The pitches I made to a couple of magazines in New York for projects I plan to do in North Africa met with *terrific* enthusiasm.'

'Did they commission anything?'

'Well that's not quite how it works. They're naturally going to want to see some stuff up front before they commission anything.'

'And have you got enough money to tide you over in the meantime?'

*No.*

'I cabled funds to a Tangiers bank before I left America.'

Among the pile of half or quarter-truths in the African scenario that Max now spread out so as to create the most favourable impression on his mother – prospects which Ella, had Max privileged her with possession of all the facts, wouldn't have hesitated to call lies – there was one consideration of central importance that Max chose not to mention. The war on drugs currently being waged by the Reagan administration had put up the price of life for those discerning folks in America who indulged, not to mention the inconvenience and discomfort which the crackdown incidentally put those discerning people to. Appalled at the prices he heard touted in San Francisco, his old school friend Piers told Max what you expected to pay for hashish and opium in Tangiers and how much more easily it could be obtained there. The price of life for a couple of days in California would see you through a couple of months in North Africa – that was the bottom line.

A week in dry dock in Arguayo had worn Max down to the state where he would have done anything for a piece of spearmint silver-foil-wrapped chewing gum. This urgent need contributed to the vigour of his exposition to his mother, adding to it uncharacteristic touches of modesty and humility. He knew Ella well enough not to believe she was taken in by it, but at least he'd been able to get things off his chest, and she had accepted his confession, even volunteered a tentative blessing. Of course he *could* do just as he pleased, but if Max was in doubt about what he *should* do there was nothing like a mixed dose of Ella's sympathy-severity followed by one of her hope-building sprees to give him the confidence he was embarking on the right course. Borderline middle-aged, he still looked back over his shoulder to check the direction his mum was pointing in.

For the moment that was Santa Cruz, the only decent-sized city on the island. Pleading preparations for the African safari, Max got on the bus that left at the junction of the Arguayo with the Guía de Isora road. George would be driving to Puerto de la Cruz the next day to pick up the selection of home movies Ella had asked for and could have taken Max with him, but Max wasn't keen on the idea of being alone with his father in the car for a couple of hours. Once on board, he took out of his pocket the *Gay Guide to Getting Laid in European Resorts*, published by a two-man San Francisco partnership, both halves of it now regrettably out of print, who until their demise had been friends of his. Checking the entries for the Canary Islands, he found the majority of them on Gran Canaria. Its speciality was a hideaway in the mountains, allegedly a riot involving manipulation of the small but tasty indigenous bananas for which the islands were justly famed, while the capital Las Palmas seemed to be, as the guide mouth-wateringly put it, 'just crawling with queers' – more gay bars in a single city than in the rest of the islands put together. A single one was listed in Puerto de la Cruz and just three in Santa Cruz, low-starred, one of them asterisked, meaning it also did dope.

'Shit! I'm on the wrong island.'

But within quarter of an hour of getting off the bus Max was installed on a high stool at the bar of Chico's, the asterisked entry, a cafe-cum-pinball-parlour located down an alley just off the main thoroughfare along the seafront, chatting intimately with the owner as if they'd known each other all their lives – as in a manner of speaking they always had.

Since his initiation into the international gay brotherhood in his early twenties, Max had come to take for granted the advantages that affiliation conferred. If you were gay you could arrive in Outer Mongolia and get same-day service, a personal guide who would assume charge of you, introduce you to the family and the camels, show you round the yurt. Within hours you would be where heterosexual foreigners might never get to.however long they stayed – inside the culture, recognised, taken on trust. That was the secret of gay power. When it came down to it, gays had no nationality, or putting it another way, they were citizens everywhere. That gave them instant access. By privilege of their sexual preference they were the first and perhaps still, with the exception of Jews, the only true cosmopolitans.

The routine at Chico's was not untypical.

'Hi.'

'Hi.'

'Fix me a Coke?'

'Sure ting. Diet or special?'

'Special.'

'You wanna come in back discuss *privado*?'

And that was all it took. Five minutes later, fifty bucks down, Max sauntered along the Ramblas with a stash in his pocket that should see him through to Africa. Briefly he had been tempted by Chico flashing his *privado*, an extremely trim little piece of arse, while bending over the sofa to straighten cushions that were already in perfect order, but arse wasn't what Max wanted just now. He wanted to snort and cruise, and in short order he was doing both, satisfying an addiction to cities which during his detox week in the rural desert of Arguayo had been starved no less than other cravings like phone calls. Max found it difficult enough to get through life without room service. His parents' houses didn't even have TV, not in Richmond, not yet in Arguayo and still not in La Orotava, where he was now heading to make some urgent calls to New York and Tangiers.

# 4

Max's version of the American dream was a so-called commercial space, a derelict factory in New York wide open to dreamers' uncommercial possibilities. Max saw the building early one spring morning, having flown to New York overnight from San Fran, where he had settled after leaving Europe, fell in love with it and pledged the for-him-enormous sum of $90,000, not so much for the bricks and mortar as for the shadows falling across the emptiness of the space they enclosed. In fact, it turned out he would have to pledge a little more, since, unlike his associates who would be on the spot to do much of the renovation work themselves, Max was still stuck in San Francisco, still en route for New York.

The reason for the delay in moving to New York went by the name of Everett Burdon, a sadistic and beautiful San Francisco art dealer. Max had never met a man who could match Everett's sophistication, wit, elegance and cruelty. No fool himself, Max made a worthwhile target for Everett's demolition skills. Max could go at least part of the course, feint and parry, provide resistance and seem to be enjoying the sparring sessions with Everett, but in the end it was Everett who always won because Max was in love with Everett while Everett's only interest in Max was as his whipping boy and slave. Max made an ideal slave, serving Everett devotedly when he got Aids, a mysterious locust-swarm disease that in less than six months could strip down an athletic young man's confidence and physique to a skeletal frame. For all that, Everett remained true to himself to the end. Max went all the way with him, lifting the cup to his mouth when Everett became too weak to do so himself, his voice too weak for his whisper to be audible, so that Max had to bend down and put his ear to his lips to be able to hear him say, 'You'll always be a loser, Max,' the last words the dying Everett said.

Max was making money right now, after Everett's death, with some of the most harrowing images documenting the attrition of Aids to have yet been published in the world's magazines. These were the fruits he had reaped as Everett's nurse in the last couple of months – intimate, moving, mysterious for the disquieting expressions on the face of a man unsentimentally taking his leave of the world. Was it mockery? Malice? Disgust? Contempt? It was all of these shadows a cynical man's soul limned in his face. 'That's what it can do to a man' – it spooked people. It was this power – people who hadn't known Everett thought it derived from the nature of the disease itself. Everett's death mask became the face of a campaign publicising the dangers of Aids – more like the dangers of Everett, said his friends, but only they could judge that.

With just a little discipline Max could have paid twenty thousand dollars off his debt in the first year. But Max wasn't thinking of his bank balance, let alone did he check it, didn't even register the pinprick of the $4,250 interest payment that became due in the spring of 1976. Weeks passed until he remembered to go home to pick up his mail, and this became such a hassle that he had it redirected to the waterfront Friends of the Earth community where he had shacked up with Jamie. With just a little straight thinking, Max might have sublet his house and creamed off a nice rent during the year and a half he was living with Jamie – by the end of the decade he could easily have paid off forty to fifty thousand dollars. But he was having too much crooked fun at work and play, in love with Jamie, happy to be in the world – nothing else mattered. What the hell, said Max, after all it was just money. He wasn't one to economise on his euphoria needs, yield one inch of his jubilant self-centredness by squandering his attention on lesser things. In the hermitic state of bliss he inhabited with Jamie there wasn't much call for news of what was going on in the rest of the world.

So people might be having to queue to fill up their cars with gas these days, but Max didn't have a car himself and as a foreigner he failed to register the enormity of Americans being subjected to fuel rationing, at some stations even being turned away. OK, so the notion of there all of a sudden *not* being more where that used to come from, no longer to be just had for the asking – this whole idea of a world shortage of oil *was* kind of unreal. But when Max was rather hurriedly called in by his bank manager on account of being in arrears with his payments, he was presented with the figures in black and white.

That Max had a whopping debt, which showed no sign of getting any smaller despite frequent cash injections in controlled, strictly homeo-pathic doses, wasn't one of his priorities at the time. When Jamie died, Max went into a tailspin and lost his appetite for life, which was replaced by a furtive death wish in anything-might-happen assignments as a war photographer in El Salavador, the Falklands ... It was in Grenada, two years later, that a colleague with whom Max had left his hotel and gone down onto the street for one last picture – the film was already in the can, the job as good as done – took a freak ricochet off the wall behind which the two of them had sought cover. The bullet smashed his spine, killing him on the spot right beside Max. *That one might have been meant for me.* Scared stiff out of his gloom, Max met Caramba at the hotel shoeshine just a couple of hours later and bounced sharply back into life. From Trinidad they flew to Caracas and travelled overland through Central America. Friends in Mexico helped to smuggle Caramba across the US border and so back to San Francisco. After his two-year absence he found the once-trim little house in a state of dereliction, a condition it now companionably shared with quite a lot of other houses in the neighbourhood.

Caramba was a kid of seventeen. Max, at twice his age, could have been his dad. It was nonetheless the kid who fixed and ran the place – the household and the householder who might have been his dad. A spindly little fellow with rickety legs, a bow-legged case of child malnutrition, Caramba resembled something that in a richer world than the one he came from might have been put out for the dustman. Were it not for his glowing eyes and a pair of shapely hands more befitting a woman's arms, which had attracted Max's attention as they plied the shoe brushes, Caramba might easily have been overlooked on his own turf, a squalid inland Caribbean backyard the tourists usually didn't get to see. But the sight of such hands at work on his undeserving shoes moved Max to shame and pity and the kind of Chaplinesque impulse to chivalrous gestures which Max in the sentimental byways of his heart was always up for. He got out of the chair, lifted the diminutive shoeshine complete with shapely brush-clutching hands and set him down in the customer's chair with the intention of shining *his* shoes, only to discover that he didn't *have* any shoes — and in the hysterical cackle the two of them then shared Max found a vessel that could soak up all the love he had to give.

But how much Max could give turned out in practice to be more than Caramba could take. He was willing to be domesticated only up to a point. When his household chores were done he wanted out, but it wasn't chores Max wanted done — he wanted love and care for the home they shared. Max was a possessive and jealous lover, expecting from a seventeen-year-old in this brave new world of unlimited fun where he had only just arrived a commitment to their friendship that was no less than his own. Max moralised to Caramba about the importance of trust in human relationships even as he kept close tabs on the boy, whose eyes were not so much roving as swivelling in their sockets at the prospect of all the goodies this toy world had to offer. Pinball machines took his fancy, drugstores, department stores, streetcars, movies, chocolate, discotheques and the obstacle courses designed by unbreakable skateboard kids even younger than himself.

Entirely taken up with his jealous surveillance of these activities, Max lost his cool. How about a bit of *gratitude* around here? How about you do something for *me* for a change? How about some *attitude*? He began to remind himself of his own stickleback father and felt miserable. Let it go, he inveighed against this prickly father presence, let it go. But he was unable to let go. Reluctant to lose track of Caramba on his roller-coaster circuit, Max was turning down assignments that required him to leave town, leaving the mail to snowdrift at the door, the letters unopened, the bills unpaid, neglecting his personal hygiene — and wondering why Caramba wriggled out of his arms when he reached for him in the dark.

With fascination he watched his ineluctable twofold doom shaping up as the runaway vehicles careered toward each other, powerless to change their course. The day Caramba was picked up for shoplifting, taken

743

into custody and deported twenty-four hours later, Max was charged with actionable neglect of his obligations to Wei-Lin Securities, now amounting to an impossible $90,000. But for the intervention of Piers, whom providence had arranged to be standing outside a tourist bar on the waterfront where Max went with the intention of drowning his miseries, Max wouldn't have had the wherewithal to pay for bail and would have gone to prison. Maybe there's more where that came from, decided Max, now thoroughly attuned to an American attitude it had once been his luxury to despise but still not rid of an old British attitude of killing two birds with one stone – and skipping bail he flew to Tangiers in pursuit of the goose that had laid him this miraculous golden egg.

# 5

In the first dozen reels of maybe as many as a couple of hundred film boxes lining the shelves of George's attic den Max could see nothing but money. Cute little coloured flashes jigged around on the fifty-four-inch roll-down screen – highly desirable rainbow-coloured bills in all the world's currencies – flashes of pixel people having fun on the beach, shoals of bright silver sixpences in the sea, gold taps in the bath, naked little bodies being sprayed with a hose and flinging precious bright droplets that glittered and changed colour in the sunlight. As soon as Max put one film back on the shelf and took down another, all he remembered seeing in it was what he had attributed to it himself – money. It took the intrusion of his father to dissolve that vision. There was George in person, a rare shot of him grinning up crookedly out of the bath as he splashed water at the camera.

Touch George for a loan? Ella was the softer touch, but he'd foolishly killed that possibility with his boast about everything being just fine. He'd been ashamed to admit the financial mess he was in. Who else was there? What was needed was a genial uncle with deep brimming pockets, a soft-hearted aunt. Where were they, those well-stacked relatives? On his mother's side there weren't any, and in the Morris colony on his father's side they were all lepers. *Touch* wasn't the word. With a debt of $90,000 it would be more like nuking George. But couldn't his father afford it? He'd written those bestsellers; the old bastard must have squirrelled something away. If George could afford to spend his life on the beach making home movies of little girls surely he must have cash to spare.

This snug, wee, high-tech den, for example. Money squirrelled away right here in this studio fitted out with equipment that must have cost tens of thousands of dollars. Just the equipment. Never mind the attic conversion. You'd never dream there was all this space up here. Max had only cottoned on to there being a room above the ceiling after crashing for a couple of hours when he got in and taking another hour to get himself back into working order. Lying on the couch and looking up. Hello, what was that? Curiosity eventually got him to his feet, picking him up and standing him on a chair to take a closer look.

Crafty! There was a handle set into the ceiling, painted white so that unless you knew it was there you wouldn't notice it.

Gingerly he pulled the handle and a trapdoor folded out so promptly that Max fell off the chair. Picking himself up, he pulled the trapdoor, complete with collapsible ladder attached, all the way down to the floor and climbed up into the space revealed. It was a photographer's darkroom combined with a studio for editing and screening videotapes.

'Wow!'

Sitting down in front of the console, flipping switches, popping all the stand-by lights, Max had the feeling of sitting in a cockpit preparing for take-off. Revving up mentally, expectations of *Star Wars* footage, and then these endless beach sequences with tots capering in and out of the sea. By reel twenty or so the two tots had begun to grow up and became identifiable as his nieces Liz and Kim, engaging little girls who already prefigured the women-in-waiting in their bodies. Kim especially. Especially on Kim the camera moved in to record her contours, her black hair and strong colours, the early delineation of her hips. Nudity was the rule. Even the boxes marked SCHOOL showed Kim and Liz absorbed in their first writing efforts, sitting or rather squirming naked at their junior desks in the schoolrooms that took up one end of George's Arguayo study. Writing seemed to involve the whole body, a foot brought up onto the desk in solidarity with the toiling hand, a tongue stuck out to the end of its tether, a face in grimace, a range of callisthenics bearing out the extremities a body could be put to when unusual concentration was required of the mind.

Then there were the sleep sequences, perhaps the weirdest footage in George's collection – hours and hours of the girls asleep. The lack

745

of any action in the images called on the resources of the cameraman. George rose to the challenge with extremely slow moving in to focus. He dissolved the image in achingly long pans from tip to toe, from a loose black curl forming a question mark in the air down over long flanks – in close-up they lost their definition, might equally well have been dunes in the desert – to a grain of sand pinpointed on a toe arrestingly brought back into focus. They were dispassionate studies, almost abstractions.

Two shelves of George's archive were taken up with INÉZ AND ESTELA. Max checked the yellow library cards. This material dated back to the mid-1970s. It was arranged chronologically, beginning with some uncharacteristic and rather shaky shots of street life around La Orotava, carnival parades and scenes of the harbour down in Puerto de la Cruz – and then there they were.

A woman and the little girl, who was evidently her daughter, seemed to be dressed to go out. The girl had red shoes and white socks on, red bows at the ends of her plaits. Her mother wore white shorts and blue sandals with gold trim, a white blouse with soft blue patterns like faint smudges of ink, rather like the Japanese cotton gown Claude had lent Max to wear the night he stayed in the house. She sat facing the camera with crossed legs, shaking the bangles down her forearms with a flick of the wrist, beautifully bronzed clear smooth skin of bare arms and legs Max couldn't help admiring. There was a clean trimness about mother and daughter suggesting to Max something along the lines of an ad for aerosol spray. Bold-faced they looked into the camera, the mother usually behind the daughter, who sat on her lap with demurely folded hands, then standing foal-like between her mother's long and shapely legs, leaning over the balcony and admiring the view. Max recognised the church tower in the background. It overlooked the square in the old town that had been almost entirely taken over by a rambling banyan tree.

'Must have been shot from a vantage point roughly the same height as the tower, somewhere lower down on the slope of the Parque Taoro, only there aren't any houses there. So it must be from one of the taller buildings standing just below the park grounds.'

Working out the puzzle of where that balcony scene had been shot from engaged Max like nothing else in the footage he'd been looking at, so it gave him a shock when he realised that the next scene had been filmed in the rooms right under the attic where he was now sitting. The camera pushed open a door leading into the master bedroom, closing in on a brightness ahead which took on the contours of the bathroom only when George raised a hand to prevent too much sunlight from whiting out the image. On cue, a woman's cello-shaped backside slid into the bath with a gentle *whoosh* as the water absorbed her body. Now there was this big luscious broad in the picture, melons and pears, fruit so ripe that the skin seemed ready to split. Everything which so far had remained suggestively implicit now bodied forth as fully achieved feminine sensuality.

Max felt his eyes popping out on stalks. He'd been sitting here since he got up eight hours ago. Putting down a line of coke on a film cassette, he snorted it to stay awake for the cake-making scenes. This cream-cake fetish of George's required full-body participation – arms, elbows, breasts and bum. Inéz and Estela worked at the counter, covering it with a layer of flour, then sitting down on it and presenting white-dusted bottoms to the camera for inspection. The imprint left by the buttocks on the counter was inspected and the procedure repeated for an imprint of bosoms.

White-bottomed and white-breasted, they got on with the business of making the cake mix – whisking and stirring in a big white enamel bowl, humouring George but also apparently enjoying the game, giggling as they cracked the eggs. The lazy yellow yolk had to stretch itself, trickling slowly out of the broken shell, just the sort of TV-ad shot a sap like George was bound to go for. Mercifully the tape ended here. He found his eyes beginning to flicker. Eventually he must have dropped off.

A noise in the room below woke him. Max looked down at his father looking up at him from the bottom of the ladder.

# 6

'OK, Dad, so now you're here – some stuff we need to talk about, don't you think? You know, this is really ... *weird* for me? I don't mean this, all this ... crap you've got here. It's being transported back into that cupboard in the St John's Wood house. Where you used to keep the DBs, remember? The dirty books with the French illustrations showing you all the ways of doing it – the box labelled *Private Medicine* – remember that stuff? Back then it was *you* catching *me* out in the DB cupboard and thrashing me within an inch of my life – well, two or three inches,

I don't want to exaggerate – for being such a little tyke, and here, boy, here I really did catch *you* with your pants down.'

George sat down with a crash on the chair at the foot of the ladder. He looked as if he might be about to have a heart attack.

Go on, thought Max, have one. Serve you right.

'Have you got a cigarette?'

Max threw down a pack with a box of matches and watched his father pick them up off the floor. His hands trembled as they struck the match and lit the cigarette in his mouth. His voice quavered when he said, 'I can't remember when you last called me Dad.'

'Don't get sentimental on me.'

George took a couple of drags, gearing up to speak.

'I didn't know about these things. I should have, but I didn't.'

'Why didn't you?'

'We were brought up differently, Max. In my generation children weren't supposed to have feelings. No one ever asked. You did as you were told. You kept your feelings to yourself and felt guilty about having them.'

'Why guilty?'

'Well, the expectation was, if you were a child in a family, that you belonged to the family. But I never felt I belonged. I didn't have the feel-ings of belonging that everyone else seemed to have, I only pretended I had. So I was a fraud, really.' He got up for an ashtray. 'But of course the question at the bottom remains the same. What is stronger, the sea wall or the sea? I could have resisted. I went along with what was expected of me because there wasn't enough in me to make resistance worthwhile. That's one of the differences between you and me. I adapted; you caused trouble. You were in open revolt. Within months of being born. You won't remember that I sometimes used to change your nappies in the night. You looked at me with hatred. You didn't want to have anything to do with me. Fuck off, you were saying. Even then. You couldn't talk, of course, but that was what your look was saying clear enough. I want this, I want that. From the beginning you always went first. *Only* you went. I don't think I've ever known anyone more self-centred.'

Max swung his feet over the edge of the trapdoor and let them rest on the ladder.

'Nifty change of subject. It was you we were supposed to be talking about, remember? But maybe you were. Maybe it was George who always

748

went first, although he *pretended* he didn't, which is why he ended up on a charge of fraud. That's crap. You didn't have a feeling of belonging, right, but then you didn't have feelings about *anything*. There just isn't much going on inside you. *Thou art lukewarm*, George. Remember your old Winchester housemaster who had a bee in his bonnet about that? That cranky old guy was still around when I passed through. How's your father? the old bastard would ask once a term, although it was obvious he didn't give a shit how you were. Why was that? I wonder. Nothing he hated so much as a lukewarm boy, that was the only judge-ment that mattered – and he had an unfailing eye for a lukewarm boy. He would buttonhole him on his way out of the refectory at the end of the term he left and tell him, *which is why I spew thee out.* That's what he gave him as his valedictory.'

'A. W. S. Brown, that was his name. He was a dandy. He wore velvet waistcoats in bright colours.'

'Waistcoats? What the fuck has this got to do with *waistcoats*?' Max came swinging down out of the attic. 'Did Brown stop you on your way out and say that to you?'

'I don't remember.'

'You don't *remember*?'

'What I remember is Brown stopping to talk to boys who were pretty. So he won't have stopped *you*.'

'Thanks for the compliment. Those were boys Brown *also* stopped. But to two generations of boys he had in his house – and that must run into the *thousands* – he was known, he was *renowned* for that sentence at the refectory door, and the boys on the receiving end never forgot it. *Thou art lukewarm and so I spew thee out.*'

'Well, those weren't the exact words, but ... along those lines.'

'So you *do* remember.' Max seized his father by the ears. 'Then what *were* the exact words?'

'So because thou art lukewarm, and neither hot nor cold, I will spew thee out.'

'Did he say that to you?'

'Well, I don't know – maybe he did. Just let go of my ears, will you.'

'Not maybe, he *did*, didn't he?' Max twisted his ears. 'That's why you remember the exact words. Didn't he?'

'Yes, as a matter of fact he did.'

Max let go and threw himself down on the couch.

George got to his feet, his fingers reaching up cautiously to touch his bright-red ears. He went to the glassed-in alcove looking out towards El Teide. There he sat down with his back to his son on the sofa that used to be in Ella's upstairs sitting room at the St John's Wood house.

'You used to twist Philip's ears when you were boys. You were a bully then. You still are. You think temperature is all that counts. You watch the mercury shooting up the thermometer and think you're hot and that being hot makes you better, creating a lot of noise and flying into a passion and generally making an exhibition of yourself. And I could live with that, up to a point. It's the bourgeois moralist in you that I can't abide: your belief that it's your right to take me to task for the sort of person I am and how I choose to live. Who was A. W. S. Brown to judge? Who are you to judge? On the basis of what happens to be your own temperament? Does that mean all people have to be like yourself? I prefer to live in a moderate climate. I don't trust extremes. I respect appearances. That's a clear-cut division; you know where you are. Here one thing, there the other. You say contradictory, I say complementary. With the people who go in for extremes you never know where you are. What's the fuss about? Privately I do other things, and I keep them to myself. You as a little bourgeois moralist would call it hypocrisy and deceit, I call it discretion, knowing there's a right time and place for everything and otherwise minding my own business.'

George lit another cigarette.

'There's nothing worse than the self-righteousness of people setting themselves up in judgement. All right, have your revenge if that's what you want, but don't be smug about it. I happen to find homosexuality repellent, but, as far as I recall, not once did I ever condemn it, at least not in front of you, or take you to task for it in the bullying and bluster-ing way you've just taken me to task for what you call my lukewarm temperament. I accept it, but does that mean I have to like it? You let me be and I'll let you be. I have in the past, so why shouldn't I continue to do so in the future?'

'Is that a deal? Will you shake on it? Do we settle for a ceasefire?'

Max got up and went over to the alcove where his father was sitting. Mollified, George held up the cigarette pack and offered him one. 'Have one of your own.'

'I will. Maybe as a bourgeois moralist I should take this pack away from you or you'll get back into the habit you wanted to kick.'

'Maybe you should. It would be an infringement of my right of choice, but it's one I would authorise.'

Max sat down on the sofa beside his father and felt the tension between them subside. He waited for his father to reopen the conversation. For a moment he hoped that other feelings would follow in the wake of their argument – positive feelings that the two of them might have got somewhere, achieved something at last – a breakthrough – the miraculous reversal of patterns that had lasted a lifetime.

No such thing, of course – after the little outburst that had briefly shaken them up, his father retreated into the safety of silence. It would be up to Max to make the going. The disappointment when he realised that nothing would ever change depressed him and made him bitter. On the rebound from the reconciliation that had petered out he went back on to the attack.

'OK, point taken. I don't want to be self-righteous or smug or to take you to task for the sort of person you are or how you choose to live. I apologise for setting myself up in judgement.'

'Accepted,' said George quickly.

'But nor –' Max put a hand on his father's shoulder '– do I want to see you go to jail.'

George recoiled.

'This is important. You've got to get this, George. Imagine any audience you like. Imagine someone you respect being privy to this, Mrs Thatcher, say,'

'God, no!'

'So how do you feel about Mrs Thatcher watching that stuff?'

'I'd really rather not. I'd find it embarrassing.'

'What's embarrassing you?'

'Well, how shall I say ... It's not the sort of thing you want to show.'

'Why not?'

'I'd feel a bit ashamed. It's the sort of thing one keeps private. Intimacy is what one wants to keep to oneself.'

'Exactly. You'd feel ashamed.'

George raised a hand. 'Not ashamed of anything I'd done, but ...' George hesitated. 'I wouldn't like someone like Mrs Thatcher to witness scenes of such intimacy and tenderness.'

'Tenderness?'

'Well this is what it's all about.' George jumped up and began haranguing his son. 'Can't you see that, Max? I don't think you can. These are my little chicks. I can be with them as I can't be with anyone else. I love them for themselves and for liberating me. I nurse them. I feed them. I wash them and stroke their fluff. Children at that age have a marvellous downy skin with a quite delicious scent, so soft and fresh that you can't help wanting to nuzzle them. And what's wrong with that?'

*Stroke their fluff?* Max looked at his father in disbelief. Was this just sentimental rubbish his father was giving him? Was it a ploy to turn the tables on him? Or was George telling the truth for once? Hard to make him out. His own indecision irritated Max. A flash of anger caught him off balance, dredging up old resentments.

'You can say that again. Not much in the way of intimate tenderness around in my time. Not much stroking my fluff that I recall. You were a God-awful father, a complete failure.'

'Perhaps for you, but that's not true of the twins.'

'What good's that to me?' If George thought he could wriggle away, he was mistaken. I'll stick you back on the hook, thought Max. 'The mother-and-daughter combo seems to have left town in a hurry.'

'Inéz was offered a better future in Argentina, better than anything I could have offered them here. I was the first to see that. I encouraged her to go. No, Max. Don't think you can bully *me*. I'm not going to let myself be pushed around.'

'No one but yourself is pushing you around.'

Max skipped out of the room.

George followed him out onto the gallery and roared after him, 'Where the hell do you think you're going?'

'To the john. I think I'm going to throw up.'

George went into the kitchen, took a bottle of wine out of the fridge and poured himself a drink. 'This is ridiculous – who does he think he is?'

Three doors down, Max took the antique Spanish mirror off the wall and laid it flat on the toilet seat. Crouching in front of the bowl, he poured a line of coke out of the packet from Chico's as carefully as if it had been a gunpowder trail he was laying on the mirror, snorting it through a barrelled thousand-peso bill.

'Boom!'

He blew off the traces of powder, hung the mirror back on the wall and sat on the toilet to collect himself before joining his father. Within a minute his mind was sparkling clear and razor-sharp. His strategy was bold but simple, as easy as baking a pie with four-and-twenty blackbirds in it to set before a king, the good old easy-as-pie lesson he remembered from nursery school.

'When the pie was opened, the birds began to sing. The early bird catches the maggot. Strike while the iron is hot.'

When he went into the kitchen he found his father on his third glass of wine, in a rather better mood than when he had left him.

'Sit down and have a glass with me, Max. There's no need for any of this to come between us. I'm glad to have you here – just the two of us – and I don't want this business to spoil it.'

Max let them pass, those Georgeisms *any of this* and *this business*. Not rising to his father's bid, he sat in silence with a subdued air.

'What's on your mind, Max? I hope you're not letting this get you down.' George sounded concerned.

Max blew out smoke and made it sound like a sigh. 'I had a call from my San Francisco bank last night, and I guess that did kind of unsettle me a bit.'

'What was it about?'

'About a loan I'm having difficulty paying back.'

'How big is the loan.'

'Around seventy-five thousand dollars.'

'How urgent is the situation?'

'To be honest, Dad, I skipped bail to get away from it. I have to raise fifty thousand yesterday. That's how urgent.'

George pursed his lips. 'The fifty thousand may not be the problem – money can be raised. Much less easy is the consequence of you skipping bail. You'll be arrested on re-entering the country. What we'll have to do is sort out the money first, and then ... Kennard still owes me one ... I rather think that Kennard may the person to call under the circumstances.'

'Who's Kennard?'

'One of my old Washington acquaintances.'

Things began popping. Max brightened.

'You still have friends in the US? From twenty years ago? That's a pretty long time, Dad.'

'Not in our line of business. A favour once done is a voucher with lifetime validity.'

There was another of those suave Georgeisms. Max began to realise how much his father's former profession had rubbed off on him.

'Wow. What exactly *was* your Washington connection back in the 60s?'

'That's a long story. Let's get you sorted out first.' George poured him a glass of wine. 'Here's to you, Max. Here's to *us*.' He raised his glass. 'It may be late in the day, Max, but when you need your father you'll find he's there for you. You didn't think I'd let you down, did you?'

'Well...'

'We're in this together. Cheers, Max.'

'Are we?'

'Cheers.'

As he raised his glass to his father's, Max was thinking what a good thing it was that a favour once done was a voucher with lifetime validity. Even better was to have the voucher in writing, and with the IOU in the form of one of the incriminating cassettes he had just taken the precaution of stashing behind the cistern in the toilet, that was what Max now had.

# CHAPTER THREE

## The Party

### 1

Naturally she objected to Playa Africana. First brought to the attention of the cabildo of Tenerife a year after Ella took up her job as director of the Department of the Environment, the new tourist town was projected for the relatively underdeveloped east coast to ease some of the load on the mass tourist centres in Los Cristianos and Playa de las Americas on the west. The department had been opposed to it from the beginning. With the infrastructure required to support the new town – the exorbitant water demands that would be made on the island's precious supply by a golf course and a freshwater lagoon, the desalination and waste-water plants, the power station, roads and landfills for rubbish – Playa Africana would put a vast area of the eastern coastline south of Guimar under concrete for ever.

The primary cause of the decay of organic diversity, as Ella had learned from the biologist Paul Ehrlich, was not direct human exploita-tion or malevolence but the habitat destruction that resulted from the expansion of human populations and activities. Mankind was destroying natural habitats by paving them over, ploughing them under, logging, overgrazing, flooding, draining or transporting exotic organisms into them, introducing toxins and changing their climate. There was an utter dependence of organisms on appropriate environments, a fragile balance very easily disturbed, and Ella empathised with that, aware how easily her own equilibrium was disturbed.

At first a mere blueprint, the ghost of an idea like many of the other short-lived schemes touted by developers which flitted through govern-ment committee rooms before expiring, Playa Africana gradually put on weight that allowed no doubt as to the size of the ecological footprint it would leave on the east coast of the island. It accrued inexorably through initial feasibility studies to more and more circumstantial plans and their acceptance by a steadily increasing majority of the municipal administration. In the end Ella was left to cast the sole dissenting vote against the construction of the new tourist facility with a projected capacity of fifty thousand rooms. In the seventh year of her tenure, when the project was finally approved and her own position damaged, to Ella it seemed irreparably, she saw no other option than to resign from her job as director of the department.

For most of her term as director her life had been dogged by her struggle with Lea Fernandez, head of the influential Tenerife Tourist Association, over Playa Africana's right to exist. For Ella the issue was always so clear that she assumed others couldn't help but see it in the same light. Saturation of space, erosion of beaches, overexploitation of water resources, loss of ecosystems, water contamination, noise and deterioration of landscapes were already existing problems that would only be exacerbated by this new burden on the environment. Unless a halt was called to the building boom that had blasted through the previous decades, the archipelago seemed likely to disappear under concrete within the next generation's lifetime. More concrete would destroy precisely what people came to the islands for. A realistic view of the future could only concur with the need for a decline in mass tourism and a paradigm shift to qualitative, meaning ecologically sustainable, tourism. Any other view was unacceptable.

The view propagated by her opponents, by none more so than Lea Fernandez, defined reality differently. It was this woman who had tried and failed to block Ella's nomination by the cabildo as the department's first director. According to the tourist association's view of reality, the Playa Africana issue turned on the desirability of jobs and profits now as opposed to the deferred and thus by-definition-dubious advantages to be reaped at some uncertain point in the future. The association was confident this view of the issue would be shared by the three quarters of the island population whose livelihood now depended directly on tourism, who would be less impressed by arguments about the need to reduce the number of aircraft arriving in Tenerife than by the depletion of their current disposable income and future investment capacity. Why should these people forgo well-deserved earnings?

Ella was distracted by legal feints and challenges to her objections to the Playa Africana project, in fact to the constitutional right of the department's director to be involved in decision-making processes of the cabildo at all. This undermined her ability to put through the many other measures she regarded as essential but found herself having repeatedly to put aside in order to deal with Playa Africana issues. In political experience, ruthlessness and venality, Ella was no match for Lea Fernandez.

The overture of the tourist association's director was so barefaced that Ella couldn't believe she had understood her correctly. Lea showed up unannounced in her office one morning and informed Ella that her opposition to the Playa Africana project was holding it up, costing the consortium which had invested in the project a great deal of money. The consortium considered that money more usefully spent in the form of a gratuity to the director of the Department of the Environment in recognition of her cooperation, with an undertaking to make over to her a share of the profits from Playa Africana — all this and more on condition that she gave up her resistance to the project immediately. Having said which, Lea Fernandez left an envelope on Ella's desk and walked out of her office.

The large brown envelope left on the desk had a long pedigree in the many receptacles that had been its predecessors — from harmless-looking shopping bags to elegant briefcases — which had occupied Ella's imagination in the decades since she discovered the suitcase crammed with banknotes in a ruined house where she sought shelter on her flight from the Russian army in 1945. The money was useless to her then and would only have weighed her down, so she left it where it was, but from this time on, a briefcase or a plastic bag full of banknotes which she found somewhere — the circumstances under which it had been discarded and where she discovered it remained blurred — began to figure in her dreams. All the more tangible, the receptacle itself and the crisp bank bills she took out of it arousing her as no erotic fantasy ever would — there might or might not be a lock on the case, in the end she would always open it, she would riffle the notes and begin counting the money, stop, make a guess at a figure she would settle for, leave the end sum to fluctuate with the needs of her mood — the fantasy born of her refugee's plight persisted as a daydream long after the plight itself had gone.

Lea Fernandez' envelope moved into this space — and Ella was so shocked that she locked it in a drawer without opening it, let alone counting the bulky wad of banknotes she could feel and see almost indecently outlined inside — bold and brassy like the woman who had put them there. Later she took out the envelope and slipped it into a second envelope, which she had a courier deliver to Lea Fernandez at her office the same day.

Not long after this incident an unsigned article appeared in an English-language magazine published in Santa Cruz, purportedly a review of news of local interest, in fact an organ of government propaganda. Under the headline GERMAN BROOM, the article discussed the projects that had been taken 'so vigorously in hand by the never less than energetic director' of the new environment agency, Ella Morris. Her forthright, not to say imperious style of leadership had caused irritation in a number of government offices, where the policy initiatives of the Department of the Environment were seen as intrusions on the prerogatives of others. Speculating on temperamental differences to be expected of a member of the administration who didn't come from the islands and was not even native Spanish, the article disclosed that *la inglesa* wasn't English either. 'Could the force of this woman's personality and decisions have been influenced by the political climate in the country where she was born and grew up — Hitler's Germany?' the writer asked. 'Could this be a foretaste of how a new German broom sweeps?'

Ella was incensed. She took the article home and gave it to Claude and George to read, expecting them to endorse her decision to lodge a complaint with the paper that had carried the piece, possibly sue the publishers for character defamation, but to her surprise they advised against. Too far-fetched, thought George. Claude said she would only be doing herself a disservice by drawing attention to something that would otherwise pass unnoticed. Expecting from them more than this in the way of solidarity, Ella felt rebuffed and hurt.

Who but Lea Fernandez could be behind the article? What had Ella done to merit such a sly attack? And how could the paper have published such an item without the cooperation of someone in the government who must have supplied them with the background information? Even if Ella couldn't prove that Fernandez was behind it, she had no intention of letting the woman get away with her disgraceful attempt at bribery. She reported the incident to the cabildo president, José Miguel Galván Bello.

But Bello was evasive. Perhaps he was indifferent or just thought her naive. What proof did Ella have of the action with which she charged Fernandez? Naturally he didn't doubt her word, the old man added, but without evidence against the accused he would consider it injudicious to confront Fernandez.

Cowards! exclaimed Ella angrily to herself.

Over the next couple of years, watching the ranks of supporters of Playa Africana in the committees steadily swell while the opposition dwindled, Ella realised how many envelopes must have been passed. Feeling isolated and helpless, she called Eduardo Rodriguez and met him for lunch. They had seen little of each other since she had taken up her new job, but Eduardo remained one of her staunchest supporters, even if he held views that sometimes conflicted with hers, as had been the case over the Playa Africana issue. But when Ella told Eduardo about Lea Fernandez' attempt to bribe her, his cynical response took Ella aback.

'There's always a quid pro quo,' he said, 'if only the sense of obliga- tion that one owes a benefactor. Envelopes are always in circulation even when they remain invisible. Morality on this island is shored up by IOUs less formal but no different from the letters of credit exchanged between banks. One has to meet one's obligations everywhere. Of course there are kickbacks to the cabildo for supporting the Playa Africana consortium. The ideals of incorruptible individuals such as yourself are a less dependable administrative alternative to having officials who can be counted on to accommodate you for a negotiable price. That's how the system works, Ella. Bribes are accepted and acceptable.'

Coming from Eduardo, it was unbelievable, but in fact just as Santana warned me, thought Ella, remembering his words on the col- lusion of interests of governments, international agencies and private business in the granting of credits to Third World countries from which they stood to gain least of all. Look at what had happened to Santana himself. Mysteriously he lost his eyesight. His health fell apart. Ella had been embroiled in the Fernandez affair, unable to make the trip out to visit her sick friend, unable to say goodbye to him as they both would have wished. All she had was the disturbing tape recording Santana sent her a couple of weeks before his sudden death at the sanatorium in San Diego where he was supposed to have been recuperating after his discharge from hospital.

'My dear Ella, when Yoshi – you'll remember him, my personal as‑ sistant, a very competent and loyal Japanese, more a friend than a PA – when Yoshi came into my room the other morning he found me sitting with my arms outstretched, exploring the ledge of the window on the wall nearest the bed. Overnight I'd gone blind. At first I was more puzzled than anxious. I asked him to come around to my side of the bed and take a look at my eyes, see if there was anything unusual about them. I could feel moisture there. Yoshi could see it, the streaks it left as it ran down my face. My eyes were oozing fluid – it seemed to be pus. He took me to see a doctor right away. It was an infection of the eyes caused by a virus, the doctor said after examining me. In rare cases this could lead to temporary blindness. He cleansed the ducts of the eyes, which were clogged up with dried pus, and prescribed antibiotic drops for the inflammation. As a result of this infection I went for my first general check‑up in twenty years. I was told I had any number of other health problems, advanced diabetes being one of the more urgent ones, but none of these other ailments concerned me as much as the loss of my eyesight. Which might seem stupid because in all likelihood the blindness has to do with the diabetes – they have a word for it, diabetic retinopathy. The consensus, at any rate, of the specialists I consulted in connection with my various health problems was that I should slow down, if not stop working altogether. A diet became imperative, not merely to lose weight – in my late sixties I weigh over two hundred pounds – but to check the advance of the diabetes. I would have to change my lifestyle, work less, sleep more, take more exercise, stop smoking cigars, reduce my alcohol intake – lead a boring life. Do I want that? I moved out of the clinic in San Francisco to a sanatorium up in the hills in the drier San Diego climate recommended for patients with the respiratory problems I was having.

'After a couple of weeks of rest in this place, doing the prescribed therapy, following the prescribed diet, my general health seems to be better but my sight remains so poor I'm unable to read or write. That's why I failed to respond to the letters you and Claude wrote me – Yoshi sent them on, and I got one of the people here to read them to me, an elderly doctor on the staff, old enough to be retired but still working night shifts. He drops in to have conversations with me from time to time. It was this doctor who broached the question of a psychosomatic background to my mysterious and sudden *affliction*, as he called it. "In the old days one might have said visitation," he said, asking me whether I was depressed as a result of the affliction or whether the affliction was a symptom of the depression. He asked me to think around my eyes. If they were not seeing, or seeing only dimly, what was it they were not seeing and perhaps not wanting to see or wanting to see only dimly? How much reality did he think I was capable of looking at without flinching? What had been going on around the time of the visitation? Had there been other visitations – times of crisis – in my life, when I would have preferred not to see what was going on – failed to recognise it – looked the other way – buried something in a back file and forgotten about it?

'This doctor – a psychiatrist – said the last thing I should assume was that I was accountable for my own actions, in charge – a laughable idea, he thought, to propose putting anyone in charge of that bundle of contradictions, deceptions, warping, insubordination, self-sabotage and other insurrections purportedly carried out in the interests of the poor deluded individual one is in the habit of taking for oneself. Since I couldn't see well enough to write or type, the doctor suggested I make tape recordings and address them to my eyes. An ode to my eyes might be nice, but I might prefer an obituary, depending on how I rated the chances of recovering my sight – a cross-examination of the service and disservice my eyes had rendered me – the complicity of my own brain, someone's brain at least, in this autobiography of a visual life. I should go back and revisit it all again.

'I followed his advice and bought this tape recorder, which incidentally has the added advantage of making it possible for me to communicate with you. And I set off on the trail. Spent a couple of weeks just getting into a view of things nearer the ground, the view that had been mine as a small child south of the border before the family emigrated from Mexico to California. Still photographs swam up out of the memory solution, fixing images of the faces of people I'd not seen in a long time – and then curious flash recordings of events and processes – stills in which whole film sequences were frozen – the essence of a phase of my life ending in some special event, a graduation ceremony, a wedding, making love to my wife Miriam for the first time, taking up a new job, moving to a new house, arriving for the first time in the courtyard in Arguayo

761

and talking with you under the dragon tree. When I imagine putting all this suppressed material out for public consumption I realise how much embarrassment and shame is tucked away out of sight, and from the vast quantity of autobiographical material how much of it would have to be edited out to get even a slim volume I would feel comfortable about putting out and allowing others to review.

'An honest autobiography – a liar's paradise.

'I began to distinguish dark and light and to pattern significance into the shapes around me. Effectively I was blind, and yet it was at this time I began to fantasise about taking a bus ride around North Africa with your son Max to see the sights. A blind sightseeing tour! We'd get on a bus in Tangiers and ride to Egypt and pass the landscape and he would tell me what was going on out there. My eyesight did improve to a point where for a while this even seemed a feasible plan. It sort of patched up – came together again – slowly, nothing spectacular. Get back in touch with your eyes, the old doctor had said to me. And whether it was as a result of those conversations or it would have happened in any case, this remains a mysterious business, even if I'm slowly getting to the bottom of it.

'You may remember – when you all came over for the twenty-fifth anniversary of the foundation – those letters we got? Those faxes that came pouring in? We had them all in a laundry basket on the floor in the canteen. Lots of complimentary things people said about the work we'd done. You put your hand in and always pulled out a plum. A lucky dip that was fixed. You couldn't go wrong. Except one. It came by mail, addressed to me personally. Yoshi doesn't open the personal mail. He leaves it on my desk – maybe a couple a day, quite a bit more around the time of the anniversary. But this one wasn't a letter, it was a newspaper article. Photostat. Not the original. Not actually an article at all. In fact it turned out to be a spoof. I just glanced through it and put it back in the envelope. If someone had asked me what it was about, I wouldn't have been able to say. Like I was under hypnosis and had been told to erase all memory of it immediately. Didn't give it another thought until a few weeks later. I'm working my way through this pile of letters lying unanswered on my desk and here's this thing again in my hand. Deal with that one tomorrow, I say without taking it out of the envelope – put it on one side – finish answering the rest of the letters – it's around one o'clock in the morning – have a few drinks – go to bed – wake up six hours later – I've gone blind. But not completely – I mean, there are still things I can see, I can see the connection – I know why and it frightens me like hell. It's like something in a horror movie. I thought, this kind of thing doesn't happen in real life. Commonplace response. Disown it. This isn't your responsibility. It doesn't have to do with you.

'The blindness itself doesn't frighten me. It's almost comforting. I take refuge in it. Settle for blindness, if that's what it takes, for as long as it takes. I stay blind. I have a physical condition, physical symptoms, pus, my system is oozing with it, detritus with an unpleasant smell is even leaking out of the soles of my feet – a virus, a pretty rare one, conventional medicine tells me, because conventional medicine is even more worried than I am – an *extremely* rare virus – how else are we going to explain the inexplicable condition of this man? But of course I know. *Only an all-powerful, all-malicious and all-evil providence could have pulled off such a stunt.* I've known that since the day I shot my wife. You and Claude have known it too, Ella. And here's the thing. I can't have spent more than ten seconds looking over that letter that night, but I have – this is the first thing to come up, over time there'll be a lot more on its way – a clear image of what the paper looks like. Dull grey colour you get with photostats. A continuous line forming a box around a double column – newspaper article, remember? But no date – no banner with the name of the newspaper – no byline underneath. It's going to take me months to get there, but it turns out that during those ten seconds I did a photographic memory blitz of the page – I don't have a photographic memory, not in the usual sense of the term – and I recorded every detail, including a blur at the bottom of the page due to a fault of the copy machine.

'*PEOPLE IN GLASS HOUSES.*

'What on earth? That's the headline, in italics – PEOPLE IN GLASS HOUSES. It's set up in a rather authoritative style to make it look like an editorial, but it's not – I had all the local newspapers checked for a piece that might have been run under that heading around the time of the foundation anniversary – negative. I'll give you the gist of it. You might like to know – that collective *you* is *me*, by the way, I'm being addressed, this article is for my eyes only – how the funds invested by the trust of the Warehouse Foundation break down. In the last decade the outstanding performers in the trust portfolio have been in what analysts now call emerging markets – what used to be called the raw-material markets of underdeveloped countries – that *underdeveloped* is not the kind of thing investors like to hear these days, so you call them emerging markets to make it sound more attractive.

'Millions of dollars the foundation has been spending on campaigns against pollution, corruption and speculation have been provided by earnings from the very companies and institutions we targeted for years for unethical business practices. To find out I'm in cahoots with logging companies from the United States, for Christ's sake, this gets to me like nothing else. This really hurts. I know how these companies work – I've followed their trail all round the world – I know how they squeeze a country down to its miserable 5 per cent share and the profits are sequestered in Bermuda or the Cayman Islands or one of those places, money abducted from the market and entering exclusive financial loops, private capital acquisition schemes on behalf of an ever wealthier, ever diminishing group of hoarders – never to see the light of useful social enterprise again.

'The foundation has teamed up with thieves and parasites.

'This is how we've been paying our way. This has been our contribution to setting up a fair deal for what used to be called the Third World before it entered the portfolio of emerging markets. We've ended up on the crooks' side of the deal. There was a lot of bad feeling around at the time of Miriam's death. I said in court at the time that her estate would be put into a trust to fund environmental projects, as Miriam would have wished – the board of trustees would run it without any interference from me – some kind of gesture like that, some kind of pledge was necessary at the time, you see. I know, I know what you'll say – this thing has been dogging me all of my life, should have seen the connection long ago. It's just that with hindsight one wonders – Yes, coming in just a minute! – They're calling me to come in for dinner – Just one more minute! – This really matters to me, Ella. Give me your honest opinion. Has it ever crossed your mind that I'm a fraud? When I told you about Miriam, the thing I first mentioned was that she was a very wealthy woman, and then the tragedy of the accident, and the imputations, the hostility of her family, the whole business of the inquest. With hindsight I did wonder if what upset me most about the inquest was not that I'd ever thought of killing my wife – I hadn't, but something even worse – I might have married her for her money. That's why I was so concerned to dissociate myself completely from the blind trust that was set up after her death – didn't want to know about it, looked away – a decision I'm not alone in finding incomprehensible now. This is what unnerves me. We're all part of this game, whether we want it or not. We're all locked into the system.

'Even when I drop off in my chair I'm always daydreaming about this crazy bus trip with Max. In my mind I guess I see the African odyssey as my great escape. Making the preparations is fun. Buying water bottles and sleeping bags, I feel I'm a kid again. But as soon as we set off it turns into a nightmare. Frightening when these African dreams start coming in the night. Never stay more than a day or two in the same place, fear of waking up because of what I'll discover when I do. I might do better to tell you right off about the bad beats – and I'm in a San Diego sanatorium, for Christ's sake – in hotel rooms between Cairo and Khartoum, where the heat gets unbelievably oppressive, sweating what appears to be a white fungus out of the walls. A cold dread comes over me at night. I have to put on a blanket. I'm that cold. Inside my frozen carcass I have this bedrock certainty of my approaching end.

'Why should the things I tell myself about myself in the night be so much worse than the things I hear in the daytime? At night it turns out the Warehouse Foundation is nothing more than self-propaganda. The end-of-the-world scenario we're all so anxious about, just something I use as a facade to indulge personal vanities, rationalise private fears. Disguise your own collapse behind the collapse of the world. It's a great place to hide.

'The nightly interrogations I'm submitted to in my dreams have a claustrophobic quality of confinement, like the Africa I peer at by day through the windows of the broken-down buses Max and I are travelling on. There are these vast spaces all around, visible to me only through a small metal window frame. I know I'm losing the battle for the control of reality. Where did the vicious circle begin? Who is doing what to whom? The people to the landscape or the landscape to the people? Or are they the same? It has the impenetrability of a dream which is mine but in which I have no say – the entanglements of a dream I can't escape. What remedy for night fears? The only remedy is to change the nature of the night. Stay out of hotel rooms where the walls sweat white fungus. Don't for the life of you go inside! Which is the moment when I wake up, thank God.

'Questions remain. Why can there be one reasonable, well-disposed being in charge of a person by day, and one whose rigidity terrorises the person into paralysis at night? Do the interrogators inhabit different parts of the brain? Why does one think well of me and one badly? Naturally because both of them are in me, the good and the evil. But if I were in there observing at first hand how the two of them behave, I'd notice above all a difference in the intensity of their behaviour, the energy that infuses them. There isn't much to remark on with the good being who's sometimes in charge. It gets on quietly with what it has to do. It doesn't make a fuss. When it's satisfied things are in order it leaves well alone. In contrast with this good being, the evil being has limitless energy. It's never satisfied that things are in order. It never leaves alone. There is always more to be done. So you see, Ella, it's in this *more* that the nature of evil lies. It's not in the nature of what is good – being essentially passive in its inclinations and satisfied with enough – to agitate ceaselessly and clamour for more. Good is moderate in its requirements – *is* moderation, whereas the evil interrogator, ceaselessly agitating and clamouring for more, can never get enough – which is why I come to the conclusion that the global altruism I used to set such store by is always going to lose out to self-interest in the end.'

# 3

With Santana's death Ella not only lost a greatly treasured friend and mentor, a phase of her life associated more closely with that friendship than with any other person, except perhaps Eduardo, also came to an equally abrupt end. The events leading up to her resignation from the Department of the Environment happened to coincide both with Santana's death and her sixtieth birthday. On the threshold of a new age, she found herself for the first time in her life with nothing in particular to do – an unacceptable notion, so she rephrased this to herself as being in need of other objectives, a new plan for her life. After seven years during which she had been constantly on the move, Ella had a longing for stillness, and where if not in Arguayo would she find it?

Twenty years previously she had laid the foundations of the garden she envisaged there. It hadn't advanced far. Now she would set about completing it. But first she would give a party, celebrating her sixty years in the world, the twenty-odd years she had been living on the island, the seven years she had spent working for the cabildo of Tenerife, the forty years she had spent with George, the thirty with Claude, as many again with children and friends, gathering up into one skein the people and memories that had contributed to her life and trying to see it in its completeness.

These thoughts of family put Ella uncomfortably in mind of her half-brothers Edward and Nico. Feeling remorse for how little she had done for them since their departure for Canada, Ella sat down to write a long letter to both of them, recounting episodes of their childhood they would have been too young to remember and anecdotes about their father and mother, and enclosing a few photographs and other treasures she sacrificed from her curiosities cabinet. Ella went on to say that in the spring she would be giving a party to celebrate her sixtieth birthday and invited them to come and stay in Arguayo with their families.

The day after she sent off this invitation a letter arrived from Edward. Evidently their letters had crossed. Edward and Nico and their wives would be making a trip to Europe in the spring. They had applied for visas to East Germany and Poland, where they planned to visit places connected with the Sieres and Winter families – the houses in which their parents had lived, the estates and at one time entire villages which their families had owned until expropriated by the new communist regimes at the end of the war. Edward wondered if Ella would like to join them.

Ella panicked. Not knowing what to reply to her brother, she turned to Claude for advice.

'Is there some reason why you shouldn't go?'

'Not really.'

'Do you want to go?'

'No.'

'Then don't.'

'But perhaps it's my duty. Edward and Nico were still so little when they left they won't know what to look for. I'm the one who ought to show them.'

Claude thought for a while.

'Are you afraid of what you'll find, or perhaps of what you'll not find?'

Ella shook her head.

'Even back then,' Claude went on, 'twenty-five years ago, when I was last over there on a lecture tour, I found the drive from Warsaw to East Berlin very depressing. Nothing was looked after, nothing repaired. The houses ... Really, I wouldn't. I don't think it's a good idea. In one old estate house that had been taken over by a cooperative they told me that once the roof began to go they would vacate the top floor, and when the damp got into the ceiling below they would keep on moving another floor down, until eventually they just abandoned the building. Those abandoned houses reminded me of destitute people. It was a landscape full of destitute old people dying on their feet from the top down.'

Claude didn't tell her that the estate house in question had belonged to Ella's family in Holm.

After a pause he added, 'Holm will be like that. I don't think you'd want to see Holm. None of those old houses will be as you remember them. All the trees will have been cut down. The gardens and parks they used to keep up around those country houses – all that will have disappeared.'

Ella took heart from these disheartening words; in fact she felt almost uplifted. They made it easier for her to breathe, freeing her from the thing she dreaded most, the paralysis of decision, an intolerable constriction when she couldn't make up her mind. Claude had got it right. She shouldn't go. Breathing more easily didn't last, however. What she had unalterably fixed in her mind after the conversation with Claude began to unravel again as soon as she sat down to put it into the words of her reply to Edward. She considered telling a lie – other engagements or something like that – but then felt uncomfortable that such an idea could have occurred to her.

Certainly she would invite her brothers and their families to Tenerife. This would mean having two parties, one in April around the actual date of her birthday for her brothers and their wives, because that was when they planned to be over in Europe in any case, and a second over Whitsun, when schoolchildren had their holidays and parents could usually get away for longer. So the invitations should go out well ahead, Ella told George and Claude, already moving into top organising gear early in the year, giving everyone plenty of time to make their arrangements. With people coming from so far away one might as well do the thing properly to make it worth their while – a week at least, for the family, perhaps two.

So far nobody but herself had noticed or at least commented on it – the fact that during the forty or so years since Ella left Hamburg on that ship for Gravesend she'd returned to Germany only once. That had been on the death of her aunt Ulia, her mother's cousin who had taken the refugee family into her Hamburg house for two years after the war. Ulia's son had written to Ella to let her know that after the funeral his mother's urn would be interred in her parents' grave in Bremerhaven. In view of the continuing rise in the cost of the upkeep of the large family grave in Hamburg, he and his cousins had decided not to renew the lease on the plot. Regretfully, they would have to let it go. During the past fifteen years no one but Ella's mother had been buried there. Her name stood on an additional stone, to one side of the two main tablets and much smaller, squeezed in rather than planned in advance, an afterthought for latecomers. Would Ella like to have it?

When she flew to Hamburg to attend the service for Aunt Ulia she went to look at the grave that was shortly to be abandoned. She couldn't bear the thought of her mother's memorial landing up on a pile of rubble in a stonemason's yard, so she had the stone transported back to England. They were living in Richmond at the time. Ella chose an elevated spot in the garden away from the river. She had her mother's stone set up there and planted some alder trees around it, which she envisaged growing into a grove where she would like to go and sit, but within a year the house was sold and the family moved to Tenerife, leaving Maria's gravestone in the Richmond garden.

This single visit back to Germany in all those years had reinforced associations that Ella wouldn't have been able to express at the time. She wouldn't have recognised or known how to put into words the feeling that her native country had become a house of the dead. Taking even the one stone out of that edifice and putting it in her garden was as much of it as she could manage. Taking it was less an act of piety than an act of exorcism – the removal of her mother from a contaminated area, breaking the last tie that still bound Ella to the country.

Everyone close to her was dead, on her mother's and grandmother's side, on her father's and grandfather's side – there they all lay, generations of them, from the stony graveyard of the cathedral in Greifswald on the Baltic coast to the plots in drowsy village churchyards in Silesia down south. In between lay fragments of Poland, puzzle pieces broken up and put together in a different way again and again by a succession of landowners, pieces in different shapes and sizes, ploughed up and allowed to stand fallow before the millionfold harvests of the dead were yielded up in such a terrifyingly short time by those estates run on the lines of modern factories at Majdanek, Belzec, Sobibór, Stutthof, Kulmhof, Treblinka and Auschwitz-Birkenau.

'The truth of it is that I fled from all that. In England it was still all around me, still too close – Paul and Sasha and Giselle. I could pretend to myself there were other good reasons for coming to live on the island, but in the end that was why I left.'

This conversation was one that she couldn't have had with anyone else, not even with Claude. Ella believed that what she could say only to herself – what was said only in the privacy of this inner conversation – amounted to the truth about herself, and this secret isolated her from all other people.

# 4

Eduard Winter, long since anglicised as Edward, was a German-Canadian much as Claude would have expected him to be – a big bluff man with pale blue eyes, a somewhat pouchy face, blond hair going white at fifty and an accent that immediately betrayed where he originally came from. He made a joke of it himself. He told them that on coming down for breakfast in hotels all over Canada – Edward travelled a lot in his job – he would say good morning to people in the elevator and someone would always ask him in what they guessed to be his native language, 'So what part of Germany do you come from?' With evident satisfaction he told jokes against himself, smiling before he reached the punchline, encouraging others to laugh to show their appreciation. Friendly, good-natured, telling his self-deprecating jokes and never imparting any information without embedding it in an anecdote, Edward might also be encouraging you to underestimate him, a strategy that might have come naturally to the unconfident boy who emigrated to Canada thirty years previously but which had since been perfected as an art in the thousands of deals he had negotiated as a breeder and trader of livestock.

'What do you think? What do you think?' Ella was in a state of hectic excitement at the arrival of her brothers in Arguayo, anxious for Claude's approval. 'Is he like me? Is there a family resemblance?'

When the visitors walked through the *portada sillería* into the court-yard, Ella secretly watched them for a minute through the chinks in a shutter. Coming into the house to look for her and let her know that their guests had arrived, Claude found her on tiptoe at the cloakroom window sneaking a look before she went out to greet them.

Both brothers had grown bigger and more stout since Ella last saw them. Both had married large women, or maybe the small and slender women they married had become so over the years. There was a large-ness about these people that George, now rather large himself, found agreeable to have spreading around him, although Ella and Claude, used to the smaller, soft-spoken, altogether less intrusive people of the island, found it cramped inside the low-ceilinged house, into which they moved with their guests after barbecuing on the terrace until it became too chilly – somehow they had to squeeze into a living room they didn't otherwise think of as small. Big-bodied, big-voiced, the North Americans displaced more air, took up more space.

Edward's wife, Amy, had a voice that could easily be heard above everyone else's conversation. 'We have these gas-powered barbecue grills, made by a company called – what's their name, Eddie?'

'Weber.'

'That's it. Weber. Now you might be interested in one of their models, George. I have to admit your barbecue was excellent – *excellent* – but watching you do all that work, getting the charcoal up to heat, using a whaddyacallit to pump air at the wood shavings – honey, these Webers make it all so much more *easy*.'

She was already slurring her words and nearly toppled off the sofa when she leaned forward with a sweep of her arm to give that last word its required emphasis. With an indulgent but somewhat concerned smile, as if keeping an eye on the erratic movements of a small child, George waited for his brother-in-law's wife to finish what she was saying.

'Well now, Amy, the charcoal, the wood shavings – they're the whole point. What kind of wood was the charcoal manufactured from? What sort of flavour do you want in the smoke from the shavings? Laurel? Mountain pine? Because seasoning meat doesn't start with the marinade or the spices you sprinkle on top. The taste is in the essences coming up from the bed of embers. Whereas whatever comes out of a gas jet tastes the same.'

'Sure, George, but that doesn't make any difference, because we get all those laurel and pine flavours out of the packet for the marinade in any case, you see, and the gas jet just does the heating, not the flavouring, not in the way you seem to do over here.'

'Well now, it may not make any difference for *you*, Amy, but it certainly does for me.'

Claude joined in the conversation, heading it in a different direction.

'I think the real secret isn't in either of those things. How meat tastes depends on what the animal eats. Lamb in Provence has a quite different taste from the lamb you eat anywhere else. The sheep graze all summer in the mountains of Haute-Provence – although who knows for how much longer – where they eat thyme, parsley and lavender, and this is the naturally seasoned meat that arrives on your plate when you order lamb at a restaurant in Aix-en-Provence. But that may be a discussion of more interest to gourmets. You all stopped over in London for a few day before coming here. I'd be curious to know what people coming from outside notice about us, what things immediately strike them – perhaps things we don't even notice ourselves.'

'The plumbing!' Amy's voice crashed in on cue and everyone laughed.

'You know,' said Edward, taking over his wife's anecdote, 'Amy and I had a helluva time in the bathroom of our London hotel trying to figure out how the damn thing worked. There was an antique – really, a genuine antique enamel bath, standing on scroll legs – with the shower apparatus attached to the wall but no means *we* could figure out to get the water coming out of the tap to change course and come out of the shower. We had to call for someone to show us.'

'So how *did* you get the shower to work?'

'There was a lever you had to pull sideways, conveniently located out of sight behind the bathtub.'

'And there was this obscene-looking thing I thought might be for washing my feet in' – Amy spluttered with laughter – 'until Marie came in and explained it was a bidet.'

'There used to be bidets in my grandmother's house in Montreal,' volunteered Marie with a tone of something like gratitude in her voice, whether for the bidet or the chance to be included in the conversation wasn't clear. 'So I kind of grew up with them, and when I moved to the west coast I really missed them.'

Before this neither she nor Nico had put in a word.

Ella wondered about this reversal. She remembered a talkative Nico and a taciturn Edward reluctant to speak because of his stutter. These were the things she would rather have been talking about at a family reunion – matters of personal interest, not this barbecuing stuff and hotel plumbing.

'But don't you remember the bath we had in St John's Wood?' she asked Edward.

'Bathtub?'

'I don't mean the one you had in the children's bath upstairs but in the bathroom downstairs – it had a lever you had to pull for the shower just like the one you and Amy have been talking about. Or the one in Schlawe, that enormous great bath the three of you used to sit in? The two of you and your sister, when you were still very little, one behind the other, sitting in the bath and playing steam trains, all of you turning around and sitting in a different order from time to time so as to give Charlotte a chance to be the driver? And when the engine overheated and needed water, it was Nico's job as assistant engine driver sitting in the middle to pull the lever, take the shower nozzle off the wall and fill up the tank – don't you remember doing that? In summer with the window open so you could watch Mr and Mrs Stork landing on the nest on the chimney on the roof to the left to feed the Stork children – and Charlotte would get down from the table and run outside to tell them they could come inside to have lunch with us when it was raining? And put plates for them down on the floor with knives and forks? Don't you remember that?'

Smile though she did throughout this spate of questions there was something strained about the way Ella asked them. The rising pitch of her voice, in which Claude heard an appeal for reassurance, had something almost desperate about it by the time she finished.

'Well of course I do,' said Nico, 'because it was me that laid the knives and forks beside the plates that Lottie put on the floor for the storks.'

'I'd forgotten that!'

Nico had hit the right button and Ella was delighted.

'And I wasn't always assistant engine driver in the middle; sometimes

I swapped with Eddie or Lottie, not so that *I* got a chance to be chief engine driver – and this was probably your idea, Ella – but so that *they* got a chance to be the boiler man and fill up the tank with water.'

Nico and Marie laughed.

'Now you must remember *that*, Eddie. Come on,' Nico said to his brother a bit impatiently. 'Ella's quite right, there *was* that contraption you had to pull on the wall to get water to come out of the shower – don't you remember that?'

Edward sat with a bemused expression on his face, glass in hand, rocking back and forth. 'You know – this is an odd thing – I don't have a single memory of Schlawe. And I must have been ... How old was I when we left Schlawe, Ella?'

'You'd have been seven.'

'So there you go. I can't remember a single thing from the first seven years of my life.'

He said this with a tone of regret, as if apologising for something he had done wrong.

'Yes, you can!' Ella jumped up and stood in front of him. 'Christmas – all right?'

Edward nodded.

'A snowy Christmas morning. Lots of snow everywhere, just like winters in Canada. You're standing in the window seat downstairs in your father's study, watching the farmers' wagons driving by. Can you see it?'

Edward shook his head.

'Concentrate!'

Ella squatted down and put her hands on his knees.

'It's a snowy morning. The wagons are packed high with snow – the farmers have cleared it from the streets of the old town centre of Schlawe on your father's orders, carting it away to dump it in the Wipper – the river flows not far from our house. Perhaps you can hear the scene even if you can't see it in your mind. Not the horses' hooves, which are practically inaudible through the double-glass window where the pots of hyacinths are wintering, but the sound of harness bells, not sweet and pleasing but harsh and discordant – can you hear them?'

Edward moved his head in what might have been a nod.

'Of course you can! This is one memory you must have, because this is all about *you* and what will become *your life*. Dozens of teams have been working through the night to clear the town of snow. Each team is made up of a large hay wagon drawn by two horses, so a lot of horses are passing by the window seat where you're standing, and although you're only five or six you can already identify every one of them by name, all of the — what — sixty to eighty horses drawing those carts. *I* can't do that! I'm fourteen and I don't know the name of a single one of those horses! You notice when the farmer changes the near-side for the far-side horse, don't you?'

Edward now nodded in confident assent.

'The first time you do this, your father doesn't believe you. He goes and stands with you at the open door. He asks each of the passing farm-ers if the names you're giving the horses are correct and he's assured that they are. You know them all! Little Eduard never makes a mistake! Your mother may not seem particularly impressed, but I certainly am and so is your father Carl. He's proud of you! We have our own *wunderkind* in the house. Eduard telling the horses becomes a Christmas speciality we lay on for the guests every year.'

Ella stood up.

'I bet you can still remember some of their names.'

'Well ...' Edward smiled. 'There was Dunga, of course, on the near side — paired with Miriam on the far side — Miriam was often trying to take a nibble at him. And then there were two grey mares it was hard to tell apart, Urscha and Flink — the name helped, because Flink was the one on the outside with the more sprightly gait, bringing her legs up more smartly than the other ... Yes, I suppose if I sat here and thought for long enough I could still come up with most of their names ...'

'Bravo!'

George began clapping and the others joined in. Stooping to kiss her brother on the forehead, touched to notice there were tears in his eyes, Ella found herself wondering at the irrelevant workings of her mind — an association that had occurred to her in connection with Miriam. Edward's horse and Santana's wife both happened to be called Miriam.

When she came downstairs early the next morning she found her two brothers already up, waiting for her, it seemed, in the kitchen. They sat on the bench at the table, dressed optimistically — the spring weather had turned unusually cold overnight, rain was forecast for the next few days — in T-shirts and shorts. But they were on holiday, and the holiday outfits declared their intention to continue as planned. Perched on either end of the bench, they seemed to be holding a seesaw in balance, reluctant to move, two large men like overage schoolboys in the air of expectancy they had regarding the business of breakfast.

Ella took the breakfast preparations in her stride as she began the conversation that for two rain-filled days would continue with only short breaks, laying a mantle of words over her two brothers in whom she still saw two boys. Somewhere she'd read that laying a mantle of words over her children belonged to a mother's foremost duties – wrapping a child in a cocoon of words, talking it into warmth, inclusion, a sense of its own worth, laying the base for a lifelong trust. Somewhere else she had read – or maybe she just knew – that as long as you continued to talk about people who had died – to talk and occasionally to have dreams about them – they remained among the living.

In the conversation the two brothers and their sister began in the kitchen the scenes of life ranged up and down the Baltic, from Stettin to Schlawe and back again, with detours to places the brothers would actually be visiting next week on their tour of communist Europe – scenes of a life they no longer remembered in country towns in Brandenburg, Silesia and Pomerania, where their father served as sub-prefect between 1936 and 1944.

Ella saw it as her task to bring this childhood back to life for her brothers. She had a total recall of detail, as if she read it off a photographic plate slotted into her mind, prompted by a name or a particular word, a no less remarkable ability to recapitulate verbatim conversations she had taken part in fifty years before, and the capacity to relay conversations which she had heard from her mother and grandmother, recalling conversations with *their* grandmothers. Under the magnifying glass of anecdotes handed down from one generation to the next, figures like Napoleon and Frederick the Great would loom up as actual people, startling in the ordinariness of the present in which they came to live with you. Edward and Nico appeared in many of these pictures Ella recalled for them in the kitchen, frequently scenes at table, where the whole family was most likely to be found in one place at one time. One of the earliest such scenes was lunch in the dining room of the sub-prefect's residence in Schlawe on the day war broke out in 1939.

Edward asked how Carl had responded to the news of the outbreak of war, and when Ella told him the sub-prefect had dismissed it as a minor affair that would be over in two weeks, Edward was pretty sure this had been the gist of what his father had said if not his actual words. But what his father said paled beside the prophecy his mother had uttered. In her matter-of-fact way, which could be so moving at moments of distress, Maria had said, No, no, Carl, it won't. *Wir werden Haus und Hof verlieren, Haus und Hof, und Du wirst sehen, auch Oscar wird man noch als Soldat holen.* Carl said she was taking nonsense and laughed it off. Ella slipped into the sing-song of her mother's original words, forgetting the boys no longer understood their native language, and she had to translate for them what their mother had said: We shall lose house and home, house and home, and, you'll see, they'll take Oscar yet for a soldier.

'He was fourteen at the time, and before the war was over he would be called up, just as Mother predicted, and sent to the Russian front. We lost all trace of him.'

How could Maria have known that? wondered Nico, and Marie, who had slipped in and was now sitting alongside them at the kitchen table, said maybe women had a better instinct for these things. Ella thought that it didn't call for instinct, just seeing what was in front of your nose. You couldn't help but see unless you were blinkered as their father had been. Blinkered? Blinkered in what way? Naturally, this question came from Edward. Knowing the conversation had taken the turn she'd anticipated but not looked forward to, Ella felt a twinge of discomfort, but having come this far there was now no turning back.

Carl Winter had been a member of the party and had chosen to work as a sub-prefect in a state run by the Nazis. If you worked for them you tended to share their views, such as the view that the invasion of Poland would lead to its capitulation within a week, which it more or less did. A member of the party? Her brothers seemed astonished. So he was a Nazi?

Ella had asked her own father this question when she visited him in Berlin the year war broke out. Andrzejewski's answer had reassured Ella at the time, but fifty years on it didn't sound as convincing to the others as it then had to Ella. Shorn of the detail that belonged to the historical context, coming out bald into their kitchen conversation, it sounded like hair-splitting. Andrzejewski had preferred to call him a National Socialist rather than a Nazi. Carl was an idealist, her father had said, in his way he was a bit of a romantic. Nazis tended to be opportunists, out for what they could get. But Carl wasn't like that, Andrzejewski explained to Ella. 'And Pappi must have known him well, because

777

he and your father used to meet regularly to discuss the upbringing of the two children who weren't his, and Pappi told me Carl was an honourable man in all their dealings with one another.'

Edward frowned. Carl's dealings as a father were one thing, his dealings as a civil servant in the Nazi state were another. Only yesterday Edward had been shown by Ella a picture of his father that made him look extremely sympathetic, a fellow lover of horses, his hand on Edward's shoulder standing in the window seat as they watched the carts passing in the snow outside. But what was Edward to make of the sub-prefect in his official capacity? Ella also told her brother how in 1944 his father had arrested a high-up in the Nazi party for getting drunk and molesting the innkeeper's wife on a visit to Schlawe, and had the man throw into jail. This action cost Carl Winter his job and ultimately his life.

But Edward was still having difficulties with the blinkered father Ella had introduced into the conversation. The memory of the horses she had restored to him had brought other memories in its wake. He remembered listening, as a three-year-old child, to the hooves of the horses passing night and day on the road to Poland throughout the summer and autumn that year the war began. As the man in charge of the province through which all those men and munitions travelled, his father must have known in advance about the invasion. But 1939 was only the beginning – Carl was still in office in 1944 before they sacked him and sent him to the front, and during those five years all kinds of other transports must have been travelling into Polish territory just east of Schlawe.

'We did lose house and home, as Mother predicted,' said Edward, 'but then maybe we deserved to. I wonder what our father would say to that. I wonder what he would say about the m-mass m-m-murder carried out by the regime he served. I mean, but for that intervention on behalf of the innkeeper's wife ...'

Having had a forgotten father restored to him the previous evening, lost him again in the course of the morning, and thrown by this reversal to a recurrence of the childhood stammer he thought he'd got rid of for ever, Edward decided at lunchtime he'd had enough and walked off through the rain with Amy in the direction of Santiago del Teide. Two years younger than his brother, Nico had almost no memories of the Schlawe years – he had sat at the kitchen table silent for the most part, listening to Ella and Edward talk. But when they were joined by Claude and George for lunch he opened up, telling them about his years in the merchant navy, how he and Marie had met on the dock where his ship was tied up in Vancouver – 'Marie tied me up too, and landlubbered me on the spot.' Family life and a desk job began in Vancouver, journey's end for Nico, and everything he had to say about that subsequent life lacked the lustre of the narratives of his earlier years at sea. He seemed content enough to have been landlubbered by Marie. Ella was happy to see him in good hands.

# 5

It was always Claude who came to pick him up at the airport, and Alex always looked forward to the hug his father gave him when he came through the gate. Claude wasn't a man disposed to hugging people. He hung back when they made to embrace him. Ella, Max and Alex were the exceptions he made, and perhaps the airport hug had become an institution because, after Alex had left home, the only place they ever met was at one of the island's two airports, through which Alex passed on his visits to Arguayo. Claude made a point of coming there alone so that they could talk about things they preferred to keep between themselves. It was not secrecy but the opportunity for a now-rare intimacy that was offered by the airport drive. Often the subject would be Ella, whose volatile states of mind Claude monitored like a seismograph, tracking her moods, anticipating the upswings and downswings, letting his son know what to expect. These conversations had become ritualised to the extent that when Claude opened with some remark to Alex like, 'Your mother's been so looking forward to seeing you,' the son already had a rough idea of what his father was going to say and moved towards it with his question.

'How is she?'

'Having to give up her job under distressing circumstances, Santana's death, a botched hip replacement I'm not supposed to mention – it's been a bit much. The letter from her father, did she tell you about that?'

'Yes, she did.'

'It activated all the war memories. And then her brothers arrive, and she goes through it all again with them. Not that there aren't happy

779

memories for them to share as well. But the boys were still small children when they set out on that trek. The core experience of their remembered childhood is traumatic. Of course it has to be talked about, again and again, as often as they feel the need to. Ella's sixty and still trapped in that circuit. She goes round and round, on and on, checking all the memories against an inventory established after countless repetitions, making sure they're all still there, until she wears herself out and is able to find her way out again ... Your arrival comes at just the right moment. It'll be a comfort to her.'

Alex recognised the familiar post-doldrums signs in his mother the moment he arrived – an unnatural effervescence, an overwrought joy. In this mood she moved more quickly, spoke more loudly, sought more physical contact, lavishing kisses and caresses she didn't ordinarily bestow.

When she introduced him to the aunts and uncles he'd never met, she stood behind him with her arms on his shoulders as if presenting a new arrival to the class.

'This is my son Alex, the youngest of my four children,' she announced in an uncharacteristically loud voice and stagy manner that embarrassed Alex.

'Why did you have to do that?' he asked irritably when they were sitting together in her belfry room afterwards.

'Because I'm proud of you. Having a son who's already a professor by the age of thirty, doesn't that make a mother proud?'

'Is that what you told them? I'm only an assistant in Graz, you know, not a professor, and my contract is only for two years.'

But in the atmosphere of Ella's room, sprawled on the bed with the clear fresh scent that seemed to be the speciality of the linen in the Arguayo house – nowhere did sheets have the freshness of scent they had here – he was too content to remain cross with his mother for long.

He liked the clarity of Ella's room, so different from the habits of his own unsettled life, which was reflected in the provisional arrangement of all the apartments he had lived in. What had changed since his last visit? This was a game they had. Whenever he came home, she took him up to the belfry so that they could play it. Through this long-established ritual they gave themselves the couple of hours alone together which they seemed to need to adjust to each other. Protracted absences from home required this adjustment. There was always some new discovery to be made, and if he found it she let him choose something to take back with him. The change might be a tiny addition to the curiosities cabinet, or she might simply have reordered what was inside it. She might have had the room painted another shade of white. They talked while Alex was looking around for what it was that had changed in the room. It wasn't easy. But there would eventually come the moment when Alex felt synchronised with Ella, his pendulum swinging on the same tack as hers, and this was when he would most likely find what he was looking for.

'Is that it? There's a stick I haven't seen before propped up by the dresser. What do you need a walking stick for?'

She admitted that several months previously she'd had a hip replacement. When Alex pressed her for details she was uncharacteristically vague, mumbling something about things wearing out as one got older. Until a few weeks ago she'd still been walking with crutches, then she could get by with a stick, but this week she had left it in her room. It was just vanity, she said. She wanted her brothers to see her as they remembered her.

'Have you heard from Max?' he asked.

'Not since Christmas.'

'And the others?'

'Not from them, either. I expect there'll be something in the post tomorrow, or they'll call.' She reached up and smoothed down the hair sticking up at the back of his head. 'I'm sure they will. They always remember my birthday.'

When they set off on the expedition to El Teide, she left the stick in her room but took Alex's arm for support whenever she had any distance to walk. They drove over to La Orotava in two cars to show the brothers and their wives the old Spanish town.

They drove through the outskirts of the Orotava valley. Cobbled streets gave way to dirt tracks leading to isolated houses among stands of banana trees on terraced slopes, then no houses at all, a coil of oily black tarmac winding up and up the wooded mountainside. Occasional gusts of scents from the profusion of roadside shrubs came wafting in through the car windows. This was where the Parque Natural de la Corona Forestal began, an extension of the protected lands around the Peak which Ella had fought for and won during her term at the Department of the Environment, she said, continuing the project undertaken with

Eduardo Rodriguez when she worked for his institute at the University of La Laguna.

Ten years of her life had gone into this. They stopped at one of the signposted spots with a view down over the forest to the ocean. If you wanted a monument commemorating how you had spent a decade of your life, thought Alex, this would be hard to beat. Ella talked animat/edly about the difficulties her campaign had faced, the many obstacles, of which there was no trace in the landscape they were looking at. To Alex it all seemed so naturally in place that he wondered what work there had been for human hands to do.

Alex parked the car alongside George's old jeep, within walking distance of the cable car that took tourists up the remaining couple of hundred metres to the summit of El Teide. This was one of the most bizarre landscapes on the islands. The plateau below the Peak, as English tourists had named Tenerife's landmark mountain, appeared to have been ploughed up by a giant tractor, leaving furrows as high as houses in the dark volcanic soil. Surrounded by the evidence of the convulsive geological forces that had been at work here apparently quite recently, Alex found his dislike for it hadn't changed. Awed by the violence of the landscape, he felt his human insignificance.

The men were already walking off to the cable car station. Marie and Amy waited for Ella and Alex to catch up.

'You go ahead without me,' Ella called after them. 'I haven't got a head for heights. The ride in the cable car just makes me dizzy.'

Marie and Amy waved and went on up the hill.

'Since when do cable cars make you dizzy?'

'Since wanting to talk to you mattered more than taking a ride in a cable car. Let's walk a bit.' Ella squeezed his arm. 'Your visits are always so short. I have so little of you to myself. Tell me about the things in your life that make you happy.'

'My work. Teaching a good class makes me happy. Or do I mean satisfied? No, I think happy. All my stars are out, as Seymour said in that moving story of Salinger's. New friends I've made, in Graz but also in Vienna and Klagenfurt. I spent a weekend there recently, met a girl I rather like.' Alex paused. 'Coming home and seeing you makes me happy. Seeing Claude. And George. Not necessarily in that order. But above all you.'

'And you mean it, I know. You don't say so in order to please me, do you, my darling Alex!'

She gave him a kiss.

'None of the others would say anything like that. Probably none of the others would *think* anything like that. Certainly not your sister. I can't remember when she last said something kind to me. She bears me a grudge. If I didn't call her from time to time I wouldn't hear anything from her. I know Felicity isn't happy. Is it my fault? What did I do wrong?' Ella stared into the distance. 'Perhaps Philip is the one of you with the best chance of leading a contented life. Philip lives too much on one level to be capable of happiness or unhappiness. Not much up, not much down. Things don't really get to him, and he doesn't need them to. Better for him like that. He's contented.'

'Maybe he *is* better off like that.'

'Felicity and Philip, you and Max – how is it possible for four children to be so different from one another? Well, in your case of course with a different father – but where does Max come from? Who are his parents? How can one's own flesh and blood be so alien to one?' Ella looked up at him. 'Does that seem to you a terrible thing for a mother to say of her own child?'

Alex hesitated.

'Not terrible, but sad.'

'It *is* sad, I know. It *is* sad. But I can't lie to myself about it. It's true. And I still hear my mother saying exactly the same thing about my brother Oscar: *Wie kann einem das eigene Kind so fremd sein!*'

She detached herself from his arm, took a few unsteady steps on her own and stood lost in the landscape. Alex wished he had an answer to his mother's question. He wished he could have come up with some words of reassurance for her to hang on to, but he remained standing where he was and said nothing, only moving to support her when he realised she might fall.

# 6

This conversation with his mother left Alex feeling uneasy. There had been similar conversations before; one could say they were becoming a regular feature of his visits home in recent years. Why had he failed to come up with a reply, not necessarily with an answer that would have enlightened Ella — he would have to be more of a philosopher than he was to accomplish that — but at least to acknowledge her concern and show her that she wasn't left alone with her question?

'I'll have to call them, all three of them, and remind them it's her birthday tomorrow.'

This too he had heard himself say in the past and failed to act on it. Part of the problem was having to make the calls from the house without being overheard. Doors and windows were always open in Arguayo. The openness the house expected of its inhabitants was one of the things Alex liked about the place. That was part of its charm. There's no Official Secrets Act in force in this house, George would say with a lopsided smile when warning first-time visitors to the house about the soundbox in the kitchen ceiling.

An alternative was to drive over to La Laguna and make the calls from Claude's house. That would mean an absence of several hours it would be difficult to explain to his mother when he was on a visit of only three or four days. She'd be hurt by it. A lie was out of the question. Ella would see through the lie at once and be hurt by that even more.

Besides, was it his business to be doing this? Max was ten years older than him. Almost another generation. They hadn't met more than a few times in the past decade. Max wouldn't take him seriously. He'd fool around, call him Pooky, his little brother, say who was he to presume to tell old Max what to do, tell him to fuck off. What's it got to do with you whether I call my mother on her birthday or not? Felicity and Philip might ask. They resented Alex's most-favoured-child status with their mother, plain for all to see from the beginning, and would probably give him the sort of brush-off they'd given him in the past. Intervening with them on Ella's behalf might have the opposite effect.

Alex could see that Max was out there on his own, different from his three brothers and sisters. As Ella had asked him up on the mountain: how could one's own flesh and blood be so alien to one? But did that matter? Was it necessary to feel kinship with one's own child? Why did Ella have to suffer on account of a son so different that there could be no bond with him in any case? Why did she have to make such a demand? Alex felt impatient with his mother. No one expected her to suffer. No one benefited from it. Couldn't she let Max be — just let go of him?

Why worry about Max? They hardly ever see each other. Why does Ella have to cause this trouble? Why is she always having to spoil things for herself? Why can't she accept things as they are?

If she were to lose her house in an earthquake, if some terrible tragedy struck and took all her family, if she got cancer or lost a leg or were to go blind like Santana, Ella would stoically bear it, yet she couldn't come to terms with her own flesh and blood being so alien to her.

But this, after all, might be what Max was looking for: Ella's flaw – the hubris of her non-acceptance, the lack of insight into there being a nature of things different from the nature she expected them to have, the imposition of her own standards, her implacability when thwarted, the stubbornness of her refusal to let things go whose nature she couldn't change.

Alex solved the problem of where to call from by driving down to the post office in Puerto de Santiago. He called Philip's office in Portsmouth first, where he got a message on his brother's answer machine.

'Please leave your message for Philip Morris now.'

The cigarette man, Max called his non-smoking brother. That still made Alex laugh. Still laughing, caught off guard by this prompt, Alex got off to a fumbling start.

'Philip? It's Alex. How are you? I'm calling from Arguayo, or rather from the post office in Puerto de Santiago for reasons I shan't go into. The most beautiful spring weather, needless to say. I know you and the family will be over later on, but that doesn't mean we're not missing having you with us now. Edward and Nico, our two uncles from Canada I've never met, are here with their wives. They're having a great time, and of course Ella's very happy to have family staying in the house at last. Look, the reason I'm calling is—'

The machine cut him off.

For some reason there was a delay in getting the second call put through, only adding to the irritation Alex was already feeling with Philip's inhospitable caller prompt, with the result that he made his message as bald as his brother's: 'Please remember to call Ella on her birthday. Alex.'

He hung up, regretting he hadn't embedded his request in a few friendly sentences to make it sound less like an order. He was wondering if he should have a third try when he turned around and saw the queue of people waiting outside the single booth for international calls at the little post office, so he dialled Felicity's London number instead.

'Kim, Liz, Felicity and Janine aren't at home but would like to hear from you if you've got something interesting to say.'

He recognised Kim's voice. Probably most of the messages got left for her and Liz. Alex had a vision of the four girls sitting around the answer machine in Felicity's house in Clapham keeping a tally of incoming calls, who got one from whom, a popularity contest, and he decided to include them all.

Last was Max. Alex called his brother's number in Tangiers. The phone picked up to the sound of Max, probably high, breezing through the message he'd left on the machine.

'OK, guys, this is *Max*. You nearly got it right but if you want to speak to the man in person your best chance of reaching him most any day of the week is at twelve noon Tangiers time, whereas if you're happy to talk to a *machine* you can do so on the stroke of the gong' — and a resonant *boing!* reminiscent of the Rank Organisation gong came booming down the line.

Alex warmed to the sound of Max's voice. He left a friendly message reminding Max it was their mother's birthday, hung up and then changed his mind. He'd like to talk to Max, after all. He looked at his watch. Twelve noon was in twenty minutes. He decided to wait.

Alex paid for the calls he'd made and went back to wait in the queue outside the booth. He collided with a woman on her way into the post office carrying a stack of parcels, which all fell to the floor.

'I'm so sorry!'

Both of them apologised. Alex stopped to help her gather up the parcels. As he stood up and placed them on top of the pile she was holding, the woman looked at him quizzically.

'Alex? Alex Morris?'

She was a tall woman with her hair scooped up behind her head and held with a comb, the sort of hairdo that probably took about fifteen seconds, slightly longer than it took Alex to recall the tousled auburn hair and the absent-minded, almost surprised air of the woman who looked as if she'd just got out of bed in a hurry when she came into class first thing in the morning, still trailing intimate scents of sleep, a natural perfume he remembered as the trademark of his former teacher at the International School in Puerto de la Cruz.

'Mirjana Stepanovic!'

'Well, you got there in the end.' She laughed. 'Have you got a few minutes? I must just deal with these. Would you mind waiting? It won't take a moment. We could have a cup of coffee or something. Would you like that?'

'I'd love to.'

Alex was about to add that he was queuing to make a phone call, but when he saw the tourists already in line to make what seemed to be rather long calls home he thought better of trying to get hold of Max in Tangiers. That decision was no longer his in any case, swept aside by the explosion of adolescent excitement at seeing again the woman with whom he'd been infatuated.

He stood outside the post office, expecting to watch her walk down the steps, but she surprised him by balancing on the rail in the middle, lifting her feet and sliding down on her backside.

'Well? What do you think?' She sauntered past him along the prom-enade. 'Am I holding up? Will I still do?'

'So you know. That I had a crush on you. You knew at the time. You knew before I did. At fifteen I had no experience of these things.'

'These things? No, and I found that very sweet.' She took his arm. 'And I still do. For you haven't changed. I could read your thoughts off your face then, and I think I still can.'

'What thoughts?'

'You're embarrassed but you're pleased. Come up and have a drink.'

A flight of steps led up from the seafront to a row of apartments that had been built on the harbour wall where Alex remembered fishermen's cottages having stood not so long ago.

'Is this your own place?'

'At weekends and during the school holidays. I live in a rather cramped flat in an unattractive spot in town, wanted to move, never got round to it, and wound up buying this place instead. It's more fun living in two places. You always have one of them to look forward to, and one of them to miss. Now tell me what you've been doing since I last saw you.'

Reluctantly Alex took her on a brief tour of his life since graduating from the school in Puerto de la Cruz, where Mirjana Stepanovic still taught, and leaving the island to study in London. He had been eight-een at the time; Mirjana must have been about thirty. He would have much preferred to sit and listen to her as he sat out on the balcony and watched her prowling around the apartment in her bare feet, padding back and forth between the living room and the kitchen until she had got together a tray of things and brought it outside, just as Alex arrived at the University of Graz and caught up with the present.

'Thank you for the postcard from University College London, by the way.' She put down the tray. 'What would you like?'

'Oh, anything …'

'Anything? Come on, Alex. You must remember how I dislike people who don't know what they want.'

'OK … then a glass of dry sherry.'

Mirjana poured him a glass and handed it to him.

'I'd have replied to your card if you'd let me have an address.' She put out her hand and rumpled his hair. 'You silly boy. Why didn't you?'

'Well … I didn't have an address at the time. I hadn't decided where to go for my postgraduate studies. And then, I suppose I preferred to be able to tell myself that you hadn't replied because you didn't have an address than to give you my address and risk not getting a reply.'

'Poor Alex!' She poured herself a bourbon. 'If you'd invited me out to tea I would have accepted, but nothing more than tea. At sixteen or seventeen how can a boy look at a woman and not think about what it would be like to have sex with her? At that age a boy can think of nothing but sex. Now I knew all that, of course. I was a young woman then, and when I was in a classroom with a group of older boys I could almost see all that testosterone whizzing around. I knew what you were thinking about when you looked at me. It never worried me because I understood it didn't have to do with me personally – you boys would have been preoccupied with sex during European history even if it hadn't happened to be me teaching it. Sex would have come into it whatever sort of woman had been standing there in front of you.'

Alex blushed. 'Was it that obvious? Incidentally, it *did* have to do with you personally.'

'Did it? Well, thank you! At that age sex is the most compelling thing in the world. You can't escape it. I found all that natural. I grew up in Tito's Yugoslavia with a much greater openness about sex than I found when we moved to Spain – or in England, for that matter, even worse, where I later studied. At the same place you went to, by the way. I wouldn't have minded inviting *you* out to tea, or other students of mine in the past, but I couldn't have done so because it might have caused expectations in a boy of that age which would only have been disappointed. So it was better for me to keep a certain distance from the boys I taught, even good students like you whom I grew ... quite fond of.' She smiled. 'So that's how it is, Alex. Would you like another drink?'

'I must get home for lunch.'

'Did I speak too freely? Are you disappointed? Have I taken the mystery out of the old memories?'

'No, no. Not at all. I admire your candour. I wish I had more of it myself.'

'How long will you be here?'

'Just a few days. It's my mother's sixtieth birthday.' Alex got up. 'And you? When will you be going back to Puerto de la Cruz?'

'The summer term begins next Tuesday, so I'll probably leave on Sunday.'

As Mirjana saw him out of the apartment she handed him her card and brushed his cheek with her lips, just a scent.

'Drop in any time you feel like it. Or you can give me a call. It would be nice to see you again and talk a bit more before you go.'

# 7

When Alex sat down to lunch with the family he told them about his chance meeting with Mirjana and was surprised how well they all seemed to remember her. During his last two years she had been his A-level supervisor, she was the teacher they talked to at PTA meetings. Ella was the one who always attended these meetings, Claude now and then, George very seldom, but it turned out that of the three of them he was the one who had the clearest memory of her. Ella had got on well with Mirjana and regretted that she'd lost touch with her after Alex left school.

'Yes, why did you?' wondered George. 'I always thought she was rather your type of person.'

'What's Ella's type of person then?' asked Marie.

'Ella's type of person is the Slav.'

'Oh, then you must tell us about the Slav. We don't seem to come across them much in Canada.'

'Yes, you do, beginning with your husband and your brother-in-law.'

'You're kidding,' said Amy. 'Edward and Nico are Slavs?'

'One of their grandparents was Polish. Another was from Silesia, a borderland where there was quite a lot of German intermarriage with Poles and Russians, so they're probably of Slav descent on that side too.'

'Well anyway,' said Marie, retrieving the point they were at risk of losing sight of, because she was a woman who liked to keep tabs on things, 'what is it about Slavs that you get on with?'

'They're hospitable. They're warm.'

'Really?' Amy sounded incredulous. 'Can that apply across the board to an entire ethnic group?'

'I think it can. Obviously there'll be individuals who are different. But in our family east of the Elbe, in all the families we knew there, people looked after one another. They helped out, gave you a plate of soup, found odd jobs for someone out of work who showed up at the door. Caring. That's what I mean by warm.'

Ella told the story of how she arrived in the Morris household in London at the end of the war and found the conversation at the dinner table dominated by Tessa's lament over a litter of kittens, a litany that dragged on for most of the meal – how one of the kittens was too weak to survive, the vets she'd consulted, what measures had to be taken on the kitten's behalf, how Tessa had been up all hours of the night but still the kitten had died.

'A kitten! I sat and listened in disbelief to this self-engrossed girl dominating the dinner table with her fuss over a litter of kittens, still grieving for my own mother who'd just died having lost everything, husband and son, house and home, everything except for the sack of potato meal and a side of bacon she'd taken with her to feed the family on the flight from Schlawe to Hamburg, which I told you all about the other day. A conversation like that taking place in a Slav family under similar circumstances is one I can't imagine.'

'Well, I find this intriguing,' said Amy, 'but I'm not sure I believe you, Ella, because I don't trust generalisations. Pity we can't have a few Slavs with us here to try your theory out and take a vote – people we don't know. Sure I find you and Edward and Nico nice warm people, but you're family, so you don't count.'

'Then why don't we start with just one?' George looked across the table at Alex. 'Do you think Mirjana would like to join us for dinner on Ella's birthday? She's a Slav. Would you mind, Ella?'

'Of course not. I'd be delighted to see her. But I think it's more for Alex to decide. She'd be his guest.'

All eyes turned to Alex, the sort of unwanted attention that still, at the age of thirty, could make him blush.

'Well, if you're all ...' He cleared this throat and began again. 'If you're all happy with the idea I can give Mirjana a call and invite her, and we'll see what she says.'

'Good,' said Amy. 'With all the men around it'll be nice to have one more woman on the team.'

Alex called Mirjana the same afternoon and invited her to dinner the following day. She said she didn't have a car — hers had just broken down — and there was no bus from Puerto de Santiago to Arguayo so he'd have to pick her up and drive her home, but if that wasn't a problem she'd be happy to come.

When Alex rang the bell at six o'clock the following evening and Mirjana opened the door, he was confronted with a stunning sight.

'My goodness!'

'Oh dear. Is it that bad?'

It wasn't a coquettish response — she seemed genuinely concerned that Alex might not like what he saw. She was wearing a sky-blue silk gown with a high waist just under her bosom, the cloth falling in one long sweep to her high-heeled white shoes. A single pearl hung on a silver chain round her neck. He was seeing Mirjana for the first time with her hair down, held in a clasp at the back of her neck and swept forward over one shoulder.

'Am I overdressed?'

'Absolutely not.'

'I hope so. One seldom gets a chance to wear this sort of thing and it's really such fun.'

'You look *marvellous*.'

Ella thought so too, and said so, and Alex wondered why Ella's praise of Mirjana made her even more radiant. The two women went off together to look around the house, talking away as if to catch up on ten years of conversations they had missed. Nico was standing alone in the courtyard and smiled at Alex when he came out of the house.

'The sample Slav is certainly warm to *look* at,' he said with a grin.

Where had such relatives been hiding all his life? Alex wished he'd met his mother's side of the family much earlier on. He was so grateful to Nico for having said exactly what he wanted to hear that he impulsively shared with him the thought in his heart.

'I was already in love with her when I was in her class. Had I been the right age, I think I might have asked her to marry me.' The urge to confide to someone his feelings for her was so strong that these words tumbled out before he knew what he was going to say. 'So I suppose specialising in Balkan studies may simply have been wanting to be close to her in another way – you know, like a fetish, possessing a garment worn by the person you admire or carrying a photograph of them in your pocket. But for her, who knows what I'd have landed up doing. Shall we go in and join the others for a drink?'

'The one doesn't exclude the other, does it?'

'Sorry?'

Nico's eyes twinkled. 'You can specialise in Balkan studies and still ask her to marry you.'

Alex laughed. 'Oh no, that was ten years ago. That's all over now.'

But sitting opposite Mirjana, who was flanked by Edward and Nico at the long dinner table in the courtyard, with Amy on one side of him and Marie on the other, Alex found Nico's casual *You can specialise in Balkan studies and still ask her to marry you* beginning to grow on him in the course of the evening.

Warm to look at – how quick his uncle had been to comment on that. Two dancing points of fire, candlelight reflected in her eyes, seemed to be winking at him when she looked across the table, even when she was in conversation with Amy or Marie. Warm to listen to as well, the mellowness of her voice warmed her words, made listening to Mirjana so agreeable, invited him to pay attention to a mellow warmth she had about her, in the texture and colour of her hair, her warm complexion, her warm mouth – unthinkable she could have cold eyes, thin lips, pale skin. Why did a person have the face they had? There might have been something – there *was* something – about Mirjana that reminded Alex of Ella. Looking at his mother on one side of Nico, then at Mirjana on the other, then back to Ella, the likeness of the two of them became so striking that he wondered why he hadn't seen it until now. The thought unsettled him.

'Alex? Could you get it?'

'What?'

'The phone's ringing.'

Alex went into George's study and picked the phone up. 'Hello?'

'Hello, Pooky. How are you?'

'Max!'

'Thanks for the reminder. That was brotherly and motherly love. Me and Ella, you've done us both a good turn. I love you for it.'

'My pleasure. Thanks for calling. Shall I put her on?'

'Just a sec. What were you thinking about when the phone rang?'

'What was I— Well, funny you should ask. We've got a guest here for dinner, a woman who was my teacher at school in Puerto. I used to be crazy about her. I haven't seen her for ten years, then I bumped into her at the post office yesterday, and today she's here, and just as the phone rang I was wondering – I mean just an idea, you know, the way one has these thoughts – whether I should ask her to marry me. I mean, not seriously of course.'

'Why not seriously?'

'Well, for a start she's twelve years older than I am. I look at her, and I look at me, and I'm just a kid by comparison.'

'You *were* a kid. Not any more. Ask her.'

'Ask her whether she thinks I'm a kid?'

'Ask her to marry you, you schmuck. It'll be an interesting experi⁄ence, and how many opportunities for interesting experiences do you expect to get in life? OK, I'll let you go, Pooky. Put Ella on.'

Normally his mother refused to take calls during meals, didn't like meals one had spent so much time preparing being interrupted by the phone. Today was different, though. She got up and went into the house without asking who the caller was. She knew – she hoped – it would be one of her children calling.

'It's Max,' Alex confided to the others, pleased it was thanks to him that this call was taking place.

'How is Max? Pity we're not going to see him on this trip,' said Amy, taking a swipe at her mouth with her napkin as if swatting a fly, and Alex suddenly felt fond of his aunt for giving expression to the feeling he'd also just had at that moment.

'He'll be coming with the rest of the family for the main event, which is taking place here over Whitsun,' said Alex. 'Too bad you guys won't be around for that too.'

'Whitsun's next month,' put in Mirjana. 'So will you be coming over again?'

'I haven't decided yet. How about you? Will you be here?' asked Alex.

'Everywhere's so crowded at Whitsun. I prefer to stay at home. Besides, I've got lazy and complacent living here. Life is so easy-going. I have to make an effort to go anywhere else.'

'Well, I can imagine,' said Amy, crunching a chicken wing and masticating with relish while managing to talk at the same time. 'Edward and I are beginning to find the winters back home awful long. Can we maybe afford to winter in Florida when we retire? A lot of people I know who live on the west coast drive down to Baja California and tie up in a trailer park by the ocean for three or fourth months. That's pretty cheap, five bucks a day, but I can't see us doing that. I mean, imagine us in a trailer park? Eddie and I are comfortable people; we like to do things in style?'

Alex wondered at this Canadian habit of making a statement sound like a question when you were just telling something in the ordinary way.

'I mean, for you guys living here the island must be ideal? I can *sympathise* with you getting lazy and complacent, Mirjana. If you live here, why *should* you want to go anywhere? I'm surprised the Europeans don't descend in hordes and turn the place into an old people's home, the way they're doing in Florida.'

'Well they do descend in hordes – the British began wintering here a hundred years ago,' said George. 'It was cheaper to run a house here, not to mention a lot healthier, than to spend the winter back home. Four quid return fare and three days by steamer from Bristol.'

'And from even further afield than that,' put in Claude at the far end of the table, where the conversation had been picked up. 'I recently heard that one of the ministries in Japan came up with a scheme to offload their surplus of old people. The plan was to find a big area in some warm dry place – not here, that would be too expensive – say, in an isolated part of Spain that nobody wants. There they would build what they call silver cities, old people's homes on the grand scale, multiplexes for tens of thousands of Japanese pensioners, and run the whole thing for considerably less than what it would cost the state to maintain all the people back home.'

794

'And how did Japanese pensioners react to the idea?'

'They were furious. How dare the state come up with a plan to turf its old people out, dump them in a foreign country thousands of miles from home? When would they ever see their grandchildren? There was such outrage the scheme had to be abandoned That doesn't change the fact that in twenty years the Japanese will have the highest percentage of old people in the world. In the long run they won't be able to afford their pensioners, which is why their civil servants came up with the idea.'

'Funny,' said Edward. 'Retiring to Spain would be just fine by me, if you had all the facilities – you know, not just leisure and accommodation but the same standard of medical care you can rely on back home.'

'Me too,' agreed Amy.

'Oh no,' said Marie. 'I sympathise with the Japanese. I'd miss home. I'd want my familiar surroundings. It's a *horrible* idea. What about your neighbourhood, the stores you go to do your shopping, your friends, your language? All those things you take for granted because they're all around you the whole time? Only when you found yourself cut off from them would you realise what you were missing, and then it would be too late.'

'I agree with Marie,' said George. 'Even when one's young, as I was when I first came here, pulling up one's roots and moving permanently to another country can be more of a risk than you realise. For a time, maybe ten or twenty years or even longer, life in the new country contin- ues to offer the attractions that took you there in the first place – you're busy, probably you're building something up, and it all seems just fine. But once that slows down, as eventually it will, you start seeing the gaps. Leisure can make you aware of a sense of displacement that never used to trouble you. You begin to miss things you never missed before.'

'What sort of things?' asked Ella, who caught this remark of George's as she came out into the courtyard and rejoined them at the table.

'Now, you'll laugh at this, but ... I miss the weather.'

'The *weather*?' asked Marie incredulously.

'The thing about English weather is it provides you with an excuse for being out of sorts which everyone will sympathise with. There are days I get up here when the sight of the sun – busy old fool, the poet said – shining away in the cloudless sky, ordering you to be in a good mood, makes me depressed. Sometimes I wish I could get up and find it raining. A nice miserable English drizzle that can be relied on to keep going until the middle of next week.'

'What else?'

'Well, I miss pubs. I miss slam-door trains. I miss houses made of red brick. Victorian architecture. Why should one be moved by that? Familiarity. Nothing special. Odd things come to mind. I miss London grime and smells. I miss English ugliness generally. More and more I've come to miss the language. And even if this is just sentimental nonsense, since I lived in London all my life and never missed the country, those crooked nooky sort of places with a village green – I could do with one of those here.'

'But you wouldn't want to go back, would you?' said Ella.

'Not really.'

'Would any of us? Claude back to France, or England?'

'If I had to go anywhere, then I suppose it would be back to Japan.'

'Amy still lives in the same part of the world where she was born and grew up, but the rest of us have all moved elsewhere. Maybe Amy's lucky not to have had to choose,' said Ella. 'Edward, Nico and myself back to a country that no longer exists? What about you, Alex? You've been on the move since you left home. Twice. Where do you think of as home now? I sometimes wonder if you'll settle down in the first place you're offered a permanent job. Or can you imagine choosing the place where you'd like to live and then finding yourself a job?'

'No,' said Alex without hesitation, 'I would only choose to live in a place if someone I was attached to also lived there. If someone I wanted to spend my life with happened to be located in Graz, and the university offered me tenure, I wouldn't mind making my home there.' He caught his guest's eye across the table. 'Your turn, Mirjana.'

'Me?' She smiled as she looked around the table. 'There's not a choice for me because I'm happiest in the present. Cádiz, where my family moved to when I was a child, is far away in the past. So is Novi Sad on the Danube, where I grew up, even further away than Cádiz. I don't dwell on places where I used to live after I've moved on. I've left no impression on them, and they leave no impression on me. When I'm staying here, in my apartment in Puerto de Santiago, I take a walk every day along a path overlooking the sea, and I scramble down to a deserted beach where I spread out my towel and lie and read. After a few hours I walk back up the cliff, and I stand there and look down at the beach I've just visited, lying on my spread-out towel all morning, but I can't pinpoint the spot where I was lying because I haven't left the slightest trace. I've already been eradicated. That's the sort of feeling I have when I think of places I used to live, or have just been, like the chair in a cafe where I've been sitting, which will be occupied by someone else within minutes of me leaving it. My presence there hasn't left any mark. I'm happiest in my own surroundings – with traces of myself, my belongings, all around me – and when I come home after I've been out somewhere, it's like picking up a conversation that's been going on while I've been away.'

A silence followed this contribution as everyone tried to work out quite what Mirjana meant. Although moved by what she'd said, Alex found something odd about it, delivered as it had been with a smile that seemed to belie the wistfulness he heard in her voice. Perhaps it was that no one apart from Mirjana figured in the glimpse she'd given them of her private life.

Edward got to his feet and tapped the side of his glass with a spoon.

'Well there's certainly nowhere Amy and I would prefer to be today, and I know the same goes for Nico and Marie. We've had a wonderful time with you, my dear Ella, the hospitality you and George have given us in your home, not least the conversations we've had together over the past few days. If we could, we'd be happy to retire to a place like this and be your neighbours, your *family*, just across the way, and see more of each other than we've managed to in the last thirty years. But, if you'll have us – and I hope this doesn't sound like a threat – we'd like to come again and visit with you more often. So let me propose a toast to Ella, with thanks for all you've done for us and with our best wishes for your health and happiness!'

The tribute was a little wooden, but there was no doubting how moved by it Edward himself was – tears in his eyes when he raised his glass and drank to Ella's health.

Amy took photographs of Ella and her brothers, Ella and George; the brothers snapped Ella and George with Marie and Amy. Then it was Alex's turn to be photographed with Mirjana, then with Ella, then standing between Ella and George. Somehow Claude was left out. Nico took pictures with a Polaroid, instant pictures he spent more time poring over, joked Marie, than looking at the subjects they were pictures of.

Nico was holding one of them up to the light from a bracket on the courtyard wall when he said, 'Strange how one parent can miss out. I

797

mean, I can see the family resemblance between Ella and Alex OK but none at all between Alex and George.'

'Ah, Nico, I think I can explain that. It's not strange at all. May I see?' Claude, who had stood rather on one side while all the family photographs were being taken, came forward and took the Polaroid out of Nico's hand. 'If you take a closer look at Alex's *ears*, for example, you won't find any resemblance to Ella's, nor to George's, for that matter, whereas if you compare his ears with *mine* – right here in front of you, take a good look – you'll spot the family resemblance immediately. Nothing strange about that, on the face of it, because Alex is my son, you see, and I'm his father.'

Claude walked over to the others standing around Ella.

'Amy? Marie? Would you like to have a look and convince yourselves?' He held out the Polaroid to Amy. 'I don't mean to make a fuss, but now Nico has brought up the lack of resemblance between father and son I'd like to point out that there *is* a resemblance, but not with George. Why should there be a resemblance with George if George isn't the father, you see. The resemblance is with *me*. We don't carry on about this, we don't trumpet it from the rooftops, but nor do we make a secret of it, do we, George? Ella? Alex? For the sake of the family it seemed to us when Alex was born that it would be easier if he was passed off as George's son, but there's a point where I think we need to draw a line between sticking with a useful social convention and telling an unnecessary lie. I don't want to find myself in the intolerable situation, as I did just now, where I'm at risk of having to disown my own child if I fail to speak up. You see? So rather than you all spending half the night making conjectures about what you may think is a scandalous business, you'll be doing me a favour if we could sit down and talk it through. Please, do all sit down and make yourselves comfortable!'

Beside himself with excitement, waving his arms, Claude was making odd little rushes forward as he tried to usher everyone back towards the dinner table.

'Sit down and continue just as you were before! I don't want to interrupt the party. There's no call for consternation. A father acknowledging his son is a perfectly ordinary matter, you know. Amy, I'd be most grateful to you if you could manage to look less *stricken*, and Edward, if you could remember to close your mouth, have a pew. Have one on me, as they say. Please!'

Ella went over to Claude and took his hand. 'Claude, calm down.'

'Why should I calm down? I've been calm long enough! It's time I got myself into a state about things that are otherwise never brought into the open. I'm entitled to that, aren't I? Why do we have to have these secrets? These are things that need to be said, Ella.'

'But who's calling this a scandalous business? You are. Nobody else thinks that. You're the one who's getting worked up about it. Not talked about, true, but not on that account a *secret*. So *let's* bring it out into the open. Let's talk about it now. Nobody here is *stricken*. You're imagining all that. Edward, Amy, Marie, Nico – are any of you stricken? Are you scandalised to learn that Alex is not George's son but Claude's? Does knowing that change anything?'

'Of course not! Poor Claude!' This burst from Marie.

There was a mumbling and shaking of heads. 'No, no ... Why on earth ...? Not in the least ...' Nico patted Claude on the back as if welcoming him into the family.

'So for all those who until now believed that Alex was my son by George we hereby set the record straight. Alex is my son by Claude, and George regards him as if he was his own son. That is a quite natural state of affairs, accepted by all the other children. In our family it has never been an issue.' Ella smiled and looked at everyone, some sitting, others still standing, unsure what to do. 'But isn't it getting rather chilly out here? Might it be better to go in?'

'I could light the braziers,' volunteered Alex, overwhelmed by what his father had just done and proud of both his parents. He still had a birthday surprise in store for his mother, one she would enjoy much more if she remained in the courtyard. But there now seemed to be general agreement it would be preferable to go indoors, so it was through the windows facing the courtyard that Ella and her guests watched the fireworks display which Alex had secretly set up with his father on the roof of the *portada sillería* earlier that day.

# 8

Unauthorised landings by African boat people on Tenerife began to take place with such frequency during the last years of the twentieth century that the government came under pressure to introduce tougher immigration legislation. Tourists reaching the island by air were un-affected by the new measures; it was visitors coming in on ferries from the African coast who now became subject to more rigorous scrutiny. The new regulations gave immigration officials discretionary powers to turn incoming Africans away or issue them with landing permits valid for as short as twenty-four hours.

Max didn't check the dates stamped in their passports. It also escaped him that it was thanks to the fact that Ali and Leila, the Moroccan brother and sister who worked for his friend Piers in Tangiers, were accompanied by a white tourist with a permanent domicile on the island that they were able to disembark without too much bureaucratic hassle — albeit only after being subjected to the body search for contraband that all arrivals from Morocco had to undergo. Passengers from Africa who were not African nationals, however, were not searched as a rule, making it no problem for Max to go ashore with a kilogram of best Moroc-can marijuana in the case which had been emptied of the typewriter it contained for exactly that purpose.

A week later the police in Adeje received a call from their colleagues at headquarters in Santa Cruz. Two Moroccan immigrants who had entered the country on a restricted tourist visa had overstepped the au-thorised duration of stay specified on their entry permits. These persons were to be picked up from the address in Arguayo they had given as their residence during their stay on the island, escorted to the San Andrés Container Terminal north of Santa Cruz — out of sight of the nearest beaches, where tourists might be disturbed by sometimes violent scenes of ejection — and taken into the custody of the port immigration author-ities for deportation back to Africa on the next available ship.

Arriving at the old bishop's residence, as the Morris house was known locally, the two Adeje policemen found no one at home. Making their way through the property, wondering if their orders covered forcible entry should this be necessary, their attention was caught by noise coming from a tent up on the hill behind the house, drums beating and the clash of cymbals to the accompaniment of clapping and laughter.

The policemen went up to investigate.

During the week the tent had been in place, the sundown ritual of *open tent* initiated by Max on Santana's model of *open roof*, which had been a much-appreciated feature of life at the San Francisco Ware-house, had become a feature of life not at all appreciated by the locals

800

in Arguayo. Everyone was invited, but they chose not to come. The Adeje police had already received complaints about the noise. However, as it turned out the source of the noise was on the private property of a respected former member of the government, they had so far done nothing to investigate.

The tent looming on the hill behind the house had a funereal appearance, attributable to the black drapes extending on all sides as awnings to provide shade – in the desert, presumably for children and animals outside. The flap accessing the tent was laced up when the inhabitants were out. *Open tent* meant they were at home to receive guests for Moroccan refreshments – water pipes, sherbet, nuts and aromatic sweetmeats, marijuana and hashish for consumption either by smoking or eating. Ali provided an occasional intermezzo with drums and cymbals, while his sister Leila did the honours, sorting and shredding the marijuana, packing and lighting the bowls of the pipes or the joints she handed to the guests, or rather guest – so far just one – George – whose uncharacteristic enthusiasm made up for the absence of others. Max and his father, and the two Moroccans whom the Adeje policemen had orders to take into custody, were the only people in the tent that evening.

In order to pass through the low, narrow entrance, the policemen had to get down on all fours and remove their caps – not an easy position from which to enforce respect for the law. The abject arrival of its representatives in the tent was greeted with laughter, deafening percussion and the smell of substances whose consumption contravened the laws of the Canary Islands. The fug inside the tent was so dense that a forensic investigator could have held up a tube for two seconds, stuck a cork in and taken it away as evidence. A placid young woman sitting cross-legged with a dreamy smile – doubtless under the influence – made no attempt to conceal from the policemen the pile of marijuana she was sorting, and continued to sort in their presence, on the cloth spread out in her lap. Should they ignore the drug offence and carry on as instructed, taking the two Moroccan fugitives into custody?

Their uncertainty as to how to proceed was exacerbated by the onslaught prompted by their entrance – not normal healthy laughter, but an uncontrollable braying – inane, hysterical waves of laughing that didn't stop. They were unable to follow the usual procedures when making an arrest, beginning with the identification of the suspects by examining their documents, because they couldn't ask for any documents until it became possible to make themselves heard. Attempting to regain their dignity by putting their caps back on – this only made them look even more comic – they set in motion another tsunami of hilarity. This provoked the policemen to take decisive action without further preliminaries. They laid hands on the two dark-skinned suspects and attempted to bundle them out of the tent via the entrance. The suspects resisted – a scrimmage ensued – six people piled on top of each other in a small space with no chance of anyone getting out, some of them having no intention of leaving because they were being so well entertained.

At this point a no-nonsense voice could be heard outside demanding to know what the hell was going on in the tent. Philip, you old wanker, roared Max, you've arrived with the cavalry in the nick of time. His brother's face appeared frowning at the flap – the frown flanked by Denis and Darren – the two boys crouching athletically on either side of him under starter's orders. Befuddled, not quite sure of the unexpected turn events were taking, George peered out at his whippet grandsons with lazy interest. Ball boys? Was the tennis still on? Hallucinations induced by the brownies he'd eaten an hour or so ago – a hilarious guest appearance by the Keystone Kops – were beginning to wear off, leaving him in a mellow aftermath. With benign amusement George beamed at the policemen, who had managed to disentangle themselves, as they ransacked the tent – Help yourselves!

'Whew! What a *fug*! No, we shan't be coming in *here*, thank you very much!' Philip's face darkened into a scowl. 'As bad as Ali Baba and the den of forty thieves!'

This was greeted by his father and his brother with convulsions of mirth.

'Look at that mug of his!' Max pointed at his brother. 'Just look at that frown!'

'Frow …' George spluttered, unable to get the word out.

Philip looked at his father with disgust. 'Come on, boys. There's nothing to detain us here.' He strode grimly off down the hill.

'Philipikins!'

'Come back, Philipino!'

'Pipikins!'

At the sight of the handcuffs being taken out by the policemen, Ali wriggled out underneath the back of the tent. The two policemen rushed in pursuit. Denis played scrum-half for his school rugby team, knew exactly what to do with an adversary trying to break out on the blind side. Ali was fleeing up towards the woods. Seeing where he could be intercepted before he disappeared into the forest, Denis took a short cut down into a steep gully, raced up the far side and brought him to the ground with a flying tackle. One of the policemen arrived panting behind him, handcuffed the fugitive lying on the ground, hoisted him to his feet and led him down the hill to the police car where his sister had already been taken by the other policeman.

Beside himself with rage, Max came up to Denis and spat at him, 'Traitor! You miserable traitor!'

'That's enough, Max. Denis did the right thing. The police wouldn't have caught up with your friend – might have taken a potshot at him. Might have winged him. Might have *killed* him.' Philip smirked. 'So you ought to be thanking Denis for saving his life.'

Max walked over and hit his brother in the face. Philip hit him back, and they fell tussling to the ground. It took the combined efforts of George and Denis to drag them apart.

Philip got up, wiping his bloody nose on his sleeve. 'That's it! I'm finished with you, Max! Never again! Not that this sordid business is any concern of mine. But now you seem to have dragged George in too. You do what you want. So shall we. There can obviously be no question of our staying here, Dad. Enjoy your opium lair. I leave you and Max to wallow with your pimps and your Fatimas in your den of vice. But not with us.'

'Don't be ridiculous, Philip,' said George good-humouredly. 'Don't get up on your hind legs and make a moralistic ass of yourself.'

His son ignored him and walked down to the house and disappeared inside. A few minutes later he came out again and walked over to a hire car parked in the courtyard.

'Philip! Wait! Where are Ann and Hilary?'

'Walking down to Santiago, I expect. They were here a few minutes ago, but it appears they've decided not to stay. So have we. I'll see if they've got rooms in a hotel somewhere.'

'Hotel? But you're staying here!'

'Not any more.'

George was aghast. 'You can't do this, Philip! We weren't expecting you until next week.'

'That's your problem, Dad. I called to say we'd be coming a week earlier than arranged. I spoke to Max and asked him to pass on the message. Which he no doubt forgot. Not that it makes any difference now. I've left a note on the kitchen table.'

He and the boys got into the car and drove off without another word.

'Oh *shit!*'

George went out into the road, where Max was arguing with the two policemen. They were packing the items they had confiscated from the tent into the boot of their car. The argument bounced back and forth over the top of the car. George couldn't hear what it was about. Finally, the policeman standing on the same side of the car as Max opened the back door for Max to get in.

'Where are *you* going, Max?'

'The police station, where else? I can't leave my friends in the lurch. I'm going with them.'

George stood watching the police car until it disappeared over the crest of the road.

'Oh *fuck!*'

As he made his way back into the house, he began taking stock of the damage. He knew his moralistic, rather priggish but at bottom kind-hearted son well enough to hope that Philip, although quick to take offence, would relent quickly when faced with sincere contrition. Would once have relented, at any rate. The influence of his broody hen of a wife, Ann, no longer made this a certain outcome. Ann harboured grudges, not only her own; she could take them over and harbour them in her insatiable wrong-brooding heart on Philip's behalf too, as George knew only too well. And sure enough, the note he found lying on the kitchen table might be in Philip's handwriting, but the archness of the style was entirely his wife's.

*As we feel we're intruding at an unwelcome moment we've decided to look for alternative accommodation in Puerto de Santiago, if not at the Excelsior then at the Mirador Hotel. Please let us know there when a visit would be convenient.*

But it was just *ludicrous*! No one in their right mind could take such a stupid business seriously. The residue of laughter still curdling inside him went cold the moment it occurred to him who else could. In an hour her plane from Las Palmas would be landing at Los Rodeos.

'How am I going to break this to Ella?'

# 9

When Ella's call from Claude's house in La Laguna was put through to Philip at the Mirador in Puerto de Santiago, Ann had already gone down for dinner with the children, and Philip could truthfully say yes to Ella's question, 'Are you free?' There was nobody in the room – he felt free to talk.

The code went back to Philip's schooldays at Sherborne. During his first term his mother had several times called the house where he lived and asked to speak to him. The first time she did so the housemaster took the call in his study and left the room while Philip was on the phone. On later occasions he didn't, making plain that mothers using his phone to speak to their sons wasn't the done thing. Talking to her with his housemaster in the background had made Philip awkward. He was unable to answer Ella's questions honestly. He told his mother about this embarrassment and she came up with a code: *Are you free?*

But he didn't like being put on the spot by his mother's question. The association with embarrassments he had suffered at school still lingered. When he left home and began making a life for himself, *Are you free?* acquired connotations with intrigue and deception. It might be a fair enough question when his mother called him at work, where it was quite likely someone would be around whom he preferred not to overhear a private conversation. Once he and Ann had moved into a flat together, however, Ella's continued use of the code became an annoyance. Ann had found out about *Are you free?* and it made her indignant. She wasn't going to allow her mother-in-law, with her dominating personality and opinions, to come between herself and her husband. It also annoyed Philip to have to say no when Ann was in the room, and it was hardly better saying yes when she wasn't. I have no secrets from my wife, he told his mother for the first time when he was thirty. She took the hint. Until this evening she had avoided asking him the code question again.

Anticipating a call from Ella, Ann had worked on Philip before she went down to join the children for dinner: 'She may think she means well, your mother, but don't you let her wriggle her way out of this one!'

Philip felt relieved his wife wasn't in the room when Ella called, just as it irritated him that relief should still be coming into this at all.

'Are you angry?'

'Yes.'

'Angry or hurt?'

It was the sort of typical Ella question that exasperated Philip.

'Both.'

'I can imagine.'

He waited for his mother to say more, but she didn't, prompting him, he didn't know why – and this again irritated him – to enlarge on what he'd said.

'It was a disgraceful scene. The two of them sitting there completely stoned, laughing their heads off. This in the middle of a police raid. All in front of the children. I felt ashamed.'

'Your father told me about it.'

'What did he say?'

'That he was sorry about what happened, and what made it worse was that he couldn't stop laughing. Marijuana can have that effect on people. But he wasn't laughing at you, Philip.'

'Of course he was.'

'I don't think so. With marijuana one sees the funny side of things; *everything* just strikes one as funny.'

'You speak from experience?'

'Well, yes, I do. It's not really laughing *at* things, you know, it's laughing *with* them. You're free of the inhibitions that stop you from laughing at things that ordinarily don't seem funny. That's why people smoke the stuff. The world becomes funny, or you can see it that way. Is that such a bad thing?'

'Not in moderation. But they were out of control.'

'Have you never been out of control?'

'Not to the detriment of other people.'

'When did you last see your father laugh like that?'

'I don't think I *ever* saw him laugh like that.'

'Don't you think it did him good?'

'I can't believe it did.'

'I think it did him good.'

'*Him* good! How about *me*? If George needs a laugh more often maybe you should be asking yourself why. Maybe he needs people to laugh with him, and there aren't enough of them around.'

'He and Claude laugh together.'

'Oh? What have they got to laugh about then?'

'What if I promise you it won't ever happen again?'

'Max *spat* at Denis, you know. He physically *attacked* me.'

'Would you forgive him this one time? Or will you go on holding it against him for the rest of his life?'

'Well if it were just this one time ... but look, Mum, you know as well as I do, Max has always enjoyed making fun of me. I got the clown's part in this family. I was the chump everyone made fun of. It was always me people were sitting on. All right, yesterday was maybe an aberration on Dad's part, something I could overlook. Given a little time. But with Max it's different. Max is vicious, an unpleasant person, a dangerous egomaniac. He always was, and he's not going to change, and I'd be happy if I never saw him again in my life.'

'Would you accept an apology from Max?'

'An apology would be meaningless. An apology only *means* something when you can take it as a guarantee that the behaviour for which the apology is tendered will not occur again.'

'That sounds like something out of a solicitor's letter.'

'I beg your pardon?'

'What if I had a word with Max.'

'It wouldn't make any difference.'

'It could.'

The thought crossed Ella's mind that Max had already left Arguayo, and that if he didn't return it would suit everyone. She might yet be able to pull the family back together.

Philip was reading her thoughts. 'You've had a word with Max more times than I can count, and it never got you anywhere. Admit it. Neither you nor Dad was ever able to handle Max.' He listened to Ella's silence at the other end of the line, and something made him go on and say, 'It wasn't only Max who was the problem. He was always so far out of line that at some point he stopped being real for me. He and I lived in different worlds and went our separate ways. I can deal with the problem of Max just by keeping out of sight of him. More of a problem for me, and to a lesser extent for Felicity, was Alex. *Is* Alex. I'm still jealous of him. I've never found out how to deal with that.'

'Jealous? What did Alex get from us that you didn't?'

'From *us*? Dad never came into this. Dad is just a man, my biological father. He's around but he isn't really there. He doesn't count. No, from *you*.'

'All right, from me.'

'Hang on a sec.' Philip took out his handkerchief and blew his nose noisily. 'What Alex got from you that none of the rest of us were ever given was truly felt love.'

He could hear his mother listening in the silence at the end of the line – eerie, as if getting the measure of him. It was a while before she spoke.

'And what you were given was *not* truly felt?' She paused, waiting for the intervention she anticipated from Philip before she went on: 'I don't understand. I'm seeing the thirteen years that you and Felicity were at home before you left for Sherborne, how you played in the garden and we all used to go out together, all the meals and the cleaning and the umpteen things one does as a matter of course as a mother, and whatever I see going on looks to me like care, and I don't know how that can take place in the absence of what you call truly felt love. There's no such thing as caring for a child unless your heart is in it. Hasn't that been your own experience as a parent?'

'Oh, absolutely.'

'Then what is it you're saying?'

'You did your duty by us, absolutely. I don't deny that. But you see, Alex was always much more your child than any of the rest of us. That's how it always seemed to us, at any rate. Do you see it differently?'

'Yes, I do.'

'Look, I'm not *blaming* you or anything. In fact I rather pity you for it. It makes me realise how fortunate I am to love all of my three children equally. A parent who loves one child so much more than the others must feel they're under a sort of curse. It must be terrible to feel yourself drawn to one child and not the others. How did you manage it?'

Ella sighed. 'Well I don't know.'

Philip interpreted Ella's sigh as the first concession he had wrung out of her. The conversation so far hadn't seemed to be getting anywhere, both of them entrenched in all-too-familiar positions, and Philip wondered if Ella was about to come around to his point of view.

'I don't know that you're right,' Ella went on to say, dashing his hopes, 'and even if it were true that I felt Alex was closer to me than my other children ... But drawn to one child and not the others, that's untrue. But everything in its time. When you and Max and Felicity were little, I loved you just as I did Alex later. But you weren't able to watch me with you and the others in the way you watched me with Alex. He was still a baby and you were already a big boy. And to you as a big boy it might have looked as though the baby was getting special treatment, but you at his age got exactly the same treatment, only you wouldn't have remembered that. You were out playing and he was in the house. You will have seen Alex being given more attention than you were getting at the age of eight, or nine, or ten because Alex went on being the baby for years, and by the time he became a little boy, you and Felicity were at boarding school, and your childhood, within the family at least, was already over.' An uncertainty came into her voice. 'How do you think I could have managed things better?'

'You should have made up your mind.'

'Made up my mind about what?'

'Whether to stay with Claude and divorce Dad or stay with Dad and break with Claude.'

Ella said nothing.

'One or the other. You should have made up your mind.'

Ella still said nothing and Philip felt himself getting angry.

'You wanted to have your cake and eat it. But you can't. You have to choose.'

'Why do I have to choose? And how can you think me being attached to two men in two so different ways, both of whom I've lived happily with all these years, has anything whatsoever to do with that smug little bourgeois remark about wanting to have your cake and eat it? How can you talk in the same breath about things that have nothing to do with one another?'

'Because both have to do with *you*. It would have been different if Alex had been Dad's son. Then I don't think I'd have minded as much as I did. It's not just that Alex was always the baby of the family everyone spoiled. I felt he had no business to be there in the first place. He came between me and my mother, and I resented that because I felt it was unjust.'

'So you *are* blaming me, after all. Your resentment becomes my responsibility is what you're saying.'

'You were always telling us, *I'm a free woman*. Fine. Go ahead. But I just want you to know that I think you've no idea how much of an egoist you are. You lived your freedom at our expense.'

'Expense? What did my freedom cost you?'

'My own freedom.'

'Freedom to do what?'

'For example, to be honest. And you were always the one so ready to preach about never telling lies. So what do you think was going on at Richmond? The rest of us all had to help support the deception that Alex was Dad's son. Alex was my brother. That was how the neighbourhood saw us. But he wasn't. He was my *half*-brother, and we had *two* dads. Maybe just as well to have a reserve dad in the house, since for most of the time we lived in Richmond George was never at home and Claude stood in for him. People outside must often have wondered what he was doing there. Who was this man? What was his role? And why did Claude put up with it? Didn't that ever occur to you? Hang on a minute.'

Ann had come into the room. Ella could hear her in the background asking why Philip hadn't come down to dinner.

'It's my mother on the phone about that business up at the house. I'm nearly done. I'll join you in a minute. Car keys? On top of the telly. All right ... where were we?'

Ella was speechless. Philip's *I'm nearly done* struck deep.

'Are you still there? Look, I don't think this conversation is really getting us anywhere, but perhaps the two of us ought to sit down to-morrow and work out an arrangement, how we can get through the week without treading on each other's toes. What say you come to the hotel tomorrow morning at nine o'clock and we talk here? Perhaps a bit early? Let's say ten. Would that be all right? Fine.'

And she heard a click as Philip hung up.

# 10

When her son hung up on her without saying goodbye it hurt Ella more than it usually did. Mostly it just irritated her. She remembered Alex being the first to complain about this habit. On a visit to his brother's office Alex spent half an hour listening to Philip making phone calls, all of them punctuated with normal goodbyes, and wondered why he treated the family differently. When they went out for lunch afterwards he asked him. Philip rearranged the salt and pepper on the table in front of him and told him he omitted saying goodbye for the same reason he didn't sign on or sign off the letters he wrote home from boarding school, still didn't on the rare occasions he wrote to his parents – because it wasn't necessary.

After this last conversation with Philip it occurred to Ella that Philip's objective as a child might have been to punish his family. Disapproving and perhaps in some way ashamed of his family, as Ella was now understanding might have been the case, his solution had been to expunge them from all the letters he'd written home as if family relationships were unmentionable, not even to be seen in company on the same page. At the time she had put it down to what she saw as a difficult phase Philip was going through, to a wilfulness of Philip's that found expression in such whims as his invention of a private alphabet or the reordering of numerals to suit his preference for secrecy – for going his own way even within the tight-knit community of trainspotters, sharing nothing even with his fellow enthusiasts. The drift of all his pursuits as a child was to shut other people out. Until Alex brought up the matter of the phone calls without a goodbye Ella had allowed all this to slip her mind. What a secretive, self-willed, cranky and solitary child her son had been.

What had struck her as self-willed and cranky in the child presented itself to Ella now as merely small-minded in the man. Was his frowning the expression of a lifetime's backlog of disapproval and resentment? Had Philip shut other people out because he felt shut out by his own family? Underneath the spoken word – which in comparison with body language counted for so little in human relationships – was this the clue he had been giving them all this time they had continued to overlook? For how prompt he had been to change the subject from Max to Alex, the resentment closest to his heart. *Was* it her fault that Philip was so jealous? What in the end was *not* somehow her fault, whatever it was that had gone wrong in the life of one's child?

The phone conversation with Philip left Ella stunned. She was sitting where she was, wondering what to do, when the phone rang. Hoping it might be Philip again with second thoughts, she picked it up and was disappointed when she heard Max's voice.

'Where are you, Max?'

'The San Andrés Container Terminal.'

'What are you doing *there*?'

'It'll take too long to explain over the phone. I'm calling from a phone box at the entrance and I only have a few coins left. Look, this is rather short notice, but do you think you could come up with five hundred dollars?' He paused for a second. 'Pay you back next week. Five hundred would just about cover it, I guess, but to be on the safe side, expenses at the other end and so on, a thousand would be even better – and courier it to me here within the next couple of hours?'

'Courier? What courier? At this time of night the only courier I'm going to find with five hundred dollars in ready cash is me. What do you want the money for?'

'I know, I know, typical *Max*, you'll be thinking, but believe me, Mum, this is in a worthy cause. Let me put you in the picture ...' Max came pouring down the line in a torrent, not letting his mother get a word in edgeways. 'The Moroccan refugees have been held here – God! what do you call this place – in a sort of *pound* for the last twelve hours, without food or even water from what I've been able to make out. No different from cattle in a stockyard. There must be about a hundred of them. Some of them have been here a couple of *weeks* waiting to be deported – the authorities only send them back when there are enough of them to make chartering a ship worthwhile, you see. Just chuck 'em in the pound and wait and see. All these people trying to make it to safety on the island. One lot even attempted the crossing in a *rowboat*. Do you know how much rowing that is from Africa? Hundreds of kilometres. Most of the boats get stopped before they even reach the shore. The Spanish authorities will be embarking them soon. They're not letting on what the destination will be, but probably Agadir. There's a chance I can bribe the captain to let me go with them. OK? Hence the cash. He insists on being paid in US dollars. Me and my Leica bird, secretly we'll be squeezing pictures on board. Think of it, Mum! The exclusive inside story on deported African refugees in—'

The payphone cut him off in mid-sentence.

There had been no opportunity for Ella to tell Max about her own reactions to a disastrous evening – the police raid in Arguayo, the conversation with Philip that had left her shaken. Max wouldn't call back, of course, so she had no way of telling him that Claude had gone to pick Alex up from the airport and would be driving from there to Arguayo, meaning that Ella had no transport.

'I *hate* the way you take everything for granted!' she yelled at the photograph of Max on the desk, 'I hate being *hijacked* by you!'

Naturally Max knew about the money Ella kept in the house. She'd had fights with him when he had plundered the cache in the past. Even a war on the other side of the world could result in Ella bunkering not only staples like salt, sugar and rice in the house but a supply of cash in several major currencies. Brought about by Ella's refugee experience, hoarding still took place forty years on. Even in an island backwater like San Cristóbal de La Laguna there were enough supplies in the cellar to outlast a siege. Even in the rural tranquillity of Arguayo there was a safe in the wall with a stash of emergency money.

She knew Max assumed she'd drop whatever she was doing and bring him the money he'd asked for; she also knew if she repeatedly gave in to such demands she was as much to blame as he was.

How timely the thought now seemed to her which had crossed her mind during the conversation with Philip – that Max had already left Arguayo of his own free will, and how well it would suit everyone under the present circumstances if for some reason he chose not to return. This made her aware of the calculating streak in herself she didn't like.

'I'll be paying Max to leave and bribing Philip to stay.'

By the time she had made up her mind and opted for the lesser of two evils, it was midnight. It shouldn't take more than half an hour by cab to reach the San Andrés Container Terminal on the Santa Cruz highway to the north-east tip of the island. From a hiding place behind a bookshelf she took a wad from an envelope, counted out seven hundred and fifty dollars in fifty-dollar bills and put them in her purse. Then she called a taxi. While waiting for the taxi she wrote a note for Claude and Alex in the event that they changed their minds and decided to return to Laguna after all. It was a warm night but it might be chilly by the sea. She put her purse with a scarf and a cardigan into a bag. When the doorbell rang ten minutes later she was ready and went out to the street, felt the pain in her hip again and went back into the house to get her stick.

The frustrations Ella felt about her family – leaving her as they so often did to sort out their problems – the righteous indignation that warmed her up when she got into the taxi, this tangle of feelings began to unwind once she made out the cause of her irritation. She realised it wasn't Philip but Max who was the particular object of her animus. It was Max forgetting to pass on Philip's message that had landed them all in this trouble. Had they known Philip would be arriving with his

813

family that afternoon the episode in the tent wouldn't have happened. Philip and his family would now be asleep in the house in Arguayo rather than in a hotel in Puerto de Santiago and she would not be sitting in this taxi on her way to the container port in the middle of the night.

How much aggression could be hidden away in a handy little ruse of forgetting! How much harm a person could do under the cover of some apparently casual slip-up, claiming innocence of any intention, disowning responsibility for what they'd done and getting away with it. He hadn't meant it! How easy for Max to get on his boat and slip off to Africa, leaving it to her to make good the damage he'd done!

It was the notion of Max absconding which particularly worked her up — Max getting off scot-free again and expecting her to pick up the tab. She realised how many unsettled scores she had with Max, how much credit she'd advanced him as a child which he would never make good. Somehow he'd always managed to get his own way. It *was* true that he'd bullied Philip. There was that mischief he'd got up to when he told Alex he was his half-brother. It was always she who had had to improvise, patching up the hurt as best she could.

Because of an accident on the coast road it took the taxi much longer than usual to reach the container terminal, part of the sprawling industrial zone stretching most of the way along the coast between Santa Cruz and San Andrés. Ella avoided driving along this road so as not to be reminded of this concrete wasteland — a memorial to one of her most bitter political defeats. Her own Department of the Environment had supported the environmentalists' campaign against this development. Planning permission went through the cabildo, of course, as it always did when big commercial interests were at stake. Ella paid off the taxi, immediately regretting she hadn't asked the driver to wait. At this hour in the morning the reception area was no longer staffed, and it might be difficult to get hold of a taxi from the public phone at the entrance.

On the vast concrete space around her there wasn't a person to be seen, although a brawling-babbling ululation became audible as she walked in the direction of the sea, a chorus of high-pitched cries punctuated at intervals by blasts on a horn, perhaps signalling the arrival or departure of a ship.

Entering a maze of alleys guarded by someone in uniform who had fallen asleep at his post, Ella found herself on the edge of a cargo unloading area now empty, fringed by illuminated tent-like stalls, where there were people still at work. A stench of rotting fruit and vegetables, a heat-stirred compound of sweetness and acridity, rose from the refuse of perishable cargo, old tyres, oil and excrement on the wharves. In the floodlit distance of the night she made out a building resembling a hangar. A signpost identified the building as the San Andrés Container Terminal. The brawling-babbling cacophony issued from this building with increasing volume the closer she got.

Through a series of doorless concrete frames she was given a view of the pen of people and animals causing the hubbub inside. In the dimly lit arena inside this building, now slated for demolition – it had once served as a pound for cattle – a crowd of several hundred people seethed, men and women, standing for the most part, small children asleep on the floor between crated doves, hobbled goats and trussed fowls. It was the women standing along the perimeter of the barred area who were ululating, a high tremolo that continued without a break. Ella had heard the sound before – Arab women making it with their tongues as a procession passed through the medina she had visited with Claude in Tangiers. An undertow of murmurs washed over the crowd, a susurrus that broke up into muffled slapping echoes chasing each other through the gloom under the high ceiling.

A man armed with a rifle stood looking down into the pen from the gallery running around the inside of the building. Was it their confine-ment the women were protesting against? The presence of this armed guard? Canisters of drinking water stood in the middle of the pound, so at least they had something to drink. But did they have food? She wondered if they'd been provided with toilet facilities – how long had they already been kept in this cage, how much longer would they have to wait here?

'This is the ugly side of the island.'

Max materialised out of the dark and was standing beside her.

'It's appalling!' She began skirting the building. 'Isn't there anyone here one can speak to about these people? You should take pictures of this place.'

'I have.'

'Didn't the guard stop you?'

'I gave him the last of my money.' Max squatted and lit a cigarette. 'Leila and Ali, the people I came with on the boat, are somewhere in there. They looked after me during the voyage over from Tangiers. I asked them to come. That was the only reason they came. That they're here now about to be deported is my responsibility. I can't get them out. But I can go with them. They haven't got a cent. I gave them the tent and the carpets, but the police confiscated it all on the pretext of defraying the costs of deporting them. They could at least have sold it and raised some cash. They're quite valuable, apparently, original craftwork from somewhere in the Atlas Mountains. But once they're dumped in Agadir, how are they going to get back to Tangiers?'

Max stood up and put his arm around her.

'Why are you using a stick? Is that new hip playing you up?'

'I fell. Nearly dislocated it, but I can manage.'

'No, you can't. Here, give me your arm.'

They took a few cautious steps.

She took the purse out of her bag and handed a wad of bills to Max.

'Here you are. Seven hundred and fifty dollars. I had no intention of giving it to you. I was very angry and very disappointed – the way you behaved here, the way you are. Always yourself first. That's why you're careless about people, why you make mistakes like forgetting to tell us Philip was coming earlier than planned. Look at the trouble that's caused. The relations between you and Philip are beyond repair. One doesn't *make* mistakes like that. Don't you see? You can't keep on walking away from wreckage for the rest of your life. A part of you stays behind in the wreckage every time.'

Ella stopped and took him by both arms.

'The good news is that you still manage to surprise me just as I'm about to give up on you. Seeing you recognise your responsibility for Ali and his sister, I feel you're making it up to me. It gives me hope, Max. Life *is* in giving more than in getting. I know, you've heard me say that often enough and it gets on your nerves, but it really is. You must *grasp* it. If you could be more aware of your actions and how they affect people, you wouldn't have to live in this narrow ego that confines you. People would respond to you differently. It could make a difference to your photography. It could get you more work. As it is, I don't see sufficient care in your pictures. Has anyone ever told you that?'

'Well, not quite in those words. But maybe you're right. Maybe that's why I'm not a particularly successful photographer.'

Still holding him by both arms, knowing she would soon be letting him go, Ella spoke to her son as if his life depended on it. 'You're not in the moment long enough because you're always in a rush to get on to the next one. The world may be accelerating, but that doesn't mean you have to too. Don't let it run your life. Step aside from time to time, stand still and look about as you're doing today, Max. Take care of your friends and send me a postcard when you all get home.'

Max smiled as he kissed his mother.

'This takes me back. The talks we had in the garden at St John's Wood, on our walks through Richmond Park and at the London flat. I was a little kid but you talked to me as if I were a grown-up. I know, one way or another I've caused you a lot of pain and trouble – and that hurts me, and don't tell me it doesn't hurt enough to make me change anything, because *this* time – like you say – there *is* hope, and I really appreciate your coming out here in the middle of the night and giving me this money, which is going to make all the difference in the world. You won't regret the investment, you'll see, and I'll make it up to you, I promise.'

By the time he had walked Ella back to the entrance it was five o'clock. The first bus for Santa Cruz would be leaving from the stop outside the cargo terminal in a quarter of an hour. The sun was still under the horizon when they reached the stop, but as Max was helping his mother up the steps onto the bus the sea began to glimmer in the dawn light. He stood waving to her until the bus was no longer in sight, turning away with a lump in his throat, stricken by the realisation that Ella was getting old and that one day, in an already not-too-distant future, she'd be gone for ever.

# 11

The moment Ella was on the bus, loose debris from the conversation she had had with Philip the previous evening started shifting painfully around in her mind.

*Maybe just as well to have a reserve dad in the house.*

*Always the one so ready to preach.*

*My own freedom.*

*Freedom to do what?*

Yes, what had he said in reply to that? Jolted roughly around at the back of the bus, she continued to hear the Moroccan women ululating in the building down on the wharves, lost track of her thoughts. Her mind went white; for a moment she dropped off.

Philip's voice cut back in, jogging her awake.

*For example, to be honest. And you were always the one so ready to preach about never telling lies. So what do you think was going on all the time at Richmond? The rest of us all had to help support the deception that Alex was Dad's son ... George was never at home, and Claude stood in for him.*

Was that a deception exactly? Hadn't it just been the way things were arranged, something they had all gone along with and not given much thought to?

*People outside must often have wondered what he was doing there. Who was this man? What was his role?*

In Santa Cruz she got off and checked the timetable for the next bus to Puerto de Santiago. She had a wait of more than an hour. She went into the cafeteria, bought herself a carton of coffee and decided she might as well walk down to the Ramblas along the route her bus would take and pick it up on its way out of town.

The promenade was deserted. She walked with the sun behind her, the vast smooth sea on her left stretching empty to the horizon. She watched her shadow fall jerkily on the pavement in front of her, trailing a thin third leg, the stick she now used to support herself. She saw herself walking alone down the promenade with no end in sight. The awareness of her solitude, that she had always been alone and always would be, pulled her up short. Tired of walking, she stopped and spoke to the sea.

'Why am I doing this? Why does it always have to be me? Why is there no one doing it with me?'

These questions pulled her up short, reminding her of Christ's question to his sleeping disciples in the Garden of Gethsemane, the scene in the New Testament that had most moved her all her life.

Perhaps, like Max she could get on a boat, if a boat would only come along, and skip off somewhere. *My own freedom.* She hugged the idea. For a moment, before she became resigned to the sense of responsibility that would never let her go, it flashed up dolphin-like, a hope far out at sea.

But already Philip's face intervened, frowning, disapproving. How could a person be wholly taken over by a single expression, like the Cheshire cat by its grin, reduced to that and nothing else? Philip's portmanteau frown, which had already become an institution in the Morris family by the time he was two or three years old – the muscles in his face contracting, not to cry like ordinary children, but to express puzzlement, doubt, disapproval or outright rejection on behalf of Philip Morris and Co., the child advisory committee he chaired with his smugly closed face and folded arms.

She saw in the wrinkled forehead the truculence of which a child was capable once it had made up its mind, stronger than any disciplinary measures she could mount against it, immune to all persuasion. It reached its apotheosis in the ghostly long-distance scowl Ella had seen glowering at her during their telephone conversation the previous night, when he had criticised her for wanting to *have her cake and eat it*. How she detested that pious little phrase! Now in his late thirties, it was this Philip trotting out his pious commonplaces whom Ella still saw when he frowned, this smug middle-aged clerk of a boy whose those-are-the-rules look sometimes bypassed her annoyance, could equally well touch her affection as spark her anger, and it was the ambivalence of her feelings that frustrated her.

All too familiar, the tape continued to unreel in Ella's head when she boarded the bus on her way to rescue a family reunion that hadn't yet begun and was already in danger of not taking place. It might be true that affection for the small boy's comic solemnity was mixed in with the mockery that Philip's pronouncements met with from his father, his elder brother and to a lesser extent, Ella didn't deny it, from herself too. It was also true, as he had said the other night, that he had taken on the role of family scapegoat for which his bookkeeping habits – the mentality of the swot, the trainspotter, hoarder of sweets and keeper of lists, most objectionably the yellow *satisfecit* scorecard ranking the performance of family members and read out to them at the end of every week – had made Philip the uncontested candidate.

'Buzz off, Philip! Stop *annoying* me!'

'I enjoy annoying people.'

She had heard him say that often enough when the children were playing out in the garden.

Had Philip acquiesced in that role, or was he never given the choice? Would it have been good for Philip if the rest of them had taken him as seriously as he took himself, at the risk of his family losing its sense of humour altogether and allowing the boy to turn into an intolerable little tyrant? Or had Ella allowed this stereotype of Philip to stand without examining it more closely, failing to look behind the dull exterior for a more sensitive child who at the age of six might have been affected by the birth of Alex in ways his mother hadn't foreseen?

Old doubts returned to trouble her.

There's a lot I have to make allowances for, Ella reminded herself, not looking forward to the conversation with her son as she got off the bus by the beach in Puerto de Santiago. There's a lot to make up on my side as well.

She arrived at the Mirador Hotel a quarter of an hour earlier than she had arranged with Philip, asking at reception where she could find the Morris family who had checked in the previous day just as Philip stepped out of the elevator, swinging a key on a chain as he walked across the foyer. He swung the key at her before giving Ella a peck on the cheek; dutiful, a kiss that didn't count. The swirling key chain carried the message.

'The others are on the beach,' he said without preliminaries. 'I wasn't sure you would want to see them till we'd talked. Alex and a girlfriend are there too. George has gone to the airport to pick up Felicity and Co. He thought they'd be down by lunch. Shall we take a stroll along the front?'

Philip looked at his watch and then noticed his mother was carrying a stick.

'Or would you prefer a drink?'

'Just as you like.'

As they settled at a table on the patio overlooking the car park at the back, Ella reached out and touched his arm. 'I'm sorry about the reception you were given at Arguayo yesterday. It's not for me to apologise for whatever was taking place in that tent, but I do regret that it happened to be going on just when you all arrived, and I can only hope it didn't upset the children.'

'Well it did. Ann most of all.' Philip frowned. 'The official line I've taken is that Dad and Max had had a few drinks and pushed the boat out a bit far.'

'Official line? Why didn't you tell them the truth?'

'That they were taking drugs? That their grandfather and their uncle were stoned?'

'Why make a mystery of it? Why demonise it? Why lie about it unnecessarily? Your children should know about it from the start. It's part of the world they're growing up in.'

'Who do you think you are to tell me about lying unnecessarily? And as long as *I* have any say in the matter, it'll certainly not be any part of the world they're growing up in.'

It was the first conversation Ella had sat down to alone with Philip since his marriage to Ann ten years ago. It disappointed her to see how quickly those years had brought about a hardening of the *petit-bourgeois* leanings she and George had combated in him as a child. Philip's opening had made clear that her endeavour to bring up her children to be independent people, tolerant of other people's right to be free in whatever ways they chose, had been lost on this son. She made an effort to conceal her irritation.

'Well, we can still speak with each other even if we disagree. Driving straight off and checking into a hotel down here, wasn't that overreacting a bit?'

'So what do you suggest we should have done? Taken the children for a walk? Gone and sat in our rooms within earshot of all the caterwauling going on inside that tent until the police had arrested everyone and carted them off to jail?'

'Why are you such a harsh judge, Philip? It wasn't *that* bad.'

'Max was. Max was completely out of hand. He called me an old wanker in front of the boys.'

'Maybe he did, but I'm sure he will have said something nice as well. Perhaps you chose not to hear that and to remember the *old wanker*. Knowing Max, I'm sure he didn't mean it unkindly. You've become so humourless. Is that your problem or his? Besides, Max is often out of order and we have to make allowances for him.'

But Philip had no intention of allowing himself to be derailed.

'Not me. Not any more. I've had to make allowances for Max since the day I was born. I'm sick of making allowances for Max. It's Max's turn to start making allowances for *me*. And for the rest of us. I'm here with a wife and three children. As their uncle, doesn't he have a responsibility to *them*? What sort of an impression does he think he's making on my kids, shacking up with those … Africans, getting Dad to smoke pot with him in that, my God, really foul-smelling tent? I'm *not* making allowances for that. The two of them just sat there and thought it was all a joke. If it weren't for Max's behaviour in that tent, and to a

821

lesser extent Dad's – I mean, this was *humiliating* – maybe I'd say OK, possibly I did overreact, we'll be up in the morning, or whenever, and move into the house as planned. But as long as that Bedouin camp is pitched on the property, Ann and I have decided we'll just be up to join the family for the day and back down to the hotel at night.'

Philip asked the waitress to charge the drinks to his room, looking at his watch and already getting to his feet. Ann and the children were waiting for him on the beach, he reminded Ella, giving her to understand that the interview was over. Ella was being dismissed before she was given a chance to discuss the issues that mattered to her.

'It might be of relevance to your plans to know that the Bedouin camp, as you call it, has been dismantled,' she said to his receding back. 'Max and his African friends have gone back to Tangiers.'

'Sorry?' Striding off across the foyer, apparently unaware of his mother limping along behind him, Philip didn't seem to be listening.

She yelled, 'Philip! Stop and listen to me!'

He turned round to see Ella standing there, her face contorted with anger. How quickly her face changed when, in George's phrase, she flew off the handle, thought Philip with disgust, feeling not for the first time how ugly his mother looked when she got angry.

'What's the matter *now*? What are you shouting for?'

'Can't you see I need *help*? Do you think I walk with a stick for *fun*? Can't you at least walk at a pace I can keep up with?'

'I'm so sorry ...' Philip came back and offered her his arm.

'It's that hip still giving you trouble, is it?'

'Of course it is. What else? Did you ever see me limping before?'

'Well, no, not limping, but handicapped in some way. I mean, you've always got one thing or another. I really don't believe I can remember a time when there was *not* something wrong with you.'

'If this is your way of getting back at me, Philip, I want you to know I think it's *despicable*, cowardly and mean.'

'What are you talking about?'

'Taking advantage of my disability. Just walking off leaving me standing there.'

'Right, so we're into blackmail now, are we? We're now cranking a regular old *physical* handicap out on parade to extort a bit of sympathy, are we? Oh good, anything for a change. Not one of those tired old emotional moans I've had to listen to most of my—'

'What have I *ever* moaned about?'

'About being a displaced person, a wife walked out on, not to mention all the terrible things that happened to those Jewish friends of yours
and the completely inadequate people it's your misfortune to have been
lumbered with as children. You think you're the cat's whiskers, don't
you? George and Felicity and Max and the rest of us aren't good enough
for you. And unlike us, you *chose* George. Oh yes, we know all about
your ideas of making family a matter of choice rather than accepting
whatever rubbish you get lumped with by your genes. Half of them are
*your* genes, you do realise? It's half of *you* you're chucking out. Do you
realise what that means? It means it's *yourself* you're dissatisfied with. It's
not what you see out there that's the problem, it's seeing it through the
problem that's *you*.' Running out of things to say, but by no means done,
he began shouting at her. 'What makes you so unapproachable for your
children, such a difficult person for us to deal with? Why do you do
this to us? What have we done to you? Why are you the way you are?'

Ella crumpled onto a straight-backed chair in a corner of the lobby,
her face drawn, a tired old woman with the corners of her mouth turned
down.

Seeing her like that, Philip backtracked. 'I'm sorry … I'd like to take
back some of the things I just said. I wish they could be unsaid. I really
didn't mean them like that.'

Ella shrugged. 'Yes you did. Better to have it out in the open. This
is how it is between us. Why are you the way you are? Some of the
thoughts I had about you on the bus on my way here weren't much
better than what you just said. Why should I have to defend myself
against you or you against me? Perhaps when this is over we should go
our separate ways. It might be better if we see as little as possible of
each other in future. It's not as if there were a law obliging us to. In the
meantime –' Ella got up and took a few steps forward '– I hope your
children will still want to come out and visit us. There's no reason why
this should concern them, is there?'

Philip hesitated before he said no.

'I know your reservations about Max, but you needn't worry. Max is
unlikely to be coming to Arguayo any more frequently than you will.
But the grandchildren – I enjoy their visits, George and I, both of us
do. We really like having them around.' She turned and appealed to

him. 'The house is large, you know. It needs guests. Without people a house begins to die.'

Coming out of the shade of the lobby, she paused on the brink of the brightness of the day outside, as if reluctant to step into it.

'Where is everyone?'

'Over there.' Philip pointed. 'Where the sunshades are. By the little hut.'

'You go on ahead. Tell them I'll join them in my own time. Walking over sand is a bit tricky for me. I'll take the long way round via the promenade.'

Philip hesitated. 'Will you be all right, then?'

'Of course I'll be all right.'

Taking off his sandals Philip ran across the beach and didn't see Ella get into the cab.

# 12

Claude got a call from Ella in mid-morning, asking him to come and pick her up from the clinic in Santa Cruz. She had been fitted with a temporary harness to prevent further hip dislocation, as had apparently almost happened the previous evening. The hip would have to be oper-ated on again. Alex had left the house early and gone down to Puerto de Santiago to have breakfast with his girlfriend, so it was George who went to pick up Felicity and his granddaughters from Reina Sofia airport.

George's enquiring look as the three of them came through the gate into the terminal was misinterpreted by Felicity. Supposing that her father, always pedantic about numbers, was puzzled that the party of four he was supposed to be collecting was missing one person, she said or rather hailed him from a distance: 'At the last minute poor Janine couldn't come. Unfortunately her father died,' giving George cause to wonder as he often had in the past where his daughter had inherited her tactlessness. The first to briefly enter George's arms was Kim. As she kissed him on the cheek she whispered, '*Fortunately* Janine's father died and so she couldn't come,' breathy with suppressed laughter, already eluding him, running on into the spreading dome of sunlight outside the terminal.

George couldn't help turning to watch her, the object of his enquiring look from the moment she had appeared in the terminal now about to disappear again. Where's she off to in such a hurry? She's got so much taller in these two years, he said to Felicity, pecking her on the cheek, and so for that matter have *you*, young lady, how nice to have you back here. Hello, Grappa, the young lady said. Liz at fifteen, quietly waiting for her turn in just the way she had when she was five, with mouse-brown hair that fell in thin strands to her collar, a placid temperament and an unmemorable face as easily overlooked in a crowd of people as her vibrant sister attracted their attention. She turned her back on George by way of greeting, but only to show him the koala bear rucksack her grandparents had sent her for Christmas before putting her arms round him and giving him a hug.

'Thank you,' she said.

'There's my girl.'

Touched by Liz in a way that he never was by Kim, baffled by the feelings that could be aroused by apparent trivia, George felt a lump come into his throat.

Felicity put on sunglasses as they walked out into the car park and said, 'It's just so *good* to be in this sunshine. Do you know how lucky you are to live here, Dad?'

'Well we do. Where's Kim gone off to?'

'Over there, Dad. Please stop fussing. She's a grown-up girl now. She'll catch us up.'

'Will she? I wonder. Car's parked in the opposite direction. Well, anyway, problem is, we're running out of water. We wonder how much longer people will be able to go on inhabiting this island if there's too much more of the sunshine and the place dries up. But talk to your mother. She'll be able to tell you much more about it than I can.'

They swung onto the highway and followed it west along the coast as far as Adeje, where they headed north-west up into the hills. Still shedding the bits of London life that clung to her, Felicity talked all the way about people George didn't know and matters that didn't interest him. While he made non-committal noises reassuring her of his atten-tion, he frequently checked the rear-view mirror to watch Kim on the seat behind Felicity making faces at her mother's back. Kim had cut her black hair short, reminding him how his sister Tessa used to wear her hair as a girl, giving them both a gamine look that went well with Tessa's sarcasms and Kim's face-pulling antics.

'Oh no, Grappa, that's unfair!' protested Liz.

The moment the car pulled up in the courtyard at Arguayo both girls flew out of the car and ran upstairs. First in the room got the choice of bed. First in the room was usually the person sitting by the door nearest to the staircase when the car came to a halt. Unthinkingly, George had parked the car with Kim on the nearside, giving Liz a handicap. She was the slower one in any case.

Felicity called up to the girls running along the gallery, 'Kim! Don't be in such a rush! We don't yet know what rooms we'll be in. Ella said that the three of us might have to be put up downstairs.'

'But we're always up here! It's our room!'

'No, it's not. The corner room is still your uncle Max's room, and if he's here and wants the room for himself then that's his right. There are lots of other people staying here as well, you know.'

While Kim was distracted by this exchange with her mother Liz quietly slipped past her sister into the corner room. 'Max isn't here, at any rate,' she called from inside.

'You girls can settle in wherever you like.'

'First in the room chooses the bed!' Liz sang out gleefully.

'That's unfair!'

'You work it out between yourselves,' said George. 'As I recall, Kim got the choice last time *and* the time before that, so I think it's your sister's turn.'

'But what about Philip's lot?' Felicity asked her father as she followed him into the kitchen. 'Where will you put them?'

'Philip's lot are staying in a hotel down in Puerto de Santiago,' said George, and gave Felicity an account of what had happened over the last few days, not without a certain satisfaction, which he concealed from his daughter.

The quarter of a century George had lived on the island had changed the values he brought with him when he moved there in the early 1960s. He had become a less sour, more supple and carefree sort of person than he would have been had he stayed in England. George's attitudes to his individual children had changed with this mellow, ing. The enmity between him and his eldest son had softened over the years – unthinkable even five years ago that he and Max would have sat smoking pot together, or that he would have sanctioned Max bringing his Arab catamite with him to live in a tent on the property.

The gradual broadening of George's own desires to encompass relation-ships that would have once shocked him had extended to tolerating his son's homosexuality. None of this would have materialised so evidently, however, had it not been for the conversation that had led to the secret deal between father and son.

George no longer disapproved of Max. He let him be. He had relin-quished all disapproval baggage in favour of the laissez-faire with which the island went about its business. Whereas the son who had once earned his approval and affection, the solid dependable boy who had become a chartered accountant, made a respectable marriage and produced two sons to carry the flag of the family name for a further generation, now struck him as an intolerable prig – in fact the sort of person George would describe himself as having been at the same age. He resented Philip boycotting the house because he disapproved of Max's morals, and it was Philip, not Max, who had scuttled the family reunion.

'If he didn't like it he could just quietly have looked the other way, couldn't he? Ella was very upset. He's spoiled this Whitsun for us al-ready.'

'Let me talk to Philip. Is Ella in Santiago with them now?'

'I've no idea where she is at the moment. Claude was going to pick her up in Santa Cruz and drive her here. She seems to have done in her hip. All I know is that she was due to be meeting Philip at his hotel this morning.'

'The girls probably want to go for a swim, so why don't we join them right away? I'll just go up and tell the girls, drop off my things and change into something else.'

Standing under the vaulted brick ceiling, George heard Felicity's question in the room overhead a few seconds later as distinctly as if she'd been with him in the kitchen. 'Would you girls like to come down with George and me to the beach and meet your cousins and go for a swim?' He'd have to remind them about the soundbox, thought George, but he got caught up with so many other things in the next few days that it slipped his mind.

Not the least of which was that no longer so innocent question *Would you girls like … to go for a swim?* He wondered if in Kim's ears it was still loaded with the memories it had for him. In the early years he had taken the girls down to the beach at Puerto de Santiago every day. Silly question – of course they wanted to go for a swim – but it was the ritual they wanted too, to wait for their grandfather to ask the question, turning it back on him when he waited too long, pretending to have forgotten. *Would you like to go for a swim, Grappa?*

These were leading questions.

Philip was fielding his beach volleyball team when George arrived with Felicity and the girls. There was no sign of Ella or Claude. Beach games under Philip's direction were organised sports played strictly according to the rules. They were in the middle of a game, Alex and Darren against Philip and Denis. Hilary doubled as umpire and linesman. Ann sat under a parasol, logging entries on the complicated scorecard Philip had devised for family games.

The arrival of Felicity's team interrupted the game. George noticed a reluctance to engage, a sort of drifting-together followed by a pulling-apart of the London girls and their Emsworth cousins. Philip seemed to notice it too, and wanted to bring them together, or perhaps it was just a part of an ongoing family game plan that the girls were immediately co-opted, Liz to play for his team, Kim with Alex and Darren. Declining offers of shade under the hotel parasol, George and Felicity sat down in the sun, Felicity to talk to her sister-in-law, George to watch the game, Ann to cast sideways glances at George, whose sunburned body resembled a charred remnant thrown up by the sea.

'You're pitch-dark, as dark as one of the natives, George.'

'No, I'm darker all over. They just do faces. So I'm told. I haven't taken a look for myself. The natives here are called Tinerfenos, by the way.'

'Don't you worry about cancer?'

'Not when I'm having a good time on the beach.'

Meeting intransigence, Ann turned the other way to talk to Felicity.

'What's happened to Claude and Ella?' Felicity asked her.

'He left to fetch Ella from the clinic in Santa Cruz. She put in only a brief appearance this morning. Apparently she was up all night and in a lot of pain, so Claude drove her back to the house.'

'Poor Ella!'

After making some half-hearted prods at the ball the girls quickly got into the spirit of the game being dictated by their male cousins. George was astonished how big these fifteen year-old-boys were. He remembered himself as being rather meagre and small at their age. Did they do regular workouts? Was Ann giving them steroids with their cornflakes? Denis, the slightly taller of the twins, was already six feet, maybe a bit over. He was broader across the shoulders and had a more athletic physique than his twin brother. Denis the physical one, Darren the brainy one – there had been an equitable division of the genes. How sensible of Philip to have put the better of the girls with the weaker of the boys. Organising team sports was the sort of thing he was good at. Darren looked quite content to lob easy balls for butter-fingered Liz, and Denis for his part clearly wanted nothing better than to slam balls as hard as possible at cousin Kim. But she wasn't going to be intimidated. She was a competitive girl and Alex dangled her at just the right height, just the sort of ball for a slam at the net, smashing the ball down at her opponent's feet. Denis and Kim paired off as naturally as Darren and Liz. No reluctance to engage now, observed George. Courting displays were in full progress.

Not much of a player of anything, George had considered himself a connoisseur of tennis and cricket while he lived in England. He enjoyed watching displays of physical skill. Alex had played this game a lot during the years he went to school on the island. He had immediately cottoned on to Kim's preference to go to the net. He put his play entirely at the disposal of her special skill. Give it to him then, said George as Kim leaped high for the ball and smashed it down, catching Denis full on the kneecap, and the ball soared off on a trajectory that carried it into the sea.

'Two–nil to Alex's team,' announced Hilary.

Philip was blowing a bit and getting very red in the face despite the precaution of a sun hat. 'I expect you girls would like to go in to cool off.'

Momentarily disengaged from a security guaranteed by the rules of the game, the quadrille of the four cousins began all over again, the boy–girl drifting-together and pulling-apart.

Denis scrunched the ball with his foot, flipping it up expertly and catching it, tossing the ball from hand to hand, weighing the options as he took a few steps towards Liz.

'Fancy a swim?'

The question was directed at his teammate but was really meant for his opponent. Kim had already turned away from the sea and was wandering off, head bent and eyes on the beach, kicking the sand, perhaps in search of something. I suppose if I were his age that's how I'd phrase it, George reflected, perfectly in tune with all this, the dissonance of entangled hormones, his grandson with the broad shoulders and handsome friendly face, his cello-shaped granddaughter with pouting lips, narrow waist and broad hips, moving in apparently opposite directions but still bound for the same place.

Alex was hailed by a woman standing by the railing along the promenade. Who was that? George wondered idly as he watched Alex wave and walk over to talk to the woman. His eyes went back to linger on Denis and Kim, and when he next looked round to check what was happening on the promenade Alex had disappeared with the unknown woman.

Philip ran splashing into the sea and dived in. Everyone followed suit. Even Ann and Hilary went in. George joined them.

As another ball game started up in the water close in to the shore, George ducked under the breakers and swam slowly, he hoped with dignity, aware that age had just been relegated by youth, to the shoal a quarter of a mile out in the bay. He could hear the shrieks becoming fainter behind him. About fifty yards to the left he watched two swimmers doing a fast crawl, ploughing up the smooth surface of the sea. They drew level. Soon they had overtaken him.

It was Kim racing Denis, no doubt to the same shoal. George trod water, lay on his back, floating with his eyes closed, meditating on the pain caused by his relegation, not without a poignancy in which he could take a kind of pleasure.

The last time Grappa had gone for a swim with the girls on their visit three years previously, Kim had been a rather pudgy thirteen, as her mother said, meaning something else, but all the more streamlined in the water for that, a powerful swimmer, all coil and spring, sleekly black-haired and sinuous as a seal. Beat you to the shoal, she said. Beyond the breakers he had tried to keep up with her in the deep water between the shore and the shoal, but he no longer could. She outswam Grappa easily. Bobbing on the tips of her toes, not quite tall enough to stand there, she bounced up and down on the concealed sandbar that ran across the bay. As George swam slowly towards her he watched her head rising out of the water and submerging again.

Resisting the currents that plucked at his legs and occasionally caused him to levitate, George could stand on the sand and breathe without having to tread water. It was an ideal place to rest, for the tremors of the body to steady after the exertions of swimming, and leisurely take aim. Looking at people on the beach, memories of rifle training as a boy in the cadet corps at Winchester came to mind. There was a rule of thumb the training supervisor had given him for estimating the distance of targets, how they appeared in your sights at fifty, a hundred, two hundred yards and over, how to adjust your aim accordingly. Let me rest on you, Grappa, Kim said to him when he arrived, and she shot up out of the sea and clung on to him, gripping his waist with her thighs. In the course of this manoeuvre her top came loose and one of her breasts spilled out. The upper half of Kim's body rose on the swell, brushing his lips with a small hard nipple that tasted of salt, rubbing up and down against him by an instinct that had now become something other than the rocking-horse game they always used to play in the sea, a harmless enough game, pretending to be two swaying sea horses glued together at the midriff, that day for the last time before the summer holidays ended and Kim went back to London.

George turned back and began to swim away from memories he could no longer take pleasure in. Jealous – at his age! Before striking out for the shore he righted himself in the water, holding out his thumb to get the cafe on the promenade lined up in his imaginary sights, estimated the target at a hundred yards and took a bead on the couple sitting under a red-and-white striped sunshade on the terrace.

# 14

A pelt of sand still cleaved to her skin in the hollow between her shoulder blades. Alex felt an urge to dislodge it. It must have stuck to her when she came wet out of the sea and lay down on the beach. Noticing additional specks of sand entangled on the fluff of white-blonde hairs along her spine, Alex ran his fingers up and down her back, brushing them off without thinking what he was doing. Mirjana Stepanovic glanced over her shoulder, raising her eyes in mock surprise at the liberties his hand was taking, and asked him what it was doing there.

'Just getting the sand off your back.'

'Yes, I can see that.' She smiled. 'It doesn't answer my question, though, does it.'

'Do you mind?'

'Not if you can give me a good answer.'

'Oh dear. This is like being back at school. All right then. I'm grooming you. And if you press me as to why I'm doing *that*, you'll shame me into admitting I wanted to touch you. Do you mind?'

'No. Have you got it all off?'

'Just about.' He inspected her. 'There's still a bit on your elbows ...'

He rubbed them with the palms of his hands. Mirjana squirmed and pulled a face. 'That tickles. You've got my funny bone.'

'Are you ticklish?'

'Not generally, but it depends on my mood. How about you?'

'Extremely ticklish, irrespective of mood. But I shouldn't be telling you, should I? That's giving a hostage to fortune.'

Mirjana helped herself to one of his cigarettes.

'I've never quite managed to work that phrase out. Have you?'

'No.'

He offered her a light with his Zippo.

'You got me there. Hoist by my own petard.'

'There's another one.'

Both of them laughed.

Alex saw to his regret that his family were packing up their gear and getting ready to leave the beach. Since he didn't have transport of his own, he would have to leave with them.

'Which reminds me. I'll come down and pick you up at about seven tomorrow evening,' he said.

'Not necessary. I've got a car.'

'You bought a car?'

'No, but I've got the use of a car for a few days.'

All this fell into place, just as everything was falling into place in his life these days without any intervention on his part. He owed the post he had taken up at the University of Graz nine months earlier to a series of coincidences, happening to be present at a particular cafe in Vienna on a particular day when a particular subject came up in the conversation. Then the riverside apartment he had serendipitously found in Graz. Bumping into Slavenka at the party in Klagenfurt. Bumping into Mirjana at the post office here, come to that, his teacher at the British School in Puerto de la Cruz he had fallen in love with as a sixteen-year-old boy and not expected he would ever see again.

His entire life, down to such details as the removal of sand grains from Mirjana's back, just seemed to drift together of its own accord – a felicitous interweaving of a magic mantle by many hands, working invisibly for the sole purpose of arranging the world so as to maximise his personal happiness.

Sitting on the promenade overlooking the sea in this perfect weather, Alex had a wish for everything to freeze, enfold this moment and preserve it for ever. The only blot on his horizon was the family row that had blown up in Arguayo. Even happiness at its most radiant didn't come unaccompanied by a shadow. If fortune favoured him too greatly, it would want something from him in return. Was that atavism, an influence of the Church or just doing a deal with your lucky stars?

'Well, I suppose I'll have to go,' he said regretfully.' There's a lot to get ready for tomorrow. And I shall have to find somewhere in the village to stay.'

'Why can't you stay at your house?'

'There are ten people staying and we're a bedroom or two short. But our neighbours let out rooms in the village so there'll be no problem finding something within walking distance.'

'I could put you up. If you don't mind making do with a pull-out bed in the living room.'

'That's very kind of you.'

Alex trundled his Zippo across the tabletop. Mirjana watched with interest, wondering where the lighter was going.

'How long are you staying?'

'I'll be flying back early on Sunday. I'm giving a seminar in Graz on Monday morning.'

'What's the seminar on?'

' "The emergence of ethnic nationalism in the republics since Tito's death", to give you its full title, "with special reference to the political consequences of Milošević coming to power in Serbia".'

'And what do you think are likely to be the consequences?'

'The break-up of the Yugoslav Federation, what else? The same thing will happen there as is already taking place in the Soviet Union.'

Mirjana stubbed out her cigarette.

'Doesn't it strike you as rather odd that a Hungarian-German Englishman brought up in the Canary Islands should be giving a seminar on contemporary Balkan geopolitics at an Austrian university?' She smiled. 'How does that sound as a list of qualifications, Alex Morris?'

He smiled back.

'I take your point. But on the other hand, where is your Yugoslav analyst, Mirjana Stepanovic, who can be counted on to jettison all the prejudices that go with their personal ethnic affiliation as Orthodox Serb, Catholic Croat or Muslim Bosnian, and give equal consideration to the points of view of all the ethnicities, providing us with an impartial account of what's happening in the country? Isn't that a much more difficult task for a Yugoslav national than for an outsider who doesn't have prejudices to jettison?'

'There's no such thing as an impartial account.'

'Well, I don't know. One person whose name comes to my mind as qualified for the task would have been Josip Broz. The adoption of the sobriquet Tito is itself an indication of the nature of the difficulties involved in establishing the pan-Yugoslav standpoint from which I'd like to believe an impartial view does become possible. Tito took pains to obscure any personal allegiances.'

'He was Croatian.'

'He may have been born in Croatia, but as a result of his experiences in Russia he was able to acquire the point of view of an outsider, and he covered up the tracks of his ethnicity so well that in the equality of all ethnic groups which he propagated as his platform for the new Yugoslavia, there was no preferential treatment given to any one of them. As another outsider, I think I can see that more clearly than, well ... the majority of your compatriots?'

Mirjana looked at him amused.

'Why are these questions of the slightest interest to you? What does any of this matter to you?'

'And you of all people ask me that!' Alex looked at her in astonishment. 'Have you forgotten? It was you who woke my interest, Mirjana. You made them matter to me because they matter to you.'

Hearing his nieces in the car park calling his name, Alex got up.

'I've got to go. See you tomorrow then,' he said, stooping to kiss her cheek before he walked off to the car park, leaving Mirjana wondering at herself for having put him down like that, ashamed of her clumsiness, wishing she could have gone back and erased her stupid question or been given five minutes more to make up for having asked it.

# 15

In the feud between Philip and his parents, which had loomed over the beach that morning, an unexpected development had taken place. At lunch Philip announced they would be checking out of the hotel and moving up to Arguayo. Wanting to be all together in the same house, the four cousins had appealed to Ella behind Philip's back to intercede with him on their behalf. This she had successfully done, using her inside knowledge – as Ann confided to Felicity – that it pained Philip to be forking out for his family to live in the Mirador when free accommodation was available up the road. What Ann didn't know was that the 50 per cent cancellation fee for the two rooms that now wouldn't be required over the Whitsun weekend had been paid by Ella as a gesture of goodwill. She felt she had to make it up to Philip. George didn't think she had anything to make up to their son and that it was cynical of Philip to have accepted her offer. Ella found it better not to tell him she had also paid everyone's air fares – Alex as usual being the exception.

Ella and Felicity didn't come down to lunch but sat in Ella's den upstairs while she made repairs to her granddaughters' clothes. She'd noticed at once that they were in need of attention. It distressed her to see the poor quality of the things they wore. Felicity didn't have much money, making it even harder for Ella to understand why she didn't take better care of such clothes as they did have. Felicity had always bought the children good-quality second-hand clothes from a local shop, but now they were teenagers they wanted to decide for themselves, so she made them an allowance and they bought their own.

'Cheap is all they can afford. This stuff isn't made to last, Mum. You shouldn't bother.'

'But you can't let your daughters run around looking like derelicts. Look at the tears on the back pocket here. It's half ripped off. Look at the seams coming adrift. Just the cheap sort of thread you get with imports from Asia. There's a top button missing on this shirt.'

'Frankly, who cares? Without the imports from Asia, what could they afford to wear? They'll be trashing the stuff soon enough in any case. Janine lets them have some of her own things they like. At least Liz wears them. She's more Janine's size.' Felicity rambled on. 'Kim wouldn't want them even if they fitted. She's become so unpleasant to Janine. Kim's bolshie – does what she wants – goes where she wants – comes home when it suits her, no matter what I say. Kim brought a boy back with her late one night and they made so much noise it woke Janine. She got up and asked them to be quiet. Kim flew at her. Who did Janine think she was, telling her where to get off?'

'Weren't you there?' asked Ella, pained by Felicity's *trashing the stuff soon enough in any case.*

'I was on night duty. Well, I come home in the morning and go to bed just as Janine is getting up to go to work. I find her in a terrible state. She's clearing out her half of the cupboard and packing a suitcase. Can't live here any more, she says. Not with Kim against her the way she is. I'm not wanted here any more. Better I clear out. And so on. So I called Kim's father and asked if she could move in with him for a while. Stephen's got two kids a few years younger than Kim by his second wife. They haven't got much space but said they'd take her in. They put a bed in the attic in the children's hobby room. Kim agreed and off she went and we all heaved a sigh of relief. But two weeks later Stephen rings up. Can't keep Kim here, he says, she doesn't make the slightest effort to fit in with the rest of the family and is a bad influence on the children.'

'Did he say specifically what the problem was?'

'Lots of problems. Just uncooperative. Didn't make her bed, refused to help around the house, smoked pot and offered it to the children, came and went just as she pleased and treated the place like a hotel. Stephen thinks she should see a therapist. Perhaps he's right.'

'Well, I find it difficult to imagine. She's not like that here.'

'There are lots of things you can't imagine, Mum. It's not like this where we live in Clapham. You don't know how sordid the world we live in is.'

'Perhaps it would help if I talked to her.'

'I'd rather you didn't. She's so easily upset these days.'

Ella was disturbed by this conversation. This wasn't how she'd brought her children up. Live every day as if it were a Sunday. The day ahead of you is yours to make up in your mind before you go down to it. You get the day you deserve only if you put your mind to it. Being short of money excused things only up to a point. Felicity lacked discipline, found it difficult to be tidy; left to herself she became slovenly. You could live frugally, as Ella had done before the war, or in poverty, as she had done after the war as a refugee in Hamburg, but your world didn't need to be *sordid* – that ugly word her daughter had used. Once you let yourself go, everything would begin to give way. Letting her children run around with holes in their clothes was a message of carelessness Felicity passed on to them. How could a child with holes in her clothes believe that her mother cared for her?

Ella decided that as a birthday present to herself she would take Felicity and the girls shopping in Santa Cruz and buy them the new clothes they all needed. As for Kim being uncooperative, it was hardly any wonder, given the lack of care her mother took with the girl. Felicity thought she could hand her over to a therapist and get her straightened out, just like that. But before seeking professional help, Kim surely needed to talk to someone close to her who would listen and give her personal support. Ella decided she would be that person, whatever Felicity said. She would sit down and talk to Kim herself.

Ann and Hilary decided to join Ella, Felicity and the girls on the excursion to Santa Cruz. Never confident of her own figure, aware of short legs that had never allowed her to look elegant, Ella was apprehensive when shopping for her own clothes. She found it more enjoyable to buy clothes for others, and El Corte Inglés in Santa Cruz intrigued Kim and Liz by its novelty, quite different from the shops familiar to them at home.

When it came to the girls trying on anything they thought boringly conservative, Ella was cunning. She gave in to them over a couple of items she didn't like in exchange for their agreement to summer frocks in which she thought they looked pretty, arguing her case convincingly enough to overcome their resistance. Helping Kim in the changing cubicle, Ella was shocked to see the state of her underclothes. She took her off to the lingerie department and bought her six sets of underwear.

'Only if you agree to throw the old ones away.'

Kim peeled it all off and stood naked in the cubicle while Ella removed the tags, pleased by her granddaughter's total lack of embarrassment, her amusement when Ella scrutinised her skin.

'Have you been drinking that carrot juice I got for you? It's cleared up your skin. See, I told you it would. Show me your back. Yes, the rash there has gone too.'

Physically, her granddaughter was much more mature than Ella had been at her age. Naturally there were temptations in the way of young girls as mature as this, but whatever Kim might already have experienced, it hadn't yet taken away from her a certain innocence which to Ella's mind was what distinguished a girl from a woman. Ella was reassured by this glimpse of her granddaughter in the cubicle. She might dress like a tart, but when she took her clothes off she had an aura of vulnerability that surprised and touched Ella.

Kim slipped on a new bra, and Ella hooked it at the back.

'It's neat,' said Kim, turning to look at herself in the mirror.

'Why are you unkind to Janine?'

'Mum told you?'

'Yes. And about the two weeks you spent with your father before he sent you back home. You don't seem to have done very well there, either. All right, Janine may be someone you don't much like, but that doesn't mean you have to be so unpleasant to her as to drive her out of the house, does it?'

Kim made a face in the mirror.

'Janine's two-faced. She pretends to be nice to me, but behind my back she's always complaining about me to my mother. They work in the same hospital and that's all they ever talk about. Janine has taken Mum over. Me and Liz don't get a look-in. Janine wants her all to herself. It's so *narrow* living in that house. It's so boring! If only I could get out!'

'Then why didn't you take the chance you were given at your father's house?'

'I wanted to punish my mother for sending me away.'

As Ella looked at her granddaughter standing there, looking so fetching in her underwear, an unsettling thought came to her. *You've no idea how sordid the world we live in is.* 'Did anything happen to you while you were at your father's house?'

'Happen? What do you mean?' Kim burst into tears. 'I don't know what to do!' she wailed.

Ella stroked her granddaughter's hair.

'Well maybe you *can* get out. You'll be leaving school this summer, won't you? Last time you were here you did the basic course in scuba diving, and you got better marks than all the others, including the boys. Remember? You enjoyed yourself. Why don't you go on and qualify as a professional diver? I know a local girl who got a job as a diver in Malaysia and now works full time in the Caribbean. Why shouldn't you do something like that too?'

Kim sniffed. 'Mummy couldn't possibly afford it.'

'Well, maybe George and I can help out.'

This was the grandchild who knew what she wanted and didn't hesitate to say so. She had a resoluteness and independence of spirit which Ella admired despite her reservations about Kim's self-centredness, but perhaps she needed that if she was to succeed in getting out. Kim was the grandchild in whom Ella could most see a kinship with herself.

'You can take the intermediate course in Santiago and live here for as long as it takes to get professional qualifications. Then you can go anywhere you want in the world.'

To get out into the world when she was Kim's age had been Ella's own dream, thwarted for so long.

'Oh yes!' Kim put her arms round Ella and kissed her.

'But don't tell anyone yet. Pass your exams first. To be fair to Liz, I'll have to come up with something for her, and maybe for your cousins too. And one other condition, Kim. When my guests come tomorrow I'd like you to wear one of the frocks we've been looking at, and if I have any say in the matter it'll be the red one with the spiral patterns. You look so pretty in it and it goes so well with your complexion. I want to be proud of you. So it's really myself I'm buying it for, you see. Will you let me do that?'

# 16

Kim put on the frock when she got up in the morning, parading along the gallery to get used to the feel of herself in a dress. She went past the open door of the room the boys were in, adjacent to the one she shared with Liz, calling out to her sister in a voice loud enough for her cousins to hear, 'I really don't think this is me, Liz. I've not worn a dress since

I was, what, *ten*? And I was shaped different then. Don't you think I look stupid in it?'

Denis peered around the door and saw his cousin standing out in the gallery wearing a skimpy sort of dress with a high waist that pushed up her breasts. Red stripes spiralled round her body, ending halfway down her thighs.

'Wow! It doesn't look stupid to *me*.'

'Do you like it?'

'You look *great* in it.'

'You think so?'

A door further down the gallery opened and her mother looked out. 'Yes, it does look nice. But it's still only half past eight, darling. The guests won't be arriving for hours. So when you go down to give Grappa and Claude a hand in the kitchen, put on something else. Ask Liz to come and help me here for a minute, will you?'

What was there to wearing that frumpy little frock with red stripes in exchange for the freedom offered to her by her grandmother's plan? It was a matter of pride. Kim wanted that freedom, but she didn't want to owe it to anyone. She didn't want to owe anything to anyone. Giving in to what Ella wanted her to wear went against the grain. Kim recognised her own stubbornness and was unhappy about it.

Although it was now long ago, she hadn't forgotten how she'd resented having to go back to London with her mother and her sister, and she'd put the blame on her grandmother, because it was her fault that she could no longer keep Kim and Liz in Arguayo. Seeking to deflect the childrens' disappointment at the loss of their island paradise, diverting from herself the blame for what her children regarded as a sell-out, this was the message their mother had been giving them ever since she carted them back to England.

After leaving the Arguayo paradise for the Clapham wilderness, it was Grappa who gradually receded in Kim's memory, Ella who came forward, although at the time Kim lived there it used to be the other way round. After their return to London it was always her grandmother who wrote to them, who sent them packages to keep them going in the months between birthdays and Christmas, made regular payments into their post-office savings books. Ella showed up unmistakably in the light. Kim could see her completely and knew where she was with Ella – on firm ground, in clear light. Because she was always in the background, you tended to take her for granted.

With Grappa, the picture was diffuse. My frogspawn, he used to call Kim and her sister during the island years, my water babies. They stuck to him, back and belly, to his playful tenderness, a grandfather who was as close to her as herself. Hard to keep anything definite in place in the swim of those wriggling frogspawn bodies together. Their weightlessness in the water, trawling the shallows off the Santiago beach. In her memory, she seemed to have spent their entire childhood in the sea. Leaving the shallows, they ventured a little further out to sea each time, boarding the frog's back, clinging on for the final ride with Grappa all the way to the bar across the bay.

Entwined with Grappa as she was never entwined with Ella, the severance from Arguayo and the severance from Grappa had hurt Kim more than the separation from her grandmother. She anticipated her grandfather's miraculous appearance in Clapham without ever quite expecting it. She hung and swung on the front gate to be the first to see him when he came down the street. But Grappa didn't come. She had still been too little when Stephen left the family – perhaps just as well, before she came to depend on him being there. She never missed her father like she missed Grappa. The weekends they went to spend with him once a month became a chore. Her mother badmouthed Stephen, idolised Grappa, and Kim followed in the grooves that by constant repetition her mother had worn in her mind, until Kim's disappointment with Grappa for failing to materialise brought her to the conclusion that it was better not to depend on anyone.

It was Grappa's voice she heard calling her name down in the courtyard.

A scent of flowers rose towards Kim as she went down the gallery stairs. The buzz down in the courtyard reminded her of a marketplace. Alicia and her daughter were sorting the bundles of flowers Paco was unloading off his mule, laying them out on tables and sorting them by colour and length to arrange in vases. Alicia told Kim to put on an apron so that she didn't mess her frock and go down into the cellar and fetch as many vases as she could find. On her way, she went into the kitchen and bumped into Rosalia, another daughter of Alicia's, with whom Kim and Liz had become great friends during their childhood on the island and not seen for years. They shrieked with delight and hugged each other.

'Come and help me bring up the vases your mother asked me to fetch.'

Chatting with each other down in the cellar, they began nibbling cheese and olives and soon forgot about the vases they were supposed to be fetching. Liz came down and said Alicia was becoming impatient. She wanted to get on with the flower arrangements. Having delivered the vases, the girls were ordered into the kitchen to help Liz and her cousin Hilary, who were making *gofio* hors d'oeuvres. Rosalia prepared *huevos moles*, yolk of egg mixed with sugar, cinnamon and lemon peel. Kim was set to work making *gofio* dessert cakes, topping them with almond paste and honey made from palm-tree shoots. This recipe, one of Ella's favourites, originated in La Gomera, where Alicia's family came from, and had been introduced by her to the Morris household.

More *gofio* was being used by George to thicken a fish stew of dusky and comb grouper which simmered in a cauldron on the other side of the kitchen. *Sancochado* stood in the pot alongside – another boiled fish stew, seasoned with oil, vinegar and hot peppers. George was head chef, and the number and variety of dishes on the menu containing fish reflected his fondness for it – parrot fish, snapper, mackerel and saupe, grilled, fried, boiled or soused. To allow George enough room for his creations and make sure that the taste of fish didn't interfere with the meat, his assistant Claude had moved into the summer kitchen, a cooler back room used during unusually hot weather. *Carne de fiesta*, chunks of seasoned pork, was a staple of festive occasions on the island as were goat's meat, rabbit in *salmorejo* sauce and *carajacas*, a liver dish served with *papas arrugadas*, small wrinkled new potatoes boiled in salty water and served in their jackets to conserve the flavour.

'When you're done here, perhaps you could come over and chop parsley for the *mojo* sauce.' George was suddenly standing beside Kim with an arm around her waist.

'I just about *am* done, but Alicia asked me to help decorate the tables,' she lied, irritated by Grappa's arm laying claim to her. 'Ask Hilary. Perhaps she'll give you a hand,' she said, detaching his arm, and left the kitchen.

In the courtyard stood a few dozen sand-coloured, broad-bellied urns with graceful handles used as flower vases. Ella had brought them over on the ferry from Morocco. Handmade, each was a little different. Over a metre high, taller than Kim was at the time the urns arrived in Arguayo, to her they'd looked big enough for Ali Baba's forty thieves to hide in. Even now, when she saw one of them lurking in the dark, she preferred to give it a wide berth. They were cheaper by the dozen, Ella explained to George when he arrived to meet the ferry and watched the urns being unloaded at the harbour in Santa Cruz, but the truth was she'd bought them because the family she saw selling them at the roadside looked as if they hadn't eaten for a week. George had hired a truck to transport the urns up to Arguayo. Seven of them had got broken over the years. When in use they always stood in puddles because of their tendency to leak.

Paco had driven up to the slopes below the snow-covered summit of El Teide that morning to cut sprigs off trees in blossom in late May at an altitude of fifteen hundred metres. Alicia put sand in the bottom of the urns, trimmed the sprigs and arranged them with flowers to make bouquets that would stand upright. The urns were heavy. It took two people to move one.

'You can put half a dozen in the courtyard,' Alicia told the girls, 'one each in all the downstairs rooms, a couple outside the gate, and distribute the rest along the gallery upstairs.'

Claude put his head around the kitchen door. 'Kim? On your way upstairs you might look in on your grandmother and ask her to come and see me in the kitchen when she's got a moment.'

Kim and Liz took hold of one of the urns and carried it between them up the stairs of the *portada sillería*. They tried to lift the urn up onto the pedestal on top of the corner post of the gallery, but it was too heavy.

'We'll have to get the boys to lift it for us,' said Kim, running off down the gallery and up the stairs to Ella's room in the old belfry. To her surprise the door was locked. She knocked. Within seconds the door opened and Alex's face appeared in the crack.

'What is it?'

'Claude asked Ella to come down when she's got a mo—'

'I'll pass the message on,' said Alex, shutting the door in her face.

'Hm! *Not* very friendly,' she said to herself and turned back to the *portada sillería* before she changed her mind and continued on around the gallery in the other direction, thinking it was time for the boys to start giving a hand too, and wondering if she would find them in their room.

## 17

'Who was that?'

'Kim. Asking if you're ready and could come down to speak to Claude.'

Ella wasn't even dressed.

The habit of imagining himself as an observer questioning his every move made his life a more complicated, secretive business than anyone would have guessed. Alex stood leaning against the door, uncomfortably aware that an hour after entering the room he was still only just inside it. He hadn't yet committed himself to being in the room – by sitting down in it, for example – and it surprised him Ella hadn't rumbled that this halfway position reflected Alex's wish to be somewhere else. He would have preferred to be with Mirjana on the terrace, from where Claude had dragged him away to go up and keep his mother company – this would have been the honest answer to a question he imagined being put to him by a disinterested observer of the scene.

He watched her face in the mirror of the dressing table by the window, where she sat sideways on in her underwear putting up her hair. She had braided the last few inches from crown to forehead, and was tucking the tips in under the hairline at the temples before inserting grips to keep it in place. The concentration required by this fiddly operation brought out beads of sweat on her upper lip.

Ella hadn't slept the previous night. The light from the window fell obliquely on her face, pitting it with tiny shadows. She had gone downstairs early and woken Claude, talking to him in his room for a couple of hours until it was time for him to get up and start cooking. Alex then saw his father in the kitchen and was requested by him to go and sit with his mother, for she was rather low, Claude said, in need of someone to listen to her sympathetically. But Alex was still standing, and that listening with sympathy which his father had asked of him was compromised by his reluctance to sit down.

The conversation between mother and son was conducted via the mirror.

'Claude and George spend all morning cooking. Cooking! As if there weren't more important things for them to be doing. What have we got Alicia and her girls for? Two grown men spending the whole morning in the kitchen, as if nobody else could be trusted with the responsibility of making lunch. They hardly ever see the children. Why aren't they doing something with them instead? Where's the festivity in what they're doing? Why aren't they being ... happy with them? *Es ist alles so alltäglich!*'

Alex stood with folded arms, watching Ella as she worked herself into a state.

'It's all so banal,' she said in a dejected voice, her face screwing up and about to break into tears.

'Alicia and the girls are busy doing the flowers,' countered Alex.

'Then they should have delegated the cooking to women in the village, who'd have been only too pleased to make a bit of money on the side. Why don't they think? What do we need all this food for, in any case? Far too much eating goes on in this house. Our whole life seems to turn on meals.' She caught her son's eye. 'Can't you say something? What's wrong with you?'

Remembering she disliked seeing him with folded arms – locking himself up and not speaking his mind, shutting her out, as Ella had said more than once – Alex unfolded his arms, surprised by the effort this cost him, and finally took a seat in the alcove at the window. There he was positioned in front of her. She could see and talk to him directly without having to address his reflection in the mirror, and he hoped the conversation between them would now flow more easily. Suppressing his growing impatience with his mother, he tried to say something conciliatory.

'Is your hip hurting?'

'The orthopaedist gave me an injection and some painkillers to see me through the day. I'm supposed to wear a harness – that monstrous thing on the bed there – to keep it from dislocating. It nearly did the other night. I tried it on but it didn't help at all.' She turned and looked at him. 'I'm so exhausted. If only I could sleep!'

Despite his irritation it distressed Alex to see his mother like this. He was conscious of the inadequacy of his sympathy.

'Claude told me what a bad night you had. That and Santana and the row with Philip ... one thing after another. It's been too much.'

Not finding the words of comfort he'd have liked to give Ella, he escaped into his own trivialities.

'I didn't have much of a night myself at Mirjana's place. We sat up very late talking. But she seemed preoccupied. I didn't feel I was getting through to her. She was wonderful when I saw her on the beach in the morning, but when I showed up at her apartment to spend the night there – she'd invited me, after all – her mood had changed. She was a bit, I don't know ... moody. Perhaps she was regretting she'd invited me.'

'Perhaps there's another man you don't know about.'

Ella was pulling a mauve band with a pattern of pink and blue flowers under the braid of hair and fixing it with snap-down buttons at the back of her head. Usually this was done so deftly he hardly noticed it, but he could see how this operation was now giving her difficulty. Alex waited for her to follow up the remark she'd thrown out, but Ella was already on another tack.

'I don't know why I'm going to the trouble of getting dressed when I've no intention of going out there,' she said irritably. 'Let the others have the party on my behalf.' She took a flannel off the dressing table to wipe the sweat off her face. 'All you seem to have on your mind is why you failed to get Mirjana into bed last night and how to manage it better next time.'

Diagnosed correctly by one of Ella's hunches, Alex remained silent until she goaded him again.

'If you're so preoccupied with Mirjana that you can't talk about anything else you needn't bother to stay.'

Alex picked up a cushion and hurled it across the room. 'All right then, since your argument with Philip is obviously the reason behind this wretched mood of yours, let's talk about it. I've only heard from Claude that you quarrelled with Philip; I don't know exactly what it was he said that upset you so much.'

Ella began dabbing cream at her face.

'I quarrelled with him? No, he quarrelled with me. He complained about having to listen all his life to what he called the same old *emotional moans*. Well, what have I ever moaned about? He said I was always wheeling out the refugee, not to mention all the things that happened to *those Jewish friends of yours* and the inadequate people it was my misfortune to have been lumbered with as children. So contemptuous! *You think you're the cat's whiskers, don't you?* he said. *George and Felicity and me and Max and the rest of us aren't good enough for you ... We know all about your ideas of making family a matter of choice rather than accepting whatever rubbish you get lumped with by your genes. Half of them are your genes, you do realise. It's half of you you're chucking out. It's yourself you're dissatisfied with. It's not what you see out there that's the problem, it's seeing it through the problem that's you.* That's exactly what he said.'

Alex didn't doubt it. As children they had all been at a disadvantage in their arguments with Ella because of her almost total recall of what they said.

'The whole thing was a tirade of hate. I know I can be trying at times, but if there's one thing I don't do, it's moan. I know my duty and I do it without complaining. Would you say I complain?'

'Not complain exactly. Sometimes you're just impossible.' You're moaning now, he thought.

'It's true I lost my temper with Philip. I now realise how much he must have hated me all his life.'

'That's just not true. If I were listening to Philip's side, I know I'd be getting a completely different story.'

Taking upon herself once again all the charges Philip had levelled at her and repeating them to Alex seemed to have an invigorating effect on Ella. Soaking up surplus cream with a tissue, she screwed it into a ball and chucked it into the waste-paper basket.

'So why should I show up at this wretched party if Philip's going to be there? It's a farce – worse, a humiliation.'

She got up, went to the closet and took out on a hanger a long mauve skirt with a subdued pink and blue flower pattern of the same material as her headband.

'Once I'm dressed, Alex, you and I can slip out the back way to avoid seeing anyone.' She appealed to him eagerly. 'We can go for a walk through the village and up into the woods. Have ourselves a secret day, just the two of us, like we used to do at Richmond in the park. What d'you think?'

Her face softening at the prospect of escape, Ella pulled up the skirt and fastened it at the back.

But you can't even walk, Alex wanted to say. 'We could,' he began cautiously, 'but it might be seen as running away, and that would be a triumph for Philip. Or he might regard it as such.'

He got up and held open the neck of the top she had chosen for Ella to slip her head through without disturbing her hair.

'One thing you must grant Philip is the right to feel as put out by you as you are by him.'

'Why must I grant him that?'

'Because then it's a mutual affair with mutual responsibility, and there's a better chance of both parties walking away without bitterness.'

Alex guided the two ends of the necklace together at the nape of her neck, holding them clear of the stray hairs there until the tug of the magnets snapped the clasp shut.

'Beyond the accident of you being mother and son, the two of you have very little in common that I can see. You and Philip might as well belong to different species. If you weren't his mother and he your son, you would have long since gone your separate ways. And even if people act as if there's a law forbidding parents from breaking off relations with their children, there's nothing unnatural about it.'

'But the other way round there's definitely no law. Children break off relations with their parents all the time. That's considered natural. Why aren't parents allowed to do the same?'

There was a knock at the door. It was Claude.

'Ella? Alex? Advance warning. The president will be arriving in a few minutes. You'd better come down.'

'Already? Isn't it rather early?'

'Well, it is. But now he's on his way there's nothing we can do about it.'

'Can't George give him a tour of the house or something?'

'George is tied up in the kitchen.'

'Then I suppose we'd better come,' said Ella without enthusiasm.

# 18

Although recently retired from the presidency of the cabildo – his third term had ended soon after Ella's resignation from the Department of the Environment – José Miguel Galván Bello had been so long in office that he conducted himself as if he still was. Now in his eighties, subject to lapses of memory he considered it beneath his dignity to acknowledge, Bello was a bald, bespectacled, stern-looking man with a professorial manner and a striking resemblance to Pope Pius XII. Had there been a reason for him to take to wearing a skullcap, his resemblance to the wartime pope seen wearing one in the portrait that hung prominently on the wall of his study would have been even more compelling.

Bello belonged to a caste of priestly men Claude had become very familiar with at the Jesuit lycée he had attended in Paris. He had an immediate understanding of this man and the nature of his vanity and how to turn it to his advantage. From the time when they became acquainted at the University of San Cristóbal de La Laguna, where the retired statesman was often called on to officiate as honorary chairman of a number of committees on which they both sat, Claude had instinctively manipulated Bello by constantly deferring to him. Impressed by Bello's success in getting budgets for higher education approved by the cabildo, committee members followed Claude's lead. Bello might not have been aware that Claude had initiated the practice – Claude might not have been aware of it himself – but a link between the youthful Professor de Marsay with his Jesuitical skill in swaying a committee and the agreeably deferential treatment he always accorded Bello was well established in the president's otherwise forgetful mind. Many things there might meanwhile have sunk into oblivion, but Claude wasn't one of them.

A second unforgotten link had been established with Ella. Although they had parted company in disagreement over the Playa Africana issue that prompted Ella's resignation, they remained on amicable terms. As the member of Bello's government in charge of environmental affairs for seven years, Ella had come to know the president well. The proximity of La Laguna to the capital made it more convenient for Claude to get into a car at short notice and drive to Santa Cruz than it was for George, who lived on the other side of the island in Arguayo looking after the grandchildren. So it was Claude rather than George who turned up as Ella's companion at receptions given by the cabildo in Santa Cruz. In Bello's mind the two of them were a couple.

Thus when the cavalcade of three cars needed to convey the former president to his lunch in Arguayo arrived at the gates of the house where Claude and Ella came out to greet their guest of honour, it was inevitable that Bello would take his host and hostess to be man and wife. Seizing enthusiastically on the children introduced to him in the courtyard – greeting children enthusiastically was a habit formed during Bello's years as a campaigning politician – he shook hands with them and made an effort to remember their names. He was under the impres-sion that these five teenagers all belonged to one fertile Catholic family.

He was particularly taken with the two elder girls. As the daughters of his host and hostess, both of whom still seemed absurdly young to Bello, naturally the girls would have grown up on the island – it never occurred to him they were anything but native Tinerfenos. That they might be grandchildren rather than children didn't cross his mind. From the bird's-eye view of a man approaching his eighty-third birthday – a statesman who had served three terms of office – the generations now queuing up in the world behind him had become impossible to tell apart. People fell into one of three general categories – children, adults and individuals his own age.

Nothing in the conversation that flowed at the table where Ella seated the president between her granddaughters, whose company the old man was so evidently enjoying, gave him cause to question any of these assumptions. Hard of hearing, refusing out of vanity to wear a hearing aid, Bello cupped his ear to follow what Kim was saying to him – it seemed to have something to do with the offshore currents in the bay of Puerto de Santiago, if he'd understood her correctly – the need to put signs up on the beach to warn unwary tourists, connected or possibly not connected with a school of dolphins she had seen sporting in the Gomera straits only the day before. The word *dolphins* fired off rows of synapses, reminding Bello to tell this attractive young woman about a bill to protect marine mammals that had been introduced during his term of office fifteen years ago, how well he and her mother had worked together on the environmental issues she'd done so much to advance as a member of his government. Kim had no idea what he was talking about, taking aboard without contradiction this *mother* for what should have been *grandmother*.

Bello was a man of fixed ideas and habits, which with advancing age and self-importance had become completely inflexible. When George, wearing the chef's regalia he so prided himself on, emerged sweaty-faced from the kitchen – platters balanced on the palm of either hand, suckling pig on one of them, marinated rabbit on the other, receiving a round of applause as he set them down on the table at which the presidential party was seated – he thought it polite to wipe his greasy fingers on his apron before shaking Bello's hand, and it was only natural the president assumed this greasy bearer of the platters to be the chef. Chefs played an important role in Bello's world. An early riser blessed with the appetite of a man half his age, he swam before breakfast at half past six – ate lunch at noon, followed by a siesta and a light supper before retiring early to bed. The world had to arrange itself around this schedule. This was why the presidential party, including a nephew, a niece, a private secretary and a chauffeur, had arrived half an hour earlier than the time stated on the invitations, leading to an unfortunate breach of protocol. Many of Ella's former colleagues, members of the Bello administration she had served in, reached the house half an hour later than their former chief. Some of these guests were still arriving as the old man was taking out his napkin and getting ready to eat. But it was already past two, and Ella saw that Bello wouldn't allow anything to intervene between himself and his food much longer.

By the time the latecomers, who had taken themselves off on a tour of the house, were assembled in the courtyard to hear the welcome address Ella intended to give before everyone sat down to lunch, it would be getting on for three and the president's lunch couldn't be delayed that long. She would have to save the speech for later and rang the bell as a sign to begin serving lunch. The guests ambling around the upstairs gallery between the belfry tower and the *portada sillería*, admiring the beauties of the seventeenth-century bishop's house, heard the bell ring and looked down into the courtyard to see food already in the process of being served. There was almost a stampede in the gallery as everyone hurried downstairs to take their place at the tables set up around the courtyard.

The tables had been so arranged as to leave triangular spaces in the corners through which the various courses would be served by Alicia and her girls. Ella, George, Claude and Alex would be so seated as to supervise operations in their respective corners, but when the guests descended in a rush from the gallery, they were busy with other things. Ella was the only one at her place, and so it was left to her to seat the new arrivals. Fortunately she had in her head a seating plan for her very mixed group of guests. Among them were local tradesmen, craftsmen who'd done work on the house, academics from La Laguna University, the Adeje postman, members of the cabildo of Tenerife, a dwarfish and extraordinarily hirsute family of whistlers from La Gomera, invited at Alex's request, not to mention the many old friends such as Eduardo and his wife Aurelia she'd not yet even had an opportunity to speak to — all these people had to be blended. By the time Ella had settled everyone alongside others she hoped they'd feel comfortable with, taking her place at the head of the table where the president was sitting, Bello was already moving on from the fish stew – having previously jumped the long queue of hors d'oeuvres – in his impatience to get to the heart of the meal, which for him was always the *carne de fiesta*. Where was the chef? The president wished to congratulate him personally.

George didn't reappear until halfway through the meal, having slipped away to change into more suitable clothes. He walked from table to table, ostensibly to make sure all his guests were enjoying their meal and had everything they wanted, actually in the hope of praise for the feat he'd carried off in providing such a variety of dishes for more than a hundred people. Delicious, they all assured him, but without his regalia they failed to establish a connection between George and the chef they'd seen bustling away in the background. Much the largest contingent of guests from La Laguna and Santa Cruz, made up of Claude's university friends and former professional colleagues of Ella's, had no idea who this man was. All the introductions that should have taken place during the half-hour allowed for people to get to know one another before sitting down to lunch had been curtailed by the premature arrival of the guest of honour.

Ella realised the proceedings had got off on the wrong foot but felt powerless to get them back on track. What was needed to interrupt the remorseless conveyor belt of food that had been set in motion by Alicia and her efficient team of helpers was a witty speech. She would have wished to give her guests something for their minds as well as their stomachs, to share with them reminiscences of some of those who were present, from the postman and the La Gomera whistlers to the members of the cabildo and the president and her five grandchildren, representing the variety she was aiming for when she invited people from such differ-ent backgrounds. She wanted to introduce a note of thoughtfulness into what she saw as degenerating into the banal routine of most parties, the mechanical provision of food and drink.

Claude wasn't the man to come up with such an address, however, and Alex was too inexperienced. George was the only one who was good at impromptu speeches. But George was so preoccupied with doing the rounds she wasn't able to catch his eye and confer with him about what she would have liked him to say. Ella was just reaching the conclusion that the only solution would be for her to give the speech when Bello pushed back his chair and got to his feet.

Bello wasn't a man to strike a glass with a spoon in order to attract attention; his eminence needed only to rise and be seen in order to command instant quiet. He stood looking sternly around the courtyard for a while, grew rather puzzled – what was he supposed to be doing here? – opening a fete? – something in connection with a birthday? Had he mistaken some birthday guests for a rebellious budget committee needing to be brought to heel? With increasing discomfort his audience waited for him to speak. Perhaps he was springing a surprise and soon the papal face would break into a beatific smile. But after a long silence during which he said nothing and the frown on his face deepened, it became clear to everybody that whatever the president had been intending to say when he got to his feet had meanwhile escaped him. The president continued to frown, aware that something had gone astray. Something had been mislaid, not necessarily through his fault – was this some sort of prank that was being played on him? With a look of indignation on his face he waited for what had been taken from him by the prankster to be given back. If he hadn't happened to glance down and catch sight of Ella signalling to Claude across the courtyard, it might have remained hidden where it had disappeared, but with this glance the link was established that brought him back to what it was he'd been intending to say.

Of course, of course! Here they were, his hostess and his host, with their charming children sitting around them! This family who had made their home on Tenerife and contributed so much to the island's life was the subject he'd stood up to address. He smiled. It was their achievements to which he wished to pay tribute – if only he could remember what those achievements were. Another long silence raised fears he might be having a relapse. Bello's secretary rescued the situation with a piece of paper he slipped into the president's hand. Bello looked with disdain at the list of underlined words. Of course! He didn't need reminding. He was off! The *dolphins* – they'd returned to the harbour of Santa Cruz after an absence of many years. The *eyesores* such as the urban landscape at Barranquera beach, the *development at Jardina* – cleaned up! The *open sewers* in San Roque and La Piterita – closed down! These were only a few of the improvements with which the island had been blessed, thanks to its first director of the environment under his administration. He burbled on.

Once astride his old political charger, there was no stopping him. Bello recalled Ella's early advocacy of landscape protection by bringing a higher percentage of the island under the trusteeship of the National Park. He praised her foresight in speaking out in favour of raising cus' toms and tariff barriers to reduce the invasion of the island by external fauna and flora that threatened the endemic species and with them one of the major tourist attractions on the islands. At the University of San Cristóbal de La Laguna her husband had done hardly less valuable work to integrate insular education policies into a larger European framework, a subject close to the president's own heart. He'd worked with Claude de Marsay at many committee meetings with the aim of putting an end to the isolation of their institutions of learning from the rest of the world. Claude's experience of the different educational systems of many coun' tries had been invaluable to the work of these committees.

'It's my very great pleasure,' Bello concluded, 'to be here on this occasion, giving me an opportunity to express my gratitude to Ella de Marsay and her husband Claude, and as a token of the appreciation of the cabildo of Tenerife in recognition of their service to present them with this gift.'

The president's secretary, who had been hovering in the background in readiness for this moment, came forward with a framed picture, much too small for the audience to be able to identify what it depicted even when Bello held it up for everyone to see. *What did he say?* It was a rare print of a map of the seven islands, explained Bello, raising his voice to make himself heard over the hubbub, from the early period of their colonisation by the Spanish during the sixteenth century. *Who?* Ella leaned across the table to kiss the president on either cheek as she received this two'edged gift, before passing it around the courtyard for her guests to take a closer look at it. *Did he say Morris or Marsay?* Watching her as she sat down again, Alex had the impression that if there'd been a hole in the ground in which his mother could have been swallowed up, she would have been grateful for it.

Another embarrassing scene occurred to him, played out only a few weeks before, here in the courtyard, on this very spot. It had met with the same awkward silence, broken here and there by a few people begin' ning to clap – an uncertain clapping that petered out a couple of times before pulling itself together and getting under way. That was when Claude had found it necessary to draw the attention of Ella's brothers and sisters'in'law to the similarity between himself and Alex in the Polaroid pictures Edward Winter had taken.

In the aftermath of Bello's unfortunate speech Alex wondered if anyone would get up and reply to it, taking the occasion to sort out names and relationships that once again had been misattributed. George or Claude were the obvious candidates for this initiative, but both chose to sit tight, passing over the incident in ways that characterised the differences between them: George laughing at his own jokes as he went around filling up people's glasses, Claude engaging the president in an academic discussion, oblivious to what everyone else in the courtyard seemed to be talking about. Perhaps his reticent father thought that having already taken a for-him-giant leap and spoken out to clear up such misunderstandings on one occasion, he could wash his hands of the matter. It was asking too much of him to expect him to start making a habit of it.

There had been a moment when Alex thought his mother would intervene, but that moment had passed. He saw his nieces and nephews in a huddle, giggling, while at another table Felicity and Philip sat side by side looking unamused, and he guessed that another row was brewing. But Bello's blunder, his identification of a non-existent Ella de Marsay, even if it hadn't quite hit the nail on the head, had nonetheless struck it a glancing blow. His mistake had a leering accuracy about it. It brought out into the open a question that at one time or another must have been in the minds of everyone present. It had shambled around in pursuit of Alex throughout his childhood and would have laid hands on him had he not managed to escape from the island.

Watching his mother hobble around the courtyard, talking to people who would be saying one thing to her and thinking another, Alex felt with extreme discomfort how exposed her position had become. He understood why Ella had always been of the opinion that men were cowards. And then something occurred to him. Now was the time for the diversion he had originally planned for later in the day – not the best move but better than none. Accordingly he went over and had a word with the family of whistlers from La Gomera. They were sitting at the end of a table in a corner, eating heartily but otherwise not involved or anxious to be involved in the party beyond the terms of their professional engagement. The mother and her son got up and went up separately into the gallery by the two staircases at either end of the courtyard while the father remained at the table. At a sign from Claude the father stood, put his fingers to his mouth and gave a whistle so piercing that everyone stopped talking. The silence of people expecting something to happen immediately settled on the courtyard.

'Thank you, thank you for your attention, everyone. For this demonstration of *silbo Gomero* I would be grateful if you could keep your voices down and refrain from reading aloud the words on these pieces of paper I shall be distributing, for that would give the game away and spoil the results of the little experiment we'll now be conducting for your entertainment.'

Walking from table to table, Alex handed out some sheets of paper.

'Here you have the list of ten questions I shall be asking Pedro to put to his wife and son in the *silbo Gomero*, and to translate for us their answers. The questions he'll be asking were unknown to them beforehand.'

He went back and stood beside the stout little man with a mop of curly grey hair and mischievous eyes. Alex had written each of the ten questions for Pedro on separate cards.

'Question one,' said Alex, handing Pedro the first card.

The first question on the list Alex had given out was what dishes had first been served at lunch. Pedro cupped his mouth and let out a series of differently pitched whistles, fluting with his index and middle finger. A swarthy boy of about fourteen leaned over the balcony of the *portada sillería* and whistled back.

'*Sancochado* and fish stew,' said Pedro, wiping his mouth with the back of his hand.

From the gallery under the belfry tower at the other end of the courtyard the woman put in a few swooping whistles reminiscent of the calls of a mynah bird.

'For my wife's taste, the *sancochado* could have done with more vinegar and hot peppers,' translated Pedro.

The audience laughed and clapped.

Alex sensed a release of the tension he had felt building around him.

'Question two,' he called out, handing Pedro the second card.

Noticing that George and Claude had taken advantage of the entertainment to slip into the house, Eduardo Rodriguez went after them. None of this escaped Philip's attention, and he followed the three of them inside.

# 19

George laughed.

'But it's a joke. Even if he is losing his marbles he remains our former president, a nice enough old chap, and it would be demeaning to correct him in front of everyone out there. You can't do that to an old man who's getting a bit senile. I was in agreement about that with the people who were in my corner of the yard. This isn't a tragic event. People have a sense of humour, you know. We had a chuckle about Ella de Marsay and drank a toast to your wife's health, Claude.' George raised his glass. 'Cheers. To Madame de Marsay. It may have diminished me a bit, but I think you've come out of it rather well. I can't understand what Eduardo's getting so worked up about.'

'It's a slur on Ella,' bristled Eduardo Rodriguez, angered by this display of levity, his protective instincts aroused. It was a slur on Ella and a slur on the house. The house had to respond, and the house was George. 'There are ways of handling this sort of thing without causing a fuss. I would do it myself. But because it's a slur on the honour of the man of the house, it can only be done by him.'

George couldn't believe his ears.

'What sort of talk is this? What century do you live in, Eduardo? You're a *scientist*, man. You're a freethinker and an atheist. You were brought up a communist, for Christ's sake — equal rights for men and women, and so on. If Ella feels offended — I haven't asked her, but I'd find it hard to believe she does — then as a modern woman it's up to her to say so. Women are in charge of their own honour these days. If she feels there's a misunderstanding here which needs to be cleared up, she's capable of doing so herself.'

'That's not how I see it at all,' said Eduardo.

'You're taking this thing much too seriously. Ignore it. Leave it to take care of itself and everyone will forget about it. If you draw it to people's attention, you'll only be encouraging gossip.'

'If it were my wife I'd want to speak out on her behalf,' said Philip. 'Of course one's got to get the record straight.'

'Well she's not your wife and this is none of your business,' retorted George, pouring himself another glass, 'nor mine, for that matter.' He laughed again. 'It's Claude's business. By all accounts, she's his wife.'

857

'You make a joke of it. This is dishonourable of you, George. Ella needs someone to look out for her.' Eduardo looked at Claude. 'But perhaps George is right. It's your name being bandied about. Perhaps under the circumstances it should be you. Don't you feel you have to say something on your own behalf?'

Claude was sitting on the sofa with crossed legs, one hand clasping his knee. 'Well,' he said, not looking at any of them, his head turned to one side as if trying to make out something on his shoulder, 'I'm not sure that this concerns anyone other than Ella, George and myself. It's a private matter. It's none of the business of any of the people out there.'

A flurry of whistles followed by laughter came in from the courtyard through the open door.

'But it's become their business, thanks to Bello's speech,' insisted Eduardo. 'You can't stick your head in the sand and pretend it didn't happen.'

'What concern of ours is Bello's speech?' Claude replied irritably. 'You call it a slur on Ella – how do you know it's a slur? Why should Ella being referred to as my wife be a *slur* on her? What entitles you to call it that? Why do people not asked for their opinion keep coming forward and thrusting it on us all the time? Do we presume on *them* in this way?'

'Well you do, as it happens.'

This unexpected intervention came from Philip. Claude was sitting with his back to him, and hadn't registered his presence in the room. He looked round in surprise.

'You'll have to explain that to me.'

'You presumed on me and Felicity from the moment you showed up in this family. You may have been invited but it was still a presumption. We weren't asked if you moving in suited us. You and George and Ella made up your mind that was the way it would be, and we had to lump it.'

'While we're on the subject, Philip,' said George, 'were we ever consulted when you decided to marry Ann?'

'That's not the same thing at all.'

'Shut up! Everyone please just shut up!' Claude put his hands over his ears. 'I object to our being called to give an account of ourselves – no, I do more than object,' continued Claude, his voice rising, 'I *forbid* it.

I'm sick of busybodies coming along and telling us what we can and can't do and how we should be living our lives.'

'Well, it's not quite like that,' Eduardo began.

'It's exactly like that! Philip coming in here thirty years on – thirty years on! – and giving us this nonsense about having been imposed on by a perfectly reasonable arrangement agreed on by three consenting adults. Or you, Eduardo, coming in here and taking us to task for not responding to what you have the effrontery to call *slurs*. Maybe Bello got it half right. Is it so unreasonable if for one part of the time there's an Ella de Marsay in this house and another part of the time an Ella Morris? Why is that a *slur*? Who's entitled to tell us we can't have both? What makes you think any of us would regard that as an *insult*?'

With an audible crack from his neck, Claude turned his head and looked at Philip.

'Wasn't Ella imposed on when the law required her to change her name from Andrzejewski to Morris? Or was Alex ever given any option to call himself by another name? Did anyone ever ask him if he preferred to grow up as Morris or de Marsay? Not that I can remember. Why should either of them have to go through life with names they didn't choose tacked arbitrarily onto them? Why should anyone be in a position to give them names branding them as belonging to him? Why should anyone have that right?'

'Well unfortunately that's the way things are,' said George. 'We all have names that have been tacked arbitrarily onto us. We all have to put up with it, and you're no exception.'

'Yes, I am. I may have started off as a de Marsay, but then I turned into a Gifford, and briefly a Gif*fort*, before I decided what name I felt I most resembled and reverted to de Marsay. I was given that choice by my uncle Louis. I admit there have been times in my life when people called me Morris, and I had to accept that, although it was against my wishes. I've had to live with Claude too, although as a boy in England I hated the name.'

'So what is it you want?'

'Everyone seems to agree that Bello made a mistake when he referred to Ella as Mrs de Marsay. But from my point of view, or from Ella's, that wasn't necessarily a *mistake*. It's an *option* she should be *entitled* to and which people ought to recognise. There are times when I've seen in Ella a greater likeness to Ella de Marsay than to Ella Morris, times when it's impossible to think of her as anyone but Ella Andrzejewski.' Claude paused. 'She is several women and she has several names.'

'Meaning you don't see any need to object?' Eduardo took his hands out of his pockets and pushed himself off the bookcase against which he'd been leaning.

'Of course not!'

Claude scowled. 'As George said right at the beginning of this wholly superfluous discussion, it's a ridiculous idea. What do you propose – going out there and distributing handbills or something?'

'I think both of you just don't have the balls,' said Eduardo. 'I'd always thought that British reserve was a mark of a gentleman, but now I've learned it's a mark of a coward.'

Eduardo left and Philip went with him, evidently satisfied to have had his point made for him.

George looked with interest at the patterns on the carpet, as if something there had caught his eye. 'Perhaps, from his point of view, he's right.'

'No, he's not,' said Claude. 'Those show-off things are easy to do. Putting up with them and not forcing the issue is what requires character.' He put an arm around George's shoulders and they followed Eduardo out into the courtyard.

# 20

'Carbon molecules could be used to construct a shaft of infinite lightness and tensile strength thirty or forty kilometres high, to boost payloads on an elevator shuttle ascending and descending within the slender molecular well connecting the earth with the stratosphere.'

'Right, and this system could dispense with conventional rockets to service a permanently manned space station for carrying out projects such as the construction of sun reflectors made of millions of crystals. The reflectors would be transported in small parts up the carbon elevator shaft and assembled in space. The sunlight deflected by this giant crystal screen and prevented from entering the atmosphere could reduce the temperature on the surface of the earth to pre-greenhouse levels.'

'Well, I don't know ... Carbon molecules could be used, you say, but tell us a bit more about just how that would be done.'

In the university corner of the yard the liveliest group at the party was having fun playing the collapse⁄of⁄civilisation⁄and⁄how⁄to⁄avert⁄it game. Ella's former colleagues from the Ecology Institute – biochemist Julio, marine biologist Domingo, the mathematician Agrippina, two lab assistants Inma and Conchita – with whom she had worked on the endemic species project ten years previously, sat at two tables. The team had since been augmented by a systems analyst and a postgraduate physicist. They'd all been in their mid⁄thirties when Alex got to know them as a teenager on his trips to Laguna to visit his father.

In those days Alex used to feel like a shop assistant participating in a board meeting, overwhelmed by the brain power around him. More than a decade had since passed. The group that Alex remembered as young was now middle⁄aged, but they could still give him that feeling. Now an academic teaching at a university himself, but a mere historian, he still felt humble in the company of scientists. He and Mirjana sat together at one corner of the table, trying to catch the projectiles whizzing back and forth. To solve the problems that had come into the world with technology, the scientists believed in still more technology. Applying technology to improve conditions in a natural environment hostile to growth or even to life at all had been so successful, Santana had said, that civilisations evolved around the principle of fighting against limits rather than learning to live with them.

Rival ideas were being batted back and forth by Julio and the physi⁄cist, who was called Carlos. You could launch cocktails of chemicals into the atmosphere from high⁄flying aircraft, said Julio, setting off chain reactions causing clouds to drop their rain. This was already a well⁄established procedure in the Soviet Union to guarantee fine weather in Moscow for the few hours of the May Day parade. Nothing groundbreaking about that, apparently, even if Alex had never heard of it. Carlos elaborated a newer variant of the same idea that involved a fleet of vessels, self⁄piloted drones, roving the oceans and injecting vast volumes of water vapour into the sky, creating an effect similar to the transpiration rising from tropical forests, which served to keep the planet cool by creating a sunshade of white reflecting clouds. And other miracles of technology, extremely sophisticated, extremely expensive, but feasible – at least according to Carlos.

Domingo took pleasure in shooting down the young physicist's more extreme flights of fancy. He thought the exclusion of sunlight from the atmosphere would more likely come from a nuclear winter than sun reflectors riding up carbon elevators. The fallout after nuclear explosions around the globe, or even just a few Pinatubo-type volcanic eruptions would reduce sunlight more efficiently than anything. Even if you mitigated the worst of the greenhouse effects, you were still left with any number of other potential wipe-out scenarios jeopardising life on earth: another ice age, for example, was predicted, which would put the planet back into the freezer some time within the next few tens of thousands of years.

'But we don't need to resort to science-fiction scenarios. It's all much closer than that. From the point of view of a marine biologist, the toxins that have got into the food chain in the oceans are ignored only because people are unaware of the nature of the problem. Plastics are the problem. The world's plastic trash collects in vast whirlpool systems in all the oceans, and it can't be broken down by bacteria. These virtually indestructible pellets floating in the sea are mistaken for plankton by fish and mammals and enter the marine food chain and eventually the human metabolism. Samples of mid-Atlantic seawater I've taken show the plankton–plastic pellet ratio to be of the order 1:10. Ten times more plastic than plankton is ingested by feeding creatures in the sea. Even if you stopped plastic production tomorrow, not to mention other industrial pollutants like heavy metals, that toxicity is not going to be reduced in the foreseeable future.'

How did Domingo think ordinary people would be living a couple of hundred years from now? Mirjana wondered. She wanted to tie all this down to fundamentals, things she could hold on to, basics that didn't change.

'Basics do change.'

'The need for housing, clothing and food hasn't changed. It's much the same now as it was hundreds of years ago. Why shouldn't it be hundreds of years from now, even if you might no longer want to eat anything that came out of the sea?'

'Anything that came out of *anywhere*.'

The megalopolis was the model of the future, said Agrippina, who'd done studies of urban conglomerations for tens of millions of inhabitants along the seaboards of China, Japan, south-east Asia, India, the east and west coasts of America. 'Maybe three quarters of the world's population will be living within fifty miles of the sea by the year 2010, increasingly reliant on a diet of seafood that will itself be reliant on Domingo's plastic-plankton diet.'

Eduardo, who had gone off for a few minutes but now returned, thought that shortages of water and energy in the future would also have an impact on the lives of people.

'They may have to accept infringements of their private space. When people look back at the privacy taken for granted in our times it will astonish them no less than the vast amounts of energy we consumed for completely trivial purposes. A premium on resources makes it conceivable we'll go to the sort of habitat design common in the Soviet Union – single-room units for individual use with cooking and washing facilities shared by all residents. Throw in sophisticated surveillance technology, and you're on your way to losing privacy altogether. Probably a decline in the cooking of food generally, the gradual obsolescence of kitchens in favour of airline-type convenience food heated in microwave ovens – to come back to your question, Mirjana. Also unisex clothing made of disposable materials that don't need washing, which wouldn't worry me, saving water and pollution by detergents, which I wouldn't mind either.'

'A loss of privacy – and beauty. No one seems to have noticed that we have less and less use for beauty now.'

This remark from George startled Alex. Arriving with bottles of red and white wine, he went around the table filling up glasses. As George stood beside Eduardo, Alex noticed how Eduardo placed a hand on the small of his back and patted him. What was that about?

Alex felt his knee warmed by Mirjana's under the table as he watched Claude and Ella standing under the *portada sillería* saying goodbye to the presidential party. In the courtyard the shadows lengthened. Something flitted past that left him sad. A new game started at the table as they began putting a list of one-liners together. The louder the suggestion was shouted, the better its chance of getting onto the list.

Dominance of global standards! Disappearance of localities, of the notion of place itself! Synchronisation! The end of individualism! Unprofitable areas of the world reduced to aboriginal reserves! Pay-as-you-go sanctuaries of primitivism preserved as tourist attractions! The rift between rich societies with technology and poor societies without it growing wider! The global player as the new tourist! Tourism infecting diversity with the bacillus of sameness! Tourism as the new imperialism! Tourism as cancer! Down with tourism!

Philip came up behind Alex. 'What's so wrong with tourism?'

'Watch out! Denis!'

A tennis ball landed on the table, bounced once and plopped into the bowl of punch in front of George.

'Hole in one!' exclaimed George with a grin, wiping punch from his face. 'What are the odds on that, Agrippina?'

Denis came over to the table. 'Sorry about that, Gramps.'

Someone said the paintings were twenty thousand years old and asked what artefacts of our present civilisation on earth were likely to survive that far into the future.

'What paintings?' George handed the ball absent-mindedly to Eduardo, who gave it back to Denis.

The appearance of the ball in the bowl of punch had an irresistible knock-on effect. Once Carlos had seen the ball he had to have it, so Denis tossed it to him across the table. Carlos took aim at Conchita as if about to hurl the ball at her, then lobbed it for her to catch. Conchita stretched up for the ball, missed it and had to duck under the table to retrieve it.

'Something conserved in mud or ice. A skeleton.'

'A skeleton's not an artefact.'

Conchita passed the ball to Inma; Carlos clapped his hands and she threw it back to him.

'Spacecraft debris in orbit.'

'That's not on earth.'

'All right then, plastic pellets drifting for all time on eddies around atolls in the south seas.'

'The atolls will have gone before them,' remarked Claude on his way across the courtyard, prompted by a memory flash of islands in the South Pacific – Henderson and Pitcairn, volcanic drops that had one day congealed in the ocean and would one day disappear back into it.

'Discarded oxygen tanks on Everest.'

'Is this a quiz?'

'Where's Ella?' wondered Claude.

The tennis ball bounced obliquely off the *portada sillería*. Kim caught it on the rebound and passed to Denis. Denis threw it scuttling in an arc across the roof and it plopped down from the belfry tower into

Darren's hands. Darren threw it across the adjacent roof. Carlos caught it, lobbing it onto the next roof, and so on around all the courtyard roofs. The game of roof ball started with the Laguna table and spread to the others. The objective of the game was something self-constituted, so natural that no one had to ask. You threw the ball to make it come off the roof at an unexpected angle, and whoever missed a catch was out of the game.

'Well...'

'Think Lascaux. Think underground. Something buried deep in the protective bowels of the earth.'

'Do you have the answer to this or are you just leading us on?'

Someone crashed into the table.

'Either we move the table or continue the conversation elsewhere.'

The three last debaters got up and carried table and benches into the middle of the courtyard.

Domingo took off his jacket, getting ready to join the game.

'A final repository for atomic waste,' said Julio, rolling up his shirt-sleeves as well. 'A midden built to last for a hundred thousand years.'

'Ah.'

'The barrels are stored in a chamber at a depth of a kilometre in-side —' he caught the ball and sent it curling up around a chimney '— the bedrock. A treasure chamber, if you like, a tomb. Our pharaoh is buried here with his radioactive jewels. Copper, uranium, plutonium. A sacred place. The entrance is sealed with thousands of tons of concrete, the site marked with signs in a hundred languages, and in case these are no longer spoken, pictograms warning anyone who happens by to keep away from this place for ever.'

The knot of people around him broke up and scattered into the ball game. It continued fast and furious into the fading light until it got so dark that George had to go inside to switch the floodlights on.

# 21

'George? Is that you?'

'Yes.'

'Could you give me a hand? This loo is so low I'm having trouble getting up.'

Ella was sitting in the dark with the door open. George put a hand under one of her armpits and hoisted her to her feet.

'We'll have to replace it with a higher one. Ideally, replace all of them, but I don't think we can afford it.'

'Perhaps not all,' George answered. 'A house really doesn't need *four* high lavatories, does it? If we replaced one upstairs and one downstairs, that would do it, wouldn't it?'

She switched on the light over the basin mirror. 'We're running out of towels. There are some more on the top shelf in the cupboard. Could you reach up and hand me down a few … No, the others. The white ones.'

Ella stacked the towels, with the fold out, on the sideboard by the basin and followed George down the passage into the summer kitchen. The wind had got up, scattering around the house fugitive jangles of the wind chime that hung above the door to the terrace.

'Is it going all right, do you think?'

'It seems to be. Thank God we've seen the last of Bello. I hope you weren't upset by anything he said.'

'You mean his getting names mixed up? He does that all the time. What does it matter? No, it didn't worry me. Did it you?'

'Not in the least. But Claude got rather agitated after Eduardo said Bello had cast a slur on your name and it was our duty to set the record straight.'

'Slur? What slur?'

'When he called you Ella de Marsay.'

'Set the record straight? Did Eduardo say that? What on earth was he talking about, I wonder?'

Noticing a loose corner of tablecloth flickering in the wind, she went outside to secure it. Whoever had been sitting there had gone inside leaving plates and glasses on the table, cigarette butts on the floor, the chairs and cushions in disarray. Unable to restrain herself, Ella began clearing up.

George saw that she'd already forgotten about the so-called slur. He went into the kitchen to fetch a tray. 'Alicia should have done all this before she left.'

'We can't depend on her for everything. She does so much as it is.' Ella put the things on the tray and sat down. 'Alicia and Paco are getting older too. How are we going to manage this place soon?'

George joined her on the trapeze sofa and with a creak they swung out into the night. Ella loved to swing. Put on a swing, she reverted to childhood. It relieved her of the responsibility for getting on with her life. Playing truant with George on the swing, they momentarily became conspirators. At the highest point of the arc they could see over the tops of the cypress trees. Lights on the island of La Gomera became visible in the background.

'You managed it all so well.'

'Managed what well?'

'All the cooking, decorating the tables, the flowers in the vases every-where ... you did it all so well. I couldn't have done it better myself. I was given lots of compliments and passed them on to you. No, no, it wasn't me, I said. George did all of this. So thank him.'

'I couldn't have done it without Claude's help. And all the others who were in the kitchen ... really.'

'Did anyone comment?'

'One or two. Aurelia. And Bello's niece, oddly.'

'Did you know that Aurelia and Eduardo have separated?'

'No, I didn't. Did she tell you herself?'

'She moved to Las Palmas two years ago. Two years! And Eduardo never even mentioned it to me.' Ella bit on her knuckle. 'How little one knows what's going on inside a person. Eduardo seemed happy having all his colleagues around him here, but without the institute in his life ... It must be lonely for him at home. His daughter lives in Argentina. His son disappeared to India years ago, Aurelia said. They've no idea where he is. They don't even know if he's alive.'

'We don't know much more about Max. We don't really know what goes on in our children's lives. My parents certainly didn't know what went on in mine, or I what went on in theirs, for that matter. Other people are mainly in the dark. Particularly those closest to one, don't you think? We get by on expectations and assumptions. But we don't really *know*. Are Felicity and Philip having a good time? Are the grandchildren enjoying themselves? Our guests? You just asked me yourself if I thought it was going all right. Well, like you, I assume so. What's the alternative to having reasonable expectations about reality? You expect to keep on finding it recognisable. You expect to find it tomorrow more or less as it was yesterday. But listening to what people around me have been saying this evening, I realise that their expectations are different from mine.

My reality has been overtaken and become obsolete. Old-fashioned is a friendlier word. All of a sudden you see this and realise how far you've drifted, how isolated you've become on your island.'

The swing slowed. Ella took his hand as they rocked, surprised to find how moist it was.

'And maybe Eduardo enjoys being on his own,' George said defiantly, as if challenging Ella to contradict him.

'My guess is that he and Inma will get together.'

'Really? And Alex and Mirjana – did you notice them?'

'No, missed them, but I did spot Kim and Denis snogging on the gallery in view of everyone down in the courtyard. That was a bit ... heavy, I thought. They are, after all, first cousins.'

'We should have invited a few more people their own age.'

Ella withdrew her hand from his, touched him on the forehead and put her hand on his chest.

'Are you feeling all right? You're not feverish, are you?'

'Feverish? What gives you that idea?'

'Your hand is damp. So is your chest. You're hot and sweating all over.'

'All that running around, I expect.'

'Perhaps *you* were upset by that slip of Bello's. Were you?'

'No. The three of us have our position on this. We stand above these things.'

'I had a conversation with Kim.'

'Oh?' George waited for Ella to follow up, but she didn't. 'What was the conversation about?'

'She's leaving school this summer and doesn't know what to do with herself. Anything as long as it gets her away from home. So I suggested she continue with the course she started here, and qualify as a professional diver.'

'A diver? You mean a *sea* diver?'

'What else?'

'Well, there are frogmen who retrieve bodies from rivers, that sort of thing.'

'I suppose it would qualify her to do that as well.'

'How long would it take?'

'A couple of years. I said we could help with the fees. And she would live here for free.'

'How would she get around?'

'We could get her a moped.'

'I suppose so.'

'You don't sound enthusiastic. I thought Kim was your favourite of the four grandchildren.'

'Well, in a way she is, but ... do you think it's a good idea for a young girl to be stuck up here on a mountain with no one her own age? Where does that lead? Snogging with her cousin. I think she's better off in London in ... the thick of things. She can do a course there.'

'But getting her away from home is what it's all about. That's what she wants – to get out into the world.'

From George's silence Ella could tell he wasn't enthusiastic about this scheme, but she felt bound by her promise to Kim.

'It's only until she qualifies. Then she can find a job anywhere she wants, and that's her dream. We can help her fulfil it.'

'All right. You do as you like. Would you mind stopping the swing? It's making me feel sick.'

Ella brought it to a standstill. 'Maybe you had a bit too much to drink.'

'Maybe I did.'

'I'll get you something to fix it.'

She went into the house.

Peculiar sensations were burrowing around inside George, not exactly pain but general discomfort all over – an unpleasant tingling in his feet, queasiness, pressure in his head.

Ella came back with a glass of liver salts. 'When did you last go to the doctor for a check-up?'

'I don't know ... a year ago, perhaps two.'

'You should see that cardiologist in Puerto de la Cruz. Perhaps your medication needs to be reviewed.'

Ella sat down and took his hand again. 'You seem preoccupied. Did something annoy you?'

'No, no.'

'Perhaps you took on too much. Perhaps it was more of a strain than you realised.'

'I don't know ... We all enjoyed ourselves in the kitchen.'

These were the conversations Ella had had with George all their married life. What was going on inside him, what he really thought, if he *had* thoughts or even took an interest in what she was talking about, it was often impossible for her to make out. *Other people are mainly in the dark*, he'd just said, *particularly those closest to one*. Ella couldn't even say for sure if it was George she was talking to or a shadow or an avatar of George, someone who could take on his likeness, someone else sitting beside her whom she'd never really known.


# 22


The party was still in full swing when Alex and Mirjana left at midnight intending to drive back to her apartment in Puerto de Santiago. In a few hours he had to be at the airport to catch his flight to Vienna. But as they walked through the *portada sillería* and saw the landscape under the light of the full moon they changed their minds.

They stood on the edge of a mysterious white stillness. It was too marvellous a night to waste indoors. The wind that had got up a couple of hours before had since lain down again and blown itself to sleep. Moonlight more like a deep frost than an illumination had settled on the mountains rolling away above them. Transformed by the full moon, the milky ocean lay poured out below, spilling languidly over the horizon.

Without an answer to the unasked question, apparently in agreement, they set off in the same direction, passing through scattered buildings on the outskirts of the village to the edge of the wood where the farmland ended. Effortlessly the path led up the mountain. In half-darkness beneath the trees Alex's sharpened sense of smell caught the scents of late spring breaking out in riot around them. Moist and heavy, dark dewy scents clung to the air. The dark and the dew seemed to draw the scents out, soaking the night.

They came out of the forest and followed a track across the mountain. Before the track went down into a hollow where it crossed a *barranco* they reached a shelter where during the heat of the day forest workers would rest in the shade. Alex had discovered the hut as a boy in the course of his explorations when he first came to the island. As a boy, in love with his teacher during his last term at the British school in Puerto de la Cruz, he used to lie with his clothes off on a cool slab of stone inside it, imagining she was lying naked beside him. He could have told her that now, but he wanted Mirjana to know without him having to tell her. Why speak? What need of speech? He was reluctant to speak, and it seemed she didn't want to either.

Alex used to see the little hut at the same moment he saw the mountain. On the far side of the ravine, at the end of the mountain range that ran across the middle of the island, El Teide suddenly flew up, a white bird on the wing, rustled out of a covert in the woods. However often he had seen this spectacle, his heart was caught unprepared. It had no choice but to soar with it. Detached from the shadows that swirled around its base, the snow-white mountain top left the earth behind it. To Alex it was a moment from the beginning of creation. At one percussive stroke the earth seemed to be made anew. To him the sound was bold and strong. But to her the peak appeared like a fugitive picked out by a searchlight, turned out of the fleece of clouds in which it had hidden, exposed by the moonlight in an empty night sky.

Mirjana was beginning to feel the cold. She shivered. He draped his jacket over her shoulders. Still without a word exchanged between them, Mirjana took his hand as they walked back down the mountain.

They got into her car and drove to Puerto de Santiago. As he followed her up the steps from the promenade to the apartment house on the seafront Alex felt that their silence became artificial, a game they were playing out of stubbornness. But the longer they waited, the harder it was to find words. Whatever he said would be banal, topple the balance, break the spell. There were no words for the rush in his blood, no time left in which to say them. Shutting the front door of her apartment, Mirjana was already clawing at his shirt, then gave up the attempt to unbutton it and pulled him into a room where the light from a lamp on the seafront spilled across a big white-sheeted bed. She ripped the shirt off him while he slipped the straps down over her shoulders, wriggled out of her dress as she pulled down his trousers, losing her balance with him as he fell, crashing down together onto the bed.

# 23

George's reluctance to go to bed made him the natural candidate for seeing that everything was locked up last thing at night. Two or three o'clock — recently it had been even later when he did his rounds.

At half past one he saw the last guests out of the house, locking the gate behind them. Was he locking out or locking in? He could hear movements in the loft over the gateway. 'Anyone up there?' He got no answer. The grandchildren, no doubt. As he crossed the courtyard to the other side of the house he again saw Kim, it seemed physically before him, swirling her dress, a spiral of patterns twisting as she turned on her heel when she stalked out of the kitchen that morning. But it was Claude who now came out of the kitchen. He was carrying a hot water bottle. George asked him if he'd like to share a joint with him in his study. Claude declined.

While still in the kitchen Claude had heard George's voice outside, talking to someone in the yard, but there was no sign of anyone when he came out and ran into him on his way across the yard, passing up George's invitation to join him in his study for a joint. Before they said goodnight, he gave George Ella's message to switch off the boiler in the basement. Claude continued up the tower stairs to the first landing, where the gallery led in both directions to rooms on opposite sides of the house. He was about to continue on up the stairs to Ella's room in the old belfry tower when he heard a door close and saw two figures retreating at the far end of the gallery in the direction of the *portada sillería*. They must have come out of the room directly above the kitchen. Just as the figures disappeared into the loft over the gateway, a door opened on the opposite side of the gallery. Philip came out in a pair of luminous white shorts.

'What the hell's going on out there? Denis? Darren? What's all this running up and down the gallery, for Christ's sake. Stay up as long as you like but just keep the volume down, will you – let the rest of us get some sleep.'

Claude saw the door close again before he went on up the stairs. The door to Ella's room stood ajar. She was sitting half undressed on the bed, still attempting to unbuckle the harness strapped round her waist to support her hip, which had been giving her discomfort all evening. She was supposed not to wear it at night but she couldn't take the thing off or put it on without help.

'What was all that about?'

'Philip, asking the boys to be quiet.'

'I thought I heard George's voice.'

'That was before. He spoke to me as I was coming out of the kitchen.'

'No, not before, after.'

'Let me help you with that.'

George was woken by the crash of the urn falling from the *portada sillería*, even if his mind reversed the order of events, persuading him he was already awake when he heard the sound that woke him. He surfaced with the familiar sense of something missing, something he had left behind him in his sleep – no idea of what it might be. Waking up to this sense of something missing was the reason why he felt reluctant to go to bed at night. Had he dropped off for a few minutes? An hour? The clock on his desk said three o'clock. There had been a tobacco pouch on the table by the chair. Where had it gone? What was he doing asleep in his study? He retraced the steps that had led him there. After seeing off the last of the guests and locking the gate, he had come back into the courtyard and said goodnight to Claude, who was on his way to bed. That must have been around two o'clock. Then he'd walked across the courtyard and gone into his study to smoke the joint he'd been looking forward to all evening but abstained from until the grandchildren were no longer around. An added pleasure – if only Gábor could have been around to see him! – was smoking the joint in his father's armchair from his study in the Hampstead house. It was the one piece of furniture George had brought out from England. Sitting in the chair while smoking pot was a defiance of his father but also the only occasion when George had fond memories of him. Why hadn't they spoken with each other more?

Then he must have fallen asleep.

Sitting in the courtyard until after midnight, Ella had got cold. She'd forgotten to take out a cushion to warm her chair. After seeing Alex and Mirjana off at the gate, she went to the loo. Peeing was painful. She recognised the familiar symptoms of the bladder infections she picked up so easily these days. Fortunately George came in and helped her up off the loo. That was when she'd last spoken with him. She hadn't mentioned the bladder pain. Claude went down to make her a hot-water bottle to put on her stomach. She switched off the bathroom light and went back into the bedroom. She noticed light streaming out into the courtyard – the kitchen light must still be on. It ought to be switched off, but perhaps George was still up. She decided it wasn't necessary for her to trek downstairs, not at two o'clock in the morning, and she went to bed.

Darren tiptoed up the staircase from the courtyard, where he'd done a recce to see who was still around. The urn falling off the post and shattering below had made a hell of a racket. His brother had been chasing Kim around the loft when she knocked it off its pedestal. Jesus, what a din! God help them if it woke his father up! Kim and Denis disappeared down the gallery and didn't come back. Liz and Darren waited and held their breath. But no one came out. The coast was clear. Darren went down again to do the dare. Gramps was still up but fast asleep in his armchair. Darren slipped into his study. Liz had dared him to nick George's tobacco pouch. CAPSTAN CUT it said on the outside – as if they didn't know what was in it! Grinning, he took it out of his pocket and waved it in her face.

'Took it off the table beside him. Carried on snoring, didn't notice a thing. Dare you to put it back without him noticing, Liz.'

Darren took a packet of cigarette papers out of the pouch and began rolling a bazooka.

The noise of the urn shattering reached Ella through her earplugs in the first deep phase of sleep, hauling her back to the surface. Her first thought was George. Getting up she went to the window and looked down into the courtyard. From the window in the belfry tower she saw the shattered urn in the light streaming out of the kitchen door. Still on? Why was the door open? Were there people still up?

Woken by the noise, missing something he couldn't quite place, George dragged himself wearily out into the courtyard to find out what had happened. He thought he heard stifled laughter upstairs, feet scuttling along the gallery overhead. A door closed softly somewhere.

'Hello? Anyone there?'

It was one of the acoustic tricks of the courtyard that noises ricocheted off the walls, making it difficult to pinpoint where they originated, but he could guess who was likely to be on the prowl at this time of the night. In the drawing room, looking at pictures with Aurelia and Eduardo earlier in the evening, he had heard the floorboards creaking as the four cousins crept in and out of their rooms – the boys into the girls' and the girls into the boys' rooms. But who with whom? While seeing the last guests out at the gate George heard whispering from the loft over the *portada sillería*. He stood straining to make out the whispers, nothing he could hear distinctly, nothing he could pin down, flibbertigibbet rumours open to interpretation. It was all in the imagination – but how much was all? The boy's arm round her waist, his hand on her buttocks, George had seen that clearly enough – but his fingers, where, exactly, had they been? What the hell was going on in this house? George walked into the middle of the courtyard and turned around slowly, looking up at the gallery.

'Hello? Anyone there?'

Something scrunched underfoot. He bent and picked it up. It was a piece of pottery. In the moonlight he saw much bigger, shockingly big fragments of one of the Moroccan urns that had shattered on the ground. It must have fallen from the corner post of the *portada sillería* where the girls had installed it that morning. George remembered thinking at the time that the pedestal on top of the post was a precarious place to put such a cumbersome, potentially lethal object. Imagine if someone had happened to be walking underneath it – himself, for instance, doing his lock-up round last thing at night. He picked his way cautiously through the shards to fetch a broom out of the kitchen cupboard.

Hearing a cry of agony, a dreadful cry – dear God! was that George's voice? – a cry torn out like a piece of the agonised gullet in which the fish hook had caught, Ella got out of bed and limped to the window. Light from the open kitchen door was still streaming out into the courtyard but there was no one to be seen. Ignoring the harness she was supposed to put on, she took her stick and laboriously made her way down the stairs.

'That'll be how it begins! I'll have to move down to the ground floor! How will we manage this house?'

The door to George's room on one side of the stairwell stood open. She saw the empty bed.

'Oh no!'

Softly she opened the door of the room on the other side of the stairwell where Claude lay asleep, clucking her tongue, the sound with which she had always woken Claude.

Claude rolled over and propped himself up on one elbow. 'What is it?'

'Something's happened to George. I'm afraid to go and look by myself. I want you to come with me.' She began to sob.

Claude got up and put his arms around her. 'Are you sure? How do you know something's happened to him?'

'I heard the most awful cry outside – he'd swallowed a fish hook – it was being torn out of him!'

'Swallowed a fish hook?'

'It was George's voice! I could feel it in my throat!'

Claude looked at the clock on his bedside table and switched off the alarm set for seven. It was four o'clock.

'Let's go and see. Or would you like me to go ahead?'

Ella nodded.

'You stay here. I'll be right back.'

As he took the broom out of the cupboard in the corner George could hear whispers, but they were so faint he couldn't make sense of them. *Guessed one of us* – was that what the whisper said or what he'd heard it say? Whose voice was it? The vaulted ceiling in the oldest part of the house was up to its tricks again. If he moved nearer the middle of the kitchen, and the people were talking in normal voices, he'd be able to hear every word they said. But not if they *shh!* whispered. Kim and Liz would know that, not necessarily the boys. *If you hadn't pushed me. What're you doing?* Laughter. Laughter couldn't be whispered. There was no mistaking Kim's laugh, which he knew so well. *Don't you like it?* She laughed again. *Shouldn't have put in the first place.* Put in? First place?

Claude couldn't find his slippers. He ran downstairs in his bare feet. When he went outside the first thing he saw in the light streaming from the open kitchen door were fragments of the shattered urn. He had to watch where he stepped so that he didn't cut his feet. Claude picked his way cautiously through the wreckage until he was able to look inside.

Broom in hand, transfixed, George stood in the middle of the kitchen, straining to make sense of these whispered scraps filtered down to him via the soundbox. *Ever had a girl suck?* He was attuned to Kim's whisper. How many of Kim's whispers had sought comfort in his ear? During their time together here, when Kim was little, he had learned to make sense of the babble of sounds she breathed into his ear. *Max, I expect.* That was her! *Someone take off comes without bra?* That was him. *Take off – shh!* Was Kim taking precautions or did she know someone was listening down in the kitchen? *Down before? Gone all away?* Was she doing one of her performances? Could she be doing it for him? *God, you're beautiful!* It felt as if someone snapped a wire around his neck and pulled it tight. He put his hands up to wrench away the wire that was throttling him, no use for beauty now, something missing – a white-hot bolt illuminated everything, seared through his darkening brain.

George lay face down on the ground with his arms stretched out, his fingertips just short of the threshold of the kitchen door, his head twisted a little to one side. Claude had to get down on his knees for a closer look at his face. The one visible eye was open, staring at the floor. Claude could see tiny contractions of a muscle in his cheek. He took George's wrist, felt for his pulse but was unable to find it.

'George?'

A slight working at the corner of his mouth seemed to indicate that George was still alive. A leakage of air, a sort of hissing was audible. It seemed he was trying to speak. Claude bent over him, his ear to his lips, to catch what he said, but the hissing had stopped. He couldn't hear anything. Claude got to his feet, picked up the telephone and called the emergency number. When he put down the phone he heard the hissing again, more like a whisper now. As he walked towards the door he located the sound. It was coming from overhead. So the house ghost was up to its tricks again! Someone in the room upstairs was whispering and the sound was amplified by the soundbox in the ceiling. He remembered that Kim and Liz had been put in there. Were they awake? Should he go up and see? If they'd heard George cry out, they'd have come down to find out what had happened. No need to wake them. He would ask in the morning. There were more urgent things to be done now. He went back upstairs to tell Ella that George was alive. Didn't look like a heart attack – more like a convulsion – poleaxed – by the look of it he'd had a stroke – but was still responding – if they acted quickly enough there was still a good chance of him coming through. As Claude phrased it to Ella now, *a good chance of him coming through* sounded a lot more favourable than was justified by his assessment of the situation he had found downstairs.

'They said the ambulance will be coming up from one of the resorts on the south coast, probably Playa de las Americas. That might take twenty minutes to half an hour. It was four o'clock when you woke me. What time was it when you heard George cry out?'

'About a quarter to.'

'So at least an hour will have passed before anything can be done for him.'

Ella shrank inside her dressing gown. 'Will that be too late?'

Claude took her other arm and helped her downstairs. Once they were in the courtyard, he went ahead to brush the debris out of the way so that Ella could get into the kitchen unhindered. George had apparently been about to do that himself; the broom was lying beside him. Ella appeared in the doorway and looked down at him.

'My poor George!'

She took a couple of steps and stood over him. Claude helped her. She wanted to kneel down beside George's body but was unable to. Claude brought a chair for her to sit on so that she could at least lean forward and touch him. Sitting on the chair was the closest she could get.

'Don't you think you should turn him on his back?'

'It might be dangerous to move him.'

'How can he breathe with his head down on the floor like that? Help him!'

Claude got down on the floor, took George by the shoulder and turned him until he was almost face up. The arm George was lying on made it difficult to roll him all the way over. Claude held his head in his hands to prevent it from lolling back over. Ella touched George's dark red cheek with her hand.

'Look at the colour of his face!'

Purplish veins stood out on his forehead, as if he were making an immense effort. White bubbles had formed on his lips. A slight contraction of the muscles was visible, tugging around the corners of his mouth. It seemed to Ella that George registered her presence. The rigid stare of his eyes relaxed as he got her into focus and she guessed she had entered his awareness. George looked up at her, his lips working as if he wanted to tell her something.

'It might be better if you waited out on the road, so that when the ambulance people reach the village, they'll immediately know which house it is,' Ella said.

But as soon as Claude let go of George's head, it rolled back to one side and Ella lost sight of his face. Claude had to move the chair again so that she could sit over him and hold his head in her hands, her forehead almost touching his when she bent forward. George was staring directly up at her, his face suddenly and mysteriously transformed, blood-gorged and ruddy, the complexion of an American Indian. She registered tiny spasms passing through his body, but the contact she had briefly established with George when Claude had held his head had now gone. It seemed he no longer recognised her. She was no longer in his gaze.

'I'm here! Look at me! George! I'm here!'

In her throat she felt the wrench a fish must feel when the hook caught in its gullet. The scream remained stuck in her throat. Suspended from the hook, unable to move, she lost all sense of the passage of time until she heard the ambulance driving at speed into the courtyard and pulling up with an abrupt thud, the same abruptness of sound she had heard in the cry when George was felled. His eyeballs rolled to the side; she was afraid his head would too, if she let go. A man in a white anorak carrying a case hurried into the kitchen with Claude. Two stretcher bearers followed. Ella let go of George's head when the doctor knelt by her chair, his hand under the patient's head as he quizzed the pupils of his eyes with a beam of light from what looked like a silver pencil.

'When did this happen?'

'Forty minutes ago?'

'He was lying like this when you found him?'

'He was lying face down.'

'You turned him over?'

'His nose was on the floor. He couldn't breathe properly. Wasn't that the right thing to do?'

The doctor didn't answer. He was busy giving George an injection, putting an oxygen mask over his nose and mouth, attaching a drip feed to the needle he had taped to the back of George's hand, holding up the flask as his two assistants moved George onto the stretcher, carried it out into the yard and slotted it on rails into the ambulance carriage.

'I shall be attending the patient on our way to Santa Cruz.'

'Is it a stroke? Will he come through?'

'There's a chance. We'll do our best. There's room for one passenger, if you want to come.'

The stretcher bearers had to lift Ella into the seat at the back of the ambulance. Claude wondered if he should dash upstairs to fetch the harness Ella should have been wearing for her hip, but there was no longer time. The doors at the back had been closed, the driver and his assistant got in at the front and the ambulance was already racing off on the road down to Adeje.

# 24

Tilting the hand cupping Mirjana's breast so that his wristwatch caught the light from the window, Alex saw that it was already five o'clock, time for them to get moving if he was to catch his plane.

'Mirjana,' he whispered, 'are you awake?'

'Mmm ...' She rolled over, raising her other arm, briefly revealing, before she let the arm fall across his chest, the little horse spreading its wings in the hollow there. Regretting the tattoo, she was reluctant to let him see it when she was awake. 'Is it already time to go?'

He nibbled her ear. A warm scent of sleep stirred up by her body as she turned over in bed drifted up towards him. He remembered it from her often late appearance for lessons first thing in the mornings, the tall sensual woman teacher with the tousled auburn hair and an absent-minded, almost surprised air, who looked as if she'd just been got out of bed in a hurry, still trailing the intimate scents of sleep into the schoolroom.

'You could fly us there on your horse.'

'What?'

Disengaging himself gently from her arm, he kissed her on the lips and got out of bed. Outlines of an apartment he had hitherto seen only in the dark emerged in the shadowy dawn light, suggesting rather than showing an alcove or perhaps a cupboard, a clothes stand that might have been a chair. A figure at the end of the corridor turned out at close range to be a raincoat on a hanger. He went into the bathroom and switched on the light, wondering about the raincoat. Raincoats were never worn on the island. How much more intimacy there was to a bathroom than a bedroom – sitting on the toilet, surveying the bottles, jars, brushes, combs, the inventory of equipment women kept there, Alex felt he was taking unfair advantage of her privacy, somehow a breach of trust. He splashed his face with cold water at the basin and turned out the light.

As he came out of the bathroom he heard someone cough in the room at the end of the corridor where the coat was hanging. The door stood ajar. A light was on in this room which had not been on when he went into the bathroom. Through the half-open door Alex glimpsed the end of a bed and a pair of feet – large white feet, a man's feet. Startled by the presence of this man he hadn't known was in the apartment, Alex made his way back to Mirjana's bedroom. She stood at the window, arms raised, drawing her hair into a knot.

'I didn't know you had a visitor.'

'Oh, is he up already?' She sounded uninterested. 'Did you bump into him?'

'No, but he's awake. The light was on in his room.'

Mirjana came over, put her arms around Alex and kissed him.

'I wish you'd told me before.'

'His being here needn't concern you.'

'It does.'

'Don't let it worry you.'

'No?'

'No. You're not jealous, are you?' She sat on the bed and pulled Alex down. 'All right. It's my ex-husband. We got divorced years ago. He showed up here the day before you came. No warning. Just turned up out of the blue. He's lost his job, doesn't know what to do, where to go. So he came here. I've given him a roof over his head. He needs time to get himself sorted out. So, there you have it.' She saw he wasn't reassured. 'Don't you believe me?'

'I do, but … is it his car you've been driving?'

'Car? What's the car got to do with it?' Mirjana laughed. 'Don't look so miserable! I'm not hiding anything from you.' She kissed him. 'If you're so interested in the car, he hired it at the airport and drove here without even calling to find out if I was in. He just rang the bell and there he was. I found him standing on the doorstep.'

She put her hand down and found his penis standing.

'Oh! Someone's up bright and early!' She took it between her fingers. 'Does that excite you?'

881

'Yes, it does.'

'I know *that* does. But does my ex-husband being here turn you on, knowing he's just down the corridor?' She fell back on the bed, lifting her thighs and guiding his penis. 'Fuck me, darling! Quickly! Fuck me hard!'

Seconds later they came together.

Hurriedly she pulled on shorts and a T-shirt, Alex stuffed his few things into a bag, they tiptoed out of the apartment and ran down the steps to the car park on the seafront, laughing at their own exuberance, the brilliance of the day lighting up around them.

'How long have we got?' she asked.

'Half an hour.'

'We'll make it!'

'You'll have to step on it.'

'I will! *Now* I know what you meant – I'll fly you there!'

As they got into the car she pulled up her T-shirt to show him the winged horse under her armpit, and Alex covered it with kisses. In the blue and white brilliance of the morning they flew down the empty road between Puerto de Santiago and Playa de San Juan before disappearing into the shadow cast by El Teide in the east. The mountain bulwark intervened between the sun now coming up over Africa and the western end of the island, leaving a long swathe dimmed in shadow. The coastal road running dead straight on a north–south axis veered east at Playa de San Juan, twisting left and right through the bends outside the little town before pulling out onto another long straight. The car was doing a hundred kilometres an hour as it approached the intersection where they would turn east onto the motorway around the southern tip of the island.

As they came out of the last bend before the junction into the full blaze of the sun rising over the coastal plain the windscreen went white. Blinded, Mirjana hit the brake pedal full on, heard the wailing siren but couldn't place where it was coming from, and went straight into the ambulance coming very fast down the Guía de Isora road to her left. According to the police reconstruction of the accident, the ambulance slammed broadside into the little car and rolled it over, then slewed back across the road, where it was hit by an oncoming car. Apart from the three vehicles converging at the Adeje junction at that early hour on the Whitsun morning, there was no other traffic on the road. Several minutes would pass before the next car reached the intersection and the driver alerted the local police, a further half-hour before ambulances arrived on the scene of the first of several accidents with fatal casualties that would occur on the island in the course of the Whitsun holiday.

# CHAPTER FOUR

⸺

# Awakenings

## 1

He was in a garish purple-lit place, struggling up out of a burning vault, his skin on fire, entangled in violently coloured toxic plants that clung to him as he tried again to escape before succumbing and going under.

Later there was whiteness, blank, still, bordered with uncertainties as to where it led; later again, in the obscurity of what appeared to be a room, something to be feared along the perimeter. He slid in and out of this image, fell over the edge, in and out of consciousness, out of exteriority and back into interiority with no notion of having been in a place that included himself. It was the first thing about his condition that seemed familiar. This kind of dislocation occurred under the influence of drugs, hallucinogenic substances he might have taken. In an absence of interiority, absence of self, distributed as he was throughout the exteriority, at one with the white room and all its shadows as if at one with himself, not separate from these, both the viewer and what was in the view, he looked across snowy wastes that gradually took shape as rows of bare-sheeted beds stretching to the border of a country in the far north.

Whether or not he should be admitted to this place was the subject of an interminable whispered discussion between two border guards in a glass hut in the obscurity at the end of the room. One of them came over to where he was lying. He wore a white uniform with something hanging around his neck which he put into his ears and pressed against his chest.

'He's awake,' he said.

'Then we can take him over,' said the other man, still in the glass hut.

'Over the border?' asked another voice, apparently his own.

'You could put it like that.'

The guard smiled down at him, patted his hand and walked away.

Intermittently there were brief awakenings in other places, brief dialogues with other people, the nurse removing the catheter, telling him to leave his penis alone when he kept taking hold of it to see if the catheter was still attached, the view of the same expanse of blue he had lain looking at for so long in a state of such pain, then a window through which he had that view, the pillow under his head, the bed on which he was lying in a hospital room.

He sat up, swung his legs encased in baggy white pyjamas over the side of the bed, and stood up. His feet skidded away and he landed painfully on the floor on his back.

Later the nurse was back with one of the white-uniformed guards, who had now turned into a doctor.

'How are you feeling?'

'All right.'

'We put railings up around the bed to prevent you from getting out and doing yourself an injury.'

'Why would I do that?'

The marvellously refreshing quality of new-mown sleep, trailing scents, a sweet heaviness that drew him down, haymaking down the hill in a soft light – briefly illuminated scenes emerged and disappeared again into the darkness.

Again someone was sitting beside his bed.

'How are you, Alex?'

'Fine. Sleeping a lot. Must be pretty tired.'

'Would you like me to bring you anything to read?'

He tried to work out the view from the window, where he was, what was going on. There were four other men on the ward. He listened to them talk, joining in from time to time, asking them questions without giving away how little he knew, and this information helped to put him back into the picture he'd fallen out of. The little old man to his left in the corner had a heart complaint. He sat all day on the side of his bed, wheezing, his face creased with pain. The three other men laughed and joked most of the time. There didn't seem to be anything wrong with them. They must have been put there to keep him and the sick old man company.

Hospital routine gave him something to hang on to. They woke him and washed him, brought meals on a tray to his bed. Every morning the same doctor came in and asked him to wiggle his toes, and he did so to the doctor's satisfaction, and there was satisfaction for him too in being able to do that. He began to take an interest in his legs, smooth and white in the bulging plaster casts he had mistaken for baggy white pyjamas. The casts were slit from the top of his thighs to the middle of his shins and the slits taped to keep the casts in place. The soles were plastered over the heel of the cast and bandaged towards the front of the foot, almost good enough for skating, only he wasn't allowed to get up.

'Not for another seven or eight weeks. It depends on how the callus forms,' explained the breezy doctor for whom he wiggled his toes in the surgery where they wheeled his bed.

'The callus is still soft. It can still be manipulated, and it will hurt, but we're going to have to do that with the left leg because it's wrongly aligned. Normally we'd keep it in position with a pin, but that requires an operation, and in your circumstances that would be too much of a risk. So we'll set the leg using a more conservative method, twisting it back into position, which we can safely do during the next couple of weeks while the callus that's forming around the fractures is still supple enough to make this possible.'

They did so twice in the surgery, two strong men, one of them holding his knee, the other twisting his leg by main force, causing him a rocketing pain that fortunately passed the moment they left off. Both legs were recased in skin-tight plaster. Looking down at matchstick legs incredibly thin and fragile in their still-wet white casing, he shivered with the cold that was creeping into him. One false step — how vulnerable he'd become, how easy it would be to snap off these spindly legs! He lost any desire to get out of bed.

Occasionally he felt unease about the things he should be getting on with instead of lying in hospital waiting for his legs to mend, but then he fell asleep and forgot about it.

Another doctor came in and asked him questions he had much more difficulty with than wiggling his toes. Asked to give his address, he wondered for which country and couldn't say for sure. Didn't he have any number of addresses in as many countries? Had he known the upshot of the conversation between the border guards as to whether to admit him to the country in the far north, he might have been able to get his bearings.

Later the same doctor came back accompanied by a thin wiry individual with a crooked, chapped mouth and a sunburned face. 'I've brought someone along to talk to you. Maybe your conversations will trigger associations that help to bring your memory back.' He was wearing a burnous. He looked like an Arab goat herder and he talked like an American. This man spoke very familiarly with Alex, as if they were old friends, although Alex had no recollection of having met him before. The doctor asked him if he had any recollection of the accident and Alex said no, and the doctor said that was their impression at the hospital too. In order to combat the embolism – a clot that had entered his bloodstream at the time of the multiple fractures of both legs and which a couple of hours after the accident had reached his brain, causing him to pass into the coma in which he had remained for the better part of a week – as a last resort the anaesthetist had experimented with a hallucinogenic drug. It wasn't yet on the market because its effects hadn't been sufficiently tested. Parts of his brain might have suffered damage. It was conceivable his memory might have been impaired.

The American in the burnous looked into the ward for an hour or two every other day. Often Alex was asleep and woke up to find him sitting on the chair by the bed. He didn't mind the man coming, but he found the conversations with him very tiring. Sometimes he dropped off in the middle of them. This didn't matter, as the conversations with the man in the burnous were often monologues. He told Alex about a fellow he knew – his brother, it turned out – and the gist of this monologue was his brother's life story. Names of places and people kept on recurring, and when they did the man in the burnous would stop and footnote the references right away. Remember him? Where we met him before? No? He would brief Alex as often as necessary, repeating anecdotes until Alex got the hang of the story and felt confident enough to make contributions to it himself.

During the first couple of weeks in hospital Alex was asleep most of the time, surfacing for intervals of an hour or two, during which he felt wonderfully refreshed. He wanted nothing. He was at peace. As he emerged from this state of pathological tiredness he slept less, remaining brilliantly and then dully awake for longer periods. Self-awareness began to grow back into those areas of his mind hitherto anaesthetised by the balm of sleep. He felt the departure of sleep as a glacial withdrawal, uncovering the rubble of the moraine it left, the raw wound that was himself. Fragmentarily his shot-apart mind began to be restored to him. A recognisable whole failed to congeal, however. He was a shredded sail through which the wind whistled, failing to carry him forward.

'You're making progress, Pooky. About time. You didn't recognise me when I first came in,' said Max.

'I did,' he lied. 'The thing you were wearing confused me.'

'The burnous?'

'What do you wear a burnous for?'

'Lots of people living in Tangiers do. The hoods are kind of neat. Burnouses are cool.' He laid a newspaper on the bed as he got up to leave. 'Claude came in to see you, and you didn't recognise him either. He asked me to give you this paper. There's an article in it about Yugoslavia he said he thought might interest you.'

Regaining possession of himself was a tedious process of investiture Alex underwent reluctantly. Accoutrements such as Pooky, the nickname he'd been given by Max, supposedly shoring up his identity, were handed over to him. Garments with an unfamiliar smell he was told were his were draped over him. It seemed he was obliged to want to have them and to acknowledge them as belonging to him – things he was supposed to take an interest in. Officially, he was Alex Morris, as stated on the name card at the end of the bed, but he felt like an impostor. As long as he failed to fill out this person from within, he remained just a dummy.

The *Daily Telegraph* left by Max carried a piece reporting on the rise of a new Serb nationalist politician. A speech recently given by Slobodan Milošević at the national congress of the Yugoslav Communist Party supplied evidence of Serbia's old territorial ambitions, held in check by Tito during his lifetime, having begun to emerge again since the leader's death, the paper said.

Alex read the article, conscious of an obligation to take an interest in it. That interest didn't ignite, however, nor did any other. He went through the motions of reclaiming what apparently belonged to him but failed to take possession of it. He remained the dummy in the bed, his name on it the only proof that he was its occupant. The dummy didn't come back to life, like so many other people he could think of who had died.

The event horizon around the accident extended on one side to a walk in the moonlight, and the white wastes of the border country to the north on the other. A week remained missing.

Max had flown in from Tangiers a couple of days after the accident. Either Max didn't know the details that interested Alex or he was pretending he didn't – reluctant, Alex suspected, to tell him things that would hurt him. But one afternoon a policeman turned up on the ward and began asking him questions. Did he have any idea what speed the car was doing when it approached the junction with the coastal road? Why hadn't the driver braked earlier? Hadn't she seen the ambulance approaching from the left? Alex couldn't remember anything, but he made an effort to appear to do so, weaving in suppositions of his own, giving the policeman an opportunity to endorse or contradict them.

'I would have thought it must have been pretty fast.'

The policeman crossed himself. 'It's a miracle you got out in one piece.'

'How is she?'

The policeman gave him an odd look. 'As I say, it's a miracle you survived. A shocking accident. As for the driver, she was a friend of yours, I gather?'

'We want to get married as soon as I'm out of this place.'

The policeman shook his head. 'I just wish for both your sakes that she hadn't been driving so fast. By now you'll no doubt have heard the details.'

'Yes.'

'As I say, a terrible business, but it was the involvement of an ambulance that makes it a particular tragedy.'

The policeman left a newspaper on the bedside table. Alex didn't look at it until he had gone. It was a back issue dating from early June, the whole of one page devoted to the accident. According to the police report, on collision with the car the stretcher with the patient's body strapped to it in the rear of the ambulance had torn loose from its rails and hurtled forward into the partition separating the back of the ambulance from the driver's cab. The resulting injuries allowed only a tentative verdict about the stroke the patient had previously suffered. He might still have been alive at the time of the accident, but even if he had reached the hospital intact it was impossible to say if he would have survived. Three dead, three seriously injured. There was a box with a picture of one of the men in the salvage crew who had retrieved the driver's body from the wreckage. They had had to cut the side of the car open to get the woman out. Her head was missing, taken clean off. It was only after they'd straightened out the pieces that they found it lying on the back seat.

The paper didn't give the names of any of the persons involved. Alex felt extreme discomfort, knowing that they must be known to him, but despite all his efforts he was unable to remember them.

# 2

In mid-July, seven weeks after the accident, a contraption was wheeled onto the ward. It was a three-sided cage on wheels. Entering the open side and supporting his weight on the horizontal bars, Alex tiptoed up and down the corridor for ten minutes before folding down the side seat to rest. He was discouraged by the effort and pain that this first attempt at walking cost him, despite having carried the weight of his body almost entirely on his arms as instructed by the physiotherapist. A week later he was taken in a wheelchair to have plaster soles fitted to his bandaged feet, and when these had dried he was given crutches to make his own way back to the ward.

During the first week of learning to walk again with the help of the cage, Alex met his father in the corridor on his way to visit him. Claude had been given leave by the university on Tenerife for the remainder of the term so that he could visit Ella in hospital on the neighbouring island of Gran Canaria. Dealing with four emergency casualties at one time had been too much for the resources of the hospital in Santa Cruz. The two who were most seriously injured, Ella and the driver of the ambulance, were taken by helicopter to the much larger hospital in Las Palmas with the best medical facilities available on the islands. Ella survived, but the driver died there the following day.

Bulletins on the state of his mother's health were passed to Alex by Max, who got them from Claude. Hurled around in the back of the ambulance when it overturned, Ella and the doctor who was attending George had both sustained multiple injuries. The doctor, who was ap-parently not seated at the moment of the impact, died at the site of the accident. The paramedic in the front and Ella owed their survival to their seat belts. Ella had suffered head wounds and a broken collarbone; several ribs were crushed, doing damage to the lungs; both hips were fractured and the thigh bone of the leg that had required a hip replacement earlier that year was also broken. Put into an artificial coma for the critical weeks after the accident, she had to lie in bed with both legs in traction, completely immobilised. Two months later Claude felt her condition was sufficiently stable for him to return to Tenerife and catch up with neglected business there while Max took over at Ella's bedside in Las Palmas.

Alex wondered at the necessity of this personal attendance on a private ward in a first-rate hospital.

'She's brave and doesn't complain. But having company takes her mind off the traction, and traction is torture.'

'What is traction?'

'You drill a hole through the shin bone just below the knee, put a bolt through it and attach weights to it on cords that hang over the end of the bed, to stretch the leg and keep it from growing back crooked. She can do nothing for herself. There are all these things she needs on the table beside the bed, but reaching over to get them is impossible.'

'What sort of things?' Alex asked without interest, feeling obliged to keep the conversation going.

'Well, where to begin ... You know your mother ... There's a jar with ointment for her dry lips, which she needs every half-hour, other jars with other ointments for bedsores, moist sanitary towels, tissue papers, earplugs ... lozenges ... rubber bands, tweezers, clips, different pairs of glasses, different cushions to help keep her comfortable ... I don't know, dozens of little things, all of them apparently essential to her well-being. A laundry ticket on a safety pin. I don't know why holding it comforts her, but it does. Not to mention all the toilet articles she would keep in the bathroom if she were able to get out of bed. Are they all necessary? With Ella it seems they are.'

' "The Princess and the Pea"?'

' "The Princess and the Pea". Well done! Seems your memory is coming back. You'll soon be as good as new.'

He watched his father cry and wondered why, if he would soon be as good as new.

'Everything seems to get to her, as you know. Her sense of smell, eyesight, sense of hearing, but it goes beyond that. I don't know ... Air pressure. Coming rain. Extrasensory perceptions. She knows what I'm thinking. It all registers with her.'

At the beginning of August the Santa Cruz police released the body of George Morris for burial. On account of the hot summer weather the service in Arguayo was held two days later, at too short notice for his son and daughter in England to be able to attend, as they would later complain to Ella, but they had gone abroad on holiday without leaving a forwarding address, and Claude had been unable to reach them in time.

It had been George's wish to be buried in the local graveyard. Alex was given leave of absence from the hospital in order to attend the funeral on crutches. Claude picked him up and drove him to Arguayo.

The enclosure stood on an isolated spot outside the village. Paco, Alicia, some of their children and all the neighbours who had been friends of the deceased were waiting outside the gates when they arrived. Claude pointed them out to Alex and reminded him who they all were. George had wanted his place in the wall, as he used to refer to it, but had expressed the wish to be buried without benefit of religion. Realising the offence it would cause inside the community that had taken George into its midst and regarded him as one of their own if he were buried in the village graveyard without any rites, Claude overruled George's wish and worked out a compromise with the priest from Santiago del Teide responsible for the Arguayo parish.

A short coffin stood on trestles facing an aperture about a metre above the ground in the graveyard wall into which it would be slotted when the ceremony was over. Alex found it hard to believe that George could have fitted into the truncated casket, let alone that the space in the wall would be big enough for it. What chance would a taller man have? Preoccupied with technicalities of this nature rather than with the funeral service itself, Alex waited for the ceremony to be over in order to watch how the men waiting by the trestles would manage the business of getting the casket into the wall. It turned out to give them no difficulty at all. Once the coffin and the aperture had been lined up with the help of wedges, which the men hammered in to give the necessary few inches of leverage, the coffin was inserted and the wall niche sealed with a thick pane of glass held in place with putty. The men were already putting the finishing touches to their handiwork before the mourners had left the graveyard.

Alex found it hard to accept that they would now all just walk off and leave George in the wall, the coffin in which he was lying visible through the glass – it seemed to him an embarrassment flagging the mourners back, an oversight, a shirt-tail hanging out of the dead man's trousers that still needed to be tucked in. To walk away as if ignoring that the coffin was still in view, the body in effect left to decompose in public, denied the privacy of concealment, this incompleteness of burial customs on the island had always seemed barbaric to Alex.

Perhaps it now struck him as particularly cruel because this was the first time it had been brought home to him by the death of someone close to him, and worse, by a dearth of feelings at precisely the moment he had expected to be moved. Aware of the inadequacy of his sorrow, Alex saw himself let down by his incapacity for grief, which could only be a measure of his selfishness. This callousness depressed him. Mirjana's death remained something abstract too, to which no feelings attached, nothing. Was it the banality of the funeral that had dulled him, George slotted into the wall, abandoned by those men with their putty fingers in altogether too insouciant a manner, as if the immuring of the deceased were merely a matter of getting their workmanship right? Nothing about the funeral left Alex with the impression that it mattered that George had died or that anybody particularly missed him. His death remained incomplete – the business of George, in a more general sense, had somehow been left unfinished – like Mirjana, just mysteriously gone.

Alex was discharged from hospital at the end of an unusually hot August. After three months the hated casts, which had begun to itch intolerably, were finally removed. When the pretty young nurse on duty peeled back the plaster to expose his skinny white legs, a revolting stench of sweat-caked unwashed rotting skin rose into his nostrils, presumably into the nurse's as well. Alex apologised and tried to make a joke of it. I'm here to do whatever's needed, the girl stated simply, washing and bandaging his legs before he returned to the ward to pack his things. The patients on the ward congratulated him on his new limbs and wished him more congenial company than four snoring men at night. Lucky dog; he'd no doubt already got a girl lined up. The friendly banter distressed Alex.

He noticed the corner was empty where the old man with heart trouble usually sat on his bed. He'd been wheeled out during the night and not come back. Before Alex left, a new patient arrived to take the old man's place. Someone else would soon come to take his own. Alex went to wait for his father at the hospital entrance, but Claude had meanwhile returned to Gran Canaria. It was Max who picked Alex up and drove him back to Arguayo. He'd thoughtfully made up a bed for his brother in George's study, so that he wouldn't have to climb any stairs.

<h1 style="text-align:center">3</h1>

From her hospital bed in Las Palmas Ella decided that with George's death the flat in La Orotava should be refurbished and put on the market for long-term rent. Otherwise they couldn't afford to keep the place. Claude entrusted to Max the removal of all personal effects from the apartment, most of them George's. Things worth keeping would be stored in Arguayo and Ella drew up a list of them, what object and what room or even in what cupboard or chest of drawers it was to be found. She had by heart a complete inventory of the moveable property in the apartment. Everything else was to be thrown out.

Alex offered to help Max with the job. The brothers shut up the Arguayo property and, for the week the rented skip stood on the waste ground opposite the house, moved into the La Orotava apartment at the top of the narrow cobbled street overlooking the old colonial town. Alex found his former bedroom dark and uninviting. The squat antique Spanish furniture he had enlisted as heavy battalions in the games he used to play there as a boy seemed oppressive now. Over the past decade the flat had been lived in by George alone. Some new admixture to the atmosphere of the house obscured its previous quality, or perhaps it was the withdrawal of whatever Ella had contributed when she had still lived there on a regular basis. It wasn't quite a smell of cheap perfume that hung in the rooms but something like it, a tawdriness he didn't remember having been there before. Alex left the windows open all week to give the place a thorough airing.

He started on the books in George's study, a miscellany with a bias towards historical and political subjects unusual for the number of languages represented. Alex had forgotten about George's background in Hungarian, German and Serbo-Croat, and he came across a number of titles relevant to his own studies. It struck him that none of these books had been published within the last twenty years. George must have lost interest in keeping up with the area after his resignation from the Foreign Office. Books of general intellectual interest dated even further back. Psychology stopped with Freud and Havelock Ellis, philosophy with Ayer and Russell. Only the genres of crime and spy fiction were represented by authors published in the 1980s. The complete Fleming oeuvre was there, naturally, and a handful of his followers in the 1970s.

In the deep shelves behind the fiction stood a second row of books hidden by the first, slim green volumes with titles like *The English Governess*, *A Bedroom Education*, *Pleasure and Punishment*, all of them printed in Montmartre in the 1950s and 1960s, a dozen authored by George Smythe, George's pen name. The once-celebrated writer of spy fiction whose works stood at the front of the bookshelf, covered up and was presumably intended to keep out of sight the eponymous author of dirty books lurking behind. Alex didn't know about this second string to Smythe's bow. Did anyone in the family? He took a handful of them through to the kitchen, where Max was clearing out the cupboards.

'Did you know about George's other career as a writer of DBs?' He handed Max *The English Governess*.

Standing on a stepladder, Max flipped through the book, lingering over a few passages before he handed the book back to his brother and turned on a cockney accent. 'It's the old *spanking* lark, innit.' He laughed. 'No, I didn't. But I'm not surprised. Our father, or rather mine, to be fair to you, was a lifelong porn addict. He had a cupboard full of the stuff at our house in St John's Wood. It gave me my initiation into sex when I was seven. I shut myself in the cupboard and wanked. At least went through the motions of doing so.'

He put his hand to his eyes and swayed. Alex grasped him by the legs.

'Hey! Steady! Are you all right?'

Max got off the stepladder and sat down shakily.

'I've been having these turns – you know, dizzy. They soon pass off. They're accompanied by this image I've been seeing all my life – not for years now, but recently he's come back – a figure in red on his way into a tunnel. Perhaps not even that. Perhaps just a sort of – what's the word, I first heard about it from a pal of Claude – Rorschach blot, behind my eyes, and the figure is what I make of it. I used to see the man in red a lot when I was a kid. Then he disappeared and I forgot

895

about him. He returned during a heavy trip I was on in Tangiers, and since then he shows up whenever I have one of these turns.'

'How often is that?'

'I don't know ... couple of times a year?'

'Have you seen a doctor?'

Max cackled. 'If I started seeing doctors about all the things wrong with me, Pooky, I'd die of worry within a month. I don't want to know about it.'

They broke off for lunch in the dark-beamed room with the glassed-in alcove looking north-west to El Teide. Missing its surplice of snow, the sparkling peak, which was usually so well turned out, looked under-dressed, as Max remarked.

'Could you imagine actually living here, Pooky?'

'You're forgetting, I did live here for ten years.'

'Yeah, but you were a kid and this was home.'

'I wouldn't mind. If I had a job teaching at the university, say, like Claude.'

'University? Here on the island? Who in the offshore world knows there's a university on Tenerife?'

'I don't mind. I'm not ambitious.'

'I'd want out. Living in a place that reminded me of my parents all the time would totally depress me. I'd go nuts.'

When he was finished with the kitchen, Max pulled down the stepladder into the attic to make room for the things they wanted to leave in storage up there while the flat was let. Alex spent the afternoon ordering the books and putting them in boxes. He made several trips down to the street with crates of rejected books and tipped them into the skip. Among the rubbish there he noticed plastic bags bulging with video cassettes.

'What's on those videos you've thrown out?' he called up to Max, who was rummaging in the attic.

'Oh, mostly crap, TV series, home movies George made. There's nothing much worth keeping. I've been through it all and kept anything that might conceivably be of interest to the grandchildren some day.'

When the apartment had been cleared, Max flew back to Tangiers and Alex caught a plane for the short hop over to Gran Canaria to visit his mother in hospital before returning to Austria for the new academic year, due to commence the following month.

He found Ella looking thin and hollow-eyed. The red flecks on the balls of her cheekbones, a filament of sweat on her upper lip, the way her glance darted restlessly from one thing to another, betrayed the hectic excitement Alex was familiar with when his mother was under stress. But he'd never seen stress illustrated so literally as by the traction machine in which she was still incarcerated. Fourteen weeks she'd been lying stretched out like this, with no end in sight because the callus was taking so long to rebuild. Her resources of stoicism seemed undiminished, however. Without ever having read any of Schopenhauer's aphorisms, she provided a living example of their application. It was a compulsion of Ella's always to imagine the opposite of any situation she happened to find herself in, as responsive to absent but readily imaginable pangs in times of contentment as she was to cheerful prospects at a time of misfortune.

There was a bright side to all this, she told Alex, taking comfort from the fact that she'd lost a lot of weight – something stranger than comfort, judging by the relish with which she began itemising even more dreadful fates that might have befallen her – she might have lost a leg – she might have lost her teeth – she might have landed up in a wheelchair. There was a white scar across the side of her head where the wound had been stitched, the hair not yet regrown, but the smaller cuts on her face had healed well. The collarbone cast had been removed the previous week, and the broken ribs no longer caused her such pain when she breathed.

Claude had been gone for two weeks. Ella was starved of human nourishment. She held her son's hand, she drank in his presence, every detail that passed his lips. She asked for exhaustive descriptions of his own months in hospital, George's funeral, the flowers that had been done by Alicia, what Alicia and her daughters had worn, his impressions of Max, clearing the apartment with him in the Orotava house, if he had remembered to clear out the things in the gallery cupboards, what changes he'd noticed with George now gone, in what things he noticed her own absence, how it felt to him to have been in Arguayo without her for the first time.

'Without you it's as if the Arguayo house has died.'

Ella's eyes glittered. 'How do you mean? What things no longer seem to you to be alive when I'm not there? In what way does the house die? Tell me! Why do I have to drag every word out of you?'

'I walk into rooms expecting to find you, only you're not there. Expectations die every time I walk into a room.'

'Expectations?' she pressed him. 'You mean that my spirit is there? Is there a ghost of me haunting the house?'

'Your presence is around me in everything I see – the beauty of things, the loving atmosphere about them ...'

'What beauty, what loving?'

'The details ... the elephant doormats outside the children's rooms, waste-paper baskets you've covered with cloth to match the curtains ... the way you've personalised the place. It's like walking into your curiosities cabinet. Presents we gave you as children twenty years ago ... those shells of mine on the windowsill, Felicity's plastic stork in the bathroom, the clarity and simplicity of things ... the scent of the bedlinen, the flowers in the vases ... the colour scheme. Just everything – the lightness of the house, which is so different from the Orotava apartment ... things that have your handwriting all over them like the cupboards stocked with emergency supplies of sugar and rice and light bulbs and –' Alex paused '– toilet paper in unbelievable quantities, whose necessity I've never quite been able to understand ... but most of all it's the *wish* that you were there, because when *you* are there the wish *isn't* there, so the wish being there sort of stands in for you in your absence.'

Ella pressed her lips together. 'Imagine I *had* died in the accident. Imagine you were in Arguayo knowing you would never walk into a room again expecting to find me there, never ever. How would it be different?'

'Different?'

'If I were actually dead rather than just not there?'

Alex hesitated.

'What would the difference be then?' Ella asked again with a morbid intensity he was beginning to find unsettling. 'What would I have left if I never came back?'

'You would have left more than I'd want to be reminded of. You would still *be* there. I would find it too painful. If you were dead rather than just not there I don't think I would want to go to Arguayo at all.'

'So is that the difference? I would still be there when I was dead, so you would rather not go there, whereas you would miss me when I was alive and wish me to be there with you?' She sounded dissatisfied. 'Isn't that rather odd? In both cases you miss my presence, but in one instance you want it and in the other you don't?'

Unable to bear this interrogation, Alex got up from the chair by her bed.

'Where are you going?'

'I'm not going anywhere. I just want to move around a bit.' He went to the window. 'Sometimes you ask questions I don't know how to answer.'

The following day Alex flew from Las Palmas to Vienna, promising Ella he would come back to visit her at Christmas. But as a result of missing the summer semester in Graz he got caught up in a backlog of work which could only be got out of the way by working through the holiday. Almost a year passed before he was able to return to Tenerife.

# 4

Ella had only recently been discharged from the rehabilitation centre where she had spent months after leaving hospital. Using crutches she could walk no more than a few steps.

During her absence from Arguayo Claude had had the ground floor of the house fitted with handrails anchored to the floor so that Ella could move from one room to another without assistance. Her bedroom had been moved down from the tower to George's former study across the courtyard from the kitchen. She was unable to do even light housework. She needed someone to help her wash, to cook and carry things for her, to get her up from the lavatory, but on most days Alicia or one of her daughters was there to help out. With furniture brought down from her room – her bed, writing desk and the curiosities cabinet – and potted plants from outside, which turned the adjacent sitting room into a con- servatory, Ella settled into her new surroundings. She had a computer installed, which Alex taught her to operate, and with the aid of the Internet she was able to follow the events that ushered in the post-cold war era – the fall of the Berlin Wall, the collapse of the communist regimes in eastern Europe, the dissolution of the Soviet Union and the disintegration of Yugoslavia. She continued to suffer chronic discomfort from her injuries but came to terms with it by projecting it onto these upheavals beyond the island, persuading herself that private pain was her only adequate expression of sympathy with the general condition of suffering in the world.

Ella watched with unease how for much of the 1990s two of her sons made their living in war zones. Max worked as a photographer in the Gulf War, in Chechnya, the Congo and Rwanda before leaving Tangiers and returning to New York and his share in the studio, while Alex was in the Balkans. The concurrent ethnic cleansing in Bosnia and genocide in Rwanda, with mass rape utilised as a deliberate tactic, tapped recollections of the horrors she had herself experienced east of the Elbe fifty years previously and added a new dimension to them. Then and now, the images of the refugee treks remained unchanged. Partly to relieve distress brought on by these events, partly out of a sense of obligation to the future interest of her grandchildren, Ella wrote an account of her experiences at the end of the Second World War, which Alex would later find among the papers relating to her will.

In his mid-fifties Claude retired from his professorship at the University of San Cristóbal de La Laguna, let his house there and moved to Arguayo. Sensing his parents' anxiety about the financial constraints that would be caused by Claude opting for early retirement and a reduced pension, Alex reassured them it was the right decision and assured them of his support should they ever need it. His father had told him it wasn't essential for him to be in Arguayo full time – he could have gone on working in Laguna during the week and spending the weekends with Ella as he'd been doing until now – but Claude worried about her nonetheless. He noticed a general decline in Ella's vitality after the accident. He anticipated it declining further over the coming years, with the impairment of her health generally, her increasing immobility and her confinement to a wheelchair inevitable outcomes. He fretted when he was away from her. Being together mattered more to them than anything. Gradually that would come to mean living in a private world and their acquiescence in the exclusion of everyone else from it.

Since the Second World War Claude had continued on the same trajectory, predictably carried forward by a momentum initiated by events that had taken place half a century before. After Ella's accident, George's death, his own early retirement and the wider disruption of the previous order he had been comfortable with, the parabola of his trajectory was broken, severing his continuity with the past. The present was a hostile construct of many instances of planned obsolescence, apparently designed to reinforce his awareness of himself and Ella having become personally superannuated. A generation of electronics had passed him by unnoticed. The first occasion he experienced this was when he went into a Paris shop to buy cassettes for a recorder he had bought there in the 1970s. He no longer recognised the shop. Only the address confirmed that it was the same place. Many of the products on sale were new to him. He didn't know how they worked, not even what they were for. An assistant dug the last box of cassettes out of the stockroom for him, relics of a bygone age.

The coordinates were gone to which he had so self-evidently belonged that he'd not been aware of his dependence on them. The accident propelled him and Ella into the backwater of Arguayo on a permanent basis. They were content to be no longer in the stream, perhaps Claude rather more so than Ella – but whether you wanted it or not the stream came to you. In cyberspace the island ceased to be isolated. A global static crackling in the background became audible, like tinnitus, and once registered would never go away. They would never need to leave the island again. Fewer people came to visit, and on the whole they preferred it that way. Claude was surprised how quickly the memory of George receded. He thought this could only be because George had already begun to recede during his lifetime.

Claude had a dream of George swinging on a trapeze in the dragon tree in the courtyard of the house. The tree in the dream was far taller and had much richer foliage than the real one. In the tight-fitting cos-tume of a circus artist, George sat on the trapeze performing gymnastic exercises. Perfectly relaxed, he rolled himself up through the branches, bar and all, ascending in a series of elegant loops until he reached the top of the tree and dematerialised in the sky.

This dream encapsulated for Claude the withdrawal of George, specifically from the ancient tree rooted in the courtyard, the centre of the life the three of them had shared in Arguayo. George had come adrift from the life around that tree for reasons Claude and Ella could only conjecture, because George was neither a very reflective nor a com-municative person. Beyond the bonhomie and suavity of this outwardly always even-tempered man, what was going on inside him? Ella didn't doubt the genuineness of the affection George had told her he felt for Claude. This affection for Claude presented a complementary facet of

George's gradual alienation from Ella. She understood that his attachment to Claude grew from the same root as his estrangement from her.

In Ella's archetypal dream about George, a dream she had dreamed many times, George was a frog squatting on her back. He sat and sat and got heavier and heavier. In the dream landscapes where she found herself with George she saw snow and wide open spaces with no place to shelter; the baby was lost or had been forgotten and if she failed to find and feed it, the baby would die. Sometimes the baby was dead already. But after George's death she ceased to have this dream. The frog was off her back. She breathed more easily. She slept better than she ever had before.

Before she folded up her life's work and put it away, she could hold it up to the light and try to see it in its completeness; the puzzle remained George. Where to put George? Peering into the old coach house of the Morris property in Hampstead, where she and George had briefly lived after getting married, Ella could see a man who seemed to her to have been extinguished long ago. By degrees he had been replaced by other men, little bits of him at a time, skin transfers subtly grafted so that you never saw by what sleight of hand the substitutions took place, never caught him in the act of this self-metamorphosis. So had that old George died? And who had taken his place? Or had the Ella she had once been now died too, bits of her at a time? When did she begin to become someone else? From what stasis could you view the wave on which you were yourself carried?

It was the same wave but it was always made up of different water, Claude pointed out to her. He noted Ella's apparent lack of interest in, or perhaps it was her independence of, the past, her early happy childhood in Herischdorf and experiences as a refugee excepted. But Ella envisaged the past, no less than the present, as being in motion all the time. Over and over, apparently explaining her husband to Claude but perhaps in order to persuade herself, she derived their reasons for marrying from their concerns at the time: for George to find in his emotional wasteland a human oasis, for Ella to put new roots down in her country of exile. It was her sense of her responsibility for George that had sustained the marriage.

Claude wondered if it had been any different then, when she had been intending to emigrate to Canada but allowed herself to be persuaded by George's tears to stay in London instead. Despite everything she would do so again, Ella was always telling Claude, a recital of self-persuasion Claude had to listen to again and again. She was still unable to sever George, probably because George wasn't to be severed from Ella's sense of belonging, which had formerly been attached to the lost paradise of her grandmother's house in Herischdorf and since then to the surrogate home personified for her by George. Only recently had she discovered the template on which George turned out to be based.

It had been shown to her in her a dream about returning to Herischdorf to find George sitting in the high chair in her grandmother Cosima's boudoir, having his mass of long silver hair combed out by Erna, her grandmother's maid. That same quiet sense of continuity flowing in the background like the stream behind her grandmother's house, a dependable presence in her life, connected her grandmother Cosima with her husband George.

His death left her with many questions.

What was the nature of that shadow Ella had always sensed accompanying George from their earliest years in St John's Wood? When she learned of his affair with a woman at the British Trade Mission who had been his lover before he married her, she thought that once the shadow had been identified it would be dispelled. But it persisted. What was the nature of the blight George had brought into her life? Did it have to do with his ready acquiescence in her relationships with other men? Had George consented to Claude joining the household because this gave him a hold over her? Because he recognised this was the only option if he were not to lose her entirely? Did he take satisfaction from a weak spot in Ella, who otherwise dominated him? Had she dominated him too much? Did he demean her in order to get his revenge on her? Did he interpret the lenience he showed to her affairs as a licence to get on undisturbed with his own? Or was his behaviour better explained by that lukewarm temper Max had always objected to in his father, the insufficient human engagement – more than that, the embedded indifference of a husband whose autistic nature Ella had learned too late was at the bottom of so many silences she had misinterpreted at the time – not George's reluctance but his inability to feel empathy with the feelings of other people or to communicate to them his own, or in the end simply his lack of substance, the emptiness of George? Was this why he had told her so many lies?

# 5

The dream stuff she had to work through at night – ancient granaries full of still-dewy dreams hung up there to dry before she could disentangle the threads and start spinning them – would later sometimes break into the reality of her daytime life. In one dream she looked down from her bedroom window. She watched as one of the branches of the dragon tree was torn off in the wind. Since she was unable to manage the stairs and had long since moved down from the belfry to the ground floor, only in a dream could she have seen such a thing happen from above. Only in a dream could such a wind have got up in the sheltered courtyard. Yet the bough lay there one morning, apparently broken under its own weight. She looked at the tree and saw it was diseased. They would have to take it out, she said to Paco, and plant another, but Paco scratched the bole, showing her a green shimmer under his thumbnail, and told her there was life in the old tree for another hundred years.

Ella felt her own mind become a porous border crossing for her waking images and the images of her sleep. The latter were usually silent, but visually they differed little. They could pass without hindrance in either direction. Passive, she felt instrumentalised, a vessel with no choice but to receive what was poured into it, a film obliged to record whatever images it was exposed to. Columns of itinerant people trekked across her dreams on journeys whose beginnings and destinations lay elsewhere but took advantage of the hospitality of her dreams while they were there, at an isolated *Landschloss*, the sort of homely chateau one might have come across in the Mark Brandenburg. She didn't recognise it but took it to be her grandmother's house in Holm. Roughly improvised bedsteads with pallets had been set up along the corridors to accommodate the hundreds of people seeking refuge. Her great-aunt, the Madame Colonel herself, in a tight-fitting Prussian-blue tunic with bright yellow gaiters and fluffy woollen bobbles in place of epaulettes, was in charge of quartering the refugees and directing operations in the refectory. Her mother turned out to be among the women serving meals. When Maria turned and smiled at her daughter, Ella felt such happiness to be reunited with her she woke up with a flooding heart.

She dreamed the return of Alicia's daughter from the Spanish mainland to become managing director of the casino hotel in Puerto de la Cruz before anyone knew she was coming. In other dreams she foresaw masonry falling from the *portada sillería*, the collapse of a terrace in the lower garden, the dismantling of the Berlin Wall — long before these events happened. She dreamed of things taking place in places that seemed further away — uprisings, violent assemblies in violently sunlit places, but also ordinary, peaceful scenes for which she found no corroboration in real life, if only because the events and the people involved were unknown to her, or she was seeing things that had happened in the past or whose time to happen had not yet come.

For the first time in her life she had no duties to discharge. This lack unsettled her for a while, until she saw the quantities of dreams she was expected to sift through and recognised what work she still had to do. When she chose to get this work done was up to her of course, and according to the biological clock she had inherited from her father, the natural dynamo of her waking cycle didn't begin much before midnight. Her intellectual appetite, the whipcord of her curiosity and the sharpness of her attention peaked at a time of the evening when most people went to bed.

Between midnight and three in the morning Ella studied what she had culled of the day's events from a list of favourite Internet sites she had worked with during her apprenticeship to computers. Not the least of these was the International Press Association's website, where she could read online the articles her son filed from Yugoslavia. Between one and two Claude would come in and sit with her, and she discussed other affairs with him even as she continued to follow whatever she was reading on the computer — two blocks of attention which she could sustain without detriment to either of them. At around two o'clock Claude would retire while Ella was still solving online puzzles or dealing with her personal correspondence. When she lay down to read and eventually fall asleep it would be past four in the morning, and sleep was even then only possible with the help of pills. She woke often in the night, got up and fell asleep again. When she didn't she wandered around, going through drawers, sorting papers, putting cupboards in order before she went back to bed and slept until late in the morning.

To Ella it seemed she had unlimited resources to accommodate the needs of people she would have been prepared to devote her time and energies to, but these resources were no longer required. She had dreams enough for everyone, but apparently they were no longer needed. Because the needs were in reality her own, she had difficulty understanding this. It didn't occur to her to question that if she had a need to give, it was also her right to do so. Even if she had once had that right, it had since been forfeited. For two years after the accident she had been taken out of service, spending the time uncoupled in a siding where she was left to recover.

Initially she tried to keep up the traditions of hospitality that ran in her blood and were accompanied by rituals she had grown up with — cooking and cleaning, airing guest rooms, decorating each place at table individually with flowers and presents for the children — but for which there was no longer the staff. For decades she had managed to keep an open house largely by her own efforts, with some support from Alicia, and it dismayed her when she discovered this was now over. Even with help she no longer could, because the will to continue was no longer there, and none of her children would keep up the traditions she had handed on to them.

The loss of culture she saw disappearing with her grandchildren's hostility to her standards, their inability to discriminate, to desire quality as individuals and not just make do like everyone else with whatever was dictated by mass consumer markets — it couldn't be helped. She knew such ideas were misunderstood as elitism. A global egalitarianism demanded levelling down to the lowest common denominator. It hurt her, nonetheless. She took it as a personal defeat. Her own imaginable end, coinciding, as she and Claude had always known it would but only latterly begun to discuss, with Claude's simultaneous extinction, she viewed with composure, even if since the accident it had suddenly drawn much closer and become more urgent. But to be conscious of herself as the final inheritor of all that had been passed on to her by her predecessors, which she would be unable to pass on in turn to her successors, distressed her. None of her children, not even Alex, could understand why this mattered to her. George had understood it, and on the night he died he had given it a name. He had called it the loss of beauty. George had experienced it as a personal loss. It pained him. Claude understood the loss only through Ella's pain. He perceived the pain, but it was not one he could feel himself.

Ella began to go out of the world. Family and friends quickly got used to her no longer being around.

'Am I looking at my life in the wrong way? Have I overlooked something? It seems to me I've given so much and been given so little back.'

Increasingly she turned to Claude for comfort. Broken as she got older, and suddenly seeming much older for having been broken, the vulnerable person Ella had always been but managed to conceal under an apparent strength that deceived everyone but Claude, she now became openly. It was left to him to take the broken bird into safekeeping, close his palms around her and breathe warmly into his sheltering hands.

# CHAPTER FIVE

## Ella's Garden

### 1

After thirteen years of working for the International Press Association, most of them as a war correspondent, Alex was invited to join the staff of a new institute for the study of geostrategic issues in south-east Europe. Financed and set up by the European Union in response to the war in Yugoslavia, the institute was to be based in Vienna. This choice was influenced as much by the city's proximity to the area as by historical connections between the Austrian capital and the former satellite countries of the Habsburg empire. The objective of the institute was to assist the incorporation into the EU of the independent republics now emerging after the disintegration of Yugoslavia, by improving trade relations and cultural exchanges. Beginning with Slovenia, the Western alliance would roll up the old map and take the recently warring states into its fold – Croatia, Bosnia, Montenegro, eventually Kosovo and perhaps Serbia as well – putting an end, it was hoped, to hundreds of years of unrest in the Balkans.

Alex's contract with IPA ran out at the end of the year, but as he was due two weeks' holiday he left the agency in the middle of December. His new job didn't begin until April, giving him three and a half months off. He was planning to spend most of that time with Nadine on Tenerife, winding up the sale of his father's property in La Laguna and sorting out the things left in the house. He had never felt entirely comfortable in Claude's rabbit warren of a house. It was associated for him with the worst period in his parents' relationship, after Claude came back from Japan.

The new job was a good solution for Alex, if not quite the one he was looking for. He would have preferred a complete break from the subjects that had preoccupied him for the past twenty years. He was restless and wanted to move on. But where to? He would have liked to work in an English-speaking country, but this hadn't happened, not so much for lack of opportunities as lack of countries where he could imagine settling down. One country that appealed to him was Canada. He felt an urge to begin something new in a place completely unknown to him, perhaps Vancouver. He would visit Montevideo, Buenos Aires and Valparaíso if only for their names. His fluent Spanish put him within range of work anywhere in Central or South America. He wanted – this was becoming an obsession – to be recycled in a new existence, perhaps a series of lives unconnected with any he had led before. He nursed vague ideas of a simple life in a solitude the contemporary world could no longer provide. Perhaps all they reflected was his immaturity, a desire to escape the sense of his inadequacy and lack of belonging.

If one's imagination alone could give one powers of self-transformation, he would go further and choose to be a pebble in a stream, pine needles on a mountain tree, the spreading feathers of a bird dropping from a cliff. There was an awareness, as he approached his forty-sixth birthday, of deeper urges having failed to articulate themselves. He had a hankering to give them one last chance. Severing connections and taking off, travelling the south seas as his father had done, sailing a boat or piloting a plane, working in a laboratory or making a film – the scope of his actually lived life seemed so narrow and had so few parts to offer him, the avatars into which he would have liked to transform himself in order to experience a closeness to life that had so far eluded him: a richer texture and density, tastes and smells and languages, beliefs and thoughts to be delivered with the package of a new life he could dream about because it would never be put to the test in reality.

That Alex put aside these daydreams and felt ready to settle for reality, resigned to remaining on the familiar treadmill of south-east European issues, even beginning to relish the prospect of remaining in the city where he'd lived without much enthusiasm for the past ten years, had to do with the refurbishing of the well-worn furniture of his life as a result of taking stock of it through the eyes of the person with whom he now shared it. As a result of being shared with Nadine it had become a different life. The break with the past that Alex had been longing for – coming up with new reasons for his existence, as he remembered Santana enjoining people to do – would not be achieved by moving to Montevideo or becoming a pilot flying mail in the North West Territories. Two months after returning from The Hague, it would happen by sitting still and letting it all configure around them in his Spittelberg apartment, beginning with the verdicts of fifteen to thirty-three years in prison to which the perpetrators of the crimes in Beli Atas had finally been sentenced.

Nadine was pregnant.

How this miraculous conception had come about remained a puzzle to both of them. The half-measures which were still as far as Nadine was prepared to go with sex, crouching on top of him, teasing the labial areas of her vagina with the tip of his penis without actually inserting it, satisfying herself before masturbating him orally, would have seemed to preclude the possibility, certainly the deliberate intention, of Nadine becoming pregnant. Yet this was what happened on the last night they spent in The Hague. Some extremely resourceful sperms must somehow have swum up the estuary to reach their berth in her womb.

'Do you want me to have this child?' she asked Alex when she told him.

'What do you mean, *this child*. Of course I do.' He was unsettled by the coldness of her question. 'Don't you?'

'I need time to think about it,' she said.

Again it was the tone of her reply rather than its content which Alex found disturbing.

But a couple of nights later Nadine turned to him in bed and said as she took his penis in her hand, 'I do! I do want the child! But I don't want it to have happened by mistake. I want us to make love properly because making a child is what we both want! So you must make love to me properly, the way I know you've always been longing to, my poor darling!'

Nadine lay back passively with her arms by her head on either side of the pillow as he got on top of her, suggesting to Alex sacrifice rather than pleasure, taking his penis into her vagina and allowing him to come inside her for the first time. But the next time it was different, and the time after that it was quite different again. Apart from the occasional phone call, nothing disturbed their intimacy, the mounting delirium of the sexual exploration that had been put off by Nadine for so long. The noises of the city, the morning clatter of bins in the yard below, the clanging of passing trams and the blast of traffic as the lights changed at the intersection below were muffled by snow collecting on the sharply

910

drawn cornices of the post office building opposite until they blurred and disappeared. Nadine wished the whole city could have disappeared with them. She wished they could have stayed all winter in hibernation in the apartment until the following spring when Alex took up his new job. But the arrangement to spend Christmas away had already been made, the flights to Tenerife long since booked, leaving them with no choice but to emerge one cold morning and fly off into the sun.

## 2

Since the events in Beli Atas Nadine had problems settling into sur-roundings she was unfamiliar with. Conscious of the thousands of previous occupants who had slept in the same bed, susceptible to traces they had left behind them, to the idea of their having done so rather than to any material evidence, Nadine felt her own presence obliterated. It prevented her from asserting her own claims on the space, disqualified her from being there. This discomfort manifested itself in a neurotic restlessness Alex had first noticed in the hotel in The Hague without knowing what caused it. Nadine displayed symptoms of what in Ella's case was known within the family as the Princess and the Pea syndrome. Recognising that similarity endeared her to Alex further.

When the taxi stopped outside the house in La Orotava and she followed him up the breezy flights of stairs to the apartment at the top, Nadine was already apprehensive about disappointing Alex's expecta-tion that she would feel at home. The rooms leading off the gallery overlooking the enclosed courtyard possessed a snugness combined with a solemn formality that didn't fit into any of Nadine's categories. She didn't know what to make of the place, and until she did wouldn't feel comfortable there. All the beds in the low-ceilinged rooms belonged to one austere set with the same heavy-jowled appearance. Originally from a seventeenth-century Spanish country house, the long dark narrow cots were built like fortresses in massive wood, impossible to sleep in but for the exuberantly sprung mattresses they'd been fitted with as a conces-sion to modern standards of comfort. The rest of the furniture was the same – chests, chests of drawers and cupboards for keeping things out of sight – all dark, dwarfish and squat, evoking for Nadine the much smaller people for whom it had been built several hundred years before.

She stood in the doorway behind Alex with her arms around him as she looked into one of the gloomy rooms.

'And you spent your childhood here? Wasn't it like living in a museum? Rather stuffy? Formidable?'

'Perhaps it was at first, but I got used to it. There's a reason for it being the way it is. Outside you live with brightness all around you on the island. Coming into the house, you're grateful for the cool darkness, the intimacy and even safety of the place. It's like going into your burrow. This was how the house was furnished when George bought it in the 60s, and this was how he kept it. This was his house. Ella never really felt at home here. Ella's house was Arguayo. But she did have a say in one part of the house.'

The dark Spanish furniture had been banished from the master bedroom. Here it was light and airy. The furnishings were modern. Nadine noticed the absence of the double bed she would have expected. Two very ordinary department-store beds with bedside tables stood side by side against the wall facing the window, which looked north towards the ocean.

Nadine sat down on one of them. 'Who slept where?'

'Ella originally slept in the bed you're sitting on. Later she moved into the room beside mine.'

'So what were the sleeping arrangements when both your fathers were here?'

Nadine watched Alex absent-mindedly undo his top shirt button and do it up again, and she wondered what Dr Jelinek would have thought about *that*.

'Well ... there's no easy answer to that question. It depends on what period we're talking about. Are you happy with that bed, by the way?'

'Yes.'

'Then I'll take this one.'

Alex stretched out on the other bed with his hands under his head.

'I'm not so sure the three of them ever stayed here at the same time. I guess they must have done. This was George's house. It was his territory. During the five years I was living here when I went to school in Puerto de la Cruz, Claude was away in Japan. When he came back he bought a house in Laguna, and that was *his* territory. So there was hardly any overlap. It was only in Arguayo that the three of them shared a common territory. They all had their own rooms there. Master bedrooms had no place in Ella's scheme of things. It's not a phrase she would have used – except perhaps in the early years in St John's Wood before Claude arrived on the scene.'

Nadine came and sat on his bed, leaning over to kiss him.

'All this still preoccupies you, doesn't it? The business of growing up with two fathers.'

With her finger she traced a contour map of his face, from the high plateau of his forehead down over his eyes, around the ridges of his cheekbones, nose and lips.

'I get the impression you have a rather negative view of George and all the bonding that took place with Claude – or should have taken place with him. Yet it's always George you're talking about, you know. Claude doesn't get much of a mention. And when he does, I don't really get an idea of the kind of person he was. I find it interesting that it's Claude's house you're selling in order to buy George's. It may be Claude you think of as your father, but in the end it's George you've chosen to move in with. It's George's bed you're lying on now.'

She took his hands and pulled him up.

'Come on. Let's go out and have some lunch.'

# 3

Nadine's remark about his two fathers hit a sore spot. *In the end it's George you've chosen to move in with.* Alex had never thought about it like that. It took him disagreeably by surprise. But how could Nadine be expected to have any idea of the sort of person Claude was when he had told her so little about him? He'd failed to do his father justice. His immediate urge was to fill in the gaps with anecdotes illustrating the special relationship he'd had with Claude, uncomfortably aware that he felt the need to speak up on his father's behalf because he could hear other voices arguing another view of him.

Claude was like a tree with a single branch, which had flowered solely under Ella's beneficial influence. When Alex tried to pin down specific memories of the things he'd done with Claude he found George tending to take over, particularly his boyhood from the age of eight to thirteen. During those five years yielding the richest store of George memories Claude had been absent in Japan. It was George who Alex saw turning up in Richmond with exotic presents from abroad. It was

George who took him out on the river in a rowing boat, went fishing with him on the quay at Puerto de la Cruz, taught him to play chess at the Hotel Marquesa and learned windsurfing with him off the beach at Playa de San Juan. Alex's memories of his early life in London were meagre by comparison. The scenes in which Claude figured were disappointingly vague, atmospheric impressions of the flat in Kensington rather than tangible happenings. It was difficult to shell his father from the memory pod he inhabited with Ella, almost impossible to fix an image of Claude which didn't include her. Only in conjunction with her had his father ever really been there at all.

After George's death his personal belongings, mainly books and papers, had gone into the attic and the apartment had been let to a local architect. When the architect died, it stood vacant for a couple of years. George's stuff had now been sitting up there for almost two decades, waiting to be dealt with. Probably Alex could throw most of it out. But that would require him to spend several days in the attic going through it all, a task he wasn't looking forward to. He got up early one morning and made a start before it got too hot under the roof. Manoeuvring cartons of files down the fragile pull-down ladder into George's study was a difficult job on his own and Nadine offered to help him, standing at the bottom of the ladder and taking them as he passed them down.

Nadine settled with a newspaper on the roof terrace while Alex sat at George's desk and began looking through. George had kept all his private letters, correspondence relating to the purchase of the flat in the 1960s, contracts, estimates, an assessment of the property by the Historic Buildings Commission of the cabildo of Tenerife. Reluctantly Alex found himself getting interested. By lunchtime he still hadn't progressed beyond the first box of files. George kept everything. Copies of bank statements were clipped to tenders from building contractors detailing roof repairs, painting, replacing the wooden railing around the gallery, an astronomic bill for bathroom fixtures which George had installed when he bought the apartment. Scrawled on the bottom of the bill was a handwritten note on the copy he had sent to Ella in London.

*It's an impressive if rather vulgar bathroom statement, featuring an outsize round tub, matching twin basins with gold taps, floor and wall tiles made of the same beautiful white marble. The sort of thing you might see in a James Bond film, minus the nymphets suitably draped. Rather on the expensive side. I was inspired by a bathroom in a Miami hotel on my last trip before ending my career at the Foreign Office, and I decided to give myself a more lavish send-off than I knew I could expect from the taxpayer.*

After reading this note Alex got up and went into the bathroom to take a look at it in detail, occasioning a peculiar synaesthetic experience. Looking at the flashy fixtures and fittings provoked the memory of a smell. It wasn't quite the perfume that had lingered in the rooms he and Max had entered after George's death, but something like it which had never struck him in the apartment before. Alex remembered leaving the windows open for days to air the place, and he felt the same urge to do so now. He couldn't reconcile this bathroom with George's fastidious tastes. What would a bathroom like that have cost? He found it all itemised in the accounts: the Carrara marble, the bevelled glass, the tub with the gold taps had cost George close to three thousand pounds – a lot of money in the 1960s. How had he paid for it?

The bestselling spy trilogy that launched George Smythe's career had brought in over a hundred thousand pounds. The film rights brought in quite a lot more. Smythe's thrillers had continued to sell well throughout the 60s and 70s, dropped off towards the end of the decade and plummeted to a few thousand copies by the mid-1980s. For about twenty years George was earning well and spending well – the Orotava flat, the house in Arguayo, a holiday apartment in a new tourist complex in La Caleta bought as an investment for his children. Bank statements he'd kept for thirty years showed remittances coming in from agents in England, the Bahamas and America, and when these began to dwindle the losses were offset by a small but steady flow from banks in Paris and Geneva. This revenue was initialled DB or UN, respectively standing for Dirty Books and United Nations, the pornography George had written for a publisher in Montmartre, presumably to make ends meet, and the translations of UN reports he appeared to have undertaken as a last resort, commissions which he probably owed to old Foreign Office connections.

What puzzled Alex was a string of payments George had made to Max, starting in the 1980s and continuing until George's death. An initial sum of fifteen thousand pounds was transferred to Max's account with a San Francisco bank, followed by smaller payments to a bank in Tangiers and a final remittance of twenty thousand pounds to the Chase Manhattan Bank in New York just a couple of months before his death. Over a period of five years George had sent Max money that added up to fifty thousand pounds.

There were other mysterious beneficiaries. For about five years during the 1970s George had a standing order with his Tenerife bank to pay the equivalent of a hundred pounds a month to someone called Cleo who had an account at the same bank. Once a year a certain Inéz received a hundred dollars paid into an account in Argentina. Alex found records of payments he had himself received from George during his student years in London and completely forgotten about. Small sums of money had gone to Felicity and her two daughters as well, but they bore no comparison to the fifty thousand that Max had received. Had it been loaned to help him out with the studio loft Max had bought in New York? If so, there was no evidence in the accounts that Max had ever paid him back.

Nadine came in and put her arms around his shoulders. 'What's that you're reading?'

'Oh, just George's old business correspondence – receipts, contracts, bank statements, stuff like that. But I can do this another time. Why don't we leave for Arguayo earlier? There are a couple of places I'd like to show you on the way.'

It was Christmas Eve. They'd arranged to stay at Arguayo over Christmas with his sister Felicity and her family. He'd last seen his sister at Max's funeral. Felicity's partner Janine, his nieces Liz and Kim and Kim's boyfriend Ahmed, by whom she'd had a baby a few months ago, were spending the holiday on Tenerife. Alex and Nadine had been invited to join them. They would have preferred to be on their own, but Alex saw no way of getting out of it. Christmas with his family held no attractions for either of them, and it wasn't much of a deal on Tenerife anyway. The sun burned it out.

# 4

As things turned out, however, Alex was glad of the company in Arguayo. Had he and Nadine been staying there alone, they'd have felt lost in the house. The property had already begun to slip in the final years his parents had lived there, and since their deaths it had gone further into decline. Standing with his sister Felicity on the grassy terrace with the double row of dragon trees that Ella had planted in the 1970s leading up to a fountain and an aviary, a netted enclosure of subtropical shrubs and trees on the west side of the house where Paco used to breed a dozen different species of singing birds, Alex was unprepared for the extent of the dereliction that had set in since his last visit.

After Ella died, the aviary was dispersed. All the birds but a pair that Paco kept for himself were sold or given away. The netting still draped over the trees was full of holes. Chronic water shortages exacerbated by the long droughts of recent summers made it hard for the eighty-year-old Paco to keep up the garden. The sprinkler system and the pump that supplied the fountain had broken down. The once-plush lawn had turned into an arid strip, host to a few yellow weeds and wild shrubs. Several trees in the avenue had died. Paco had chopped them down but not replaced them, leaving gaps it was painful for Alex to see. Alicia was confined to her house by near-blindness. Like all the young people Alex had grown up with in the village thirty years ago, their children had left home and found jobs in the tourist belt along the coast.

Glad of someone she could share her troubles with, Felicity recited the catalogue of woes Alex usually found himself listening to when she called him in Vienna. With Ella and Claude now gone and all the others abroad, she herself living in London and unable to get to Arguayo for more than a few weeks a year, there was no longer anyone left in the village to look after the property, even if she'd been able to afford a caretaker.

'What can I do? Please, Alex. Say something that'll cheer me up.'

'Well, for a start we could get saplings to replace the dead trees, couldn't we? I know a mechanic in Puerto de la Cruz. I'll ask him to come over after Christmas to sort out the sprinkler system and fix the fountain pump.'

'But I'm only here for ten days.'

'Don't worry. I can deal with it. Nadine and I will probably be staying until the beginning of March.'

'Lucky you.'

Seeing Felicity's anxious face, Alex added, 'And if it's the money that's worrying you, I don't mind paying. I'll make it my Christmas present to you, if you like, so you'll be helping me out too.'

She put her arms around him and kissed him. 'That's sweet of you. It *is* the money I'm worried about. I didn't realise what I was letting myself in for. Look at the state of the wall on the weather side of the house. The windows, the gutters, the roof ... I don't know where to begin.' They stood looking up at the house and he felt her helplessness. 'Talk about an inheritance!' she burst out. 'Just look at what I've been saddled with! It's all right for you and Philip, living in apartments that are easy to keep up. But I've been lumbered with this white elephant.'

'It's what you wanted,' Alex reminded her without sympathy, wishing his sister could see the little she thought she'd got in the perspective of the very much less that most people had.

'I never understood why Max was interested in La Caleta. The resort flopped. It was such a derelict sort of place.'

'Max liked derelict sorts of places.'

'Why are you selling your house in Laguna?'

'I couldn't otherwise afford to buy the Orotava apartment off Philip.'

'Perhaps I'll have to let this place go too, eventually.'

'Let it go?' Alex was horrified. 'What do you mean, let it go? These are the crown jewels, Felicity. Look at what you've got here! A historic building with vaulted ceilings going back to the seventeenth century. The belfry tower, a courtyard with perhaps the oldest dragon tree on the west side of the island, a courtyard with a *portada sillería* – almost unique. Not to mention Ella's garden, over thirty years in the making. It's yours to look after, not to give away. You *can't* let it go.'

'It's all very well for you to talk. That heritage stuff is fine so long as you're not the one paying the bills. How do you suggest I raise the cash to maintain the place? I'd no idea we'd been left so little *money*. I'd assumed, what with three properties knocking around the island, four if you include Claude's house, which went to you, that there'd also be something in the kitty to help us with the upkeep. I'm sorry, but I just can't afford it.'

'OK, so you were done out of the inheritance you deserved,' snapped Alex. 'Poor you. No money, just this crappy old house. If you were always so eager to have this place – and I remember you saying so when we first moved here – why didn't you give some thought to how you were going to maintain it? If you can't afford a second house, why don't you leave London and move here?'

'That's out of the question.'

'No, it's not. Be a bit more flexible! Be just a tiny bit imaginative! You and Janine with your background in nursing and hospital administration – there are lots of opportunities on the island. I know. Not just at state hospitals. I was talking to Dr Vargas the other day. The private-health sector here is booming. With affluent elderly Europeans wanting to winter on Tenerife, a lot of expatriate money is moving here, and clinics have opened to cater for them – private nursing homes for rich old people. The two of you might even run a place yourself.' He looked at the house, and a thought struck him. 'Here, for example. You could run a nice little retirement home in this place.'

'It's not a possibility that had occurred to me.'

'Then check it out.'

'Maybe I should,' Felicity said reluctantly.

'Sell that place in Clapham and move here full time. If Ahmed is out of a job, he and Kim might even help you run the place. Where better to bring up a child? Bring the house back to life. Deckchairs for the old folks up on the sunroof of the *portada sillería*, croquet down on the lawn in the avenue of dragon trees, perhaps with a peacock or two on parade, meals served in the courtyard – you'd have people queuing up, I bet you.'

'Still. We might make enough to keep us and cover running costs, I suppose, but I got an estimate for the roof, and that alone was *horrendous* – a hundred and fifty thousand euros!'

Alex put his arm around his sister's bulky waist and gave her a squeeze into which he put as much annoyance as affection.

'You're full of *buts*. Come on! Don't be so negative! How much would you get for your house in Clapham? Add to that your share of what you'll be getting from the Kensington flat when we sell it. So what's this nonsense about there not being enough money in the kitty? Felicity, you're *rolling*.'

'*Me?*'

She looked unhappy at the idea.

# 5

*Where better to bring up a child?*

Only afterwards did Alex realise that the advice he had been handing out to his sister was the blueprint for a future he secretly imagined for himself and Nadine. To return to the island where he had spent such a happy childhood was a dream he'd like to realise for his own wife and child. What better place, not only for his daughter, as he was already convinced she would be, to grow up in, but for Nadine to put behind her the ordeal of the last five years?

He had hoped that, once the trial in The Hague was over, Nadine would be less preoccupied with what had been done to her and embark on a new life, but since their return to Vienna two months ago the old symptoms had started to reappear. She found excuses not to leave the apartment on her own. She had gone back to sleeping in a chair with a lamp shining full on her face, to discourage the nightmares, which she persuaded herself were worse when she lay down in the dark. The chronic sore between her fingers which she used to chafe with her nails, since healed, broke open again. Most of all it distressed Alex how offhand she was about her pregnancy, as if she didn't trust it, didn't want it. Since she avoided talking about it whenever he raised the subject, that seemed to be the only conclusion.

How had Ella come to terms with the rape and terror she had been subjected to by the Russians in 1945? She had told him in detail about those experiences, but that had been thirty years after the event. He had never asked her about traumatisation; Ella had only even learned the word in connection with the Vietnam War. How had *she* dealt with it? Ella more than anyone would have known how to help Nadine, but Ella had died before Nadine arrived in his life.

Nadine had stopped seeing her psychiatrist in Vienna before the trial. When Alex became worried about the recurrence of Nadine's symptoms, he suggested she start therapy again. Nadine didn't want to. All there was to be said had been said already; nothing would come of repeating it. So Alex went to see Dr Jelinek himself. This was when he first learned about red-towel syndrome. The psychiatrist had found this symptom so remarkable that she discussed it at length in the account of

920

Nadine's case history she wrote up for a scientific journal, and 'red-towel syndrome' entered the literature.

At the Medica clinic in Zagreb where Nadine aborted the rape child the towels were the standard white. But Nadine had a phobia of contagion, didn't want towels that had been used by other people, and bought her own – red ones, so there was no risk of the clinic's towels being confused with her own. Dr Jelinek had established that Nadine chose red rather than pink or blue or any other colour because red was the colour of blood. Traces of blood were least likely to be detected on red fabric, and it was to absorb blood that Nadine later bought red towels on her return to Vienna.

Once a week – for years it became her Sunday ritual, displacing churchgoing with her mother – she soaked in a bath and used a razor to shave her body from top to toe. The full-body shave became an addiction. A year after she left Medica red towels were still in use at her mother's apartment in Leopoldov. She took her baths there because her own tiny flat didn't have a bath, but she managed to conceal from her mother what she was doing to herself. When she eventually confessed it to Dr Jelinek, Nadine took off her top to show the psychiatrist the skin trouble that had prompted the shaving ritual – tiny blemishes, protuberances, not even that, microscopic irregularities in the surface of the skin, or in her imagination, thought the dermatologist Dr Jelinek sent her to for a second opinion. But they were still so unbearable to Nadine that she felt compelled to slice them off. In the course of the week they insisted on growing back, or so she persuaded herself. Her body was lacerated with the scars, making it impossible for the dermatologist to establish the original state of the patient's skin. Bleeding was unavoidable; indeed bloodletting seemed to be its purpose: purgation.

It had taken Dr Jelinek a couple of years to wean her patient off self-mutilation, so when Alex told her he was worried that Nadine was suffering a relapse, her first question to him concerned the colour of the towels in his apartment and if Nadine had brought any of her own when she moved in with him, and if so, did they happen to be red? Alex couldn't recall any towels having arrived with Nadine. Besides, he had the evidence of the smoothness of the body he saw, which his hands passed over every day. Dr Jelinek warned him not to underestimate how resilient and cunning Nadine's post-trauma neurosis could be. He should keep a lookout for the appearance of red towels, as that would be an indication she had fallen back into old habits, which she would go to great lengths to keep hidden from him. Dr Jelinek didn't find it surprising that Nadine might have had a relapse after being obliged to relive her experiences at the trial, but the recurrence of nightmares, fear of the dark and the other symptoms Nadine showed were within the margin of tolerance that distinguished normal resistance from what Alex was alarmed to hear the psychiatrist call pathological defence strategies.

As for the pregnancy Nadine showed little enthusiasm for, Dr Jelinek told him that similar reactions ranging from apathy to hostility and extending to self-mutilation belonged to the profile of war rape victims treated in clinics. She might have chosen of her own will to have this child, unlike the baby that had been imposed on her by force and she had aborted, but in all other respects the symptoms of pregnancy were the same. It was not unnatural if Nadine's second, if wanted pregnancy reminded her of the first, unwanted one. Rape pregnancies might cause a woman to react negatively to subsequent pregnancies for the remainder of her childbearing life. It was a form of imprinting she might never escape.

As he listened to Dr Jelinek, Alex found himself reconsidering his mother from this new point of view. He wondered if Ella's later brusqueness, her irritability and her increasingly low opinion of men, a generic downgrading of the quality of maleness as such, provided evidence of the effects of such imprinting.

An uneasy foreboding he preferred to keep to himself prevented Alex from raising with the psychiatrist the question of what was to be understood by her phrase *chosen of her own will to have this child*. For Nadine certainly hadn't reckoned on getting pregnant; she had conceived under circumstances that seemed rather to suggest she had chosen *not* to have a child. The awkward half-measures she adopted in bed with him even suggested an unwillingness to have *sex*. She had gone through with it to please him rather than herself, and this had begun to rub off on Alex. He felt guilty about wanting to have sex with Nadine. Regrettably he chose to exclude such thoughts from his discussion with Dr Jelinek.

Before they arrived in Arguayo Nadine had made a point of asking Alex not to mention to anyone that she was expecting a child. Eight weeks into pregnancy, her body showed no trace of it. Alex waited with interest to see how she would respond to Kim's three-month-old baby.

Sitiawa was a radiant little girl, happy to be passed into anyone's arms, beaming at whoever wanted to hold her – at her grandmother Felicity, her father Ahmed, at Liz and Alex; she even charmed a soft expression not otherwise often seen from Janine's dour face. She passed the baby on rather reluctantly to Nadine, the last in the round of Sitiawa admirers at the table where they were sitting having lunch, but the moment she entered Nadine's arms, the baby screwed up her face and began to squall.

'Da da da da,' cooed Felicity.

'Siti Siti Siti, what's the matter?' Ahmed got to his feet.

'It seems *I'm* the matter,' said Nadine, frowning as she held the baby awkwardly. 'I'm sorry. I must have done something she didn't like.'

Ahmed hovered at her side. 'Shall I take her off you?'

'Perhaps you'd better.'

'How odd,' said Kim. 'She doesn't normally do that.'

'She's tired, that's all it is. I can hear from the way she's crying.' Felicity smiled reassuringly at Nadine. 'It's got nothing to do with you, dear. She's just had enough of being passed around.'

'She's hungry is what it is,' said Kim, taking the baby from Ahmed and undoing the buttons of her shirt. The baby's lips closed on the proffered nipple, and she quietened down. 'See?'

Momentarily shaken, Nadine rallied. 'Well, if that's all it takes, I think I shall manage when the time comes.'

'When the time comes?' queried Felicity. 'Do you mean to say you're expecting?'

'I am, or rather we are. It's partly Alex's fault.'

'Nadine!'

The women got up and crowded around her. They showed such obvious pleasure at this news that Nadine felt it almost as a reproof that she'd so far managed to come up with so little enthusiasm for her pregnancy herself.

Whatever had prompted her to go public with her pregnancy, the effect of Nadine's announcement was to enrol her in Alex's family, getting her accepted as belonging much more quickly than she might otherwise have been. She no longer had a secret to brood on by herself, undecided whether it was something she wanted or not. It was no longer just her property. It became a prospect that involved the rest of the family, one they so obviously looked forward to that it reinforced Nadine's cautious pleasure.

The announcement also seemed to trigger a burst of activity around the house – cleaning, painting and repair jobs which everyone had put off since Ella and Claude had committed suicide there. Nadine had noticed that the family avoided sitting on the terrace overlooking the garden on the west side of the house. This was the scene of the suicide, and until now it had remained a taboo area. But when Felicity and her daughters took off the furniture covers there to wash them, and Alex and Ahmed set about repainting the wooden chairs, it was as if the family had tacitly reached an agreement – it was time for the house to move on.

Ahmed took the shutters of the doors and windows off their hinges and lined them up in the courtyard, where he rubbed them down with sandpaper before repainting them. Kim and Liz went around the house emptying cupboards, throwing out food that had long passed its sell-by date, emptying drawers and shelves and wiping them clean, while Nadine stood at the sink washing the contents of a huge kitchen dresser, including sixteen-piece sets of fine porcelain and cutlery with matching linen table covers which had sat unused for no one knew how long. Alex arranged for his handyman in Puerto de la Cruz to come over and repair the defective watering system for the garden. Within a couple of days the fountain pump was working again, restoring to the garden the sound of splashing water that Alex had missed on his recent visits to Arguayo.

The terrace walls in Ella's lower garden had been damaged by storms, and with a view to restoring them to their original state, Alex searched through some photograph albums to remind himself what they had looked like. There were no photos, but it occurred to him they might appear in one of the home videos that used to sit on a shelf in Ella's linen room. He went up to see if they were still there and found Liz at the sewing machine, repairing cushion covers and pillowcases. He admired how deftly she handled the machine.

'Where did you learn to do that?'

Liz laughed, her chin bobbing up and down. 'What do I do for a living, Alex?'

'You work for a fashion designer.'

'So? I don't just draw, do I? I also make things. I make all my friends' clothes. Being a good seamstress is part of it.'

'I suppose it is. Is that what you always wanted to do?'

'You sent me an allowance to help me through the course, remember?'

'Did I? I'd forgotten that.'

'But you didn't come up here just to talk to me, did you?'

'No, as it happens. How did you guess?'

The machine purred away. Liz took her time answering.

'Here we are in Arguayo for Christmas, just as we all used to be when I was growing up. But that stopped ages ago. Apart from the funeral for Ella and Claude last year, I can't remember when we last saw each other. You've become just a man. I don't think you were ever much interested in us. You never wrote letters. You never visited us in Clapham.'

Alex smarted. 'I visited your mother there earlier this year.'

'Just the once. And that was on business.'

'I suppose I have been a lousy uncle.'

'I'm not complaining. Why should you take any particular interest in us? And I'm really grateful for the financial help. All I'm saying is that you never looked me up when you were in London, so I imagine there must be some other reason why you came up.'

Alex wondered how this niece of his could have reached the age of thirty without his ever having realised how astute she was.

'Actually, I was wondering what happened to the videos which used to sit on that shelf behind you?'

'Ah. Well, no one knows. We had a look for them after the funeral. I think they were moved to George's apartment in Orotava, but they seem to have disappeared from there too.'

Alex was struck by a thought.

'Now that you mention it, I remember helping Max to clear out the apartment around the time of George's death, before the place was let to the architect. I've been looking through some of the things Max and I left in the attic. He threw out bags of videos and film. He said there were piles of the stuff and he'd looked through it all. Some was worth keeping but the rest might as well go, and I took his word for it.'

'Why would Max have chucked it out? It wasn't his to get rid of.'

'Well, someone had to clear the stuff out if the apartment was going to be let. Ella was in hospital and Max was around, and he had to make up his mind on the spot what to keep and what to throw out.'

Liz stopped the sewing machine and snapped the thread with her teeth. 'Do you mind if I ask you a personal question?'

'Fire away.'

'What about that teacher who was your girlfriend?'

'What teacher?'

'The one you brought to Ella's birthday party.'

'Oh, Mirjana. What about her?'

'Were you planning on marrying her?'

'Marrying ... Well, she died, didn't she.'

Alex got up and opened the window looking towards the Teno mountains. An irritating déjà vu impression of having done this before, with his mother sitting at the sewing machine instead of Liz, warped his perceptions.

'She was killed in the accident.'

'The accident Grappa and Ella were involved in?'

'It was Mirjana's car that collided with the ambulance.'

'I'd forgotten that. Who was driving?'

'She was.'

'Poor Alex.' The sewing machine began purring again. 'Her death shook you up, didn't it?'

# 7

He remembered the party had still been in full swing when he and Mirjana had left to drive back to her apartment. In a few hours Alex had to be at the airport. But as they walked through the *portada sillería* and saw the landscape spread out around them under the light of the full moon, they changed their minds. Moonlight like a deep frost had settled on the mountains rolling away above them. A milky ocean lay poured out below. Transformed by the full moon, the lake of milk spilled languidly over the rim of the horizon.

Alex slipped out of bed very early without waking Nadine and took the road he had taken with Mirjana that morning sixteen years ago. It had been midsummer then; it was the winter solstice now. In the blue sheen of the early morning he remembered Mirjana with the winged horse tattooed under her armpit flying down the bright road between Puerto de Santiago and Playa de San Juan before entering the shadow cast by El Teide in the east. The car must have been doing a hundred kilometres an hour approaching the junction where they would turn east onto the motorway around the southern tip of the island. They came out of the curve into the full brilliance of the rising sun. The windscreen went white. Mirjana panicked and stamped on the brake pedal. They heard the wailing siren but couldn't place where it was coming from, went straight into the ambulance they didn't see coming down the Guía de Isora road. Thereafter everything was a blank.

At this time of year the sun rose at a different point on the horizon. Had the car approached the junction a little earlier or a little later or at another time of year, Mirjana wouldn't have been dazzled by the sun. She would have seen the ambulance in time to brake. She would still be alive and his life would be different. Perhaps Ella would still be alive too. He wondered about all the stillborn possibilities of that foregone life, his own no less than hers.

Alex pulled over to the side of the road and parked the car.

He walked across the road and looked for the cross in the undergrowth on the verge. He found it with his foot, the tip of his shoe striking the stone plinth on which the cross was mounted. He stooped down and bent back the grass with his hands. MIRJANA STEPANOVIC 1946–1988. Verdigris obscured the inscription. He rubbed it with his handkerchief. Casual passers-by wouldn't be able to decipher the inscription; people who came knowing what they were looking for didn't need to, so why have it?

There was a story he remembered Mirjana telling him on two separate occasions about the beach where she went to get away from the tourists in Puerto de Santiago. When on vacation she often spent the morning on this beach. Then she scrambled back up the cliff to the road and looked down at the beach, trying to figure out where she'd just been lying on her spread-out towel, but she could no longer pinpoint the spot because she hadn't left any trace. She'd already been eradicated, she said. That was the feeling she had when she thought of the places she used to live, Novi Sad on the banks of the Danube, where she grew up, Cádiz, London, Madrid, or just places she'd very briefly been, like the chair in the cafe where she had breakfast, which would be occupied by someone else within minutes of her leaving it. That must have been why she had told him the same story twice – because it made such a deep impression on her that her presence had left no mark.

# 8

When Nadine woke up in the mornings, she wondered if she had forgotten something. Had something she was supposed to be doing slipped her mind? This question accompanied her for the first few days she spent alone with Alex in Arguayo. It always came up first thing in the morning – an odd sort of question. Had she mislaid something in the night? Mislaid the night itself? Another dreamless night, slept all the way through – where had all the sleepless nights gone that had once been so familiar to her?

Alex had already left the night behind him and moved on: 'What do you feel like doing today? Would you like to go somewhere? We could go to the end of the world.'

She was amused by his somewheres.

'We could drive up into the mountains and have lunch in Masca.'

'Where's the end of the world?'

'A peninsula in the north.'

'Does the end of the world have a name?'

'Caleta de Bastian.'

'What else?'

'We could drive in the other direction, down to the sea. Fancy a day down on the beach? Perhaps take a boat over to La Gomera and check out the whistlers.'

'Or?'

'We could stay here.'

Every morning, after making love, Alex would suggest such outings. They would lie in bed thinking about them, discussing the options and deferring a decision until the following day. For the time being, so far at least, they both preferred to stay at home. Staying at home was their natural condition. Home was where they naturally gravitated. Where else could they be with each other better? What else if not home was being with one another? To do what they knew they would be doing in any case, but to do so with the relief occasioned by not having to do the something else they pretended to discuss, this game they played made the foregone conclusion more precious.

Nadine felt the days before returning to Vienna were slipping away from her. She tried to put a rope around them and make them fast.

'I'd always expected happiness would be a presence. There would be something there. It would be *about* something. But it's not. It's more like an absence.'

'An absence?'

'The absence of what otherwise prevented happiness.'

'And what prevented it?'

'Beli Atas. All those years waiting for the trial to happen. Now it's over, there's an absence inside me. It's no longer any concern of mine. Unbelievable! But it did take getting used to. And you were so patient with me.' She put her arms around him and kissed him. 'You thought that when we came back from The Hague I'd be able to put it all behind me, didn't you, just like that?'

'Well, not just like that.'

'But the next couple of months were almost the worst. It was like trying to get free of an addiction, this ... thing that had taken possession of me. It belongs to you, and you belong to it, but you've got to let go. I was afraid of that. Who would I be without it? I was scared, and I found myself backsliding.'

'I know. It worried me too.'

'The miraculous thing is the baby arriving and taking its place inside me – all this being worked out without my knowing, in fact resisting it, doing everything I could not to get pregnant, actually not to have sex, because I was still in possession of the thing and it wouldn't let me. Naturally it resented the baby, because then it would lose me.'

It was already early February, with the first breaking of spring blossom on the fruit trees above Arguayo in the upper reaches of the Santiago valley. A mildness in the air, an exhilarating softness of the air she had never experienced before, made Nadine reluctant to leave and go back to Vienna. The swooping bird call she heard in the woods behind the house, a long-drawn-out sound dipping and scooping towards the end, lured her up into the forest with the hope of catching sight of the bird. The head of the call was as bright as the tail, and that was how she imagined the bird to be, its head and tail feathers bright, the dipping and scooping body in between as dull and lacking in colour as the middle of its song. Perhaps it was a mating call. Nadine was allowed to hear the call but not to see the bird that made it. Still, this was the guardian spirit of the place. This was the sound of her happiness, and this was its texture, with the delicious softness of the valley air, and it only came to Nadine with the superstition that once she left Arguayo she would relinquish the happiness she had experienced there too.

# 9

They got married at Easter in a register office in the 7th District of Vienna. Ten weeks later a girl was born. She had the same long matted strands of dark hair her grandmother had at birth, and they called the child Ella.

The other grandmother was a jealous woman, still insistent in her mid-fifties on privileges she had learned were her birthright as an only child. Offended they hadn't called the girl Annemarie after her, Nadine's mother affected to take little interest in her granddaughter, but the open, trusting nature of the child won her over just as quickly as her own mother had once overcome her resistance to Selim's child.

Nadine went to the patisserie every day with Ella to visit her grand-mother. The exhausted, dreary, ill-lit apartment over the shop in Leo-poldstadt, where nothing had changed in half a century, was lit up by discoveries the little girl made there – pulling a cord and watching with fascination as light mushroomed inside a yellow lampshade, arranging leaves she brought up from the street in bright patterns on the carpet. She sat contentedly on the sofa beside her grandmother going through albums of family photographs. Quiet and self-contained, Ella was like her namesake grandmother, Alex noted, in that she was not demonstrat-ive in her affection towards anyone except her parents, sometimes not even with them, but she seemed aware of a duty to be responsive to the needs of others even if she didn't share them, allowing herself to be picked up and kissed by visitors unable to resist taking the little girl into their arms.

It was a long time since Annemarie Lersch had taken anyone in her arms. It seemed to be an effect of doing so with her granddaughter – the risk of showing tenderness that might be rebuffed was one she could afford to take with a little girl – that the hard-edged shopkeeper softened and learned, as it were, to take herself in her arms. She became ready to acknowledge feelings she hadn't permitted herself since the early years with Selim, before she took over the business from her parents and it came to dominate her life, pushing into the background everything but the jingle of coins she heard in the till. Jealous of Nadine's closeness to her father, Annemarie had withheld herself from Nadine too. Now they had Ella, through whom they could touch one another, the stunted relationship between mother and daughter cautiously blossomed again.

Alex observed all this and wondered how such changes could have been wrought in their life almost instantly by the arrival of their daughter. Nothing in twenty years of his life as an academic and a journalist had touched him comparably. He liked his new job at the institute well enough, but these days work occupied his thoughts much less than the well-being of wife and child. The centrifugal urge of his previous life, always pulling him out to the public periphery, always away from himself, was replaced by a single point enfolded within his family. He sank without regret into a bourgeois condition of life he had previously despised, surprised to find it less narrow than he had feared. Often working from home, he eavesdropped on Nadine and Ella in the background of strategic studies, learned to gauge instead the threat potential of squawks and yells he had never heard in the apartment before, a language in which he was illiterate. Looking up when they came into the room where he sat at his desk, still not quite believing in their presence, Alex continued to be surprised that they shared his life and were always at home with him. Once he ceased to travel, there was nowhere else. Home was where the three of them belonged. He hardly dared admit it to himself. He hardly dared think such a thought, let alone say the words aloud, for fear of undoing a spell. They were a happy family. In a world of uncertainty and unhappiness, he was certain about the miracle of the happiness of their family life. How was this possible? Was it extraordinary or banal? Could it decently be mentioned in public? Having seen all that he had seen, wasn't his claim to happiness in an unhappy world something to be ashamed of, which he would do better to keep to himself?

'Nonsense,' said Andro and Mirsad when he tried out such views on them. He listened with respect for their experience, which he'd never given a thought to until now. They had raised two daughters, said Andro, without detriment to the refugee organisation they had run from their home.

'And vice versa,' added Mirsad.

It now seemed miraculous to Alex.

Five years after their last meeting at the trial Drita kept the promise she had made to her cousin in The Hague and came to visit them in Vienna. She swept into the Spittelberg apartment like a squall, turning everything upside down for a few days, before she moved on to shake up more of her Kosovo-Albanian relatives who had meanwhile made their homes in half a dozen cities across north-west Europe. As a parting present to Nadine, Drita left her some photographs of Beli Atas that must have been taken in the 1960s, around the time Selim left home to work in Austria. He was to be seen in one of the portraits of the family, squinting on a bench in the sun with seven of his brothers and sisters on either side of their mother and father. The photos showed the three houses of the Kelani *zadruga* up on the hill, the yard behind them, children playing with goats by the well, the view down over roofs to distant hills. Nadine remembered seeing some of these pictures projected onto a screen in the courtroom in The Hague.

After looking at the photographs with Drita, Nadine left them in a pile on the chest of drawers in the hall. The next day they had dis-appeared. Alex noticed they'd gone and wondered if he'd ever see them again but didn't mention it. A week later Nadine sat down with Ella and began sticking them into the album where all her old pictures were collected, and Alex listened to her talking to the little girl in Albanian as she did when she was alone with her, just as Alex made a habit of speaking English with his daughter whenever the two of them were on their own. Ella loved picture books. The puzzle of the black-and-white photographs of people who were there on the pages but somehow not quite here, in the same room with her but in another colour, another time and place, completely absorbed her. Looking at the photographs she began to talk, entering the mystery of language.

'Is that Selim?'

'Yes, it is.'

'Is he there?'

'That's him sitting on the left on the bench.' Ella touched the figure, tinier than her finger.

'Is he *there*?'

The reality of it being and not being Selim in the picture. In this new world of his daughter's there were insights to be gained with her every day, discoveries he hadn't bargained for.

Straightening out his life, tidying up his old one to make room for the new, Alex came across his ancient Sony recorder in a bottom drawer. In another box he found a stack of tapes his mother had recorded for him and sent instead of letters during the final years when she was no longer able to write. The format of the tapes for Ella's more recent Olympus was slightly different from the microcassettes that fitted his Sony, so he had had to buy another recorder to listen to them. He selected one of the cassettes in a bundle dated September–December. These must have been the last she'd made with her own recorder before that final message on the Sony Alex had inadvertently left in Arguayo on his visit the following year.

Reconstructing the scene on the terrace, arriving there in his imagination as the forensic investigators of the Santa Cruz police had arrived on that perfect spring morning, Alex saw the little white wrought-iron table on which the cylindrical metal object lay. Ella had had his name, telephone number and address inscribed on a plaque glued to the side of the recorder, so that if it got lost like so many of its predecessors it could be returned to him. And the police had returned the recorder to him. It took them a year, but they did eventually post Ella's message, a reminder from her that finding something her forgetful son had lost was one of the last things she'd done in her life, restoring it to him as she'd restored countless other things he'd mislaid in the past – putting something as a surprise in one of his shoes or under his pillow, some place he wouldn't expect to find it, no doubt smiling to herself as she imagined his pleasure when he did.

# 10

'September the first, five o'clock in the afternoon. My darling Alex, where will you be listening to this, I wonder – at home in Vienna or in a hotel somewhere, or maybe on a plane? I thought I'd take you for a spin around the garden. Off we go. Hear the leaves crackling? A carpet of them under the tree in the courtyard, unusual this early in the year. Very hot weather we've been having all summer. Hardly any rain. As

I mentioned to you on my last tape, water reserves are sinking more quickly than expected. We're getting into shortages. One wonders how much longer people will go on being able to live up on this dry hillside. Thank God for my scooter! Or rather, thank you children who gave it to me for my birthday. What a wonderful idea that was of yours! I can get around the garden on my own now. I even went all the way up the road to Santiago del Teide. Under my own battery power. Claude or Paco used to have to push me, and of course I was grateful, but I dislike being so dependent. But fortunately— Whoops! That was a bigger stone than I'd bargained for ... We're on our way to the tropical garden at the end of the lower terrace, which is where I keep what I call my exotics, trees and shrubs. Paco terraced this part of the garden twenty years ago. You and I went down together on your last visit. I'll record some of the trees as we pass them ...

'Here's an orchid tree in bloom, with the most beautiful overlapping petals, magenta-lavender, hundreds of them. The flowers spread their wings. They really look like butterflies milling, about to take off. What you have to imagine is that tenseness about to release which you can almost hear just before a big swarm of them flutter off the boughs, wings beating as they rise ... then a bank of poinsettia and on the other side great bushes of hibiscus. It's temperamental further up the hill, but flourishes like a weed down here, I've no idea why.

'Here's one tree I'm rather proud of because he gave us so much difficulty when he was young. Perhaps he was trying to push his roots down into a stone or some obstacle. A cockspur coral tree seven or eight metres tall, which is about as high as they grow. A grateful tree, as if he knew what we'd done for him and wanted to give us something in return. Some trees have to struggle to get up off the ground, just as some children do, and then to everyone's surprise they really take off, unfolding the most spectacular foliage and flowers. We called this one Sandro after a boy in the village who was always getting into trouble with the law. Everyone had written him off. He's now doing extremely well, running his own marine sports store down in Puerto. Nobody expected anything of him, and so he was under no pressure to make something of his life.

'The cockspur coral started flowering in mid-April and is still going ... red cockscomb flowers, not large by tropical standards, but pretty. I wish you could see them. And here's a cutting we took from the candlenut tree that began growing into the window of the house in

La Laguna, remember? You used to climb down it rather than go by the stairs to get into the yard. The tree was all over the place in Laguna but hasn't done so well up here – the altitude, Paco thinks – and the whole point of putting it here was to provide shade on hot afternoons. Claude still has his hammock underneath, but he has difficulty getting in and out of it these days, so it's only used by the occasional visitor ... Just a minute ...

'There! I've got myself installed on the bench. Until the acacias on the terrace below began to get so tall, we used to be able to see La Gomera from here. We put in a dozen of them, not realising just how tall they grow. They've just begun to flower and will go on through the winter. Little yellow flowers, not much to look at, but with a very sweet perfume. Sweet acacia, that's how it got its name ...

'What was special about this morning? When I woke up and saw the date on the calendar clock on my bedside table, it reminded me that sixty-three years ago today the war began with Germany's invasion of Poland – that's how conditioned I still am. For my generation I suppose it'll always be *the* war, because it was the war we lived through when we were growing up. It was the war we experienced personally, and there's been no war like it since. At lunch my stepfather Carl told us it would all be over in a couple of weeks. He laughed when my mother said that by the time it ended her son Oscar would have been drafted into the army – he was thirteen at the time. Well, you know what happened ... all that happened ... and when people judge me I feel it should be taken into account, that we lost our home and became refugees. Hardly a day passes without me thinking about my mother, mainly her but my grandmother too, linking me with people who lived a hundred and fifty years ago. Aunt Cathy, who was ninety when she taught me English in Herischdorf in the 1930s, she grew up in England during the early years of the reign of Queen Victoria – the stories *her* English grandmother told Aunt Cathy, and Aunt Cathy told me, must go back as far again. When I was first taken to see her, it must have been a weekday, she served us tea and biscuits. I was only six or seven. It amused her to see me perched on one of her best chairs with my legs dangling and a monogrammed napkin on my lap, so beautifully folded I didn't dare open it. When I told her that at home we had biscuits with tea only on Sunday, she said, "*I* make *every* day a Sunday." I thought her way of eating biscuits not

935

very ladylike, crumbling them on her plate and dabbing at them with her fingertips. But *Make every day a Sunday* entered the family language.

'I used to wonder how my mother always managed to come up with such memorable ways of putting things, and I still remember the first occasion she said them. *If in doubt about doing something, ask yourself if it would be all right for your children to see you doing it* – nothing I ever heard from my mother has given me such guidance whenever I felt unsure. Countless practical tips she gave me have accompanied me all my life, and I now realise they must have been handed down to my mother by her predecessors as well. *Sit down and think before you get up to start hunting around for something you've lost* – you were forever losing your latchkey, and you've heard me say that so many times you must have got fed up with it. But it *did* help, didn't it? I got it from Cosima, your great-grandmother. And who did *she* get it from? I still have dreams about her and my mother and Aunt Cathy dabbing at her biscuit crumbs, and as long as I continue to, they remain alive, and we still go on trying to make every day a Sunday. Some time I'll get down to writing an account of the world I grew up in, but I keep on saying that to myself and I never do. So I'm telling you some of the stories on these tapes just in case ... At least they'll live on with you when I'm no longer around.'

'Hello, Alex. Ella left the tape recorder with me when she came up to the house on her way into the village. She thought I might like to leave you a message. I know she's been making these recordings about her early life. She's been talking about it a lot to me as well. As the only surviving member of her family old enough to remember, she sees herself as the treasurer of a store of family stories it's her responsibility to account for. You can't have failed to notice how this is becoming something of an obsession with her. It's left to me to tell you about our *present* life. She's guarded about what she reveals of herself. It has to do with that self-discipline of her Prussian background, which all of us have had cause to complain about at one time or another. She won't tell you a word about her health, for instance. As if it could have escaped you that her urge to put together this chronicle of her life wouldn't have arisen without a qualifying *while I still can*.

'It's still early days, and so far we've consulted only one specialist in Santa Cruz, but the first diagnosis we've been given points to muscular dystrophy. Loss of motor control has begun in Ella's case with the fingers and toes. The first symptoms of this go back to her accident. That was when she began to feel occasional numbness in her feet. I remember her asking me at the time to take off those tight-fitting stockings they make patients wear in hospital as a safeguard against thrombosis. Well ... she didn't have any on. The socks-on feeling is one of the symptoms of a condition that was diagnosed as polyneuropathy at the time. It's quite a mouthful of a word but it tells you practically nothing. The numbness in her toes, which later began to affect her fingers, may have to do with damage done to the spine. Or it may have had to do with the antibiotics she was on which hadn't been tested for side effects when taken for longer than a month – Ella was on them for well over two. They were manufactured by an American drug company taking advantage of laxer standards outside the US. If something goes wrong, and someone sues, the damages awarded by courts over here are negligible compared with those in America ... That, at any rate, was what I was told by a microbiologist friend of mine at the university. Or it may be that this new illness isn't connected with any of that business at all.

'My guess is that this is a pathological syndrome we don't have an explanation for, don't have a name for, don't really know anything about at all – something that has been the matter with Ella since the war. There was no one to look after her on her wanderings across the war zone east of the Elbe, a girl in her teens taking her life in her hands to get back home because her mother was on her own with three small children and needed her help. Even the experience of being hunted down and raped, terrible as that was, was not something on which she could dwell, because there wasn't the time. In the face of the catastrophe she witnessed unfolding all around her, her personal trauma was almost incidental. She had no choice but to take all the horrors into herself – those country-estate houses full of her relatives committing suicide as the Russian army got near, poisoning themselves, shooting themselves, hanging themselves from the stairs, bodies everywhere, dead people and animals in their thousands lying around the countryside and rotting in ditches, refugees on country roads being strafed by aircraft, mown down before her eyes, refugees discarding their dead and wounded and enfeebled old people by the wayside – everyday occurrences she must have seen hundreds of times. She opened her mouth to scream but no sound came out. That unheard scream stuck in her throat would give voice, if it could, to the burden she's been carrying around with her since 1945.

'What can she say? What can she do? What can she feel that is com‑ mensurate with such scenes? She can do almost nothing to relieve any of this suffering, but she needs to relieve it, if only to help herself. If she can help others she will help herself. She can paste pictures of disaster victims into cupboards. There is even a feeling of guilt that she has survived. Those fortunate enough to stay alive didn't fuss about what they'd been through. They got on with life, married, had children and so on. Outwardly they're like everyone else. But the scream remained stuck in her throat. This is an image I have of Ella's trauma from the very beginning – a young woman in a state of speechless shock. Remember the circumstances under which we first met. I was up in the mansard of my uncle's house in Paris when I smelt gas. I ran downstairs to find out where it was coming from, and there was Ella walking towards me in the mezzanine, pale as death, opening windows as she went. It wasn't until much later she told me she'd switched on the oven in the kitchen and tried to gas herself – not for the first time, and it wouldn't be the last. In peacetime she comes up with her death wish, her mysterious illnesses for which the doctors are unable to find an adequate cause. Inexplicable pains have pursued her all her life. Some of them have been tracked down to illnesses we could understand and deal with, others eluded us. Like this muscular dystrophy supposedly creeping up on her now.

'How come she's begun talking to you *now* about the war? We've agreed to respect each other's privacy with you, and not to listen to what the other is telling you on this tape, but I can guess. From the moment she woke up this morning, she has talked of nothing else. Just a date on the calendar is sufficient pretext – bang, and off she goes. I've listened to her wartime memories so many times they've become my own. It's the scream still on hold. Muscular dystrophy – maybe, maybe not. For me it's the scream tightening its grip. Maybe the same thing. She's losing her mobility. She's freezing up. How well will she be able to walk and talk a year from now? Six months? I just heard her arrive back, by the way. We'll talk soon, OK? We'll open the tape to let you in for supper.'

'Ella just got back from the village and we're having supper outside. She has some news to tell you, so why don't you sit down and join us here?'
'You'll remember Felipe, Alex. You and he were the same age when we arrived here in the 60s, and you used to play together. He now runs a plumbing business with his son in Adeje. Well, he happened to be

up here on a visit when I looked in to see Alicia and Paco, and he told me something I think you'll find touching. What's happened to the salt, Claude?'

'It's behind your glass.'

'You'll remember that, because the two of you were old friends and Felipe lives in Adeje, I asked him if he'd mind going to the road junction once in a while to clear the grass around the memorial for Mirjana on the side of the road. And Felipe did that, didn't he, Claude?'

'He did. Whenever I happened to be passing that way I'd stop and take a look and it was always cared for.'

'Well, Felipe happened to mention that the Adeje council will be doing roadworks at the junction, installing new lights and broadening the approach to make room for the increased traffic coming down the coast road over the last ten years. Apparently, quite a lot of accidents have happened there since. Which means that the grass verge will have to go to make way for more tarmac ... So Felipe wondered what to do about the memorial. His idea is to put it on the wall of the building alongside the road. He spoke to the owner of the house and she had no objections. Felipe asked me if I'd like him to do it. He says all it needs is some cement to fix the stone to the wall, and he asked me at what height it should be attached. Whether chest height wouldn't attract the wrong kind of attention to it. He says that if he placed it a foot above the ground it would be less conspicuous, and I rather agree with him. I told him I'd ask you. By the way, he said the woman who owns the building mentioned to him that a couple of months ago somebody left a wreath on the memorial, and Felipe wondered if that might have been you.'

'I don't know, somehow another week seems to have passed. Time goes so much more quickly than it used to. It's over a year since I moved down here out of my room in the tower. Getting up and down those stairs became too much. So we've brought my bed down and set it up in George's old study because it's too big to fit in the little bedroom. The drawing room adjacent we've kept as it was, only we've put in a sofa that converts into a bed for Claude when he spends the night down here. He often does that now, as I need help to get out of bed when I go to the loo. On top of the long-term effects of the accident, I've got arthritis. I've seen several doctors about it, but there isn't much to be done. Those cold damp beds we slept in for years during the war, I expect. Living in this dry climate helps to keep it at bay. I'm no longer able to lift my hands up to my head to do my hair. So we had to sacrifice it. I gave Claude a pair of scissors and asked him to cut it off. But what to do with the hair? It seemed such a waste. Alicia's daughter Inma plaited it in a coil and sealed the ends with wax. The coil is four and a half feet long. We were quite proud of it. Inma says there's a coiffeur who makes wigs in Santa Cruz, and I could probably sell it there for hundreds of euros. For the time being we've put it in the curiosities cupboard. We brought the cupboard down from the tower a few days ago, by the way, because we want to go through it and decide which of you should get what, and I can only do that when I can see what's in it. So much of you children's lives seems to have collected in this house that we'd like to start dividing it up between the four of you. Claude has made an inventory of all the moveable goods. He'll be along in a minute. We thought we'd make a start on the cupboard this morning.

'Just between ourselves. I haven't yet spoken to Claude about it, but there's a tremor in his hands I've noticed recently, plus he has a moment of hesitation when he's about to talk – a hiatus, you know, the sort of pause you sometimes come across in people who've got a suppressed stutter. Eduardo developed exactly the same mannerism when he got Parkinson's. I suspect Claude has got it too.

'Yes? I'm in here ... What? Whenever you like.

'He's also going a bit deaf. He's sensitive about it, so I'll have to catch him in the right mood to tackle him on the subject. Anyway, he'll be here in a moment, so I thought you should be informed and know what to do in case of a ... deterioration, you know, should that crop up some way further along the line, which could land us with other problems.

'Would you like some more coffee? A drink?'

'I wouldn't mind a glass of wine if you'll join me.'

'Here's a copy of the list I just printed out. Back in a minute.'

' "Inventory of disposable items in the Arguayo property to be divided between Max, Felicity, Philip and Alex". There are several pages of it. Perhaps I ought to tell you in advance, Alex, that most of what's here will be going to your brothers and sister. Quite a lot from this household in the way of sheets and bedding, small items of furniture, vases and whatnot has already been moved to the La Laguna house, which you will be inheriting. So when Claude and I make a provisional division of the house inventory into lots, and send the list round to the four of you,

940

don't be disappointed if yours is less than what the others are getting. There's no reason for you not to be listening in on what Claude and I will be saying when we discuss the lists, but I'm not sure you'll find it of much interest to hear us going through this inventory. It's going to take us all day. I know I shall find some of it heartbreaking. Here ... these barred children's beds, for example, complete with little mattresses and bedclothes, the stacks of children's clothes and toys, which have been sitting in mothballs up in the attic. Things like the collections of stones and shells. I couldn't throw them out, so I packed them all away when Kim and Liz left the island to start school in England, and they've been sitting there for the last quarter of a century. Will our grandchildren need them for their own children? Will they want any of this old stuff? We've accumulated so much during the thirty-five years in Arguayo which I was quite sure one of you children would find some use for when the time came, but now it has I don't know what to do with it. I've asked people in the village, but no one seems interested. And what are we going to do with bigger pieces like the six pinewood cupboards, or was it seven, we originally had made for this house? I look at them and ask myself what on earth we've got all these things for. Well, there was a time when we needed them. They belong here as linen cupboards for the bedrooms upstairs and as general storage space downstairs, but is Felicity going to need them all? Does she need that much linen or that many cupboards? It seems a pity to break up the set, but I'm afraid that's what we're going to have to do.'

'That's another thing I've been meaning to tell you – a couple of books by Kaser I saw reviewed recently, one on Albania, one on Kosovo. I can send you the reviews if you're interested. But you probably know the books already. Wasn't he a colleague of yours at Graz? And one other thing I wanted to say now that your stint with IPA is coming to an end: I'm proud of you for having taken the decision to get out of university life. Surviving ten years as a war correspondent was a hell of an achieve- ment. And you wrote good dispatches. Watching you when you were a young man, barricading yourself behind books, I was reminded of myself at the same age, and I can say now that I felt a bit uneasy. When I applied for my first position as a lecturer in London I still had it in my nostrils – the smell of the cloisters of the Jesuit school where, you remember, I went to school in Paris – the smell of safety and privilege.

That was why I took on that advisory work for the island government, sitting on reform committees and so on. Looking back, I realise I should have got more into that kind of work sooner. Maybe more into being a father too. If it was sometimes difficult for me to acknowledge I was one of two fathers, your position can't always have been easy either. Did you and I talk about those things enough? I think George managed better than I did. I'm left with a feeling of inadequacy – having let you down as a father. I don't know if you have any ideas about what you're going to do when you leave IPA. But if you want to come back and work on the island, now's the time.'

'October the twenty-third, a cooler day for once.

'The blue of the sky isn't the blue I remember. Is it the blue that's changed or is it me? *Wäre das Auge nicht sonnenhaft, die Sonne könnt es nie erblicken.* If the sun were not in us, in our eye, our eye could not see it. Goethe. Ferdinand lent me his copy in Schlawe, still with me. A breeze I don't feel but can hear in the wind chime on the terrace where I'm sitting.

'There! Came in on cue. Did you hear it?

'I want to tell you about my last day in the garden a week ago. I drove around with Paco to see what needed doing. He showed me his aviary, which I thought looked run-down, the nesting boxes dirty, rips in the netting not properly mended – so unlike Paco. Perhaps it's getting too much for him. I rather hope so, because I hate keeping birds in captivity. He's very pleased with the blue chaffinches he's managed to start breeding. There seemed to be as many chiffchaffs as canaries in the aviary. Paco is puzzled how the riffraffs, as he calls them, are getting through the netting. He's still selling a lot of his birds. When the wind is right we can hear them up here on the terrace singing their hearts out. So then we had a look at the dragon trees, several of which are ailing. He thinks it's due to a fungus and gave me a specimen to send in for analysis at the Institute of Horticulture. It would grieve me if we were to lose them. Because they grow so slowly, they were the first trees I put in when we came here in the 1960s, a double row of saplings, thirty-two in all, and all these years later they're still not more than eight feet high. So losing even a couple of them would destroy the symmetry of the avenue, effectively for ever. Those forty-odd years can never be made good. You can replant the trees, but not the years. So what do you think? Would

942

it be better to leave it as it is? As we were coming back up the path and turning onto the road, the two right wheels of the scooter sank into a ditch I'd failed to see and it tipped over, depositing me on the road. I broke my left wrist. I felt like an upended tortoise, helpless, knowing I'd cracked my shell and it was my own fault for not watching out. No more runs in the garden for the foreseeable future. The foreseeable future is that bit by bit things move away from you, do you know, Alex, out of your sphere.

'As a young woman I thought the end always came quickly to people, as I saw it come to them in the war, but now I'm finding out that it comes slowly, in many little stages, lots of little things one is deprived of and gets used to doing without, lots of *little* deaths, as it were. As for the accident – it wasn't *just* an accident, I believe nothing's *just* – Claude was running towards me to help me when we first met, George was walking up a flight of stairs away from me when his mother called and he looked round. That was how we were introduced. When the accident happened, I wasn't paying proper attention to what I was doing, because I was still preoccupied with my ailing dragon trees. But what's proper? I was in sympathy with them. If there'd been nothing wrong with them, nothing would have happened to me. I believe there's a synchrony and a sharing taking place between events beyond anything we can even begin to imagine.'

'December the tenth. It's Christmas in another fifteen days. Claude wants me to talk about this without him because he's not sure he would get through without breaking down. Gradually we're coming round to what it is we want to do. That's nothing to break down about. On the contrary, these years have been the best, but tears come more easily to Claude than they do to me. These last years here have been the happiest of my life. The first years and the last. I've had more time for myself than I've had since I was a child. Claude and I have been more there for each other than ever before. The passing of the days in Arguayo reminds me of life in my grandmother's house. The days would just slide by, and nothing hindered them from doing so. There was always an abundance of time. A man called Mr Engels used to come in on Saturdays to wind up the clocks, keeping account of the time that passed in the house week by week, noting it down in a little book that was kept on the mantelpiece. There was always that abundance of time, and if we ever doubted it we could look it up in Mr Engels' book. If we fell short of it or overspent, Mr Engels made it up for us. He might put a clock a minute forward or a minute back, but as a child that was the extent of my awareness of our expenditure of time. The same spirit lives in Arguayo. Claude and I feel we could go on like this for ever. Unthink-able that the two of us wouldn't be able to manage here on our own for as long as it takes. So now's when to stop. In the late afternoon, while the going's good, no more than the tip of the first shadow encroaching on the garden. Time to go indoors.

'My handicaps have got worse over the last six months. Claude has deteriorated too. Neither of us wants to continue without the other. We made this decision long ago, or rather, we never had to make it. We've known it all our lives. We're packed and are ready to leave. I'm learning that there are different shades of readiness. There's a readiness to leave that's long been established, months ago, all the letters and documents, the arrangement of things we shall be leaving behind. What I have to put behind me is not so hard for me to do. But what I have to put in front of me — that's a different readiness — neither of us are ready in that sense. Leave for where? Even nothingness is a place, and I have to go there without Claude. This stands before me. We can be holding hands and go out together, but in that moment he and I are severed. I am not ready for that. Will I ever be? How can I be ready for that parting? Which is why I think it will just have to come over us, on the impulse of a moment. The probable truth about the *moment* is that despite all our expectations and carefully laid plans, it will take us by surprise. Because the *moment*, when it comes, will never have been here before, and we shall not recognise what we see.'

# ACKNOWLEDGEMENTS

Mindful of Dr Johnson's dictum that a man will turn over half a library to make a single book, I would like to acknowledge the contributions that have gone into the making of this one.

My information for the wide-ranging and complex background to *Ella Morris* has been gleaned mainly from historical and scientific works on specialist subjects I was unfamiliar with.

Some of the details shoring up the activities of George Morris as a courier for the British Trade Mission in eastern Europe as described in the *St John's Wood* section of Book One, were supplied by S. Dorril's history of the British secret service, *MI6: Inside the Covert World of Her Majesty's Secret Intelligence Service.*

For the account of the meeting in Budapest between Eichmann and Joel Brand and the details of Eichmann's offer to sell Brand one million Jews in exchange for ten thousand trucks, as alluded to in that *St John's Wood* section, I am indebted to Alex Weissberg's book *Die Geschichte von Joel Brand.*

Episodes from Sasha Borowski's life relating to his experiences during Stalin's Great Purge, described in the *Paris* section of Book One, were inspired by Weissberg's magnificent, now regrettably neglected work *Hexensabbat.*

The quantum physics as expounded to Ella Morris in the same *Paris* section owe a considerable debt to two works by a former Heisenberg pupil, Hans-Peter Dürr: *Wir erleben mehr als wir begreifen: Quantenphysik und Lebensfragen* and *Auch die Wissenschaft spricht nur in Gleichnissen.*

Descriptions giving detail, substance and colour to Paris in the 1950s as contemporaries experienced it were provided by J. Campbell's *Paris Interzone* and S. Karnow's *Paris in the Fifties.*

The ecology of Tenerife features on many websites, among them

945

ATAN (Asociación Tinerfeña de Amigos de la Naturaleza) and a Heidelberg University research project on Tenerife devoted to *Element cycles and socioeconomic dynamics: Understanding global processes on a local scale.* A study by D. Weaver, 'Sustainable tourism: is it sustainable?', which was published in *Tourism in the 21st Century: Lessons from Experience*, provided a template for the discussion of $CO_2$ emissions on Tenerife in *A delicate Balance* in Book Three. Fundación Encuentro's *Espana 1998* and Faulkner, Moscardo & Law's *Tourism in the 21st Century: Lessons from Experience* provided useful general guides.

But for my good fortune in coming across K. Köpruner's *Reisen in das Land der Kriege,* the extraordinary episode that took place in Zadar just prior to the outbreak of the Yugoslavian Civil War would have remained unknown to me, and *Pogrom*, the fourth section in Book One, would not have been written.

The following sources, listed in alphabetical order, have been essential as guides to a better understanding of the wars in the former Yugoslavia.

J. Cigelj, *Appartement 102 – Omarska* * B. Hoti, *Entkommen: Tagebuch eines Überlebenden aus dem Kosovo* * *Human Rights Watch* March 2000, Vol.12, No.3 (D) * K. Kaser, *Familie und Verwandtschaft auf dem Balkan* * K. Kaser and H. Eberhart, *Albanien: Stammesleben zwischen Tradition und Moderne* * H. Kramer and V. Džihić, *Die Kosovo-Bilanz* * H. Loquai, *Der Kosovo-Konflikt* * M. Rüb, *Kosovo Ursachen und Folgen eines Krieges in Europa* * T. Schmid, *Krieg im Kosovo* * T. Schuller-Götzburg, *Erinnerungen an Jugoslawien* * *Washington Post* Report from Dragacin, Yugoslavia, 22 June 1999.

In the discussion of evil at the beginning of the section *Nadine* in Book One, there is a lengthy examination of the case of Goran Jelisić, then on trial at the International Tribunal in The Hague. I am indebted to Slavenka Drakulić and her book *Keiner war dabei: Kriegsverbrechen auf dem Balkan vor Gericht* for much of the background quoted in this discussion. At the end of *Nadine*, the predicament of rape victims during Yugoslavia's Civil War draws on information in *Leila: Ein bosnisches Mädchen* by A. Cavelius. In *Information on the Support Unit of the Victims & Witnesses,* W. Lobwein et al. give us a look behind the scenes at the International Court of Justice in The Hague.

The section *Les Événements* in Book Two distils and merges many sources into a unified narrative. Although works such as Guy Debord's *La société du spectacle* give a useful overall view of the May 1968 events in

Paris, when it comes to the hour-by-hour reconstruction of street battles the best eye-witness accounts were given by the students themselves, whose POV is the one taken in the novel. Many of these reports are or at the time of writing were available on the internet.

One of the fullest, originally published by Solidarity in a pamphlet 'Paris: May 1968. Non à la Bureaucratie', is to be found at: www.marxists.org/history/france/may-1968/libertarian-communist-account.htm.

An eye-witness account, 'On the barricades in May 1968' by Karen Moller is at www.swans.com/library/art12/moller02.html; Andre Hoyles' 'General Strike: France 1968' at www.prole.info/texts/generalstrike1968.html; 'France '68: The wild days of May' at http://revcom.us/a/v20/960-69 /961/fran.68.htm.

Le Monde's chronicle of headlines, 'Dates and Principal Events', can be accessed at www.marxists.org/history/france/may-1968/timeline.htm.

In many instances, where it seemed to me that cited quotations did not intrude on the narrative, use of them has been acknowledged at the point where they appear. This was the case with Christopher R. Browning's book Ordinary Men: Reserve Police Battalion 101 and the Final Solution in Poland, Rachel Carson's Silent Spring and Donella and Dennis Meadows et al., The Limits to Growth: A report for the Club of Rome's Project on the Predicament of Mankind. The extended quotation from this work has been reproduced with the kind permission of Dennis Meadows.

In cases where I judged that that they might well intrude, this being a novel and not a non-fiction work, there has been no mention of them within the text. This Acknowledgement is an attempt to make good the deficit. It applies particularly to material used in Book Three, notably from Sing C. Chew's World ecological degradation and J. Diamond's Collapse: How societies choose to fail or succeed. I am indebted to E. O. Wilson's epochal anthology Biodiversity (1988), specifically to contributions from: P. R. Ehrlich, 'The loss of diversity: Causes and consequences' * R. Norgaard, 'The rise of the global exchange economy and the loss of biological diversity' * N. Myers. 'Tropical forests and their species: Going, going...?' * M. Plotkin, 'The outlook for new agricultural and industrial products from the tropics', and E.O. Wilson, 'The Current State of Biological Diversity'.

A special first-readership thanks goes to Joebug, Longo and Squillo, friends who have accompanied the progress not only of this book but of quite a few in the past.

There remains of course a vast invisible debt beyond what any such book-keeping can encompass. In the course of the thirty years between the inception and the conclusion of what eventually emerged as *Ella Morris*, the infusion of other written and spoken influences of which I have not even been conscious – one might call them the much larger half of a library turned over in my sleep – is immeasurable.

Without the persistence, patience, good sense and good will of the editors at Weidenfeld – Celia Hayley and Sophie Buchan, assisted by Jennifer Kerslake – who had the task of giving shape to a very long and unwieldy MS, this book would not have appeared in its present form. Without the loyal support of Alan Samson and Tony Holden, it wouldn't have appeared at all.

JDM, Munich 2014

# W&N

*blog and newsletter*

For literary discussion, author insight,
book news, exclusive content,
recipes and giveaways, visit the
Weidenfeld & Nicolson blog and
sign up for the newsletter at:

## www.wnblog.co.uk

For breaking news, reviews and exclusive competitions
Follow us 🐦 @wnbooks
Find us ⓕ facebook.com/WNfiction